PAT BOOTH

THREE COMPLETE NOVELS

PAT BOOTH

THREE COMPLETE NOVELS

MALIBU

BEVERLY HILLS

PALM BEACH

WINGS BOOKS

New York • Avenel, New Jersey

This omnibus was originally published in separate volumes under the titles:

Malibu, copyright © 1990 by Orcam Corporation
Beverly Hills, copyright © 1989 by Orcam Corporation
Palm Beach, copyright © 1985 by Pat Booth

This edition contains the complete and unabridged texts of the original editions. They have been completely reset for this volume.

This 1994 edition is published by Wing Books,
distributed by Outlet Book Company, Inc., a Random House Company,
40 Engelhard Avenue, Avenel, New Jersey 07001,
by arrangement with Crown Publishers, Inc.

Random House
New York • Toronto • London • Sydney • Auckland

Printed and bound in the United States of America

Library of Congress Cataloging-in-Publication Data

Booth, Pat.
    [Novels. Selections]
    Three complete novels / Pat Booth.
      p.   cm.
    Contents: Malibu—Beverly Hills—Palm Beach.
    ISBN 0-517-10065-7
    1. Man-woman relationships—United States—Fiction. 2. Upper classes—United States—
Fiction. 3. Love stories, American. I. Booth, Pat. Malibu. 1994. II. Booth, Pat. Beverly Hills.
1994. III. Booth, Pat. Palm Beach. 1994. IV. Title. V. Title: 3 complete novels.
PS3552.O646A6   1994
813′.54—dc20
                                                                                            93-41487
                                                                                                CIP

8 7 6 5 4 3 2 1

Contents

MALIBU

To Ansel Adams, Robert Mapplethorpe, and Man Ray—
thanks for the memories

~ *Prologue* ~

T
HE HEADLIGHTS OF the Porsche probed the winding road, and the hot
wind moaned through Malibu Canyon. There were other sounds in the
still night and the purr of the engine didn't drown them—the howl of a
coyote, the throbbing staccato of a fire department helicopter patrolling the
Santa Monica Mountains, the roar of the faraway surf. The driver wore
gloves of soft red leather, and the wheel twisted and turned as the car powered higher into the hills, leaving Pacific Coast Highway below, a neon ribbon of traffic along the moonlit beach.

A hand reached for the Blaupunkt and the creamy voice of Gladys Knight
sang of a man who was leaving L.A. for a simpler place in time, leaving on
the midnight train, never to return. Now the driver laughed—a cruel laugh,
far from humor. The song was an omen. Because tonight there would be
leaving; tonight there would be heartbreak; tonight there would be fear,
loathing, and a terrible destruction in Los Angeles County.

The driver looked up and watched the eagle swoop across the moon, its
wings magnified in silhouette against the silver backdrop. Then the wicked
eyes turned back to the road. A shuddering sigh merged with the music. It
was an adrenaline sound, full of excitement and tension, and a foot pressed
down on the accelerator as driver, car, and its murderous cargo hurried
toward their destination.

On Mulholland Highway the Porsche slowed. A graveled view site
platformed from the roadside. The sleek car nosed onto it, tires crunching,
and the headlights played across the gorge below. The gloved hand killed the
engine, and the sound of silence was broken only by heavy breathing. Next,
the hands reached for the empty gasoline can. It flew from the car, clattering
against the rocks, before coming to rest in a crevice where tomorrow it would
be discovered. The moonbeams caught it, and again the maniacal chuckle
erupted from the throat of the driver. It was only a can of fuel, but it was also
a death warrant. And it was the path to power, billions, and a horrible revenge.

Now the driver moved fast. The hands reached for the garden hose that

5

lay against the red leather of the backseat. The door opened and closed. The pipe was thrust into the gas tank of the Porsche, and soon its other end was snaking down the precipice. The pungent smell of high-octane fuel merged with the scent of sage and eucalyptus on the night air, and the trickling sound was as innocent as genocide as the gas ran in rivulets among the tinder-dry brush of the canyon. There had been no rain. The earth was parched. The chaparral was dying of thirst at this, the dangerous end of the Malibu summer when the desert winds roared through the canyons to the sea.

The driver returned to the car, flicked the ignition switch, and the eyes watched the fuel gauge as the gas siphoned in a slippery stream down the hillside. When the tank was nearly empty the flow was stopped and the hose was gathered up and stowed in the trunk of the car. The driver walked to the brink of the canyon and scanned the valley for the house. There it was, tucked down low among the rocks, adobe calm, its stucco draped with climbing jasmine. The victim was asleep in there, and the Santa Ana wind was gusting, searching for the flames it longed to carry.

A simple Bic lighter, cupped in the gloved hands against the hot breeze, flared unsteadily in the phosphorescent moonlight. Down it went, toward the ground already wet and dark with the gasoline. The flame burst into life and the wind fastened onto it and made it its own.

The driver stood back from the heat, and then the door of the Porsche was opening, closing, and the engine was gunning, the tires screeching as they spewed gravel into the already flaming canyon. In seconds the car was gone, speeding down toward the safety of the coast, leaving behind the holocaust its driver had unleashed.

The orange ball rolled down the hillside and the sky was alive with marmalade flames. Smoke curled around the football moon, and the brush evaporated, its burning cinders floating on the crazed breeze. The roar of the flames and the searing heat were the only warning of the firestorm as it raced at seventy miles an hour toward the unprotected home, and the person inside.

The flames engulfed the house. They reached into the open windows and probed the courtyards. They consumed the creepers, and they feasted from the beams that projected from the stucco. They exploded the plate glass of the picture windows, and rushed up the wide wooden stairs to the bedroom. The victim was awake now in the short seconds before the longest sleep— back to the wall, eyes wide with the vision of infinity, hands raised in horror to prevent the unpreventable. There was no time for prayers to God, for mother, for mercy from the fire. Instead there was death by murder in Malibu, the heaven that was so suddenly burning in the flames of hell.

~1~

PAT PARKER CREPT through the state-of-the-trend New Yorkers, well aware that she was the only person in the pulsating auditorium who was permitted to carry a camera. Crouching low at the edge of the stage, she knew that her black jersey Alaïa microdress was sliding up her long legs to the point where sculpted thigh became jutting buttocks, but she didn't care. She only cared about getting the shot. It was moving fast, as it always did. The magic moment wouldn't wait. There was no time for dress adjustment, slow focusing, or meter confirmation of the fast-changing light. Here, on the cutting edge of photoreportage, she was flying by the seat of her pure silk bikini-brief panties, guided only by long experience and endless practice. The battered Nikon twirled in her fingers as if attached to them by flesh, blood, and nerve fibers, and the glorious image filled the ground-glass screen as she eased her forefinger onto the shutter release.

At the Brooklyn Academy of Music's "Don't Bungle the Jungle" fund-raiser, Madonna and Sandra Bernhard were acting as if they were coming out of the closet in public, and the Olympus Pearlcorder on Pat Parker's hip, and the Pan-X film in the bowels of the black Nikon were capturing it for posterity. She could feel her heart pounding in her chest, and, beneath the wool dress, her taut breasts were sticky with sweat and excitement. As she always did at such moments, she prayed that the image would find its way onto the celluloid, and that no mistake would ruin the picture.

Inside her head, behind the aquamarine eyes, behind the perfect nose with its flared nostrils, behind the full slash of the edible mouth, Pat Parker was computer cool as she made her calculations. She had thirty-six exposures. A fast reload would take thirty seconds. How far were the two girls on stage from a climactic moment? To motor drive or not to motor drive—that was the question. Should she rattle out the film now, and risk missing a hot shot later as she juggled the reload—or should she stay on single snaps like a sniper in the grass, making every bullet count as it banged into the target?

"Sit the fuck down," hissed a five-hundred-dollar ticket holder in the front seats.

She didn't turn around. She didn't even *think* of obeying. Nothing could come between her and her objective, the picture in the can. Nothing ever had. Nothing ever would. She waited, her luscious body draped over the sharp edge of the stage, as she stared up the endless Sandra Bernhard legs to where her bottom bumped and ground against Madonna's.

"I got you . . . *babe*," they sang to her tape recorder and to the vibrating audience, and many who heard them thought they knew *exactly* what they meant.

Pat Parker caught her breath. The stage was exploding. The steam was rising. She hadn't seen anything so hot since Mick Jagger and Tina Turner at Live Aid. The surprise duet hadn't been announced and the more impatient of the fashionable New York art/design/model-world crowd had already left for Indo- and Undo-chine, where dinner was to be. But Pat Parker had heard the rumors. She always did. So she had hung around to the bitter end, and it was turning into the sweetest media event she had ever experienced. Madonna and Sandra had been provocative on the Letterman show, and in an *Interview* interview the megastar had hinted that she had entered a new stage in her sexual development.

In the banter before the rip-roaring performance of the Sonny and Cher song they had introduced themselves as a couple of dy . . . big, pregnant pause . . . namos. And while Madonna, smiling broadly, had told the audience not to believe the rumors about their relationship, Sandra had capped it with a heartfelt, *"Believe them."*

Now, before the all-seeing Nikkor 105mm telephoto, the audiovisual event peaked.

The two girls changed the lyrics of the song.

"Although we may not have a cock . . .

At least we're sure exactly what we've got . . ."

In unison they clamped their right hands to the crotches of their identical cut-off floral jeans, and as they did so, hips thrusting, heads flung back in glorious defiance of convention, Pat Parker's waiting finger pounced on the button of the motor drive.

The sophisticated downtown art-scene audience erupted behind her. The save-the-rain-forest benefit at the newly trendy Brooklyn Academy of Music was a million miles from the traditional Big Apple charity bash, and the Suzy crowd—the nouvelle-society Trump types, the Euro-trash, and the patrician Astor/Buckley set—were safely tucked away at the Tiffany Feather ball at the Plaza. Here were long-legged models like Iman, black and hot as the May night; Elle MacPherson parading the best body in the world bar none, way above 10; and the spellbinding Christie Brinkley melting down minds with the brilliance of her smile. These people, the ones who gave the famous energy to New York, cared that every second the world was losing a football-field-size area of trees. Madonna herself had told them about the fatal carbon dioxide that only plants could remove, and explained how it was creating a greenhouse over the world that would one day warm the globe, melt the ice caps, and burn up their grandchildren.

But right now Clementes, Harings, Lichtensteins and Schnabels, Olden-
burgs, Mardens, and Ruschas were thinking about something else. They were
cheering, whooping, and waving their hands above their heads in delight at
the gutsy irreverence and brave honesty of the once virginal, once prayerful,
once material girl.

Pat Parker hugged the camera, crushing it against her breast as she
looked quickly at her watch. It was past eleven. It had happened later than
expected. Damn! This would miss the early morning papers. That meant the
story would break in the news no-man's-land of the later editions. But that
was just thinking New York—the *News* and the *Post*. Nationwide, *USA Today*
would run it big on Thursday morning, and there was always TV. "Entertainment Tonight" could show stills to back up a news item, and of course the
tabloid shows like "A Current Affair" would be fascinated. As a backstop
there were always the more happening magazines like *US* and *Details*. Right
now she had to get the film into the developer to see if the image was safe.
No photographer, however great, however professional, took that for
granted.

The crowd was surging toward an exit crammed with paparazzi, a colorful
sea of psychedelic T-shirts, rap fatigues, baggy pants, and rainbow string ties
that were the trendies' interpretation of the invitation's "casual evening at-
tire." Now the faces ran the gauntlet of the Sony cameras and the phallic
directional microphones as they muttered platitudes for the sound bites. Nobody would get more than seven seconds. Network research had shown that
to be the average attention span of the TV audience. Pat Parker, however,
skirted the photographers, and as she hurried down the steps she was looking
out for Jed, her driver, and for the Range Rover parked out there somewhere
in the oily black sea of limousines. She saw him and shouted out Jed's name,
which was when she bumped right into Kenny Scharf.

The graffiti artist was tall and good-looking, with short cropped hair, and
he seemed nervous as hell. The jungle bungle evening was his production.
He had badgered Madonna into doing it, and everyone else had fallen into
place—Bob Weir from the legendary Grateful Dead, the B-52's, and, of
course, the sharp-tongued temptress Sandra Bernhard, whose duet with Madonna had elevated the evening from the memorable to the legendary. On
stage Scharf had given a rambling speech. His hand had shaken, and it had
been clear that the strain of it all was beginning to tell. Now he had something else to worry about. Who the hell had given the Parker girl photographic privileges? It hadn't been him, and Madonna had insisted on "no
cameras." The signs were up all over the auditorium.

Scharf looked at Pat's excited face. His eyes fell toward the Nikon
clutched in her hand.

"You didn't . . . take pictures of Madonna's duet . . . did you . . . ?"
he mumbled hopelessly.

"I sort of did, Kenny," said Pat simply.

Kenny looked desperate. Pat Parker stood her ground. He was far too gentle to make a grab for the camera. If he had she'd have fought for it, and probably won.

"Pat, please don't do this to me. Don't publish those pictures. I mean, I promised Madonna, and she did it all for the conservation thing, and . . . and . . ."

Pat Parker took a deep breath. Kenny's approach was the only way to play her. All her life she'd been tough as nails. She'd had to be. She'd had to survive her childhood, her adolescence, and growing up in the hard city. And she'd had to get where she was today, the up-and-coming photographer to watch, the beautiful one, who looked so much better than all the hard chargers who sat for her portraits. Macho men she ate for breakfast. The sensitive ones at least had a chance.

"I don't know, Kenny. I mean, I didn't gate crash. Medina gave me the okay to shoot. He even put it in writing."

Kenny desperate metamorphosed into Kenny destroyed.

"He had no right to do that. It was agreed 'no photographs.' It was part of the deal."

"Yeah . . ."

Pat Parker shook her head and her blond hair swirled in the warm air of the New York evening. She knew all about show business ambivalence, the love/hate relationship with publicity. You had to do it, or the flame of fame might flicker and die in the fight for success. But you resented the invasion of privacy, the endless hassles, the uneasy symbiosis with a press you despised but needed if you were to keep reality in your dreams. Why had Madonna done that duet? As a secret revelation to a roomful of friends on a "not beyond these walls" understanding? Hell, no! She was a dedicated professional who changed her image with the calculation and split-second timing of a symphony conductor. Was this the unveiling of a new Madonna, a surreptitious trial run of a brand-new persona to see how it might play? It was highly possible. And yet . . . and yet . . . Madonna *had* made mistakes, and they had been emotional ones. Perhaps the film in the belly of the Nikon had recorded one of those—an outpouring of genuine affection that had been totally spontaneous and that would be later regretted.

Pat Parker sighed. "Kenny, she wanted everyone to know."

Kenny ran a hand through his hair. "It was a joke, Pat. She was teasing."

The Parker eyebrows arched and her lips relaxed into a wide-open smile. "Oh, Kenny!"

"I'm asking you, Pat, as a friend. If you don't make it happen, it'll sink. You know New Yorkers. They're so wrapped up in themselves the outside world hardly exists for them. They wouldn't know a story if it sued them."

Pat laughed a bittersweet laugh. It was true. The audience had been so frightened of committing the cardinal Big Apple crime of being the last to leave, that many had missed the climactic duet. Those who had stayed were already wondering where they would be seated at dinner. Upstairs at Indochine, or tucked away in the basement? At the A table with the Joels, the Wenners, and the Kleins, or languishing in outer Siberia at the back of the restaurant, far from the warmth of Brian McNally's smile? They had limo problems, and how the hell did you get out of this place called Brooklyn, and did they have the staying power for the late-night/early-morning appearance at Rudolf's Mars? None of the city papers would have bothered to assign a reporter to cover the show. They relied on their syndicated columnists for that. The whole shebang wouldn't rate the column inches of the Plaza party. At best the gossip writers would pull a few names off the press release and say they'd been there. So Middle America would be starved of the juicy tidbit, and quite suddenly Pat Parker found herself thinking that might be no bad thing.

She shrugged her broad shoulders. The hell with it. Who cared?

"Okay, Kenny," she said at last with a weary smile. "You win. I'll bury it."

"You're a sweetheart," he said, relief all over his face. He hugged her quickly and disappeared into the people graffiti of the milling crowd.

Pat Parker slowed down as the adrenaline fountain faltered. Wow! It had been a biggie, but she had let it go. What did that *mean?* Last year she would have had to have been ripped from the story by saber-toothed hound dogs. Yet she had just surrendered it, because a nice guy had asked nicely. Was she losing it? Getting weak? She bit her lip, chewing at it gently in the middle of the frantic crowd. But already she knew the answer. She was bored with her life. In the early days of deadlines and graft, and dangerous streets, there had been something to prove as she had run the gauntlet of male sarcasm and disbelief that a woman—a beautiful woman—could do the job better than they. Back then, she'd had no time and less inclination to question the worthiness of what she did, because until she succeeded there was a sense in which it had not yet been done. Now it was. She wasn't the most celebrated photographer in New York, but she'd already had a one-woman show at the Staley-Wise, Crown was talking a book, and her network of contacts among the glitterati and the night fungus was something everyone envied. She knew the city and New York knew her, and she had reached the stage of technical expertise where she could forget about the science of photography and concentrate only on its art. Art. That was it. That was the place she wanted to be. She had surrendered her scoop so easily because winning was no longer enough. What she wanted to do now was to *create* beauty.

Jed leaned over and opened the door of the Range Rover. Adoration shone from his eyes.

"How did it go?"

Pat Parker clambered in like a trucker into the cab of an eighteen-wheeler. Thigh, underpants, garter belt, everything hung out. She flung the Nikon with its once-precious film onto the backseat as if she had gotten it as a gift in a McDonald's Happy Meal. She let out a deep sigh of regret/satisfaction and she shook her head from side to side to let the air at her overheated scalp.

"Only brilliant, and I blew it."

"Bob Weir was that good? The crowd was stiff with Deadheads."

"No, silly rabbit. Madonna just about did it with Sandra on the stage. I got it." She jerked her thumb over her shoulder at the Nikon as Jed eased the car out into the limo soup.

"That's great, Pat. You want we go to the lab an' do the prints right away? Where will they go? The *Post*?"

Pat shrugged.

"The filing cabinet. The wall of the john. Under your pillow, I guess, red-blooded male."

She turned her smile on her assistant, lighting him up in the street glow. Poor Jed looked his usual dear, sweet mess—the wire-mesh glasses, the wire brush hair, the jungle rap, jungle brother clothes—but he smiled back at her, pleased that the boss he loved was pleased with him.

"Whaddya mean we're not going to *use* them?"

"I just promised not to. Guess I'm going soft in the head."

"They *leaned* on you?"

Jed's tone was incredulous, prepared to be indignant. Nobody pushed Pat Parker around. Not while five-foot-nothing of uncoordinated nerd look-alike was rooting on her team.

"In the nicest possible way. Kenny's friendship with Madonna was on the line. He'd promised no pix. Somebody screwed up giving me the okay."

"Jeez!" Jed said it all. Was this the Pat Parker who'd pay in blood for a hot picture if that was its price?

She reached up and stretched, like some sleek, sleepy cat in one of the jungles about to be saved.

"Oh, Jed, I don't know. I just think I'm at some sort of career crossroads. I can feel it coming on. Like, who *cares* about reportage anymore? There has to be more to life than illustrating gossip. Maybe if I'd taken some shots of the disappearing rain forest *that* might have made a difference, but Madonna and Sandra rubbing butts . . . I mean . . . I mean . . . it's hardly *crucial*, is it?"

"Maybe not *crucial,* but I guess it is sort of interesting."

"Yeah, men like that, don't they? Women, too, maybe."

Pat Parker's bright eyes went dreamy, but she wasn't really thinking about the bi-girl duet anymore. She was thinking about her future. Was New York over for her? Had she cracked it open? Was there nothing left to find, nothing more to prove? And if she had scooped the meat from the claws of the world's most complex city, what the hell else was left for an encore? One thing was certain. The challenge would have to come from a different direction. She scratched absentmindedly at her crotch, oblivious to the leaping Adam's apple of her boy Friday.

"Indochine?" he managed in a squeezed voice.

"I suppose."

"You've got a ticket. You get to eat. Table twenty-nine," said Jed. He was her secretary, too, and his information was important. She needed to know where she stood in the dangerous forest of the New York night. Was she just the photographer? Or was she a guest? If the latter, then the famous would relax around her. It would be easier. Brian and Anne McNally, inventors of

Odeon, Indochine, and the Canal Bar, were Pat's good friends, but they had to walk the thin line between guarding the privacy of their star-spangled clientele and providing them with the publicity outlets that were so vital to their careers.

Jed snaked through the deserted downtown streets like the native he was. Not many people could do Brooklyn to Indochine without running directions on the cellular phone.

"I'll be outside. No hurry. You want a thirty-five an' a wide angle for the inside stuff? The 400 ASA should be fast enough without flash. I seem to remember there's light in there, upstairs anyways."

"Yeah. Thanks, Jed. Tomorrow's yours. Come in on Friday. You're fabulous." She leaned over and kissed him quickly on the cheek, scooped up the couple of Nikons he pulled from the glove compartment, and opened the door as the car came to a stop outside the restaurant.

She pushed through the knot of photographers, waving to a couple she knew, ignoring the scowls of the many who knew her. Most of them didn't like her. The Big Apple chauvinists had perfected their art. They were jealous of the contacts they hadn't the charm or the brains to make, and they excused their career failure and Pat Parker's fame by attributing it all to her beauty. The broad got in by putting out, they whined. Was there any other way for a woman? In the early days, in the war zone between a job and a union card, some bright spark had once filled her car with grass cuttings to pay her back for getting a picture published. Finding that much grass in the inner city had probably been the most creative thing he'd ever done. For a while, the meaner and more jealous of her colleagues had taken to calling her "the lawn." They didn't do it anymore because even the most myopic could see that the towering beauty was now a towering success.

Pat waved her ticket at the door police, and soon she was inside, her practiced eye sliding around the long thin restaurant, sizing up the scene, sorting it out.

The hot table was stretched out along the wall and the heavy hitters were already there. Billy Joel and the luminescent Christie were sitting with Mick Jones of Foreigner, and Pat knew that Jones was producing the new Joel L.P. *Rolling Stone* publisher Jann Wenner formed dangerous liaisons with crophaired Glenn Close, and the seriously attractive and footloose Lori Singer. Sweet Kelly Klein wore the 1.2-million-buck duchess of Windsor's ring, and Calvin, the man who had bought it for her, sat neat and tidy in an immaculate suit of old-fashioned cut, one that looked like it might have belonged to the duke. The art scene was represented by stayer Brice Marden, currently showing in the Whitney Biennial. Model, musician, publisher, couturier, movie star. It was an interesting meritocrat mix. The aristocrats were all at the dull Plaza party, and they were the only thing missing. Apart from Lee Radziwill and Tatum O'Neal, most of the BAM "faces" had come on to the restaurant.

People bounced off Pat Parker like Ping-Pong balls in a wind tunnel. They didn't stick. Half a sentence was heavy-duty social intercourse to a professional party player in this town. Maybe it was the coke. Maybe it was the propulsion pressure in the cooker of the city. There seemed to be so little time, so much to say. Or was it so much time, so little to say? Whatever the reason, the fervor of the game-show-host greetings unfailingly failed to follow through as the hungry eyes searched the room over Pat's padded shoulders for fresh social prey.

"Shoulder pads, darling? I know it's difficult to go cold turkey and give them up, but we've all got to try . . . I was just saying to . . . Oh, hi, sweetheart, are you renting Bridgehampton this . . ."

The wife of the arbitrageur charged on, blowing a soundless kiss at Pat to cover her retreat as she fastened onto Di Cummin, a fabulous-looking girl in a Rifat Ozbek multicolored top, whose houses in the Hamptons, Sun Valley, Fifth Avenue, and the Virgin Islands were *Architectural Digest* regulars.

"Pat Parker! Working? In Alaïa? It's not allowed."

Jacqueline Schnabel, fabulous ex-wife of the painter Julian (canvas), had left her husband for another type of painter (houses, the town). The ebullient boss of the Alaïa shop looked ravishing in a leopard-spotted low-cut dress, again by Ozbek, hot designer of the millisecond. In answer, Pat ducked down and took her friend's picture.

"There, now I made money out of you." She laughed. "Come on, Jacqueline, let's go eat. Come and sit at my table, wherever it is."

Number 29 was a good one, making an L with the A table. Pat squeezed herself onto the banquette from where she could shoot right down the corridor of celebrities as they picked at the prawn balls and sucked at the iced Chablis. It was funny. On the East Coast the famous drank. On the West Coast they didn't. But then of course they didn't eat much here, whereas on the other side of America they were always jamming in the fuel for their endless aerobics sessions. She peered around her table, giving Jacqueline a little squeeze to tell her that she loved her. Hmmmm. Mainly queens. In the old days the homosexuals had dressed like women. Not anymore. The macho heteros were dolled out in the frock equivalents. The gays wore wall-to-wall Wall Street. Above their boxlike British-style suits, their pink faces were scrubbed till they shone, not a hair out of place, not a kind sentiment allowed past flossed, bleached, water-picked teeth. At first the tailored brigade affected a lofty disdain for the two great-looking chicks who had invaded their table. They melted a bit when Kelly Klein waved at them, a bit more when Brian McNally came by and cracked a few jokes, and then they rolled over, legs in the air, when Lauren Hutton blew heavy kisses. The Indochinese food that had been embargoed at the far end of the table began filtering through. The repartee began to flow. The New York evening was loosening up.

Pat Parker fired off a roll of Kodak at the laughing faces, called for an outsize can of Sapporo, the hot cold Japanese beer, and wondered why it was okay for the famous to enjoy themselves in the Big Apple but uncool for them to do so in L.A. Somebody should write a dissertation on it. Undoubtedly, in Ph.D.-rich America, several already had. Suddenly, she was having a good time as the existential career doubts of the earlier evening began to fade. Iman and Bond Girl Talisa Soto, trailing a string of black-clothed liquid lovelies, their impossibly long legs draped by implausibly short skirts, dropped by to kiss "hello." So did chic Anna Wintour, editor of the new and more "now" *Vogue,* allowing her glacial façade to drop just an inch or two for the photographer she admired. Jean Pagliuso, fashion photography's Pat Parker and hot from the altar at the Bel-Air Hotel, stopped at the table. She was followed by Peter Beard, the Kenyan conservationist cult figure whose "I-was-discovered-by-Iman" badge hinted at his sense of humor. In a few significant moments, the social center of gravity began to shift imperceptibly toward the Pat Parker table to such an extent that Ian Schrager, Steve Rubell's partner, whose whole life was an exercise in the recognition of such things, actually felt the need to comment on it.

Then, quite suddenly, she saw him. The fingers of alarm ran with Jerry Lee Lewis abandon up and down her back. She caught her breath. She looked again as her stomach tightened. Across the room, partially hidden behind a column, a man watched her. His pallor was not the legacy of the long Manhattan winter. It was the haggard paleness of the terminally ill, and his devastated good looks, his crumpled, listless skin, mocked the memory of the man he had once been. But he was dead. She had been at his funeral in March. She had wept bitter tears for her lost friend. What was he doing, this ghost at the feast? She stood up. Her shaking fingers reached for the edge of the table, to push it back, to squeeze out of the cramped space. Her eyes never left the eyes of the man who watched her. A glass of wine toppled onto the white tablecloth, but Pat Parker didn't stop. Her body was moving but her whole being was on hold. Her essence was frozen over with the ice of dread. Around her, the party chatter was wrapped in a fog of unreality as the faces became Magritte faces, surreal symbols, stereotypes, the flesh and blood of individuals no more. She felt a hand on her arm, but she brushed it away. She had to go to him. She had been sucked from her seat by a super- natural force that terrified her, and she was a free agent no more. How had he escaped from the cold grave? What was he doing at Indochine among the bourgeoisie he loved to hate? Why was he watching her, his hands gripping the arms of his wheelchair, his dear head held high as he questioned her soul across the sea of frivolous laughter, his expression troubled, quizzical . . . mocking? She pushed across the waves of table hoppers, and the vision dis- appeared from view. He was behind the column. She was nearly there. She steeled herself. She went around it.

"Robert!" she gasped.

But it wasn't Robert. It was someone else, of course. Someone who looked so very like him.

The mists blew away from her eyes, as common sense came back to banish emotion. The man was Robert's double, and in a wheelchair, and clearly so very ill. She stood foolishly before him, looking down at him, and he up at her as she tried to put her experience into words.

"I'm sorry . . ." she blurted out. "I . . . ." Her hands splayed apart to say this couldn't be said. For an age the sick man stared into her face, and she into his as the differences multiplied and she saw that he was not Mapplethorpe, was not really him, was not nearly him. She had invented the similarity. In the midst of the frivolity, her unconscious mind had spoken to her. It had taken her back to the last time she had seen him, wrecked and so near to death.

"Pat," he had whispered as he had held out his frail hand to her.

"Oh, Robert, are you all right?" She had asked her hopeless question as she had dropped down beside his chair, and she had held his hand as her eyes had filled with tears at the sight of his suffering beauty.

"There have been better days," he had replied with a watery, rueful smile. And then he had asked her if she remembered Bond Street.

How could she ever forget it?

It had been five long years ago, and she had been down and out in the big city. She had had no direction, no skills, no money, just the power of her personality, her beauty, and the iceberg of her talent. It seemed like yesterday—a bar downtown, a black guy who'd made her laugh, the accepted invitation to go see some photographer who lived nearby. She had crammed into the rickety elevator and it had been like traveling in a mobile prison as she had headed upward, the uncertain light streaming through the grille of her cage. At seventeen she had known she was not being wise, but she had learned from her childhood that wisdom was a luxury that only the rich and secure could afford. Her new friend, who'd said he was a dancer, had knocked on the door, and the leather guy who'd opened it had seemed so small, yet so perfect, and he'd been pleased to see them in a laid-back kind of way. Pat had flopped down on the black leather sofa and slung her feet onto the fifties glass table with the arrogance of the very young and the very beautiful and she'd looked around the small studio, taking in the oak chest of drawers, the crucifixes, the single lily in the slim vase.

"Christ, it's like a church in here," she had said irreverently, and the guy in the leather pants had laughed and agreed.

"I make altars all the time. It's my Catholic past."

It had started there. She'd admired the flower prints all over the walls and the frames he'd made and designed himself, and he'd watched her carefully with the professional detachment of a man who desired only men. She hadn't been shocked when he'd pulled out the beautiful pictures he'd insisted on describing as pornography, despite their obvious status as supreme art, and she hadn't minded, although she hadn't joined in, when he'd smoked a joint and told hair-raising tales of how the pictures had come to be taken, and about how vitally important it had been for him to be a participant, not merely a voyeur, in the wild S&M world in which he lived. It had been her very first lecture on the value of artistic integrity, and despite the bizarre nature of the subject matter, she had learned the lesson. To record it you had to become it, to be it. You had to be involved, to have a point of view. Otherwise you were just another tourist in town, there to milk the moment of a fast buck, and to live vicariously from the experiences of others. They had talked into the night, and he had liked her, and the very next morning, he had offered her a job as his assistant, and in a moment of inspiration she had accepted. It had been the time and place that her life had begun. At their last meeting, dying of AIDS, he had needed oxygen to help him breathe, but he had fought to talk to her.

"I see your stuff all the time. It's good, Patti. It's very good," he had whispered.

He called her Patti, and Pat had often wondered if that was why he had been drawn to her in the first place. Patti Smith had been the wind beneath his sixties wings.

"It's shit, Robert. You know it. It's meaningless shit."

She had been surprised by the vehemence of her own self-denunciation. It was as if she had realized it for the first time. The clouds of hypocrisy had been blown away, as they were around Robert, and she had been left with nothing but the rude truth of her artistic inadequacy.

"It's a transition," he had said softly. There had been a calm in his words, and they had been full of the wisdom of the end of life. There had been the sad feeling he was talking about them both, voyagers on a journey to the greater beauty, speaking of all the unfinished business and the joy and the angst of all the unfinished business to come. You had only to keep the faith. You had only to struggle and not give up, and out of the weakness would come strength and out of lies would come truth.

Pat had felt her eyes fill with tears. He was a reproach to her, this dying friend from long ago. She had drifted from his world to find her own as he had encouraged her to do. She had thrown herself into the demimonde of the New York night, and she had taken his advice and submerged herself in its creative frivolity, in the dark brilliance of its social satire. This soft underbelly of the great American Empire was as real and as vital as Astroturf, and she had chronicled it faithfully, lending it the eye of her mind, and pulling beauty from the shallows, and plucking art from the lush thickness of the drug- and sweat-scented air. At one time it had seemed to her the most important work in the world. At her last meeting with Robert she had realized she had been wasting her life.

"What should I do, Robert?" she had asked.

He had laughed, the sound affectionate, not humorous.

"Oh, Patti, if there was ever a way to answer that."

She smiled now as she remembered. Robert of all people had offered no easy answers. He had known about the agony and the ecstasy that he had refused to separate from his art. The artist had to find his own way. It was a vital part of what he did, perhaps the most important part of all.

"Are you still able to work, Robert?" she had asked.

"In my mind."

He had smiled at the girl he had always loved and admired. Then he had asked her for a favor.

"Patti," he said, "do something for me, will ya? For the old days."

Pat Parker had felt the tear roll right down her cheek. For the old days. For the wonderful mind-bending old days when she had learned the slippery feel of film in her hands, the snap of the lens as it attached to the camera, the sensual touch of the shutter beneath her fingers. She had bathed then in the soft glow of tungsten and caught images against the hard edge of strobe, and she had wandered deliciously in the gloom of the darkroom cooking the chemicals until the magic moment that the image was born. They had lived at night and slept briefly by day, and the man the world would one day remember as perhaps its most original photographic artist had taught her all the secrets that were possible to impart. For the old days . . . ? Anything.

She had leaned in closer to find out what she was being asked to do.

"Go to California," he had whispered. "Go to Malibu, Patti. Go see Alabama. Do it for me."

Pat Parker's face crumpled at the memory. The sob exploded from her heart. Beneath the bright lights of the big city, she was crying for her dead friend and for all that he had meant to her. She stood there wracked with sorrow, dimly aware that the man who had conjured it all up was looking at her in amazement, a worried expression creasing his parchment skin.

She backed away from the stranger as the tears came from the tap of regret, and she pushed through the party people toward the door. As she did so, she recognized the turning point within her. At Indochine she had discovered her own road to Damascus. Her old life was over. Her new one was about to begin. She would go to see Ben Alabama. She would look for her future in Malibu.

~2~

THE NOTES FROM the blue piano hung in the heat of the New Orleans
evening, sitting sweet on the sticky wind. Across from the building, the
L&N tracks still rumbled with the memory of the streetcar, and Stanley, dirty
with sweat, scratched at the stubble of his beard. He was a caged animal, all
wrapped up in the heat and the boredom, and he looked across the room at
the woman he loathed, at the woman he so suddenly wanted.

The ambivalence shone from him, like the moon over the muddy river.
He wanted to hurt. He wanted to love. And he wanted revenge for all the
insults and the airs and graces, revenge for all the high-blown lies. In the sex
dance he would be as powerful as the muscled arms that sprang from his
tank top; as strong as the lean, hungry legs that lived in his grease-stained
pants; as triumphant as the taut, tense buttocks that would punish this vain
woman who stood before him.

The faded Southern belle tried not to look at him, but she couldn't avoid
his eyes. It wasn't decent, yet she had to watch him because she could sense
his want, and it merged with hers. God, she could smell his sex. It dripped
from him, the sensual drops burning in her brain as the summer night breeze
plucked at her damp clothes and the blue piano lied that it was all just fine.
She wanted to go to him and rub herself against his barbarian body. She
wanted to hear his foul mouth yell the coarse things it would find to say. Her
pretty yellow frock stained with his sweat, that was what she wanted. But she
couldn't tell him. He mustn't know those things. He must never be allowed
that triumph, never suspect that anything as common and uncouth as he
could light the light of a lady.

So she turned away from his smoldering eyes, and she dabbed at her brow
with the cologne-soaked handkerchief and tried to escape from desire in the
comforting world of make-believe.

—

IN THE FRONT row of the Juilliard Drama Theater, Emma Guinness shared
Blanche DuBois's dilemma. She sat on the edge of her seat, and a smile of
outrageous joy played across her pert features. God, he was *fantastic!* The

19

moody boy was a dream. His black lank hair was messed up all around his face, and his grimy skin glistened beneath the hot stage lighting. It was the face of a fallen angel. It was long, aquiline, far from the Brando prototype, and the straight nose flared down deliciously from a high brow into the fullest lips that Emma had ever seen. He looked so dangerous. Physically and emotionally, this boy could wreck hearts, bodies, peace of mind. Around him there would be no relaxation, only love and fear, passion and pleading, only the fierce excitement of undreamed-of pleasure and pain.

She half turned to the flame-haired woman on her right.

"Who *is* he, Dawn?" she hissed.

Dawn Steel, one-time toilet paper designer and now in turnaround as the most powerful woman in Hollywood, the studio boss of Columbia, didn't know. But she was going to find out. She leaned back in her chair and asked the minion in the seat behind her.

"He's apparently called Tony Valentino. Not only great-looking, but the name hints at a sense of humor," she said to Emma with a laugh.

Emma Guinness allowed herself a small, tight smile. Goodness, she'd expected to be bored out of her pants by this Juilliard play for the agents and casting people. Instead, someone was setting them on fire. The nobody student actor had his fingers on her sexual rheostat and, boy, was he twisting it in the right direction. She turned to her other side. The girl sitting next to her jumped to attention.

"He'd be wonderful for our 'Stars of Tomorrow' section, wouldn't he," Emma stated. It was not a question. Although Guinness was not her real name, Emma tried to act as autocratic as she thought a British brewery heiress might. Disagreement with the editor of about-to-be-relaunched *New Celebrity* magazine was simply not an option. Samantha du Pont, who headed up Features, hurried to admit that Tony Valentino would be just perfect for any role that Emma might suggest.

"Shall I talk to him about it at the reception afterward?" asked the subservient Samantha.

"No," said Emma Guinness, quite loudly in the hushed theater. "I will."

As she spoke she tingled inside. God, the body! They didn't have things like that in England. He was tall, about six foot, and he must have spent an age with chest expanders or whatever they called them over here. But it wasn't just the muscles and the face, it was the total package. There was an insolence, a brooding, screw-you James Dean vibration about him that just had to extend beyond the role he was playing and into his private life. That meant Tony Valentino was a Tennessee Williams man, full of contradictions and fascinating dead ends, the aggressive surface masculinity, the primal colors, the overt sexuality masking delicious layers of subtle complexity.

Emma wanted to possess him. She wanted to tame him. She wanted to break him like one might a wild and dangerous mustang, and then to show him off in some safe corral, walk him about, tell everyone casually, "Oh, he's mine."

She looked around to see if the audience were seeing what she was seeing. Yes, they were. And this was the toughest crowd in the world. Every May the fourth-year drama students at the prestigious Juilliard School put on a play in the 206-seat drama theater for Broadway's and Hollywood's finest. The tickets were two hundred bucks apiece, and were strictly invitation-only so that the hottest talent spotters in the business could have a chance to preview the raw material. Now, the agents and casting people sat entranced by the stage presence of the novice genius as he played the part of Stanley in *A Streetcar Named Desire*, the role that had launched Brando's career.

For a second or two, Emma Guinness was sorry that her own impressions were so dramatically confirmed by the knowing audience. She would rather have discovered him all by herself. She didn't fancy having to barge through a checkbook-toting crowd of industry and theatrical hustlers to reach the boy wonder at the reception. But immediately she relaxed. This was the theater. There were no jobs for unknowns. Certainly there was no money for them. The hard-nosed players might be enjoying themselves right now, but they would not go out on a limb for a nonpro when ninety percent of the track-record actors were out of work. She smiled. There was no doubt in her mind. She could have him. The latter-day Valentino would crawl all over her like a hot rash in summer when she told him who she was, and what, if cards were well played, she just *might* do for him. Mmmmmmm! It was a delicious thought.

Tony was lost in the world of his character, but he was detached enough to realize his performance was a triumph. He had it. It was working for him in the way he had always known it would, on this, the most important night of his life. The adrenaline stew was just right, simmering, spiced, bubbling up to the rim but not boiling over. In the superreality he could feel the emotions of Stanley Kowalski, but up there, layered above them where they should be, were his own. He knew exactly what he felt about uptown Allison Vanderbilt/ Blanche DuBois so pretty and demure in her yellow dress, because in real life he had taken time out to experience her firsthand. He had seduced the patrician millionaire's daughter simply because he had known that they would be playing this scene together, and for no other reason. He had wanted the chemistry to be right. He had wanted her to want him so that it showed on the stage, the only place it mattered. It was his version of Method acting. While the rest of the twenty students who made up his "year" had gone to bed early, and tossed and turned in discomfort through the steamy New York night, he had taken Allison Vanderbilt, a Vanderbilt whose lineage predated the Commodore, as Stanley would have taken Blanche—cruelly, greedily, mouthing lewd curses and leaving the marks of his fingers as bruises on the smooth white skin of her butt.

Now was the payoff. He could see her tremble as he swaggered toward her. He could see the naked need in her frightened eyes. His body was taut like the strings of an instrument and for a brief moment his own desire threatened to derail his precision. So he reined it in and allowed himself to see not the beautiful, reserved Allison Vanderbilt but the defeated Allison/ Blanche of the previous night, her long legs thrashing in the liquid aftermath of his crude invasion. She had wept in the lull after the storm of bodies, and she had tried to communicate with the Tony who had, unbeknown to her, become the Stanley of the drama. But he had cut short her string of words, as Stanley would have done. He had nothing against the upper-class innocent who had tried to talk of love. It wasn't personal. It was strictly business. Because Tony Valentino was off and running to the place he had to be. To the spotlight. To the pinnacle. To the fame that only movie stardom could give him.

Dawn Steel leaned in toward Emma Guinness.

"Good chemistry, no?" she said.

Emma Guinness growled her assent because, unbelievably, she was jealous. Valentino had made love to the girl who played Blanche. There was no doubt about it. Emma felt less certain that the sun would rise tomorrow. Yes, they were lovers—real ones, and tonight while Emma Guinness slept alone between the Pratesi sheets in the triplex on Fifth she would dream of the young stranger in the pale girl's arms. She could hardly believe what was happening to her. Could it be anything to do with jet lag? Had the power and prestige of her new position in the New World unhinged her? Sex had always been something she used. Now here it was popping up, out of the blue, for no apparent reason. It was deeply, deliciously unsettling.

Tony reached out for Allison, and she leaned against his chest as if all her life had been a long journey to this destination. She could feel his heat. She could hear the beating of his heart as it thumped against hers. The acrid smell of him was alive in her nostrils, as the warmth of his cruel, beautiful body lived in her memory. She tried to think about what she was supposed to be feeling, but the counterfeit emotions warred with the real ones. Blanche was drawn to this lowlife as a flirt to the flame of masculinity. Blanche didn't know about love and caring and commitment. Blanche was too caught up in hysterical illusion to have time for such meaningful emotions. Now she was supposed to swoon Southern style in the arms of the macho hero. But Allison Vanderbilt didn't feel like swooning. She felt like crying. All her life she'd been protected. That was what Daddy and the trust funds had been for. Here, in the middle of the raging drama called love, she was beginning to lose the plot. Tony's hands were so rough and uncaring on her shoulders, just as they had been on her naked body the last terrible, wonderful night. For four long years she had harbored her secret crush on the unresponsive Tony. They all had. It was the students' private joke. None of the girls had managed to break through the wall of icy politeness that surrounded him. In the safe distance from him, the feelings had grown until every girl in the class was ripe fruit on the tree of lust. But Tony, single-mindedly relentless in his pursuit of artistic excellence, had noticed none of them. Then three weeks ago he had noticed Allison Vanderbilt. When he had beckoned, she had come running, and in the madness that followed she had fallen in love with him. Last night, however, in the fury of bodies, it had seemed not so much the end of the blissful beginning as the beginning of a horrible end. So now she clung to him like a limpet, aware that this might be the last chance she ever got to hold him. The adoration shone from her eyes. The devil-may-care indifference lasered back from his. His voice rasped into the magic of the brilliant theatrical moment.

"We've had this date with each other from the beginning!" he whispered as the weeping Allison sank to her knees before him. The curtain swept in from the wings, and the audience dissolved into a massive wave of applause.

TONY VALENTINO stood next to the bust of Dvořák in the reception hall of the Juilliard, and the crowd clustered around him. He knew what had happened. He had triumphed. The play had passed in the blur that to performers was an infallible pointer to success. The audience had hummed in tune to his acting like a high wire in a brisk wind, and then there were his own feelings —the lightness that was lifting his feet from the floor, the almost sexual sensation below his waist, the tingling at the tips of his fingers. He had been brilliant and everyone had recognized his brilliance. From this precious moment on, the world would give him the things he must have. He peered at the smiling faces. Which packet of human skin and bone would give him the first gift? Who would offer him work? Should he stay "pure" for a little longer and stay with the theater, perfecting his art for the silver screen that was his real target? Or should he take the plunge now and sign with a Hollywood agent? He could tell which were the Hollywood players. They had the suntans. They held back at the edge of the crowd, happy to bask in the gravitational field of the man of the moment, but biding their time. The Broadway people had no such scruples. They leaned in hard, not above hustling, happy to point a shoulder to clear the way. Tony got the message. In the Big Apple, his home for the last four years, life didn't wait for you. In the Big Orange, it did little else.

Then he realized that someone was missing. He turned to Allison, standing beside him in the packed crowd.

"Allison, have you seen my mother? She wasn't there when the curtain went up."

Allison shook her head. It would be weird for Maria to miss the performance. Tony's mother, Maria Valentino, was a regular at all the plays. She had herself been an actress of sorts, and the young actors were drawn to her fierce independence, her jaunty humor, and the touching way she handled her prickly son. Allison had often wished her own mother, a patrician emotional prune who wandered through life as if it were a purgatory sent personally to plague her, had been more of a free spirit like Tony's mother.

Tony's eyes searched the crowd. If there was room among all the excitement, he was a little worried. It was his big night. His mother wouldn't have wanted to miss it. She had intended to come. She'd said so. Yet punctuality was not his mother's strongest suit. Nor predictability, for that matter. It infuriated him sometimes, but it was also a part of her he loved. All their lives together they had wandered across the slippery surface of America, coming to rest briefly in rented apartments as the schools and the jobs came and went. The only continuity had been the perpetual motion. A flower-power child of the sixties, his mother had believed with Donne that change was the nursery of music, joy, life, and eternity, and so home had been the open road and the tacky rooms with their tattered metaphysical books and torn Beatles posters, a cockroach-and-grime soup that was always too hot, always too cold, always a billion miles from the security Tony craved. His father hadn't bothered to hang around for his birth. "Not good enough to marry," his mother would say bravely with a dismissive wave of her hand and a vivacious smile, but Tony would not smile, and his hands would clench in anger as he thought about his father's betrayal. It was so difficult to understand. His mother had been so beautiful. The photographs of her proved it. More important, she had charm, that indefinable quality that intelligence tests didn't measure, but which was as vital as it was rare in the sparky war that went by the name of life. How the hell could anybody ever leave her?

Tony turned toward the first-year student who was hovering nearby, the girl who had acted as his dresser. "Tina, would you be really kind and see if you can find my mother? Tell her where I am. Thanks a lot."

The girl hurried off, pleased to be asked a favor by the man she secretly worshiped, as the crowd jostled closer to Tony Valentino.

Across the room Emma Guinness watched him, and her eyes shone as she waited for her moment. It was almost time. The lover boy was preening himself as if the admirers of the nanosecond would be around forever. How deliciously, wonderfully, predictable. He had strutted his brief moment on the stage and the first whiff of success had gone to his head like hard liquor to a teenage brain. Goodness gracious, why didn't people realize that the struggle was forever, and that the higher you got the more important it was to try harder, to appear more humble, to ignore the increasingly gushing PR? Surely some cheap doctor must have written a book about it. They had about everything else. She took a deep breath. Short and squat, she pumped up her chest, and cut into the edge of the crowd, trailing her retinue behind her.

Dawn Steel hung back. She wasn't a follower, and although she liked the sword-tongued Englishwoman, her sixth sense told her that something unexpected was about to happen. You didn't get to run a studio without at least six senses. The three *New Celebrity* employees, however, clung to their peripatetic boss like Saran Wrap. Already they had learned that the Guinness court made that of the Borgias look like a nunnery. Daggers and gift horses were distributed with a Machiavellian cunning that made it difficult to distinguish one from the other. It was important to stay close to the boss. Over her shoulder Emma Guinness said, "I'll do the talking." The comment was unnecessary. She always did.

Tony Valentino saw the crowd around him do a passable imitation of the Red Sea as the woman stalked through. She was coming on strong and her whole persona screamed "power," but what Tony couldn't take his eyes off were her extraordinary clothes. She was a fashion tragedy of enormous proportions. She was a complex joke, an aesthetic affront, a dreadful, appalling terrorist act of taste. Whoever she was had succeeded in looking like a cross between Little Bo Peep and the Sugar Plum Fairy. Her great bosom heaved

out of the tulle, her waist strained against a yellow satin belt that was covered
in bows, a tutuesque frock surrounded short, thick legs like the frill on a ham
bone. Tony felt the wind whistle from his lungs. Clothes were things he
noticed. In all his life he had never seen anything so dreadful. Laughter and
tears, tears of laughter, fought for possession of his eyes. He had no idea who
she was. He couldn't know that clothes had always been Emma Guinness's
problem. He couldn't have dreamed up the paradox that had put the ultimate fashion victim at the head of a magazine dedicated to the single-minded
pursuit of style. But he could recognize a disaster when it was aiming at his
face.

"Hello, Tony. I'm Emma Guinness," she said, thrusting out her hand at
him and smiling lasciviously. Tony took the hand carefully, with minimal
enthusiasm. His expression said the touch of a wet fish would have been
more welcome.

For a second, her smile dimmed. The Guinness name had scored no
points. Drat. That was the problem with nobodies. They were no one. And
they didn't know anybody. It would all have to be spelled out.

"I'm the editor of *New Celebrity* magazine." She waved a dismissive hand
at the three minions that flanked her. "These people work for me." The "for
now" hovered in the air.

Tony couldn't think of anything appropriate to say. The dress filled his
vision. Had it been intentional? Was it kitsch? Was it *good* kitsch? He looked
at her face. She wasn't ugly, wasn't even plain, but neither was she good-
looking. The owllike eyes were round and brown, the nose big and straight,
the chin far more than determined, absolutely certain. Her mouth, however,
was small and mean, and two pointed ears stuck straight out from the sides of
her head, giving the unsettling impression of some distant Spockian relative,
the other-worldly genes diluted by a few earthly generations. Her breasts
were the main event. They were huge and rather fine and, strapped into the
Patrick Kelly party frock horror in *Dangerous Liaisons* style, it remained a
distinct possibility that they might pop out like twin rabbits from a conjuror's
hat.

"You've heard of my magazine," she barked.

Tony splayed open his hands and laughed. His gesture said he didn't know
where to begin. The stranger was over the top in every direction. What did
you say to thunderbolts, tornadoes, and other high-energy natural disasters?

The woman was smiling again. Her eyes bored into him. First his face,
then his chest and torso, and then, unbelievably, the rest of him. She was
looking him up and down. The whole thing was surreal.

"You can act," said Emma Guinness. Her tone was patronizing, and at the
same time vaguely indecent. Tony was left with the distinct impression that
she had wanted to ask, "What else can you do?"

"Thank you," he said coolly. For some reason he sensed that his crowd
was listening to the dialogue. Did they know the girl from the top of the
Christmas tree? Were they subscribers to her boring magazine? *New Celebrity? New Celebrity?* Wait a minute. Wasn't that the one that Dick Latham

was about to relaunch in a media blitz? *New York* magazine had done an article on it. This must be the Brit he had imported to run it. Okay. It was an important, mainline magazine. She could probably do him some good. He tried to calm the screw-you vibes that were running through him.

"We might be able to do something with you." Emma Guinness's laugh was that of a coquette as she dangled the bait before the loser. She peered into what would be his upwardly mobile heart through the limpid pools of the Valentino eyes. Valentino! Really! What had he been christened? Fellatio, probably. I thought Fellatio was an Italian footballer until I discovered Smirnoff. Ha. Ha. Ha. Emma was enjoying herself. This was what it was all about. *This* made all the insults, all the bottom licking, all the social climbing worthwhile. Here she was, using the power of her position to score the most beautiful piece of trade she had ever set eyes on. And there was an audience, and not just any audience. Dawn Steel, her brand-new best friend, was behind somewhere. Then there were the various *New Celebrity* office girls whom she allowed, as a magnanimous gesture, to use meaningless titles like fashion editor and art director. On either side were people who had whole suites at CAA, ICM, and Morris. She was making an impression, and it wasn't on horseshit. Tomorrow quality tongues would be wagging. And tonight it was baked in the cake that the Valentino tongue would be putting in time and a half.

Tony Valentino didn't like it. He was not someone that people did something "with" or "to." He did the doing. He always had. He always would. Once again, he was being underestimated. Yet once again, the underestimater would have to be reeducated. It was a wearying process, but it had to be done. Now he felt that for once it could turn into a pleasure. The puffed-up would-be temptress in the catastrophic frock was an accident waiting to happen.

He swayed back, and an insolent hand found the bone of an insolent hip.

"Just what did you have in mind?" he drawled.

They leaned forward to catch it. The casting couch? What was the New York magazine world's equivalent? Surely not cash?

Emma Guinness knew exactly what she had in mind. The problem was how to get it into words in front of all these people. What she basically wanted was to take this thing home. She didn't even mind if the greasepaint stayed on, as long as the dirty clothes came off. Then she wanted to play with his body, and even more than that she wanted him to play with hers. Of course, before she could get to that she would have to endure a wordy foreplay during which, basically, she would promise to make him a star in return for services rendered. It wasn't such an old transaction, or such an unusual one. The gender reversal was the only topspin.

"A gentleman should never ask what is in a lady's mind," she said and turned the force of her full frontal smile upon him, pushing out her breasts, standing up a bit for badly needed extra height, and letting her tongue play over her scarlet lips in a gesture of unmistakable suggestion. All the time her eyes stripped him. They lingered lovingly on the sallow, grime-streaked skin, on the delicious beads of sweat that stood out on his upper lip, on the mouth that had been made with pleasure in mind. By her side the *New Celebrity* cohorts shuffled in acute discomfort. The boss was excelling herself on the downside. They recognized the potential for disaster, and they exchanged glances among themselves as they dared to hope for a social tragedy.

"You want to put me in your magazine?" said Tony. His tone was still mocking, but he had injected into it a hint of interest, the veiled insinuation that, despite his self-confident pride, appearing in her magazine might be a clever career move.

Emma Guinness smiled an indulgent smile. My, was he pleased with himself! But then this was America and he was an actor, albeit an unknown. In England to be an actor was irredeemably common. It was what the gays did. And the incompetents. Here, of course, actors were aristocracy in the society whose bones, muscles, and joints were constructed of celluloid film stock. She must never forget the difference.

"Yes, we have a section called 'Stars of Tomorrow.' I pride myself on the fact that it is a self-fulfilling prophecy." She wondered if she should have spelled it out for the thick simpleton. "Fuck me for fame" would have gotten through the neuron mess all right, but it wouldn't have played so well with the agents, the staff, and dear old Dawn.

"So you put me in your magazine, and you make me a star," he said, as if he had followed her reasoning with some difficulty, but had managed to reach the bottom line all by himself. He was leading her on. Somehow he couldn't help it. Curiosity was too strong.

Emma gave the laugh she would have described as tinkling, the one that came out like tearing tin foil. She had him. He'd wear briefs, wouldn't he? Not boxer shorts. Perhaps those hideous French-style ones that all the greasy studs wore on the beach in the South of France. Yes, it would definitely be Club Méditerranée in the underwear department. Would they be colored? Red! God! Surely not black! The crowd began to recede. She moved closer. Yes, she could smell him now. No-nonsense masculine. The sweat of work. A million miles from the acrid underarm sweat of fear and excitement. She wanted to reach out and touch his arm. That might be a cool move. Seeing is believing, but touching is the truth. She laid her fingers on his arm, feeling the merchandise. It didn't withdraw from her. It was warm, and grubby, and very, very firm.

"And what would I have to do in return?"

He let the flirtation in among the words like a butterfly loosed in a tense stomach. The slow smile started at the outside of his lips, lit up his eyes, creased the greased skin of his forehead. Was his arm pressing out against her fingers?

Emma Guinness opened up like a flower in sunlight. Boy, for a second there, she'd been worried. Confronted directly by his presence, she had wondered briefly if she was trying to put the bite on more than she could chew. The guy had an aura about him, a distance, the sweet but daunting whiff of charisma. Now, however, she was inclined to think that the whole package might be nothing more nor less than a cunningly disguised stupidity. Good. Great! The thicker they were, the harder they came. Anyway, the contract was all drawn up. It only needed to be signed.

She breathed out, her sigh suggestive, and she lit the fires in what she imagined were her smoldering eyes. She gripped the skin of his forearm, hoping that it wasn't a pinch, and she drew him toward her as she swayed, or was it tottered, toward him.

"What would you say to a candlelit dinner for two?" She laughed to show that she knew it was a cliché. She laughed to say that they were grownups and that beating around the bush was for lesser mortals, not for the gods and goddesses of desire. She laughed to show the world that she could joke, and to cover, with the thin cloak of decency, her naked invitation to fuck.

Tony could hardly believe his ears, but he knew she was serious. He had played her along to see just how far she would go, but he had never expected this. Now he was irritated, but he was not the first to react. Allison was. She had been beside him all the time.

When she spoke her voice was shaking with ice-cold anger. "Tony will be a star without your magazine, or your 'candlelit dinner for two,' " she said. The rebuke was in the words, but it was also in the accent, in the haughty tones, in the body language of the upper-class girl. Two hundred years of history and ancient money peered down the Vanderbilt nose at the parvenue who had dared make her moves on the man Allison loved. The patrician eyes bored into Emma's soul, effortlessly seeing through her social pretense and recognizing her for the class impostor she was. High on the alabaster cheeks of Allison Vanderbilt twin spots glowed red.

Emma turned on her rival. Her eyes narrowed. Her mouth tightened. "Listen, sweetheart, get a transfusion before you mess with the grownups. You look like you've given your last pint of blood. If you could act your way out of a paper bag I'd say you were playing a corpse."

Tony Valentino took a step forward. "Don't you *dare* speak to Allison like that," he exploded. "Who the *hell* do you think you are? You prance in here, like some Christmas decoration come to life, and you make the most disgusting and unprofessional suggestion I have ever heard. Are you on something? If you are, for God's sake go get some help."

Emma Guinness took one short, fast step backward. Her head rolled on her shoulders, her face was wiped clean of expression, and for a second or two it just hung there, pancake flat, as it prepared for various depictions of shock. A hand flew to her open mouth. Breath rushed into her lungs. "Oh!" she heard herself say. "Whooooooooh," agreed the listening crowd. The adrenaline sluice gates had opened inside her. She was sinking. She was falling. Her insides were an elevator on the move. The words were still whacking into the target, but they hadn't yet acquired the meaning that would cause the pain. It was numbness time, but already it was ceasing to be. *Unprofessional!* In America, the ultimate abuse. *A Christmas decoration!* He was being rude about her frock. He had sussed her Achilles heel. He had realized that she was the trendsetter who didn't know how to *dress.* He was suggesting that she took drugs, that she needed a psychiatrist. The thoughts tumbled over themselves and they added up to one word. *Humiliation.* She had been publicly humiliated in front of an audience who would not forget. Tomorrow, tonight, there would not be an employee of *New Celebrity* who hadn't heard the story. In Hollywood, she would be the joke of the week. In speedier New York, the joke of the day. It was the worst moment by far in a life that had not been short of them, and as Emma Guinness tried not to cry, she was already beginning to hate.

In front of her was the boy who had done it. There was no answer to his insults. There was a time for words, and a time for retreat. She was aware that her face was on fire. She knew that they could all see the thick film of tears in her eyes. She realized that her shoulders were sagging. But she still had to get away. Eyes downcast, her heart thumping, her mind already obsessed with vengeance, she turned her back on her tormentor and pushed through the crowd toward the exit. As she did so, she muttered her promise. It was low, inaudible, but to her the words she spoke were the most important she had ever uttered.

"I will destroy you, Tony Valentino, for what you have just done to me. I will destroy you . . . destroy you . . . destroy you . . ."

She was dimly aware of a girl pushing past her in the opposite direction, but she was so taken up with the vehemence of her promise, with the solemnity of her dreadful threat, that she didn't notice that this girl was also on the verge of tears, also shrouded with the aura of misery and defeat, also consumed by vast sorrow.

Tony's smile of triumph died as he watched Tina's path cross the line of Emma Guinness's retreat. He could recognize the body language of emotion as easily as he could portray it, and both the back of the departing girl and the front of the advancing one said the same thing. Anguish.

"What is it, Tina?" he called out to her across the few feet that separated them. But already he knew. Tina had gone to find his mother.

And his mother was dead.

TONY VALENTINO could do every emotion in the book, but he had never been able to cry. Now he was learning. The tears rolled down the proud cheeks, and his chest heaved with the sounds of his sorrow. He sat, his head buried in his hands, and he swayed backward and forward, and then from side to side as if somehow he could shake the misery from him. The boards of the stage were hard beneath his harder bottom, but the outside world had ceased to exist. It was all inside, where the memories were, the memories of the only person he had ever loved.

"Don't. Tony, please don't . . ." said Allison. She reached out to touch his shoulder, to tell him she was with him, to let him know she cared. And she did. Love made the loved one you. More than you. Through crying eyes she watched his grief, and she prayed for something to say that would make it better. But all she could think of was what she had seen outside the theater. Tina had brought the news of the accident and Allison and Tony had rushed to the sidewalk beneath the underpass. Maria Valentino had seemed so frail, her white frock stained with blood, a rag doll of a former person crushed to death as she had hurried across the road, hopelessly late as usual, to catch her son's triumph. Allison had stood there, bathed in shock and swathed in sympathy for the boy she loved, as he had held his dead mother tight in his arms, kissing her, washing her with his tears, and murmuring helplessly all the things he had longed to say to her but had never said. Eventually she had led him away from the tragedy, and she had taken him back to the deserted theater. He had walked beside her in a daze. Now, Tony's rich voice was small as he spoke through the sobs.

"We were together," he said. "It was us against the world, always. She was on my side. Whatever happened. When I was bad, when I was good, when I was cruel . . . whatever . . ."

He gulped in great lungfuls of air, and he let them out in shuddering gasps, his whole body, so strong and powerful, given over to the emotion the world considered weakness.

"I know . . . I know . . ." said Allison Vanderbilt, who could never know. When she had been bad as a child she had been punished, or rather banished to the wings where nannies ruled. Her parents had smiled distantly and said, "I think Allison is tired . . . perhaps a little bed . . ." and the next day they would be gone, to Kentucky for the horses, to Virginia for the fishing, to Palm Beach.

"She was wild and she was free . . . and she wanted what *I* wanted, not what she wanted for me. She used to say if I killed, she'd hide me, and if I wanted to be a fucking *accountant* she'd be proud of me, because she loved me. She loved me . . ."

Again the wave of sorrow shook him. He had been poor. He'd never had a real home. The high-school diploma from Tennessee actually contained spelling mistakes. His father had abandoned them. Yet he had never been emotionally deprived. His mother had been the foundation on which he had built the mighty edifice of his ambition, and in the tempests of life, she had held firm for him. Always.

"She wanted to be an actress, too . . . she'd talk to me about that and about how all the assholes tried to score her, and how she'd laugh in their faces and she never played the game . . . never. She was better than everyone. She was so good . . . and she was the only one who could make me fucking *laugh.*"

Tony slammed his hand against the dusty boards of the empty stage. Somehow the memory of the laughter made the sorrow worse. Was fun gone forever now? Would the struggle for greatness take place against a gray backdrop, the scenery always drab in the darkened auditoriums in which he would be doomed to seek his dream? He didn't resist as Allison hugged him in the solidarity of sadness. She had known his mother, too. She was a link. She knew a tiny part of the things he was saying.

"I took her for granted. I never told her how much I loved her, how much I needed her. She gave her whole life to me. To me, some bastard son by a bastard who walked out on her, when she could have thrown me away with the garbage and made something of her own life . . ."

"No. No." Allison couldn't take that, and she couldn't allow Tony to take it. Maria Valentino had created him, and he was the most wonderful thing Allison had met in her sheltered life. He was her hero. His arrogance, his focus, his ambition were what she aspired to, born as she was in the wild desert of the rich. She had floated through the best schools, through Smith, through the chummy, plummy Anglophile world of WASP America on a cloud of cash and carelessness. When she'd discovered her talent for acting, the family had clucked, and smiled patronizing smiles, and gone out of the way to hide the fact that they were impressed when she'd been among the two percent accepted annually by the Juilliard drama school. But Tony wanted. Tony *was* his desire, and his ambition was a laser so concentrated that it melted anything that stood in his way as it had melted Allison Vanderbilt's tender heart.

"You are her memorial, Tony," she sobbed through her own tears. "She was so wonderful and all she wanted was to make you wonderful, too. I loved her. I wish she had been my mother. I wish . . . I *wish!*"

Tony melted against the body he had used so cruelly. His triumph was empty. The movers and shakers might have watched it, but one had not. His mother had not seen his greatness. And it hurt like *hell* in places he never knew he had, in his heart, in his soul, in his essence.

"I can't believe it . . . There's no point in going on . . ."

But Allison wouldn't permit the self-pity. Not from Tony. Not ever. He was strong. He was brutal. He was cruel, and she loved those characteristics, because they were worn on his sleeve for the world to see. Take me as I am. Leave me alone. Don't mess with me, if you can't stand the heat of my fire. There was an honesty about him that made everything else unimportant. What were the mere feelings of mere mortals in the white-hot crucible of purpose? In the glory land that was his destination there would be rewards that eclipsed the mundane longings for peace, quiet, and comfort, for security, self-respect, and a normal life. The sly nastiness of her own family was another matter altogether. Around her, words were liars. "I love you" had been used so much it was the cheapest currency, and it bought no satisfaction when it was the substitute for the loving actions that alone would have given it meaning.

"Tony, don't ever say that. You'll go on and on, because you're you, you're the 'you' your mother made, and she made the most beautiful person in the world."

She hugged him tight, and for these peak moments of sorrow, he was the little boy he had never really been. He tried to see the future through the black clouds, but there was nothing out there.

"I don't know what to do," he said.

It was a question. For the first time in his life he needed help. Allison Vanderbilt took a deep breath. Did she dare to say what she had been dreaming? It was May. Their final term was over. Juilliard was finished forever.

"Tony, let's go away together. Let's go far away, while you feel like this. Maybe I can help. I want to . . . so much . . ."

He looked up at her then, his face stricken, the tears tracing great rivers of grime and grease down his cheeks. It was as if he was seeing her for the very first time, her beauty, the blueness of her eyes, the determined cut of her chin. He said nothing, and his silence encouraged her to carry on.

"We could go to California," she said. "My family has a beach house there that nobody ever uses. We could go to Malibu."

~3~

T HE BRIGHT MALIBU sunlight poured in through the French doors from the beach. Power-bleach strong, it played over the already faded Sheraton furniture, sucking the brown from the wood. It ate voraciously at the Clarence House chintzes that covered the sofas and chairs, hungry for their still sharp color. It even threatened the vibrant shades of the Mirós, the Kandinskys, and a lingering Egon Schiele whose misfortune it was to have been hung too close to sand. Mostly, however, the sun shone on the face of Richard Latham and he inclined his head toward it, basking in its rays as if recharging a solar-powered battery.

He shifted easily on the golden chair and fingered the only tie in the room. He hadn't gotten used to Malibu informality yet. But then, in this life, he didn't have to get used to things. Other people did. He looked around his vast John Stefanidis-designed drawing room at the small crowd of celebrities who were his guests. There were maybe fifty named faces, and nearly all would have been asked for an autograph on a street in Peoria. It was flattering that they were there. But soon they would realize it was *they* who should be flattered.

The chairs had been arranged in a semicircle around a lectern to avoid the problems of precedence that could upset sensitive show-business egos. Martin Sheen, brand-new honorary mayor of Malibu, was giving the speech and everyone was wishing that his predecessor, Ali McGraw, hadn't decided to swap Malibu Cove Colony for Pacific Palisades. The speech was a rambling, sixties time-warp affair, full of pseudolove, flower-power idealism, and slack intellectual associations. The good news was that it was nearly over.

"And so I now declare Malibu to be a nuclear-free zone, a sanctuary for aliens and the homeless, and a protected environment for all life, wild and tame."

He smiled around the room aggressively, well aware that his hippie seeds were falling on stony ground, and not caring a bit. The muted, polite applause had stopped by the time he had returned to his seat. Latham stood up.

He ambled toward the vacant lectern, his movements slow and unhurried as he let everyone know he was totally unfazed by his "power" audience.

"Thank you, Martin," said Richard Latham. His smile was unconvincing, but his whole demeanor insisted that nothing disturb the outward harmony of the meeting. "I'm sure that none of us in Malibu wants to be blown up, and luckily there are no plans that I know of for a missile base on the Pepperdine campus . . . everything else certainly, but I'm assured nothing nuclear . . ."

He paused to accept the relieved laughter. The actor/activist was getting his from the billionaire, but in a way that couldn't cause offense. They liked the Pepperdine crack. Malibu was always fighting with its university. The seat of learning wanted to expand while the Malibuites wanted everything to remain the same. In the most recent skirmish the Pepperdine growth plan had been given the go-ahead despite the vociferous complaints of the home-owners, who objected to the flowering of the groves of academe in the intel-lectual desert of the beachland. He peered around the immaculate drawing room. Would the fireplace wall take the Hockney? Would it be happy so close to the Bauhaus painters? He'd have to give it a try.

"And I know we all feel for the plight of the homeless, and, perhaps to a lesser extent, for the predicament of the aliens . . ."

Again he hesitated. This was tricky ground. There were Republicans in Malibu like himself, but not many, and the celebrity activists who crammed the drawing room of his Broad Beach home had voted solidly Democrat. They cared about the homeless all right, but they didn't want them cluttering up the beach, causing accidents on the already life-threatening highway, or cooling the steam heat of the property boom. And the aliens, of course, were the Mexicans. These were irritating when they came from East L.A., bran-dished stilettos on the beach, and got sick on Corona and Tecate while they swayed to ghetto blaster salsa rhythms. However, there was the garden to be done and the kitchen to be cleaned and the high-end cars to be washed. Somebody was required to hose down the roof when the brushfires started in the late summer; to house-sit and lug sandbags in the winter storms when the sea threatened; and to cook and serve the quesadillas at the Ali McGraw-designed Malibu Adobe restaurant, which was the slick place to lunch.

"But I think we'd all agree that this is a national problem, not to be solved by Malibu alone. I don't think any of us would like the media to encourage a massive exodus of the homeless and the aliens to our little neck of the woods. Unless, that is, Martin and Charlie and Emilio can find room for them all up at Point Dume . . ."

Charlie Sheen laughed loudly at that. He loved and respected his father, but didn't fully share his ideals. Emilio Estevez, not a loud laughter, permit-ted himself an enigmatic smile. Perhaps the hardest worker in Hollywood was wondering how he'd found time to attend this meeting.

"But we can certainly all applaud Martin's last sentiment. All life must be sacred here, wild or tame, including the life of the coyote who just ate your dog."

Now Dick Latham laughed, and it was a deeply wonderful sight. His sunburned face dissolved into a liquid of charismatic charm. His blue eyes sparkled like the ocean the audience could see over his left shoulder, and the gull-white teeth, a dental dream, shone in the sunlight that beamed across the dunes. His hair, Brylcreemed in a patent-leather patina, was flecked with the gray of his fifty years, and the weathered mahogany of his skin, firm and tight, was wrinkled only by the exuberant warmth of his smile. Even the sound he made was a turn-on. His laugh hugged you. It was intimate, soft, yet masculine, the laugh of the co-conspirator, of the man who secretly wanted to steal your heart. The women just loved it, and the men really liked it, and the special feelings he gave out came winging back, amplified, in the bonhomie soup that was now the room's atmosphere. Even Martin Sheen, chastened by the gentle chastisement, could hold no animosity.

Of course, Dick Latham was far more than his handsome exterior. He was not merely the immaculately cut cashmere blue blazer with the bright burnished Marine Corps buttons; the gray worsted pants with the Wilkinson sword creases; the spit and polish of the Bass Weejun tasseled loafers. He was the richest, randiest man in America. He was the Rhett Butler robber baron who had had the balls to build an inherited fortune into megabucks. And he was single. That, too, was a factor to be taken into consideration as the room shared his little joke with California enthusiasm, the bleached, bonded teeth baring in the money mirth of the early Malibu summer.

Dick Latham flicked into "seriously, though" mode, cutting off the laughter as if turning a spigot.

"Well, what I really wanted to do, apart from responding to Martin's generous and undoubtedly heartfelt sentiments, was to thank you all for coming to my home today. Many of you I don't know personally, but of course your fame and your talent, and your warm hearts have made you public property to some extent, and so, on one level, I know you all."

Flatter them. Go over the top. Beyond. The famous could never get enough of it. To succeed in the movie industry you had to believe in yourself through all the failure years when nobody else did. If you didn't have an ego, you didn't have a prayer.

"Nobody ever accused J.R. of having a 'warm heart' before," laughed Larry Hagman from the back of the room. Hagman had lived in the Colony forever, and there was no Malibu resident who gave more to the community or laughed louder at the cantankerous pomposity of some of his fellow citizens.

"Well, *j'accuse*," Latham laughed. "I saw you working your guts out for the emergency-room benefit a little while back, and I don't believe it was because you were worried about cold heart failure."

The clapping drowned his words. Malibu's twenty-four-hour emergency room was always in danger of closing down. Residents Johnny Carson, Dyan Cannon, Olivia Newton-John, and Michael Landon had all helped Hagman raise money for the Nighttime Medic charity.

Latham held up his hand shyly, the little boy diffidence quite clearly nothing but a charming act. He had them. All of them. They were on his side.

"I'm a newcomer to Malibu, but already I love it, and I share your concerns about its future. I wanted to meet you today to let you know that my . . . resources . . . such as they are . . . and any expertise I may have, are at your disposal in the fight to get Malibu incorporated as a town and in the battle to preserve it from those who want only to make money for themselves while they destroy one of the most beautiful places on earth."

It was a tour de force of understatement. The Latham assets, the "resources such as they are," were estimated by *Forbes* at around ten billion bucks. The Latham lawyers, arm in arm, could have spanned the borders of Malibu from Sunset Boulevard to the Ventura County line. The Latham media empire, newspapers, magazines, books, TV, and radio stations, peddled influence that presidents envied. Here, before their eyes, the money mountain was pledging himself to fight on their side in the war that now they would win. It was a magic moment, but it was about to get better.

"And I wanted to tell you, as evidence of my commitment to Malibu, that apart from this little house"—he paused while the property-wise audience appraised it at around six and a half million—"I am negotiating to buy a thousand acres, in various parcels in the Santa Monica Mountains, most of it in what will soon, I promise, be the town of Malibu. It goes without saying that this land will be used in the spirit of preservation, conservation, and total environmental respect. We must look after the land with the same dedication with which we look after our own bodies."

They undressed him with their eyes. What did *his* body look like, this plutocrat from heaven who would help preserve their precious privacy from the hoi polloi? It was why they were all here, difficult miles from where they worked, safe from the prying eyes of the tourists who had wrecked Beverly Hills and Bel Air. In Malibu there were no maps to the stars' homes, no buses full of gawping gapers, no riffraff to disturb the gilded privacy. The nine million visitors who came each year thronged Zuma, and Topanga, and Leo Carrillo, and were far too busy contracting skin cancer to bother the Shirley MacLaines, the Benatars and the Van Halens, the Stings and the Rob Lowes, who made Malibu the star capital of the Western Hemisphere.

The group X-ray vision liked what it saw. If Dick Latham looked after the Malibu hills with the same loving care he expended on himself, then they were home free. His shoulders were square and broad and they indented, via a triangular torso, to a flat, hard stomach. He was tall, and he stood well, with the posture of an athlete, the gorgeous brown skin of his expressive hands merging happily with neat, expertly manicured nails. Were the rumors correct? Was it true that he was in love with all the women in the world, but that he wanted only to break their hearts? Was there an ounce of truth in the stories of his hard, cruel lovemaking, of the callousness of his subsequent rejection, of the suicides and the nervous breakdowns of the girls who had dared to fly too close to the Latham flame? The delicious speculation rolled around the room. Goldie Hawn and Kurt Russell wondered about it, and so did Robert Redford, all Broad Beach neighbors of the billionaire. Over in the corner, nursing the James Dean loner talent, Sean Penn bothered to think about it, while Steven Spielberg and Kate Capshaw, who had walked across the dunes from their rented house, speculated on what Latham would be like to love.

But Latham hadn't finished. With the flair of the natural showman, he had saved the best till last. "One other thing before I let you get on to the champagne and the Calistoga. I have made one other little investment in the Southland, and I wanted you to be the first to know about it, because I hope that many of you will be working with me at some time in the future."

Working with him? *For* him? And nearly everyone in the room a movie person. It couldn't be. It was.

"Two days ago, I bought Cosmos Studios. As you know, times have been hard there. Somewhere down the line, with your help, I know I can make it once again the very best studio in Hollywood. Thank you very much."

He opened his hands in a gesture that said the formalities were now over. On cue, red-jacketed waiters bearing trays of champagne and mineral water erupted through the French doors from the terrace, whose terra-cotta stone merged with the white sand of the beach.

All around the room his guests stood up. If the heavens had opened and he had ascended publicly to the right hand of God the Father Almighty, Dick Latham could not have produced a more impressive finale to his speech. The redeemer of Malibu, and now, at least potentially a career doctor, too. In L.A. County there was more than enough of all but one thing. There was more than enough sun, sushi, sin, and sexual fantasy. There was far too much money, and material goods, and men with genes as perfect as their jeans. The whole place was awash with a plethora of wine, and wishes, and wall-to-wall women with the wild wind in their perfect blond hair. What there was *not* enough of was work. For every "go" project there were hundreds of thousands of insubstantial dreams. The deals were so seldom "done" deals. The lights were hardly ever green, and the favorite word was *no*. And without the work, where was the fame, the success, the power? Cosmos had been making bombs for the Air Force for the last ten years, and there was no sign of a turnaround. It was rumored that the studio was on the verge of bankruptcy, and if it went under, a vital source of "work" would be removed. Now, with Latham as the billionaire owner, Cosmos would arise phoenixlike from the flames of failure. The collective imagination had been well and truly fired. The moment they got home they would call their agents. Cosmos was back in the game. Overnight, Latham had become numero uno of the two hundred or so "players" in town. Despite the reputed dangers, a couple of the braver women decided then and there that they would risk playing with him.

Dick Latham scooped up a Baccarat glass of '81 Cristal from a silver salver offered reverently by a great-looking actor/waiter. He didn't usually drink, but the room was screaming "celebration." He didn't like to disappoint them. Oddly, at the very moment everyone wanted to engage him in conversation, there was a disinclination to do so. The famous Malibu cool demanded it. These people were genuine stars. The starlets who wouldn't have hesitated to make their pitch hadn't achieved Malibu yet. They were still pigging it in the Hollywood Hills. And the prestarlet beach girls, who hung around the public Malibu, the most beautiful girls in the world bar none, hadn't been invited to this particular Latham party. So the heavy hitters talked among themselves, waiting in sophisticated mode for the billionaire studio owner to approach them first.

The great-looking woman who *did* walk up to Latham was difficult to recognize as one of the world's greatest rock and rollers.

"Hi," she said easily. "Malibu's lucky to have you. I'm Pat Giraldo." She put out her hand.

Latham took it as if it were her heart, holding it for a millisecond longer than was necessary with the delicacy of someone who feared it might break.

"No, you're not," he said. "You're Pat Benatar."

"Only on tour and in the studio. Here I'm Giraldo and I'm Mom."

"When you're as beautiful as you, it doesn't matter what you're called." He laughed to show that he knew it was just an L.A. compliment, but that he couldn't resist it anyway.

Pat Benatar was drawn to him. He seemed totally relaxed. There was no tension anywhere near him. He was apparently devoid of the vaguest hint of neurosis. So few people were totally without anxiety around the famous. Still, as a no-nonsense person of considerable morality despite the raunchiness of her stage image, she couldn't help feeling that there were parts of Richard Latham that were vaguely disreputable. His eyes were too intimate, the touch of his hand too light, too strangely insistent. She was well and truly married, but he was coming on to her. No question.

"I hear you're building on a plot above Zuma." His eyes said that he knew most of the thing she needed to know—about her, about everything. At fifty he was too old to be a fan, but he would know that her *Heartbreaker* album had done five million, that she was married to her lead guitarist, that on stage she was the leather lady.

"Yeah, we move in by Christmas, hopefully. Building in Malibu is a nightmare. Seems like you have to get permission from ten different organizations. It took a couple of years to get zoning on the plans. Still"—and she paused and cocked her pretty face to one side, her expression quizzical—"that won't be a problem for you on your thousand acres if you're not going to build on it. What'll you do, pitch a tent and watch the sun set?"

Dick Latham laughed. The supersuccessful were shrewd. When you could work a stage and take home millions, you had to know a thing or two about human nature. Was she on to him? No. She was just firing on instinct. That was cool. *She* was cool in her dressed-down, washed-out, trendily ripped blue jeans, steel-tipped black cowboy boots, and long pink sweatshirt. He took in the tiptop ass, and the tranquil, knowing eyes, and decided there and then that he liked the Benatar/Giraldo split personality, and the hard rock body that contained it.

"I thought I might allow myself *one* house." His voice was mock pleading and his eyes smiled soothingly at her, as he seemed to sway just a little bit closer to the edge of her space, so that she, involuntarily, found herself swinging back away from him.

He reached out for her and took hold of the brass key chain that hung around the rock star's neck, squinting up the eyes that were too vain for glasses as he read the inscription.

" 'Heartbreaker,' " he read. "Do you break hearts, Pat Giraldo?" His voice was creamy, like a low ballad, but it was urgent, probing, asking for some less than neutral response.

"Only the hearts of fantasists, *Mr.* Latham. If you've just bought a movie studio, you're going to have to learn about illusion."

There was a rebuke in the words, in the subtly emphasized *Mr.* But there was admiration, too, for the superb execution of the pitch.

For a second she glimpsed the steel behind the smiling charm of the billionaire. She had patronized him on purpose. He wasn't used to that. But at once the chink in the smooth armor closed.

"It's a pity you're in the wrong line of work, and I can't offer you a job," he said. *It's a pity I can't own you, use you, break you,* said the eyes that watched her. The thought occurred to him suddenly. "But I could offer you an in-depth profile in my magazine *New Celebrity* when you next have an album to plug. I think schizophrenic mom/rocker caught between male groupies and the PTA would be great copy. I'll have a word with the editor. Get your PR people to get in touch with her."

It was Pat Benatar, not Pat Giraldo, who laughed. She had seen him want her, seen him look for the angle, the way to control her. That was what you did on a gig. You had to find out what they needed, and then you gave it to them, and then they loved you. But she didn't want Dick Latham, didn't need his magazine, wasn't interested in the things his eyes offered. He was too cocky by half. He underestimated people. He needed to be put in his place.

"I heard *Celebrity* was a bit of a disappointment, after all that money you spent on the launch."

The arrow quivered in the center of Dick Latham's psyche. His eyes narrowed, his heart speeded, his fists clenched. Suddenly the attempted flirtation had turned sour. There was only one thing that Dick Latham cared about more than beautiful women, and that was business and winning at business. His father had done that to him. Every day of his childhood he had been told how weak he was, how stupid, how incapable of measuring up to the crude old meritocrat property millionaire. There had been two alternatives in the shadow of the oak. Perish, or grow into the sunlight with a greater vigor and determination than the parent until the young plant was a taller and bigger tree than the one that had fathered it. Latham had chosen the second course. As a result he was *seriously* rich, and his father's "fortune," the one that had always been rammed down his throat, was now barely the income on the income on the income. That was reality, but what mattered in life was how you felt inside. The hungry and the poor never forgot their hunger and their poverty despite any riches the world might shower on them. So Latham could never forget those early days when he had been made to feel a failure by the only person he had ever wanted to think him a success. As a result every business reversal, however inconsequential, cut him to the quick. In his wounded heart he saw every loss as the beginning of the end, the day when the triumphant ride up the mountain became, overnight, the slippery descent down the other side. *Celebrity* had been his baby. He had conceived it. He had watched it grow. He had borne it. Others had expressed their doubts. Did America need another *People,* another *US,* another *Interview?* Yes, he had said as he had put his reputation on the line. No, had said the subscribers, the advertisers, and anybody else whose opinion was remotely of value. *Celebrity* had bombed. It was moribund. It needed the kiss of life. He had given it everything, plowing money into PR, into cover price reduction, and even, in desperation, into giveaways. But money had not changed *Celebrity*'s terminally ill status, and the world in its wisdom knew it. They didn't even want it for free. Okay, so Benatar didn't know about his plans to relaunch a revitalized magazine under the leadership of Emma Guinness, the new and brilliant editor he had just hired from England. But that made no difference. The beautiful rock star had reminded him of what was still, right now, a personal tragedy, and it made him madder than hell.

"Magazines take time," he whispered between suddenly clenched teeth. It was true, but who cared? In Malibu everyone recognized the whiff of failure. It could clear a room. Quite suddenly, Dick Latham turned away from her and plunged into the relieved crowd, leaving the singer wondering just what particular chord she had struck deep in the personality of the strange billionaire.

The Malibu that now surrounded Dick Latham was an impressive group. Sartorially they were a million miles from Beverly Hills, aggressively underdressed, ostentatiously casual. Jewelry was minimal, Adolfo and Galanos conspicuous by their absence, not an Armani suit in sight. Instead there were tennis clothes, Ralph Lauren shorts, Levi's, Top-siders, and Cole-Haan loafers worn Palm Beach style with no socks. The women were exercised, the younger ones happy to show the results in Lycra, Day-Glo, and supercasual stuff from Agnès B. and Katharine Hamnett, body-conscious gear, often of faded denim, that looked its best on the edge of a beach. Those who had dressed up had done so in the clothes of cutting-edge designers, light-years from the safety of Valentino, Bill Blass, and Oscar de la Renta. There were a couple of Rifat Ozbek shirts, three great girls in Gaultier, and a long-legged model in a heart-stopping Isaïa sex skirt, which singlehandedly restored Dick Latham's good mood. He gravitated toward her, through the Paul Young men and the unscented women, noticing the sobriety, the cold sense of purpose, and the almost tangible self-control of the group. Boy, he thought, if California is first and Malibu leads the way, watch out, America. In a year or two the fun and games will be over.

A hand at his elbow deflected him from his tawny-haired target. Its owner was *not* cool. No way. He was small and fat and bearded, and it seemed like he was on blow or booze or both. He thrust his sweaty hand into Latham's and massaged the Latham elbow with his other, as he leered up into the billionaire's face.

"I'm Fairhaven," he barked, "the agent at CPA. Phil Struthers. Grace Harcourt. Fritz Silverberg." He rolled off the second-string clients he represented as if they were a potted curriculum vitae. "I live down the beach. We're neighbors. And I want to congratulate you on the Cosmos thing, and on all your success, and your *beautiful* home." He released the Latham hand and waved an arm around the drawing room, encapsulating the yellow "Benin" fabric-covered walls, the Bessarabian rugs, the Solia carving and the exaggerated swirls of the Grinling Gibbons looking glass that the David Hockney would soon replace.

"It's just a beach house," said Latham dismissively, hoping his cold water would wash off the creepy crawling thing that clung to him. Across the room, the girl with the micro-mini was watching.

"Listen, beach house, schmeech house. Who's gonna head up that broken-down studio you bought? I got some scripts he'd like. Maybe I could run 'em by you first. You want breakfast tomorrow? I could walk down the beach."

Fairhaven grabbed a passing glass of champagne as if it were a life jacket in a rough sea. His nose was beginning to run. The Latham stomach was beginning to turn.

"We're here to discuss the incorporation issue, not the movie business," he said sharply. Jesus. The girl with the skirt had just cocked her leg forward and Latham could have sworn he had seen a patch of white panties flash against a sun-browned leg.

Fairhaven's skin was not quite thick enough to miss the rebuke.

"Listen, Latham," he said with a surly smile of what he hoped was patronization. "You listen to me. You're the new kid on the block down here. I been here a lifetime. I moved to the beach five years ago, so I know the score. In Malibu you're rich, an' you got a studio, an' you live in a real classy, real expensive home, but when it comes to things like incorporation an' preservation an' all that bullshit, you're blowing in the wind. When people wanna talk all that crap they talk to Alabama." He peered ostentatiously around the room before delivering his coup de grâce. "An' Alabama ain't fuckin' here." He leered pugnaciously at Latham to see how his words had landed. He didn't care. He felt good. He had a mill of equity in the house, business was "mustn't complain," and the Maserati was almost as much fun as the chick he kept in West Hollywood to sit on his face.

For the second time in ten minutes Dick Latham froze. It wasn't the crudeness of the industry bit player. During the long march to the crock of gold, Latham had lunched off nastier specimens. It was what he had said about Alabama. That had hit home, because it was the truth. Ben Alabama, biker, art genius, arch conservationist—the most respected and acclaimed photographer in America. Nobody in the know used the "Ben," of course. Alabama was bigger by far than first names. He was monumental, an institution, mightier than the mountains in which he lived, loved, and protected. Alabama had taken over the Sierra Club when his friend Ansel Adams had died. He was president of the Santa Monica Mountains Preservation Society, and when he wasn't brawling with the bikers he loved up at the Rock House in Seminole Hot Springs, he was lunching at the White House, being fêted by every Democrat congressman and senator on Capitol Hill, and selling his landscape prints for a hundred thousand bucks a pop, and his rarer portraits for more. Alabama wore a red bandanna and a ponytail, and Willie Nelson looked like him, only Alabama was tougher, and despite his sixty years, Alabama had muscles where they had no right to be. But all that meant nothing beside the central point. Alabama was not there. He had been invited, of course, but he hadn't showed, and without him Dick Latham's attempt to hijack the Malibu preservation movement for his personal, private use was nothing more nor less than a pathetic failure.

Failure. Once again the word did the scenic ride of the Latham mind. Once more the music began to play as the adrenaline squirted. A second time he turned around and walked away from an unwelcome Aladdin who had unleashed the failure genie to plague him. First, *Celebrity*. Now, the absence of Alabama. For chrissakes. An environmental party without him was Malibu without the goddamn beach. Why hadn't he come? Latham knew the answer. Because of Paris, twenty-five years ago, and the thing that had happened there. Apparently Alabama hadn't forgotten. Already it looked as if the enemy of old was destined to become the enemy of the future.

Suddenly Dick Latham had had enough of his party. Any gossip columnist would have sworn on his mother's life that it was the best roomful that Malibu had seen in years. George Christy from the *Reporter* looked as if he'd died and gone to heaven. It was stellar fusion, no question. Yet Latham wanted out. Ignoring the ripe parted lips and come-on California smile of the simmering model, he headed straight for the sand. He kicked off his loafers and the silk Saks socks, and threw the thousand-buck blazer on the grass of the dunes as if it were a girl's broken heart. He strode across the beach in the vertical midday sunlight and he kicked aggressively at the surf, not bothering to turn up the bottoms of his once immaculate pants. Pat Benatar had told him that *Celebrity*, his pride, his would-be joy, was a washed-up rag. And some disgusting nobody from nowhere had gotten it right. His party had been blowing in the wind. Alabama was somewhere else.

ALABAMA SAT bolt upright, his hands held high on the bars of the Heritage Harley, and he leaned into the turns so that the burning chrome pipes of his bike were millimeters from the melting tarmac. His fearsome goatee and the trademark red bandanna streaming out in the canyon wind emphasized his role of easy-riding ruler of the road, and now, ponytail flying free from his helmetless head, he turned to shout over his shoulder at his passenger.

"We coulda been sipping champagne and nibbling canapés right this minute, King. I delivered us from the fate worse than death."

The guy who sat behind Alabama was impressive too. His high concept could be summed up in one word. *Muscle.* There was very little else on his body, less than six percent fat, khaki shorts and a tank top, the minimalistic clothes straining desperately to contain sleek bundles of actin and myosin that looked as if they had come straight from a Leonardo da Vinci anatomical drawing. At medical school they could have taught off him. There would have been no need for corpses. Every bundle of fibers stood out in sharp relief from its fellows, and King could name them all.

He leaned over Alabama's broad shoulders. "What's Latham like, Alabam?" Alabama's assistant, friend, and brilliant printer of his photographs was the only person alive who was allowed to pronounce his name with only three a's.

"He's an asshole."

"A rich asshole."

"Yeah, rich and smooth. Let's just say his mother knew a thing or two when she decided to call him Dick."

The two friends lapsed into silence, both tacitly agreeing that conversation was too difficult against the background of the throbbing engine and the hot wind. As he threw the bike into the chicanes, Alabama thought back to the time he had last seen Dick Latham. It had been Paris, in the mid-sixties, and Alabama had been staying with his friends Juliette and Man Ray in their tiny apartment in Montparnasse. Alabama had just branched out into portraits, on a brief holiday from the brooding landscapes that had made him famous, and Dick Latham, heir to a large fortune, had made an interesting subject as the traditional American playboy in Paris who kissed the girls and made them cry. Alabama's photograph of Latham had caught all that—the haughty pseudopride of the little boy lost as he tried to be the ultimate sophisticate; the surface arrogance; the almost feminine good looks. They had hated each other on sight, of course, and the crackling bad vibes had produced a great portrait, as they so often did. Latham had loathed the print and had refused to pay for it. In the normal way that would merely have been intensely irritating, but Paris had been a difficult time financially for Alabama. He had laid out francs on the Latham shoot, and it was cash he could ill afford. In the normal way his prickly pride would have prevented him from asking for money, but he already owed his friend Man a few hundred dollars, and so, biting the bullet, he had gone to Dick Latham and told him that he needed to be repaid for his film and processing costs. The haughty playboy had turned down the perfectly reasonable request and had laughed in his face. Even after all these years the memory of the humiliation was more than enough to send the bile bubbling into the back of Alabama's throat. To have his precious work scorned was infuriating. To be forced to beg, and then to be rudely refused was worse. It was behavior that could never be forgotten or forgiven. For three days Alabama had actually gone short of food and booze. Hunger had been a minor inconvenience, but forced abstinence had been as intolerable to him then as it would be now.

There had been revenge of sorts. Latham had been going out with one of Alabama's favorite models, the speedy, lovely, and incredibly beautiful Eva

Ventura, and the playboy had met his match in the sparky girl. He had fallen in love with her, and the alien emotion had threatened to turn his spoiled-brat life-style upside down. Eva had heard about Latham's appalling treatment of her friend Alabama, and had apparently hurried to his apartment to give him the hardest of hard times, only to catch him in flagrante with an old girlfriend. The strong-willed Eva hadn't hesitated. She might have been able to forgive his faithlessness alone, but on top of the character flaw revealed by his behavior toward Alabama, it was too much. She had walked out on the playboy who was supposed to do the leaving, and she had never returned. Latham had searched everywhere for her, hiring detectives, taking ads in the papers, even daring to badger a hostile Alabama, but she had disappeared without trace. Finally, Latham had given up and returned, heartbroken and devastated, to America.

Alabama had not seen him from that day to this, but he had heard about him. Everyone had. In twenty-five go-go years the playboy had metamorphosed into the hard-nosed entrepreneur and the inherited loot had been transformed into media megabucks. Now he was in Malibu, apparently trying to buy huge hunks of Alabama's beloved mountains and to muscle in on Alabama's unquestioned role as top friend of the environment and chief scourge of all developers. For the last two weeks Alabama's house had been under telephone siege as Latham tried to get him to come to his party. Well, screw him! Paris was not forgotten, and Alabama chuckled to himself as he thought of one investment the financial shrewdini had blown. He had refused to pay Alabama a hundred bucks for his portrait. Today it was worth a hundred and fifty thousand and change.

"I need a six-pack of Mexican," shouted Alabama.

"You always need a six-pack of Mexican, and you always drink a twelve-pack, man," screamed King into the wind as Alabama nodded. "An' I get the Sprite so's I can drive you home."

"Mexican don't agree with your muscles, King," roared Alabama. He was having a good time. He was sixty and at last life was getting simpler. It was bikes, beer, and the mountains now, and nothing else. He hadn't shot a photograph for ten years. Not that anybody knew, of course. It was a carefully kept secret. For thirty years he had taken photographs of the nature that he loved, and he had sold only a tiny fraction of his stockpiled prints. It had been more than enough to establish his reputation. So now, when he needed money to finance the environmental wars he ceaselessly fought, he merely pulled a few fifties or sixties negatives from the vault and had King print them up. The sun rising over the mountain in 1955 looked much as it had this morning, and the 1989, together with the scrawled Alabama signature, was good for a hundred thousand minimum any day of the week. When the critics traced the stages of the development of his work in prestigious magazines like *Artforum*, Alabama would laugh like a drain.

He could remember the actual day the thought had occurred to him. He had read somewhere that there were more photographs in the world than bricks. The idea had zapped him right between the eyes. All he was doing was recording beauty, drawing people's attention to it in an interesting and novel way. But all around, nature, the ultimate raw material of that beauty, was being destroyed by greedy, unthinking people in the name of profit, progress, or profligacy. Surely the true artist, the person who really cared about beauty as he did, should make it his mission to preserve that beauty rather than merely recording its disappearance. From that moment on he hadn't taken a photograph. Instead, he had become the champion of every leaf, every branch, of every animal and insect that existed in the beloved hills in which he had always lived.

But if that was the main part of his life, this was another. It was the weekend, and L.A. County was a hundred degrees hot rather than the usual seventy-eight that Neil Simon maintained was the same number as the interesting people that lived there. So today he was doing what he always did on a Saturday. He was going to the Rock House in Seminole Hot Springs to hang out with the bikers, drink cold beer, and eat glutinous chili in the sun-drenched canyons.

As the Harley turned the corner in the road, the shining vision unfolded. There were maybe two hundred bikes parked in line abreast along one side of the highway, a hundred more on the other—two long, luscious ribbons of chrome and paint, gleaming and glistening in the bright sunlight. Over to the right, set back from the road, were a couple of nondescript wooden buildings, one approached by high steps. A sprawling courtyard joined them, in the middle of which stood a magnificent sycamore tree. All around this central tree swirled a black river of leather. The bikers were everywhere, swarming like flies over the picnic tables, arguing, roaring, shouting, swearing, and each man, each biker girl, held in his or her hand a can of beer. Strangely for such a gathering, the floor of the courtyard was clean. No human detritus marred it. There were no cigarette butts, no beer cans, no napkins stained with ketchup, no nastier items. All these unwanted objects were stowed in the two or three vast bins that were strategically placed throughout the eating and drinking area.

As Alabama rode into view, the crowd acclaimed him.

"Hi, man. Hi, Alabama," roared the bikers in raucous unison.

He raised a gnarled hand to acknowledge them, and, riding right up to the door of the restaurant, he parked next door to the sign that read NO PARKING. It was his slot. Somewhere in Detroit the chairman of General Motors had one. Well, so did Alabama.

"Okay, King, my man. I'm drinking Dos Equis. What are you eating? Biker burger, like forever?"

He barged into the Rock House restaurant as King set off to the next-door Rock Store where they sold the cold beer.

Inside, the filthy cubicles quieted briefly as he walked in, and then erupted again with a muted howl of universal welcome. They didn't throng him, they just let him know that they knew he was there, and were glad, and then they were back to the boasting and the baiting and the banter that bikers loved. Alabama noticed Mickey Rourke at one table, surrounded by the nobodies who were his equals for this one day. Gary Busey, Leif Garrett, and Justine Bateman leaned over to wave "hi" from the upper level of the diner. It was like that, this place, and it was older than most of the restaurants within thirty miles of the center of L.A., the city that wasn't supposed to have one. They shot movies at the Rock House from time to time, and celebrities like Jon Peters who loved bikes dropped in and acted ordinary, but mostly everybody hung out in the sun and enjoyed being around people who were just like them.

A guy sidled up to Alabama as he put in his food order. He palmed a Nikon onto the counter.

"Hey, Alabama, you shoot good pictures. What's my best lens for this, man?"

"Throw it away," growled Alabama pleasantly. "It gets in the way of your eyes."

"No, I'm serious, man."

"So am I, man. Take too many photographs and you forget to see. The Japanese are totally blind. Near as they get to nature is photo albums."

The greasy bacon/cheeseburger they called "biker" hit the counter. The bowl of chili—cheese, onions, and green peppers added—came next. Alabama scooped it all up.

"But I want to make some serious art, Alabama," said the Rock House regular. What he meant was some serious bucks like Alabama.

"Art, fart," said Alabama, smiling. "God's the only artist around, man. I never met a human could compete with him. Look around you. Relax. Sit back and enjoy it. Trade in the Nikon and send the money to me. I'll try and make sure there's some nature left for you to enjoy."

He slapped the embryonic photographer hard on the shoulder to show that there were no bad feelings, and he wandered out into the sunshine to get started on the beer.

King beckoned him from Alabama's favorite vantage point, a scuffed, brown plastic-covered banquette at the back of the garden where the bikers were gathered. He mumbled some greetings as he pushed through the crowd, but he didn't stop. He was thirsty.

He flopped down and took the beer that King handed him, nipping the neck of the Dos Equis between thumb and forefinger where the lime was wedged.

"Nice day, King," he mumbled, burping his satisfaction at the brightness of the sunshine and the hazy heat blanket that had settled over the canyon. He scratched the lobe of his ear, and then at the T-shirt where it clung to his full stomach, and he thanked the Lord he wasn't having to endure the industrial-strength bullshit that right now was being ladled out at Richard Latham's "Hello, Malibu" party.

"Jeez, Alabam, take a look at that," said King suddenly.

Alabama squinted into the sunlight.

A vast man stood in the middle of the courtyard over by the central sycamore tree, and he was not a sight for weak stomachs. He was a great beast of a person with a mountainous ass, powerful legs, and glistening, bulbous muscles. The tattoos that ran along his arms were Nazi in origin, swastikas in red and black, crosses, eagles, skulls, crossbones, and other skeletal objects. He was naked above the waist and in large letters across his broad, sweaty back was tattooed the slogan FEAR THIS WHITE SUPREMACIST. He wore a peaked cap and black pebble sunglasses. A pair of handcuffs dangled from the back pocket of his leather jeans and an enormous "Crocodile" Dundee knife swung from his belt. On his scuffed black boots were silver spurs. He gripped a can of Budweiser in his right hand. In his left was an outsize polystyrene cup. By his side stood a thin bleached blonde. On the edges of good-looking, she wore a denim jacket over tough, braless tits, and a pair of cutoffs. It was clear that she belonged to the white supremacist who was to be feared. It was also clear that the incredible hulk wanted to emphasize this fact.

"Fill me up, slag," he boomed.

The local bikers exchanged glances, and some sort of silence descended on the previously rowdy crowd. The man mountain was in trouble mode. They could recognize the symptoms. He was cruising for a bruising and in any fight he looked to be a likely winner. One or two of the regulars looked across uncertainly at Alabama.

The girl took the Budweiser from his right hand and the cup from his left, and poured the one into the other in a gesture of total and unconditional subservience. Please and thank you were not in the stranger's vocabulary. He took the cup and the empty can, and he tossed the latter into the air. It arced through the sunlight and landed, clattering on the ground, a few feet from Alabama. Next he lifted the cup to his mouth and he downed the beer in one gurgling swallow.

Alabama stood up. He stepped forward, bent down, and picked up the empty Bud. Saying nothing at all, he dropped it into a nearby bin. He returned to his seat. The silence was now complete. The Rock House regulars were quiet as the grave. Only strangers and masochists dropped litter around Alabama.

The stranger seemed to sense the unease. He looked around and followed the direction of the eyes until he was staring straight at Alabama. He smiled, a hideous, leering smile because he had worked out what was going down. The old buzzard on the bench was the guy who had picked up his discarded Bud. Obviously he was some environmentalist freak, and clearly, too, he was some sort of respected figure around here. That was why the milksop bikers were eyeballing the old crone. He let out a rumbling guffaw. Shit, the guy was *old!* Late fifties, maybe even sixty. Who *were* these chicken noodle California bikers? The sun had clearly burned the balls off them. They took their orders from the Geritol Kid. Well, he'd give them a lesson in the eating of humble pie. He dropped the empty cup. Then, carefully, his eyes never leaving Alabama's, he ground his heel on it, laughing defiantly as he did so.

"Pick it up," said Alabama. He spoke softly, but he didn't need to shout.

In the pregnant silence his words lanced across the space that separated him from the white supremacist.

In response, the stranger smiled a loathsome smile. He reached down and he pulled out the knife, and he turned it around in the sunlight as if he were roasting it on a spit. "I would, old man," he rasped, "but I'm saving energy to carve my initials on that tree."

He ambled toward the sycamore.

Alabama stood up once again. He put down the Dos Equis on the seat. He breathed in deeply, inflating his barrel chest, and he pushed out both his arms to the powder-blue sky, stretching them, flexing the ropelike muscles. Now he exhaled, his sigh weary, resigned to the *que sera*. He moved slowly, like a sunburned snake on a hot highway.

Out of the corner of his eye, the stranger watched Alabama's approach, sizing him up. He was old, but he was big, and he was cool and there was something about the confident way he walked. There was no fear near him. None at all.

The stranger held the knife up to the tree, and he ripped at a poster pinned to it—one about fighting the new helmet law.

"Don't touch my tree," said Alabama.

They were close now, and the stranger could see the glint in the old man's eyes, saw the flexing of his sinewy muscles, but again he laughed because, of course, he had the knife.

"I don't take no orders from no grandfathers," he sneered.

Alabama spoke slowly as if to a lesser form of life, and his voice was arctic cold in the midday heat.

"Listen, shithead," he drawled. "You touch my tree an' I'll carve my name in miniature on your needle dick."

The stranger's mouth dropped open as the words began to wander around his brain. He was only halfway to realizing that he had been insulted, about a quarter of the way to realizing exactly what had been *said*. But already he knew that he would have to cut the old boy open. The knife jerked up from his side, as his mind fought for the appropriate response.

Twenty paces behind Alabama, King wondered if his friend and employer had bitten off more than he could chew. But long experience told him not to worry. All around, the others felt the same. In the quiet, the expectation shone from their faces. How could the stranger know about Alabama and trees? It had taken them a while to learn.

"You fucking corpse . . ." started the stranger, but he never finished. Alabama's cowboy-booted leg had liftoff. The instep, dusty and nail hard, met the would-be sculptor's crotch at the point of its maximum upward momentum. As the irresistible force of the Alabama boot collided with the immovable object of the stranger's pelvic bone, the unfortunate bits of flesh between them were crushed to pulp. The biker sank to his knees as the sky danced around in the heavens and the pain promised to come later. He dropped the knife. "Aw shit," he said on the tide of air that rushed from his lungs.

Alabama took his leg back. He stooped down and he picked up the knife. He leaned forward and he placed the tip against the distended jugular vein of the white supremacist who was to be feared.

"You dropped your Styrofoam cup on the ground," hissed Alabama. "An' it ain't biodegradable."

"Aaaaaaah," screamed the stranger. The pain had arrived, elbowing out the numb void that had gripped his crotch. His head shook from side to side, his eyes swam, and in his ears was a word he'd never heard before.

Alabama ignored his scream as his own would have been ignored if he'd lost the millisecond fight.

He whispered into the ear of the wounded psychopath. "The plastic is made of these long-chain hydrocarbons, man. Don't nothin' break 'em down. I'll show you. Eat it."

It took a bit of getting used to, but he managed it. In many ways eating the remains of the plastic cup was the most impressive thing he'd managed in his miserable life so far.

Alabama stood up and he tossed the knife into the trash as he went back to his seat. But he didn't feel like drinking anymore, and somebody else could pick up the pieces. He signaled to King, and in a minute or two the Heritage was gunning, and the old street fighter, the biker, the beer guzzler, the environmentalist, and the most famous photographer in the world was going home.

$-4-$

PAT PARKER ROARED past Sunset Boulevard in the open Jeep Islander, and her blond hair streamed behind her California-style as it was supposed to. The late afternoon sun burned hot on her face, and to her left, along the beach, the surf was up, and the wetsuited teenagers were still riding the waves. She held on to the wheel tightly as she played the dangerous video game called Pacific Coast Highway, where the prize was a safe arrival, and the penalty was the fire department chopper ride to the hospital in Santa Monica. Boy, was it a long way from New York! She had been out of the Big Apple for seven hours, and it felt like a lifetime.

She flicked the switch of the radio, found a surfing station playing vintage Beach Boys, and wondered if she dared attempt the death-defying application of total block to her exposed nose. No way. Of the various life-threatening options, melanoma looked deeply attractive. So she shook her head, exhilarated by the sun and the warm wind, and the new mood that flowed through her. This was what she had needed. A fresh beginning. A challenge. A change of direction. She felt like singing, and she laughed into the breeze as she ran over in her mind the events that had brought her here.

It was three months since the dying Mapplethorpe had made his enigmatic suggestion that she go see Alabama in Malibu. At first she had dismissed it. What would the grand old man of American photography want with the trendy chronicler of the "vitally important" New York night scene? Alabama was a legend. He was landscapes and portraits and one-man retrospectives at the Whitney and the Met. She was prancing poseurs and posturing pansies in hellholes that rejoiced in the inventiveness of their ugliness. He was medals in the Rose Garden, groveling reviews in the *Times,* sleek Fifty-seventh Street galleries, and megabuck collectors. She was five hundred dollars a throw if she was lucky, spreads in *On the Avenue* and *Details,* Amaretto di Pat, loose talk of a cooperative effort with the ubiquitous Tama. They couldn't be further apart . . . and yet . . . and yet. Wasn't that what she needed? A total turnaround. Had Picasso shrunk from the journey from blue to cubes? Had Goya allowed himself to be stuck at naked duchesses, and forsworn the new frontiers of madness and black Satans? Had Gauguin slaved on in the Paris stock exchange, Michelangelo balked at the roof of the Sistine Chapel? The list was endless of artists who'd risked change, but it was longer of those who hadn't. Pat Parker didn't want to be in the last category, and the weird experience at Indochine, when she had seemed to see the ghost of her dead friend, had helped make up her mind.

Over the next weeks she had gone through the entire body of her work and had selected six prints. With her heart in her boots, and the prospect of ridicule hanging over her head, she packed them up and Fed-Exed them, with a short note, to Alabama.

> Dear Alabama,
> Robert Mapplethorpe suggested that I do this. I think these six prints are my best work, and I'm not sure that I even like them. I'm at a sort of crisis—photography-wise. Would you see me? I could come to Malibu.

She hadn't expected an answer. At the very most she supposed there might have been a short, polite note from some patronizing administrative assistant. But the Western Union telegram had not minced its words. It had said simply, "Come. Alabama." And she had obeyed.

Now she was in Malibu, and soon she would meet the mythical figure who had issued the incredibly cryptic invitation. Her heart speeded. Would it be a disaster? On paper, almost certainly. But what did paper know? One thing was going for her. Alabama was known to be an eccentric, and, of all the people in life, Pat Parker got on with those best of all. She looked out to the beach. God, the sea was blue. And so was the sky, dotted with gulls and swooping brown pelicans fishing lazily in the stiff breeze. To her right the cliffs rose roughly, their face scarred by countless landslides that would have closed the road she now traveled. A sign saying GETTY told her where the richest and dullest art was, and soon she was cruising into the heart of old Malibu past the pier of Alice's Restaurant, where Arlo Guthrie maintained you could get anything you wanted; past the gates to the Colony where the movie stars had once lived; past the Hughes Market, its architecture brand-new ancient Spanish mission; past the bleak neatness of Pepperdine University, whose hilarious mission impossible was to push mind stuff in Malibu, where the only thing that anyone cared about was bodies.

She knew only vaguely where she was going. Someone at Alabama's called King had told her where to turn right off PCH. Then she was to head straight up into the mountains. She could see them now, stretched out against the skyline, battleship gray in the sunlight, massive, mighty, majestic. He lived somewhere up there in the heart of the hills that some called Malibu and others called Santa Monica, and it was rumored that he acted as if they belonged to him. Pat took a deep breath. Everyone she had spoken to had agreed on one thing. Alabama either liked you, or he didn't. You were his friend, or his enemy. Toward nothing and nobody was he neutral. So she hadn't packed much in the way of clothes. If things went badly, she would just walk away. In the pocket of her faded Levi's the ticket was round trip.

Malibu was changing. The speeding highway now whizzed past small shops whose neat neon said serious beach and body—pastel T-shirts, Day-Glo swimsuits, tone for the copper people. There were sexy-looking restaurants with names like Something Fishy, Zooma Sushi, and the Coral Beach Cantina, and there were designer gyms and adobe mini-malls, their lots well stocked with Samurais, Wranglers, and Porsches, those potent icons of the Southland dream. On either side of her, fellow death dancers on the freeway, were the product of the fabulous California gene pool. The impossibly pretty girls tossed their American hair in time to the thundering basses of their Blaupunkts, while blond surf supermen posed, pouted, and powered their cars into nonexistent spaces in the teeth of the oncoming traffic like kamikazes in search of an honorable end. Bearded agents in black Beamers looked suitably serious, as they creamed past wetbacks in bangers from East L.A. Creepy, crawling families of Hertz tourists rubbernecked the roadside as they searched for the elusive spirit that went by the name of Malibu, while bearded bikers, their sunglassed eyes set in time warp on some vision of a Peter Fonda past, rode proudly, heads and handlebars held high, on their endless journey to nowhere.

Pat Parker eased the Jeep into the right-hand lane as the horns of her fellow travelers blared in universal irritation. Some of the beautiful people even found the energy to shout indistinct abuse into the ozone as they rushed past her on Narcissus errands to the star-studded futures that they knew would be theirs.

Pat hung the right and laughed at the angst so surprisingly revealed. In New York being pissed off was a way of life, an intelligent response to the crime, the temperature, and the noise. What was the excuse here? The souring of dreams? The blandness of perfection? The predictability of yet another wonderful day in Paradise? Maybe she'd find out. She climbed the winding road, and each S bend delivered its visual feast as she snaked higher and higher into the hills. Above her, hawks rode the thermal currents of the canyon, searching the scrub of the chaparral for mice, while on either side patches of brilliant color lit up the brush. There were tall white-plumed yucca plants, blazing red patches of wild fuchsia, and clumps of creamy yellow bush poppies. Mustard, wild tobacco, and castor beans grew along the roadside, while the air was heavy with the scent of purple and black sage. It was a beautiful wilderness, dotted with outsize sandstone rocks, and all the time life erupted around her; the flash of a blue jay, its harsh cry preceding its brief appearance; quarrelsome groups of jet-black crows disputing the ownership of telephone poles; the sudden disturbance of the vegetation by an unseen animal—a coyote, a deer, a rare bobcat?

All around her was naked beauty, and Pat Parker, who understood such things, vibrated in tune to it. It was what she had been looking for. Here in Alabama's mountains she would make the photographs that would matter. She knew it with absolute certainty. Everything that had gone before was dress rehearsal. In a thousand sweaty stink boxes of the night she had perfected the technique of photography. Now, she could afford to forget about the skills she had acquired. The only thing that mattered was the vision, and God had given her the eye to see the wonder of the nature he had created. On an impulse, she slowed down. She steered the Jeep off the road, and, at the edge of the cliff, she stopped, turning off the ignition and basking in the warm wonder of the silence. She got out and reached into the back for the

Nikon, clipping on a 28mm wide-angle lens. Way below her was the dark blue carpet of the ocean, the specks of the surfers tiny against the white peaks of the waves. The canyon framed it, dark gray and rusty brown, and the birds soared on the hot wind against the ceiling of a cloudless sky. On remote control, she flicked the f-stop to 11, the speed to 125, the distance to infinity. The light reading was in her head, the lightness of being was in her heart. This would be the first photograph of her new life.

Then she saw the movement. Below her, in the thick bushes beneath the shade of a giant oak, something was stirring. It was big, threateningly big on the lonely roadside, and Pat Parker caught her breath as the beauty of the moment receded to be replaced by sudden fear. At once she was aware that she was a stranger in these rugged mountains. Mean streets, with their well-known dangers, were her natural habitat. Here she was a foreigner. She lowered the camera. She looked over her shoulder toward the Jeep. She looked down at the continuing disturbance, and her legs were already asking that they be allowed to run. What animals lived here? What kind of *people?* Red-necked mountain men, dangerously unpredictable in their interbred remoteness? The sort of person who might enjoy frightening a long-legged New York photographer halfway to her grave?

The voice that wafted up from below, however, was not scary. Instead, it was scathingly cynical.

"Good idea. Good idea for a chocolate box," it boomed. "Or one of those postcards to send the folks back home."

The face poked out from the bush. It was pugnacious, its leathery lines cracked up in a patronizing smile, and the small goatee jutted up at Pat like an exclamation mark. In answer, Pat Parker's Nikon flashed up like a mugger's Saturday night special, and her finger darted down on the shutter.

"There," she exclaimed, her voice heavy with sarcasm, "now I've got myself a garden gnome."

Alabama had never, ever before been described as a garden gnome. Of all the things he didn't want to be, a garden gnome had to be high on the list. In the Rock House unwise bikers had called him ostensibly ruder things, and facial rearrangement had followed to the satisfaction of all. But this insulter was a woman. A very good-looking, very feisty, very quick-witted woman, and it was with a frisson of surprise that Alabama realized that he wasn't angry at all.

He continued his act of physical revelation, and, as his massive bulk exploded from the plant that had hidden him, Pat Parker realized that a garden gnome was not what she had "got." What she *had* got was the side of a house, a land whale, a menacing mountain man whose T-shirt, dirty and torn, read unequivocally, I SHOOT PHOTOGRAPHERS.

She took a step back. He took a step forward. Her supercilious smile faded from her face, as one of genuine amusement crept over his.

"A garden gnome?" he said, his voice thick with incredulous humor.

"It was just the way your head poked out of the greenery, I mean . . . I mean . . . I didn't mean . . ."

But already she could see the laughter in his intelligent eyes, and her pseudoapology petered out. It wasn't every day that Pat Parker was accused of taking a boring photograph, especially by some ignorant, superannuated biker in the Santa Monica Mountains, who should have bothered to take time out to grow up.

"Well, I guess I deserved it, but from here your photograph did look major-league dull," said Alabama.

"From there isn't from here. It's lesson one in photography," said Pat evenly. It was. Millimeters made the difference. Washington Square only looked good if you were Kertész looking down on it.

"Oh, it *is*, is it?" chuckled Alabama. He continued to advance upon her. She held her ground, chin stuck out in defiance. "And what," boomed the greatest photographer in the world, "is lesson two?"

"Don't criticize someone else's work unless you have *some* idea of what it is you are talking about," said Pat.

Alabama's smile broadened. She was getting angry again. Her eyes were sparkling. The indignation was heavy in the words. Lord, she was a looker, and her anger made her more beautiful. He just had to wind her up one more turn. A garden gnome, indeed!

"Work!" he guffawed. "*Work!* Jeez! If that's work, so is jerking off."

"Don't," said Pat with all the coldness she could muster, "be so disgusting."

A disgusting garden gnome. It was a first. At Alabama's stage of life, not many things were.

He had reached her now, clambering up onto the edge of the road, puffing slightly from the exertion of the climb. Up close she was better than from down below. Her eyes were wide with righteous indignation, and huge blue irises swam in a white sea beneath no-nonsense bushy eyebrows. Her voluptuous mouth was peeled back in a snarl over perfect teeth, and her whole body, from the top of her lustrous hair to the toes of her scuffed cowboy boots, leaned toward him as if it longed to become an offensive weapon. Her blue denim top was open to show the cleavage of clearly braless breasts, and her ballet dancer's butt strained against the indigo of faded 501's at the top of rainbow legs. To Alabama, it was definitely time to make up, if not to kiss. She was old enough to be his grandchild, but there had been younger.

"Listen, I'm sorry. I'm teasing. Are you a photographer?"

He pushed out his hand at her. She didn't take it.

"Yes," she barked at him.

"In which case it may be that you have heard of me," he drawled. "They call me Alabama."

"They do?" said Pat Parker in a voice that seemed to come from at least another mountain range.

This would be an excellent moment for the earthquake, she thought. The earth could open now. She could swallowtail in, and then it could close again, and that would be that. Alabama. Alabama, the disgusting garden gnome. Alabama, to whom she had just taught lessons one and two in photography. She recognized him now, of course, from the photographs. But it was a tad too late. That she hadn't expected to meet him erupting from the canyon bushes would hardly do for extenuating circumstances.

There was a rushing noise in her head.

"Listen, I'm most terribly . . ."

He waved away her apology as if swatting a fly.

"And you are?"

"I'm the Pat Parker who was coming to see you." Her voice was strangled. The past tense seemed absolutely inescapable.

For a second he paused. Then his massive hand pumped up and landed on his broad thigh with a resounding *thwack*. The peal of delighted laughter exploded from the depths of his bull neck.

"Well, that's wonderful, Pat Parker," he boomed. "For a moment there I thought I was going to miss out on lesson three."

DICK LATHAM slid into the New York boardroom of Cosmos Pictures like a little boy late for assembly. His shy smile said he was so sorry for hanging everyone up, for the rudeness, for the personal inefficiency. He shrugged his shoulders in apology, and he sidled toward the Hepplewhite chairman's chair, motioning for everyone to continue as if he weren't there. The man who leaped up to pull back his seat was nodded down again by the Latham eyes. Oh no, he didn't want to put anybody out. He'd just sit down and shut up and let the boys get right on with it.

The CEO of Cosmos, however, had acquired a speech impediment. His formerly smooth delivery was now a spurting, staccato affair full of half-finished sentences, cul-de-sacs, and mysterious nonsequiturs. He fished around with his finger in the collar of his Sea Island cotton shirt and the words of the TV bite went round and round in his mind. "Never let them see you sweat." Well, he'd blown it. Here in the boardroom, beneath the heavy-duty art, the cunning John Saladino lighting, before the eyes of the superboss, the moisture was dripping from him like dew on a Smoky Mountain morning.

"Like I was saying . . . I mean . . . oftentimes . . . oftentimes . . . when a studio changes hands the slate is looked at . . . is gone through with a view to . . . I mean, so that the new management might want to change direction . . ."

He stared in desperation down the mahogany table as if the gleaming wood could help him escape from his verbal mess. *Oftentimes* was a word he had never used before. Now it filled up his mind like a football. The dictionary had just been boiled down. There was nothing left but "oftentimes . . . oftentimes . . ." And what did he mean "the new management"? He was the *old* management. The whole table was the old management. That there might one day *be* a new management was why the gardenia-scented air was tinged with the unmistakable smell of fear.

Dick Latham smiled. He sat way back in his chair and his immaculately manicured nails drummed on the shining table. He looked up at the Titian, over at the Rembrandt; his laughing eyes scanned the stricken faces of the Cosmos management. They tried to smile back. God, how they tried. Mouths were ripped back over bonded teeth, eyes tried to scrumple up in some pale imitation of warmth. It was as if the executioner, on a whim, had decided to spare the victim who managed the best smile on the edge of eternity. Hearts were simply not in it. Latham reached forward and pulled the Limoges coffee cup toward him, as the waiter materialized at his side.

"What is it?" said Dick Latham.

The Cosmos CEO stopped. At last someone had said something interesting. For brief seconds he could relax. Mr. Latham was inquiring about the brand of coffee.

"Kenyan, sir. From the Rift Valley, Mr. Kent says. Will that do?"

Latham nodded, as the stream poured sedately into the porcelain from the Georgian silver pot.

He waved a hand in the air, the hand that lied "Don't let me interrupt." He looked carefully at the two-bit agent, one-time lawyer, and general Hollywood hanger-on whom he had inherited as his studio boss. God, he was disgusting. Small and fat, built for a foul-smelling cigar and for the game of musical chairs that was job hunting in Tinsel Town. What deals had he struck with the devil to reach his moment of mini-fame? From the series of box-office bombs he had presided over, talent was clearly not one of his attributes. Nor, apparently, was public speaking.

"So, as oftentimes we do this . . . sort of review . . . oftentimes we should do it now."

He sat down suddenly as if he had been sandbagged, and he nodded to the bearded, bespectacled man at his side.

This man now stood up, adjusted his glasses, coughed, and began to speak in a small, thin voice. His eyes were fixed on the open manila folder on the table in front of him.

"In the usual way I have divided the projects into those currently in production; the definite done deals that are presently green lighted; and the preproduction development deals that have either reached step status or in which we have significant upfront exposure. I won't deal with projects in turnaround." He paused. The roomful of eyes were on Latham. The billionaire was magazines and publishing. Would he understand the movie jive? Would it matter? The head of production droned on.

"But I should just start by saying that CinemaScope test marketing of *Home Fires* is extremely encouraging. They're getting sixty-five percent A's from the preview audiences, which is blockbuster bullish. We're hoping for a huge opening on Memorial Day."

"How many screens?" said Latham suddenly. His smile had gone. The laughing eyes were narrow.

They all sat up straight. It was the right question.

The studio boss discovered an enormous interest in the intricate plasterwork of the ceiling, then in the state of his nails, finally in the design of the Chinese silk rug.

"A thousand, I think," said the production guy unhappily. "We're going for a slow, steady build," he added in desperation, aware that this did not exactly gel with the hoped-for "huge opening" on Memorial Day.

"Budget?" snapped Latham with killer speed.

Oh, dear! He'd gotten there. He knew. He was on top of it.

The production head was beginning to fall apart.

"Over the line or under the line?" he tried, in a forlorn attempt to stave off disaster.

"Both," said Latham with asplike deadliness.

"Thirty-five/forty," admitted the broken man.

It was no good. A forty-million-dollar picture, whose stars alone had cost five million, could not afford to open on as few as a thousand screens. Two thousand plus and the marketing surveys might be meaningful. A mere thousand and the picture was doomed.

In the silence they all thought first of their careers. Where would they go when the music stopped? Where would they find the seats for their asses that would enable the game to continue, the platinum cards to remain in play, the people who now loved them to love them still?

"So *Home Fires* is burning," said Dick Latham in summary. "It would appear that Cosmos has not yet ended its losing streak," he added.

They didn't move. Would it be quick? Would it hurt? Would he do them all at once? Here. Now. Or would he leave a few of them around to keep the offices clean, to hang out the welcome mats for their replacements.

"But it just so happens, this is no big deal," said Latham, "because, as from this minute, Cosmos Pictures is no longer in the movie business."

What! They were history, but so was the studio? That wasn't how it happened. Studios, like cans of bad sardines, were for trading, not opening and closing. The cast of characters changed, but the studios remained the same. They were owned by conglomerates, or soft drink companies, or by superrich individuals who fancied movie star ass. Currently, the Japanese were sniffing around. Tomorrow maybe it would be Martians. You could do anything to a studio—you could rape it, ransack it, polish it, cherish it—but you couldn't close it down. It was an unAmerican activity, like burning the flag or sandblasting Mount Rushmore. Dick Latham, apparently so smooth, suave, and well informed, had clearly gone off his rocker.

The CEO, from the relative safety of unemployment, actually found the balls to say it. "You can't do that," he blurted out.

"Well," drawled Latham, "I think you'll find that I can. Cosmos is sitting on around a billion dollars' worth of prime L.A. real estate. If I were to sell it off, close it down, and put the billion with the Treasury, I'd be seeing close on a hundred million a year . . . against a retrospective five-year average profit of . . . well, you tell me."

His eye found the Cosmos finance man, the only one in the room apart from Latham with a gleam in his eye.

"Twenty million, tops, depending on how you account for—"

"Precisely," agreed Latham, cutting off the accountant in midsentence. "And what I say is, 'Why bother to make bad movies when you can be making good money?'"

There was no answer to that, or rather the right answer could not publicly be admitted. The truth of the matter was that it was far more *fun* to make bad movies than good money. A billion in Treasuries was no fun at all. A billion financing your fantasies was fascinatingly fantastic. This was the bottom line that Hollywood always denied, as it preached instead the propaganda of business efficiency. None of the has-beens in the room was about to articulate it now.

"So, gentlemen, I am afraid it only remains for me to ask you all for resignations, and of course to say that which goes without saying, that all contracts will be scrupulously adhered to."

He stood up. He smoothed down the nonexistent creases in the jacket of his immaculate suit, and he smiled once more as he cast them into the outer darkness.

"Good luck," he said, as he walked quickly to the door.

He closed the oak doors behind him and stalked briskly through the anteroom. The secretary, nearly pretty, smiled hard as he passed.

"Mr. Havers is waiting in your office, as you asked," she said breathlessly. "And then you have a one o'clock luncheon appointment with Emma Guinness at the Four Seasons."

"Good," snapped Latham. He ignored the elevator, and instead took the stairs to his penthouse office. He moved fast. That had been fun. Twenty-six executives all executed at one sitting. Must be some sort of a record for face-to-face firing. Lord, how he hated incompetents. God, how he loved the Guinness tits.

He burst into his office. Havers jumped up from the sofa.

"How did it go?"

"Great! They tried to give me some bullshit about *Home Fires* turning Cosmos around. Can you believe it?"

"Yeah," drawled Havers. "I imagine there'll be a few people out there who'll prefer to go see Indiana III."

Latham laughed. He liked Havers. He liked the fact that he was ruthless and dispassionate in his sincere pursuit of profit. It was why he had elevated him to the number-two slot at Latham Communications.

"So shall I go ahead and hit the wire services with this?"

"Give Liz Smith an hour or two first. I owe her one. Okay?"

"Who gets the real estate? Fred Sands? Douglas?"

"No, give it to Steven Shapiro at Stan Herman. Give him a two-month exclusive, then you can open it up to the others."

Latham walked over to the partners' desk, to the picture window with its view over Central Park.

"Tell Steve that he should come and see me at Broad Beach over the weekend. I'm going down to Malibu tonight."

"I'll have the 727 stand by."

"No, don't bother with it. Let's economize. I'll do an MGM. I want to check it out. Never done it before. Book me a private room. Guinness will be coming with me."

He didn't mind treating Havers like a gofer. In the Latham world they were all gofers, whatever the fancy titles on their doors.

"When do we go to the second phase of the Cosmos deal?"

Latham sat down, shooting the cuffs of his blue poplin Bonwit-Teller shirt. He swung to the right in the swivel chair. He swung to the left. He checked himself out in the Chinese Chippendale mirror. Yeah, he looked good. The New and Lingwood neckties were so White's. The tan was beginning to fade, though. He'd have to work on it over the weekend.

"Yes, phase two, Cosmos. The hornet's nest," he mused over his long, sensitive fingers. He breathed in deeply. He wasn't sure about the Calvin Klein Obsession. It wasn't at all subtle, was in fact rather sickly. He'd throw it out. Go back to Royal Yacht. It wasn't so sensual, but it was effortlessly correct.

"We're close to closing on the Canyon tract. It was peanuts. Five million bucks, six hundred acres. The old fart wanted a nondevelopment clause in the contract. He got an extra five hundred thousand instead." Havers sneered visibly at the weakness of humanity, as he smiled at the awesome power of cash.

"And it runs next to Alabama's land," said Latham to himself, a faraway expression on his face.

"Yeah," said Havers. "I wonder what he'll do when he finds out you're going to build a movie studio next to him."

Latham chuckled as he contemplated the enormity of what he was planning. He was going to build a brand-spanking-new Cosmos studio slap bang in the middle of Alabama's Malibu hills. The famous Cosmos trademark, the spinning globe against the star-spangled universe, would live on. The name of the legendary studio would not die. He would build it for nickels and dimes on the Malibu land he had just bought for small change. And most of the billion dollars he realized from the prime real estate on which the studio now sat would sit safely on loan to the United States government. It was a deal created in heaven, a dream deal that made the juices bubble and flow inside him.

But one thing was quite certain.

When he discovered that Dick Latham, posing as an ecological savior, was in fact an environmental rapist, Alabama was going to go stark, staring, raving mad.

—

"SHE DIDN'T!"

"She *did!*"

"In front of *everybody?*"

"Of everybody. I was standing right there. So was Jennifer. Like *ask* her."

"Omigod . . . I can hardly believe it really happened. It's just so deeply . . . crucial."

"And he said . . . I can't remember the exact words. But he told her she was disgusting and unprofessional and that her clothes were a complete *mess.*"

"What was she wearing?"

"A dreadful tulle thing—like a ballet dancer, with this humungous yellow belt and Alice in Wonderland shoes. She looked like Doris Day dressed for

Halloween, or one of Cinderella's sisters. I can't *tell* you what she looked like. You know the kinda thing she wears."

"What did she *say?*"

"Nothing. I mean, she was blown away. She was totally destroyed, and this great-looking guy had pissed all over her. It was unreal. Totally and completely *unreal.*"

"I'd just die. I'd have to hide. How can she come in and like . . . carry on, when she knows we all *know?*"

"Amanda says that's what used to happen in England when she was working at *Class* magazine. She was unfazed. They were real mean to her, you know how the English can be with all those words they use. Apparently she came from the North, which is like coming from 'Joisey,' and she changed her name from Doreen something-or-other to Emma Guinness, which is like being called Whitney or Cabot Lodge, and she took all these lessons to get her accent straight. Amanda says they were merciless with her. They found out she'd screwed her way to the top job at some out-of-town magazine, and they used to call her the British Open, after a *golf* competition."

Samantha du Pont and Mary Polk, the fashion editor, dissolved into laughter, scattering the colored pencils, the layouts, the transparencies, and the empty coffee cups across their desks. In the lunch break at *New Celebrity* the atmosphere of manic delight was building fast. Samantha, who headed up features, had actually been *there* on the infamous Juilliard evening when their hated boss had been so gloriously humiliated, and she was milking the fact for every last drop of its dramatic potential.

"Anyway, for years Emma just took it all. Never said a thing. Never laughed, never cried, just hung in there and swallowed it. Amanda says Victoria Brougham, the editor, used to ask her about the working classes. You know, like 'How will the working classes react to this, Emma, you're the expert, how will they feel about that?' They used to put bottles of Guinness, which is some kind of beer, on her desk and laugh about her 'cousins,' and they were so cruel because she was so gross and pushy and brash, exactly like she is here.

"And then one day, the magazine changed hands and before anyone knew it, they made Emma editor."

The manic buzz of excitement quieted. The sun of the collective pleasure was suddenly obscured by cloud.

"Amanda says Emma tape recorded Victoria bad-mouthing the new owner. Apparently he'd made all his own money, which is not at all the thing to have done in England. Emma played the tape back to him. Victoria had mimicked his accent or something. That's what Amanda says, anyway. She says they're real sensitive about that kind of thing over there."

"And then they all got fired."

"They sure did."

An uneasy silence descended. It had been three weeks since Emma Guinness had been imported by Richard Latham to take over his rapidly fading *Celebrity* magazine, and so far Samantha and Mary were still there.

They were not, however, including pensions in their longrange financial planning. They were working on the last edition of the old-style *Celebrity* magazine. *New Celebrity* had been conceived, but was in embryo and no one in the magazine's offices could cross their hearts and say they truly believed they would be present at its birth.

The two friends tried to stay "up." There had to be some more mileage in the Juilliard debacle somewhere.

"What was the guy's name?"

"Tony Valentino. Forget Rudolph. This was the real thing. I mean, he was adorable. It's the only time I've ever seen Emma show any taste. It was incredible hunk time, and I don't even *like* muscles."

"God, we ought to do something for him. I wonder how he'd feel about . . . he'd feel about . . . marriage!"

The laughter was back. Not for long.

"Who is marrying whom?" said Emma Guinness from the door. Somehow the pompous accuracy of her grammar was more sinister than the snarl of her voice. She stood there, her owllike eyes scanning the room for treachery, heresy, for lèse-majesté.

Mary Polk, whose life was fashion, did a double wince. Once for the unwelcome presence of the boss at the moment they were ridiculing her. Twice, for the clothes she wore, a gruesome magenta matching coat and skirt and an identically colored cloche hat.

"Oh, I was joking about someone Samantha met," she managed at last.

"Yes, I'm sure Samantha's friends are an unfailing source of humor," agreed Emma Guinness, advancing into the office. "Her articles are pretty funny, too . . . funny peculiar, rather than funny ha-ha, I should say."

"You didn't like spa burnout?" said Samantha.

"One doesn't like or dislike spa burnout any more than one likes or dislikes antiwrinkle cream, plastic surgeons, and how-to-be-happy books," barked Emma Guinness. "It is merely that one is transcendentally *bored* by them. They are part of the reason *Celebrity* went down the loo, they and the 'brilliant' people who write about them."

Emma leaned into the insult, wrapping the word *brilliant* in a patchwork quilt of sarcasm, cynicism, and irony. She knew these girls. She had their number. They were the transatlantic cousins of the bitches who had made her life hell at *Class* magazine. In the battle for upward mobility, she had swallowed about every insult the daughters of the British aristocracy could dream up. And social cruelty was their blood sport. Hundreds of years of training in the defeat and repulsion of social climbers had been distilled into their genes. They knew with surgical accuracy how to inflict the worst possible pain with the smallest word, the most economical gesture, the apparently careless smile. Compared to Victoria Brougham and her army of class fellow travelers, these Americans were amateurs in the art of the putdown, but despite that, and their position as her employees, they still tried. And when they did, like now, they were punished, as their English predecessors had been. She had repaid *their* social violence with her own medal, the grand order of the sack, and now the New World snobs were in line for a similar investiture.

Emma sat down at the desk, flicking with her fingers through the trash that littered it. She picked up a transparency between thumb and forefinger as if it were a dead roach, and she held it up to the lamp.

"Lord Almighty, I didn't know we were using *Penthouse* photographers these days, mary. And the girl looks like a hooker. Am I missing some deeply meaningful social trend here, or is it just the tit-and-bum it appears to be?"

Mary Polk's mouth dropped open. They hadn't talked to her like that during hazing when she was a sorority pledge at Brown. Damn it, the *judge* hadn't even talked to her in that tone of voice after the little lapse from grace with cocaine in the early days at Area. The trust funds existed to protect you from experiences like this. So did Uncle Willie's law firm, and all the cousins, and the appalling mandibular discomfort of the Boston Brahmin accent. Now some jumped-up Brit was as good as telling her she had no taste. No taste! Mary Polk. Her ancestors were so grand they hadn't come over on the *Mayflower,* they'd met the boat. Jesus, her family had the import monopoly on class. She stuck out the family chin, and flashed the family eyes, as she prepared to do battle.

"Those photographs were taken by Claude Deare, and the girl is Sam Acrefield." She intoned the names of the star photographer and the supermodel as if they were the death sentence on Emma Guinness's artistic judgment.

"Exactly right," said Emma with a wicked smile, throwing the trannie back on the desk. "A pornographer and a hooker. The question is what are they doing in the magazine?"

"Listen, Emma, everyone uses Claude, and Claude uses Sam. You must know that." Samantha's adrenaline was on the move. She had to stand by her friend.

" 'Everyone uses Claude,' 'Everyone uses Claude' . . ." mimicked Emma cruelly but accurately, setting her jaw in concrete to catch Samantha's accent. "Of *course* I know that. Anyone in the Western Hemisphere not already dead from déjà vu knows that. That's the problem. Listen, love, it's impossible to tell one *Celebrity* fashion layout from another, or the *Celebrity* layouts from those of any of the other drossy magazines, and why? Because 'Everyone uses Claude,' and because the blinkered fools who tinker around pretending to work in this industry are too lazy or too blind to see that Claude Deare is a superannuated, impotent old lecher and Sam Acrefield is a high-class call girl."

"I don't see what their sexual behavior has to do with it," intoned Mary haughtily. For all sorts of reasons Boston liberals liked to leave sex out of things.

"Then I'll *tell* you, fashion guru," hissed Emma Guinness. "Obvious sex," she intoned, "is last year, and so, I fear, are you."

She threw down the gauntlet. It was High Noon. Emma, gun drawn, was about to fire. If the Bostonian moved a muscle in retaliation, she would be dead.

"Who would *you* use, Emma?" Samantha rushed in with her diversion.

"Pat Parker." Emma shot out the name without a second's hesitation.

"Pat Parker?" both girls intoned in unison.

"She's reportage," said Mary dismissively.

"She's trendy," said Samantha, giving the word pejorative topspin. "I mean she's underground, not mainstream, hardly *Celebrity.*"

"Boy, are you right! Hardly *Celebrity,* but very, *very New Celebrity.*" Emma Guinness's voice was triumphant. "Pat Parker is 'now.' She's 'happening.' She's where it's at. I don't give a damn if her lighting's off, or she hires the 'wrong' hairdresser, or if she hasn't worked for the correct magazines. You don't get excitement in this world without exciting people. That's what it's all about. Safe is dull. Let's get the hell out there on the cutting edge and dare the readers to catch up. They will, but we've got to wake them up first. Wean them off the visual Halcion."

"Visual Halcion? Thank you, Emma. Thank you very much," said Mary, wilting under the criticism and well aware that sarcasm was the lowest form of wit.

"Maybe we could get her to shoot the 'Stars of Tomorrow' section. Perhaps she could persuade that Tony Valentino to change his mind about doing the slot."

Samantha smiled as she unleashed the verbal missile with the nuclear head. Almost certainly she herself would perish in the blast, but it would be worth it to let the dreaded Emma know that everyone in the office knew the smallest details of her humiliation.

Emma's world stopped in its tracks. Once again her antennae had been right. She could have sworn that they were discussing her when she had walked into the room. Here was confirmation. The blush exploded up from her neck and expanded from the center of her cheeks, like ripples from the splash of a stone in a pond. She clenched her fists, and her heart speeded. In her mind she could see all the amused, astounded faces, feel the scornful words dripping like acid into her psyche. The fire of embarrassment burned in her anew as she remembered the face of the boy god, so full of scorn, so utterly sure of himself, as he demolished her publicly before all the people that mattered. It was the story of her life. The battle to reach the position in which no one could touch her. The hard work, the sacrifice, the scheming, and the eventual victory. Then what? There was always another person to plague her. First an army of the socially powerful, and now, at the height of her success, a nobody from nowheresville called . . . *Valentino?* The rage was sucked into the vacuum of shock that had opened within her. Her eyes narrowed, and the malice lasered out at the girl who had dared to mock her.

"Do you two know . . . can you have any idea, why I kept you in your jobs? Well, I'll tell you. I wanted you to produce one last issue of your moribund magazine, an issue more dreadfully dull and cunningly complacent than any you had ever produced before. Why? Because it will show back to back with my first edition of *New Celebrity*. Everyone will get to compare the sublime with the ridiculous. That's why I left it all to you. I could never have produced anything so startlingly mediocre. You two have the rarest talent. You bore for the galaxy. You invented banality. When the Lord created lack of creativity, he was dreaming of you. Now I'm just off to the Four Seasons to have lunch with Dick Latham, and I'm going down to Malibu with him for the weekend. And I'm going to tell him that I'm going to sack the lot of you. Every sodding one, do you hear?" Her voice rose in both decibels and pitch.

The tears of terminal irritation glistened in her eyes. The boot was too good for them. These girls would never starve. They would never be too hot, never too cold. They'd go to the Hamptons for the summer, or to England where some grand WASP publisher would have them head up his PR department when the weather turned nasty in the fall. They'd never go away. Instead they'd truck on and on, telling and retelling the saga of how Emma Guinness, despite her position and her fame, got hers, in public, at the Juilliard Theater from the beautiful actor whom nobody had ever heard of.

She walked to the door. When she reached it, she turned, and her face was twisted with a terrible rage. "I hate you," she hissed. "I hate you all. And one day I'll show you just how far and how high I'm going to go."

—

TONY VALENTINO lay back in the bubbles, shielded his eyes against the sun, and tried desperately to have a bad time. He scowled, he flicked his head from side to side in irritation, he ran through his repertoire of miserable, fed-up expressions and gestures. Usually that was enough. Make the body do it, and the mind followed. Not this time. No way. Malibu was too powerful. It had crept inside his brain and was rotting it with the alien sensation called pleasure.

He twisted around in the Jacuzzi, and the water jets followed him, plucking deliciously at his hard body. Through the low glass barrier that bordered the compound he watched the surf barely fifty feet away across the beach. The Southern California waves came in lazily, as mellow and unhurried as the citizens of the dreamland who wandered by the side of the sea. Pelicans and gulls practiced their nosedives in the hazy heat. Sandpipers cavorted on the caramel sand. He reached for the glass of iced San Pellegrino, and as he crushed the fresh lime into the mineral water, he sang along to the Milli Vanilli song that wafted from the poolside speakers of the Sony sound system.

"Glad you came?"

She hovered above him, her graceful body silhouetted against the sun, and he squinted up at her, both his arms stretched out around the rim of the Jacuzzi. He smiled to say yes, that despite everything, he *was* glad, even though he knew it was an interlude, an opiate for pain that had been dulled but would never go away. Malibu was numbing his feelings in the way he had intended, but reality wouldn't hide forever. Nor did he want it to.

Allison took the smile gratefully. For the poor little rich girl, who had lived forever beneath the emotional poverty line, it was a precious gift.

"What do you want to do about lunch? I got some stuff from Hughes earlier. You want to help me do a barbecue? It's the California thing."

Again he didn't answer. He scooped up the Oliver Peoples horn-rimmed sunglasses from the wooden deck that surrounded the Jacuzzi and slipped them on, masking the eyes that could give away his feelings.

"Only 'healthful' food, I hope. No salt. No cholesterol. At least no low-density lipoproteins." He laughed, surprised that he still could.

"What do you think I am, a murderer? Listen, in the land of wheatgrass juice polyunsaturated fat is poison. We've got asparagus, and then chicken breasts and spinach salad. Strawberries and blueberries afterward, if you like."

The laughter danced in her words. She was so happy, thought Tony. And so very good. She had spirited him away from misery, and now every move she made, every word she spoke was designed to make him feel better and to encourage him to forget. She was in love with him, of course, but why, that was the question. Why would an angel, rich, beautiful, talented, born with a whole canteen of platinum cutlery cascading from her mouth, fall in love with a cold, uncouth psychopath in whose veins iced ambition had replaced warm blood? He had been cruel to her. He had used her. He was using her still, and she had repaid him with kindness, generosity, and good humor. The strange feeling inside him just had to be guilt, but already it was merging with something else.

She stood over him, straight and proud, like an actress should, and the patrician cut of her genes showed at each curve of her body, every contour of her face. The one-piece Donna Karan thong she wore was, however, the class enemy. It gave the lie to her aristocratic Ralph Lauren/Calvin Klein model looks, the haughty height of her brow, the thick bushiness of her eyebrows, the pencil straightness of her nose. Black as night, it bisected her full bottom and spoke eloquently of her longing for the low life. Wrapped tight around her hourglass waist and the nipples of small, firm breasts, the sheer black Lycra, slinky sexy in the bright sunlight, told the truth about Allison Vander-bilt and the things she wanted when she crawled at bedtime between the faded cotton of ten-year-old Pratesi sheets. The girl needed love, but she had never been loved, and somehow, over the years, she had concluded that she wasn't lovable. So now she no longer looked for admiration and respect, for warmth and consideration and tenderness. Those things, unlike the houses, the horses, the jewelry, and the servants, had never been part of her birth-right. Instead she saw it as her role to dispense pleasure, not to receive it, and gradually, as time passed, lust had filled the vacuum where love should have been, and subservient desire had become the fuel for her nocturnal fantasies.

"Get in, Allison," said Tony Valentino. His voice was husky, urgent. He took off his sunglasses and laid them on the weathered wood.

For a second she paused, but then the smile of satisfaction crinkled up the corners of her mouth. Her eyes sparkled, and she tossed her hair in the beach breeze like a young pony. She stepped toward the edge of the Jacuzzi

and slid quickly into the foaming water. Across from him, she watched him
and he made no move toward her, as their eyes met. She swallowed hard. He
could see her throat bob beneath the skin of her long neck, see the perspira-
tion standing out on her upper lip, and her eyes snaked away to the safe sky
as his lasered into her mind, reading her passion like the big-print storybook
of a child. He knew! Oh, God, he knew her secrets, and her whole body
shuddered beneath the warm currents as it prepared itself for the delicious
insults that would be the making of their love. Over his shoulder a surfer
strode down the beach, his board slung beneath his arm. He was barely ten
yards from them. The Colony beach was private to the high water mark, but
in a fierce democracy there was no enforcing of that mobile boundary. Whatever happened now would take place in public, and Allison Vanderbilt's heart
hammered against her chest in delightful panic at the thought. Once again
she dared to look at him. Both his hands were below the surface of the water,
and his eyes were hooded, his head to one side, his expression hungry. As she
watched, he straightened his back, and he wriggled down and then his swimming trunks were bubbling on the surface of the Jacuzzi.

Again Allison swallowed. Her eyes widened. Her stomach tightened. The
breath trembled in her flared nostrils, and her lungs shook as the currents of
air rushed in and out in long, unmeasured gusts. The blanket of unreality
descended, and the day receded from her, here at the edge of total passion
where the desert met the sea. Her mouth was dry as the canyon wind. The
thong of her swimsuit bit into the part of her that was now commanding her
body and ruling her soul. In the wetness, she was melting, wetter somehow
than the water that surrounded her. She was slippery inside, as her ass
pushed against the rough seat of the Jacuzzi and her breasts tingled as the
bone-hard jet current caught them, tensing her already taut nipples. Across
from her he was naked now, naked and stiff with the longing it would be her
privilege to satisfy. But still she didn't move. He would tell her what to do.
He would know, and whatever he wanted would be right. She reached for
her breast. Her fingers fumbled at the edge of the material, scurrying inside
to feel the blood force itself into the throbbing cone of her nipple. She
squeezed tight, as it thrust back at her thumb and forefinger, and all the time
the pleasure fountain played within her, lighting up her mind, soaking the
velvet walls of her secrecy, mixing with the waters that cocooned the soon-to-
be lovers. Her butt tightened. Her back arched. Her pelvis contracted and
relaxed, opening and closing in anticipation of the pleasure to come. Now
with her left hand she felt for her other nipple, and she watched him, proud
and defiant as she played with herself, lewd and abandoned, as she turned
her body for him. She crushed her ripe breasts beneath the flat of her hand,
and she rubbed from side to side, pulling them from the black material so
that they floated on the surface of the Jacuzzi—lost, revealed, then lost again
—in the froth of the steamy water. Strawberry pink and vanilla they pointed
at him, their pure white in contrast to the delicate rose of her sun-teased
torso. She cupped them, pushing them up so he could see his gift. She
pinched the rock-hard nipples, thrusting the blood into them until they

swelled to bursting point, oblivious to the sharp pain, wanting only to inflame him to the point where there could be no turning back. She was burning. The flames of lust were alive inside her. And now her right hand dipped down, drawn to the core of her by a force far stronger than her will. Her legs splayed out and her forefinger hooked beneath the narrow strip of fabric. She moaned gently as she found the pleasure source, and she abandoned her humanity as she became the animal she longed to be.

"Yes, Allison," he whispered gently. "Do it. Play with yourself. Do it to yourself."

His words opened the floodgates of passion. She bucked out at her hand, desperate for the surrogate satisfaction. She reared against herself, thrusting, pushing, crushing, as she ground against stiff fingers. Her mouth fell open. The breath rushed past perfect teeth. Her head lolled to one side on the frothy sea of abandonment. Her hands raced up, down, back behind to the dark, trembling skin of her buttocks. Now her fingers moved forward again, chasing the ecstasy, milking the cream from each spine-chilling moment of joy. She felt so crude. She was rude and without shame as she masturbated for the man she worshiped. The expression on his face was her reward.

She was inside herself now, her hand sucked into the dripping smoothness, and the silken walls clamped down on the tearing fingers. Slowly her greedy, inaccurate movements acquired a rhythm and she arched her back as the music built within her to the awesome crescendo of release. Her eyes were hazy with the closeness of the orgasm and her hand moved cleverly, in and out, up and down, in the piston purpose of desire. All the time she watched him. This was for him. Everything was for him.

He launched himself across the watery space that separated them, and she was surrounded by the steel ring of his arms. His face was against her face, and his breath was hot on her sweatsoaked cheeks. His body was plastered tight against her, and she wrapped her legs around him, her hand still buried in her own core. Then, against the flatness of her lower stomach, she felt the part of him she longed for. Impossibly large, harder than mountain rock, he reared against her skin, and she smiled in triumph at what she had created, and she dared to imagine what it would do.

But first he wanted to drink from the moisture of her lips. His mouth found hers, and the stubble of his beard rubbed wonderfully against her smooth skin. There was no delicacy in his kiss. It was the kiss of the barbarian conqueror who had fought long and hard for the spoils he now claimed. Trembling, she surrendered to him, striving to divide herself into two separate parts, the better to savor the two distinct areas of ecstasy that were now her body. In the clash of teeth, in the merger of mouths, in the bruised battery of lips, she lived at the pinnacle of joy. But against her stomach, against the back of her hand still clasped against her throbbing mound of love, she could feel the source of his power. It stabbed at her like a dagger; it was heavy, angry, like a club; it thrust at her, the spear that must impale her in the thousand deaths in which alone she would be reborn.

His hands were lost in the luxuriance of her hair, twisting, pulling, forcing her mouth against his. His tongue twined with hers, and their liquid merged to lubricate the slam dance of slippery love.

He drew back from her, and his wild eyes bored into her. They signed the pact then. He didn't love her, but he needed her so badly that he would take her now, whether or not she wanted it. He made no promises to her, except to fill her body to overflowing with his pent-up lust. There could be no consideration for her, no tenderness, no commitment. She would have to take what she could find on the bleak steppes of his emotions, and he would not be held responsible if she starved in the emotional wilderness. She understood that. She loved him. Her body would be her gift to him. In the giving of it she would find her ultimate pleasure. She had wanted more, but it would do for now, because bodies had unfinished business, and because reason was the poor relation of almighty emotion.

He reached down roughly, and he plucked her hand from between her legs. He bent at the knee, and she felt faint as he positioned himself to take her. There at her opening, he waited. She could feel his sharpness nestling dangerously in the slippery hair, throbbing tight against the supreme softness of her quivering lips of love. Her hands floated to the surface and she gripped the surround of the Jacuzzi to steady herself for the wonderful, vicious assault that he was about to unleash. She wanted to touch it, to marvel at its hugeness, but more than that she wanted it to own her. She wanted to ride it. She wanted it thrust up inside her. She wanted it buried so deep in her body that it could never, never escape.

Her legs trembled beneath her, and she forced them farther apart until the whole of her lower body was an abyss demanding to be filled. In all her life she had never been so wide open, and the juice of her love ran like a river over the pulsing walls of her heartland.

"Please, please," she moaned.

It was enough. He thrust forward at her, and his vastness slid inside her. She cried out in joy as he filled her. She shook as he rammed into the roof of her, lifting her whole body with the crude, cruel force of his invasion. She gasped in awe at the wild feeling, and her eyes widened in wonder at the size of the intruder. On the borders where pleasure met pain she hung on to him, pinned to the wall of the hot tub, her whole body a mere envelope to the power of his desire. Now he stood up straight, his legs straining beneath the weight of her, and dripping, the thong of her swimsuit rudely displaced from the midline, she emerged from the foaming water impaled on the still expanding point of him. Her breasts thrust out from the top of the Lycra swimsuit, and he buried his head between them, his strong hands cupped beneath her buttocks, as he manipulated her whole body around the fulcrum that was now the center of her universe. She clasped her legs around his waist and hooked her ankles over each other, clamping herself down over the pleasure source, and as she did so she knew that she couldn't stop the orgasm.

The breath rasped from her lungs, and her muscles lost their coordination. She cried a short sharp cry of painful satisfaction, and the world turned on its axis, the blue sky kaleidoscoping into the battleship gray of the mountains, merging with the aquamarine of the sea. She was a surfer, her firm body writhing and twisting on the cresting wave. She was a bird, soaring, swooping on the thermal currents of the canyons.

Twitching, convulsing, her body shuddered with the spasms of her climax and her legs untwined, jerking in a crazed rhythm of release amid the fine spray of her sexuality. The air was thick with the musk of her. Her love was heavy on the warm breeze. The longing cascaded down her thighs as it soaked his stomach and conjured up the look of wonder in his faraway eyes.

"Ooooooooooh!" she howled at the heavens as she danced the threshing dance of the dying, her legs the legs of a hanged man windmilling frantically as they sought the platform they would never find. He didn't free her. He paid no attention to her little death. He moved through it and beyond it as if it had never been. And so, inexorably, did she. The source of her crazed delight reverberated still, but on the other side of the hill Allison Vanderbilt wanted only to climb it once more.

He twisted around, spinning her on the tip of him, lifting up her leg and pushing it past his muscular chest. Then he was behind her, yet still inside her, and she could see him no more. Now she was supported only by the stick of hot flesh that joined them. He arched his torso away from her back until she was balanced on the point of him, hanging in midair, steadied only by the tips of his fingers at her narrow waist. She could feel only the place where he surged into her and her body hurtled upward at each powerful thrust of his hips, before crashing down with its own weight as he relaxed. For long minutes of eternal bliss he rode her. He was anonymous, invisible, known to her only by the baton of his lust, and once again the music inside her was building to a crescendo as her whole body howled for release. This time he seemed to hear it.

Once again he spun her around until she faced him, her eyes thick with tears of longing, her lips bared, her chin thrust out in helpless defiance. Her hair, wet with sweat, was plastered across her forehead and the breath rushed in angry torrents across her parted teeth. She had melted down. She had become liquid. She flowed toward him on a sensuous sea of sexuality, and he could drink her, do with her as he wished, as long as she could watch his eyes at the very moment he flowed into her. That was all she wanted now. She wanted to feel the truth of him, soaking her own fountain, drowning her own waterfall, submerging the ocean she was with the one he was about to become. In the lust land, he responded. It was time. He stopped. He was still. Her rocked and rearing body was motionless. There was only the fullness, the enormous presence, joining him to her in the bondage from which she wished never to be freed. She tried to conjure up the vision of it, buried in her warm depths, to capture in the eye of her mind the beautiful thing it was about to do. In the heart of her there was the tiniest movement, the vibration of a hummingbird at the face of a wide-open flower. Then, once, twice, three times, she felt it, a spurt, a silken caress, three delicious discrete splashes of molten love that signaled the moment of union. It was the lull before the storm. He exploded, rushing forward, his hands clutching frantically at her thighs, as he followed through into the heart of his orgasm. As he did so she clamped down over him, strangling him with the soft noose of her love lips, and her own climax collided with the exuberant force of his. On and on it went, fearful in its intensity, and his rumbling groan of pleasure merged with her sharp cry of release, as the gulls swooped overhead, and the majestic mountains stared down at the lovers.

"I DON'T know how to take a great photograph. I don't even know how to recognize a great subject, but I do know where beauty is an' it's here. The thing to do is to hang around and sooner or later something good happens."

"You're saying it's luck, Alabama?"

"No such thing, sweetheart. Just hard work. Just being ready for the moment whenever it comes. You have to master the technical side until you can do it in your sleep. The most important thing then is to forget it, and let the mind see. The moment you start to think, you're lost. First develop the instinct, then trust it. There's not much else."

"You don't think it can be taught?"

"Only to the person who has it already. It can be developed, refined, polished, but it has to *be* there. The talent can be raw, but without it there's no art. Just another boring photograph."

Pat Parker winced in pain, not at Alabama's optimistic/pessimistic analysis of what made a photographic artist, but because the inseams of her jeans were now two tight balls of material chafing the skin of her inner thighs. For the umpteenth time that afternoon she attempted to smooth them flat, knowing that in a minute or two they would ride up and the agony would start all over again.

She debated whether to tell him. No. She didn't want to be a city girl whining in the great outdoors. Alabama, up ahead of her, looked absolutely monumental, indestructible like the vast rock formations they were riding past. To complain about something as essentially trivial as pain was out of the question.

"Now I understand why people wear those riding pants. I always thought it was to turn everyone on."

He didn't look back. He wasn't interested. And his blue jeans, for some reason she didn't understand, hugged the ankles of his battered brown cowboy boots. Apparently, like taking photographs, riding was an art you mastered and then forgot. She gripped the reins and thought of the prized Japanese trait of "gamay"—perseverance. If it had projected the yen into the stratosphere it might be useful on a horseback photographic field trip in the Santa Monica Mountains.

"You know there's only one enemy in these mountains," said Alabama over his shoulder, his face shielded from the overhead sun by the brim of his snakeskin-rimmed, black leather Trilby hat. "An' that's human. They light the fires that burn them, an' they build the tract trash that litters them. Never met a developer I didn't want to shoot."

His hand lingered longingly on the pearl handle of the Smith & Wesson .45 that dangled from an intricately tooled holster at his hip. Pat was glad she wasn't a builder. She breathed in deeply, and the scent of the sage and the pine on the superheated breeze hurried into her head. She adjusted the wide-brimmed hat that Alabama had lent her, and felt the sweat trickle down between her breasts, beneath the already saturated white camisole top. Jeez, this was worse than the World, Mars, and M.K. rolled into one. It seldom got to be a hundred degrees in the slime pits of New York City. At least there were no cigarettes here. In the Alabama world of the high chaparral, smokers probably rated right next to developers in the popularity stakes.

"Is that why Malibu wants to become a town?"

"It's the main reason. If we incorporate, then the people who live here can decide what the place gets to look like. Not a bad little idea. It's called democracy. Used to be quite popular."

"But not with the developers."

"Yeah. Right now, for the most part, the people who make the zoning decisions aren't residents. An' they can be 'influenced.' Development means more tax dollars, and more tax dollars equals bigger bureaus for the bureaucrats. They don't have to live in the mess they permit, so what happens to Malibu doesn't affect them."

"The local papers seem to talk about nothing but sewers. That's hardly the Malibu image."

"Sewers are shorthand for development. Right now every house in Malibu has a septic tank, and I'll tell you when the sea comes in, those fancy beach houses in the Colony are knee deep in it. But the residents are happy to put up with the inconvenience because without central sewers nobody can build hotels and restaurants and convention centers. So the homeowners want to kibosh the sewers, and the county politicians and the developers want to put them in. The whole thing comes down to what to do with the shit."

He laughed, his great belly wobbling in the sunlight, at the thought of all the movie stars and the millionaires, the rock stars and the writers, the painters and the piss artists fighting for the God-given right to dispose of their own waste.

"Who's going to win?" asked Pat.

"I am," said Alabama simply, and he laughed again and dug his heels into the flanks of his horse, sending the animal scurrying up a steep slope beneath an overhanging rock.

Pat smiled as she attempted to follow her leader. It figured. Alabama was as far from losing as he was from grace. Already she was beginning to love him as the father she had never had, and his prickly impossibility, his drinking bouts, and his eccentricity were charming idiosyncrasies that enabled her to relate to him as some sort of an equal. There had been no formal lessons, but each time he spoke she learned something about photography, and more important, about art. Beneath the banter and the baiting, Ben Alabama was a Zen soldier. Everything was intertwined. All was related. The way you lived your life, the values you held were every bit as vital as the direction you pointed your camera. "Every man has a photograph in him," he was fond of saying. "And it's the best place for it to remain." Even his apparent weaknesses, he sold as strengths. Drinking beer was to mock the seriousness of life. Fighting was good clean fun, and part of an American tradition the sweeping away of which had led to a weaker, more dependent society, one that suffered from a soul-sapping deficiency in self-respect. His social abrasiveness was really only self-assertion, and that was the duty of anyone who lived by a moral code and was proud of it.

They had reached a peak that looked down on all the others, and Alabama reined in his horse and turned in his western saddle to savor the extraordinary view. Pat did the same, the wild beauty of the hundred-mile vista taking away her breath. To one side stretched the San Fernando Valley, the houses and the "civilization" dwarfed by the majesty of the mountains. To the other, the Malibu hills were bordered by the sea and in the crystal clarity she could see Catalina, the south side of Santa Monica Bay, and north way into Ventura County. The sun played across the colors, shading rock and shrub, the hills and the valleys in subtle grays, browns, and sage greens, while over it all, separating earth from sky, hung a hazy layer of purple and magenta, of lilac and burnished orange, mixed in the magic of the constantly changing light.

"Knocking on heaven's door," said Alabama, in awe of the beauty.

Pat slung her legs gratefully over the saddle as she dismounted. She reached for the crumpled Mark Cross canvas tote bag that contained everything in the world she cared about. She fished out a Leica and an 85mm telephoto lens, which she clipped to the battered body of the camera. Her eyes searched the distant horizon, computing the light. Next she thumbed open a pack of Ilford HP3, and without looking she loaded it, snapped the camera back closed, and ran off three exposures with the lens pointed at the dusty scrub.

"You need a five-by-seven view camera," said Alabama. "You'll get nothing with a Leica. An' it's a color photograph. You want Kodachrome, an' maybe a red filter to bring out the shadows. Sun's overhead. Vertical light's no good for landscape. You wanna go wider than eight-five millimeter. Way wider for a halfway decent picture."

He leaned pugnaciously from the saddle toward his protégé. She was disappointing him. She was going for the obvious, and in a not very well thought-out way. He didn't mind telling her so. He didn't mind telling anybody anything about photography.

She whirled around on him, and the long lens zeroed in on the jutting point of his aggressive chin. Her fingers twirled on the serrated edge of the viewfinder. His irritated eyes swam into focus as his tree-on-a-blasted-heath saddle stance melded perfectly with the rocky backdrop in silhouette against the harsh overhead light of the sky. *Click* went the shutter.

"Oh," said Alabama.

"I think you'll find that *that* is the photograph," mocked Pat Parker.

"I think that maybe I will," agreed Alabama, laughing at himself and his presumption. He should have known. The girl was a genius. From the moment her six prints had cascaded onto the pine of his kitchen table, he had known that she had the X factor. It had been years since he'd seen such good photographs, and the alien subject matter hadn't made an iota of difference to the excitement that had gripped him. The girl could visualize, and she could seize the moment. She could compose, she could cut, and she could print. In short, she had the knack, and he had immediately invited her to Malibu. He wasn't sorry. The photographs she had taken while staying as his guest had confirmed her brilliance. On two occasions only had he doubted her, and for the second time she had turned the tables on him. The garden gnome picture, as he now referred to it, had made a superb print. Elliott Erwitt funny, it defined elves, pixies, and little people in the forest and the fact that hard-as-nails Alabama was its subject merely added to the joke. Now, she had duplicated Karsh's Churchill trick. The Canadian photographer had deliberately made the statesman angry to capture his definitive belligerence. The resulting portrait had been one of the greatest ever taken. There was no doubt in Alabama's mind that this picture, too, would be a revelation. He turned to check the background, the light, the sky, and his mind's eye conceptualized the angle he'd have made with the horse, the expression that must have been playing on his face, the one that the telephoto lens would have captured perfectly. He could actually "see" the print, in the way that Mozart could "hear" the music he wrote, and it was superb.

He swung himself out of the saddle.

He walked over to Pat, and he put his arm around her shoulders.

"I'm sorry," he said. "I've got to stop doing that."

She laughed. "You don't have to stop doing anything. You're a legend."

"I used to be." The strange feeling welled up in Alabama. Good God, he was going to tell her the secret that only King and he knew.

"What do you mean, 'used to be'? I went to your Metropolitan show last year. I saw your recent photographs, Alabama. They're as beautiful as anything you've ever done. I mean they're the *same*."

He had surprised her. The humility, the self-doubt were totally out of character. Surely he hadn't been fishing for anything so mundane as a compliment. He *must* have had enough of those by now.

"I'll tell you why they're the same, Pat Parker. They're the same because I haven't taken a photograph for ten years, and I don't intend to take another. I just print up the old negatives and stick on today's date. What do you think of that, my friend?"

Pat knew she was being tested. Shock/horror/reproach was not the correct reaction. Either it was some complex joke, or there were perfectly good reasons that would explain the unthinkable. She was being asked to believe that Bacon had given up painting, that Carson had stopped cracking jokes, that Reagan had refused to appear on television. It was bizarre, but then the truth often was.

"If it's true, why are you telling me?"

Alabama looked puzzled, *was* puzzled.

"I'm not quite sure," he said at last. "I think it's because I like you. I think it's because I think that in time you'll understand."

Somehow the subject had closed itself off. It was on the back burner, to be investigated and discussed as part of the ongoing process of friendship development. He did like this girl, but more than that, he trusted and admired her. She was his own speed. In Los Angeles County, precious few were.

"Anyway, talented girl, we should be getting back if we're going to make that Latham lunch. How do you feel about billionaires? They do anything for you?"

"Not yet, not yet," Pat Parker laughed.

— 5 —

THE BUTLER, HIS whole life a complicated training in unflappability, had lost the plot. He stood in the open door and wondered whether to shout for help, to call the police, or to stand back and welcome the extraordinary duo into his house.

"Alabama and friend for Dick Latham," growled Alabama in threatening tones. The beer smell and the beer belly preceded him, and behind the tree trunks of his Levied legs the pipes of the Harley still crackled and creaked from the heat of the furious descent from the mountains. The English majordomo had heard about bikers, remembered Brando in *The Wild One*, but he had never expected to see one this close.

"Mr. Alabama?" he managed, his question mark vast. A Mr. Alabama had been on the guest list for lunch.

"Yeah," grunted Alabama, not bothering to put the butler straight on the small print of his nomenclature. He pushed past the gate guardian, and Pat, smiling at the confusion, followed in his wake.

Fait accompli and *savoir faire* were about the only French that Englishmen understood. If the house was to be raped and pillaged, then the surrender should be handled with decorum.

"May I take your 'hat,' sir?" said the butler, allowing himself a liberal measure of sarcasm to cover the defeat he had just suffered.

"No," said Alabama. "It's grown onto my head." That looked to be true. It was battered enough to have been slept in for several years, and where brim met forehead there were nutrients that would have supported growth of sorts. The Englishman winced. In America it was the limeys who were supposed to have the monopoly on dirt. Lack of cleanliness and their legendary meanness were far better known national characteristics on this side of the Atlantic than the phlegm and sophistication that the British liked to think they were famous for.

Pat Parker looked around at the serious money. It was everywhere—in the museum-quality furniture, in the serious art, in the superb architecture—and her aesthetic vision lasered in on it, melding it in her journalistic mind with the bits and pieces she already knew about Richard Latham. He lived most of the time in New York, and he owned magazines for which she had occasionally worked. She had seen him around at the grander parties she had covered, but mostly they had lived in parallel but distinctly separate worlds, and she had never actually met him. She knew he had a reputation as a ladykiller, and he was very good-looking for an older man. That, and the megabucks, made him interesting, even to a girl whose heroes and heroines were photographers, painters, and writers, not superrich robber barons with Don Juan complexes. Alabama had told her the Paris story, and that had added depth to the one-dimensional character of the press clippings. Latham might have behaved badly all those years ago, but at least he had had the balls to stand up to Alabama, and the heart to break when the girl he loved had walked out on him. Many of the men she knew possessed neither.

The Mexican-tiled foyer in which they found themselves was full of flowers. Geraniums cascaded from terra-cotta pots, pink and mauve impatiens sprouted from hanging baskets, bougainvillea climbed around stucco columns. In the center a fountain, tiled in ancient Spanish tiles, tinkled pleasantly, and eyes were drawn past it to a courtyard in which a forty-foot pool sparkled in the midday sun. The walls were heavy with paintings—Dutch seventeenth-century still lifes, Van Dycks of serious soldiers, what looked suspiciously like a genuine Franz Hals. Mozart's Violin Concerto in E minor, soft and harrowing, warbled from hidden speakers.

"Can I offer you a drink, madam?" tried the chastened butler as he attempted some kind of recovery from social shock.

"I'd love a Coke," said Pat.

"Classic . . . or . . . otherwise?"

"Oh, Classic, I guess."

"Diet . . . or otherwise."

"Diet."

"Caffeine free . . . or . . ."

"Otherwise," said Pat sharply.

"Sir?" said the butler.

"Beer. Dos Equis, Corona, or Tecate, in order of preference. Bottled. Slice of lime. Cold. Quickly," said Alabama.

He leered pugnaciously at the hired help, as he covered the options.

"Welcome, welcome," said Dick Latham, leaking the oil of affability onto the troubled waters. "Alabama, at last. And the beautiful and talented Pat Parker."

He creamed forward, his over-the-top smile happy on his sun-burnished face, his teeth flashing and shining in the bright light. He was Polo casual, pink on blue, the Guess? watch a gentle joke on his muscular forearm. His shoes shone and his pants cut, and, as he reached for Alabama's hand, he devoured Pat with amused, solicitous eyes.

"You owe me a hundred bucks," grumbled Alabama, shaking the hand that Latham offered with minimal enthusiasm.

"How clever of you to remember," Latham laughed without missing a beat. "Paris, wasn't it? A lifetime ago. Youth is wasted on the young, don't you think so, Alabama?"

He smiled at her as he spoke, aware of his social smoothness, of his formidable self-confidence, as he deflected the aggression with his so-subtle apology. Despite herself, she smiled back. The articles in *Time* and *Forbes* hadn't captured the charisma, hadn't mentioned the lean, hard body, the Anglicized accent. He was fifty going on forty, and the charm juice sprayed from him like scent from an atomizer in the perfume department at Bloomingdale's.

Alabama's belligerent eyes narrowed. Latham might have gotten his act together, but the boy was the father of the man. Inside he wouldn't have changed that much. People didn't. And he wasn't going to get away with making his slimy moves on Pat Parker.

"Oh, I never thought youth was wasted on Eva Ventura. Do you remember that beautiful girl? I wonder whatever happened to her."

The sexy smile vanished from Dick Latham's lips. They were tight now, and devoid of blood, drawn in a pencil line across his jawbone. His eyes shut down and he froze as his shoulders stiffened and the breath whistled into his flared nostrils. He hadn't heard that name in twenty years, but scarcely a twenty-minute period passed during which he didn't think about her. Eva Ventura, who had floodlit his heart and given new meaning to his jaded life. She had been all the fun and the gaiety and the spontaneous energy that had been absent from his dark childhood, and he had loved her more than he had known it was possible to love. All the disparate chords had merged in a secret harmony of beautiful music as, in Eva Ventura, his future had made sense at last. But his devils had never been completely exorcised. When an old girlfriend had made her play for him, he had gone through the sexual motions more out of habit than anything else, and because he had forgotten how to refuse. Eva had found them together. She had laughed in his face at his fickle faithlessness, and she had vanished into thin air. The nausea welled up in his stomach as he remembered the dreadful loss, and he gritted his teeth in rage at the wrong that could never be made right. Now, his feelings extroverted once again, he turned in ice-cold fury toward Alabama. It was clear that the old biker had brought up Eva's name to irritate him. He could tell from the jaunty way the weather-beaten head was tucked to one side, its eyes fascinated by the effect of its tongue's action, the half smile of revenge puckering up the corners of the chapped lips. Alabama hadn't forgotten Paris, Latham's rejection of his work, and the millionaire's callous refusal to pay him the money he was morally owed.

In Latham's mind the potential insults queued up for consideration. Then the training of the last twenty-five years reasserted itself. In the rarefied money maze he inhabited there was no room for petty emotion. Tit for cheap tat was for losers. It was a revelation of weakness. The need for retaliation pinpointed the precise location of your Achilles heel, and where you had been hurt once you could be hurt again. So the trick was to disguise the pain but never, ever to forget it. Revenge was a dish better served cold, but Dick

Latham had acquired a taste for it deep frozen. He didn't merely get even, or marginally ahead. Instead he leap-frogged into other worlds as he put distance between himself and his enemies. Then, when they were eaten away with jealousy at his success, he lobbed clever bombs at them from outer galaxies, wrecking their lives and humiliating them, while making sure they were well aware of their destroyer's identity.

But with Alabama there was another angle. He needed him. He had to have him on his side during this crucial period. Alabama ran the Santa Monica Mountains Preservation trust singlehanded from his abysslike pockets. He was the money source, and he had the ears of the politicians, the public, and the vital media. He was the thrust behind Malibu's antideveloper cityhood application. He would be a difficult friend, but an intolerable enemy. Without Alabama, Dick Latham's land purchase, the site of his secretly projected Cosmos studio, would be derailed. If for one second he thought Latham would be an ecologically unreliable neighbor, Alabama could use his influence with the landowner to block the sale, or to write antidevelopment clauses into the contract even at this late stage of escrow. He might persuade the government to buy the land. He might even mobilize the money to buy it himself. Now was not the time to antagonize him, whatever he said, however he behaved. Latham took a deep breath. "Yes, she was a wonderful girl, wasn't she? Sometimes I think I should have married her."

He bit on his lip as he forced the banality through it. He stuffed the jauntiness back into his step, and he dragged on the debonair mantle once again, reloading his charm gun, as he fought to camouflage the wound he had suffered. He turned toward Pat. "Pat Parker, I've got someone here who's dying to meet you. She's my secret weapon. I've brought her over from England to revamp my magazine *Celebrity*. You'll love her. She's full of ideas. Name's Emma Guinness."

He laid a hand on Pat's shoulder, and she was aware of his touch as he steered her across the pool patio to the double doors of the main house.

"Of course, Alabama's far too grand for magazines anymore, I'm afraid. Too frivolous, I expect, after MOMA, the Whitney, and the Met. By the way, Alabama, I love your recent work. So fresh. *So* original. Not that you have any reason to respect my judgment after my sad little performance in Paris. Have you still got that portrait? I'd swap it for a quarter of a million to the Sierra Club."

He turned over his shoulder to watch the effect as he dangled the cash carrot. It was way over double the rate for an Alabama portrait, even an early one. And the Sierra Club wasn't as rich as it had been in Ansel's day. Yosemite could do with the bucks, and it was a subtle hint that he, Latham, was an environmental friend. But his stomach tightened. He could do without a physical reminder of that time. Maybe, he'd be spared it. Alabama had probably used the print as a dart board.

Pat turned also to see the effect of the windfall on her friend, as the Latham hand, exerting an intriguing pressure, continued to linger on her arm. She knew Alabama disliked and mistrusted the billionaire. How would he deal with the dilemma? Would the Sierra Club's gift horse be looked in the mouth to satisfy his prickly ego? It would be a close call.

Not for Alabama.

"Half a million," he said.

"A million," countered Latham perversely, "on condition that Pat Parker keeps my portrait on the table beside her bed."

He laughed as he spoke, and they all stopped in their tracks. But the Latham hand was still on the Parker arm.

"You're joking." She smiled as the red exploded high on her cheeks.

"I've never been more serious in my life." His smile was changing. His eyes bored into her. He was telling her something she wasn't quite ready to hear. Inside, she felt the drums begin to beat, as she realized he did mean it. He wanted to see her in bed. He wanted to see her curled up and sleepy, catlike and vulnerable in the early morning, see her rubbing the dust from her eyes, hear her yawn, smell the earthy scent of her as she tumbled beneath the cheap sheets after the too-late nights in the too-loud clubs. For a mere million his picture could see all that, and she could see him, and she wouldn't forget him because she was the sort who would keep a promise, however frivolous, however bizarre.

"It's up to you, Pat Parker," growled Alabama. "A lifetime of nightmares in exchange for a million for the mountains." He had forgotten how rich Latham was, how capricious, how consumed by the need to conquer beauty. The chase was on. He had seen it start. His brand-new friend was the quarry and she had better watch out.

"Listen, a bedside Alabama of Mr. Latham would be no hardship at all. Certainly more appetizing than one of my folks."

They both heard the cheerful banter of her first sentence tail off into the pathos of her second. For a brief moment the pain was visible, almost tangible, and she paused, seeming to hear hidden voices, to see invisible demons.

But there was a distraction. The doors before them were flung open. A small bundle of humanity was all wrapped up in a frilly bikini, the upper portion of which struggled to contain vast breasts, while the lower bit served both as wrapper to a broad-beamed butt, and launching pad for short, stocky legs. The brilliant white of the swimsuit offset the lobster pink of her skin. Whoever she was had economized on the sunscreen.

"Emma!" said Latham, wincing at the visual. "Come and meet the famous Alabama, and the beautiful Pat Parker. I've just bought a portrait Alabama did of me in Paris when I was young. I'm hoping it's going to perform the same function for me as a similar one did for Dorian Gray."

"On my bedside table? Thanks a lot!" Pat laughed. She held out a hand to Emma Guinness. "Hi, I'm Pat Parker," she said.

Alabama waved a halfhearted greeting, his hand firmly by his side.

"I know you are. I'm a fan. I love your work," said Emma. "If they'd used people like you, *Celebrity* wouldn't need to be turned around."

"Thanks," said Pat. A compliment was a good way to start. Already she liked the girl in the dreadful swimsuit. There had been no pretense that the ghastly *Celebrity* had been a success. The truthfulness added weight to the Englishwoman's flattery.

Latham smiled in satisfaction at the promising beginning. Both Emma and he had different plans for Pat Parker. Emma's would dovetail neatly with his. His would certainly not harmonize with Emma's. He turned to Alabama.

"Alabama, let me spirit you away for a few minutes. I want to show you some plans I have for building a house on that land I'm buying near you in the mountains. I want it to merge with its surroundings. I thought maybe you'd have a few ideas. You two girls get to know each other, and we'll meet later for lunch."

Alabama grunted his acquiescence. He hadn't looked forward to this lunch, but he had accepted out of curiosity and because any knowledge of a potential enemy was better than none. Now he had already scored a million dollars for the high Sierras and was about to get a preview of the monstrosity that the high roller was trying to build in his mountains. Great! It would be ammunition for the Coastal Commission hearing on the zoning when he later objected to the Latham plans. He grabbed at the cold Corona that had just materialized on the butler's Georgian silver salver, and he shuffled off with the billionaire.

Emma Guinness flopped onto the slubbed-silk sofa, and Pat Parker into an armchair.

"So, Pat, why Malibu?" She watched the photographer, taking in the good looks and the powerful fashion statement. The T-shirt she recognized. It was by hot new English designer of the moment, John Richmond. The tattoo motif—God, America, Mom, Elvis—was very "now," Harley biker chic, as the trendsetters tired of Chanel and conspicuous consumption and began to look for their fashion statements among the lowlife of the wild side. She must remember that for *New Celebrity*. Earthiness was coming back. Roots, the working class, dressing down were coming up in a modified sixties rehash after the rampant materialism of the fifties-style Reagan years. The Parker boots, battered, comfy, would run and run like the endless Parker legs, and the jeans, baggy, faded, would make sitting down a pleasure rather than an ordeal.

"I'm here because Alabama's here. I'm working with him. Developing a new perspective. I was stuck. He's helping me."

"You didn't look stuck to me. I loved your work."

"Yeah, well, it's what you feel inside, isn't it? I wanted to move on."

"To what?" Emma wasn't discouraged. The new Pat Parker might be more exciting than the old. Brand-new photographs for her brand-new magazine. She prayed it wasn't watered-down Alabama nature shots, though. More or less anything would play but those.

"Oh, I don't know, really. That's why I'm here. To find out. People still, I guess. I can't get away from them. They fascinate me. But not frothy people. I want to shoot deep people, dangerous people. You know, people who *care*."

"Yes, I know what you mean. More than Warhol died with Andy. 'Wows' and 'goshes' aren't enough as conversation. Frivolous is passé. But will you find those sorts of people in Malibu? I've only been here since yesterday and I'm on the verge of coma. I can't stay awake. There's this mellow yellow poison gas drifting in from the sea that bleaches out all the dark, brooding, productive thoughts into pretty, pale pastels. A week or two of this and I'll be the Day-Glo girl."

Pat laughed, not least because the Day-Glo girl would be a dramatic improvement on the frilly lobster. But she liked the rapid-fire conversation of the English girl, liked her unashamed trendiness, her analytical mind.

"Listen, color's a relief after all that New York black. And sleeping at night is a weird experience. I'm trying to get used to the noise of the quiet."

"Yes, but the sea makes such a racket. I keep thinking it's coming in the bedroom window. Apparently it's only a matter of time before it does." Emma laughed, and then she seemed to make a decision. She leaned forward, her arms on her knees. "Listen, Pat, I want you to work for *New Celebrity.* How would you feel about doing that on an exclusive basis? You'd get a retainer, a big one, and total artistic freedom to produce anything you liked. That might be just what you need right now. Cash, but no deadlines. An outlet, but no directions. I'd be buying your judgment and your vision, because I trust them."

Pat sat back in the chair. Despite Andy's death she wanted to say "wow." But she was enough of a New Yorker not to let her enthusiasm show.

"The trouble is, I'm sort of blocked right now. You say 'no deadlines,' but you'd have to see something for your money. And how much money were you thinking, anyway?"

She laid her head in her hand and smiled to disguise the hardnosed negotiating position.

"Say one hundred thousand for two big spreads a year."

"Wow!" said Pat Parker, despite herself.

Now Emma smiled. She had cleared the deal with Latham, and he had suggested adding twenty-five thousand to the retainer. Pat Parker would never have been offered a contract like it. But Emma had learned that in life you had to pay over the top for excellence. If you had the guts to do it, it always looked cheap later.

Emma Guinness leaned forward. "Are you on?" she asked.

"I'm not off. I'm not off." Pat laughed, playing for time. There was probably extra juice to be squeezed from the deal, but she couldn't think where. Ritts, Weber, and Newton didn't get offered contracts like this. Now, out of the blue, and at the very point where she was considering throwing in the towel on photojournalism, she had been offered the moon and the stars. How like life. Already she was wondering just what the hell she would choose as a subject for a *New Celebrity* photo essay. Her mind was blank. Writers weren't the only artists who got blocked.

"And I could choose whatever I did? I mean, you're not hoping for New York nighttime reportage and all the stuff I've concentrated on so far."

"It's up to you. If you want to do more of that, fine. If not, that's fine, too."

"You say two spreads a year, but you say 'no deadlines.' How would that work?"

"It'd be loose. Of course, I'd really like something yesterday, for my first issue, but if you haven't got anything in the can, I'll live with that. What I mean is that you won't be pinned down too tight. I just know we can work together. I can work with anyone I admire. The trouble is there aren't many who fit that bill."

"I accept," said Pat. There was a time for chatter and a time for action. She had a dream job. She was artistically underwritten. "Scorpions of the Santa Monica Mountains" would get a five-page spread and earn fifty thousand, at least in theory, at least in the contract. Okay, she wouldn't do that to Emma and Latham, but in a pinch she could. It was major-league freedom and it meant she could stay on in Malibu with Alabama. She could be a humble assistant, a gofer to the guru, and yet retain an outlet for her work and a magnificent income. All she had to do was what she did best. She had only to take photographs.

Emma jumped up.

"Great. Terrific. That's wonderful." She rushed over to Pat and hugged her tight. Inside she was bubbling, too. Her success had been built on the backs of the brilliant people she employed. Recognizing greatness in unlikely places and then hiring it was her chief talent—perhaps her only one. Now she was on the road and running. Michael Flaubert, the trendsetting black fashion journalist, had already agreed to take the vital fashion portfolio, and Kit Jacosta, the young, hip novelist, had been bribed to step down from his intellectual ivory tower to head up features. The Parker-Flaubert-Jacosta triumvirate was the stuff of magazine legend, and the adrenaline sang in the Guinness arteries as she contemplated her magnificent future.

"Come on, Pat, let's have some champagne to celebrate. I'm *so* excited."

"I'll stick with the Coke. I don't drink." Pat laughed, infected by Emma's enthusiasm and still trying to acclimate to the amazing thing that had happened to her.

"You don't? God, I do, and I feel like getting absolutely plastered." Actually, in all her life Emma had never once been drunk. She was a control freak, and that included self-control. But she had learned that people were not naturally drawn to those who were fearful of letting go. So she cultivated the appearance of looseness and pretended to enjoy the pointless business of having a good time. "Come on, let's go for a walk on the beach, then. I'm your boss, you've got to humor me," she said breathlessly, jumping up.

Pat stood up too, and, laughing, the two brand-new friends walked out through the French doors onto the sand of the private volleyball court that bordered the terrace of the Latham home. The sun scorched down on them, angling in sharply across the tranquil ocean. The smog-free air was fresh in their nostrils.

"Jesus, I could do with a surfer," said Emma suddenly.

"What!"

"A surfer to play with. Wouldn't that be nice? All slippery muscles and speechless, blond hair, brain dead, and tasting salty. Stamina of a horse, called Ricky, with parents my age. Ever since I've been in Malibu I haven't thought of anything else." Emma laughed to show she was serious.

"Oh, Emma, you're joking. He'd bore you rigid. 'Ricky' would be the kind of guy who thought a double entendre was a strong drink. How about Dick Latham? More your speed, I'd have thought," she added shrewdly.

"That's the alternative," agreed Emma with a smile. She sat down on the corner of a windsurfer that lay across the dunes.

"But he *is* a little too good to be true, isn't he?" Emma's voice went reflective as Pat sat down beside her. What she meant was that Latham liked girls who were ten times more beautiful than she—girls like Pat Parker, from whose face and body the Latham eyes had not strayed during the brief moments since they'd met; girls like Pat, whose salary he had suggested increasing by twenty-five percent; girls like Parker, whose photographic career had seemed so very well known to the satyrical billionaire.

"Listen, once in a blue moon they're allowed to be good."

"Mmmmmm. I don't think Dick's really very 'good,' do you? I mean, it's good that he's rich, and he's not gay, and it's good that he's interesting and bright and it's good that he's good-looking and knows how to make a woman feel incredibly good, but I'm afraid, really, he's very, very bad."

"Are you having an affair with him?"

Pat had never met such a wide-open English person. She must have died the death in her emotionally constipated homeland, have found nirvana in the mood incontinence of America. She was getting to know her at breakneck speed.

"Not unless you call a mile-high fuck in the loo on MGM Air an affair."

"Emma, you didn't!" Pat sat down on the serrated platform of the windsurfer. The incredulous amusement was thick in her voice.

"Oh, yes, we did."

"Why, I mean, how . . ."

"With very great difficulty and a certain amount of perseverance," said Emma, her voice mock serious. "He said he'd always wanted to try it, and as an employee, I felt it was my duty to accommodate him. Joy was minimal, but afterward there was a certain sense of achievement. He seemed chiefly concerned with the fact that it gave him the right to wear some sort of club tie. Oh, and he said it was good for the calf muscles on a long flight. You're supposed to exercise on aeroplanes nowadays. But then, being an American you know all about that. Health is something that hasn't caught on in Europe, you know."

"God, Emma, that's just unbelievable. I always imagined Latham to be so cool. I can't imagine him . . ."

Pat Parker tried to imagine what she couldn't, and as she did so she wondered what she felt about it. Clearly Latham had a problem. He had to have women, had to humiliate them, wasn't *that* fussy what they looked like. Emma Guinness's sharp mind and quick tongue were attractive, but she was very far from the drop-dead beautiful girls that hung on the Latham arm in the glossy magazines. Then there was the venue for the assignation. Original? Daring? Tacky? Bad manners? It was difficult to say. When she had first met him she had been flattered by the attention he had paid her, despite the subterranean feeling that he was not entirely wholesome. What should she make of that in light of what she had just learned? One thing was certain. With Dick Latham what you saw was not necessarily what you got. Emma's revelation had added surprise to his list of attributes/defects.

"Anyway," laughed Emma, "surfers permitting, I am hoping for a rematch in slightly more salubrious surroundings. Afterward, I am hoping for an exchange of sentiments more meaningful than remarks about aerobics and club ties. What are you after, Pat Parker, surely not Alabama? He looks like the proverbial old man of the woods, and I'd be *very* nervous about the state of his underwear."

"Oh, God, no, I mean not like that. He's my hero, that's all. And he's kind beneath all the bluster, and he's the most honest man I've ever met in my life."

"How awful." Emma shuddered. "Honest people are so brutal."

"Well, he *is* a little brutal, but only to those he doesn't trust."

"He doesn't trust Dick, does he?"

"No, I don't think he does. He hates businessmen, and then there was some fight they had in Paris a long time ago."

"Well, all I know is that Dick wants to buy up all this land in the mountains, God knows why, and he needs Alabama to okay it. Alabama's the godfather around here, apparently . . . and Dick reckons *he's* the godfather everywhere else. They're probably up there now, each making offers the other can't refuse. There shouldn't be any trouble finding horses' heads to stick in each other's beds. Malibu's stiff with them. More nags than beach boys . . . unfortunately."

She looked transcendentally saddened by the deficiency of human flesh, the oversupply of the equine variety, and Pat had to laugh, despite the less than flattering press Emma had given Alabama.

"How did you get to meet Dick Latham, Emma?"

"Anglophilia is one of his perversions. He has a house in Chester Square, which is where all the grand Americans live. Member of White's, debentures at Wimbledon, fittings at Anderson and Sheppard, the whole nine yards as you'd say, whatever that means. He was looking for someone to pull *Celebrity* out of the shit, and I'd just done that with a rag called *Class*, so he offered me a million a year and the use of his brownstone on Fifth, and I said yes, of course. I'd been dying to get out of England."

"What can you possibly mean? England sounds wonderful. I'm longing to go there."

"The tourists enjoy it. The English are quite nice to them, and they don't have time to get fed up with the food and the weather. It's the English that the English don't like. The whole place is in a state of constant undeclared civil war. The accents are the uniforms of the rival armies, and the different classes rape and pillage and take no prisoners. The 'workers' steal, the aristo-crats drink, and the bourgeois suffer. It's vicious stuff, believe me. For you Americans class warfare is an ethnic affair. You know . . . black hardhats playing rap music on building sites to irritate redneck foremen who are play-ing country music to infuriate the blacks, and they're both cranking up the volume to madden the Jewish doctor across the street who's trying to listen to Strindberg. It's child's play compared to England, where everyone really *cares* about the class struggle. People work for peanuts all their lives to score a knighthood that the real aristocrats giggle at."

"But hasn't Thatcher changed all that?"

"God, she's tried, but they'll change her first. Until they get rid of the royals, it'll be business as usual."

The bitterness was beginning to show, and from the ashes of the amusing, irreverent, self-confident Emma Guinness a new animal was emerging. It was a wounded one, a hound at bay, dangerous, frightened, angry, hurt. Her lips curled over her words and her eyes were narrow, her lips tight and mean. She clenched her fists, and her knuckles were white against the red of her skin, as she relived the pain and the cruelty of the words that had clearly hurt more than the proverbial sticks and stones. Pat saw it all, and filed it away in her memory. As with Dick Latham, first impressions of Emma Guinness were misleading. The girl she saw now was one who had to be handled with caution. The hatred was alive in her. Pat could almost touch it.

"You're not allowed to feel like that in Malibu," said Pat gently. "It's against the law."

Emma started, as if emerging from a nightmare sleep.

"What? Oh yes, England." She laughed unconvincingly. "I was on my hobby horse. It's a bad subject for me."

"You should hear me on parents." Pat felt the need to show solidarity. There was no pain that she couldn't cap with the pain of her childhood.

"Bad parents?"

"Only the worst." Pat bit her lip as she dared to remember.

But Emma Guinness, not even a sounding board, was certainly no wailing wall. Other people's lives were deeply uninteresting to her. To that extent she was thoroughly British.

Her eyes went dreamy. "I *suppose* I had parents," she said at last. "I could never get very interested in them."

She stood up. "Come on, I'm hungry, and I ought to change for lunch. Let's go and join the others before they bore themselves to death."

Pat stood up. A new job. Dick Latham, member of White's, the Forbes 400, and the Mile High Club, his laughing eyes probing her. Alabama, a bomb on a short fuse in the billionaire's lair. Emma Guinness, Pat's new boss, a witty, vicious trendsetter who talked of surfer's bodies and schemed secretly to become the Latham wife. One thing was certain. It was going to be one hell of a lunch.

—

"WATCH OUT for the salsa," said Pat. "It's red hot."

"Good," boomed Alabama, scooping a mound onto a tortilla chip. "If you can't insult your stomach, what the hell can you insult around here?"

"Oh, I'm sure that finding something to insult isn't a problem for you, Mr. Alabama," said Emma Guinness pertly, sipping gently on the white Napa Valley chardonnay from the Jordan Vineyard.

"We must all call Alabama Alabama," said Dick Latham pleasantly. "It's like Sting . . . or Cher . . . only different, of course." He allowed himself the gentle jab. His earlier meeting with Alabama had gone far better than expected. The mock plans for the house he never intended to build had been impressive, and expensive. He'd hired Richard Martin to design a low-slung contemporary that had melted into the mountain landscape. There had been detailed plans for solar heating, underground power lines, and rich landscaping so that the whole modest ten-thousand-square-foot compound would be all but invisible, and yet at the same time would make a low-key artistic statement destined to appeal to an aesthete like Alabama. The old boy had grunted and groaned but, reading between the lines of his token protests, Latham had known that he'd been impressed.

"If you must, I suppose you must," the prickly environmentalist had concluded, and Latham had known that all objections to his buying the land would now be withdrawn.

He smiled gently around his lunch table as he dreamed of the real-estate coup he had pulled off. Cosmos Studios in all its ancient glory would be reborn in the mountains that looked down on Malibu, and Alabama would go ballistic. There was no fool like an old fool. There was nothing sweeter than revenge on a long-time enemy, especially if you were enriched by the process.

"What do you think of Mr. Latham's house, Alabama?" asked Pat. He was glowering at Latham, his brow darkening at being mentioned in the same breath as a pop star and an anorectic actress whose proudest possessions appeared to be her belly button and her butt.

"Not bad for a gin palace. You know, a cross between ancient Rome and 2001. Press a button and the swimming pool turns into a think tank."

"Surely not that bad," laughed Latham easily in the tones reserved for an unruly and overindulged child. "You had to admit that it was environment-friendly, Alabama. It *is* rather modern, but I think Martin's going to win a prize with it, and after all, we are living in the present, aren't we? I can't stand the idea of trying to build something old."

"Yeah, that was the problem with *Celebrity*," said Emma, demonstrating that she was not afraid to irritate her boss.

Latham frowned. With great deliberation he eased a small piece of butter onto a tiny sliver of melba toast.

"Well, let's just hope that the trendsetter from across the water doesn't repeat the old mistakes . . . and that she doesn't replace them with new ones."

The temperature sank a couple of points. Alabama looked up, encouraged.

Pat watched Emma, saw the two red spots high on her cheekbones. The English girl was living dangerously. Intimacy at thirty thousand feet clearly provided no easement into the billionaire's good books. The prenuptial agreement looked light-years away. Lantham's sense of humor did not extend into his business dealings.

"I hope *I'm* not going to prove a mistake," said Pat suddenly. "But I want to say that I'm really looking forward to working with Emma."

"What?" The question shot from Alabama.

"Emma offered me a job working exclusively for *New Celebrity*. I'm on a generous retainer, and I do two spreads a year of my own choosing. Isn't it wonderful? It means I can stay on with you without being a burden, and have an outlet for my work at the same time."

"Why on earth do you need an outlet for your work?" said Alabama.

He was thoroughly put out. Pat had expected it. She wasn't frightened of him, but she knew this would take some handling. Across the table she sensed Latham's eyes upon her. He wanted to see how she handled pressure. Why did she feel that he wanted her to fall apart beneath it?

"An artist needs an outlet. You know that, Alabama. How many exhibitions have you had over the years, how many print sales, how many books?" She looked straight into his angry eyes. She knew what was coming.

"No pretty pictures in silly, glossy magazines," he barked.

"When you were my age you were selling wedding photographs in Kentucky." Pat Parker's jaw was set. Her bright eyes flashed. She would have to use her temper. She could do that, because in all her life so far she had never lost it. It was a survival trick she had learned during the bloody battles of the war that had been family life.

"Lucky you," crowed Emma Guinness. "Weddings are almost as much fun as funerals. People make such glorious fools of themselves."

Alabama ignored her. The Kentucky crack was up under his ribs like the blade of a blunt knife.

Dick Latham's eyes were in Wimbledon mode. This was turning into serious spectator sport. Rows were *such* fun to watch. But which way to bet? Alabama, the sore-headed bear veteran of a billion such encounters, or the spunky girl with the breasts and the legs and the thoroughbred personality? He shook his head. It was no good. It was too close to call. He reached for the wine and settled back in the Chippendale carver to catch the fun.

"I'm not ashamed of that. Why should I be? It was honest work and I did it well and I made people happy . . ." Alabama stopped, suddenly aware that he had been forced onto the defensive. Now he had left himself open to an unanswerable counterattack. Nor was Pat Parker ashamed of the job she had taken; it, too, was honest work that made people happy. His eyes flashed. He would cut her off at the pass. "*Celebrity* magazine is a trivial pursuit run by parasites and poseurs that panders to the worst instincts of the neurotic and idle rich," he spluttered.

"I *hope*," said Emma Guinness with a brittle laugh. "If it doesn't, it won't be through want of trying."

Latham, despite the insult to his baby, laughed too. The ball was deep against the Parker baseline.

It was to be effortlessly returned.

"That," she said dismissively, "is both patronizing and elitist. In a free society the people decide what gives them pleasure. They are more likely to be right than a group of hypocrites with egos too big for their hatbands. Living life isn't so easy that you can do it for others. Intellectuals always make that mistake."

Alabama went red. He went redder. He went reddest. He began to pulsate. Latham swore he could hear him hum, see him throb, feel the heat that burned from him.

"I'm not a fucking intellectual," he boomed. The word infuriated him. It was the ultimate insult.

"I know you're not, but you should try to avoid sounding like one."

"Don't patronize me," he howled at her.

"Don't patronize the public," she shot back.

"I don't have to listen to this," screamed Alabama. "You charge into my life uninvited, unwanted, because you needed my help and here you are telling me what to say and think, like the mind quacks in the godforsaken magazine that's hired you. Maybe you deserve each other. Maybe you should go back to the stink zone and scurry about taking snaps of the roaches. And maybe you should get the hell out of my life, and not come back."

He stood up, pushing out his butt at the chair. His gesture was so sudden, so precipitous, that he caught the butler as he moved forward with the tray of iced gazpacho Andaluz. The glutinous soup had liftoff. It left the silver tureen and it flew like red-wine vomit, rich in bits and pieces of vegetable, tomato cubes, onion, croutons, red pimentos, straight at Emma Guinness. She took the direct hit in the cleavage of a sequined Beverly Hillbilly bolero top, across the front of which was the legend NEW CELEBRITY. The gritty first course surged down between her tits, dyeing the ghastly garment blood red, and saving it instantly from sartorial disaster. She who had looked fashion tragic, now looked fashion bright.

"Oh *fuck!*" she screamed.

They all looked at her in horror. The butler darted in, shrunk back from the enormity of the task that confronted him, summoned up the courage to approach once more. He dabbed delicately at the mammary mountain with a damask napkin, well aware that the only appropriate response would be with a fire hose.

"I'm sorry," lied Alabama.

"Oh, *Emma!*" gasped Pat.

"Oh *shit!*" added the soup target.

The silence that followed was broken by two sounds. The first was the gentle drip, drip, drip of gazpacho onto the priceless Kirman Persian carpet. The second was the gentle tones of Dick Latham's laughter.

They were soft at first, but they strengthened, and slowly his whole body began to rock with the emotion. He put both hands onto the soup-splattered tablecloth and his eyes creased up as he beheld the angst and confusion of his lunch party. Emma Guinness, so full of herself, so quick and sharp, was now a clawed lobster swimming in her own bisque. Alabama, the Rock House and White House regular, was the clumsy klutz who had dropped the food. And there, floating above them all in the star slot, was the girl whose body he suddenly wanted more than his next breath. So what if there was soup on the John Singer Sargent, gazpacho on the four hundred-knot-to-the-inch silk rug. They could be replaced if they couldn't be cleaned. But the highnoon drama of his luncheon could never be repeated. In mellow Malibu such an event could not have been staged. It was brilliant. It was beautiful. And it was breaking him up.

Alabama was the second to chuckle. Pat Parker wasn't far behind. It took Emma Guinness longest to get to the joke of which she was the punch line, but get there she did. The butler alone, appalled by the *Valdez*-size spill and the cleanup it entailed, remained isolated from the gales of laughter that now roared around the room.

"There's a girl in my soup," tried Alabama.

"Don't let on. They'll all want one," Pat giggled.

"The soup's deep in me," Emma laughed.

"Pass the girl," howled Dick Latham.

"Don't be a Dick," they all roared at him in unison, quoting the T-shirt.

"Oh, my . . . God . . ." Latham laughed through his tears. "What a fabulous bloody lunch."

~6~

PAT PARKER WALKED slowly across the dunes, the Nikon dangling loosely from her arm. She was full of Mexican food, and she felt at one with the beauty, her whole life in tune with nature, with the beach, the mountains, with the pale blue of the sky. Beneath her feet the sand was warm but not burning, and the Malibu sea breeze ruffled her hair and cooled her skin. The salty air licked at her. The heat haze wrapped her. The bright brilliance of the colors floodlit the inside of her mind. It was one of those moments of transcendence when life fitted into place. The jigsaw was no longer a pile of unconnected woodwork on the floor, promising only frustration and hard work in return for some unspecified later reward. Instead everything had merged in a visual feast of total satisfaction. It all made sense. The doubts and fears had melted in the burning kaleidoscope of the heatscape.

She stopped at the crest of the dunes and looked down Broad Beach, all the way to Zuma, a sun-bronzed crescent of oiled humanity. There it was breast-to-face intimate. Here, where the plutocrats hung out, it was as crowded as Central Park in the wilding dusk. She smiled as she remembered lunch, and how the harmony had replaced the discord. It was a metaphor for how she felt right now, the good coming out of the bad, the struggle and the strife metamorphosing for no apparent reason into the pleasure of peace. Her fight with Alabama had strengthened their relationship, not harmed it. The bully in him had tried to cow her, and she had not allowed it. She had seen the respect grow in his eyes, the admiration for her artistic talents merging with admiration for the strength of her personality. And Latham's interest in her was deepening. It was flattering, and nicely disturbing, because there was a sense in which now she was his employee. The billionaire media king would be looking out for her and her work. He had begged her to stay for the afternoon, and when Alabama had left after lunch, she had remained. But her trigger finger was itchy. Out there on the sands of Malibu pictures were waiting, photographs that might one day form part of a spread in the Latham/Guinness magazine.

Now, she looked around her. The surfers were busy in the waves, and the girls who watched them were lost in Walkman sound as they basted their bodies with Coppertone and revolved spitlike in the ultraviolet rays. A windsurfer knifed through the water. A girl-watching chopper pilot droned overhead. Joggers jogged, lovers lingered, and the only sounds were the waves, the gulls, and the *plop-plop* of bat against ball as the eternal beach tennis battles raged in the dreamland. There was nothing there that would look better on film than in reality. It was almost too perfect, and not for the first time in her life Pat speculated that the photo opportunities in heaven would pale beside the ones in hell.

Which was the moment she saw him. He stood like a god against the crest of the dunes, a foot thrown forward, his head held back, Viking proud, and the sun lit him from the side, casting his long shadow like an omen across the sand. He wore baggy jeans of faded blue, and a washed-out shirt of a deeper color, beneath which a brilliant white sweatshirt ringed a long, powerful neck. He was totally preoccupied, staring into space and yet seeing nothing, lost in the scary, wonderful world that Pat knew instinctively would be his dreams. His body seemed taut, poised for perpetual motion, some action of single-minded purpose that he was scared to commit to. Pat's Nikon rose from her side like the stealthy rifle of the hunter, unwilling to disturb the prey, yet hungry for the kill.

In the lens she had him, a proud and dangerous animal in her sights. The ball of her forefinger twirled the focus. She gasped in excitement as his profile clarified. God, he was extraordinary. He was an eagle, and a lion, the strong brow racing down the proud aquiline nose to a sensuous, knowing mouth. His chin poked out at the world like an exclamation mark, his broad shoulders supported the head where the violent will would live, and his muscular chest, triangular beneath the navy-blue cotton of his shirt, parceled the heart that wouldn't know how to love. His image was sharp now, and Pat could see the honey brown of his lightly tanned flesh, see the lustrous glow of his midnight hair. Although she was forty feet from him, she had the mad sensation that she could actually smell the masculine musk of him, the scent of his liquid charisma borne like a love potion on the erratic breeze. Deep in her soul the molecules rearranged themselves.

Her finger strengthened on the shutter and it hovered at the point of release. And then he moved. His head swiveled around suddenly, and, through the telephoto lens of her camera, he was staring deep into her eyes. They lanced into her, searing in the majesty of their total disapproval, and her finger froze at the point of fire as she was numbed by the weird intensity of his gaze. The camera was the glass through which she saw him, but she did not see darkly. This was face to face. It amplified him. He had become his eyes and his whole body poured into the scorn that lasered out at her. Pat was stuck at the edge of her picture. The viewfinder was still jammed tight against her cheek, and yet she couldn't move. She couldn't shoot him. She couldn't fail to do so. The thoughts rushed through her mind—desire, confusion, excitement, and yes, shame. In Africa they believed that photographs robbed you of your soul. That was what the magnificent eyes were accusing

her of. And she was guilty—of impoliteness, of voyeurism, and of lust in the
first degree. She lowered the camera. She lowered her gaze and, full of the
most wonderful foreboding, she walked slowly toward him. He didn't move
as she approached, but he watched her carefully. Pat Parker had never
thought much about her beauty. Usually she took it for granted. Not now.
For the first time in her life she was grateful for it. It would be the shield that
would protect her. And it would be the open sesame to the closed book with
the gorgeous cover that she had found on the sands of Malibu.

She smiled shyly as she got closer, and she splayed out her hands in what
she hoped was a disarming gesture.

"I'm sorry," she said. "I should have asked your permission. It was rude of
me."

He didn't answer. He didn't smile. He stared through her, haughty, cold,
clearly unmoved by her apology. She was near to him now, standing on the
brink of his aura, and the aggression and the pride, the insolent self-righ-
teousness were so real she felt she could reach out and touch them.

"May I take your photograph . . . *sir!*" she added with a laugh.

"No!"

"Why not?"

"I don't have to explain myself to you." His head notched back. He
seemed to be watching her from a distant planet.

Pat's heart quickened. She hadn't expected that, and why was her stomach so suddenly without a bottom, and her mouth dry as the low desert, and
where was the reflex anger that at any other time would be bubbling through
her body?

"You don't like having your photograph taken?" she said simply. It was
halfway between a question and a statement of a fact.

He looked away from her, back toward the houses, as if her remark didn't
deserve an answer.

"Why do you suppose they all live here?" he said suddenly. "I mean the
actors."

"Because it's the most expensive beach in Malibu. Why Malibu? Because
there's peace here? I don't know. Are you an actor?"

He waved away her question as if *he* was not the point, in a gesture that
somehow emphasized that he was the only point.

"I think it has to do with revenge," he said.

"Revenge? As in 'living-well-is-the-best . . .'"

"Yeah." He turned toward her, and the sun behind him paled to a yellow
irrelevance in comparison to the warmth of his totally unexpected smile. His
whole face launched into it like a swallow diver from a high board, and Pat
Parker was sucked up into its liquid intimacy, thrilled beyond any reason that
she had found the right answer to the mini-riddle he had posed.

"You see, nobody believed in them till it was too late," he said. "Not too
late for success, but too late for it to matter."

"Do people believe in you?"

She wanted to get away from "them." She wanted to get to "him."

"*I* do."

"Is that enough?"

"For now." Again he smiled. Or rather the intensity of the original one strengthened.

"I still want to take your picture."

"If you let me take yours."

He laughed as he spoke, aware that she wouldn't want that. Already he seemed to know her.

"I'm a photographer. Nobody shoots the photographer."

"Okay, so now you know how I feel."

Pat gave up. On the photograph. Suddenly it didn't seem so important. Other things did.

"Are you from here?" she asked.

"Nobody's from here. I live in New York. And I *am* an actor. I just finished at the Juilliard. I'm Tony Valentino." He held out his hand to her.

She took it, and his firm grip closed on her, tightened, and then left her. There was no flirtation in his touch or in the eyes that watched her. His whole demeanor said he was above and beyond such mundane things. But Pat remembered the feel of his flesh, the first fleeting brush of bodies, and there was a tingling at the base of her spine, and a lightness in her heart.

"I'm from New York, too. Isn't it weird we're not friends," she joked.

"Yes, it's a big place," he said. His answer was strangely literal, and it was with a shock that Pat realized that he possessed no sense of humor. People were supposed to have that. It was something the world considered important. Not that she had ever rated it. Those who laughed at themselves were usually a joke. It was the people who took themselves seriously who ended up getting things together. Revolving bow ties and whoopee cushions were the mortal enemies of houses on Broad Beach.

"Do you want to walk along the beach a bit? Big Apple refugees should stick together in Wonderland. We can keep each other nervous."

"Sure," he said.

"You want Zuma and real people or Broad Beach and vengeful fantasy ones?"

"If I'm talking to you I won't need to worry about the other people," said Tony Valentino.

She cocked her head to one side to show that she hadn't quite fathomed what he meant. It sounded suspiciously like a compliment from lips that were obviously a stranger to them. On the other hand it might have been a remark about his concentration, as in "When I'm talking to someone, whoever it is, I focus exclusively on them."

"Let's do Zuma. Beach Boys, Gidget, and Frankie Avalon. My mom would have died to be here." She winced as she thought of her. Perhaps the most valuable thing she'd done for Pat in her entire life was to lend herself to this conversation. She looked up at Tony, and she started in amazement at what had happened to him.

He had fallen apart. His square shoulders were slumped, his high head was low, and his fine features, so proud and glorious, were stricken with a terrible sorrow. The change of mood was devastating in its suddenness and in its totality.

"What's the matter?" said Pat quickly, as the alarm bells sounded within her.

"My mother died last Friday," he said, his voice shaking. His face was pointed at the sand. She couldn't see it. But she knew it. Mist would shroud the arrogant eyes. The sensual lips would be trembling. She reached out. She had to touch him. Her hand found his forearm.

"I'm terribly sorry," she said. And she was. It was extraordinary. This stranger had moved her with his beauty, and now he was moving her with his sorrow. She had been wrong about his unfeeling heart. Before her eyes, it was breaking.

He looked up at her, haggard, haunted, unashamed of his weakness as before he had been oblivious to his strength. The tears filled his eyes, hovering at the brim, at the base of his long lashes. He took a deep breath, forcing himself together through a stupendous act of will.

"I'm not used to it. I never will be."

"Time helps." Pat mouthed the platitudes that were all language offered at moments of supreme importance. She linked her arm through his, surprised and pleased that he allowed it.

"I guess." His laugh was bitter, as he acknowledged her attempt at comfort, recognizing the inadequacy of words, and yet their necessity. "The trouble is that I was too busy wanting things to tell her I loved her."

"I think she knew." Pat would have known. She had never seen anything so expressive as this man who stood before her. His feelings were on his forearm, beneath her fingers where his sleeve would have been. They exploded from his forever eyes. They beamed out in the charisma that clothed him. His feelings might not be nice, or kind or comfortable, but they would always be impossible to ignore. And the target of his love would be illuminated in a light so bright it would melt the heavens.

"Thank you," he said.

And as he said it, Pat Parker knew just exactly what was happening.

She was falling in love.

—

PAT PARKER sat all alone in the crowded restaurant, and once more she looked at her watch. It was seven thirty. He was half an hour late. She sipped at the Calistoga mineral water, but the ice had melted and it was losing its fizz. So was she. The clientele of Zooma Sushi didn't help her mod. They were young and hip and great-looking, and they were having the good time she wasn't. They laughed, and they giggled, their lustrous brown skins vibrant against predominantly white clothes, and it was perfectly clear that they all stood close to the movies. Outside in the lot the Jeeps and the open Corvettes, the Mondiale Ferraris and the convertible Jaguars confirmed it. There was money to burn here in this Malibu hot spot, networks to be set up, parts to be gotten, deals to be done.

Pat sighed. Jeez! Could she have been so wrong? It was the oldest mistake in the book. A good-looking boy on a beach. In *Malibu!* A short conversation. High-speed getting to know you. Emotions emoted. He had even admitted to being an actor. They had walked hand in hand on the sand and they had stopped for a cold Coke at the food stall on Zuma, and she had listened spellbound to the history of his life, but mostly she had watched him, bowled over by his beauty, and the extraordinary expressiveness of his face and gestures. His personality had been so real. There had been no hint of a line being shot, no whiff of a come-on. Pat had not hesitated to become a believer. Now she wasn't so sure. Distanced from the power of him, there was a place for doubt. The clock said he was half an hour late. That was fact. It was entirely possible that this was the first half hour of life without Tony Valentino. She held up her hand and grabbed the sleeve of the passing waiter. He stopped, and smiled, his blond hair, male-model good looks, and his ponytail giving away his Thespian dreams.

"I think I'll eat," she said. "I guess I've been stood up."

"No, you haven't," said Tony Valentino.

He stood over the table like Heathcliff on a blasted moor, brooding, moody, black as a thundercloud against the pastel colors of the restaurant and its diners. He wore a leather jacket, faded but totally clean, and beneath it a simple legendless T-shirt, crisp and white against the olive skin of his neck. A buckled cavalry belt held up standard-issue faded 501's. Black cowboy boots peeped from their bottoms, on one of which was a matte-black spur. He lowered a battered crash helmet onto the small table, and outside, through the picture windows of the restaurant, Pat could see the red-and-white striped Kawasaki Ninja bike that had clearly been his transport. The light was above and behind him, as it had been earlier at the beach, and his features were obscure, as if he specialized in mystery, his whole being a complicated essay in disguise, camouflage, and the delicious excitement of the unknown.

"Hi," said Pat, her tone neutral, waiting for the apology. But already she was losing it. The nasty half an hour was already a memory. The exotic now had wonderful promises for the future. It was the way he held the weapon of his body. It was a spear, hovering above her, ready to strike at her heart. It was so strangely dangerous. The threat was not overt, but it was everywhere. It hung in the air, it steamed from the corners of his broad shoulders, it hammered its jungle rhythms in the pit of her stomach.

"I'm sorry I'm late," he said. There was no excuse offered, just the bare apology. He reached for the chair opposite her, and he sat down. As he did so, his face was fully visible. He didn't look very sorry. He looked deeply wonderful.

"Is lateness a problem for you? I imagine it must be complicated to be unpunctual—as an actor."

"No, it's not a problem for me." He smiled at her irritation. His eyes dared her to keep the subject alive. The "for me" was almost, but not quite, a taunt.

Pat felt the anger fuse begin its slow burn inside her. Her head told her to cool it. She didn't know this guy well enough to quarrel with him. If all she wanted to do was fight with him, she should walk right out of the restaurant. They had started like that, with some sort of confrontation. Now it was happening again. But he was so damned pleased with himself. It wasn't fair that anyone could be so cocky and so beautiful. Okay, so she fancied him, but it wasn't enough. She wanted to control him, and the place to establish that was square one.

"Well, it's a problem for me. I've been waiting here for thirty goddamn minutes. The least you can do is make up some excuse. It's called manners."

"Do lies make you feel better?"

Again he smiled the marvelous, infuriating smile. Lies were for little people, it said. They were for cowards; for those who were not proud of themselves and their behavior; for the weak, who cared what the world thought. His eyes bored into her. He wanted an answer. She was on the defensive, and yet *he* was in the wrong. Or was he?

Did lies make her feel better? Yes, they did, but it wasn't the sort of thing she could admit. Yet to deny it would be to hand him victory on a plate. In an attempt to conceal her Catch-22 predicament, Pat said nothing.

She swept up the menu, furious and yet at the same time weirdly elated. Never in her life had the two paradoxical emotions existed side by side.

"I'm going to have salmon, tuna, and yellowtail, and a California roll wrapped in cucumber rather than seaweed," she said. "What are you going to have?"

"I don't know," he said. "I've never had sushi. You'll have to help me."

Pat smiled her surprise. He had done yet another 180-degree turn. Total vulnerability had replaced the screw-you macho almost-insolence of the previous moment. But then Pat realized that was merely on the surface. Actually, his behavior was in character, and the salient features of that character were honesty and fearlessness. He had been late, had no excuse, and had apologized for it. He wasn't ashamed of that, and he didn't need to lie about it. He'd never had sushi before. That was merely a fact. He didn't care that it might imply a lack of sophistication. He could have come up with another restaurant when Pat had suggested they meet at Zooma Sushi, but he hadn't wanted to. He wasn't afraid of his own ignorance, nor of asking for help even from a person to whom he had just given both the motive and the ammunition for an attempt at a mini-humiliation.

"Oh, well, it's raw fish," said Pat. A part of her hoped he would recoil from that, the godlike face crumpling in the disgust of the mere mortal.

"Yeah, I know. I've been waiting for an aficionado to show me the way."

"Why do I get the feeling that not many people show you the way?" Pat laughed to show that he was forgiven and that they were friends again, friends on a journey to something else.

"Because I know where I'm going."

"And where is that?"

"To the top."

"Of?"

"Acting. Movies. The world."

He leaned in toward her, daring her to laugh at his presumption. But she didn't want to. Maybe it was a laughable ambition, but not when it tumbled from those lips, not when it was allied to the fire of those eyes. Certainly there was no doubt in her mind that it could be achieved. Pat knew about the will and what it could do. It was the faith that blew away the opposition, and atomized the obstacles. It was the fuel that kept you going when the tank was on empty. It was the motive force that loved nothing more than the word *impossible* because of the opportunity it provided for proving the silly world wrong.

"Do you have a game plan?" Pat dared to ask the question. This boy was no run-of-the-mill Hollywood and Vine dreamer, a hapless soldier in the army of the hopelessly hopeful who would end as cannon fodder in the Tinsel Town wars. But there should be substance in his powerful dreams. Laser purpose could not be pointed merely at the stars. It must have earthly targets, too.

"I'm going back to New York. I've got a small part in an off-Broadway stage adaptation of *East of Eden.* I need more experience. It's too soon for out here."

It was the right answer. The determination to win and the belief in himself had not interfered with his judgment. Hollywood didn't want you if it knew that you wanted it. It preferred to imagine it did the discovering, because it was the most insecure, paranoid, and aggressive place on earth.

"And after that you'll get an agent, look for more parts in the theater?"

"Yeah."

"Do you need photographs, for when you're job hunting?"

"Yes, I do." He watched her.

"Can I take them?"

"Are you expensive?" His smile was enigmatic. "I haven't got much money."

"I'm free. For you. And I'm very, very good. As good a photographer as you are an actor. Maybe even better."

She smiled to show she meant it, and that it was a challenge. She was daring him to take something for nothing, this proud man who wouldn't usually do that sort of thing. But already she was thinking of the photographs she could take of him. If she could capture one-quarter of his essence on celluloid she would have made a masterpiece. Already she was laying him out in her mind, choosing the backdrop, arranging the lighting. He was tungsten, no question . . . and he was naked. God, yes he was, naked as the dreamy day he was born, his skin glistening with sweat, hot beneath the lights, the juice of him staining the white background paper, his steam rising like mist from the floor of her studio. Would he be shy then, at last, as she moved with the precision of the surgeon around him? Would he avert his eyes from hers as they plundered his defenseless body, raiding it, pillaging it for its visual splendor without shame or mercy? Dispassionate, she would capture him;

the cool professional, she would use him; untouched by his beauty, she would order him about, move this way, turn that, and "Oh, what a pity your legs are a little too short for your torso, your feet a tad too large for your legs."

The sushi hit the table, flattening Pat Parker's fantasy. In confusion, she picked up the chopsticks, poured some low-sodium soy sauce into the bowl, and transferred a small mound of green horseradish from the plate to the soy.

"Watch out for this stuff. It can tear the top off your head. What you do is dunk the fish in the sauce, add a sliver of spiced ginger, and a touch of horseradish, then go for it. Here, like this."

She reached forward for the glistening salmon, the wedge of raw fish nestling on a small tight mound of white rice. She rolled it in the soy allowing the rice to blot up the sauce, dressed it with horseradish and ginger, and held it out across the table to him.

He leaned toward her and allowed her to feed him, but his eyes never left hers, and the moment was not about food. It was about taking, and being given, and about tenderness and looking after people, and, unmistakably, it was also about eating and being eaten.

"Mmmmm, it's good," he murmured. "Like smoked salmon. Thanks."

Pat felt the feeling explode in the middle of her. It was too strong. He was too much. She was jealous of the fish. She wanted to be it, deep in the recesses of his mouth, all mixed up with his saliva, about to be swallowed into the delicious darkness of his body. She knew that she was just staring at him, her mouth half-open in a smile of serious longing. She knew he would notice that, and probably he would think it her weakness, but there was nothing to be done about it. It just was. Mr. Honesty would have to deal with it.

"What kind of pictures do you take?"

Pictures? What did he mean, pictures? Oh, yes. Reality, not the steamy jungles of lust.

"Reportage mainly. Portraits, too. I've just made a deal with *New Celebrity* magazine in New York."

"The billionaire's magazine that the English girl edits?"

"That's the one."

"Do you know her?" he asked.

"Emma Guinness. Yes. She was lunching at that house on Broad Beach where we met."

"She *was*?"

"Yes. Why?"

"I met her the other day. She was at the end-of-term production at the Juilliard. She came on to me, with an 'I'm-going-to-make-you-a-star' pitch."

"Emma Guinness? She didn't!"

"Oh, yes, she did."

"And?" God! Surely it was too early for jealousy.

"I was a little hard on her." He smiled the understatement.

"What did you say?"

"Whatever. Rough stuff. She'll be an enemy now."

"Quite a powerful one, no? I mean career-wise. Was it a real casting-couch thing?" All sorts of ideas were streaming through Pat's mind. Emma and her surfer fantasies. Short, squat Emma with her designs on the Latham empire. Big-titted Emma who would have squawked while she came a mile high over America. But mostly she was trying to visualize Emma putting the moves on Tony Valentino. It was not an exercise for a squeamish stomach.

"Yeah, it was for real. I didn't imagine it, if that's what you mean."

"Well, I'm glad you rained on her parade," said Pat with a conviction that came easily to her.

"I wouldn't like to have to work for her."

"I hope it's easier for a woman." Pat laughed. "Actually, she's quite funny, and she's very bright. Latham thinks she can turn the magazine around. She's hiring some pretty impressive people. Myself included."

"What's Latham like?" said Tony suddenly.

Pat paused. She had to think about that.

"Sort of sleek, dangerous, rather charming." She paused. "A bit like you, really."

"Older. Richer. More powerful."

"For now," agreed Pat.

Their eyes were gridlocked. Emma and Tony had unnerved her. Was it possible that Latham and Pat were unnerving him?

"I heard he's a bastard."

Pat smiled in triumph. It was definite. There was a spark of jealousy.

"Only if he's allowed to be."

For a minute or two they ate in silence.

"Did you know he just bought Cosmos Studios?" Pat floated the bait. If money was the flame that attracted the mothlike women to the Latham persona, a movie studio might well be the sticky paper to the Tony Valentino fly.

"I didn't know that," said Tony slowly.

"Would you like to meet him?" She knew she was playing with fire.

"In what capacity?" So did he.

"Oh, as my friend. As an actor. What else?"

"On the off chance he'd stick me in a Cosmos movie?" The sarcasm was up there on the surface. There was accusation in his voice. He was hinting that Pat's suggestion was not a million miles from Emma Guinness's. The expression on his face said he was disappointed by her.

She retreated fast. Aggression was her reaction of choice when she was caught playing unworthy games.

"Oh, come on, Tony. You know that's not how things happen. Studio owners don't handle casting. He might be a lot of things, but I hardly think Dick Latham's unprofessional."

Would he be humbled by the putdown? Would he ever!

"Then why the hell would 'your friend, the actor' want to meet the old fart?" His lip curled on the question.

"Lighten up, Tony. It was only an idea. I thought he might be a useful contact, that's all. This *is* California. We're in Malibu, for God's sake. It's how things *work*."

"It's not how I work, Pat Parker," said Tony simply. There was no anger in his voice, only a patient desire that she should understand. "I'm good at what I do, and I'm going to be the best at it. Sooner or later everyone will recognize that. It's just a matter of time. I don't have to push and pull, and hustle and lick butt. All I have to do is what I do. Don't you feel that way about your photographs?"

"No, I *don't*," said Pat, her voice raised with the vehemence of her emotion. "Listen, the world is littered with undiscovered talent. People squash it on the road. There are photographers out there who make me look like a blind woman. But they're unknowns, nobodies, and they'll stay like that if they subscribe to your philosophy. You've got to sell yourself in this life in this land, otherwise for sure nobody's buying. You've got to have charm. You've got to catch them with honey, not vinegar. It's not enough to be brilliant. They've got to be persuaded to look, to see, to *understand*. And if an artist can't handle the self-promotion shit, then for sure he'd better latch onto someone who can."

She leaned across the table to emphasize her point.

"If you *really* believed in yourself, you wouldn't feel like that," he said. "You push because you're insecure about your talent, and because you don't trust the public to recognize it. That's a mistake. They're always right. They always know. Every ounce of energy has to go into the work. There should be none left for the bullshit."

Pat took a deep breath. There was something so magnificent about his naïveté. The world hadn't touched him. Perhaps it couldn't touch him. There was something awesome about that. A blinkered vision made you narrow, but it made you singleminded. The Valentino will was aimed directly at the eye of the bull. Not many people's were.

"Tony. Tony," she pleaded. "Listen to me. If you were producing your art simply for its own sake, for your personal satisfaction alone, then maybe you'd be right. You could paint your pictures or act your dramas in secret and then, of course, nothing would matter but how good you thought you were. But you want more than that. You need the world to recognize you. You want fame. Hell, you want to be a movie star. To *want* that is artistically impure. It's like wanting money. I'm not saying it's bad. I'm just saying that you want to compete in the marketplace, and if that's what you want, then you've got to roll up your sleeves and start to peddle the dreams and shovel the shit. Otherwise, however great you are, you're going to lose out to a slicker salesman with better PR. Can't you see that?"

"You don't believe faith can move mountains."

"I'd rather put my trust in nitroglycerine."

"Faith and high explosive. That's a good combination."

"Yeah, we could be a good combination, Tony Valentino," said Pat Parker, and her hand snaked out across the table to touch his arm.

IN ALABAMA's studio the chaotic confusion was skin deep. The polished wood of the floor was littered with the foil and discarded cardboard of dead Polaroid packs. Background paper, pink, white, and russet brown, hung drunkenly from poles, from the backs of chairs, from drawing pins on the black-painted walls. Through the skylight streamed the sun, and hard rock, Tom Petty and the Heartbreakers' "Full Moon Fever," amplified the excitement in the shaking, vibrating air. The trolleys of film were piled high with lenses, and Hasselblad backs, jars of vaseline for soft-focus effects, lens brushes, cans of Diet Coke. And through it all, like a gunslinger on a lead-soaked street, Pat Parker ducked and dived, as she picked off the photographs, her camera swiveling as it fired, a twelve-shot six-gun that never missed her man.

He was totally unself-conscious, and she hadn't expected that. It was yet another surprise in the magical process of getting to know him, and as Pat positioned herself to find a new angle on him, only part of her was a photographer. The rest was already a lover.

He was naked to the waist, and his skin glistened beneath the heat of the photofloods, the thin wisps of hair that formed a T from his chest to his navel damp with his sweat. He lay back against the black leather of the chair, his hand to his chin, his blue-jeaned legs stretched out straight, and he stared away in the distance just as he had done at the moment she had first seen him.

High on the balcony that ran around the top of the studio, Alabama watched them. His girl was as good as he had known she would be as she conducted the complicated orchestra of the shoot. Every nuance of light, every contrast, every motion had to be recognized and used. What was not there had to be created, what was not wanted had to be abolished. Film speed, shutter speed, focus, depth of field had to be fed into the mind computer, and all the time the subject had to be relaxed, excited, directed, manipulated as the moment was milked of its artistic possibility and greatness was coaxed onto the film. She had the knowledge, but she had more than that. She was involved. She was not merely a voyeur. She was engaged in the process. A part of her performed the technical tricks, but the more important part was allowing herself to feel. Photographer and subject had merged in the magic whole that allowed each to transcend himself. Their souls had gone from their bodies and hung in the air between them, melted together in a throbbing harmony of feeling. And it was as clear as the daylight that streamed through the skylight that they were falling in love.

He chuckled to himself. Once he had lived there at the cutting edge of feeling when the world had been alive, and full of the intense meaning that went by the global name of "youth." At that precise moment she looked up at him, aware of his presence in the heightened sensitivity of the creative process. He put his thumb into the air, and he nodded once, twice, smiling down at her, as she smiled back at him in thanks for the confirmation of what already she knew.

"Stand up, Tony," she said. "Look away, chin up, right arm forward a bit, left arm back—as if you're walking but don't move. That's great. That's wonderful. You look terrific. Oh, God, you look just great."

The stream of talk was a caress that pulled him closer to her, and his body responded to her commands automatically. He was a natural, accepting direction intuitively, his movement anticipating her desires as he struck the poses that would conjure up the dreams. No model could do this. No weak person could. This boy was in harmony with his body, and the gravitas that dripped from him gave weight and depth to attitudes that would otherwise have been narcissistic, almost effeminate. Here was male beauty—raw, undiluted, blatantly masculine, and devoid of any hint of softness or subterfuge. The honesty would be in the print, and all who saw it would know that Tony Valentino was as hard and as real as the steel in his eyes.

Damn! She was firing on empty. She tore the back from the Hasselblad, reached for another, and clipped it on. She looked up at Alabama, but he had gone. She looked back at Tony. He smiled at her, angling his body in the light as if moving it beneath a waterfall. Good. He was deep into it. He was with her. The magic moment hadn't gone. And now they were alone.

She peered down into the viewfinder, allowing the lens to roam over his body. Where next? She swallowed. Suddenly she knew. She paused, and once again she looked up at him. Could she ask him that? Would he understand? Would he get it wrong? The question was in her eyes, but she knew it would never reach her lips. It didn't have to. On some secret wavelength he heard her, and on another he answered. Slowly, deliberately, with all the time in the world, Tony Valentino reached for the buckle of his belt.

—

DICK LATHAM clapped his hands and leaned back against the wall of his office. The scale model took up most of the room. It sprawled across a vast metal table, and it was detail perfect to the tufts of sagebrush, the model cars in the lot, the miniature security house at the gates. Dick Latham's Cosmos Pictures studio was a functional scar across five hundred acres of the most beautiful mountains in the world, and his heart leaped for joy in his chest as he beheld it.

Across the room Havers smiled at him. "Good, no?" he said.

Dick Latham didn't have to answer. His expression said it all. He was following in the footsteps of the legends. When had anybody built a brand-new studio from scratch? People traded them. Nobody built them. It took a Goldwyn, a Mayer, or a Warner to do that. Or a Latham. His father would be turning in his grave with jealousy. *His* vision had begun and ended with shopping malls. Now his son, the one he had always despised, was boldly treading where no latter-day celluloid visionary had trod before. The Latham media empire was about to expand into the areas from which it had so far held back—feature film and television production, and the icing on the cake was a property deal richer by far than his dead father had ever dreamed of being.

"So where do we stand, Tommy?"

Havers preened himself. "Tommy" was a Latham departure. It meant an unusually good Latham mood.

"It's going well. We closed on the land. No antidevelopment clauses in the contract. Alabama gave the nod to the landowner. It seems like you turned him around at lunch the other day. Your intervention made all the difference. So now we're moving as fast as we can on the zoning. As you know, it's a business. We'll need environmental impact reports, have to deal with landowners' groups, the California Coastal Commission, the cityhood people."

"Does the development fall within the boundaries of the proposed Malibu city limits?"

"At least eighty percent of it."

"So we want cityhood delayed as long as possible?"

"You bet, and obviously we want the sewers. You can't run a studio on septic tanks."

"How does it look for planning permission?"

"It'll be tough, but we're winning. Our attorneys are getting together a powerful case. The moment we go public with this they'll be off and running. In the meantime they're planning all sorts of lawsuits to delay the incorporation thing until we can ram the zoning through. We're spreading money around like muck and the politicians are feeding fine. Political contributions. Freebies. Favorite charities. Every which ways."

"Don't underestimate the land lovers, Havers. They're zealots. And Alabama's a leader if ever I met one. I don't like him, but hell, I respect him. He'll want our balls when he hears what we're up to."

"Yeah, we're not overconfident. If it was a country club, we wouldn't have a prayer. But a studio. In Malibu! It has to have a good chance. I mean, it's a movie colony. Always was, always will be. The guys that pull the strings here have to be at least ambivalent about it. It'll be work for them, for chrissakes, and no commuting. The studio/Malibu round trip can be four hours on a bad day, worse if PCH is blocked in the slides. They'll pretend to be anti, but they'll be busy when it comes to the fundraising and they won't call in their IOU's on this one. My gut says we're home free, but I could be wrong."

"The plans are on the money," drawled Latham, drooling over the Cosmos model. "And Grossman knows what he's doing on the nuts and bolts?"

"Yes, he's good. We've cross-checked him with the industry pros. The sound stages, the studios, the back lots are all state of the art. The recording stuff alone is twenty-five million. It's Swahili to me, but the technical boys are on top of it. Grossman can put it together all right. No way he can run it, of course. Making the right movies will be the toughest part."

"Jesus, I'm going to go from vandal to savior to environmental rapist faster than a roller coaster," said Latham, far from displeased at the thought. "When I closed the old Cosmos and turned their land into bucks, I was a philistine moneymaker with no sense of history. Now half the world will see me as a soulful Cecil B. DeMille, and the other half as an ecological barbarian."

"Well, you know what Ricky Nelson said—you can't please everyone, so you'd better please yourself."

"Who *are* we going to get to run it?" said Latham suddenly. Since the death of the last mogul it had been the question to ask in Hollywood. "I never saw a sorrier crew than the old Cosmos management. Firing them was one of the better moments."

"It's tricky," said Havers. "The Peter Principle applies. You know, people rise to the level of their own incompetence. However slick the show business attorney or agent, however brilliant the producer or director, they all screw up on the main job. You go business, you go creative, and the bottom line *still* makes itself up independent of the boss-man and his team. I don't know whether random walk applies to Wall Street, but it seems that you can only pick hit movies with a pin."

Dick Latham moved toward the model and ran a finger over the gleaming roof of an outbuilding.

"Don't worry, we'll find a winner. I always do. And I'll give Cosmos some personal input. I know traditionally that's supposed to be a disaster, but I don't buy that bullshit. When you put together a ten-billion-buck media business, you've got to have some idea of what the public wants."

He smiled lazily. It wasn't often he said things like that. Ten billion bucks, give or take a few hundred thousand million. If you knew exactly how rich you were, you weren't.

"Listen, Mr. Latham, you could do it in your sleep," lied Havers, who was of the opinion that nobody could. "The only question is how much time you want to put into what will only represent ten percent of the company."

"A bit, a bit." Latham laughed. "Cosmos is my new toy. I want to put it together. Make it run. You'd be surprised how often ten percent of a business becomes fifty or more. There are a whole load of people I want to bring back into the spotlight. Puttnam could make some heart art movies after we've stitched his tongue. *Miss Saigon* sounds interesting, and *Aspects of Love* is a must. Wouldn't you just love to see Whitney Houston in anything? And what about that Melissa Wayne? She's dynamite. She lights up the screen. She'd have to sign a contract. I'd want her long-term."

"I heard she was big trouble."

"She's big sex appeal. That's always trouble. It can be handled." Latham spoke softly. Melissa Wayne was a target. She was his own size.

"Do you know her?" Havers's question was cautious. He had gotten where he was today by tuning his antennae to the subtle vibrations that emanated from Richard Latham. Powerful men didn't like to spell things out. They preferred everything to be cloaked in the reassuring cloud of ambiguity. That way you could preserve mystique while insinuating your wants and needs, desires that if spelled out in black and white might demean you, or return to haunt you. Watergate burglars, arms-for-hostage conspirators, the murderous knights in Becket's cathedral had all made a business of interpreting the whims of the masters they served.

"No," said Latham slowly.

"If she's going to work for Cosmos, perhaps we should meet with her . . . maybe in a social situation."

Latham admired the "we," the way the suggestion had come from his lieutenant. It was why Havers was his number two.

"I was thinking of taking the yacht over to the islands on the weekend. That might be a good opportunity. You come too, Tommy. You could fly back to New York tonight, then come back on Friday. Take the helicopter out to us on Saturday morning. We'll anchor off Catalina. Oh, and Tommy, invite that photographer, Pat Parker. I want to keep tabs on her, now we've got her under contract."

"Fine. I'll do what I can. Can I dangle a career carrot at the Wayne girl?"

"Dangle what you like," said Latham shortly, flicking his hand in a gesture that said he didn't need to be bothered by the procedural niceties. "What did you think of the ten million that conglomerate paid for *Interview?*"

"It was brave money. I don't reckon Andy's ghost will hang around for long."

"Yeah, I agree. It makes the two Condé Nast paid for *Details* look cheap. The four American Express shelled out for *L.A. Style* was about right. We looked at it, didn't we? I remember speed reading a boring memo."

"It was too small."

Latham nodded.

"You're off, then?"

"I've got the plane standing by at LAX."

"Okay, let's do a quick lunch at La Scala, then you can take the Rolls on to the airport. I want to go over the Cosmos financing, and I want to talk to you about getting David Mlinaric to redo the Chester Square house. We'll use two cars. I'll take the Porsche. That suit you?"

Havers's head bobbed up and down. Suicide suited him if Dick Latham suggested it.

"Oh, what was the name of the photographer again?" said Havers as he walked toward the door.

"Pat Parker," said Latham quickly. But it wasn't quite enough. It seemed to require emphasis. "Yes, Pat Parker," he said.

———

THERE WAS silence in the semidarkness. The red light shone dully in the gloom. Pat leaned forward and reached into the water, taking the print by the corner. She turned it over and peered down into the basin.

"How does it look?" growled Alabama. He leaned over her shoulder, and he couldn't hold back his enthusiasm. It was years since he had felt like this. He had seen her take the photograph and he had sensed the excitement of the shoot. The lighting had been inspired, the subject had been inspiring. The angles, poses, the nuances of expression had been picture perfect. If the focus was right, the camera hand steady, the exposure congruent with the speed, the print would be a masterpiece. It had stood out on the contact sheet, a priceless gem among fine jewels, and now he couldn't wait to see it washed, dried, and mounted.

"It looks good. Very good," murmured Pat almost to herself.

She fished it from the bath and stuck it, dripping, on the wall where it hung by capillary action. Tony Valentino stared back at them in the dim, religious light. She felt the breath seep from her body. The print was magic, and it was only the first roll of the ten she had taken. If it was a harbinger of things to come, she had had the shoot of a lifetime. And there was always that last roll—the one she had marked with the big red cross. If this was brilliant, there was better by far in the can, and the goosebumps stood out on Pat Parker's arm as she dared to remember the pagan beauty of Valentino's naked body. Her finger had trembled on the viewfinder as she had fought to focus in the emotional noose that had gripped her. Somehow she had managed it, she'd never know how, and at the end, when something had badly needed to be said, there had been nothing at all to say. He had pulled up his pants as if lowering them had been the most natural thing in the world. He had buckled his belt, and flopped down on the sofa, and asked her how she thought the session had gone as if making a comment on the weather. She had gulped and muttered "real good" and fought to clear her mind of the steamy vision as, at the same time, she had battled to fix it forever in memory. And there, on the bench, undeveloped, were the results, and up on the wall was the charismatic face of the man who obsessed her.

"It's not bad," said Alabama. The guilt welled up in him. "I mean, it's good. It's excellent." He was pleased, thrilled even, by the portrait she had made. But he was also envious. It had been so long since the creative juices had flowed, and now, watching the image emerge, he dared to remember the intense pleasure of the darkroom.

"*Why* is it so good, Alabama?"

"Ah, the great American question. The 'why' question." He laughed. "We always assume there's an answer to it. It's our optimism. The Europeans who deal in pessimism say there seldom is. Let's see. Well, it's technically good. That's maybe a quarter of it. The sharpness, the light illuminating one side of the face, casting the other side into shadow. That gives starkness, and that harshness matches the expression. Mostly it's in his eyes, isn't it? You've captured the longing, the desperation, the loneliness, and even the cruelty. Valentino is dangerous. He could hurt you. He'd rather enjoy it."

"You mean hypothetically?" Pat was anxious that Alabama not read too much into her relationship with her subject. His last bit had sounded suspiciously like a warning.

"Whatever."

"He does look terribly unhappy, doesn't he? His mother just died. He was real fond of her."

"What's he doing out here? Hustling the movies?"

"No!" Pat's denial was far too partisan, too emphatic. "I mean, he's just finished at the Juilliard in New York. He was a drama student there. He's staying with a friend in a house in the Colony."

"Girl-friend?"

"A friend who happens to be a girl," said Pat, not at all happy at the way the conversation was turning out. The sex of the Valentino host rankled. "She was at the Juilliard too. She asked him out here to help him get over his mother."

"Must be rich if the family has a house they don't use in the Colony. What's her name?" said Alabama. He knew most of the longer-term residents in Malibu.

"Vanderbilt. Allison Vanderbilt. I think she's big money."

"Yep, she is. Genuine American aristocracy. Not many of them around here. 'Specially not on the beach. A few scattered landside in the hills in places they can keep their horses. Jews on the sand, gentiles in the mountains is the rule in Malibu."

"I don't think that Tony is very into money." She looked at the eyes on the wall. What *were* they into? The career success he craved? Or was that just a line thrown out to catch the fish he really wanted. A golden fish like Allison Vanderbilt, perhaps, with her millions, her pedigree, and her WASP-ish Lily Pulitzer wraparounds wrapped around her waspish waist.

"Maybe. Maybe," said Alabama. "But take a tip from an old one, Pat Parker. Don't listen to what they say. Watch what they do."

"He's not a beach bum, Alabama. He's not on the make."

"You met him on the beach. He's living with a rich girl on the beach. He's an actor. He's ambitious. Jesus, this is Malibu, not Lourdes."

"You don't understand," she said coldly.

"Listen, honey, you can handle it. Have fun. What's life without a little angst? I'm just reserving the right to say 'I told you so.' It's one of the few advantages of being my age. You get to say it quite a lot."

He scratched himself, suddenly bored with the role of solicitous uncle.

"Anyways," he added, "however it turns out, you got some great pictures. You used him first. Should make a wild spread in that magazine of yours."

"I'm not going to publish these. They're for Tony's portfolio. They're for him." For us. Damn it, for *me*.

"Oh, I see," said Alabama with a chuckle.

"Anyway, he's already tangled with Emma Guinness. She wouldn't publish his photographs even if I submitted them." The Valentino face stared accusingly from the wall, dramatic in its uncompromising beauty. Yes, she would. Anybody would. Whatever her personal feelings, Emma Guinness would override them when she saw the material. She was an editor first and foremost, and *New Celebrity* was what mattered to her. Pat had thought about it. Now she was thinking about it again. Her conclusion was the same. The stumbling block to a Tony Valentino photo spread in *New Celebrity* would be Tony Valentino, and nobody else.

"I thought your famous contract gave you the right to submit your own material and insist that it be published."

Pat said nothing. He was right. It did.

Soon she would have to confront this. The dilemma was building inside her. All her life, work had been her fuel. She had lived for it, and it had been her crutch in all the times of her trouble. And it was so seldom that the work was "right." Sometimes it was passable, sometimes good, but so very rarely great before the unforgiving jury of artistic self-judgment. But here, now, in front of her, was perhaps the very best photograph she had ever taken, and there on the bench were the others . . . and the roll of film marked X. They couldn't be held back. They had to be published. Sounds in the forest unheard were for the Alabamas of this world. He might be big enough, confident enough, to create masterpieces for his eyes only. She wasn't. The photographs should be forced into *New Celebrity,* if necessary by invoking her contract. Her art demanded it. All resistance would have to be swept away. Emma's resistance. Tony's resistance. She took a deep breath as the immobile mountain felt the touch of the immovable object. Could she possibly publish Tony's photographs without his consent? He hadn't signed a release, yet he had agreed to the shoot. He wasn't the kind of guy who'd know about attorneys, but their relationship in embryo would be aborted with night-follows-day certainty. She would lose him before she had won him, and for what? For the glory she craved, perhaps more than the uncertain love he could provide. But maybe he could be persuaded to say yes to publication. After all, he, too, was powered by his dreams. The photo spread would do wonders for him. If the world shared half her enthusiasm for the pictures, he would become that rare-as-a-mockingbird's-teeth phenomenon, an overnight star. There would be deaths in the stampede of agents and casting people. Then he would thank her, because she would have been good for him. They would have used each other, and love and ambition could merge in the potent synergy that would fuse them together, body, soul, and mind . . . forever and ever.

She turned toward Alabama, and he smiled at her in the twilight of the darkroom. He knew what was in her mind. In the early days he had wrestled with problems like that before the god of fame had touched his shoulder with the sword of success and elevated him to the mountain from which he could laugh at the preoccupations of the lesser mortals. It was the age-old photographer's dilemma. When did you betray the trust of a subject? When did art matter more than keeping the faith? Did the ends justify the means in the name of supreme beauty?

"Of course, maybe this print is the only good one," said Alabama slowly. "Then the whole thing's academic. Anything else in this lot? What about the one marked X? What's that for? Hidden treasure?"

She blushed in the darkness. Alabama's instincts were phenomenal.

"Oh . . . he . . . took his clothes off for that one," she said, looking away.

She shouldn't be embarrassed. She hadn't asked him to. It had been a million miles from a come-on for either of them. But Alabama hadn't been there. He couldn't know how "right" it had been in the context of the shoot. Now it sounded tacky. Why had she told him? It had slipped out, as the truth did around Alabama. She prayed he wouldn't take a cheap shot at her.

He didn't.

"That would be the logical conclusion of this one," he said simply. "I suspect the chronology of the pictures would be the sequence of the layout." He paused, lost in thought. "It *will* be dynamite," he added.

"But Tony wouldn't want them published," she said.

"Yeah," agreed Alabama. "But he'd be wrong. Maybe not with just any pictures, but with these he'd be wrong."

Pat leaped at the chance, thrilled that Alabama agreed with her.

"Alabama, could you talk to him? I mean, when you've seen the other prints. He knows I've got an interest in this. He'd know you were objective."

Alabama shook his head. "I'll tell him I like the photographs. I do. I won't tell him how to run his own life. I don't do that."

"You tell me all the time," said Pat ruefully.

"You ask all the time, and anyways, you came to learn, and you're a photographer. I actually know a little about that."

She laughed. "You're right. I'm sorry. It *is* my problem, and it comes with the territory. A month ago I couldn't take a photograph I liked. Now I've got an outlet, and a wonderful print, and I'm blocked by conscience and/or a guy whose feelings I care about."

"It's happened before, Pat Parker. It's called a moral dilemma."

"What do you do about those?"

"I wait and see what I do. It's quite interesting. You argue the case for and against, and then you sit back and wait for the verdict. It seems to come from somewhere else, and it's impossible to predict."

"Oh, great. Thanks, Alabama. I'm a spectator, not a player."

"Relax, honey, and try a little gentle persuasion. Take him away for the weekend. Work on him. Show him the prints. Tell him he'll be a star. Plead. Beg. Blackmail."

"Latham's CEO called, a guy called Havers, and asked me on Latham's yacht for the weekend. They're going to Catalina. I said a definite 'maybe.' Do you think I could take Tony along?"

Alabama paused. Latham made him nervous. He was a neighbor now, largely because Alabama had withdrawn his objection to the huge land purchase. But he didn't like him and he didn't trust him, and he was suspicious of the interest he was showing in his protégée. Still, the presence of the uncompromising Valentino on the Latham yacht would for sure spike the billionaire's guns. The prickly Tony, young, virile, and fiercely proud, would be the author of some supremely unsettling on-board moments.

"Yeah," drawled Alabama. "You do that. Moon on the water, salt spray in the hair, beluga in the belly. You should have a magic time. An' I feel sure that Dick Latham and Tony Valentino are going to be the hottest item since Batman and Robin."

"Holy bat-boats," laughed Pat Parker.

~7~

PAT SAT CLOSE behind him, closer than she needed to, and her arms wrapped tight around his waist as he leaned into the sharp turn. It felt like Alabama's bike, but they were miles from a road, and a thousand yards from land. On either side of her bare legs, the water funneled up as the wave runner forged through the crystal clear waters of the Pacific off the deserted western side of Santa Catalina Island. She laid her head against his back to hide it from the wind and to smell the scent of him, and she looked up at the barren cliffs that pointed ruggedly at the royal-blue sky. She couldn't remember when she had been so happy, but with the greed of the lover she wanted to be happier.

"Let's go explore one of the coves," she shouted into the stiff breeze above the buzz of the engine. The sun beat down on her shoulders, tickling the skin beneath the brand-new tan, and she shook her salt-stained hair behind her, as she scanned the coastline for a sandy strip of beach.

He slowed down as he heard her, and raised his hand to shield his eyes from the glare. He turned the vessel toward the harsh coastline, his eyes searching the shore for a landing place. He half turned and pointed to where the canyon cut into the mountain. She nodded, and the wave runner nosed toward the pocket beach, as a bald eagle swooped from the jagged rock face and painted its shadow on the shimmering water of the ocean. A few yards from the sand she swung her legs across the red saddle and prepared to guide the craft through the six-inch swell. He cut the engine. The silence crowded in on them. He jumped into the sea and steered the Yamaha up onto the sand.

For a minute or two they pushed it, using the tiny waves as rollers, until the wave runner was wedged safely on solid ground. Then, exhausted by the effort and drained by the heat, they collapsed onto the sand.

"No people," said Tony. He laughed at his understatement. They were miles from anywhere, as they had intended to be, and they were deliciously trapped. On either side the 165-million-year-old metamorphic rocks reached for the sky. Ahead of them lay a wall of stone, maybe a hundred feet high, jagged and unclimbable. Behind them stretched the vast ocean. The beach on which they lay was barely thirty feet wide, fifteen feet deep, and the sun covered it with a hot blanket, the warm air isolated from the ocean breeze by sheer cliffs.

"Not a good place for engine failure," said Pat, looking at the red-and-white striped wave runner with apprehension.

"Oh, I don't know," said Tony. He said it quietly, and Pat felt the thrill she was meant to feel. She turned to him, squinting in the brightness to see if his expression was adding to, or subtracting from, his words. But he lay flat in the sand, the ocean playing around his feet, and his arms were stretched out like Christ's on the cross, as he buried himself in the beauty of the moment. She saw the wisps of black hair beneath his arms, damp with the sea and his sweat, and she watched his muscular chest heave as he breathed. His eyes were closed. His face was a mask of peace. His feelings were an enigma.

Pat felt the stab of disappointment. "I hope the others aren't worried about us," she said, forcing reality into the Treasure Island illusion. In her mind she could see them. It was nearly lunchtime. They would be spaced out decoratively on the aft deck of *The Hedonist,* as smooth stewards dispensed the canapés and the Taittinger Rosé, and Beethoven did his bit on the Technics sound system. Dick Latham, formidably casual in L.A. Gear sneakers, white cotton slacks, and a plain white T-shirt, would have his battered Topsiders up on the Jon Bannenberg-designed banquettes that surrounded the vast deck. He would be effortlessly maintaining his outer calm, but inside the irritation would be growing. He was an obsessive beneath the cool veneer. Pat had picked that up. Lunch was at one. And two of his party were missing.

"Who cares about them? They're in another world," said Tony lazily.

"You don't care about Allison?" Pat bit her lip. She hadn't meant to say that, yet she hadn't been able to resist it. Allison Vanderbilt would be sitting across from Dick Latham, and already she would have turned down the champagne in favor of something more aristocratic, like Coke. She would be uncomfortable among all the conspicuous consumption, and she would be eying Latham with all the suspicion that the very old money reserved for the relatively new. Mostly, however, she would be sick with worry because Tony Valentino was missing . . . and because he had taken Pat Parker with him.

He didn't answer her, and there was a rebuke in his silence. Pat looked down. She picked up a handful of sand and let it slip through her fingers. Allison Vanderbilt was a problem. Havers hadn't been enthusiastic when she had made Tony Valentino a condition of her presence on the Latham yacht. She had hardly been wild with joy when Tony had made Allison Vanderbilt a condition of his.

"I'm staying with her," he'd said simply. "I can't take off without her." The implication had been that she was a friend and a kind one, nothing more nor less. There had been no amplification on that theme, nor would there be. Pat had not needed to be an amateur psychologist to get the picture. Allison Vanderbilt, her fawnlike eyes wide with vulnerable wonder, was head over heels in love with Tony Valentino. He was not in love with her. But there was a courtesy in his treatment of her, a kind of solicitous care, that Pat found alarming. He was always wondering if Allison was too hot or cold, whether she was comfortable, and he asked her from time to time if she was "all right." That last was an understandable question. Allison Vanderbilt looked stricken, brave, permanently at the edge of tears, and only her patrician genes and stainless-steel upper lip prevented her from dissolving into a sea of liquid misery. But if it was quite certain that Tony and Allison were not lovers, it was far from definite that they had not, somewhere along the line, made love. Now Pat Parker's stomach formed a tight knot as a wave of panic passed through her.

"Latham wants you," said Tony suddenly, his voice piercing Pat's thoughts like a spear.

"You're crazy!" He'd surprised her. Yes, Latham *was* interested in her. Of course he was. Why the hell hadn't she admitted it? It wasn't the biggest deal in the world. Latham fancied everyone.

"I'm not crazy. He wants you." Tony Valentino sat up. He looked at her. He was serious. He took everything so seriously.

"No, he's just interested because he's employed me. I'm the new kid on his block. The new toy. He flirts with everyone. It's his style. He does it with Allison. He *certainly* does it with Melissa Wayne. *She's* the target of the weekend."

"No, you are."

"*Tony!*" She emphasized the last syllable in mock reproach, and she threw the sand at him halfheartedly to lie that this was embarrassing. Why was he going on? Was he jealous? Could such an emotion possibly exist behind the disinterested eyes?

"What do you think of him?" he said.

"Weeeeell, he's difficult to ignore, isn't he? I mean, he's larger than life, and not just because of the money. I don't trust him. I haven't a clue why. I don't even know if I like him, but he's funny, and smart and interesting. I guess all that counts for something."

"He can't look at me," said Tony.

"I haven't noticed you look at him yet."

Pat laughed. It was true. Latham, the man who loved women, had reacted to the startling good looks and the youth of Tony Valentino with all the enthusiasm of a farmer for the presence of a fox in his hen coop. In return, the tortured, focused Tony, his faraway eyes set on his faraway dreams, had treated Latham like an elderly pedophile at a children's picnic. Latham, aggressively charming and dangerously urbane, had missed no opportunity to patronize his youthful rival. Valentino, his lip curled in a semipermanent snarl of superciliousness, had treated the billionaire like a joke in bad taste. Pat Parker had become their natural battlefield.

"You know, in some ways he's like me," said Tony.

"*What?*" Pat's mouth dropped open.

"Yes, he is. He's in pain all the time. He wants. He tries to disguise the fact that he does. He's addicted to proving something. All his bits and pieces, the trains, the boats, the planes, mean nothing to him. He's haunted. That's what he is."

Pat took a deep breath. He hadn't talked like this before. It sounded like a weakness he was discussing, but from his lips it was majestic too, like the suffering on the cross, pain for a higher purpose, a greater good.

He sat before her, and the water lapped around the faded blue cotton of his swimming trunks. His hands were splayed out Buddhist style across his legs, their palms imploring her to understand what he was saying. He was revealing himself to her. It was personal. She should realize that. His eyes cut into hers. He was talking about Latham, but he was also talking about himself.

"I hate him. He disgusts me. But it's me I see. He has to have the spotlight, but it's mine. I must have it, but he thinks it's his. He's pathetic. I'm pathetic. But the world thinks he's wonderful, and that's what it's going to think about me. Can you begin to understand that, Pat? Does it sound crazy?"

"Yes," said Pat suddenly. "It does. Crazy, but majestic. You're talking about the opposite of comfort. You're talking about antisecurity, and screw happiness, and the awesome power of the will. It's having your own way, isn't it, Tony? That's what you and Latham want. The stuff of your dreams are different, but it's the dreams that fuel you both. It's obsession that binds you together underneath."

He seemed calmed by her vehement profession of understanding, but he was still troubled by something. Pat knew instinctually what it was. He was troubled by her. He was troubled by them.

"And you, what do you want?" he said at last.

"Thanks for finding the time to care," she said gently.

She meant that. It wasn't a rebuke.

She looked up at the sky. What did she want? Him? Yes, but more than that.

She spoke haltingly as the thoughts came. "I guess I want in the abstract. I want like the little people want. I want to be happy. I want to be loved. I need to love. Working and making beautiful things seems to deliver the goods best. So that's what I do. But it's a means to an end, and the end is satisfaction, and security, and belonging and having someone belong to me . . ."

She peered up at him to see how her thoughts had landed.

"That's right," he said. "That's the right way to feel." He seemed unaware of his patronization, and the fact that he didn't recognize it made it go away. "It makes us opposites." He smiled to show that he'd hoped for that, because it meant they had a chance.

"The kind that attract?" said Pat, smiling back at him.

"The kind that attract," he said, and his voice was lower as he spoke, and his eyelids sank down over his suddenly smoldering eyes.

She couldn't resist it. It was crazy, but she just couldn't. He had to be teased, despite the dangers. Nobody should take himself that seriously.

"An opposite like Dick Latham," she said.

His voice stepped back from the edge of intimacy.

"Don't play games with me, Pat Parker," he said.

"Oh, but I *want* to play games with you, Tony Valentino. Sometimes I feel you've been seriously deprived of games." She laughed to taunt him, and she scooped up another handful of sand and she threw it onto his thighs to show that she wasn't afraid of him, but that she liked him more than was entirely safe.

For a second the war raged on his face, and then she saw herself win and the triumph surged within her. His smile was little-boy-sorry as he admitted to his crippled sense of humor. But it didn't linger long. Fun was to him an alien world. Lust wasn't. He leaned forward and he reached out to touch her.

She didn't move. She was frozen in boiling ice. Only his finger could release her from the numbness that gripped her. It was on her arm, and its touch was more real than mind and body, than the bright sun in the heavens, than the cold ocean that had turned them into a volcanic island of passion, waiting to explode in the bliss of union.

His eyes danced in her soul, and she made the music for him. It was slow dancing, clear and low, and the notes of the melody were sweet in her body. Lazy, loving, far now from the panic to come, the sounds of desire built within her. They cascaded out through her own eyes, and they swayed in tune to his. Her fingers tingled, the sweat rushed to bathe her upper lip, the salt air was deliciously nervous in her flared nostrils. His finger traced the contours of her arm. It wandered across the smooth muscle, lingered on the hot skin, reached up to her shoulder. There, the flat of his hand rested, feeling her gentle motion. She was breathing for his hand. It rose and fell, so near the loveliness of her neck, waiting there, with all the time in the world. She turned toward his hand, and she leaned her head to one side to capture it, her cheek crushing it softly like a flower in a book. He could feel her warm breath on his face. It was the beginning of the negotiation of bodies, the give and take, the threat and promise, the war and peace that would abolish all boundaries and obliterate all distinction, until there was only surrender and togetherness in the awesome harmony of eternal joy.

He inched across the sand toward her, until his face was close to hers. She was bathed in his breath, and she inclined toward him, eager for all that he would do for her, greedy for his love. He cupped her head in his hands, holding it reverently. The wonder shone from his eyes into the love light that blazed from hers.

"Tony," she whispered, her voice breaking. "Tony," she murmured again, loving the sound of his name, lusting for the intimacy he offered with his eyes.

His finger was on her chin, lifting it up to him. His thumb was at her lower lip, slippery on the sweat there, washed by the currents of her breath. She opened her lips to taste his salty skin, and she put out her tongue to touch the finger that hurried to be touched. Her mouth was parched as the summer canyon, but her tongue was wet still, and it licked him gently, painting his sensitive fingers with precious saliva in the tender prelude to the making of their love. His finger waited, passive, and she played with it, nuzzling it with her teeth. She eased it deeper into her mouth, pushed it back again, clasped it tight to tell him about the prison of her body, and how it longed to hold him in its velvet walls. She moved her head from side to side and her neck swayed to the secret rhythms of romance, craning nearer, stretching back. And all the time the messages from her body came winging in, the delicious fear in her stomach, the rushing blood in her taut nipples, the aching void at the core of her.

His hand moved behind her neck, and the finger she had tasted burrowed into her hair. He drew her toward him, and she pushed back against his hand, making him force her, forcing him to admit that he wanted her as much as she wanted him. She was still fighting him. She was his equal, courageous, determined, giving nothing away. Her resistance made him stronger. His hand was rough now as he drew her in, and his lips were tender no more. They closed over hers, crushing her mouth, and his tongue pushed into her, invading her rudely in the way that part of her longed to be invaded. She reached for him and drew him to her, bruising his lips with hers. He pressed against her, battling her tongue with his, using his wetness to slake the thirst of her longing. Their teeth clashed in the kiss. Their mouths became one. It was war. But it was a conflict that both would win, and they gave no quarter and demanded no mercy as they battled for the pleasure victory that each must have. His whole body was plastered against hers now, the power of his muscled chest heavy against her breasts. Slowly, inevitably, he forced her back until she was prostrate beneath him, her back buried against the hot sand, his body above her, framed by the beauty of the pale blue sky.

At last his mouth freed hers, and she lay still below him, captured, as she had been in her dreams, by the man she loved. She smiled in triumph, and the breath rasped between her throbbing lips, her chest rising and falling beneath his. She could smell him. She could taste him. Oh, dear God, she could feel him—rock hard against her hips, his legs heavy on hers, his dripping, sweat-soaked skin melting on her body. But there was a new expression on his face. No longer was he the cruel conqueror. The harshness had left his features. There was a softness in his eyes that she had not seen before, and she knew that now a more subtle, more delicate wind was blowing, one that would whip her to a frenzy of ecstasy more complete than she had ever known.

His hand was on her chest. He reached for her breast, tracing its lines to the nipple. Beneath the cotton of her swimsuit, her flesh quivered beneath his touch. She pushed out at his hand, and her eyes pleaded with him to be bold. He heard her. He hooked his finger beneath the material until she knew what he would do, and he paused to use up the moment. Memory must have this. It must never go away. Through all the years of familiar intimacy, this second would be remembered. Slowly, almost sad that there would never be another first time, he unveiled her. The shuddering sigh rushed from him.

His eyes were filled up with the vision. She lay flat, but her breast did not. It rose up at him, a white triangle of perfection, pure and lovely as snow on a distant mountain. The paleness in contrast to the syrup brown of her skin, its firmness against gravity's invisible pull, the crowning glory of the shell-pink cone that capped it—all merged in the mist of passion, and Tony Valentino bent down in homage before its savage beauty.

With his tongue he touched the tip of her nipple, and it reared against him, impossible in its tightness. He waited there, vibrating with her, feeling her blood course against his, amazed by the rhythmic thrusts of her pulse. He could feel her heart beating through his own delicate skin, as her nipple expanded and contracted, pushing out, retreating, ebbing and flowing against his wetness. Gently, in wonder, he licked at her, moving his tongue across the slippery surface of her throbbing breast. He nuzzled against her, rubbing the silken softness with the roughness of his cheek. He took the petal pinkness between his teeth, threatening it, loving it, pressing down, marveling at how the tautness sprang back against him, at the power of her fragile skin to cage the blood that rushed so furiously beneath its surface. And all the time he listened to the low moans of satisfaction that sprang from her, as his body caught fire, and his roaring mind planned new acts for the drama of love.

She pulled herself up, supporting her body on her elbows in the wet, warm sand, and her breast thrust out at his mouth. She groaned her pleasure, but all the time she was wanting more. How could this go on forever? How could it be speeded, how slowed, how, dear Lord, could it be intensified? She reached behind to untie the top of her swimsuit, but already the focus of her mind was moving away from her pulsing breasts. She threw the strip of material onto the sand and, exhausted by the effort, she fell back, half-naked, totally open to the man who now owned her body.

He buried his head between the firm mounds of flesh, and his mouth roamed over them, feeding from their fullness, his tongue sliding deliciously over the creamy skin. They were wet with his wetness, gleaming and glistening with his moisture, and damp, too, with the sweat of her desire. He burrowed in, losing himself in the warmth of her, as if he wanted only to be buried inside her body, to merge with her, to become her so that his terrible need would be a need no more. But there was no turning back in the dance of commitment. There was no standing still. There was only the headlong advance toward the moment of glory.

His arms were pylons in the sand beside her. He pressed himself up above her, and then his head was moving down toward the place she longed for it to be. His tongue weaved a slippery track on her stomach, pausing at her navel, heading down again to the edge of her bikini bottom. She knew what would happen now, and her heart raced as the lust fountain exploded inside, making a river of the silvery stream that slid from her.

She arched her back, and she pulled her bottom upward. Her hands found the elastic of her bikini briefs. She thrust them down, without shame, without guilt. They straddled her thighs, a sensual bridge between her straining legs, and she thrust out at the material as she fought to open herself up to him. For long seconds he hovered above her, a hummingbird eager for the nectar of the dew-soaked flower. The wisps of her shining hair were watered with the scented juice of her. Her pouting pink love lips nestled in the liquid, downy sea. He breathed in the steam heat of her, as she sizzled on the burning plateau of desire. Then he lowered his face to taste her, to please her, to love her, and her moan of acquiescence was the music for their sweet communion.

His lips touched hers in the alien kiss. Shy, she pushed out at his mouth. He breathed gently against her. Her radiant heat beamed back at him, the musk of her passion floating into his mind.

"Yes, yes," she whispered, her voice husky, her eyes closed tight to seal in the excitement. She was melting for him. All the warm wetness of her body was drawn to his lips. Her essence lingered in love at the edge of his tongue.

She felt the still tip of it, soft against her softness, and then it began to move. She shuddered from the shock of his touch—the enormity of what he was doing, the wonder of what it meant. In the ultimate intimacy, his tongue was speaking to her in the language more honest than words.

There would be no retreat from this. It was the firm foundation on which everything would be built. It meant everything, yet its meaning was a slave to the feeling of it. Sensation and commitment had merged in the magic of the moment.

His tongue slid upward, swimming on the flood tide of her, and it came to rest at the throbbing center of her world. It stopped, aware of where it was, knowing so well what it could do now. She moaned to reassure him, but he needed no reassurance. His bones, his muscles, his mind were there for her alone. Over the nerve-racked minutes he must build the mighty castle of her ecstasy, and then he must demolish it in the explosion that would set the sky on fire.

His tongue moved against the millimeters of her sexual flesh. Gently at first, then harder, his tongue grew firm, more pointed, more insistent. He swept against the core of her, licking at her, milking her of joy, and his whole face bathed in the bath she had become, as it submerged itself in the sole purpose of her pleasure. Rhythmically, his tongue rubbed at her. It darted, random, in her depths. It slipped against the slick of her, and his hands snaked beneath her. He reached for the tight skin of her buttocks, and he drew her toward him, increasing the pressure of his head in the heart of her, and she shouted out sharply on the breeze as ecstasy blanketed her mind.

He picked her up and forced her to his mouth, like a chalice to the lips of a desert traveler.

His tongue was desperate now in its quest for her. It left the pleasure center and dived down into the molten sea, plunging into the dark recess of her, drinking, exploring, licking, as it loved her. His mouth closed over the opening of her, sucking the sweetness from her, and then every part of his face joined the battle for her joy. She arched her back and thrust her pelvis at his head, greedy for sensation, wanting only more. He thrust back at her wonderful, airless prison, and he listened to the music of their love, the wet sounds, splashing, dripping, foaming, as he swam on the river she had become.

"Oh! Ooooooh!" she moaned. It was running away from her. She was out of control. Her legs heaved against the bikini bottoms that straddled them, and she heard the material tear as she fought to open herself wider to his mouth. Her stomach was flat as iron, the muscles of her ass tight, as she battled for the strength to squeeze yet more pleasure from his tongue. Her mouth was dry, as all the liquid of her body turned into the love that was drowning him. Soon, so soon, it would all dissolve and the steel purpose would fall apart in the thrashing dissolution of her orgasm. And she would be empty. The void that ached in her depths would not be filled. Fanned to a furnace by his lips, the fires would grow cold all alone, isolated from *his* pleasure by the separateness of her body.

"Tony," she whispered. "Make love to me. Put yourself inside me."

She opened her eyes and stared into his. He must know how much she wanted this.

She wanted to see his face at the moment they were joined together forever.

In answer, he rose up above her, and she was aware of his hand at the waist of his swimsuit. She felt his body wriggle once, twice, sensed the wonderful touch of him against the slippery skin of her thigh. She reached down, unable to stop herself, and she stared into his soul as she held him for the very first time. With both hands she clasped it, and her heart seemed to stop as the wave of adrenaline broke within her. It was so big, vast and angry, its tautness pulsating against her fingers, threatening her, promising her fulfillment beyond the reach of wild dreams. For a second, in the conspiracy of lovers, they fought to hold the moment. But already the head of him was straining at the mouth of her, and she was opening, wide, wider than was possible. The muscles of her legs heaved against the bikini bottoms, and the ripping, tearing sound of the material was the signal for the union. Her legs snapped apart, and her bottom rocketed upward from the sand. With a cry of delight, he plunged forward. He rammed into her, filling her full, bursting her open with the hugeness of his lust. Her mouth opened, as the breath rushed from her lungs. Inside she was delirious, as the most intense pleasure flirted with the sharpness of pain. She opened wider, but there was nothing left, and still he reached in, deeper and deeper, farther and farther, more and more. He forced her apart, making the space for himself, and her sleek sheer walls stretched around him, her skin merging with his in a closeness made possible only by the abundance of her liquid love. Now at last he was at the roof of her, and it seemed as if there was nothing else but him in her body. He had taken it over. The rest of her was isolated in some forgotten corner of the envelope that was flesh and bone. He was her child, growing in her womb. He was the unforgiving marauder, pillaging her bowels with the cruel delight of his alien invasion. He was her lover, stiff and wonderful in her belly, in his rightful home at last, safe in the land she prayed he would never leave.

Her eyes were wide as the part of her that held him. In wonder, she watched him. Pinned on the point of his purpose, she looked down from the brink of the abyss. He moved inside her, and, as she was acclimating to his presence, he began to withdraw. But before the panic of emptiness could replace the joy of fulfillment, he was back. Her whole body shook with the rhythm of his strokes. Out to the brink, back to the ceiling of her world, the piston action was terrible in its reassurance, conjuring up blissful visions of the release that was its goal. She clamped down on him as far as her body would allow and she moaned her pleasure as she welcomed the climax she feared. This first time was too intense. There was no controlling it. Later they could become clever lovers. Now they were hungry novices, enslaved by the experience that was stronger than either of them. Faster, harder, he tore into her. Softer, more welcoming, she relaxed for him and their stomachs slapped together, greased with sweat and love, in the musical rhythm of lust.

His eyes told her of his moment, as her body howled of hers. She was rigid at the second the music soared to its crescendo. Every part of her sang in harmony. She was whole. She was perfect in the time before the truth was told. She was dimly aware of his furious body, but her inner eyes were staring at the brilliant light that had illuminated her mind. At the peak the breath was full in her lungs, and the message from God was alive in her heart.

"I love you. I love you," she screamed at the heavens and at him, and then, happy now to die, she leaped from the cliffs into the boiling sea of her orgasm.

—

DICK LATHAM peered over the stern and his smile was as natural as the Joker's. Below, the crew were attaching the davits to the wave runner. Pat and Tony stood on the afterdeck, their fingers intertwined loosely, and they talked quietly to each other, oblivious to the orderly confusion around them. Latham's knowing, suspicious eyes roamed over them. He noticed Pat's ripped bikini bottoms, tied at her hip by what looked like the drawstring of a man's swimsuit. He took in Tony's trunks, held up by a rough knot formed from the loose material that had somehow lost its means of support. They had missed lunch. Hell, they had missed tea. And it didn't take a Sherlock Holmes to figure out why. Somewhere out there, on the sands of Catalina, Pat Parker and Tony Valentino had been doing it on the beach.

Through clenched teeth, Dick Latham called out to them. "Where were you? We missed you. We were beginning to get worried."

They looked up at him, but the breeze had taken his words.

"What?" said Pat. Tony Valentino said nothing, his sullen face turned up in disdain at his rival.

Latham wasn't the sort of man to repeat himself.

He beckoned them, his arm darting up and down in a gesture that gave away his irritation.

They took their time. The back of *The Hedonist* was layered like a cake. The lower deck was where the toys were loaded and unloaded, the Riva ski boat, the windsurfers, jet skis, the small sailboat, the wave runners. It was used for swimming, skiing, and scuba diving, and its transom doors opened to the ocean where a vast platform extended out into the swell. The deck above was indented back and comprised the outside dining area where lunch and dinner were eaten on the few days when the coastal Southern California weather rose above its normal Mediterranean climactic range. Latham stood on the deck above that, the sitting area where communal drinks were taken before meals, and where batteries of telephones kept him in touch with the outside world. Precisely sixty steps would deliver the lovers to his face. About a minute. He waited at least three.

Tony came first. He swaggered into Latham's view, holding his hips like a dangerous weapon, and the pseudosmile around the corners of his mouth spoke volumes. Pat followed, languid, lazy, her body relaxed, moving with the sleek, liquid motions of a well-fed cat. Latham had intended to be coolly supercilious, but the sight of them revised the emotional possibilities. He was deeply pissed off. The trick would be to hide it. At first he said nothing, hoping for the apology that wouldn't come.

"I wish you'd told us you were taking off on that thing. It would have been polite. There were four of them last time I counted. Some of us might have liked to come along," he tried.

"We wanted to do a bit more than just make circles around the boat," said Tony. The words plus the gestures could have run as a short play off-Broadway. He twirled his fingers in the air in a circular motion to signify the fatuous route that all the safe, silly fatuous people would have taken as they trolled around the safety of the floating gin palace with its wall-to-wall crew. People like you have no guts, he was saying. Your idea of adventure is boats in the bathtub. You're old, old man. You're old and safe and secure, and your money has drained you of excitement and interest as surely as the years have drained away your youth. The only thing that was missing was a middle finger raised in mockery . . . and Dick Latham spinning on it like a nursery top.

Latham watched him. It was personal now. It wasn't just Pat Parker. It was everything. It was the generation war. It was sexual combat. It was the vital necessity of winning, whatever and wherever the conflict. The excitement welled up inside him, replacing the anger. In the oceans in which Latham swam, *he* was the great white shark. There was no competition anymore, just smaller fish to eat. Now, here, swimming among the plankton and the groping grouper, he had found a killer whale. It was wonderful. He could flex his mental muscles, get back in shape, and experience the satisfaction of humiliating someone who was very nearly his own size. There was even a prize, as there was in all the best contests. It might have the Valentino fingerprints on it now, but they could be gotten rid of in the wash. Then, polished, retooled, and carefully engraved with the Latham initials, Pat Parker would take her rightful position on the Latham mantelpiece, with the other trophies. Who knew, she might do a couple of months there, before he hit her with the sledgehammer he used for breaking the hearts. Yes, she would be a glorious victory in the endless war he waged against the female race.

He laughed, and this time his face read "mirth."

"God, Tony, you make me feel like a geriatric. Any minute now you'll be calling me 'sir' and pulling out chairs for me. Let me just say right now that if it comes to the kiss of life, I'm allergic to men."

They all laughed at that, Pat in relief, Tony in victory, Latham inside. "Anyway, you two must be thirsty," he continued. " 'Boating' is thirsty work!" He smiled to show he knew. He pulled the cellular phone from his waistband and pushed a button for the steward. He flopped down in a chair, Fred Astaire casual, and made a motion for them to join him. Their "impoliteness" was apparently forgotten. Latham had slid on, creamy smooth, to a role other than that of offended host.

The lovers joined him. Tony sprawled confidently against the cushions, Pat by his side, her hand resting casually on his leg. She had to keep the contact. Inside she was still full of him, and her heart sang as she thought of it. She felt deliciously and uncharacteristically passive. Tony was in control. Of himself. Of the mighty Dick Latham. Of her. The gulls soared overhead. Strauss warbled from the sound system. The only problem in the world was what to order to drink.

"When I said we were worried, what I really meant was that Allison was worried." Latham smiled easily as he dropped the note of discord into the lovers' harmony.

Was that a flash of guilt in the surly eyes of the Adonis? Was there a tinge of green in those of the photographer?

The steward padded across the deck to take the orders.

"Oh, Johnson, have someone tell Ms. Vanderbilt that her friend is back. I think you'll find she's in her cabin," he said casually over his shoulder. The veiled insinuation was unmistakable. Vanderbilt and Valentino had been an item. Valentino and Pat had cheated on her. It was no big deal, but it *was* a little shabby. Not at all the sort of trick that the Lathams of this world descended from the moral high ground to play. He had effortlessly cast himself in the part of the responsible adult, patiently explaining about right and wrong after the kids had pulled the wings from the fly.

Tony shifted on the white terrycloth of the banquette. Pat's hand drifted from his suddenly restless leg.

"Allison's a big girl," he said, cutting through to Latham's meaning.

"But a little vulnerable, no?" Latham smiled. He looked at Tony. His laughing eyes found Pat's. Accusation lingered amid the humor.

"I have a feeling you'd know about the vulnerability of women," she laughed, in retaliation.

"What would you like to drink, miss?" asked the steward.

"I can recommend the peach juice. I had a Bellini before lunch. Of course they'd make it fresh," said Latham, ignoring her jibe as he swam easily in the undercurrents of the conversation. She was sticking up for her man like a lover should. He liked that. He liked her, liked the salt-matted hair, the jutting breasts, the hard boy's ass that platformed out at the top of her long, luscious legs.

"Yeah, okay," said Pat. "What are you having, Tony?" In answer, Tony waved the steward away, shaking his head from side to side. It wasn't the time to be accepting a glass of water from Latham. That his butt was on his boat was a compromising enough position.

"So, Tony, apart from riding the dangerous waves, what other activities can we find for your amusement?" asked Latham, baiting the trap. A wave runner was no problem for a biker with a sense of balance. There were toys down below that would be. How would the Big Apple Thespian play on a mono-ski with Dick Latham at the wheel of the boat? Would he score points at skeet shooting as the clay pigeons curved and curled in the wind off the stern, and the Latham Purdey's blazed inaccurately at his shoulder? How complete would be his downfall on the windsurfer, that graveyard of a novice's self-confidence? Dick Latham excelled at all of the above. He had endured long hours at the Holland and Holland shooting school near Heathrow, and wet, longer ones in Scotland Augusts as the cunning grouse flew in waves above his guns. He had windsurfed with Baron Arnaud de Rosnay before his death, and he had taken lessons with his beautiful widow, speed windsurfer champion Jenna, off her beach in Mustique. Ivana Trump had been his instructress on the mono. Oh, yes, years and billions were not the only things that Dick Latham had over the cocky Tony Valentino. The name of the game would be to demonstrate it.

"What I'd really like to try is scuba diving," said Tony easily, picking his way through the Latham minefield. Strong lungs and a stronger body were all it needed.

"Yeah, we can do that," said Latham, trying to hide his disappointment. "The best place is Santa Cruz, a few miles up the coast off Santa Barbara. They have some amazing caves. We can go up there this evening, while we have dinner. Go out first thing in the morning if that sounds like fun."

"Fun? Fun? I'm not against fun," said Melissa Wayne.

In all her short sharp life, Melissa Wayne had never said a truer word. Fun she knew about, and pleasure, and the inflicting of cunning, delicious pain. She stood there on the edge of the group, and as she spoke she became its center. It was as if some celestial spotlight had picked her out, and as it lit her, she began to shine with a brilliance of her own. She was small in stature, but in no other way, and her multifaceted beauty gleamed like a priceless cut diamond bathed in starlight. She wore Chanel crocodile sneakers, velvet soft jeans around her drum-tight butt, a silk Yves Saint Laurent shirt falling away from pert, pushy tits. But clothes were not her point. Her personality was. It dwarfed her body, reaching out like a tentacled aura to touch her audience. The perfect face, the freckles around the turned-up nose, the heart-shaped mouth, the neat little ears were merely props for the main event called Melissa Wayne, and the three who watched her sniffed at her X factor with the fascination she had come to regard as her due.

"Ah, Melissa," murmured Latham, visibly affected by her presence. "I don't think you have met Tony Valentino and Pat Parker. Pat is a very famous photographer"—he paused—"who works for one of my magazines, and Tony is . . . Tony is an 'actor.' And Melissa is, well, Melissa is Melissa, isn't she?" He laughed easily.

"Hi, Tony," said Melissa Wayne. She didn't deal in women, period. If the entire female sex vanished in a flash, leaving her the sole survivor, to Melissa it would be a slow news day. She walked forward quickly as she put out her hand to him. When he reached up to take it, she didn't give it back. She kept it, as if it were a painting on loan. Her tongue snaked over lipstickless lips.

"I don't know your work," she said.

It was a masterpiece. She was deadly serious, matter-of-fact, her words as far from flirtation as her body was close to it. Her message was unmistakable. Tony was an actor. That meant he was a serious artist, as she was. The female "photographer" and the billionaire had ceased to exist. In the world there were only two people—she, and the boy who should be on the menu for dinner. The fact that Melissa Wayne was bought by the households of America as sexual breakfast cereal was overlooked. In this role, she was Streep and Fonda in Oscar combat. Somehow her presumption elevated Tony to Nicholson and Hoffman status. That was exactly what she had intended.

Tony smiled his pleasure, his hand happy in the Wayne one. He stood up.

"I've just finished at the Juilliard," he said. "Next stop is Steinbeck's *East of Eden* off-Broadway." He ran off the attenuated curriculum vitae as if it were Olivier's. He was completely unfazed by its shortness. Latham had to admire it. Belief in yourself was contagious. He'd always known that about himself. Now, with a modicum of surprise, he realized it could be true for others.

"The Juilliard's the best, and improving on James Dean should be a challenge," she said. "If I'm in town I'll come to the opening night."

"Hi, I'm Pat Parker," said Pat coldly. "I'll see you there . . . if you're in town."

"Hi," said Melissa Wayne with a half nod in the direction of Pat's hello. She didn't turn around.

"How was the trip? Did they look after you?" asked Dick Latham, enjoying himself thoroughly.

"Fine," said Melissa. She continued to stare at Tony. He continued to hold her gaze. She had tuned into his wavelength with the expertise of the woman who lived for men. That was flattering, and it was flattery with topspin, because the actress had long ago dropped the *-let* from her *star*.

With reluctance Melissa relinquished Tony's hand. She sat down on the edge of a director's chair, knees together, legs splayed out, her hands resting on the faded denim. She was silent, but her quietness did nothing to detract from her stunning appeal.

"Did you helicopter in?" asked Pat. The instant jealousy was receding. She liked women. They were at least innocent until proven guilty. The Wayne come-on had been a work of art, but then she was famous for that. It was why she was a box-office creamer. It was why she got two-point-five per pop. She was a pro playing a pro, and she had to practice. After all, Pat had to take photographs. Anyway, Pat was the one in possession. The body memories said so.

"I didn't swim," said Melissa. She turned to face Pat, and scorn for her small talk was all over her face. She smiled to take the sting out of her rudeness, effortlessly emphasizing her patronization.

"I thought maybe you'd been beamed in from fantasy-land," said Pat.

"You're not a paparazzi, are you?" said Melissa in retaliation. She wrinkled her nose.

"Pat's a very brilliant photographer," said Tony Valentino.

He was absolutely definite about it. There was no compromise. His tone was not angry, but his sentiment was clear. If Melissa Wayne didn't climb down, she would be pushed, her fame notwithstanding. He liked her. He respected her. But Pat Parker was off-limits.

Melissa looked at him, back at Pat. For a second or two she was undecided. Fantasy-land! Jeez! The dreamy boy won. God, he was sure of himself. That was good. It made it better during the sex games when they crawled across the room wearing the saddle she kept in her closet. This one might even take the bit. Whatever, sooner or later, she would make sure the photographer girl got to see the Polaroids if not the videotape. She wouldn't be best pleased by the insight into the Wayne fantasy-land they provided.

"That's a relief!" she said with a laugh. It wasn't totally clear what she meant. That Pat wasn't paparazzi? That the conversation was over? That she and Tony had avoided a falling-out?

"Well," said Dick Latham. "I'm going to get a bath, have a massage, and then we'll meet back here for drinks before dinner. Say about seven?"

He stood up.

"*What* fun!" he said, and with a chuckle he was gone.

———

"GOD, DINNER is going to be rough," said Pat. She stared into the mirror to check her makeup, but she was watching Tony, as he lounged in an armchair catching Diane Sawyer fresh via satellite on the ABC news.

"Yeah, Melissa's a loose cannon. But I admire her. She's taken some shots to get where she is. I suppose she feels she has the right to hand out a few. You can't judge people like her by the same rules."

Pat turned around. She knew what he meant. Hard-chargers put up with a lot of bullshit on the journey to their place in the sun. Sweet dispositions got left behind. Humility, generosity, sense of humor got discarded with the other excess baggage. Right now, however, it suited her *not* to understand. Tony had stood up for her when Melissa had gone on to the offensive, but he had been flattered by the star's attention.

"You mean one law for the Melissa Waynes, another for the rest of us," she said, letting the sarcasm hang out.

Tony sighed. He closed his eyes. It was a part of life he didn't like. Pat was on the verge of picking a fight, because she had seen him shine out to the girl who shone at the world. Big deal. Why did she have to be so predictable? Neither her body nor her mind were.

"Okay, she liked me. I liked her. There's no need for a philosophical discussion about it."

He crossed a blue-jeaned leg over the other one. He raised his arms above his head. He didn't actually yawn but he went through the body motions. In a test of attentive powers half the audience would have described the sound he wasn't making.

Pat started to frown, but it turned into a laugh. She loved his refusal to be drawn into games. Around him, everything was simple and honest. All was on the surface—the good, the bad, and the ugly, although there was precious little of the latter. It was true she'd been jealous of his liking Melissa Wayne, but what sort of a guy wouldn't fancy her? The girl made Basinger look like a hot dog. Compared to her, Meg Ryan had all the vulnerable charm of a leper in a Jacuzzi. Side by side with Melissa Wayne, the Playmate of the Millennium would have possessed the subtle sensuality of a road drill.

"Okay, okay, I'm sorry," she said. "Actually she *is* a turnon. And it would be great if she showed for your opening. It'd for sure help with the PR."

Pat regretted it immediately. They'd had this conversation before. But hell, he was so other-worldly, and she was so worldly-wise. To get by in this life you needed a little help from your acquaintances. You didn't get much from your friends, unless you were in a mess and short of an enthusiastic audience.

He looked like he'd respond—a staccato blurb about not needing a tart to help with his art—but he passed on it. "Why do you think she's here?" he said instead.

Pat cocked her head to one side. Tony so seldom asked a "why" question. "I'd have thought she was just Latham's speed. I mean he bought Cosmos, even if he raped it for the real estate."

"You think he's a star-fucker doing coitus interruptus on Hollywood?" mused Tony. "I wonder. Somehow I don't think so."

"Well, he can't stick her in a movie. Now that he's dismantled Cosmos, he doesn't have a studio. And I don't think Latham's the sort of guy who'd stoop to finance indie production. Melissa's box-office performance means there's money for her films anywhere. Maybe he just likes her. Maybe she likes him. After all, you two did."

Tony smiled at her halfhearted attempt to resurrect the argument in embryo, as he continued to think out loud. "I mean, Latham's still got the Cosmos logo, the library, the goodwill. All he's missing is the buildings, the product, and the people. Plenty of those in L.A."

"Cecil B. de Latham? I don't think so somehow. He's too WASP . . . East Coast . . . too smooth. Most likely he'll sell the bits and pieces to the Japanese. They've already got the banks, and a rising sun over the Cosmos spinning globe would look real dandy. Jeez, wouldn't it have been wonderful to have lost the war?"

Tony wasn't persuaded. Latham was up to something.

"We'll see. But I can't help feeling that something's going down. That guy Havers helicoptered in with six or seven suits who had to be bankers or lawyers or both. They've been stuck below deck like they were cabin class since yesterday morning. I walked by the communications room this morning and there were fax machines going nuts."

"It's probably like that all the time. We one-fax families don't understand how the other half lives. I mean the relaunch of *New Celebrity* is probably worth a message or two."

Pat was proud of herself. That had segued in nicely. Sooner or later she had to bring up the question of the photographs. The deadline for the prestigious first issue was approaching. The lead time could not be chipped away indefinitely. If the photo spread was to have maximum impact, it should coincide with the barrage of publicity that would accompany the launch. Already the awesome Latham PR machine was grinding into gear. The gossip columns were full of it, each morsel placed lovingly by Marilyn Evans or Rogers and Cowan where it would show best. Billy Norwich, Liz Smith, Suzy carried it most weeks, and the seminal incorruptibles, the George Christys of this world, were passing the message in the rarefied grapevines that twined across the heavens joining star to star.

"Have you thought about what you're going to do for the magazine?" said Tony suddenly.

She took a deep breath. He'd brought it up. This was the moment. There were two ways to go. She could tell him the naked truth or she could dress it up. The second way would be easier. The trouble was that Tony would rip right through the packaging to the bare flesh, and she would be left looking devious.

"I thought maybe . . . you," she blurted out.

He said nothing. He looked down at his hand. He looked back at her.

"And when did you have that idea?" he said.

Before or after the photographic session, he meant. Before or after this afternoon. "Are you using me, Pat Parker?" asked his eyes. "Are you for real? Or are you for yourself?"

She bypassed the question.

"They're just so *good,* Tony. You know that. Alabama said so. When something's that great, you have to use it. It's a responsibility."

"It's a *responsibility* to show America my dick?"

She shook her head from side to side. Oh boy! It was going to be worse than she'd thought. "Listen, Tony, I don't know how to explain this but—"

He held up his hand to cut her off. "Don't shoot me some crap about the photos making me a star, okay? I know you're hung up on that stuff. If they're as good as you think, they'll make *you* a star. That's the bottom line, isn't it? Maybe it always was."

Pat tried to stay calm. Part of what he said was true. The spread would be good for him. It would be better for her. But so what? They were technically lovers. If that meant anything, and she wanted desperately to believe it did, then he should be as eager for her success as she was for his. Art was beauty. It could do no wrong. It would be brilliant for everyone—for her, Tony, Latham, Emma, for *New Celebrity.* She was going to fight for it.

"Why do you object?" She launched into the attack.

"They were personal, Pat. They were mine. They were me. You took them for *me*, remember? Not for the world."

"Yes, I did, and they're still yours. I won't use them if you tell me not to. I just want to change your mind. I want to stop you from making a mistake, because I do care for you, not because I don't. They started out as pictures, but when they were printed—when I saw them—they were something else. It's like Ansel Adams's *Moonrise* photograph. The stupid moon's there over Hernandez every night. It never misses. But the photograph is more than its subject. The beauty is in the angle, the point of view, the emphasis on some indefinable part of the reality that only the artist sees. Artists make the others see. They open their eyes. It's like you, Tony, in that *Streetcar* you told me about at the Juilliard. How many schoolkids have murdered those same lines you spoke? But you made the words live. When you said them the audience *understood.* You gave them your perspective, Tony. You made them art. I've done that to your face and your body. Those photographs have captured something that's bigger and more fundamental than you. It's the *idea* of you and what you represent. Anyone can look at them and they know you, they feel you, they have a relationship with you. Maybe they're sad and lonely and fed up with their lives, but when they see those photographs they'll feel better inside for just a moment or two. And they'll pick themselves up and hold their stomachs in, and maybe they'll remember what it was like to dream in the days before the music died. That's what I'm talking about, Tony. You've got to understand. You've got to believe me."

She sat forward, her whole body leaning into her words as she fought for what she must have. But at the back of her mind she had made an awful decision. She might not have persuaded him, but she had persuaded herself. If he said no, she was going to betray him. She was going to publish and be damned.

Tony's face was quizzical. He'd heard her pitch, and she was sure he was impressed by it. It had weakened his resolve, but it hadn't turned him around.

"I wonder if you're right," he said at last. "I don't know that the world's ready for mainline male pinups. I don't know that I'm ready for it, whether it's me or not, whether it's art or not. Look at the fuss about the Mapplethorpe photographs. People *can* disagree about art, you know."

Pat took a deep breath. The Mapplethorpe name could stop her heart.

"Listen, I knew Robert. He was my friend. I loved him. When he was alive he was just another photographer to the rest of the world. Now that he's dead, the art crowd wants to make him a hero. *He* used to make the distinction between his art and his pornography. *He* knew they were different. 'That's my pornography,' he'd say. I heard him say it a thousand times. But the portraits of you are beautiful because your body is beautiful and because you're pure and untouched by crassness and mediocrity. And that makes you difficult as *hell*, and impossible, and cruel sometimes . . . and it makes me love you."

There were tears in her eyes. For her dead friend. For her so-new lover. For the art that must see the light of day.

"You're more like me than I thought," said Tony, and he stood up, and he walked across the room to her.

─

SEARCHLIGHTS PICKED out the silvery wake, and the moon shone down on the ocean, bathing it in a phosphorescent glow. The hum of the engines made the deck vibrate gently, but otherwise there was little sensation of motion. That the 120-foot megayacht was powering through the swell at close to forty miles an hour was a well-kept secret. On the aft deck of *The Hedonist* the dinner table gleamed with Georgian silver, the starched linen was Four Seasons pristine, and the Waterford crystal appeared to have been cut yesterday rather than at the tail end of the eighteenth century. Scented gardenias flown in from Florida swam in individual bowls in front of each place setting, damask napkins sat sedately on Crown Derby side plates, and a low conversation-friendly orchid centerpiece crowned a table that would not have looked out of place at Buckingham Palace, but which here, on the Pacific Ocean off Catalina Island, looked like very hard work.

The group drinking Krug on the afterdeck had made a sartorial effort, with one notable exception. Tony had come as Stanley Kowalski. His one concession to the opulence of the setting was that he had washed. Nobody seemed to mind. After all, the nearest mainland was Malibu, where overdressing was a criminal activity.

"Ready for the caves of Santa Cruz?" said Dick Latham, the banter beneath his words. He was dressed in the Palm Beach uniform of navy double-breasted blazer, bright green pants, highly polished Cole-Haan loafers, no socks. He sipped pensively at the vintage champagne.

"Are you?"

"You bet. They're pretty deep, you know. We'll dive sixty feet, maybe more. We'll have to be careful. I've ordered a decompression chamber, but it won't be installed for a month or two."

"Tony, are you sure you should be doing that? You've never dived before." Pat knew Latham was using psychological warfare. It might not be working on Tony. It was beginning to faze her. She held on to his arm as tightly as the hour-glass Anne Klein jacket clung to her torso, above the full-length see-through Perry Ellis silk chiffon skirt.

"It's just swimming. I'll copy Dick. I'm sure he'll be doing all the safe things."

Latham laughed. The guy didn't stop. He was fearless. "That's right. Follow the old man and you can't go wrong. That's the ticket, isn't it, Havers? You're the expert."

Havers, white-tuxedoed, white-faced from the hours below deck making the empire work, laughed at his own expense. He was Gromyko to his boss's Khrushchev. The top Russian had once boasted that his henchman would drop his pants and sit on a block of ice if ordered to. But then Gromyko had been there to crack a rare smile at Khrushchev's funeral.

"It's always the clever thing to do," agreed Havers as he gulped at a neat Glenlivet.

"I'm always looking for clever things to do," said Melissa Wayne. It didn't look to be a lie. She had come as the Golden Girl. Her shoulders were bare, and her toffee-brown lickable skin slid into a matte gold sequined mini-sheath dress. The best legs in the business ended in Isaac Mizrahi gold rubber boots. Gold and rubber! Peaches and cream as a harmony cliché was history. Her hair was piled up on top, waiting only for the word to come cascading down. Conversation faded away in her presence, as it was supposed to.

Dick Latham's eyes ate her as a first course, despite the iced silver bowls of packed beluga that waited on the table. A movement on the edge of the group broke the spell.

"Ah, Allison, there you are. We're complete. What have you got down there in your cabin? *War and Peace?* Ha! Ha! Now, I don't think you've met Melissa Wayne, a fellow Thespian. Allison was a student with Tony at the Juilliard, Melissa. She's a bona-fide member of the American aristocracy stooping to conquer, despite familial lack of enthusiasm. That's about it, isn't it, Allison?"

Allison Vanderbilt was pale as snow, but she made a beautiful ghost. If Pat was on-the-nail stylish, and Melissa Wayne at-the-edge trendy, then Allison Vanderbilt was cashless class. She wore a simple black cocktail dress that might have been Yves Saint Laurent or Givenchy, but was actually run together by a little woman in Seal Harbor, where her parents, who thought the Hamptons common, kept a summer vacation home. She was barefoot. She knew about teak decks. The Vanderbilt twelve-meter had been a contender for the Americas' Cup.

She looked hopelessly at Tony, helplessly at Pat. Her unseeing eyes played in panic over the golden condom that was Melissa's dress.

"Hi, Allison, you look just wonderful," said Pat.

"Doesn't she just?" said Latham.

"Terrific," agreed Havers, hoping he would draw her at dinner.

"Mm," said Melissa Wayne, a noise that might have meant very nearly anything.

The only person whose opinion Allison cared about said nothing at all. Part of her thanked God for that. One more "Are you all right, Allison?" and she'd have burst into tears.

"Some champagne for you, Allison?" asked Latham solicitously. The connoisseur in him loved her look, vulnerable, pure, transparently good. The snob in him liked it even more. He had come a long way since his father had stuck his first mall together. Yale had been okay, and now of course there was the Racquet, the Union, and the Knick. But he was short of a good prep school, and the cradle-to-grave buddies that the old money had. And the Brook had never let him in. That hurt. Lots of things did. The megabucks could make most things right, but they couldn't give you the belief in your own superiority that a Scottish nanny could. If you hadn't fought with the upper classes as kids on the dunes of New England, if you hadn't learned to dance with them, slept over, stood next to them as an angel in the nativity play, you would remain forever an outsider. You might be invited to their houses, befriended, permitted to marry their daughters even, but only your children would be considered their equal.

"What I'd really like is a glass of scotch," said Allison.

Latham heard the secret class language. It was the sort of thing he picked up from the British in the bar at White's. You didn't say "a scotch." You said "a *glass* of scotch." It was the aristocratic mistrust of conversational shorthand, the suspicion of champagne as a nouveau-riche drink, the total lack of concern about whether or not others might think whiskey an unladylike choice. If she'd felt like drinking piss, Allison Vanderbilt would have asked for a *glass* of it, and everyone in the room would have somehow felt themselves to be with the wrong drink. You had to admire it. The girl was in emotional pain. A peasant had let her down, but the safety net of her background had caught her. She might have fallen, but she still dangled in the air above the heads of the rest of them, superior, ultimately untouchable, and, at the end of the day, aware of it.

"A glass of Famous Grouse for Miss Vanderbilt," said Latham.

"What I want to know," said Melissa Wayne, irritated by Latham's solicitous attention to the powder-puff drama student from the East, "is why you are keeping a whole barrel load of men in the bowels of the ship. I saw a couple of them come up for air. Are they reserves or something? I think we should be told." She laughed flirtatiously, eying Tony, as she let him know what men were for.

"Ah, my guilty secret is out of the bag." Latham laughed mysteriously. "I was saving that for the dessert, or rather the pudding, as my English friends would say." His eyes flicked toward Allison in an attempt at forming class solidarity. She continued to stare forlornly at Tony.

"Well, I have to admit there *is* a deal cooking. Rather an exciting one as deals go. But let's wait. As this is still L.A. County and we're not allowed to eat anything fattening, it'll do as the bombe surprise."

He ushered them toward the table.

"Now, let's see, Melissa here, on my right. Pat, if you could bear to take my other side. Then, what about Tony next to Melissa, and then Allison, and last but not least Tommy, between Allison and Pat. Isn't this fun—the grown-ups get to eat with the children." He laughed as he spoke to show that he at least was a child. Somehow he allowed the impression to linger in the air that at least one of the children was as old and as serious as God.

Six stewards moved forward to draw back six chairs, and drop six napkins into six laps. The glistening caviar, served only with quarters of lemon, stared up at them. Crystal shot glasses were filled with freezing, viscous Absolut vodka. San Pellegrino burbled into the Waterford tumblers.

"I hope the caviar is all right," said Latham. "It came down with Tommy from Petrossian and then with Melissa in the helicopter. If it's not, we'll blame them." He chuckled as he small-talked his guests, scooping a spoonful of caviar onto a slice of butterless toast.

"I had a call the other day from someone named Emma Guinness," said Melissa Wayne. "She claimed to be the editor of one of your magazines, *New Celebrity*. I didn't know there was an *old Celebrity*."

"We're revamping it," said Dick Latham pleasantly. "Emma's from England. My new broom. I suggested she do a profile on you, Melissa. What did you tell her?"

He turned to the star. She smiled provocatively.

"Ah, a hands-on owner. I like that." Her expression insinuated that the Latham hands were already on her. "I said 'maybe.' I never trust Brit journalists. Anyone who's a success is an outcast in England. The papers make their lives hell. I have it in my contracts I won't tour there. Several of us do. I hope she's not going to turn *Celebrity* into a watered-down *Spy*."

"That's certainly not my plan," said Dick Latham, banging back the vodka in a single gulp. He didn't like anyone bad-mouthing *Celebrity*, especially a hot star like Melissa Wayne. These days when the name agencies—CAA, ICM, Morris—ran the town, gossip and hearsay could metamorphose instantly into the gospel truth. A magazine that depended for its lifeblood on star access could be blackballed out of existence in seconds, and then the only people who would appear between its covers would be desperate unisex bimbos from the daytime soaps. "But don't ask me about it, talk to Pat Parker. She's on the masthead. She's under exclusive contract. Hers and Emma's hearts beat as one."

He gestured extravagantly to Pat, as if introducing a prize-fighter. He had set up round two.

Melissa turned slowly toward her former adversary. Pat stared back at her across the table, an anticipatory smile playing around her lips. She didn't intend to start anything, but if something was started, then she was going to finish it—with or without the help of Tony Valentino.

"So, Patricia," said Melissa. "*Tell* us about *New Celebrity*."

She sat back in her chair like a studio boss waiting for a minion to pitch a script. The impression was left that whatever was now delivered would be found wanting. Her right hand twiddled a lock of hair, her left drummed impatiently on the immaculate tablecloth. Her sultry eyes fastened onto Tony Valentino across the table. "Watch me," they said. "Who do you want? The woman or the mouse?"

"Emma would be able to tell you better than I can—but I know what she's aiming for. It's going to be a fearless magazine—not bitchy, not gossipy, but artistically dangerous, cutting edge, something entirely new. It's going to be very visual, and the 'people' articles are going to dig deep into motivation, into weaknesses and strengths. You know, like, What made you want to be a movie star? What does it mean to you to be famous? How do you cope with it? What terrifies you? What turns you on? What turns you off?"

Melissa Wayne laughed. She threw her head back to do so.

"Well," she drawled, "I'd have no problem at all answering the last two questions." Her meaning was unmistakable. To emphasize it, her eyes flicked to Tony and her tongue slipped out to moisten her upper lip. Then they swiveled back to Pat, and the wet lip curled.

Pat took a deep breath. Okay, she'd tried. Now she slipped off the gloves.

Dick Latham stepped metaphorically between them. A catfight would be fun, but he didn't want Melissa Wayne painting herself into a corner in which she would be honor-bound to refuse to appear in the magazine. Social blood sports and business were better not mixed.

"On a more specific level, have you given any thought to your first photo spread, Pat? I'm just longing to see it," he said.

Pat's mind stopped in its tracks. The confrontation had been avoided. A far more significant one was brewing. This mattered. Was the dinner table the place for it? Who knew? When at last she spoke, she herself was quite surprised by what she said.

"I want to do a photo essay on Tony. The prints are brilliant, but I'm having problems persuading him to let me use them."

She couldn't look at him as she played her dirty trick. She was using the others against him. It was unfair, but it might just work. Her heart hammered in her chest. Their relationship was on the line.

Melissa Wayne came right in on cue.

"My God, how wonderful," she said. "I was beginning to wonder about *New Celebrity* from what you said. Now I'm converted." She patted the Latham arm as she stared at the furious face of Tony Valentino. "Write me down for a subscription. Does my piece get to rub shoulders with his?"

Latham smiled. "Sounds great. Tony as the spirit-of-a-generation. Focused, drug-free youth, and something the women can relate to. I like it. Yes, I like it very much."

Despite himself, he did. Tony was unique. The fact that Latham would have liked him atomized was beside the point. He was visual dynamite, and the chemistry that bubbled between him and Pat would have lit up the photo session. He looked at his rival, and there was curiosity on his face that mirrored the ambivalence in his heart. Tony would be good for *New Celebrity*, and therefore good for Dick Latham. It was a new angle on the young actor, and it jelled with the grudging respect Dick already felt for him. The guy was powered by ambition, but had never crawled. On the contrary, he had gloried in being confrontational. In the ordinary way Latham would have put that down to the unthinking bravado of youth. But with Tony, it seemed to spring not from a denial of insecurity, but from an extraordinary self-confidence. You didn't have to like it, but you had to admire it.

"Why the objections, Tony?" asked Havers.

Tony said nothing, and for a second it looked as if he would ignore the intense interest that now sparked around him.

"Maybe Tony felt that the photographs were personal," said Allison Vanderbilt suddenly.

Her face was white, her knuckles whiter. The mist in her eyes was tears. Her voice was heavy with accusation. She was accusing Pat of betrayal of trust, of disloyalty, the ultimate crime in the code of the upper classes. And as a subsidiary felony, a misdemeanor really, she was accusing Pat of stealing the man that Allison loved.

"They were," said Tony. His eyes were daggers in Pat's as she dared at last to look at him.

"Oh, nonsense, you mustn't be so bourgeois," laughed Melissa, flicking her head at Allison, but talking to Tony. "That kind of thinking is for the silver-spoon brigade with nothing to protect but their privacy. Those of us with talent have an obligation to display it, be it beauty, brains, or both." She pushed out her pointed breasts at the table and giggled to show that she came in the last category.

Pat fought back the temptation to come to the rescue of the distraught Allison. But Melissa, for all the worst reasons, had ended up on Pat's side. And she was bringing her powerful cannon to bear on Tony.

"Would you take your clothes off for *Playboy?*" asked Tony, zeroing in on Melissa. His question tried to be hostile, but ended semiserious. He admired Wayne, and he fancied her. She was what a woman should be—up-front, determined, and with something to aim at.

"I did," said Melissa simply. "It was how I got my first part." The humor had gone from her voice. She had moved on. "Did you take off your clothes for Pat's pictures?"

There was silence at the table. It was broken only by Allison Vanderbilt's sharp intake of breath. Pat looked up at the starry sky. Its peace was a dramatic contrast to the dinner for which it was the ceiling. Havers coughed. Dick Latham sat forward, alert, waiting for the reply. On Melissa's face was a half smile of anticipation. Tony Valentino had become a thundercloud full of hidden lightning.

"Yes, I did," he said at last.

"Good for you," whispered Melissa Wayne. Her breath was coming faster. "I can't wait to see them," she added.

"That was brave," muttered Havers, horrified by the male lapse of taste.

Latham digested it. Artistic danger. Cutting edge. Emma had gone on and on about that. Pat had just mentioned it. Well, apparently they all meant what they said. He thought fast, and as he did so the printouts cascaded from the computer of his brain. And they all ended up in the tray marked "brilliant."

"I think it sounds very, very interesting," he said. There was no trace of sarcasm in his voice.

"You do?" said Pat. If he felt like that *before* he saw the photographs, he would be over the moon afterward.

She had feared his ridicule, first because of the publishing risk involved, second because he so obviously disliked Tony. Clearly she had underestimated him. He wasn't an ordinary man with ordinary prejudices like Havers. He was an original. He thought for himself. He didn't let his feelings get in the way of his judgment. It was as if she were seeing him for the first time.

Dick Latham had made his billions the newfangled way. He had earned them.

"I would consider it a very great privilege to be allowed to see them," said Latham. He looked straight at Tony. Man to man. Equal to equal. Professional to professional.

Tony looked back at him. It was a powerful pitch, especially as it came from a man who had no reason at all to like him, and every possible reason to rejoice in his humiliation. Latham had been handed the perfect ammunition, and he had refused to use it. Instead the billionaire was asking for a personal favor. Already he had paid Tony a difficult male compliment by predicting that the world would enjoy the sight of his body. It was an impressive and unexpected turnabout, and it had taken courage. Tony liked that. You had to dare to change. You had to seize the moment. You had to lose the past, and look only to the future. Inside, a weird feeling was on the verge of being born. Could he end up *liking* Dick Latham? Anything was possible. Because he was well on the way to hating Pat Parker for the unforgivable thing she had done.

"I think Pat's decided to publish them, anyway," he said at last, letting the bitterness hang out. He turned toward her, and his words were cold as ice when he spoke. "I didn't know who you were," he added.

Pat shook his eyes from hers. She had won. She had lost. She had sold him for her art. The photographs would be used now. Latham would ram them past Emma Guinness, if she objected, and it was far from certain that she would. The deed had been done, and she had lost her lover. She wished he would understand. She had been ruthless, as he was ruthless. There, across the table, weeping gently, was Allison Vanderbilt, whom he had used. But he wouldn't see that. He wouldn't take it into consideration. With blinkered vision, he would hold this against her, despite the fact that in the same situation he would have done precisely the same thing. The crazy part was he would benefit from this. Her pictures would launch his career as they sank the relationship they shared. It was so mad, so bad, yet so deeply necessary. Never before in her entire life had getting her own way felt so pointless.

She looked up at the sea of blurred faces. The caviar had gone, but the halibut bonne femme and the Puligny Montrachet had landed. Dinner still had to be endured. So did the rest of her life. She straightened herself up.

"Perhaps this is the time for my little announcement," said Dick Latham into the curious mood that had descended over the table.

They tried to look interested, but they didn't succeed. Allison was way past surprises. She looked like she was about to faint. Havers was clearly in on the secret, whatever it was. Tony was lost in the proud fastness of his private world. Pat suffered in hers. Only Melissa Wayne retained the energy to register excitement.

Latham wasn't fazed by the poor response. The expression on his face said he had the cards. When he played them everyone would sit up and take notice.

"You may remember that recently I bought Cosmos Pictures. When I took advantage of a real-estate play and closed down production, people concluded that my interest in the studio was over. That is not the case. Far from it." He paused to allow the message to sink in. Tony drifted up toward the surface from the depths in which he'd been swimming. Melissa cocked her head to one side. Pat slipped her mind into forward gear.

"In fact it is my plan to rebuild Cosmos—to create a brand-new studio from scratch in the style of the old Hollywood. I intend to turn it into the best and most influential studio in the world. I'm counting on you to star in some of my pictures, Melissa, and who knows . . . maybe Pat will one day direct, and perhaps Allison and Tony . . . will act in a Cosmos movie . . ."

He opened his arms to all of them, as he signaled the wide-open possibilities of the future and his eagle eyes inventoried the faces at his dinner table. He had them all now. They were hooked. He could reel them in. He could throw them back. He could fillet them and cook them and eat them up.

Melissa let out a whoop of excitement. More work. More glory. More cash and the cachet that could be turned into sex. All the studios courted her, but Cosmos was special. Despite its string of flops, it was old Hollywood aristocracy, and she had never worked for it before. Allison heard the siren movie call across the rocks and ruins of her life. The word *director* spun in Pat's mind, as moving images replaced the stills. But the most dramatic effect of the Latham words was on the face of Tony Valentino.

He seemed deeply shocked by the news, and yet it was impossible to tell whether he thought it good or bad. His expression defined ambivalence. In his eyes shone the light of excitement. At the same time his mouth curled down in an expression that could only be disgust. His other features alternated uncertainly between the two extremes of emotion. Fascinated, Pat watched him across the table, acutely aware of his dilemma. Latham, a man he despised, had offered obliquely to make Tony's dream come true. Would he accept? Would he put career before principle, as she had just done? Yes, he would. Pat knew that. And in his brilliant future there would be no place for her. The anger flooded through her. Damn! It was so unfair, so hypocritical. He was just like her. He would betray his own feelings to get what he wanted just as she had allowed her own ambition to turn her into a traitor. Didn't two wrongs cancel each other out, even if they didn't make a right?

Then, suddenly, another thought occurred to her, cutting into her mind like a thunderbolt from the blue. "Where are you going to build the new studio?" she said.

"Oh, somewhere in the desert," said Dick Latham with an airy wave of his hand.

—

"Isn't pat coming?" said Dick Latham, pretending a surprise he didn't feel.

"No idea," muttered Tony, as if he hardly knew who Latham was talking about. He picked his way through the piles of diving apparatus that were laid out on the bottom deck of *The Hedonist*. "Do we really need wetsuits?" he asked.

Latham smiled. It was beginning. Tony was trying to score an early point. The Pacific water off Santa Cruz Island was around seventy. It was cold, but not *that* cold. If Tony could shame Latham into leaving the rubber suit behind, the older man would have an uncomfortable morning. Tony's younger and more efficient body-temperature-regulating system would give him an advantage.

The diving instructor, who was a full-time member of the yacht's crew, answered for his boss. "The surge tides can throw you against the walls of the caves. You can rip yourself to shreds in there if you're not careful. You need wet suits, boots, heavy gloves, especially if you want to pick up a lobster."

"Oh," said Tony with a smile. "I see we'll have to be *very* careful."

Latham and the diver exchanged glances. "You *have* done this before, haven't you, sir?" asked the diver warily.

"In my sleep," said Tony, ambiguously.

The summer fog lay like a blanket across the sea, wrapping Santa Cruz in a cotton wool mist. It was warming already, though, and the blurred ball of the sun was fighting to peep through the haze. The water was calm, the swell rolling in gently, but the diver seemed nervous. His anxious eyes scanned the water.

"Going to be okay, Joe?" asked Latham.

"You know how it is, sir, it's unpredictable, and the tide's really too high. Are you sure you don't want to try this later?"

He was aware of Tony's eyes on him.

"Can't. We've got to get back to Santa Barbara this afternoon. I'm in New York first thing in the morning."

"Well, I'll be right behind you," said Joe.

"To hold your hand," laughed Tony.

The muscles rippled on the forearms of the diver. He turned toward Tony, his eyes flashing.

"No need for you to come, Joe," drawled Latham. "Our young friend likes to live dangerously. I think we should accommodate him." He laughed. The caves were not to be trifled with. It was crazy to explore them without an experienced diver and speleologist.

But that was what a part of life should be about, wasn't it? There should be a time for excitement, and pitting your wits against the elements, and for doing things that weren't strictly sensible. It was a lesson the old could learn from the young.

They climbed into their wet suits as Joe checked the bottles and the regulators. The small diving boat, lowered already into the water, bobbed off the stern.

"I'll be anchored off the Lobster Caves, if you're doing them first, then I'll move across to the Bat Cave when I see you swim over. Look after yourself."

"If the asshole gets himself into trouble, leave him behind" was the unspoken message. Professionals loathed glory boys. They were always having to clean up their messes.

Dick Latham nodded. It was exactly what he intended. A half-drowned

Tony Valentino being sucked from the water by the unforgiving Joe would make an excellent end to the morning.

"Okay, Tony, let's do it." They climbed into the boat and Joe manhandled the heavy bottles into the stern across the swimming platform of *The Hedonist*. He started the outboard, and soon the dive boat was cutting across the swell toward the Cavern Point shore of the island.

"Let's do the Bat Cave first," said Tony.

"Fine, in at the deep end," agreed Latham.

They hauled on the bottles as the boat anchored, adjusted their masks and mouthpieces, and took up their positions on the edge of the boat. Then, together, they toppled over backward into the water and the bubbles and the dark ocean swallowed them. The cold took away their breath as they cartwheeled in the water, but soon they were oriented and swimming strongly toward the jagged opening in the cliffs. Dick Latham felt for the underwater light at his belt, and he tensed his shoulders, adjusting the air bottle on his back. Bat Cave was the second largest on the island, and, he remembered, a safe one, but you could never tell. Here there would be no minions to smooth his way. His billions would be as relevant as bird droppings.

The entrance loomed up, black against the brown cliff, and his flippers caught briefly against sharp rocks that guarded the cave's entrance. His head broke the surface of the water, and he turned around to see Tony's beside him. He reached down for the light and shone it above his head into the cave. The interior seemed at first to consist of a single chamber, at the back of which was a dry platform of pebbles and piles of rotting wood. He half swam, half walked into the cave, ducking down low in the water to keep his air bottle beneath the surface so that the ocean's buoyancy would take its weight. He aimed his light at the ceiling, and there, hanging upside down in the darkness, were the reason for the cave's name. A bat, caught in the spotlight, uncurled its wings and in seconds the air of the cave was full of them, darting and jinking in the gloom above the heads of the explorers. Tony, too, reached for his flashlamp, and for a minute or two they tried to catch the furious bats in their beams like fighter planes in the fingers of wartime searchlights. Tony laughed and Latham joined in, two boys locked in an adventure, boys who had been rivals, even enemies, minutes before. Away to their right, a narrow passageway led off from the main atrium of the cave. The water lapped near its ceiling, leaving little headroom above its surface.

Dick Latham pulled out his mouthpiece.

"Let's try that." He pointed at the internal exit to the cave. "I'll go first." He ducked down below the surface, holding the light in front of him in the blackness, and began to swim toward the opening. As he did so, he felt an underwater current suck at him, pushing him off course. His shoulder touched the rocky wall of the cave. His head brushed against it. Damn! You couldn't predict the swell. They should have been wearing helmets with mounted lights. Thank God for the heavy gloves. He turned around. Tony, too, had been caught by the unexpected motion of the sea. His thumbs-up gesture said it was no big deal. For a second he paused in the opening, but he felt Tony's shoulders on his fins. It would have been wise to wait. Swells came in sets. The smart diver would hang around to see what would unfold before pushing on. But, caught up in the atmosphere of male competition, Latham didn't wait. He took a deep breath of air, and he pushed into the narrow passageway between the rocks, Tony following close behind. There was no space to turn around. The only way was forward.

The light pointed ahead, reflected from the sharp, ragged walls, disappeared into the darkness of the tunnel. Dick floated toward the surface, but now the roof of the channel merged with the surface of the water. There was nothing to breathe but the bottled air on their backs. For long minutes they swam on, and Latham tried to calculate in which direction they were heading. It was no good. The tunnel twisted and turned. It was impossible to know if they were running parallel to the sea, heading back toward it, or burrowing deeper into the ancient rock of the island. Dick Latham felt the first fingers of alarm, in the pit of his stomach, at the nape of his neck. He wasn't frightened yet. It was a pleasant feeling, with the advantage of strangeness. His body was tingling, on maximum alert, and his mind was cool, running faster than it did in a tough negotiation with a worthy opponent. To his right the light picked out another tunnel, heading off at right angles to the main channel. His gut told him it might cut through to the ocean. Or it could be a cul-de-sac. If they made the turn they would have to be careful. A few more and they could get lost. They had used maybe fifteen minutes of air. There were fifteen left. He angled himself into the opening of the tributary, which was when it happened.

The slapping water began to boil around him, and a powerful jet erupted from the tunnel. It picked him up like a leaf in a hurricane and hurled him bodily at the wall. It was as if he had taken a direct hit from a hidden fire hose in a riot at night. The pain exploded in his shoulder where he banged against the rock. His left flipper was torn from his foot. His mask was sucked from his face, the mouthpiece of his air line was dragged from between his teeth. He tried to right himself with his hands and to protect himself with his feet, but the rocks sandpapered against him. A glove disappeared into the boiling caldron of water, and his hand was crushed against the sharp surface of the wall, ripping the skin from his fingers and exposing the bone of his knuckles. A light exploded in the middle of his mind as the nightmare began, and around his brain a ghostly voice was repeating what he knew. "You're in trouble, Dick Latham. You're in deep trouble, and it's your own fault."

He righted himself in the lull as the current subsided, but he knew as he did so that it was the end of nothing but the beginning.

He reached over his shoulder to grab at his floating mouthpiece, and he jammed it back into his mouth. He steadied himself along the wall, noticing the cloud of blood that spiraled from his injured hand, and he tried to hang on for dear life against the countercurrent that he knew was coming. He moved his arm frantically to signal Tony to keep back from the entrance to the side channel, and then he tried to find a purchase point on the jagged rock face.

The water sucked at him. It plucked at his legs, drawing him away from the rock face. Stronger and stronger it pulled at him, peeling his bleeding fingers from the wall to which he clung. He looked over his shoulder into the black hole that wanted him, and suddenly he knew with the certainty of the damned that he would die. There would be no escape from the vacuum trap. Once inside the churning hellhole, he wouldn't have the strength to swim against the swirling currents. If he wasn't battered unconscious against the sharp rocks, he would be held captive beneath the water, watching in panic as the gauge of his breathing tank flicked toward empty. Out there on the deceptively smooth surface of the ocean, Joe would be waiting, oblivious to his danger. Even if Tony was able to turn around in the narrow passageway and get back to the dive boat, there would be no time for the rescue. Dick Latham held on, but as he did so he could already feel his fingers, and his life, slipping away.

His past didn't flash before him as it was supposed to. Instead, the black bile of anger surged up within him. Damn it to hell! He wasn't ready yet. There were too many people out there to be glad about this. There were enemies to be destroyed, women to be devoured, magic deals to be done. He would never get to see *New Celebrity*, never cut the ribbon on the Cosmos studio, never hear the noises that Pat Parker made in the final surrender. So he threshed with his feet, and he tore with his hands, and he filled his lungs with air for the superhuman effort to avoid his fate. Shit! Tony Valentino would watch him die. There was nothing else he could or would do, and Dick Latham didn't blame him. So much for the generation game. He hadn't expected it to end like this. Game, set, and match to love with no replays on the first encounter and in record time.

The surge tide scraped him off the wall. It bundled him into a ball of chaos and swallowed him up. He corkscrewed into the darkness, and his head crashed against a rock, sending bright stars fireworking into the blackness of his mind. There was a terrific blow behind his shoulder, and suddenly there was no air in his mouthpiece. In panic, he realized what had happened. The collision with the rock face had knocked the entire first stage from his air bottle. The only breath he had left was already in his lungs, and now his mouth was full of salt water. His heart drummed in his chest, as he fought to stay calm in the short seconds before death. He had one chance. If he could wait for the ebbing current to flow once again, it might catapult him through the narrow opening he had just entered. Once outside, he could share Tony's air. He peered through the gloom as he tried to get his bearings. He grabbed for the light, but it was no longer on his belt, swept away in the maelstrom that had engulfed him. In desperation he braced himself to plunge into the unknown, and he pushed down hard with his heels to gain forward momentum. The sharp pain shot up from his ankle, crowding into his breathless brain. He was stuck. His foot was caught in a crevice. His last chance was gone. Dick Latham gave up. It was supposed to be a pleasant way to go. You drifted away as if falling asleep. You took a deep breath and the water bubbled in. You floated above your body in the famous death experience, glad to be shot of it, free at last from the flesh-and-bone prison that foolish mortals were so attached to.

The hand gripped him. A face loomed up against his. A mouthpiece was thrust against his lips. Dick Latham bit at it, and life flowed into his lungs, as relief and oxygen coursed through his blood. It was Tony. He'd braved the whirlpool to join Latham in the watery grave. In an act of superhuman courage, generosity, and foolishness, he had sacrificed his own future so that a man he hated could have a few more minutes of his. The thoughts kaleidoscoped in Latham's mind as warmth and gratitude battled with fear and hopelessness. But Tony Valentino had other plans. His fingers were buried in the flesh of Latham's upper arm, and it wasn't the grip of panic or desperation. It was the grip of determination. His other hand hovered in front of Latham's face. His finger jutted out, pointing back over his shoulder in the direction of the bottleneck entrance. His finger jabbed emphatically. They were going to attempt the impossible. They were going to try to swim against the force of the current.

The urgency of Tony's fingers and the emphasis of his gesture stiffened Latham's backbone. The young man had always looked strong, but Latham had imagined his muscles to be designer ones, all pumped up for show in some narcissistic Manhattan gym. Now they would be put to the test. Tony jerked Latham's hand down toward his belt, and he crunched up his body, placing both feet on either side of Latham's midriff to get maximum thrust from the wall. Latham hooked his other hand into the belt and, steadied by the younger man, he maneuvered his trapped foot free of the crevice that held it. Tony reached for the mouthpiece, took a lungful of air, and passed it back to Latham. His hand jerked up. His hand jerked down. His legs pistoned straight. He shot like a bullet into the foaming water, and Latham was dragged in his wake, kicking furiously to provide additional forward momentum. They arrowed toward the exit, into the teeth of the countercurrent. Every millimeter they achieved, their speed slowed. Then, three feet from their target, they stopped. Tony's arms churned the water. Latham's legs threshed up and down. It was no good. They weren't moving. Once again the wave of fatalism passed through Latham. So near. So far. Thirty-six inches in some godforsaken cave was the difference between a glorious future and oblivion.

Latham realized that Tony had a decision to make. Without Latham in tow, Valentino would have a chance. Carrying the excess baggage, he was doomed. Latham should let go of the belt. It was the right thing to do. Already Tony had done too much for him. Whatever. He didn't let go. In fact his knuckles tightened on the belt that was his lifeline, and in extremis Dick Latham smiled grimly as he realized what a very unpleasant man he was.

Tony turned to look at him. He could see the Valentino eyes through the foaming gloom. They bored into him with all the scorn of the winner for the loser. I've won, they said. I was right. You were weak, and I am strong. If we die now it will change nothing. You didn't even have the decency to let go. It was the most effective message. Somewhere in the depths of Dick Latham's soul the fountain of adrenaline began to play. Damn it! Damn him! The power coursed into his legs. Suddenly they were light as feathers, and they thrashed the water with renewed vigor. Together they inched forward and Tony, encouraged, redoubled his efforts. His arms hammered at the sea. His legs crashed up and down beneath Latham's body. Then, quite suddenly, like Jonah from the whale's mouth, they were vomited through the opening. They tumbled forward, cascading over each other, and crashed into the wall outside.

Their velocity, and the shock of the impact, threw them sideways out of the suction of the deadly side cave. In the calm, they sank to the sandy bottom, and the joy rushed through them. They hugged each other, holding on tight in mutual congratulation, and the tears of gratitude sprang from Latham's eyes. They shared the mouthpiece, and it was the pipe of peace between them. They were friends now. Whatever happened, they were joined together by a bond more powerful than any other. Latham owed Tony his life. Tony had risked his for the billionaire in his arms. Their closeness was more than physical. Later there would be words, but now they were not necessary. Through the mist on the inside of their masks, their eyes were talking.

~ 8 ~

*E*MMA GUINNESS SAT behind the desk in the thronelike chair and peered around the meeting she was taking.

"I'm into class," she said. "It's going to be the new American thing. I want writers from Harvard and Yale, but they've got to look good enough for a Calvin Klein ad. Brains without beauty isn't going to hack it in the 1990s."

She leered pugnaciously around the room. Was there any dissent? Who dared raise the flag of rebellion at her court? Who wanted the order of her boot? Not anyone. Their silence was golden.

"And I want lots of subtle sex. The fact that you and I don't like it means nothing. Everybody's terrified to screw, and yet the urge hasn't gone yet. One day it will, and we can ride a nice Puritan wave, but the early nineties will be glossies with naughty bits. So I want art dirt, okay? You know, whoever's the new Newton. *Playboy* with sex. Look, don't touch."

She tapped on the table as an accompaniment to her stream of consciousness, and all the time she wondered how best to wound, to sow the seeds of misery among the best and brightest she had hired.

"Now I don't want anything too camp, Howard," she said sharply to the art director she had stolen from *Vogues Hommes*. "Camp's okay for the odd article as long as it's haute camp, but not for the visuals. Eyes-wise, *New Celebrity*'s strictly straight. Fashion?" She paused. As always, the curtain was descending. "Well, fashion's Michael, isn't it? Just keep it young and energetic and not too *dull* . . . but not too daring either . . . I mean, like, use . . . Oh, God, use whomever you like, just don't screw up, okay? . . ."

Michael smirked. It was the Guinness blind spot. In the whole magazine he would be the only person with carte blanche. He tried not to look at her clothes, but his eyes kept scurrying back to the red-button booties that kept peeping from beneath her desk. What was so fascinating about the disgusting? It took real originality to be a genuine fashion victim.

"Now, novelizations. We need a few of those upper-class privileged kids wittering on about how dreadful it is to have cash, nice parents, and a rich education that allows them to get paid for tapping out drivel on typewriters.

You know, lots of drugs, sordid bits about bodily functions, and the hopelessness of life when you've got it all. That's *definitely* nineties stuff. 'Downhill All the Way' type rubbish, 'Straight Run to the Grave,' 'Dead in the Night'—if you can't find an author, hire an Ivy League Social Register model and I'll rattle off his autobiographical first novel during my lunch break."

"What about Maria Gonzales?" tried Jacosta, the sharp features guy.

"Okay. I don't mind her. At least she's young, and young's coming back. She doesn't even seem to share the journalistic horror of adjectives. She doesn't copy that lush Hemingway, even if the rest of America is hanging on to him as if he invented writing. I can't quite work out whether the fear of descriptive passages is to do with a short attention span or dislike of reading period. I know readers are supposed to use their imagination to fill in the blank spaces themselves, but I've always considered books to be a spectator sport. Anyway, give Gonzales a go. Is she still screwing that girl at Ford's?"

Jacosta thought she was. Howard from Paris hadn't been in the Big Apple long enough to know. Michael was able to provide a definite yes.

"Good for her. Go up to five for a first serialization. She's a 'serious' writer, so she shouldn't cost more than that. If she's greedy, come back to me and I'll call her agent. It's Mort, isn't it? He loves me. Don't you all?" She laughed to show that she knew they loathed her, and that she didn't mind. It was the friction she needed. It brought out the best in her, and her best was brilliant.

The telephone rang. She frowned. "I said no calls," she muttered, sweeping it up and scowling out over Central Park.

"Oh, Dick, well . . . *hello!* I thought you were in Malibu. How nice . . ."

She beamed around the room. They all knew who Dick was. Now they'd get to see how close she was to the boss.

"Why that's *wonderful!* So *soon.* I never thought Pat would come across this early. Great! Yes, the first edition. Absolutely. What's the subject? I didn't know there was one in Malibu." She laughed, and her whole face shone with an other-worldly vivacity. A Pat Parker spread for the relaunch. Dick Latham sweet-talking her on the telephone in front of a room full of minions. It was turning into a delicious day.

"Oh . . . oh . . . a boy, you mean they're all of a boy . . . the same one . . . I see." The bounce had gone from her voice. A boy, a *Malibu* boy, didn't sound too kosher. But then, Pat Parker had shot the pix, and photos didn't translate well into words. "Anyway, *you* like them, that's the important thing. No, you've got an incredible eye. I mean it. I'm not bullshitting you . . . okay . . . in five minutes, terrific. I'll get right back to you."

She eased the receiver back onto the phone as if she were tickling Latham's back with it. She peered around the room. It was time for an update, an interruption to normal programming. A big story had broken.

"We have a Pat Parker photo spread for the first edition. Dick's got the prints upstairs. He's sending them down. He's wild about them."

"Of a boy from Malibu?" said Michael, whose fashion portfolio came with built-in bravery. He let the sarcasm out.

"Yeah," said Emma defensively. "I don't think Mr. Latham is likely to be wrong," she added icily. The "Dick" had become "Mr." for the hired help.

"Now, where were we? Oh yes, trendy writers. Well, the trouble is the lead time. They'll be out before we get them in, but one has to try. Just remember nasty is nice, okay? Babies are history, families are dull, singles are back. The world hasn't caught on yet, but *we* know, don't we, campers? Booze is dying, health is hot, and we don't take orders from Euro-trash anymore . . . except . . ." and she laughed a brittle, threatening laugh, "from me."

"I don't know that you're totally right about families," tried Jacosta. "I mean *parenting* is a pretty seminal issue, especially fatherhood." He shifted in his chair, waiting for the lash of the Guinness tongue. Sometimes he experienced a modicum of pleasure from pain. He must talk to his shrink about it. Trying to keep the old buzzard interested was a problem these days.

"Seminal? *Sem*inal? Balls! Semen is more seminal than 'parenting.' Forget all that Spock schlock. Now semen skin rejuvenators, *that's* an issue. Didn't Jackie Bisset have one in that Beverly Hills class-struggle flick? Whatever. Somebody write me a memo on semen, okay? Well done, Kit. There you are, all those long words paid off at last."

The knock on the door interrupted her. The secretary who entered the room was beautiful and haughty as befitted God's handmaiden. She didn't wait to be invited in. She held a manila envelope.

"Mr. Latham asked me to deliver this," she said. She walked across the room like a model on a catwalk and laid the envelope in front of Emma Guinness.

"Thank you," said Emma with the coldness she reserved for good-looking women of a lower status than herself.

She reached for the envelope and eased open the pins that held the flap.

She pulled out the handful of prints and leaned forward eagerly to look at them. The face stared back at her. The face, the body, and Jesus Christ, the dick. It was one of the most beautiful photographs she had ever seen. The dangerous eyes held her. The shades of black and white sang in the sweetest harmony. It was magic. It was brilliance. It was hotter than the burning fires of Hades. She swallowed hard, because it was other things, too. It was searing memories. It was chaotic discord. It was the plucking fingers of dread trampling up and down her suddenly sweating spine. The print swam before her eyes. A red mist had descended. Her heart was hammering beneath her heaving breasts. Never, ever again had she expected to confront this face, this body. She had wiped it from the forefront of her mind, and it lingered only in the dark place where all the humiliations lived—in the basement of the id, from where the occasional muted scream taunted her. Tony Valentino! The name exploded in her brain as the sweat leaped to her upper lip. The lowlife who had crossed her was to be the photo spread in the very first issue of her magazine.

"Are they a disaster?" asked Michael hopefully. He couldn't hold back his enthusiasm for the promising situation. Emma Guinness was white as the ghost she had clearly seen. The print trembled in her hands. Her unseeing eyes wandered over it in panic.

Emma didn't answer. The points that pricked at the skin of her butt were the horns of a dilemma. As she handed the photos across to the fashion editor, she was already confronting it. On the one hand, the photos were wonderful. They were pure art—heart art, not dirt art, and they would be an asset to the magazine. Alone, they would guarantee the success of the re-launch. *New Celebrity* and Emma Guinness's career would be off and running. But at the same time Emma was determined not to use them. This boy had humiliated her. He had spurned her advances. He had insulted her in public. No way did she intend to help him. The photo spread would appear over her dead body, despite the fact that Latham, whose word was law, loved them, and that Pat Parker had the contractual right to demand that they be used. And there was another angle. It was crystal clear from the photographs that Tony and Pat were lovers. Their chemistry sizzled from the surface of the prints. They were a celebration of sensuality, the ultimate gift to the voyeur who would not stoop publicly to snoop. So jealousy was added to revenge, and both battled self-interest, as Emma wondered just what the hell she would do.

"Wow," said Michael. "These are hot." They all crowded around him, looking over his shoulder as he flicked through the prints. The chorus of acclaim was as predictable as wasps at a picnic. The people assembled in that room had only two things in common. They had all been picked by Emma Guinness, and they all knew how to pick winners. It was back to square one. The hirelings she had personally assembled were against her, and so was the ultimate arbiter upstairs.

"Too strong . . . male nudity . . . too sophisticated," she tried.

"Nooooooh," they all chorused.

"Not the first issue . . . sets an unfortunate precedent . . . upset the straight men . . ." Her wild eyes scanned the room for support.

Those who normally would not have dared to disagree with her, did now. United they stood. Divided on these photographs they had no desire to be. Their voices rose in a Tower of Babel refutation.

Emma Guiness shuddered. She breathed in deeply. There was no time like the present. She picked up the phone and punched three numbers.

"Emma Guinness for Mr. Latham," she said.

SHE WENT in at a trot, as if physical momentum alone would give her the psychological edge. He sat back at his desk and smiled his welcome. He looked as if he had been born again. The life positively vibrated from him, despite the bandaged hand, and a colorful bruise high up on his brow.

"Emma, sit down," he said, standing up and waving her into a chair. "Aren't they great? That was what we needed, wasn't it? It's a wrap now. I couldn't be more pleased."

"That's what I wanted to talk to you about, Dick. I know they're good photographs, very good actually, but I don't think this is the right image. I mean the boy looks a bit Latin, I mean a bit cheap, I mean he looks a bit too . . . oh, Malibu. You know, sort of obvious, don't you think? I'm sure Pat can do better. It is the *first* issue, and he's not exactly a celebrity, is he, whoever he is."

She realized that her syntax had fallen apart. She realized that he realized it. Words were her transport through life. Usually she kept them in tiptop working order. Now, at the moment she needed highly greased grammar, her motor mouth had seized.

"What on earth are you talking about?" Dick Latham laughed, eying her tits. "You sound as if you're on Dexedrine."

"The pictures," blurted Emma. "I don't think they're right for the magazine."

"He's called Tony Valentino," said Dick Latham, cutting through to the bottom line. He was still smiling, but he was watching her like a cat—her face now, not her chest.

Emma paused. He couldn't know, could he? But why the fuck were these pictures coming through Latham? Why hadn't Pat Parker submitted them to her? That would have been the right way to do things.

"Well, whatever he's called, I don't think he's *New Celebrity* material, and I don't think his bits and pieces are either." Her eyes slipped away from his as she spoke.

"There's a theory that you met him once," said Latham. His voice was amused.

"Tony Valentino? I don't think so. He looks sort of male bimbo-esque. I guess I could have seen his head shot if he was a model. Was he ever in England?"

Emma shifted in the chair. She knew her face was giving her away. Her cheeks were on fire. She had to brazen it out, but he knew. He knew. Would he let her off the hook?

No, he wouldn't.

"He was an actor, at the Juilliard. Word is you visited his end-of-term play, *A Streetcar Named Desire.* He played Stanley. Odd that you don't remember his face. It's rather a memorable one, don't you think?"

"I vaguely remember," muttered Emma, gazing out of the window in desperation. "I hadn't put the two together."

"The only reason I mention it is that Pat was worried because apparently there was a falling-out between you and Tony over something or other. She thought you might hold it against him vis-à-vis these pictures. Of course, I told her that you were far too professional for that. Business is business in this company, I said, and nobody believes that more than Emma Guinness. She'd shoot her grandmother for circulation, sell her son for the right advertising, said I." He paused, and he leaned forward across the desk. The smile had gone. His expression was cruel. "I wasn't wrong, was I?" he added.

Emma Guinness swallowed. There was only one possible answer to his question. She laughed a gallows laugh.

"Of course not," she managed through strangled lips. "How did you get to meet Valentino? Through Pat?" She struggled to change the subject.

He ignored her question.

"So now what were you saying about these photographs?"

"Yes, I see, well on second thought they're very dramatic, and, of course, they *are* beautiful. I wasn't questioning that. I think maybe my initial impression was a little hasty. They're so strong, maybe they just took some digesting. Thank you, Dick. You've opened my eyes on this one. Pat, too. Isn't she clever? Yes, the more I think about it . . ."

She was dying inside. Tony Valentino had wounded her soul. She was going to make him a star. His career would be launched in her magazine. What she had promised to trade for his flesh, she was about to give him as a reward for his insults. And no longer would it be a piddling quarter page in the all-but-invisible "Stars of Tomorrow" section. Now it would be page after steamy page of celluloid charisma burning into the eyes of every agent and casting person coast to coast.

But Dick Latham's mind had wandered on. He had bludgeoned his employee into submission. His objective was achieved. Now, in his own time, he was prepared to answer her question.

"You asked about myself and Tony Valentino," he said. "I'll tell you. Do you know what he did?"

Emma didn't know.

"He saved my life," said Dick Latham.

—

"You're not happy, are you?" Alabama gazed out over the mountains, their lower slopes wrapped in coastal mist. He didn't turn around as he spoke.

Pat Parker kicked out her legs and lay back on the outsize sofa as she planned her answer. No, she wasn't happy. She was miserable. She felt like an orange from which someone had sucked the juice, leaving her dry, empty, all used up. The last few days she had gone through the motions of living, but it had passed like a bad dream, full of cul-de-sacs, traps, and things happening to her that she couldn't help. Unrequited love might not be the most original feeling in the world. Knowing that didn't help.

"No, it's not a good time," she said at last, smiling bitterly at her understatement.

"You did right," said Alabama. "When fame hits the fan Tony will be grateful."

"He thinks I betrayed him."

"You did, but it was an end-justifies-the-means thing, you know, like Arnold Newman's portrait of Krupp. The kraut thought he looked just fine, and Newman had turned him into the pictorial symbol of evil. The moment you stop shooting trees and get into people you catch all the ego rubbish. Blast through it. Keep your eyes on the art, and everything ends okay."

"Happy endings?" Pat laughed doubtfully.

"I've seen less promising situations turn into happy families," said Alabama.

"For*get* it. Mrs. Tony Valentino would have to have the moral purity of Joan of Arc, *and* the strength."

"The girl was a schizophrenic," said Alabama dismissively. "Listen, are we shooting today? You wanna go down to the Rock House and do some bikers?"

"You mean do some beer."

"Whatever." Alabama smiled, turning around to face her.

"Nah," said Pat. "I just feel like hanging around and having you tell me photography stories—like about Kertész, tell me about Kertész." She curled up her legs like a child waiting for a favorite story at bedtime. Alabama, tough and terrible to the outside world, was so soothing to her. He was chamomile tea, warm muffins, and woolly bunnies at dusk. Was everyone like that—showing different faces to different people, not really a single person at all?

"One day everyone will say Kertész was better than Steichen, Stieglitz, and Weston. He could find beauty where no one else could see it. *That* is the ultimate genius. I cheated. I took obvious beauty, and I made it more beautiful. André saw a leaf in the wind, snow on the ground of an ugly square, and his lens made it something else. Cartier-Bresson and Brassaï both acknowledged their debt to Kertész. The world didn't know him till Szarkowski's MOMA exhibition in the sixties, and poor old André never forgave the world for its oversight. He was one of the most bitter men I have ever met, and with the least reason. Imagine, inventing the photoreportage style, and then worrying about whether or not people give you credit for it."

"I can sympathize with that. It must be so *frustrating* to know that you possess something that nobody else can see. Tony feels like that. It eats away at him. He hasn't mentioned it, but I can see it in his eyes." Pat couldn't stay away from Tony for long.

"Like everything else in life, the emotion can be used or abused. You can make it work for you, and use its energy to help you get what you want. Or you can point it inward rather than outward, and let the acid drip away at you until there's nothing left. Toward the end André could talk about nothing else but how the Americans had failed to appreciate him. He was the unhappiest artist, but the greatest. I find that the most unbelievable paradox." Alabama shook his head.

"Except that dissatisfaction is the sharpener of your art. You judge it yourself, and the more harsh your judgment the harder you try. I suppose that in the end only by thinking your work is rubbish do you get to perfection. The trick is to be able to live through the discouragement, and not pack it in."

Immediately, Pat wished she could take back her words. Alabama turned back toward the mountain. He said nothing. She hadn't meant to, but she had struck a chord within him. Had he really stopped taking photographs because there were more of them in the world than bricks?

"Yeah," he said at last. "It was the other way around for me. Everybody loved my stuff. I just wasn't so sure about it myself. The fact they all went belly up for it, made me doubt it. They trash the mountains, pollute the rivers, and screw the trees and then they shell out hundreds of thousands for my pictures of the things they're ruining. It seemed a good joke to plow their money back into the environment, and con them at the same time."

"Take my portrait, Alabama."

"What?"

"Take my portrait." She jumped up, excited. "I want you to. I want you to work again. Please. Do it for me. Just one portrait. That's all I'm asking for. Will you? Please, Alabama. Please."

She ran across to him, as he turned toward her framed by the picture window against the mountains.

"It's not a small thing," he said, avoiding her eyes.

"I know that. I know it. You're frightened. You're nervous. You think it might turn out like *shit*."

She dared to goad him. It was dangerous, but he responded to that.

"What the *hell* do you mean? Nervous? Of a photograph? Me? Jesus, girl, have you forgotten who I *am*?"

"Have *you*?"

"Listen, I never wanted to be a Picasso—a 'paint-till-you-faint' artist. I gave up because I was fed up. If I wanted to, I could take a better portrait than you've seen in ten years with the frigging lens cap on."

"Do it. Prove it!"

"I don't have to prove anything to you."

"I wasn't talking about me. I was talking about proving it to yourself."

He was pacing up and down now, irritated, hesitant, and yes, fearful.

"And what the *hell* would you do with this portrait? Peddle it for a stinking Porsche?"

"No," said Pat simply. "I'd send it to Tony."

~9~

Tony Valentino stared into the mirror and scowled. It wasn't the reflection that made him do that. It was the stuff inside his head. To do this part he had to hate, and to hurt. He had to feel the raw emotions that gave Cal his exposed-nerve personality. Then he had to project them outward so that all the world could feel how it felt to be rejected. Everyone must know for themselves the dread reality of a world without love. He had read Steinbeck's book half a dozen times. He had walked the fields and the hills of Salinas, smelled the scent of the hot grass, lain down gratefully on the rich earth as he would sink into the lap of his beloved mother. "Mother"—the word lasered into his mind as he meant it to, and it set light to the feelings that were Cal's feelings. This dressing room was no longer on Broadway. No more was he an actor waiting for a curtain call and a hushed, expectant audience. He had ceased to be Tony Valentino. He was Cal Trask. He was Steinbeck's Cain on whom the Lord had set his mark. He was Adam's son, Eve's offspring, and he dwelled in the land of Nod, to the East of Eden.

The tap on the door was insistent.

"Two, Mr. Valentino," said the disembodied voice.

In the cunning artificial dream Tony Valentino stood up. He sleepwalked to the door and opened it. He ambled into the corridor and loped along the passageway toward the stage. His shoulders were hunched to protect himself from the slings and arrows that humanity liked to throw at him. He flicked his fingers as he lied that he didn't care, and a smile of scorn played around the edges of his mouth. He caught sight of himself in a mirror, and he hated his beauty, so he crunched up his face into a crushed cardboard expression that was supposed to mock his good looks but only succeeded in emphasizing them. The women would love him out there, damn them. They always loved Cal. They were frightened of him. They were in awe of his unpredictable moods, yet fascinated by the way he recoiled from them until the very moment of their knee-trembling surrender. He despised them for loving him. He was so unlovable. That great truth he had gleaned from the stony ground of his childhood. He kicked out at a rubbish bin that was a metaphor for the

150

world, and he heard the muted hum of the audience behind the heavy curtains. The men out there would loathe him. They knew his secret. They recognized that he was deep-down bad, and, although they would always be his enemies, he respected them for being right. They were the half of humanity who had his number. They were the gender of his father, and his ambivalent love for them lay curled up tight in the womb of his hatred.

In the front seat of the darkened auditorium, Pat Parker's gut was tangled as Medusa's hair. James Dean had played this role in the famous Elia Kazan movie, and Pat could understand why girls committed suicide when he'd died. Tony's Cal was deeper than Dean's, and it wasn't just that she was involved with him still, and therefore the very opposite of a disinterested spectator. There was all the vulnerability of Dean's character, the shy, wounded charm; the touching eagerness to be accepted, standing beside the brittle defensiveness of the boy-man who had learned in the hard school of childhood that grownups could not be counted on for love. But there was more than that. Tony's Cal was strong in the midst of his weakness. His scars were deep inside and the battles he fought were not with the world, but with himself. He was walled away from people. They could whip his flesh, but they couldn't touch his soul. His essence was unavailable to them, and it was his essence that she wanted. Pat breathed in deeply, astounded at the depth of the emotions that sloshed around within her. She was part critic, part psychiatrist, and all the time she was the one-time lover who recoiled from the possibility that the boy she still worshiped would never love her again.

"What do you think?" Dick Latham leaned in toward her like a priest in a confessional.

"I can't describe it," said Pat.

She cocked her head to one side, rolled her eyes to the ceiling, and splayed out her hands in her lap to emphasize the inadequacy of mere words.

Dick Latham chuckled. Tony Valentino's virtuoso performance was hardly a peak moment for the male sex. All around the auditorium husbands had lost their wives, boys their girlfriends, women their hearts. But for Latham it was different. He wasn't wearing the hat of Romeo competitor. He was wearing the halo of successful angel. On his return from Catalina, reborn as a result of Tony's unexpected and selfless bravery, he had attended the rehearsals of the off-off-Broadway stage adaptation of *East of Eden* in which Tony was appearing, and had been electrified by what he'd seen. Hours later, he had bought the whole production, closed down a struggling mainline musical by making its grateful backers an offer they couldn't refuse, and moved Tony's play lock, stock, and barrel to Broadway proper. His personal PR, Jay Rubenstein, had overseen the play's prelaunch publicity, and the vast advertising budget had done the rest. The first night was a major social and literary event. Every critic in New York was there, and the literary lions had prowled the aisles before the curtain had risen. Mailer, Vidal, Wolfe had shaded into Plimpton, Didion, and Dominick Dunne. Society had run the gamut from nouvelle Gutfreund greenbacks to the A and B class of Astor and Buckley. And everyone knew that they were present at a triumph.

"He's playing himself, isn't he?" said Latham.

Pat shook her head, half in denial, half in wonderment. It wasn't as simple as that. Tony was *using* bits of himself, but Cal wasn't him. Cal's prostitute mother had deserted him. Tony's beloved mother had defined decency and faithfulness. Cal struggled to win the approval of his distant father. Tony had been a fatherless child. Yet, despite the differences, Latham was right. It was the similarities that had her nerves on edge. It seemed that Tony had somehow been bathed in lovelessness, and that his aloofness, his untouchability was the result. There was something almost psychopathic about him—a cruelty, a single-minded sense of purpose that excluded others, even lovers, perhaps especially them. He pushed people away, and the closer they came, the harder he pushed. Pat knew. She had experienced it. Okay, maybe she had behaved badly. She had done the "wrong thing," but did she deserve to be excluded from the life of the man she loved? Wasn't that overreaction by a person who took himself and his ideals far too seriously? Then doubt bubbled up inside her. Could it be that Tony had used his uncompromising moral code as an excuse to ditch her? Men did that. No! She recoiled from the possibility. Tony didn't need excuses. Only the weak needed those. Tony, above all else, was strong. It was what she loved most about him. There was even a part of her that admired the way he had reacted to her betrayal of him. He hadn't stood for it. She hadn't measured up to his high standards and he had rejected her because of it. She respected him for that, but it didn't make life any easier. It wouldn't be long before she was face-to-face with him at the Canal Bar party. What should she say? How should she behave? What the *hell* should she feel?

"What do you think, Emma?" Pat turned to her right. Somehow the more people who got into this conversation the better. It would dilute its strength.

"Not a lot, quite frankly," lied Emma. "It reminds me of those plays we had in England in the fifties. It was part of a trend called 'kitchen sink' drama. This is the same sort of thing, only with fields instead of sidewalks. You know, nasty people doing nasty things to each other in nasty surroundings. You get art points for the degree of nastiness achieved on the principle that only degradation is real and anything fine is false."

"Emma doesn't like the play, Dick," said Pat immediately, dropping Emma deep into it. It was a reflex action. Emma was her friend, but nobody was going to get away with criticizing Tony or the play that was his vehicle.

"What?" barked Latham.

Emma's cheeks reddened. "What I meant," she spluttered across Pat at her boss, "was that personally, for me, the subject matter is a little depressing, but the play itself is *very* powerful. Very. I think it's going to be a huge success. I *know* it is. And of course, synergizing with Pat's pix in *New Celebrity*, it's going to make Tony the toast of the town. No question." She bit on her lip as she uttered the unwelcome words. The worst thing of all was that they were true. The evening was turning into a disaster of cosmic proportions, and it promised to plumb deeper depths. Latham had coincided the play's opening night with the *New Celebrity* launch party at the Canal Bar.

The moment Tony had taken the bows at this triumph, they would all be traipsing downtown to watch him taking them at a second. At the instant of her magazine glory, Emma Guinness would be upstaged by the nobody she had turned into the biggest somebody in New York. Even the Almighty wouldn't have had the nerve to dream up a script like that. The man who had humiliated her had saved Latham's life, and become a star overnight. To add insult to injury, he actually had talent. The only good news was that his relationship with Pat was on the rocks. Maybe that would provide some consolation bad tastes amid the sugary menu of wall-to-wall congratulations that looked destined to be the diet of the evening. She took a deep breath. Soon she would have to confront him for the first time since her humiliation in the Juilliard. Their respective situations could hardly be more different. What on earth would happen?

"I hope you're going to be able to learn to think American, Emma," said Dick Latham coldly. "England has produced some great writers certainly, but precious few of them *this* century. I don't know how anyone can fail to appreciate Steinbeck."

He knew he was misinterpreting what Emma had said, but he did so on purpose. No hireling could get away with trashing his play.

"No, I agree," babbled Emma. "Hemingway, O'Neill, Fitzgerald, Faulkner, Tennessee Williams, Steinbeck—I mean, they're tremendously impressive. Shaw, Maugham, goodness, Wilde, are minnows by comparison, drawing-room stuff against the power of the American greats. The English admire your writers *enormously*." She leaned across Pat, her expression absolutely slavish in its subservience.

"The *middle*-class English, maybe. The upper classes have never heard of them," said Latham curtly.

Emma Guinness recoiled from the tongue lash of the Latham whip. He was one of the few Americans who could make an English class crack, like that. Obviously he had learned a trick or two in the White's bar, because his comment was right on the money. The British aristocracy were enormously proud of their intellectual poverty. They left the business of writing to the dreaded middle classes. When the king had been introduced to Gibbon, author of the monumental *Decline and Fall of the Roman Empire,* his only comment had been: "What is it, scribble, scribble, scribble, eh, Mr. Gibbon?" At a stroke, Emma, by her erudition, had revealed herself as a card-carrying member of the bourgeoisie rather than of the upper classes to which she had always aspired. Americans weren't supposed to know the difference. This one did. Latham, her boss, the most powerful man in her world and the one she dreamed of marrying, knew her social secret. Salt burned in the old wounds.

"Thanks a *lot*, Pat," she hissed sotto voce.

But Pat wasn't listening. Quiet descended on the audience. The curtain was going up.

Tony Valentino stared across the room toward the desk where the woman sat. She was bathed in shadow. Brittle blond hair wreathed her small, sharp features and the black lace dress, so prim and prudish, lied about the lewd woman she was. He peered through the gloom, and his heart stopped as he saw her for the first time. A lifetime of longing hadn't prepared him for this. On the one hand was fantasy, the world of his desperate childlike dreams, as he had constructed the perfect woman from the void of fact. But here was reality. Here, in the "proper" Victorian study, among the ferns and the spotless antimacassars, was the whore who was his mother.

"What do you want from me?" she said, her voice harsh.

"I don't want anything." It was the biggest and most grotesque lie of all time. What did you want from the woman who had borne you? It wasn't as simple as "love." In the love desert he had learned to do without. There were ways to survive its absence. You pickled yourself in the vinegar of hatred and you learned not to trust. You schemed and you planned and you skulked in the dark places among the dark people who were your kith and kin, and laughter was a sneer, and happiness was just an illusion. The dearth of love was the death of hope, but you could live with hopelessness and it gave you a wild courage because you had nothing left to lose and nowhere to fall.

"Why come then? Why follow me? How long have you known?"

Her voice was petulant. She wasn't pleased to see the son she had hardly seen. She wanted information that she could use. Even now her wants had precedence over his, as they always had.

"Why did you leave us?" he blurted out, but it wasn't the right question. "Why did you leave me?" he added. It was right now.

He waited for the answer as if for the kiss of the ax's blade, and he knew it wouldn't satisfy. It was the abandonment. That was the source of the pain. He had been so small, so defenseless, so innocent and yet, even in the first hours and days, so deeply unlovable that the woman who had borne him would all but kill to escape from him. She had shot his father because he tried to stop her from leaving. She had risked murder to get away from him. What mark was upon him? What dread aura signaled his worthlessness? For God's sake, why was he so impossible to love? Tony felt the tear swell in his eye, felt his heart heave in his chest because he knew this agony. It was his. It always had been. His father had left him all those years ago. Even now, he could scarcely believe that it was not his own fault. There must have been some deficiency in him that had pushed his father away and condemned his beloved mother to a lifetime of poverty and loneliness as she struggled against all odds to bring him up on the open road.

The tear squeezed out and ran down his cheek as he drew the emotion from the reservoir of pain. But at the same time his white-knuckled fists clenched by his sides because there was room for another feeling now. There was space for anger. Whatever the cause of their leaving, deserters were traitors. As such, they were enemies to be hated and punished. Cal and Tony had learned how to survive in the cruel world, but their crippled hearts cried out for revenge as others lusted for happiness and security and the love of families. Cal needed the idea of his mother, but already he was beginning to loathe the fact of her. Tony wanted his father, but there was a part of him that dreamed of patricide.

"I left you because you were in the way of what I wanted."

She lifted up her chin, and she smiled as she said that, showing the sharp incisor teeth of the wolverine, her eyes flashing in the dull light.

"I was a baby, Mother. I was just a baby."

The reproach was solid in his words, and his heart was breaking for the helpless thing he had been, and for the helplessness that lived on, buried deep beneath the veneer of his toughness. But, as he spoke, he knew that he was not reaching her. There was space where her heart should be. She was psychologically deformed, as stunted and as warped as if her limbs had been twisted and misshapen in some terrible disease or by some accident of birth. There were words for it. Evil. Wickedness. The devil. But they had no meaning, because she was still his mother.

She didn't answer. Instead she looked down and studied the back of arthritic hands, their skin dotted with brown spots, hands aged before their time, hands that his father said had once been beautiful.

"Did you leave us for this? Are you glad?"

He signaled with his hands to summon up the bogus gentility of the brothel, the disgusting tawdriness of the shame house that his mother had preferred to him. He was giving her a chance to apologize. Long after love had gone, and after all the years on the emotional rack, he wanted her formal admission that a great wrong had been done. But she didn't know how to say sorry, because the sorrow she knew did not involve the insubstantial shadows who were other people. It only involved her, and the decay that was the legacy of her rotten life.

She leaned forward and both her hands were on the green leather of her businesswoman's desk. Her face poked out from the shadows into the mind of her son.

"Yes, I'm glad. I'm rich and I'm free and I do what I want. I'm free of snot-nosed kids who only want things, and I'm free of your saintly father and his selfish goodness, and I'm free of all the cant and the hypocrisy of the slime that run this world. I see them in here, you know. I've got photographs of the rubbish who rule us, writhing under the whips, lusting for pain and humiliation at the hands of big, dull women who only want to eat chocolate and rest their feet. They ask for our votes, but they want the heel marks of my girls on their crotches. Do you realize that? Have you any *idea* about the world out there? Yes, I left you for this, because this is *mine* and in the hell of families, women are *owned*. They're slaves to the babies they produce and the men who father them. Drudges. Victims. Servants. Do you hear? Do you hear?"

She was screaming now. Cal recoiled from her as he was directed to do, but then Tony felt the feeling deep within. Her words touched him. He had read them a hundred times in the script, but he had not been emotionally prepared for them as he was now. His intellect saw a poor, psychologically damaged woman. But his heart saw the mother whose blood was his blood.

And there was a message in her words that he understood. She was talking about freedom. She didn't mean freedom to vote, freedom under the law, freedom to speak freely. She meant *real* freedom. His mother was talking about freedom from conscience, from responsibility, from guilt. She had wanted to be free of babies and poverty, from worrying about what other people thought, free to create her own personal, idiosyncratic world in the land of the supposed free where in fact conformity was the universal goal. At a stroke, she was no longer evil. There was an odd logic in her behavior, that only an anarchist like Tony could understand, that only an outsider like Cal would appreciate. A hundred years separated the two men, and it was the difference between walking toward the woman who had just spoken and walking away from her. The stage directions called for the latter. But Tony Valentino wanted with overwhelming strength to take her in his arms.

He walked across the stage, and the surprise was there in the eyes of the actress who had become the father he had never had.

Pat Parker was dimly aware that her feelings were the feelings of the entire audience. It was as if in the silence, emotion had become universal. She knew what she wanted. With all her heart she wanted the mother-and-child reunion. But at the same time, the stage was electric with a sense of terrible uncertainty. The immediacy was total. There was no predicting what would happen, because the characters were as alive as life itself, and because there were no scripts in the real world. This was the ultimate in the art of acting. Tony had lifted them up in the palm of his hand, and they had journeyed through the vale of his emotional sorrow. Most of the crowd had forgotten they were in the theater.

Pat was excited. Now that she had seen Tony act, so many things made sense. She could see where the charisma came from. It flowed from an otherworldly ability to communicate dramatic art. Deep in the theatrical experience, she was hardly able to see Tony as the boy who had once been "hers." He had become public property like the ocean and the beach, and the wide-open sky. Later, as the thrill subsided, there would be time for memory of ownership, and for regrets at the loss of it. Right now, she could only admire him.

Emma Guinness was beside herself with rage. She shifted about on her seat and cursed the thing that was happening all around her. He had been good at the Juilliard. Here he was brilliant. Then, she had thrilled to his performance as she had dreamed of his body. Now, he was an untouchable. He was in the process of being anointed with the success that would take him beyond her reach forever, and the revenge she wanted so badly was receding into the dim distance. Next to her was Pat Parker, the girl who had loved him. The relationship might be over now, but Pat had experienced the flesh that Emma wanted. Somehow that made her a rival—a *successful* rival. And it wasn't just Tony. Latham had chosen Pat to sit next to. Latham's eyes never left the beautiful photographer, as he laughed at her jokes and hung on her words. Yet Latham was Emma's target, and Pat knew that. Maybe she wasn't encouraging the billionaire, but she wasn't discouraging him either. The mean little business of repeating Emma's criticism of his play was an example of the undercurrent flowing beneath the surface. Pat Parker had better watch out. She was creeping toward the Guinness enemy list. Those who reached that, lived to regret it.

Five seats farther along the front row, Melissa Wayne was ecstatic. She hadn't forgotten the moody nobody on the boat off Catalina who had had the luck and the good judgment to save Dick Latham's life. There had been chemistry between them, despite the fact that he had belonged to the photographer who was too good-looking by half. When the invitation to *East of Eden* had arrived in tandem with the one to the Canal Bar launch party for *New Celebrity*, she had immediately accepted. Somewhere down the line she was due to give Emma Guinness an in-depth interview for the already successful revamped magazine. That, and the fact that Dick Latham was apparently planning a new schedule of movies at Cosmos, made the evening interesting from a career point of view. Seeing Tony Valentino again was to have been just icing on the cake. Not anymore. He had become the main event. She couldn't take her eyes off him. Anybody could recognize the power of his performance, but as a professional she knew exactly how difficult it was. Not for one minute did he seem to be acting. He had become Cal to such an extent that one could be forgiven for thinking the whole thing wasn't very clever at all and that he had simply had the good fortune to find a part that was the mirror image of his own personality. Melissa, however, was sophisticated enough to know that was not true. His brilliance was to make it *seem* so. It was a whole new dimension to the boy whose chief attributes until now had seemed to be his flesh and blood and his touchingly insolent self-confidence. So Melissa Wayne licked her lips in the darkness and squeezed her legs together, as she waited for all the good things that would surely happen to her on what promised to be a memorable evening.

Directly behind Dick Latham, Allison Vanderbilt's eyes sparkled through the mist of her tears. She was glad that her date, Jamie Leavenworth, hadn't made it back from the bar. That was good because it meant that she was alone with the man she loved. All around her the audience thought they had a lease on Tony Valentino as he seemed to show the public his most private feelings, but Allison Vanderbilt knew it was a sham, perhaps the most beautiful, brilliant confidence trick that had ever been played. Alone in the crowd she knew him. She had crawled inside his wounded soul and wandered in wonder in its secret places. Oh yes, Pat Parker had been with him, but she had only wanted to use him for her own career purposes. Allison's love was pure. She needed nothing from Tony. His dreams were her dreams. She would die for him, do anything for him, and the magnificence of her selfless obsession filled her up. He didn't love her, but that didn't matter. The only thing that mattered was Tony and the things he wanted. Two days ago they had walked in Central Park and he had held her hand in a gesture that said she was his dearest friend, as he had told her of Pat Parker's mean betrayal and of how upset he had been by her disloyalty. It had hurt to hear him talk of the woman he had loved, but it had been wonderful once again to be so close to him. Later on, they would sit at the same table at dinner and she prayed to the Lord that she wouldn't cry, like now, damn it, because it was so hard when you loved so much . . .

Dick Latham wondered if he had ever had such a good time in all his life. In his heart there was an odd affection for the massed humanity that surrounded him. He loved them because they were reacting in the right way. He loved them because they so obviously agreed with him. They were wise and wonderful because they loved the play that he had backed and because they loved the boy who had saved his life. *East of Eden* would be sold out for months. On his first foray into Broadway investing, he had struck gold. Once again the Latham touch had been the Midas one. Later, they would celebrate the first sellout issue of *New Celebrity*. Already there was an advertiser's feeding frenzy as the upmarket products queued to get into future editions of the magazine. Subscriptions were going through the roof. God was in his heaven and his hated father was spinning like a top in his grave. He felt invincible. He was the man who could do no wrong. There wasn't even a problem about finding something for an encore. He had backed a hit play and launched a wildly successful magazine. Making a blockbuster movie would be a cinch. Tony Valentino would star in it. He was made for a celluloid crossover, and it would be no problem to pull him from the play that Latham owned. It didn't matter that he was unknown. His talent transcended such petty considerations. Melissa Wayne could carry that part of the deal. All that was needed was for the man of the moment to dream up the package, and the lights sparkling in the Hollywood firmament would all be green.

He turned toward Pat. She was on the edge of her seat, leaning in toward the stage. He had been going to say something, but he didn't want to interrupt her intense concentration. So he watched her, in the stage glow, as she stared at the boy she loved, and an even better feeling wafted over Dick Latham. The worst thing about happiness was wondering how it could be improved upon. Now, suddenly, he knew.

Tony Valentino had reached his mother. He knelt down. Tears poured down his cheeks. She didn't pull back from him when he took her in his arms. Instead, she rocked from side to side in the alien embrace of tenderness. All her life she had never known she had needed comfort. All his days, he had yearned for it. He looked up at her, his face dissolving in hope and longing for a better future.

"I forgive you, Mother," he whispered. "I understand. I understand."

~ 10 ~

TONY VALENTINO SAT back in the limo and poured himself a large drink. He knew intellectually that he had produced the performance of a lifetime. He had seen it in the eyes of the audience. They had clapped till their hands were numb and the curtain calls had gone on and on. In the dressing room afterward, the congratulations had been transparently truthful, and yet, the bizarre feeling that made no sense gripped him. Tony Valentino couldn't escape the weird sensation that he had bombed. It had happened a couple of times before, and he had discussed it with his teachers at the Juilliard. They hadn't been much help, because they hadn't been used to dealing with talent like his. Tony had tried to analyze it, and unhampered by false pride, had concluded that perhaps it had to do with genius. For most people, doing things really well was a reward in itself. To the tortured genius, everything was an uninteresting stepping-stone toward the perfection that could never be achieved. Horowitz had endured nervous breakdowns and addiction to tranquilizers in an attempt to escape the pain of creation. Goya and van Gogh had lapsed into madness. The majority of America's literary Nobel laureates were alcoholics. The fact that he had done well was pushed to the back of his mind by the agonizing thought that he could have done better, and the places he had failed filled his brain at the expense of the moments in which he had triumphed. The applause of the crowd and the hyperbole of the critics meant nothing to him. His jury sat in silence inside. It handed down its verdict, and the verdict was guilty. He could think only of the rare times when his words and gestures hadn't matched, and of the tiny instances when there had been a time lag between body and tongue, and more important, between heart and mind. By his own stratospheric standards, his performance had been a failure, while by any rational ones it had been a stupendous success. The trouble was that only his opinion mattered. His art had never been the trick of instilling confidence in others. So he drank deep on the neat Glenfiddich, allowing the alcohol to burn against the lining of his empty stomach. He caught his breath and stared moodily from the car window at the steamy streets of the darkened city. The gloom filled him. It was going to be a bad evening. He felt evil. The trendies at the Canal Bar had better watch out. So had Melissa Wayne, who sat beside him, thin and lovely on the fat cushions, and tricky Dicky on his other side, and busty Emma Guinness with her sandpaper tongue, and Pat Parker, too, Pat who had made love to him on the sand and traded his trust for a slick career move. He had thought she was special, but she had shown herself to be like all the other rats in the stinking city, buying and selling each other, foraging for advantage in the sewers and gutters as they turned their faces away from the stars. In their fashion they had all made their moves on Tony Valentino. Well, tonight the devil was in him. Future moves had better not be false ones.

Melissa Wayne sat quietly, surrounded by the aura of her spectacular beauty. She wore a richly embroidered black velvet jacket over a torso bare except for a purple moiré bra top, from which African coins dangled on beaded chains. A faux emerald necklace separated her exposed upper body from the pallor of her exquisite face. Her blond hair was piled up high in a young Barbara Hutton cut, and her eyes were hidden by diamanté-rimmed sunglasses above pert scarlet lips. A pencil-thin black crepe skirt hid the rest of her above Manolo Blahnik gold lattice grosgrain shoes. She reached out and hooked her hand inside Tony's thigh in a gesture that was both a threat and a promise. "This belongs to me" she was saying.

Tony ignored the Wayne hand. Not many people could do that. Melissa's fingers resting on an inside leg were not usually a take-it-or-leave-it phenomenon. They set wheels in motion, hormones bubbling, the blood rushing headlong to places from which it couldn't escape. But he genuinely didn't mind. Okay, so the bitch wanted him. Way down on the list of priorities, maybe he wanted her. If it happened, it would be cool. If it didn't, the world would keep on turning. He was aware that his indifference was turning her on, but that wasn't the reason for it. His mood was. Black as the night outside, it sat on his shoulder, full of thunder, tight with lightning, thick with the storm of pent-up irritation that must erupt before the evening's end.

"Can I get you a drink, Melissa?" said Dick Latham, his eyes fastening onto the errant hand. The diversion was a reflex action. The man who loved to defeat women couldn't bear to watch another playing his own game. He had other plans for tonight, and Melissa was not part of them, but still it rankled that her hand was stalking somebody else.

"Is there any champagne?"

"There usually is. Let's see." Dick Latham didn't move a muscle. In the rare air of his plutocracy he had only to speak. Actions were for others. In New York State the limos were no longer allowed to serve alcohol, but that law applied only to the *hired* limos that the mere millionaires used. This stretched Mercedes was a Latham possession. So was the blessed Dom in the icebox. So was the bodyguard, huge on the tiny bucket seat, who now reached for it. The *pop* of the cork unglued Melissa's hand from Tony's leg, as if the mini-explosion had occurred beneath her fingers. She accepted the

wine and put it to her lips provocatively, leaving a scarlet half-moon of lipstick on the Baccarat flute.

"Have we taken over the whole restaurant?" she breathed.

"Yes and no," said Latham, precise in his assault on the law of excluded
middle. "I told Brian to let in a few of the better-looking regulars. I find that
adds *tension* to a party. The best ones need loads of that."

"Somehow," said Melissa Wayne, "I don't think lack of tension is going to
be the problem tonight." With the skill of the really good actress, she insinuated both that she knew Tony Valentino was a ticking bomb, and that she
didn't mind a bit.

"Our little table should be fun," said Latham. "You remember Pat, don't
you, Melissa? The photographer who took the wonderful photos of Tony."

"Is she a lesbian?" said Melissa suddenly. Her ambush had the virtue of
total surprise, as it was supposed to.

Dick Latham choked theatrically on his glass of chardonnay. Tony Valentino sat up an inch or two from his slouched position. Even the bodyguard,
giving his "hear-no-evil" impression, seemed to perk up.

"No!" Latham laughed. "What on *earth* gave you that impression?"

"Oh, I don't know. Just her vibes. She seemed sort of sexually indetermi-
nate, and on the boat she was hostile in that way that people in gender
turmoil often are."

"Pat wasn't hostile. You were," said Tony Valentino.

Melissa smiled. It was *exactly* what she'd wanted—a reaction from the
target. He flashed his accusing eyes at her. She smiled radiantly back.

"Oh, I'm so sorry, sir. I was *hostile*? That's very unlike me. How gall*ant* of
you to stand up for the wronged lady. Quite the knight in shining armor."

She laughed as she mocked him, far from fearful of his dangerous mood.
She implied effortlessly that his championing of Pat Parker had nothing to
do with setting the record straight, but everything to do with the way he felt
about her.

Tony shifted in his seat. God, she was hot. It was like sitting next to a
radiator. He could smell her sex beneath her Paloma Picasso. The Rifat bra
was losing the battle to hold back her breasts. They were weapons in offensive mode. He could just about see her nipples. Despite himself and the
memory of Pat Parker, the feeling began to build within him.

"Actually," said Latham, "Tony and Pat don't get along."

He sounded far from worried about the falling-out.

"She went back on her word." Tony was irritated. He didn't appreciate
comments on his private life.

"That's something I can't *bear*," said Melissa enthusiastically. Her hand
sneaked back. She licked wet lips. In the real world, word-breaking was her
second favorite exercise.

"Here we are," said Dick Latham.

There they were. The street outside the Canal Bar looked like the dangerous part of Gotham City—tack on seed on sleaze—the perfect camouflage
for New York's hottest restaurant. The sidewalk was littered with paper, old

pizza, and paparazzi. The latter swarmed around the limo, sensing the serious money from the cut of the carriagework.

Melissa sighed, adjusted her underwear through the crepe skirt, and waited for somebody to open the door. She pretended to hate what she loved. Being an actress made her good at that.

On the pavement she stood her ground, making no effort to push through the milling crowd. The flashbulbs lit the night. A cocklike mike sidled up to her lips. " 'Entertainment Tonight,' " said Leeza Gibbons unnecessarily. Melissa turned quickly to Dick Latham, smiling on her arm. Her expression flashed a "well done." The prime-time nationwide show didn't do a lot of hanging around outside restaurants. It was a neat PR move. Now she looked around for Tony. She wanted him in frame. He would be grateful for the coast-to-coast exposure. He wasn't there. She looked back. He wasn't in the limo either. He'd slunk around the crowd, in the classic Penn pincer move. She shrugged. It was a way to go. She slipped into gear for the sound bite, mentioning her current movie in every sentence so that it couldn't be edited out. Then, microseconds before they cut her off, she smiled a full frontal good-bye, and sliced through the blazing cameras toward the Canal Bar.

Inside, Dante and the gang were already on fire. The room was packed, the decibels were on positive feedback, and the Run-D.M.C. rap music sprayed over the black-uniformed crowd like machine-gun fire.

A Greek god loitered at the *maître d*'s lectern. At the sight of Dick Latham and Melissa Wayne, he metamorphosed into a body servant.

"Sir, Ms. Wayne, welcome to the Canal Bar. I'll show you your table."

As it was supposed to, the sound faded as they made their entrance. But New York wasn't as impressed as L.A. The vast, dirty city was a great leveler. Star status hardly protected you from the accusing eyes of the beggars and homeless, the static and the neurosis, the beady eye of a Saturday night special. In Beverly Hills by now, the boys and girls would be polishing their pitches. In the Big Apple they were too busy getting high.

There were three empty places at the table.

"Hi," crowed Emma Guinness from the depths of a nerve-racking Isaac Mizrahi silver sweatshirt.

"There you are." Tommy Havers smiled from a too-well-cut Cerruti suit.

"Hello." Allison Vanderbilt waved, stylish in a no-name navy-blue sheath dress. "May I introduce Lord Leavenworth."

Jamie Leavenworth tried to stand up, but with difficulty. He was drunk. He burped once, laughed, burped again, and sat down. He looked like a chinless cherub, shining bright, lost in terminal self-admiration as he reached for his gin and tonic. Melissa Wayne ignored him. Dick Latham nodded. His father, the earl of Swinley, was a fellow member of White's.

"Hi, Dick," said Pat Parker.

His eyes zeroed in on her. The rest of the table receded. Dick Latham took a deep breath. She looked like she had invented animal magnetism. Her hair was lion wild, back-combed into a tawny mass of jungle excitement. She wore a Katharine Hamnett shaded leather jacket bearing the ecological legend CLEAN UP OR DIE above a black velour body suit, and the material gripped her skin like it wanted to *be* it. She stood up, like a skyscraper growing in time-lapse photography, and her unusual height was emphasized by the Cuban heels of her black patent leather ankle boots. Dick Latham reached up to kiss her with the reverence of a communicant.

"Where's Tony?" hissed Melissa Wayne.

"Is he sitting with us?" whined Emma Guinness.

Pat Parker's leonine eyes scanned the room over the Latham shoulder, wary, like those of the animal she resembled.

"I think I see him over there," said Havers.

"Tony who?" slurred the incapacitated aristocrat.

"Ah, Tony, there you are. You gave the photographers the slip, and after my publicity people had sold grandmothers to get the right ones to turn up. What shall we do with him?" He aimed an affectionate punch at the shoulder that had appeared next to his.

"Hi, Tony," said Pat.

"Hi." His voice was flat, dull, devoid of emotion. It was a duet. The room was no longer the set. It had become the distant backdrop.

"You were great in the play," said Pat simply. She smiled, giving him an opening, opening the rest of her life to him. Boom, boom went her heart— ram, bam against her ribs.

He waved away the compliment. His eyes shut her out. "Hi" was all she was going to get. In her memory his stomach was against hers. She could smell his sweat. She could hear him moan while he came.

"Hello, Allison," he said. He walked over to kiss her.

"Careful," growled Leavenworth, putting his hand over his drink as if Tony had endangered his most valuable possession.

Tony's eyes flashed fire at him. "How have you been?" he said to Allison.

"Oh, okay," she laughed bravely to show she had handled it. "Loved the play. You were really cooking, especially in the second act. It was a difficult part. You were great."

"I wasn't happy with it," he said. There was a bond between them stronger than the "love" they'd made. She would get his true feelings, because she deserved it and because she would listen.

"I thought it was even better than your Stanley Kowalski," said Emma Guinness. Tony looked at her for the second time in his life, and she stared back at him, her face expressing an extraordinary mixture of emotions. She was defiant, determined to put a brave front on the unpromising meeting. She was trying to be cute—"We-can-rise-above-this" style. There was a carrot—"Like-me-and-I'll-forgive-you." There was a stick—"Keep the feud going and I'll bury you under my words in front of all the people who invented you."

"I like the silver tent better than the ballet-dancer rig," said Tony, his voice thick with sarcasm.

"I think we should get hold of some wine," said Dick Latham cheerfully.

"Fab," gurgled Lord Leavenworth.

"Don't you think you've had enough, Jamie?" whispered Allison quietly to her date.

"What?" said Leavenworth loudly. He spun around on her. "Don't dare . . . ever . . . tell me what to drink. Do you hear? Mind your own fucking business."

"What did you say?" said Tony into the shocked silence.

"It doesn't matter. Please, Tony," said Allison to avert disaster.

"Tony," said Pat.

"People, people," admonished Dick Latham, far from disturbed by developments.

"He told her to mind her own fucking business," said Emma Guinness, oiling oily waters.

"Yes, I did," agreed Leavenworth, a fatuous smile on his face. He leaned back in his chair belligerently.

Tony hovered above him. He lowered his head until it was inches from the Englishman's.

"Apologize," he barked.

"Tony, he's zoned," said Pat.

"So what?" said Melissa Wayne.

"Piss off, you fucking wop," said the fifteenth Viscount Leavenworth.

Tony hit him. It was a vicious blow. Starting from the shoulder his arm pistoned out, downward, at an oblique angle, and his fist collided with the cheekbone of the lush. It didn't stop there. It traveled on. The nose was a definite obstacle, but not an insuperable one. It disappeared. The lower lip didn't fare much better. It was a ripe mango falling from the tree, and the seeds that spilled from it were a couple of teeth from the already depleted lower jaw of the chinless wonder. A fine spray of blood wafted across the immaculate table, and a particularly large globule attached itself to one of the understated white daisies that formed its centerpiece.

"Oh, dear," said Dick Latham. Thank God the English upper classes disliked their children. Otherwise Swinley could have caused all sorts of difficulties for him in the bar at White's.

"Direct hit," crowed Melissa Wayne, enormously impressed. The last decent fight in Morton's, Richard Zanuck's, had been an age ago. L.A. didn't approve of them.

"Fisticuffs? Before the soup?" said the cheerful voice of Brian McNally, who had materialized at the table with the sixth sense of the superb restaurateur.

Lord Leavenworth hadn't finished bleeding. He slid gently off the chair and continued to do it on the floor.

"I wonder, Brian," said Dick Latham, holding the arm of the restaurant's owner, "if we could find someone to scoop him up and chaperone him to Lenox Hill."

"I'll go," said Allison. "He's my second cousin," she added by way of excess explanation as she dabbed with a napkin at the place where her relative's nose had been.

"I'm sorry, Allison," said Tony, rubbing his skinned knuckles.

"It's okay," she said, as two large men arrived from nowhere to pick up the comatose peer. Her tone of voice implied that it would have been just fine if he'd confessed to being the Night Stalker.

"He ought to use Hoefflin," said Melissa Wayne enigmatically.

Even her impenetrable remarks carried weight. Everyone looked at her.

"For the plastic surgery," she amplified. "He's the only man. Even better than Michael Hogan."

"Will he sue? Assault charges, maybe?" asked Emma hopefully. A viscount bleeding on the floor was bliss to her. The possibility of bad things happening to Tony Valentino was even better.

"The English don't go in for that kind of thing," said Latham. "But it may well be that Tony is asked to resign from some of his clubs." He laughed at the ridiculous thought, as the divine waitress from an Ethiopia-equivalent country removed the bloodstained flowers. He beamed around the depleted table. The surreal feel was tangible. The earl's heir was disappearing through the disinterested ranks of Manhattan haute café society, leaving a trail of blue blood on the linoleum floor. The trademark McNally decorative minimalism had paid off once again. Tommy Havers escorted Allison and the unconscious body.

The eaterie entrepreneur still hovered at the table, thoroughly at home in the atmosphere of transcendent sangfroid. That his countryman had taken a pratfall didn't faze him. Male East-Enders liked nothing better than to knock the noses off earls' sons, not least because female East-Enders liked to go to bed with them. In Bethnal Green there was permanent open season on hooray Henries. Anyway, to give good restaurant you had to deliver drama, and so far this evening it was lights, camera, action all the way.

Tony sat down at last. Dinner had officially begun.

"You didn't have to do that, Tony," said Pat. She dared to accuse him across the table.

"No money in it, you mean?" He smiled insolently back at her.

Her cheeks reddened as they signaled the hit.

"He was drunk. He didn't know what he was saying. He couldn't defend himself." She tried to stay calm, but the anger was rising inside. The money crack was *so* unfair. But *was* it? What he was really saying was that he was spontaneous, direct, honest, while she was devious, calculating, cunning.

"Who cares that he was drunk? Who cares that he couldn't defend himself? He was insulting. I like men who don't put up with that." Melissa Wayne's tongue sneaked out to emphasize the last bit. Her eyes daggered into Pat's.

"We all know you like men, period," Pat shot back at her.

"And you don't. There. I was right all the time." Melissa smiled triumphantly around the table.

"*I'll* handle this," snarled Tony. He didn't need a champion.

Pat felt the bile explode at the back of her throat. She didn't know what the hell the hooker meant about her not liking men, but the remark insinuated that she had been discussed behind her back, and in a not-very-flattering way.

"The trouble is," said Pat slowly, "that you're not very civilized, are you, Tony?"

"That from the wild animal look-alike."

"At least I don't *behave* like a wild animal."

"No, you behave like a roach. Creepy, crawly, and always getting into places it's not wanted."

"Like your pants?" said Pat.

"Goodness," said Emma, "this is the first X-rated dinner party I've ever been to."

"Shut the fuck up," said Tony.

"See!" said Emma, mock demurely.

"Like my *life*," he added, turning back toward Pat and spitting the words at her across the table.

"Now. Now. Tony. Pat. Let's all calm down. We're all excited. I know I am. And let's remember we're here to celebrate *New Celebrity*, and Tony's success, and Pat's pictures. Let's have some food and learn to love each other again. Okay. *Okay?*"

There was steel in the last okay. Latham liked to walk on the wild side, but there was a limit. Now he was letting everyone know it had been reached. The fight had had one welcome dividend. It had scared off the massed table hoppers who had been gathering on all sides.

Havers walked back to the table.

"It's all under control," he said. "I sent Allison, the Englishman, and one of the bodyguards in the limo to the hospital and I alerted the company medical people to smooth things along. Also, the lawyers. Another limo's on the way in case there's a mess in the Mercedes. I'll have someone talk to the limey in the morning when he's sober so there are no complications." He sat down, fixed a smile to his face, and prepared to act as if nothing had happened.

"I don't want anybody covering up for me . . ."

"Relax, Tony." Latham's arm was firm and definite on the arm of the man who had saved his life. "It's detail stuff. It's no big deal. Forget it. These things happen."

He waved away the Leavenworth nose as if it didn't exist, which of course it no longer did.

"Now," he continued, "let's get these chairs cleared away. Pat, you move in closer to me. Tony, you shift around a bit so that Melissa isn't so isolated. There, that's better. And Tommy, you let Emma in on all the company secrets, okay? All the ones that you keep from me. She's such a gossip, I'll pick them up from her later on."

He chuckled to camouflage what he'd done, but everyone at the table knew. The couplings he'd suggested slipped on the mantle of inevitability, as beneath the surface the subplots raged.

Emma Guinness drank deep on the bitter cup. She'd drawn Havers, who was as interesting and as appetizing as old broccoli. The guy wasn't a man, he was a thing. He was the engine that made the Latham companies go, and as such was well oiled, powerful, and in perfect working order, but compared to the captain on the bridge, he was nothing. Across the table sat the man she wanted. Sure, it was aiming high, but she had always done that. And she had the brains for the job, the nerves of steel, the rubber-ball ability to bounce back. Not many who aspired to Latham had her attributes. They might be better looking, more charming, sexier, but they couldn't run his magazines. At the end of the day when Latham crawled between his sheets, it was his business, not romance, that he thought about. Anybody who made it success-ful would be his close friend.

The trick would be to turn the dreaded *F* word into something else. There had been no action replay of the mile-high coupling, but she was counting on the advertising figures and the *New Celebrity* subscriptions to rekindle his interest in her. Then, once the sexual bridge had been well and truly crossed, she had plans for the rest of it—the relationship; the live-in-lover stage; heck, wedding bells and the leverage of bloodline kids before the supersettlement. Yes, that was it. Marriage was not her end game plan for Dick Latham. Divorce was. She would cut him in half and walk away the richest woman in the world, pushing the queen of England into second place. Then, dear God, the streets of Belgravia and the hills of the Cotswolds would be red with the blood of those who had humiliated her. And most of all, a terrible fate would be found for the jumped-up actor on the other side of the table.

But as the wonderful daydream peaked within her, it began the slow fade. Across the table was the reason. Dick Latham's head was inclined toward Pat's. He was talking intensely into her face. She was nodding back at him, engrossed by his pitch. His hands waved before her eyes in a myriad of clever gestures. He smiled. He frowned. He ran through his entire repertoire of expressions. It was clear what he was doing. He was trying to pull her. Emma Guinness, wife to be, mother of his children, future recipient of fifty percent of his fortune, simply did not exist in his world. She swallowed hard and the malice flowed out of her toward Pat Parker. The girl was making a move on her guy. Already the photographer had captured the actor Emma had wanted, and then proceeded to turn him into a star and a Latham protégé, safe from the Guinness revenge. Pat was playing a dangerous game. Emma had wiped people out for less.

"What do you think of the plans for Cosmos?" said Havers, cutting into her thoughts.

It was just about the only remark in the world that could have gotten her attention. She turned toward him and her face lit up.

"I'd like to know more about them."

"Specifically?"

"Specifically, personnel, as in Who's going to run it?"

"No decision yet. Any ideas?"

Emma pretended to be thinking. It wasn't difficult. She was going to run it. She hadn't been in the States long, but she had America's drift. America was about movies. It always had been. It always would be. Movies were what the country cared about, movies, and their watered-down surrogate, television. America was bound together by celluloid muscles. Its skeleton was made in Hollywood. It was fueled on dream power. The movies made Montana like Manhattan, and allowed Americans to know and understand each other in a country too big for intimacy. Stars were what Americans had in common. They loved them. They revered them. They were fascinated by them. In Hollywood two hundred players controlled the movie game, and there was a sense in which they were the most powerful people in the land. They manufactured the country's self-image. They ran the propaganda machine. In the free world they, more than anyone else, controlled the minds. To run Cosmos would be to be an integral part of that elite. In comparison, the editorship of *New Celebrity* was nothing.

"What about me?" she said.

"You?" He laughed. "You're not serious."

"Maybe I'm not." Emma laughed too. She wanted to sow a seed, nothing more. "But I could do it better than the usual team of suspects—the agents, the lawyers, and the movie politicians they always end up with."

"Aren't you a little short of experience?"

" 'The name men give to their mistakes,' as Oscar Wilde used to say. Yes, thank God, I am. That would be my saving grace. Listen, the only thing that's important in running a studio is picking movies that the public likes. Nobody knows how to do that for certain, okay? But who are the experts on trends? Who makes their living from anticipating what the public wants and giving it to them, all glossily packaged, dripping with style, and with no rough edges?"

"The editors of successful magazines?"

She patted his hand. "How did you ever guess?" she said. "Actually, it's not even a new idea. Disney has been sniffing around *Esquire, Premiere,* and *New York* magazine for lower-level executives."

"Don't call us, we'll call you—when *New Celebrity's* winning awards." Havers laughed dismissively.

"That won't be a very long wait," said Emma Guinness, staring moodily across the table at the man who could make all her dreams come true.

Dick Latham was letting himself go. He could smell Pat's breath, strawberry sweet in his nostrils. He could see in her eyes the ambivalence, the tough vulnerability, the defensive sense of humor that she used to deflect the pain. He was under no illusions. She didn't like him, but at least she wasn't indifferent to him. There had been less promising beginnings. Occasionally her eyes would flick away from his, and although he didn't turn to follow their direction, he could sense where they were aiming. She was watching Tony, Tony and Melissa, Tony with whom she could only fight, Tony whom she wanted only to love. Dick Latham was a veteran of all the lust wars. He knew what was going down. Tony and Pat, their hate and their love merged in the most explosive mixture of all, were trying to make each other jealous. Latham and Melissa were the tools of the time-honored game. It was an invidious position, but it could be used. The rules said that Pat must appear fascinated by Latham. For greater credibility, it would help if her feelings could go halfway toward matching her actions. So she was allowing herself to like him more than she did, and Dick Latham was taking advantage of the situation for all he was worth.

"Any thoughts about your next spread for us? I can hardly wait." He stared deep into her eyes, a dreamy expression on his face. He meant it. In the chase, everything must be meant.

"Not really. It just happens. Keep the mind prepared and the eyes open. Give luck a chance to kick in." The half smile around her lips said she knew his game, and that she didn't mind. He could keep going. He'd have to do very well, better than he'd ever done before, but she wasn't shutting him out. She could surprise herself, if he could surprise her.

She was hot in the catsuit. Her body itched. The whole of her was sensitized to everything. She was still cross, still indignant, hell and damn it, still in love.

Across the table the impossible Tony was allowing Melissa to vamp him. She was draped over him like a cloak, and Pat knew without hearing it the sort of shit Melissa was ladling out. It would be movie-time stuff—the big names littering the floor around her neat little ankles as she tried to impress Tony with the bits of her that he couldn't see. Which didn't leave much. She was Parental Guidance at the least, and that was just her clothes. The body language was hard core. Her fingers fiddled with the nape of his neck. Under the table her foot would be footling with his. Already she had spooned some of her avocado mousse into his ridiculous open mouth. Had he *any* idea what a fool he was making of himself?

Pat forced her eyes away from him. What was slick Dick going on about? Lord, he was as smooth as an actor playing a middle-aged God—authoritarian, all-knowing, deeply caring, supremely self-confident. He kept running his fingers through his graying hair, as if proud of the fact that he wasn't vain enough to dye it, and every time he smiled he seemed to think he was dishing out a present. But he *was* good-looking. And powerful. And he was enormously easy. She never felt he was going to run dry, say something that jarred, or do something uncool. In a situation like this it added up to quite a lot.

"You know I've never met anyone like you before."

Pat smiled as she watched him notch up the rheostat of his come-on.

"Me neither." The way she said it wasn't necessarily a compliment.

He sensed it.

"What do you want, Pat Parker?"

"Can you give it to me, if I tell you?" she said at last.

"Try me!"

Her eyes flicked across at Tony. For a second they faced each other, their expressions saying they wanted only to hurt and harm. Neither gave an inch. There was no mercy, just the cold steel of revenge. He turned toward Melissa, and she leaned into him, red lips parted, her hands playing with his thigh. It was certain what would happen. In hours they would lovers. Pat's stomach turned on the wave of nausea.

She decided fast. This dreadful game was for two players. Tit for tat. The sacrifice of the nose to spite the face. But first there were concessions to be won and conditions to be agreed.

"Do you remember, a few weeks ago, in Malibu . . . ?" she began tentatively.

He finished her sentence for her. "I told you about my plans for movies at Cosmos . . ."

He smiled in triumph, as her eyebrows arched up in amused surprise. He was on to her. He knew before she knew.

"Okay, yes, Cosmos, and the movies and me getting a chance to direct . . ."

"You want that?"

She took a deep breath.

"Yes, I do."

"Do you think you could do it?"

"I know I could."

"Yes, I think so too."

For long seconds he said nothing, as he savored his victory. The deed was as good as done. Pat Parker was on the verge of surrender.

"Do you mind my asking why you want it?"

Pat took a deep breath.

"Because it's there. The challenge. It's a way to move on, to get bigger, to have more effect. Every still photographer dreams of it. They seldom get the chance, and most of them would be terrified if they did. But they all want it, in their beds at night."

"Is that what *you* think of in your bed at night?" Dick Latham allowed himself the gentle sarcasm, and he glanced quickly across the table at his one-time rival.

Pat didn't answer. She was about to make love for revenge, and in addition she would get something she wanted. It didn't have to spelled out. A strange detachment wafted over her. Mentally she inventoried her body. Was it ready for this? Could it be done convincingly? What was this business called? Prostitution? Could it be *enjoyed?*

He smiled a cruel smile as he read her thoughts.

"Do you keep my Alabama portrait beside your bed?" he asked suddenly.

"Yes, I do. It was a promise, wasn't it? You gave the money to the Sierra Club?"

He nodded slowly. They were both people who kept their word. Perhaps that was all they had in common, yet they were about to be lovers.

"The directing thing is no problem," he said. "You can have that." He waved a dismissive hand. He stared hard at her. His voice was harder.

"I have an overwhelming desire to see my portrait again," he said. "Tonight."

~*11*~

*H*E PICKED UP the portrait and peered at the person he had been. Twenty-five years melted away. Dick Latham was back in Paris.

"Why didn't you like it?" asked Pat. She stood in the doorway of her bedroom, and the feeling of unreality deepened.

"I didn't like many things in those days." He was quiet as he remembered. God, he'd been good-looking, and cruel, like some Nordic prince. It was all in the eyes. Alabama had trapped the truth in the molecules of the film. He could feel the feelings he was feeling then—contempt for the crusty, low-born photographer; disdain for the fellow American in Paris who hadn't been to the right schools, hadn't a "family," wasn't rigid as cardboard with cash; disinterest in the artist who wasn't dead—that potent contradiction in terms that labeled the poseur photographer as nothing but a jumped-up pavement performer, unknown to museums, collectors, and ancient money. It was all there on the face that Pat Parker woke to in the morning and went to bed with at night.

She walked to his side and watched him with him.

"You look kinda cocky," she said, laughing a little.

"I was," said Latham. He didn't laugh. He was still back in the distant days. Already his mind was reaching out from the photo session to the other memories.

"What happened to the girl Alabama told me about?" said Pat. It would help if she could get to know him. This would be the shortcut.

He looked up at her, then back at the photograph.

"She walked out on me. Wouldn't you have walked out on this son of a bitch?"

"Oh, I don't know. You looked like fun."

"If you were into sick jokes." She had never seen him like this. The confidence had gone. He was humble. It was as if he loathed himself, the veneer of his self-confidence covering nothing but a gaping vacuum. He hated the part of him that the picture revealed, because the careless boy of the portrait had blown *his* future happiness. All these years later, Dick Latham still loved the girl who had left him.

"She was that special?"

There were tears in his eyes, no question.

"Yes," he said simply. "She was that special. And I took her heart in my hand, and I . . ." His voice petered out, but his hand clamped down tight, and his knuckles whitened as he made the fist. Then his arm shot out, and his fingers opened and his crushed love flew away across the room, as the bird had flown so many years ago.

"Nobody since then?"

"Nobody since then . . ."

They both wondered whether he would add "till now."

It would have been so easy and so cheap to tell the lie. Say it and I'll despise you forever, thought Pat.

He stopped. He sat down on the bed, the portrait across his knee. He looked up at the girl he wanted, and the guilt pricked at him. He was amazed by the alien emotion. Others had such feelings, not he. So many people led lives thinly buttered with fear. Terrified of the world they lived in, they were slaves to fortune and hostage to the whims and caprices of others. They were shackled by the chains of their own conscience, too. When they couldn't find others to make rules for them, they made petty rules for themselves. Life to them was pain. The stick of the world's disapproval was laid semipermanently across their shoulders, and when nobody had the energy to punish them anymore, they scourged themselves with the whip of guilt. Mea culpa had never been a Dick Latham problem. His rule was to take what he wanted without thought, hesitation, or the expectation of remorse. He had bought the beauty who stood before him. The price was around fifteen million, the cost of a risky, bomb-able movie at his brand-new studio. The tag was the highest yet, and he had promised to pay it. Not to collect would be unthinkable. But now, on the edge of yet another meaningless conquest, he held back. Why the *hell* was he waiting?

Standing in front of him, Pat sensed his dilemma. Her head was on one side, her expression quizzical, as she watched his conflict.

He looked up at her, and suddenly, there was desperation on his face. "Listen," he said. "We don't have to do this. . . . I mean . . . the movie's fine anyway. You've got that. You'd be brilliant . . ."

But Pat Parker had already made her decision. She was in the driver's seat. Perhaps she always had been. Dick Latham would never know how well he'd done. Vulnerability, sensitivity, decency had never been part of his arsenal. His best performance had been an accident.

Pat reached beneath her arm, and her fingers closed on the zipper of her catsuit.

MELISSA WAYNE picked up the photograph and stared at it suspiciously.

"Who's this?" she asked, her remote-control jealousy sensing a rival.

Tony took it out of her hand.

"It's my mother. She's dead."

His tone was matter-of-fact, but Melissa could tell it was a big deal.

"I'm sorry. She was very beautiful." As a rule she never spoke well of her own sex. For dead mothers she could make an exception.

Tony looked at the photograph as if seeing it for the first time. There was a longing in his eyes.

"Yes, she was beautiful, but she never used it. She didn't even know it."

Melissa sensed the accusation in his words. It wasn't a remark that applied to her. She wished she hadn't brought up the subject. It was extraordinarily unpromising. Sympathetic small talk was a million miles from her forte. Now she had to dredge up more.

"How long ago . . . was it?" she tried, without much enthusiasm. She couldn't get the *D* word out. She peered in desperation around the dingy apartment, searching for a diversion. Most things looked like roach haunts. It was best not to pick anything else up.

Tony didn't answer. He realized she couldn't care less about his mother. He didn't mind. The sorrow was his, not hers.

They sized each other up like two pieces of steak on a butcher's slab. Then, quite suddenly, the spark was back. Electricity fizzled in the fetid air of the room. There was danger, excitement, and there was the unknown.

"Come here," he growled.

He had stolen her line. This was supposed to be a Melissa Wayne production. As the star she had precedence. He was the bit player, not the director. Part of her wanted to get that straight. Another deliciously unfamiliar part wanted only to obey. She sashayed toward him, a smile of patronization on her face. "I'm indulging you," said her expression. "We'll start your way. We'll end up mine." Inches from him, she stopped. The points of her breasts nudged at the cotton of his shirt. Her breath fanned his face as she mocked him with her closeness. Her threat was everywhere, in her jutting hips, in the firm aggressive stance of her legs, in the tongue that slicked over heart-shaped lips. Any second he would reach for her, and from the touch of his fingers she would know at once whether he was man enough to control her. One hesitant move, one lapse from surefootedness, and he would be on the knees that God had given him, the better to worship her.

Tony wasn't thinking about any of that. Her feelings didn't matter. The minds of others scarcely existed for him. They were unknowable, and uninteresting. They were academic distractions. To spend time investigating them was to waste energy, and dilute the force of his will. In front of him was the movie star, ripe as a wet peach. She was cocksure and sassy. She was uncomplicated and ruthless, and as pretty as anyone had a right to be. Most of all, she was *there*, on his tacky carpet, next to his unmade bed with its grubby sheets, ready, willing, and fantastically able to make him feel good, to make him forget the pain—the death pain, the art pain, the Pat Parker pain.

He put out his hand and grabbed a handful of her hair. His touch was not rough, but it was absolutely masterful. He drew her head toward him, until the skin of their lips were millimeters apart. Her eyes drowned in his, and he could see the lust in them, and the wonder, and yes, the fear that would be a newcomer to the Melissa Wayne sexual repertoire.

He lowered his savage lips to hers. It was the kiss of an enemy, terrible in its intensity and ruthless in its aggression. He invaded her mouth. His tongue ransacked her. His teeth ground remorselessly against hers, as he fed from her. It was close to pain, far from gentleness, and, ravaged by him, her head a prisoner in his powerful hands, she stood stock-still in awe of his lust. His body was crushed against hers. His male smell was thick in her flared nostrils. The throbbing heat of him thrust rudely against her stomach. She couldn't breathe, but breathing was not important anymore.

One hand twisted in her hair, the other reached behind her back for the strap of her bra. He unhooked it, and it fell away from her pulsing breasts. He drew her into him, plastering her chest against his.

"Tony!" she tried to say as his mouth freed hers. *Slow down. Be careful. Don't hurt me.* But she didn't want any of the things for which her eyes asked. Her body was calling the shots. Her mind was a mere servant. She needed more cruelty, more passion, more of his gloriously selfish lust.

He knew that. She was a mustang to be tamed, and first there must be the hell and the heaven of ecstasy before she trotted meekly into the corral, happy to be led, delirious beneath the saddle of her rider. So he put both hands on her shoulders, and stared deep into her eyes as, firmly, he pushed her down. She sank to her knees, full of wonderful despair, and reveled in the alien humility. Nobody had done this to her. Not like this. There had been no one to dare. Her face was tight against the burning heat of his blue-jeaned crotch. She could see the shape of him, enormous in its threat, rock hard with its promise. She rested her cheek against it, and her fluttering hands reached for the snare-drum tightness of her nipples. She pinched them until she could recognize pain in the sea of pleasure that engulfed her. She was full of dread, stuffed tight with longing, proud to be made to do the deed she would do. She reached for the straining muscles of his thighs. She ran her hands against the soft cotton. Her fingers found the buttons. She moved reverently, bravely taking this small initiative, fearful that he would forbid it. His strength hovered over her, threatening, formidable. Slowly she undid him. It sprang from the tightness of his jeans, leaping and rearing from the shorts that draped it. Like a dagger it glistened against her cheek, radiating heat, big, vast, pulsating with purpose in her face. She held the base of him in her hands, and she took a deep breath, filling her lungs with the precious air she would need. Around her fingers, his hair was wet with sweat, the shaft of him slippery in her grasp. She moved her hands upward, her skin burning with his heat. She could feel the blood pounding through the arteries that stood out on the shining surface. Up toward the tip she traveled, close to the angry point of him, and she bent in close and breathed in his musk as her lips moved toward their destination. At the back of her head she felt his hands take up their position. They rested there gently, but their presence had purpose. There would be no turning back from this. No second thoughts. There would be no avoiding the sweet conclusion. She shuddered at the thought of the delicious coercion.

There was the slightest pressure behind her head, propelling it forward. It was a command. She moved to obey. Her tongue snaked out and rested against the point of him, bathing the heat, but fanning the lust. She moved it against him, savoring the taste, sliding it gently over his tense flesh. Round and up and down, her tongue traveled, darting into the opening, lapping lovingly at the still miraculously expanding shaft. His low moan encouraged her, and the jerky movements at the back of her head and neck ordered her to the next stage in the slow dance of desire. She opened her mouth wide, so wide, and he slid gratefully into her. At first just the tip entered her, but already she knew his plan. Behind her the hands were tightening. Before her, the hips were thrusting. In panic she tried to look up at him, to tell him no, but the eyes that reached his screamed only yes, and the cruel eyes that stared back agreed. He slid deeper into her, and she opened wider to take him, until there was no mouth left for his hugeness . . . only throat. But still he didn't stop. Remorselessly, he advanced until he owned her space, and there, locked between his hands and his hips, she was nothing but the soft wetness that wrapped him.

For long seconds he stayed there as the air in her lungs vanished, and she fought to breathe through nostrils drowning in the sweat of his stomach. Then, at last, he was retreating and the oxygen howled into her lungs. She reached out to push him away, the flat of her hands thrusting against his pubic bones, but her mind and body wanted different things. The desire to breathe and be free of him was replaced by the far more powerful need for his return. So her hands snaked around to the firmness of his buttocks, and she drew him in toward her once again, throwing back her head to receive him. She heard him laugh as he speared her, pushing to the farthest recesses of her throat, pulling back, pounding once again into the velvet softness. Now they were in rhythm and her panic receded as her passion grew. There was a time and a tide, an ebb and flow, a time for breathing and emptiness, a time for stillness and fulfillment. He was making love to her mouth with the same intensity that others had made love to her body. The only difference was the part of her he had chosen for his entrance. Already she was thinking of one thing. How would she deal with the bittersweet ending? As if sensing her concern, he showed her. There was little warning. He didn't speed. He didn't slow. Quite suddenly, he withdrew to the opening of her, and there he waited.

Behind her head his hands were rigid. She was trapped in the vice of him, helpless as she secretly longed to be. All her ecstasy would be his ecstasy, every shuddering spasm of his delight would be her surrogate joy. She stiffened for the moment and her mouth was dry around him as fear and wonder merged before the pent-up torrent that would be released. Everything had stopped in the lull before the storm, all was calm in the hurricane's eye. She didn't dare to move. He didn't deign to. Her eyes, wide with fright and excitement, twisted up toward his face. His, hooded with cruel lust, peered down at her.

And then he nodded. His head jerked up, jerked down, and she knew what it said. He was giving himself permission. This was the advance warning of the honor he would bestow.

Her mouth was a surge tide at sea. It was an undammed mountain river. The waterfall was inside her, and she was drowning in the flood of his liquid desire. There was no time to taste him. It was hardly possible to feel him. There was only the battle for survival in the storm, and the mad, clashing emotions as he pumped her full of the passion that would never be love. She tried to swallow but she couldn't, and he flowed out of her as he poured into her, soaking her, anointing her with his blissful essence. He soared against the walls of her throat, thrusting, pushing, spending himself in her, washing her with the sweet feed of his soul. And all the time his fingers twined in her hair as he rode her mouth, twisting the reins in time to the rough rhythms of his climax.

It was over. Like a rag doll she sagged on the stick of him. Her head lolled sideways, and breath sucked into the vacuum of her lungs. The present was past, but it would never cease to exist, and Melissa Wayne shuddered with the sublime feeling that was as near as she had ever been to commitment.

He slipped from her mouth, and she smiled up at him, awash with his intimacy. Now he would subside, and there should be some small pretense of tenderness, a touch, a caress, in the gentleness charade that manners required. She started to get up, and she reached behind her neck to hold his hands. They had been introduced to each other at last in the most fundamental way possible, in the clash of bodies. Now it was time to build some kind of a relationship on that firmest of foundations.

She opened her mouth to say something. But he held up his hand, demanding silence.

He placed both hands on her shoulders and he turned her around, until she faced away from him toward the edge of the bed. Once more, her heart hammered against her ribs, forcing the blood through her reawakening body. Before, there had been time only to monitor the feelings from the top of her. Now, the messages screamed in from below. She was still half-clothed, but she was damp with desire, hot as the fires of hell in her panties beneath the skirt. Had he the strength to do this now? She dared to hope for it, and the butterflies flew in her stomach as she prepared to obey his most outlandish request. He pushed her forward, firmly but gently, and she lost her balance as she was supposed to, falling toward the edge of the bed. She steadied herself against it, and she waited, bobbing on the adrenaline sea of superreality that surged within her.

He lifted her skirt, unveiling her legs, pushing it up roughly over the back of her thighs, where her stockings merged with the black garter belt. She tried to visualize herself in his eyes as he unwrapped her. Apart from her face, her bottom was her best feature. Pert, rounded, firm yet resilient, and basted honey brown by the sun. The snow-white silk panties, cut like a

Brazilian thong, ran in the thinnest pencil line across the divide of her buttocks. He paused to savor the sight of her and she was pleased. And then,
quite suddenly, she was frightened as the thought occurred to her. Surely
not. Surely he wouldn't . . .

She twisted around to forbid what he had made no move to try, but his
hand was on the back of her head, pointing it forward, disallowing her attempt to assert control. Whatever he wanted, he would have. The choice was
his alone. She swallowed, and the taste of him lingered, giving her strength at
the moment of her passivity. Strung out on the edge of the ultimate abandon,
she tried to let go of herself, to give herself to him totally, to do with as he
willed. She would ask nothing so that she could receive everything. She must
trust that there was mercy in the man that ruled her, and she thrilled with
delicious horror at the thought that there might be none.

His hands were on her buttocks. They traced wet patterns on her skin,
making circles on the soft surface. They wandered freely into the divide,
hooking beneath the silk of the thong, dipping boldly down to feel the shy
entrance. Down, down between her trembling legs went the fingers that
ruled her, skin diving into the treasure pool, shameless as they investigated
her, rude with their boldness. At the lips of her they paused, separated, and
then his finger dipped inside, and his thumb reached back to hover at the
brink of her most alien place, pushing down gently into the furrowed, yielding skin. He held the core of her, and she couldn't see his face. She was
trapped as she had never been trapped before, defenseless, wide open, utterly and completely unable to influence what would happen now.

"Tony, please," she murmured. She didn't know what she meant. She just
wanted to say his name. It wasn't a plea for cruelty or kindness. It was a
hopeless request for both. Until this terrible, marvelous moment, Melissa
Wayne had never known the true meaning of ambivalence. She could actually
feel herself pulse beneath his fingers. They would be burning in the caldron
of her, melting in the bubbling Jacuzzi fountain of her lust. She pushed back
at them, and in response they thrust at her, luxuriating in the welcome of her
passive passion. Then, suddenly, they were gone. She was untouched by him,
and she pushed out her bottom, searching for some part of his body, arching
her back as she thrust her butt into empty air. She ground her pelvis in the
void, pleading with him not to leave her alone on the brink of union. She was
without pride now, the movie star no longer, just a victim of a need more
awful than she had ever known.

"Please, Tony, please," she pleaded, groaning as she ground herself
toward him, pushing back with both hands on the edge of the bed to find
some part of him to touch her. She looked down, through silver-slicked
thighs, and she could see his blue-jeaned legs, the scuffed suede of his ankle
boots. He was still there. He hadn't left her. There was still hope. Surely he
wouldn't be that cruel. He wouldn't walk away now, would he, leaving her to
conjure up her own understudy orgasm? In answer to her unspoken question, Tony Valentino lowered himself into the divide of her buttocks. He
didn't slip off her panties. He left them where they were. Throbbing with

heat, rock hard once more, she felt him push into the cleavage, down into the wetland, and she moaned her encouragement as she swayed her pelvis from side to side, the better to grip him. The length of him lay against her, bathing in her steam, sizzling on the platter of her bottom. Then, it slid lower until the tip of him threatened her illicit place, hovering above the pulsing ring. The dread filled her. She shook her head in hopeless defiance and in alien longing. There was nothing she could do. It was his decision. Already she was relaxing against his touch. Her muscles were his friends, not his enemies, and slippery with her longing, they were barriers no more. For long seconds he paused at the forbidden entrance, flirting with the pain, playing with the possibility, sampling the pleasure of the humiliation. He leaned against it, felt it give, heard her juddering moan of acquiescence and terror. She felt his stomach muscles tighten across her butt. She sensed his body draw tight like the string of a bow. All his energy and power seemed to surge into the part of him that threatened her, and she readied herself as best she could for the assault to come. He lifted away from her, the hammer drawing back for the mighty blow, and her whole body was the nail . . . and the nether place where the tip of him rested was its quivering, defenseless head.

When he came at her, it was as if he had been shot from the barrel of a gun. The breath was crushed from her lungs as his chest crashed down on her back. Her bottom shook with the force of his momentum, and she fell forward pinioned to the edge of the bed by the power of his velocity. But at the very last millisecond he changed his direction. He swooped down, and up, and the weapon of his passion rampaged in glory into her dripping core. She was spared. But at the same time she was executed. His sword had speared her to its hilt. She was split apart. She was full, wrapped tight around the invader like the second skin she wanted to be. No longer did she have a body of her own. She was the clothing of another's body. She was his home and his shelter. She was the flesh-and-blood prison for the part of him that must never leave.

The orgasm was the sky through which she flew. There was no waiting, no savoring, no building toward a conclusion. There was only the truth of the climax. It was instant. It merged with the moment of his entrance, and by the time he collided with the roof of her world, the celestial choirs were lost in descants of swooping, soaring ecstasy. She was on her knees as she should be at this moment of supreme beauty, and she screamed into the wild music, burying her head in her hands, as the tears poured down her cheeks.

Then, in the jingle-jangle aftermath, there was a new feeling to be felt. Slowly but surely the sobs of joy turned into something else. Her head was buried deep in the far-from-clean Valentino sheets, but Melissa Wayne had something to say.

"Tony . . . you bastard," she growled.

~ 12 ~

MELISSA WAYNE LAY back on the sun bed on the pool terrace of her home and looked out over Beverly Hills. It was hot at the top of Benedict Canyon, but the air was fresh and clear and she could see a patch of silver ocean across the rolling hills. She adjusted the volume of the Walkman until the Stones were rolling into her mind on muffled steel wheels, and she tried to make sense of the chaos that had turned her world upside down. There was only one word for it. Actually two. Tony Valentino. She had never thought it would happen. She was too selfish. She was too ambitious. Her career came before sex, before everything, or at least it had until the extraordinary *East of Eden* evening when she had finally met her match. She ran her hand across her flat stomach, her fingers trailing among the downy hairs over the brown skin and the firm muscles, and she remembered the touch of him. It was so cruel. It was careless. It was rough and unloving, devoid of respect. It was hungry, greedy, completely lacking in tenderness. When he touched her his hands roamed free like marauding conquerors, interested only in gratification, and she felt helpless and unloved. It was dreadful. It was humiliating. But it was also the most exciting and erotic sexual experience that she had ever had. She knew what was happening. She was experiencing what her former lovers had known. In her increasingly exotic S&M world, the boys had always been the toys. She, the superstar, had always been the S. They, the miserable males, had inevitably been M. A touch of the whip, the key turning in the lock of a handcuff, lovers chained to the foot of her bed while she slept with a rival, had been the stuff of her games. There had been tongue baths, and cunning torture, tattoos saying embarrassing things in embarrassing places, and always the beautiful boys of beautysville had queued up to be used by the star for the status it bestowed and for the wild, alien delights of submission.

Tony had forced her to make the switch. She had fought against it, but desire had been too strong and the power of his persona had thrust her into a sexual role she had never imagined she would play. She was obsessed by him. He was there all the time, in her dreams at night, in the more fevered

179

dreams that came by day. Latham had pulled Tony out of the Broadway play, and his part had been taken by an understudy to the fury of the ticket holders. He had moved to Malibu to help with the preproduction of Latham's first Cosmos movie, and so now he could and would swoop down on Melissa's house, stride into her bedroom, and drag her from bed to make "love" anywhere, anyway, anytime he chose. Then he would leave. He would simply disappear, and she wouldn't be able to find him to scream at him and tell him what a pig he was. The hours would pass, and then the days, until she could only pray that the noise in the driveway was the crunching of his bike's wheels, that his was the hand on her door, that the rough voice in the dark night belonged to him, ordering her to please him as if she existed to do nothing else. Sometimes he would have her standing up by the side of the bed, not bothering to undress, merely undoing his fly and using her like a cheap envelope to receive his lust. At others he would take her on the floor of her clothes closet and then leave her, locked in for the rest of the night, awash with his sex, until her embarrassed maid freed her the next morning. He made love to her in the pool; leaning over the leather seat of his bike; in the kitchen, standing against the cold door of the kitchen fridge. He wouldn't wait for her orgasm. He would leave after his, and the delicious humiliation tied her up in the silken chains of human bondage as it was destined to do, until her very mind was a prisoner and her will enslaved. For two terrible, wonderful weeks the sensual torture had continued, and Melissa Wayne was unhinged by it.

She took a deep breath as the sun beat down on her gorgeous body. Every sound made her start. Every noise made her salivate. Every cracking twig, each creak of furniture, every footstep turned on the capricious fountain inside her. She was a Pavlovian dog, and her bell was no longer Tony Valentino. It was the thought of him. But at the same time, Melissa Wayne had reservoirs of strength. She was flirting with the boundaries of love addiction, but she had not yet reached them. She was that toughest of all creatures, a successful actress in Hollywood. And there was a part of her that could still say no. Right now, the game of obsession suited her. She was between parts, and she liked to use her brief vacations for mind and body expansion of one kind or another. It was all part of the vital life experiences that no actress could afford to miss out on. You needed range in your repertoire. So, although Tony Valentino loomed over her mind like the Phantom of the Opera, there was an extent to which she was playing the role of love slave rather than actually living it. And that had one curious, but absolutely compelling, result. There was a part of Melissa Wayne that would never forgive Tony Valentino for the way he was treating her. Her body might lust for his passion. Her mind vowed vengeance for it. Somewhere down the line, when the time was right, the star would punish the zero for his lèse-majesté. It might be achieved in a groveling role reversal, in which Tony himself was forced into the part he had cast for her. More likely, it would take another form. She would simply destroy him. It wasn't personal. It was a power trip. It would be fun to blot him out and watch him hurting. It would be nice to see him cry, as his world fell apart and bad things happened to those he loved. It would be delicious to watch his dreams die and his soul burn, to see his essence wither and perish like a leaf in an oven. Yes, he should realize that the stakes were high in any game he played with Melissa Wayne. And her heart beat faster as she contemplated the trouble she could cause for the boy who had dared to be her sadistic lover. The intercom by the sun bed buzzed once. She picked up the receiver.

"Damn! I forgot. Okay, send her out to the pool. Oh, better bring some coffee, and some champagne about an hour later."

She banged the receiver down and reached for the terry bathrobe. Jeez! What a time for an interview. But was any time good? She sat up and pulled on the robe as a small, determined figure erupted from the dark of the house.

Emma Guinness marched across the grass toward the star. She wore a floral dress whose vast rhododendrons dwarfed anything that could be found in nature. An outsize flower tried unsuccessfully to cover each enormous breast, and the unfortunate pattern was continued on hideous shoes. She tripped over a sprinkler head but didn't take her eyes off her target as she narrowly failed to fall.

"Hi," she said cheerfully.

"Hi," agreed Melissa, with less enthusiasm.

"I'm sorry I'm early," said Emma, hovering over the star like a human bouquet.

"Actually, I'd completely forgotten you were coming," said Melissa, who liked to get the upper hand early in an interview. Later you could always stoop graciously to the level of the interviewee. At the start, it was best to establish superiority.

"Is it a bad time?"

"It's always a bad time for an interview, but no, it's fine." Melissa laughed to take the sting out of her words.

She motioned to the chair beside her, and Emma sank into it, notepad across ample lap, the Beverly Hills sun threatening to wilt her flowers.

"How's Tony Valentino?" said Emma Guinness.

"What!" said Melissa.

"I heard you were seeing him." Emma Guinness never accepted the role of second string for long. She had known her question would put Melissa on the defensive.

"I hope this interview hasn't started yet," said Melissa coldly.

"No, of course not. We're off the record. I only asked out of personal interest. It fascinates me how a little guy like that can travel so far so fast."

Melissa's face relaxed into a smile. The Guinness girl was refreshing. It was very un-Hollywood to give so much away. Being rude about a Melissa Wayne boyfriend was a dangerous game. Guinness couldn't have known that Melissa would share the sentiments she had just expressed.

"You think Valentino is a little guy?" said Melissa. "After selling all those magazines, the rave reviews on Broadway, and saving the billionaire's life?"

"Listen, he's got a pretty body, loot fixed the reviews, and saving Latham was luck. He can act a bit, I admit that. But you know the media. He's this month's flavor. Not next month's."

Emma's face twisted as she spoke. She couldn't keep the bitterness out of the words.

Melissa laughed. "I'm not so sure you're right about that. It looks like he's going to star in a Melissa Wayne movie."

Suddenly, all Emma Guinness's color was in her dress. Her face was white.

"What?"

Melissa smiled to see the effect of her words. Emma Guinness might run the most successful Latham magazine. Informationwise, however, she was clearly out of the company loop. And what the hell had Tony done to upset the flower bed? Something pretty unspeakable, that was for sure. Melissa was beginning to enjoy herself. Who was interviewing whom?

"Yeah, it's sort of secret, but you work for Latham, so I guess you can know. He's scheduling a new slate of movies at Cosmos, and the first one is a Melissa Wayne vehicle, with Tony Valentino supporting. He has some crazy idea about getting that dyke bitch Pat Parker to direct, but I'll undo that part of the deal."

"You can't allow that," spluttered Emma Guinness.

The Wayne eyebrows arched up. People didn't tell her what she could and couldn't do.

"What I mean is, surely it isn't a very good idea to risk your career appearing in a movie with an unknown like Tony, and especially with Pat. They were together, you know . . ."

The horror was behind Emma's eyes. Tony as a rave centerfold was one thing. Tony as a hot Broadway actor was another. But Tony as a movie star was something else altogether. It couldn't be permitted. It mustn't be.

"I think," said Melissa grandly, "that it would take more than one poor movie to 'risk' my career. Anyway, I think Tony would be very good in the part. It's made for him. The chemistry between us is . . . well, interesting. It's about a young would-be actor who gets obsessed with a successful actress he meets in Malibu. Hardly a reach for Tony, I would imagine, and the younger-man/slightly-older-woman thing is hot right now. I think it'll play. My box office'll make sure it opens. It'll be the first production of the revamped studio. That means there'll be no skimping on the advertising budget and no problem with distribution. Billy Diller's done a steamy script. Could have been hotter, I guess, but one can always get those things right on the night . . ."

As if to emphasize that aspect of the deal, Melissa threw back the bathrobe and allowed the sun at her body. Emma's eyes crawled jealously over it. It was another flesh field that Valentino had harvested. Those hands had felt this body. These hips had ground against his. Was his seed in there now, the legacy of last night's passion? She shifted in her seat at the unsettling thought, and the Wagnerian music began to play inside her head. God, not

The Ring. It was bad news when she heard that. It was so real. It wasn't like a song in her head, a tune on her brain. It was like a whole sodding orchestra in there, tuning up. The shrink in London had been quite interested in her orchestra, especially the fact that she heard it loudest when things upset her badly. He had wondered if it was an auditory hallucination, and had put her on a quietener pill called Fluanxol. She'd only gone to see the silly old fart because she'd had trouble sleeping and the stupid G.P. had suggested it. But the tablets had helped. It was a pity she hadn't brought some with her to America.

"It might make him a star," said Emma Guinness, her voice wrapped in horror.

"Why would that matter? What have you got against him? He's not very nice to women, is he?" Melissa sounded amused, but her tones were soft and inviting. With the skill of a superb actress, she intimated that any confessing that Emma might do would be to a sympathetic and far from powerless ear.

Emma cocked her head to one side as she picked up the message. *The Ring* had become *Tannhäuser,* loud and insistent, the horns blaring dangerously in her head.

"He behaved very badly to me once," she said at last.

"Sometimes he tries to do that to me," said Melissa in the understatement of her week. She actually had his finger marks in bruises on her butt. Her tongue licked nervous lips at the thought of it.

"He does?" said Emma carefully, trying to hide the hope in her voice. Two important women had been treated badly by a man. It was the stuff of which evil alliances were made. One thing was certain. Emma and Melissa working in tandem could bring tears to the Valentino eyes. *Tannhäuser* was louder now, its strains soaring grandly through her mind. She almost wanted to conduct the music.

"Sometimes," said Emma softly through the Wagner, "I dream of paying him back."

"Do you ever think of how you might do it?" said Melissa with anaconda innocence.

"Just dreams," laughed Emma mirthlessly. "Unlike you, I'm not in a position of power over him."

"Power?" said Melissa.

"Yes, the ultimate power. You're the star. The only thing he wants is to be one. You can stop that. You could ruin his movie career before it ever takes off . . . if you wanted to."

"You mean in the movie we're making together."

"Yes." Emma laughed.

"Ha. Ha," laughed Melissa, "that would be funny."

What a good joke, they agreed. Nothing had been said. Nothing had been promised. No commitment had been made. It was just two girls laughing about a tricky boy who was a bit too big for his boots. No more. No less. Like *hell!*

"What would be *really* funny," giggled Emma, "would be if Pat Parker had to direct you and Tony doing steamy love scenes. She's potty about him, and deep down I think he's still gone on her. Can you just imagine that?"

Melissa's smile had gone cold. Yes, Valentino probably would still love the serious-minded photographer with her artistic airs and graces. His treatment of Melissa certainly had nothing to do with love, and much more to do with disgust. It was as if he were punishing her for her role as a female sex symbol. By humiliating her, Valentino was avenging himself on all the women, perhaps especially on Pat Parker, with whom he was still deeply involved despite some silly lovers' tiff. Pat Parker. What was it the cow had said to her on the Latham boat? "I thought maybe you'd been beamed in from Fantasy-land." She'd topped that by screwing Valentino on the beach. Mmmmm . . . Pat Parker was not a favorite person. There was poetry in the suggestion of the limey who looked like a wreath.

The coffee arrived, but already Melissa Wayne felt like champagne. She said so, and she wasn't at all surprised to find that Emma Guinness felt like it too. The interview remained, but the interview was no longer important. The secret alliance was.

"Okay, Melissa, what do you want me to say about you in my magazine?" said Emma.

"Whatever your magazine wants to say about me," said Melissa.

And they both laughed in the bright Beverly Hills sunshine, because both had received good news from each other, the good news that would be bad news for Tony Valentino and Pat Parker.

⸺

"YOU DELIVER on promises, don't you?" shouted Pat above the noise of the helicopter's engine.

"Only when they make sense." Dick Latham mouthed the words, refusing to compete with the roar of the chopper. He slipped his hand into Pat's and they watched as the jet-copter came to rest on the graded pad, the wind of its blades ruffling their hair and fanning their faces. The pilot cut the motor. Silence descended on the canyon. Doors opened, and in seconds the passengers were walking down steps to the bright red dirt of the newly bulldozed landing strip. They peered around in the blazing sunlight as they accustomed themselves to the alien environment of the deserted mountains. They carried briefcases, cameras, notepads, and, with the brittle bonhomie of their species, they tried to pretend that they were at home when they weren't. Jesus! What a place for a press conference—stuffed up in the heavens, so near to civilization and yet so far. Latham had better deliver on his promise of hard news. If there was any letdown they would rain on his parade for a year and a day—despite the freebies and the handouts, the bribes and the bountiful bimbos and all the other arm-twisting, mouth-watering delights that the Lathams of this world showered on the fourth estate.

Dick Latham walked toward them. Behind him Tommy Havers consulted his clipboard. The mountaintop press conference was coming together like clockwork. This was the fifth incoming flight of the morning, and there were two more on the way. Half a mile up the hill fifty journalists were already getting plastered on the Krug and bourbon in the sort of high-end tent a genuine Bedouin would never want to leave. It looked like a hundred percent turnout and this wasn't just a California thing. The nationals were there in force and it hadn't been easy to get them there. Havers had walked the tightrope between whetting jaded press appetites and giving the game away. Luckily, over the years he'd never squandered the capital of believability, and the media had learned to trust him. Even NBC had sent a crew. Soon, with luck, Brokaw's locked jaw would be struggling to tell the world what Latham wanted it to hear.

"Hi, Lawrence. Comfortable trip?" Latham called out to a *Wall Street Journal* scribbler he recognized. The journalist screwed up his eyes in the glare and peered suspiciously back. He wasn't particularly impressed at being singled out for recognition by the billionaire. A few years back he'd scored a Pulitzer, and in the American pecking order writers who'd won those deferred to nobody. Anyway, one thing was clear. In laying on a bonanza like this, Latham was admitting that he needed something. The *Journal* scribe was about to be a brown-nosee, not a brown-noser.

"I hope this isn't some environmentalist shit," he said, threateningly.

Latham laughed. If they only knew. "No, Lawrence, I can safely say that this hasn't to do with the environment, and that's the way I'd like it to remain."

Havers shepherded the press toward a trio of jeeps that would carry them on the bumpy half-mile ride to the mountain-peak marquee.

Pat kicked at the red soil. "Is this where you're going to build your house?" she said. "It's one helluva pad."

Latham avoided her eyes when he answered. "Yes, it is big," he said evasively. Before the day was over she'd know the truth. How would she deal with it? She thought the purpose of the press conference was to announce publicly the reincarnation of Cosmos, and to reveal the details of its first daring movie schedule, including the film that she would direct. She didn't know that the dynamite had been saved for the punch line. The real news would be the studio's location. They would all be standing on it—back lots, front lots, wardrobe, props, production offices—all nestling happily in the middle of the once beautiful Malibu hills that Alabama had spent his life trying to protect. It wouldn't have to be spelled out. These ink merchants might look like a load of street people, but they had the noses of claret connoisseurs when it came to sniffing out the information that would sell the papers for which they worked. The moment they hit Pacific Coast Highway, they would telephone their offices and the story would break. The next person they would all call would be Alabama, Pat Parker's friend and mentor. It would be make-your-mind-up time for the girl whose body he could still feel against his. On the one hand would be the friend she admired, the moral high ground, the nature she now loved to photograph. On the other would be the billionaire she had bedded, and the brilliant career in movies he could open and close like the covers of a book. He smiled grimly as he mapped out her dilemma in his mind. Which way would she go? With a frisson of surprise he realized that he really cared.

"What style are you going to build in?" asked Pat.

Damn! The house again, the house that would be a sound stage.

"Come on," said Latham, hurrying toward one of the jeeps. "We ought to get back to the others. Melissa can't be left alone for a moment without making a scene, and God knows what Tony'll be saying to the news hounds— something uncomfortable, uncompromising, and uncalled for, I expect."

He watched her wince as he played the Tony card. When that hit the table, all desire for architectural discussion should disappear. It did.

"You made Tony's dream come true. Was it because he saved your life?"

"Does there always have to be a reason? Don't you think he's right for the part? I do. I thought you did."

He spoke sharply to emphasize that he was looking at things objectively, that he was a businessman, the kind of guy who wouldn't let personal factors influence an important decision. Pat laughed to show she saw through the bullshit.

"Listen, Dick. He's incredibly talented. But there are lots of actors out there who are that. Ditto directors. You're way out on a limb, and everyone knows it. I happen to think you're right, and the trust you've put in us won't be misplaced, but you're winging it. You must have reasons for doing that. Personal ones."

She squeezed his arm like a lover could. Not that she did love him. She still wasn't sure whether she even liked him. But she *was* close to him. The body memories said so.

Dick laughed ruefully. It was a new feeling to have someone around who could see inside him. Normally that might be irritating . . . and dangerous. With Pat Parker it was fun . . . and dangerous.

"Listen, motivation is pretty much of a mystery, despite what the psychobabblers say. But yes, I suppose there are noncommercial reasons for using both you and Tony. I guess I want to show everyone, and myself, that I can do this thing. Making movies is supposed to be rocket science, but it's really smoke and mirrors. I reckon my gut is as good at predicting how something will play as anyone else's. Okay, I could guarantee an opening by using Cruise, Hanks, or Murphy, but that hardly makes me a hero, just a megabuck banker. And ultimately an opening doesn't guarantee a flick will have legs. If my show runs, *our* show, I'll be the only one on the planet who predicted it. Sure I'm taking a hell of a gamble, but there's a window of opportunity here, and I'll only get this one chance. It's the first movie of the revamped Cosmos slate. The distributors, the reviewers, even the public will have to suspend common sense and give believing a try, just this one time. The curiosity quotient will be phenomenal. At least it'll get sampled. That's in the cake. If it's brilliant, I'm a star. If it's not, I'm a rich hick who went Hollywood, to give his glands and his ego an outing. That's the way I like to live. On the edge, but with insurance. Your skill, Tony's skill, are my secret weapons. And it ain't insider trading to profit from the information."

"It should be. I'm going to reinvent the movie genre. I'm going to teach the world how to watch. They'll see things they've never seen," said Pat excitedly.

She climbed into the back of the jeep, swinging her long legs up, the blue denim of her shirt sweeping open to show most of her braless breasts. Dick Latham swallowed. Her peep show was totally innocent, but it added emphasis to her words. Teaching the world the art of voyeurism seemed suddenly well within the Pat Parker reach.

They set off, bumping, grinding, winding toward the sky. Pat was quiet. Saying it was one thing. Delivering the goods was another. You had to believe in yourself, but at the same time the memories of past artistic struggles lingered to highlight the difficulties. She would have to learn a new medium on the job. She would have to handle Melissa Wayne, whose reputation as a troublemaker was as legendary as her mistrust and hatred of women. And she would have to deal with Tony Valentino—deal with his prickly pride, with his hatred of her, deal with the pain of the past, and the certain pain of the future as she directed his on-screen passion with the woman who was already his off-screen lover. Then there was Allison, psychologically wounded by Tony, as she, Pat, had been wounded. Why the hell had someone stuck her in the movie, and why did the script call for her suicide? Jeez! Life had better not imitate art on this one. And moviemaking was a deadline business. There could be no luxuriating in the angst of "block," no hanging around while inspiration slept late. She would have to crack her whip, and the wild celluloid animals would have to jump on cue if the whole shebang wasn't to end in blood, tears, and a horrible destruction. So she took a deep breath and hung on to the side of the jeep as it threatened to wobble off the corkscrew road, and the delicious dread and the terrified excitement filled up her mind.

"*New Celebrity* went off with a big bang," said a journalist, turning around from the front seat of the Wrangler.

"Yeah," smiled Dick Latham, as if it was no big deal. "We're way ahead of the old one on subscriptions and advertising already. It's a hit, and you ain't seen nothing yet."

"What's Emma Guinness going to do for an encore after male nudes?"

"You'll have to ask her. She'll be at lunch."

Pat swung around. "What's Emma doing here?"

The spear of guilt lanced into her. She hadn't forgotten the time on Broad Beach when the feisty Englishwoman had admitted her plans for surfers and Dick Latham—not necessarily in that order. Emma had been her friend, and she had hired Pat for more money than she had ever imagined she was worth. In return, in the Canal Bar, Pat had allowed the man that Emma daydreamed of marrying to make his moves on her. It hadn't needed a Columbo to get the picture. While Emma had been bored to death by Tommy Havers, Dick Latham had poured his charm all over her. The Guinness eyes had narrowed as they registered the slight, and without being able to do anything about it, Pat Parker had watched an enemy in embryo grow in front of her. It made her uneasy. Emma Guinness was a dangerous woman to cross. Beneath the joky malice of her exterior lurked the iceberg capacity for genuine hatred. When talking about her English class enemies, Pat had seen its tip. Now Pat herself was a Guinness target, no question. It was only a matter of time before the arrows came winging in.

"Emma likes to be where the action is," said Dick.

"Likes to be where you are," corrected Pat. If Emma was to be an adversary, Pat had better start her own undermining operation.

"Same thing," said Latham easily, no stranger to the sin of pride.

"We'd better keep her away from Tony," said Pat.

"And you," added Latham with a laugh. His response was purposefully ambiguous. Emma away from Pat? Pat away from Tony?

"Here we are," said Pat, ignoring the double entendre.

The Jeep crunched to a halt at the very top of the world. The marquee had been set up on a graded platform at the tip of the mountain ridge. The vista that unfolded around them was spectacular. You could see to Santa Barbara, west to the coast of Catalina Island, east across the Valley to the Santa Susana and San Gabriel mountains, south to the sparkling Santa Monica Bay. It was a forever view, breathtaking in its bright loveliness, and the hills shimmered in a heatscape cooled at the edges by the blue of the ocean. Down below, in the canyon, another helicopter was winging in, and hawks rode the thermal currents in competition, swooping and soaring above the chaparral in lofty disdain for the outsiders who had disturbed their tranquillity.

The hum of animated conversation erupted from the tent, as the tongues of the word merchants loosened with the booze. Nobody was much concerned with the breathtaking view, despite the rolled-up sides of the marquee. Latham and Pat plunged into the melee, the jeeploads of semifresh journalists led by Havers in their wake.

A large conversational knot separated to reveal Melissa Wayne at its core, incredibly edible in a Gaultier pin-striped miniskirt and soft leather jacket.

"Hi, Dick," gushed Melissa. "Hello, Pat," she managed in an entirely different tone of voice. She hadn't forgotten the confrontations on the yacht trip and at the Canal Bar, but all sorts of things had happened since then. She had signed for the Cosmos movie that Pat would direct. She had been used and abused by Tony, who'd had some sort of relationship with the photographer. And Pat, and presumably Tony, clearly had unspecified secret deals with the billionaire, which explained his dangerous decision to stick them in his movie. It was enough of a psycho minefield to make walking carefully a necessity. Later, when she was carrying the flick on the broad back of her name, there would be time for starry fireworks. In the meantime, she would keep her usually stratospheric profile at sea level.

"Hi, Melissa. I'm really pleased we're going to be working together," lied Pat. She looked around. Where was Tony? The bitch had screwed him. He'd screwed the bitch. Which one did she hate the most?

"Tony's over there," said Melissa with psychic accuracy.

Pat's eyes followed the Wayne finger as if they were attached to it by string. Immediately her head snapped back as she realized too late that she had been wearing her feelings on her sleeve.

Melissa's smile of triumph said most of it. Tony Valentino's screw-you expression of disgust as he caught her eye had said the rest.

In retaliation, she slipped her hand into Dick Latham's. The moneybags are mine, said her gesture.

Inside, she was worried. How the hell would this get done? She had to make peace with Wayne for the sake of the movie. She had to mend bridges with Tony for the sake of . . . Well, never mind.

"What did you think of the script?" Pat turned to Melissa. "Please, let's be professional," said her eyes. "Let's bury the crap. Let's make a movie they'll all remember."

"I signed, didn't I? It's okay. It's not great, but it's fine. We can redo a lot of my stuff."

Pat shuddered. The script of *Malibu* wasn't set in cement—no script was —but Melissa Wayne wielding a pen was a nerve-racking thought. Melissa Wayne rewriting her own part was far worse. Still, this wasn't the time to say so. Press receptions were about harmony. If it couldn't be faked at this early stage, then a disaster of cosmic proportions was definite.

"There you are," said Emma Guinness. She smiled the smile of the Damien child. "Pat and Dick. Dick and Pat. All my favorite people. Hello, Melissa. Where's the brilliant James Dean remount? Pouting in a corner somewhere, I expect, besieged by kamikaze women who saw his willie in *New Celebrity*. *What* a success they were, those pictures, weren't they, Pat? Didn't you just love them, Melissa? Almost as good as the real thing, I imagine, but I'm no expert. Dear me, no! Ha ha! I have to defer to others on that one. Goodness, what fun this is. Movie time. The big league. The genuine nitty-gritty. And us poor journalists allowed to hover around the edges of the action. *What* excitement! I feel quite *faint*."

"Can you get me a drink, Emma," ordered Dick Latham abruptly, ignoring the waiter who hovered at his shoulder. "Oh, and get a glass of champagne for Pat, will you?"

The dismissal was absolute. Nobody made fun of Dick Latham and his friends, however well the abuse was camouflaged in the clothes of humor. Emma's face fell like an elevator, as she realized her miscalculation. But inside she was strangely elated. She felt weird, detached, other-worldly. It was as if, at some fundamental level, nothing mattered anymore. All the scheming, all the cunning plans had added up to zero. She had arrived but she still wasn't *there*. She had made a brilliant success of the magazine. She was the toast of New York. Yet she was the gofer who got the drinks for the billionaire and his screw. She had money, acclamation, minions to serve her, but her true objective had eluded her. She was no closer than she had ever been to the global revenge she wanted so desperately. Her enemies survived and flourished—all those hated English girls who had humiliated her, Tony Valentino for whom she dreamed of a special hell, and now Pat Parker, who had hijacked the money mountain that Emma had intended to marry. It wasn't enough to be brilliant. Mere brutality didn't deliver the goods. While she played the game by the rules, however well, she could never win. The realization broke over Emma Guinness like the surf on a lonely beach. To get her own way she would have to up the ante. There was room for moderation no longer. Drastic situations demanded drastic solutions. From this moment on, she wouldn't shrink from them. She would sign her personal pact with the devil, and whatever the price she would pay it. So she smiled to cover the evil that bubbled so suddenly from her soul, and she walked away through the crowd to collect the poison chalices for the enemies she would destroy.

"Dick!" Pat's tone of voice said he had gone too far. The smile on her lips said he had hardly gone far enough.

He smiled back at her, proud of his cruelty, secure in his strength. East Coast people weren't supposed to be like this. Up-front ruthlessness was an L.A. thing. Way out West, brutality was the instrument that measured the diameter of your balls. But Dick Latham had already adjusted to life on the rim. He was in Rome and he was out-Romaning the Romans.

"So, Melissa, I'm thrilled that we managed to talk your agent into letting you do our movie," said Latham. He smiled at his conceit. When the old owl had seen the size of the check, he'd had to pop a popper for his angina.

"It'll be *fun*," gushed Melissa. She smiled seductively at Latham, wickedly at Pat. Her "fun" sounded like the kind cats had with mice. "Where will we be shooting? Right here in Malibu, I guess."

"For the location scenes, yes. Until we can build a new studio, the inside stuff'll happen at Universal. I've done a deal with MCA."

"Where exactly in the desert are you building the new Cosmos?" said Pat suddenly.

"Yes, yes," said Latham, rubbing his hands together to conceal the inappropriateness of his response.

"Where?" said Pat sharply. The premonition was pricking at her.

"That was a topic I wanted to save for the press conference," said Dick Latham after a pregnant pause.

Pat frowned. His eyes had flicked away from her. He was hiding something.

"I think we ought to mingle a bit," he said. "Spread the good word about how brilliant we all are. Remember, this is L.A. County. Understatement is a sign of mental instability. When you're talking telephone-number money, don't forget the area codes. The locals always divide by six anyway. Tell the truth and they'll think you're a minus quantity."

He laughed brightly and disappeared into the crowd.

"Isn't he great?" Pat laughed.

"Isn't he *rich!*" countered Melissa.

"Look, Melissa. We've got to work together," said Pat, taking the bull by the horns. "Can we try to be friends, for the time it takes to make the movie at least?"

"Friends! Friends?" Melissa Wayne curled her tongue around the word as if it were a dirty one. "There are only two sorts of people in my life." She sneered. "The ones I don't like, and the ones I go to bed with. Sometimes they overlap."

Pat shook her head as if the cause were lost. She stuck out her chin. If Wayne wanted hardball she could have it. Bullies often reacted better to the stick than the carrot.

"Is Tony Valentino an overlap?"

Melissa Wayne's head shot back. Her cheeks reddened. Damn! She'd been trying to keep that part of her life under wraps.

"Mind your own business," she replied. She turned and walked away, but as she did so, she was running over the plans she had made for the beautiful boy who had dared to abuse her.

"Your drink, madam." Emma Guinness's voice was thick with sarcasm. She held out the glass of champagne to Pat.

Pat debated whether to apologize to Emma for Latham's rudeness, but the glint in the Guinness eyes told her not to bother. A sign of weakness might make things worse. "Thanks, Emma," she said, reaching for the glass. The champagne never got to her outstretched fingers. Emma pitched forward, pretending a passing waiter had caught her from behind. The Krug splashed from the glass as it was meant to, soaking Pat's hand, her wrist, and the John Richmond tattoo on the long sleeve of her shirt.

"I'm *so* sorry. I'm afraid I'll never make a waitress," intoned Emma Guinness theatrically, the smile twisting her features. "Where's Dick? Has the lord and master deserted his mistress?"

Fire blazed in Pat Parker's belly.

"Listen, Emma, don't give me that bullshit. You and Dick had nothing going. You work for him, that's all. Anything that existed was all in your mind. It's the best place for it."

She waved her hand up and down to shake off the champagne. God, the girl was a chameleon. She was fun, and bright and amusing . . . and then she was this.

"You work for him too, Pat. I just hadn't realized you did it on the horizontal. There's a name for that kind of job, isn't there? For sure it isn't photographer—but it does begin with a *p*."

"Careful, Emma. Your ugliness is beginning to show. I mean the inside stuff." Pat's eyes dusted the horrendous purple silk bugle-beaded coat-and-shirt disaster that was Emma's sartorial statement of the day. Thank the Lord, Guinness had nothing to do with her movie. No way could Pat have been diplomatic after a remark like that. She'd been called a few things in her time. A hooker had never been one of them.

Emma Guinness started to contract. She made tight fists. The color drained from her champagne-reddened face. Her lips were tight and mean around her mouth. She'd gotten the message. It was a taste dig. Through the years she had acquired a hypersensitive allergy to those. She searched the word processor that was her brain for the appropriate insult, but already she was moving past mere language. The bitch was daring to defy her, after throwing a wrench into the delicate machinery of the Guinness future. All the ancient hated ones were suddenly lumped together in the parcel of flesh and bone that stood before her. Pat had become Victoria Brougham and the *Class* enemies of England. She was Tony Valentino and the Nantucket/Vassar girls of old *Celebrity*. She was the entire world that existed only to thwart Emma Guinness and to deny her her rightful place in the sun. The conversation roared and receded in Emma's mind. The Wagner thundered in her head. Nothing seemed real anymore. There were only blood-red colors, and bright sharp smells, and at the tips of her fingers the space-program lacquered nails tingled like the talons of a tiger at bay. She could rip this girl apart. Before they hauled her from the twitching body, she could rake those cheeks past plastic surgery. It would feel so good to plow the bleeding furrows, to gouge the eyes Shakespeare-style, to hear the screams of the stricken enemy. That was where she was going. She didn't care anymore about cheap, clever remarks. They were for silly, civilized people who played the game by the rules. Now, she was black as the night, and in league with the devil and his secret ways. She was going mad, of course. But she was embracing her madness. That was the point. To be superhuman you had to soar above convention. You had to dream crazy dreams, and you had to dare to do dreadful things. You didn't fear retribution, because society's miserable revenge was painless compared to the agony of not having everything that you wanted. She was free at last, swimming unencumbered in the icy lake of pure hatred, and, at the moment of her weird epiphany, Emma Guinness cooled down.

"I'm sorry," she said. "I didn't mean all that. I think I must have had too much to drink."

Pat, astonished, tried to catch up with the mood change.

"That's okay. I understand. Forget it." She managed a lukewarm smile.

"I'm sorry Dick wasn't here. He'd have loved that little conversation." Emma Guinness laughed. The charm was back. The poison gas that had bubbled from the swamp of her id was blowing away in the wind.

Pat could hardly believe the character change. Mentally, she filed it away. One thing was clear. Emma Guinness was near to some sort of breakdown. Underneath the brilliance, her psyche was in ruins. She was terribly unstable, and yet nobody who hadn't witnessed the outburst could be made to believe how dangerous she had become. Should she try to warn Latham? Hell, no! He'd be suspicious of her motives. Anyway, Latham needed about as much protection as a black widow spider needed from its unfortunate mate.

For now, however, she would hold out the olive branch.

"Listen, Emma. You know Dick and I aren't really . . . an item. I mean . . ."

"Well, you did a little better than a john in a cloud over Wisconsin." Emma laughed, dreaming of deathrays, smelling the blood.

"Less novel. More mundane." Pat laughed, conjuring up visions of straitjackets, men in white coats, Thorazine syringes.

"Hi, Pat. Hi, Emma. Remember me? Allison Vanderbilt." Allison Vanderbilt did not look like someone who would be easily forgotten, nor did her tone assume she had been. She was coolly beautiful in a cream Alaïa pantsuit, and her ostensibly humble demeanor was a class weapon she carried like a club.

"Hello, Allison. How wonderful to see you," said Pat, grateful for the interruption. "Isn't it terrific you're working on the show? I love your part. You're going to be perfect. Is your family pleased?"

Somehow the Vanderbilt family was a topic that hovered like an aura around Allison.

"Oh, they think it's a tremendous joke. Deep down, I think Mommy's quite impressed. She has this crush on Sylvester Stallone, and now she imagines I'll be inviting him to stay. Daddy keeps boasting about some starlet he used to take to El Morocco way back in the Stone Age, and he's threatening to turn the orchid house into a screening room. He actually warned me about casting couches, you know . . ."

"It's great to see you so happy," said Pat.

"Have you seen Tony?" said Emma Guinness, congenitally opposed to happiness wherever she found it.

The fleeting expression of pain across the Vanderbilt features was her reward.

"Yes, he's over there. I'm so pleased we're going to be working together," said Allison with unnecessary sincerity. Pat was much easier to like now that she and Tony were no longer lovers.

"You and Melissa should be great chemistry," said Emma, "especially with Pat stirring the mix." Nobody felt the urge to agree with that.

Pat had had enough. "I haven't said hello to Tony yet," she said quickly. "I mustn't ignore my leading man."

Her heart bumping around in her boots, she cut loose from Emma and Allison and aimed herself through the crowd at Tony.

Tony Valentino was equal parts agony and ecstasy. The press reception was a hell constructed with him in mind. The reason for it was sweet dreams. He shifted from one foot to another and tried to say things that were both true and inoffensive, while around him the hardboiled press veterans lobbed their bombs. What did it feel like to be a male pinup? What would his dead mother have thought? Were male sex symbols airheads, like female ones? Why did the possession of a passable body suggest that the boy bimbo should be able to *act*? He sipped on the tomato juice, breathed deeply, and tried to keep the Latham faith. His instructions had been straightforward. Don't blow it. Don't bust nose. Play Saint Sebastian until there were no arrows left. Dick Latham's advice had been polite, but there had been a threat in his words. Tony didn't mind. He was where he dreamed of being. He was in his rightful place at last. Here, on the brink of fame, he could take anything that they threw at him.

"What's *Malibu* about, Tony?" sneered a columnist. He wanted to find out if the idiot could *speak*.

"Obsession. It's a film about wanting—about the pointlessness of ambition, and yet its absolute inescapability. It's an essay on success, fame, making it, and their relationship to happiness and contentedness. It contrasts quiet lives with noisy lives, peace with war, the struggle to reach goals that never stay still with the passive acceptance of fate. It asks the question, 'Which is the better way?' "

"And which is the better way?"

"There are no answers in films or in life. There are just worthwhile, carefully drawn questions."

"Like, 'Why the hell are we all stuck up this mountain listening to psychodrivel from rent-a-dick?' " said someone in a slurred voice from the edge of the crowd.

Valentino's fists whitened. He swirled around to locate the endangered lush.

"Because of the emotion that killed the cat—curiosity," said Pat Parker. "And what Tony just said is very far from drivel. It's the most intelligent statement of the film's highest concept I've heard. You should write it down, if you're still capable of writing."

She stood beside him, and when their eyes met the old solidarity was back. Whatever they had been to each other, whatever they would become, they were the same people on the same side. They were out there, on the limb, living dangerously. They were taking the shots and hunting for the rewards, daring, dreaming, gambling with life. Unlike Cohen's bird on the wire, his drunken midnight chorister, Tony Valentino and Pat Parker were free. It wasn't pleasant. It wasn't comfortable. Perhaps it wasn't even wise. But it was inevitable. Around them clustered the fact men—the experts on the status quo, on what could be done, on what was impossible. Short on will and long on education, they dealt in the currency of safety. They constructed their lives on apparently firm foundations from the bricks and mortar of security and they paid for predictability with the hard cash of boredom. Here was the dilemma at the heart of *Malibu,* the movie. Should you embrace an obsession, or recoil from it?

Imperceptibly, Pat and Tony moved closer to each other. Their shoulders touched, swayed away from each other, touched again. It wasn't the tightness of the crowd. It was the passion they still shared. Surrounded by the sea of mediocrity, they clung together, and both realized at the same time that the second stage of their lives was beginning.

"You haven't directed before. The only brand-name star in the movie is Melissa Wayne. What makes you think this isn't going to be a disaster?"

"What's Dick Latham up to?"

"How long have you known him?"

"Is this going to be a trend at the new Cosmos—using unknowns?"

The questions came in fast and furious, and Pat held up her hand to fend them off.

"Please, gentlemen, be patient. There are press people who haven't arrived yet. There's going to be a formal question-and-answer session later on. All your questions will be answered then. Let's do this thing right."

She slipped her hand into Tony's, pleased that he didn't resist, and she led him away from the gadflies who had been tormenting him.

"Let's go outside for a while. I need to talk," she whispered.

He went with her. Outside the tent, the heat and the quiet closed in on them. Pat walked to the edge of the hillside, and the vista stretched away from them like a magic carpet. They could see to the Sierra Madres and beyond, the majestic mountains shimmering in the heat haze.

"God, it's beautiful here," said Pat. "It's moments like this that I feel I really know Alabama."

"How is he?" said Tony. Alabama was neutral ground, safe, unthreatening. Tony liked him. Pat loved him.

"The same. He never changes. He's furious I've agreed to do this movie, but he's not really mad, he just pretends to be."

"He doesn't believe movies are art? Maybe he's right," said Tony.

"Some are, some aren't. Ours will be." She turned toward him and smiled. Our movie. Yours and mine. A joint project for two people who had been joined together before fate had separated them. Her eyes hinted she was thinking that. His recognized her thought.

"It's going to be tough as hell," said Tony suddenly. The pain of future torment flashed across his face.

"Me and you . . . and Allison . . . and Melissa?" she both said and asked.

He nodded, staring out into the brightness of the heatscape.

"We need to be friends," said Pat. "You need to forgive me. You need to trust me."

Again he nodded, avoiding her gaze. Pat took a deep breath. Would words make it better or worse?

"Should trusting be so easy?" he said at last. There was reproach in his voice, but not terminal reproach.

She reached out and took his hand once more, and she stared deep into his eyes. She would only have this chance to state her case. Her heart was on trial.

"Tony, listen to me. I'm not proud of what I did, but I *had* to do it. You of all people must understand that. When I took those beautiful photographs, I had no idea of what would happen to them. Please believe me. It wasn't a calculated thing. It just happened in the most natural way in the world. It was the sort of thing that could never have been forced. You must have felt that. I never asked you to do what you did. You did it yourself, because it felt so right. That's how great art happens. And when it does, you can't ignore it. I couldn't, anyway. It's too rare. It's too important. It's bigger than people and their feelings, because without it people can't grow. Am I making sense? Okay, maybe I was wrong, but look what's happened because of what I did. I knew it would. *New Celebrity* is a sensation because of us. This movie's happened because of it. Everything you ever wanted to happen has happened. I may not have done the right thing, but can't I take some credit for all the good things that are showering down on us?" She squeezed his hands.

"Tony, look at me. Tell me it's okay. Tell me *we're* okay. If not the same, at least friends, close friends."

His face was a mask. She searched it for clues. Nothing stared back at her. Deep down she knew he was playing with her. She was being forced to predict the expression that would come next. The embryonic director in her had to admire it, as the woman and the lover screamed their dissent.

She couldn't leave it to chance. She had to influence him. So she stepped close, into his space, until her body was close against his. She was risking rejection. She knew that. He could humiliate her for this, and he was good at that. Far too good. Still, he remained an enigma. His emotions were locked away. But they were there. Millimeters beneath his skin, she could sense their presence. He had not moved back. He had stood his ground. In the absence of straws to clutch at, she squeezed the hand he was allowing her to hold.

"I thought the leading man was the star's perk," said Melissa Wayne.

The cold water of her sneering words poured over Tony and Pat. They snapped apart as if separated by a steel spring.

"I'm sorry to interrupt such a . . . private moment," snarled the star, "but as at least three photographers have captured it for posterity through their telephotos, and as you are standing in full view of most of California's paid gossips, I thought I should swing by and say hello. I know you're new to the movie game, but on a set we have no secrets. We'll be one big happy family of professionals, doing our job, oblivious of personal feelings, having no favorites." Her lips positively curled with malice as she cast her sarcasm at what she firmly believed were the born-again lovers. Her threat was everywhere. She wouldn't forgive this. Her face had been publicly slapped. The gauntlet had been thrown down. She was picking it up for a duel to the death.

Pat cursed inside. Melissa Wayne had only one attribute. Her sex appeal. She hated only one class of thing. Women. She had jumped to the premature conclusion that Pat had stolen back "her" lover. It was a capital offense. As the result of this misunderstanding, the director and her star were set on a collision course, and principal photography was weeks away. There were no words to explain what had happened. The body language had done the talking. Pat couldn't apologize. So she just stared at Melissa in helpless defiance.

Melissa glared back. Then suddenly she laughed, throwing back her head and tossing her hair in the sunlight, pushing out her pert breasts.

"I'm going back to the party. Dick is limbering up for some kind of an announcement." She turned as if to walk away from them. Over her shoulder she let rip with the Parthian shot. "See you in the love scenes, Tony," she said, but she was looking at Pat Parker as she spoke.

"Don't worry about her," said Tony. "I can handle Melissa Wayne."

"You've had practice?" Pat bit her lip, but she could not resist the jealous dig.

"That won't help." There was anger in his voice. Melissa might have forced them into some kind of alliance, but he hadn't forgiven Pat. His tone said she shouldn't assume too much.

"I know. I'm sorry," she said. "Maybe you can handle her, but I wonder if I can."

"Melissa's a bully. You just have to stand up to her. She's ambitious. At the end of the day she won't wreck the movie. She can't afford to be in a stinker. Nobody can."

"I hope you're right." Pat's mind was whirling. "See you in the love scenes," she'd said. It was a loaded remark, because everyone had heard the rumors about Melissa Wayne, about how she was a reality freak, believed in the whole Method bit, couldn't stand faked sex. Directing steam and sizzle was difficult enough without having the guy you loved on the wrong end of the lens . . . with a souped-up nympho who didn't believe in briefs and G-strings beneath the sheets, whose box-office clout could deliver the things she wanted.

"We can control her," repeated Tony, his voice hard and forceful, as if saying it would make it true.

"Yeah, I guess so, and Dick'll be a help. We can always lean on him."

"Yeah, we can always depend on Dick," he sneered.

She felt the coldness. Nothing had been forgotten. Up ahead, there would be only stormy waters. Dick Latham and Melissa Wayne were hot topics that could not be avoided.

Pat reached out to hold the arm that had just left her.

"Come on, Tony, let's go and hear what the old boy's going on about." The "old" was a concession. She'd wanted to come up with more of a putdown to show that Latham wasn't important to her, but at the last minute she hadn't been able to find one. Why? But this was no time for self-analysis. Life was off and running. She and Tony weren't back together again, despite what Melissa thought, but they had achieved some sort of armed truce. For the sake of the movie? As a prelude to something more? It was difficult to know.

They walked toward the tent.

Dick Latham was on the rostrum, talking into a microphone.

"I expect some of you are wondering where I am going to build the new Cosmos studio," he said. "Well, I'm proud to be able to say that the answer is . . . here. We are standing on it now. Cosmos Pictures will be built in the Malibu hills."

The roar of interest exploded around the room as the meaning of his words sank in. A studio in Malibu, in the mountains where war raged between the developers and the environmentalists. Dick Latham was about to carve up the canyons. He was going to try to build the new Cosmos slap bang in the middle of Alabamaland. Armageddon was about to be unleashed.

The words rushed into Pat Parker's mind. Her mouth opened and her hand flew to it.

"What!" said Tony Valentino by her side.

"Cosmos! In Alabama's hills?" she whispered, half to herself, half to him.

Already she was beginning to understand the implications. She was working for Cosmos, for Latham. She was on their side. Her whole brilliant future, Tony's future, their future together was bound up in the success of the movie that would be the keynote for the revived studio. If it failed, everything would fail. But Cosmos in Malibu meant that Alabama, her friend and mentor, would become her bitter enemy. He would fight with all the fearful force at his disposal to derail Latham's plans. She would be forced to choose between the hare and the hounds. No way could she run with both. In desperation she looked at Tony. In shock he stared back at her, as gradually he, too, became aware of her dilemma.

She looked back at Latham. Surely it was a joke. He'd told her Cosmos was destined for the desert. He'd gone on and on about his concern for the environment. There had been the model of the house he was intending to build in the canyon. But even as she tried to hope that it wasn't true, Pat knew it was. Deep in her heart she had sensed that something like this was afoot. She had never trusted the billionaire she had allowed to love her. His eyes had avoided hers earlier when he had ignored her questions about the home he never planned to build. He had conned them all. The bastard had bought, used, tempted, and manipulated her, and now he was laughing as he dared her to fight back. The anger flared up inside her.

She pushed forward through the excited crowd. As she did so, Dick Latham's eyes caught hers. He had been looking for her, and now across forty feet their faces locked together. It was clear from his expression that he wasn't proud of the trick he'd played. He wasn't crowing, mocking the dilemma he had forced upon her, as he rejoiced in yet another hollow victory over a woman. Instead, he looked frightened, and the sight of Dick Latham's fear stopped Pat in her tracks. She had never seen it before. Probably no one had. She understood immediately. Latham still wanted her. He wanted her more than he had wanted anyone since Paris all those years ago. He had been unable to resist the Cosmos-in-Malibu deal, because it had made brilliant business sense, but now he was terrified that it would cost him the woman he loved. Across the heads of the boozed-up journalists, he was pleading with her. His face was talking with an eloquence that even Tony would envy. Pat took a deep breath. Anger had been so simple. On its wave she could have ridden toward the decent thing—the mountains, Alabama, and the goodbye to Hollywood dreams. But now, melted by the humanity of Dick Latham's bizarre love, anger was going, going, gone.

For the first time in her life Pat Parker was a spectator. She hadn't a clue what she would do next. She turned to Tony, who had caught up with her. Tony looked at Latham. Tony looked at Pat. He saw the communication that Pat and Latham shared.

When he spoke, there was sadness in his tone—sadness and resignation. "The bastard's got you," he said.

~ 13 ~

ALABAMA TWISTED THE top off the Corona with his teeth and spat it into the fireplace.

"The dentist told you to stop that," said King absentmindedly.

"The *dentist*," growled Alabama, "is praying that I fall off the Harley and catch a mouthful of road. That way he can spec the house on Winding Way *and* stick some concrete caissons under that broken-down piece of shit he's bought under the landslide at Big Rock. Bottlecap damage is merely a new Porsche."

He burped to accentuate dentist scorn, and stared out over the panoramic view.

"So what do we do today?" said King.

"Same as always. You print some more money, man, and I dream up ways to spend it."

King laughed. His eyes flicked back to the paper on his knee. "Some chick named Finke's written an article on Malibu in the *Times*. Says it's in danger of turning into Miami Beach." He sat back to enjoy the fireworks he had lit, flexing his pecs and stretching his quads. Alabama loathed Malibu exposés written by glib outsiders who thought of themselves as seers.

Alabama puffed himself up. "I've read more of that bullshit than you've done chest repetitions, man. A little history, lists of celebrity homeowners, interviews with a gossip of verbally incontinent rent-a-mouths, a couple of eyecatching headlines, and it's another deadline met in mediocrity land. All you need for that crap is press clippings, a jaundiced eye, and a paper with a name that gets you the entrée to people who otherwise wouldn't piss on you if you were on fire. What I can't understand is how some reporter—"

The telephone cut into his diatribe. He ambled across to it and scooped it up. "Hello," he barked.

"This is Richard Brillstein of the *L.A. Times*. Is this Ben Alabama?"

"The *Times*? Jesus, I was just talking about the *Times*. Yes, this is Alabama. What do you want?"

"Well, uh . . . Mr. Alabama . . . I've just attended a press conference given by Richard Latham, the new owner of Cosmos Studios . . . you know who I mean?"

"I know Latham." Alabama was suddenly wary.

"And he's just announced . . . I mean, literally an hour ago . . . that he's intending to build an entire studio right here, next to your ranch, in the Malibu hills."

"WHAT!" Alabama shouted the word down the line. King sat up.

"That's what I imagined your reaction would be. It was mine, too. There would have to be considerable environmental impact. He's talking about hundreds of acres of sound stages, back lots, front lots, you name it. Then there'd have to be access roads, whole mountaintops graded, and central sewers, of course, which would put him on collision course with the cityhood people. I wanted your reaction, Mr. Alabama. I'm glad I'm the first to give you this information, although I realize it must be bad news for you . . ."

But Brillstein didn't get the scoop of the Alabama response. In the middle of his sentence, Alabama put down the phone. He stood still. Movement was impossible as the fury built. Anger for him was a way of life, an affectation, even. It was seldom personal, nothing more than a useful character ploy that paid dividends in terms of people intimidated and his own way achieved. This was different. This was rage. It was hot and cold at the same time. It was the freezing ice block that plucked the skin from bleeding hands on some snowy steppe. It was the branding iron hissing and sizzling on bare flesh in macabre ritual torture. The fury tore at his ancient gizzards. He clamped his fists tight. He screwed up his eyes, and great gusts of air billowed in and out of his bellows lungs. The blood was everywhere. He could see it as a mist before his screwed-up eyes. He could hear it rushing in his ears. He could feel it pumping like a fire hose in the cavern of his chest.

"What's the matter?" said King. Alabama's face was red. Now, before King's eyes, it was whitening. "What's Latham done?"

"He's a dead man," breathed Alabama. "He's committed suicide," he whispered. "He's gone, history, he's an ex-person," he wheezed.

He faced King, as if seeing him for the first time. His voice was incredulous, as he amplified his answer.

"He's dared . . . he's *dared* . . . to try and build his godforsaken studio in the middle of my mountains."

He stared in defiance at his assistant. There! He'd gotten it out. He'd actually said it in words. It was a considerable achievement. There ought to be applause. Inside, the idea was scurrying around his brain like a rat in the night. A studio, a *movie* studio, sitting like some hideous neoplastic growth in the heart of the beautiful hills. Never in his entire life had he contemplated such a perversion. All the horror in the universe was encapsulated in it. Cosmos was the epitome of the tawdry tinsel of cheap illusion. Latham was the disgusting devil of capitalism rampant, the crass cash mountain, the symbol of the mammon and materialism that Alabama had spent his years decrying. Now they had come together to threaten the love of his life. It was mindbending. It was the firm foundation on which a crusade could be built.

The billionaire must be stopped. It didn't matter how. The cost was immaterial. If it took murder, then so be it. The gas chamber was an incidental detail. Alabama's own life was an inconsequential irrelevance, in contrast to the monumental abortion that threatened to color the world blood red. His eyes darted around the room, mirroring the ideas that darted across the computer screen of his mind. What should he do? What must be done? Resolve wasn't enough. Superhuman cunning would be needed to defeat the billionaire's evil. He must calm down. He must think.

"He can't do that," said King, appalled.

"No, he can't. He won't. I won't let him," muttered Alabama.

He walked across the room and threw himself down on the outsize sofa. Good. His thoughts were sorting themselves out in some form of sequence, as his brain recovered from the chaos of shock. Latham had made a public announcement at a press conference. That meant his ground would have been carefully prepared. Billionaires didn't stay billionaires by failing to deliver on their promises. Staying megarich was a confidence trick. Billions were a banking pyramid. For as long as they remained believers, the moneylenders would hold it up. When doubt crept in, Kashoggi-style, they pulled the rug. That meant Latham had gotten permission to build Cosmos in the mountains. He wouldn't actually have the zoning, but he would have the secret promise of it. Clearly he had worked miracles at the normally environmentally conscious California Coastal Commission. Was it already too late to intervene? That was the first question. How could the die be uncast? That was the second.

"Do you think Pat knows about this?" asked King.

Alabama sat up. He hadn't thought of that. The Cosmos thing had wiped everything from his mind. Pat had agreed to direct a Cosmos movie. She was thick with Latham and the dreadful English girl who ran the stupid magazine. It seemed impossible that she wouldn't know about Latham's plans for the studio. That made her the very worst sort of person, a traitor. No! Alabama recoiled from the idea. She couldn't have known. She was an artist. She'd learned to love the mountains. Heck, she'd photographed them. She wouldn't be a party to their brutal rape. After all, he, Alabama, who usually knew everything, had heard nothing about the diabolical plan. Latham knew how to keep a secret. He must have kept it from her. There was a way to find out. He would call her. She would tell him how horrified she was. She would back out of the movie, tear up her *New Celebrity* contract, and she would never speak to Richard Latham again. She would volunteer her support, and she would work with Alabama to undo what must be undone. But as he laid out the scenario in his mind, Alabama already knew it wasn't as simple as that. Pat Parker was a go-getter. As far as it was possible, she was on the side of the virtuous, but when good clashed with the ambition that fueled her, which would win? Then there was the joker in the pack, the one called Tony Valentino. More than grace, Pat wanted him. Would she give up her own and her lover's fame and fortune for the flora and fauna of some parched hillside? Like *hell* she would. Valentino and Latham would work together as the magnet sucking Pat Parker toward her dreams. What could Alabama offer as a counterattraction to a lover's gratitude and artistic acclamation in the minds of the masses? Snakes and doe-eyed deer, hawks and canyon mice, stark rocks, barren land, and the still heat of the high chaparral. To side with him, Pat Parker would have to be more than a saint. She would have to be the angel she so closely resembled.

"I don't think she knew," said Alabama. "But I think she knows now."

King was silent as he thought about it. He idolized Pat. Somehow he sensed she was on the verge of exclusion from his world, that the decision would be hers, that it would not be an easy one.

"How can you stop Latham? Call the president?"

King could never get over the fact that Alabama and the president were friends. Alabama was *his* friend. He was real. He could be touched. He smelled. He got drunk. The president, however, was, well, the president, like God was God, the pope was the pope, and Orel Hershiser was Orel Hershiser. The concept of Alabama and the president was for King the place where reality met illusion. Okay, so the president had run on an environmentalist ticket, and had once owned an Indian motorcycle, and loved to take bad photographs, but that still didn't make his friendship with his boss any more believable.

"Yeah, I can call the president, and my friends in the Congress. I can spend days on the telephone calling in the IOUs. I can do the media, and put a bomb under the PR people, but all that takes time. It's my guess that time is something I don't have too much of. Latham knows that a lot of powerful people won't want this. If he's ready to go public with it, it's because it's on the verge of happening."

"So what can you do?"

"I could kill him."

King laughed. Then he laughed nervously.

"Seriously, Alabama."

"No, I'm serious. I could blow the bastard away. I could waste him."

King said nothing. He had never seen Alabama in such a dangerous mood.

"Or I could do something that would mobilize public opinion in a way that it has never been moved before. Something that nobody could ignore. Something that would get through to people, make them visualize the potential tragedy, make them feel it in their hearts and minds, make them see it . . . see it . . . make them *see* it . . ."

There was a Damascus light burning in Alabama's face. It was illuminating him. In its clarity, he saw. At once he knew what he must do. In the purity of his personal epiphany, he was filled with an awesome resolve. He stood up.

"Where's the Linhof?" he said.

"It's in the camera room. In the safe. Why?"

"Is it in shape?"

"Yeah, sure it is. All the cameras are, Alabama. They always have been. You told me to look after them."

Alabama felt the shudder run down his spine. He had never imagined he would reach this moment. He had longed for it, dreaded it, recoiled from it, and now he was on the brink of embracing it. For so many years he had made his excuses. Bricks, he'd said. Nature, he'd lied. Too many photographs, too many photographers, he'd bleated. He'd dreamed up all sorts of reasons why he'd given up photography, and they had all had one purpose— to hide the real one. Fear. Now, he faced the truth. He had put away his cameras because he was terrified that he had lost his artistic skill. Ten years ago there had been a bad patch, a period when nothing had seemed to work visually. For most artists that was a daily demon to be wrestled with. For Alabama, however, it had been a first, and it had scared the living daylights out of him. He had gone dry, and he had reacted to the cessation of the fountain by refusing to try to turn it on. Days without working had dragged into weeks, months, years, and, as each second passed, his artistic courage had drained away. The excuses and rationalizations had gained in strength. He had learned to live with the lies and the cheating, and in King, the brilliant printer, he had found the willing codependent. Together they had constructed the façade that hid the truth so well. And what was the truth? That the mighty Alabama, the art hero of three generations, was a fake, a cheat, and a coward. Beer helped disguise that. So did the bikes and the brawls. So did the protection of the mountains that he had made into his own personal cause. Well, now it was over. The time had come to confront the demons.

"Do you know what I'm going to do, King?" said Alabama.

King knew the answer was coming.

"I'm going to make photographs. I'm going to make pictures of that canyon that Latham's trying to wreck, and the world will weep when they see their beauty. I'm going to make photographs that I've never made before. I'm going to take all the photographs that for years I was too terrified to take. I can do it. I must do it. I will do it."

He stood there, shaking with the power of the moment, wanting to shout out in joy and pain at this, the instant of his rebirth. As King watched, in awe of his friend's transformation, tears of determination and relief poured down Alabama's cheeks.

THE SUN came up over Saddle Peak, sending sleepy fingers of light poking into the canyon. It hung there, underlined by the mountain, as if pausing for breath after the long night journey to the top of the world. The ground stirred at daybreak. The blackness softened, the shapes formed, and the valley, cool and moist from the dew of the sea, gathered its strength for the heat to come.

Alabama was ready for the magic of the new beginning. For two hours he had clung to the mountainside, his feet wedged in a rock ledge, his shoulder numb against a bleak boulder. In front of him the mahogany view camera had all the space. It gleamed in the glow of the earliest light. King had not forsaken it during the barren years. It was polished, oiled, and loved. Now, the 10/8 plate nestling in its bowels, it was ready to be used. Alabama took a deep breath. This was a million miles from Nikon land, leagues from Hassel-blad territory, where motor-drive was a dirty word and where there were no second chances. He had the picture in his head, where it needed to be. Nine-tenths of the work was done. But still there was the mechanical part. It mustn't be allowed to destroy the consummate beauty that was alive in the eye of his mind.

He processed the information, using Ansel's zone system. He didn't have to think. Experience thought for him. Luminance value of the weak sun, say Zone VII. So, if 250 candelas per square foot was on VII, 60 candelas per square foot would fall on Zone V. He was using Isopan film which indicated a basic exposure of $\frac{1}{60}$ of a second at f/8. The 3X yellow filter, which he now added, would reduce that to $\frac{1}{20}$ of a second. He let the pent-up breath whistle through his nostrils, disturbing the silence. He could almost see the sun grow. The moment would be gone almost before it arrived. It had to be anticipated. The second it was experienced it would already be too late. Alabama reached forward. He stopped down to f/32. His finger hovered on the release. Then, quite suddenly, he seized. A wave of panic broke over him. He was numb, paralyzed, bathed instantly in clammy chaos, and the cool professionalism that ruled his mind degenerated into discord. A voice boomed in his brain. "You can't do this," it said. "You've forgotten how." It laughed—a horrible, mocking laugh. "You remember all those bad photographs you despised, Alabama? Well, join the club, you old phony. There's another one coming up. Moon in June. Red sails in the sunset. Say cheese and watch the birdie. Into the drawer with it, Ben, baby. Stick it in the family album. Bore the relatives with it on a wet Sunday afternoon." The voice was cackling with helpless mirth in his mind. "You got up in the middle of the night to shoot this shit? You climbed the mountain to blaze away at the mediocre? Oh, Alabama! Stick to the beer and the memories and the might-have-been. Leave the photography to those with balls that still work."

"No," he said out loud, wiping the sweat from his brow with the back of his hand. He fought to concentrate. The pastel shades were painted onto the hills now. The light was growing in the womb of darkness. His gut said, "so soon"—but his gut didn't know anymore. How could he break the block? How could he make the confidence grow like the beauty that was erupting all over the canyon? He searched for allies in his loneliness. But in the art void, there were no friends, only doubts and fears and the ghostly intangibility of the feckless muse.

Then it came to him. Through the mystery of the magic moment, he saw the vision across the canyon. It was white stucco. It was squat. It was ugly. Smoke billowed from its chimneys. A vivid red neon sign uttered the obscenity. Cosmos Studios it read, and it seemed to Alabama that the sun itself recoiled from the ugliness of the mirage. His mind cleared. The voice in his head receded. Here was something worse than failure and the scorn of the world. Here was the prospect that the mountains he loved would be destroyed. Once again he could "see." Once more he could "feel." It wasn't too late. The time was now. He squeezed the shutter release and gave the picture a "long" one-second exposure. Even as he captured it, he knew what he had. This would be better than *Moonrise Over Hernandez,* more dramatic than Ansel's glorious *Black Sun.* Already he knew that it would need waterbath development to preserve maximum density in the foreground. Even now he could see the cut of the print, calculate to the last millimeter the photograph's depth of field. God, he had done it! He could *do* it! The goblin of doubt was no longer perched on his shoulder. And in the bag on his back were twelve virgin plates.

Ben Alabama let himself go. He entered the nature he loved, and at the same time he opened up to allow it to enter him. The sun was rising over the mountain, but the sun was also rising in his heart.

—

SPLOSH! THE pelican dropped from the sky like a thunderbolt and disappeared beneath the surface of the sea. He reemerged instantly, and the flash of silver at his beak said he'd scored. Beneath the balcony, a forty-five-year-old beachboy adjusted the fishing rod that stuck up from the sand. Apart from these competitors, Carbon Beach, the one they called "Deal Beach," was deserted.

"What am I going to do, Allison?" said Pat. She turned back from the balcony. Allison Vanderbilt was stretched out in a chair, her long legs hitched up on each other. She wore dark glasses as a concession to California. Otherwise, she was pure New England from the cut of her classic hair to the tips of her perfect toes.

"God, Pat, I don't know. Isn't it what people call a moral dilemma?"

She laughed helplessly. Manners replaced morals in the upper-class high ground from which she operated. Appropriate and inappropriate courses of action were laid down in the unwritten constitution of the aristocracy. Murder, rape, arson, torture were all covered by the shadowy rules you learned from Scots nannies in the nursery. Things were done. Things were not done. In every conceivable situation you knew how to behave because the regulations had dripped into you by osmosis during a thousand tailgate picnics, a hundred horse shows, at scores of balls as you danced with class fellow travelers in shoes that were always too tight. If Pat herself didn't know what to do, Allison wouldn't be able to tell her.

Pat screwed up her eyes against the brightness of the early morning sun, and she sighed. She had gotten to know Allison, and she really liked her, but the beautiful rich girl's relationship to the real world was as close as that of a dyslexic to a dictionary. On her Alice in Wonderland planet a career was what you had to irritate your family, money grew in trust funds, and friends were nearly always cousins.

"The way I see it," said Allison, trying hard to be helpful, "is that Mr. Latham is rather ruthless. I mean, he's the sort of man who would . . . who would . . ." She cast around in her mind for a definition of ruthless behavior. "Who would . . . haggle in a store," she managed at last. She wrinkled her nose in disgust at the thought. Arabs did that. And nouveau riche people like Latham. *So* demeaning. After all, it was only *money.*

Pat laughed at the touching naïveté. Allison made her laugh, and at this particular point in her life, there were few enough people who could do that. It was amazing that the friendship had developed at all. Allison must have despised the way she had treated Tony, and, as a would-be rival, she had reason to be jealous. But it hadn't turned out like that. Instead, Allison had been drawn to her precisely *because* she had loved Tony, and because Allison sensed that she still did. In the Vanderbilt book, loving the same people as they did meant you had good taste. And people with taste could be forgiven anything.

"Okay, so he's an iron man, a hard charger. How does that affect what I do?"

"Well, perhaps you should be tough with him yourself. You could tell him you think that his plan to build Cosmos in the mountains is a *really* bad idea. You could tell Alabama you've told Mr. Latham that. Then Alabama would know that you'd done your best, and he couldn't be cross. If Mr. Latham doesn't listen, at least you've tried and it's not your fault."

Again Pat laughed. The thought of Latham giving up his deal because Pat thought it was a *really* bad idea was about as funny as the bad-tempered Alabama being satisfied by her weak-kneed intervention.

"And do you think I should go on working for Latham? Should I go on directing the movie as if nothing has happened, while they pour concrete all over the hills and Alabama has apoplexy?"

"But the hills are Alabama's charity, aren't they? Not yours. I mean, if he wants to blow a fuse it doesn't mean you have to hold his hand while he goes up in smoke." Allison knew what she meant. Charities weren't interchangeable. If Aunt Miffy was spina bifida, then you bought a table at her party. You didn't bother with the retinitis pigmentosa Eye Ball, because that was run by the awful pushy woman who kept pretending she was a Whitney when she wasn't.

"Alabama would think I was disloyal," said Pat, wondering why she had to explain the obvious.

"Oh," said Allison, puzzled. She cocked her head to one side as she tried to understand it. *Loyalty* was a class buzzword. It was the most important attribute of all. Dreadful deeds were done in its name. The most extraordinary things were left undone because of it. But somehow it was out of context in this conversation. Why?

"Surely they don't really *have* loyalty in California," she said at last.

She knew it sounded a bit odd, but it was sort of true. Out here, people prided themselves on their lack of sensitivity and their toughness. Nothing was allowed to get in the way of their bottom lines, whatever those were. Conscience and codes had been what they'd come to California to escape. There were no school friends here, no family, and the only thing familiarity bred in the Southland was contempt. Alabama was one of "nature's gentlemen," that potent English euphemism for someone who was likable, but of inferior social status. He had the insubstantiality of servants, inhabiting that strange buffer zone between reality and illusion that existed beyond the green baize door. Of course, he was feisty and wonderful, and admirable because he loved okay things like art and conservation, but at the end of the day he was a shadowy figure who was in no position to ask for loyalty, let alone demand it. It was funny that Pat Parker felt otherwise, but then she *had* been born in New York, which was careless of her.

Pat peered out at the pounding surf. Allison had rung a bell. Maybe she did understand things after all. Sometimes ostriches had a better view from the sand than the shrewdinis from the treetops. She was right. This was California, Los *Angeles*, damn it, not Lynchburg, Virginia. And it was the movie business, where people gambled, where they won and lost. She looked down the beach. There weren't very many losers on Carbon, where Latham had rented her a house for the duration of the shoot. Bruce Willis. McEnroe. Disney honcho Jeff Katzenberg. All-purpose mover and shaker Freddie Fields. Hard Rock Café owner Peter Morton. Over the years, they'd probably stepped on the odd toe. Hypersensitivity was the mortal enemy of high-end property on Deal Beach.

It was time to get "real." If she wanted to commit hara-kiri and give up her dreams for somebody else's, nobody would care. Tinsel didn't know how to cry off camera. If she walked out on the Latham flick, she'd never work again in Hollywood. And for what? Mickey Mouse points from a rag bag of environmentalists, who'd never pay her bills or remember her name? The gratitude of an old man who didn't have the balls to take photographs anymore? The moral glory of doing the right thing? Whatever she did wouldn't make any difference. The mountains would be raped with or without her. She wouldn't even be an accomplice. Like Pilate, she could wash her hands of the whole sorry business. She took a deep breath and tried to ignore the guilt that pricked at her.

"Yeah, you're right, Allison. The hills are Alabama's fight, or 'charity,' as you put it. Not mine. Why should I throw over the movie just to show solidarity with him? It's too much of a sacrifice. And, hell, how do I know that if I quit I won't be dropping everyone else in it? Latham might just hire another director, but he might shelve the entire project. Then you wouldn't get your chance, and Tony wouldn't get his . . ."

Pat recoiled at the thought of Tony's terrible disappointment, but not so far and so fast as Allison Vanderbilt.

"God, I hadn't thought of that. Tony might not get the movie." Quite suddenly, Allison had been touched by the conversation. No longer was it mere social metaphysics and ethical philosophy, it was flesh and blood. The color drained from her face. Her expression was haunted.

"Perhaps you should say nothing to Latham," she added in a strangled voice. Deviousness was as foreign to her as soul food, but this was life and death.

"No, I'll call him. Why not? He's conned me. I'll tell him he's got no taste and less manners and that he's a jumped-up bastard who wouldn't know a fine feeling if it sat on his face. I'll get it off my chest, and then in the morning I'll punch in as if nothing has happened. He won't mind. He likes people who stand up to him, especially if they intend to back down when it's time to count the cash."

Allison wasn't sure. These people were aliens, Pat Parker included. How could anybody predict their behavior?

"Whatever you do, you wouldn't put Tony's career at risk, would you?" she pleaded.

"You love him very much, don't you?" said Pat.

Allison nodded. She didn't trust her voice to say those words.

"So do I," said Pat simply. "He thinks I don't, and that I just used him for my career. You probably think that, too. But it's not true. I love him as much as I ever did. Perhaps more."

"I know," said Allison. "At least I think I know. You're like him in many ways. You want. You need things. I respect that, but I don't really understand it. I just want whatever he wants."

"What if he wanted me?" Pat's question popped out.

Allison paused. It was a test. Whose love was the greater? It was like the story of Solomon and the baby and the rival mothers.

"I'd want him to have you. I'd help him to get you. If that was what he really wanted . . ."

It was true. Tony was her obsession. Possession wasn't a part of the deal. Her feelings were too strong for that. They soared in the high sky far above such petty considerations as jealousy and greed, beyond ownership, togetherness, and reciprocity.

Pat walked toward Allison and knelt down by the side of her chair. She took the patrician hand in hers as she would the wing of a wounded bird.

"I think he does love me, Allison. Deep down I think he still does," she whispered.

Allison stared straight ahead. She knew what she was being asked for. She was being asked for help.

"I'll be seeing him tonight, at the Getty," she said.

Pat's breath flowed out of her. Nothing had been said, but she knew Allison had granted her silent request. The relief filled her up, but at the same time there were other things to worry about. She, too, was going to the mysterious party at the Getty Museum. So was everyone else. Especially Alabama. He was giving a surprise showing of his "latest" work, presumably King's rehashes of his vintage sixties stuff, passed off as new. There would be no avoiding him. He would force her to take sides, and by the end of the evening he would be her enemy. Latham, too, was a guest, and the president of the United States, Alabama's old friend, was coming down from the vacation ranch he owned in the Sierra Madre mountains. His presence guaranteed a Malibu media beanfeast of epic proportions. Every star in the heavens would be turning out for the party at which Alabama and Latham would meet for the first time since the announcement of the billionaire's plans for the studio in the mountains. For sure, fireworks would be on the menu. But most important of all, she would be seeing Tony again. Could Allison make things right between them? Would they once again be lovers?

DICK LATHAM pushed back against the jets of the Jacuzzi and watched the gulls wheeling over a sea in which a school of dolphins played. His East Coast friends would laugh at this kind of decadence—a hot tub on his bedroom terrace with a view down Broad Beach all the way across Zuma to Point Dume—but secretly they would envy it. It had to do with the finely tuned survival instincts of the old money. Those who had made their loot the original way, by inheriting it, had never forgotten the lessons of the French Revolution. Conspicuous consumption made the peasantry restless. These days they didn't need to chop off your head. Their weapon was the ballot box, and with it they could cut off your assets when the party got too boisterous. The new-money arbitrageurs of Wall Street had discovered the truth of that when they had shown the unacceptable face of capitalism. It was something Mellons, Vanderbilts, and Rockefellers bent over backward to avoid.

The intercom buzzed.

Latham flicked open the channel. It was amusing to do business in the Jacuzzi while watching babes on the beach. A tub with a view was *so* California.

"Yeah," he drawled.

"It's Tommy. Can you spare a minute?"

"Come right on up."

"Great! I'll be up there in two."

Latham reached for the Lalique decanter of Joy de Bains. Why should bath essence be a female thing? It was too good for them. He upended a generous quantity into the foaming water and twiddled the knobs to increase the power of the jets. What brilliant news would Havers bring? More millions made? More rivals cast down? More personal triumphs for the man with the platinum-plated everything?

Havers advanced across the acreage of the Latham bedroom. He winced at the prospect of a tubside interview. A cerebral child, he had always felt out of place in the jocker-room. There, male nakedness, and the way you dealt with it, was some kind of a subterranean test of character.

As if reading the Havers mind, Dick Latham readjusted himself ostentatiously below the bubbles. It was his mission in life to amplify male discomfort wherever he found it.

"What have you got, Tommy?"

"I just wanted to bring you up-to-date on the fight about the Cosmos zoning. I thought you should have the latest before the Getty party."

"Yeah, how's it playing? Seems the opposition are a load of pussycats. They haven't got their act together. Instead of mobilizing the opposition, Alabama's kissing up to the president and throwing some boring retrospective at the Getty. The old goat must be all shot to pieces by the booze. Full of sound and fury signifying nothing. All mouth and trousers, as my British friends would say."

"That's the message I'm getting. I've just talked to Fingleton at Coastal. They had their heads down, expecting all kinds of heavy artillery, but there's next to nothing—two or three liberal congressmen sounding off, a few extra letters in the politicos' mail bags, a couple of scathing articles in the left-wing press. Nothing heavy duty. It just isn't orchestrated. What I can't understand is Alabama. He issued one over-the-top statement and then disappeared from the face of the earth. Unless he pulls a hat rabbit, we're home free on this one. We'll have the go-ahead in a week or two, and the bulldozers up there in three."

Dick Latham stared out to the sand. A girl was pushing a windsurfer into the waves—G-string bikini, a taut body, snow-white hair. God! Why did anyone live anywhere else? At eighty thousand for an undeveloped oceanfront foot, the land was a steal. Hell, you only needed 125 feet of frontage to build something respectable. Then there was nothing to do but sit back, watch the women, and count the capital gains until the tidal wave took you away—easy come, easy go in the Southland where "security" was an expletive you deleted, and where the game's name was "reach-for-the-sky." Then, in the midst of his reverie, he frowned. A cloud had appeared on his spotless horizon. Formed from instinct, it was growing fast, darkening, moving toward the center of his mind. It was wishful thinking to categorize Alabama as a lush and a loser. Underestimating enemies had never been a Latham failure. Somewhere, out there, Alabama was up to something. Sooner rather than later, he would find out what it was. His gut told him it would not be pleasant.

"What's the schedule for the weekend?" asked Latham, forcing the anxiety from his mind.

"Well, Emma Guinness and the *New Celebrity* people are coming down tomorrow. I guess they all want to be patted on the head, given raises, etcetera. I must say they've done a fantastic job. The magazine's doing gangbuster business."

"That's Emma's work. It's all due to her. And she's all due to me."

Dick Latham spoke sharply. At the end of the day you followed the flow of money to find out where the credit belonged. It wasn't an infallible pointer, but usually it was accurate. Credit was something he could never get enough of. It was his father's legacy.

"Yes, that was a brilliant hiring, Dick. Absolutely brilliant."

"Listen, I'll have all the hired help over for lunch tomorrow, but keep dinner free, okay? I'll take Emma to La Scala. The sea bass is great there, and it'll be fun to hear her being beastly about the Saturday night celebrities. How are things at Cosmos?"

"We desperately need to find a CEO. Did you see the short list I sent you?"

"It's shorter now. I crossed everyone off. They're all losers, Tommy. They're the sort of guys who only know two words. Yes, for anyone above them. No, for the guys below. I need someone who isn't afraid to take a measured risk. Lawyers and agents don't like doing that, and the so-called creative people are happy with risks but aren't too kosher at calculating them. What about hiring a celebrity shrink? At least they'd know where the bodies are buried, and they might have a line on what'll play in Pomona."

"Maybe you'll find one at the Getty this evening. All the usual suspects'll turn out for the president," said Havers.

"I wonder why the president's turning out," said Latham.

"Isn't he some sort of photography buff?"

Latham didn't answer. The world and his wife knew that. The old boy had actually had an exhibition of his rubbish at the Corcoran Gallery in Washington when he'd been a senator. Latham had been to the opening night and had tittered behind his hand with the rest of the glitterati at the brazen presumption of the politician's ego. Okay, so the posturing old fake fancied himself a celluloid aesthete, and had been a friend and admirer of Alabama's from way back. It still didn't explain the presence of the most important man in the Western world at an elitist museum in Malibu.

"Anyway," said Latham, "if I get a chance to talk to him, is there anything I need to bring up? What about those TV license applications in Chicago? Aren't they up before the FCC?"

"Yup, it wouldn't hurt to mention those. The chairman of the FCC was at Yale with him, and he's a new appointee. You never know what a word in an ear can do."

Dick Latham frowned. A very unpleasant thought was forming. Into whose ear was Alabama whispering?

~14~

FOR AN ORDINARY mortal the gates of the Getty were more difficult to
enter than the eye of a needle, but Alabama was not ordinary. He had
been waved through them as befitted the God he was. Now, he stood like
Colossus on the brick-paved entrance to the peristyle garden of the museum,
and he peered grandly down the pool toward the main building of the repro-
duction Roman villa. He hadn't bothered to dress for the party. He had come
as himself.

All around him the heavy hitters whispered like the scheming courtiers of
ancient Rome. In traditional Malibu style, they had arrived on time, so that
they could leave early. What was not traditional was the nervous tension that
crackled in the crystal air. You could feel the angst. The president was coming. And there was Alabama in the clothes that Oxfam would have turned
down, with his muscle-bound sidekick and his art armor all around him like a
halo. Any minute now, the billionaire would show up to join Streisand, Cher,
Spielberg, and Johnny Carson, and everyone would watch as the cold war
that had been raging in Malibu for as long as anyone could remember burst
into flame. There, before their eyes, in the museum that tried to be tranquil,
Latham and Alabama would square off for the fight of the millennium, with
the president of the United States of America as referee. A studio in Alabama's mountains! It was as inflammatory as the famous brushfires that raged
at the end of the Malibu summer.

"King, my man, this is going to be just like the old days," said Alabama.
His heart swelled in his barrel chest. On the edge of war, he had never felt so
at peace. The reason was upstairs, on the walls of the photography room.
After so many years of art infertility, he was potent once more. In the early
morning, as the sun had come up over the hills, he had fought his demons
and won. A part of him was actually grateful to the philistine money man.
Latham had provided the tough going that had enabled the tough to get
rough. When the devil had driven, all Alabama's psychological creative blocks
had melted away and the work that had sprung from his soul was the best he
had ever done. Right now, the doors to the exhibit were locked. Presidents

liked to have something to open, and the impact would be greater that way. The photographs would have a dramatic effect as the opinion makers feasted on the visual banquet he had prepared for them. He had distilled and concentrated the beauty of the mountains. It shone from the surface of his prints more brilliantly than it did in the nature that had been his inspiration. There, in black and white, was the wonder that the wrecker was planning to destroy. No seal beneath the hunter's club, no child staring at the barrel of a murderer's gun could have spoken more eloquently for the cause that was his, and would become the world's. He knew he would win. The pictures were too powerful for the billionaire's billions. The environmentally conscious stars would rise up on the tidal wave of their fame and sink Dick Latham like a toy boat at sea. He never should have messed with Alabama. Not in Paris all those years ago. Not now. Not ever.

The Secret Service men were scattered among the crowd like raisins in a fruitcake. Transmitters pressed to their ears, sunglasses glinting in the late afternoon light, their eyes darted that way and this as they waited for the arrival of the president. A helicopter clattered overhead, drowning out the party small talk as its pilot monitored the progress of the presidential motorcade down Pacific Coast Highway. Some bothered to look up. Most didn't. Malibu cool demanded low-key response to everything except major disasters like dented cars, invasions of personal privacy, and weaknesses in the property market.

"Good luck, Alabama," said Cher.

Alabama smiled and held out a gnarled hand. She was renting in Malibu right now, but she would buy soon, and she was persuasive, and environmentally sound.

"I can count on your support?" he asked with a smile.

"Anytime. Anyplace. I'll sing. I'll act. Have you seen me tap? Who does the loonie think he's messing with? Mere money doesn't cut it around here. He should wise up and go home."

"Maybe we can arrange that. The president's in our corner. When he leans, you feel the weight."

"You're not exactly light, Alabama."

"We'll see. We'll see." Alabama chuckled. He felt so good. It was like a biker rumble in the old days, a poker game when you had the cards. Any minute now, Dick Latham would cream through the doors on his charm cloud, and Alabama would let him have it right between the laser beams of bogus sincerity that would be shining from his eyes. He hadn't rehearsed his speech. Righteous indignation would do the talking. When the dust settled, Latham would know both that it was personal and that he had lost. Paris would be avenged. The mountains would be safe.

"Would you like a glass for your beer, sir?" said the waiter hovering beside him. Clearly, he was new to Malibu.

"Naw," said Alabama, placing the bottle to his lips and drinking deep. His eyes scanned the crowd. They had all showed up as he had expected them to. Norman and Lyn Lear's Environmental Media Association were well represented. Its thirty-five high rollers paid around twenty-five thousand a year each for ecological causes such as Alabama's. Redford was there, over by the Flemish marble figure of Bathsheba, talking to Disney boss Michael Eisner and his wife Jane. All were EMA members. The rival Earth Communications Office was represented by Tom Cruise, John Ritter, and its evangelical founder, the charismatic Bonnie Reiss. And the hard-core environmental agitants-litigants had showed. Alabama noted members of both the Natural Resources Defense Council and the Environmental Defense Fund deep in conversation with Bob Hattoy, L.A. regional director of the Sierra Club, as they rubbed shoulders with a nude Greek youth from around 530 B.C.

But Alabama was looking for someone else in the crowd, and he couldn't see her. Pat Parker had been invited. Would she come? What would she say? What would she do? The doubt welled up inside him, as his exhilaration faded. He could deal with the president. He could handle Latham. But how would he fare with Pat Parker, the only person on earth he considered an equal? She had stood up to him before, a hundred times, and mostly she had won. But in those days she had always had right on her side. Would she now? She had much to lose by doing the moral thing, and a lot to gain by avoiding it. If she stood by him, he would admire and respect her more than ever. If she didn't . . . well. Alabama tried not to think about the awful thing that would have to happen. Then, on the edge of the crowd, he caught sight of two people who might not be far from Pat Parker. Tony Valentino and Allison Vanderbilt were deep in conversation.

"She still loves you, Tony," said Allison. "Really. I believe her."

"Did she ask you to tell me that?"

Allison Vanderbilt wasn't good at lies. There were so few people, apart from her parents, that she could be bothered to make them up for.

"Not exactly. But she probably knew I'd tell you." She stared straight at him, unafraid of his sarcasm, because she wanted him to be happy and because she believed that Pat could make him happy.

"She just wants the movie to go smoothly. She's only interested in her career, and what I can do for it. She's proved that already. Now she's trying to use you. That's probably why she made friends with you in the first place."

"Is it so terrible to want things, Tony? Is it so awful to use people to get them? Haven't you ever done that?"

She didn't spell out her accusation, but it was there between the lines. Allison didn't mind his using her. Allison prayed that he would. But it didn't alter the fact that he had.

Allison saw the mini guilt cloud scud across his features. She pressed home her advantage.

"Sometimes, if you love very much, it's an honor to be used. And ambitious people can genuinely love people who are good for them. Perhaps it's the only way they can love. I know love is supposed to be pure and without ulterior motive and all that stuff, but that only happens in romance novels. In the real world, people love the people who help make their dreams come true."

"So says the great expert on the 'real' world."

Allison had set herself up for the rebuke, but she didn't mind, because she knew she had gotten through to him. Tony and Pat were soul brother and sister. For them, career and love would never be separated like church and state. If such a love was their goal, then each was destined for a loveless life.

"Maybe I understand the world a bit better than you, Tony," said Allison. "At least I think about it from time to time."

"Meaning I don't?" He smiled to show he wasn't picking a fight. Allison was no fun to fight with. Winning made him feel like a jerk.

"I mean you don't really care what other people think, so you're not the world expert on human motivation. It's fine not to be. It's not a criticism."

She smiled at the ridiculous concept of her criticizing Tony.

"You're right," he said ruefully. "People are Martians. They're a total mystery to me."

Allison laughed. "And to other people, too. It's just that most people have all sorts of clever theories about what makes other people tick, and they pass them off as fact. Nobody knows the truth, so nobody can prove them wrong. How else do you think shrinks make their money?"

"I guess Pat's less of a mystery than anyone else," he said, almost to himself. What the hell did he feel about Pat Parker? He found it so hard to analyze things like that. A part of him still loved her. Another part believed she had betrayed him. The trouble was, he didn't have much of an angle on love. Sympathy, empathy, and understanding didn't loom large in his emotional life. When he thought about her, he wanted her. Her body had set him on fire. He had always felt good when she was near to him, less good when she was far. She made him feel strong. He loved to fight with her because she stood up to him, and she wouldn't put up with his bullshit. He admired her spunky determination, her quick temper, her artistic talent, and he really liked the greedy way she ate, the clothes she wore, and the jokes she told. She never irritated him, and nearly everyone else did. He actually *liked* her. That was the most remarkable thing of all. She had been the friend who could become the flick-of-a-switch lover, and he had never known when some ghostly finger was going to turn on the current. Was that love? Or did the Greeks have a more subtle word for it? Whatever! For good or ill, those seemed to be the feelings inside him.

"Forgive her, Tony. She didn't mean to do a bad thing, and only good things have come out of it. For her, yes, but for you, too. And for me."

Tony said nothing. He trusted Allison. She was so pure and she loved him purely. Nothing she said was ever intended to mislead. Anything she wanted for him would only be wonderful. Why the hell couldn't he love *her?* She was beautiful, incredibly beautiful, and she made love with an intensity he had never experienced in any woman. To love her should be so easy, and yet something made it impossible.

"Is Pat coming this evening?" he said at last.

"Yes, she is."

"What's she going to say to Alabama?"

"God, I don't know. I think she's going to tell him she can't help him."

"She shouldn't do that."

"Why? What do you mean?" There was alarm in Allison's voice.

"It would be the wrong thing to do. A studio doesn't belong in those mountains. Alabama's her friend. She shouldn't let him down. Hell, she's supposed to be an artist. She should care about those kinds of things."

"But if she doesn't side with Latham, she'll be off the movie, and then the movie might not get made. You'd lose your big chance. She can't risk that."

Alarm was becoming panic. Allison only cared about Tony's dreams. Nothing must wreck them.

"Screw the movie. At the end of the day, it's just entertainment. And screw Latham. He's a bastard. He always was. He always will be. All he cares about is his stinking cash. Somebody ought to tell him that."

Allison looked at him in horror. Maybe she didn't understand him after all. She had always thought he cared only about becoming a star. Now, he seemed to care more that Pat Parker shouldn't betray her ideals. Heavens! Had her pep talk been *that* successful? Perhaps the man she loved knew how to love after all. He had actually expressed a selfless emotion, or so it seemed. Well, if he wanted Pat Parker more than his name in lights, that was fine by her. It would just take some getting used to.

But their conversation was over.

"Look, it's the president," said new hot realtor Lori McGovern.

And it was.

President Fulton was pulling off a "low-key" entrance that was effortlessly high profile. He swept through the doors of the Getty on a wave of Secret Service men and he pumped hands and exchanged greetings with half a dozen potential campaign contributors en route to Alabama.

Alabama walked forward to greet him. Anyone else of his appearance would have been gunned down before he had taken another step. He looked far more sinister than an assassin, but he was the president's oldest friend.

"Alabama, my old buddy," said the president, arms open wide for the bear hug. Really powerful men knew the value of public admissions of friendship.

"Fred, Fred, it's good of you to come." Alabama didn't stand on formality. A Fred was a Fred, not a "Mr. President." He'd actually gone biking with Fred Fulton in the days when he'd owned an Indian, before he'd ever thought of politics as a career. They'd drunk beer together, and shared dreams of earning a living from photography. Even in those ancient days, they'd worried about the environment, way before it was cool to do so, and before there was much to worry about. Now old friends had come together in the face of a threat, in the greatest tradition of friendship. On the telephone, Alabama had laid it on the line. He had asked for help in the expectation of getting it, and he hadn't been disappointed. In the ordinary way, a billionaire like Latham would not be a man that even a president would want to cross. But this wasn't the ordinary way. The life or death of Alabama's mountains was at stake.

"Where are the photographs, Alabama? That's what I want to know. And what are we going to do about this guy who's trying to steal away our birthright?" Fulton liked to dramatize. His trumpet always sounded certain. That was why his followers won so many battles for him. He looked around the crowd, clustered about the Roman garden, and his words floated over them so that they would be in no doubt where he stood on this matter—shoulder to shoulder with Alabama. Fulton's finely tuned political antennae picked up the message that the crowd consisted mainly of Democrats. They were his people. Many of the stars had turned out for his campaign rallies. They would do the right thing. Or would they? After all, it wasn't a theme park that Latham was planning to build in the hills. It was a movie studio. It would be a potential source of work to people who could never get enough of that. To side against it would be to put ideals before career. It was a choice that film people found difficult to get right.

"Come on, I'll show you," said Alabama. He led the way through the parting crowd, the president in tow, and the Malibu celebrities trotting along behind. Excitement was mounting. Exhibitions usually contained few surprises. They were advertised, reviewed, and expounded upon until everyone knew exactly what to expect. This one, however, was surrounded by secrecy. The doors to the photography room had been locked for two days, and no one had the faintest idea of what was inside. Soon they would know.

The crowd surged through the Roman columns of the recreated Neapolitan villa into the marble-floored entrance vestibule. Following their leader, they filed up the stairs. The oak doors of the photography room were locked. A large key materialized in Alabama's hand. Now he opened them. He stood back, gesturing to the president to pass him. It was not a large room, and there were not many prints on its plain white walls. There didn't have to be. They were original Alabamas. The president looked around at his friend and smiled.

"Where should I start?" he said.

Alabama gestured to a nearby wall. The president walked up to the print. He stood back. He stood up close. He leaned in to savor the detail. He stood back once more. Alabama was at his shoulder. The president repeated the performance for five more prints in total silence. Then, at last, he turned toward Alabama. His eyes were alight with excitement. He opened his mouth to speak, but for once words failed the old campaigner. His hands were dragged in to the rescue. They splayed open. They fluttered, they hovered, they dropped back to his side in the gesture that said what was coming would be woefully inadequate.

"Never . . . never . . ." he mumbled, "have I seen such beautiful pictures. Is this . . . is this . . . the canyon that Latham is trying to destroy?"

Alabama nodded. Malibu leaned in to hear the great man's sentiments. They were not long in coming.

"Well," said the president of the United States, "he won't be allowed to, will he?"

Dick latham was late. He jumped from his car and he hurried across the gravel toward the doors of the Getty. Havers and a couple of lawyers scurried at his side. He was immaculate in a pin-striped white and dark gray worsted suit, and only the worried expression on his face hinted that all was not well with his world. It was instinct. Things had been too quiet out there, beyond the perimeter of the Latham Enterprises wagon train. Had the Indians been gathering in the silent darkness? Was this Getty Museum cocktail party/exhibition in the presence of the president the perfect place for an ambush? If so, he was prepared. He had brought his own law, not in the shape of six-guns, but in the form of their latter-day equivalent, a brace of shiny attorneys with the notches of rich court settlements on their butts. Whatever harsh words were said, they had better not be slanderous. There should be no hint of impropriety, and no veiled insinuations that anyone would attempt unduly to influence the zoning decisions of properly authorized agencies. Simple abuse he could deal with. It was water off a duck's back. All he cared about was winning. And the way things looked at the Coastal Commission, who had the power to give the final yes or no, he had as good as won. And yet, and yet . . .

The garden of the Getty opened up before him. He stopped. Apart from a few wandering waiters, it was deserted.

He grabbed the nearest one by the sleeve.

"Where is everyone?"

The waiter pointed. "Up there in the photography room, looking at the photographs," he said.

Dick Latham set off again at a furious pace. Damn! Why the hell hadn't he allowed for the PCH traffic and the added disruption of the President's motorcade? Everyone else had. It was a beginner's mistake in Malibu. Presumably the president was up there already. The shiny-suited hit men hanging about had "Secret Service" in neon on their chests. They watched him suspiciously but didn't approach. He'd passed the door check, and he looked vaguely familiar.

He clattered up the stairs. The line to the photography gallery snaked along the passageway.

"Hi, Dick," said the appalling Broad Beach agent who had once told Latham his party was a nonevent because Alabama hadn't showed. "Alabama's inside with the president." The bearded freak name-dropped loud and clear, and Malibuite Rich Little, standing a few feet behind, couldn't help mimicking him.

Latham fired himself toward the head of the line. He wasn't waiting for anyone. If things were being said behind his back, he wanted to hear what they were. He barged into the packed room, pushing ahead of Olivia Newton-John, who was far too polite and charming to object. There, he all but collided with Alabama.

He bounced back. Their eyes locked like the antlers of rutting stags.

"Tricky Dicky!" barked Alabama.

"Ben Alabama," countered Latham. He was off balance. He'd rehearsed this in his mind, but here was reality. Alabama looked as mean as ever. The difference was that this time he had good reason to be.

"You lied to me," said Alabama fiercely, between clenched teeth. It was the deep end. Before everybody who was anybody in Malibu, i.e., the entire movie industry, Latham was being publicly branded as a liar.

"I have attorneys here," said Latham coolly. "That's a slanderous defamation."

"That's the gospel truth," growled Alabama. "You told me you wanted that land to build a house on it, not a stinking studio."

"I changed my mind," said Latham.

"You're gonna have to change it back," said Alabama, leaning forward menacingly, his eyes small with his vast hatred.

"That's for the California Coastal Commission to decide," said Latham. He wasn't going to be bullied. If Alabama lost his temper, Latham would win. He looked to be on the verge of doing just that. He was acutely aware of the silence in the room. Everyone was catching every word of this. Hundreds of versions of the conversation would be circulating the Southland within the hour.

"That studio will go up over my dead body." Alabama's voice was quivering with scarcely suppressed anger.

"I hope not, but if that's what it takes . . ."

Latham smiled a tight smile. It was shifting his way. He could feel it.

"You always were a bastard, Latham. You haven't changed. You're still the same snot-nosed little rich kid you were in Paris. You think the world is one of your nursery toys that you can break if you wish, don't you? Well, it's our world too, and we're not going to let you touch it."

"Hello, Latham," said the president. He had materialized at the billionaire's elbow.

"Hello, Mr. President," said Dick Latham, wilting slightly at the production of the biggest gun of all.

The president smiled a threatening smile. His pseudofriendly manner was the most dangerous thing Latham had ever seen. He had met the guy three or four times before, and he'd never thought much of his leftist politics and folksy style, but he had never underestimated the toughness of the man. Fulton had a reputation for furthering his friends and burying his enemies. Latham's policy had been to steer clear of him and work for the future election of a Republican. But there was no avoiding him now.

Quickly he introduced Havers and his two legal eagles, managing to mention that they were attorneys. He saw the old boy's eyes narrow as they sensed the point he was making. Anything said now would be on public record. Words would have to be chosen carefully.

"Have you any idea what I've just seen?" said the president. He leaned forward, clearly expecting an answer to his impossible question. It was one of those maddening "Guess-what-I'm-thinking" interrogations to which pompous superiors subjected their inferiors. Latham hadn't a clue. A partridge in a pear tree? The beauty of holiness? The CIA file on Gorbachev's mistress?

"I don't know," he blurted into the silence. A mist of unreality was descending.

"I'll tell you," said the president as if to some small and willfully stupid child. "No, better than that, I'll show you." He reached out for Latham's arm and he gripped it firmly. Then he dragged him through the rapidly parting crowd to the wall of the room. "On these walls," boomed the president, "are some of the finest, most beautiful, most moving photographs I have ever seen in a life at least partially devoted to the study and practice of photography. These are not snaps. These are art. Fine art. The finest art I have ever seen. Look at them, Latham. You look at them."

Latham knew what was coming. He looked at the photographs with the enthusiasm he reserved for messes on roads. The beauty stared back at him. In the normal way it would have touched him, as it was supposed to. He had never seen the mountains look like that before. They were revealed. Before, he had seen them through the biblical glass darkly. Now, it was face-to-face. He recognized the canyon, of course. It was the Cosmos back-lot-to-be. The strong, silent photographs had accomplished an extraordinary feat. They had painted a gory red sign above his head . . . and it read ATTILA THE HUN.

"Well?" boomed the president.

Latham swallowed. The old fool might be a left-wing hooligan and a class enemy, but he was still America's leader. The power of his office was draped around him like an aura. There was an extent to which he *was* America, the country that Latham loved. He had to be answered. But how? He was aware of the Malibu crowd pressing around. Necks were craning, ears were flapping, tongues were preparing to wag.

"They're very good," he managed at last. His body had stopped. His lungs were still. His heart, if it was still pumping, was keeping a desperately low profile.

" 'Very good'? 'Very good'?" said the president in incredulous tones. "Damn it, man, you're planning to stick your movie studio slap bang in the middle of this beautiful canyon. These pictures actually *show* the damage you're going to do. And all you can say is 'They're very good.' What sort of a guy are you, Latham? Have you got a heart? Have you got a soul?"

The president was puffed up like a balloon. His eyes were staring. Latham could have sworn he was beginning to shake. It was an awesome sight. Fulton had wound himself up into one of his famous and much-feared furies. All that was needed now for stratospheric lift-off was a word—any word—from Dick Latham.

The Latham mind was starting up again. He had been lured into a trap. He had underestimated Alabama, and now the devious old buzzard had turned the tables on him. The photographs were a wonderful idea, but they were brilliant chiefly because they were so beautiful. They spoke directly to the gut. Intellectually, one might be for or against development in the hills. After seeing these prints, there was only one possible emotional verdict. Hell, Latham felt it himself. Still, he mustn't be beaten. He must never be defeated. This was business, and he had to win. Right now, what was needed was damage control. He fought to find the words that wouldn't blow the presidential fuse.

"The last word is with the California Coastal Commission . . ." he tried. It was as far as he got.

"The *Coastal* Commission . . ." sneered the president, his voice thick with amazement. "The Coastal Commission," he repeated, as if it were a hilarious joke. "Listen, Latham," he barked, "I carried California, and I didn't carry it small. California's my state. The people that make California work are my friends. Now, *you get this.* I can't influence a zoning decision. That would be improper. But no two-bit local bureaucrat who votes for your stinking studio in Alabama's mountains is ever going to end up a friend of mine. You hear what I'm saying? And another thing. I've got a state-of-the-union coming up and a press conference, and the environment's a hot issue, and you know how the media loves examples. Well, there wouldn't be a better one than Alabama's prints on blackboards around the room. And a mug shot of yours for good measure. How's that going to play at the newsstands where they sell your ink, Latham, and with the FCC, where they license your TV stations? You tell me that, Latham. You just tell me that."

But Dick Latham didn't want to tell the president how it would play. Dick Latham knew exactly how it would play. It would not play well. He was cool now. He was back on target in his mind. Cosmos was only a small part of his empire. Latham Enterprises itself could not be jeopardized. There was no telling where a thing like this could end. The president had done his homework, and he had slipped in a spine-chilling threat. He knew about the Chicago TV licenses. Latham, imagining a harmonious meeting, had actually been going to bring them up himself. Now it was crystal clear just what message would be whispered into the ear of Fulton's old chum who ran the FCC. It wouldn't have to be spelled out. Nothing incriminating would be said, but the net effect would be the murder of the Windy City cash cow that figured so prominently in the profit projections of Latham Enterprises. And the threatened presidential press conference would not be the happiest of moments. The editorials of his rival newspapers would tear him apart. So would the liberals who peopled the publishing industry. In the Park Avenue drawing rooms, the shoulders would be as cold as the buffets.

One thing was certain. To press ahead with his plans for Cosmos in the mountains would be criminally stupid. But even as he admitted that to himself, Latham knew that he couldn't give up. It was personal. It was him against Alabama. It was Latham locked in the infinite war with his father in the grave. Hell, he could fight the president. The old fart was hardly God. And he could survive the media and the loss of the Chicago deal. What was the point in having money if you couldn't afford to lose it to get your own way? His last words had been correct. It was down to the Coastal Commission. If they said yes, as still looked more than likely, he would get what he wanted after all.

He drew himself up. It was High Noon. He was facing the commander-in-chief, the most powerful man in the world, but he didn't flinch.

"I have listened to what you have said, Mr. President, and you must do what you must do. But it doesn't change my plans. History is full of those who have fought change and resisted progress. I don't intend to be one of them."

The president's eyes narrowed as he listened to the totally unexpected Latham response. The robber baron had taken his best shot, and he hadn't surrendered. That it was crazy didn't detract from the billionaire's courage. Fulton was the supreme political animal. He had used his temper. He had bullied and blustered to get his way. It hadn't worked. That meant losses must be cut. Presidential power and prestige must not be squandered in a squalid public slanging match. He turned on his heel without saying another word, and, surrounded by his entourage, he stalked from the room.

Alabama hadn't caught the last bit. He had left when the president was ahead and Latham on the ropes, because he had seen the face in the back of the crowd that he had wanted to see. He pushed through the people toward her, coming at her obliquely so that she would have no warning of his approach. As he did so, he palmed the Leica that swung from his belt. He wasn't worried. He knew it would be all right, but he had to hear it from her. He had to know that Pat Parker was on the side of the angels, was on *his* side. Three feet away from her, and behind her, he paused. He bent down and caught her in the viewfinder, angling for the best position as the computer in his mind calculated the light. Then he waited. She would have the portrait she had asked for, the one he had suggested she would flog for a Ferrari or was it peddle for a Porsche, the one she said she wanted for Tony Valentino. She was more beautiful than ever in the lens of the Leica, her proud head held high, the animated sparkle shining in her eyes. Something was making her smile. It reminded Alabama of the sun coming up over the mountain, and, as it broke around the edges of her mouth, he called out softly to her, "Pat!" She turned toward him as he had intended, and her smile deepened as she saw him and what he was doing. *Click!* There it was. A perfect portrait by the man who had rediscovered his art.

"Alabama, you've taken a photograph!" she said.

He laughed as he stood up, letting the Leica fall to his side.

"I've taken several," he said, throwing out his arm to the prints on the wall.

"I know," she said simply.

"You could tell they were new?" he said.

"I could tell. They're magnificent. They're totally different. They make me want to cry."

He laughed. She was the only person in the world apart from King who knew his secret, and the only one whose magic eye would have known for certain that these photographs were new, not old.

"You like them?"

"It's beyond 'like,' beyond love, Alabama." She reached out and touched him. "How did you do it? How did you break the block?"

"You helped. You softened me up. You told me the truth I hadn't dared to tell myself—that I was scared—that I was a coward. But Latham pushed the button. He had to be stopped. He still does."

He watched her closely. Decision time was near. They were pleased to see each other. For how long would pleasure last? Which way would it go?

Pat swallowed. She still hadn't decided. She was on the edge of the razor. There was Tony. There was Alabama. There was Latham and the movie she would direct, and there were the photographs of the mountains, haunting in their precarious loveliness, on the walls of the John Paul Getty Museum.

His eyes glinted. She didn't have long. It shouldn't be that difficult. The jury in her heart should need no extra time. Then, over her shoulder, Alabama saw him. Tony Valentino stood close, watching them, and Pat Parker had no idea that he was there.

"Where do you stand, Pat?" he said.

Pat took a deep breath. Even now she didn't know what she would say. She was about to find out.

"With you, Alabama," she said.

The relief flooded into his heart. He wanted to take her in his arms and bear-hug her until she cried for mercy. But before that, he wanted more. He wanted chapter and verse. He wanted it spelled out so that there could be no room for doubt, and no going back.

"You won't work for him? You'll give up the movie, and the *New Celebrity* thing?"

"Unless I can persuade him to drop his plans for Cosmos in Malibu."

"Latham might scrap the movie. Tony might not get his chance. You'd risk that?"

As he spoke, Alabama stared into Tony Valentino's eyes over Pat's shoulder. Tony's lasered back fiercely, giving no inkling of the feelings inside.

"Tony's talent will get him where he wants to go. He doesn't need my help," said Pat. Nor my hindrance, she thought. Had she betrayed him a second time? Could you betray people by doing the right thing? She tried to work out what she felt, but she couldn't. There was relief that the decision had been made, but it was balanced by anxiety about her suddenly so uncertain future. Her old job was gone. So, most probably, was her new one. And she had lost Tony forever. It was a stiff price to pay for virtue.

Alabama moved toward her, and she leaned into his embrace. That, at least, felt safe and good. It was wonderful to be back, in the base camp of his arms, after the no-man's-land of moral uncertainty.

"Let's go and tell Latham now," he said. "He can't stand up to all of us. We'll make him give in."

Over her shoulder, Tony's eyes still held his. Alabama smiled gently. Was his premonition correct? Time would tell.

He steered Pat through the stars to the place he had left Latham, impaled on the subtle spear of the president's threat. Now, he stood alone with his henchmen, shell-shocked and forlorn amid the fascinated crowd. The president was nowhere to be seen.

"Hello, Dick," said Pat.

He smiled wanly. "You, too?" he asked. He seemed to know.

"Give it up," she said. "It's bad. It's the wrong thing to do. Everyone can see that now. Alabama's shown them."

"I can't," he said. His eyes dropped from hers. He didn't seem angry, or even stubborn. It was as if his hands were tied by his past, by his personality, by all the forces that had shaped his extraordinary life.

"I can't work for you, Dick, if you do this. I can't work for *New Celebrity*. I can't even be your friend."

Did he shudder at the very last bit? Had that at least touched him?

"Whatever," he said.

The anger welled up in Pat. "Whatever"? Hell! "Why do you always have to play God, Dick Latham?" she exploded. "You'd be better off playing the little boy that deep down you are. You tear the wings off flies. You lie and you cheat and you steal to make miserable money when you've got an obscene amount of it already, and you make me *sick* with your pride and your power and your terrible emotional poverty. You ought to learn how to *care*, Dick Latham, because otherwise, nobody, but *nobody*, is ever going to love you."

"Hear, hear," said somebody in the crowd. It was Robert Redford. Dick Latham looked up and saw him. Redford had played the mountain man, Jeremiah Johnson, in a movie once, a character who looked a lot like Alabama. He had fallen in love with Utah and, through his Sundance Foundation, he worked harder to preserve the beauty of nature than he did at his career. Now, publicly, he had sided against Latham.

"Don't be a hick, Dick," said someone else. It was Martin Sheen, unofficial mayor of Malibu, and once the recipient of Latham's gentle scorn at his Broad Beach party light-years ago. He was the soul of the beachland, or at least its conscience. *He* knew how to care. He had given the world lessons in it.

The stars crowded in on him, pushing closer.

"If you do it, I'd never work for Cosmos," said Mel Gibson.

"None of us would," agreed Barbra Streisand. The chorus was taken up. "We won't work for you." "We won't work for you." It was becoming a chant. At the back of the crowd, arms began to sway in unison.

Dick Latham swallowed. There was a time and a tide in the affairs of man that, if taken at the ebb, led straight down the john. Such a time was now. Such a tide was surging all around him. Before him, plastered tight against him by the mass of stellar humanity, was the girl that he had come nearest to loving after the only true love of his life. The words of the president still reverberated in the air. The threat to his media empire still rang in his ears. Now, he had started a celebrity strike. The stars of Malibu were about to picket his studio. If he continued on his disastrous course, he would be risking everything he had ever created, and then Pat would be right. Nobody, not *anybody*, would ever love him.

He held up a hand, and the voice that sounded hardly seemed like his.

"It seems I have miscalculated," he said. "I have decided to withdraw all plans to build a studio in Malibu."

The howl of approval rent the air, as, slowly but surely, the anger started to form in Dick Latham. It burned softly at first, but then it burned brighter, and soon brightest, banishing his disappointment like the sun dissolving the marine mist from the midmorning Malibu shore. Alabama had won. He had lost. But he didn't have to like it. And the word that kept going round and round in his brain was *revenge*.

He pushed toward the exit, thrusting roughly at the crowd. He brushed past Alabama, whose face was alight with the smile of triumph, and Latham's voice was tight as a noose around the neck of a dangling man as he spoke. "I wonder if you'll ever take another photograph," he snarled.

Pat Parker watched him go, and the relief at his surrender was at war with the fear of what would happen now. She had blown her top, in public. Latham would never forgive her. From this moment on he would be her enemy. That frightened her, but it also saddened her. There was a part of Dick Latham she liked very much, perhaps too much. It was the part that reminded her of herself.

Suddenly, she wanted to get away from all the people. She didn't even want Alabama's congratulations. She didn't want to hear him crowing in triumph, because his victory was also her defeat. She wanted to be alone. She wanted to think, and to get things into perspective. She had to make plans. She had to adjust to the fact that her world had been turned upside down and that she had nobody to blame but herself. So she allowed herself to be sucked through the exit on the river of fame, and, in the corridor outside the photography room, she turned right when everyone else turned left toward the stairs. The sign on the door ahead said simply—PAINTINGS AND SCULPTURE —but the most important thing was that the gallery into which she walked was empty.

Or rather, it had been, because now it was full of her, and of the man who had followed her into it. She realized she was not alone when she heard four footsteps on the marble floor instead of two. She spun around. He stopped.

"Tony!"

He said nothing.

She stared helplessly at him. Would the recriminations and the accusations start now? Should she try some kind of explanation, some sort of apology? It was all too much, too soon. She felt drained, but she still cared—God, how she cared! She tried to read his expression. What was there on the face of the boy she loved? Would she ever know? Would it help to know? But his face was blank. Long and hard, he looked at her, the perfect mask of his expression hiding the mystery of his persona.

And then, quite suddenly, he began to smile.

The smile started like a spark of fire in the high chaparral. It caught from the corners of his mouth, and it spread inward and upward to engulf his lips, his eyes and his suddenly wrinkling forehead. Fanned by wind, it burned across his face, until the smile was a furnace, brighter than sunlight, warming Pat's heart with its radiant heat.

"Oh, Tony," she murmured, and she fell forward into his arms. He was ready for her. He caught her, and held her with a strength that said he would never let go. He hugged her to him, squeezing out the doubt and the pain, and she buried her head in his power, smelling the warmth of him, nestling down deep in the body she loved.

"It's over," he whispered. He meant the anger, the frustration, the bitterness.

"Is it starting? Is it beginning again?" she said softly, meaning their future, the union that would be their marriage, the eternity they would share. His eyes said yes.

For long seconds they were happy merely to be close after the long parting, but then their bodies began to stir. The greed was growing. Touching had made them hungry. She pulled her face from his chest, and she looked up at him through the tear mist that filled her eyes.

"Tony!"

His fingers ran through her hair, feverish in their hurry to experience her once more. His eyes roamed over her beauty, desperate to capture it forever. Then he drew her to him, and he bent toward her, and his lips rushed to her lips. In the cool gloom of the art temple, the kiss was their wedding ring, as their soundless mouths screamed the vows of faith. Their moisture merged. Their hard bodies clamped close. Their tongues lapped together. She clasped her hands around his waist and, in reply, he thrust his hips against hers, grinding into her. She felt him grow. She felt herself open. Bigger, wider, harder, softer, taller, wetter, oh dear, so very wet. Beneath her skirt, she was burning. Beneath his jeans, he was on fire. His leg forced itself between hers, and she bent down, half sitting on his thigh, rocking on it, hungry for friction. Her heart was hammering, her mind was roaring. She pushed against him, caressing his throbbing heat with her crotch, teasing it, urging him on, thrilled by the pounding blood that rushed next to the core of her. Her hands squeezed him in toward her. Her thigh jammed itself between his legs, and she swayed from side to side, rubbing him as her tongue searched the back of his throat, and her breasts flattened against his chest. Through the denim of his jeans she could feel the tip of him. Through the folds of her skirt, through the silk of her panties, he could feel the slicked velvet of her heartland. Molecules of material separated them. It was not enough. They had dared to reach a rhythm now. They danced in time to the music of lust, and they knew what they wanted. They wanted orgasm. Somehow that mattered more than anything else. In the crash of souls the past would be forgotten. Forgiveness, explanation, the hollow excuses—all the shallow, sullen tricks of words—would be rendered unnecessary by the shower of liquid flesh. Their new day would dawn in the glorious explosion of bodies. It was so very near. She held her breath as she tiptoed close to her conclusion. He was rigid on the edge of his. They clung together at the brink, determined to drown in each other. Closer, harder, they forced themselves together. They must be each other, become each other's skin and bone and blood. Later, their child would formalize their union. Now, there was only the promise of all the happiness to come.

~15~

THEY WANDERED BACK from the sea, savoring the fading heat of the late afternoon sun. The beach was quiet on the Malibu, a lazy, laid-back place of strollers, old friends and young lovers, and the surf washed the sand clean as the mountains watched and the birds wheeled in the powder blue of the sky.

She took his hand, and he squeezed hers, as they reached the steps. He stood back to let her past, and she walked up to the faded wooden terrace of the beach house, her long legs pointing to the hard perfection of her butt, and the strong slope of her back. He noticed her beauty, and he swallowed as he followed her.

She turned and smiled to show that she knew his thoughts, and she loved them, and then she walked across the balcony that separated the house from the beach, and she leaned over it, certain that he would join her there. For long seconds they said nothing.

"I couldn't forgive you, and I couldn't forget you," he said at last. They hadn't discussed this.

"And now?"

"It's moved on."

"What do you mean, 'moved on'?"

She smiled calmly. The language they both wanted was the language of bodies, not these words and sentences.

He laughed to show that he hardly knew what he meant, and that it didn't matter now.

"You were incredibly brave . . . with Latham. I've never seen a woman do that."

Again she smiled, in gratitude, in relief. She had done the hardest thing. So often, it was the right one.

"I thought he'd fire me, fire you, fire everyone. And then he calls me and says 'Nothing's changed.' I still can't believe it. What is he, a masochist or something?"

"Nobody ever told the bastard how to behave. No one ever cared about

227

him enough to bother. He respected you for what you did. *I* respect you for it."

"You do?"

"I said I did." Tony smiled lazily. Compliments didn't come easily to him. Repeating them was harder. He tried, as he had tried a hundred times, to work out why he had forgiven her, why her betrayal no longer mattered to him. Was it her incredible courage with Latham? Her decision to put Alabama's mountains before her career? Was it Allison, who had made him see that Pat really loved him?

"Did Allison speak to you about us?" said Pat, reading his thoughts.

"You mean, did she tell me what you told her to tell me? Yes, she did. She was word perfect. She believed you."

"Do *you* believe me?"

"Believe what?"

"Who's fishing now?" She reached over and poked him lightly on the brown skin of his forearm. "Believe that I love you," she added, her voice lower, husky.

"*Do* you love me?"

"Yes. Very much. Very, very much. I never stopped." She looked into his eyes.

"In your fashion." He was beginning to understand that Pat and he loved in a different way from everyone else.

"In our fashion." She realized that, too.

Her eyes probed hungrily into his.

It was almost time, but there was something she wanted to do first.

"Hey, I've got a present for you," she said as if she had just remembered it.

She walked to the edge of the terrace and picked up the photograph from beneath the shirt that had covered it. She handed it to him.

"Alabama took it yesterday at the Getty," she said. "He sent it over this morning. I want you to have it."

He looked down at the photograph, then back at her, then once more at the image of her.

"It's beautiful," he said. "There's only one thing in the world I want more than this." He laid down the photograph.

"What?" she whispered.

"You."

He smiled a slow, easy smile. The current was running. He played with her fingers as they reached for his. He ran his hand gently across them, as if he had never felt them before. Her shoulder was heavy on him, and she leaned over and lay her head against the side of his neck, nestling there, warm and wanting. He breathed her in, the sweet aroma of her merging with the salt breeze, with the subtle scent of sun oil from bathers on the beach. Then he bent down until his head was against hers, and for long seconds they were content to be close as the surf crashed on the sand beneath them and the gulls wheeled in the sky above. Waves of alien tenderness coursed

through him. The pulse of total love beat within her. They were more together than ever.

"Tony," she whispered. "Tony . . ." But he put his finger to her lips,
telling her that this was no time for words. Her uneven sigh hurried past his
fingers. He could feel her breath, heavy with its message of desire. Inside, he
knew her heart would be in time with his, rapping out the dangerous drum
riff of body purpose and flesh longing. Her eyes were languid—wide and
willful as they laid bare her dreams. She longed for him. She would have
what she wanted.

They drifted into the kiss. Mouths open, tongues so ready, they fell
toward it. Nuzzling at dry lips, they were content to wait for wetness in the
luxury of so-slow love. They bit at each other with all the world's tenderness,
their teeth roaming over the vulnerable skin. Then their hands were allies,
reaching for each other's heads to fine-tune the passion. Their fingers en-
twined in each other's hair, rubbing, pushing, pulling to make the magic
grow. Malibu went away, the beach beauty receding into a backdrop of beige
and blue. Now it existed only to frame them, and, in the forefront of the
photograph, they breathed their love into each other's mouths.

They clung together. Their hands had become arms, and already their soft
bodies were tensing as they feared to lose the moment they had. Rougher
now, they tied each other tight in ropes of limbs, and the delicate kiss was
already hungry, greedy for more, determined to have it. They dived into the
sea of lust, refreshed by the abundant wetness, as the liquid intimacy swallowed them. Tongue on tongue, they swayed together. Hip to hip, they
shared the hardness. Souls on fire, they trembled at the gates of ecstasy.

He pushed her away, and she allowed the parting because she knew what
it promised. He led her back from the sun's glare into the darkness of the
house, and she went like the willing victim of a pagan sacrifice. In the gloom
at the back of the room, he stopped, turning once more to face her. He
reached out and unbuttoned her shirt. He watched her closely, savoring
every nuance of expression as she stood so still, so passive, at the mercy of his
unhurried fingers. He peeled back the cotton shirt, and her breasts stood
there, humble in their defenseless beauty. He touched them, to show he
owned them, and his hands were the masterful hands of the general inspecting the spoils of victory. He cupped her breasts. He held her nipples between his forefinger and thumb. He ran an insolent finger up the gentle
slope of their curvature, down the underside, where they sprang vertically
from the hot skin of her torso. These are mine, said his gestures. These are a
piece of the property that you have sold to me. You have no rights anymore,
apart from the right to give pleasure, and the right to receive it. She shuddered with delicious acquiescence. Her breasts trembled beneath his touch.
Her chest heaved with the effort of breathing, as her blood surged in the
adrenaline high.

His hands dropped lower, to the belt of her blue jeans. He undid it.
Gently but firmly, he lowered her pants. She didn't help him. He didn't want
her to. She moaned as the material slipped below her butt, and she looked

down past her bare stomach to the silk panties. She was ashamed that they were already wet in front, and yet she was pleased too, because he'd done that. It was his fault. The spring of lust and love that spilled from her was his creation as much as hers. So was the heady scent of her musk that wrapped them both in the cocoon of intimacy. Her upper body was still tented by the shirt. Her lower legs were still clothed by her jeans, but the heart of her was now nearly revealed. Its damp warmth was on the silken surface of the bikini briefs, exposing the guilty secret of the throbbing core it covered.

He reached into the elastic of her panties. He pulled them down, until they were buried in the rumpled denim that veiled her upper thighs. His hand hovered near to her, basking in her radiant heat, tantalizing the glistening down beneath it. Her love lips shone in the triangle, coral pink, gleaming in the slippery ocean of lust. They were so shy, so beautiful, so desperately in need of his touch. Again she moaned on the edge of abandonment, and she pushed out, her hips moving millimeters toward him in the gesture of surrender. Her body was pleading for his, yet still he held back, knowing that every millisecond of joy postponed would multiply a hundredfold in the bliss to come. His hand crept closer. It touched the soft, soaked hair, withdrew, touched it once more. He stared into her eyes, and she nodded the permission he didn't need. Again she moved out at him, more insistent now, as shame faded into the urgency of desire.

He lay the flat of his palm against her. She groaned her pleasure at him, throwing back her head and showing him her long, white neck. He massaged the abundant wetness, and she rubbed herself against his hand, loving it, demanding more. Gently, he explored the brink of her, hooking his finger into the edge of the silken opening, laying it back, pushing in deeper. She bent down at the knee, following his finger, as if trying to capture it inside her, encouraging it to explore further the secret parts of her that belonged to him and always would. In answer, he moved higher, until his fingers rested on the place that had become the center of her body. Reverently, he moved against it, exploding the stars in her mind.

"Oooooooh," she moaned as he milked the ecstasy from her. Her legs were weak. Her knees buckled. Her whole body pivoted around the pleasure source. The sweat sprang from her upper lip, trickled in drops around her breasts, stood out in a sheen of passion around her tense nipples. Still he moved against her mystery. He seemed to know the privacy of her. He was roaming across her body, unlocking its forbidden places. He had keys to all the doors. Already, he had stolen her heart. Now he was taking the rest of her.

Her hands reached for him. She must have more than this. She must have all of him now. She reached for his jeans, but he stopped her. There would be only one leader, only one led. His hands were on her shoulders. He guided her backward toward the sofa, and she sat down, half losing her balance, falling back across the cushions. Her legs splayed open. She was pleading with him to take her, fast, hard, as cruelly as he wanted, as cruelly as *she* wanted in the desperate limbo in which he had left her. He stood over her, staring in awe at her conquered body. The smile of longing played across her lips, and danced in her wondering eyes. Her hand reached for her nipple. The other moved between her legs. In the full frontal power of his gaze, her finger slipped inside. She was daring him. She was showing him what she wanted. He must do this, or she would. It had to be done. There could be only one escape from the steam pressure that filled her body. Release must come. He had to understand that.

For long seconds Tony Valentino left her alone on the plane of her longing. Joined only by eyes, their need grew. She could see the might of him expand. She could see his passion pounding and throbbing. Please, her eyes asked. Do it now. However you want to. I exist for you. I have no other purpose.

He reached for his belt. He undid it. He flicked open the buttons of his 501's. He was free. He slipped out of his jeans and shorts and walked toward her. He knelt beneath her open legs and rested his hands on her thighs. She eased herself down toward him, tears of love misting up her eyes. He rose up to meet her, and they slid into each other, each in their natural home at last, joined together, as they were meant to be.

"I love you, Pat," he murmured.

"Always love me," she whispered back.

EMMA GUINNESS dropped the microphone between her breasts. It disappeared, and for a second she wondered if she would ever find it again. Thank God for the wire it was attached to. She peered into the mirror. Nothing showed—neither the hidden microphone already warming up in her cleavage, nor the angst in her mind. In half an hour she would be having dinner with Dick Latham, the target in which she'd once dreamed of being embedded. Days ago, marriage had existed as a distant possibility in her imagination. It existed there no longer. Latham had humiliated her in public, before a rival, before Pat Parker, her employee, and the Guinness world had turned nasty. From that moment on, she had changed. She had surrendered to her darkest dreams. Now, the world that specialized in plaguing her was about to find out that when the going got tough, the clever got evil.

She picked up a bottle of Paloma Picasso and splashed it over her shoulders. Damn! She was already beginning to sweat through the Dior underarm deodorant. It took super glue to block her armpit pores when the Wagner was tuning up. She picked up the belt with its Velcro attachment and its little pouch. The Pearlcorder nestled inside. She attached the jack plug to the microphone socket and bundled up the spare wire, tucking it into the belt. The high-tech industrial counterespionage shop off Grosvenor Square had been quite specific. The recording device was voice activated. Running time on the super-long-play tape was three hours. If a mouse farted during dinner, it would be captured for posterity in quadraphonic sound. She smiled a vicious smile. She had played this game before in the old *Class* days and Victoria Brougham had bitten the dust as a result. Even now she could see the hatchet-faced bitch doing her takeoff on the owner's North Country accent. She'd sat in the chair, legs apart, knickers showing, in the English upper-class way, and she'd looked like a milk-laden Guernsey in a wet field, as she'd bad-mouthed her employer and social inferior with the earthshattering arrogance of her species. Emma's hidden Phillips recorder had caught it for posterity. Things were better now. These days, she could afford a state-of-the-art Olympus for her electronic eavesdropping.

Her smile broadened. It was quite possible that nothing would come from the dinner-table conversation. But the harder she worked, the luckier she got. The prepared mind was chance's friend. One fine day, if she was ready for it, the words would be dropped that would change her future. She pressed RECORD. "One. Two. Three. Testing. I hate you all." She said it softly. "I hate you all." She repeated it loudly. "I HATE YOU ALL." She pushed the rewind button, and then the replay, and her smile was Cheshire cat wide as the recorder repeated her truth. She looked at her watch. Dinner was at eight. Drinks on the sand first. She must hurry. What the hell should she wear?

She waddled to the closet, blissfully unaware of the mirror's view of her copious rear, her dumpy legs, her bull neck. She sighed. There wasn't a cheap dress in there. The labels were cutting-edge trend. Nearly all of them had appeared on slinky models in the better glossies. But as she looked them over, she knew that on her they would fail. Over the years she had tried to analyze it. She'd never succeeded. Was it her shape, her deportment, the awkward way she moved? Perhaps it was her skin, her personality, the pheromones she gave off. Maybe it was simply that her aura clashed with clothes, although to be frank she didn't look right when she was naked either. Again she sighed, as she reached at random into the dress rack. The Bruce Oldfield number she pulled out looked a dream on Princess Di. The flowers that bloom in the spring, tra! la!—light, summery, frothy as a well-timed soufflé. Pah! On her, it would look like an over-the-top floral tribute at a nouveau riche crematorium.

She climbed into it, as she would a turnip field in winter. She ripped up the zipper, breathing out as she did so, and she smoothed down the protesting silk, before resuming normal lung activity. Good! Nothing had actually torn, although it was far too tight. She'd been eating for comfort and putting on weight. It wasn't hard to do in America, where the major addiction was sugar, and where sweet things tasted best. The tape recorder bulged noticeably. She rooted around for some kind of a shawl. The sun had gone down. The Malibu evening would be cool. She might look a trifle dowdy, but that wasn't the point. Dick Latham had already had his last shot at her.

She was ready. In her mind she ran through a list of possible subjects for blackmail. Anything to do with tax would be promising. Rich people couldn't bear paying those. "Only the little people pay taxes," Leona Helmsley had said. If she could trick Latham into revealing a Swiss bank account, a Liechtensteinian company, or something shady in a sunny place like the Caymans, she would be on a winner to nothing. Then there were all the run-of-the-mill billionaire crimes—like parking, stock manipulation, insider trading, breach of fiduciary trust, and more exotic peccadilloes like antitrust shenanigans, illegal campaign contributions, bribes to foreign governments. It wouldn't be easy. Latham was an American, not a loose-lipped European, who would trade any secret for an easy laugh. It would help if she could get him pissed. Again that would be no problem back in the old country, where nondrinkers were regarded with the suspicion reserved for acquaintances who called you by your first name.

Once more, she checked the inventory in the mirror. Did she look like a spy? No. She looked like a sack of potatoes that some lazy sod of a gardener had left in the flower bed. The hell with it! She was ready for dinner. Dick Latham, Pat Parker, and Tony Valentino had better watch out. Their guts would be her garters as she danced on their graves.

—

"I'M NOT taking any more calls. I don't care who the hell it is. Do you understand? The Speaker, the governor, especially not the president, okay? I'm out. I'm taking a meeting. I'm dead. Tell 'em whatever you like, but don't bother me with it."

Dick Latham slammed the telephone down, and thrust out his glass toward Havers. "Fix me another scotch," he barked.

Havers hurried to obey. He had never seen Latham like this. The guy was on fire with rage. He could all but see the smoke pouring out of his ears. And he was drinking. This was his third in the half hour that Havers had been in his office. He had good reason. The moment he had gotten home from the Getty the evening before, the storm had broken. The telephone was ringing off the hook. The courier vans were lined up on Broad Beach Road. The press were beginning to gather like vultures on the sand. Already there were a couple of live TV vans parked outside, and one of them was CNN. Alabama's photographs had exploded into the consciousness of the country's opinion makers with the force of a nuclear blast. All three network breakfast shows were clamoring for an interview with the would-be environmental rapist, and recently the calls had become more sinister. The bankers had started appearing on the line. Their tones carefully couched in lawyerly financial-speak, they had said one thing and meant another. They were worried, not by anything specific, but just worried in the way that perennially anxious people were when anything abnormal occurred. The Latham PR machine had moved smoothly into damage-control mode. Already some underling had been accused of masterminding the "Cosmos in Malibu" idea and had dutifully fallen on his sword.

Latham himself had televised a two-minute segment that was being made available nationally in which he had reassured everyone that the hills would not be touched. In a gesture of good faith, he had decided to give his entire mountain land holding to the Santa Monica Mountain Preservation Trust. They would be park lands forever—nature and horse trails for the people to enjoy. He personally apologized to everyone he had upset, and particularly to Alabama, the grand old man of the mountains, whose vigilance and artistic genius had narrowly averted environmental tragedy. Latham admitted with all the considerable charm at his disposal that the buck stopped with him. He took personal responsibility for the near disaster. Yet, at the same time, he managed to insinuate that this had been a lower-echelon decision made by lesser mortals who had been prevented in the most final way possible from making the same mistake again.

He grabbed the glass from Havers and gulped at it.

"Jesus, Tommy. All these years of image building. All the work and the contacts. All the crap from the politicos, the payola, and the pretense, and now, at a stroke, I'm public enemy number one. This is going to cost us, believe me. Licenses, circulation, subscriptions, God knows how much influence. That broken-down old idiot up in the mountains has bent my business."

"It'll blow over," said Havers. "It's bad now, but people forget. A week, a month, and it's history. We've contained it. We were fast with the response. We've given something away, admitted we were wrong, had the balls to do that. It could even turn into a plus. You know . . . we're open, we're responsible, we don't cover things up like the oil boys and the chemical companies. We make our mistakes and we pay for them . . ." He petered out. From the fire in the Latham eyes he could see he was not making his point.

"Don't *give* me that bullshit," exploded Latham, sucking greedily on his Glenfiddich. "He's cost me. A hundred million. Maybe two. He's turned me into Slippery Sam. I'm in there with the toxic wasters, the polluters, all the cheap hustlers and scammers who'd sell their mothers to turn a buck they don't need. Me! Dick Latham! Shit, Havers, yesterday morning I was a *gentleman*. What do you think I am now? An untouchable. A zombie, creeping around under stones with the rest of the social undead. My father will be laughing in his grave . . ."

Dick Latham had gone pale. The thought of his father had done it. He white-knuckled his fist around the cut glass of the tumbler. His hand began to shake. He stared, his eyes unseeing, through Tommy Havers. Somewhere down deep in the fires of hell, his father would be chuckling at his misfortune. All the billions, all the success, all the power, and still he could be thwarted by a mere mortal while his father gloated, the father who had made him what he was . . .

"I want Alabama wiped out," said Dick Latham, his voice shaking with hatred. "Whatever it takes. I want him ruined."

Havers looked doubtful. "I'm not sure it would be wise to move against him now. Perhaps later. Right now, he could finger you. It could upset a delicate situation. The spotlight's on us. Anything we do will be noticed."

Dick Latham nodded. In the midst of his fury, in the woozy booze mist that was beginning to fog his mind, he could see that Havers was making sense. There was a time and a tide for revenge as well as fortune. It wasn't now. It would be later.

"Do you want me to stay here for a day or two?"

"No," said Latham. "Get back to New York. Life's got to go on." Through the red haze of anger, the thought occurred to him. Did Alabama's life really have to go on? Would the crusty old scarecrow live forever to enjoy the memory of the time he'd bested the billionaire? Was it possible for Malibu to contain the two of them?

"Okay," said a relieved Havers, nervously looking at Latham's scotch. He hadn't seen his boss drink like this before. His words weren't slurred yet, and for sure he wasn't stumbling about, but there was a wild look in his usually calm eyes. There was electricity in the evening air, a contained desperation, that Havers, who didn't usually vibe in on such things, found deeply disturbing.

"You're sure you don't need me to take some of the heat?" he added.

"Meaning I can't?" snarled Latham.

He turned on Havers like a wolf at bay. The steam that had been building inside was coming out.

"No, Dick, of course I didn't mean that. I just meant—"

"I don't care what the hell you mean, Havers. Just go, okay? Earn the money I pay you."

Doormats didn't like to be walked on. Luckily they didn't possess voices that could frame complaints.

Havers hurried from the room. For the first time in his life he actually felt sorry for Emma Guinness. She was going to have the nastiest evening of her life so far.

—

DICK LATHAM exploded onto the terrace. Emma Guinness was there already. She turned to greet him.

"Oh, do look, Dick, there's a seal out there in the shallows. I haven't seen one before . . ." Across her face was a girlish smile as she posed awkwardly in the unaccustomed role of nature lover.

"Fuck seals," said Dick Latham. His momentum carried him toward the drink tray that the butler had laid out. He grabbed the Glenfiddich by the neck as if about to strangle it, and "freshened up" a drink that was way too fresh already.

Emma Guinness watched him. She could see he was drunk.

"Bad day?" she attempted.

Dick Latham let out a kind of growl as he pressed the cutglass tumbler to his lips. He swallowed a mouthful of malt whiskey.

"Have you any *idea* what has happened today?" The words held together, but their emphasis was unusual, and their unnatural definition told the truth about the Latham mental state. He was zoned. He was also furious.

Emma took a deep breath and the hidden microphone rubbed against the clammy flesh of her cleavage. She aimed herself at him like a reporter on "Eyewitness News." Her tape recorder wanted to know *exactly* what had happened to the billionaire's day.

"I gather there's a certain amount of fallout from Alabama's counterattack on the Cosmos thing," said Emma.

"Do you limeys still think understatement is cute?" rasped Latham. "The bastard has screwed me." He spat out the words as if they would exorcise ghosts. They were thick with disbelief. He'd been screwed at last. Through all the deals, the wheels, and the haute finance, it had finally happened. The shafter had been shafted by a broken-down old man of the woods, who wouldn't know a leveraged buyout from a discounted Third World loan. Jesus! Was this the turning point? Was this the moment when the sweet turned sour, when the harmony became discord, when the long march up the mountain turned into the head-over-heels descent down the other side?

"You mean you're going to have to build Cosmos somewhere else? Is that the end of the world?"

Emma was living dangerously. Her gut told her to.

"It's not the point. It's not the point," shouted Latham, his voice pitched curiously high. "I was made to look like a fool. The president of the United States actually threatened me. Can you believe it? . . . The *president* talked to me like I was a child of ten. Just about every movie star in America lined up to dump on me . . . and all I'd done was gone to the Getty to look at some dreary photographs because I thought it was a Malibu thing to do." An intense feeling of unreality was gripping Dick Latham. It was like an appalling dream.

"What did the president say?"

The tape was listening.

"Who *cares* what he said? It's what he made me do. It's what that scumbag Alabama's made me do. He's wrecked my plans. *My* plans. My *plans*." The outrage was everywhere. It hung in the cool night breeze. It scurried around on the dunes of the beach. Out there in the shallows, the seals would be sharing it. Nobody crossed Dick Latham. It was what the billions were for. It was the sole and simple reason for their presence in the world. But how could he revenge himself on Alabama? He couldn't sell the old biker's stock short. He couldn't bamboozle his bankers and pull the rug from the bottom of his debt pyramid. Alabama was outside and above Latham's financial world, and he was beyond the reach of his media one. He had never envied the Mafia before. They might never be able to spend the riches they possessed; might never do more than eat their wife's spaghetti in some tract home in Miami; might never graduate past platinum-plated playmates and heartless, low-end tarts; but by God, they could enjoy their revenge. They had people who would kill for them. They had minions who enjoyed it. They had people who specialized in providing genuine unpleasantness for their victims before the merciful release of death. All it took was an oblique word, a packet of petty cash, a cryptic call to some psychopathic hit man in the dark, and the deed was done. And what could Latham drum up in the revenge department? A gaggle of lily-livered lawyers who actually believed the brazen lie that the pen was mightier than the sword; a shrill of silver-tongued leader writers whose words would end up lining drawers if they were lucky; a drink-soddened circus of talk-show rent-a-mouths bleating on to an anesthetized TV audience with a nanosecond attention span and a couch-potato world view. It wasn't good enough. It was a disaster. The man who had everything couldn't afford to buy his enemies a really bad time.

"It's amazing that some broken-down old fart like that can have such an impact," said Emma, showing solidarity as she tried to loosen up his tongue.

He slumped down on the beach chair, and some of the scotch slurped out of the glass onto the white linen of his pants. "I'd like to kill him," he said suddenly. "Maybe I will."

The drink was talking, but the recorder didn't know that. It didn't have eyes. It only had ears.

Emma laughed softly. Inside, her heart was singing. She'd never expected this. Latham, Mr. Tight Lips himself, was running off at the mouth, and the magnetic tape between her tits was eating his words.

"I think I'll have a gin and tonic," said Emma cunningly, walking to the drinks tray. Drinking encouraged drinking. With her back toward Latham, she poured a tiny measure of Tanqueray into the bottom of a glass and filled it up with Schweppes. She turned around, sipping at it, and screwed up her face in an expression that said "strong." She smiled ruefully to show that she could never get measures right. Then she slid across the terrace and sat down next to him. The Pearlcorder could have nailed him at fifty feet. Half a dozen were safer.

"Where are you taking me to dinner?" she asked in what she hoped was a disarming, little girl voice.

"Dinner?" said Latham. "Oh, La Scala," he mumbled.

His glass was empty. He was feeling a bit better. Evil, but better. Grandiloquence was expanding inside him. The Mafia did it, and who the hell were they compared to Dick Latham? They were two-bit hustlers with funny names and ugly faces who would never smell the Rose Garden, or get to be threatened in front of superstars by the president in the John Paul Getty Museum. They were outsiders compared to him, small-change artists who wouldn't rate a halfway decent table at Mortons, Le Cirque, or San Lorenzo in London. They slipped and slid around the bottomland amid the ooze and the slime, and nickels and dimes could buy and sell them. Okay, so he'd never before attempted serious revenge, but it wasn't too late to learn. Nothing was. Leveraged buyouts had been Swahili to him a year or two back, yet he'd financed a couple of the bigger ones through the boys at Kohlberg, Kravis. If he could handle a heavy-duty LBO, he could pass some pain Alabama's way. He merely had to turn the might of his mind to it, and the job was done.

"Can I get you another drink?" asked Emma.

He stuck out his glass to her, saying nothing. She was an employee. As such, she was roach slime. From now on, the people who worked for him were going to have to learn a few serious things about loyalty. If they wanted to bask in the stellar rays that shone from him, they would have to start striking Faustian devil deals. When he said "Jump!" the traditional "How high?" response would no longer be enough. In the future he would be looking for an "Off which cliff?" type reply. He wanted Henry II's knights drawing his paychecks, the kind of people who weren't averse to a little murder in the cathedral if that was the whim of his day. Yeah, Alabama was a sort of souped-up California-style Thomas à Becket—a tough cookie on a morality jag and a collision course with a king. The more he thought about it, the more he liked it. He was feeling much better. He was feeling pretty good. Hell, he was feeling fantastic. What he needed was another Glenfiddich, and forget the rocks.

Emma upended the scotch. She'd already established her reputation for pouring outsize drinks. She didn't blow it now. The caramel-colored booze was way past finger measurement. It looked like a long drink. She spirited it toward the wobbling Latham hand. He embraced it as if it were an antidote for poison. Perhaps it was.

"Will we be taking a driver?" she asked. "If you didn't want to bother with one, I could drive you."

Latham didn't answer at first. He was drinking and thinking. Would Havers kill for him? Could he ask him? He laughed bitterly. Havers would happily falsify a tax return, handle an inside trade; he'd even live dangerously and bribe the odd official, but that was all. No, if the walk was to be on the wild side, he'd have to discover some cats that were at home in the dark. But he had no idea where to look. His money had insulated him from foul people and kept his hands squeaky clean. Now, when he wanted to dirty them, the billions were an obstacle. Once again, the gloom cloud began to descend. He drank deep to keep it at bay.

"We'll take a driver. Always take a driver," he mumbled. "Let's go. I'm fed up with sitting here on this goddamn beach."

He stood up too suddenly. He staggered. He righted himself. A fatuous smile played around his lips. He picked up a telephone.

"Is the car waiting?" He slammed it down. "Okay, we're outta here," he said. He was conscious as he spoke that he was trying to sound like a gangster.

He stalked through the house, ignoring the butler, the maids, and the chauffeur who loitered in the courtyard inside the front door.

"La Scala," he barked rudely as he passed the gray-uniformed driver.

Outside, he climbed into the navy-blue Rolls-Royce with the discreet R.L. painted in dark red on the front door. He pushed into the back. There was no nonsense about ladies first. Emma piled in next to him. The door clunked shut. In seconds they were nosing out onto Pacific Coast Highway by the Trancas Restaurant.

"What's that place like?" said Emma in bright conversational tones. She could relax. The Pearlcorder was going to get an earful tonight. There was no hurry.

"Cowboys and rock 'n' rollers. It's about as rough and tough as Malibu gets." Rough and tough. It was how he felt. It was how he wanted to be. It reminded him of Paris. He'd felt like this then, when women had taken the brunt of his aggression. Alabama floated back into the gunsight of his mind. Right now he would be up there in the hills, gloating and guzzling beer. He'd be reading the articles, catching the afterburn of his victory via his satellite dish, taking the calls from all the weak-kneed, bleeding-heart lefties who cared so desperately about nature from their high-rise condos in Metropolis. He pressed the button that wound the window down. Lights blazed from the Malibu Cove Colony beach houses, the surf crashed against the sand of Escondido Creek, the lazy breeze melded with the smell of tiptop leather. It was a perfect evening in Malibu. The Santa Anas were blowing, and the night was sultry, here by the ocean, the freshness of the salt air merging seductively with the hot, dry wind from the Mojave Desert. At moments like these, Malibu was heaven. But the drumbeats of Hades, deep and insistent, were already throbbing in Dick Latham's drink-sodden mind.

The Rolls purred sedately on, oblivious to the hatred it harbored in its bowels. The moonbeams were bright on the water by the side of the highway, and the lights of fishing boats shone on the horizon. They passed Pepperdine, snug and smug against the dark outlines of the hills. They made the left at Cross Creek, and the sleek car eased itself toward the restaurant lot, through the knots of late pizza-filled surfers, the wandering lovers, and all the other clever people who knew that late-summer Malibu was where God would choose to spend his vacation.

At La Scala they were ready for them. Jean, the son of the owner and the maître d', was hovering at the lectern as Dick Latham stumbled through the door. Emma followed in his wake.

"A very great pleasure to see you again, sir."

At La Scala, there was nothing they didn't know about status. Latham was up there in the rarefied air where Marvin Davis lived. So what if he'd just been forced to climb down on his studio location? He was still a social ten in Malibu, and anywhere else, for that matter. The best table was in the window overlooking the Serra Retreat. They headed there now. On every side, conversations quieted.

As they crossed the restaurant, a table to their right looked as if it was occupied by several different species of rat. There was a large albino, a very common brown, and a couple of mongrels. The whitest one of all said, quite clearly, "Alabama."

Latham stopped in his tracks. He twirled around, losing the maître d', who sailed on oblivious to the fact that he had lost his valuable convoy. He stalked over to the table, and its occupants looked up expectantly. Surely not. This was too good to be true. They were about to receive a megabuck table hop. If so, stock would rise; points would be scored. They exchanged glances. Which one of their number had been secretly harboring a billionaire acquaintance?

Latham hovered over the table like an avenging angel. Emma stood behind him. "Who mentioned Alabama?" he growled.

The rats exchanged furtive glances. This was not to be a friendly meeting. This was a visit from the exterminator. They said nothing. The brown rat managed a nervous laugh. If an effusive greeting from Latham was money in the bank, to be publicly insulted by him was negative cash flow. The snow-white rat who'd condensed the Alabama/Latham/Cosmos story for the table went a whiter shade of pale.

Latham's furious eyes twirled like tank turrets. He was way past sense. It never occurred to him that these guys might be developers who wanted the Alabamas of this world buried as badly as he did. That wasn't what his gut said. Paranoia was striking deep. The universe that had existed as his personal plunder ground now seemed peopled exclusively by enemies. This was the new Dick Latham. This was Danger Man and Captain Power, the guy the wise didn't mess with if they wanted to stay healthy. It was a brave new cosmos of blood and twisted bodies, of concrete overcoats and offers that couldn't be refused. That it existed only in his drunken fantasy was unimportant. The unreal could be made real. In Southern California it happened all the time.

"You can tell your friend Alabama," he hissed, bending over the table like a tree on a blasted heath, "that he hasn't got long to enjoy his minimouse victory. Tell him that Dick Latham personally guarantees it. You got that? Personally. I guarantee it." The delusions of omnipotence swirled in the Latham psyche, swimming free in the malt whiskey sea. He felt like a god. He could cast thunderbolts down from the sky. He could wipe out lesser mortals with a flick of his fingers. It was no longer a question of how. It had become a question of when.

The maître d', reaching the empty Latham table, turned to discover the disaster that was unfolding at his rear. The tourists from Vegas and his star customer were on a collision course. He darted back to avert tragedy. He grabbed the Latham arm and tugged deferentially at it. He hadn't realized that Latham was wasted. He hadn't ever been before. On previous visits to the restaurant, his cool had dropped the room temperature a couple of notches.

Dick Latham shook off the man's hand. He had said his piece. The law had been laid down. Everyone knew where he stood. What he needed now was a drink. He allowed himself to be steered to the table.

"Bring me a bottle of single-malt scotch," he said as he sat down in the window to the hum of reanimated conversation.

Emma eased herself onto the banquette opposite. Food should be kept to a minimum if the Latham stream of consciousness was to be kept flowing. She made a mental note of what she had gotten so far. Threats. Violent, public threats against Alabama. It was titillating, but words were cheap. In bars from the redwood forest to the Gulf Stream waters, macho Marlboro men were mouthing similar promises they wouldn't have the nuts to keep.

The pretty waitress came back to wonder if Famous Grouse, a blended rather than a single malt, would do. Latham was past the connoisseur stage. He nodded curtly, and in a minute or two he was back in whiskeyland.

"I think we'll need a little time for the menu," said Emma to the waitress. She gave a conspiratorial smile that said she knew her date was zoned, but that she could handle it.

She looked around. The faces were out in force. Neil Diamond was dining with his realtor Carol Rapf, spirit of the Malibu, doubtless celebrating the sale of his Colony home for $5.6 million cash to buyers who'd closed escrow in an unheard-of twenty-four hours. Rob Lowe, Mr. Midnight Blue, was eating with another realtor, the spectacular-looking Betty Graham. Was Mr. Clean turned Mr. Dirty thinking of trading places? Up or down would be the question. Farther along the prime-table line, Batman Jon Peters, former hairdresser, Streisand friend, and now Hollywood's most powerful producer, held hands with a beautiful actress.

Dick Latham slumped like an oily rag against the banquette, nursing the glass in his lap. His unseeing eyes stared out across the creek and up toward the Serra houses, their lights twinkling in the darkness. He knew he was drunk, but he didn't know the significance of it. Drink melted insight, and he didn't realize that the strange thoughts that ebbed and flowed within him were an ethanol production. All he knew was that he felt alternately powerful and impotent. The scotch seemed to keep him positive. Abstinence had him veering toward the negative. There was a simple enough solution. He took another gulp.

"Why is it," he said, in the whiny voice of the spoiled child he had once been, "that I give everything, and I get nothing in return?" He leered at Emma, his face lopsided. He wanted an answer to his fatuous question.

Emma held back the smile. Dick Latham getting nothing in return for his bountiful generosity was a hilarious idea.

"Maybe you don't ask for enough," said Emma. Her words sort of slipped out, but as she uttered them, the idea came to her. It cut through her mind like a knife through butter . . . and it took her breath away.

"Ask for enough . . . I don't ask for enough?" slurred Latham, as if trying to translate a dimly remembered foreign language. "Must one spell everything out . . . chapter and verse . . . to everyone? Don't the people who live off me have enough initiative to anticipate my needs and get the job done that needs to be done? I pay enough fiddlers. Why the fuck should I fiddle myself?"

"What job needs to be done, Dick? I don't understand."

Dick Latham sat to attention. Quite suddenly, he banged the glass of scotch on the table. The whiskey leaped from it, soaking the white cloth. The sharp sound of tumbler on table hushed the deal talk all around.

"Alabama needs to be blown away, wasted, put to sleep. I want him dead, super dead, so dead they have to invent a new word to describe it. Is *that* clear? Can there be any room for doubt about that?" His eyes were narrow. Spit darted from tight lips. His knuckles were white. He had shouted the first bit. He whispered the second. "And because nobody I employ has the *guts* to do the job for me, I'm going to waste the bastard myself."

The microphone between Emma Guinness's breasts was in no doubt at all as to the message it had received.

—

EMMA GUINNESS winced as she remembered Dick Latham's Technicolor yawn at La Scala. It had been a problem getting him out. Thank God, they'd taken the chauffeur. His semicomatose body had been dragged through the thrilled diners. It had reminded the old-timers of the golden days when Flynn and

Co. had dared to raise hell before Hollywood had been sold lock, stock, cock, and barrel to the gray corporations. He had parked another cookie of humongous proportions in the back of the Rolls, and now he summoned up a third as the butler and footman carried him up the marble stairs to his bed. Emma stood at the foot of the staircase, fingering the pouch at her waist, and chuckled to herself as the retching, puking billionaire disappeared from view.

"When you've put him to bed, you can leave everything," she called up to the retreating trio. "I'll look after Mr. Latham."

"Very good, miss," said the puffing butler over his shoulder, relieved to be shedding responsibility for what looked like an extraordinarily unpromising situation.

Emma looked at her watch. It was early, not yet nine o'clock. She walked through the house toward the beach, and out onto the sand. The wind was picking up. It plucked at her hair, hot and caressing, blanketing her face with its valley heat. Today Malibu had changed. It was Santa Ana season. The freshness of the air was still there, but now there was the promise of something else—of sauna sunshine, desert dryness, of the crisp unrelenting warmth that would make you sweat and toss beneath your Porthault sheets.

The plan was coming together in her mind like a child's jigsaw. It was incredibly simple. All she needed was steel nerves, and the world would be handed to her on a silver salver. As she walked out onto the deserted dunes, she hitched up her skirt and fumbled for the pouch at her belt. The sleek brushed-chrome recorder that she reached for was the ticket to an earthly Paradise. She pressed REWIND, and almost immediately she pressed STOP, and then PLAY. Dick Latham's dire death threat against Alabama was crystal clear. He didn't sound drunk. The adrenaline of his fury had overridden the tranquillizing effect of the booze as he had made his vicious promise. The motive for murder was already established beyond reasonable doubt. So, now, was a murderous state of mind. Probable cause remained. And the crime. That needed to be committed. No question. Murders always needed a victim. It was a sine qua non. Ha! Ha! Oh yes, it was. A corpse was required. A corpse like Alabama. Now, Emma Guinness laughed. She rocked and roared with laughter out there on the lonely sand in front of Dustin's place and Bernie Brillstein's and Spielberg's rental that had burned to the ground so soon after he traded in Amy for groovy Kate Capshaw. She held her sides to keep them from splitting. She held the Pearlcorder tight in her hand like the lottery winner it was.

Slowly her laughter subsided. She felt so good—so crazy, but so wonderful. She had slipped her moorings forever now, and cut the rope that tied her to mundanity. She was adrift on the mad, wild seas, where anything could happen and the danger and possible disasters paled beside the infinite possibilities that were opening for her. By morning, she would be in a position to make all her hateful dreams come true.

She stood still in the wind. She was thinking, remembering. Like everyone else in the world, she had planned the perfect crime. Unlike the world's wankers, she would carry hers out. It all hinged on one memory. A couple of days ago, when she had been driving with Latham in the Testarossa, it had run out of gas. Luckily, they had been only minutes from the Cross Creek Texaco. Latham, laughing and enjoying the pretense that he was a mere mortal, had paid his deposit like a regular guy and walked out of the gas station with a gallon can of gas. He'd stuck it in the tank, thrown the empty can in the trunk, and headed straight home to Broad Beach to give the chauffeur a hard time. The can would be there now, where he'd left it—a can of gas carrying the fingerprints of a man with murder in his heart.

She hurried back into the house, and headed through it toward the five-car garage. She stopped and listened, but all was quiet. Dick would be unconscious upstairs. The servants would be tucked away doing whatever servants did when they could not be seen. She had all the time in the world. The keys to the Ferrari were on the board by the garage door. She took them, walked over to the gleaming red car, and opened the trunk. The empty can stared back at her. It was where Latham had thrown it. She picked up a clean rag from the bench, and lifted it gingerly from the bottom, being careful not to touch the chrome handle where the billionaire's fingerprints would be. She placed it next to the car's gas tank. She looked around. Shelves lined one wall of the carpeted garage. They were bursting with automobile goodies. A parts store would have given anything for the inventory. She selected a piece of hose, stuffed one end in the tank of the Ferrari and the other end in her mouth. She sucked until she tasted gas and then she transferred that end to the empty can. The high-octane fuel bubbled into its new home.

She picked up the can and carried it over to the white Targa Porsche, placing it carefully on the leather of the backseat, next to the red leather gloves that Latham wore when driving his toys. Again, she looked at her watch. Nine fifteen. She had several hours to lose. She didn't want the butler and the chauffeur testifying that Latham had been too drunk to stand. He would need a few hours to recover before a jury would deem him capable of doing the deed that she was about to do. Anyway, the middle of the night would be the best time. People slept then. People who were about to be framed slept; witnesses slept; victims slept . . . the sleep of the dead, the sleep of the damned.

She tiptoed out of the garage and made her way through the deserted, dimly lit house to her bedroom. She changed quickly into jeans and a black polo-neck sweater, and then she climbed into bed. She would not sleep, but she closed her eyes to cover her racing mind. Step by step she went through the plan, the left on Malibu Canyon, the right on Piuma Drive up to the Saddle Peak. She knew exactly where Alabama lived. She knew exactly where he would die. And in the morning, when the world woke to the smell of flames, she would claim all the prizes that were rightfully hers.

And then the world would darken for the people who had crossed her— for Dick Latham who had spurned her, for Pat Parker who had dared to be her rival, and, most of all, for Tony Valentino, who had humiliated her and left the terrible scars on her soul.

ALABAMA KNEW that it was the middle of the night but hadn't a clue what time it was. It was like this when he was working. The world went away. Nothing existed then, but the images, the magic, and the wonderful surprises in the darkness as he astonished himself with the astounding talent that seemed to belong to someone else. The image was coming through now, a ghostly shape forming itself on the paper, and Alabama filled in the gaps from memory—a tree here, a shaft of light there, the brushed texture of the bushes on the mountainside. The photographs of the canyon had done their job, but the memory of their beauty had lingered on, lighting up Alabama's art-starved mind. That afternoon he had returned to the place that would now be safe forever, and he had taken more photographs in celebration of his victory. It had been more complete than he had imagined. Overnight, Latham had become a pariah. His social life was dead. His businesses were badly wounded. Oh, he would survive. But never again would he shine like a newly minted penny. He was used up, tarnished, yesterday's man, and Alabama had organized it all . . . with a little help from his friends.

He walked across the darkroom and looked at the clock: 3:00 A.M. That was good. Another hour or two and he'd turn in. Maybe he'd sleep late tomorrow. The GMA satellite interview he'd done that morning had worn him out. He rubbed his eyes and returned to the bench. He had forgotten the joy of printing. Even in the early days when he had been taking photographs, King had done most of that. It wasn't that Alabama was bad at it, merely that subcontracting it left more time for shooting. He thought of King, fast asleep in his room upstairs. The excitement of the last few days, and Alabama's return to photography, had proved too much for his muscle-bound assistant. Drained by the nervous tension, he had crashed out early, popping a couple of rare sleepers to guarantee him the unconsciousness he needed. Alabama smiled. How like life that was. In the days when he had lain artistically fallow, King had never faltered. He had been a tireless source of strength and encouragement over the years as the doubt and the guilt had swirled around in the beer mist, and Alabama had wrestled unsuccessfully with his demons. Now, as Alabama had burst into the sunshine of his brand-new day, King had allowed himself to fall apart. Well, that was okay. Alabama felt strong enough to rise to any challenge. It would do him good to look after others for a change. He had been too selfish for way too long.

The sharp crack brought him back from his thoughts. It had sounded like a whip, and it had come from beyond the closed door of the darkroom. Something had fallen over. A brush? Whatever. The possibility of burglars didn't enter his mind. It was too remote out here for the lazy robbers from the urban ghettos, and the local variety would have sooner raided the devil in hell than Alabama. Could King be cruising around looking for something? No way. He was deep in his chemical land of Nod, and he'd deserved his escape.

The second noise was louder. It sounded like a gunshot. Damn! Alabama looked at the print. It was at a critical stage. It couldn't be risked, and bumps in the night were always a disappointment. He'd kick himself if he ruined a masterpiece for the pleasure of scaring off some inquisitive coyote. He bent over the image, screwing up his eyes in the dim infrared glow, and then he smelled fire.

That was different. It was what hill dwellers dreaded. At this time of the year the canyons were powder dry. The daily prayer was for the rains to begin. Alabama hurried to the door. He paused. He listened. He breathed in deeply. Should he open the thick, light-tight door? The thoughts were coming fast. If the house was burning, he might be opening the door on an inferno. The alternative wasn't attractive either. He could leave the door closed and bake in the oven of his darkroom. He tried to stay calm. It was probably nothing. Most things were. And he'd survived fires in the mountains before. Hell, in retrospect, they'd been fun, and the chaparral recovered eventually. It was nature's way of fertilizing the soil and clearing out the rubbish.

He put his hand on the inside of the door. It wasn't hot. That was a good sign. He filled his lungs with air. He crouched down. He opened the door. The flames licked at him. Long and thin, like the heads of snakes, they shimmied toward him and the wall of heat crashed into his face and filled up his mind with its danger. The room was burning. The house above it would be burning. All around the canyon would be burning in the fire of hell. The noise of the fire roared in his ears, crackling, hissing, sizzling across the neuron pathway to understanding. He slammed the door shut, buying himself only precious seconds, as he tried to think what to do. He stared around him in the bogus safety of the gloomy womb. There was an apron hanging on a hook. The water bath was full of ice-cold water. He grabbed at the apron, plunged it into the water above the glorious print the world would never see, and wrapped it around his head and shoulders. Crouching once again, he headed back to the door. Smoke was more of a danger than the flames, and hot air rose. He would stay near the floor where the oxygen still was, and he would try to make the stairs. He mapped out an escape route in his mind. Halfway up the stairs was a glass window. If he could break through that, he might be able to get out of the house. But the mountain would be burning. There would be no place to hide. Except the pool. Yes, that was it! Some of the old-timers who lived in the hills waited out brushfires in swimming pools. It was considered a macho thing to do. You put on tanks if you were a sissy, and you sat out the blaze in the deep end. If you were a real man, not the imitation variety, you saved on the cost of the bottled air. A foot of hose would hack it if you didn't mind your air smoky—one end in the mouth, the other an inch above the surface of the water. An hour or two of that, and you had a story that guaranteed attention for a year and a day. The pool was about a hundred feet from the house, and Alabama used it as a reservoir. He remembered it was at least half full.

He tensed himself at the door. He reached for the knob with one hand, and he clasped the wet material around his head with the other.

He opened the door and sprang forward into the fire. He didn't have to see. This was his home. The heat seared at him, plucking at his clothes, but he ran on, praying the stairs would not have been destroyed by fire. The bottom step gave way as he put his weight on it, but it held him—just— disintegrating with a sharp crack as his foot left it for the one above. He climbed the burning ladder, one step ahead of disaster, until he reached the turn in the stairwell. The window would be to his right. He didn't feel for it. His hands would melt in the heat out there. He kept them wrapped in the damp cotton. Like a linebacker shoulder-charging an opponent, Alabama threw his whole weight sideways. The window exploded against his arm, and amid a shower of glass and fiery frame, he shot through it. It was a six-foot drop, and he knew he wasn't positioned for a safe landing. There would be damage on contact. There was. He crashed down to earth on the shoulder that had atomized the window. There was a sickening wrench as he felt it dislocate, but the pain was bearable, because pain was a luxury this close to death. He peered out into the firestorm. Up ahead, the orchard that led to the possible safety of the pool was a furnace, but the scrub had been cut back to bare earth as a fire break. Unless he was unlucky, he would make it. He set off, loping through the sparks and the flying cinders like the wounded bear he was. He had traveled a distance of about thirty feet when he remembered King.

He stopped as the dreadful thought hit him. He turned back toward the house. It was burning from top to bottom. It was blanketed in flames, swathed in a marmalade bandage by the all-consuming fire. And King was inside, in a drugged sleep. Alabama's mighty heart heaved in his chest. He calculated the odds. Most probably, King was dead already. Nobody could have survived the inferno. To enter it and to try to save his friend would have only one result. He should hurry on to the pool while he still had time. It was the only sensible thing to do.

Like *hell* it was! Alabama didn't think anymore. Thinking had always been a bad business. It confused you. The gut was a far more dependable organ than the brain. He turned around, and he charged toward the house.

The back door had conveniently disappeared, and Alabama aimed himself through the halo of flames into the bowels of his burning home. The stairway to the upstairs bedrooms was a more serious affair than the basement steps he had just climbed. The sturdier oak could resist the flames longer. He took them two at a time as he plunged into the flaming hell, and he knew that his clothes were burning because he could feel the darts of pain against his skin, feel the skin peel away, feel the flesh bubble as it melted on the inside that had become the outside. He struggled on, aware that he was slowing as the wall of fire in front of him thickened. But there was no going back. There was only onward, and upward in a journey toward the eternity that he knew was his destination. King would already be walking there—King, who had given his life to Alabama, as Alabama was dedicating his to King in this gesture of ultimate solidarity. The pain had stopped, and the wall of fire was beckoning. His feet were lighter as he reached the landing, and there was a new spring in his step, because now he was at one with the fire. He was in tune with it, floating on it, a blissful, wondrous part of it. Here, at the end of life and the beginning of death, Alabama had *become* the flames. He staggered, but still he sailed on and his mind was full of love for the world that had given him such a wonderful existence. There would be others after him to march the arduous marches to beauty. Others, like Pat Parker, would travel his path through the long nights of sorrow to the light that he was on the verge of knowing. They would fight, and strive and suffer and enjoy as he had endured those things, and then they would merge as he was merging with the nature source in the endless sleep of ultimate peace.

Brighter than the brightest part of the fire burned Ben Alabama. He sparkled in the heart of the hills that were his home, and the light that shone from him would never die. It would live on forever in the beauty he had created, and in the beauty he had saved.

~16~

THE WATER HAMMERS crashed in Dick Latham's brain. He'd forgotten what a hangover was like. In the old days there had been lots, but he'd been young then. This was a vicious killer. The room swam when he stood. His stomach churned when he lay down. He wanted water, but he couldn't face the trip to the bathroom. He needed aspirin, but he wouldn't be able to keep it down. He longed for death, but he hadn't the energy for anything so exhausting. The metaphysical element was a minor problem. Through the banging in his head, there were fragments of memories. In La Scala, embarrassing things had been said, inappropriate deeds done. The hell with it, even in extremis Dick Latham didn't worry about the idiots. What they thought of him was their problem, not his. Nobody ever said unpleasant things to his face, and he couldn't care less what was said behind his back. He held on to his forehead to prevent it from releasing his brains all over the bed to go with the other nasties that had accumulated through the night. He turned his head to left and right, wondering if movement would help. The wave of nausea rushed through him. The sun was peeping through the blinds. From the degree of brightness it was early, maybe seven o'clock. He groaned, but that, too, was a mistake. The ticking of his bedside clock was deafening. He was reminded of Bob Newhart's plaintive cry. "*Please* don't fizz, Alka-Seltzer."

Then he remembered. Oh no! Any minute now the television was going to turn itself on. It was the way he woke up, to Bryant and Co., and dishy Deborah Norville, who always made for a sexy start to the day. God, that would be the last straw. Willard's heartiness, and all those geriatric birthdays would be a cruel and unusual punishment. Where the hell was the remote control? The preprogrammed TV turn-on could be aborted . . . if you had a master's degree in computer engineering from MIT, and a head that didn't hurt when you thought.

He tried to sit up. As usual, the remote control had vanished. He flopped down again. Resignation crashed over him. He had as much control over events as the man at the stake before the firing squad. At least that lucky guy would have a pain-free future.

Click! It had happened. The room was full of Toyotas and why you should hurry to buy them, of toothpaste that made you taste good, of a breakfast cereal that saved your life. Then there was Deborah Norville, queasily self-confident as she wrapped her luscious lips around the news.

"A brush fire in the Malibu hills claimed the life last night of famous photographer and environmentalist, Ben Alabama. Mr. Alabama, known to everyone simply as Alabama, died when fire destroyed his ranch house in the Santa Monica Mountains. Recently Alabama won a notable victory when he prevented the siting of the Cosmos movie studios on undeveloped land next to the Saddle Peak ranch where he lived. Police suspect arson. The president, a long-time friend of Alabama's, said that America and the world had lost a great artist and a great man. He will be attending the funeral later this week in California.

"In Lebanon . . ."

Again Latham sat up. This time he stayed up. His hangover had disappeared. Alabama had been burned. God had granted his wish. He'd never believed in prayer. He did now. He reached for the telephone. He should be thrilled. He *was* thrilled. No, he wasn't. Hell, he wasn't thrilled at all. Last night he'd wanted Alabama dead. Now that he was, Latham missed him. Somehow Alabama had been a part of his life. He had been a comfortable enemy to hate, and he went back a long way, back to Paris when life had meant something. There was nobody else in the whole world who had known Dick Latham in the good old days. It counted for something. Damn it, he was sorry the old buzzard was dead. Wasn't life extraordinary? Wilde had been right. The only thing worse than not getting what you wanted was getting it.

The telephone beneath his hand was ringing. He picked it up.

"Dick? Tommy. Have you heard about Alabama?"

"I just caught it on NBC. I can't believe it."

"I never believed in coincidence before," said Havers. His tone said that he was not totally prepared to believe in it now.

"Yeah, amazing." Dick Latham's mind stopped in its tracks. What the hell had he said to all those guys in La Scala last night? He'd threatened Alabama. And now Alabama was burned to death in a fire the police believed was started by an arsonist. The two and two made four. He might be a suspect. Thank God, he had an alibi. His skin was suddenly clammy. Sweat sprang from beneath his arms. What alibi? Someone had poured him into bed around nine. He had slept alone. And Alabama's ranch was only a twenty-five-minute drive away.

"Listen, Tommy, can you slip down here to California? I'd like you to be around. Drop everything, okay? Just get here, and bring that slick lawyer from Kruger, French. You know, the young guy with the sharp suits, Felderman or Federman . . ."

"Feldman? The one we used when the accountant at KBAC had his hand in the till? He's criminal law."

"Bring him anyway, okay?" said Latham. The premonition was building inside him. He tried to put the bits of the evening back together. He'd played most of it as Al Capone, the Mr. Big who could not be crossed without exacting a terrible retribution. His timing had been way off. Thank God there was no hard evidence of the things he'd said. The table of tourists in La Scala had seen him being carried out. Nobody would have taken him seriously. Everyone would have reckoned the drink was talking. Anyway, one thing was for sure. *He* wasn't the firebug. If the cops had evidence of arson, it wouldn't point the finger at him. No way, could it. No way.

"Are you all right, Dick? You sound like you've got the flu."

"Yeah, no, I'm fine, maybe some virus or something. Anyway, hurry on down and we'll see if we can salvage any of this Cosmos thing. Maybe now that the old boy's history, everyone'll relax on it. I wouldn't count on it, but we ought to explore it."

"I'll be there in nine," said Tommy Havers. He hung up. So did Latham. For a second or two he was thoughtful. He should get more information, perhaps call Arnold York, the publisher of the *Malibu Times*. He was a helpful guy and he'd have the police version by now.

The door of his bedroom opened. Nobody had knocked. Emma Guinness stood in the doorway. She was in blue jeans and a black polo-neck sweater. She looked like a dumpy cat burglar. There was something in her hand.

"What the hell are you doing in here? Didn't anyone teach you how to knock?"

The expression in her eyes stopped him. It was triumphant. The smile devoured her face. In all his life Latham had never seen anyone so transcendentally happy.

"Well, Dick Latham, aren't *you* the man who keeps his promises," she said.

Latham opened his mouth to pick up where he left off, but as he did so, his premonition began to focus itself. The blurry feeling was clarifying, taking shape, and the vision that it formed uncaged the flying insects in the pit of his long-suffering stomach.

"Exactly what do you mean?" said Dick Latham. But in his guts he knew. Emma Guinness was insinuating that he had killed Alabama, or at least had him killed, but it was more than that. Her whole manner suggested that she had something that could tie him to the crime he had never committed. He tried to get his mind working as he covered the possible angles. It had to be more than his drunken threats, but what? He had done nothing. He was innocent. The only crime he was guilty of was wanting Alabama dead. But the look on her face was curdling further his already curdled stomach. It was a spine-chilling look of the purest evil. Her face was twisted in an expression of total wickedness, and the blood ran cold in Dick Latham's veins as he realized that he had made a fundamental mistake that he might pay for with everything. He had always known that Emma Guinness was cruel and vindictive. Those attributes had counted for nothing, because of her incredible talent. He had failed, however, to understand the most important truth of all. He hadn't realized that Emma Guinness was mad.

"What I mean is that you burned Alabama last night," said Emma. She took a step into the room. She closed the bedroom door behind her.

"You know I didn't do that," said Latham, his voice shaking.

"Does it matter what I know? It's what the police know that counts, isn't it?"

"There's not a shred of . . ."

"Evidence to suggest that you did it?" Emma finished his sentence. She was standing at the end of his bed now. He could see her glow. She was radiant. She was totally in command. She held up her hand so that he could see the tape recorder.

"This heard you," she said simply. "It was listening when you told it what you were going to do to Alabama."

Not for one single second did he think she was lying. And he knew this was only the beginning. There was more. There was worse to come. He felt the blood drain from his face. His stomach turned. Over her shoulder Willard Scott was wearing something camp and cuddling an embarrassed Okie at a senior citizens' picnic.

"The cops will have found a can of gasoline up there on Saddle Peak," said Emma. "The one you picked up the other day when the Ferrari died on us. Remember?"

Latham swallowed hard. He remembered. He'd carried it a hundred yards. His prints would be all over it. The tape plus the can equaled a case, if not a conviction, and an arrest would be more than enough to destroy him. The psychopath at the foot of his bed held his future in the palm of her hand. He could take the recorder from her by force, but the tape would be long gone and well hidden. The can would be with Homicide. It would take nothing more than one call to link the prints to him. Dick Latham could feel the handcuffs on his wrists.

But even as he dared to contemplate the bleakness of his future, he recoiled from the horror of what had happened.

"You did it," he said, his voice quiet but shaking. "You started the fire that killed Alabama."

She laughed then, a hideous, vicious laugh, and it was more than enough as an answer. She had flipped. She'd gone crazy. God, he should have seen the signs. People were always talking about her paranoia. Several people, including Tommy Havers, had warned him that she was teetering on the brink of insanity. He simply hadn't listened. It wasn't a side of her that he saw, and there were always a ton of men to bad-mouth a bright, brilliant woman, especially when she was a success and had power over them. But that was then. This was now. He was in mortal danger. A murderess was standing in his bedroom, and she was threatening to frame him for the crime she'd committed. Facts winged into his mind. He had the motive. He'd declared his intent, both publicly and privately. His threats were on tape. If

Emma had driven up to the mountains to start the fire, she'd have taken one of his cars. The tire prints would be up there somewhere. He had no alibi. He'd slept alone. His fingerprints were on the can. If she had the will, she could do it . . . and the will was painted in blood all over her face.

"What do you want from me?" he said at last. There was always a deal—always was, always would be.

Emma paused to savor the moment. Her request would be granted, and it would be the first of many. She had the stuff of which blackmailers dreamed. She puffed herself up. She was going to enjoy these words, because of all the things they meant and they would mean.

"I want Cosmos Studios," she said. "I want total power to run it as I wish."

———

"EMMA GUINNESS? Running Cosmos? You're joking, Dick."

"I'm not joking," said Dick Latham. He wasn't. He had never been more serious. He looked out of the window to avoid Havers's eye. At this moment he would have gladly traded places with any one of the impoverished surfers on the beach.

"But she wouldn't have a clue how to run a major studio. I wouldn't. You probably wouldn't. I mean, she'd be a disaster. We'd be the laughingstock of Hollywood, and everywhere else, for that matter."

"I've made up my mind," said Latham. "This isn't a discussion, it's a statement of fact."

Havers looked desperate. He wasn't about to give up, whatever the risk to his career of disagreeing with the boss.

"What about *New Celebrity?* It's running great, and it's Emma's baby. You've admitted that she turned it around singlehanded. If she leaves to screw up Cosmos, what the hell will happen to the magazine? Don't do this, Dick. At least explain the logic of it. It just doesn't make sense."

Dick Latham kept his eyes on the sea. "She's a trendsetter. She knows what the public wants. If she can pick fashions, she can choose movies. There's nothing else to the job. Some lawyer can second-guess her on all the business stuff. It'll work. Trust me. My instinct says it's right."

Havers had never heard Latham sound so unconvincing and so unconvinced. He remembered the conversation he'd had with Emma in the Canal Bar when she'd pitched him the idea of her running Cosmos. He hadn't bought it. Apparently Latham had. Why? What the hell was going down? Maybe there was a grain of truth in what Latham was saying, but overall it was naïve. There was marketing and distribution, the vital business of setting up a film, costing it, anticipating the problems up front. And you had to have believability in the industry, a network of relationships with the people that counted, with the stars, the packagers, and the vitally important banks. It helped to have shake-hands integrity, or rather the ability to fake it, and it was a plus if you could develop an on-the-lot esprit that would get people working for less money and keep the unions sweet. Emma Guinness excelled in none of the above. She was ignorant of moviemaking, and she was psychotoxic on top. Dick Latham would regret his decision from day one. The interesting question was why he was making it.

"Well, Dick, you know best," said Havers. "It's your show, but I've always considered Emma Guinness to be dangerously unstable." It was his way of washing his hands of the whole business. "When does she take over?"

"She's taken over," said Latham. His voice seemed far away. He was strangely detached. "She's hard at work right now."

Havers couldn't resist it.

"Doing exactly what?" he asked.

Dick Latham turned to face him.

"Rewriting the script of *Malibu*," he replied.

There was a long silence.

"I didn't know that project was still on the go list," said Havers carefully. He had heard the Pat Parker diatribe against Latham at the Getty. It had been the catalyst to the explosive reaction of the Malibu movie stars. There was a sense in which it had been Pat Parker, not Alabama, who had finally derailed Latham's plan. At the very least, Havers imagined that she'd have been off the payroll together with Tony and Allison and anyone else who might have been guilty through their association with her. Apparently not. Why?

"There comes a point beyond which personal feelings shouldn't enter into these things," lied Latham. "If *Malibu* and Pat Parker were a good idea before our little setback, then they're still a good idea after it. I called her and told her so." He turned away to the relative safety of the sea. Pat Parker and personal feelings were *not* separate. She might have crossed him, but God, she'd looked magnificent doing it. It had taken his breath away. Not much did. At the moment of his groveling defeat it was the one bright spot. She'd called him a child. She had his number. That made her unique. She was the club to which he wanted to belong, the one with the guts and good taste to pitch him out. It was almost as simple as that.

"And what does the new studio boss think of *Malibu*? Wasn't there bad blood between Guinness and Valentino? What the hell's she doing fiddling around with the script? That's hardly what studio heads do. It all sounds pretty weird to me . . ."

Dick Latham took a deep breath. He hoped Havers would never know how weird it really was, that Emma Guinness was the only thing separating him from a murder-one conviction. Compared to the importance of that, who the hell cared what she was doing at Cosmos?

Havers, however, in the unaccustomed role of dog with a bone, couldn't let go. "I mean, what's she *doing* with the script?"

"She's beefing up the sex scenes," said Dick Latham, with a nervous laugh.

THE HELICOPTER swooped low over Saddle Peak. The charred remains of the Alabama ranch, still smoking in the early light, lay like a black carpet below. Pat Parker leaned out of the window, and the tears rolled down her cheeks in the gusting wind. She could see the remains of the house now, a gutted shell against the rocks of the canyon wall. Nothing could have survived the terrible blaze. She tried to picture his last minutes, tried to imagine his thoughts as the hellfire devoured him and the home he'd loved. Already she missed him. There was a void in her life where he had been, and she knew it would never be filled.

Pat leaned over to the pilot and signaled with her hand for him to go lower. All morning they had been scouting locations for the movie, but this pilgrimage had always been at the back of her mind.

"Can you land?" she shouted above the roar of the rotor.

He nodded and swooped in, the *wop-wop-wop* of the engine rebounding from the dense walls of the canyon.

As soon as the helicopter was still, Pat jumped onto the scorched earth. The path of the fire was clearly visible. It had started from the road, high above, and rushed down, cutting a swath of destruction across the valley as it headed for Alabama's house. It had probably been started by a cigarette thrown by some careless driver as he headed home, oblivious to the havoc he had left behind. Certainly nobody could have done such a wicked thing on purpose, despite fire department and police theories of arson.

She walked toward the deserted house, so well remembered, and once again the grief gripped her. The funeral was tomorrow, and it would be a media event of vast proportions. The presence of the president alone would ensure that, but so would Alabama's personal reputation. Today, she would say her private farewell, in the place where his ghost would linger, here in the hills whose beauty would last forever in his photographs. At least the prints were safe. Nobody who lived in the Santa Monica Mountains could ignore the possibility of brushfires, and Alabama's precious negatives were locked in a fireproof vault at the Bank of America in Century City. What would become of them? Alabama had no family. Presumably they would be left in trust to some museum, although he had hated those and the besuited art-business men who ran them.

She walked toward the gap where the big oak doors had been, and looked in. She could see right through the house, past the frames of the melted plate-glass windows to the vista that Alabama had loved. It was a forever view, big and grand like the old man who had watched it, and more than anything it reminded Pat of the friend she would never see again. The stair-case had vanished, and there was no way to get upstairs to the place he had died. But she could sense him. She could feel the spirit of him in the place his soul would never leave. It was a comforting feeling. She was close to him, and there was warmth in her heart beside the sorrow for the surrogate father she had lost.

King had died too, near as always to the master he loved. Once again tears sprang to Pat's eyes as she thought of the gentleness of his strength. His muscles had not saved him from the flames. Nothing could have done that. It must have descended like a thunderbolt, total in its surprise. But there would have been time for panic in the frantic seconds before the end, and Pat tried to close off her mind to the horror of those moments.

On an impulse, she knelt down on the singed tiles of the floor, and she closed her eyes and clasped her hands before her in prayer.

"Dear God, protect them," she whispered. "Wherever they are, love them as they loved me."

EMMA GUINNESS looked out to sea. The Santa Ana wind had picked up the San Fernando Valley smog, pushed it through the Malibu canyons, and deposited it—a thin layer of yellow fuzz—over the surface of the ocean. But Emma couldn't have cared less. What was a little pollution when all her blackest wishes had been granted? She leaned over the edge of the bluff and looked down to the jagged rocks ninety feet below. Surfers were riding the waves. A girl sunbathed topless on the private beach. The crash of the ceaseless surf caressed her ears. She breathed in deeply and turned around toward the state-of-the-art Point Dume contemporary home that Cosmos had leased for her. Here on Cliffside Drive the real estate was real. Down on the sand a tidal wave would one day drag the stilt homes out to sea. Most of the land-side houses would be consumed by fire. But the bluffs would survive for a thousand years, until the rock-eating sea eventually triumphed over them.

The platform on which she stood was built on a promontory that jutted out from the cliffs. It had been organized as a sitting area with a Santa Barbara umbrella and some high-tech Tropitone sun beds. Compact-disc music warbled gently on the outside loudspeaker system. The portable laptop word processor sat expectantly on the table. Emma sighed. She'd taken a few minutes off from writing to savor her wonderful world, but she couldn't stay away for long. There was too much to do; too much misery to sow; too many enemies to be cast down.

She walked back to the Balans chair that spared your back and knelt down at it, flexing her fingers in the speckled sunlight of Malibu's Indian summer. She adjusted the page and ran off a riff of sentences to start the flow. It was the third day of her tenure at Cosmos, yet she had hardly been near the place. She had her priorities, and the birth pain of the new studio was low on the list of them. At the very top was revenge. She had spent the time here on the bluff, writing, while the trucks unloaded her meager possessions onto the marble and granite floors of her spectacular rented home. Somewhere inside, a brace of secretaries fielded the calls. Here on the cliff face, the temperature was a few degrees hotter than anywhere else in Malibu, and the steam heat was coming from the green screen of the Smith-Corona. She had never written sex before, but, boy, had she got the hang of it. The visions flowed freely across a mind alive with make-believe sensations as the smells and the sounds, the tastes and the touches, tumbled over each other in her fevered brain. She held back on the euphemisms—the proud urgency of his desire, the shy ventricles, the illicit amulets of love. Instead, she named names, crude, rude, and deadly shrewd, as she spelled it out so that nobody would need to use any imagination. This, after all, was a script. It was her direction to the director. When she called a spade a spade, she wanted there to be no mistake about recognition of the implement.

She chuckled to herself as her fingers flew across the keyboard. Sometimes writing was like this. At times like these she seemed to be tuned to some inner stream of consciousness, and her fingers could hardly work fast enough to keep pace with the manic dictation that spilled up from her creative well. It was rare, but wonderful when it happened, a total contrast to the gray, sad days when every word had to be chiseled from stone. But she wasn't surprised. Everything was working for her. It was coming together. The moment she had surrendered to her darkest dreams, she had triumphed. A little murder had been the smallest price to pay.

The ugliest secretary in Hollywood, chosen by Emma for her spectacular homeliness, called out across the lawn. "Mr. Richard Latham on the telephone, Ms. Guinness."

"Take a message," Emma shouted back. Tony was beneath, Melissa was on top in the cowgirl position. Camera pans across the lovers, then zooms in for close-up. She could see Pat Parker's face, see her tense body hunched in the director's chair, as her lover made love to the legend before her eyes. Melissa had to thrust up, had to push with her finger into Tony's half-open mouth, had to moan and groan with crazed passion as she readied herself for her celluloid orgasm. Close-up on Melissa's face. Soundtrack. Wind up the music. Close-up of Tony's face as he lost it in the sea of sticky ecstasy. Would Pat be watching through the hand lens to frame the shot? Would Melissa be coming for real as she performed the on-set party trick she was famous for? And what would Tony Valentino be thinking as the sexpert balled him, as his girlfriend watched, wondering how soon she dared yell "Cut"? Emma could actually feel the angst. It jelled with the groovy sweat beneath her arms. It hovered in the bright air. It fingered her spine with its delicious anxiety.

She whacked out the words with renewed intensity, and as she did so the switch flicked inside her. She was turned on. She was warming up. The juices were on the move, like the ones she was writing about. She had become Melissa Wayne, throbbing and pulsating beneath Tony Valentino's piston power. She had him at last, nailing her to the floor. She was wrapped around his hard body, sucking him dry as he surged into her. Ooooooh! She shifted her shins on the chair and waved her rump in the air, wiggling it from side to side as the screen rocked to her autoerotica. Jesus! She was melting as she wrote about them melting. She was all revved up, gunning in neutral, and the typewriter keys beneath her fingers were the substitute for the bits of bodies she so suddenly needed to touch.

Merely reading this would make Pat Parker cry. Directing it would drive her mad. And Tony, proud, arrogant Tony, wouldn't he just love playing a piece of meat? The scene was X-rated. The "serious" actor would be a Harry Reems dead ringer. The guy who'd already bared it all for Emma's *New Celebrity* would be doing it in the movies and the talkies. He'd be typecast for a hundred years. As a geriatric they'd be offering him senior citizens' sex-instruction videos. The laugh burbled up from her stomach, as she savored the magic moment and all the ones to come, and she tapped away like a woman possessed as she dreamed up the scenario of her fiendish retribution.

They had to get from the floor to the bed, from wide-open spaces to the secrecy of sheets. It was beneath the Pratesis that Melissa Wayne, queen of closed sets, could wreak the havoc she was so very famous for wreaking. She didn't like jock straps and bikini bottoms and all the bits and pieces the professionals used. She liked to do away with them for the greater glory of the "art" she performed. When Melissa Wayne did her orgasm in close-up, there was only ever one take.

Emma's fingers shifted the lovers.

He picks her up, roughly, as if she is weightless. He walks to the bed. He throws her down. He tears back the covers and the sheets. She rolls gratefully between them. She turns to watch the lover she longs for. Her lips are parted, moist with lust.

There. They were there, where the damage could and would be done. Next, she would draw the sheets over them. She would melt into his arms. Her hips would thrust eagerly toward his. Emma stopped typing. It was almost too good to be true. Pat Parker and Tony Valentino's relationship would not survive the *Malibu* she was creating. The sizzling script would see to that, and so would the sexual athleticism and Method acting of Melissa Wayne. Then, when the relationship was in ruins, she would make her move, and Tony Valentino, who had turned her down once and humiliated her, would not do so again. He would crawl on his hands and knees across the floor to satisfy her. He would plead to please the studio boss, because, if he didn't, she would take away the future that was his obsession. She would have him where she wanted him at last, humble at her feet, and in his gritty, groveling surrender she would transform the hero into the body slave she had always dreamed of owning.

Emma's fingers snaked back to the keyboard, and once again the letters began to dance across the screen. They formed the language of erotica, but they spelled the death warrant for Pat and Tony's happiness.

Only one thing was needed for the great and glorious conclusion she planned, and the strains of Wagner surged suddenly in her head as she thought of it.

Melissa Wayne was already her ally. Tonight, when they met, they would sign their pact in Tony Valentino's blood.

EMMA SAT behind her desk in the power position. Covered in rhinestones from head to toe, she looked like the Lone Ranger in drag, but the invisible sign above her head read STUDIO BOSS, and it was Melissa Wayne who had made the journey to Malibu. She sat across from Emma in a blue-jeaned tangle of limbs, and she licked luscious lips as she spoke.

"Well, Emma, I won't say I wasn't surprised, but I *do* say I'm pleased. It's wonderful for you, for me, for women in general."

Melissa Wayne purred like the cat she was. She had never liked a woman, dead or alive, and she didn't intend to start now. But she had been around

Hollywood long enough to appreciate the value of the right noises. The bitch across the desk had come a long way from magazine land. Clearly she had balls. She had to be humored, at least while she sat in the CEO's musical chair. Anyway, they had already established a common interest—the punishment and humiliation of the impossible Tony Valentino. If that item was still on the agenda, Melissa was Emma's enthusiastic ally.

"It's fun, isn't it?" warbled Emma Guinness, shifting around to avoid a rhinestone that had impacted her butt. "I mean, everybody's all caught up with the science of moviemaking, yet everyone admits they don't know how to do it. I plan to enjoy myself. That way the public will, too."

Melissa laughed. "That's always been my motto. I get on pretty well with my leading men."

Emma joined in the laughter, glad that Melissa had brought up the subject. She was aware that it hadn't been accidental. The interview she had shared with the star at her Benedict Canyon home had been "no holds barred." It had stretched over a couple of bottles of Krug and mostly it had been about Tony Valentino. They knew each other pretty well for two people who didn't believe in friendship.

"Are you still seeing Tony?" said Emma.

"No," said Melissa. She bit her lip at the thought of him, and the way he had behaved toward her. Their bizarre relationship had hardly defined tenderness and commitment, but there had been the closeness of bodies. At least he had bothered to be beastly to her. That took effort and energy. It had been an involvement of sorts. Then, out of the blue, it had stopped. There had been no explanations, no apologies, and no goodbyes. One minute he had been her pirate lover, cruel, crude, and unpredictable, but at least *there*. The next moment he had gone. She hadn't been able to reach him on the phone. Her letters, faxes, and Fed-Exes had gone unanswered. His agent had given her the Hollywood runaround. For a time she had wallowed in hysteria. She had dreamed of sending him dead chickens and skewered dolls, and she had left terrible messages on his answering machine promising retribution, and then begging him to return. Finally, the heat of her feelings had cooled and, in the unforgiving light of her new dawn, she knew exactly what she wanted for her sadistic lover. Even in the days when she had lain used and abused on the floor, hosed down by his lust, she had wanted to hurt him. Now, deserted and discounted, she planned far worse things for the boy who had dared to humiliate Melissa Wayne, the star the sane world yearned for.

"He went back with Pat, I heard," said Emma.

"I heard that too," said Melissa through tight teeth.

Their glinting eyes locked together.

"But he's still the supporting actor in our movie, isn't he, Melissa? It's his one shot at fame, isn't it? Wild horses won't make him give that up."

Melissa smiled. She liked the "our movie" bit, and it was true. Melissa was the box-office legend. Emma was the studio boss. Between them they owned the film. If they stuck together, they couldn't be defeated.

"Meaning?" drawled Melissa, her smile deepening.

"I'm just stating facts," said Emma. "Tony's going to have to realize that we're the boss. If he wants the movie, he pleases us."

Melissa Wayne squirmed in her chair, pushing her pelvis down on the heel on which she sat. The *boss!* She was going to be Tony's *boss!* She was going to get control of him at last. Her bit would cut into *his* mouth; her whip would crack against *his* flank. She leaned forward into the conspiracy.

"That will be very nice," she said quietly, with an intensity that Emma could almost touch.

"I should say that I've made a few changes in the script," said Emma, a half smile playing around her lips.

Melissa was vibrating on her wavelength. The changes that Emma had made would be good changes. There was no question about it.

"What I've done basically," continued Emma, "is to beef up the love scenes between you and Tony. And I've strengthened the obsession element. Before, there was a certain equality in the relationship. Now, we have a struggling young actor, infatuated with a cruel and capricious megastar. Does that sound like you and Tony, Melissa?"

The expression on Melissa Wayne's face said that it sounded like sweet music. Her mind was racing deliciously, but there was a question she needed to have answered.

"What does Pat Parker think of that?" she said.

"We don't have to worry about Pat Parker. I don't subscribe to the 'auteur' theory. She's just the director. She does what I tell her to do. What *we* tell her to do. So far she knows nothing, but if she doesn't like it, she can walk."

"And Latham?" Melissa wanted to cover all the angles. In moviemaking it was vital to understand where the ultimate power lay. She could hardly control her excitement. A beautiful idea was forming in her mind. Could Emma Guinness be thinking it, too?

"Latham will give me carte blanche. My control at Cosmos is total. He's promised me that." Emma waved an expansive hand in the air for emphasis.

"So we're going to make a very steamy movie," whispered Melissa. Her pink tongue darted out to moisten already damp lips.

"Oh, yes, we are," agreed Emma. "A very sexy, very *realistic* movie."

Melissa had been given the opening. She had hardly needed it.

"In a couple of my shows," she said, "when the chemistry has been right, I've found that a closed set can do wonders for a love scene. It helps if you can really let go—keep the acting to a minimum, if you know what I mean."

"I know *exactly* what you mean. Keep the acting to the *bare* minimum," Emma laughed.

"I wonder if Tony could be persuaded . . ." said Melissa wickedly, the lewd images already dancing in her mind.

"I feel absolutely certain that he could, if it's put to him in the right way . . ." Emma's X-rated thoughts were steaming up her brain. "Of course, Pat Parker would have to direct the scene, wouldn't she? There'd probably be fireworks!" The glee positively creamed from Emma's words.

"Yeah, she'd go wild, wouldn't she?" agreed Melissa, delighted. "But if we sort of insisted on it, and didn't back down. If we stuck together and issued ultimatums and things, then everyone would have to fall into line . . ." Melissa twiddled her fingers in her hair like the willful child she was.

"Pre*cisely.*" Emma Guinness leaned back in her chair. Her voice was thick with satisfaction.

They were singing in harmony. They were joined to each other at the hip. They were glued to each other by the intensity of their hatred for Tony Valentino, and by the force of their weird lust for him. It was an unholy alliance. It was an invincible one.

"Have you by any chance got a copy of your revised script? I'd like to take a look at it tonight."

Melissa Wayne was a throbbing beacon of perverse desire. Lust bubbled in her blood. Loathing foamed in her soul.

Emma picked up the blue-covered script from her desk. She held it out toward Melissa. "Take a look at page one," she said.

EMMA GUINNESS was taking the meeting. She sat behind the vast desk and peered around the room like a scientist eying a cage of experimental rats. Her audience had the expectant, hang-dog appearance of Hollywood hotshots in the presence of someone hotter than themselves. They smiled a lot, shifted about, and behind their nervous eyes you could see them dreaming up clever things to say. The executive producer, fat, blond, and forty, was clearly a candidate for gallstones. The two junior production execs in identical Montana-type brown leather jackets, 501's, and boots, seemed thin and worried as well they might be with bank repo orders threatening on the serious cars they couldn't quite afford. The scriptwriter was desperate, and with excellent reason. He was facing the firing squad. The producer, pulled into the project both because he had an on-lot deal with the old Cosmos and because he had a mahogany-brown nose, was tuning up.

"I'd just like to say—on behalf of us all—that Mr. Latham has made a brilliantly original choice in hiring you to run the studio. I'm a great admirer of your new magazine, and I just know that wonderful times are ahead for Cosmos. It's a thrill to be part of them." He pulled out a large handkerchief and wiped sweat from his greasy brow. Had it been enough? Was his producer deal safe? He hadn't had a sniff at a hit in five years. He was about as expendable as it was possible to get.

Emma nodded curtly. "We're here to discuss the *Malibu* script," she said in a way that made it sound like an all-purpose rebuke.

She picked it up from the desk between thumb and forefinger as if it were contaminated. Then she dropped it. It fell, and lay there among the pencils and telephones, half-open, half-closed. "I think you should all know that I'm rewriting it."

Everyone looked at everyone else. Power went to heads in Hollywood. Delusions were always grandiose. The fawning subservience of inferiors and the inventiveness of their flattery unhinged even the most stable, and there were few enough of those in town. However, it usually took a week or two to happen. The guinness chick, having pulled the job from the hat against odds that were far greater than astronomical, had apparently succumbed to Tinsel Town's occupational disease with earth-shattering speed. Now, she thought she could write a script. Clearly, she was a frustrated "serious" writer. A lot of people who ended up running magazines were. Starved of a Nobel, the intellectual manqué had her sights on a screenwriting Oscar. They all groaned inside. This was a textbook example of how movie stinkers got born.

"Major rewrites?" tried the jumpy scribbler who'd done the first draft.

"Not so *very* major," said Emma. The writer brightened visibly. His credit might still be safe.

"What I've basically done is strengthened the sex. We're lucky enough to have Melissa in this movie, and you don't hire a Streisand unless she gets to sing."

Tweedle Dum and Tweedle Dee, the nervous young Turks, laughed obsequiously to show that they'd got the joke. Melissa's love scenes were the stuff of legend. They were what her box office was all about. Then there were those rumors—the ones about her liking to do it for *real*.

"Is that wise?" tried the producer. "I mean, the sex has been understated in this summer's movies, and they've done great."

Emma laughed her nastiest laugh.

"Well, you have vast experience, Mr. . . . Mr. . . ." She petered out, rudely insinuating that she had forgotten the man's name. "And we must all listen to what you say, but at the new Cosmos we are going to *try* to escape the old thinking. That was why Dick hired me. The safest thing to do, supposedly, is to copy the movies that worked last year. We are going to try to live a little more dangerously, and with a little more imagination. I happen to think that *Malibu* needs hot sex. It's a movie about obsession and about love. Love and sex go together, you know. You ought to try it sometime."

The producer was eager to show that Yes was his middle name. He did a 180-degree handbrake turn.

"Yeah, Emma, you're right. 9½ *Weeks* might not have hit big domestic, but it was hot as hell on video, did a hundred million overseas, and made Basinger an international star. They're making a sequel. And *Sea of Love* did gangbuster business. In an age of look-don't-touch sex, I think the public wants sensuality. No nasty diseases from watching it. I'm game, up to and including . . . if you know what I mean. Is Valentino?"

"Valentino will do whatever it takes," said Emma, drifting away into the reverie called "revenge."

She had never forgotten, nor would she ever forget, the things he'd once said to her. This was the payoff from the pact she'd signed with the devil. Her new life was running clockwork smooth. Murder and blackmail had been swapped for a studio, and ultimate power over those she hated. It was the perfect deal, and it had taken steel nerves of a strength they didn't know about in Hollywood, where they were supposed to have invented the things. These losers in her office had no idea what she was allowed to do. The poor fools thought that Latham was the bossman. How could they know that she owned Latham, far more surely than if she had married him? A single phone call and he would be booked on a murder one. She could do it right now. She could pick up the phone on her desk and say to the cops, "Latham did it." They had only to take his fingerprints, and it would be Hello, San Quentin. Later, she'd make him give her money, and all the other things. Right now she had what she wanted—people to play with, and power over the boy who had done her wrong, and over the woman who loved him.

"I get the feeling that you'll be taking a day-by-day interest in this show," said the producer carefully.

"You feel right," snapped Emma. "Pat Parker reports to me. Everyone does, okay? Of course, we will respect *all* Melissa Wayne's opinions. She's the engine on this thing. It's her vehicle. She gets what she wants when she wants it. Understood? If there are any problems, anytime, day or night, somebody contacts me. I can't emphasize enough how badly I will feel if anybody upsets Melissa."

She peered around the room for nonexistent dissent. She knew she was encouraging a breach of the usual chain of command, and that it was totally unorthodox. But that didn't matter. These idiots thought the name of the game was to make mere money. They hadn't a clue that it was called "revenge."

"SEND HER in," said Emma. She took a deep breath. This was going to be fun, but it was going to be dangerous fun. Pat Parker was her own size. She felt like putting her ankle boots up on the desk as a power play, so she did. What a pity she never smoked. For the first time in her life she saw the point of cigars.

"Listen, Emma, what the hell's going on around here? I've just heard from some gofer that you're rewriting the script. Why wasn't I told?"

Pat came in at a run and shooting from the hip. She was furious. Her words splattered like bullets into the armor-plated shield of the Guinness aura.

"Yeah, I did some rewriting. You know how it is. Nobody can write out here. On this side of the Mississippi, words are things you use on telephones."

"Don't be clever. Explain why I was out of the loop."

"Heavens, Pat, you're so *direct*. This isn't a John Wayne movie. Calm down, for goodness' sake."

"I'm not calm. Why the hell should I be? The studio boss rewrites the script and holds a script conference without me, and I get to hear about it on the grapevine. It's incredibly unprofessional . . . at the very least."

She towered over the Guinness desk, her cheeks red, her eyes flashing.

"Ah, yes, we movie old-timers must remain professional at all costs, mustn't we? As a veteran studio chief, I salute your concern as an experienced director." The sarcasm didn't last long on her mean lips. Emma's eyes narrowed. "Actually, I didn't tell you because I thought you might object, and I wanted to sound out the others first, the ones who've actually made a movie before. I know it doesn't count for much, but I thought I'd pick what passes for their brains."

"The rumor is you want to make a porno flick," said Pat, cutting through the bullshit to the bottom line.

"Pat! Pat! Do me a favor, will you? I mean, *really*. Please don't underestimate me. It's true that I've made the movie more sensual. It needed that. And I've made some changes to emphasize the obsessional aspect of Tony's feelings for Melissa . . . but that's it. I don't think you should be overreacting like this. Why don't you sit down and relax?"

Pat didn't want to sit down. She wanted to find out what was going down. Something was. From the moment the bombshell had been dropped that Emma had gotten the Cosmos job, Pat's antennae had been twitching like crazy. She had seen the vicious side of the English girl, and she knew that Emma hated Tony, and disliked her. Now she was taking a personal interest in *Malibu* to the extent that she was actually fiddling around with the script. She must have a billion more important things to do in her new job. The whole thing was deeply sinister. She was hotting up the sex—between Tony Valentino and the nympho star he'd been involved with while Pat's relationship with him had been on hiatus. Pat couldn't avoid the bizarre feeling that this was personal, that the entire movie, the script, the casting, the weird choice of Emma to run Cosmos, were all part of a plot to drive her mad. Of course, she also realized that was impossible. The movie would cost twenty million bucks minimum. Nobody would risk that kind of cash to work off private grudges. Anyway, this was Latham's show. He was first and foremost a businessman. Although he had reason to hate her, he had seemed to love her, and the fact that he had kept her on the picture was a powerful indicator of the respect he felt for her. Then there was Latham and Tony. Tony had saved Latham's life. That would count for something when the chips were down, if it ever got that far.

Despite all that, Pat knew she was going to be baited. It had started already. The script changes were part of it. Later it could get worse. But she was in a tricky position. How did you object to something as nebulous as love scenes without sounding like some souped-up Jerry Falwell? She needed to know where she stood.

"Just how strong are the new scenes?" she said.

Emma smiled. She'd been waiting for that one.

"Let's just say that nobody is going to ask 'Where's the beef?'" She paused. "Of course, it may be that you won't feel up to directing them, Pat. That's what I was worried about. That's part of the reason you were momentarily 'out of the loop,' or whatever it was you felt out of. I mean, given that you . . . and Tony . . . and Tony . . . and Melissa . . ." She stopped. She tapped with her pencil on the leather of the desk. "I had hoped," she continued, "that we'd all be able to rise above personal differences and difficulties, but if there are going to be problems, I think we should confront them now."

"Listen, I can handle personalities," barked Pat. "What I want to know is who's directing this movie. Me or you?"

"You or I," said Emma, congenitally unable to ignore bad grammar. "You're the director, Pat. But you direct my script." There was steel in her words.

"And what happens when we disagree?"

"It's Frank Sinatra time. We do it my way."

Pat was furious. Her voice quivered as she spoke.

"Listen, Emma, I'm not a grip or a gofer on this show. I'm the director. Okay, so I'm not the most experienced person in the world and I believe in teamwork and all that stuff, but I'm not going to be your servant on this thing. I have artistic control or I walk, understand? So can the Harry Cohn line and start learning a little civility. You're a woman, remember, not Genghis fucking Khan."

Emma's eyes narrowed.

"Let's get one thing straight," she snarled. "This is a new-style studio, but I'm going to run it the old-fashioned way, as a medieval kingdom, and you can like it or you can lump it. I'm sure," she sneered, "that there are studios all over town just dying to pick up a box-office legend like you. Be my guest. Give them a try. Go across the street. It'll take you a couple of years to find an agent, let alone a job."

Pat jumped up. That was it. She was history. The movie wasn't worth it. She'd nearly betrayed Alabama to do it. Now she was being manipulated by a psychopath. Okay, she had wanted it desperately. She still did. But there were limits. They had been reached. As far as she was concerned, it was over.

"You go, Tony goes," said Emma Guinness.

Pat stopped in her tracks, but her mind whirred on. At the very last minute, the Guinness bitch had raised the stakes. Tony was apparently tied to her deal. In her mind she could see his stricken face. Pat might want this movie, but Tony would sacrifice his life for it. Pat knew that. So, apparently, did Emma. If she walked out of the door, she would not only be destroying her own embryonic movie career, she would be callously aborting Tony's. She loved him. Hell, she wanted to marry him. Could she stamp on his dreams to satisfy her self-respect? What would he think of her if she did that? What would he feel about her if she didn't? Carrots and sticks filled her head. She grabbed at her one lifeline. It was time to bring Latham into the equation. He had wanted her on this movie. He had made a deal and he hadn't broken it, despite her diatribe against him at the Getty. They had an unwritten contract, signed by bodies in the oldest agreement of all. She wasn't particularly proud of it, but she didn't regret it. Especially now.

Yes, Latham was her trump card. The moment had arrived. There was no question. This was the time to play it.

Pat walked back to the desk. She sat down, folded her arms in her lap, and said quietly, "I think we should discuss what you have just said with Dick Latham."

"Do you?" said Emma Guinness. "So do I."

Her face was wreathed in a horrible smile that turned Pat's stomach. It wasn't the response she'd expected. She'd imagined that Emma had been indulging in a personal power trip and that the mere mention of the Latham name would bring her to heel. It hadn't had that effect. Apparently Emma knew something that Pat didn't.

Emma pushed a button on the intercom.

"Get me Latham," she said, and the absence of the prefix "Mr." was the most worrying development of all.

Latham's voice came over the intercom quickly. Too quickly. Usually, he would have kept her waiting for a minute or two behind the secretary wall.

"Yes, Emma?" His voice sounded strange.

"Listen, Dick, I've got Pat in my office. I just wanted to get something clarified, and she's listening in right now. Do I have complete control of this thing—hire and fire, everything? Can I replace Tony and Pat and deal with any legal problems along the line, all on my own say-so? Can you confirm it so that she can hear?"

She beamed across the desk. She wasn't asking a question. She was giving a demonstration.

"I hope that won't be necessary, Emma," said Dick Latham in a distant voice. "I hope Pat will see things your way, but yes, you have complete control. Cosmos is your baby. Whatever you decide will have my complete support. My votes are your votes. You have my word on that."

"Thank you, Dick." She flicked a switch and cut him off without bothering to say good-bye.

She leered at Pat, her eyes gleaming with pleasure at the demonstration of her awesome power.

"So, Pat Parker, it's make-your-mind-up time," she said.

It was. Pat tried to understand the extraordinary conversation she'd just heard. Latham had come across like a Guinness lapdog. It was the most bizarre thing she'd ever witnessed. What on earth had happened to him? But there wasn't time for that sort of speculation. The fact was that her trump had been effortlessly trumped. It was down to her. It was down to this. Could she destroy Tony's dream for a matter of her own personal principle? The answer was quite simple. No. She couldn't. She loved him too much. He wanted too much. There was only one thing to be done with her pride. She must swallow it, even if it choked her.

"I'll direct on your terms," she said.

~17~

PAT BURIED HER head in the towel and shifted around in the sand as she tried to get comfortable in the ninety-degree heat. She'd felt like Zuma, and boy had she gotten it. This wasn't the sophisticated dunes of Broad Beach or the semi-private sands of the Colony. This was Togetherness, Love, and the Beach Boys in a Coppertone plastic paradise of hard young bodies and the dreams of teenage queens. All around, beachland throbbed. Bats whacked against rubber balls, Frisbees skimmed the hot sand, and rock blared from ghetto blasters as the Angelenos enjoyed their escape from the sticky city. Beside her, Tony Valentino screwed up his eyes as he read the script. From time to time Pat noticed him wince.

"What do you think?"

"It's a great part. Could be a neat movie. It's just the sex bits. They're porno. Hard, not soft."

"We can tone them down. Words mean nothing in a visual medium," said Pat with a bravado she didn't feel. She agreed with Tony. *Malibu* was a fascinating study in obsession. The characters were the plot. It explored the neurosis called "love" in a spellbinding way. But the sex was true blue. For years Hollywood had been flirting with the idea of hard core with name stars, and the best that it had managed was the watered-down *9½ Weeks*. Well, *Malibu* was straight up and there was little or nothing Pat could do about it. The day before she had surrendered to Emma Guinness, and a foot or two away, his bronzed body slicked with oil in the bright sun, was the gorgeous reason. The fact that her gut instinct told her the movie would make him a star was both the good and the bad news. The question on her mind was this. How the hell would she be able to direct the sex scenes that Emma had dreamed up?

"But how much *can* you change if Latham told you both that Emma has total control?" said Tony. "I wonder how the hell she conned him. It's funny, I thought the guy was tough. I thought he was brutal, but wise. But he's a fool, and a weak one. Guinness has hung him out to dry."

266

He was puzzled. Latham had surprised him. It seemed as if he'd undergone a dramatic character change. It was difficult to explain.

"It's not going to be easy to handle this," said Tony.

"I expect Melissa will find it easy enough to handle."

Pat wanted to bite off her tongue. She hadn't meant to say that, but she had a lot on her mind. They were back together again. The past, however, didn't vanish overnight. They hadn't discussed Melissa Wayne, but Pat and the rest of Hollywood knew they'd had an affair. How had it ended? Hell, *had* it ended? There were unanswered questions and now the script called for on-screen reincarnation of the off-screen lust. If he had been the boy next door, Tony and she would have spent the rest of their lives talking about it, *communicating*, sharing their feelings in the way that was universally supposed to be healthy. But Tony had never lived next door to anybody. He came from some Spockian planet. The normal rules didn't apply to him. It was a reason to love him.

"How will *you* handle it?" He threw her remark right back at her. If they were to survive the Guinness/Wayne assault, it would have to be together. If they were divided at this early stage, they would fall fast.

"I'm a big girl," said Pat, feeling like a little one. "It's only acting. I'm not a popcorn muncher from Peoria who thinks it's real. Kissing someone for twenty-six takes before breakfast isn't fun. It's work."

"Kissing isn't the problem," said Tony, throwing the script down onto the sand to the envious glances of half a dozen Valley girls. "Emma is. Melissa is."

"You worried she'll try her famous let's-forget-the-acting routine?"

He didn't answer. He remembered the Wayne body draped over the bed while he used it for his angry pleasure. He had been in control then. He wasn't now. This wasn't his show, and, despite her title, it wasn't Pat's either. The movie belonged to the only two women in the world who had reason to hate him.

Pat sat up. "I've got a great idea." She laughed. "Actresses always want to direct. Melissa and I could swap. That way you'd get to do all those dirty things with *me*."

He smiled at her gallant attempt to lighten up. He touched her shoulder, letting his finger rest on the oiled skin, tracing a *P* on the firm flesh.

"We ought to be working," he said. "I should be learning lines. You should be scouting locations. What the hell are we doing on the goddamn beach?"

"I love you," she said.

"I love you back."

"You send my love back?"

It was their joke. She rolled over to be closer to him. She could smell him, and he smelled so masculine, as if his body contained all the strength in the world. She wanted to lick it, to taste the saltiness of him. She did.

"Hey, this is a public beach."

"There's no rule against eating," said Pat, her voice soft and silky.

"Oh, yes there is," he said. A few feet away a trio of tanned teenagers were giggling at them.

Pat stared up at the brilliant sun. It was the lull before the storm. Yes, she should be working, but work would be her life for the next year, and there would be no fun in it, only blood, toil, sweat, and tears. She had come here with Tony today because in her heart she knew it would be their last togetherness. Soon they would be on the set, buffeted by storms and the raging sea and all the perils of the celluloid deep. They might not survive it. At least they would be able to look back to this day, and remember when life had been simple—suntan oil, hot dogs, cold Cokes—with the low surf rasping at the beach and kids all around who didn't know the meaning of care. She smiled to herself. They were the director and the star of a major studio movie. There wasn't a person on the sand who wouldn't have traded places with them. Yet she envied *them*, their simplicity, their freedom, the security of their tomorrows. The dice man, as usual, was dealing out his paradoxes and his oxymorons. The failures were happy. The successful were miserable in the prison of their fame. Why not, then, try to fail? Why, then, try to succeed? There was no sense in the conundrum. Life, as always, hoarded its mysteries and defied those who sought to understand it.

"I wonder if Alabama can see us now, and King," she said, and her voice caught in her throat as she remembered them.

"Alabama'll be too busy sampling the cold Mexican in heaven," Tony laughed.

But it seemed that he was wrong. The portable cellular telephone was ringing in Pat's Mark Cross tote bag, and when she picked it up the voice on the line was quite clear.

"Pat Parker? This is Pete Withers. I'm an attorney at Withers, Salisbury, Caldwell, and Carruthers. I wanted to talk to you about Mr. Ben Alabama's will."

"His *will?*" said Pat.

"Yes, it seems that he has appointed you the sole beneficiary of his estate, and the curator of his entire photographic legacy. I think we should meet as soon as possible," said the man called Withers.

Pat's mouth was wide open, but she managed to make it work.

"I think we should," she said.

―

TOMMY HAVERS paced up and down on the carpet of Latham's study.

"I don't think Mary Grossman is up to the job at *New Celebrity*," he said. "Maybe we should try to poach Tina Brown from *Vanity Fair*, or get Emma Soames to come over from London. We'll be okay for an issue or two, but then it'll start to unravel."

Dick Latham waved away the worries as if they were of no account. Havers looked at him, astounded. This was his *baby*. The magazine had topped their conversations for the last year and a half.

"What have the police got on the Alabama arson thing?" he asked abruptly.

Havers shifted gears. He appeared distracted. A sixth sense told him that his boss was losing it. That mattered. If the business started to slide, *he* would be blamed for it.

"Oh, I don't know. Let me think . . . oh yes, the police say it was premeditated. They've got the prints of the suspect. And they think he was driving some high-end sports car. There were tire marks on the gravel. They've got casts. They seem to think it was a Porsche."

"One or two of those in L.A. County," said Latham.

"Only one guy's prints on the gas can, though," said Havers.

He was impatient. He wanted to get on. There were important things on the agenda, like Cosmos and the behavior of the volatile Emma Guinness in the preproduction of its first vital movie.

"They can hardly fingerprint everyone with a Porsche, can they?" said Latham. He didn't sound very sure about that.

"Hardly," agreed Havers. "I wonder if Alabama was really a target or whether it was just some well-heeled fruitcake who likes to start fires."

"I'll buy the nut theory," said Latham. "It's safe to do that in California."

"Speaking of which," said Havers. "Emma Guinness has got them all bobbing like corks over at Cosmos. She's spent her first five days rewriting the *Malibu* script, for God's sake, as if there wasn't anything more important to do. Turned it into an haute-porn skin flick, by all accounts. The only good news is that Wayne's thrilled. Maybe that's a clever move. Parker and Valentino aren't exactly Fellini and Cruise. If the movie opens, it'll be because of Melissa."

"How are Parker and Valentino taking it? I mean, you know, they're an item."

"Who cares?" said Havers. "Let 'em walk if they don't like it. They need the movie. The movie doesn't need them."

"As Alabama's heir, Pat Parker doesn't need anybody," said Latham shortly. She had become rich overnight. People like Havers underestimated the power of serious money. Those like Latham, who had it, didn't.

"No, she's staying put. Her guy's got stars in his eyes, and she's hot for him. And Cosmos is putting up twenty million to finance her directing debut. That's a lot of Alabama prints on the block at Sotheby's and Christie's. She's not going anywhere . . . unless she gets pushed."

Havers sounded hopeful. He didn't know much about the making of movies but, like the business pro he was, he was learning fast. People were telling him things. The cognoscenti agreed that if the movie was to have a chance in hell, the clever move would be to ditch the unknowns.

"Don't underestimate her, Tommy," said Latham. His voice was gentler now. "She's tough, and she has more talent than you think. Valentino, too. He's got what it takes."

"Yeah, and he saved your life." Havers, the perennial servant, sensed a new weakness in his usually masterful master. It encouraged him to live dangerously.

"That's not the point," snapped Latham. "The guy can act. He's got the X factor. I'm surprised you can't see it, but then it's not exactly a profit-and-loss statement, so I suppose you can't be expected to. Tony's an original. He doesn't give a damn about other people, and he's motivated. When people cross him, they get to see the terror of his ways. In fact," mused Dick Latham, "he rather reminds me of myself."

EMMA GUINNESS erupted onto the tangled chaos of the set like a hurricane hammering into the Gulf Coast. Secretaries, personal assistants, and junior studio executives flew about in her wake. They scribbled as they half walked, half ran, trying desperately to pick up the pearls she was unloading before the swine.

"I want the studio lease deal with Universal tied up tight as a bondage freak, okay? Tell the lawyers they're history if there's an 'out.' Somebody write it, I'll sign it, if anybody *can* write these days. I know the telephone murdered word ability. Maybe the fax'll kiss it to life."

"What's the news on the Malibu site?" dared a lowly assistant.

"Shit, I don't know. They just buried the old fart who kyboshed it. The least we can do is stick a sound stage over his grave. Beats rosmaries for remembrance. But that's a Latham thing. Depends on whether or not he's got the nuts for a fight."

The underlings exchanged glances as they scurried along. Guinness was flying high indeed if she could afford shots at the boss of bosses. How soon would it be before flight turned into a free fall? Not long, was the collective prayer.

"I don't want there to be *any* problems with the studio space. We're trying to make a sodding movie here, and I don't want any pissing around. Understood?"

They got the message, but only just. The plummy Guinness vowels and the odd British usage posed problems for Southern California shorthand on the run.

Emma jumped over the wires that ran like varicose veins across the floor, dodged the boom microphones and the camera tracks for the dolly shots, sped past the wardrobe people and the makeup crowd. She headed for the middle of the set, toward the vast double bed. When she reached it, she stopped.

"Christ!" she said. "These are nylon sheets."

"No, they're not *actually* nylon, they're a combination . . ."

"Lose them," barked Emma, cutting off the assistant executive producer as if he were corn in a field. "When I say Pratesi," she thundered, "I *mean* it. And when I say fired I mean that too."

They cowered around her. There was no resistance. It wasn't just the money and the mortgages, the mistresses and the Maseratis. It was more than that. She had hire-and-fire ability for sure, but she had power over people because, ultimately, she was so bright, and so vicious and so utterly convinced she was right. To stand up to her was to be humiliated. She was a masochist's dream, a sadist's worst nightmare. Compared to Emma Guinness, Elm Street's Freddy Kreuger was a friendly old man.

A couple of grips stripped the bed.

"For God's sake, wash your horrid hands before you put the Pratesis on," she grumbled at the gofers. "I don't want my star catching communicable diseases."

Even the surly union members took it, and they weren't in the taking business. On any other set that remark would have closed down the picture.

"Where's Melissa?"

"I'm right here," said a voice from behind her. Melissa Wayne was indeed there. She was undressed to kill. The outsize Ralph Lauren Polo dressing gown was half-undone. Her naked breasts poked provocatively from it. She wore plain white cotton bikini briefs, and nothing else at all but a look of steamy expectation.

"How clever of you, Emma," she pouted, "to run a love scene with the opening credits."

"Well, you look just *wonderful*, Melissa. If I was a fella I'd be in love. Listen, I think I'm in love anyway."

Emma smiled a greasy smile at her secret ally. Sex objects weren't fussy about the gender or the species of their compliments sources. Animals would do. Plants at a push.

"Well, thank you, ma'am," simpered Melissa. "And where, I wonder, is my lover of the morning?" she added.

"Thanking God for his good luck?" joked Emma.

"I'm not so sure." Melissa smiled. The conspirators laughed. In a few moments, when the cameras began to roll, a start would be made on the dish of revenge.

"Okay," said Pat Parker. "We'd better go through this."

She had arrived unnoticed, and it was clear that she wasn't in small-talking mood. She looked pale, short of sleep, and her let's-get-on-with-it manner didn't hide the anxiety that wrapped her like an aura.

"I think," said Melissa, "that we ought to wait for the other half of the love unit. Otherwise, you'll only have to repeat yourself."

Her words were innocent. Her tone wasn't. The "love unit" was invested with the most lascivious connotations.

"Somebody go tell Valentino he's late," barked Emma.

"Late for love," giggled Melissa.

They stood in silence as a minion went to fetch the star. Then Tony was threading his way across the set in a dark red silk dressing gown.

"Hi," he said to no one in particular, tossing his head in the air with a nonchalance Pat knew he didn't feel.

"Well, good *morning*, Tony," purred Melissa. The catlike sound was leopard rather than Siamese.

Pat started talking fast.

"Okay, as you know from the script, this is an under-the-credits shot. The idea is to set the scene for the movie's sensual/obsessional themes. We want the audience to know there's going to be lots more where this came from. Isn't that right, Emma?"

"Oh, yes, that's right. Lots, lots more."

Pat winced at the delight in Emma's voice. "Of course, the usual view is that you introduce the characters before you have them make love, on the principle that sex between strangers is either dull, pornography, or both. However, on *this* occasion Emma's script calls for the ignoring of that particular convention. Ours," she added sarcastically, "not to reason why."

"Ours but to do and die . . . until we drop." Melissa Wayne laughed, demonstrating a surprising knowledge of Tennyson's poem.

"So you start on the floor, and we pan across the room before hitting some close-ups. Then Tony picks Melissa up, walks across to the bed, and then there's the bed bit."

Pat was aware that her bare description hardly did the scene its full erotic justice. She couldn't bring herself to go into more detail.

The silence was expectant. They wanted more direction. They were waiting for her to spell it out.

"The script is quite explicit. I know you've all read it. So perhaps I can leave the mechanics up to you two, and concentrate on the photography and the lighting. Obviously, if there's anything that needs to be changed, I can help with that as we go along," said Pat defensively.

"I like to be directed all the way. I find it helpful. When I'm fucking in public, I need feedback," said Melissa, definitely.

"We're *not* fucking. We're acting," said Tony, angrily.

"Sometimes I get confused between the two," said Melissa, totally unfazed by his irritation. A nearby cameraman suppressed a laugh.

"It was a *façon de parler*," said Emma. "That's French for a manner of speaking." She smiled a superior smile. Melissa smiled back at her.

Melissa and she were singing in unison. It was turning out far better than she had dreamed it could be. Both Pat and Tony looked furious, miserable, and, best of all, totally impotent.

"Is it direction you're after, or a congratulatory running commentary?" Pat sneered at Melissa.

"If you can't handle the one, the other will do," said Melissa wickedly.

"Let's get the hell on with it," said Tony.

"Isn't he romantic?" Melissa giggled. "Thank God I'm a pro."

"You said it," growled Pat.

"Do we need all these people around?" said Emma. She didn't want Melissa to be inhibited.

"No, don't worry, it's fine. I'm not ashamed of my body. If they're going to see it on Main Street, why shouldn't the guys here? We'll save the closed sets for later when it gets a bit more intense."

As if to emphasize her point, she threw back her shoulders and dropped the terrycloth robe on the floor. Her breasts stood there, pointing straight out at the eyes that ate them, in the way the breasts were supposed to do, but never did. It was like a party trick—clever, unexpected, and performed with panache.

Pat couldn't help watching them. Emma gazed in open admiration at the twin weapons of the war that she and the star were waging.

Tony took a deep breath. In the past he had used Melissa Wayne as mercilessly as she would have used him, if she'd been able to get away with it. He didn't feel guilty. She was diamond tough, and the bars of Hollywood were full of beaten-down guys with angel faces who'd been broken on the wheel of her capricious lust. Body dancing with Melissa Wayne was a cardinal terror for all but the very brave. He'd not only survived it, he'd enjoyed it, and best of all had been watching the biter bitten. Now the roles were reversed. She was the one with the power. Only by giving up his dream could he deprive her of it. But still he had feelings, and the seminaked Melissa Wayne had stirred them up as she had intended. No man could remain neutral in the presence of her beauty. The script called for their lovemaking. Across the short space that divided them, he could all but smell her sex. He would have to lose himself in the role as he always did. To seem to love it, he would have to live it. To feel it, he would have to be it. It was his method. It was what he would do now. Pat Parker would have to be banished from his mind. Emma Guinness must disappear. Then there would be only the heat of bodies beneath the hot lights, and the intensity that made his acting so much more real than dull reality.

He, too, looked at the breasts on which Pat and Emma focused.

"It's rude to stare," said Melissa flirtatiously.

Pat walked across the set. "I want you to start here," she lied. "There are three camera angles. Directly above, left oblique, right oblique. We start from above, and that should be Tony on top, naked butt please, with Melissa's legs intertwined in his. Forget the soundtrack, that's heavy classical or some shit. You're kissing passionately, openmouthed with lots of tongue action for the side cameras to catch. I want mouth moisture, lots of it. If you want, that can be artificial. Somebody sponge down Tony's back for the sweat."

"Don't worry, I'll make him sweat. I've done it before," said Melissa.

Pat groaned inside. "*Please* try to remember we're making a movie here," she said sharply.

"I *have* made the odd one or two before," said Melissa, "which is more than can be said about you."

Tony slipped the dressing gown off his shoulders, letting it hang around his belt. A production assistant sponged his back. Pat signaled for lights. The floods came on, bathing the set in instant heat. Pat and Emma retreated to the relative darkness at the edge of the set, leaving the two "lovers" alone.

"I'm looking forward to this," whispered Melissa. "And to the next time."

She sat down on the floor and watched him. He would be new to doing this in public. However good he was, and she sensed he would be very good, it would not be easy for him. He reached for the knot of his belt, and he stared away into space as he undid it. He flung the robe away out of camera.

He was naked. Melissa's eyes feasted on her target. It would be her barometer. She had one purpose in this scene, one single purpose in life. She had to excite it, make it firm, make it strong, make it want her as she already wanted it. She focused in on her objective, willing it to be, to become, to live and to love her, and her hands reached for the elastic of her panties. Convention dictated that she keep them on, that her costar's body be draped carefully over her to hide the fact that she was wearing them. But that wasn't the Wayne way. Real was real, and fake was fake, and flesh must touch if hearts were to beat faster. It was the surefire way to turn the box-office cash flow from a trickle to a raging river. It had worked before. It would work again.

She pushed her panties down her legs and kicked them free. She lay back on the floor, her legs tantalizing inches apart, the perfect triangle of blond pubic hairs framing delicate lips of pink.

"Okay, Tony, get into position, please." Pat's voice was strained as she tried desperately to be businesslike.

He lowered himself onto her, and she thrust up to meet him. The warmth of her downy hair pushed gratefully against his still sleeping flesh. He shuddered at the tender touch of her as he was supposed to. She reached up, putting her arms around his neck, and drew him in toward her, capturing him in the closeness trap where minds deferred to bodies and the will was weak. The scent of her wrapped him. She was so soft and yielding, so firm in her purpose. The cameras were not yet rolling and already she was making love to him, warming him up, preparing him for what was to come.

"Action!" shouted Pat Parker, and Melissa Wayne's lips rose up to feast from his.

Pat began to sweat. She could feel the wetness beneath her arms, and it wasn't the arc lights that were causing it. It was what they were bathing. On one level this was just a kiss. It was neither the first nor the last of a billion such celluloid lip meetings, and it should have had about as much significance as an arms control chat in Geneva. Except that this was Tony, and that was Melissa, and the only thing parting the bits of them that rubbed together was skin. Pat looked away. She looked back. She fought back the clammy nausea that gripped her. It had hardly started, and she herself had called for "action." Now all she wanted to do was to scream "Cut." She tried to calm down. She was the director. She had to think like a lens. She did it all the time in photography. Usually it was second nature to her. It wasn't now. She fought to be objective. Was the kiss too long, too deep, too open, too closed? Hell, it was perfect. It was perfect hell. The on-camera lovers meant it. Tony was eating Melissa. She was devouring him. They were as close as two pages of a scented letter in an envelope, and it was as welcome to Pat Parker as a tooth in a pumpkin pie.

It was Melissa who came up for air.

"How are we doing?" she murmured through soaking, bruised lips.

Melissa smiled across at Pat. She pouted up at Tony, his face inches from hers. All her plans were working. God, it was wonderful. Tony was entering into the spirit of the love scene as she had hoped he would, and the damage was all over the face of the director. The mouth action was the hors d'oeuvre, but it hadn't existed in isolation. The lower half of her body had been wriggling and writhing with snakelike sensuality. Already it was having its inevitable effect on the flesh and blood of the boy she hated to love. For now it was invisible. Soon it wouldn't be. In a few minutes they would all know that he wanted her. They would be able to see his lust. Pat Parker would have to watch the undeniable evidence of his desire.

How were they doing? Melissa had asked.

"Fine," mumbled Pat. "Are you okay, Tony?" she said, aware that it was a ridiculous question. She desperately needed some warm response from him. "I'm suffering for my art"; "I still love you"; "The cow's got bad breath"—any or all of those would have been music to her ears.

"Maybe we should get on with the scene," he answered coldly, after a long pause. He hated being brought back from the superreality of his illusion. That was why the stage was so wonderful. There, he was on his own in his private make-believe world. The critics came before and after, never during the performance. But he could sense Pat's pain. It filled the set. He should care about it, but he couldn't because this was work. This was his art. The only thing that mattered was that it be good. Anything else was a distraction. In the story he was a lover obsessed with a legend. That meant for now, for these brief moments, he *was* that person. He wanted to get back to Melissa's body. He wanted to drown in the juices of Melissa's love. The fact that he despised her in real life was a dangerous, art-crippling thought. As such, he fought to banish it from his mind.

Pat heard what he said. She understood him well enough to read between the lines. She knew what he was thinking, and it hurt like hell. But there was no going back. There was only one thing she could possibly do, and so she did it.

"Okay, let's go to take two," she said.

"What a *terrific* idea," said Emma Guinness from somewhere behind her back.

PAT PARKER stormed into the Winnebago, slamming the door behind her. Tony, sitting at the dressing table, wiping makeup from his face, spun around.

"You fuck rat," she shouted. "You were making love to her."

"Don't give me that shit, I was acting . . ."

"Acting. You weren't acting. I could *see* you weren't acting. Jesus, you had a . . . everyone could see it. I mean, Tony, really . . ."

He jumped up. "I was acting, damn it. Don't do this, Pat. Don't do this to me. Don't do this to yourself. You're playing into their hands. Emma wants it. Melissa wants it. Don't give it to them on a plate."

"It's you. Hell, it's *you,* Tony. Don't lie to me. She was turning you on out there. Admit it. Go on, admit it."

"It doesn't mean anything, Pat. It was nothing." He knew he wasn't giving her the answer she wanted, and he couldn't, because her accusation was true.

He was human. It was blood that ran in his veins, not water. Nobody could have carried off a scene with Melissa Wayne and remained sexually neutral. Yes, she had turned him on. She understood a man's wiring. She had a map of the male circuitry. And that was good. So did the Melissa in the movie. It was why his fictional character had fallen for her. The scene had been real because both actors had wanted to make it real. That was the way he operated. If Pat didn't understand that about him, she understood nothing.

Neither sweet reason nor sweet charity, however, were the emotions playing stage front in Pat Parker's mind.

"It might mean nothing to you, but it means one hell of a lot to me," shouted Pat, her voice breaking. Her eyes were misty. She didn't want to cry, yet tears were close. The heat from the coupling couple had warmed the set. Okay, so it was wild footage and it would be great cinema, but it had tied Pat's stomach in knots. She hadn't had to direct, as threatened. All she'd had to do was watch, and it had been the worst ten minutes of her life so far. In vain she tried to cut herself off from reality, and to retreat into some private world of dissociation, but she hadn't pulled it off. She wasn't an introvert. She was all up front. She always had been and she always would be. Her feelings lived neither in her head nor her heart, but on her sleeve. Well, here they were—the disgust, the jealousy, the anger, and the terrible, horrible pain.

"Pat, please, try to understand . . . you know how it is, we're trying to do something big here, something important. This movie can be totally original. You've got to rise above the pettiness—you've got to."

"Don't tell me what I've got to do. I'm telling you what *you've* got to do. You've got to get the hell out of my life, forever, okay? And I mean it. I don't love you anymore. I don't even like you anymore, because you're a cheap, hustling, egotistical sex maniac. You can't love anybody because you're too in love with yourself."

"Pat, listen. Listen . . ."

But Pat wasn't in a listening mood. What she wanted was action, and not some steamy kiss. Her wild eyes searched the room. She was looking for a weapon, a missile, anything that would escalate this ridiculous word-fest to something genuinely painful. But Tony's dressing room was as bare as his soul, as sparse as his emotions. Then she saw the Sony Sports Walkman. It sat on the chair beside him. He didn't listen to music on it. He listened to himself, saying the godforsaken lines that were the only things he cared about. She bent down, scooped it up, and backed away from him. The wire was wound around it.

"Pat!"

"You fucking *bastard!*" she screamed. She whirled it around her head until it twirled in the air above her like a bright yellow bomb. He didn't duck. He wouldn't would he? Too much bloody dignity. His one concession to self-defense was to raise a half-hearted arm. It didn't stop her. She let fly. The plastic sound machine snaked through the air and whacked into his arm. Then it unhitched itself from the black lead that had held it, and sailed on to catch him a glancing blow on the side of his head above his ear. It didn't stop. It flew toward the dressing table, and made direct contact with the framed photograph that sat there, smashing it to smithereens. The girl in the picture didn't look surprised by the fate that had overtaken her. Maria Valentino was smiling a warm, open smile, full of love and tenderness, through the broken glass that now swathed her. Her beautiful face stared across the years through the devastation and seemed to be talking directly to Pat. "Don't hurt my Tony," said the deep blue eyes. "He's difficult to understand, but you must try to understand him. He's good, and he needs you. You need each other."

Pat's hand flew to her mouth.

"Oh, Tony! Oh, Tony, I'm so sorry."

He walked to the table. His eyes filled with tears. He picked up the wounded portrait, clearing away the broken glass with his fingers, and he stared into the eyes of the mother he loved so desperately. Her picture was torn, down at the bottom, near the soft hands that had so often comforted him; that had rubbed his back to send him to sleep as a child; that had bathed his wounds and held him close when he needed the love he could accept from no one else. A tear squeezed out, a tear for the memories and all the love that had gone unspoken until the dread night when it was too late. Now, there was just his mother's picture, and out there, somewhere in the still heavens, her spirit was watching over him as it always had.

He turned to Pat, and his face was full of sorrow. He wasn't angry. On his grief-savaged face were all the regrets of all the children through eternal time. Why, when you loved so much, were the words so difficult to say? Why, when it was too late, was it so easy and so painful to feel? There were no answers to the past, only ill-learned lessons for the future, but in the present there were the tears of regret that streamed down the cheeks of Tony Valentino. His shoulders crumpled. He sat down hard in the chair, and he buried his head in his hands. From between them came the sound of his sobs.

For a brief moment Pat stared at him in wide-eyed shock. It was a moment of total revelation. She was looking through a window into Tony's soul. Now at last she knew what it was she wanted. She wanted this, the quivering heart of him wrapped in the beautiful, heartless package that was all he would allow the silly world to see. On the table lay the photograph of the only person he had genuinely loved, and Pat knew with a terrible certainty that she wanted to be her replacement more than she wanted life itself. Light-years ago, Pat had been angry with him. Now she adored him with a greater intensity than she had dreamed possible. She knelt down beside him, and she held him tight in her arms as his mother would have held him. She drew him close, to squeeze out the sorrow, and her fingers reached up to caress his neck, to give comfort, to say sorry.

"I love you, Tony," she whispered. "Oh, my God, I love you so much."

⸺

"I NEED to talk to you."

Melissa Wayne climbed into the passenger seat of the studio golf cart and stared straight ahead. The fact that she didn't look at Tony as she spoke made two points at once. She was going to say something that was difficult to say, and she was going to say something important.

Tony Valentino took a deep breath. Off the set he didn't want to have anything to do with Melissa Wayne. She was big trouble, and any interaction at all could disturb the vital on-camera chemistry he was working so hard to get right.

"Okay," he said, without enthusiasm. "I'm going over to business affairs. Want to come for the ride?"

"I want to do it for real," said Melissa. Bushes were not things she beat about. Still, she didn't look at him.

Tony swallowed hard. He'd wondered when this was coming. He knew exactly what she meant.

"What do you mean?" he said.

"I mean on the set, making love, for real. It's the best way. It's the only way. I've done it before. It works."

She talked fast, as if afraid he'd interrupt her.

"You're joking," he said.

Now she turned toward him. He leaned over the wheel and faced her.

"No, Tony. I'm not joking. You know that. I'm serious. It's vital for the movie. It'll give it total believability. Trust me. There's no problem. We've done it before . . . and it was fun." She allowed herself a provocative half smile. Fun was what it hadn't been. It had been wild, painful, ridiculously intense, but it had never been fun. Time and again he had treated her like a slut in an alley, a shuddering, juddering stand-up trick, five bucks' worth at the most in the poor part of town. To be used like that had been a first for the movie star—a delicious, humiliating first that must and would be paid for with Tony Valentino's peace of mind.

"You're crazy," he said, and the disgust was in his voice. The old anger was building, overriding the delicate politics of the shoot. Melissa Wayne might be a famous actress, but at heart she was a two-bit nympho.

"I'm not crazy," said Melissa Wayne evenly. "I'm the star."

"Drop dead, Melissa," he said.

For a long time she looked at him, and her face ran the gamut of emotions from initial shock, through irritation, to a frighteningly self-confident calm.

"I wonder," she said at last, "just who will end up getting dropped."

—

"CONGRATULATIONS, TONY. I saw the dailies last night. Your scene with Melissa was a blast."

Emma Guinness stood up as Tony Valentino stalked into her office. He sat down in the chair opposite her before she had a chance to offer it to him. He made no reference to her pseudocompliment. Instead, he slid his eyes up and down the cream silk coat and skirt she wore, and his expression said he'd like to throw up over it. Emma's most senior personal assistant had delivered the summons to the meeting. There had been no way to avoid the one-on-one, but he didn't have to like it.

"Which brings me to the little problem that has arisen."

She sat down again, smoothing the skirt over her fat thighs.

"It seems," she said, a smirk on her lips, "that our star is not happy. By 'our star' I mean, of course, Melissa."

Tony stared at her aggressively. He'd guessed it. Melissa had gone whining to Emma. Had she told the truth? Or had she invented some other complaint? The latter, most likely. She could hardly have gone bleating to Emma that her costar wouldn't screw her on the set. He said nothing.

"It seems that her initial enthusiasm for you has waned, if you will forgive my British understatement," said Emma carefully. "She's produced a long list of grievances ranging from . . ."—she peered down at her desk seemingly to consult some list—". . . from 'lack of professionalism,' whatever that means, to . . . to 'bad breath.' " She laughed heartily. "I guess after the kissing scene yesterday she is in a position to know about *that*, although judging from her performance, it didn't seem to put her off."

The twin spots of anger sprang up on Tony's cheeks as they were supposed to. He was a vain man, and he didn't like being made fun of. In all his life he had never been accused of anything as deeply wounding as having halitosis. It didn't matter that it wasn't true. It was the cruel falsity of the accusation that enraged him. Body odor, dandruff, greasy skin, dirty ears were things that other people had, not Tony Valentino. He didn't mind being thought a bastard, cold and aloof, mean and uncaring. They went with the turf of obsessional ambition. Supermen suffered those afflictions. Only nerds, however, had bad breath. He wouldn't deny it. That was beneath his dignity. So he glowered in silence, and he waited for the other things that he knew were coming.

"I suppose I owe it to you to let you know what else she said. It's a real litany of grievances, I'm afraid, and the bottom line is that she's badly upset. Let's see, oh, I don't know, 'ignorance of fundamental movie techniques, bad acting, lack of consideration for colleagues, unfortunate personal habits, hygiene'—that's apparently *apart* from the breath problem—and, last but not least, she said you embarrassed her dreadfully by getting . . . sort of . . . excited . . . during the lovemaking. She says that's happened before with amateurs and that it always makes her 'sick to her stomach,' yes, that was the actual expression she used."

"She wanted me to screw her for real on the set. You've heard the rumors. She has a reputation for it," Tony exploded. "I told her to forget it, and now she's come to you with all these lies."

"Ah!" said Emma Guinness, with the wisdom of the sage. "So *that*'s it, is it?" She managed to insinuate that she half believed Tony, but that there was room for doubt. "Argue your case," said her eyes.

"No way," said Valentino's. The "I don't have to explain myself to you or to anyone" was written all over his face.

"Tony, I'm not quite sure that you appreciate the situation in which I find

myself," said Emma Guinness in the tones of a kindly schoolmistress address-
ing a dull student. "I'm trying to run a studio here, make a movie, an important one, a *vital* one. Cosmos is new. I'm new. We're both going to be judged
on how this show turns out. If it's a stinker, nobody in town will want to bring
their people and their scripts to us. We'll be the Mickey Mouse outfit of the
minute. It'll take years to rebuild the studio's reputation . . ." She paused as
if she had a lot further to go.

"So?" said Valentino rudely.

Emma smiled indulgently. *God,* she loathed him. He'd learned nothing.
She had more power than the Almighty, and still he patronized her. Heavens,
she wanted him. Right now she wanted to rip off his blue jeans and eat him
till she was full. She wanted to drown in his wonderful breath, and experience firsthand the state of his personal hygiene. Dirty, clean, and everything
in between, she wanted to taste and enjoy him, until the itch that plagued her
was so well and truly scratched it would never trouble her again.

"So, as I said, I've got big problems. You know how things work. The
nearest thing to a guarantee that a picture will open is the star. That's Melissa, not you, I'm afraid. She's serious box office, and she's not happy. If she
walks, we're gone. Everybody knows everything in this town. They'll be talking 'on-the-set' problems. The movie could become a bomb before it ever
gets made. I can't allow that to happen."

"You want me to screw her?"

Tony stuck his jaw out as he dared her to come clean. If she admitted it,
at least she'd be honest. She'd also be a greasy, brown-nosed bottom dweller
who was prepared to sacrifice every last principle of professionalism to the
demands of turning a buck. And, not least, she'd be making a movie without
Tony Valentino. Method acting had its limits.

"I'm not saying that," said Emma cunningly, as she wiggled out of his
trap. "I couldn't, could I? But I'm asking you to have a little sympathy for the
dilemma in which I find myself. Melissa's the star. She's unhappy with you.
You're the unknown. You get the drift?"

"You're going to fire me because some slut tells you lies?"

"Oh, Tony, Tony, life isn't so black and white," laughed the wryly philosophical Emma. "I haven't said that . . . yet."

The "yet" came as a whiplash, and it brought Tony Valentino up short. He
had retained a naïve belief in the power of truth, that right triumphed in the
end over wrong. Of course, he remembered times it hadn't happened, but on
the whole it did. Suddenly, it looked as if this was going to be yet another
example of the exception proving the rule. His career was at stake, the shot at
stardom that was as vital to him as the air he breathed and the food he ate.
He was under no illusions. If they broke his contract and forced him from
the film, he was finished. He knew that. Emma knew that.

"Frankly, Tony, the business people here are worried. They worry a lot
about you. They worry about Pat. I can handle them, of course. They belong
to me, these people, but I can't ignore what they say entirely. And it's not
just the marketers and the distribution people, it's the guys at Latham

Enterprises, too. Tommy Havers rings me three times a week. He wants you fired, Tony. He thinks that's the safest thing to do, and safety is all he cares about. I spend more time than I have available to spend fighting for your job in this movie, and now Melissa comes howling out of the woodwork, screaming for your blood. What do I get from you in return? I get scowls, and bad tempers, and scarcely veiled dislike. Does that sound like a fair deal to you? What would you do in my position?"

Emma sat back and watched her missiles fall on the enemy position. They were deadly accurate. It would soften him up a bit for the next assault. Emma ladled on the powerful imagery. She was his champion, fighting off the dragons to save his life, her brave sword arm seared by the flames of the filth. It should twang the heartstrings. Bullshit so often did.

"I can see you might have problems," said Tony with minimal generosity. "They don't sound quite as serious as mine."

Emma laughed to show she appreciated his scrawny olive branch. "Other people's problems seldom do," she said. She tapped a pencil on the table. She always did that before she escalated the nastiness.

"I was wondering, in view of everything, if you might find yourself able to meet Melissa halfway, if indeed it is possible to get a little bit pregnant." Again, she laughed to camouflage what she was asking. "It seemed the love scene was going so well, and that . . . to say the very least . . . you were not repulsed by it. Perhaps you could find it in your heart to indulge her, assuming, of course, that your version of her real grievance is true."

"Do you honestly think that I could do that to Pat?" snarled Tony. The disgust was back in his voice.

"Would Pat be happy to see your career go up in smoke?" said Emma.

Tony said nothing. It would certainly be a price that Pat would pay. The question was could *he* pay it. After all, *he* knew that he despised Melissa Wayne. Making love to her had about as much emotional significance for him as brushing his teeth. His problem was his pride. He couldn't stand being manipulated into doing something he didn't want to do. But on the other hand, could he live with the death of his dreams? What did you do without them? What could life mean when they were gone? When he finally got around to dying, at least he wanted to be alive.

"Because it *would* destroy your career," Emma continued. "You do *know* that, don't you? Gossip circulates like blood in Hollywood. They'll have you down as a temperamental no-talent asshole who was a giant-size pain in the butt on the set. 'He believed his own PR,' they'll say. 'He did a cheesecake spread in some magazine and thought he knew how to act. He had the good fortune to get to play opposite Melissa Wayne, who never met a man she didn't like, and he managed to turn off the turn-on queen.' Tony, you won't just be gone, you'll be gone like you'd never been."

"Yeah," said Tony Valentino. It was a time-stretching word. Hell, he needed time to think. This was all too fast. He had to talk to Pat. He had to talk again to Melissa. Something had to be done to stave off the Emma Guinness disaster scenario. Every word of her dire prediction was true. He believed it implicitly. He had one chance. This one. If he didn't take it, the only noise he would hear for the rest of his life would be the sound of doors slamming in his face. Could he do what he was being asked to do? He'd done it before. For *pleasure!* But he'd be destroying his relationship with Pat, and he'd be signing a deal with the devil that would undermine his self-respect forever. On the other hand, how would self-respect survive among the un-dead where he would be spending his zombie future? His marked card would probably extend to Broadway, off-Broadway, up to and beyond reper-tory in the Styx. He might have to give up acting altogether. He recoiled from the thought. Melissa Wayne's body formed in his mind. He could see its curves, smell its alluring smells, hear the wet noises it made when it was excited. Then the vision faded, to be replaced by Pat Parker's accusing eye, large in the viewfinder, as he betrayed her in public.

He shifted from side to side on the chair.

"Yeah, what?" said Emma. She leaned forward, gauging him, sizing him up. When was the correct moment to strike? Now? Milliseconds later? Life was timing. You had to read it right.

"You could order Melissa to back off," he said. Not for one second did he think that was a remote possibility.

Emma smiled the smile of the almost-victor. She was so nearly where she wanted to be, and still Tony Valentino had no idea of her real destination.

"I'm not sure that Melissa is the sort of person who takes orders," said Emma. Inside she was smiling. Every word of Melissa's golf-cart ultimatum had been discussed and planned by the conspirators. Melissa's goal had been Tony Valentino in flagrante delicto on screen. Emma's was slightly different.

Tony felt the cloud of gloom descend, blotting out false hope. It was true. Melissa had the ultimate power. He was being asked to sacrifice his career or his pride. Either way he would lose.

"Of course, as you say, it *would* make all sorts of difficulties for Pat," mused Emma, as if thinking aloud. "I wonder, I just wonder, if we might be able to work something out . . ."

He said nothing. He just stared at her. There was a creepy feeling at the base of his spine.

"I guess if I *really* put myself on the line, I could save you from this. I don't know . . . I could try."

She looked down at her pudgy fingers. She looked up slyly at him. "I could read the riot act to Melissa. Play hardball. Call her bluff. If I say you stay, and dare her to walk, she might not. She'd damage her own reputation if she did. Not fatally, of course, but she'd lose brownie points. And I could hang in tough with Havers, Latham, the people at Enterprises, and the turds in the basement at Cosmos. I could say, 'He stays or I go,' and see how it plays. Of course, they might get rid of *me.* I'm hardly indispensable around here. Studio bosses in this town have the life expectancy of hibiscus flowers. But I *could* try it. I *could.*"

She looked out to the Hollywood Hills, a dreamy expression on her face as she went through the motions of considering the self-sacrifice.

"Of course, if I *did*," Emma continued, "I'd expect a little something in return. If not necessarily your friendship, at least your gratitude. We'd have to work very closely together to minimize the damage, and I'd have to count on your absolute support and your total loyalty. We'd have to be a team, you and I, and nobody would need to know about that. In fact it would be much better if they didn't. It would be our little secret, between you and me. I think it would even be better if Pat didn't know about it . . . or Melissa."

She looked up to see how she was doing. Had he caught the drift? Did she need to spell it out more clearly?

"What *exactly* do you mean?" said Tony Valentino. He had an overpowering sense of déjà vu. He'd been here before—in the auditorium at the Juilliard all those light-years ago. Suddenly, he could see it. It was a gigantic conspiracy. This thing in front of him had created this moment. He had imagined that he'd been running his own life, that Pat had been running hers, that Latham was in charge, that events were random. But he had been wrong. All the time, *she* had been in control. They were flies caught in the net of the web that she, the spider woman, had spun. Emma had never forgiven him for the humiliation she had suffered at his hands. Now she wanted revenge. The *New Celebrity* spread, the role in the movie, Emma's job as studio boss, the hiring of the impossibly sexual Melissa Wayne, the choice of Pat as director—all had been carefully planned. All along there had been only one objective, only one goal, only one target. Him. To save himself, he was being asked to give himself to her. It was his only way out.

Emma Guinness smiled.

"Let's just say," she drawled, "that if I put myself on the line for you, I would expect us to get to know each other very well indeed."

—

"WHAT DID you say?" said Pat, her eyes glinting with fury.

"I told her the only person she'd get to fuck her would be herself."

Pat smiled a wintry smile. She would have signed away her soul to have been there. She had never wanted to kill before. She did now. And not just Emma Guinness. There was Melissa Wayne, too.

"And the Melissa business?" she snarled.

"We didn't go into it. I think she got my message."

Pat laughed a bitter laugh.

"So it's over."

"Yeah, I guess. Either we jump, or we're pushed."

They looked at each other, and the love they were both learning to feel took the edge off the anger and the disappointment. This was where someone was supposed to say, "You know, I'm glad." But neither of them was saying it, because neither was thinking it. Disaster had struck. Denying it wouldn't help. Tony had done the good thing, the right thing, the decent thing, and it had cost him the thing he wanted most, his movie career. Pat, too, was desolate, both for him and for herself. Her one chance at directing was history, and all because of the evil of two women.

She threaded her hand into his.

"We've got each other," she said. "We wouldn't have us if you'd done what they wanted you to do."

He smiled a strange smile that almost looked like tenderness. Pat wanted him to do it again.

"Say something to me," she said.

"What?"

"Think!"

He laughed.

"I love you?"

"No!"

"I love you."

"Right second time. You've got to practice," she joked, nuzzling into him as the irritation began to fade in the reality of their new togetherness. There was a bond between them now. It was deeper than it had ever been, strengthened by the disasters they had faced, and all the future ones they would survive.

"What are we going to do, Tony?" she said. In the closeness it seemed safe to talk about the uncertainty of their future, of his future.

"Well, you'll be up to your eyeballs sorting out Alabama's estate. That has to be a job for at least ten people."

"At least we'll have all the money we could ever want."

"I'm an actor, Pat. I have to act."

It was a gentle rebuke, but already the problems were surfacing. Their love was going to be tested.

"What will you do?"

"Oh, I don't know, knock on doors, beg, plead, act somehow."

"In L.A.?" It would be where Pat was, where Alabama's estate was. But it wouldn't be where the stage jobs were. She knew that. So did he.

"In New York, I'd imagine."

She took a deep breath. It was happening already. Their ambitions would separate them physically. How long would it be before the spiritual bond weakened? Whatever the logic, in his soul Tony would blame her for this. If she hadn't existed, if *they* hadn't existed, Tony could be riding to glory by now. At the stage doors of the icy city he would remember that as the rejections piled up, and the dreams dissolved, leaving only the empty obsession behind. If Tony had traveled light, he'd still be swimming. She was the emotional baggage that had sunk him. Damn it! She wasn't going to lose him like this. Not again. There had to be a way out. How could she smash through the evil and the darkness to the light? Emma Guinness floated across her mind, a simpering, billowing target of taffeta and lace, and the bloody mist of Pat's loathing wafted like a veil before her eyes.

"Tony, we've got to *do* something. We could sue, I don't know, go to the press, anything. We can't just sit here and let them do this to us."

"Forget it," said Tony. "It's gone. Sue Cosmos? You'd need a billion dollars just to get someone to file the complaint. The media'd love it, and the joke'd be on us."

Pat walked over to him. She knelt down.

"Tony, I'm not going to let them break us up. I'm not going to let *us* blow this. I'm not. I'm not. Help me." There were tears in her eyes. She rested both hands on his knees. He covered them with his, and he tried to smile at her.

"I could sell insurance, and we could have two-point-five kids," he said. It was the best he could do.

She smiled determinedly through her misery. Her mind tumbled over itself in search of the elusive solution.

"I'd try Latham," said Tony bitterly. "I saved the asshole's life. But you heard him on the phone. He's given Cosmos to Guinness as her personal toy. I'm for sure not begging to that son of a bitch."

Pat froze as he spoke, and immediately she knew what she would do. Tony couldn't ask Dick Latham to save him. She could. After all, she had asked him for something before.

~18~

Dick Latham strode along the beach as if getting to the far end of it would solve the problems of his life. He spoke fast, and Pat Parker had to strain to hear him as his words blew away on the desert wind.

"Don't even ask me, Pat. I had it all yesterday. Faxes, telexes, my telephone occupied all day. Emma is crazed. I don't know what Tony said to her or did to her, but she's a basket case. She wants him dead, obliterated, wiped off the face of the earth. Firing him from the movie is just an appetizer as far as she's concerned. You're a target by proxy. You're gone, too. She's adamant, and I can't change her mind. I've tried, and I can't."

He strode on, his guilty eyes avoiding Pat's suspicious ones.

"That's bullshit, Dick," exploded Pat, "and you know it. You invented Emma Guinness like some Frankenstein monster. You made her. You're responsible. You can blow her away. You owe it to the world to do that. Cosmos is your toy train set. Fire her, not us. She was a crazy choice anyway. Everyone thinks that."

"Don't tell me how to run my business!" He looked at her now. She had touched a raw nerve. Nobody told Dick Latham he'd made bad choices. Not anybody.

"I'm sorry, Dick, but I'm just so angry and so sad, not for me but for Tony. You know the story. Melissa wanted him to screw her for real on the set, and then Emma wanted body visiting rights for reining in Melissa. If you believe that, and it's true, you can't let them get away with it. It's not . . . it's not . . ." She paused. She was going to say *right*, but with the Dick Lathams of this world that wouldn't be powerful enough. "It's not professional," she spat out at last.

Latham walked on. He didn't answer her right away. He couldn't tell her that Emma owned him. There was no way even to intimate that he was a blackmail target because he was a murder suspect. Of course Pat was right. She always was. Emma was a psychopath of the most dangerous and violent kind, and she held his beating heart in the palm of her hand. The game she was playing on the set of *Malibu* wasn't just unprofessional or immoral. It was downright evil. He knew all about Tony's obsession. He'd had obsessions of his own. He knew, too, that if he didn't intervene, Valentino's life would be over. But it was Tony's life, or his. Someday there would be a way to deal with Emma Guinness. At the top of the money pile there always was. But it would take precious time, and planning, and the careful covering of tracks. Right now, he was under the gun. Emma was insisting on his written endorsement of her firepower. That, or else. He had to give her what she wanted.

"Pat, this isn't personal. This is business. I have to choose between my studio boss and the unknown director and star of *one* movie. It has to be you and Tony that go. If I fire Emma after a few days on the job, I'll pick up a reputation as a man who can't make up his mind, and a guy whose word can't be trusted. That's death in this town. In any town." He winced as he thought of it. That much was true.

"Is your reputation so important, Dick? Isn't there anything else in your life, like decency and morality, and goodness?"

Her voice was sad, accusing, as she felt her hopes slipping away from her.

He was strangely subdued when he answered her. "There was once, a long time ago," he said. "In Paris there was someone who was decency and morality and all the stuff you talk about, but I lost her. Then there was nothing but making money and building . . . building the company because it was the only thing I had that couldn't hurt me. There was no peace of mind after that, no relaxation, no enjoyment, because everything was strictly business. It was profit, not pleasure. The bottom line, not happiness. If I couldn't turn a profit on a person or a thing, I simply threw it away. Then there was you. You were different. You made me feel different. I thought I had a chance with you, Pat, but you always loved Tony." There was no accusation in his voice, just a world-weary sadness for what might have been.

"And now you're throwing me away, and Tony?"

"I guess I am."

"Don't do it, Dick. Try to do the right thing just this once."

"I can't. It's out of my control."

She was silent, angry, and miserable, but still she walked beside him on the beach.

"What are you going to do about Cosmos?" she said suddenly. "Now that Alabama's dead, are you going to try to build it in the hills after all?"

His pace slowed. "You'd fight me if I did, wouldn't you? As Alabama's heiress."

"Yes, I would. For the right reasons, *and* for the wrong ones. I'd fight you until I burned in hell."

He laughed a bitter laugh. "And you'd win," he said, "like Alabama won. I respected him, you know. I respect you."

He turned toward her, and there was longing in his eyes, longing for the sort of girl who reminded him so much of the love he'd lost. But he had to tear his eyes away. He could never have her, not after what he was about to do to her and to Tony.

"Will I have to fight you?" she said.

He paused.

"No, you won't. I *can* give you that. I'll build Cosmos in Palm Desert, just to show you I can do a decent thing."

The mini-surge of relief was lost in the flood tide of Pat's general disappointment. How could this man *be* like this? What did he mean—"I *can* give you that"? Her next words came out direct from her instinct.

"Dick . . . is there some problem . . . I mean between you and Emma?"

"What do you mean?" he shot back at her quickly, too quickly.

"I don't really know what I mean. It's just that she seems to have so much influence over you, and nobody else does . . . it's weird, because she's so wicked and you have so much power."

"When you're responsible for a company the size of mine, power is an illusion," he offered. "The business decisions make themselves."

Pat had reached the end of the line. There was nothing left. He still wanted her. That she knew. But he didn't want her enough. There was something else that he wanted, perhaps needed, more. He said it was business success. She didn't buy that. Beneath the surface, things weren't as they seemed.

She stopped and he slowed, but he kept going. Both knew it was the parting of the ways. Both knew that each shared at least some regret.

"Good-bye, Dick," she said.

"Good luck, Pat," he replied.

She took a deep breath as she watched him walk on.

—

IN THE fireproof vault of the Bank of America in Century City, the temperature was precisely seventy degrees. It had been seventy degrees for ten years now, and it always would be. Pat sat at the long table and sighed at the enormity of the task ahead of her. The entire room had been rented by Alabama, and the steel shelves had been built especially to house the collection of his lifetime's work. Here, the beauty was safe from the world; from the fire that had consumed his poor, dear body; from the mudslides in the hills; from burglars, vandals, and earthquakes. Now it was Pat's responsibility. She had to decide what to do with it. The possibilities were endless—traveling exhibitions; a permanent, revolving exhibit at some gallery in L.A. or Malibu; the sale of some or all of the work to finance the environmental causes that Alabama had loved. She couldn't begin to make a decision on what to do until she had seen exactly what was there. That meant weeks, if not months, going through the prints and the negatives; putting some order into the chaotic cataloguing system; sorting through the photographs that were a bittersweet essay on her old friend's life.

In front of her were ten hatboxes. All of them were stuffed with pictures. No wonder he had stopped. The photographic desert of his later years was more than compensated for by the unbridled fertility of his earlier ones.

She flipped the lid from one of the boxes and began to work her way through the images. These were personal photographs, Alabama's snaps, if the extraordinary originality of the composition, lighting, and point of view could be described by such a word. He had made his name as a landscape and portrait artist, but his street reportage was the equal of that of Brassaï, Lartigue, and Cartier-Bresson. No wonder the French photographers sprang to mind. Because this was Paris, Paris in the sixties, Paris at the time Alabama had taken the famous photograph of the young Dick Latham.

The relaxed faces of the boulevardiers sprang to life across the years. Man Ray kissed his wife Juliette by the banks of the Seine. Jean-Paul Sartre held hands with Simone de Beauvoir in a flower market. André Malraux and Teilhard de Chardin sat, talking earnestly, at a roadside café. Some of the faces Pat recognized instantly. With others she had to turn the prints over to see Alabama's scrawled inscriptions on the back. "Man Ray and Pat Booth looking at his prints. 1966." "Juliette, furious, May 1965." "Brigitte Bardot and Roger Vadim at La Coupole, Summer '64."

Pat sighed. This was fun. She was losing herself in the past in a wonderful escape from the pain of the present. The gaiety of the sixties was alive on the shiny surface of the prints, and she could picture her dear friend, stoked up on absinthe or Kir Royale, crouching behind the camera as he spied on the friends who would have loved him.

She picked up the photograph, and quite suddenly her world turned. Goose bumps sprang from her skin. Electric fingers probed her spine. The print swam before her eyes. Her breath caught in her throat, and shock squeezed at her neck as the flood of adrenaline welled up inside her.

Dick Latham stared at her from the distant past, but it was not Dick Latham that she was looking at. It was the girl by his side. Pat recognized her instantly. Not for one single second did she doubt who it was. The girl beside Dick Latham, smiling out at the world with a calm, self-confident loveliness, was the girl that Latham had loved. But she was also somebody else. She was the girl in the broken photograph in the trailer of Tony Valentino. She was his mother . . . and she was pregnant.

Pat's trembling fingers turned the print over. Alabama's handwriting was quite certain.

"Dick Latham and Eva Ventura," it read, "with their baby, Paris 1965."

Pat's mind was on fire. She turned the print over once again as the pieces of the puzzle slotted into place. Ventura. Ventura. Pregnant with Dick Latham's child.

Her hand shot out to the telephone on the table in front of her. Please, God, let him be in. She punched the number. Tony's voice answered.

There was no time to say hello.

"Was your mother ever called Ventura?" she shouted into the mouthpiece.

"Yes, why? She changed her name to Valentino so my father couldn't find her."

"Stay where you are! Don't move! I'm coming over," screamed Pat as she banged the telephone down.

Dear God! It was true.

Tony Valentino was Dick Latham's son.

PAT ERUPTED into the room. She held the print in front of her, brandishing it like the ticket to heaven it was.

Tony jumped up.

"What the hell's happening . . . ?"

"Tony, omigod, Tony, look, look . . ." The excitement was all over her face.

She couldn't get it into words. There was too much to say and nowhere to start. What was the most important part? That he'd found a father? That his father was a billionaire? That his father was the sole owner of Cosmos Studios? On the helter-skelter drive from Century City she had sorted out some vague priorities. Now, confronted with the reality of Tony, all she could do was thrust the photograph into his bemused face.

He looked at it and a wave of tenderness broke across his face as he recognized his mother.

"Where did you *get* this?"

Pat fought back the excitement and the exasperation. The most important thing that had ever happened to Tony Valentino was happening right now, and he hadn't gotten to the point.

"*Look* at it, Tony, look at it!"

Once again Tony looked at the picture. He looked at his mother. He looked at the bulge in her belly that she was wearing like a badge of honor. And then he looked at Dick Latham. Still, he didn't speak, but his face was changing. The bloom and the excitement of early spring, of light, bright summer, faded through a fast fall to the depths of dead winter. Pat watched the extraordinary barometer that was his expression, and she knew she had to help him understand the importance of what she had discovered.

"Tony, turn the photograph over. Alabama took it. Look what he's written on the back." He did so in a dream, a cold, bleak dream.

Pat decided. He was in shock. His brain had gotten there, but this discovery of his father was so strong, so vast, he was unable to think and to act on the information.

Her voice was patient now, as quiet and careful as was possible when your world had changed.

"Tony, it says 'with their child.' 'With *their* child.' It's your mother and Dick Latham, with their child in Paris, in the year you were born. It's Alabama's writing. He never made mistakes. Not with his precious pictures. Don't you see? Dick Latham is your *father*. You're his son."

She wanted to reach out and touch him, but she was too fascinated by what would be the wonder of his reaction as the truth sank in at last.

He looked up from the photograph. He looked at her, and his face was curled up with a bitterness she had never seen before.

"I know," he said simply.

"You WHAT?"

"I know," he repeated. "I know Dick Latham's my father."

Pat's mouth was wide open. So were her eyes. She closed both as she spoke. It was she who didn't understand.

"You've always known?"

"Yes."

"But, but . . . why . . ." The words drifted away into silence. Her hands tried to do the talking. Her whole face attempted to display her disbelief.

"Why didn't I tell everyone? I'll tell you. Because I never wanted to give the bastard the pleasure of knowing he had a son." His face was brutal. The words were spitballs of scarcely suppressed rage.

Pat was coming back from the no-man's-land of numbness. There were so many questions. Which first?

But Tony was talking.

"That prick walked out on my mother. He got her pregnant, and he left her without a penny, with nowhere to live, with nowhere to go, with nobody to love her. He wrecked her life, because he's a callous, vicious, mean-spirited *bastard*. And the only thing in the world that I've got over him is that I know who he is, and he doesn't know who I am. He's never had a child. Now he's older, he probably wants one. Hell, he's picked up all the other toys along the way." Tony's fists were white. His teeth were bared. He was beginning to shake. "The only thing I regret is that I didn't let him drown. I wish I'd *drowned* him."

"No!" Pat almost shouted her denial. It wasn't like that. He had it wrong. Alabama had told her the story. So had Dick Latham. And the versions had agreed.

"What do you mean, no? What the hell do you know about it?"

"I know what Dick told me. I know what Alabama told me. Dick didn't leave your mother. She walked out on *him*. He tried to find her. She disappeared. Okay, he behaved badly and she found out, but he worshiped her. He wanted to marry her. It's why he's never been able to love anyone else. It's why he's so horrible to women."

The vehemence of her words reached him.

"What?" he said at last, doubt creeping in around the corners of the hatred.

"It's true. You trust me, don't you? I wouldn't lie to you. I love you, Tony. Latham behaved really badly to Alabama in Paris, and your mother was Alabama's friend. Then Latham was unfaithful, and so she left him. Alabama says she was the ultimate free spirit, a real child of the sixties. She wasn't impressed by all his money and his class. When he was mean and low, she just went away, and she took his baby with her. She took you with her, Tony."

"But she couldn't have done that—I mean, she had nothing. We never had anything. There were times when there wasn't enough food, and it was cold, and all those apartments and always moving . . ."

"She was proud, Tony, and she was free. Christ, can't you understand that? Where the hell do you think *you* got all that stuff from? You're

constructed of it. You'd have done exactly what she did. You don't take anything from anybody. You'd die in the gutter rather than ask for help. Look at
you. You're doing it now."

"I'm not," he said, and never in all the time she had known him had Pat
heard him sound less convincing.

"Oh, yes, you are." She laughed as she spoke, because it was funny that he
could even *think* of denying it.

"He could have found her if he'd tried. If he'd really wanted to."

"Tony, she *changed her name.* You said it yourself. She went on the run,
and you ran with her. The point is she didn't want him to find her. She didn't
want the millions and the houses and the neat little schools with their neat
little uniforms, and all the WASP shit, and the cotillions and the cradle-to-
grave security that sucks those people dry of all their feelings, and desire, and
possibility. She didn't want that for you. She wanted to bring you up herself,
with all her wisdom and love, and it didn't matter that it was hard and
uncomfortable, because it was honest and good and right, and because it
made you into what you are."

"What did it make me into?"

"The man I love," said Pat simply, and she walked over to him now and
held both his hands. She lifted them up to her mouth, and he didn't resist as
she kissed them. But his eyes were still haunted. It was hard to give up the
hatred that had sustained you. It was hard to acknowledge that the assump-
tions on which you had built your life were wrong. Inside, Tony was in
turmoil. Dick Latham had been the devil of his existence. At first he had
been a shadowy figure of evil, and then, through Pat and Alabama, he had
taken human form. It had been difficult to deal with him as a mortal man,
but there had been a strange poetry in using him as he loathed him, in
holding the vast secret so close to his hating heart. Then there had been the
time in the sea cave, when his blood had overridden the cold command of his
intellect and he had risked his life to save the man who had been so indifferent to the baby he had been. Day after day he had watched Latham, and
recoiled in disgust at the similarities he shared with him, the gestures, the
aloofness, the callous ambition, the need to win. They had even wanted the
same woman. They had even *had* the same woman, and Tony had felt a weird
ambivalence about that too, as he had seen Pat drawn to both of them by the
siren call of the genes. But what now? If hatred was based on illusion, what
was left to be felt?

"What should I do?" he said, when he meant, What should I feel?

"We've got to go and see Dick," said Pat. "We've got to tell him." She had
never in her life felt so strongly about anything. She squeezed his hands for
emphasis. "He's got to know. It'll change his life. It can change yours. He's
your father, damn it. What do you think will happen to Emma Guinness
now?"

The smile broke through the gaunt features, like a weak sun over hard
snow.

"Yeah," he said at last, and his smile broadened. "He can throw Emma Guinness back in the shit she came from. What the hell else are fathers for?"

DICK LATHAM buried his head in his hands, and the sound of his sobbing filled the room. He had never cried before, but it was all so overwhelming, there could only be tears. They poured through the fingers that covered his face, and they washed him clean. It was the moment of his rebirth. He had a son. The lost had been found. The empty had been filled.

Tony Valentino stood beside his father and he was determined to hide his own emotion as Dick Latham succumbed to his. He hadn't known what he would feel at this moment, but he hadn't expected this. The incredible strength of his father's reaction proved everything that Pat had said. He had loved, all right. He had worshiped. He had adored. It was more than blood that tied them together. It was the love of his mother. What would come next? Where would the brand-new relationship lead? Already he was aware of a ridiculous sense of competition. Who would handle the scene best? Who would steal it? Jeez! He smiled through watery eyes at his cold ability to introspect at such a time. But at least he hadn't thought of the reunion as visual software for some future stage performance.

Dick Latham's shoulders heaved with the strength of his feelings. Tony could feel their intensity. There needed to be touching, but neither of them were any good at that. Despite himself, Tony's hand reached out and laid itself against the immaculate cashmere of his father's blazer. There it stayed, exerting no pressure, in an ambivalent gesture that fell short of commitment, yet was clear in its desire to comfort. Through the emotion that wracked him, Dick Latham recognized it. His hand closed over his son's, and at last he looked up at the man to whom he had given life, at the son who had saved his own.

"I can't believe it," he said, but he did. The photograph on the desk before him said it all, but it was his heart that was certain. There was no reasonable doubt, because he didn't feel any. He knew, and, now that he knew, there was a sense in which he had always known. Why had he, the cold lover of women, the hater of men, been drawn to the prickly boy with the daggers in his eyes? Because of Tony's obsession. It hung around him and Dick Latham had recognized the aura whose colors were the same as his. They had shared dark dreams of greatness; they had shared the body of the woman who had brought them together; and in their rivalry there had been the mutual respect of those who were more similar than perhaps they would have liked to be. Why else had Latham believed in the novice actor? Why else had he put him in his movie against all sense? And why, in the caves of Santa Cruz, had the boy who pretended to despise him risked his life to save him?

The sudden lump in Tony's throat stopped the sentences that were trying to form. He swallowed, but it didn't go away, and the mist in his eyes was denser now, the pressure of his fingers stronger on the shoulder of his father. There was no script for this. The writer was the heart, and words were a language it had never learned. In his mind, the thoughts tumbled over themselves. He was glad, but he was sorry. He felt warm, but there was resentment, too. Why should he be pleased to have found the man his beloved mother had spent a lifetime trying to escape? Yet, how could anyone not be moved by the moment when flesh met blood?

"I'm . . . sorry . . . that Mom wasn't here for this," he said at last, as a large tear made its escape from the corner of his eye. It scurried free, and rolled down his cheek, giving away the secret of his feelings, as tears were supposed to do.

"She changed her name," said Latham. "So I would never find her. If only you could ever know how much I loved her."

He buried his head again, and his tears came harder now as grief crept to the center of his stage, elbowing out shock and joy and hope for the future. He would never see Eva again. All the years he had hoped for that, and time had dulled the pain, but not the memory. That had remained, shrouded in glory at the altar of his heart, irreplaceable, always to be worshiped. Now she was dead, and he could never say sorry. How many times had he rehearsed the speech that would never be spoken? But she had left her legacy. Before him stood the son he had last seen in the body he'd loved. There, before him, was Alabama's evidence of his vivid memory. Here, beside him, was the living proof, the living product of the only happiness he had ever known.

Tony was being asked to forgive. He felt it strongly.

"I thought you deserted her," he said. "I didn't know she left you." He was still trying to get it straight in his mind. The earth was round, not flat. It took some believing, some getting used to.

"Yes, she left me, because I was a bastard who deserved to be left . . ." He paused. He had to know. "Did she ever talk about me? Did she ever say she loved me?"

Latham looked up. Hope bathed his face.

Slowly, Tony nodded. He wasn't certain that it was the truth, but deep down he knew it had to be. His mother's reaction had been too extreme, for too long, her silence too quiet. In this life lack of faith, the cruelty of youth, were not so rare, perhaps not so heinous. But Latham's lapse from grace had changed his mother's life, and uprooted his. Until the day of her death it had affected her. Yes, she had loved him—been obsessed by him anyway, and that was the strongest love of all.

He was aware that he was issuing absolution, and strangely touched that it should be so desperately needed. In the early days, fathers existed to look after you. But the early days had gone. In the latter years, fathers were for looking after. Had those days already arrived?

Latham stood up. The future would not be easy, but God, it would be so wonderful. He was alone no longer. He had an heir, a tough, straight, resourceful son. Perhaps it was better like this. Tony had been spared the weed-killer of Latham's overbearing personality. He had not been stunted by the emotional poison of power-seeking and moneymaking. He had been raised by an angel in poverty and physical insecurity, and he had learned strength and resilience in the hard-knocks university of life on the road. Now they stood shoulder to shoulder as equals, joined by the accident of birth, but not hampered by it. No garbage would be dished out, no shit taken. Hypocrisy could relax in this father-and-son relationship, and the innocent love of the gullible child would never founder on the disappointed rocks of grown-up judgment.

On an impulse he reached forward and hugged the man who was his child. All the warmth he had was in the embrace, and Tony, wrapped in his father's arms, felt his own respond. The spigot of tears turned with his world as he joined with the father who had made him. He began to sob, letting it all go at last. As his tears splashed down onto Dick Latham's shoulders, he was lost in an incredible joy.

IT WAS a war council. Pat Parker sat on the edge of her chair. Tony, on red alert, sat on the corner of his father's desk. Behind it, Dick Latham was finishing the unbelievable story of Emma Guinness's blackmail.

"So you see, there was nothing I could do except the right thing, and I was too weak to do that. Whatever happened, I was going to be ruined. I was going to jail. Your careers seemed a small price to pay for avoiding that. Now, of course, it's different. I'll stand up to her, whatever the cost. She might destroy me, but I'll take her down too, and you'll be safe . . ."

He seemed happy that it had come to this. Dick Latham was about to do a fine thing. He was about to make a sacrifice, for the son he had found and the girl that his son loved. It felt extraordinarily good. Was the cliché really true? Was Schweitzer at Lambarene *really* more content than Donald Trump?

"No!" said Tony and Pat in unison. They looked at each other, and smiled at the synchronicity of their unrehearsed reaction. They had heard the story, and their minds were still whirling at the extraordinary invention of the wickedness, but at gut level they recoiled from Dick Latham's solution. Pat tried to keep her thoughts on course, to hold back the forces of incredible hatred that threatened to derail them. In her mind's eye, she could see the flames of the fire that Emma had set, see it racing down the mountain to devour the man she had admired and respected more than any other on earth. It seemed impossible that there could be a more terrible crime than that, but Emma had constructed one. She had compounded it. She had added blackmail to her disgusting, devilish stew and used casual murder as an instrument of revenge. That it was the action of a madwoman didn't lessen the crime. It was the callousness that made it so evil. Emma had no reason to hate Alabama. She had hardly known him. He had never crossed her. Yet, to avenge a personal slight, she had rubbed him out as if he were no more important than a chalk scribble on a child's blackboard. It was as forgivable as genocide. It demanded and would receive thunderbolt retribution. The only questions were when and how.

"She tape-recorded your conversation that night at La Scala," said Pat. She was thinking out loud.

"Yes, she must have wired herself for sound like in some James Bond movie."

"You could do the same," said Pat slowly.

"What do you mean?"

But Tony had gotten there.

"Yes, that's it. When you tell her you're not going to fire us from the movie; when you stand up to her and call her bluff, you could be tape-recording her reaction."

"Tapes aren't admissible evidence," said the lawyer in Dick Latham, but already he loved the idea. Emma's La Scala recording wouldn't have been admissible either, but its psychological effect on him had been devastating. Together with the other evidence, it would have given the cops the motivation to nail him to the wall. Emma Guinness was clearly unhinged. When he confronted her, she would rant and rave like a Billingsgate fishwife, as she painted her dark threats. What's more, he could arrange for Havers to be in the next room, with maybe a notary public, a cop, hell, a whole worship of bishops as witnesses. If it was handled correctly, he would be off the hook and Emma would be impaled on it.

"You're right," he said at last. "It's a wonderful idea. I guess I need a voice-activated recording device or something. I probably haven't got an employee who isn't wearing one." He laughed, but not at the thought of his wall-to-wall minions being wired for sound. He laughed because he was happy; because he was no longer alone; because he had a son.

And Pat laughed too, because she had just learned about revenge and the beauty of it; and because soon, so soon, the fiend who had burned Alabama and tried to destroy both her and Tony would be getting hers at last.

Tony laughed loudest, because he was allowed to be in love again; because the hideous girl in the hideous clothes would never again sit like a monkey on his back; because he had a father; and because now the world would get a chance to see the brilliant art he longed to show it.

It was coming together. They all knew that. They were close to an end that would also be a glorious beginning.

＊

EMMA SAT across from Dick Latham where, a few hours before, Pat Parker had sat. The self-confidence oozed from her. She sat in the chair the way Victoria Brougham would have sat in it; legs wide apart, arms draped casually over its wings, her head lolling easily against its back.

"So it's 'Good-bye, Tony' and 'Good-bye, Pat,' and the only thing left to say is 'Good riddance.'"

"No, you're wrong," said Dick Latham with counterfeit innocence. "There's one more thing left to be said."

Emma smiled. She liked guessing games. She was rather good at them. She thought she might try "Congratulations." Someone like Dick Latham wouldn't be much more imaginative than that.

"Good-bye, Emma!" said Dick Latham, before she could answer him.

She laughed. "What do you mean?"

"I mean that's what's left to be said—'Good-bye, Emma.' "

Emma's laugh wasn't so relaxed now.

"Meaning?" she said, waiting for the explanation of what was clearly a ponderous Latham joke.

"Meaning," said Latham, "you're fired."

"What?"

"Fired, sacked, out of a job, out on the street. You're finished, Emma Guinness. I can't answer for the Third World, but in the first two you're history."

Her small eyes got smaller. Surely he wasn't going to take her on. Surely he wasn't fool enough to doubt her resolve. Maybe it was just a dealer's ploy to test her. Yes, that would be it. He'd try standing up to her, and then fold like a pack of cards the moment she didn't back down. How *pathetic!* Sometimes the powerful behaved like children. They held out their knuckles and they wanted them to be rapped so that they could find out where their limits lay. Oh, well, if bib-and-tuckered Dick wanted strict nanny Emma, then that was what he would get. With knobs on.

"Listen, Latham," she snapped. "I didn't burn that old fart Alabama because I liked setting fires. I did it so that you could take the rap for it. I can finger you for his murder and you know it. The can I stuck up there is locked up where you can't get at it, and when I call the cops and play them that tape, they'll want your prints, billionaire, and they'll want to know what the tires of your Porsche look like. And you won't even have time to change them, honey, 'cause unless you get very wise very fast, I'm going to give them a call right now."

"And tell them what?"

Emma looked at him like she might a beach bum. She'd never thought of Latham as being thick before, but why not? Most people were, and making megabucks didn't require intelligence, just creativity, the two being totally different things.

She put on her I'm-trying-to-say-it-as-simply-as-I-can tone and, in true English fashion, she raised her voice as if talking to a foreigner. "I'll tell them that you murdered Alabama, Dick," she said.

"But I didn't. You did."

She shook her head from side to side. Good Lord, wasn't Alzheimer's supposed to be a gradual process? "*I* know that, dear," she said in a voice dripping with patronization. "*You* know that. But the clever bit is that the *cops* won't know it."

"Oh, yes they will."

Emma opened her mouth to blast him out of his complacent idiocy. At that precise moment, he drew back the blue blazer that reminded her so much of Lord's in June.

The words died in her throat. The vision seared into her eyes. A recorder was strapped across his chest. A smile of triumph was plastered across his face.

Emma Guinness was dimly aware of a door opening at the back of the room. She was in shock, but she knew what had happened. She had walked straight into an ambush, and she would pay for her mistake with her life. In front of her was the tape recorder. Behind her, there would be witnesses.

She heard herself speak. Her own voice seemed to come from light-years away, but she had to have the answer to one question.

"Why?" she said.

"Because Tony Valentino is my son," said Dick Latham.

—

EMMA GUINNESS stood on the edge of the cliff and looked down to the rocks below. Her party was over. It was time to call it a day. The pretty balloons drifted over her head among the black clouds of doom, and the bright sun laughed at the misery she would feel if feeling was possible. Even the surf sounded strange inside her head. It whooshed and crashed, but it carried a weird echo, and the gulls that soared on the Santa Ana wind were like swooping bats in the twilight of her life. Malibu mocked her. It was straight and light, so clean, crisp, and monumental as the mighty mountains met the sea in a place shorn of care and short on sorrow. Here she stood, in contrast, beaten and alone, as far from all the things she wanted as from the state of grace she would never know. The wind picked up the hem of her short skirt, the one that strangled her fulsome thighs and ringed her ample waist like a hangman's noose. Was she dressed to be killed? Who knew? Who, any longer, cared?

The surfers were riding the waves out there—sun-bleached brains directing sun-faded boards to the sun-drenched beach. How she envied them their hard bodies and their soft minds. She was hovering at the gates of hell, full to the brim with hatred and despair, while on the ocean humans like her asked only for a white-topped curler to carry them in, thought only of Coke and pizza and Mary-Lou as they planned their open jeep ride home. She took a deep breath as she blotted out the peace of Malibu. It was time for her own demons. Her head twisted from side to side, as the Wagner played. Tony Valentino was Dick Latham's son. His heir. The man who would one day own the billions. He was safe from her. He always would be. He was safe to love and be loved by Pat Parker; safe to soar above the world in the firmament of fame; safe to savor every one of the dreams he had dared to dream. His obsession was satisfied. Hers was doomed.

She laughed now, at the joke that had been her life, and the bitterness cackled in the sound. They had let her go, because they had suspected that it might end like this—suspected it and wanted it. Well, it was the least she could do. At the very end she would do something for others. Her last act would be her first generous one.

She took a step nearer to the edge, and peered down into the abyss. A hundred feet below, the rocks looked so clean. Would it hurt? Nothing could hurt more than the hurt now. Would she bump on the cliffs on the way down, breaking things, before the final oblivion? It was a thought. She ought technically to have forward momentum. Mmmm. That would entail a run before takeoff. She looked back over her shoulder across the steam-ironed lawn. Yes, that would do the trick. She walked back twenty paces toward the house. Was this the long jump or the high jump? On school sports days she had been lousy at both. She crouched down, like you did at the start of a race, and she stuck out her jaw to intimidate the competitors who weren't there. Inside her head she was waiting for the gun. But *she* was the starter, and the finisher, the producer, director, the star.

And she was also the audience. As she launched herself forward, she realized just how ridiculous she must look, especially from above. The gulls would see her short, squat frame as it tore across the lawn to the cliff edge. They would be catching the piston action of her pumping legs, watching her straggly hair floating in the warm wind, wondering at her heaving breasts as they bounced up and down on the journey to destruction. She was almost there now, and already there was no turning back. She braced herself for takeoff, the sadness gone as she immersed herself in the business of orchestrating her death. She would sail like a bird to Paradise. Arms outstretched, she would swallow dive from the cliff, dumpy and awkward no longer as she flew toward destiny. For one brief moment in time she would soar on the wings of angels in the light and wind, and then it would be over and there would be no more pain and hatred, only perfect peace.

But she hadn't factored the garden hose into her equation. Green and surreptitious, it was a snake in the grass at the edge of the bluff. Emma's speeding ankle caught it. The top half of her body rushed on. The lower half slowed dramatically. But it was too late to try again. It was far too late for that. The cliffside launch, however, was not to be a serene occasion. Instead of a graceful descent to a stylish death, Emma Guinness was doomed to go out like the sack of potatoes she had always so closely resembled.

Headfirst, tumbling over herself in an uncontrolled jumble of flailing limbs, Emma Guinness shot from the cliff. Upside down, downside up, she cartwheeled through space, and the surfers below turned to watch as they heard her final comment on the life she'd loathed.

Emma's last will and testament shivered on the Santa Ana wind.

"Fuuuuuuuuuuuuuuuuuck!" she screamed.

~ *Epilogue* ~

THE MOON LICKED the long beach, casting silver shadows on the surf. High in the sky the stars shone in the cloudless sky, and beneath their feet the sand was cold and damp as they walked to nowhere. The mountains, massive and dark above the deserted highway, glowed in the twilight, and the rush of waves, loud on soft, serenaded the love of the lovers.

"Every time I walk here, I think of us and how we started," said Pat, slipping her hand into Tony's. She sighed against the salt breeze, in love with Malibu and the ocean and the caramel sand, in love with the man it had given her.

"It's like the edge of the world here, isn't it?" he answered. "It's so near to infinite space. You feel you're part of the universe. That day, when I came here, when you wanted to take my photograph, I needed that feeling. I was so sad, so beaten, but the beach gave me perspective. Life, death meet here. I was dying, then there was you."

"Oh, Tony." She squeezed his hand, because he so seldom said things like that.

He turned to face her, and the moonbeams illuminated a face that was already alight with love.

He stopped. She moved closer to him, and he opened his arms to take her in. There on the beach she clung to him, merging with him as life and death merged, and she wanted to stay where she was forever. There could be no happiness like this. On the sands of Malibu, her Paradise had been found, lost, and found again at last. "I don't hate anymore," he said suddenly, as if some dark screen had been lifted from his eyes and he could see once again. "I don't hate Dick. God, there's even a part of me that loves him. I don't even hate poor Emma."

She looked up at him through misty tears of adoration. "The beach cleansed the world of her, didn't it?" she said. Pat couldn't forgive. Emma's broken body on the rocks of Point Dume had been perfect justice.

"She'd have been driven crazy by the movie's success, wouldn't she? I mean, an Oscar nomination for the picture, for you, for me. And Allison replacing Melissa. The chances of that happening were as small as finding a lost grain of sand on this beach." Tony shook his head in disbelief.

Pat laughed. "It wasn't luck," she said. "It was a little thing called talent. The world will know that the next time it happens, and the next, and the time after that . . ."

"I thought I was supposed to be the one with the ego," he said, smiling down at her. "So do I get to be the star of the next Pat Parker production?"

"No *way!*" said Pat. She had been waiting for the right time to tell him. It was now, and the moonlit Malibu beach was the perfect place. "Either he does . . . or she does." She stood back from him. She laid her hand on the flat of her stomach.

"Pat?" The question exploded from him.

"Yes," she said.

His eyes were on fire with wonder, with amazement, with delight. And he bent down, and she reached up, and his lips closed over hers, and they joined forever in the child they would share.

BEVERLY HILLS

To my husband, Garth,
with all my love

~ 1 ~

PAULA HOPE WAS numb with tiredness, but she had never been more determined. On sun-washed Melrose Avenue, half a mile from the Hollywood freeway, the street people didn't know that. All they could see was an exhausted girl in dirty blue jeans and a dirtier shirt. They saw only her dramatically beautiful face, and her straggly blond hair, matted with dust and held in a ponytail bob by a plain red elastic band. Those who looked longer noticed the limp, of course. That was something to watch in the caldron of the L.A. summer evening, as the wind from the desert waved the fronds of Paramount Studios palm trees against the sun-bleached sky.

Paula sighed as she struggled on. She was used to the steam heat of the Everglades, but this was a different kind of hot. It was the relentless heat of the fan oven, the crisp, brittle heat of the sauna. It was clean and clear like a bright white flame, and she could smell its burning ozone in her nostrils. Blowtorch sharp, it scorched her, and beneath her feet the paving stones shimmered like a mirage. She stayed to the north of Melrose because she didn't have the strength to cross to the shady side, and anyway here she was closer to the Hollywood Hills, their famous sign visible at the street intersections, swathed in the fluffy brown haze of the heatscape. The words of the psalm came back to her. The hills, from whence cometh my help. She smiled grimly and stopped. She would have to ask directions, but on the L.A. sidewalk everyone looked as if they belonged somewhere else. "Which way is Beverly Hills?" she said to a passerby.

"Keep going," he muttered, hurrying on.

How long? How far? But up ahead she could see the answer. God had made a glorious crown for Beverly Hills. To the left the sun was dying, and before Paula's eyes the heavens were alive with color. The clouds, stretched out in layered ribbons against a powder-blue sky, were tinged with pink. Now, as she watched, they deepened to a burnished orange, silhouetting a thousand finger-thin palm trees against the pastel painting of the early sunset. On a whim she turned to look back, and over her shoulder, ghostly pale against the distant San Gabriel Mountains, was the moon. At once Paula

307

recognized it as a symbol of the hell that had been her past, while up ahead was the paradise of Beverly Hills, the place where she would find her future.

Paula knew with crystal clarity what she wanted from it. She wanted to be loved. She wanted to be adored. She wanted someone to take care of her forever and wrap her in a cocoon of happiness in which there would be no more tragedy, no more loss, no more wickedness. In her brave new world there would be security, safety, and excitement, in the arms of someone who would hold and never let go, who would love but never leave, who would be brimful of life and would never die. In her magic future she would *be* someone, respected and admired, and she would have friends like ordinary people and she would have the luxury of leisure and the time simply to *exist*. She wanted to surround herself with beauty, and at least to see if not to own some of the wonderful things her teacher Emily Carstairs had told her about. Most of all she wanted never again to be poor and hungry, and at the mercy of a cruel world in which evil had stolen away the precious people she had loved more than her own life.

And then she wanted the revenge she had promised Seth Baker. Only in the music of his screams could the squatting toad of hatred be banished from her mind. Only in the river of his blood could her loathing be washed away. Only as the foul breath rattled in death from his lungs could she be reborn.

But Paula was a realist. Before she could have any of the things she desired so desperately, she would have to create a future for herself. God knew how, but she had to escape from the bottomland of life where she had always lived. Right now, however, the problem was to find a place to sleep, somewhere safe and free if that wasn't a contradiction. Luckily on her long walk from the freeway the neighborhood had steadily improved, and Paula hoped that it was a metaphor for her life. The boarded liquor stores, ninety-nine cent movie rentals, and poverty-stricken Hispanics of early Melrose had been replaced by delicious-smelling restaurants and frivolous boutiques, as low-end retro-punk merged imperceptibly into credit-card-crunching chic. Now, as she hauled one bejeaned leg in front of the other, past the fruits and the nuts and the flakes of the muesli that was Southern California, the storefronts were getting grander by the minute. One in particular caught her eye, and she walked over and gazed through its broad windows.

It was an antique store, but that description was ridiculously inadequate. It was an Aladdin's cave of beauty that sent Paula's tired heart leaping in her chest. Ornate mirrors, gold leaf, ancient smoky glass hung complacently over delicate half tables of faded, highly polished wood. On the walls rich tapestries danced with color, their needlework executed with the intricacy of the painter, depicting heroic scenes of glory and triumph. Multicolored rugs, dusty and dark with messages from distant lands, were scattered like giant postage stamps over the floors and on them languished furniture the likes of which she had never seen. Great bow-fronted chests covered with ornate giltwork merged happily with severe geometrical ones, and the infinite varieties of the wood shaded into each other beneath the glow of a discreet lighting system. On and on the "store" went. Over the years it had consumed its neighbors and now the marginally different, yet at the same time homogeneous, storefronts stretched the entire length of the block.

Paula stopped. The wall of beauty had brought her up short. She stood close to the gray glass, smoked to keep out the harmful rays of the sun, and she pressed her face against it as her eyes roamed over the trove of treasures. Apart from the artwork there seemed to be nobody inside. No human marred the splendor of the ancient Roman busts as they stared grandly from their columns in their terra-cotta marble tunics. Their unseeing alabaster eyes seemed to peer back at Paula, mocking her from their positions of eternal security. On an impulse she stuck out her tongue at them and their haughtiness, leaving a little wet mark on the immaculate window of the storefront.

Winthrop Tower wondered why the street girl was bothering to stick out her tongue at him. He arched an eyebrow as he watched her, and his practiced eyes slid over her visuals. The fact that women were not his bag did not diminish his interest. Neither was Sheraton, but he could still spot a fake secretaire at forty feet across a coal cellar in the dead of night. She was certainly beautiful, if in need of a little cleaning, perhaps a tad of judicious restoration. She would need polish and wax in terms of makeup and all the funny things that women wore, and if he allowed himself to be perfectionistic with a capital P, then some cunning sculptor might improve the line of the nose. But if in profile, and to the connoisseur, her features were marginally less than classic—face on, she was stunning.

The eyes and the mouth, both partially hidden from the side, were the jewels in the crown. Her eyes were great marbles of blue light glistening with irreverence and interest, and Winthrop's gaze was swept down the bridge of an upturned nose, to the slash of the voluptuous mouth.

And the cheekbones! Oh dear, they were very good. A touch of the Eurasian? Well not *really*, but the hint of that sort of thing, all high and proud and in marvelously happy triangular relationship to that pouting mouth from which the pink tongue had so surprisingly protruded. Her hair was a mess of course, but it was obviously American hair, which meant it was the best stuff in the world. Which left the teeth—tombstone correct; and the jaw—no-nonsense, jutting geometry; and things like the neck—swans, pedestals (Carrara marble ones)—and the skin, smooth, honey-brown basted; and those pretty, neat little ears. In his orderly mind Winthrop Tower ticked off the inventory, and with a frisson of surprise he added up her score. My oh my, she *was* good. Take away the tiredness and sharpen her up a bit and she would sparkle and shine in mint showroom condition. Park Avenue Winter Antiques Show quality. No question. Had she been a Longton Hall owl at a Sotheby's sale he'd have bought her. He chortled to himself and looked down again at the catalogue on his knee. The girl was forgotten.

Paula wondered at first what the store was called. The Tower Design plaque was discreet—simple black roman letters on a highly polished brass plate, the legend partially worn away by daily polishing over more years than a town like L.A. was supposed to have existed. The feeling inside her was overwhelming. She wanted to go in, and so she did.

Inside it was quiet and cool and apparently she was alone in what might easily have been a Pharaoh's tomb. Up close, the things were far more lovely: the textures, the subtlety, the workmanship; the shades, the architecture, the amazingly sensitive juxtaposition of the art. The cavernous rooms were crammed with priceless objects and yet there was no sensation of overcrowding. Her eyes picked out a group—a painting, a chair, a table, a rug, which made up a whole far more interesting than the sum of the individual parts. Each set seemed to bear a relationship to a neighboring grouping until she could not escape the feeling that everything was related by progressive degree to everything else. The room made sense to her eye. If you moved anything the fairy castle of visual pleasure would fall.

The chair next to her spoke directly to her soul. It was a great throne of a chair standing majestically on sturdy, bowed feet. It was upholstered in a pink silk damask, but the intricacy of its wood carving scoffed at the necessity for that. "I'm for looking at," it seemed to say. "I am a statement. The fact that I am a chair is merely incidental. Rest on me and you will *become* someone."

Paula couldn't resist its siren call. She was sucked toward it, and to reach it she squeezed her taut bottom past a table on which sat a large, complacent Chinese vase.

For a second or two she paused, her denim-encrusted butt poised over the pink silk. Should she be doing this in someone else's store? The hell with it. The worst they could do was throw her out, and it would be so wonderful to sit, and to be a queen . . . for just a minute.

Winthrop Tower stood up and dropped the Christie's catalogue onto the green leather top of the Chippendale desk. The important furniture sale in New York looked vaguely interesting. It was difficult to know whether to bother to go or not. He might get one of the girls to ask the Algonquin if they had his usual suite. That would decide it. Right now it was about time to close.

He walked to the front door of the store, which was when he saw her. The rude street beauty with the irreverent tongue had her grubby blue jeans in the only piece of furniture that wasn't for sale. She was sitting in Queen Marie Antoinette's and Tower's favorite chair. It was lèse-majesté.

The girl saw him and the fright passed across her beautiful face like a cloud scudding across the fullest of full moons. It didn't last. The moment it arrived it was gone, to be replaced by a devil-may-care insolence all wrapped up in the spicy aroma of irreverent charm.

"I wanted to know what it felt like to be a queen," she said simply.

"Oh, it has its moments," said the most famous and successful designer in the Western world. Tower stood back, hand on hip, and struck a pose. Inside, he was already beginning to laugh.

Paula cocked her head to one side as she tried to sum up the situation. She had followed her natural instincts and showed no weakness when the stranger had confronted her. Now she smiled back at him, because she felt somehow that he was kind, and because she needed kindness.

He was tall but lopsided in a seemingly intentional way, as if he wanted to catch you off balance and felt he was more likely to do so by setting a good example. He was around sixty, but Paula was picking up much younger vibes, and his face had the well-worn look that could have come from either speedy living or anno domini. His eyes sparkled but the bags beneath them said "booze" while the reading glasses perched on the end of his Roman nose looked like they might be merely a prop. Small tufts of hair grew from commodious nostrils and although he was shaved he was hardly "clean shaven." The male process had obviously been hurried, perhaps always was, and there was a clump of untouched hairs beneath a receding chin. His mouth, thin but not mean, was maybe a little merciless.

Now he smiled as he spoke. "First you put out your tongue at me. Next you sit in my favorite chair. You're not, I hope . . ." and he wrinkled up his nose in pseudodisgust, "a kissing telegram?"

Paula smiled. "Gee, no. Of course not." The thought suddenly dawned on her. "Oh God, no I wasn't sticking out my tongue at *you*. I didn't know you were in here. I was doing it at all those Romans. They looked so pleased with themselves."

She stood up. Somehow that seemed the proper thing to do. The stranger's whole manner was casual but his clothes indicated clearly that he wasn't the hired help. His shirt was button-down gray linen, and the tie looked like that of a college that would mean something to people who knew, but the rest of him was far more impressive. He wore a suit of the palest brown corduroy, and, although he looked completely at home in it, it didn't really fit him. The shoulders of the jacket were round and it ballooned out at the waist to accommodate a healthy paunch. The pants of the suit were voluminous. Baggy and a little threadbare at the knee, they were turned up where they met ancient, highly polished brown brogue lace-up walking shoes.

"Are you Mr. Tower?" she asked. "Is this your store? I think it's the most wonderful place I've ever seen in my life."

Once again his eyes appraised her, as the honest compliment hung in the air. The girl was liquid glory. She flowed into his mind like Rodin, the curves of Moore, Michelangelo, and da Vinci on a good chiseling day. Her breasts weren't large, but they were far from small, and in terms of perspective they sang in harmony with the belted waist he might enclose in the palms of two hands if he squeezed tightly enough. For a butt man, like Winthrop, it was a good day, too. Inside the filthy Levi's the proud bottom was snare-drum tight. And then there were the legs. Away they went, zipping like good news down to the dirt-streaked Adidas sneakers, but why was the thigh of the left noticeably thinner than the one on the right? An injury? A leg in plaster recently? After some accident?

Winthrop Tower stroked at a droopy earlobe. "You're right about the Romans. Ancient yuppies, really. Dreadfully nouveau, and no sense of humor. I'm glad it wasn't me. And thanks for the compliment . . . about all this, I mean." He waved a lazy hand to encapsulate several million dollars' worth of museum pieces, and the pleasure swooped from his face. He didn't know why he was pleased. Compliments about his "taste" from the art arbiters of the globe were usually about as interesting as small earthquakes in Chile in which nobody had been hurt.

"Oh, and yes, I *am* Winthrop Tower. And you're *not* a kissing telegram or anything like that?"

Paula thrust out a grubby hand. "I wish I was," she said with a laugh. "That would mean I had some money. I'm down to my last ten bucks." It was a billion miles from a pitch.

"What made you sit in *that* chair?"

Paula looked at it carefully. "Oh, I don't know, it's sort of unique, I mean, it looks as if it's *used* to being a seat, but only for special people. It sort of rises above being a chair, but isn't ashamed to do the job if it approves of the sitter. Sounds silly doesn't it, but that's what I felt when I saw it." She laughed self-consciously as if she were almost ashamed to say such pompous things, but not quite.

Winthrop Tower's wise eyes widened. He didn't often experience the spark of intense artistic interest. Once a year, less, when at the back of some crumbling Scottish castle a grubby unidentified Rembrandt peeped shyly from some damp wall. Occasionally, very rarely, when he met some "new" artist whose work transcended Madison Avenue bullshit and dealer hype. Now, it had happened. The girl from nowhere, with the tongue, the tits, and the dirty jeans, had told the "truth" about his chair. She had plumbed his secret fantasy as if it had been written above his head in blood-red neon.

"How did you know?" he asked simply. Was this some joke? Would the girl now reveal herself as the great-niece of the immortal designer Sister Parish, sent on a whim to plague him?

Paula laughed, pleased by his agreement, a bit puzzled by his question. "Well, I didn't *know*. I mean, that's just what the chair made me feel."

"So you're not a furniture expert." The gray-painted Louis XVI fauteuil, *à la Reine*, was museum quality. It bore the stamp of Dubois, and the carving of its channeled seat rails, and the fluid lines of its down-curved arm supports transcended mere beauty.

"I'm not an anything expert."

"I wonder," said Tower slowly. It was just possible. Only just. There was a way to find out.

All along the back of his neck the flesh was crawling with the premonition. Was it about to happen? At long last. "Come with me," he said, and he took her arm as he steered her safely past the green T'ang dynasty urn that a little old lady from Pasadena had been using as a table lamp before he had liberated it.

Paula went with him. If she handled this well, she might get some food. At least a drink of water. Perhaps even some sort of help.

He hurried into the bowels of the showroom toward a set of dining-room chairs arranged in a semicircle about a round table. They were made of a peculiar milky wood, with black horsehair seats, and on their backs mythological figures were carved on a darker and more traditional-colored wood.

"What do you think of those?" he asked.

"I think they are magnificent. Very simple. Very secure. They're beautiful."

"They're German Biedermeier. Eighteen-ten. We call that wood 'blonde.' The ones with the arms are sometimes called 'carvers.' I've never seen a finer set." He watched her like a lynx. She would need a hint. The curator of the Smithsonian would. "I should say . . ."

But she cut into his speech. "Except for that one, over there on the left. It seems out of place. Sort of sad, by comparison, but it looks like all the others . . ."

Winthrop Tower felt the thrill of excitement. Of course it *looked* like the others. It was meant to. The skills of the greatest restoration firm in the world—Oxford Restorers of Long Island—had *made* it look like all the others. But it didn't *feel* like all the others. To the eye that could feel, it was wrong. It was a fake, a great big bogus lie in the middle of the purest beauty. But only half a dozen people in the world had that aesthetic vision, and they were all titans in the field of fine furniture. Now, this girl, apparently a kid from nowhere, had picked an impostor at the Biedermeier feast, only seconds after she had divined the truth about the two queens' chair.

He took a step back and opened his mouth to speak, but still he could not believe it. He wanted confirmation. "Which rug is your favorite?"

The glorious pistachio-green Tabriz from the late Shah's collection—it was not perhaps the most expensive carpet in the world but he had never walked on one more beautiful.

"This drawing by Fragonard . . ."

Yes, of course, it was Angelica's hands that weren't quite right as they reached for Orlando—great frankfurter fingers from the supposed brush of the master of feminine delicacy.

"Let's rearrange this corner of the showroom. I'll do it. You direct me. Now let's put a picture in place of this Chinese Chippendale looking glass. You pick it. From anywhere in the room. And let's find some different objects for this little table. No. Let's find another table altogether. You choose it. You just say."

He couldn't keep the enthusiasm from his voice. All his life, since the flowering of his artistic brilliance at Yale, he had believed that beauty existed despite the opinion of the observer. All that was required to recognize it was a person born with eyes that could "see." This was a talent, he had always maintained, that could not be learned or taught. It could be refined by experience and by endless exposure to great art, but it predated education. It was more fundamental. It had to be there first. Now, of course, it was too late to demonstrate that *his* monumental taste had been innate. At the height of his fame that could hardly be proved, and in the early days when his raw genius had been plain for anyone to see, nobody had known him and no one had wanted to. His fellow countrymen, obsessed by the value of "learning" and with an instinctive belief in the value of "expertise," had always scoffed at his theory, and he had been unable to provide evidence for its truth.

At last here before him was the living proof, a blue-jeaned Venus hot from heaven, the ultimate untrained "eye" who would show the world that he had been right all along. Paula didn't hesitate. "Well, I think perhaps that horse picture would be good there, with that gilt wood table and perhaps that clock. Of course we'd need to change the rug to that one with the tree design with all the things in the branches . . ."

"Oh God. Oh God," Winthrop murmured to himself as he struggled with the Sartorius equine painting that had cost him a quarter of a million dollars at the Bridport sale. Could he manage to move the fabulous Venetian marble-topped baroque side table he had found in the Brandolini Venice palazzo, and swapped with the Fiat heiress for a tired Guardi? Probably not, but his mind's eye could already see the Thomas Eardley tortoiseshell table clock sitting beneath the head of the Derby winner. And of course the girl was right. The whole needed nothing more than the Persian Isfahan depicting the traditional tree of life. The exquisite grouping would bring tears to the eyes of a half-switched-on beholder. The corner of some Beverly Hills drawing room would remain forever a shrine of beauty and the photographers from *World of Interiors* and *Architectural Digest* would home in on it like Navy missiles on a Libyan jet.

He stood back. There was no point in carrying on. It had been proved. Beyond reasonable doubt. She had it. She knew nothing, but she could do it all. Goddamn it, he had been *right*.

"What's your name?"

"Paula Hope."

He laughed and held out his hands in a gesture that said for once in his life he didn't know what to say. "Do you know what you have just done, Paula? Have you any *idea* what you can do?"

But as he spoke, he saw she didn't know. He looked quickly at his watch. It was getting late. He had agreed to meet a client for cocktails. It would have been a big commission. A million, maybe one point two. But he didn't hesitate. "Paula, if you're not doing anything else, would you let me take you somewhere to eat?"

Paula's eyes widened. God, food! She'd almost forgotten. Now she remembered and her stomach screamed at her to accept. "I'd love to," she said.

∼2∼

I'D LIKE YOU all to give me a minute or two before I make up my mind."
Robert Hartford picked up the horn-rimmed glasses from the Barce-
lona cut-glass coffee table, and he breathed in deeply. All around him was
the pungent smell of fear. It wasn't physical fear. The six men who sat on the
edges of the comfortable Osborne and Little chintz-covered sofas and chairs
were not afraid of bodily injury. It was a more comprehensive fear than that.
All of them stood very, very close to a deal that would reinvent their careers.
A yes from Hartford and they were home free, movie heroes in La-la Land,
up-to-the-millisecond Oscar creamers with the best tables at Morton's and
Spago to prove it.

A no and they were yesterday's men, the crowd for whom the big time
had been just too hot to handle. Their personal reputations would be shot in
the town where image was money, where money was power, and where
power was sex. Six careers, six mighty mortgages, three and a half mistresses,
fleets of high-end cars, love, respect, and marriages were suspended in the
Havana cigar smoke of the Sunset Hotel bungalow, and fingers of panic
plucked at the studio executives as they waited for the star's decision.

Robert Hartford gave them the little-boy smile—the one that turned on
the moviegoers coast to coast—and he watched the Galaxy top management
sweat.

He didn't look like a fifty-six-million-dollar man, but he did look far too
good to eat. His face was simply perfect. No more, no less. Women thought
so. Men thought so. Children thought so. Animals given the gift of speech
would have said that they thought so, too. There was just no possible argument about it. To say that he was not beautiful was to brand the judge insane,
blind, mendacious, or a blend of all three. The emotions in his eyes depended on the perspective of the person watching him. They were sad eyes,
shy eyes, laughing eyes, strong eyes. They were all of those things at once
. . . and none of them, their infinite variety confusing as it excited, shocking as it soothed. Although he was thirty-six, the crow had not landed. In fact
the crow hadn't even flown overhead, and the skin at the corners of his

315

remarkable eyes was a smooth honey color, totally devoid of wrinkles. The Hartford hair, dark brown and unfashionably short at the top and sides, was nonetheless long at the back, reaching down the nape of a graceful neck. Its cut was geometric, offsetting the square, dimpled jaw, the high cheekbones, the glint of the cobalt-blue eyes. It was these last that saved the face from a bland perfection. He didn't look like a model, nor did he resemble some Marlboro man, a swaggering macho pseudocowboy with two left feet and ten-minute reflexes. It wasn't even, in the end analysis, an "interesting" face —the sort of good looks that depended on shock value to deliver, a crooked nose, hooded eyes, an overly ripe mouth. But although it was none of them, it was all of them, merged in a secret harmony. It was the face of a man that women, all women, would love. His clothes didn't detract from his visual splendor. Their simplicity emphasized it. His plain white T-shirt was squeaky clean and free of mindless chatter, and it covered a lean torso from which brown, wiry arms protruded, the muscles rangy and businesslike—far from the designer triceps and biceps of the bodybuilder crowd. He wore pressed blue jeans, colorless Nike sneakers, and simple white socks that drew attention to the length of his legs and the tautness of his bottom. In short, Robert Hartford's beauty had an edge that could cut, and all around the immaculately decorated Sunset Hotel bungalow, his captive audience knew it.

"If there's anything we can say to influence you in any way . . ."

Bos Liebowitz's voice was shaking. He couldn't bear the silence. You were supposed to have learned how to deal with it in the sixties when it was a measure of your "cool." Well, he hadn't. Right now he cared more desperately than he had ever cared before and it was pointless to hide it. What could he do to make the superstar say what he wanted to hear? What could he give him? How could he flatter him? Hartford had more girls than he could ever use, and Bos had told him a hundred times that he loved him more than God. Galaxy had broken its piggy bank to offer the record-breaking guarantee that the studio was floating at the movie hero, but perhaps he could have lined up a little more bank finance, hocked a few more old movies from the studio library, begged for it, stolen it.

Robert lifted up a bronzed hand and waved it in the air in a gesture that said "shut up."

"Just a few minutes. Bear with me, Bos. And I'll let you have my answer."

Again he smiled the shy, unassuming smile, and inside he laughed at the enormity of his assumption. He knew what he was going to say. He had known for two weeks, but the beauty of life at the top of the heap was that you could shower it down on the ants who lived at the bottom. That was what he was doing right now. It was better than sex. Almost.

Bos Liebowitz, too, held up his hand in the universal gesture of surrender.

"Forgive me, Robert. Forgive me. It's just I can't help thinking of all those wonderful movies we could make . . . all those wonderful movies . . ." And those rentals, and tie-ins, and video rights, those sequels and the lists in *Variety* and the *Reporter* and the angst at the other studios.

Robert Hartford movies didn't just "open." They never closed. They had legs that went on forever, and first-weekend theater returns so large they looked like misprints. Why couldn't the bastard just say yes? Seven pictures, ten percent of the producers' gross, eight big ones guaranteed per movie. It was unheard of. It might never happen again in the history of the industry. It certainly hadn't come anywhere near to happening yet. But whatever it cost it was worth it, because Hartford was more bankable than the banks, the nearest thing to certainty in the Hollywood dice game, with a profit graph on his last four pictures that aimed straight at heaven.

Robert Hartford's baby-blue eyes had gone dreamy. He seemed to have left them. Oblivious to the mutterings of the mere mortals, he peered imperiously around his Mark Hampton-designed drawing room. How clever of Mark to decide on the tetrad color scheme, rather than the boring monotone, monochrome, or analogous schemes that the West Coast designers slavishly employed. The four hues melded in a perfect mix—the delicate pink and russet reds of the sofas; the creamy yellow of the lampshades against the tan walls; the rich browns of the Sheraton furniture; and the turquoise blue of the garden-of-paradise silk rug from the Persian holy city of Qum. The style was aristocratic, but it was not a cold room, and the important early cubist Picassos, daughters of the Demoiselles d'Avignon, were at home amidst the ambience of understated tradition. Yes, it was a beautiful room, dripping with good taste—and crowded with some of the ugliest men Robert had ever seen.

Robert tugged at an ear, placed his glasses on his perfect nose, and cleared his throat. "I'd have artistic control, script, casting approval and final cut, and veto over choice of product."

It was a statement posing as a question. Bos nodded quickly.

"Which shall not be unreasonably withheld," added Cal Brewer, who headed up the Galaxy contracts department.

Robert Hartford's eyes narrowed, his sensuous mouth thinned, his jaw jutted.

Liebowitz's heart stopped. He whirled on the attorney. "Shut up, Cal!" he hissed.

The explosion of his command roared around the room, vibrating the Limoges coffee cups on the three-quarter-inch-thick coffee table and bouncing off the beige of the Thai silk walls. "Sorry," he added almost immediately. It had been an overreaction, a potentially disastrous loss of control, very un-Hollywood. But, God, he was nervous. Later, if Hartford didn't accept their offer, Cal Brewer could and would be let go. For now, it was more important that they all appear one big happy family, riding to glory on the back of the legend's name.

"What I meant to say was that what Robert finds reasonable, *we* will find reasonable. We always have in the past, and we always will in the future. You have my personal word on that." Bos actually rubbed his hands together as he made oil for the suddenly troubled waters.

When the contract was signed they could fight with Robert Hartford until he was boxed, but until the ink was dry on the contract there would *be* no deal. And no deal might mean no studio, or worse, a studio with a boss whose name was no longer Liebowitz.

He leaned forward, acutely aware that sweat was staining the front of his Sea Island cotton Bijan shirt. He watched Hartford like he would the Maker on Judgment Day.

Robert Hartford didn't even bother to look pacified. He flicked his head away from all of them and began to study the ceiling, his long, sensitive fingers reaching up to massage the back of his neck.

"Do you know this place is for sale?" he said at last into the anguished silence.

Six minds whirred to a stop. What place? For sale? What the hell was he talking about?

Robert Hartford beamed around the room. He seemed to want an answer to his totally out-of-context question at the very moment when the only thing anybody else wanted was an answer to theirs.

The vice president of production, insulated to some extent from the general angst by his relatively lowly position, got his mind together first. "You mean the bungalow?" he tried.

"No. No. The whole thing. The whole hotel." Robert waved a languid arm in the air to encapsulate it all—the late afternoon Beverly Hills sun knifing through the open window, the hiss of the lawn sprinkler on the emerald grass outside, the muted rumble of a room-service trolley from beyond the ivy-covered wall that bordered the Hartford compound.

Bos Liebowitz alone knew what was happening. Robert Hartford was playing with them. They were mice to his cat. He knew exactly what he was going to do, but was enjoying the fact that they didn't. It was a Hollywood power trip pure and simple, and all they could do was tag along.

"Must be a bit of a worry . . . I mean, you living here and not knowing who the new owner's gonna be," he said as casually as he could. He had never been able to understand why Robert Hartford chose to live in a hotel, however splendid, when he could have afforded any estate in Bel-Air or Beverly Hills.

"Weeeell," Robert drawled. "I mean, I imagine the new management wouldn't throw me out!"

An explosion of anxious laughter rocked the room.

Amused, Robert Hartford watched the awesome manifestation of his power. It was moments like this when it was all worthwhile—the careful legend building, the loneliness that erected the myths, the sacrifices and the hard work as brick by brick he had constructed his mighty career. He'd never wavered from his objective; he had never varied his methods. In fashion and out of it he had plowed his furrow, and now, at last, the whole world wanted him.

The Galaxy contract on the shining glass coffee table said so. Robert Hartford. A seven-picture deal. Fifty-six million bucks, big points on the gross, and no artistic indulgence "unreasonably withheld." Money had long since ceased to mean much to him. He already had far more than he could spend. But it was a method of keeping score, and in Hollywood it was the language of love, the dialect he would always understand.

He smiled carefully around the tuberose-scented room, his beguiling eyes snakecharming the studio players one by one. His smile dried their counterfeit mirth and soothed their jangled nerves. It was the smile that made the housewives feel all right, and the teenagers feel themselves. It was the smile that posed the mystery, and the sphinxlike smile that promised the conclusion would satisfy. It was the smile that pried into the magic of motivation, and the smile that gave no clue to its own.

"It's make-your-mind-up time," he said softly in the voice of a lover. "With this contract I thee wed . . ." and he picked up the Bic pen with its chewed end, and the ink running down the inside of the plastic.

He talked as he wrote, destroying the importance of the moment with the willfulness of a child. His voice now was matter-of-fact, devoid of the charming playfulness that had taken the edge off his earlier banter.

"You know the best thing about this place? The staff. I don't know where the hell Francisco gets them. They look like the usual wetbacks, but they all speak immaculate English, and they have this instinctive way of anticipating what you want."

He paused. He'd gotten as far as *Hart.* . . . He looked up.

Not a whisker moved; not a muscle; not a joint creaked. Their expressions were frozen in horrendous half smiles of anticipation. But he had the antidote in his hand: . . . *ford.* With the stroke of a Bic he could make the studio top brass come alive. Of course it wouldn't be as much fun then. It was the same with women. Climax and anticlimax; the chase; the games, and the fury of the coupling; and then the little death and the relative dullness of the life thereafter.

So, like lovemaking, he was eking it out. But, like lovemaking, too, there was a limit beyond which things could not decently be prolonged. Robert Hartford let out a sigh and leaned forward once again. With no more ado, he scrawled . . . *ford.*

Cal Brewer remained rooted to the spot. The contract had five copies. All needed the Hartford signature. Bos, however, came off the sofa like a brain-damaged boxer at the sound of a doorbell. He was a bottom-line man. Hartford had just signed on it. It was a done deal. A man like him wouldn't bother to sign again. There were photocopying machines to relieve one of drudgery like that. If the photocopying had to be witnessed at great expense by the equivalent of a panel of bishops to validate the signature and the facsimile, *that* was mere detail.

Right now, the trick was to glorify the moment. The blissful second when he, Bos Liebowitz had, at the stroke of a broken ballpoint, become the second most important man in the most important town in the world.

The tears were thick in his eyes as he waddled across the four-hundred-knots-to-the-inch pure silk rug toward the man who had made him so happy. It was time for celebration, time for the laying on of hands. His money had been accepted. There was a sense in which it was only right and proper that he should be allowed to finger the merchandise.

Robert Hartford, however, was way ahead of him. The man who loved women could not stand the touch of men.

He was on his feet, his movements fluid, as he distanced himself from Bos. In a flash the sofa was between him and those who jostled to congratulate him. He picked up the telephone from the sun-faded sofa table and dialed once.

"Ah, Conchita," he sighed his relief. A female. "You have a cold!" His tone was intimate. He scolded. He was alarmed. The whole focus of his attention was on the disembodied Mexican voice that took the orders for food and drink. "Vitamin C. Honey. And a tequila before bed tonight," he prescribed, his words creamy with solicitation.

The senior management of what had just become the most successful studio in Hollywood were forced to put their joy on hold, as Robert Hartford sweet-talked the anonymous woman. A few of them bothered to wonder who she was.

Bos Liebowitz, however, didn't find it odd at all. He had seen this happen before, and it was part of the reason he had just promised Robert Hartford fifty-six million dollars. The movie star had the knack. It was by far the most important thing he had. Perhaps it was the only one. From dusk to dawn, and from dawn to dusk he thought of women. He thought of pleasing them, and of their softness, and he daydreamed of their divine smells, and the way they held their heads, and the funny things they worried about. He planned his conquest of them, and he worshiped their beauty, and loved their plainness also, their specialty and their ordinariness. Robert Hartford adored the stars in their heavens but he adored, too, the clerks at the Ralph's check-out counters, and the tender-age night kids outside. The Roxy or Gazzarri's on the Strip and the fifty-year-old agents, and the sixty-year-old casting directors, and all the crazy girls on the Santa Monica freeway with the wild wind in their hair. He was mesmerized by them all, and they were beguiled by the bizarre intensity of his interest. In turn he vibrated to their reaction in an endless dance of positive reinforcement, until the whole world he inhabited had become a spinning vortex around his body and his bed and the secret places of wonderful strangers.

"Conchita," he murmured the name like a response in church. "Can you send me along some of that 'seventy-nine Pol Roger Rosé. Oh, two or three. And some bits and pieces, those dates rolled in bacon, smoked salmon with brown bread, the usual things. Oh, and I'll have some peach juice. Yeah, a celebration you could say . . ." He laughed a tinkling laugh, full of conspiracy and comradeship, as he let her know that she was more important than all of them put together, all the hairy, horrible things with their smelly socks and their sexual inadequacies, with their halitosis and their hernias, their dandruff and their disgusting toes. He cradled the telephone against his cheek and clavicle, freeing his other hand, and he peered at his new partners over the edge of the horn rims.

"Now, you watch that cold. Early to bed. Promise?"

He eased the telephone back onto its holder.

"I thought some champagne," he said. "Congratulations! You boys have done a good deal."

Nobody quite knew what to say. They were all caught up in Robert Hartford's letdown. They, the rubbish, would be drinking his champagne. He, the sophisticate, would be doing the peach juice. They wanted hugs, and declarations of undying affection, and proud promises for the future. He wanted to make someone called Conchita burn up with desire at the Sunset Hotel's switchboard.

It was too soon to talk of the projects ahead. It was too late to rehash old ones. In short, there was not much to say at a time when something badly needed to be said. It was Bos Liebowitz who said it. "Well, Robert. How are you going to spend the money?" he asked.

Robert Hartford looked him straight in the eye. "I'm going to buy this hotel," he said.

—

ROBERT HARTFORD hurried across the faded Mexican tile of the pink-and-white impatiens-lined walkway to the adjacent bungalow of his compound, and already he was feeling better. He could tolerate a roomful of men for only so long, and he had been dangerously close to running out of emotional breath.

He knocked on the door, but he opened it as he did so, and the delicious scent of her wafted out onto the evening air. She was sitting on the edge of the bed, and she smiled up at him as he stood in the doorway. She had been waiting for him. Her expression said that. And so did her body, and the clothes that underdressed it. The girl's forehead was propped against her hand, and long black hair burrowed through her fingers before cascading down to frame the sculpted arm. Her elbow rested provocatively on the milky paleness of her thigh, indenting the creamy skin. Her lips were moist, her head leaned seductively to one side, and her eyes were ablaze.

"Hi, Robert," she murmured.

He didn't answer. He was in church. He wanted to kneel. This was the communion that gave meaning to his life. She was so white—white as light in the town of brown women—and that made the black so much better. Her midnight stockings were turned down at midthigh, and the straps of her garter belt lay loose against her skin. Her silk nightdress was short, circling her in a black band that was in contrast to the snowy slope of her back and the flesh strips of her upper legs. But it was her breasts that took Robert Hartford's breath away. The flimsiest brocade fought to contain them, the material forming a sensual latticework over the firm flesh as the girl's crouched, catlike position magnified their fullness.

He smiled at her.

"You're so beautiful," he whispered. He breathed the words, as he willed her to believe him, and his smile, and hers, deepened as she did.

"Thank you." It was a murmur, brimful of pleasure, but it was also the "thank you" of a little girl. The hint of formal politeness in the prelude to the storm of bodies delighted Robert. He moved toward her.

She sat up and turned to face him full on. Her tongue crept out to moisten her parted lips, and she swallowed hard as she prepared to be the lover of the man who loved women.

He stood before her and reached for her hands as his eyes reassured her, and her fingers played lazily with his. He drew her up toward him, and she flowed into his arms, silky smooth and sweet smelling, soft as the black material that clothed her, her body supple and willing. His hands caressed the velvet skin of her back, and she shuddered against his chest as the sensation flowed through her, and he drew himself in closer to lose himself in the tense flesh of her breasts.

She turned up her face toward his, and she closed her eyes as she willed him to love her. "Kiss me, Robert," she murmured.

In answer, he ran his hands through her hair, twining its strands through his fingers. Then he bent toward the long whiteness of her neck, and his breath fanned her. He paused, deliciously unhurried, and his hands traced the contours of her head, holding her hostage to him, she who only wanted to be his prisoner. Then his lips descended, warm and humid on the dry desert of her skin, and their landing was butterfly soft, hovering between presence and absence in the delicious mixture of threat and promise.

A sigh of longing slipped from her, and she reached up to take what he was so tantalizingly slow to give. Her hands cupped his cheeks and she opened her eyes wide in the stricken gaze of the frightened fawn as she moved his lips to hers.

He sensed she could wait no more and, excited by her desire, he matched it with his own, allowing the wonderful girl to draw him into the sweet trap of her lips, parted hungrily to receive him. He closed his eyes, the better to feel her, and his mouth melted gratefully against hers. There was a time for control, and there was a time for letting go. Robert Hartford was no longer a conscious being. He had become an instinct, the most subtle and sophisticated sensual animal in the world, and now his every motion was designed only to capture the elusive prey of pleasure—pleasure for himself, pleasure for the goddess he was worshiping.

She fought him in the kiss, and he rode her desperate mouth, swaying, retreating, advancing, in the abundant wetness and the heat of lips. For long seconds he allowed her savage onslaught, and then as the wild passion gripped her, and the low whimper murmured in her throat, as her hands reached out to draw his buttocks in against her thrusting hips, he slowed the pace once more. Languid, liquid, his mouth captured her quivering tongue, and his hands played her hair, her neck, as if both were the reins of a crazed mustang that must learn to be ridden. His touch was gentle as he guided her to the easy calm she would learn from him. Gradually she relinquished her greedy, headstrong assault, as she allowed him to guide her to the sensuous shyness of a more delicate love. Their tongues swayed together in a velvet embrace, and she experienced at last the taste of him as she sucked the nectar from his lips with the patience and calm of a honeybee at the heart of a wide-open flower.

Now his mouth lingered on the high pallor of her cheeks, caressed the dark line of her eyebrows, slipped down to taste the fluttering lids of her nut-brown eyes. But always he returned to her lips and, like a parched traveler in the desert of her face, he drank from the fountain of her. Then, strong enough to explore once more, he set out again in the search for satisfaction: out to the lobe of her perfect ear; up to the broad brilliance of her forehead, where the glory of her face met the mane of lustrous, scented, jet-black hair.

He breathed in the perfumed essence of her and he laughed in his heart as he smelled the secrets of all the soft, seductive beauties with their beguiling ways, their brilliance, and their superhuman strengths. It was always different, so endlessly the same, as the doe-skinned wonders lent him their bodies to thrill and be thrilled. It was the way to handle women. To love them was simply not enough. They had to be adored. Only then could they give the gift of joy that was always theirs to bestow.

Her face was wet with the tracks of his tongue, and her cheeks were moist with tears of passion.

Her long legs were weak with excitement. He could feel it, as she shuddered in his embrace, as her hands picked pleadingly at his body.

She sank down against the creamy ivory of the Pratesi bed cover, until her head rested on the outsize pillow, and he smiled tenderly at her, as the love light blazed in her big round eyes, and the musky, majestic aroma of her need seeped into the scented air. She lay back, and her hands wandered to her breasts, to the fevered skin framed by the black brocade, to the pink pulses that were her nipples.

He reached out and he slipped one black strap over her shoulder, then the other, unveiling the twin monuments to terminal beauty for the eyes of the man who understood.

She lay back, and she smiled at him as she watched her reflection mirrored in his delighted eyes. The consummate sculpture had at last met the supreme aesthete. She was more beautiful than all the beautiful girls she knew, but he was more beautiful than she. And he knew how to love. He was showing her, and in the dawn of lovers' wisdom she realized that she knew nothing at all. For an age of anticipation he simply watched her. His eyes feasted on her, speaking to her, roaming lovingly over her, until her hot flesh crawled with sensation, and tingled with longing. His look was liquid intimacy. His eyes said the words that his tongue would never speak—that he loved her more completely than any perfect woman had ever been perfectly loved—and the lies of his eyes didn't matter. There was only the present, only the agonizing nearness of him.

She swallowed hard and her eyes, round with disbelief, gazed into the mystery of his. His hand moved toward her, and his touch was so feathery in its lightness, that she could hardly comprehend the crashing vibrations it sent coursing through her. "Oh God, Robert . . ." she moaned.

His finger hovered on the borders of her nipple, and his eyes asked the tender permission, as they watched for the telltale signs from her body that each stage of arousal had been filled up to its potential, and that no tiny area of sensual possibility remained unexplored.

She could feel it pulsating at the edge of his finger. All the blood in her body was there, forcing the skin into the geometrical point of the triangle.

"Touch me, touch me . . ." she pleaded.

And he did. But it was not his finger that touched her.

He leaned in toward her, and he bent down as if to the sacrament, and the tip of his tongue, wet and warm, merged with the sharp point of the center of her world.

~3~

T HE GEORGIAN CRYSTAL chandelier ruled the room. On either side, flanking it like a Praetorian guard, were its lesser fellows, showering down pearls of brilliant light on the up-market swine below. The crowd was tense, and packed together on gold-painted chairs in the ballroom of the Sunset Hotel. The hum of their excited conversation waxed and waned like the Santa Monica surf, merging in uneasy harmony with the metallic Ravi Shankar sitar music that burbled from the concealed speaker system.

"Christ, Kristina, I've just signed the movie deal of the century and now you've dragged me off to some psychedelic sixties time-warp rally. What *is* this? Who on *earth* persuaded Francisco to let these fruitcakes use his hotel?"

The indulgent smile on Robert Hartford's face gave the lie to the sentiments he was expressing. He leaned toward his daughter, into the sweet aura of Dior's Poison, close to the swanlike neck with its clusters of Tina Chow astraltrip aquamarine stones, up against the shoulder-pads of her black Giorgio Armani jacket. His velvet-soft whisper was intimate, and totally unrelated to the words he spoke. Kristina Hartford was to some extent insulated from the industrial strength of his charm, but she was also a woman.

"Oh, Dad, relax. Let it all *go*. Caroline Kirkegaard could change your life if you let her."

Robert laughed dismissively. Then his nostrils began to twitch. "What's that funny smell," he asked, suspiciously.

"They've smudged the room," said Kristina, as if talking to a small child.

"They've done *what?*"

"They burn leaves from a cedar, and bits from sage bushes to 'clear' the room. It removes all the stored vibrations and leaves everyone receptive for the message from the crystals."

"Good God," said Robert cheerfully in a seen-it-all-now tone.

She reached for his hand and twined her fingers in among his, squeezing affectionately to show that she could live with his skepticism and appreciate

325

his good humor. Robert squeezed back, pleased by the contact and the unconditional affection it symbolized.

He ran his practiced eye over the woman he had created. It was difficult to be objective about her, but he tried. The body was superb, and she was well dressed, even if the couture was a little unadventurous. That was a function of the ludicrously large allowance he paid her. Cash was the enemy of cachet, and cheap so often the friend of chic. There was too much of her mother in the face, a certain bland flatness that looked passable as a whole but lost points on a feature-by-feature analysis—the ripe mouth and sparky eyes scoring high; the too-large nose, the high forehead, and the fleshy cheekbones failing to deliver absolute beauty. But Robert adored her. For him Kristina represented the difference between love and sex. If it hadn't been for her, he wouldn't have had a clue that they were not the same thing.

"Listen, sweetheart, there can't be two people called Caroline Kirkegaard in this town. If it's the one I threw off my movie five years ago then I'm telling you she's really bad vibes. Believe me, *really* bad."

"Vibes, Dad. *Vibes!!!* God, it's getting to you already. Like no way was Caroline Kirkegaard ever an *actress.*" The putdown was as unintentional as it was unmistakable. In Kristina's scheme of things, psychics ranked higher than movie people.

The laughter was bubbling through Kristina's words. She'd only heard about the Kirkegaard channeling meeting an hour or so before, and she'd rushed over from the UCLA campus in Westwood and had only just made it in time. If she'd known earlier she'd have made a point of dropping in on her father, but the way things had turned out she'd bumped into him anyway saying good-bye to a tearful, dark-haired beauty in the lobby. Kristina had immediately captured him and dragged him along to the meeting, as he pretended to complain. It was fun teasing him, and basking in the glory that always accompanied public appearances with her famous father, and she was also enjoying introducing him to the New Age movement that was becoming such a large part of her life. Of course, she *expected* skepticism. If you couldn't count on a dad for that, what *could* you count on him for?

"Well, I'll recognize her when I see her. Once seen never forgotten."

It was true. He'd never totally forgotten Caroline Kirkegaard, and now, as he thought of her, he couldn't suppress the shudder of revulsion. Big, butch, ballsy as hell, she had stood out from the faceless crowd of bit players in the movie that had been constructed as his own personal vehicle. She had towered above all the rest, both literally and figuratively, and in the scenes they had done together she had all but stolen them. That in itself had been unforgivable, but it had been much more than that. Robert Hartford had found her deeply unsettling. There had been an impossible-to-ignore quality about her, and in watching her he understood about moths and flames, and the compulsion of male spiders for fatal union with black widows. She had the hypnotic immediacy of a particularly violent traffic accident, of a plane falling in flames from an angry sky.

He had acted with surgical speed and precision. The director and the producer had been summoned to his office at the studio, and he had told them—just like that—that she was history. He hadn't asked that she be given the soft soap in terms of some let-you-down-gently-excuse, and she hadn't been given any. She had been told, quite simply, that she was off the movie, because Robert Hartford had ordered it and he had never been told—although he could imagine—what her reaction had been.

He shifted in his seat, suddenly uncomfortable on the little red cushion, and he looked around the room. For all his talk of freaks and weirdos the crowd in the ballroom was actually platinum-card-carrying Beverly Hills: exuberant suntans, silver hair, buckets of gold for the predominantly middle-aged males; brave, brittle lifted faces, bright colors, and pendulous semi-precious Kenneth J. Lane necklaces and bracelets for the marginally older women. Scattered among the agents and lower-level studio-production people were a couple of screen "writers" that Robert recognized, a trio of actors that he almost did, and a swathe of support people like the doctors who made the tits and the faces stay up, the lawyers who handled the divorces, and the dentists who were responsible for the unearthly whiteness of the wall-to-wall teeth. Then there were the starlets with their expressions of desperate expectancy and their wide-open bleached, bonded smiles that belied their ugly interiors, their gold-bullion souls, their computerized hearts.

"Look, it's beginning!" said Kristina.

As if on cue the lights dimmed, stilling the roar of conversation in the Sunset ballroom. At the same time somebody turned up the tuneless music, and twin spotlights lit the stage.

Robert couldn't help being caught up in the almost palpable excitement of the crowd. "These people ought to know better," he muttered to himself as a mantra to ward off the electric enthusiasm that surrounded him on every side.

Two porters walked briskly onto the stage, carrying three black Doric columns, made of papier-mâché, each about five feet long. They searched around on the floor, looking for chalk marks, and took great care to position them with total accuracy at the points of an equilateral triangle. A third man entered from the left carrying a simple straight-backed metal chair, which he placed at a point equidistant from the columns. Then all three withdrew. The mystical music stopped. There was no sound at all in the audience. The Testarossa and Countach keys were quiet in their pockets. The thick, creamy scent of Giorgio still in their nostrils, they forced all thought of box-office returns to the back of their minds. Any minute now the channel herself would walk onto the stage, and soon they would be in touch, across vast stretches of eternal time, with the people that once they had been.

The girl who hurried onto the stage now was clearly *not* the main feature, but to Robert Hartford she was a more than acceptable trailer. She was extremely pretty. Her red hair was cut in a flashy, slightly old-fashioned Farrah Fawcett, and it framed an enthusiastic, pert face whose main features were a surgically perfect nose and pouting heart-shaped lips. She wore standard-issue 501s and a checked shirt that looked like it was from an L.L. Bean catalogue. In L.A., where they knew about such things, it was obvious that she was heavily into exercise, and from her superconfident walk, and the way her rock-hard ass stuck straight up, it was also clear that Narcissus was a close relative.

She carried a large tray strapped around her neck, holding three outsize clear quartz crystals. Each was about nine inches high, brilliant and translucent, rising from an irregular base to a uniform point. Making light of what was obviously formidable weight, she placed one carefully on the top of each column. Immediately the spotlights sought them out, and there was a murmur in the crowd as three beams illuminated their beauty. The light seemed to blaze from the surface of the stones, haunting, mysterious, and totally alive. For a second the girl stood back and allowed the crystals to speak silently to the crowd. Then she walked to the center of the stage. In a soft, silky voice she said, "My name is Kanga. I am Caroline Kirkegaard's disciple. The mistress of Destiny is ready for you. May the truth of the crystal live in your hearts, and the love of the Great One illuminate your minds."

Then she turned quickly and left the stage.

"She's muddled that up," whispered Robert. "Surely she meant truth in the mind and love in the heart."

"Ssssssssh," hissed Kristina, irritated. Parental skepticism was one thing, literary criticism was another, especially from her father, whose I.Q. equaled his diastolic blood pressure.

"Is the Great One God?" he persevered, beginning to enjoy himself.

"We're *all* gods," whispered Kristina.

"Ah," said Robert. "That one."

"Don't think, feel," exhorted Kristina in her role as metaphysical navigator, blissfully unaware that she was mouthing a line from a sixties musical.

"If I don't think, I won't know what it is I'm feeling," said Robert.

"Be *quiet!*" ordered someone loudly from the row behind.

Robert twisted in his seat, ready, willing, and fantastically able to do battle with the shadowy bastard who had *dared* to give him an order. But Caroline Kirkegaard forestalled him. She was striding across the stage, and she was as impossible to ignore as nuclear war.

Robert felt his eyes sucked toward her by some power beyond his control. Oh yes, it was "his" Caroline Kirkegaard, all right. He recognized her instantly, and a packet of dread exploded inside him. This woman had reason to hate him, and one thing was certain. She wasn't the sort of enemy that anybody should have.

Caroline Kirkegaard sat down on the chair in the dead center of the crystal triangle. She sat quite still, her spine straight, head held high, eyes wide open, and her long pale neck stretched upward, as if longing for the kiss of some Druid's knife. The black Saint Laurent cocktail frock she wore—cut low in front, and slashed surgically up the side of the pencil skirt—had the effect and purpose of an exclamation mark. It wasn't there to hide. It was there to reveal. Her milk-white body exploded from it like toothpaste from a punctured tube, oozing out in a tight stream of flesh, and as it did so it was sculpted into muscle perfection and bone brilliance by some Valkyrian artist who had never heard of bourgeois self-control. Her yellow-blond Bryl-creemed hair was slicked back from her high forehead in a fifties Tony Curtis cut and chopped off mercilessly at the back where the skyscraper neck met the Nordic head.

Her face was disturbingly beautiful. Below dangerous brows her eyes were an unnatural metallic blue, quite unlike the blue of the sky or sea, as if the color had been invented by a chance clash of the elements in a freak electrical storm. They held her eager audience with the irresistible power of cosmic blue-black holes—beckoning, demanding, insisting that they watch her if they dared. Down, down into the eyes they went—all the movie men and the groovy women, the medical mavens and Rodeo matrons—spinning gratefully into their depths. It didn't matter that they were unable to breathe. The important thing was to *be* there, safe in the sanctuary of her mysterious purpose, womb-warm in the glow of her vision, rammed up tight against the luminous knowledge of her stellar brain. Caroline Kirkegaard's wet lips dripped promises. They were vermilion, but, unlike her eyes, color was not their point. It was their lushness. They were mangoes, and papaya and kiwi and loquat, exotic in their tropical come-on, twin pads of glistening mem-brane parted in the unmistakable statement that they were ready to eat . . . and be eaten.

Her torso alone would have had the muscle-pumping bodybuilders of Venice Beach weeping in their steroid soup. Her shoulders, broad and strong as a rigid steel joist, supported arms that could have won wrestling matches on bars. Her breasts headed straight for the audience, shameless in the enor-mity of their statement, and were separated from each other by a cleavage that, in more ways than one, conjured up visions of Silicon Valley. Across the crack-of-doom divide stretched the milky way of the Caroline Kirkegaard mammary land. Most of it was visible above the low-cut black dress, and the acreage that wasn't was merely shrouded in thin cloud by the sheer silk material. Two tight nipples, icepick sharp, fought mano-a-mano with the Saint Laurent dress, and for a good reason. The half-cone tips of her bra had been removed, and the brown pigment of her areolae was a mere wisp of silk away from total visibility.

As if carved in stone, she received the homage of the audience, her hands clasped around two crystals that rested in her lap.

"She's like a goddess!" Kristina's breathless whisper was saturated with awe, and beside her in the semidarkness Robert Hartford was uncharacteris-tically lost for words. He swallowed hard in the somehow noisy silence. Caro-line Kirkegaard had always been difficult to ignore, but this was ridiculous. Heavens, she was big! Not so much a goddess as a praying mantis, hovering over the stage, burying the chair in which she sat, and dwarfing life itself with the sheer size of her personality. She wasn't really a woman at all. She was an *event*. She transcended gender, a great statue of androgyny that spoke alike to men, women, and children in the Esperanto of universal sexuality. Robert could feel it. It was a fine mist enveloping his delicate sensual antennae, and all around him he knew that the Hollywood power people were giving up the struggle to retain their jaded indifference as they plopped, one by one, gasping and gulping, into the sexual stew that was now the room's atmosphere. It wasn't just the men. It was the women, too, sinking gracefully into the seductive sea of the Kirkegaard charisma.

"Look, the crystals," said Kristina.

Perfectly still on their pedestals several feet from Caroline Kirkegaard's Viking head, the crystals seemed to have come alive. The spotlights played over them as they had before, but it was the way the light reemerged that now fascinated the audience. Before it had been reflected in uniform diffusion from the facets of the stones, but now it was on the move. It began to choose direction, and it gained in strength, cascading out, as if it had been born again in the heart of the cold geometry. As the crowd watched, their bodies humming like tuning forks to the subterranean vibrations, the light that streamed from the crystals began to aim itself at Caroline Kirkegaard. Gradually the beams became more focused, until at last they were lasers darting like spears at the bone sculpture that was her head, giving off a ghostly, incandescent glow at her forehead, high up on her cheekbones, deep in her bottomless eyes.

Kristina heard her own sharp intake of breath. Her whole body was full of the absolute certainty that something wonderful was happening. She wanted to *be* that light. There, inside the vision, lost in the crystal moonbeams, she could find herself. There, bathing at the knowledge fountain, she could get drunk on meaning. There, in the warm heart of Caroline's loving mind, she could find all the truths at last.

But the light had changed direction. Funneling in from the crystal-topped columns it flowed down both sides of her, indenting at the waspish waist, caressing her thighs, lapping lovingly at her stiltlike legs. It hugged Caroline closely like an aura, and Kristina, her willing ears tuned to hear such things, fancied she could hear the humming of the light, high pitched and resonant, that signaled the end of the beginning.

Caroline Kirkegaard closed her eyes. Then she breathed in deeply through her nose, inflating her majestic torso. Next the breath rushed out of her and the sound filled the room, until everyone could sense the currents of air that she was creating. Slowly, a crystal in the palm of each hand, her arms rose up from her sides until they pointed straight at the audience.

"She's directing her kundalini energy through the crystals, and using the force of the other crystals to energize her," whispered Kristina, leaning in toward her father, but keeping her eyes fixed on the stage. "Can't you feel the power in the room?"

Robert shifted in his chair. He could feel something, but it was impossible to say what it was. Irritation? The contagious enthusiasm of the gullible crowd? The appalling discomfort of not being the center of attraction? There was a sensation of strangeness, of being on a voyage, the weird exhilaration of finding yourself in a foreign country that you weren't sure you liked.

He jumped suddenly as the music struck up again. It was a hideous aural

experience, loud and dissonant, tuneless and disjointed. There were synthe-
sizers, gongs, bells and droning, chanting, Eastern voices repeating meaningless sounds amid the chaos.

"God, what a dreadful noise," said Robert.

"You're just not in *tune* with it," hissed Kristina. *"We* are."

"It's not in tune with itself," protested Robert.

"You can't *'hear'* it."

"I can. That's the problem."

"It's shamanic music. They play it all the time on that radio station, the
Wave. It opens your consciousness to higher planes and it potentiates the
power of the crystals. This one is called Wakan-tanka."

"Now, *that* I can believe."

She looked at him sharply, as she sensed the ridicule.

But the dialogue was over.

"Link hands," commanded Caroline Kirkegaard.

Her voice, pure Southern California, silky smooth, was a million miles
from the fjords where she came from, but despite its softness it cut through
the silence like the crack of a whip. No one in the audience considered
disobeying her, not even Robert Hartford, who thanked the Lord in heaven
that he had chosen an aisle seat as he reached for his daughter's hand.

Caroline watched them obey her, and the thrill of excitement coursed
through her. This was what it was all about. Power over people. She worshiped it. The audience, however, recoiled from it. They wanted release from
their responsibilities and the awesome decisions that they endlessly had to
make. They wanted to retreat from self-determination to a simpler world
where they danced to the tune of a piper who was no longer themselves. It
was a straightforward transaction, as old as time, as old as ruler and the ruled,
as ancient as leaders and the led. All their problems would melt away if they
would give Caroline the control that she longed for with every fiber of her
mighty will.

Holding hands made it easier. Feeling was believing but touching was the
truth, and other people's flesh was the most powerful medicine. If they were
linked together, then they were *connected.* To some extent they were no
longer discrete individuals. They had become a crowd, an entity with a personality that was dramatically different from those of the individual human
beings who combined to form it.

Caroline stood up, well aware of the psychological impact of her unusual
height. She raised a hand to focus the eyes.

"I am who I was," she intoned.

"I am who I was," they dutifully responded.

"I am who I was," said Kristina.

"Bullshit," said Robert Hartford. "Reincarnation bullshit," he repeated,
quite loudly.

But Kristina wasn't listening to him. She smiled to herself. They had all
existed before, and somehow those past lives lived on in them right now. It

was reassuring to feel that life stretched back endlessly into the distant past. It made her feel bigger, more important, *part* of something.

"I will be who I am," said Caroline Kirkegaard.

Robert Hartford was beginning to get irritated. The Kirkegaard bitch had just said that everyone would experience an infinite number of future lives, and the life they were leading now would be incorporated into that endless future. Dear old reincarnation. Original as sin. No, the maddening thing was the smiles of wonder on the faces of the audience. On *Kristina's* face. It was unbelievable. They were looking at age-old soft soap, and seeing the Holy Grail. It was totally ridiculous even in bone-from-the-neck-up Beverly Hills where the nearest things to intellectuals were screenwriters and shrinks.

"The future and the past," said Caroline Kirkegaard mysteriously, "are one through me."

Robert Hartford stood up. It was garbage. He didn't bother to say good-bye to Kristina. She was too busy mouthing her responses to the High Priest-ess to notice that he was leaving. He would make as much noise as possible on the way out, as he voted on the whole incredible charade with his feet, and he vowed to recommend to Francisco Livingstone that in future all Destiny meetings be banned from the Sunset Hotel.

Caroline saw someone making a high-profile exit, but she wasn't fazed. There was always somebody in the audience who couldn't stand the competi-tion, who resented the power she exercised. It was good he was leaving. There was room for only one force source at a Destiny meeting. She peered out over the flushed faces, and the glorious feeling exploded within her. God, it was magnificent—asserting the control. They would say anything now, be-lieve anything. They were committed, not to truth, not to knowledge, not to wisdom—but to her.

"Raise your hands above your head," she ordered, as maybe a thousand hands reached for the sky. "We are the brothers and sisters of eternity," said Caroline Kirkegaard.

Robert Hartford tried to shut his ears to the meta-claptrap that was un-folding in his wake as he made for the exit, and he avoided the eyes of the crowd on the way out. His instinct told him that the audience was too enrap-tured by the Kirkegaard charisma to spare a thought for a mere superstar, even one of his stature. That added insult to the intellectual injuries he had just sustained. But as he approached the exit, he noticed a man he had seen somewhere before, who seemed to be trying to communicate with him, al-though it was not certain what his expression meant. Despite himself Robert couldn't help returning his gaze and the corners of his mouth turned down in irritation as he realized that some sort of acknowledgment might have to be made. The familiar stranger's look seemed to be saying that he understood why Hartford was leaving while at the same time insinuating that his depar-ture was the result of all sorts of ego problems that weren't totally admirable, were even slightly humorous. The Hartford jaw set in concrete as he sailed past the maybe acquaintance. Screw him, whoever he was. Fifty-six-million-dollar movie stars could afford to ignore people they didn't know they knew.

At the back of the room, beside the exit, and beneath a brooding, romantic landscape of the Hudson River School, the man was quite unmoved by Robert Hartford's failure to either recognize or acknowledge him. He leaned nonchalantly against the oak-paneled wall of the Sunset ballroom, wearing an expensive single-breasted dark blue worsted suit, a nondescript blue-striped tie, and an unfashionable but far from cheap white silk shirt. The jacket was tightly buttoned, and that seemed a symbol for his entire appearance—from the tips of his patent-leather hair to the soles of his highly polished thick-soled tasseled loafers. His face, like the rest of him, was giving nothing away. It was relaxed in an expression that was not quite a smile, hovering on the borders of both disdain and patronization. Broad, bushy eyebrows, black as night, bristled over wide-set eyes, and a determined, snub nose tapered off into a mean mouth, which in turn was lost in a square, aggressive jaw. His features warred with each other, suggesting he was a creature of deep contradictions, and his fastidious appearance bore that out, existing as it did in contrast to the lack of style that characterized his choice of clothes. Right now, behind the enigmatic face, David Plutarch was fighting back the all-but-uncontrollable desire to laugh.

He had arrived late to find that it was standing room only and for a second or two he had wondered whether to leave immediately. Now, however, crazed Arab stallions couldn't drive him away. It wasn't what she said, it was the way she said it, and of course it wasn't even that . . . it was who she *was*. He had never seen anything like her. Anywhere. She was a dream come true, a wild fantasy figure from his unconscious mind, and the desire bubbled up from the cess and the muck to drown his reason with its decaying, infinitely alluring aroma. But although he was aware that all sorts of slumbering giants were shifting and grunting in the early dawn of arousal, his cutlass-sharp mind was still analyzing the extraordinary spectacle he was watching.

The woman called Caroline Kirkegaard was clearly a control freak. It took one to recognize one. But whereas he had built the fourth largest fortune in America to satisfy his craving for power, this girl clearly preferred something a little more immediate. She liked to *see* the effect of her charisma. She liked to touch it, to taste it, to smell it, to hear it, and the frisson of excitement rushed down his powerful back as he admired the supreme virtuosity of her performance. It was incredible. The grownups all around him were holding hands like soppy teenagers on a first date as they mouthed the meaningless metaphysics, filling the room with the sound of their chanting.

"You are the flowers, the birds, the corn in the fields . . ." Caroline Kirkegaard paused for the sting . . . "You are the *worms!*"

There was absolutely no hesitation when the crowd reached the "worms" bit. In this context there was clearly no shame in being a worm at all.

"We are joined together in the protoplasm of infinity," said Caroline Kirkegaard definitely.

Plutarch's mouth dropped open. It was far better than brilliant. She was playing the childhood game of Simon says, and the crowd would do anything for her. But where would it end? "Give me your money and become my slave?" "Renounce your family and deny your friend?" "Torture this one, kill that one in the name of the brotherhood of transcendental rubbish?"

Plutarch loved every bit of it. If only the charisma could be distilled, bottled, *sold.* That was how business worked. Create a need in people for something that isn't basically good for them—drink, cigarettes, candy, game shows—and then peddle it with high-octane energy and adventurous advertising until they were hooked and you were rich. This load of losers dressed as winners were all the same. They were lost souls longing to be found. They were searching for elusive happiness, or trying to escape intolerable loneliness, and they were reaching blindly into every bizarre avenue to fill the void in their hearts. All of them, in one sense or another, had failed. Some had successful careers but were universally loathed. Others were loved but no longer had money for the rent. Some would be depressed, some anxious, others still would be deep in long-term relationships with booze or drugs. All were at a low ebb, all vulnerable, all clutching at straws, desperate for quick fixes, cheap promises, and instant transports to delight from the terminal angst that plagued them. The Kirkegaard woman would know all that. She was merely giving them what they wanted. It was the great American way.

Plutarch's lips curled in a smile of the deepest satisfaction, as he tried to climb inside her intriguing mind.

He nodded to himself. Oh yes, he could see it all. The poor lambs were lining up for the slaughter, little lost sheep who had gone astray. Not for a moment did he identify with them. After all, he was only there because he had been passing by on his way from a business meeting in one of the Sunset bungalows. He had seen the crowd, and he had popped in to take a look. Boy, was he glad he had. What a *star* she was! Clearly she adored what she was doing. Her lips were parted in a kind of sensual anguish, and her hips were thrusting out at the losers who loved her. She was throbbing with pleasure as she massaged the audience. He could see the excitement at the points of those mind-numbing tits, and he could dream about it tingling in the hot bed between those divine legs as she stretched her arms upward to impale the flock she led on the sharp shaft of her enormous will.

David Plutarch swallowed, noticing that his mouth was suddenly dry, and that he was warm in the cool of the air-conditioned ballroom. He could sense the thin film of sweat that had sprung from nowhere to coat his upper lip and he felt his heart speed up in his chest, the moths start their frivolous dance in the pit of his stomach. God in *heaven,* she was attractive. . . .

In front of Plutarch, in the body of the room, Kristina was a flower, and a worm, and was now publicly admitting that she was a part of the protoplasm of infinity. She was not sure why, but it just felt so *good* to be all those beautiful things. She didn't ask for proof. It was true because it *felt* true. It was true because Caroline Kirkegaard said so.

But Caroline Kirkegaard was flailing her arms from side to side and her mighty breasts were heaving around like twin storms at sea. "Silence!" she screamed.

Kristina's mouth, still muttering about protoplasm, shut tight.

The silence that the mistress of Destiny had ordered now filled the room. On and on it went, longer and longer, as its creator stood motionless on the stage. Kristina felt the collective anxiety. They had been on an emotional roll, strange in its intensity. Now they were all strung out in the alien territory of the unaccustomed quiet. Kristina could actually hear her heart beating as she waited.

"You . . . . are . . . . NOTHING!"

The last word erupted from the stage like a missile, and the contempt, and the accusation exploded in an air burst over the crowd.

Kristina's head shot back and her eyes widened. She was stunned, her mind shocked into blankness by the completeness of her surprise at finding herself suddenly a nothing. If *she* was nothing then perhaps all those other intriguing things were really nothing, too. Yes, that must be it. God, how clever! She'd nearly fooled herself, but at the very last moment faith had rescued her. It was true. She was nothing. Sad, but true, and it sort of gelled with the feelings she already had about herself deep inside.

"What are you?"

"Nothing," said Kristina and everyone else.

"LOUDER!"

"NOTHING."

"Again."

"NOTHING."

Kristina screamed into the growing chorus, and the louder she shouted the better she felt. She squeezed tight on the sweaty palm of the nothing beside her and she howled her nothingness at the gleaming wooden panels of the ballroom, at the high ceiling with its intricate plaster molding, at the extravagant arrangements of white phalaenopsis butterfly orchids, at the Chinese Chippendale mirrors. In her eyes there was a glistening, luminous zeal as she went for the peak experience, and the fervor and wild excitement cascaded from her bared lips, because now she knew who she was.

Relief flooded through her, shaking her with the intensity of an orgasm. She belonged at last. She was joined to everyone else in the room. They were a great and glorious team of nothings. Nobody had been picked out for special treatment. The hands they held said so. It wasn't like life where people were big failures, little failures, and all sorts of grades in between. Instead here was an equality of nobodies, a humming, throbbing conglomeration of nothingness. From this point anything would be possible. From the bedrock of nonexistence that Kristina and all the others now so cheerfully embraced there would be only one way to go: up. Then, who knew, with Caroline Kirkegaard as the spirit guide they might, one fine day, actually become something.

"NOTHING! NOTHING! NOTHING!"

Kristina's voice filled up her own ears as the sensation of listening and shouting merged into one, and she traveled on the sound surf to the grotto where she could lose the identity that plagued her. It was a wonderful place, full of light and wisdom and absolutely devoid of responsibility. In it she could swim free, unencumbered by the paraphernalia of herself, her credit cards, her matte black BMW convertible, her Cartier Panther watch, her pride, her presumption, her prejudice. As she howled the desperate hymn to her own inadequacy, she sensed that she was about to be reborn.

"NOTHING. NOTHING. NOTHING."

Once again the Kirkegaard arms were in the air, signaling for quiet, and slowly, like some ponderous oil tanker ordered to stop in the Gulf, the cacophony of sound began to fade. The nothings who would be somethings were shutting up on cue. A few couldn't stop their hysterical chanting, and their brand-new brothers cradled them in brotherly arms, and their brand-new sisters slapped them hard with sisterly palms until they obeyed the instruction.

"You have gained great insights here today," breathed Caroline into the expectant silence. "Together we can go on to learn larger truths. But first you must make a commitment—to Fate, to each other, to yourselves. Join with me in Destiny. Merge with the Cosmic Force. Please come forward if you are ready to inherit the earth."

Kristina jumped onto feet that didn't seem to belong to her anymore. All around everyone else did the same thing. Then they rushed toward the stage, jostling, pushing, pulling at the other members of their instant family as they fought to sign on. They *were* ready to inherit the earth. It sounded like the best possible deal for a gang of wall-to-wall nothings. And yes, they *wanted* the Cosmic Force on their side—in script conferences, on the tennis court, and in the bedroom, where any force at all would be enormously welcome. They thronged the edge of the dais and they tried to reach up and touch her and to speak to her, but somehow, without doing anything at all, she held them at bay. It was as if a magnetic force field surrounded her, a barrier that the uninitiated couldn't cross. There was no keep-your-distance body language, and nothing was said, nothing gestured. Somehow they recoiled from her at the very moment they wanted so badly to make contact with her, and so they stood before her in their foolish ranks, smiling stupidly as the love beamed out of their eyes toward her.

In all her life Kristina had never felt so vitally important, and yet so completely impotent.

Towering above them, Caroline Kirkegaard moistened her silky lips as a half smile of pleasure played across her face. Then, decisively, she turned to one side and stalked imperiously from the room, leaving Kristina and the others spaced out on the plateau of their own enthusiasm, the place where they so desperately wanted to be.

THE CORRIDOR stretched out in front of Caroline Kirkegaard and the thick pile of the carpet sucked at her like quicksand as she strode along. She smiled as she walked, at the thought of the Destiny converts she had left behind. By now, they would be desperate to put their names down on some list, to write the checks, to "belong." But that was another trick she'd learned. She made them work for it. That way you separated the real cannon fodder from the bogus kind. Leaving them all stretched out on their adrenaline jag was another vital ingredient in the mix of their conditioning process. In half an hour's time the real enthusiasts would be besieging the Destiny offices in Century City, while others would be burning up the telephone lines with their commitments and their cash.

The girl called Kanga half-ran, half-walked beside her. It was the only way she could keep up.

Caroline Kirkegaard looked straight ahead, but she inclined her head toward her assistant as she spoke. "Good, no?"

"It was awesome, Caro. Totally awesome." The redhead's voice was full of respect.

"Who was there? Anybody worthwhile?"

"Only Robert Hartford, no less. The bad news is that he walked."

"Robert Hartford at one of *my* meetings? Which cat dragged *him* in?"

"His daughter, Kristina. Great body."

For a second or two Caroline Kirkegaard stalked on in ominous silence as she digested the information. "Fuck Hartford," she said at last. "Anyone else?"

"Oh, Silvers, the hot agent at CAA. And that actress that got eaten by the extraterrestrial in the Lucas film. Or did *she* eat the extraterrestrial? No above-the-title people. No 'go' execs. No real heavy hitters." Kanga paused, wondering if she dared to live dangerously, then decided to go for it. "Except Robert Hartford," she added.

"You missed the most important one of all."

The Kirkegaard words were heavy with accusation.

"Who?" Kanga's voice was nervous.

"Plutarch."

Caroline shot the name out like the ace of trumps.

"Plutarch?"

"He's two-point-five billion and change. He was standing at the back, and *he* didn't walk." The last bit she said reflectively, almost to herself. "Good-looking guy . . . if you like them brash and common. You should be able to recognize people like that, Kanga. You're my assistant, remember. The others are shit. Plutarch's the real thing. He just sold Stellar Communications to United Electric. Read the *Journal, Fortune, Forbes.* Forget all that mystical crap from the Bodhi Tree."

"Yes, Caroline."

" 'Yes, Caroline.' 'Yes, Caroline,' " mimicked Caroline cruelly, stealing a quick look at her crestfallen assistant as she hurried along beside her, trying valiantly to keep up. The famous wallpaper of the famous hotel—pink palm trees set in three-dimensional relief against a setting sun—gave way to a section of mirrored wall around an alcove, and Caroline Kirkegaard slowed down to catch it. The sight of herself was one of the few things on earth that had the power to stop her in her tracks. She allowed it to do that now.

She angled herself for the sideways reflection, throwing back her head and peering at herself out of the corners of her eyes. She had changed backstage into a sleek black full-length Bill Blass dress and she stood six foot three inches in her Karl Lagerfeld at Charles Jourdan black satin high-heeled pumps.

"Do you think they realized I wasn't wearing any panties?"

"*I* for sure did."

In the looking glass, Kanga Gillespie was watching the Kirkegaard reflection with the same concentration as Caroline.

"Ah, but then you're paid to notice such things. That's what you get presents for, isn't it, Kanga?"

The redhead blushed, all over her neck, up onto her cheeks, at the tips of her ears. She made no attempt at all to do anything about the Kirkegaard hand that had reached out to squeeze her heavily muscled thigh.

"I don't notice you because of the presents, or because you pay me, Caro."

"Tell me why you notice me."

"Because you're beautiful."

Kanga Gillespie chewed on a suddenly nervous lip. She knew what was coming. It often started like this. Out of nothing, in public, in totally impossible situations. Any second now and a waiter with his trolley would come bustling around the corner, or a bevy of hotel guests would erupt into the corridor from one of the rooms.

"No, the *real* reason, Kanga."

She towered over the younger girl and the cruelty merged with something else in the weird blue eyes. Her powerful arm snaked out and caught Kanga by the neck, her fingers intertwining roughly in the backcombed hair. A ripple passed along her biceps, drawing her assistant's face upward, backward, nearer to hers.

"Because I love you." Kanga's voice was little-girl quiet, as if the words had been forced from her at gunpoint. Her lips trembled as she spoke.

Caroline Kirkegaard moved closer, without relaxing her viselike grip, and her breath fanned out over the pert, pretty face. "You love me because I gave you your tits and your cute little nose, and because you want me to fix up your eyes so they're big and round like mine."

Kanga Gillespie took a deep breath as she felt the delicious wave of passivity flow through her. There was no resisting Caroline. From the very beginning it had been like this, from the very first day when she had been summoned to Caroline's house for the one-on-one aerobics session, and the whole of her life had been turned into wonderful, spine-tingling chaos. She had been the instructor on that occasion, but she had been learning lessons ever since. How to obey, how to serve, and yes, how to worship.

The luscious lips hovered above her, wet and wide and ripe and ready.

"I loved you from the beginning," murmured Kanga. "Please kiss me. Please, Caro, please."

Caroline Kirkegaard had seen her desire, but she would not fulfill it. She stood back and released her grip, and she laughed.

Kanga tried to stop herself from shaking, as the hot and cold sensations

danced over her suddenly clammy skin. She attempted a smile. God, she had
never been a lesbian. She hadn't even had crushes on other girls at school.
But within three weeks of meeting Caroline Kirkegaard she had left her
husband, given up her job at the gym, and moved into Caroline's house in
the canyons. From that day to this, over two nerve-jangling years, Kanga had
been obsessed by her—sexually, intellectually, spiritually—and there wasn't a
thing on earth she could do about it.

Caroline Kirkegaard set off again. At the elevator station she found another mirror, and she devoured her image as she waited for the doors to
open. Her body *was* amazing. God and surgery hand in hand had created the
scaffolding, and two or three hours a day of blood, toil, sweat, and tears had
done the rest. She went through instructresses like Kleenex on a cold mountainside in Aspen. They could last maybe an hour with her, maybe more on
the aerobics, but on the weights she blew them away. All except Kanga. She
had been special. Not on the Nautilus. Not on the circuit training, but on the
floor. Oh yes, on the floor she had been the best, which was why she had
taken her on, and trained her to do all the things she did so very well.

"I love this place," said Caroline suddenly. "I always have, you know. It *is*
Hollywood. It *is* Beverly Hills. If you owned this, you'd own them all, all the
players, all the studios, all the dreams . . ."

Her voice trailed off, and she stroked at herself like a sleepy cat, as the
Sunset elevator rose to meet her.

"There's some old guy who's had it forever. They're always doing pieces
on him in magazines. He looks like Father Time," said a distracted Kanga.

She had to look away from Caroline as she spoke.

"Yeah, Francisco Livingstone," said Caroline. She stuck both hands on her
head and smoothed down the golden hair so it looked like it had been
sprayed onto her skull, high gloss, heavy lacquer, sleek and lovely. "There's a
rumor he wants to sell it," she added reflectively.

The doors whirred open. The elevator had arrived, and already the eyes of
the operator were bulging. Caroline ignored him. She strode into the elevator, hitched up her skirt, and adjusted her garter as if the man weren't there.
"Lobby," said Caroline. She didn't say "please." Vast expanses of her milky
muscled thigh merged with the black stockings below. The younger girl tried
not to watch it. The elevator swooped downward from the fifth floor where
their dressing room had been. "You thinking of buying it?" Kanga tried to
lighten up. Caroline couldn't stand it when she moped.

But Caroline Kirkegaard didn't laugh. She leaned backward against the
ancient oak paneling that Otis had imported from a Scottish castle to wall the
Sunset elevator. "Destiny could buy it . . . someday," she said.

"Destiny? In the hotel business? What next? Fast food?"

"Shut up, Kanga."

Kanga Gillespie bit her lip and cursed her stupidity. She had made the
cardinal error. Making fun of Destiny in public. Okay, only the elevator man
had overheard her, but the George Christys of this world paid good bucks for

gossip. If the word got out that Destiny didn't take itself seriously then it would be the end of everything.

In the lobby, Caroline heaped salt into the wound. "Never, ever do that again, Kanga, or you're history, understand?" she hissed. "I'll wipe you out, sweetheart, you'd better believe it."

But the mood was gone like mercury on a marble floor as Caroline Kirkegaard marched across the Carrara stone of the Sunset reception area.

When she spoke again her voice was alive with enthusiasm, almost before Kanga Gillespie's eyes had a chance to fill with tears.

"Don't you see, Kanga? It would be a perfect move. Think of it. Destiny owning the Sunset Hotel. The prestige. The PR. The instant worldwide recognition. We'd keep the hotel side going, but we could use part of the building for residential training seminars, and rallies, and channeling sessions. I mean it would be *brilliant*—the guests would be intrigued by the whole thing, and we could have good-looking chicks like you out by the pool to get people interested. And they wouldn't be just any people. They'd be the sort of people who stay at the Sunset. I mean, look at them. You can *smell* the money."

She waved a hand at the crowded lobby. It looked like Louis Vuitton had married Gucci and Mark Cross had been best man. The luggage alone was worth a few hundred thousand dollars. Only God's accountant knew what the people were worth.

Kanga objected to being one of the poolside chicks, but she was thrilled to be called good-looking by Caroline, and even more pleased that her anger was gone. "It's a cool idea, Caro. I mean it's *really* great, and it would be *so* fun. But this place would go for megabucks—and we're doing terrific, but not that well . . ."

"Okay, we're not there yet, but we will be, baby. You trust me. Just believe in me. We're closer than you think. Much, much closer."

She swept through the doors of the Sunset Hotel, scattering porters and valet parkers like a fox in a chicken coop. The metallic gray convertible 560 SL Mercedes was already there, parked by the curb as she had ordered it to be, but Caroline Kirkegaard wasn't thinking about such mundane things. A name sang in her brain. Plutarch. David Plutarch.

He had been there at the meeting where they had all but worshiped her. Had he, like Hartford, been immune to her power? One thing was certain. He hadn't walked out. And at the thought of that, the adrenaline sizzled through her arteries, and the joy reached out to every distant corner of her immaculate body as she contemplated her glittering future.

~4~

"GOOD LORD, WHAT on earth have you done to your leg?" said Winthrop Tower as he shepherded Paula through the traffic toward Morton's.

Paula laughed unselfconsciously. "I had an accident when I was very young. I've had it all my life. The leg, too, I guess," she joked.

Winthrop wasn't the sort of man to be embarrassed by the things he said. Nine times out of ten his remarks were supposed to be embarrassing. If she could laugh about something as awesome as a limp, then so could he.

"They shoot horses," he chuckled.

"Where I come from they *eat* horses."

"Where *do* you come from?"

Pain flashed across her face, wiping away the smile. "Grand Cypress—a place called Placid," she managed at last. "It's in Florida. In the Everglades. It's taken me a year to get from there to here."

They had reached the other side of the street, and Tower could see the change in her. It was as if she were a rag doll crumpling before him. There were tears in her deep blue eyes and her lips were trembling as she spat out the spare description of her home. The lump would be growing in her throat. Her sudden sorrow was so real he could almost touch it.

He reached out to her, and he took her small hand in his big creased one and he squeezed the support that he couldn't put into words. He felt the tenderness well up inside him, and the unaccustomed emotion both surprised and excited him. Here at last was someone he could relate to. Not right now, perhaps. Not quite yet. But one day he could and would talk to this girl, and she to him. Then he would learn of the source of her sadness, and he would help her, and they would become friends, good friends, close friends in Temporary Town where relationships were career moves, and shifting sand was considered a firm foundation. What was she running from? What horrors had she left behind, this girl who understood the things *he* understood, this stranger who walked with beauty and knew its secret ways?

The Morton's parking lot was filling already with high-end cars, and the Mexican valet parkers were unashamedly arranging them so that the most exotic and expensive achieved the most prominence, Rollers and Beamers and Mercs to the fore, rented Chevys and Fords consigned to the anonymity of the side alley. It was cooler now but the legacy of the heat remained, sucking the scent from the night flowering jasmine, while the dry desert wind rustled the palm fronds against the discreet green neon MORTON's sign on the stucco building. The whole restaurant was diffused in a warm, welcoming pink glow from uplighters carefully positioned among the lush green foliage of the palm and banana trees.

It was undeniably pretty and totally unthreatening, but at the same time Paula picked up the vibration that all was not as it seemed. The people erupting from the cars were good-looking and better dressed but somehow they were not completely at ease. The men laughed too loud as they smoothed down the material of their cashmere jackets over spare asses, and they looked nervous as the Hispanics clambered behind the wheels of their proudest possessions. "Ding it, and I'll sue your ass," snarled one hard charger. The women smiled brittle smiles and shook their hair in the night breeze as they looked around expectantly, checking their fellow diners, checking who was checking *them*. Tower eased Paula through the tightening knot of people that thronged around the French doors to the restaurant.

Inside the war between tension and relaxation continued. To the left of them, a large square opening showed chefs hard at work in the spotless kitchen, hinting that this was an unpretentious place where food was the major concern. Directly in front of them, however, like an interrogation team at Moscow's Lubianka prison, stood the welcoming committee. A darkly good-looking girl, tall and thin in a stylish red dress, was flanked by an unbelievably handsome man in a well-cut but casual navy-blue suit. It was Saint Peter and his assistant at the gate. Goats and sheep were about to part company. For those unfortunates unprotected by the Grace of success, it was the moment of reckoning. But not, apparently, for Winthrop Tower and Paula.

Twin smiles showed twin sets of perfect Southern California teeth.

"Good evening, Mr. Tower," they both chimed, their enthusiastic deference tinged with a hint of anxiety. "We weren't expecting you. Are you joining someone else tonight?" added the square-jawed Adonis.

That was the point. Morton's tables, even more than Spago's, were the Holy Grail in trendy L.A. One booked them via Peter's sister, Pam, at least two or three days in advance. Tonight, as always, the restaurant was full. Unless Tower was joining somebody, there was technically no room for him. But here, of course, the irresistible force and the immovable object collided, because it was completely unthinkable that a man of Tower's prestige and importance be turned away. What's more, he could hardly be kept waiting. Anything more than five minutes and he would be gone. The practiced eyes of the receptionist scanned the table list, and the maître d' hovered at her side lending moral support, as she rated the tables in order of the industry status of the bookers. Tower must have one of the top ten tables. That meant someone who had scored a "good" table before would now be shifted to an intermediate one, and some hapless intermediate would get the bum's rush to the outer Siberia that was the back of the room, where an extra table would not have to be created out of thin air. Anywhere else on earth this would not have been a disaster, but here on the edge of Beverly Hills, where appearance and illusion were the only reality, it might mean the difference between career life and career oblivion.

"Any problem?" said Tower with anaconda innocence.

The implied threat concentrated the minds of the gatekeepers. The receptionist's eye fastened on to a pseudocelebrity who lurked at the bottom of the "good" table list. Her eyes flicked the question to her boss as her pencil hovered over the unfortunate's name like a hawk above a canyon mouse. He nodded, and the pencil swooped.

She turned toward Tower, her smile bright. "Yes, we have a table for you right away, sir. Please follow me." She set off down the wooden walkway into the restaurant.

"It matters where you sit," whispered Winthrop loudly, in a tone of voice insinuating that it mattered only to people who were not him. "The rule is stick to the areca palms, and avoid the bananas like the plague. Anywhere near the Francis Bacon or the Ed Ruscha is a tragedy. The serious art is the consolation prize for the losers!"

Paula took it in. She could see what Winthrop meant. The back of the room was already full, mostly men eating together, with the occasional older woman. On either side of this grouping were two pots containing miniature banana trees. A huge and very beautiful Francis Bacon hovered over them, bordered by a painting that read THINGS TO EAT. That must be the Ruscha. These people had obviously come early, and they were noticeably less attractive than those who were scattered among the front tables between the areca palms. Paula had time to notice champion dieters Dolly Parton and Oprah Winfrey sitting together as she was swept through toward the tables for two arranged along the windowed right wall of the restaurant.

Winthrop pulled back the rattan chair and she sank gratefully down, taking in the pristine pink tablecloths, the small earthenware pots of flowers, and the little candles burning in glass jars that gave a warm, romantic glow to the room.

A great-looking waiter, white jeans, white apron, white shirt, black tie, asked them if they wanted anything to drink.

"A Coke'd be fine," said Paula. She was too tired to be made nervous by the swank of the place, too hungry to be intimidated by the clean, crisp napkins, the bewildering array of knives and forks, and the heady aroma of hard cash and harder fame that bounced off the Mexican-tile and wood-inlaid floor, the rattan ceiling, the long, glittering bar. She knew she looked a mess, but somehow the exalted status of her brand-new friend made that unimportant.

"I'll have a scotch and soda. Famous Grouse. No ice. A very large one," said Winthrop Tower. "You're not supposed to drink in this town," he said to Paula. "Only Perrier, or Chardonnay if you must. Anything else is considered 'unhealthful,' and by palm-tree sushi logic that makes you less lovable, and ultimately less rich. In Beverly Hills it's as close as you get to serious crime. Personally, I side with the English on the whole business. Never trust a man who doesn't trust himself to drink."

"You're not English, are you? You sound English sometimes."

"No, just pretentious." Tower giggled. "Although I did have an English period. In the sixties, I think. Can't remember much about it, but I worked in London for about seven years with a guy called John Fowler. The only people who can remember the sixties are the ones who missed the party. I'm told I had a *great* time."

The scotch arrived, and Winthrop attacked it as Paula sipped at her Coke.

"It sounds silly, but I don't quite know what it is you do, Mr. Tower. I mean, I know you sell all those beautiful things and . . ."

"I'm Winthrop, darling, actually Winty to friends like you, and I'm in the protection business. I protect the rich from their appalling taste."

Paula's laugh was incredulous. "Why would the rich have bad taste?"

"Why wouldn't they? It shows bad taste to spend all one's time making money."

"Aren't *you* rich? You *look* rich. You'd better *be* rich, 'cause no way can I chip in on this check."

"Well, there *is* a certain amount of money, but the serious stuff I made the old-fashioned way. I inherited it." Again he giggled, and he signaled for another scotch. He sat back and watched her as the whiskey wandered into his bloodstream through the lining of his mercifully empty stomach. It was the best shot of the day. None of the other drinks would be as good, but he wouldn't be discouraged by that.

The piercing voice cut into his pleasant mood like a knife through skin. "Winthrop, darling. How *are* you? Why don't you ever return my calls? Well, I've got you now, haven't I? Listen, you've just *got* to do my house. I've had a disaster with a Chilean. A decorator, dear, not a husband. Anyway, it all has to be redone, top to bottom. *You've* got to do it."

Winthrop Tower winced visibly. The Cruella de Ville figure hovered over the table, in a shimmering Galanos gown and a cloud of cloying Joy. The clinging dress emphasized the spare tire around her slack stomach, and as she gushed at Winthrop a fine spray of saliva wafted over the table.

"Before you decorate your house, Miranda, don't you think you should have yourself done first?" he said.

Paula gasped.

"What do you mean?" said the dreadful interloper, her eyes wide with horror as the Tower meaning sank in.

"I was thinking of liposuction," said Winthrop Tower with a wicked smile. "Do you know that over five thousand liters of human fat are removed each year in America? I'm sure most of it comes from here, dear. It's no coincidence that 'shrivel belly' is the anagram of 'Beverly Hills.'"

She was gone, as she was intended to be. Her head held high, her jaw set, no stranger to abuse, she rejoined her ancient husband of the nanosecond at a poor table too near the bar but beneath a superb Chuck Arnoldi collage of multicolored twigs.

"What!" said Paula.

"Oh, don't worry about her, darling. She's the void beneath the Beverly Hills veneer. She's been through hundreds of husbands. Her children can't stand her. She tried to adopt a baby once. Sent it back because it wasn't a boy. Lives in an Alberto Lensi house on a hundred geologically suspect acres in the Santa Monica mountains. Very fitting. Did you know that the anagram of Santa Monica is 'satanic moan'?"

Winthrop took the second scotch fast. "Listen, Paula. While I'm still sober, can I offer you a job?"

Paula's eyes widened as she crammed a huge piece of bread into her mouth. God, a job! What kind of a job? Cleaning probably. Polishing all that beautiful furniture, in a cool store, safe, and well fed, and with a base to build on.

"What job?"

"Oh, I don't know. You'd troll around with me, and we'd talk about what I was doing, and we'd just do the sorts of things we were doing earlier across the road. What would you want? Five hundred? Five-fifty?"

"A month?"

"A week, sweetheart. A week."

"Omigod!"

Winthrop could see her enthusiasm. He swept up the menu, and his heart was singing inside. It was all going to be all right.

He'd never worried about dying, not even after the coronary, but the idea of the ultimate full stop saddened him. There was a lot to be said for death, and nothing at all to recommend eternal life, but somehow it was the waste that was so irritating. All that time and effort, all that accumulated wisdom stuffed down the gullets of the worms, or blown up into the ubiquitous L.A. smog that played such havoc with his sinuses. Had it all been for nothing, the "life sucks and then you're dead" of the T-shirt legend? If so, then it was a monumental confidence trick played on humanity by a God with a warped sense of humor, to say the very least. Tower Design would be dismembered to pay the bureaucrats of whatever dreadful charity eventually starred in his will. Certainly he had no competent relatives to take the business over. But worse than that, far worse, was the loss of all the brilliant knowledge that was stuffed inside his head. If only there was someone to pass *that* on to. He looked into Paula's innocent, eager face.

"Have we dealt? Is it a deal? I'm your boss?"

"Mr. Tower, Winty, I'd love to work for you, but I mean . . . I haven't got anywhere to stay, and believe it or not, these are the only clothes I have. The rest got ripped off in New Mexico. I don't know how to do anything pretty much, and I might have given you the wrong impression in there. I was kinda winging it, you know . . ."

Winthrop Tower held up his hand to silence her. "Darling, for goodness sake don't *ever* tell the truth. It's too obvious. Anyone can do *that*. Creative lying is the name of the game in Beverly Hills.

"Seriously, though, the beauty of you is that you don't *know* that you have the thing you have. Trust me. Humor me. Patronize a silly old man. It's my money, and these jaundiced eyes are wide open, believe it or not. Clothes"— he flicked a dismissive wrist—"are a credit card away. As for somewhere to stay, that's no problem at all. You must stay with me."

"Well, with my wages I could find a room somewhere pretty nice. I wouldn't want to be a nuisance."

"Nonsense, my dear. Of *course* you must be a nuisance. All the very best people are, and I feel sure you have the makings of a superbly creative nuisance. Later on, darling, you will discover that the greatest enemy of fame and fortune is boredom, and the greatest foe of success is ease. What I need is stimulation, irritation"—he paused, his fingers together, his eyes laughing at her, as he thought out loud—"and yes, competition. I think you might be my own size, Paula Hope, and believe me when I say that not many people are."

"Well, if you pay me and feed me and house me I'll do my best to cause you some problems, and the first one is I don't understand this menu so you'll have to choose my food. What's mozzarella?"

"It's a tasteless cheese that Beverly Hills people use for dieting when they can't afford cocaine."

Paula cocked her head to one side. "You're joking."

"I'm not. Just try using a bathroom in this town. They're permanently occupied. This is *not* a place for those with weak bladders."

"Well, I'm not on a diet, and I'm starving. Maybe you should order for me. What should I have?"

"Protein, dear. What you need is some grease on the inside of your arteries," whispered Winthrop conspiratorially, peering suspiciously around the restaurant. "It's heresy to say such things in a place like this of course, but I'm a great cholesterol man. Red meat and plenty of salt to thicken the blood. That's what these people need. If they all worked a bit harder on their souls and not quite so much on their bodies there'd be a little less angst among the palm trees. Now, prawn cocktail, some of Peter's fabulous beef, potato skins with sour cream and chives, a selection of vegetables. Maybe some ice cream later. How does that sound?"

"Sweet music. Listen, Winty. You're going to have to teach me one helluva a lot. I mean, I really want to learn about everything."

"Winty!" The large pussycat of a man loomed over the table in an immaculate tuxedo.

"Merv! Hello! Do you know my new assistant, Paula Hope? Paula, this is Merv Griffin. Gave up TV to become a Master of the Universe. How are you, Merv? Love the way the Hilton's turned out."

Paula held out a hand and basked in the famous smile. She *supposed* this wasn't a dream, but she was no longer completely certain.

"Winty, I wanted to ask your advice about my place out in Palm Desert. Can I get my people to fix up a meeting sometime?"

"Sure. And what's this I hear about your place here being twenty thousand square feet bigger than the Spellings'?"

"Yeah, and it's got a view, too." Griffin displayed the stylish chuckle.

"All poor Candy gets to see is the old folk putting on Armand Hammer's miniature golf course."

Again he laughed, and he patted Winthrop's shoulder affectionately.

"Nice to meet you, Paula. See you soon, Winty." He wandered off to join a bevy of Japanese at the best table in the room, beneath the right-hand areca.

"How do you *know* all these people?" Paula laughed.

"Oh, you know, it's a small town. Like Mamet says, 'It's lonely at the top, but at least it ain't crowded.' " He laughed to show he was laughing at himself.

"Who's Mamet?"

"A brilliant playwright who among other things described all these people as 'secure whores.' " He waved his arm around to encapsulate the movie industry. The room was full of its heaviest hitters.

"And are they whores?"

"Well, as he says, 'The movie industry is like an affair—full of surprises and you're always getting fucked.' "

"Is that really true?"

"Listen, the only things that are really true about Hollywood are the things one makes up. You take Tinsel Town people as they are. Live with them, lie with them, cry with them, die with them. God, I need another scotch."

The drink came and went. Another accompanied the prawns, while number five preceded the côte de boeuf. Before the meat was finished Winthrop Tower was zoned. It didn't seem to affect the substance of his speech as much as its form. His words slurred and came more slowly, and he slumped down at the table, his eyes glassy. The sumptuous meal was punctuated by the periodic implosion of the L.A. table-hopping elite, some like Griffin, sexy Michelle Pfeiffer, and handsome, laid-back Peter Morton, the restaurant's owner, welcomed and cherished, others unmistakably encouraged to "walk on." Stuffed shirts, the insensitive welcome outstayers, the pompous and the presumptive all got their marching orders, and Paula, marginally embarrassed at first, soon got the picture. The cruel wit was far from blanket bombing. It was surgically accurate. The good guys were insulated from it. The others were taken out one by one.

But still the scotch came, and Paula's eyes widened. She hadn't seen drinking on this scale. It wasn't the redneck Bud swilling of an Everglades Saturday night as the diner shook to the roar of the football replays and the whine of the country music on the jukebox. This was a headier, steadier, altogether more serious business. Now, before her eyes, her new boss was slipping into the next stage of drunkenness. The glass in his hand was no longer straight, and the whiskey threatened to spill out onto the tablecloth. He sank deeper into his chair, and his eyes were hooded, his movements suddenly slow and clumsy.

Paula realized that she would have to take charge. "Mr. Tower. If I can really stay overnight at your place, would you mind if we left now? I'm real tired." She said it quite firmly.

"What?" His eyes narrowed belligerently.

"Home," she said simply. Then, "Now."

"Don't piss on my party. I decide when . . ." But there was something in her eyes. Something so sad, so strong, so deeply appealing. It cut straight through the swirling mists of aggression and grandiosity that were welling up inside him.

He stood up, swaying slightly. "Quite right, Paula. Home. Yes, quite right, my dear. You must be tired. *I'm* tired. We're all tired. Let's go home."

"Where's home?" asked Paula. She didn't even know where he lived, but she prayed it was close.

"Sunset Hotel," he mumbled.

———

THE STRETCH LIMO erupted into the Morton's parking lot from the alley that ran along the south side of the restaurant. It squealed to a stop, and a man jumped out from the driver's seat. He was in a hurry and he strode toward the brick walkway where Paula struggled to support Winthrop Tower and the monstrous glass of Kümmel-on-the-rocks that he had ordered as his last semiconscious act, and insisted on taking with him as he left.

The man was dressed in a nondescript black suit, cut tight and nipped in at the waist, and he wore black socks, black shoes, and a black tie against a snow-white shirt. He was neat, seemingly obsessively so, but it was not the suit of a boss or even of a businessman. It was the suit of a servant. The clothes emphasized the body. He was thin, but strong looking, as if every ounce of fat had been burned away, and the muscle had been kept to a level that would permit maximum movement, while retaining maximum strength.

"Mr. Tower! Cor blimey, strike a light you've 'ad me pissing roun' the cafs like a bleedin' lunatic," he said cheerfully as he approached.

He looked like a fallen angel. It was a powerful, cruel face, perfectly proportioned, with wide spaces between the eyes, a short bobbed nose, and a square jaw. His hair was blond and cut short so that his features were emphasized. His narrow lips revealed straight white teeth, but it was his eyes that rang alarm bells. They weren't a cherub's eyes. They were Damien's eyes, blue but vacant, pretty but effortlessly unkind. They glinted and gleamed in his baby face, and they lied about the innocent smile he smiled.

Tower waved a limp hand that fell back almost immediately. "Graham," he said, "dear boy . . . where's my Mercedes Bass . . ." The stranger smiled at Winthrop. Then he turned toward Paula, and the smile disappeared.

" 'oo are you when you're at 'ome?" he asked rudely.

It sounded like an English accent. "I was going to ask you the same thing, but more politely," said Paula coldly.

"Paula's with me . . . coming home with me to stay . . . new assistant . . ." That was all Winthrop Tower could manage. With a grunt and a groan he lolled sideways onto Paula's shoulder, the glass of kümmel still balanced in his hand.

"I'm sorry, miss. Very sorry. I didn't know you was with Mr. Winthrop. He's a bit Brahms, ain' he? Lucky I found you. I bin all roun' the 'ouses."

" 'Brahms'?" said Paula.

He laughed an easy laugh. "Oh yeah, there I goes again. Brahms and Liszt. Pissed. That's what we say at 'ome. It's rhymin' slang. 'ere, let's get him in the Merc."

Paula went through the motions while the man called Graham did the heavy lifting. "I was supposed to meet Mr. Winthrop at the shop, but he took off like, an' I 'adn't a clue where he pissed off to," he said, effortlessly shouldering his boss's limp body. "Tried the Dôme, an' the Ivy an' that chinky Chinese on North Camden an' blimey O'Riley I didn't think of Morton's till ten minutes ago."

He cocked his head to one side and looked at Paula, smiling saucily. Then the smile was replaced by a look of concern. "Your leg all right, darlin'?" he said.

"Oh yeah. One leg's a bit shorter than the other. It's always been like that. I'm used to it."

"Oh." His voice was flat, like his face. But it wasn't a dull flatness, nor a boring face. Both were disturbingly attractive. This man might take orders but he belonged to nobody but himself.

"I'm his wheels, dear, and I sort of smooth 'is path through life, you know. Like tonight I'm 'is bleedin' legs."

"Does he often get this drunk?"

"Does 'e ever? Never 'appier than down the boozer, crusin' for a brusin'. An yet durin' the day he's got nobs eatin' out of 'is 'and. Bloody fantastic, ain' it? That's what I calls it, any rate. You ever think of 'avin somefink done wiv that leg? Seems a shame to be left with that limp, an' this *is* America—the medical promised land."

Paula blushed. Most people were embarrassed by her limp and clammed up about it. Today the only two people she'd met had waded right into it. In the Everglades they took things like that for granted, like the skeeters and the hurricanes, the floods and the TB. If those were the cards you'd been dealt you played them. It took money to change them, and there wasn't any of that. Obviously in Los Angeles they saw things differently. Bodies were like cars. They could be rebuilt and redesigned, and the really strange thing was not to bother.

"It would cost thousands of dollars," she said. "It's no big deal. I'm not an athlete!"

"No, but you're very beautiful." Again he looked at her, but it was a peculiar look this time. Intense. Deep. As if he didn't say things like that to everyone.

She turned away, but her blush deepened. Her limp was the most personal thing about her. It was as if he had seen her naked and was talking about the shape of her body.

He propped Winthrop Tower among the pillows on the vast rear seat of the Mercedes. "There you are, Mr. Winthrop. Now you keep it buttoned till we get 'ome. All right, sir? That's the ticket." He winked at Paula, and she felt a little shock of surprise at how fast his mood could change. They had hardly met and yet he had revealed an emotional range that would have shamed an experienced repertory actor. Did he really feel all those things, or just some of them? Or none of them at all? Only the eyes said the last was true.

" 'op in darlin', and we'll beetle over to the Sunset. It's quite a joint. Impressive, that's what it is." In the driver's seat, he slipped on dark glasses despite the blackness of the night. Did he know about the out-to-lunch eyes? Did he want to shut the trapdoor to his soul? Why on earth did Paula want to know the answer to that?

"I didn't know Mr. Tower was takin' on no assistant," Graham said as he gunned the engine.

"Neither did I. I sort of wandered in off the street, and we got talking and I admired his store, and he offered me a job. Then he took me to that restaurant, and drank all the scotch they had, and then you showed up."

"Seventh cavalry. Well, anyway, I'm glad. Your face around'll be nice. More than nice. Bloody fantastic."

"Thanks."

"You don't look like you're from L.A."

"I'm from Florida. The Everglades."

"An' you wanted to get out?"

"I *had* to get out."

He heard the bitterness, the sadness, the anger, and the hatred. "Bad things?"

She bit at her lip.

He looked at her quickly. "We're not bad people here," he said. "We'll look after you. You see if we don't."

He put out his hand to touch her arm, a gloved hand, black leather, soft and slinky and at war with the sentiment he had just expressed.

From the back, through the glass partition that divided the car, came the faint strains of a song.

The Tower voice was fine, although the drink had taken the edge off the intonation. "Gentlemen songsters off on a spree, doomed from here to eterniteeeeeee . . ."

Graham nodded over his shoulder. " 'e always sings that when 'e's pissed. 'e used to be something called a Whiffenpoof at somewhere called Yale. More pouf than whiff, 'e always says. It goes on about black sheep and gentlemen. Just about sums Mr. Tower up, that does."

"He said he'd inherited some money."

" 'e wasn't lying, darling. 'is family's from Boston. One of the richest in America. 'e always said he became a designer to irritate them, and moved to L.A. to drive them mad. Anyway, the ones with the loot died off an' they left it to Mr. Tower 'cos 'e was the only family left. There, that's the Sunset up ahead."

The Sunset Hotel loomed out of the night, like a good deed in a naughty world, and instantly Paula was mesmerized by it. She actually heard herself gasp as the reality of the "hotel" collided with her meager expectations of it. There was a wrench at her heart, and fingers clutched at the depths of her stomach as its beauty exploded all over her, taking away her breath. This was not a hotel. It was the pastel fantasy of some manic cakemaker on an icing jag; it was a latter-day Xanadu, light blazing from the windows of its pleasure dome, searching the velvet darkness for defectors from its delights; it was big and proud and wild and wonderful and it beckoned the lovers of all things bright and beautiful to experience the marvelous mysteries of its womb. Its tall central tower hovered, maybe ten stories high, above the dark section of the Strip, and a sign in green script said simply THE SUNSET HOTEL.

All around it, like an honor guard in the glow of its aura, stood tall, thin palms. Their trunks, painted ghostly white by uplighters from below, were in dramatic contrast to the vivid green of the treetops, and their height and old age emphasized the quiet statement of the ancient Spanish mission architecture. It was a dream of delicate balconies and intricate wrought iron—at once deliciously public and tantalizingly discreet–and it glowed its excitement into the night sky, and throbbed its exotic energy into the foothills of the canyons that were its backdrop. This was no parvenu. There was nothing nouveau about the Sunset's riche. It had endured, and it would endure, and its grandeur would mock the failure of those who entered its portals to do the same.

Nestling down at the base of the tower, a rambling series of buildings sprawled off into the night. Through the open window of the car came the creamy scent of gardenias. The rich aroma was thick in the balmy air, and Paula could see the dense bushes on either side of the driveway, bearing thousands of the milk-white blossoms that had turned the warm darkness into the most potent perfume. She could hear the Sunset, too. It hummed with impossible-to-identify vibrations that spoke to her heart, not her ears. It was talking to her, and Paula wanted to shake her head and get rid of the cobwebs that were inside, so that she could hear the thing it was trying to say. Even as she listened with her soul, her mind said this was ridiculous, but the message was there. "I am your future," said the stucco walls. "Within me, all things will happen to you. You will love me and you will loathe me, but you will never ignore me. I promise you that. I promise you that."

"Not a bad little pub," said Graham.

They had arrived beneath a covered portico, which allowed three lanes of cars to park side by side. From the one nearest the hotel, a blood-red carpet led toward banks of revolving, highly polished brass-and-mirrored doors. Half a dozen young men, apparently hot from the centerfold of *Surf* magazine, loitered around the entrance waiting to park the cars. The door-man, resplendent in full gold braid commissionaire's uniform, marched for-ward crisply to open the back door of the Mercedes.

"'arf a mo', Fritz ol' son . . ."

But Graham wasn't quite quick enough. During the ride Winthrop Tower had shifted position. Now he was leaning against the inside of the door. As Fritz opened it, he fell, very gently, very slowly, onto the deep pile carpet. The glass of kümmel was still miraculously attached to his hand. It didn't break but its contents, largely melted ice cubes now, spilled out to form a little puddle on the immaculate carpet.

From what appeared to be the corpse the sentiment was firm. "Fuck," said Winthrop Tower, quite loudly, lying where he lay, and making no effort whatsoever to get up.

"Christ!" said Graham.

"Oh no," said Paula.

"Good evening, Mr. Tower," said the doorman. Not one syllable of his greeting contained an ounce of reproach. Nor did it go one inch toward admitting the undoubted fact that Mr. Tower was lying, apparently uncon-scious, on the floor of the hotel's main entrance.

By now Graham was out of the car, and he was already hauling Winthrop into the air like a drooping flag up a pole. Paula, too, hurried out to help, and at that precise moment she saw him.

He had been standing there, where the car had stopped, and as Paula jumped from it, he moved quickly to help Graham as the doorman stood back. He looked old for a busboy, and he wasn't dressed like the others. In fact, clothes-wise he looked like a drycleaned version of Paula—crisp Levi's, brown tasseled Bass Weejuns, a soft, faded brown leather bomber jacket over a plain white T-shirt. His eyes caught hers and lingered for a second, regis-tering a spark of interest before he bent down for the Tower rescue opera-tion.

"I'll give you a hand," he said simply to Graham.

"Thanks, mate," Graham replied.

With Tower hanging unsteadily between his two human crutches, the unlikely group set off toward the lobby. The doorman, dripping gravitas, the finally empty glass of kümmel held like a chalice in both hands, marched ahead of them.

"Home at last," slurred Winthrop Tower before letting out a burp of around seven on the Richter scale. He filled his lungs. "Lord have mercy on such as we . . . Ba! Ba! Ba!" he sang.

The stranger chuckled as the revivified Whiffenpoof song rent the scented night air, and Paula, bringing up the rear, laughed, too, at what she now recognized as high farce. The guy must be hotel security. He seemed really cool. Together Graham and he looked like they were out of a Calvin Klein Obsession advertisement. If all the guys in L.A. looked like this, Help!

Paula was hardly ready for the beauty of the marble-columned lobby. It had the feel and look of a vast private living room. There were inviting sofas, and chairs and more flowers than she had ever seen in one room in her entire life. It was almost empty, apart from two crisp, gray-suited ice maidens manning the reception desk, and two or three uniformed bellboys placed at strategic points across the vast space.

As the odd convoy made its way through, no one batted an eyelid. It was clear what the party line was going to be. Doorman, busboys, security, bellboys, receptionists, all would play this straight as a die. Whatever Winthrop Tower sang, said, or did, he and his entourage were going to be treated as if their behavior was totally and completely normal. Perhaps it was. With the exception of the security guy's smile there was no hint of mockery in anyone's demeanor, no patronage, no supercilious condescension at all. It was quite brilliant, the more so for being so utterly unexpected. No computerized Hilton or Westin could have carried it off. No funky inn or trendy watering hole, no fancy hostelry or fashionable crash pad could have possibly known how to do it. It was effortlessly upper class in its unflappability, and its easy transcendence of rules and regulations. One thing was completely clear. In this place Winthrop Tower was not a lush, a loser, or a joke. He was a gentleman, and the gentlemen's gentlemen, and woman, who were ministering to him in his hour of need were not forgetting it for a second.

Paula wondered if there were any arrival formalities to be completed. If she was going to be staying, shouldn't she check in? Apparently not. The caravan didn't stop. It swept through the palatial lobby, clippety-clop across the white Carrara marble to the halting melody of the Whiffenpoof song, past the Henry Moore sculptures, the Modigliani paintings, past the carved columns and the graceful Ming vases toward the bank of elevators.

The elevator boy, too, appeared not to notice the state of the guest. He nodded politely and pressed *P.*

"Watch out! Be careful."

The security guy had relaxed his grip and the Tower head, suspended only by its India-rubber neck, rolled sideways and collided sharply with the oak paneling of the elevator's interior. Paula's voice was full of reproach, and the security man's head snapped around toward her as she spoke.

It was the first time she had seen him head on, and once again she was caught short by the visual. Forget the Calvin Klein ad. He was achingly good looking, despite the irritation that had flashed into the extraordinary eyes at her outburst. But just as soon as it had appeared it was gone. His face softened, and he smiled again as if puzzled by something.

He caught the lolling Tower head, still watching Paula. "Sorry," he said. There was something strange about the way he said it. He seemed surprised, almost amused by himself, as if he weren't used to apologizing to anyone, let alone scruffy girls of uncertain origin and unspecific identity.

"It's okay. I just don't want him to hurt himself," said Paula.

" 'e's feelin' no pain, luv," said Graham.

"She's right," said the guy.

It was a rebuke. No question. He was putting Graham down for his frivolity, commending Paula for her concerned attitude. Again she tried to make sense of it. He seemed very sure of himself for an employee. Certainly rubbing a guy like Graham the wrong way was not for the faint-hearted. She'd worked *that* out.

"Yeah, 'course."

Graham had swallowed it. Not with the very best grace in the world, but he'd taken it. Paula felt the metaphorical temperature drop. There was a coldness between the two men, and it had followed some sort of subterranean clash in which the stranger had come out on top.

Again the fascinating eyes sought hers. "See," they said. "Did you catch that? You got me to apologize, and now I've made him back down. You're doing well, but you haven't a clue just how well."

They had arrived. The doors drew back, and they were in the anteroom of the Tower apartment.

"Here, I'll let you take over from here, Graham," said the stranger. But he walked out of the elevator, into the foyer of the apartment, and stood there as if he wanted something.

"Thank you very much for helping like that," said Paula. "It was very kind of you."

He didn't want to go. Again he was smiling at her, as if he was enjoying a marvelous private joke.

Paula felt the flash of irritation. "I think we all ought to be going to bed," she said, as Graham struggled past with the stuporous Winthrop.

"I think that's an excellent idea," said the security man, but still he didn't move. At his back the elevator door remained open. The boy in charge was pressing no buttons until he got his instructions.

The idea came to Paula quite suddenly. God, how crass of her. The guy wanted a tip. It must be that. There were ten bucks in her pocket. The last money she had in all the world. It was way too much, but she could hardly tear it in half, and anyway the Sunset Hotel was not small time. The battle raged in her mind only briefly. The hell with it. Mr. Smarty Pants with his outrageous face probably deserved it. She fished in her pocket, hoping that it wouldn't be too impossibly crumpled. It was. She pulled it out and thrust it at him quickly to cover her embarrassment.

He looked down at her outstretched hand, and the filthy ten lying in the middle of her palm. In all her life she had never ever seen anyone look so surprised. He was dumbfounded. He was absolutely and completely astonished. If she had pulled a samurai sword from her jeans and started to cut off his toes he couldn't have been more comprehensively flabbergasted. There was shock all over his face, and disbelief, and his wonderful mouth dropped wide open to reveal even better teeth.

From behind her came the cockney accent, too late, far too late. "Oh no, luv. Oh dear me no," said Graham.

Without knowing exactly what had happened, Paula realized she had done the wrong thing. Perhaps security guys weren't allowed to be tipped. Was the tip too big? Too *small?* Maybe tipping was a male business. Whatever. Her face registered her confusion.

But the receiver of her bucks was already undergoing a transformation. The phenomenal surprise he had clearly just experienced was apparently not an unpleasant one. There was wonder on his face now, and the humor was coming back, and there was that other thing, that intense interest, as if the rest of the world had frozen into a backdrop that existed only to frame her.

"What's your name?" he said, clutching the bill in his hand.

"Paula Hope," said Paula, thoroughly bemused, and at the same time weirdly excited by the unpredictable chain of events.

He transferred the money into his left hand, and he extended his right one.

"I'm Robert Hartford," he said, "and I want to thank you for your extremely generous tip."

~5~

PAULA WAS TOO tired to sleep—tired, confused, depressed, elated. She
had expected a hard sidewalk as a mattress, and yet here she was
suspended like a lily on a pond on the softest bed in the world. The gentle
whir of the air-conditioning merged with the muted hum of the Sunset Boulevard traffic and in her nostrils was the delicious smell of the bedside free-
sias. She was safe, but for how long? She had been given a future—an exciting, infinitely possible future, but would it still be there in the morning?

Along the corridor, the man called Winthrop Tower would be lying comatose. In his jingle-jangle morning would the job he had so capriciously offered her be available? Maybe he was one of those enthusiastic artists who
promised the world, but who found it more difficult to deliver. She had liked
him so much, and trusted him instantly, but she had never expected him to
dissolve so comprehensively into unconsciousness. Then there was Graham,
with his wiry body and his chirpy cockney-speak, and his unpredictable
changes of mood. She felt ambivalent about him, drawn to him but unsettled
by the aura of menace that hovered around him like a shroud. He had
seemed to like her, but was he what he seemed?

Round and round it all went in a whirligig of doubt and hope, as the good
faded into the bad and optimism merged with pessimism, murdering sleep,
and sending her naked body tossing and turning beneath the cool cream
linen sheets. It was creeping in, the memory that she was trying to banish.
God! How could she have done it? Robert Hartford. Trying to tip him. In the
darkness the sweat rushed to her skin as she allowed herself to remember the
ultimate embarrassing moment. Talk about a hick from Hicksville. She had
defined the term. Like the rest of America she knew what he looked like.
Why the *hell* hadn't she recognized him? Okay, so she wasn't expecting him,
and he wasn't supposed to be hanging around any place *she* was staying at, in
blue jeans and a bomber jacket at eleven at night, but to push a ten at him
like he was some servant when he'd been kind enough to help out! She
buried her head in the pillow and groaned out loud in the blackness as she
tried in vain to forget what she'd done. Why hadn't Graham *told* her? It must

have been done on purpose. It was almost as if he'd wanted her to insult the movie star for mysterious reasons of his own. Certainly there had been a coolness between them, right from the beginning, and Paula couldn't get out of her mind the totally mad idea that in some weird way the bad vibes had been partially to do with her.

Apparently he lived there, in the hotel. For sure they would meet again if all the offers of the day before held good. But even as she shied away from the horror of that, she was drawn toward it. He had been so utterly charming, and even before her faux pas, he had been impossible to ignore. All the time she had been aware of him, of his movements, his gestures, of his otherworldly beauty. She had noticed him notice her and the lazy searchlights of his eyes had played across her, taking their time, not ashamed of their interest, pleased that she knew he was watching her. He had taken her money. He had folded it, lengthwise, as he had introduced himself, and the memory of his laugh and his exaggerated thank-you were vivid in her mind. As the meaning of his name sank in, she had tried to say something, but the words just hadn't come. She had turned and fled, muttering goodnight despite the fact that she had absolutely no idea where she was, and where she was going. She had closed some door behind her and died in the darkness until Graham's gentle knock had signaled that Robert Hartford had gone.

"Sorry, luv," he'd said. "Shoulda told ya. Sort of imagined most people knew 'artford."

"Graham, I *tipped* him."

"Yeah, doll, you did. Did you see his boat?"

"His boat?"

"Boat race. Face."

"Oh God!"

"Listen, luv. Serves him right. Thinks 'e's God's bleedin' gift to women. Blimey, I bet no one's ever done *that* before."

"Mr. Tower will be furious."

"No way. Them two's good mates. They'd think it's bloody funny. But you watch out for 'artford. I saw him looking at you the way he does. Most girls in this town go at him like kamikazis, 'cos of who he is, like. The way you treated him'll really get 'im goin'."

Graham had looked discouraged at the thought. He had showed her her bedroom, and the glorious wall-to-wall marble bath with more potions and lotions than Paula had ever seen before, and he had said goodnight.

As she had lain back in the bubbles and the boiling water, Robert Hartford had not gone away. He had hovered there in the steamy scented air, exciting, embarrassing, listening, looking, and later, as she'd climbed into bed, she had felt his lingering presence. But now, in the dead of night, it was difficult to make sense of anything.

She lay back on the soft pillow and squeezed her eyes shut as she struggled to still her racing mind. Damn! It was no good. She might as well get up, walk around, read, maybe watch some TV with the sound turned way down low. But paradoxically, as she decided to stop trying to sleep, she felt the first gentle waves washing over her. The thing she wanted most was being given to her only as she stopped trying to achieve it. How like life, she thought, but the tide had turned, and now she was being swept out to sea, away from the nerve-racked shore, out, onward, backward to the wide oceans of memory and the lost continent of dreams.

—

PAULA PUT up her hand.

"Please, Miss Carstairs, what is 'art'?"

"Whatever I say it is," said Emily Carstairs, firmly.

The giggles erupted around the schoolroom and Paula realized that she had somehow been worsted in the exchange. Not that she had been trying to score a point off Miss Carstairs. She worshiped her.

"But what if you're wrong?" persisted Paula.

"Then it will be your duty to expose me, Paula Hope." There was a smile on the crinkly, kindly Carstairs face.

"How will I know when you're wrong?" Paula could feel the initiative running away from her.

"By trusting your heart, dear."

"Oh."

Paula's twelve-year-old mind tried to sort through her teacher's words. There were rules in art, and Emily Carstairs, her beloved teacher, knew them. But at the same time teachers could apparently be wrong, which seemed to imply that the "rules" were not really "rules" at all. Bad art, or bad artistic judgment, should be exposed—even when the person producing it was a teacher, or a so-called expert. Then there was the amazing implication that a small child could do the exposing, simply by trusting her heart. Apparently you judged art with your feelings, not with your intellect. You should not be afraid to learn from the learned, but you should always reserve your right to disagree with them.

Paula peered around the schoolroom to see if her friends were picking up the same message. The blank faces stared back at her, the dirty, bored, inbred faces of the swamp. If Emily Carstairs had been talking in Mandarin Chinese they might have understood her better. It was at that very moment that Paula came to realize she was different.

It was a turning point, and the recognition of it zipped through her body to explode in a hot flush of excitement all over her cheeks. Emily Carstairs had been talking to an "art" class of thirty children, and Paula was the only one who had the remotest idea of what she was saying.

The two vases stood side by side on the table in front of Miss Carstairs.

"Now, children," she said in a weary voice. "What do you see here on the table?"

They didn't answer. It was the last class before the bell. They were thinking of food, and catfish in the shallows, and all the Mark Twain things that deep-country, waterlogged kids thought about, and they prayed collectively for merciful release from Miss Carstairs's peculiar games.

"Two vases," said Paula. She already knew what was coming. She could *"see" it. For three blissful years she had been soaking up the Carstairs message.*

"Yes, dear, two vases. One of them, I'm glad to say, is mine. The other, I am far more glad to say, is the proud possession of the Pahokee County school board."

They twisted their heads that way and this, as their little bottoms shifted on the hard wood seats, and they picked at their noses and willed the bell to ring. There were two more or less identical vases on the table. Big deal. Who cared?

"Now, it is the task of you budding . . . aesthetes . . . to decide which vase is 'art' and which is most decidedly not." She sniffed, and she flung her head back in a gesture that seemed an attempt to ward off terminal despair. She stood foresquare behind the table, scrawny, frail, but to Paula absolutely magnificent as her scorn flew over the heads of the children she addressed. Her face was wrinkled but her eyes were bright, flashing with life above the bags of flesh that underlined them. Her dress had clearly once been fine, but was now a little faded and not quite clean, but it was not the main event. Miss Carstairs was. Proud and valiant, she transcended her lowly position as art teacher in the Placid school. Like a colossus she hovered above the swamp. Like a soaring eagle she flew high above the bars of poverty, ignorance, and mundanity that formed the walls of their prison.

"Think of it," she added as she took in the vacant gazes, "as a quiz show on TV."

The children immediately perked up. "Ah, the flame of learning burning bright at last," mocked Emily Carstairs. "The God of the tube has not forsaken us in our hour of need. Blessed be 'Jeopardy,' and the son of the 'Wheel of Fortune.'"

Boy, did she have them now.

"Here," she said, "is the red vase, on my right. There is its fellow. Now, what color should we call that? Tan? Beige? Nasty words, I know, but I think they will do. Now the name of the game is to choose the vase that we think is beautiful. That should be roughly the same as choosing the vase that we think is 'good art,' 'has artistic value,' etcetera, etcetera." She paused patiently. "Now, children, hands up those in favor of the red vase."

A set of hands reached for the sky. Red was the color of Dad's boat, of the dress Mom wore on a Saturday night to the bingo in Ochopee, and anyway it was the color of blood.

Paula pushed her hand down toward the floor, and she thought she caught the sharp, flinty edge of a Carstairs smile as she seemed to notice her adamant decision. Paula did a lightning inventory of the room. Three other children had not put up their hands.

"It may be," said Emily Carstairs, her lopsided face slipping into a look of intense cunning, "that some among you consider both vases to be beautiful. Let us see the hands of those particular 'connoisseurs.'"

"Con a what?" said one child, as the hands of the three dissenters shot upward, their wise-ass eyes sure that they had identified the "catch."

Still Paula's hand remained solidly by her side.

"You are the only vote for the sand-colored vase, Paula Hope," said Emily Carstairs, her voice giving nothing away. "Maybe you could tell us why you choose to be in a minority of one."

They giggled again now, thoroughly enjoying what they imagined to be Paula's acute discomfort. Silly old Paula with her airs and graces and always top of the class in everything had it wrong at last. Twenty-nine to one. Ha Ha Ha.

But Paula didn't hear them. She was looking at the vase, at the beautiful stoneware vase.

"Its color is so unusual. It's delicate, and it's not uniform. I mean, the color has different shades as if someone mixed it by hand and then painted it on themselves. The red vase is just red, a dull, ordinary red." Her button nose wrinkled in distaste. "But that one has a wonderful, flowing shape that's elegant, and the red one is short and squat and its lines are just . . . well . . . boring. It's as if the red one just wants to hold some water and some flowers and be done with it. The sand-colored one wants to be looked at for itself. It wouldn't mind holding things, in fact it would be brilliant at that, but people would always look at it first." She stopped. The words had flowed from her, but at the same time her mind had filtered them. All those picture books, the slides that Emily had shown them of Chinese porcelain, of Florentine vases, of Japanese ones, had left their surreptitious mark on her memory.

"It's the red one, ain't it," said a loud-mouthed boy from the back.

"Ah, the red one. What shall we do with the red one?" said Emily dreamily. She picked it up, between thumb and forefinger like one might a very dirty, very nasty rag that just cleaned a squashed cockroach off the kitchen counter. Then she extended her arm to the side of the table, and then a little bit past it.

"I think we should put it out of its misery, don't you," she said, and she dropped it on the linoleum floor. The sound of the explosion as it shattered sent twenty-nine heads flicking back, and Miss Carstairs's and Paula's peals of laughter merged happily with the death rattle of the Pahokee County school board's hideous red vase.

In the thunderous silence that followed the crash, the school bell rang insistently. Art class was over. School was finished. Bemused and vaguely resentful that some trick they didn't quite understand had been played on them, the children began to file from the room.

"Paula Hope, can you stay behind for a word, please?"

"Yes, Miss Carstairs."

Paula walked up to the front.

"You were the only one who saw my vase."

"It's beautiful, Miss Carstairs."

"You're beautiful, Paula, and you can recognize beauty. That's a very rare combination in this world."

Paula blushed. "Where did it come from?"

"China. It's a Kuan-yao vase. Southern Sung dynasty. Nine-sixty to twelve seventy-nine."

"I remember you telling me about Sung, and how they invented a new glazing process."

"Yes, the monochrome feldspathic glaze. You remember everything, don't you?"

She seemed to make a decision. Her voice was suddenly excited. "Paula, I want you to come home with me now for an hour or two. I want to show you some things like this vase. Lots of wonderful things. You have a rare talent. I'm going to teach you how to use it. You're not a child anymore. You're not like all the others. You deserve more, and I'm going to make sure that you get it."

Paula looked at her and listened, and as she did so she believed. There and then, as the belief in herself flooded through her, her childhood ended. When she walked from the classroom, her teacher's arm around her shoulders, she was a woman.

THE WARM afterglow of Emily's memory lit up the darkness as Paula slipped out of the dream. She lay quite still, as if by doing so she could prolong the vision that was already beginning to fade, but it was impossible. It was going, and Paula sighed in the blackness as she thought of the nightmare that so often took its place. She tried to force the awful thoughts from her mind, to hang on to the happiness, but she knew as she did so it was pointless.

There was no escape from what was to come. Once again she was going to relive the past. She took a deep breath—the diver above the murky, icy pond —and then she plunged down into the depths of sleep to confront the demons that she could never slay.

LAZILY, THEIR wings set, the mosquitoes zeroed in on Paula. She lay across the crumpled sheets, and surrendered her naked body to them, as her tears dripped onto the grubby pillow. The damp heat wrapped her up, sucking the sweat from her glistening body, and the sound of her sobbing filled the miserable room. Outside the cabin of the houseboat, the Everglades swamp provided the background music: bullfrogs croaking their raucous melody; warm wet sounds as the forest oozed and dripped; the drone of a distant pickup truck carrying a nobody to nowhere.

A moonbeam found her through the open porthole, and played over her soft skin, painting the loveliness of her body. Like some peeping voyeur the finger of light darted across her breasts, and roamed gratefully over her strong, proud shoulders, her muscular arms, her flat stomach. Then, suddenly, it was gone, obscured by some prudish cloud. Once again the blackness blanketed her.

"Damn! Damn! Damn!" she whispered with a terrible intensity as the memory of the horror howled like a hounddog in her soul.

She shuddered in the steamy heat. She could still feel the arms of the men tight around her neck and shoulders, hear their hideous laughter, smell the

smoky beer hell of their breath. But mostly she could see. Holding her captive, they had forced her to watch the rape and the murder of her friend.

She had read about things like that before—some people up north in a bar
somewhere, an enthusiastic audience as their friends had committed the heinous crime, but things like that didn't happen around you. Until last night,
when they had happened to Laura. Laura had been the regular waitress in
Seth Baker's diner, and Paula had been helping out to earn some extra
money, as she often did. Seth Baker, mean and ugly, owned the liquor store,
the gas station and the only "restaurant" in town, which meant he controlled
the only things that anybody wanted in the place called Placid. It gave him
the power of God over the drunken drifters and losers who passed for his
friends. Last night, as the blue smoke had hung heavy in the fetid air, curling
between the checkered tablecloths and the sawdust-covered floor, he had used
it. He had raped Laura, while some drunken hero had held her by a belt
coiled tight around her neck, and Paula had seen it all. And at the end poor
Laura's eyes had been frosted glass and she had lain so still—so very still—on
the filthy floor.

Paula had been the first to understand what had happened.

"She's dead. You've killed her. You pigs have killed her," she had screamed
at the top of her voice.

They had let her go then and she had rushed to Laura and bathed her
poor defiled body with tears of helplessness as they had stood back, spectators
now, no longer big, no longer strong, just men at the bottom of life with
nowhere further to fall.

"She was a drifter. We'll put her in the swamp. Weren't no one's fault. She
did it to herself," the man who had made it happen had said at last.

Paula had turned to Seth Baker and called him a murderer, and she had
promised him personally that she would watch them all burn for the hideous
thing they had done. They had all recoiled from her fury, and they had
drifted away. But Paula had seen the beginnings of fear creep into Baker's
eyes as he had watched Paula carefully, as if weighing the possibility of her
keeping her promise. She had run from the diner, as she had sensed her own
danger, and, slaked on violence, they had let her go.

Now she clutched the sweat-soaked sheet around her as she shivered with
fear and rage. Even as she had run through the outskirts of the town, down
the old dirt track to the edge of the lake where the houseboat was moored, she
had realized that she herself had become a target. There was no point going
to the sheriff—Baker owned him, and Paula knew that if he had been in that
dreadful room, he would have joined in. Emily would have helped her, but
Emily had died six months ago. No, in Placid she was powerless and at risk.
She had to escape.

Paula took another deep breath, as she tried to concentrate. She had no
money. She had no job. And in the next room, piled on top of each other on
the tiered bunks like brand-new tools in an old woodshed, were the twin
brothers to whom she had been a mother for the last five years. They were six
years old—"Cool Hand" Luke, and reckless Jake—and when she had put

them to bed earlier, their happy, love-filled faces had shown no inkling of the shadow that was about to fall upon their little world. They had been asleep before the bedtime story had been finished as they always were, exhausted by the cheerful war against poverty that they all fought by day, and Paula had hurried to the diner for the evening shift, the boring evening with the card-board-cutout alcoholics, hopeless, hapless, harmless. . . .

She fought against the tears, biting at her lower lip, as once again Laura's pleading face flashed from her memory. Again the rage consumed her, wiping away the sorrow from her mind.

In Placid there would be no justice for the fiends. Nobody would miss Laura. She had been a runaway, a nobody floating on the slippery surface of America, a nonperson to everyone but to Paula, who had loved her. In Baker's town they would pretend that they vaguely remembered her if any-one bothered to ask after her. Was that the waitress that moved on a few weeks back—Lana? Lori? Laura? One thing was for sure. They would stick together rehearsing their booze-wrapped lies until everyone believed them, or was too bored to care.

Quietly, Paula slipped both feet to the scuffed linoleum of the cabin floor, and she moved toward the door. On the deck it was hotter than it had been inside, as once again the silver-white of the moonlight bathed her nakedness. There was no one there to watch her. The rotting wood of the jetty had long since led to its abandonment, and the hulk that was her home was the only "boat" tied to it.

She tossed her head in the super-still air, stretching her long neck, and sending her tousled blond hair dancing in the moonbeams. She looked back toward the aft cabin where the twins were, and then she tiptoed gently to the porthole and peeped in. They lay like dead soldiers slain in battle across the bunks, their small limbs abandoned in the deep commitment of children's sleep. Their little chests rose and fell and their parted lips smiled the content-ment they had no right to feel. In the dreamland they would be frolicking like spring lambs, unaware of the tragedy that had already engulfed them. To-morrow they would all have to leave Placid forever. The killers knew where she lived, and she had seen in Baker's eyes that he wanted her dead.

Paula sighed as she stared at their beauty, and she felt their tiny fingers clutching at her heart. God, how she loved them. Luke, quiet, brave, honest, and shy—the one she called Cool Hand after the old movie because he kept it all inside. Jake—the extrovert who kept despair at bay with the powerful weapon of his smile. The Mr. Bear he slept with didn't really look like an animal at all—it was a sad, shapeless thing that Paula had thrown together from a bundle of rags—but it was Jake's most prized possession.

She walked back to the guardrail and peered out over the lake. Beneath the shimmering light of the full moon it stretched out before her like the glassy sea of the hymn. At once, as they always did, the fond memories came winging back. The lake was Daddy, and Daddy was fun, and happiness and safety in those far-off days before the laughter had died. A huge tear trickled down Paula's cheek, and she knelt down, squatting near the splintered, bleached-out wood of the deck, touching it so that she could remember better those far-off days.

"Oh, Daddy, darling Daddy," she whispered. "Help me. Tell me what I should do."

Her voice broke on the hopeless words and she began to sob once more as the loneliness crowded in on her. But only the forest was listening—areca and sable palms bending solicitously to catch her words; tall royal palms reaching straight to the sky impervious to human grief; the buttonwoods and tangled mangroves at the water's edge with sad, dark tales of their own to tell.

There below her, tethered to the gangplank, was the boat he'd built, its wood rotting, its green paint faded and peeled. Six years ago next month her mother had died giving birth to the twins, and five short months later a hit-and-run driver had killed her father as he had returned from fishing a creek off the Miccosukee Strand. At fifteen she had become both a mother and a father instead of the sister she had been intended to be. The rented house had gone, and the meager savings of a carpenter had left nothing after Paula had bought the rundown houseboat. From that moment to this she had battled to keep it all together. And all the time, pushed down deep in the undergrowth of her mind—the loss of her beloved father lived on to plague her.

She wanted so much to be near him, and she moved to the gangplank, and looked down into the small boat he had built. She could see the heavy rock, and the coil of rope attached to it, sitting in the bow. It was the anchor they used to hold the boat still in the shallows off the mangroves. She could see him now as he heaved the rock into the lake—and she could hear her own squeals of mock irritation as the water from the splash soaked her.

She stepped carefully down the rusty ladder, into the boat, and sat down on the seat that had always been hers. It seemed to comfort her, this link with the past, and suddenly she moved forward, picked up the paddle, and untied the bowline from the ladder. Reaching out over the side she pushed hard with the paddle against the sandy bottom, propelling the boat out into the darkness, as green parrots shrieked overhead and bonefish plopped in the shadows that danced at the water's edge.

For a minute or two she was lost in the rhythm of the movement as she paddled the boat toward deeper water until the houseboat was small behind her, and was soon cut off from sight behind a low ridge of mangroves that jutted fingerlike into the lake. She knew this place so well. How many times had they come here for long lazy afternoons of fishing and philosophy in the golden age of her childhood? Paula stopped paddling. She picked up the stone—so light now, so heavy then—and heaved it into the water. Then she sat back in the stern and peered up at the stars. In the morning she'd be gone. Now she would say good-bye to the sacred places to which she would never return. So she cuddled up tight, wrapped in the night and the old days, naked as the baby she wished she still was. She squashed her full breasts against the skin of her forearms and pushed her knees to her elbows like a child in a womb and the comfort coursed through her at long last. Then she pulled the *ancient tarpaulin around her and, gloriously, the horror and fear began to fade into the woolly haze of sleep.*

Paula sat bolt upright as she crashed into terrified wakefulness.

She knew with absolute certainty that something horrible was happening. But what? Where? Then she saw it. In the sky. Above the place where the houseboat would be. The sky was glowing. The sky was red. The sky was alight.

She tore up the anchor and grabbed at the paddle, thrusting it like a dagger into the gleaming water. A cry gathered at the back of her throat.

"Fire," she whispered.

"Fire!" she shouted.

"Fire!" she screamed across the empty lake, at the teeming, careless forest.

She tore at the smooth surface of the water, and the old boat groaned with the power of her strokes as it began to obey. She was separated from the houseboat by a small mangrove island, and in minutes she would be around it. Long, endless minutes as the fire burned. God, let it be the jetty, or some camper's fire igniting the undergrowth farther inland.

She broke around the edge of the island, and the flames lit up her eyes. It was a torch. The old boat was on fire from its bow to its stern, from its water line to the roof of the two cabins on its deck. The still, hot air was full of the crackling roar of the flames, and the smell of the smoke, campfire clean, wandered with the innocence of Satan amidst the streaks of silver moonlight.

"Luke! Jake!"

Her body trembled with the effort of the scream as she tried to alert them to the danger. Her wild eyes combed the banks of the lake for the twins. Surely they had escaped. But the dread filled her, strangling hope. There was only the sound of the flames. Only the shadowy, deserted shoreline. Only the searing heat plucking at her eyes and melting her heart. Her home was an inferno. Bright, infinitely bright it burned, the old wood glowing and sparkling as it had never done before. Exploding, falling, crunching in upon themselves the timbers surrendered to the fire, and bits broke away, burned to a crispy lightness, as they spiraled upward toward the sky.

Paula paddled furiously, but the wall of heat was rock solid against her face as she approached the blaze. It singed her, angry against her exposed nipples, cross against her sweat-soaked stomach, enraged against her bare thighs, but still there was no room for pain in her racing mind.

"Noooooooo," she howled at the moon to forbid the disaster.

"Jake! Luke! Oh, dear God, noooooo!"

The flames roared back. She looked around desperately. What should she do? No way to stop the burning. No possibility of getting closer. Then, on the edge of vision, she saw the movement. Out near the old towpath, where the jetty met the bank, something was moving. Her heart leaped for joy. It was all right. They were there, safe on land. Her little brothers had been delivered from the fire. She peered desperately into the shadows and tried to focus through the crazy patterns of light. There was something, someone in the bushes, half hidden, half revealed. Then, as she watched, the figure began to move. It was the figure of a man and he was hurrying away from the fire.

"Help! Help!" she screamed.

But he ran on, turning only once to look over his shoulder as he heard her shout. It was the precise moment that a shaft of moonlight caught him, illuminating him plainly in the phosphorus glow.

Seth Baker was running away from her burning home.

Seth Baker! In the midst of her panic she knew instantly what had happened. He had done this. He had started the fire. He had tried to murder her, thinking that she would be asleep inside. To protect himself he had tried to kill her.

Helpless, she turned once again to face the agonizing vision, as her life burned before her. The twins' cabin was a red ball of flame. Nothing could live in there. Nothing. Paula clenched her fists and she beat on her knees as the nausea gripped her, the bile rose in her throat, and the horrible world danced before her eyes.

Then it happened.

The door of the cabin where the twins slept disintegrated. There was a muffled explosion, and a tongue of flame speared out through the space where the door had been. Flame . . . and something else.

Two small marionettes, their puppetlike arms outstretched, stumbled through the door. They walked in slow motion, their movements jerky, and sometimes it looked as if they would fall, as they swayed from side to side. From top to toe they burned. They were tiny beacons of flame, small torches of flickering light as they struggled away from the fire they had become. One led the other, his blazing arm held high, and on the end of it was a blob of flame that burned brighter than all the rest. Rooted to the spot by the glue of horror, Paula knew instantly what it was. It was Mr. Bear. It was Jake's Mr. Bear, and he was carrying it with him to Paradise.

Despite the heat Paula paddled closer, and, as she did so the twins gave up their doomed march to freedom. Jake staggered and toppled and the animal he loved flew away from him as he fell, his hands still reaching for the grown-up arms that would never comfort him. Luke fell at the same time, crashing into Jake, merging with him in a burning fiery embrace and together the twins who had been born together died together in a crumpled heap of flames at the edge of the deck.

Like a stricken animal, moaning softly, Paula crouched down in the bottom of the boat, her hand raised above her head as if to protect herself from the evil she had seen, as a part of her died forever with the little brothers she loved.

For an age she was still, locked in anguish, her soul tossed on the sea of her torment. Then, at last, quite quietly, her voice shaking with a transcendent conviction, she made her promise.

"I swear on the blood of my family that you will die, Seth Baker, for what you have done. You will die in horror and terror as they have died, and you will scream for the mercy that you never gave."

~ 6 ~

*I*T WAS ONE of those days when you could see forever. L.A. was clear and crisp and across the valley the mountains were sharply focused—massive, brooding, complacent as they watched the San Fernando matchstick men and women doing the bizarre things that humans did. David Plutarch peered out at them from his poolside gazebo before turning slowly to savor the other half of his panorama. On one side lay the humble valley with its magnificent mountains, on the other the proud palaces of Beverly Hills and Bel-Air, the boxlike towers of Century City, and out there in the distance across the Malibu hills, Catalina Island and the sparkling ocean, the water already polka-dotted by the white sails of yachts.

He smiled to himself as a strange happiness wafted through him. Days like this made it all worthwhile.

Here he was, high above the City of Angels, safe in his twenty-million-dollar estate above the old Sinatra house, with Caroline Kirkegaard by his side.

He walked toward her and flopped down on the terrycloth sun bed next to her, his lean, oil-slicked body the color of a newly minted penny against the pure white background. He looked down at himself. Not bad for the mid-forties. Tight, but not stringy; creased but very far from wrinkled; the tan exuberant but not the mahogany dark of the obsessive sunbather.

Now he looked over at Caroline, and at once the music began to play inside him. She was magnificent in a jet-black Norma Kamali nylon-and-spandex one-piece, a slingshot thong steamy from the sands of Ipanema that bisected her buttocks with geometrical precision. All the ends of her seemed to be blood red, her toes; her fingernails; her glistening, half-parted lips. She lay flat, on her side, her eyes open, but although they were pointed in Plutarch's direction they didn't appear to be watching him.

"Pretty special, huh?" he tried, half meaning the day, half meaning her.

Caroline Kirkegaard ignored him, but the beginnings of a smile flirted with the edges of her lips. She knew what she was doing. She wasn't answer-

367

ing when spoken to; she was injecting a bolus of angst into a serene situation; she was being predictably unpredictable.

Plutarch was acutely aware that she hadn't responded to his innocent remark, and although this should be no big deal, somehow, maddeningly, it was.

"What made you want to make so much money?" asked Caroline dreamily, noticing how eagerly his eyes darted toward her, how hurt they'd been when she had blocked him out before. Her question was conciliatory. At the same time there was a leitmotif of mockery in its background, the veiled insinuation that making money was a pretty tawdry ambition.

"I never wanted to be rich. I just wanted to create things, and to have my own way." He smiled a childlike smile when he said that. It was true. He'd never wanted to stare complacently from the covers of *Fortune* and *Business Week*. He'd never longed for the trains and boats and planes and all the other toys of the Forbes 500 boys.

"You were wise. Only losers try to make *money*. It's like working at being happy. Do what you have to do and everything falls into place—the loot, the contentedness, everything."

"And if you don't *have* a goal, or a talent?" Plutarch asked.

"Then get one, quick, or it's all over."

He laughed. People who lived by the will had a way of taking it for granted that the rare commodity was available to everyone.

She sat up, her stupendous torso emasculating gravity. Then she leaned forward, resting her breasts on her knees. "Have you got your own way now, Mr. David Plutarch?" she asked, staring deep into his hungry eyes.

The question was laden with innuendo. She leaned forward farther, squashing her breasts into her knees, then rocked back, then forward again, squeezing, pushing, relaxing, and all the time watching him, watching . . .

He swallowed hard. Did he have his own way? It was impossible to say. Yes. She was there beside him, inside his life, filling it up with anxious excitement. No. Because he didn't own her. He had not broken her, defeated her, dominated her. And he had never touched her. That was the worst bit of all . . . the waiting, the planning, the hoping.

"Partly," he answered, turning his face from hers. "Do you want a drink?" he added as camouflage.

"No."

Again Plutarch recognized the power play. How often had he played the same game himself, hovering on the verge of rudeness to assert his superiority, and to show that he didn't feel he had to be polite? The evening he had first set eyes on Caroline he had recognized a virtuoso performer in the exercise of power. She was as good as he was, as strong as he, possibly even more single-minded, and all his life he had never met anyone who was those things. From that moment he had longed to control *her* and in doing so to win a contest of will with perhaps the only person on earth who was a match for him.

"So, how did you do it, David? How did you put it all together?"

"Oh, I don't know," he mumbled casually. "I just built a little company and sold it to United Electric for two point five. U.E. paid too much. It was maybe worth two." David Plutarch couldn't help the evasion. It was second nature to him, coded into his genes. Winners hoarded information like fine jewels.

Caroline smiled as she watched him shortchange her. He was almost good looking, the brooding brow, the deep-set green eyes, the aggressive jaw. But there was something undeniably crude about him. It wasn't just the bikini-style, Club Mediterranée swimming briefs, or even the heavy gold ring with its vulgar diamond; it was more fundamental than that. There was something mean about his soul, something crass about it, some fundamental absence of class that all the millions would never ever quite dispel. She had wanted something from him—to pick the brains of the billionaire, and unlock some of the secrets of his success, but he had seen what she wanted and he had automatically backed away from giving it to her. Not that it mattered. In a little while she would pluck him like ripe fruit from the tree. And afterward, he would beg to be allowed to make all her dreams come true.

"So, now your only problem is to know what to do with the money." Again her voice had that mocking lilt, because she knew she was on target. The Plutarchs of this world did not thrive on spare time. It might have been a shrewd financial move to peddle Stellar to U.E. It almost certainly hadn't been good for his peace of mind.

"It's the kind of problem I like," lied Plutarch.

"Sometimes when your life changes it's not so easy. Despite money. Despite all this." She threw out a statuesque arm to take in the world spread out like a magic carpet around them. "Then you have to have a spirituality to fall back on."

"New Age?"

"Destiny."

"Yes, of course, Destiny."

In his former life as the hard-nosed entrepreneur, Plutarch had had no time for such things. Now he was definitely interested. All around him the material world seemed to be in retreat. It was the first thing he'd noticed when he'd cast off his business blinders. Everywhere there was a new interest in the metaphysical, and he had set out to explore that alien world as an antidote to the vast stretches of spare time that threatened to engulf him. It had been an eye-opening journey. Unbeknown to him there existed a parallel New Age culture.

It was a sensual world of massage and messages, of Maharishis, mediums, and mind-trips, a world of passive passion and steely gentleness as gurus filled up the vacuums of empty lives and dreamers dared to experience their elusive dreams. Hypnotists, telepathists, clairvoyants, and astrologers were guides on the supposed journeys to the center of self. Channelers, numerologists, psychics, and metaphysicians led the group gropers to peak experiences that gave new meaning to the bittersweet sigh between two mysteries that went by the name of life.

He had not embraced the counterculture entirely, but he had been at least partially seduced by it.

Then he had on a whim decided to go to the Kirkegaard meeting, and at once he had realized that all the disparate elements of his life could come together in her persona. The woman had it all, and something more. He had never seen anyone so beautiful, and he was drawn toward the flame of her unapproachable sexuality. In her, mysticism and Mammon merged deliciously as Plutarch hoped that they would in *his* life. He wanted more of her. In his dreams that night they had been joined together into a cohesive force that would transcend this world and reach out into uncharted, unconquered realms of cosmic time and space.

Caroline watched him carefully as she reached for the Mario Badescu number thirty sun-block. She squeezed a huge blob onto her hand and massaged it languorously onto her legs, her inner thighs, up high where they vanished into the minimal swimsuit, as his eyes roamed over her. She had recognized him early on at the Destiny meeting and although he didn't know it she had been doing it all for him, analyzing his every reaction. She had noted the bits that seemed to excite him, the parts that didn't, and slowly but surely the jigsaw had fitted into place. He loved her when she was dominant. He became alive when she insulted the crowd of which he was a part, as a demonstration of her power over them. The ultimate voyeur, he couldn't take his eyes off her when she strutted, macho and masculine, across the stage.

At last the picture was perfect. Plutarch was obsessed not with Destiny but with her, and it was a sexual obsession. The man who had so recently dealt in power had discovered the alien delights of subservience.

Over the past couple of days she had noticed that he loved nothing more than to watch her lithe body cutting like an otter through the waters of his pool; her muscles ballooning deliciously on the Nautilus machines, the oiled leather belt biting into her straining waist; and most of all he loved to watch the sweat-soaked aerobics lessons with little Kanga, as their bodies melted and the smell of them merged deliciously in his twitching nostrils. It wasn't so very strange that a powerful man had at last discovered the awesome world of sexual desire, but Caroline's knowledge was the key to owning him, and soon she would be turning the key in a padlock around his heart.

Plutarch seemed to sense her thought process. He wanted to get back to more tangible things, but he couldn't take his eyes off the legs. "The computerized astrological-chart thing . . . It's a good idea. The guy came up with a neat program and the advertising people think it'll play . . ."

Caroline laughed inside. It had been merely a ruse to get to him, and boy, had it paid off. The moment she had seen him at the Sunset Hotel she had decided to meet him. She hadn't bothered to make an appointment. First thing the next morning, she had simply banged at his door, or rather at his security-guarded, TV-monitored, Door King-communication-rigged, electronically operated gate. He had rushed to see her, and her calling card had been a business scheme—computerized astrological charts. You feed in the birthdate, time, and place at one end, and your future pops out at the other.

Ground-breaking idea. Neat. Surefire. And neither Plutarch nor Caroline had mentioned it again until now, because it had served its purpose—by allowing them to meet. They had circled each other like gladiators in the Roman arena, but it had been no contest. Caroline had already discovered the Achilles' heel of his sexuality, and she had held her glorious body over him like the unanswerable weapon it was. By the end of the meeting, Plutarch had trotted in front of her like a broken mustang, and it had been merely a question of slipping into the saddle.

"Good," she said dismissively, banishing astrology, computers, charts, and all such mundane things from their relationship. "David?" Her voice was husky. It was almost time.

"Yes."

"Come here."

He stood up, wanting to ask why, ashamed to be doing her bidding, not daring, not wanting to refuse.

"I want you to rub some of this into my feet," she said.

He moved toward her. "Your feet . . . ?" His voice was strangled. It was the first invitation to touch her. But her feet! He knew what it meant, yet he couldn't fight against it.

She didn't explain. She handed him the Chanel Hydrafilm Protective Moisturizer, and her whirlpool eyes were hooded, as she lay back and sent her legs snaking out toward him. He couldn't sit beside her. There was no room. There wasn't meant to be. He took the cream, and he knelt down before the feet that he was to serve.

With shaking hands he reached out to do her bidding.

Plutarch's whole body was tingling. It was like super-reality—those moments when fear or excitement made everything crystal clear. The smells amplified in his bared nostrils—the heady scent of the Chanel, the crisp ozone of the midmorning canyon air—the soothing aroma of the pines. Beneath his trembling hands was the body of his dreams, the feet of the woman who obsessed him. He worked reverently at them, rubbing them gently, neither too hard nor too soft, as he struggled to prolong the moment.

Her voice melted into the maelstrom of his mind. "David," she said, "I have a fantasy and I'd like you to indulge me."

He couldn't answer. There was no room in his crammed brain for fantasies other than his own. His hands lay still on her, unable to move in the thunderstorm of sensation that had engulfed him.

"I want you to give me dinner. In one of the bungalows at the Sunset Hotel. Pink champagne, flowers, beautiful music . . . everything."

He fought to concentrate.

"We could do it here," he managed at last.

"No, it has to be the Sunset," she insisted dreamily. "Tonight." Her feet moved lazily, encouragingly, against his hands.

"Of course," he mumbled. "Of course I can arrange that."

"Oh, and David," she purred, "I almost forgot. The dinner should be for three."

CAROLINE KIRKEGAARD stepped into the gardens of the Sunset Hotel and was immediately enveloped by the lush foliage—pink and white double hibiscus, oleander, banana trees, schefflera, Benjamina, ficus, cypress, acacia, and Washingtonia palms.

Here, near the lobby, the restaurant, and the Star Room, waiter and guest noise was loudest. It was where the cheaper bungalows started, where the relatively impoverished stayed, able to afford only a miserly thousand dollars a night, there but not really *there* in the shadowy world of Beverly Hills scorekeeping. As she headed along the azalea-lined walkways, down worn stone steps, past bowls of bougainvillea and tinkling fountains, beneath Spanish-tiled arches, the houses got grander. The one to the right of her was more a compound than a bungalow, and Caroline knew that behind its faded terracotta wall was a pool that would have done credit to estates in Brentwood, Bel-Air, or Holmby Hills.

She jerked an accusing finger at the wall. "Robert Hartford lives there," she hissed, the pilot light of her permanent loathing bursting briefly into flame.

"Asshole," Kanga murmured in a conciliatory tone of voice, imagining that Caroline was irritated that Hartford had walked out of the Destiny meeting. "Does this guy we are going to meet have anything to do with Destiny?" she tried, knowing as she did so that it was hopeless. If Caroline had intended to tell her more, then she wouldn't have had to ask the question.

"He will have . . . after tonight."

Kanga sighed, but she said nothing.

The door said BUNGALOW 9, and to reach it you passed beneath an archway of ficus, and another of wrought iron on which white roses twined. There was a heady scent of jasmine, and the faint sound of what might have been Wagner filtered through the carved oak door. Caroline Kirkegaard pressed the bell.

He opened the door himself and the stirring music surged past his stocky body. He looked nervous, and yet elated. He didn't speak.

Neither did Caroline. Nor did Kanga.

The room was full of flowers, all of them white—lilies, orchids, gladiolas, gardenias.

The TV, set in a mahogany mock Chippendale cabinet, was switched to CNN, and stock prices ran along the bottom of the picture, but the sound was switched off. The Wagner, *Tannhäuser*, exploded from twin speakers on either side of one end of the room.

On the coffee table stood three bottles of what looked like pink champagne nestling in the traditional plastic Sunset Hotel ice buckets bearing the setting-sun logo of the most famous hotel in the world. There were three Baccarat flute glasses, and somebody had bothered to frost them in the fridge. A huge silver ice bucket contained a bowl packed to the brim with beluga caviar, and three spoons protruded from the top of it.

Caroline walked quickly across the room and flicked the switch of the Carver amplifier. Wagner died.

Plutarch broke the noisy silence. He licked nervously at dry lips and said, "You don't like Wagner?"

"I like champagne," said Caroline as she smiled at him.

His eyes never left Caroline as he picked up a bottle, eased the wire and gold foil from the neck, and pressed the pads of both thumbs beneath either side of the cork.

The tiny *pop* seemed to surprise him, but not nearly so much as Caroline Kirkegaard's next remark.

"Get undressed, Kanga," she snapped.

"What . . ."

"DO IT!"

Caroline smiled sweetly as she issued the extraordinary command, and her serene facial expression was totally at odds with the explosive force of her words. She held out her hand and watched David Plutarch swallow nervously as the drama she was directing began to unfold. Next he would fill a glass with champagne and hand it to her, and his mind would boil as he anticipated the enormity of what was to come. She threw back her head and laughed as she saw that she had him. His eyes were wide, and his hands shook as he tried to control the bottle. The crushed pink petals of the champagne spilled onto the walnut table and it took him long seconds to fill the flute to the correct two-thirds level. Was that sweat breaking out around the careful lips? Was that the thumping of his heart beneath the navy-blue Polo shirt? Yes, yes it was, and she laughed some more as the liquid power flowed in her veins, and the drums began to pound in the pit of her stomach.

She took the glass he offered and her eyes watched his as he stared first at her . . . and then at Kanga. Now, as she sipped delicately on the champagne, she turned to see if she had been obeyed.

Kanga's mouth was half open as she tried to make sense of what was going on. The surprise was all over her beautiful features, the upturned nose, the trembling lips, the firm set of her brave chin.

The Kirkegaard eyebrows arched upward, questioning why she had not been instantly obeyed. Then her features softened in a smile of encouragement as she added the carrot to the stick.

Once, just once, she nodded imperceptibly. Go ahead, Kanga. Trust me. Do it for me. Because you love me. Because you must.

Kanga's arms moved slowly, serpents to the flute of the charmer, toward the buttons of her shirt. All the time she stared straight at Caroline, as if to say, "I don't know what's going on, but I'll do this for you. Only for you." One by one the bone buttons surrendered until they were all undone. Now, draped by the soft linen of the pure white Calvin Klein shirt, the divide of her breasts was visible, her freckled, suntanned skin painted by the faint glow of embarrassment, anxiety, and, despite herself, the warm flush of early desire. It was quite obvious that she wore no bra.

She paused. Then with a sudden movement she took the plunge, throwing back the shirt, and at the same time thrusting her chest forward at the hungry eyes in a gesture of hopeless defiance.

Caroline had never seen her quite like this, so shy, so afraid, and so very appealing. Kanga stood foresquare, her legs apart, one hand hiding coyly behind her back, the thumb of the other hooked with make-believe bravado behind the tight leather of the belt, and her breasts, two unutterably lovely documents of surrender, seemed to fill the room. The curve of their upper slope ran from the tense turned-up tips of the pink triangular nipples to tighter pectorals, and below the contours formed a smooth, flattened U from the apex of the breast to the vertical, high-tone muscles of her chest wall. There was a voluptuous fullness about them, a sort of pendulous tension, that underlined their defiance of gravity.

Caroline walked toward her, as Kanga stood her ground, her head held back, and angled very slightly away from the woman who was her obsession. She reached out with her left hand and she ran a lazy finger along Kanga's upper lip, catching the moisture that had gathered there. Then, languorously, she transferred the finger to her own mouth, all the time staring deep into the young girl's eyes. Now, she reached down to the cold champagne and she dipped her thumb and forefinger into the pink bubbles and her hand moved toward Kanga's breast. Pink on pink, cold on warm, first one side and then the other, she anointed them with wine as the breath shuddered from Kanga's lungs and the sigh of want rustled between her desert-dry lips at the intimacy of the gesture. Then Caroline bent down slowly, cupping one breast with her hand as her tongue slid out to taste the warm tightness of the champagne-and-sweat-drenched nipple. For delicious seconds it lingered there, soft and slippery against the murmuring flesh, and Kanga's moan of ecstasy filled the room as she reached in desperation, first for her own free nipple and then for the buckle of her belt.

Caroline drew back, and her voice was hoarse with desire as she breathed the words. "Yes, darling. You're so beautiful. Yes, my darling. Take off your jeans." Kanga's fumbling fingers tore at the belt, and ripped at the buttons of the Levi's. She squirmed from side to side as the skin-tight denim thwarted her and she pushed down to release the hot heart of her to the eyes of her must-be lover. Caroline smiled. Like some lovely ice creation, the girl was melting in the sizzling heat of her lust.

"Come here," she ordered. Kanga did as she was told. Stumbling across the carpet, her movement hampered by the pants she hadn't time to remove, she struggled toward Caroline.

A reigning monarch now, Caroline placed one hand upon the hot skin of the girl's naked shoulder, and gently, but firmly, she forced Kanga to kneel before her.

For a second Caroline paused, then she, too, bent at the knees and, reaching down with both hands, she took hold of the hem of her skirt. Slowly, she began to lift. It seemed that her legs themselves were moving inexorably upward. The thighs elongated, slinking toward the ceiling, long and luscious and full of wicked promises. The tops of her stockings gripped them firmly, black on cream, and in turn the pure white of the garter straps clutched at the dark silk and all the time the knowledge of what was to come scrambled the minds of her two eager victims. At the uppermost edge of her thigh she paused and Kanga's heart stopped with the dress that had become a veil. She couldn't hold herself back. The groan of abandonment floated free of her.

"Please," she murmured.

"Do you want it?"

"Yes." Kanga's voice was soft, defeated.

"How much do you want me?"

But Caroline didn't wait for an answer to her question. She raised the dress to her waist.

"Oooooh," murmured Kanga, leaning forward eagerly.

"Wait for my permission."

At the moment of truth Caroline Kirkegaard had not forgotten her ultimate objective, and now she turned toward him, and a smile of triumph broke across her face. David Plutarch lay slumped across the sofa. His breath was coming fast, and, lost in wonder at what he was seeing, it was clear he could think only of what was to come. Caroline was turning his ultimate fantasy into reality. She was in control of the man she had set out to dominate, and the expression on his face was the eloquent confirmation of her victory. It was time.

Her hand came up slowly, undoing the still life she had created, and her forefinger beckoned to him. It pulled him up from the sofa, and across the carpet, and he hurried toward his fate.

"Look at her, David Plutarch. She's mine, isn't she?"

Standing awkwardly beside the two women, he nodded his assent.

"She'd do anything I asked. She'd steal, she'd kill for me."

It was strange. Caroline had won but she still wanted to prove her power. Plutarch was beneath her, but in some way he was still an equal to be impressed as he was being humiliated, to be pleased while he was being punished.

"Kanga!" Caroline's voice was taut. "Undo his fly."

The redhead came out of her dream, her face suddenly stricken.

"Now, Kanga!"

Plutarch held Caroline's eyes as the fumbling, obedient fingers sought him. He understood at last. Caroline would not be touched by him, nor would she touch. And it didn't matter that the one he wanted wanted nothing to do with him. It was right. It was fitting. She was a superior being. It was enough that he would be allowed to stare into her eyes as the business was concluded. Kanga's fingers had obeyed their mistress. He was exposed.

"Go ahead, Kanga!" ordered Caroline Kirkegaard.

There was a pause. So short. So unthreatening. Because of course she would be obeyed. And she was.

Plutarch's eyes, glassy with ecstasy, locked onto Caroline's as the sublime sensations flowed through his body. "Is it good? Do you like it?" asked Caroline, her tone triumphant.

His voice was hoarse as he spoke.

"How do you do it, Caroline Kirkegaard?"

"Better than you, David Plutarch."

He stared at her helplessly, already rushing toward the conclusion that could not be delayed. She saw it in his eyes.

"I'll tell you when. Not before." Caroline's voice was sharp.

Yes, she wanted to control that too.

But she couldn't. Surely she couldn't. Not that. His whole being was hovering on the edge of the chasm. He only wanted to float free on the wild wind of release. In this one thing he would assert independence. No mere spectator could control the mystery of his orgasm. In the very last round of all he would save face with a minor victory.

But he couldn't do it. He remained there, poised on the brink of the cliff, unable to step forward, unwilling to step back. Time and again he steeled himself for the leap into the pleasure space, but each time the invisible wall forced him to retreat.

He heard her laughter. He saw her smiling face. She knew. She could sense his struggle, she could predict its outcome. The moment would be hers, not his.

"Please," he murmured as he admitted it.

Again she laughed, and she threw back her head, reveling in her absolute authority. The pause seemed like an eternity.

"Okay, David Plutarch. Do it," she said at last.

Her words unlocked the gate and David Plutarch flowed through it. His knees buckled and he staggered sideways as the mighty river of pent-up lust rushed from him. Kanga reached for the carpet to steady herself as she recoiled from the incredible force of his orgasm, and the triumphant smile shone from her face, as she looked up at her mistress for the reward that surely now would be hers.

Caroline's lips broke into a soft smile as she glanced down at Kanga, and her voice, caressing yet still commanding, was urgent. "Kanga. Go! Now! Right this minute! I'll call you later, but only if you do what I say *immediately.*"

There was no time to dress properly. There was time only to grab her shirt and pull up her blue jeans before the door crashed shut behind her and she was outside the bungalow, half naked and alone in the jasmine-scented garden.

David Plutarch staggered toward the sofa and fell onto it, burying his face in the pillows. He half turned toward Caroline. "What do you want?" he murmured.

"I want you to buy me the Sunset Hotel," she said.

~7~

ROBERT HARTFORD LOPED across the Star Room of the Sunset Hotel like a wolf who had just fed. He looked neither to right nor to left, because he knew what he would see if he did. The clientele were the most sophisticated in the world when it came to celebrities—and small-town gawkers and gapers were conspicuous by their absence—but there were limits, and Robert Hartford transcended them. It had to do with rationing, with mystery, with the careful attention to career building that had always been his trademark. Robert didn't do the coast-to-coast chats. He wasn't rent-a-mouth for the glossy magazines. The details of his private life were shrouded in the mystery that only great care, and a carnivorous Century City law firm on a monstrous retainer, could guarantee.

So now the eyes of the women devoured him. They sniffed at the air to savor the smell of his charisma. They willed him to look at them, to shine the light of his countenance upon them, and give them, not peace, but wild hope. What they wanted from him was fuel for the fires of their daydreams, gasoline for the furnace of their night ones. That they wouldn't get it simply added to the potency of the Hartford myth.

The men watched him, too, the Hollywood men, short on short and long on longing. They watched him carefully, like small children a conjuror. They wanted to know how he did it. What was the trick? Could it be learned? Could it be performed? It was his sexuality. That was what they wanted. They wanted to bottle it, to distill it, to concentrate it. They wanted to pour the delicious charm juice all over their hairy chests and their short little dicks and to smooth it liberally all over the shiny skin of their bald, glistening heads. Then, then, one fine day, they, too, would achieve superstud status in Star Town, and the wall-to-wall women who ignored them now would howl at the moon while they came.

Everyone knew exactly who he was. His recognition factor was at least one hundred percent, possibly more. If he'd had a buck for each murmured "Robert Hartford" his meal would have been free.

Francisco Livingstone half rose to greet him. He smiled, crinkling up his leathery, heavily suntanned face as his fingers pulled at a neatly cut, snow-white mustache.

"Morning, Robert," he said.

The tones were mellifluous, the accent upper class. That went with the clothes. Francisco looked like a walking fashion plate transported from an era when even to *think* about male "fashion" demonstrated a lack of good taste. He didn't, therefore, buy his clothes from the obvious places, expatriate stores like Dunhill and Kent and Curwen that specialized in the Beverly Hills idea of the "English" look. He didn't get his shoes from Church's or his sweaters from Carroll and Co., and he avoided Ralph Lauren's Polo store on Rodeo like the plague. Instead he fitted himself out in London, where the genuine articles were, thus establishing himself as the ultimate in Beverly Hills aristocracy, that rare creature who was totally at home outside its city limits. His silver hair, slicked down with Royal Yacht hair oil from Thomas's in London's Duke Street, was parted at one side in a line that was the shortest possible distance between two points. The herringbone-tweed hacking jacket from Savile Row's Kilgour, French and Stanbury was patched at the elbows with worn, dark green leather, and it enclosed a pale blue cotton Harvie and Hudson shirt, knotted at the deep collar by a blue-and-white polka-dotted silk tie. One and a half inches of cuff peeped from the sleeves of his coat, showing plain, oval gold cuff links engraved with the faded remains of some indecipherable family crest. His trousers were dark gray worsted, belted around his thin waist by a navy-blue belt that sported a single brick-red line along its middle, and they broke over the laces of forty-year-old Lobb's shoes, cracked and weathered by years of diligent polishing. A red-and-white handkerchief cascaded in careful confusion from his breast pocket.

Robert Hartford took the parchment hand, noting the firmness of the old man's grip. "You're looking well, Francisco," said Robert. "Sometimes I think you've found the fountain of eternal youth." It was a fantasy of Robert's that such a thing existed. The aging process was one of the few things he had not been able to control.

"Hah, it's called Lafite, dear boy. And do you know I'm doing a *very* wicked thing." He chuckled charmingly at his naughtiness. "I'm drinking up the 'sixty-ones. I'm told it's a capital offense as they won't peak for years yet. But when you reach my age time is of the essence, isn't it? Yes, it is, my word, it is." He nodded sagely to himself, his gimlet eyes twinkling, as his old head wagged up and down.

Robert Hartford was seldom on this side of a conversation, and there were few people that he would allow to put him there. Livingstone knew exactly what the lunch was all about, but he would take his time before he got to the bottom line. Men like him hated bluntness. Instead they dealt in manners, and courtesy, in rituals and in delicacy.

"Are you a claret man, Robert?"

Robert Hartford laughed. The question assumed so much—that the world was divided into "claret men" and "Burgundy men"; that any civilized person would be a drinker of fine French wine; that "both" was no possible answer.

"Actually, I'm a great lover of the better white Burgundies. Corton Charlemagne. Le Montrachet. I've been meaning to ask you to beef up the Century Room's list in that area. Otherwise, and I know you'll disapprove, I'm rather fond of champagne."

Francisco Livingstone threw up his hands in mock horror. Few old people could drink much of that. "Dear me, no! I can't be doing with it. Girl's drink."

Robert laughed. "In that case, Francisco, I suspect you have quite a store of it tucked away in your bedroom cooler."

It was no secret. Francisco had never let the weakness of his flesh stand in the way of the willingness of his spirit. In the fifty years since he had bought and built up the fabled Sunset Hotel he had ground his way through most of distaff Hollywood. Few women were safe from his gallant conversational sallies, and those who signaled their interest were, there and then, investigated by his courtly fingers. Robert Hartford had never quite understood how the old boy managed it. Admirers of women such as he could seldom see the charms of another man. But although Francisco Livingstone had been a widower for thirty years, he seldom slept alone, and hardly ever with the same person. If anything had changed, it was the age of his bedmates. This seemed to vary in inverse proportion to his own. As Livingstone got older the chicks got younger. Now he slept with women less than half his age. And that made him, in Robert Hartford's eyes at least, a very impressive figure indeed.

"Aha, you know my secret. Dear me, have the chambermaids been talking? Is that the gossip?" He appeared delighted, leaning forward in his chair for corroboration of his virility. He wanted chapter and verse.

Robert Hartford froze a little inside. Women were for loving, they were not for leering over. They were too wonderful for that, too gentle, too delicate, too strong, too resilient.

He reached for a piece of bread, broke it, and scooped on a dollop of saltless butter. He said nothing, but his talkative eyes registered their disapproval. A man's man would have given the old boy his moment of male pride, but Robert Hartford was not a man's man, and he didn't care who knew it.

Francisco Livingstone picked up the rebuke, and the sunshine left his face. He did not hold it against Hartford. He held it against himself. That was how he had gotten to be the most admired and respected hotelier in America. Hotels required sensitivity. You had to vibrate in tune with them, as you anticipated every whim of your guests. You had to charm your staff, and retain the demeanor of the aesthete as you moved with fashion, and yet never forsook good taste. A second or two ago he had allowed his creaky hormones to dictate a remark that lacked delicacy. Most men in Hollywood wouldn't have recognized that.

Robert had, and he hadn't liked it.

The old man swept up the menu, the gesture symbolically closing the subject.

"Now, dear boy. A little luncheon, I think, don't you? The smoked salmon is always fresh from the Dee, but then you know that. Can't think why I'm selling the stuff to you. You *live* here!" He waved for the waiter, and the hovering servant shot forward to the most important table in the room.

"A bottle of Krug—yes, I think Mr. Hartford would approve of the 1969. Now, not too cold. Don't murder it." He turned to Robert. "I'm told Krug needs bottle time, isn't that right?"

Robert smiled back, letting the silence linger a bit. In business, as perhaps in life, the trick was to be a watcher, a listener, a collector of the facts. It wasn't necessarily a way to be liked, but it was the way to win.

"Sounds good to me," he drawled, well aware that Francisco had deferred to him in the choice of the wine. He leaned back against the comfortable upholstery of the banquette and looked around the familiar restaurant.

It was an endlessly fascinating place, the hub of Beverly Hills deal talk since Francisco had opened it maybe forty years earlier. It existed on all sorts of secret levels that were not apparent to the majority of its customers. The nub of the Star Room was the four or five tables at one of which they now sat. These power tables controlled the entrances to the glass-enclosed loggia, which was the *only* place for breakfast, and the charming al fresco courtyard that was *the* only place to have lunch.

From this pole position, anyone who was anybody could be checked out, and as they left they had to run the gauntlet of the Livingstone/Hartford table, from which they could either be graciously acknowledged or cruelly snubbed. Robert ticked off the "faces." Sleek Whitney Houston lunching with bright Jodie Foster. Ex-skier Ivana Trump eating à deux with tennis star Martina Navratilova. Superproducer Jerry Weintraub and Sylvester Stallone, doubtless discussing their new movie *Polo* that Stallone would direct. Robert peered over to his left, toward the Outer Mongolia that was the entrance of the room where nobody but the cameramen, the Japanese, the Eurotrash, and the single ladies sat. The hungry eyes stared back, as the outsiders looked in, as far from the real Star Room as the Devil from Grace. He smiled to himself and to the cooled-out pianist, who was running through a selection from *Phantom* for the inattentive restaurant.

Vibing in on Hartford's detachment, Livingstone decided to start flirting with the point. "I shan't really miss it, you know," he said wistfully.

"It was about a year ago I first heard you were thinking of selling. Now it's definite. Is that right?" Robert had known immediately what Francisco was talking about.

Livingstone gazed dreamily around the room, filling up now with the lunchtime power brokers. As much as anyone, he had created this industry. Not the studios, of course, but the *style* of it all. The Sunset was a symbol of Hollywood. It was the center of Los Angeles, the city that wasn't supposed to have a center, and its majestic aura of unflappable calm defined Mellow Yellow Land.

"Yes. I'm going to sell it. I've had enough. I want some peace. I want to travel. I need a rest from Beverly Hills. The whole place has changed. The traffic's a disaster. All the old houses are being pulled down. Nobody talks about anything but crime, cholesterol, and couture. The bookshops have gone. So have the toy stores, and there's nothing *cheap* anymore. It's just car phones with call waiting, the boredom of the endless real-estate boom and all those perfect bloody palm trees and steam-ironed lawns. And the Sunset's such a responsibility. It's like a banana republic—I feel I can't leave without either getting deposed or the whole place falling to bits. The *real* cost of living here's about half a million brain cells a day. More if you drink."

He laughed to show he wasn't serious. Beverly Hills was still paradise and the Sunset was no Panama. It was a superbly functioning machine. Every rule in the hotel was made to be broken, but you had to know who to allow to break the rules. No dogs for the salesman from Ohio. A pack of beagles if Robert Redford or Warren Beatty expressed the wish for them. And the hotel was never, ever "full," even when all the bedrooms had people sleeping in them, never "full," that is, to the "right" person. On one memorable occasion Francisco Livingstone had moved out of his own apartment to accommodate Princess Grace of Monaco, and on another even more auspicious one he had personally supervised the erection of a tent in the hotel gardens when Onassis and Callas had asked for a room. So luxurious had been its appointments, so lavish its decoration that ever since guests had been asking if they, too, could be afforded the privilege of sleeping in one. Little things like that made the difference, and decisions of that sort could only be made by an entrepreneur, a man who knew the powerful people he entertained because he was one himself.

"Do you have a buyer?"

"Not yet." An enigmatic smile.

"Are you advertising it?"

"Well, *you've* heard it's for sale."

The champagne arrived then. Two waiters. A bucket of ice. The cork made no vulgar *pop*. There was no nonsense about tasting it.

Robert raised the glass to his lips, and he watched Livingstone carefully as he drank. "I might be interested in buying it."

"Ah!" It was Livingstone's turn to drink. He paused. "If I have to drink champagne it must be Krug. I know everyone swears by Moët's Dom Pérignon and Louis Roederer's Cristal, but I think it's because the bottles are pretty more than anything else. I've blind-tasted all of them—here and in France—and Krug wins. In my book, anyway. Of course, most Americans are drawn to wines like Taittinger that are made predominantly with the sweeter Chardonnay grape. I prefer champagnes like Krug that rely on the dryer Pinot noir."

"It's very strong, very rich, Francisco."

Again there was a silence. Who would break it? Who was more interested? Buyer or seller? Interest would cost money.

"Forgive my asking, Robert, but why on earth would you be interested in buying the Sunset Hotel?"

Robert Hartford knew there was no way to tell him, and he knew also that it would be unwise to try.

How could he describe an obsession? How could he talk about a childhood fantasy that had bubbled and fizzed within him since he had been old enough to walk? He had come to the Sunset for children's parties and even now he could remember the sticky pink cakes and the wonderful ice creams piled high on the groaning buffet tables, festooned with streamers and balloons and all the things that made life worth living. Magicians and party favors, rabbits popping nervously from silk top hats, the jugglers and the clowns, and the wonderful sprints along the endless corridors as the old retainers turned a blind eye to the screaming antics of the children of the Hollywood elite. Later, as he had grown, it had come to mean other things.

When his father and his mother had fought, which they did with the regularity of a metronome, his father would move out of the Rexford Drive house to take up residence in the Sunset Hotel. Then he would do what all bad parents did. First he bribed his only child in an attempt to turn him against his mother. Second, he cheated on his wife. Third, he spent money with a wild extravagance, both to assert his individuality and to hammer his partner's share of the often precarious family finances. Thus, through his formative years Robert had come to associate the Sunset with excitement and with scenes of spectacularly conspicuous license and consumption.

Breaking glass and drunken oaths in the middle of the night would signal the parental row. Next morning he would tiptoe down to find his enraged mother packing up his father's things for the Sunset. "This is the last time," she would scream. "That pig is never coming home again." All of which meant that his father was already ensconced in a bungalow at the hotel. The telephone calls would come later in the day, after school, and sooner or later one of them would sneak past his mother's defensive screen. "Darling, it's Daddy. I'm at the Sunset. Why don't you walk over for tea. The icebox is full of good things, oh, and I've bought you some things I know you'll like."

The bungalow would be stuffed to bursting with extravagant presents, and room service would be a never-ending source of good things to eat. He would pretend to listen to the antimother propaganda, but mostly he would just have the time of his life until his father slunk back home. And during the blissful ten days or so, the girls would come and the girls would go. He'd find them, long-legged beauties barely twice his age, douching themselves in the marble bathrooms, or turning sleepily in darkened bedrooms, the half-empty bottles of Dom Pérignon guarding them on the mahogany bedside tables. Some ignored him as if he didn't exist as they made their cryptic phone calls in the living room, their white panties poking out from beneath outsize T-shirts. Others would try to befriend him, muttering flattering things about his father in little-girl voices, in a transparent attempt to do themselves a bit of good in the industry in which his father's influence waxed and waned.

And a few, very few, had noticed how beautiful he was and had not held back from showing it. They had stroked his hair, and breathed their sweet breath over his face, and they had allowed their silken, half-clothed bodies to rub gently against him as they had talked about the color of his eyes and the straightness of his teeth, and about how big and strong he was, how more like a man than a boy . . .

Had it started there? He had loved them all. The indifferent hookers, so hard and strong and single-minded in their pursuit of cash; the soft-brained doe-skinned starlets, so tenacious, so exotically ambitious in their search for fame; the lust-driven sensualists, on fire with the unscratchable itch, so determined to please themselves in the act of pleasing others. Each one he could remember. The haunting scent of them, their sleepy gestures, their sex-soaked eyes. And he had wanted them. He had wanted to own them all and have them do for him the dreamy things they would do for his father, and above all he wanted to worship them, and they to return his adoration until they sank deep into the vortex of the physical and the wild world went spinning round.

Later the Sunset had marked the milestones on his path to fame. He had married at the hotel, the terrible, fruitful marriage that had been the first step on the road to stardom, and when he had divorced the legend who had briefly been his wife, he had moved into a small room at the Sunset as his father had before him. He had never left. When his own movie career had hit, he had attended the Oscar night parties there, and the banquets for the visiting celebrities, the fund-raisers and the charity balls. As his career had headed into the stratosphere, he had taken over a suite, then adjoining suites, a bungalow, then adjacent bungalows, until he had achieved the compound he had now—four thousand square feet of Spanish hacienda in the grounds of the most expensive hotel in the world.

He loved the Sunset because it was his life, and he wanted it because he wanted to own himself. That was the truth, and, as always, the truth could not be told.

So Robert Hartford looked Francisco Livingstone directly in the eye, and told him the story he had prepared.

"You see, Francisco, running a hotel and making movies are really the same business. You have the set, and endless plots and subplots, and you have the cast—the guests and the all-important staff. I want to direct *The Sunset Hotel*. I want to tell the beautiful visual story, and I want to write the script and I want the crew to harmonize and to improvise and to reach new heights of technical excellence. I want it to be a bigger hit than it has ever been and to make more money, and to be critically acclaimed until the world agrees that it is a work of art so complete, so brilliant that it is the standard against which all others are judged."

Francisco laughed out loud and his laugh managed to be both respectful and disparaging at the same time. It had been the sort of thing he'd wanted to hear. Almost. The Sunset turned into a hundred miserable condominiums had not been his plan for the extraordinary hotel he had created. Yet, Robert Hartford *daring* to imagine he knew how to do something as impossibly difficult as running the greatest and most exclusive hotel on earth just had to be a joke. God, people were amazing. Their gall. Their effrontery. Their sheer bloody chutzpa. He had never suffered from the sin of pride. Gluttony, maybe; lust, definitely; and lots of other ones. But he would never, for instance, in his wildest dreams, imagine that he could carry off a few supporting roles in Robert Hartford's pictures. Here, however, before his eyes, the best-looking man in the world was cheerfully boasting that he could pull off the part of best hotelier, too. He filed it away in the voluminous drawer that was his life's experience. Never underestimate the power of the famous to overestimate themselves. Was it their strength or their weakness? Perhaps both.

"Well, why not?" said Francisco. "God knows the place could do with a few new characters and plot twists." He peered around the clockwork-smooth restaurant, the perfectly operating bar, the waiters drilled to Prussian parade-ground standard. To his practiced eye it looked like the top. The only place to go from here would be down. Still, flattery was what the Hartfords of this world understood. They could never get enough. That was what drove them on. To excuse any disrespect in his earlier laugh he added, "I couldn't imagine anyone I'd rather sell to."

Nobody had mentioned money, but then nobody had picked his nose.

Robert watched him with hawklike eyes. Was this the moment to mention it?

His gut said yes.

"How much are you looking for, Francisco?" said Robert casually. He paused. "From a friendly buyer, like myself."

Livingstone sipped at the champagne, rolling it around his mouth as if he were at a professional tasting. He swallowed, and he smiled as he watched the movie star bobbing like a cork on the sea of nervous anticipation. "Oh, I don't know, Robert. I'm not much good at things like that. Jack Douglas and Fred Sands say one thing, Drexel, Burnham says another. You know how it is. Who do you believe? The realtors or the banks? You pay everyone for advice, and the advice cancels itself out. What do you think it's worth?"

Robert laughed. It was the oldest trick in the book. It didn't matter what the sums were. You got the *other* person to come out with a price. "I don't know, what, a hundred million?" he said, after a short pause.

Livingstone knew all about the Hartford contract with Galaxy. Fifty-six guaranteed over seven pictures. Seven years? A bank would lend him around thirty on that sort of security. His net worth before the deal was probably ten, give or take a few. He could put up around forty million cash for his equity interest and raise a mortgage of an additional seventy-five. He wouldn't be able to afford any more than a hundred and fifteen million, and that would be stretching him.

"To be honest, Robert, I'm looking for around a hundred and seventy. It's a lot I know, but the Sunset's unique, isn't it? You couldn't build it, and the goodwill must be worth a third of that."

Robert Hartford's face was expressionless, but inside the sinking feeling had taken the bottom out of his stomach. Okay, so Francisco would drop from the asker, but probably not much more than fifteen percent. It seemed there would be a gap that financially he couldn't bridge.

"That's too much for me." Robert's voice was quick, matter of fact. Livingstone shrugged.

Robert Hartford stuck out his dimpled jaw. The blue eyes flashed and the famed nostrils flared. He leaned forward across the table and his suntanned fingers gripped the powder-pink cloth. "I'm not messing around, Francisco," he said. "I don't do that."

"Good heavens, dear boy, I didn't think you were for a minute. Lord no, never entered my mind. It's just that I owe it to my old age to get the market price, don't I? I know you understand that. You better than anyone."

Robert was not placated. "I don't blame your trying for a fancy price, but asking isn't getting. Frankly, the hotel needs a facelift. It's looking a little tired, Francisco. When you live in a place you see these things. A buyer would want to spend big bucks doing it up. I certainly would."

Francisco snorted his derision. "Oh, you would, would you? And are you quite sure your 'improvements' would *be* an improvement? You make marvelous movies, but I didn't know that interior design was a 'hobby' of yours."

"I'd have Winty do it." Robert floated the trump card onto the table with the innocence of an asp.

"Ah, yes. Tower. Yes."

Winthrop Tower, the taste arbiter of America. Winthrop Tower, the West Coast designer who had single-handedly shifted the style center away from New York, if not quite to Los Angeles then at least to some indefinable place in the middle. Tower was beyond reproach. If you didn't like his work, then you were wrong. It was as simple as that.

"You could get Tower to do it?" Livingstone had to ask the question. After all, he'd tried and failed on occasions far too numerous to remember, despite the fact that Tower had been living in the hotel for the past five years. "Sorry, darling, hotels aren't my thing. They're for living in, not designing," the designer had always replied to Livingstone's increasingly desperate entreaties.

"For sure he'd do it." Robert paused. "For *me*. We've been friends for a very long time," he added enigmatically.

Livingstone knew that. Tower was drawn naturally to a man as beautiful as Robert. Whether it was animate or inanimate, Tower loved beauty wherever it existed.

Inside the old man's head the glorious vision was falling into place. The Sunset, remodeled by the best designer in the world. The Sunset, a style Mecca, transformed by the hands of the guru into a work of extraordinary art. He might not own it then, but at least he would live to see it, and everybody in the world would always think of the Sunset as Livingstone's monument. Yes, that would indeed be something. He could even continue living there, powerless maybe, but rich beyond dreams and with the respect for the founding father shining in everyone's eyes. That would be better than an extra million or two in the bank and the horror of watching them tack up a cheap neon sign on the hotel tower.

Robert Hartford had just discovered Francisco Livingstone's weakness, but with the instinct of the born dealer he immediately backed away. He waved a dismissive hand in the air. "Anyway, Francisco. Enough of all this business. Let's enjoy our lunch. Keep me in mind, and if you can't face the other potential buyers then you know where to find me."

He picked up the menu that he knew by heart, and he studied it as he might the early box-office returns. But he couldn't resist the last word. "My God," he muttered, almost to himself, "old Winty would do an amazing job on this hotel."

"OMIGOD, MIRRORS," said Winthrop Tower, holding on to his forehead as if trying to keep his brains inside. "Why on earth do people want to keep looking at themselves? I mean, I could understand it if *Robert* walled his bungalow in mirrors. But the *Coriarchis*. It makes one wonder how on earth they keep their food down."

Paula fought back the blush, but it was hopeless. She shifted her weight onto the other foot, trying not to sink completely into the quicksand of the vomit-colored carpet. The very mention of Robert's name was more than enough to paint her red all over. Winthrop cocked an all-seeing eye in her direction. Colors were his thing. He never missed a change in one. "What-*ever* you do, dear, don't tip Antoine Coriarchi's butler if he brings you a drink. He's British. He'd be appalled. On the other hand you have my permission to tip Mr. Coriarchi. He's so obsessed by money he'd be thrilled."

"That's enough of that, Mr. Tower, sir. Any more of that an' I'll remind you what you said to that nice Mr. Stallone in the St. James's Club last night," said Graham cheerfully.

"*Thank* you, Graham," said Paula, as Tower groaned theatrically, and her embarrassment at the memory of her first meeting with Robert Hartford subsided. She had only known them all for a few weeks but already she was part of a team that shared private jokes, a boisterous camaraderie, and an easy acceptance of each other's strengths and limitations. But although Tower and Graham were now her friends, she couldn't help feeling somehow that the whole thing would soon be revealed as a gigantic mistake. She had landed on her feet so rapidly, and the memories of tragedy and despair were still fresh in her mind. She had no right to be there, standing beneath the monstrous oil painting of Corelli Coriarchi in the huge drawing room as part of a design team whose commission on this job alone would top three-quarters of a million dollars. She might have lucked out, but she still had so much to learn. The mirrors were a case in point. What was wrong with them? They made the vast room even bigger, and it was true that they were a rather yucky shade of gray and sported some nasty engraved twiddly bits, but she couldn't quite understand the global objection to mirrored walls. That was no problem. She would ask.

"Why are mirrors a no-no, Winty?"

"Last year, dear, and one tries to forget last year as hard as one tries to forget last night. Then of course they're faux, and we're off 'faux.' And they're pretentious, trying to give the impression that the space is bigger than it is.

We don't allow pretension unless it's *us* pretending, dear. What else? They're too easy. Much more fun to get light into rooms using lovely lacquers and glosses, and windows, and skylights, and Florida ceilings. I'm *definitely* going to bring those back. You probably had one in the Everglades, didn't you, sweetheart?"

"We didn't have electricity, let alone electrically operated ceilings."

"Good Lord, how did you keep the booze cold?"

"Mr. and Mrs. Coriarchi will be joining you shortly," boomed the butler from the huge double doorway. "May I get you something to drink?" He sounded enormously pleased with himself. His lip curled over the "Mr. and Mrs. Coriarchi" as if it was a subtle, but enormously funny joke. At the same time he managed to raise an eyebrow in muted disdain at the appearance of the trio in "his" drawing room. A footman had shown them in and he, as head servant, was viewing them for the first time. Mr. Tower he knew, and approved of. The girl, however, didn't look at all at home. Very pretty, but definitely an outsider, in those odd beige trousers and funny brown jacket, and those hilarious old shoes. The other one was definitely a servant. It took one to recognize one. It took one to despise one.

"I'll have a glass of champagne," said Winthrop Tower, adding no non-sense about "if you have any," "if you have a bottle open," et cetera.

"Miss?" Again the surreptitiously witty delivery.

"I'll have a root beer, please," said Paula.

"A root *beer?*" said the butler. His mouth was open. He was incredulous. Had Paula asked for a glass of piss he couldn't possibly have been more appalled. "I'm very sorry, 'miss,' but we don't have any . . . such drink . . . in the house."

Paula's face registered the direct hit. She deflated visibly before the su-percilious servant's eyes. "Why on earth not?" said Tower, peering ostenta-tiously around the room. "You seem to have stocked up on most of the other disgusting things."

"Miss Paula'll have a Coke," said Graham quickly. "I'll 'ave one, too." He was acutely aware that the butler had rumbled his lowly status and had no intention of even *offering* him a drink.

"Very well," said the now thoroughly disgruntled servant, as he withdrew from the room.

"Imagine having to live in the same house as a butler with a personality that could ice champagne," said Winthrop loudly at the Englishman's disap-pearing back. "Apart from wanting to look at themselves in mirrors we must now add masochism to the list of the Coriarchis' perversions."

Paula could have sworn that she saw the Englishman's back wince.

"What's that about our perversions?" said Corelli Coriarchi.

She stood there in the doorway, where the butler had been, and more than anything else she looked like the cracked crab salad they served at the Bistro Garden. Her skin was faintly pink from an injudicious and halfhearted exposure to the vicious August sun, and she had chosen to clothe herself in variations of that color. A pastel pink chiffon scarf hid the scrawny neck and clashed exuberantly with the darker shade of the unfortunate suit. She wore stockings that themselves glowed pinkly, and her large feet were crammed into frankly orange shoes. Blood-red talons, layer upon layer of some plastic material almost certainly developed in the space program, were the claws, and her hyperthyroid eyes bulged menacingly from a small, pinched face. Her upper lip said "electrolysis time" quite clearly, and her hair, tortured, maimed beyond retrieval by years of wicked chemical warfare, would have settled gratefully for being straw. Pendulous bracelets, solid gold, platinum, and silver, drooped from her undernourished forearms, a potent testament to her strength and determination rather than to her irrelevant wealth.

If she was cracked crab, the man who stood by her side was crème brulée. He'd gone the whole hog on the sun. His skin was baked mahogany brown, George Hamilton-style, as if he had been attempting suicide and had chosen skin cancer as his method of self-destruction. He wore a seriously unpleasant cream suit, a red shirt, and in the hairs that sprouted from its open neck a hilarious medallion nestled complacently on a thick gold chain. He looked Levantine, and indeed he was, his mighty fortune founded on the sale of very cheap movies to cheaper people. Despite his burnished exterior, his whole persona reeked of an almost unnatural softness, a sort of sybaritic hedonism, and it was quite certain that inside the caramel-coated brulée the texture of his crème would be just right. When he farted, thought Winthrop Tower, there would be absolutely no noise at all.

But it was the frightful wife who wore the pants, and right now the expression on her face said that she was going to give them an outing. She had caught the "decorator" in an unguarded aside. Now she would make him pay for it.

Her expression was quizzical, almost haughty. She wanted some kind of explanation.

Winthrop Tower looked her right in the eye. "I was just saying," said Winthrop evenly, "that living in this house, and employing that butler, indicated that you must derive a certain pleasure from pain."

Paula's hand rushed to her face to cram the laugh back inside. Graham tried to keep his mouth straight. Tower stared pugnaciously at the Coriarchis.

It was simple. Either they could take offense, and Tower and his employees would walk there and then—or they could pocket their pride, and be allowed the privilege of paying the best interior designer in America three-quarters of a million dollars. The debate raged in Corelli Coriarchi's eyes, as the neutral smile flitted backward and forward across the face of her husband. It didn't rage for long. She had tried to score a point, and she had been outgunned by a far higher-caliber social confidence. And she had been left an "out." It would be possible—*just* possible—to write the Tower remark off as a joke.

"Ha. Ha," she said rather than laughed.

"Ha. Ha," agreed her husband.

"Good," said Winthrop Tower. "May I introduce my assistant, Paula Hope. She'll be working closely with me on the design."

Mrs. Coriarchi edged forward in a curious sideways approach that gelled perfectly with her crab persona. She extended a claw toward Paula as if probing a possible piece of food. Paula shook her hand, but the fish eyes evaded hers, circling instead to fasten on Winthrop in an expression that said she was going to make one last attempt to even things up. "So young," she said to Winthrop. "Has Ms. Hope had a lot of experience?" Her eyes swiveled back to take in the absence of Hope heirlooms, the dubious appearance of the Hope wardrobe, the slightly scuffed leather of the Hope loafers.

"Good God, I hope not," said Winthrop. "Experience is the name we give to our mistakes."

"Ha. Ha," said Antoine Coriarchi mirthlessly. "Oscar Wilde."

"He got it from me," said Tower without missing a beat. "So you've decided to do away with the 'work' of poor Hugh Gates," he continued, flourishing an expansive hand to take in the safe-but-sorry California oatmeal/ficus/abstract painting school of interior design.

"How clever of you to recognize Mr. Gates's work," said Antoine Coriarchi in an attempt at reconciliation.

"Oh, we designers are like dogs," said Winthrop. "We recognize each other from the smell of the messes we leave behind."

"You don't think you can work around the existing design," tried the male Coriarchi.

"Work around it? Work around it? Good God, don't you realize this stuff is *dead.* It's crying out for a decent burial." He stalked over to one of the two Greek-style mock columns that flanked the doorway in a pretense at holding it up. He pointed an appalled finger at it. "Do you know what we call that? We call it a Gates post. And do you know its only use? To piss against when you're too drunk to make it to the john."

Mrs. Coriarchi took one step backward. She couldn't take much more. But with the steely determination of her breed she was not going to let go of her objective.

She had dragged her husband halfway across the world to America, and she had chosen Beverly Hills because it was the only place in the whole country that remained vaguely grand while at the same time quite definitely preferring money to class. Now she was here, but a few million dollars later she had still not arrived. Winthrop Tower would change all that. If he could be persuaded to "do" her house, to take her money, then she stood a good chance of graduating to be insulted by a superior brand of person. It was that glittering prize into which she had sunk her bonded teeth, and she was not about to let go. "I'm not feeling very well, Mr. Tower. If you'll excuse me, I think I'll go and lie down. Antoine can deal with everything. He knows what I like."

"Fine," said Tower, removing a glass of champagne from the silver salver that a footman, not the butler, had offered him. He made no reference at all to the supposed Coriarchi indisposition.

"I hope you feel better," said Paula.

"*Thank* you, dear," said Corelli Coriarchi. With a flick, sniff, and a pout she was gone.

Antoine Coriarchi poured himself across the carpet. "Where do we start?" he said.

"With the cash," said Winthrop easily. "Just like the movie business."

"We don't get to explore your ideas for the house to see if they're compatible with ours?"

"That," said Winthrop Tower, taking a deep gulp of the champagne, "would be an exercise in futility. I can tell you here and now," and he peered, horrified, around the room, "that our tastes will *not* be compatible. It is because you have zero expertise in this area that you are buying mine."

Paula could hardly believe her ears. In the Everglades Coriarchi would be either a murderer or the coward of the county by now.

"I suppose I wouldn't expect you to know how to make my movies," he managed at last in a desperate attempt to excuse his abject lack of pride.

"Good," said Winthrop. "I'm glad we've got that settled. Now, what happens is this. You pay me a design fee of two hundred and fifty thousand dollars, half now before I give away all my secrets and half on submission of the detailed design scheme. In addition I pocket thirty percent of the wholesale cost of the entire job. You get a house designed from top to bottom by me." The "with all the social benefits that such a deal implies" was unspoken.

Tower chuckled inside. It was far from the way he usually did business, but this was different. The Coriarchis were beyond the pale, and he had decided to take the job for the money, not because he needed it but because he *felt* like it. In this life it was vital to practice one's whims. They were an antidote to old age.

Normally Tower's relationship with a client was not nearly so autocratic. It didn't have to be. His godlike status in the design world meant that he could pick and choose who he worked for, or rather with, and he insisted that all his customers have at least the rudiments of taste. Conflict over his suggested schemes was rare, because a filtering process had occurred before he was actually hired. People came to him because they had seen his work, liked it and admired it—either in the shelter books (*Architectural Digest, HG, World of Interiors*) or in the homes of friends. Already, therefore, there was invariably some form of meeting of the minds before the design schemes were submitted and discussed. At this point Tower would meet several times with the clients and form an impression of the sort of people they were, of their artistic psychology, of the type of life they led. Did they own a billion cats? Then, detachable slipcovers for the sofas and chairs. Did they spend all their lives watching TV in bed? The concealed video systems and bedroom cabinetry could set them back a quarter of a million dollars. Were they grand entertainers with a wide circle of friends/enemies? If so they would be given imposing vistas, expensive art, drawing rooms like aircraft hangars. Did they like to hide from the world surrounded by clutter and the wife of the moment in dark wombs? In which case he would provide them with textured fabrics, rich colors, deeply subtle lighting. The Tower Design schemes were works of art all by themselves, and some had already changed hands for money at Sotheby's in New York. There would be hand-painted room interiors, intricate cards showing swatches of materials for the curtains, the carpets, the sofas, the chairs, glossy color photographs of pieces of furniture and paintings, intricate line drawings of the innards of closets, the fine details of cornices and moldings, diagrams of hydraulically operated hidden TVs, mobile walls, sliding panels. There would be examples of the vitally important details, the door furniture, the light-switch panels, the covers of the electrical boxes, things that lesser designers ignored.

The client would be allowed to pass judgment on the design scheme, and within reason, and more important "within taste," modifications would be made. Rigidity was not a Tower problem. If there was more than one way to skin a cat there were an almost infinite number of ways to design a room. The limit was the border of his artistic vision, and he hadn't reached it yet.

The Coriarchis, however, were a different kettle of oily fish. It was quite possible that they had never set eyes on a single example of his work. They had hired him for his social cachet, for his vaulting reputation, the way people sometimes gravitated toward infinitely grand designers like Henri Samuel (Rothschilds, Wrightsmans, and, oh dear, Gutfreunds), Mrs. Henry Parish II, a.k.a. Sister Parish (the Kennedy White House, the Duke and Duchess of York), or Mark Hampton (everyone else). What the Coriarchis wanted was not a beautiful environment but a rocket up their drooping social life. In exchange for giving them that, Tower would exert upon them maximum artistic discipline. Like unruly, rude, and ill-educated schoolchildren they would be taken severely in hand. They would be given what was good for them, and by God they would like it.

He smiled to himself because there was one more reason he had agreed to take the Coriarchi commission. He was going to leave it to Paula. He'd supervise her closely of course, but basically the job would be hers.

"You'd like the check now? Right here?" asked Coriarchi in a gloomy voice.

"That's right. Then we can get cracking."

The moviemaker mooned over to a large, almost certainly fake, Queen Anne walnut bureau, peddled, definitely, by the dreadful Gates as the real thing. He wrote out a check for $125,000 and, walking back, his shoulders sagging, he handed it to Winthrop, who peered at it suspiciously.

"Now I'll tell you what, old luv, why don't you potter off and administer to poor Mrs. Coriarchi while I take my rescue team on a lightning tour of the disaster area. We can leave the bedroom until another time. Don't worry, we'll find our way around. Shouldn't take more than half an hour." He waved his champagne glass in the air like a flag ordering the troops into line. "Come on, gang. We come to bury Gates not to praise him," he chortled. "Death to the California style. Onward to designing glory."

He set off at a brisk trot, Paula and Graham hurrying behind, as Coriarchi slunk from the room.

"Always start in the hallway," he said. "Back to the front door. Actually it's better to stand *outside* the front door and look into the house through it, but we'll stand here rather than on ceremony."

The trio stood crammed together, their backs plastered against the fussy carving of the massive mahogany front door.

Tower winced theatrically. "Well I'm glad I did *that*. Graham, make a note to scrap this terrible, fussy door. I'll have scenes from the rites of spring imprinted on my back for weeks.

"Okay, Paula. Away you go. What are we going to do with all this, short of bulldozing it?"

The white marble hallway stretched away toward the "Gates post" columns that flanked the double doors leading into the drawing room. To their left a wide corridor ran for about a hundred feet before joining at a T junction with another corridor, which crossed at right angles to it. The top of the T, they all knew, contained the bedrooms, which looked out over a sumptuous pool to a splendid city view of Los Angeles. The wall on either side of the passage was dotted with an untidy arrangement of assorted ultramodern prints, predominantly homegrown California artists—Ed Moses, Billy Al Bengston, Bob Graham, Richard Diebenkorn.

Paula swallowed. How had Emily Carstairs told her to do it? "First you have to look, dear. But much more important, you have to see. Clear all the rubbish away. Block it out. Look at the space. Feel the architecture."

"Well," she started hesitantly. "I think it would be wonderful to open up the ceiling, and let some sunlight in. Then I think the marble floor is too severe, and too white against the white walls. I'd . . . maybe . . . leave the marble at the edges but perhaps scoop out the middle and inlay some oak boards, quite dark, if we had the skylight. I'd carry that floor design through to the cross bar of the T where the other passageway meets this one. Then, where they meet there could be an alcove . . . square I think, and rather classical with a fine piece of Renaissance sculpture, big, male probably, and carefully lit from below, with the natural light coming in on it from above."

Winthrop Tower's smile was that of the proud father for the winning child.

"Wonderful. Perfect. And your metaphor?"

"What do you mean?" said Paula, pleased but bemused.

"Dear God. You do it, but you don't know it. It's scary. It frightens me. The cross," he said.

"I still don't get it."

"Dear girl . . . Christ on the cross is your metaphor. Crucifixion actually took place on a T bar. You've put in the dark wooden bars of the cross. You've hung a godlike figure at the intersection. You've made it open air. It's out-of-this-world brilliant. And you didn't know. I really don't think you knew what you were doing."

Paula saw it at once. He was right. There was a unifying theme to her design suggestion, and it was religious.

The wise old eyes were on her now, boring deep into her, proud but also vaguely suspicious. "Okay, Ms. Superdesigner. Own up. Where did it come from? Where did you learn all about inlays, and Renaissance statues, and mixing textures like wood and stone? You didn't learn that in the Everglades. They don't know about things like that . . . in . . . 'Florida.' "

"Oh, but they do," said Paula. "My best friend in the whole world knew all about those things, and we both lived in the swamp."

"What friend?"

"Her name was Emily Carstairs. And she was a drunk. A lovely, wonderful, kind old drunk, who taught me everything she knew about design. She worked in New York once, and then she sort of dropped out, and she ended up living in Grand Cypress."

"Emily Carstairs . . . ? Emily Carstairs . . . ? *I* remember Emily Carstairs. She had a store in the nineties on Madison. Wonderful fabrics, and a few bits of odd furniture. Must have been fifteen years ago. God, we all used to go in there and steal her stuff from her. No idea at all about what to charge. She used to drink more than I did. She'd fall asleep on an ottoman in the store window and forget to lock the door at night. You could see her in there sleeping as you motored past. And although that shop was on the edge of the civilized world, she was never robbed. Can you believe it? It used to shake my faith in the evil of the human race."

Paula laughed, thrilled to find that her new friend had known her old one.

"That's my Emily. She could fall asleep in the middle of a sentence. Well, she lived in the Everglades. She taught the art class in the school at Placid, and I used to just about live at her house, going through all her books, and her drawings, and listening to her stories. I guess that was where I learned whatever it is I've learned. She used to fascinate me. You know what she used to say about gin. 'Gin doesn't destroy your art, it just destroys your ability to profit from it.' "

Tower laughed.

"It may be true about gin but I haven't done so badly at turning a buck on scotch."

"*And* the rest of it, Mr. Tower."

"That's enough from you, Graham. We're talking about *art* here." He turned back to Paula. "What happened to dear old Emily? Is she still in the Everglades getting the mosquitoes plastered?"

"No. She died nearly two years ago."

"Oh, I'm sorry."

"So was I. Devastated. But she was longing for it. 'So exciting, dear, don't you think, to find out the answer to *that* one,' she used to say to me." Paula mimicked the patrician Bostonian nasal twang.

"Know what she meant. Know what she meant. Hell sounds like great fun. Not so sure about heaven. Not at *all* sure about that. Oh, and talking of hell, are you organized for Livingstone's ball tonight? You know he's calling it a black ball and everyone has to dress in black. Can't think where he got the idea from unless he's just had mumps. You can get that in the balls you know, and they go black and drop off." He paused deep in reflection on the serious subject of Livingstone's potential testicular problems.

"Oh, Winty, you are dreadful. Livingstone's a lovely old man. People give white balls. Why shouldn't he give a black one? Anyway, yes, I am ready for it. I picked up a great dress at that store you told me about on Rodeo."

"Wonderful, darling. Wait till you see mine!" laughed Winthrop. Then his expression went wicked. "Can't wait for the rematch," he added.

"What rematch?" But Paula knew. The color high up on her cheeks said so.

"You and the bellboy, dear. The one on seven million a year. Whatsisname. The actor. Tip of my tongue. Made a movie or two." He smiled wickedly.

"Oh God," said Paula, her heart thumping suddenly in her chest. "He won't be there, will he?"

"Oh yes, he will. I promise you that. And I'll tell you something else. He'll be all over you like a hot rash, or I don't know Robert Hartford."

"He won't remember me." How could you dread a thing you hoped for?

"Yes, he will. Bellboys *never* forget good tippers."

"Winty, *stop* it! God, how awful! That was the very worst moment of my life. I mean . . . should I go and try to apologize? He must have thought I was such a hick."

" 'e thought you was beautiful, Paula." There was a trace of bitterness in Graham's voice. At Tower's ribbing of Paula? At the memory of Robert Hartford's eyes?

"Yes, Graham, I'm sure you're right. I do believe he would have thought that, darling, and I'd advise a chastity belt beneath your pretty black dress, although the last time I looked for one of those in Giorgio they'd been out of them for some time."

She gestured as if to hit him, but he ducked away from her.

"Listen, you two, I'm off to track down the rest of that champagne. You don't need me. You and Graham wander around the house. He'll take notes for you, dear. See you later."

He was gone. Paula and Graham were alone.

"Blimey," said Graham. The boss was on form today. " 'e's a brutal little bugger isn't he?"

"You'd better believe it."

A different mood had descended. It was as if Winthrop had been the sun and had darted suddenly behind a cloud, plunging the world into shadow. Or was it Graham's undiluted presence that had cast the subtle gloom? There was an intensity about him when they were alone that was not apparent when he was locked in his role as the Tower foil, the straight man to his master's voice. It was difficult to pinpoint, a brooding, know-what-you're-thinking camaraderie that Paula found unsettling, yet very real. When she was alone with Graham, Tower's irreverent jokiness faded into illusion. Possibly he was a brutal little bugger, but he was a pastry-cake pussycat compared with the brutality of the world, the brutishness that *she* knew about, that Graham knew about, too. She was ashamed now of her flustered little-girl act when she had confronted the thought of meeting Robert Hartford again. Did she honestly care what some movie star thought of her? How could she stoop so low, she, Paula who had seen her brothers burn before her eyes? How could she play the pathetic film fan at the idea of being confronted by Robert Hartford at Francisco Livingstone's silly, frothy "black" ball? The frivolity she had allowed herself mocked the solemnity of the sacred memories.

She tried to say it, but it wouldn't be said. There was no way. She waved an impotent hand. "Sometimes I wonder how I got here . . . I mean . . . after everything . . ."

"Yeah. I know, doll."

They both knew that. It was the thing they had in common. They couldn't talk about it, but they were joined in the conspiracy of those who had experienced genuine poverty. Not the cosmetic kind—one TV, an ancient car, and no holidays—but the real, dreaded thing. The cold for Graham, painful in his damp bones; the East End flat with its leaking roof and the outside khazi down at the end of the backyard through the dripping, stinking eel boxes, its walls lined with frozen corrugated iron. The mosquito-laden heat for Paula, sucking at her sweaty skin, as it turned her mind to fire and her soul to cinders, unrelieved by air-conditioning or the electric fans that the merely poor enjoyed. Dirty clothes, shoes that couldn't keep the outside out, Christmas and birthdays carefully and cruelly spaced-out reminders of the nothing that they had, of the nothings that therefore they were. And the hunger, worst of all by far, the rumbling anxiety in the pits of stomachs that didn't know the feeling of enough and only knew the desire for more. There was no nobility in such suffering. It didn't make you fine and admirable as you learned to survive. It made you mean, and vicious, and callous, and insensitive. It made you angry, and tense and nervous, and fearful. You could think only of escape, and of the blood of those who stood in your way, and you longed and wanted with a terrible intensity that the haves of this world would never, ever understand. And worst of all, the poverty and the suffering lived on to plague you in the land of plenty. There they were standing in the middle of one of the richest houses in the richest town in the richest country in the world, and yet the poison of terminal deprivation still coursed like venom through their veins. So poor Mrs. Coriarchi's feelings had been hurt, and Tower had insulted the porno-movie millionaire, and Paula had thought of an imaginative way to blow some of his ill-gotten gains. So what? At the end of the day, so what? Because the only thing that really mattered was that neither Paula nor Graham would ever, ever have to go back to the places they had been. No word had passed between them, but in the fellowship of the damned it hadn't had to. It was the kind of thing that eyes spoke about far more eloquently than tongues.

For a second they watched each other, daring to think back, their memories horrified yet fascinated by what once they had been.

Paula broke the moment. She smiled wryly. "Come on, Graham. Let's get to work." And then, her smile lightening, brightening—"And Graham . . . let's pretend it's ours."

— 8 —

WHY IS LIVINGSTONE giving a ball, Dad?"
Robert Hartford winced despite himself. The word *Dad* could do
that to him, because although he was one technically, he had never *thought*
of himself as one. That had always been his problem with Kristina. He loved
her deeply but in his own special way—a way that was light-years from normal paternal affection.

"Francisco's been giving balls all his life in this town . . . They help
decide whether you are dead or alive socially. Some people find it useful to
know."

Robert Hartford peered at himself in the mirror. The famed annual Livingstone ball at the Sunset Hotel had black as its theme this year, but he
hadn't really bothered about that. He never did. A dinner jacket was black, so
were a bow tie and a pair of velvet slippers. About the only concession he had
made to the "black" party spirit was a double-breasted waistcoat his father
had always worn. Even now he could visualize it, slung across the back of a
chair in the sitting room of another dim distant bungalow in the same hotel.
The rest of his father's clothes would be in a heap around it, and in the
bedroom the gentle moans of some soft-skinned dream would be the evidence that his father was "entertaining." Robert smiled as he remembered
him. He, too, had never been a "dad."

"Did you know this is your grandfather's waistcoat? Whenever I saw it
hanging over a chair, I knew he was on the job in the bedroom."

"That's gross, Daddy." Kristina Hartford didn't mean the rebuke, and
there was laughter in her words. Just to make sure he didn't get it wrong, she
shook her short blond hair and let him see her smile in the mirror.

Robert smiled back.

"You look good, Kristina. Very beautiful. That dress is perfect. Is it Chanel?"

"Thank you, Daddy," she said. "You look pretty good yourself. And how
do you know about things like Chanel?"

396

"It's my business to know such things." Then he laughed. "No, really. I may not be much of a father, but I still pay the bills."

It was true he never had been much of a father. Most of her life Kristina had been brought up by the mother that Robert himself could hardly remember. His marriage to the famous actress hadn't survived the fact that he had become better box office than she—that potent reason for Hollywood marriage breakdown—and she had slunk off to the East Coast, taking the baby Kristina with her.

Now, he walked over to his daughter and he put his arms around her waist, and he felt her melt in them, with all the love she had never had, with all the love he didn't know how to give her.

"Oh, Daddy, it's so great to be with you, sort of *properly*. Not just visiting. Thank God, UCLA accepted me."

He squeezed her to him, but even as he did so he was uncomfortable. He could feel her breasts against his chest, firm and hard, and her tiny waist, and the heat of her and the glorious smell. Christ! Why couldn't he be like other people? They experienced normal emotions like warmth and tenderness and sympathy. They empathized and they comforted, and they used tough love, all the myriad of decent human feelings that made parenthood possible, and allowed children to be childlike. But he had only one means of communication. He could speak only the language of sex. It was the sole emotional dialect that he could understand. Already, he had felt her respond to the siren call of his sexuality. Everybody did. The animals did. The flowers did. The servants were always remarking on the fact that flowers lived twice as long in his rooms as in anyone else's. The guilt coursed through him and merged with satisfaction in the soup of his ambivalence. He could do it. Always. He had it. But it meant he was a failure while he was winning, a freak at the pinnacle of his success, a loser at life in the middle of the endless victories of lust.

There was a gentle knock on the door. "Who is it?" he called out.

"It's Joe, sir, with the drinks you ordered." The disembodied voice of the servant wafted into the bedroom.

"Okay, Joe, I'll be right out. Wonderful." He patted his daughter lightly on the bottom. "Go and say hello to Joe, darling. He'd love to see you."

Kristina smiled wryly at him. "Don't be long," she said.

In the bedroom Robert Hartford stood back to admire himself in the mirror, and the vanity began to smooth the worries away. He practiced a smile, and then another, and then one that merged with a little frown, before springing back again. Yes, it was all there. The tricks were packed away in the box ready for use. He would conjure his way to what he wanted. He would use his magic to win the Sunset Hotel.

Since the Star Room lunch with Livingstone he had thought of little else but the hotel and the buying of it. That was why he was going to the party. In the ordinary way he wouldn't have bothered. Parties were politics, and he floated above that in the Milky Way where the serious stars lived. Tonight, however, it was different.

Without naming names Francisco had intimated that there was another bidder in the wings. That might be a negotiating ploy, but if it wasn't then it was more than likely that the rival would be at the ball, and Robert would be on the lookout for someone who appeared to be dealing in ulterior motives. The sultan of Brunei, maybe, always a great buyer of up-market hotels. Or it could be anyone of half a dozen megarich wheeler-dealers like Perelman, Merv Griffin, or Donald Trump, who were into buying quality, uniqueness, and prestige wherever they could find it.

He straightened his tie. What he needed was one of Joe's cocktails to get him into the party spirit. Kristina's enthusiasm already had him heading in that direction.

Robert strolled casually back into the drawing room.

"Joe, how are you? You're looking well. Who is Livingstone allowing you to make drinks for this evening?"

It was an in-joke. Joe had been the barman at the Savoy in London under the immortal Harry Craddock of *Savoy Cocktail Book* fame, until Francisco Livingstone had spirited him over to Beverly Hills. Now he occupied an illustrious position as adviser to the barmen at the Sunset Hotel, and as cocktail maker to Mr. Livingstone himself. On special occasions such as this Joe was allowed to wait on carefully selected guests. The whole hotel had been taken over for the party, and the rooms allocated to out-of-towners or to L.A. residents who preferred to stay the night rather than drive home in the small hours. It was a potent symbol of importance to be allowed the services of Joe.

"Good evening, sir. Thank you, sir. Well, sir, I've been to Mr. Tower sir, of course. I always do him, as well as yourself. And a Mr. Trump, sir. He's from the East Coast, I think, sir. Some sort of businessman there, I'm told. Then, Mr. David Plutarch over in bungalow nine. Apart from Ms. Streisand, that's about it, I think, sir. Isn't Miss Kristina looking beautiful? It's been ages since I last saw her."

Kristina blushed as Joe held the silver salver out toward Robert.

"What have you got here, Joe?" Robert put the drink to his nose. "Peach juice. Gin. Cointreau. Angostura?"

"Nearly sir, nearly."

He tasted it, and as always the elixir lifted his spirits. It was an extraordinarily delicate cocktail, the balance perfect, colder than ice, its top still frothy. The fresh fruit harmonized perfectly with the alcohol, bittersweet, strong, and satisfying.

"How did Harry Craddock say you should drink a cocktail?"

"Quickly, sir, while it's still laughing at you."

"Well, it's certainly a pleasure to obey him," said Robert, downing the delicious drink. "Who is in Mr. Tower's party?"

Normally Joe would be the soul of discretion, but Robert Hartford was Sunset Hotel family. So was Winthrop Tower.

"Just that man who does for him, Gordon is it." The old servant wrinkled his eyes up in distaste. "Oh, and a *very* pretty young girl, sir. Absolutely gorgeous, in a very stylish dress. She was ever so nice, sir. Miss Hope I think she was called." Joe knew where Robert Hartford's interests lay.

"I've met her. You're right, she *is* beautiful. The last time I saw her she tipped me ten bucks."

"She did what?" Kristina exploded her disbelief.

"Surely not, sir," said a scandalized Joe.

"Yes, she did. She put it right in my hand, after I'd helped Winty upstairs one evening."

"She's very young, sir," said Joe. He'd really liked the girl.

"I think she sounds absolutely divine." Kristina laughed.

"She thought I was a security man, or something," said Robert thoughtfully. "Anyway, she's going to the party?"

"Oh yes, sir, she is. Looks like a film star, sir. More than the real thing."

"If you're nice to her, perhaps she'll slip you a twenty next time. I don't know how you struggle by on your income," teased Kristina.

"Mmmmmmm," said Robert absentmindedly. "Joe, be an angel and do me another one of these in about ten minutes, could you. Oh, and while you're here could you bring out some canapés. The room-service people put them in the refrigerator a little earlier."

They were alone, sitting opposite each other across the glass table with its neat piles of blue bound scripts, its Waterford bowl full of floating gardenias, its exquisite Rodin bronze.

"Is Galaxy really paying you seven million a picture, Dad? That's what they say on campus."

Robert tried to put on his weary "it's only money" expression, but it didn't quite come off.

"Yes, as a matter of fact they are."

She leaned forward, and clasped both hands around her face. "That's *amazing.*" Her enthusiasm didn't quite ring true. Kristina wasn't very interested in cash. Too tangible.

Robert Hartford felt the sudden surge of adrenaline. "Actually, it *is* rather amazing. Shall I tell you why? Do you know what I'm going to buy?"

"A fantastic estate."

"Well, yes and no. I'm going to buy the Sunset Hotel."

"You're not! I mean, I heard a rumor it was for sale, but . . ."

"I can't afford it? Apparently I can. My accountants have been over the figures, and my business people say it will be a disaster, but they all agree I can do it. The bank's falling over itself to lend the money. No creditworthy people left in America apparently. The Galaxy contract I've just signed is better security than any of their Third World loans and most of their farm ones. In the worst scenario, if I default, they'll end up owning a totally prestigious asset that's worth more than money in the bank. They say I can afford to bid a hundred and fifteen million, if I gear myself up to the hilt."

"Are you going to *do* it?"

Robert sipped deep on the drink, as Joe reentered. He took a carefully rolled brown-bread-and-smoked-salmon canapé from the tray and popped it into his mouth.

"Yeah," he drawled, "why the hell not?"

"When do you bid?"

"When the moment's right. The credit lines are open now. The offer document is drawn up. It's just a question of dealing with the psychology. I think there's going to be some sort of announcement tonight."

He put a surreptitious finger to his lips. Joe wouldn't know what they were talking about. He'd been out of the room when he'd mentioned the hotel. It was best to keep it that way.

"My *God,* it's the most exciting thing I've ever *heard,* Dad. Can I come and work for you? I'd do anything. PR. Accounts. The linen."

"What, and drop out of UCLA?"

Immediately he relented. Responsible father was not a favored Robert Hartford role. "Yes, of course you could come and work for me. *With* me. You're my only child. Part of it would be yours."

Kristina clapped her hands together in glee. "I just knew this whole weekend was going to be exciting karma," she said. "The sun and the moon are in a tight relationship with Jupiter any minute now. That means it's make-your-mind-up-time for Pisceans."

"You don't believe all that crap."

"Of course I do. Everyone does. It's a new age dawning, Dad. Ultimate knowledge didn't end with the sixties."

Robert groaned out loud. He'd forgotten that side of Kristina. The problem was that the sixties hadn't ended with the sixties.

"Don't knock it, Dad. It's commitment time for Virgos, too. Maybe you'll meet a woman who isn't just a tooth on a circular saw."

Usually Robert couldn't stand jokes like that, but now he laughed. He was in a good mood that wasn't just a sexy mood. It was going to be fun. He was taking his only daughter to a ball, like the best father in the world, and there was a hotel to buy, and an old boy to sell it. Maybe Kristina was right, and Virgo was rising or falling or whatever. And, at the back of his mind, there was something else. The girl with the proud, sad face who'd paid him ten bucks to go away because she was tired, and she hadn't known what else to do.

He stood up. "Come on, you," he said cheerfully. "Stop making fun of your father, and let's go to the party."

THE SWIMMING pool at the Sunset Hotel had been transformed into a steaming caldron of Hades. Smoke rose from it, and the surface bubbled with tantalizing menace, as if it longed only to claim the black-and-midnight people who clustered around it. Occasionally, through the mist, loomed one of many huge black swans, its back alight with candles. For a moment or two each would hover, partially visible in the constantly moving vapor clouds, before disappearing once more into the darkness.

The orchestra, too, was consumed by smoke, but the music transcended it. It reached out into every corner of the ghostly gathering, trembling, rising, falling, swooping onto the ears of the guests, filling them up with delicious dread, and touching their quivering spines with fingers of ice. It was Wagnerian in its grandiosity, rococo on Gothic on baroque, and as they sipped nervously on their '79 Perrier-Jouët Rosé champagne everyone agreed that Francisco Livingstone's black ball was exceeding expectations.

The sweet scents of the night flowering jasmine and the gardenias argued that this was in reality paradise, not hell, but the flaming, fiery torches that hung from the darkened fan palm trees allowed the exotic myth to live, as they painted anxious shadows on the faces of the partygoers. And there was something else out there on the lake.

A figure of unearthly gloom was ferrying his boat across the sulfurous surface of the water. He was stooped, cloaked in black, and his face was hidden beneath the wide brim of his hat. About his movements there was an otherworldly weariness, as if he were doomed forever to ferry souls in torment to the burning gates of external damnation. Now, suddenly, he burst into song, and his words filled the music of the orchestra as they sank into the psyches of all who listened. It was a magnificent voice, powerful, compelling, a cry from the heart, the message of the collective unconscious demanding that it be obeyed.

> "Come to me now, now that life here is ending,
> Come to me now, now the death knell is sounding . . ."

"It's so *spooky*. I mean, that guy is just wonderful. How do they get all that smoke?"

"Dry ice, luv. Packed on wooden platforms on the swans' backs. They've each got little clockwork motors underneath." Graham answered Paula quickly, as if he had been waiting for her to speak.

"God, Francisco's really gone for it tonight, hasn't he? Looks like he's practicing for the Grim Reaper. Hellfire, damnation, and purgatory. Deals with the devil. It's just like Spago on a Thursday night," said Winthrop Tower.

They stood on the edge of the crowd, a party within the party, thoroughly enjoying themselves.

Especially Paula. Unbelievably, she felt she had a new home. Certainly she had a dear new friend. By day he was kind, charming, and infinitely wise, and he moved through the world of interior design on a cloud of brilliance that everyone recognized and all respected. At night the alcohol would unleash the poet in him and for a while his wit would sparkle and he would declare unconditional war on hypocrisy and the tawdry values of the society in which he had chosen to live. Then, usually quite suddenly, he would go over the top, and at lightning speed it would all be over. Next morning, however, he would be back on line, a little rueful maybe, mildly apologetic, but hard at work in the business he had elevated to a fine art form.

He had kept his promise, and Paula knew that she had more than fulfilled hers. He was teaching her everything, and she was storing the information away and merging it with her uncanny natural eye to excel in every area of the trade. Together they trolled what "antique" shops L.A. possessed and they talked to the cabinetmakers and the fabric manufacturers, and they went through swatches and sat down with architects, and they endured endless sessions with bemused clients.

But if Winty was a joy, Graham was an enigma. Only one thing was for sure. He had become very interested in her. His eyes never left her, and when she caught them she couldn't help but recognize their burning intensity. She liked him, but his quicksilver moods unnerved her, and often his gaiety seemed merely a cover for darker feelings that blackened the water around the tip of his emotional iceberg.

> "So death takes all, and life bows down to serve her,
> In black we die, and in despair we surrender . . ."

The hellish gondolier's voice sailed above the crowd.

"Dear, oh dear," said Winthrop. "All this talk of death is giving me the most *marvelous* appetite. *Such* an underexposed topic. How very *clever* of Francisco."

"Hello, Winty, gloomy enough for you?"

"Hi, Kelly, sweetheart. Yes, darling, I'm feeling incredibly optimistic about it all. Death's so reassuring, isn't it? Imagine the *horror* of endless life. It'd be like that torture, you know, when they won't allow you to sleep. Have you ever done a transatlantic economy class?"

Kelly McGillis had done several. In the days when she'd been a waitress. Not anymore. "Do you think there's anything *wrong* with Livingstone?" she asked.

"Nothing that death can't fix, dear."

"Winty!" they all chorused.

"Well, all I can say is that I hope this isn't the last party he ever gives," said Winthrop. "This is the fourteenth I've been to, and I can't remember any of them, which is the ultimate test of an excellent host."

Francisco Livingstone's parties at the Sunset Hotel were legendary and when they happened, Hollywood talked of nothing else for weeks before and didn't change the subject for weeks afterward. It wasn't just the inventiveness of the food and drink, of the bands, of the exotic themes and the superb timing with which they were stage-managed.

The real action was in the guest list. It wasn't a total disaster not to be invited. But then earthquakes weren't total disasters, and there were those who maintained there could be life after nuclear war. Leprosy, the Greenhouse Effect, Black Monday were all examples of things that *could* be survived, and so life went on after the Livingstone invitations had failed to arrive. Shrinks, however, saw their income spike upward, and post-office workers encountered a whole gamut of the strangest emotions in the month or two that preceded a Sunset Hotel ball.

The European invitations would go out first, followed ten days later by the East Coast ones. Finally, four days later, out would go the invitations to the ones who cared the most. To minimize nervous breakdowns they would be posted simultaneously at the baroque Beverly Hills post office on Santa Monica Boulevard. Then the trouble would start. As anxiety rose, fueled by unkind calls from "friends" in Europe and New York, the tougher and more desperate wives would contact Livingstone's office, to wonder if their invitation had "gone astray" because of their "change of address," or whether it had been among the batch of mail destroyed that very morning by the dog. This was L.A., so the guest list was an infinitely mobile one. Old friends were safe, but meritocrats were judged on merit, or rather box office, it being Hollywood's idiosyncratic tendency to confuse the two. This was why everyone cared so much. To be a new invitee meant you were on the way up. To be culled from the list meant you were dying if not dead. Thus the absence or presence of the black engraved card on the hall table had potent messages for the future. It told you what you would or wouldn't be able to afford, who might or might not cut you dead at the hairdresser. There was one rule, and it had only been broken twice. The list would be neither added to, nor subtracted from. Princess Margaret, passing through New York from her house on Mustique, had once been added at the request of Drue Heinz, a mutual friend of hers and Francisco's. She had been one exception. On another occasion there had been a call from a Beverly Hills psychiatrist ringing from the house of one of his patients. He had been trying to talk her down from the roof. The only thing that would prevent her suicide would be a Livingstone invitation. Francisco had thought about it long and hard before capitulating. No way, however, would she get away with the ploy again. Next time she could jump. From Elsa Maxwell, Livingstone had learned that in planning a guest list there was no place at all for pity, sentiment, or a sense of obligation.

The superb baritone was finishing his aria. His voice breaking with transcendental doom, he slipped away into the mists, to the thunderous applause of the partygoers.

"Paula! You're not going to have a glass of champagne? It's a '79. You ought to *try* it."

"Okay, Winty, if you think there'll be enough for you."

A waiter rushed past and Paula spun around to get his attention. "Would you bring me a glass of champagne?"

"With the tips you give, it would be a positive pleasure," said Robert Hartford.

He was standing beside her, so close they were almost touching. He leaned in closer, and his eyes were dancing with her. She could smell his warmth, she could sense his heart, she could hear the things his body was saying to her.

I've thought about you. I've remembered you. In bed at night I have dreamed of you, he was saying. You've been to my secret places, and walked in my forbidden cities, and I know you and you know me, and we will know each other.

His seductive power lasered in on Paula. In his sultry gaze there was the ultimate intimacy—quiet, intense, targeted solely at her. Despite the crowd, they were alone, communing together in the first sweet moments of the thing that could be love. She did not know what to say, but it didn't matter. Now she realized that he had been with her every moment since their first meeting, as his sex-ray eyes told her she had been with him. Somewhere just beneath the surface, they had been joined together.

He put out his hand and he touched her arm, and she fought back the desire to hold on to him, and to pull him toward her, and admit to the world what was going on.

But the world already knew. As they recognized the moment, nobody spoke. Winthrop Tower saw it through the prism of ambivalence. Kristina saw it, warped by the spectacles of daughterly possession. Graham felt it, like a knife in his heart.

"We haven't been properly introduced," said Robert.

"Paula Hope," said Paula.

"God, I thought you two had met. Now, where on earth did I get that idea from? Paula, this is Robert Hartford, the man the Lord created with women in mind."

Winthrop Tower's introduction was way too late. "You know the good Graham, our friend from across the water," he added.

Graham's nod was curt. Robert's was curter.

"*Omigod,* now I know who you are. You're the girl who tipped my dad," said Kristina suddenly.

Color rushed into Paula's cheeks. At the memory of her faux pas, at the far more unsettling reference to Robert Hartford as a "dad." The blonde could have been her sister.

"I didn't recognize him!" Paula's response was *not* an apology.

"Where have you been *living?*" Kristina's incredulity was cunning. She said it with a laugh that hid most, but not all, of the scorn. "You're a hick," she was saying. Now, Paula's only real escape would be to say something about how there was no law about people having to recognize Robert Hartford. To her dad, who'd made it his life's work to be totally recognizable to everyone in America, that would be bad vibes. She would have succeeded in driving a wedge between them. Such a move was out of character for her, but she only had one father, and this girl was *startlingly* beautiful.

"There's no law that says I have to be recognized," said Robert with an incredibly lazy smile. "Maybe Paula's had more important things to do with her life than paint her nails, watch movies, and generally carry on like an empty-headed mall Val with an inexhaustible supply of plastic."

"No, Kristina's quite right. It was incredibly naïve of me, and anyway I *have* seen most of your movies. I just never expected to meet you. Not then, not ever."

She held out the olive branch to the defeated daughter without thinking, without any ulterior motive, just at the sight of her crestfallen face.

Her reward was Kristina's look of surprised gratitude. "What sign are you?" asked Kristina.

"Taurus," said Paula warily, not entirely convinced that the attack was over.

"It's a good time for you. There's only the moon in your sign this month. And there's a brilliant aspect between the Sun and Neptune."

"Oh," said Paula, wanting to say "thank you" but feeling somehow it would be inappropriate.

The Hartford eyes were probing her deeply. "Now that we more or less live under the same roof we can go *on* meeting each other," he murmured.

"Yeah, on an' on an' on . . ." said Graham. He made it sound cheerful, but his cockney cockiness was heavy with sarcasm.

Robert half turned toward him, his eyes blazing with anger, but there was nothing that could be said. Graham stared evenly back. They knew they were rivals now.

"I'd like that very much." Paula ignored the bad feelings that had swirled up like the mists over Francisco Livingstone's swimming pool. She was still in psychic touch with him, and, in the delicious metaphysical clinch, she didn't want to let go. They were getting to know each other at lightning speed. She was tuned into him and already she felt like a lover, quivering at the brink of him.

Winthrop Tower understood it all. Graham had fallen hard for Paula. That Tower could live with. Robert Hartford, however, was something else. He specialized in making women unhappy, *after* the most blissful happiness of all. Nor could Tower control him. Nobody could. If Paula was sucked into the whirling Hartford girl pool, which looked far more than likely, she might easily drown. As her protector, he wasn't about to allow that.

"Robert, what's all this I hear about the hotel being for sale, and you being a potential buyer?" he said quickly.

It was the only thing that could have broken Robert and Paula's communion. Robert had wanted badly to have this conversation with Winthrop, and now the best thing of all had happened. Tower himself had brought the subject up. "If I bought it, would you redesign it?" Robert went straight for it. His gut told him it was the thing to do.

"If I had a choirboy for each time Francisco asked me to do that, dear, I could have the 'Hallelujah' chorus whenever I snapped my fingers."

"But what if *I* asked you, Winty?"

Winthrop laughed, as the spray of fine charm wafted over him. It *would* be different if Robert asked him. He had known and liked him for years. Francisco, however, was from an older generation. One of the things he had learned in the design business was to pick out the clients who would be potential trouble and those who would not. Livingstone would have been trouble. At every stage of the design process he would have resisted change. He would have given up the old with the greatest difficulty and he would have resisted the new with every fiber of his being. Despite the fact that intellectually Francisco Livingstone knew that Tower would transform the Sunset into a design masterpiece, emotionally he would not be able to deal with it. Robert, in contrast, would let him get on with it. That was the only way he, Tower, would ever agree to take the job.

"I'd say a definite 'maybe.'"

"How would I get you firmer than that?"

"One of your famous candlelit dinners for two, sweetheart."

He struck the famous Tower hand-on-hip pose as he laughed outrageously at the double entendre. So did everyone else. Laughed, that is.

"No, come on, Winty."

"I'm coming, sweetheart, I'm coming. Don't rush me. Not at my age!"

More laughter.

"You'd have carte blanche."

"Loo seats to lampshades?"

"Finger bowls to toothpicks."

"And Paula is my design assistant on the entire job, working as liaison between us?" said Winthrop, quite unable to resist the temptation.

Then an amazing thing happened. Robert Hartford began to blush. The twin spots appeared like headlights on the sunburned cheeks, but then they became bloodstains spreading out to cover his entire face. He put a finger in the neck of his shirt, and he looked down in confusion, as if completely dumbfounded by the alien feeling that had suddenly overcome him.

To those who saw it, it was remarkably charming, so much so that Winthrop actually wondered whether it was a secret weapon, a newly unveiled armament in Robert's constantly expanding romantic arsenal. If so, then he should learn how to duplicate it on the screen. He would have been showered with Oscars.

Still staring at his shoes, Robert mumbled, "Well, that's settled then," and he looked up again at Paula.

A crashing, booming noise reverberated over the loudspeaker system. "Dinner is served," intoned an extravagant English accent.

"Saved by the gong," said Winthrop Tower.

He hurried off, encircling Graham's elbow in the classical older man's steering grip, bearing his servant away with him. Somehow Kristina was sucked into their wake.

Robert didn't move. Neither did Paula.

"I'll enjoy working with you," said Paula. Her cheeks were rosy red as she spoke, and the smile she wore lit up the words. It was as far from the traditional remark at the end of a successful job interview as the moon from Mars.

He didn't answer at first. He simply turned the light of his countenance upon her. The blue of his eyes, surreal, hypnotic, shone bright beneath the hooded, lazy lids, and his mouth softened at the corners in a smile that was a million miles from humor. He leaned his head to one side, in a gesture that said his whole mighty concentration was focused exclusively on her. He appeared to be about to speak, and the smile that wasn't a smile seemed to broaden as his whole face shone with an otherworldly warmth.

Their silence was an island in the middle of a sea of noise, and although no words were spoken they were speaking at the most fundamental level of their being.

Paula swallowed hard as the magic moment wrapped her up.

She knew what she was doing. She was falling in love. With the most famous movie star in the whole wide world. It was crazy. It was mad. It was deeply wonderful.

When Robert Hartford spoke his voice was low, husky, frighteningly intense.

"We're going to be lovers," he said.

⸺

THE GREAT banqueting hall at the Sunset Hotel had never looked so evil. It was like a black hole sucking you into its ghostly intrigue and delicious spookiness. The Georgian central chandelier was still there, the one that had adorned the ballroom of the Duchess of Richmond at her dance before the battle of Waterloo. From all around it, huge areas of black damask swooped out in folds to tent the entire ceiling. It formed the walls, too, and at strategic points flaming torches burned, sending tongues of flickering light dancing across the smooth oak of the floor. Thirty tables, each seating ten, were clustered at one end of the room, their tablecloths black, their Wedgwood Colonnade bone-china dinner services milk-white and black, their centerpieces Waterford crystal bowls of floating gardenias in which Rigaud candles drifted on rafts of midnight blue. The scent from the flowers was heavy in the ethereal air, and from hidden loudspeakers the soft strains of the poolside death aria reminded everyone of the theme for Francisco Livingstone's extraordinary ball.

The atmosphere of another world, however, had not entirely succeeded in diverting the Hollywood elite from the priorities of this one. They wanted to know who else was there and what this meant about *their* status.

Everyone knew that these days the A-list/B-list grading system for L.A. parties no longer applied. The old guard—the Gregory Pecks, the Charlton Hestons, the Lew Wassermans, the Ray Starks, the Robert Stacks, the Irving Lazars—were slowing down and staying home while the new party people— the Marvin Davises, the Leonard Goldbergs, the Deutsches, the mighty Quinns, the proud peacock Tartikoffs, foxy Barry Diller, artful Doug Cramer, Mr. and Mrs. Barbara Walters, the revivified Sue Mengers, Princess Zsa Zsa von Anhalt, and the increasingly more beautiful and vivacious Cristina Ferrare and her husband, Tony Thomopoulos—couldn't replace them. New blood was required, and the name of the up-to-date game was to fill one's parties with a judicious balance of up-to-date people who were strangers to Beverly Hills. So, apart from the new and the old party people, Livingstone had invited top rock band Guns N' Roses; George Bush's brother, Prescott Bush, who had been a fellow Whiffenpoof of Winthrop Tower's at Yale; Michael Crawford, soon to open *Phantom* in L.A.; top black Jesse Jackson;

top gun Tom Cruise, and top party bikers Justine Bateman and boyfriend Leif Garrett, who'd pitched up on their Heritage Harley. Culture was catered for by beautiful Baryshnikov, the other coast by Tom Wolfe, and couture by the dashing Kleins. It being Beverly Hills rather than New York, everyone who'd been invited had turned up, and now they were all marveling at the "mix."

But if being invited to the Livingstone party meant that you had jumped the first hurdle into the inner sanctum, there was still a final fence to be negotiated. Those who had at last relaxed on the invitation obstacle were now experiencing varying degrees of adrenaline surge as they confronted the placement one. At which table were you sitting? And with whom?

Believing, with the divine Elsa, that a good host should treat his guests like children, no matter what their age, Livingstone had erected a huge blackboard at the entrance to the room with a diagram showing the position and seating arrangement at each table. Around this oracle of triumph or doom, three hundred of the most important people in the entertainment business were crammed like Japanese commuters waiting for a train. Livingstone had expected that. That was why the blackboard was so big. It had taken him two glorious weeks to plan the seating of his guests, fourteen spite-filled days in which old scores were settled and new alliances cemented. He had not shrunk from the incendiary task. He was too old and powerful for that. Instead, he had reveled in it. Former partners in feuds, sour business deals, marriages and dissolutions (Beverly Hills's new word for divorce) were stuck mercilessly together, on the principle that high tension provided party energy. To add insult to injury, the tables were named shamelessly from one to thirty, and it didn't take a professor of mathematics to work out which one was the most important . . . and which the least.

Robert Hartford stood back from the milling crowd. The hand on his elbow confirmed that he had been right to do so. It was Martin, an assistant manager at the hotel. "You and Miss Kristina are at Mr. Livingstone's table, Mr. Hartford, sir. If you'll follow me, I'll lead the way."

All around the room this little scenario was being repeated. The real movers and shakers were holding back. Barbra Streisand didn't look at blackboards. Nor did the Armand Hammers, the Mike Ovitzes, or the David Plutarchs of this world. Sunset Hotel employees had been surreptitiously detailed to look after the people who weren't used to anything else.

The first table, Livingstone's, was in the middle nearest to the dance floor, and apart from the fact that it wasn't actually raised on a separate dais and lit by multiple spotlights, it was quite apparent that it was the place to be. Livingstone was already there, standing proudly behind a chair. He made little waving gestures of greeting to Robert Hartford.

"Robert, my dear chap, glad you could make the arduous journey. And this must be Kristina, who I haven't seen for *far* too long. You used to sit on my knee, m'dear. Oh, yes, a long time ago. Robert, you're over there, one away from me, and Kristina, you're three away from me on the other side.

Yes, that should do it. A billionaire on each side and you the filling for the sandwich. Dear me, *isn't* this fun?"

Robert peered over the table. There were no name cards. Both his dinner companions remained a mystery. In the normal way that would have been irritating, but potluck at a Livingstone party was like a lucky dip in which all the tickets scored Rolls-Royces. Who would it be? Whoever was immediately to Francisco's left would be good business, good fun, possibly both. He was enjoying himself. It was a wonderful party, and the face of the girl called Paula still lingered hauntingly in his memory.

"Ah, there's Barbra. Darling, don't you look divine? How did a poor old wreck like me end up sitting next to a goddess at his own party. My, my, isn't this just fantastic."

Barbra Streisand did look divine. Wearing a Scaasi dress, yellow diamonds, her hair piled high by Victor Vidal, she sat down in the pole position on Livingstone's right like the genuine superstar she was.

"And there's David. You found us. Good. Next to Barbra, old boy. You two know each other of course, and I'm sure you both know Robert, and his daughter, Kristina. David Plutarch made his fortune by keeping us in touch with the heavens, or was it the other way around? Stellar communications of one sort or another anyway, which means he should get on well with Robert and Barbra. Ha, Ha! Yes! Ah, there you are, my dear. Another of our great communicators. In between myself and Robert, please. Do you all know Caroline Kirkegaard?"

She hovered above the table like a genie released from Aladdin's lamp. She, too, wore a tuxedo, but there all similarities to the men's dinner jackets disappeared. The Donna Karan creation flowed over shoulders rendered even more than usually massive by rounded pads. The silk facings were curved as well, but it was all but impossible to notice their cunning shape because of the vision they framed. From her long bare neck to the slash of her belly button, Caroline Kirkegaard was exposed; from the edge of one melonious breast to its rock hard companion she was visible. The great expanse of delicious whiteness was in dramatic contrast to the jet black sheath of the "dress" that stuck to her body, defining a gigantic double hourglass— the top of which nipped in at the waist, the bottom one at the knees. Her Hemingwayesque lashes and brows were emphasized with mascara, and her drowning-pool eyes, under- and overlined in vivid amethyst, sang in tense harmony with the powerful red coromandel of her lips. Despite the stylish sophistication of the Chanel makeup and the fashionable inventiveness of the couture evening dress, the nervous fallout from her presence settled over the table like radioactive dust.

Robert Hartford took an involuntary step back, recoiling from her. Livingstone was motioning her down beside him. She was an honored guest at the top table in the room. Caroline Kirkegaard, whose fledgling movie career he had personally ruined. Caroline Kirkegaard, who had apparently risen phoenixlike from the flames of the defeat he had engineered, to a position of undoubted power once again. Since the Destiny meeting he had walked out

of, her squalid little cult had gone from strength to strength, but what the
hell was she doing *here?* With him. With Barbra Streisand. With Livingstone.
With Plutarch. The thoughts stopped there as the man who majored in passion read the neon eyes. Plutarch! He was watching Caroline the way the
bewitched watched their mistresses. There was hunger in his look, and a
slavelike devotion mixed in with the pride of the possessed for the possessor.
It was plain for all to see. David Plutarch and Caroline Kirkegaard had,
through the workings of the devil, come together, which meant that now she
stood close to his billions, to his power, to his possibility.

Robert took a deep breath. He was caged with her for a couple of hours.
There was no way he could walk out. Not on Livingstone, at this time. It
would not be forgiven, and the thing he so desperately wanted would be
denied him. Livingstone's table placements were notorious for their cruelty,
but why Kirkegaard next to him? Did Livingstone, who knew everything,
know the story? And if so, what wayward perversity had encouraged him to
thrust them together?

"Now, Caroline, I'm not sure that you have met Barbra and perhaps you
don't know Robert Hartford, because I think this is the first time you have
been to one of our little get-togethers. We have David to thank for that."

"Hello, Robert," said Caroline Kirkegaard.

There was amusement in her voice, the amusement of the surpriser for
the predicament of the surprised. She flicked her head down, looked hard at
her chair, and Robert reached out toward it and pulled it back for her.
Immediately he was aware of what he had done. He had behaved with reflex
gallantry toward a woman who must be his enemy. Somehow she had
"made" him do it. The first point was hers. The second wouldn't be.

"Not since *Angels in Heaven,*" he said.

"Yes, you destroyed my acting career, didn't you, Robert? All by yourself.
But perhaps you did me a favor."

She turned on her smile at him—unfazed, seemingly unfazable.

With the curiosity of the connoisseur he tried to work out what he felt
about her. Physically, she still repulsed him. She was too hard, too tough, too
menacing. He didn't bear her much personal animosity. He had dumped her
from the movie because he found her vibrations deeply unsettling, because
her charisma made her a rival, and because he had wanted to exercise his
power and his hypocrisy at the same time. Exercising those were as much a
part of making it in Hollywood as the money and the fame.

"I was surprised to see you at one of my meetings. In this very room,
wasn't it?" said Caroline. Again she smiled serenely, and the message was
clear. The past was ancient history, "forgotten" not forgiven, by a person who
had moved on to bigger and better things. She had audiences of her own
now, and people like Robert Hartford sat in them.

"Yes, my daughter dragged me along to it." He paused for the putdown:
"She's going through an impossible stage. I was able to resist the message."
The last sentence dripped sarcasm.

"I'm glad there aren't many like you." She smiled an enigmatic smile. Their eyes locked in combat.

She leaned forward to reach for a glass of water, and her cleavage opened wide. Robert's eyes crawled right in. He couldn't help it. Neither, on Caroline's other side, could Livingstone.

"What's all this I hear about you selling the hotel, Francisco?" said Barbra Streisand.

"Ah, Barbra, you've preempted me. I was going to make a little speech about it after dinner. You know how I love to 'say a few words,' and it would quite spoil it if I let my secret out of the bag too soon."

"Well, all I can say is that if it *is* for sale then someone very sympathetic must buy it. I couldn't *bear* it if it went to some faceless hotel chain." She beamed around the half-empty table for potential buyers with taste.

"Now, why doesn't nice Mr. Plutarch buy it? I'm sure he wouldn't change a thing and we could all keep coming back as if nothing had happened. We could even embalm you, Francisco, and put you in the lobby, and then, each night when we went out to dinner we could stroke your foot for good luck like they do the statue of the horse in the Hôtel de Paris in Monte Carlo."

An icy silence descended on the table. Plutarch studied his linen napkin. The half smile of the Sphinx played around the lips of Caroline Kirkegaard. Robert Hartford's sensuous mouth was pencil thin across his face.

"Or, Robert, what about you? You live here. You must love the place as much as anyone, and now that you're so rich, couldn't *you* buy it? I think that would make *so* much sense, don't you, Francisco? I mean, Robert's a part of your décor around here. It would be like selling the hotel to itself."

The silence got even colder.

Francisco Livingstone's laugh was gentle, but not entirely kind. "Just in time, Donald," he said, as he stood up. "Barbra is auctioning my hotel here at the table, and you're just in time for the bidding. Ivana, how lovely you look, as always. Now, I know everyone knows the Trumps, because the Trumps know *everyone*."

Caroline Kirkegaard did the math. The table was approaching the four-billion-dollar mark. It made her feel warm inside, the more so because nearly three billion was hers. Plutarch was hers. He'd caved in more comprehensively than she had dreamed possible, and after the fun and games with Kanga in bungalow 9 he wanted more and more. He was fascinated by her, dangling on her sexual hook, like a recently hanged man. She had asked for the hotel, and he had promised it to her, but even in his obsession his business sense had not totally deserted him. He would retain a controlling interest and nearly all the money would be borrowed against the asset of the hotel itself so that his own downside risk was strictly limited. How much would it cost? So far Livingstone hadn't named a price, but at the meeting the three of them had had the night before he had intimated that there was another serious bidder. Caroline didn't necessarily believe him, but she was worried, and the warmth in her gut at the proximity of so much money was tempered by anxiety that Donald Trump could be just the sort of person to be interested in the hotel. He owned hotels already, casinos in Atlantic City and the Bahamas; his recent acquisition of the Plaza in New York, the mention in his book *The Art of the Deal* that Ivan Boesky had once offered him the Beverly Hills Hotel. The Sunset might fit well into his empire. It was prestigious enough, and more than anything else the high-profile developer dealt in prestige.

Behind the Trumps were the last two guests, and in many ways they were the most surprising of all, because they were totally faceless. Nobody had the remotest clue who they were.

"Now, last but not least," said Livingstone, with the barest and most subtle indication that here *were* the least among the gathering, "are Henry and Freda Cox of Cox, Cox and Playfair, the very best attorneys on the West Coast, in my humble opinion."

Everyone arrived at the same conclusion at once. Livingstone was going to sell the hotel. The buyers were at the table. So was his lawyer. Could it be conceivably possible that the deal was going to be done here, now, in the middle of dinner in the Sunset ballroom?

Francisco's next remark did little to dispel the speculation.

"I have an idea," he said as ten silver tureens packed tight with beluga caviar hit the table simultaneously, and as ten waiters leaned forward to pour Stolichnaya vodka from bottles frozen into foot-square cubes of ice.

"Why don't we play a little game? We go around the table, and we all say what we would do if we owned the Sunset Hotel. How we would change it. How we would do things differently. Oh, I forget. I don't get a turn. I *do* own the hotel, and of course I'd change nothing!" He laughed pleasantly. "Barbra?"

"I'd throw out all the guests and have the whole place running exclusively for me. A staff-to-guest ratio of about four hundred to one would suit me fine."

They all laughed at that. Some with relief. At least *she* wasn't a serious buyer.

"Caroline?"

"I'd bring the Sunset triumphantly into the New Age. I'd hold Destiny seminars here, and spread the word to the other guests until everyone was caught up in the excitement of the future, the glory of the past, and the infinite possibility of the present. It would grow and grow until it was the center of the universe, the paradise for the brave new world that I know will come to banish all sorrow and to bring new hope to humanity."

"David?"

"Caroline has just said what I would have said had I the power and the knowledge . . . and the brilliance." Plutarch's face gleamed with wild enthusiasm as he spoke.

"Ivana?"

"I'd keep it just as it is, as you would, Francisco. If it ain't broke, don't fix it."

"Thank you, my dear. I can't believe you really mean it, because I know you have wonderful ideas about interior design, but thank you anyway."

"Donald?"

"Gambling in California? I don't think the economy needs it, do you? Now, Florida . . . that's another question entirely. No, I think that the California game is real estate. I'd buy it, hold it, get someone good to run it, trade it. The money'd be safer than in the Bank of America, if I didn't have to pay too much."

"Henry?"

"I have to be very careful what I say . . ." Lawyers often started out like that. "Because I'm the only one at the table here who couldn't afford it." He got a bit of a laugh, but heavy hitters didn't laugh hard and long at lightweights' jokes. "I guess I'd just soldier on, and hope that Livingstone didn't open up down the street. In fact I'd have a clause in the purchase contract about that."

His wife wasn't asked. "Kristina?"

"I'd give it to my father," she said at last, but her eyes were fixed on Caroline Kirkegaard as she spoke. All around the table there was a little ripple of applause at her generosity.

It was Robert's turn. He tried to separate the fact from the fiction. Was this just games, or was Francisco in earnest? It was difficult to say. Would his speech be important, or just meaningless chitchat at the whim of a cunning, courtly old man? He paused, sipped pensively at his vodka, and his voice was quiet when at last he spoke.

"I'd have Winthrop Tower draw up plans for a total rebuilding and redecoration of the Sunset Hotel," he said, "and I'd build a house for Francisco on the grounds and make it part of the agreement that he remained in a consultant's capacity until the day he died."

"And boy, would you be praying for *that*," whispered Caroline sotto voce.

"I didn't think you believed in death," he shot back out loud.

"It's a transition."

"Can it," said Robert rudely.

If Francisco Livingstone had heard the interchange he chose to ignore it. He sat there like a bird on a perch, a wise old owl, and the spoon of caviar hovered at his blue-tinged lips. He was deep in thought.

"Moonies, loonies, bucks, and bores," he said at last to no one in particular.

There was ragged laughter. Everyone, with the egos of the supersuccessful, imagined he was being rude about someone else.

Caroline felt the excitement build within her. Francisco was going to sell for sure, and the other serious buyer was almost certainly Trump. She knew as much about the New Yorker as anyone else, but no more. One fact stuck in her mind. He liked to buy assets cheap, from sellers who were hurting. He was a patient man who would wait for years before striking. Plutarch, however, was a different sort of businessman. He saw a deal and went for it, happy to pay over the top now for something that he truly believed would be worth much more later. Trump would come in low, and wouldn't chase it because there were hundreds of other irons in his fire. Plutarch, awash with cash, and besotted by her, would pay Livingstone his asking price or damn near it. And as for Robert Hartford, well, she had never thought of him as a joke before. He might be a power in Hollywood, but he wasn't serious money. He was out of his league at last, a dilettante movie star with delusions of grandeur and sexual complexes that made Don Juan seem as psychically wholesome as an astronaut. It would be more fun than she had had in years to dump on his Mickey Mouse dreams, if indeed he dared to entertain them.

She took the caviar fast, rolling it around her cavernous mouth, and her eyes sparkled their encouragement at the bankroll across the table.

She turned toward Robert, eager to patronize the man who had so capriciously destroyed what she had once wanted more than anything. Intuitively she knew where he would be weakest. "Is that your daughter across the table?" she asked.

"Yeah."

"She's a lovely girl, isn't she? We had a little talk earlier, out by the pool." Robert turned to watch her, the way he would a serpent.

"Yes, she is." His voice was flat, noncommittal. "Who introduced you?"

"She did. She's been to more than one of my meetings, you know."

"Yes, I gather they're very profitable. You should be proud. Cash from weakness. Money from losers." Immediately he regretted his last words.

"And is Kristina a loser, Robert? Surely not."

"My daughter has no money of her own, Caroline."

"Just a rich, doting father."

"Do you see much of *your* family, Caroline?"

Twin specks began to glow high on the alabaster cheeks. She laughed, but there was no humor in the sound. "Touché, Robert. Yes, families are difficult, aren't they, when one wants things so badly."

In the silence they both called the truce. Happy families was a game that neither of them had played. Somewhere back in Scandinavia, there would be a Kirkegaard family—proud daddy, sad mummy, a Kirkegaard boyfriend, husband, child? There, in some safe suburb she would have existed for a while and then, when lofty ambition soared above the dreary status quo, it would have been make-your-mind-up time. To stay or not to stay? Was it nobler in the mind to batten down and heave to on the sea of promises and responsibility, or braver and better to take up arms against dull decency and fly away? She had chosen flight. So had he. That made them allies against mediocrity at least, and it made them both sinners against themselves and against those who had trusted and depended on them. Robert had often wrestled with the dilemma. There was only one life to lead, and for so many the question had become not how did you live, but how would you die. For such people the future was the place, and the present merely the valley of the shadow, where you made your dispositions, and did the right thing, and hoped that in some far-off one-day world you would be repaid for your sacrifice.

Or there was his way, Caroline's way. Their goal had never been safety, security, the absence of pain. Those things frightened them, because they clipped their wings and caged them. Robert's power was sexual. Hers was the force of her extraordinary will. They were oil and water, but together they dressed the salad of life. They gave it taste. They made people want it. They gave surrogate hope to the dreary survivors. They were the soapiate of the people.

She was thinking that, too. Her wry smile said it, and then, mysteriously, it changed until it was saying something else entirely. His antennae trembled in the path of her smile, and he couldn't help returning it to say he knew.

She was so big, so beautiful, so hard. She was a diamond, an icicle, a mountain peak in a cold, bleak range, and she would be incredible, this half woman, this half man, with her muscles and her madness, her cunning and her inventive cruelty. Could he have her? Just once—screaming for him, in the way some did. Could he throw her out, and hurt her badly for the crime of being like him? Could he exorcise the ghosts within himself by conjuring up her orgasm, and killing her with the weapon of his attraction?

"No," said her eyes. "But try, do try. We deserve that contest, and I will win and you will lose."

The caviar had gone, and so had the Dover sole bonne femme, flown in that day from the North Sea. And now, inexplicably, before the beef Wellington and the soufflé Grand Marnier, Francisco Livingstone was on his feet, and the major domo's booming voice was praying for silence.

"My lords, ladies and gentlemen, pray silence for your host, Mr. Francisco Livingstone."

Slowly the hum of conversation faded.

He stood there like some immaculate scarecrow, the kind some nouvelle society billionaire would buy for his King Edward potato patch.

His dinner jacket hung like a sentence of death from his scrawny shoulders, but it was as perfect a fit as Huntsman of Savile Row could arrange within the confines of good taste. His bow tie was droopy enough to reassure everyone that it was tied not clipped, and his perfectly plain cream silk shirt was what you would expect from New and Lingwood, the Eton tailor's shop, understated, devoid of horrible frills, and with a soft, deep collar. There were plain bone buttons down its front and pretentious studs were mercifully absent. The simple, worn links, eighteen-carat gold but wafer thin, were just visible at the cuffs that protruded from the sleeves of the dinner jacket he never, *ever*, referred to as a tuxedo. A cream silk handkerchief tumbled untidily from his breast pocket, and his ancient, patrician voice creaked as he spoke.

"Dear friends," he lied. "Dear, dear friends, thank you for coming to my party." He paused like a hound sniffing the track of a fox. "We have had so many of these balls, over the years, haven't we? Wonderful evenings. So much fun. Some of you have been to all of them. Others of you are marvelous *new* friends. But tonight, I am so very sad to say, is the last one of all."

The murmur rustled around the room like wind in the willows.

Caroline leaned forward in her seat, her lips parted in anticipation. Plutarch fought for, and found, her eye. Robert, too, was alert, a runner at the starting gate, waiting for the gun.

"What I am going to say now may surprise some of you. You may think I am being unnecessarily dramatic, and the last thing I want to do is spoil the delicious dinner that I planned for you, but here it is. I live alone. I am an old man. Funny as it may seem to many of you, I have no one to talk to and yet I have something very important to say. So I thought I would tell you all—all at once—all my friends who have made my life so very happy and the Sunset Hotel such a joy on this earth . . ."

Spit it out, thought Caroline.

"I went a while back to see my doctor, as I do from time to time, when the man at the bank says I can afford to go . . ."

They all laughed uneasily.

"And do you know what he told me?"

In the silence nobody knew, but a few had guessed.

"He told me I was dying."

"Ooooooooh!"

"Noooooooh!"

Mumble.

Rumble. The murmuring earthquake of shock and disbelief shook the room. Livingstone waited until the sound had subsided. When he spoke again his tone was cheerfully conversational. "In fact, he was quite specific. He said I had only a couple of years to go. Maybe three at the most."

Caroline Kirkegaard's eyes were alive with excitement. Across the table Plutarch's calculator mind was humming. Both had reached the same conclusion. He would sell fast to the man who could put the money on the table first. Plutarch fought back the compulsion to grab the old boy's arm and put in his bid then and there.

Robert Hartford was thinking what the others were thinking as his heart sank, and the prize slipped away from his outstretched hand.

"So I thought, as my little joke, that I would give a black ball, so that I could enjoy an evening of my own mourning. Not, perhaps, in the very best of taste, but it tickled my fancy, and when you haven't long to go one wants that tickled as much as possible . . ."

There was the odd nervous laugh. Francisco Livingstone's reputation as an eccentric was certainly being lived up to tonight.

"So, reluctantly I have decided to sell my life's work. I have decided to sell the Sunset Hotel. So wish me well, and bon voyage, and I love you all." Quite suddenly he sat down.

The tears rolled down Barbra Streisand's cheeks. "Oh, Francisco . . . I'm so sorry. I had no idea . . ." The others, too, struggled to find the appropriate words.

But Livingstone's hand was up. He was still in control and he wanted action. "Now, which one of you buggers is going to buy my hotel?" he said.

—

ROBERT HARTFORD's right hand was tingling, and his feet weren't touching the floor. He could remember the parchment touch, the arthritic fingers, the little squeeze that had said, "I'm pleased. I trust you. Don't let me down." And he chuckled to himself as he weaved among the black-draped tables toward his destination. All around him rose the flak of would-be friends, business acquaintances, former lovers, all united in their aim of deflecting his purpose. They bounced off him. He nodded and smiled and made little warding-off gestures with his hands, but he didn't stop, he didn't even slow down. It was too important. Things were far too wonderful. He had to find Winthrop Tower. He had to tell him he had just bought the Sunset Hotel.

The crowd around the tables was breaking up now, with the coffee and liqueurs, and people were beginning to dance to the Lester Lanin orchestra that Livingstone had flown in specially from the East Coast. Some of the tables were half empty, a few deserted. Where the hell was Winty? He was hardly a dancing man. He would be sticking tight somewhere to a glass of the genuine 1812 Grande Fine Champagne Napoleon Cognac that Livingstone was offering among the liqueurs.

There he was. Sitting all alone. Doing what came naturally.

"Winty!"

"Robert! Hello, old dear. Good God, what a bombshell! The old boy sure has balls even if they are black. Poor old Livingstone. The Big C, I imagine. Awful thing is, it didn't spoil my appetite. Amazing dinner. Didn't you think?"

Robert grabbed Tower by the shoulders. "Who is the owner of the Sunset Hotel?" he asked.

"Heavens, Robert, I didn't think you drank. I mean, not seriously. Mind you, I can understand the lapse from grace. The Haut Brion was out of this world."

"I am!"

"You are what, dear? Pissed? Yes, I can see that. Good for you. I've got about half an hour to go, if I can get them to bring me another cognac."

"Listen to me, Winty! Listen to me! I've just bought the hotel. I shook hands with Livingstone, in a verbal agreement witnessed by his lawyer. It's legal. I've done it. I'm the new owner."

In his mind the glorious vision danced. Plutarch had been the first to respond to Francisco Livingstone's bombshell when most of the others at the table had thought that the old boy was joking. "I would be interested in making an offer," he had said. "Do we know the price?" He had sat back, calm and confident in the certain knowledge that whatever the price was he could easily afford it, and he had smiled across the table at Caroline, his face reassuring, smug, totally at ease.

"I would like to hear your offer first, if you don't mind indulging me," Livingstone had replied.

"A hundred and sixty million cash."

Robert's heart had headed south as he had realized he could never match Plutarch's bid.

The Plutarch eyes had gleamed their triumph, as Livingstone had turned to Trump, but Trump had simply shaken his head from side to side.

"Robert?"

Robert had been aware of Caroline Kirkegaard's eyes upon him at his moment of defeat. "I can't match it," he had said, his head low, his spirits far, far lower. Across the table, he had felt Kristina's sympathy. There had been tears in her eyes.

"What would be your very best offer, Robert? I'd like to know."

A hundred and fifteen, he had said.

The old fox had smiled then, a slow, lazy, self-confident smile. "Subject to certain conditions, I accept."

"WHAT?"

The Plutarch/Kirkegaard question had not been a harmonious duet. It had exploded into the previously genteel dinner-table atmosphere, hers high pitched, piercing; his strangled, disbelieving. And it had been the wonderful beginning of Robert Hartford's first major nonsexual high.

Tower's expression said the message was beginning to sink in. "Robert, that's incredible. Were there other bidders? You mean he did the deal there and then, at the table?"

"You'd better believe he did. He was all ready for it. He had some lawyer sitting there. Plutarch bid a hundred and sixty million."

"Christ, Robert, you didn't top that?"

"I didn't have to. Livingstone told Plutarch that he wouldn't sell to him for a billion dollars. Didn't want the Sunset to fall into the 'wrong' hands. I thought Plutarch was going to have a fit."

"So, what'd you pay for it—if you don't mind my asking?"

"A hundred and fifteen million, with strings."

"Strings?"

"I, or my family, hold it for ten years minimum. Within a year you submit plans to redecorate and redesign it."

"I *do*?"

"You do. You shook my hand on it earlier, in front of that beautiful girl. . . ."

He looked around quickly. Where was she? He'd wanted her to be there to hear of his triumph.

"Robert, you're on. I said I'd do it. I'd love to do it."

"Where's your assistant?"

"Around somewhere. There, there she is. Over there with Graham. God, she's going to be thrilled."

"What on earth's the matter with her leg?" asked Robert.

She was limping. She'd hurt herself. He felt the concern well up inside him, and he was surprised that there was room for any such emotion at this the moment of his triumph. He walked quickly toward her, his worried look conflicting with her open smile of welcome.

"Are you all right? Have you hurt yourself? What's the matter with your leg?"

"Oh, that. It's nothing. I've had it since I was two. I had an accident. One leg's shorter than the other. It's no big deal. I'm used to it." She laughed to prove it.

"No, it's not," he said. "It can't be."

Paula looked puzzled. She didn't reply, but her expression was asking for elaboration.

"I mean, you can't have one leg shorter than the other. You can't have a limp."

"What do you mean, Robert?"

In the face of the question he wasn't sure. The women he liked were perfect in their way. If not perfectly beautiful, then perfectly powerful, or perfectly amusing, or even perfectly rich. He liked Paula very much—more than he'd realized—and she was supremely beautiful, so she couldn't possibly be . . . crippled. The word burst in his mind like a bomb, and he was completely aware of the wave of irrationality that had so suddenly submerged him. But the awareness didn't change anything. His intellect had been completely blocked by his emotion, and outside it was beginning to show.

"I mean . . . I mean . . . that you should have something done about it," he blurted out at last.

It seemed a wildly callous thing to say, but it was the way he said it that did the damage. There was disgust in his voice. The disgust of the aesthete for the ugly, of the clean for the dirty, of the virtuous for the sinner. His words meant that he was repulsed by her deformity, that he couldn't ignore it, that it actually made a difference in what he thought of her.

It happened so fast that everyone was astonished, but the pain and the hurt hadn't made it to Paula's eyes by the time Graham's lightning reactions allowed him to speak.

"Limps upset you, do they, Mr. Hartford? You look like you seen a bleedin' ghost. 'ad a friend once who felt like that about 'ospitals."

"No. I didn't mean that . . . I meant . . ." But he *did* mean it. The horror in his eyes said so. It was done. He had revealed the flaw within him, as he had beheld the flaw in her.

"I was going to ask you to dance," he said, and his hands splayed out to show their helplessness at the ridiculous inadequacy of his response, at its inevitability.

There was no way for him to make any sense of it. There *was* no sense. Only feeling. Only emotion. Only his naked self. So he backed away from her and then turned his back, and he hurried away through the tables, toward the big double doors, and in seconds he was lost in the bowels of the hotel he had so recently bought.

⟶

THE MUTED roar of the party wafted out into the scented gardens of the Sunset Hotel. It waxed and waned on the idiosyncratic night breeze, now loud and insistent with aggressive merriment, then muted, a soft, surrogate happiness blowing on the wind. Around Paula, however, the sounds of

Francisco Livingstone's black ball were crashing against a massive breakwater of solid misery.

She sat, still as a dancer in repose, on the weathered seat beneath the jasmine-entwined arbor, and the white, moonlit flowers seemed to weep in sympathy with her. All around her the black chiffon of the Mary McFadden skirt billowed out. Its folds, plucked by the warm air, danced up around the thick black suede belt and rustled about her ankles and the plain black Chanel satin pumps that until this evening had been her pride and her joy. She shivered with sadness, and despite the heat of the far from silent night, her skin was chilled beneath the skimpy material of the black camisole.

Next to her, formal, uncomfortable, like a suitor in a stilted play, sat Graham. As a concession to the "black" theme of the party he wore a frock coat, pinstripe trousers, a wing collar, and a black silk stock in an attempt at period style that succeeded only in making him look like a cockney music-hall villain.

"I can't believe what he just did," said Paula.

There were tears in her eyes and her voice broke, as she fought to hold it all together. All through dinner she had been thinking only of Robert. He had haunted her, and she had hovered on the delicious brink where intense physical attraction merges with something else. Now, distracted in the moon-softened darkness, she tried to tell Graham what she felt.

"It was weird," agreed Graham. He sat close to her, and his face was turned toward hers, his eyes wide with wonder at her beauty, with alarm at her agony.

"I mean, nobody's ever reacted like that before. Ever. It was as if I were a leper. He couldn't even look at me. You saw it, didn't you? It wasn't just me."

"It weren't just you, Paula." He spoke softly, as if he didn't want the words to hurt, and as if lowering his voice would take away some of the pain. But his sympathy for her was tinged with satisfaction. Hartford had behaved like a pig. It was quite extraordinary. His legendary sophistication and charm had vanished into thin air. He had hurt Paula badly, and she wasn't the sort of girl who would put up with that. It was an ill wind, and it had brought Graham luck.

"Listen, luv, forget it. They're all nuts here. They're not real people."

"I never think about it anymore—the way I walk. I've never thought about it. It's just there." She picked at the delicate material of the skirt, rolling it between her thumb and forefinger in a forlorn attempt to comfort herself. She had done that as a child, to the red satin dress her mother wore.

"I know, luv. I know. *I* don't notice it. There's too much else to look at."

"Sometimes my little brothers would joke about it, but they were just tiny kids."

Graham was instantly alert. All he knew of Paula's past was that there had been some terrible disaster, and both he and Winthrop had somehow known not to probe too deep. He moved closer to her.

"I never told you about my family," she continued. Her voice had a dreamy, disembodied feel to it. It was painted in sadness, but it was a sorrow somehow too fundamental for the obvious symptoms of grief.

Again Graham was silent. It seemed the most likely way to unlock the secret gates.

Paula gazed up at the stars twinkling in the satin sky, at the clouds hurrying across the complacent moon, as she looked for answers she would never receive. Was it time now, to let it out, to unleash all the horror? He liked her, this blue-eyed boy who sat beside her, and he wanted to know all the things she hadn't been able to bring herself to tell. She didn't make the decision. Somehow, like all the important ones in life, it made itself.

"I'll tell you about it, if you like. If you can believe it . . . if you can stand it . . . if I can . . ." said Paula, but she wasn't really talking to Graham anymore, she was talking to herself.

Graham's face was close to hers, close to the tears, and the soft regret, and the hatred that flowed from her as she told her story—told of the poverty and the happiness; of her dear, dead father and the struggle to bring up the twins; of Laura's terrible death and the holocaust that Seth Baker had wreaked on her little brothers; of the night her world had died.

She was dimly aware of his face, and now, as her cup of sorrow emptied, she noticed for the first time the extraordinary change that had come over it.

He seemed frozen, his attention absolute, but somehow he was separated from her by a wall of feeling that she couldn't cross. His eyes were without bottoms as they stared into hers, and his mouth, so often cheerful, was now a slit trench across his chiseled jaw. His brow was furrowed, and he leaned forward, his hand clasped tight against his thigh, his knuckles white.

"What did you do, Paula?" His voice was arctic cold; soft and deadly as he asked the question.

"It rained in the early morning, and they never sent the fire engine. But they sent a truck with two little coffins, and they pretended to find something to put inside them. It was funny, nobody seemed to mind very much."

"You didn't go to the sheriff?"

"Seth Baker owned Sheriff Mardon. Oh, I thought about it, as far as I could think about anything. But I didn't see him light the fire and it was dark, and he's important there, and I never was. . . . Maybe they'd even have blamed me. You know, what was I doing on the lake in the middle of the night. . . . And even if they'd believed me, and arrested him and found him guilty, what would have happened to him? Nothing, most likely. The lawyers would have gotten him off with a few years in jail."

"Yeah," said Graham softly, and he reached out to touch her, to comfort the girl he loved. "I'm sorry, darlin'," he said. "I'm very sorry."

He *was* sorry, but far more he was angry, and he was good at that. There were villains in the East End of London who could swear to it, and had. But he was also puzzled, and the surprise was up there with the icy fury all over his beautiful, cruel face. Inside him the strange emotion felt all wrong. He had never felt like this about anyone before. Not about his mother who had brought him up and whom he thought he "loved"; not about the tough, talkative cockney girls with their brittle glitz and their sparky humor who'd catered to the lusts of his formative years; not even for the mates who'd drunk with him pint for pint from the Elephant and Castle to Green Gate— the villains he'd called "friends" in the old days. Now, however, he felt strangely protective. He wanted to touch this girl, but softly. He wanted to stroke her, feel her skin, and conjure up a smile in the so-sad eyes. Above all he wanted to be with her. Just sitting side by side was almost enough, so that they could be together against the world that had mistreated them. It was called "love," and Graham smiled to himself like a foreigner in a strange country as he saw it for the very first time.

"You really understand it all, don't you?" said Paula.

"Yeah, doll, in a way I do." He squeezed her hand and he looked away, embarrassed that she had felt him care.

"Did terrible things happen to you?" she asked.

"Yeah, a few. But it's different, ain't it?"

He knew what he meant. It *was* different. She was a bird, wasn't she, and a wounded one. In the East End, men who attempted rape were outcasts, and those who harmed children were doubly so. A fella was fair game in the life contest, but a bird wasn't. Baker was roach slime, and he, Graham, longed to hurt him for what he had done to the innocents. Yeah, it would be good to see him hurting, and screaming and doing the things they did when they could see in your eyes that you didn't know what mercy meant.

"Why is it different? Because you're strong and I'm weak?" said Paula.

"Something like that."

"Well, I'm not weak. Nobody will ever understand what's going on inside my mind. One day I'll kill him. It's all I think about."

Her eyes flashed her determination, and her brow furrowed with the intensity of her desire for vengeance.

"Don't think about it, Paula. Try not to think about it."

She bit on her lip and tried to stop the tears, but they rolled on down her cheeks anyway, great big round tears of accusation and despair.

He put his arm around her and squeezed her tight, as if his strength could stop the memories, and she leaned in against his shoulder in the gratitude of the comforted. The sweet scent of her was in his nostrils, and her soft blond hair was warm against his neck, and so he turned his face toward her and nuzzled down, allowing his half-open lips to roam across the surface of her, and he shuddered with the alien feeling as he touched the only person who had ever felt to him like a human being.

"Oh God, I wish I could kill him," she sobbed.

Graham reached up, and his fingers brushed at the tears on her cheeks. "You know what, luv," he murmured. "I got a funny feelin' someone will."

～*9*～

"*I*'VE BEEN WATCHING you."

It was far more than a statement of fact. It was an invitation to conspiracy. Caroline Kirkegaard's searchlight eyes flicked up and down the girl as if she were dusting her.

"You have?" said Jami Ramona, her voice breathless. She had been to countless Destiny meetings, but never for one second had she dared imagine she was anything more than a face in the crowd. She smiled her satisfaction —the famous Jami Ramona smile that breathed new life into the covers of *Elle* and *Vogue;* that alone guaranteed the mortgage payments on the Elan model agency's flashy Madison Avenue office; the megabuck turn-on smile that sent the cosmetics leaping from the counters of a million malls. Although she was only fifteen, they didn't come much bigger in the modeling world than sweet Jami Ramona, but all she could think was that Caroline Kirkegaard had been watching her.

"Yes, I know you well," purred Caroline.

She lay back on the cushions of the chintz chair—one leg crossed over the other—a pale python-skin, sling-back Manolo Blahnik shoe dangling from her foot. Her relaxation was so profound you could almost touch it. Her whole being vibrated with terminal truth, twitching in tune to the cosmic tremors that seemed to Jami to fill the room.

"You do?" said Jami, mystified but impressed.

Caroline allowed herself the deepest of sighs, and her magnificent chest shuddered beneath the Valentino silk-lined linen blazer. There was no acting like this. It was the best, because it hovered on the very borders of reality. The trick was to be half there, half absent. The absent part made it so completely believable, but at the same time, in order to control the process, you had to remain at least partially conscious of it. "My spirit guides have told me much, and I have asked them more, the better to know you."

The formalized, rather stilted speech was second nature now. She had stolen it from Jach Pursel, trance-channeling "Creator" of Lazaris, and grand old man of the genre. In the trance it would be amplified as the guide "took over" her vocal cords to impart the wisdom of timeless times. That at least was the public explanation. The other possibility was just as plausible: that the words and sentiments were Caroline's own—separated from the normal ones by a conscious act of dissociation that could be switched on and off at will. Sometimes even she wasn't sure which explanation to believe. But here, now, she did.

She had a job for Jami Ramona. And when it was done, she, Caroline, not Robert Hartford, would own the Sunset Hotel.

Jami moved to the edge of the sofa. For months she had been trying to arrange a private channeling and a psychic reading with the charismatic founder of the Destiny movement, but the wall of secretaries and followers had been impenetrable. The mistress did not grant private sessions on request. They were an honor she bestowed as a gift. Then, out of the blue at Greg Gorman's studio, she had received the call when she had been shooting an *Elle* cover. A person called Kanga had said Caroline Kirkegaard would see her that evening at her home on Callejuela Drive, in Coldwater Canyon. She was to be there at six sharp.

"Can you tell me what the spirits said?" Jami's eagerness was palpable.

"They will tell you directly, through me, later. But already I sense what you want to know. You are searching, aren't you, Jami, searching to find the self that you have lost."

Caroline watched and listened for the young girl's aura, damping down her intellect and tuning in her antennae to Jami Ramona's desires. What did she want? What did she need? Only when those questions were answered could she be used.

"What should you do about your mother? Yes, you must find your answer to that. And the deep doubt you feel about yourself, and the path you have taken. Why does it feel so bad, Jami, when it was supposed to feel so good? I think I know. I know, I know. The spirits have talked to me. They will talk to you."

Jami Ramona gasped. Wow! Jeez! It was scary. Double scary. How had Caroline known? How could she know? Jami had never told a soul. There had never been a soul to tell.

"Your spirit tells me of this. All your spirits, from many lives, from many ages."

The pushy mother was common knowledge in the media. It was almost a public debate. How far should you thrust a daughter? In the material world was it all right to turn looks into cash at the expense of a childhood? The hatchet-faced harridan had sat beside Jami Ramona and reeled off the justifications to Bryant Gumbel on the "Today" show as her daughter had squirmed beside her in blue jeans identical to the ones she was wearing now. Did the trust fund excuse turning a kid into a sex object? Was look-but-don't-touch cool when teddy bears were stashed behind the background paper? And what about the Arab munitions billionaire and his parties and his fleshy-faced sons, and the late nights at Boer 2 and Les Bains in Paris, and the N.Y. night fungus at M.K. and Au Bar, at the impossible to find Club O and the all-but-impossible to enter Velvet Box? Was that a fair barter for the cheer-leading and chocolate of the manqué homecoming queen? Caroline smiled. The TV sound bite had defined the meaning of the term *ambivalence*. Jami Ramona would hate her powerful mom with the same intensity with which she loved her, and the problem would loom over her little life like a total eclipse of the heart.

There were tears in the aquamarine Ramona eyes. "Those . . . are the things I feel . . . the things I worry about. How did you . . ."

Caroline's hand was in the air, demanding silence. Her copper bracelet, with its fingerlike polished quartz stone, flashed in the light from the table lamp. "I asked you here for a reason. I sensed great sadness, and I feel it now, but beyond there is magnificent possibility. You are blocked, Jami Ramona, you are blocked from your future. The spirit guides can open the way. They have told me as much. They can save you for a success that the world has seldom seen before. But you must hurry. There is something to be done, and time is running out . . ."

"That's what I *feel*. I know I can do great things, but I don't know what to do, or how. I feel that something is holding me back and I don't know what it is." Jami wrung her delicate hands, and the film of tears thickened over the cover-girl eyes as she spoke.

"Be patient, Jami. You are *so* special. So unique. I don't just mean your beauty or your success—those the world recognizes even though you don't. I mean your spiritual glory. I see you astride the universe and talking with the purest spirits. I see you walking in the garden of God as his most valued and special servant . . ."

Caroline paused for the apparent throwaway that was in fact the bottom line.

"Of course, the *material* success will be fantastic. I see you moving here to L.A. and I see screens, big screens, not just television, although there will be a lot of that. Because nobody will be able to refuse you anything when you finally reach the light that you have always so deeply deserved. They will give you anything, everything. They will ask you what you want to do, and they will plead with you to name your price, and everyone who has stood in your way will bow down before you and beg the forgiveness of your mercy. And I see your mother . . . at your feet, silent at last."

Caroline stared into the misty gleaming eyes of the beautiful child she had captured. It was all there. Belief. Greed. The desperate longing for the promises to come true. Jami Ramona was sitting up straight cuddling her lovely knees, tossing her jet-black hair that way and this, and her tongue darted nervously over pale peach lips, wetting her pouting mouth as she quivered on the edge of her wonderful future.

But again the Kirkegaard hand was in the air. "If a way can be found to right the wrong. . . ." she said.

Jami stammered her response. "How can I right . . . the wrong. What can I do?"

"You must ask the spirits," Caroline replied calmly. "I will prepare my body for them."

Jami Ramona held her breath. Watching a channeler position herself for a trance was usually no big deal for her, although it always managed to quicken her pulse. After all, she'd seen most of the star turns—channeler to history's famous, Elwood Babbitt, J. Z. Knight and the spectacular Ramtha; plump Penny Torres and the bean-spilling Mafu—but this was different.

Caroline stood up. She smoothed the soft cream linen over her steel-strut body, watching the child model as she did so. Then she peered quickly around the room. The drawing room of the house that had supposedly once belonged to Hedy Lamarr stared back at her, reassuring in its Beverly Hills rented unreality. Some mock antique furniture, a few deeply indifferent hunting prints, the odd potted plant with mildewed leaves, a big screen Mitsubishi and the obligatory VCR. Only the outsize quartz crystal rock on the table in front of her was clearly not hired. It had cost Plutarch $160,000 from the Isis gallery on Rodeo Drive, and it was the key to everything.

Caroline looked at it lovingly. Impersonal and inanimate, it was her friend, because it was the source of the power she worshiped. She had possessed many stones—rubies to open the first chakra at the base of the spine and to allow the energy flow from the earth to enter the body; pink coral and pink jade to open the heart center and lift depression; carnelian, agate, and Madeira citrines to increase sexual energy—but when she had seen the mighty, clear quartz crystal she had fallen in love. It had spoken to her, as the crystals that were right for you were supposed to do, and intuitively she had known that she must own it. It wasn't just its size, its clarity, its brilliance, although all these things added to its amplifying force. It was the inclusion. Deep in its center there was an internal fracture whose prismatic light effects formed a miniature landscape with a doorway that seemed to draw you inside the crystal. Caroline could lose herself in its depths. She could climb inside it and vibrate to the heartbeat of its cold geometry. She could hide in its mystery and she could shine like a beacon from its thousand facets, from its perfect tip. It was her shelter and her springboard; her solace and her life source; it was her strength—and it asked for nothing in return. She had cleaned the crystal of all prior influences with smoke from wild sawgrass, and by immersion in sea salt for seven days and nights. Next she had recharged it by leaving it out for seven months of nights, allowing the feminine moon energy and the soft light of the stars to fill it up with their subtle power. Then she had wrapped it in pure silk, and surrounded the silk with soft leather, and the leather with fine Egyptian cotton and she had stored it away, untouched by anyone else, in the wall safe, to await the work it would be called upon to perform.

That morning she had taken it out, and now she stooped to pick it up, noticing as she did so that baby Jami's blue eyes were focused tight upon it.

"Will you travel with me to another world to find out who you are?" asked Caroline, intercepting the young girl's gaze.

"Oh yes," whispered Jami. To the magical place where the cash secrets were. To the fantasy realm where Mommy dearest lost her tongue.

Caroline swept up the crystal. Cradling it against her massive bosom, she walked back to her chair, sat down, and immediately closed her eyes.

Her voice was businesslike. "I will be going into a deep trance, and during that period I will have no knowledge of what the spirit guides are saying. At the beginning and at the end the trance will be lighter, and then I will have some awareness of the messages they bring. I am a clear channel—perhaps the only one—and the voices you will hear and the sentiments they express will not be influenced or filtered in any way through me. This you believe."

She paused, her eyes still closed, as if she needed confirmation.

Jami nodded at the unseeing eyes, and they seemed to sense her affirmation. She tried to hold on to the excitement bubbling inside her.

Caroline took a deep breath. The channeling process never varied. The sandalwood joss sticks burning in the circle of infinity around the room had "cleared" her. Next, she needed to "center" herself—the state of calm receptivity that was the feeling of being collected at her center. Without a proper centering it was impossible to focus correctly on the crystal. Deep breathing and concentration alone could achieve centering, but Caroline preferred to use a shortcut. She picked up the bell from the table beside her and, her eyes closed, her spine perfectly straight, she rang it once, twice, and then continuously—allowing the steady, rhythmic sound to carry her calmly toward her heart. After "centering," came "grounding." Unless you were securely tethered or grounded, it was impossible to achieve the balance that was such a vital ingredient in successful crystal work. Now, therefore, Caroline imagined a golden cord of light traveling downward, through her spine, down through the floor and into the earth. She exhaled deeply, sending energy down the cord, and as she became attached to the mass of the world, she felt the familiar heaviness in her lower body and a pleasant tingling sensation over her bottom.

She was ready. In her mind she threw the switch. As she did so, the force of her will merged with that of the crystal and together they beamed out at Jami Ramona.

She lifted the crystal above her head, holding it with both hands, and inclining it toward her target. "I am going to balance my body, aligning the energy centers to receive the spirit. When the crystal rests on my knees I will have opened myself as a trance channel."

On purpose Caroline had omitted the prayer. Most of the other channelers prayed before the trance that the gatekeeper would permit only the wise and enlightened spirits to use their bodies. But Caroline would not pray for that. Long ago she had attained a more fundamental perspective.

She was God, as much as God was God. Therefore Her will and His will were one. The spirits who would enter her body would say the things that she wanted them to say because they existed to serve her as they had always done, and in that service the cosmos would ultimately benefit as her enemies were cast down.

She took another deep breath, and her body shuddered as if shaken by a giant invisible hand. Down, down went the crystal, between her closed eyes, over her nose, brushing past the wet, parted lips to bisect her jutting chin, to run like a dagger down the white swan's neck to the rigid, mountainous breasts. For a second it paused there, sparkling with darting light, and Jami's eyes were drawn toward it, and to them, the triumvirate of the guru, who would change her life.

Caroline's breathing was heavy now, deep and rhythmic. Lower, steadily lower, sank the crystal, past the muscular midriff and the leveled stomach to the lap that was its destination.

The voice when it came was a surprise. Its accent was impossible to locate, its loudness and its pitch difficult to place on any scale. It was the voice of a woman.

"From the ancient empire of Atlantis I salute you, Jami Ramona."

Caroline Kirkegaard's head was thrown back, and her lips moved with the words that were not hers. Her eyes were tightly closed, but her hands had left the crystal in her lap and now they spread out in a strange gesture of openness that could have been some kind of a greeting.

"Who . . . are . . . you?" Jami's throat was dry as she tried the question. She had to talk to the spirit.

"I was your sister in the distant days when you were Vamara, daughter of Vanya, child of Ton. Greetings, dear one. I live in your heart, but now I can hear your voice."

"There was a wrong . . ." blurted Jami.

"You talk of the great wrong, of the sadness that surrounds your heart like a cage the sweet bird of your youth."

"Yes. Yes," stammered Jami Ramona.

"You can make it right, soul of Vamara. Now, in your age, in your place, at your time, the window of opportunity has opened. You will pass through the vale of your sorrow, and, in the wonder of the land beyond, you will become every possibility. You will be everything you have dreamed of being and far more, my beloved sister. I am here to tell you of these things, and the distant events that caused them."

Jami's mouth was open, but it didn't know what to say. Adrift on the sea of her longing, she could do nothing but wait.

"You loved Per more than your own life, and in return he worshiped you. He was older, and he was a brave warrior, but when he was with you he became the child that you were, and together you were so pure, and so strong that it seemed the sun shone from your eyes and the earth existed only as a platform for your feet. . . ."

Jami's heart thrilled as she thought of the great love that she had once experienced. Certainly the fumbling sons of the Arab billionaire didn't hold a candle to the mighty soldier of whom she was hearing for the very first time. Nor for that matter did the jaded yuppies in the Surf Club or the impoverished photographer's assistants, who sometimes made their inexpert pitches in the dressing rooms of New York studios.

"You were one with him and he with you, and your eyes belonged to each other, and you owned each other's ears and tongues and your hearts beat together. . . ."

"Like, what actually *happened?*" said Jami, unable to hide the trace of irritation in her voice.

Her celestial sister seemed totally unfazed by her sibling's earthly impatience. "You were married to Per on the eve of a great battle, and you had kept yourself for him as he had remained pure for you. That night you were to exchange the precious gifts of your bodies, but you were sad and greedy for him and fearful that he would be harmed in the coming conflict. Headstrong and selfish, you demanded that he withdraw from the combat to preserve himself for you, and until he promised to do that which he could never promise, you said your body would be forever a foreign field for him. He cried bitter tears to weaken your resolve and he pleaded with you through the restless night, but you were hard and cold when you should have been soft and warm. You withdrew from the touch of his hand, and you gambled that his desire for you was greater than his loyalty to the great Empire of Atlantis that he served. But he could not make that promise, and the great love you shared was not consummated on that wedding night, nor was it ever before the spear that found him on the morrow separated his soul from yours through light-years of eternal time. . . ."

Jami Ramona blinked through the tears, and the truth pierced her as the spear had smitten her long-ago lover on that ancient battlefield. Yes, it had been like that. Now she knew it. The greatest of all loves, frozen, unconsummated, had lingered on, suspended forever on the brink of blissful union. From that moment to this in all her lives the awful blockade had held her back. She had stopped herself at the second she should have moved on to glory, and the pattern had been repeating itself ever since.

She and Per must live and love again. She must discover him somewhere on the winding roads of eternity, and the terrible wrong that she had done him must be made right at last.

"Oh, Per," she murmured. "Forgive me. Please forgive me."

Caroline Kirkegaard's hands were once again on the crystal, and Jami fought back the panic as she realized what that meant. The spirit was about to leave. The trance of the channeler was about to lighten. And nobody had told her what it was she had to do.

"Don't go yet. Please don't go. How can I meet Per? Where can I go to find him?" She blurted out the words.

"It is the reason I asked to speak with you. He is here, now in the City of the Angels. At this the crossroads of all your infinities you have a chance to meet with him and to give him the gift that in Atlantis you once denied him. But he is old in this life, and he is preparing himself for a great journey. There is not much time. . . ."

The voice was fainter. Caroline Kirkegaard's body was twitching as if struggling to be rid of the spirit that had briefly possessed her.

Jami Ramona was on her feet. "Where? Where is he? What is his name?" She howled her questions at the other world.

"I must go now. I have to leave, but you and Per will meet and love, and the gifts of a million past lives will be showered upon your head, gifts stored through eons of ultimate time are about to be released as you cement the union that once so nearly was, and once again is about to be . . ."

The voice was a whisper and the convulsions that shook Caroline's body were the curtains drawing steadily across the spirit's stage.

Jami Ramona rushed across the small space that separated them and grabbed at Caroline's massive shoulders, and she shook them as she screamed her anguish. "Who? Where? Oh, please, dear God, please tell me . . ."

"In the sunset. You will find him in the sunset . . ." murmured her spiritual sister from long ago.

—

JAMI RAMONA stood in Francisco Livingstone's Mario Buatta-designed drawing room, and she shook with desire. She moistened her dry lips with her all-but-dry tongue, and she tried to stay calm on the verge of ecstasy.

She stepped forward, fearing that she would fall, her limbs hardly hers anymore as she walked toward her destiny. On her face was a half smile of lust for her glittering future, for the lover of all her lifetimes, for the act that would transport her to the astral plane where only gods and goddesses lived.

It had been so easy, when she had feared it would be so difficult. At the channeling session an hour before, "You will find him in the sunset" had been the ultimate in enigmatic predictions. But Caroline Kirkegaard, shaking herself like a sleepy dog as she emerged from the depths of the trance, had saved the day. The spirit guide had spoken her last words in the light phase of Caroline's dissociation. She had been able to interpret the cryptic message. The sunset must be the Sunset Hotel, and the old man preparing for a journey had to be its terminally ill owner, Francisco Livingstone.

Quickly, the dominoes had slotted into space. Per, Vamara's doomed husband, lived on in the millionaire. The spirit had intervened to bring the two lovers together once again. In this life Jami could break the spell that held her in limbo. But time was moving on. The chance must be taken now. Or never.

Jami had not hesitated. She had felt more alive than at any time in her life, more certain, more bold, more single-minded. Livingstone was an old man. She was fifteen. But they were married before God, and he was her great love and she was his. The present didn't matter. Only the future mattered. Only the past.

The drive down Coldwater to the Sunset Hotel had seemed eternal, but the dry wind from the desert had plucked at her hair as the moonbeams had caught the palm trees and her heart had filled with the enormity of what was to be. The Mercedes roadster had stopped sharply in the side street that ran along one side of the hotel's grounds.

Jami had opened the car door, as she would open her heart and her body, and Caroline Kirkegaard had whispered once again the thing that she would do. "Bungalow seven, Jami. For your wedding night."

She had rung the bell, and eventually it had been answered. An ancient man, silver haired, but sweet smelling, had been wrapped in a big terry dressing gown bearing the braided legend of the Sunset Hotel on its breast pocket. He had looked like an actor auditioning for the role of God, and it was clear that he had just gotten out of the bath. He had been surprised to see her, but he had recovered quickly. When she had said, "Can I please come in?" it had seemed the shortest of times before he had answered. "Yes."

Francisco Livingstone walked before her wearing nothing but the bathrobe and an expression of bemused anticipation. Who was this marvelous-looking girl, who had presented herself at his door at bedtime? Had she been sent as a joke from a friend? Or had she simply knocked on the wrong door? The first of the two possibilities he discarded quickly. In this town, he had no such licentious acquaintances. Some variation of the second possibility was much more likely.

He turned to watch her over his shoulder and he caught his breath. She was gorgeous. Her whole face was afire with an otherworldly animation, and her big blue eyes flashed and burned. She wore pressed 501s, a navy-blue jacket, and a cream silk shirt that struggled to handle what looked like wonderful breasts, and her mane of black hair flowed and streamed in chaotic disorder as if she had driven down from the canyons in a Mercedes roadster to meet the lover of her dreams. Her makeup looked like it had been painted by an artist. Just the minimum, restrained, delicate, immensely stylish. He cleared his throat nervously.

Jami Ramona saw herself happening in his eyes. She had a speech ready. She would welcome her ancient lover, while trying to acknowledge that her words would seem strange to him. But events were moving too fast inside her, within him. Apparently words could wait.

She saw, not an old man, but the warrior of Atlantis, soon to die, strong and brave and deeply in love with her. There was so little time to give the gift, and it must be so beautiful to sustain them both through infinity and to unlock the treasures of her future. This was the stuff of the truest lust, and in all her life Jami Ramona had not come close to it. The wet desire gripped her.

She stood there, on the Aubusson carpet, and she cocked her left leg, the knee thrown forward, the heel of her crocodile-skin loafer a half inch from the ground. As it was meant to, the professional model's pose threw her body into the shape that unleashed the dreams. Her eyes never left Livingstone's for one moment as she eased the immaculately tailored navy-blue Ralph Lauren blazer from her shoulders, allowing it to fall in an untidy heap at her ankles. The cashmere, and the bright brass buttons, wrinkled, rumpled against the pastel colors of the rich carpet, seemed to emphasize the abandonment that was to come. Next her fingers found the buttons of the cream silk shirt that was already wide open at the neck, framing the outer reaches of her naked breasts. She undid them quickly to the big brass buckle of the cavalry belt, but she did not draw back the creamy silk. It stayed there, held by the buttons no longer, held only by the firm mounds of throbbing, thrusting flesh.

The Livingstone breath was on hold. The Ramona fingers were on the edges of the material. With all the time of many worlds she drew it back.

She was perfectly still, perfectly perfect, like an unveiled statue. Her breasts pointed straight ahead, browned gently by the California sun, and the pouting pink of their turned-up ends was the color of sea-washed shells on a Caribbean shore.

Jami reached up and cupped the tight flesh of her breasts in her hands, the tips of her fingers reaching for the taut nipples, and she squeezed gently, forcing the blood into the cul-de-sac, making the peach-pink cones bulge deliciously as the stretched skin fought to contain the fullness. Then the palms of her hands moved away, letting her fingers linger lightly at the very tips of her breasts, brushing the twin points, seeming to marvel at their sharpness as they swelled to the bursting point.

Almost dreamily her hands moved toward the buckle of the belt. Languidly, she flicked it open. Still her eyes never left her target. It was all for him as she unwrapped his present, and the amazement in his beaten face was confirmation that every move she made was making more certain the union that must be.

The buckle clinked against the clasp and dangled free at her waist. She reached up with her body, and wriggled once, twice, three times as she thrust down on the jeans with both hands, stripping away the soft blue denim that clung to the heat of her like a second skin. The shirt cascaded out, tenting her flat midriff, and draping the neat line of her belly button, drifting across her pulsing breasts.

Surrounded by the crumpled denim the pure whiteness of the Bloomie's bikini briefs merged delightfully with the honey-roasted skin of her taut, adolescent thighs, already streaked with desire.

"Do you like me?" asked her eyes. "Do you like the look of my body? Do you want me now as you wanted me once before in a distant life at a distant time?"

She tossed back her head, proud of the visual banquet that she was, as her thumbs found the elastic of her panties. She eased them down, allowing the dripping, shining hair to emerge with tantalizing slowness. As she did so she pushed out from her pelvis until there was nothing in the room but the perfect triangle of love and the pouting pink lips nestling at its center. Jami pushed away the panties, draping them like a rope bridge across her straining thighs, and she moved, and thrust, sending the denim jeans slipping toward her ankles. For a second or two she stood quite still as the air filled with the scent of her passion, and then her right hand moved toward the thrilling core of her. Her finger ran through the slippery, downy hair and she rested her hand against the hot, velvet softness, soothing her sensual anguish as she swayed with longing.

She pushed against herself as her eyes impaled her victim. He was hers more completely than he had been anyone's. His slumped shoulders said it, and his parted lips, his heaving chest proclaimed it.

It was time. Time to reclaim all her yesterdays and to make possible all her tomorrows.

"Come here," whispered Jami Ramona.

~10~

PAULA NUZZLED HER chin against her white T-shirt and hunched the shoulders of her black blazer up around her neck. Carefully she studied the knees of her faded Levi's and her ice-cream-for-the-feet L.A. Gear candy-striped laceless high tops. She burrowed her back against the blue glazed Deco tiles of the wall of the Mann's Plaza cinema in Westwood, and she prayed to heaven that nobody would recognize her. The sign on the marquee above her head gave away her game. STARRING ROBERT HARTFORD . . . it read.

She had gotten there early enough to find a place to park in the lot opposite, and already the line was snaking around the side of the cinema. She breathed in deeply, steadying herself for the ordeal of the surrogate meeting with the movie star, and she looked up at the pink-and-blue mackerel sky, the clouds arranged in shoals like the aquamarine sea off the Florida Keys. Soon it would be dark, thank the Lord, and nobody would be able to watch her doing the thing she was ashamed of doing—seeing Robert Hartford again.

For the millionth time she tried to make sense of what had happened between them, before the dreadful confrontation. Something? Nothing? Not much? He had seemed far more than intrigued by her, and it had grown in intensity—in the extraordinary emotional closeness by the pool at the Sunset. While the gondolier sang, and Paula's heart leaped in her chest, Robert had made his earth-shattering prediction that they would be lovers. But his reputation as a pursuer of women was legendary. Maybe he had just been practicing on her. Maybe it had all meant zip to him. No! Paula rejected the idea out of hand. Of all the problems she had faced, self-doubt had always been toward the bottom of the list. She was beautiful, and she was good, and one day she would be wise and the world would know that she was the winner she felt herself to be. Robert Hartford had seen those things in her, and he had reacted to them.

"Paula?"

The voice cut into her thoughts, and Paula's head snapped around to find out who had spoken her name.

"Kristina?"

"Hi, what on earth are you doing here?"

Kristina Hartford was already amused, but her question wasn't unkind. She had recognized Paula Hope immediately. It wasn't the sort of face, or body, that you could easily forget.

"Oh . . . just catching a movie," Paula laughed.

"*Daddy's* movie?" Kristina cocked her head to one side. One or two of the kids in the line pricked up their ears at that, but this was L.A., and they pretended not to be listening.

Paula wasn't going to stay on the ropes for long. "Are *you* going to see it?" she countered.

She injected just enough disbelief into the question to suggest that going to see your father's movie was a little unusual, too.

"Yeah, I always do. He likes me to sample the audience reaction." Kristina admired Paula's rebound. She liked the girl. Paula was determined but not pushy, and Kristina hadn't forgotten how she had come to her rescue the night at the ball when her father had put her down. "Hey, are you alone? I am. Could I join you? Like we could see it together."

Paula tried to make sense of her ambivalence. Seeing Robert Hartford again was one thing. Doing it with his daughter was another. Yet it was always more fun with someone else, and the suggestion had come from Kristina. Their first meeting had hardly been peaceful coexistence. It would seem ungracious not to accept.

"Sure." Paula moved sideways to let Kristina join the line. "Looks like a pretty long line. If you'd had to go to the back you might not have made it."

"I could have pulled rank as the star's daughter." Kristina laughed, but she was only half joking. Then her voice went conspiratorial to show she hadn't meant to be flash. "*You* could have gotten in as the star's girlfriend."

A blush exploded all over Paula's face.

"What do you mean?" She blurted out the words.

"Just joking," said Kristina. "But aren't you?"

"Aren't I what?" asked Paula. The couple in front turned around to look at her. Behind her she could sense that the couple was already looking.

"Daddy's girlfriend." Kristina's eyes were twinkling.

"Of course I'm not. I hardly know your father."

"You could have fooled me. I was *there*, you know, at Livingstone's party. By the pool. Remember? Listen, it's no big deal. I didn't mean to embarrass you." Kristina's smile was friendly.

Paula smiled back, allowing the conspiracy. "I'd only ever met him once before that night, and I haven't seen him since."

Kristina looked relieved—then a little suspicious—then relieved again, as she studied Paula's transparently honest face and decided to believe her. Now that she knew Paula was not one of her father's conquests, she somehow wished that she were. God, he could do a lot worse. She felt a surge of warmth toward the pretty young girl.

"Well, all I can say is that I've seen most of Daddy's moves and, boy, was he shining out to you that night. You'd better believe it."

"He was?"

"I'm *telling* you."

"I imagine he comes on strong to quite a lot of people. I don't mean to criticize, but I guess he has that reputation. . . ."

"For screwing everything that moves!"

"Kristina!" A laugh exploded from Paula's throat at the irreverence. There was a titter from the people in front. Another from those behind.

"Well, it's true. That's why this line goes around the block. But you're pretty special. Young and beautiful and sure of yourself. Daddy likes girls who are perfect."

Paula's smile faded fast at the last bit. Yes, Robert Hartford would like perfection. He would hate the things that marred it.

"You make him sound as if he thinks of women as objects."

"He does. And the funny thing is it's mutual. Sometimes I think he's a bigger sex object than Marilyn Monroe. Most girls want to score him just to say they've been there. I don't think he's ever had a grown-up relationship with anyone."

"Surely with your mother."

"*Especially* not with Mom." Kristina laughed. "The marriage was so short I sometimes wonder where they found the time to conceive me!"

"Gee, Kristina, that's your parents you're talking about."

"Oh, listen, I love Dad. It's just that he's got this one area of weakness that's also his greatest strength. Like, he's a teenager, emotionally locked in a time warp, as if nobody ever taught him how to feel. I can't imagine him falling in love like everyone else, you know, getting married, settling down, having kids. Sometimes I feel like I was a giant mistake. I call him 'Daddy' and he looks at me as if I'm absolutely crazy. It's weird!"

"Must be," said Paula, not at all sure that Robert Hartford as a father would be very nice at all, not even sure that Robert Hartford was very nice, and yet at the same time wanting to hear more and more about him.

"How's the movie doing?" Paula eased the conversation into less personal territory.

"Awesome. The opening weekend was a slam dunk, and that's how you measure a star's box-office power. It did seven and a half thousand per screen the first week. The second week was only off six percent, can you believe?"

"That's good?" asked Paula.

"That's like *totally* rad. If the second week's off anything less than twenty-five percent, it's good. Six is brilliant. It's the way you tell if a movie's going to be a hit or not. This'll do a hundred million domestic. Easy." Kristina's voice was full of infectious enthusiasm. And pride.

The line had started to move in earnest.

"Here we go," said Kristina. "Let's go see how he earns the money."

In the darkness they rearranged the food. Paula wasn't thirsty, and she certainly wasn't hungry, but to steady her nerves she had bought an outsize Cherry Coke and a cardboard box of peculiarly revolting-looking nachos with a glutinous half-cold melted cheese sauce. Over the corn chips she had ladled jalapeños, ketchup, mustard, *and* pickle relish. Kristina, who admitted to already having done a burger at Stratton's Grill, had ordered melted butter with the large carton of popcorn and a Diet Pepsi. All this junk they placed carefully at their feet, knowing as they did so that at some stage of the movie they, or the people who pushed past them, would of course spill the stickiest bits, which would then become attached to the soles of their shoes.

ROBERT HARTFORD's above-the-title credit was vast. At last the movie had begun, and the butterflies were free in Paula's stomach. Who was it up there? The man she knew, who lusted after feminine perfection with a fervor that was as crippling to his emotional life as her limp was to her body? Or the celluloid lover, as flawless as the women he sought, slinky smooth, and creamy sweet, fantasy fuel for the theaterful of escapists who watched him? Both? Neither? A subtle amalgamation of the two? Paula couldn't decide. At times he veered in one direction; then he seemed to change course; alternating between nerve-racking familiarity and equally disturbing obscurity. She tried to get a bead on it, and slowly it dawned on her that her differing impressions of him were not subjective. They changed with the roles he played on the screen. It was basically a father/son AIDS movie, the first of its kind. Robert Hartford was playing a rich conservative senator with a fading, insecure wife and a gorgeous, focused ballet-dancer mistress, whose whole world begins to crumble when his beloved son and potential political heir gets ill with AIDS. What he finds impossible to come to terms with is the implication, soon to be dramatically confirmed, that his son is a homosexual, a way of life that the screen Robert Hartford has spent the whole of his public life bad-mouthing. The timeless subplot, whether or not he should break his marriage vows and leave the wife he respects but no longer loves for the younger woman who could light up his life, shared equal screen time with the father/son tearjerker. Paula could sense immediately that the father/son chemistry was a disaster. The Robert Hartford who recoiled from the exuberantly good-looking AIDS victim was the Robert Hartford who had rushed from the room at Livingstone's ball. In those scenes he was a star no more. He was the man she knew—the good and the bad, the one who had plumbed the depths of her eyes, the one who hadn't been able to cope with her deformity. On the other hand, with the ballet dancer and the wife he was exclusively the legend, the myth, the one-dimensional Robert Hartford that she had never met, would never meet. And the fascinating thing was that it was to *this* Robert Hartford that the audience related. They squirmed almost visibly in their seats in the father/son bits. They blossomed like flowers in sunlight at the subplot scenes. The message was inescapable. Robert

Hartford and men was the worst possible karma. Robert Hartford and women was sweet, fantastic dreams.

So the two sections of Paula watched the two pieces of Robert Hartford. The public stargazer drooled over his celluloid lovemaking as it winced at his "heavy" emotional conflict with the gay son, while the private, infatuated girl identified wildly with his tortured reality as it was repelled by his stylized Don Juan male/female interactions.

What neither part of her was ready for was the man in front saying, quite loudly, "If you ask me it's the father who's the fag."

She turned to see if Kristina had heard. Her new friend's resigned expression, eyes rolling up to the ceiling, said she had.

Paula stared daggers into the back of the bull neck in front of her, outraged that anyone beside herself was even thinking in such analytical terms about Robert Hartford. Immediately she got the picture. The big bodybuilding stiff had lost his girlfriend to the screen lover. She was stretched out beside him, feeding her face and dreaming X-rated dreams. So he had put the boot in. Not that the chick seemed to have heard him. Now he leaned over, and he said it again.

"Ssssh, Bill," she said, without taking her eyes off the screen.

Paula felt the rage well up inside her like a spring of boiling blood. Nobody could talk about Robert like that. It was disgusting. It was untrue. It was out of order. In her anger she forgot totally that he was in the public domain; that the idiot in front had paid good money and was entitled to an opinion; that he was anyway talking about the role, not the actor. She ignored the fact that she had no possible claim on Robert; that Kristina was the person, if any, who could rightfully take exception; that the remark was a private one addressed to someone who was not her. None of those things occurred to her. There was just the vast buzz of dreadful irritation, the shock of the intensely personal insult, and the absolute determination to avenge it.

Paula reached down quickly and she gathered up the Cherry Coke, and the nachos in their appalling box, swimming in the tasteless bright yellow cheese and covered with congealed relish, mustard, ketchup, and peppers. Then she scooped up Kristina's drink and her popcorn with its melted butter. For a second or two she balanced the food like a novice juggler. Then she stood up, leaned over, and emptied it all into the lap of the man in front.

His shriek of enraged surprise shot through the theater.

"Good God," said Kristina, half to herself, half out loud. "The girl's in love."

—

ROBERT HARTFORD sat bolt upright on the chintz sofa, and the expression on his face registered acute discomfort. It was bad enough being alone in a room with a man, but it was far worse when that man was on the verge of tears, and on the edge of revealing all sorts of dreadful personal secrets. Quite apart from anything else, it was so unexpected. Granted the old boy had sounded a bit strange when he'd asked if he could drop by for a drink, but he had given no indication that he would be bringing his amateur dramatic kit with him. So Robert coughed, and craned his neck, and crossed his corduroy-panted legs as he prayed that the unwelcome storm of sentiment would quickly blow itself out.

Francisco Livingstone sat slumped in the green upholstered Hepplewhite shield-back chair opposite, and he tried visibly to hold it all together. There was a thick film of moisture in his rheumy old eyes, and his face looked like the side of an Alp after an avalanche. It was damp and lopsided, and weirdly twisted as if one side was paralyzed, the other in spasm. He held on to the silver-headed cane propped between his legs with both hands, as if it were the precarious support on which his whole life rested, and he spoke in a quavering, reedy voice. "I've done . . . an incredibly stupid . . . thing," he said.

Robert adjusted the famous horn-rims on the equally famous nose, sipped petulantly on his neat Glenfiddich, and prayed for his ordeal to be over. At least priests in the confessional didn't have to *watch* the spilling of the beans.

"Can I get you a glass of Armagnac, Francisco? I've got a bottle of Bas Armée, 1848, open. Year of revolutions and all that. Come on. Cheer you up."

Livingstone waved a hand in an ambivalent gesture, but his mind was far from brandy. "I'm afraid . . . Robert, I don't know how to say this. . . . I'm going to have to renege on our deal."

"What do you mean, Francisco?" The Hartford voice, usually soft, was hard as Sheffield steel. There was only one deal.

"I mean the hotel. I can't sell it to you. I have to sell it to Plutarch and Kirkegaard. I have no choice."

Robert Hartford could actually feel his temperature dropping. Inside it was already arctic cold, and the freeze was moving upward and outward at lightning speed. He could feel the icy frost fingers playing on his skin, on the nape of his neck, along his back, pricking like needles in the pits of his arms. Already he was in a new dimension, all fastidious homophobia on hold, all unimportant preferences and dislikes forgotten. This was reality. This was the bottom line.

"We did a deal, Francisco," he said coldly. A deal. In Hollywood, where deals were the Holy Grail. His voice emphasized that fact.

"I know we had a verbal agreement, but I want . . . you to let me out of it. If you don't I'll have to renege anyway. You'd have to sue me. . . ."

Robert shot to his feet. "Francisco! What the *hell* is all this about? What *is* all this bullshit? A deal's a deal. Of all people in this godforsaken town, you should know that. You're the only honorable man I know."

"No, it's finished, Robert. It's over. I can't sell the Sunset to you. God knows I wanted to. But something terrible has happened and it's all my fault. I've blown it. My reputation, a young girl's career. I'm going to jail, Robert, if I don't do what they say."

Robert walked across the intervening space, as he tried to calm down inside. Already the anger was receding, and into the vacuum poured the torrent of his cool, clear intelligence. Things were not as they seemed. They seldom were. All sorts of things had happened to make Livingstone change his mind. Young girls. Jail. A reputation in ruins. The one, two, three added up to blackmail. He walked across the room and placed a hand on the old man's bowed shoulder, and he squeezed gently in a gesture of solidarity.

"Tell me what's happened, Francisco. Tell me everything," Robert said quietly. But already he knew some answers. Livingstone liked young girls. How young? Perhaps, too young. And somebody had found out about it— someone who didn't want Livingstone to sell the Sunset Hotel to Robert Hartford. Someone who would do anything to get what she wanted. Someone exactly like Caroline Kirkegaard. Yes, blackmail and Caroline Kirkegaard would go together like beluga and Stolichnaya. A ray of light burst through the storm clouds as the thought cheered him. Once before he had dumped on Caroline Kirkegaard. But things had changed since then. In those days he had merely had a lease on Hollywood. These days he as good as owned it freehold—sunshine, sushi, and pseudosex. It was his village, his cabbage patch, and in it people could be made to do things, made to leave things undone. That was the whole point of being at the top of the anthill. There was no other point at all. Power was the game's name, and the trick was to *use* it.

"She just rang the doorbell, around eleven o'clock last night. . . ." He paused. "I think I will have that glass of brandy, Robert."

Robert walked thoughtfully toward the Sheraton sideboard, and he poured a generous measure of Armagnac from an 1845 Dummers Jersey City works decanter into a wafer-thin balloon glass. He swirled the caramel-colored liquid around the glass once, twice, and then walked back to Francisco.

"I can't tell you how beautiful she was. All my life I don't think I've seen a young girl as lovely."

"How old *was* she, Francisco?"

"Ah, yes. How old? That's the right question, I'm afraid. She was jailbait, all right. Apparently she's fifteen."

"And you didn't know her? Didn't know where she'd come from? She just knocked on your door out of the blue?"

"Yes. Yes. I know it was madness. That's what I feel now. And that's what I felt at first last night. I was going to call security after I'd heard her pitch, but Robert, I mean, you understand things like this, she was special, out-of-this-world lovely, and she just stripped off her clothes. I mean, before I could say anything. She didn't even say her name."

Robert Hartford's eyes widened perceptibly. There were enough bullshitters in Hollywood to tell lies about what girls looked like and what they'd done, but Francisco Livingstone was not one of them. Despite his age, he was a connoisseur. Almost certainly the girl was as special as he maintained. His heart speeded imperceptibly as he contemplated that kind of beauty.

"It sounds crazy, Robert, but somehow I feel you're the only man on earth who could understand what I did. I mean, it was the *moment*. One struggles to get through life despite it, and how many times are there moments like that? You can count them on the fingers of one hand. I was crazy, but somehow I felt that nothing mattered beside the vital importance of owning that beauty, just for an hour or two. Can you begin to comprehend . . . ?"

Robert nodded slowly. Yes, he understood that. Too well.

"And, you know, there was something else. She talked a lot of nonsense about being together in another world—you know the Shirley MacLaine stuff —but it felt so right one could almost believe it. Almost." He lowered his head to shield himself from the Hartford eyes.

"You made love to her?"

"Yes."

"And you didn't know how old she was? You didn't ask?"

"No."

At last he parted with the glass of brandy, handing it, almost unwillingly, to Livingstone. "And now she's filed a complaint with the BHPD?"

Livingstone took a long pull at the fiery liquid, and a deep breath before he answered. "No. It's worse than that. If that's all it was I could have brazened it out, bought her off, hushed it up. In the hotel business you do that all the time for others. There'd have been someone to do it for me. No, the awful thing is the girl was used. She's completely innocent. She was set up, and now she stands to lose even more than I do. That's what makes it so damn dreadful." The tears were in his eyes again.

"But what's the problem? You both deny it. It didn't happen. Your word against somebody else's. Easy."

"It's not as simple, Robert. They've got photographs. They sent them round to me this morning."

"Photographs? Christ, Francisco, this isn't a *movie*. This is real life. What on earth do you mean, 'photographs'? You and the girl took photographs?"

"No, no, of course not. Oh, I don't know, Robert, but they've got some damned photographs. I screwed the girl. I wasn't looking around for bloody photographers. Someone must have got hold of a master key, and either hidden in the room earlier or let themselves in while we were in the bedroom. They shot a roll—on infrared film probably—and slunk out again. I really don't know, but I can't think of any other explanation. I *do* know they have the negatives because they sent the prints round this morning. There's absolutely no mistaking the pair of us. We're clearly identifiable."

"Who sent the photographs?"

"Caroline Kirkegaard."

Again Robert nodded, frowning as he concentrated. "Who's making the complaint? The girl's mother? If the girl's not complaining, why should the cops worry? They can't know how old she is from the photographs. All they'll know is you're a dirty old man."

He couldn't resist the oblique dig, but immediately he regretted it. Cheap shots made *you* cheap, not anyone else.

Livingstone ignored it. The things on his mind were more important. "It seems she's rather famous and that the whole world knows she's only fifteen. Apparently she's one of those hotshot teenybopper models."

"What's her name?"

"Jami Ramona."

Robert Hartford's eyebrows shot up.

"*The* Jami Ramona," he said quickly, his tone incredulous.

"You've heard of her?"

Robert Hartford took a deep breath and he looked at Francisco Livingstone as if he were seeing him for the very first time. "Good *God*," he said at last, as if in the front pew at church, "*you* screwed Jami Ramona?"

Livingstone, however, didn't appreciate the nuances of what he had achieved. He plowed on. "The photographs would tell the cops that, and if they showed them to the media as well, the pressure on them to act would be enormous. They'd have to indict me. They'd have to send me down. The girl apparently has product endorsement contracts coming out of her ears. They all have morals clauses these days. Her career would be history if this came out, quite apart from what happens to me."

Robert Hartford felt the anger rushing back. Livingstone was a big boy even if an ill one and an old one. If he chose to sail close to the wind, despite all his years of experience, then there was a sense in which he deserved what was coming to him, but the girl, the beautiful young girl—Jami Ramona— ruined at fifteen by Caroline Kirkegaard in a scheme to do Robert out of the hotel he dreamed of owning. *That* was something else.

"Don't worry, Francisco. There's a way out of this. I know there is. There always is. This is our town. Between us we know everyone. Chief Terrlizese, Senator Chilton, the newspaper people. We can keep the lid on it."

Livingstone shook his head. "The story'd go nationwide. It's too big."

Again he bowed his head, as if ashamed of the words he now spoke. "I'm not proud of it, but you know, Robert, I've always *cared* what people thought of me. All my life I've had a reputation as a gentleman, and I've never really been one, not by birth, not by behavior. But it's been my vanity to create that image, and the Sunset Hotel has been a part of it. Grand, upper class, effortlessly 'correct.' Now I am exposed as a molester of children. At the end of my life I would become a disgusting joke and all the enemies through the years would have their revenge. It's too much to ask of me, Robert. I can save my reputation and a young girl's reputation by doing what they want. I know I promised you the hotel, but you're young, you have another career, a brilliant one. I'm sorry, but you have to help me."

Robert didn't answer directly.

"Has Kirkegaard contacted you, apart from sending the photographs? Was there a note?"

"She telephoned. She said that she had the negatives, and that the police and the media would get the photographs unless I agreed to sell her the Sunset Hotel. She gave me forty-eight hours to make my decision."

"How on *earth* did she get Jami Ramona to do what she did?" That was *really* worrying Robert, and not just because it was a loose end in the story.

The memory of the Ramona body was fresh in his mind from the Herb Ritts photographs in the latest *Vanity Fair,* from the Bruce Weber ones in last month's *L.A. Style.*

"I just don't know. But I think it's to do with all that Destiny business. Caroline Kirkegaard has total control over some of those followers of hers. It's like Scientology, or Jim Jones, and all those Moonies. You know, cults and charismatic leaders and people looking for answers and meanings, and a way to irritate their parents. The only thing I can think is she filled her full of rubbish about us being lovers in a past life or something and the girl believed it. It's not our world, Robert, but it's Kirkegaard's and Plutarch's and apparently Jami Ramona's. That's why I never wanted to sell her the hotel in the first place."

"You're sure Ramona's not in on it."

"I'm certain. And if she is, and she's prepared to blow her entire career and be exposed to public ridicule just so that Caroline Kirkegaard can get what she wants, then she's been brainwashed and she needs help badly. Either way, it's not her fault."

"I agree." Robert seemed relieved by that. He buried his head in his hands and for a few seconds gave himself over to the contemplation of Caroline Kirkegaard's wickedness. Ripping off the gullible was one thing. This was quite another. It showed a murderous ruthlessness. In shark city that was not unheard of, but Robert Hartford didn't like it to happen around him. That was for the early days when the career was vulnerable as a newborn baby, and when the rules had to be bent by whatever tool came to hand. But now, in the rarefied echelons of haute Beverly Hills life, it was totally unacceptable. And the poor young girl, little Jami Ramona with the body of an angel and the face of a goddess. He twisted his hand up into a tight ball and he buried it in the other one, as if grinding something in a mortar.

Then slowly, like a beautiful vision forming from a vapor cloud, the idea came to him. There was a way out. A wonderful way out. One that would use the most powerful weapon that he possessed. At a stroke he would win back the hotel he coveted, save the reputation and career of a beautiful young girl, and allow a poor old man to die in peace and dignity. And once again he would cast down Caroline Kirkegaard into the dirt where she belonged. Yes, he would use his most fearsome weapon.

He would use himself.

THEY CIRCLED each other like gladiators in some ancient arena. But although they knew they were adversaries, locked in a battle to the death that only one could win, there was a closeness they shared: the hate that one further twist of the wheel could turn to love; the universal scorn of perennial winners for the losing lost; the common ground of those who wanted with the desperation of the obsessed.

"I wasn't sure you'd come," said Robert Hartford, his smile laden with impish charm.

"How could I refuse red roses from the latter-day Valentino?" replied

Caroline Kirkegaard. She smiled too, a ripe, sun-filled smile, that balanced the Hartford flirtation ounce for precious ounce.

Both knew that the charade was a lie, and, paradoxically and to the surprise of each, they knew, too, that it was no such thing.

She watched him as she might a lion, a healthy dose of caution mixed in with the respect, and she wondered as she did so just what it was she felt. For so long it had been so easy to loathe him. In those distant days he had destroyed her with the casual disinterest of a child pulling the wings from a fly, because she was strong and because she was a competitor. For that, and for that alone, he had capriciously ruined her movie career. In the early days of desert wound-licking, out by the Salton Sea, she had fed on her hatred, as she had discovered that her friends were impostors and her acquaintances had acquired a selective amnesia with regard to her name. Later she had learned that the open expression of anger was not the L.A. way. To become powerful you had to be cool, at least on the outside. It had been part of her growing up, and since then she had left her own victims strewn casually across the dreamscape in which only the strong survived and only the strongest triumphed.

Her smile turned inward as she took the laughing cocktail from his hand, and placed its frothing wetness against her lips. Was there anything more beautiful than an old rival setting himself up for the biggest fall of all? The roses had come straight out of the blue, and the card had said everything in the bold, straightforward handwriting of the superstar: "Dear Caroline, No hard feelings. Have dinner with me, and let's start again. Tonight at eight?" It had been signed "The new owner of the Sunset Hotel."

So Francisco Livingstone hadn't had the guts to tell him the deal was off. So he didn't know about Jami Ramona and the extraterrestrial lovemaking. So he was blissfully ignorant of the glossy photographs rubbing up against each other in her Coldwater Canyon safe, and the license they had given her to buy the hotel the idiot thought was his. Well, that was fine, because any moment now she would reveal him as being the biggest fool in Beverly Hills, where, to say the very least, the fools did not come small.

She sipped at the drink, her eyes sparkling, her tongue playing at the rim of the V-shaped cocktail glass. Already she had taken in the scene. It was to be that Hollywood institution—a Robert Hartford candlelit dinner for two— and her heart was singing as she realized what it meant.

"I hope you don't mind it being just the two of us. I should have mentioned it before. I just thought that we had so much to discuss . . ." He left the rest of it hanging in the air where it hung best, allowing the glass candlesticks of the arched dining alcove, the elegant Waterford crystal, the effortlessly patrician Limoges china to speak for him.

The waiter hovered in the background, seen but not heard, fussing with the table, reorganizing the cymbidium orchids, turning the frosted white Burgundy in the silver bucket, refolding the already immaculately folded Irish linen napkins.

"Dinner alone with Robert Hartford. Is there any other way?" She couldn't quite hide the element of mockery, didn't really try to.

He held his glass up toward her. "To my hotel," he said, in retaliation. "Can you drink to that?"

"Of course, Robert. Any night. Any day. To the Sunset Hotel and its new owner." Caroline smiled mysteriously.

Both shared the identical thought. What fun it was to drink to yourself when your audience thought you were drinking to it.

"Let's sit down for a minute or two. I asked for dinner at eight-thirty if that's okay. It's not really cool enough for a fire, but I think they're one of the great pleasures of life, don't you?"

He steered her toward the flickering fire. Real logs. No nonsense with piped gas. The essence of scrub oak and eucalyptus flavored the air. They sat down side by side on the huge sofa—black and white, oil and water—held together by nefarious purpose. And something else? The attraction of opposites? The mutual attraction of the stupendously attractive?

"You've come a long way, Caroline."

"You, too, Robert."

Both smiled. Meritocrats were always proud of their journeys, in contrast to aristocrats, who rejoiced in the lack of them.

"If I made it more difficult for you in the early days, I'm sorry." He looked down at a perfect fingernail as he delivered the almost-apology.

"The early days are supposed to be difficult. If it hadn't been you, it would have been someone else."

They were moving around the edges of it. The conciliation had a purpose. Everything was occurring on two quite different levels.

It was the body that was getting to him. Somehow it defined a new type of woman, perhaps a new age of femininity. It was a milestone, like a Rubens *grande dame,* or an anorectic sixties model, symbolic of things to come, and of a violent break with the immediate past. As a connoisseur Robert Hartford wanted to see it, to feel it, to taste it, to smell it. He wanted to hear the sounds it made when it did the things its predecessors had done—and yet there was something so dreadfully unwholesome about her, so wicked, so alarmingly "wrong." As he watched her, his whole being seemed to be split down the middle. His intellect was well aware that she was deadly, a woman who had and would stop at nothing to get what she wanted, but at the same time his emotions drew him mothlike toward her flickering flame. What did he want? The destruction of the blackmailing woman who had dared to cross him, or her superhard body melting against his? Could he allow himself to want both?

The mist of ambivalence was floating across Caroline, too. In a few hours he would know how she had triumphed over him, and her first act would be to rub his face in the dirt as he had rubbed hers so many years ago. Like a thief in the night, he would be ejected from her hotel, where he had lived for years, and she would personally supervise as her employees piled his possessions on the lawns and walkways for any passing nobody to gawk at. But right now, this minute, there was no denying the animal urgency of his attraction. The legend wafted among the liquid charm, the boyish charisma oiled the magical gestures, the scent of his sexuality insinuated itself into her nostrils. Would he take her, after dinner, as he was supposed to do—unable to resist doing the thing he was famous for doing so well? And would it be wonderful? Would he ring the bells that nobody had ever really rung, and, if not, could she then close forever the chapter of sex, that fifties, sixties, seventies thing that the eighties had been unsure about, and the nineties would do without?

He turned toward her, and his concentration was immense. She was the only woman in the room, but she was also the only person in the world. His expression said he was fascinated by her, and there was no point in hiding it.

"I'm so *glad* you came tonight," he murmured, in the voice that made womankind feel all right.

THE FINGER of the flashlight poked around the darkness. At first its attention seemed random, but then its motions became more regular, the searchlight of the guardpost sweeping the blackness with remorseless efficiency. The bits of the room came together, pieces of a puzzle forming the picture—the arm of a chair, the corner of a print, the edge of an Indian dhurrie. There was total silence. Nothing moved, except the thin beam of restless light.

It was looking for something, and now the slight sound of footsteps insinuated itself into the quiet as the intruder began to move around the room. It was the walls that seemed of most interest. The beam combed them from ceiling to floor, lingering on the postage-stamp pictures, before discarding them and moving on.

The fireplace flashed into view, with its plain mahogany mantel and its cargo of engraved invitations. The light lingered hopefully, and then it moved upward. The large oil painting was less valuable than its ornate frame, and the flowers it depicted looked like they could use some water, but the beam was pleased. It steadied, and the intruder moved toward it.

A hand, gloved in black, reached up to touch the intricate carving of the wood, before running along the borders of the picture.

In the stillness, the sigh was an explosion, as breath whistled from lungs that had been holding it too long.

CAROLINE PUSHED the plate a symbolic inch toward the center of the table, and she wondered when she had last eaten so well. Succulent clams, not too big, not too small, with lemon, pepper, and the delicious shallots in vinegar that were so difficult to find outside France; a tender, juicy chicken Kiev crisp outside, soft and creamy inside with lightly cooked spinach in which she could *taste* the iron, and the newest potatoes she had ever had, painted with mint, brushed with butter, firm and round; finally, a raspberry tart, the pride of the Sunset's world-renowned pastry chef, washed down with a nectar-sweet Château Coutet from the vineyard south of Bordeaux.

It wasn't however the pleasant sensation of fullness in her tummy that was in the forefront of her consciousness. It was the far more substantial feeling deep in the depths of her.

Across the table was its cause. His face bathed in the candlelight, the twinkling eyes of the star searched hers for the evidence of his effect. All through the delicious meal he had shone out at her, and the rheostat of his attraction had been turned endlessly upward. It had been a virtuoso performance as he had run the gamut of his seductive skills, melding the different roles brilliantly, discarding one at the very point it had peaked, replacing it with another that merged in perfect harmony with the part relinquished. The enthusiasm of the child, touching in its eager simplicity, became at the very point of its maximum effect the vulnerability of the little boy lost on the sea of pointless fame. The ruthless businessman retreated at the pinnacle of his success into the altruistic philosopher, wise and kind, as the man of Mammon became in turn the artist, the pragmatist, the dreamer. He hinted of his riches as he laughed at them, and he talked of his power as he scorned it— and all the time his beauty shone on her, like the light reflecting from a many-faceted gemstone, always different, ultimately the same. Despite her valiant efforts to remain objective, Caroline Kirkegaard was hypnotized and the feeling within her said that it mattered not at all that at long last the biter had been bitten.

One thing she knew. Never again would she have a chance to sample this exotic fruit, and when he discovered what she knew, Robert Hartford would regret this evening with every fiber of his being for every second of his life. So she relaxed and allowed the wonderful feeling to build beneath the expert gaze of its creator.

The waiter seemed unnerved by the electric currents that crackled in the warm air of the room. "Can I offer you a glass of champagne, ma'am?" He held the already opened bottle, its glass misty with the cold, so that Caroline could see the label and the year.

"No, thank you," she said.

He moved around the table to Robert Hartford. "Sir?"

"No, thank you, Klaus. I think that will be everything. Oh, and Klaus, can you thank Monsieur Bosquet for me? Tell him he surpassed himself."

"Certainly, sir. Have a pleasant evening, sir. Madam."

"Thank you, Klaus. Oh, Klaus, on your way out can you leave the front door ajar. It's a little hot in here and I can't bear the air-conditioning. I'll close it later."

"Of course, sir. Thank you, sir."

He was gone. They were alone.

"It was a wonderful dinner, Robert."

"It's a wonderful evening, Caroline."

"Shall we go and sit by the fire?" This time it was her suggestion.

He stood up.

"Of course," he murmured.

—

The safe was behind the painting. The flashlight picked it out. It was small, with a combination lock, and the gloved hand moved over it eagerly, flicking the dial with the practiced ease of the expert. Two wires, two microphones emerged from the darkness, and soon their black suction caps were stuck fast to the dull bronze of the safe and the dial was spinning beneath the knowing fingers. It happened fast. A click. Another. A third, and the door was open.

The light exploded from the safe, reflected by the quartz crystal that seemed to fill the interior. But there was something else inside, and it was for the manila envelope that the hand reached.

━

ALL THROUGH dinner Robert had played her like a fine musical instrument, and he had watched her fall through cold cynicism, warmer amusement, and dawning interest into hot desire. Now, on the sofa, she was ready for him and the unescapable truth was that, despite himself, he was ready for her too.

She didn't move away as he moved nearer to her. They never did. If anything she leaned toward him like a flower toward light, inclining delicately toward his face, and his moist, inviting lips.

"Were you always as beautiful as this?" he murmured, his words wafting over her, fanning the flames that flickered in her eyes.

It wasn't a question that needed an answer. It was the delicate lubricant that would ease the slide to surrender. His hand on the back of the sofa behind Caroline's head moved imperceptibly, ready, willing, but not finally committed until the response had been received.

Caroline Kirkegaard felt herself letting go.

For the last two and a half hours she had wanted this, but she had never discarded her alternative plan. One false move, one heavy-handed gesture, and she would have struck back with the weapon of ridicule. If making love to Robert Hartford was the best way to end an evening with him, then turning him down after a clumsy advance would be its equal. So she waited to the very last moment to see how it would end.

But it never ended. One moment merged into the next. There was no actual moment when the lovemaking began. Perhaps it had started the second she had walked through his front door.

One moment they were apart. The next they were together. No decisions. No choices. Just the inevitable union.

His mouth melted against hers, and his fingers landed on the warm skin at the nape of her neck. Both touches were light, soft as the touch of a hummingbird at the face of a flower.

At first it was just his lips, millimeters apart, moving against hers, touching, ceasing to touch, touching again as they moved across the surface of hers, breathing out, breathing in. It seemed she was washed by his breath, as it rippled in waves at the gates of her nostrils. His scent was inside her, strong, and clever, full of the reassuring maleness that so very few men possessed, and, as she lay tight against him, allowing him to orchestrate the sensual dance, she felt his left hand at her breast.

It was enough. Deep inside the burning fuse reached the tinder box, and the explosion of lust shook her body. A spectator no more, she reached for him, one hand grabbing his neck, the other tearing at the breast he touched. Her mouth opened to devour him and her tongue darted out to find the wetness that his lips concealed. With her left hand she drew him into her, grinding his beautiful face against hers, and with her right she reached down into the bodice of the loose cotton dress, ripping back the flimsy material and freeing the magnificent breast for the fingers that sought it.

PAULA HURRIED along the jasmine-scented path, clutching the folder of transparencies beneath her arm. She wasn't looking forward to this, and at the same time she was longing for it. As she walked, subconsciously trying to hide the limp that had so appalled Robert Hartford the last time they had met, she rehearsed what she would say to him: "Sorry to bother you, Mr. Hartford, but Winty wanted me to drop these transparencies around right away . . ."

She would keep it businesslike and brisk. Winthrop had been offered a whole series of the most fabulous David Hockney lithographs, but the artist wanted a quick answer. If Robert liked them, then they could be a major feature of the redecoration plan at the Sunset.

Winty had been adamant that Robert should see the transparencies right away, and he had asked Paula to drop them off at his bungalow. Reluctantly, she had agreed. Now she wondered if he could look her in the eye after the weird business at the Livingstone ball, and she wondered too, if she would be able to look him in his. She spent all her days thinking about him, but she still hadn't worked out what she felt. Above all, she remembered his beauty and his so-casual charm, the wonderful things he had said to her and the care-filled way he had said them and, although she wasn't sure she could forgive him, she was already certain she couldn't forget him.

She had arrived, and she took a deep breath as she reached for the door, noticing as she did so that it was open.

On an impulse she didn't bother with the bell. Instead she walked inside.

Her spirits rose as she tiptoed across the gray marble of the entrance hall. Where would he be? What would he be doing? Making himself some scrambled eggs in the kitchen? Catching an old movie on TV like the rest of the world? Flicking through a script with those wonderful glasses perched on the end of that wonderful nose?

The big mahogany double doors to what would be the drawing room were closed, and Paula, straining her ears for conversation, heard nothing. She took a quick look around, intrigued to find herself in the superstar's home. The walls stared back at her, giving nothing away, a reasonably good Picasso bullfight etching in a fine frame on one, and a walnut-and-gilt mirror, safe but unexciting, on the other. The stippled terra-cotta paintwork was surrounded by a bright floral-patterned orange-and-yellow material border, and the restrained, understated feel of the hallway was emphasized by the plain stone of the floor. The light, not quite enough of it, came from a run-of-the-mill china lamp with a flat, cream triangular shade.

Paula suppressed the frisson of guilt that she was trespassing. He wouldn't mind. She was there on his business, and anyway, surprising him in his own lair might help to even up the scoreboard. She crept toward the doors, and turned one of the brass knobs gently.

The visual hit her right between the eyes. Both their backs were to the door, but they were turned to face each other, and the roaring kiss had reached the critical stage. She was big and blond, and it looked like she was actually eating him. Her wide wet mouth ripped at his, and the muscles on her bare forearms stood out like ropes as she forced his head in toward her. He would certainly need dentistry to recover from the ferocious onslaught, at the very least stitches, possibly major surgery. But it was also obvious that Robert Hartford was a million miles from pain. The thing that clinched it was the vast breast overflowing from his left hand. It was a milk lake, a butter mountain, a mighty mound of smooth vanilla with a hot tip, chocolate dark, and it sent Paula's stomach on a roller-coaster churner as the nausea gripped her.

She was rooted to the spot, but inside all sorts of things were happening, all kinds of questions were being answered. Mainly anger, and frustration and disbelief and all the other myriad of human emotions that went under the umbrella heading of "jealousy."

Her voice was sharp as an icepick when at last she spoke. "Don't you just wonder where those lips have *been?*" she snarled.

He spun around, the shock all over his face, his lips bruised and wet with Caroline's saliva. "What on earth . . . ?"

"You should close your front door," she said with a sickly smile that barely disguised the murder in her heart.

Robert Hartford went through the motions of trying to stand, but his position, twisted around, off balance, his hand still locked behind Caroline's neck, was against it. He half rose, half fell back, and all the time his face changed color—pale pink, red, vermilion.

"What the *hell* are you doing in my house?" he finally managed to explode.

But already his anger lacked conviction, subdued by the pleasure he felt at seeing her.

She stood there, absolutely furious, her beautiful face beautifully twisted with rage, and he knew that she was cross because she was jealous and that made it all right. Women in Robert's world were allowed to feel such things. They were positively encouraged to do so, because it meant that they *cared.*

Paula knew she had no prior claims on Robert Hartford. At the most they had exchanged a few looks, a few meaningless phrases. It wasn't any of her business whom he kissed, and anyway she had absolutely no right at all to come barging into his home. But her emotions told her reason that Robert Hartford belonged to *her.*

"I'll tell you what the *hell* I'm doing here. I'm working for you, in case you hadn't realized. I brought these over for you to have a look at." With great deliberation she emptied the contents of the folder onto the floor. The transparencies cascaded into an untidy heap on the thick pile of the carpet.

"How was I to know you were trying to swallow Silicon Valley?" she added.

"Listen, sweetheart . . ." Caroline Kirkegaard's face was halfway between amusement and irritation as she tried to speak.

"Oh, shut up, you freak, or I'll report you to your plastic surgeon."

"Don't you dare come sneaking into my house and insulting my guests and me. Don't you know how to knock? Couldn't you ring the bell?" said Robert, his tone milder than his words.

Inside he was in love with the plastic-surgeon crack. The girl was full of spunk. She was terrific. And most of her anger seemed to be directed at Caroline.

But not, apparently, all.

"Listen, you're the one with the reputation for knocking, and ringing bells. Although from your vacuum-cleaner act it looks like you're more of a marshmallow than a stud."

His mouth dropped wide open. Nobody spoke to Robert Hartford even halfway like that. If they did, and got away with it, it would mean that his starlight was dimming.

"Don't talk to me like that. Don't talk to me like that." He was standing now, shaking with a newborn rage, and his face pulsated as he spat out the words. Who did this girl think she *was*?

Beside him on the sofa Caroline Kirkegaard's smile returned. Robert Hartford was getting his at long last.

"I'll talk to you exactly how I *want* to talk to you," said Paula quietly. "And you'd better watch what you say or maybe I'll *limp* all over you."

"Get out! Get out of here or I'll fucking throw you out!" He took a step toward her.

Paula held up her hands in mock surrender. "Okay, okay, I'm going quietly." She smirked as she backed toward the door. "Apoplexy can't be healthy at your advanced age. I wouldn't want to be responsible for that . . ."

She paused for the Parthian shot.

"*Or* the kiss of life. . . ."

~11~

THE CANYON DAWN was crisp and foggy, the mist clinging to the foothills, the soft rumble of the traffic blanketed by the moist air. Caroline shuddered in her dressing gown as she walked across the bedroom. The condensation was thick on the windows and she peered out into the early morning, her mind stiff with resolve despite the cold. It was the best time for meditation, before the day had begun and the night had ended.

She walked quickly to the bathroom and threw off the robe, allowing the icy air to touch her nakedness as she watched herself in the full-length mirror. All around the room, the walls were covered with photographs of the Sunset Hotel. They were everywhere, taped to the mirror, piled high on the marble surfaces around the basin, propped up around the bath. It was the same in the kitchen and the den, and the other rooms that people never saw. Caroline was surrounded by the thing she wanted, so that she could never forget it. The pictures kept her focused on her obsession, seeping into her mind by osmosis. She called them her treasure maps, and she encouraged her Destiny disciples to use them, too.

Maybe an actress wanted a part in a sitcom or movie. Okay, Caroline would tell her to wallpaper her house with the symbols of what she wanted—photographs of the producer, the casting guy, the writers, and the stars. She should have the name of the show made up in neon shining from the wall of her bedroom; have the theme song play on endless loop on the piped stereo system; run the repeats time after time on the VCR. That was the treasure-map trick. Live it, love it, be it, become it, until Fate surrendered and Luck gave up. Pray for it, breathe it, dream it, die for it, until they tired of resistance and welcomed you home. Aim for it, relax in it, enjoy it, experience it, until you controlled the destiny you were destined to control.

She took a deep breath and walked out, across the bedroom, along the landing, down the stairs to the den.

The crystal was always locked away in the safe, and now she pulled back the picture from the wall and reached for the combination dial. Usually the crystal was alone in there—the only truly valuable thing she possessed—but today it had company. The manila envelope and the incriminating Livingstone/Ramona photos it contained *was* the Sunset Hotel. Her hotel. The one she now effectively owned.

Caroline dialed the combination. 10123. The number of her bank account at the Crédit Suisse in Zurich.

The crystal shone back at her dully in the almost-light. But before she touched it she reached for the photographs. A quick look at the teenage raver and her heart-stopping body would be better than a six-alarm electric fire.

The smooth bottom of the safe slipped beneath her searching fingers and a shaft of panic slithered into her body as she realized that the folder was no longer there.

It had gone, but a single photograph had been left behind. The crystal swayed away to the wall of the safe as she ripped out the glossy photograph on which it rested.

In the gloom it was clear. It wasn't Jami Ramona and it wasn't Francisco Livingstone. It was a photograph of Robert Hartford, and there was writing on it. The mauve pen was quite definite. "To Caroline Kirkegaard. Thanks for an unforgettable evening. A memento from the owner of the Sunset Hotel."

———

ROBERT HARTFORD loved the spa at the Sunset Hotel in the early morning. It wasn't just the wall-to-wall women, although they were the main attraction. It was the high ceilings and the lack of space meanness; the immaculately clean beige carpeted sprung floor of the aerobics area; the acres of sparkling mirrored glass that allowed him to see how very beautiful he was. Of course there was Nautilus, but there was also the full range of Eagle equipment for those who preferred to torture their muscles that way, and there were hydraulic water-resistance machines for aficionados of muscle pain, and weights, and bars and swimming machines and Stairmasters, treadmills, and bicycles. Machines read your blood pressure and printed out your physiological truths, and they took your pulse through the palms of your hands, telling you when to work harder, when to relax, and how many of the dreaded calories you had actually burned. And through it all, like angels in paradise, wandered the women whose bodies he wanted to *have*. The instructresses wore identical leotards so that he could pick them out from the clients who would otherwise have resembled them. They were cut high to show lots of thigh, and the mind-bending bodies they enclosed, all strutting muscle and sleek brown skin, were out there on the surface setting the example that just had to be followed.

"Hi, Lisa," said Robert as he loped through the entrance foyer into the temple of the body beautiful.

"Good morning, Mr. Hartford. Those new towels you wanted have come in. They're real neat."

The receptionist glowed at the sight of him.

"Well done, Lisa. I'll try one out today. Is Grace in yet?"

Big and butch, a Beverly Hills police officer who worked at the Sunset gym in her spare time, Grace was the nearest thing to a man that Robert Hartford could tolerate.

"Yes, sir. She's in the staff room. I'll call through immediately and say that you're here."

He nodded briskly, pleased by the beautiful girl's deference.

He walked over to the rack and selected a pair of twenty-pound weights. "Hi, Robert. Is it true you're to be the new landlord?" said the wonderful-looking girl next to him.

He smiled enigmatically. "Would you promise to keep coming if I was, Heather? I could make it a contractual obligation of the seller to deliver you."

Heather Locklear was a star with a *really* good body. In Hollywood, mockingbird's teeth were more common than that.

"Try to keep me away from the Sunset. I want to be buried here."

"Not a bad idea. Live, love, and die at the Sunset Hotel."

The sound of a commotion wafted in from the lobby, puncturing the pleasantries. "Where *is* he? The front desk *said* he was in here. *Show* me where Robert Hartford is or I'll break your neck . . ."

Caroline Kirkegaard strode into the room close on the heels of her furious words. She wore a one-piece Dance France leotard, jet black with red ankle socks. Chains were draped from a black leather band around her neck and twin thongs ran across her bondaged chest to an identical belt. Her furious searchlight eyes scanned the room and settled on Robert. The moment he saw her, a smile of beatific anticipation lit up his face.

"You cheap crook," she hissed. "You had some criminal rob my house." She rushed up to him, but two feet away she stopped, as if deflected by an invisible force field.

"What on earth can you mean, Caroline? What was stolen? What did the cops say? I thought I was having dinner with you last night."

"That's what I'm saying. You knew the house was empty," she hissed. "You arranged for someone to rob my safe. I'm going to bring charges. You're history, Robert. You're going to do time." She was trembling with a terrible anger, her lush lips, the ones he could still *taste,* working the syllables of hate.

"Money? Jewelry, Caroline? Surely not bearer bonds." He rocked backward and forward, his eyes twinkling, as he savored his moment of triumph.

"Personal things . . ." she spluttered in desperation. The defeat was all over her face. She couldn't file a complaint about the burglary of porno pix that she was intending to use in a blackmail attempt. Anyway, Robert had an alibi. And there had been no forced entry, no damage to the safe, no evidence of an intrusion of any kind, still less any information that tied Hartford to the shadowy "crime." The best she could hope for from the cops would be a polite "don't waste our time," and at worst she could open a hornets' nest if Hartford, Livingstone, and Ramona teamed up against her.

"So you lose again, Caroline. It's getting to be a habit," he said quietly. She leered at him horribly.

"So the dear old Sunset becomes a knock shop for jaded movie stars," she said.

"At least it'll be safe from the storm troopers of the Destiny movement," he replied.

The sweat stood out on the Kirkegaard skin like dew on a Smoky Mountain morning. Her treasure maps. Her future. The future that *must* be. It suddenly looked about as certain as a sure thing in the second race.

She tried to turn the venom in her mind into liquid form as she hissed her words at Hartford. "I hate you, Robert Hartford. God, how I hate you. And I *swear*, you will be sorry you ever crossed me."

Robert reached for one of the telephones that were strategically placed around the gym. He spoke into the receiver lazily, unhurriedly, but his voice was thick with power.

"Security? Robert Hartford speaking. Get a couple of your biggest boys up to the spa, will you? There's a thing posing as a woman up here and I want you to throw it out of my hotel."

PAULA SLUNK into the room like a thief in the night, her head held low, her spirits lower. She hadn't slept a wink. When jealousy had pushed her to one side of the bed, shame had tossed her back to the other. All night long she had wondered how she could have behaved as she had. After all, if Robert Hartford couldn't kiss who he wanted to in the sanctity of his own drawing room it wasn't much of a world. How had she summoned up the gall to think that he owed her any sort of fidelity? He probably had forgotten her name, even her face, and yet she had behaved like a wronged wife, or a crossed mistress. In retaliation, probably at this very meeting, he would blot her out as if she had never been. Thank God, he hadn't arrived yet.

"Hello, darling. Goodness, you look like you've just donated your last drop of blood. You make me feel positively 'healthy,' not at all a pleasant sensation. Are you all right?"

Winthrop Tower stood up as Paula slid into the boardroom. So did the owllike figure in the big round red plastic sunglasses.

"Sweethearts, do you know each other? This is Paula Hope, my assistant, and this, of course, is David Hockney, who actually prefers Southern California to Bradford, despite the shortage of Marmite, Weetabix and bloater paste. Shows you how perverse he is, doesn't it, dear?"

"Morning, Winty. Hi, David," said Paula, sinking down into the chair that Tower had pulled back for her as if she wanted it to swallow her whole.

The boardroom of the Sunset Hotel seemed to have been designed to enjoy the short silence that followed. The carpet was so thick it swallowed sound and threatened to drown ankles. The shining mahogany of the table was a hymn to order, as were the Sheraton dining-room chairs, and the Thomas Eakins oil of boats on a river that hung over the Adams fireplace. Only the tinkle of the coffee cups on the sideboard, receiving hot Kenyan coffee from a pear-shaped eighteenth-century silver pot, disturbed the rather aggressive calm.

"You all right, luv?" asked Hockney in an accent that sounded to Paula just like Graham's, although any Englishman would have been able to put 350 miles between them.

"Sort of," said Paula. "I didn't sleep last night," she added as explanation.

"Nights aren't for sleeping. Mornings are. That's why God made curtains —to keep out the sun while one's asleep," said Winthrop definitely.

"Is Robert Hartford coming?" asked Paula.

"That's why we're all here, dear. Waiting breathlessly for the landlord and master. Have you met him, David?"

"Course not. Otherwise I wouldn't be wearing my best sunglasses." He struck a pose, and Paula had to laugh despite herself.

"I am afraid I behaved rather badly to Robert last night," she confessed.

"Omigod. You didn't turn down one of his passes, did you? I've always maintained he'll marry the first girl that does that."

"You know, when you told me to take David's transparencies over last night? The door was open, and I caught him kissing some girl."

"Goodness, that's a bit like getting to watch the pope at his bedside prayers, isn't it," said Hockney with a laugh.

"My word, how wonderful. Is he any good at it? I mean' does he *measure up*?" trilled Winthrop.

The performance of the male sex symbol was of enormous interest to the two friends.

"I behaved terribly badly. I can't figure out why, but I was rude." Somehow the understatement of the decade seemed necessary.

"You mean, you didn't applaud," said a straight-faced Hockney.

"Don't say you didn't have a ticket," said Winthrop.

Paula tried to laugh. The welcome irreverence was thick in the air. "No, seriously. When he gets here he's going to be furious. He'll splatter me all over the walls."

Winthrop peered around. "Well, that would be a great improvement on that sick-colored silk," he intoned professionally. "Brighten it up no end. Don't you think so, David?"

"Certainly would, and if we could persuade him to get a bit of her over the carpet, then bully for Robert."

Robert Hartford's arrival could be heard in the corridor outside. "They're already in the boardroom, Mr. Hartford," said an obsequious voice from behind the door. "Yes, Miss Hope is in there, too."

Around the table the joking stopped. The door opened. In the doorway stood the new owner of the Sunset Hotel.

"Good morning, gentlemen," he said. There was absolutely no acknowledgement at all that the room contained a woman. For Robert Hartford that alone was worth an entry in the *Guinness Book of Records.* He stalked over to the table and pulled back the chair at its head, motioning to the waiter that he'd have a cup of coffee.

"You know Paula, don't you," said Winthrop Tower with a broad smile. He wasn't afraid of anyone. His talent ensured that he didn't have to be.

Robert's head shot up. "Yes. I'm afraid I do." He paused. His eyes avoided Paula's when he spoke again, as hers were avoiding him.

"I wanted to say this in front of you, Winthrop, and I'm sorry that Mr. Hockney has to listen to what is essentially among the three of us. Last night Miss Hope broke into my bungalow, uninvited and unannounced, and was incredibly rude and insulting both to myself and to my guest. I want an explanation, and I want action, at the very least a verbal and a written apology." He arched his neck and peered at the ceiling, in a gesture that was supposed to be magisterial, but made it seem as if his shirt was too tight at the neck.

"Good God," said Tower. "At long last love."

"I *was* unannounced, but I didn't 'break in' because the front door was wide open, and that made me think that nothing particularly *private* was in progress. And I *was* sort of invited because Winty asked me to drop Mr. Hockney's transparencies by as a matter of urgency." Paula's voice was full of defiance. She was in the wrong, but not *that* wrong. And where was the reference to the kiss? God, he was good looking. How could he possibly want to kiss that androgynous thing on the sofa?

"Nobody asked you to drop them on my floor," said Robert with all the coldness he could muster. The girl was amazing. As far from cowardice as from dishonesty, she was a whiter shade of pale, but she wasn't intimidated by him.

"Dropped by trannies on the floor? A capital offense. Off with her head," David Hockney pitched in, ever the enemy of hypocrisy wherever he found it.

"Who was the lucky girl, Robert?" asked Winthrop shrewdly.

"That's not the point," said Robert, a speck of red high up on each cheek.

"I saw that Kirkegaard woman around eight, heading past the pool in your direction. Surely not her, Robert."

The hunted look flashed into the Hartford eyes. This was ridiculous. The topic of conversation was being changed completely. Paula was being spirited out of the dock, and he was being surreptitiously sucked into it in her place. Paula had seen Caroline. He could hardly deny it.

"Listen, stop changing the subject. Paula was extremely rude to me. She ought to apologize." He was aware as he spoke that his demands were already well watered down, and no concessions had been received from the other side. He was losing. In the ordinary way, that would have been intolerable. Somehow, now, it wasn't.

"I'm always leaving my door open," said Winthrop. "And nobody *ever* comes in. Just my luck!" An expression of monumental sadness played across his drink-ravaged features.

Robert felt the beginnings of a smile. He fought against it, but he didn't win. His three opponents saw it. Their feet were in the door of his bad mood.

"I'm sorry if I was rude," said Paula.

" 'If'?" said Robert. "You were *incredibly* rude."

"I *said* I was sorry."

He laughed. "Well, I accept your apology. I can't imagine why."

"It won't happen again," said Paula.

To Robert that suddenly sounded more like a threat than anything else.

"Thank God for that," said Winthrop. "It reminded me of Yale, and I can't *bear* to be reminded of that."

Robert craned his neck, but he made no response to the friendly jibe. "Now," he said. "Mr. Hockney's lithographs. Well, they're marvelous, aren't they?"

"It just so happens," said David Hockney in theatrical mode, "that I have brought some lithographs along with me, trannies perhaps not doing the work justice." He pulled up a portfolio from the side of his chair and began laying the lithographs out on the huge table.

For a moment or two there was silence as they sifted through them. They were all on the same side once more.

"What do you think, Paula?" said Winthrop.

"I think the tentative decorative scheme for the rooms would match them perfectly. I'm less sure about the one for the corridors."

Winthrop beamed at his star pupil. She was right of course. A disaster in the hallways. Perfection in the bedrooms.

What he was most proud of was the sensitivity with which she had handled the famous artist. Painters of Hockney's caliber were enormously wary of interior designers. Their paintings were works of art, objects in their own right, and a million miles from "decoration." Any insinuation that they were merely part of a decorative scheme, along with the color of the armchairs and the texture of the carpets, would be guaranteed to annoy. She had put it beautifully. It was a lucky coincidence that the bedroom décor would not have to be changed to accommodate the Hockney lithographs.

"Paula's right," said Winthrop, with the certainty of someone stating that two plus two equaled four. "Incidentally, Robert, do you actually *own* the hotel yet? I mean, have you signed on the dotted line?"

"Ten minutes ago. Livingstone and I tied it up at breakfast."

"Congratulations," said Paula.

"Thank you," said Robert.

For the first time since the "misunderstanding" they looked full into each other's eyes, and the crackling communication was instantly visible.

"I hope," and he smiled, "that at my 'advanced age' God will spare me for a year or two to enjoy it."

She blushed as she remembered, as she was meant to do, and she smiled back, a smile no less brilliant, no less meaningful. "If death threatens in the interim, it would be more than a pleasure to perform the kiss of life," she said.

Winthrop Tower jumped up. "Come on, gooseberry, I mean David," he said, smiling broadly. "Now that the landlord has spoken we can get off to my office and talk money, and gossip, and other boys' talk. No point sitting around here when we don't understand the private jokes."

David Hockney stopped briefly in the doorway to blow a kiss. "Bye bye, Robert. Bye, Paula. Now, you two be sure and have a very nice day."

They were alone.

Somehow that made things altogether more difficult.

For the first time in his life Robert was not quite sure what to say to a woman. The alien feeling filled him up. Doubt. Uncertainty. Goddamn it, panic. He studied his fingernails. There was an enormous tenderness inside, a great longing, all soft and gentle and full of strange emotions that he vaguely recognized but couldn't fully understand. Usually his mind was sharp, his feelings sharper. He was definition man, focused like a laser, certain of where he was going, of where he had come from. Now, inexplicably, he was an unguided missile rocketing off into uncertain space, and it was wonderful while it was frightening, disturbing while it delivered the peace of which he had always dreamed. Locked tight in the grip of paradox, he did nothing, said nothing, in case the alien experience should go away.

"We drove them out," said Paula. It was the truth, but the naughty excitement in her voice was full of childlike pride. They had shared something together, something important and instantly recognizable. Two of the greatest artists in America had seen it. They wouldn't be wrong.

She wanted him to acknowledge it, too. She wanted it out in the open where the sun could warm it and the rain could nourish it and where it could grow and grow like no love had grown before.

"Yes, we did," he said, and his laugh was nervous as he stepped into the conspiracy of hearts.

It made her bolder, and her face was alive with the courage of youth. "Last night . . . I was jealous, that's why I said all those things I didn't mean." She was daring him to talk to her like a lover, or would-be lover, as he had by the pool on the night of Livingstone's party. Her face was begging for it, on fire with desire, glistening with longing. A part of him tried to respond. There was so much to explain. But speech would break the moment, and the moment was already too precious to be broken.

"You had no reason to be jealous. Perhaps I can make you understand that one day." It was as far as he could bring himself to go.

"Listen, I should have rung the beastly bell."

The sheeplike smile was magic. Robert Hartford was already halfway under its spell. It was remarkable. All these feelings, and they had scarcely touched.

He stood up, pushing the chair back gently, and Paula's heart raced in her chest as she dared to hope that it would happen. So many things were clear now. There was an intensity between them that could no longer be denied. Sometimes it had worn the mask of hatred, sometimes of attraction, now it appeared as it really was. She had no reason to, but she loved him. It was as simple and as impossible as that. The crippled orphan from nowhere, and the sexual hero of a generation who dealt in human perfection, who could choose any woman in the world. On the edge of triumph Paula could think only of failure. He had recoiled from the limp she had forgotten she had, and now, inside, he could be laughing at her extravagant presumption as he mercilessly led her on to become the greater fool.

But Robert Hartford had never been so far from laughter. At the other end of the spectrum where he was, there was only an explosion of affection, and a desire to release it.

She was only a foot or two away and he walked to her, and knelt by the side of her chair. She sat still, well aware of his presence but looking straight ahead in case she would frighten away her almost-lover. He reached out to touch her forearm, tracing a pattern on the brown skin, ruffling the blond hairs as he stared up at her profile. Then he reached up and laid his finger against her neck, as if taking the pulse of her, the temperature of the passion that lay hidden beneath the surface of her. Then he reached upward as still her face pointed away from his, and he followed the contours of her proud chin, and he lingered below the pouting lips as if afraid to be more bold without some sign of her acquiescence.

The shuddering sigh leaped from between the lips he threatened, and her breath fanned his questioning finger, but still she looked ahead, still she didn't turn toward him. So, he touched the part of her that her sigh had signaled for him to touch. The tender flesh of her lips pressed deliciously against his finger, and then at last she responded. Here in the slow dawn of commitment, she opened her mouth and gripped his finger lightly, nuzzling the explorer, her lips running along the length of it as she breathed out, coating the millimeters where their bodies joined with her damp moan of longing.

More bold, he moved at the verge of her body, pressing in gently against the teeth that were closed against him. For a second he stayed there, at the gates of her, knowing that soon she would allow him to enter, soon she would beg for it. And in response to his self-confident patience, her mouth opened wider in the escalation of the war that would be love, and the dry became wet, the desert the oasis, as her tongue bathed the part of him that she could see, the only part of him she could feel.

At long last she turned to him, and their eyes met in the contract that soon their bodies would sign.

They stood together and she melted into his arms. But there was lost ground to be reclaimed. On the edges of intimacy they had hidden from each other's faces; now all must be admitted. He gazed down into the eyes of the first woman he had seen, and she gazed back into the eyes of the first man she had loved. Her face was awash with the messages of her body, and her eyes were hooded with longing, her lips parted in the half smile of desire. Above the mouth that he had touched, two tiny beads of sweat stood out, and her breath came quickly, unashamed of the raging feelings within her.

Above her, and so close, was the face they all wanted. It was covered with a mantle of gentleness she had never seen before, an otherworldly glow that spoke of angels, and of the paradise that soon she would know. He paused before the mutual surrender, as if reviewing the past life that was now ending, silent before the future that soon would unfold. Then, reverently, he bent in toward her and the lips she dreamed of sank gratefully against hers.

~ *12* ~

"IT CAN'T BE economical to do all the beds with Pratesi sheets." Kristina was honestly appalled at the idea.

"Money isn't the issue here, Kristina. Excellence is. The people who stay at the new Sunset will want the best of everything. If they don't, they should go somewhere else. It's a question of getting the costing right. The sheets are three hundred dollars apiece. Work out how long they last and factor the expense into the room charge. Wilton carpets, interlined curtains shipped over from Sadlers of Pimlico, Avery Boardman sofas and chairs, four coats of paint—the rooms will be the best anywhere. They must be."

She spoke with the zeal of the fanatic, but she could see that she wasn't really carrying Kristina with her. That was the problem with a conventional background. There was always a shortfall in the imagination department. Still, that was what she had to learn. That was what Paula was teaching her. Since the day they had met by chance at the movies in Westwood the two girls had become close friends. Kristina had been fascinated by Paula's brilliance at interior design, and when she had begun to take an interest in it, Paula had immediately suggested that she work with her on the Sunset Hotel redecoration. Kristina had jumped at the chance, and Robert and Winthrop had quickly agreed.

Paula walked over to the bed and bent down to run the rose-patterned sheet between her thumb and forefinger. "Feel how soft it is, Kristina. It gets even softer the more it's washed, and it lasts four times as long as any other sheet. In the end it's probably cheaper."

"I just keep wondering if Daddy can afford all this."

Paula heard the implied criticism and rose above it. She liked Kristina and Kristina liked her. It was the way things were going to stay. It was cool that the elder girl would feel hostility. Kristina, a college kid and Hollywood "royalty," was effectively working for a nobody from nowhere with nothing but a diploma in self-confidence from the university of life, and a little thing called unlimited talent.

Their friendship was an unlikely one. Paula had never known people like

Kristina. In the poverty trap they didn't exist, because there toughness was the norm and character was stripped to its basics. Kristina, however, preserved from difficulty in the aspic of ease, was infinitely complex. All the effort and energy that the Paulas of this world had spent on staying warm, or getting cool, on feeding and clothing themselves, the rich Kristinas had blown on making themselves more "interesting." On the surface self-confidence reigned supreme. But underneath the brittle heart was obviously vulnerable, conditioned by years of the casually brutal neglect that the rich pretended was "good" for their children.

Paula was intrigued by her and her automatic mistrust of the straightforward approach. She loved her world-weary pessimism and her tongue-in-cheek tendency to put herself down. Then there was the wonderful way she could use words to make smoke screens and confuse the most simple situation. All the weapons and armor that Kristina possessed were designed for wars that Paula had never had to fight. Similarly, Paula's strengths—her belief in herself, her brave honesty, her formidably useful short-fuse temper— were effective in battles that would have had no relevance at all to Kristina's looking-glass world. In short, theirs was that strongest yet most volatile of mutual attractions—the attraction of opposites.

"Listen, sweetheart, your father wants the Sunset to be the envy of everyone. It will be."

"I still can't believe it, can you? It's strange that Livingstone would give up all that money just to have Daddy own the Sunset. I mean, I never really thought of Dad and Francisco as being close." She paused, lost in awe at the thought of her father's being close to *anyone.*

Paula heard what she was saying. "I think they're rather alike in some ways. Neither would be a great guest on 'Wheel of Fortune,' would he?"

They both laughed. It was true. Livingstone was a private person, hidden beneath the dense fog of his arm's-length politeness. Robert was more overtly reclusive. Both held their emotional cards close to their chests, so that nobody ever knew what they were thinking or feeling.

"Okay, I agree on the sheets. You're right. Go for bust. So how many do we need? Three sets per single and a twenty percent reserve." Kristina whipped out her calculator. "That's 432 times three equals 1,296 plus around 260 . . . God that's about a hundred eighty thousand for the single sheets, probably the same again for the kings."

"Given away," laughed Paula. "Wait till we start on the pillowcases, the shams, the bed covers, and the towels. We could blow two million bucks on the linen. Maybe more."

The model room stared back at them, unashamed in its extravagance, as far from a hotel bedroom as it was possible to be. Paula and Winthrop had avoided creeping anonymity by designing every single room in the hotel slightly differently, and the enormous amount of extra work had paid off. The room that was already finished looked as if it belonged to someone. Sleeping in it would be like sleeping in someone else's bedroom. For the night you had been lent the room of a perfect stranger, but one whose houses regularly appeared between the covers of magazines as excellent as *HG* and *Connoisseur*. Even though you could afford the price of your overnight stay you would think twice about shelling out for the Audubon bird engravings that hung over the fireplace, and you would have never thought to ask your designer to put a white terrycloth-covered sofa and an NEC color TV in the bathroom for after-tub relaxation, nor to hide the combination adjustable wall safe behind a hinged Biedermeier mirror. People were used to refrigerators in their hotel bedrooms, but the Sub-Zeros at the Sunset Hotel contained pink champagne and the nuts were macadamias, cashews, and pistachios, not the regular "mixed" variety, the bottled water Badoit, not Perrier, the chocolates from the Queen's chocolatier, Charbonnel and Walker in London, rather than the more obvious Godiva brand. They were little things in themselves, but little things that meant a lot. There was no more abused word in the English language than *luxury,* but the Sunset Hotel, paradoxically far too grand to aspire to the word, would come closest to defining it.

"It's going to be so beautiful," said Paula, the enthusiasm shining in her eyes. "Imagine the dreadful things that Kirkegaard woman would have done to it."

Kristina was standing at the window that looked out over the Sunset pool. She didn't turn around. "I like her," she said.

"Kristina! You *can't.* Nobody could. She's a monster!"

Kristina turned to face her. "I admire her. There's something so strong about her. People are frightened of her because she knows what she wants and because she's spiritual and she's wise, and she exists on so many different levels."

"Oh, bull, Kristina. She's a fake. And she's evil. Look what she tried to do to Livingstone. If it hadn't been for Robert, the old boy would have been destroyed. I can't believe what you're saying to me."

"You're too black and white, Paula. Nothing's as it seems, you know, in this life. I mean, maybe that model and he *had* met before in another life. Maybe they were meant to make love. And if Livingstone was ashamed of it afterward, then he shouldn't have done it. And if he wasn't, then why should he care so much about the world knowing? I think Caroline's pretty magnificent. I mean, she's made a whole new life for herself, and everyone lines up to dump on her. Daddy, you, everybody. It's no sin to want this hotel. My father does. Why shouldn't Caroline?"

Kristina felt the words flowing more freely as she spoke. Despite what her father had told her and Paula about the blackmail attempt, she found it impossible to blame Caroline Kirkegaard. At Livingstone's ball when she had finally met her, she had not been disappointed. Now as she thought of Caroline her mind filled with strange, warm feelings of respect, of admiration . . . and of something else, indefinable, unsettling, very far from unpleasant. It was irritating that Paula misunderstood her, but it wasn't difficult to understand why. Paula was a Taurus and both her feet were firmly planted on the ground, making her a perfect match for her father's obsessive Virgo. She didn't understand the Piscean, Aquarian world that Kristina and Caroline inhabited, the world of the seeker, the traveler, of the dreamer. But why couldn't she just admit that? Why did she have to be *right,* and Caroline wrong? Why did the blinkered realists think that they had a monopoly on wisdom?

"I didn't know you were a Destiny supporter," said Paula thoughtfully. She frowned. That was the flip side of Kristina, the vulnerability, the lack of focus, the weakness. Although they were endearing qualities, they were also dangerous. A cloud-obscured head was not the best instrument for seeing through Caroline Kirkegaard.

"I'm not a 'Destiny supporter.' I just think Caroline Kirkegaard gets a raw deal. That's all." Kristina's tone said she wanted to change the subject.

Paula walked through to the bathroom. In many ways this was the most remarkable part of the whole redecoration plan. Very few people had bathrooms as grand as the ones they found in an expensive hotel, and certainly nobody had ones as clean. It had been Paula's idea to double the size of the Sherle Wagner-fitted bathrooms and to turn them into a cross between a den and a recreation room, effectively making each single room a mini suite. They had telephones, and piped-in music, cable TV, and an intercom to the front desk. The shower doubled as a steam cabinet, and in its marble walls there were water jets for a pummeling massage. In front of the sofas were glass tables on which sat crisp copies of *L.A. Style, California Magazine,* and *Condé Nast's Traveler.* Beside the bath a marble recess contained vast jars brimful of Joy pour les Bains, and dishes were laden with Dior soap. The usual "luxury" hotel detritus of shower caps, sewing kits, spare buttons, and shampoo was conspicuous by its absence. At the Sunset people didn't do their own sewing, the women didn't do their own hair, and the something-for-nothing ambience of its "competitors" was a must to avoid. Everything that could possibly be needed was a telephone call away. No request was too outlandish, no demand sniffed at, no naïveté patronized, no ignorance punished. The guests were kings and queens for a night and a day, for the entire length of their stay. Unbeknown to them, they were watched from dawn till dusk, and more important still from dusk till dawn. The KGB would have drooled at the efficiency of the Sunset's information-gathering service, the CIA murdered to obtain it. From a thousand different directions, information on each and every guest was fed into the mainframe IBM computer. What did they like for breakfast? When did they go to sleep? When did they wake? Did they entertain "disreputable" guests, were they noisy; in what state did they leave their rooms? What did they look like in the lobby, and how much did they spend in the bar, on the telephone, in the restaurants? Their career status was monitored, and their taste in flowers noted. This secret system allowed the Sunset to excel. A hotel was only as good as its clientele. So the weeds were removed, and the trees pruned, and the survivors were nourished in a way that ensured they returned again and again to the immensely subtle welcome they had come to expect. They would be greeted by name, and the room would already be scented with their favorite flowers, the icebox packed with their favorite drinks. A persistent regular would receive the cleverest gifts—a leather-bound copy of her latest best-seller; a complimentary hour and a half's massage for the busy executive who, the computer said, had ordered one before; a dinner for two, on the house, in the hotel's restaurant, the menu already written out in italic script, the dishes chosen from past preferences stored in the infinitely knowledgeable memory bank. For others, the hotel would always be "full," and they would never fathom the reason why. How could one such former guest imagine that the computer knew about that time when, in a frantic hurry, he had cleaned his shoes on the bedroom drapes? And if another's wife didn't know about the hookers he'd entertained in the late-night Star Room, how could the hotel hold it against him? Nobody would remember that another had helped himself to a few coathangers, abused the chambermaids, and left no tip. But the Sunset did not forget . . . at least until a non grata became so successful, so famous that he or she had to be allowed a second chance.

"How much has the room cost, Kristina?"

" 'bout seventy-five thousand."

"It looks it. Oh well, only about another two hundred and twenty to go," said Paula.

"I don't think there's going to be any time for the honeymoon," said Kristina suddenly, her face wreathed in a wicked smile.

Paula blushed and then frowned. It had been three endless days since Robert Hartford had kissed her, and she had not heard a word from him. It was driving her crazy but no way was she going to tell Kristina that. "Listen, Kristina. Your father and I are just friends." Her face relaxed in a smile. "But do you honestly think America would forgive him for not taking a honeymoon if he ever *did* get married? There'd be a revolution"—now she laughed—"led by me. . . ."

Kristina sat down on the bed, bouncing up and down as if to test its softness. "Okay, Paula. Tell the truth. What's he like? Go on. Tell me!"

"Kris*tina!*"

"No, really. Go on. I'm your best friend. Friends are allowed to talk about those things." Kristina's laughing smile was alive with fun, but there was more to it than just girl-talk. Robert's whole career was in some way based on his legendary sack-artistry. Kristina's entire school career had been a succession of endless jokes on the subject. She had constructed an encyclopedia of stock responses to the ongoing jibes, but at the end of the day she was as curious as anyone else.

"Kristina, you're gross. We're talking about your *father.*" Paula laughed to show she didn't mind.

"Is it the quantity or the quality?" Kristina giggled.

Paula scooped up a Pratesi pillow. She advanced threateningly on her suddenly cowering friend.

"Or is it, 'never mind the quality, feel the width!' " Kristina laughed helplessly, falling over sideways to avoid the inevitable blow.

Thwack!

In seconds the immaculate room was in chaos as the pillow fight raged.

ROBERT HARTFORD's arrival at New York's Carlyle Hotel reminded Paula for some strange reason of the Spanish Inquisition. The limo she sat in was so stretched it looked like it had endured long hours on the rack for failing to make the right religious noises, and the green-uniformed porters hovered reverently about it like priests at a deeply significant ceremony. They made little darting motions with their hands at the still-moving limo, drawing back, then swooping in again as they tried to lay their groping fingers on the door handle at the precise moment the car actually came to a stop.

Next to her on the backseat, Robert gave new meaning to the term "vehicle role," and now as the limo finally halted at the curb he melted through the door ahead of her, because he was sitting nearest to the sidewalk. Wraithlike, he drifted across the pavement, his head held low and his eyes downcast to avoid the full frontal smiles of the priest/servants. His mid-calf-length navy-blue cashmere coat swished in the crisp wind-chilled air, and his perfect features hid shyly beneath the rim of a dark brown trilby hat, the trademark tortoiseshell glasses, and the folds of the Cambridge blue tasseled scarf that was knotted casually around his neck. To Paula he looked exactly like a god, and her excitement, building steadily on the trip from Kennedy, at the sight of the Manhattan skyline, and the tense, tingling streets of New York, now kicked into overdrive.

"Hi, Peter," murmured Robert at the porter called Frank and the one called Joe as he headed for the polished brass doors of the Carlyle.

"What about the luggage?" asked Paula, smiling. She just wanted to hear his voice. She just wanted him to know she was loving every second of this, every moment of him.

"It finds its way upstairs," he said with a shy laugh and the casual wave of a black-gloved hand. Then he stood back and motioned for her to enter the already revolving door.

The lobby of the hotel opened up in front of her, slotting effortlessly and immediately into the category labeled "good taste" in her mind. The black-and-white marble here was deliciously weathered, and the stone had not seen the quarry for a good thirty years, possibly more. There were flowers, but not too many flowers, and they weren't pretentious orchids but instead white azaleas and hydrangeas. No brass. No "clever" lighting. No cheap tricks. There was no magazine stand, just a discreet hole in the wall through which you would be passed more or less anything you asked for, and the gilt mirrors, the French tapestries, and the Beauvais-style rugs were all the sorts of things that would have been completely at home in Brooke Astor's apartment on Park Avenue. The staff stood about in uniforms that clearly did not embarrass them, and they looked as if they were proud to be doing the job they were doing.

The pinstripe-panted man hurried across the floor to greet them. "Mr. Hartford, sir. Welcome home. It must be two and a half months since we saw you last, sir."

The assistant manager was more than usually friendly. Robert Hartford had owned a pied-à-terre at the Carlyle for around seven years now, and he was always welcomed specially by the management, but in the last few days he had ceased to be "just" a movie star. Now he was the brand-new owner of the Sunset Hotel, the nearest equivalent on the West Coast to the formidably grand Carlyle. That gave cause for mild concern—would he try to poach the best staff in America? With the reticence of the first rate, he gave no hint of his thoughts, making no mention of the story that every newspaper in America had covered.

"Sullivan, may I introduce Ms. Hope, who will be staying with me. Perhaps you could arrange a key . . ."

In the elevator, he replied noncommittally to the old retainer's routine inquiry about his health. There were other things on his mind. There was Paula.

She stood beside him, tall and proud amid the unaccustomed luxury, and somehow she fitted in better than he did in her jet-black Azzedine Alaïa that clung to every molecule-moving curve of her delicious body; the wide brown crocodile belt, the silk stockings that defined eternal legs before disappearing into black Maud Frizon shoes.

He slipped his hand into hers. "I'm so glad you let me come, Paula."

"Robert, what on earth do you mean, 'let you come'!"

He smiled at her. "It's true. You're here on Tower Design business. I'm here because of you. Okay, I meet a couple of movie people for a tax write-off, but you're the reason. You know that."

It *was* true, and Paula could hardly understand the speed with which it had all happened.

Their kiss had changed everything—while it had lasted. Later, separated from him again, the doubts had come thick and fast. What did a kiss mean to Robert Hartford? It had *felt* important, but then that was part of the knack, wasn't it, the famed ability to make every woman feel like she was special.

The days had seemed like years, but there had been no call. Nothing. For the very first time in her life Paula had experienced the unique pain of torture by telephone. Watching it, rushing back home at every possible moment to sit by it, calling the switchboard endlessly to track down hoped-for messages that might have "gone astray." Luckily there had been the work to distract her, the Coriarchi house, and Tower's arch humor and Graham's nerve-racking and increasingly hungry eyes. Just when the pain was beginning to fade, and the memory of the kiss to lose its sharp edge, the telephone did what life did, it gave her what she wanted at the very point when she didn't want it quite so badly.

"Paula? Robert."

"Hi, Robert." Oh so very casually friendly.

"I've been locked in an editing room day and night."

An excuse.

"Oh." No possible correct answer to that. "I hope you got what you wanted."

"Not yet."

Deliciously ambiguous. Paula realized he wasn't talking about the cutting room or his movie.

"Listen, Paula. I gather from Winty that you and he are going to New York next week to look at some furniture and design some apartment."

"Yes. I've never been. I'm really excited."

"Well . . ." he had paused, and Paula could almost see the little-boy gestures that defined "appealing"—the hand darting through the immaculate hair, the glasses trick, the surrogate uncertainty. "Well, I have an apartment up there, and I haven't been for a while and it would be nice to go . . ." Again the heart-melting pause. ". . . And I wondered if perhaps you would sort of 'be my guest' and I could show you New York at the times you weren't working."

There, said the voice, it's been on my mind and I've spat it out, and now, beautiful woman, I am at your mercy—poor Robert Hartford, accommodation provider, tour guide, and general gofer to the stars of the world like Paula.

"I'd love it." The words had tumbled from her.

Now they had arrived at the front door of his apartment.

"Here we are," said Hartford. "I'll let myself in," said Robert over his shoulder to the elevator man.

The door closed behind them, and in front of them the view opened up over Central Park.

She peered around the apartment with an eye that was half professional, half looking for clues that would reveal bits of the mysterious man who fascinated her. Why did he love hotels so much? For their anonymity? Efficiency? A flight from responsibility? Didn't he want to *own* things? Or did he just want to own people? Would he be able to tell her if she asked? Could they have that kind of conversation? So many questions. So much to learn. Such joy in the learning.

"It's just beautiful, Robert. I mean, that view . . ."

The room itself was giving nothing away. Nondescript mahogany furniture, stylish Ackermann prints depicting naval battles from the Napoleonic wars, correct chintzes with a basic reddish-brown motif. There were pleasant lamps judiciously placed, a pure wool gray carpet, and a perfectly acceptable Persian runner in the small hallway. A smart black Sony TV with a matching VCR seemed the only concession to the twentieth century in what was a basically Georgian-style room—all of which served to emphasize rather than diminish the persona of its owner. Perhaps that was its real function.

"I'm glad you like it." He flopped down in an armchair and watched her as she toured the small apartment. "What do you think of New York so far?"

"Well, I think the people who live here must be the luckiest in the world. All these stretch limos and private planes and views of Central Park." She laughed as she teased him, and he, who hated to be teased, laughed back.

"You'll see the other New York, the real one, soon enough."

"When?"

"Whenever."

"You know what I've always dreamed of doing?"

"No idea."

"Going skating."

"We can do that." He paused. "Can you skate?"

She felt the hidden question. It was the time to confront the thing that must be confronted.

She sat down opposite him. "You mean with my leg?"

"No, I just meant . . . can you skate . . . ?"

"It really bothers you, doesn't it, Robert? Is it so bad? I just don't think about it. I'm so used to it. That night at Livingstone's party you really freaked, didn't you?"

He twisted around in his seat and tore his face away from hers. "I didn't freak." He hated the word and its implications. "I just hate . . . untidiness," he managed at last.

"And my limp is untidy?" She tried to feel for what he meant.

He wanted out of the conversation, but she had to get to the bottom of it.

"Not untidy . . . I mean, is it necessary? Can't you do something about it? It's such a terrible shame—you're so beautiful, Paula." He seemed suddenly irritated at being forced to fight the demons he would rather ignore.

"I think I could. I had an accident when I was very young. My leg got caught between the dock and a boat and I had something called a compound fracture of the leg bone. It was just about half an inch that was damaged but it was so badly fragmented that when it healed my left leg was just that little bit shorter than the other. It would take a lot of expensive operations to correct it, bone grafts, putting in bits of metal. . . . There was never any money for that. I just got used to it. Everyone did. I can move around as well as I want to, and yes, I can skate."

Her smile was soft, kind—seeming to say that she realized that the disability they were *really* discussing was his.

He was acutely uncomfortable. "I know it's ridiculous, but it seems so wrong. I mean, it's a crime against nature. You're so wonderful looking . . . and then there's this . . . thing. If it's only money I'd be more than glad . . ."

"To fix me up, so's I don't embarrass?"

He heard her mild rebuke. "I'm sorry, Paula. I just can't help the way I feel. I know it's crazy . . ." His voice, desolate, trailed off. How could he possibly put into words all the things he felt about beautiful women? They existed as goddesslike reflections in the eyes of a little boy in his father's suite at the Sunset Hotel. They weren't just people, they were symbols of life's perfection, of its possibility. He loved women. He loved everything about them, and he dreamed of a manless world in which only he existed to worship them. Every flaw they possessed was an insult to the natural order, because they were meant to be unblemished, untarnished, undefiled. But how could he say all that without sounding like a madman?

"You can't just love me as I am? *I* think I'm pretty special."

"I don't want to change you, Paula."

"What do you want to do with me?"

Her voice was husky.

She took one step toward him. And another.

The breath crept from him like a thief in the night. He didn't want to disturb the moment, but his body was saying the things it loved to say. She stood between his open legs, her leg was against his, and the scent of her was in his nostrils. Her lips opened as her eyes widened. She was there to be touched. She expected it. She wanted it. The permission was in her eyes. The command was in them.

He sat stock still. He was mesmerized by the promise of what she would do. His coat was still on, his scarf, everything, and yet he was wide open to her.

For a second he paused. In past lives he had not had to think about this. Instinct had guided him. Now, in the alien world called love, he was frighteningly responsible.

His hand was on her stomach, his other against her hip. Hardly touching her, he signaled her toward him. She sank down, her eyes not leaving his, and, as she did so, her skirt slid upward to reveal the brown skin at the top of her black-stockinged legs. Her lips were parted and her breath came fast. Her fingers found the bone buttons of his coat. She freed the material and pushed it away from his body.

Together they crossed the dangerous divide into intimacy. Now their collusion translated into longing, as his desire took physical form. He reached forward to touch the side of her head, in awe of her beauty. He stroked at her silky, soft hair, feeling the warmth of her beneath his fingers, and he moaned quietly in anticipation of the pleasure to come.

She smiled at his acquiescence, and the love flowed freely from her face to his as she reached down to unloose the buttons that strained to restrain him.

He closed his eyes as she freed him, and she sighed as she reached for him, holding it gently, clasping the fingers of her right hand around its base, running those of her left up and down the shaft of it, amazed by the beauty of the symbol of his need for her. With both hands she held it, then, letting go, she tortured him with the soft touch of her fingertips, exploring him, as she grew more bold and the wonderful sensation soared within her. She reached down to the depths, and her hand pushed beneath him, gamboling in the secret places, before reemerging to stoke the flames of his lust. Up and down and around about her fingers moved, prowling like a tiger in the night fires of the forest, sometimes hurrying, sometimes stealthy, always tantalizingly unpredictable. And she watched him, as each precious touch, each deliciously threatened absence, winged to the fevered forefront of his mind.

"Paula, Paula," he murmured and he reached out to hold her, crushing her to him, as he dedicated his life to her. Then, slowly, he stood up, and he drew her up with him. They stood there, their bodies painted against each other, locked tight in the embrace from which there could be only release.

Still she held him, and he was alive against her hand, expanding, thrusting, growing, becoming, and she sighed as she pressed harder against him at the eagerness she could feel. Her lips parted, and her teeth bared as she knew that she must have him, and his eyes flashed and his head moved from side to side as he, too, surrendered to the union that must be. Now her mouth closed across his neck, and her tongue snaked out to taste his flesh, as below he bucked and reared against her hand. Tenderly yet jealously she kissed him, standing up on the tips of her toes to reach him, and as she did so she thrust her pelvis out and guided the rock hardness of him to the place where stocking and garter met, to the baby-soft skin of her upper thigh. All the time her eyes questioned him, and told him all the truths they had waited so long to tell. He heard her, and his, too, had messages for her as the moan gathered at the back of his throat, and his throbbing blood rushed like a waterfall so near to the core of her.

Nuzzling in against his neck, she soaked him with her saturated breath and still she held him, tightening her grip on him as he expanded, relaxing it as he ebbed, loving the life she could feel in her hand, against her leg, in the howling center of her mind. She moved him against her, pointing him at the subtly different parts of her upper leg, rubbing him against the sheer silk of her stocking tops, pushing him daringly against the elastic edge of her panties. There at the brink of her she played with him, allowing him to rest briefly among the downy, wet hairs before guiding him back once more to the outside.

"Oh, Paula. Oh God, I love you," he whispered.

But she reached up higher and her lips trembled before his as they told of her own love. He bent down toward her, and his tongue slipped out to the tip of her chin. For a moment it lingered there, and then rhythmically it began to move. It traveled upward to her lower lip, brushing across her teeth, then hooking beneath her upper lip, pulling it away and allowing it to fall back, before resuming its journey. It traced a wonderful, wet pattern at the edge of her nostril, flirting lazily with the borders of the entrance before hurrying on to the bridge of her nose. It was a brush, softer and finer and more laden with sweet wetness than any had ever been, and it moved with deft strokes to paint the beauty of Paula's face. It sank daringly into the valleys of her now closed eyes. It roamed free across cheek and forehead and chin, and it drank shamelessly from her eager lips.

The groan of abandonment broke in Paula's throat. Before she had been an explorer in the foreign country of passion, but now she was a veteran in the love war. Her lips merged with his, and she fanned his mouth with her breath as her tongue invaded him, taunting his with the sharpness of her teeth. All the time she shared the universal predicament of lovers. How far? How fast? How to capture the elusive physical moment so that the wonder would never die? Only one thing was certain. They must become each other. They must fuse. They must merge. Later, in marriage, but now in the commitment of total ecstasy. Afterward, during forever, there would be time for tenderness and bittersweet words and for all the promises and poetry of the romance they would create. But here was reality: two bodies sizzling with the heat they had made for each other. She wanted him to take her, standing up, before any words were spoken. She wanted him to fill her with his love, and spray her with the purity of his intentions because words were liars that had kept them apart and must do so no longer. It was what he wanted, too.

She arched her back and braced herself, and she thrust up at him, reaching into the kiss as she pushed her hips forward. At the same time she eased down her panties and she guided him to the wetness of her. Now his hands looped down behind her and his palms cupped her buttocks, drawing them toward him, as he positioned himself for the sublime moment. She felt the pressure and her hand moved to place him at her entry as she opened up to give him the gift that would always be his.

There was a void within her, a vacuum of dripping, boiling need, and the lips of her love were pink petals of longing in the rain-soaked jungle of desire. So she reached up once again for precious height, and he bent down low and the tip of him strained at the shy entrance, and it closed over him, touching him with its velvet promise. Then he pushed out at her and she at him and his fingers sank into the firm flesh of her bottom, and he drew her in and she enclosed him.

Deep within her she could feel him. She drew back and she watched him as he invaded her, the half smile of desire all over her face. She was pinned against him, his strong hands on her buttocks as he thrust into the heart of her body, hard and high and deep. Paula cried out in happiness. She felt light, and lighter and lightest as her feet parted from the floor and suddenly she was in midair, held on the spear of his longing. She wrapped her legs around his waist and drew them tight together, using them to force him even farther inside her. Tight against the roof of her, he waited and they lived for pleasure, existing for the seconds that seemed like light years on the pinnacle of passion. Then he moved across the narrow hallway, carrying her with him to the bedroom, and he laid her down on the bed.

Now the length of him began to move within her and the wet sounds where their bodies touched made music for the celebration of their love. Even before he had found a rhythm, she knew that she couldn't hold back her orgasm. It was too much, too soon, after far too long. Her whole body was poised for the moment. Beneath her breasts, in her stomach, in her wide-open heartland, she felt the muscles tense. Inside she was wet like a river around the invader. She could feel the fountain spraying down the inside of her legs, falling back into the divide of her buttocks. The fresh musk of her need was hot in the air, and she reached down with both hands to feel the place where he surged into her, where his sweat-soaked hair rubbed deliciously against her melting, sliding mound of love.

But it was hopeless. She was lost. It was running away from her toward the inevitable conclusion. She tried to warn him, her damp hands pushing gently against his heaving chest, her eyes telling him, her lips murmuring soundlessly the great truth of what was to come. But he wanted it, too, because he, too, was ready—poised to melt down his heart and his mind and his soul and to feed it into her forever. She heard the thickening of his breathing as his lungs raced to fuel his coursing blood, and she watched him hungrily as his expression signaled the ecstasy of despair at the brink of bliss. I love you. I love you, she told him with her heart, and he heard her on that wild plain where lovers spoke. I love you, too, my darling, said his faraway eyes.

So they leaned in together, bathed in sweat and swathed in love, as they sought the strength for the sweet communion. He had pulled out from her, almost all the way, and he hovered there in the entrance of her, caught between the slippery pink fingers that framed his pulsating heat. Neither dared to move, eager not to disturb the intensity of the moment, eager to contrast the stillness now with the explosion that was to come. In the silence they were together, floating high above the canyon of the orgasm like hawks on the wind, stalking it, hunting it, waiting to possess it. How long could they stay there, untouched by it? It was a glorious game as they flirted with the ultimate ecstasy, easy lovers in flight above the abyss.

She felt it first in his hands. They tightened, they tensed, and then they reached for what they must have.

She felt her whole pelvis being dragged into him, as his fingers dived down into the depths of her buttocks as if they would draw her inside his body. At the same time he launched himself forward and plunged into the heart of her.

Like an arrow quivering in the target, she felt his shuddering surrender at the sublime moment of his conquest. The dammed-up torrent of longing cascaded from him, soaking the silken walls of her with endless ribbons of love. It was a jumping, rearing feeling of total satisfaction as his body shook against hers and still it came, ceaselessly abundant, filling her, falling from her, whipping her senses into a frenzy as the tropical tempest drowned her in the flood of crazy joy. His whole body was a fountain, existing only to bathe her in love and he pushed against her, and she pushed back, as his desire collided with her excitement and their world changed forever in the truth of the orgasm. The walls of her clamped down over him, and pleasure fell on them like hard rain on a lonely road as she milked him of his precious gift. And now her waterfall was added to the sensual sea, and together they poured into each other, drowning as they had meant to drown in the beauty of eternal love.

In the quaking aftermath, deep inside her still, Robert leaned forward to find her lips and Paula leaned forward to find his. Nuzzling into each other they kissed, full of happiness and the sure knowledge that what had passed between them was the end of nothing but the beginning.

~ *13* ~

ROBERT HARTFORD WAS watching Paula, and she was almost, but not quite, oblivious to him. In the Peter Purcell showrooms in the D & D Building, the beating heart of the chic New York decorator scene, the action was hotting up and Paula was in the thick of it. She stood there, in the simple sand-colored Christina de Castelnau dress, its formal lines in love with the curves of her body, as she argued her point with the fervor of someone who knew she was correct.

"This furniture *is* right, Winty. In fact, it's perfect. More than perfect. It's just what the Montmorencys need. I know you're off trompe l'oeil and the distressed look, but try to separate the furniture from the rest of it. It's the *association* that's throwing you off course."

The rounded, avuncular figure at the end of the table chuckled at the irreverence. As pioneer of the Maxwell Parrish-meets-Magritte style of intellectual, Mediterranean-influenced design, Peter Purcell was the colossus of New York interior decoration. In L.A. people died for a Tower-designed house. In the Big Apple they were equally happy to lay down their lives for a Purcell apartment. Like Winthrop, he picked and he chose. Mere money was not enough. He had to like you. And now, despite her shortage of tact, he very much liked Paula Hope.

Robert smiled as he watched her. Purcell and Tower were rivals. They respected each other, but they couldn't afford to actually *like* each other, although each was scrupulously careful to avoid anything at all that would bring that out into the open. However, there were points that each wanted to make, and as the pressure of irritation built up a head of steam beneath the surface, outright confrontation remained a distinct possibility. Paula, Robert realized, was in the middle, and he had never seen anything more magnificent.

Tower tugged at his spaniel's earlobe and peered around the cluttered but immaculate showroom. "You see, Paula, you have to remember that the Montmorencys are basically as old as France, which has been around for a year or two. That means that all their European houses are not exactly new,

475

and it also means, despite their loot, that they know what a damp wall looks like. They're not Rothschilds, you know. They're aristocrats."

"Yes?" Paula, in full spate, and in love with the fabulous Purcell furniture, was impatient to get to Winthrop's point.

He ignored her exasperation, although when he spoke again, there was a new I'm-talking-as-slowly-as-I-can-so-that-you'll-understand quality to his voice.

"What I'm getting at is that the Montmorencys don't really need their New York apartment to be done up at great expense to look like the west wing of the château after the leaves have blocked the gutter in the heavy rains. It's fine for the nouvelle society people—they're sick and tired of everything looking brand new and working perfectly—but the Montmorencys like the idea of having something a bit slick and sleek for a change. That's why they've chosen a penthouse at the Metropolitan Tower, rather than some stuffy triplex in a co-op on Fifth. They'll tell all their friends that of course they realize it's frightfully common, but actually they'll be tickled to bits with it."

Robert drew in his breath. So did Purcell. Battle lines were being drawn. Paula, however, knew what she wanted.

Purcell spoke up. "I think Ms. Hope's point, Paula's point, Winthrop, is that the furniture can and does exist perfectly well in isolation from my particular design point of view. If the 'Montmorencys,' or anyone else for that matter, finds *that* laughable in any way, then it doesn't of necessity extend to the furniture."

"Precisely," said Paula.

Tower scowled. Paula had committed a cardinal sin. She had sided with a rival against him, and in public. "Mr. Purcell is not the only person in New York designing 'excellent' furniture, Paula. There's Jay Spectre and Mario Buatta and Juan Montoya. Maybe you'll fall in love with them, too." He flicked an eye over at Robert in the corner. "At your age you're young enough to fall in love with everyone."

"Isn't she lucky," jousted Purcell. "At our age we're too old to fall in love with *anyone.*"

"Except ourselves," said Winthrop.

An uneasy silence descended.

Robert caught Paula's eye. She caught his. At last she seemed to realize that hornets were shifting about in their nest and that somehow, unwittingly, it was she who had stirred them up.

"Well, I know I'm just the casual observer," said Robert diplomatically, "and I find it all terribly interesting, but what I'm longing to do is to see the actual apartment. Is the plan that we go there now, and then I get to take Paula out to lunch?"

Winthrop Tower raised an eyebrow. "On the principle that in America and India designers defer to movie stars, I suppose we should fall in with your plan," he said dryly, and stood up. "Yes, I think we've seen just about everything," he added. The "worth seeing" was very nearly said. "Thanks a lot, Peter. We must break bread sometime."

"Open a bottle, anyway," said Purcell with a smirk.

Break it over your cheap little toupee, dear, thought Tower.

"Listen, I really enjoyed meeting you. I think your furniture is divine," said Paula.

"Yes, and when she's taken over my firm I expect she'll be buying lots of it."

A pained expression rushed across Paula's face.

In the limo outside she came out with it. "Winty, I'm sorry, have I upset you in some way?"

He capitulated immediately. "No, darling. Of course not. You know me. Couldn't bear you going on and on about his furniture. The smug old tart looked like he'd had his first orgasm in years."

She laughed, but she still couldn't give up. "But it *is* wonderful."

"Seen worse," conceded Winthrop.

She punched at his arm and laughed to show it was all over.

"Believe it or not, I was your age once," he responded ruefully.

"Stick around and you will be again," said Paula.

"Can I stick around too?" asked Robert. She was right. She did make time go backward. There was ozone in the air around her, and sparkling electricity. She made the colors sing, the smells more real, and the sounds vibrate. If that wasn't an elixir of youth, what was?

She snuggled into him, and he could feel her breast firm, infinitely appealing, against his chest, and he could smell the sweetness of her breath as she laughed up into his eyes. "You can stick as close as you like for as long as you like."

"Now come along, children, not in front of the adult," admonished Winthrop Tower as the limo swept past the Plaza and onto Central Park South.

But they didn't hear the joke. They were together in the private world of lovers. They knew each other now, not each other's minds, each other's souls, but far more significant, each other's bodies. In the love furnace of the night they had bathed in passion and the memory of ecstasy lived on. She slipped her hand into his and he squeezed it hard as he savored the intense excitement. He had watched her in Purcell's office, and she had taken his breath away. Her bravery, her self-confidence, the accuracy of her taste. She had confronted the two famous designers as an equal and emerged unscathed from the contest. Before she had always been just a beautiful little girl in his eyes—the goddess from the backwoods who had burst into his world, but who remained a lesser mortal to be humored, and patronized perhaps, before the shuddering surrender. Now she was an equal, a superior in what was to him an alien scene, and it made his conquest more poignant. That was part of it. The other part was more important. To achieve the ultimate conquest you had to be conquered yourself. He hadn't known that before. Last night he had learned the lesson.

As she fell Paula could feel him falling. She could see it in his tender eyes, she could feel it against her breast in his speeding heart. So she crept nearer, plastering herself tight to his body, and he leaned back toward her in the conspiracy of closeness as they both dreamed of the skin beneath the clothes, of the lust and love just under the surface.

"I'm thinking of last night," she whispered softly.

"I'm thinking of tonight," he whispered back.

At the Metropolitan Tower they were expected.

The doorman leaped forward and two or three people who had just lunched at the Russian Tea Room next door stopped to see if the limo contained any "faces." The "look-isn't-that-Robert-Hartford?" chorus erupted around the trio as they went inside.

"Mr. Tower for the Count de Montmorency," said Winthrop to the pretty girl behind the reception desk. "What do you think of the Léger?" he said over his shoulder to Paula and Robert. A vast Léger black-and-white tapestry dominated the exquisite entrance hall, with its understated azaleas, and minimalist black leather armchairs.

"It's great. I love the whole look."

"Andrée Putnam. Works out of Paris. Very big in the sixties. Coming back now. Did Rubell's Morgans. The Léger belongs to Harry Macklowe, who built the building. There's another one, in color, at the Fifty-sixth Street entrance. We'll catch it on the way out."

The receptionist was talking into the intercom. "Yes, sir, I'll send them up."

A tall, diffident Frenchman was waiting for them in the foyer of the penthouse apartment. He pushed forward a ramrod hand. "Edouard de Montmorency."

Winthrop made the introductions. "And this is Robert Hartford," he paused for effect. "He's my assistant's assistant."

The aristocrat looked a bit confused at what was clearly a private joke. "I can't offer you anything . . ." He made a feeble gesture at the totally empty space that stretched out for acres, seventy-five stories above New York.

"That's fine. We just wanted to get an impression of the apartment. Obviously we have floor plans and photographs, but seeing is believing, touching is the truth."

Paula and Robert wandered over to the glass wall, a mural of the best view in New York. "God, this is magnificent," said Robert. "Both rivers, the Park, New Jersey, La Guardia. What a skyline."

"Paula. What do you think?" said Winthrop. "What would old Emily Carstairs have thought of this? Actually, we're so high up, we could probably ask her." He looked at his watch. "Perhaps better not. The sun's over the yard-arm. She'll be plastered by now if paradise lives up to its name."

Paula snapped into action. She talked fast, as if plugging into some stream of consciousness. "Obviously the view is the main attraction, but I think we should avoid maximizing it. It would be too much. It's so strong all by itself that to point chairs and things at it would be to detract from the living space.

The thing to do is to aim everything in that direction so you balance the inside against the outside and end up with some harmony."

Robert watched in awe as she set off on a lightning tour of the five-thousand-square-foot apartment. Walls crashed down, new ones sprang up as she bulldozed through the space, dreaming of what it could be, what it could mean. Colors rushed from her mouth and textures danced in her eyes as she painted the verbal picture of the beauty that was screaming to be created. Occasionally she would turn to an at first confused and then progressively enchanted Montmorency to ask him how he liked to live, what his family consisted of, their ages, their hobbies, his preoccupations. As they all listened, mouths half open in bewildered admiration, the dream apartment came together before their eyes. It was a visible thing, and it bore as much relation to the rooms in which they stood as space appeared to have to time.

Even Winthrop Tower was astounded. "Dear me, I think she's got it," he said, Professor Higgins-like, from the ranks of the spectators.

"Wonderful," said Montmorency, his eyes shining. "I accept," he added enigmatically, in an utterance that sounded suspiciously like the "I do" of the marriage ceremony.

"How on earth can you *do* that, Paula?" said an impressed Robert, oblivious to the presence of the others in the room.

"Did you like it?" she said.

"I loved it."

Do you like *me*, asked her eyes.

I love you, howled his.

Mmmmmmmmmmm, said her body.

He moved toward her.

"Listen, you two. I'm sure that it's around time for that lunch or whatever you were both planning. Why don't you hop off, and I'll stay and sort out a few of the boring details with the count," said Winthrop quickly. He gave them an enormous wink.

Almost before the wink was over, the two lovers were gone.

THERE WAS an almost unbearable pain somewhere at the bottom of Robert Hartford's legs.

None of the other skaters seemed to be suffering as he was. They glided by, contented smiles on their faces, and their cheeks were ruddy as they waved their arms in time to the waltz that blared gaudily from the loudspeakers. But Robert wanted to rest, and so he swerved clumsily to the red barrier that surrounded the Wollman rink.

When they had erupted out of the Metropolitan Tower, onto 57th Street, Paula had had the idea. "Oh, Robert, let's go try the skating rink we could see from the penthouse. Please."

He had immediately succumbed to her enthusiasm.

Now, the roar of skates, a blur of color, and the shout of enthusiastic welcome signaled Paula's arrival.

"Christ, where did you learn how to do that?"

"My dad taught me when I was very young. There was a rink in Miami. He'd drive me over on the weekends sometimes. I haven't done it for years, but it seems like yesterday."

His face veiled over with a sudden sadness as she spoke "How old were you when your old man died?"

"Fifteen." She pushed the reply out fast as if she hoped that would end it.

Robert lay across the barrier like a beaten prizefighter, but even in his skating getup he looked like someone from a superior planet. Blue jeans, the thick lambswool sweater, black as night, and the trilby hat of the day before, softly folded, yet as crisp and as neat as any that Lock's of St. James's could produce. His face was alight with the cold and the exertion, and Paula's closeness was filling him up with a sense of power and grandeur that he had never felt before.

All his life he had considered himself a connoisseur of lovemaking. Sometimes he felt he had invented it. Now however, he realized that he knew nothing at all about it. Bertrand Russell had once said that to recognize that was the beginnings of wisdom. If so, then Robert's life so far had been blissfully ignorant. In retrospect it was simple. The vital ingredient in the mix had always been absent. He had left out the love. Now, with this girl, the fatal deficiency had been rectified. He loved her, but he hardly knew the person he loved, and now every time she spoke he would learn more of her. Her body he had explored, but that, too, had mysteries in reserve, to be revealed in breathtaking installments over passion-filled years. And there was her past—the family, the strange void, the aura of tragedy that hung around her like a phantom of the night. What had made her as wonderful as she was, and what could he do to ease the pain that summoned up a tenderness within him he had never known he possessed?

"You loved your father very much, didn't you? I can see it in your eyes."

"Yes, oh yes. I loved him." Paula leaned over the balustrade. She cupped her chin on her red woolen mittens, and tears filled her eyes. "Do you know what he did?" she said, and her voice caught as she spoke. She swallowed and then she patted her chest with her right hand. "He reached inside . . . and he put a string of fairy lights around my heart."

He reached for her, his hand useless on her arm but there for her, in the gesture that said he always would be. "But not your mother?"

How did he know that? The leap of intuition was effortless, as if she was speaking to him on several levels all at once. Was this what love was like? Shorthand? "No, not my mother. Poor Mama. Somehow she never measured up to Dad. He was my man."

She gave a little half laugh of disbelief, and a tear dislodged itself, tracing an uneasy pattern down her flushed cheek.

Robert reached for it, wiping it away. "I'm looking after you now."

His words said more than that. Your problems are over, sweet Paula. Those days are gone. Anything you want now you will have. Because you are with me, and I am strong, and I have power and I control the people who control this world of ours. Let me please you. Name what you want. Let me show you my strength.

She smiled up at him, hearing what he was saying, grateful for it, despite the fact that she knew he could not right the ultimate wrong that tortured her.

"I loved last night," she said simply.

"So did I."

She moved toward him on the barrier and pressed her shoulder against his.

"I want to do it again."

She peered up at him, and her smile was no longer sad, but it was teasing, full of affection, hovering on the borders of desire.

"Here?"

"We could skate real close," she murmured. "I mean *real* close."

"Paula!" His voice registered mock shock. "I've got cramps in my legs." He laughed.

"Beats a headache!" She dug him in the ribs, laughing too.

"Omigod. Is it Robert Hartford?"

A huge girl with zits more or less crashed into them as she went into recognition mode. "It is. Oh it *is*," she spluttered. "Marie!" she screamed over her shoulder.

Robert cursed the fame he loved. Most of his life was spent avoiding this in public, even as he schemed and worked for it in private. His neck seemed to shorten and his face retreated beneath the brim of his hat. Celebrity recognition took several forms, each as inexplicably weird as the others. Some people were just plain rude, believing that to insult fame was a good method of preserving precarious self-respect. "Hated your last movie." "You don't look so hot in the flesh." "Is it really true what they say in the *Enquirer,* that you've made arrangements to be preserved in ice when you die?" Others went mute, staring with baleful eyes. Some demanded autographs, but possessed no pen or paper and ended up with a scrawled "hello" in lipstick on the back of their hand. Some, mercifully few, played amateur critic and ran through the plots of several movies, only a few of which he had actually starred in. All started from the assumption that he was a creature so far removed from them that the ordinary conventions of polite human intercourse could and should be suspended. In the absence of rules, anything could happen, and that made Robert Hartford extremely nervous.

The fan stuck out an accusatory finger at Paula. "Is that the actress who played the hooker in *Past Master?*"

"If you'll excuse us," mumbled Robert. He grabbed Paula's arm and pulled her toward the nearby exit.

Over his shoulder wafted an excitable, "I had a dream about you once."

"Did you hear that? You had her in her dream." Paula giggled at her accusation.

"On that basis, I'm afraid there have been several others!"

"On *any* basis there have been several others." Again she laughed to show that it was another joke. Somehow the laughter this time wasn't *quite* so spontaneous.

"And now there's you." He turned to look at her, and his eyes were full of concern as he surprised himself. "There's *only* you," he added.

She looked at him quizzically; then she slipped her hand into his.

"Let's take it minute by minute," she said at last, wondering what on earth she meant.

"Let's," he said, and his arms were around her. Then his mouth crushed down on hers and he kissed her as if he were never going to be allowed to touch her again. She tried to gasp but his hungry lips had other ideas and so she just tingled with the thrill of it as her feet reached up on tiptoe so that she could be that little bit closer than close to him.

"Let's go back to the Carlyle." Robert's voice was thick.

"Please," she murmured.

They hurried from the rink, but the skates and the cramp had made Robert's walk stiff and awkward.

"Who's limping now?" whispered Paula.

—

THE TELEPHONE was ringing when they walked into the apartment.

"Let's leave it," said Robert.

"No, you can't," said Paula.

The really young could never do that. He smiled, indulging her. The desk would have taken a message.

"Hello," he said.

"Mr. Robert Hartford?" said the bright voice of a young woman.

"Yes."

"Can you please hold the line while I pass you on to Mr. William Kentucky, personal assistant to Mr. Hank Marvel." She spoke the names in a very definite, very careful way, as if they were deeply impressive.

Robert Hartford groaned. It was bad enough that the call was from Marvel, but this sort of corporate game playing drove him crazy. He wasn't against ego building, but he liked the bricks to be made of something substantial, like Oscars or box-office returns. Anybody with a mill or two could hire an army of wet-knickered, hair-lacquered, overmanicured bimbos to keep people waiting on the telephone. He sent his eyes up to the ceiling to tell Paula it was a bore, that he wanted to be with her, and she smiled back as she began to unpeel the layers of clothes that wrapped her.

The male voice that came on the line now was full of self-importance. "I'm sorry to keep you waiting, but the president of Moviecom International wishes to speak with you, and he is presently on a call to the Coast."

"Tell Marvel," said Robert Hartford in the voice he reserved for out-of-line males, the lowest species in the evolutionary hierarchy, "to call me back, in *person* please, when he is finished with his call to 'the Coast.'"

He slammed the telephone down. "Asshole," he said, as Paula watched him. He didn't move from the telephone. It rang almost immediately.

"Hartford? Marvel."

"Yes," barked Robert rudely.

"*Hank* Marvel," said the gravelly voice, chastened, but irritated by the Hartford response to the most valuable thing he had, his name. "I believe we're having dinner tonight."

Robert winced, as he beheld, albeit at the end of the telephone, the nastiness of Hank Marvel. He was the classic Napoleon type, a short man with a shorter fuse who had fought his way from the gutter, piled up the bodies, and then climbed on top of them to reach the pot of gold he was now plundering. He was no longer small in the eyes of the world, but as he pulled the covers over him at night he would *feel* small and he would be forever on the lookout for those who had sensed his *real* net worth—people like Robert Hartford, whose patrician vision could peer effortlessly into the dark recesses of the Marvel poisonality.

"My people booked a table at Le Cirque." He sounded quite pleased about that. Very nouvelle society. Kravis and Roehm. Erteguns and Trumps, Steinbergs and Kluges. It was where they all went when they felt like something a little grander than Mortimer's. A very rich man like Marvel would be at home in Le Cirque, where he could be sure of meeting a person or two who was quite a bit richer than he. Marvel would probably have his own table there.

"Can't stand the place," said Robert in a definite voice.

"Why on earth not? It's a very good restaurant."

"Oh, you know how it is. One has one's likes and dislikes."

"Well, where do *you* want to go?" Marvel was thoroughly disgruntled. The yes-men he surrounded himself with didn't have likes and dislikes. He had them on their behalf.

"What about the Russian Tea Room?"

Since the distant days when he had been a struggling actor Robert had always loved the beautiful restaurant next to Carnegie Hall on West 57th Street. The fact that it had always been Hollywood's home away from home in New York was almost incidental. It was a marvelous no-nonsense restaurant that had never made the fatal mistake of allowing its age-old trendiness to go to its head. It seemed to be open all day and all night, and anyone with the price of its meals could and would get a table there. Perhaps alone in New York it was where middle America could actually hear the dreary things that celebrities said to each other. The food was safe, not brilliant, with a few notable exceptions, but the ambience, the luscious red leather chairs, the enormously well-framed, well-hung paintings, and the attentive but far from overzealous service made it a classic that had never lost the cutting edge of its chic.

Marvel laughed a nasty patronizing laugh. "Ha! I should have guessed. That's where all you movie stars hang out, isn't it? They make a big fuss of you there, do they?"

"Sort of. You might bump into the odd studio owner as well. You know, the *mainstream* ones."

Marvel had deserved that. Moviecom was a pushy little studio that was traveling fast but hadn't yet arrived. They made commercial movies but they had a reputation for cutting corners and double-dealing. Robert had accepted Marvel's invitation out of basic curiosity. A dealer like Marvel, a businessman rather than a moviemaker, had to want something.

"Listen, Moviecom's on its way up. It'll be there," said Marvel bluntly, cutting down into the deeper layers of the conversation. "I have plans for the company. That's why I wanted to meet up with you tonight."

Robert paused. To cancel or not to cancel. That was the question. Curiosity versus pleasure. Curiosity won. "Well, I look forward very much to hearing any of your business proposals." Robert managed to emphasize the word *business*. What he meant was, "Stay away from the artistic side, philistine. The nearest thing you get to creativity is in the morning when you dump."

"Yeah," growled Marvel. "Okay, you book a table at your place. See you at seven."

"Seven-thirty."

"Whatever!" Marvel slammed down the phone as if he were crushing it into Robert's face.

"What was *that* all about?" said Paula.

"I'm afraid," said Robert moving toward her, "we're in for a terrible evening."

"But that's not till tonight."

Paula's message was unmistakable.

—

ROBERT SPIRITED Paula under the blood-red canopy through the polished-brass and carved-wood doors of the Russian Tea Room, past the line that waited patiently for a table, to the place where the suited manager hovered.

"Hello, Mr. Hartford. How kind of you to come and see us. Your guests have arrived." He turned around and made little ushering gestures toward the number-one semicircular banquette just inside the main room, the place where all the real stars sat. Three people were there already. Two, Robert Hartford had expected. Hank Marvel, charming as genocide, and a bleached, birdlike thing that was obviously his wife. The third man was a total surprise. It was David Plutarch.

Robert's cool was his most valuable asset after his looks. He didn't lose it now, even though his mind was on red alert. Plutarch! Caroline's Plutarch. There was only one thing that was certain. His presence here, despite any bullshit excuses, would be no accident at all.

Marvel rose like scum to the surface to greet them. "Ah, Robert. There you are. Good to see you. Yes, good." He seemed to be trying to convince himself. "You don't know my wife. This is Marie-Lee, a big fan of your 'work,'" and I hope you don't mind my bringing along my great friend, David Plutarch. David was at loose ends in New York, if you can believe that, and I insisted he join us."

The Plutarch expression was a mystery wrapped in an enigma inside a question mark. He raised himself an inch or two from the seat, in a gesture that said he didn't stand for anyone, and he extended a tentative hand toward

Robert. An inscrutable half smile played across his lips. "Robert, how nice," he said. "Not since Livingstone's black ball."

"Hello, David," said Robert, taking his hand. Then he turned his dazzling smile on Marie-Lee Marvel. "I'm very pleased to meet you," he said, investing the *you* with a special emphasis that brought a blush to Mrs. Marvel's cheeks. He stood back to reveal his prized possession. "And this is Paula Hope."

Paula felt the eyes rake her. Robert had briefed her about the Marvels. The roughly good-looking man in the dark suit called Plutarch she didn't know, although his name seemed vaguely familiar. God, they were really giving her a going-over. She fought back the desire to look down and check her dress. Inside, she was still making love. Did it show!

They all stood up and moved about, working out some unspoken placement, and then they were huddled around the table, the massive egos rubbing up against each other, fighting for space.

"David was the underbidder on the Sunset Hotel, darling," said Robert, turning quickly toward Paula, who sat close by his side. She must know that fast. It would be an evening for careful conversation.

"Hardly the *under*bidder," said Plutarch sharply. "Let's just say the losing bidder."

Robert just smiled.

"Well, it's a great pleasure meeting you at last, Robert," said Marvel with the sincerity of a sociopath.

"It's a great honor, dear," said the wife.

Marie-Lee Marvel had seen better days, but she could still remember them. Her beauty, or rather her prettiness, had long since fled, but it had left traces behind, hints in the bone structure, insinuations in the almost stylish cut of the bleached brittle hair, faint suggestions around the hard mouth and the heavily mascaraed eyes. She had married the pushy Hank Marvel when he was less than nothing and had stood by him on the harrowing journey from crass via cash to some pale imitation of class. The secret they shared was that they were the only two people alive who knew just exactly how awful he was.

"It's not an 'honor,' " said Marvel crossly, contradicting his wife and annoyed by the implications of her excessive humility. "It's a pleasure, as I said."

"I wonder if you'd mind not smoking that cigar," said Hartford calmly, ignoring the undercurrents of the conversation completely. "It would spoil my food and I don't think it would be fair to the other diners either."

Hank Marvel looked down at the unlit Montecristo No. 2 cigar that sat like a torpedo between his fat fingers. He seemed surprised to see it there. He looked up at Robert, at his wife, at Paula, at Plutarch, at the restaurant where the "other diners" were, and his small eyes narrowed to keyhole slits. Slowly, deliberately, he reached for his inside pocket and pulled out a leather cigar case. He stowed the offending weed away beside its afterdinner fellow, and his lips were tight against his uneven teeth.

"Thank you," said Robert coolly. "I hope you didn't mind my asking."

Paula pushed her knee hard against his in the gesture that said "well done." She felt the little thrill inside, and the warmth of her lover's leg pushing against her.

"Do you come here often, Mr. Hartford? I know it has a reputation as a watering hole for the movie industry. Publishing, too, I think," said Marie-Lee.

"Call him Robert," said Marvel rudely.

"Yes, please do, Mrs. Marvel, Marie-Lee," said Robert smiling suavely into the heavily made-up face.

"Good Lord," said Paula suddenly, "look at that marvelous Picasso."

Four heads shot around to follow the direction of her pointed finger. The painting she referred to was on the opposite wall. A red-haired lady sat in profile, and at the same time head on, holding in her lap a cage in which two small birds cavorted. Her right breast, large and round, formed the dead center of the canvas, while her left breast simply didn't exist at all. Instead, the viewer's eye was drawn to a muscular forearm of dubious anatomical accuracy. The vivid red of her dress matched the red leather of the banquette below her, and was relieved by two cunningly placed stripes of jet black. The background, arranged in layers of progressively darkened green, wandered away to the plain gilt frame in waves whose shape suggested the outline of the lady herself.

"That's not a Picasso," said Hank Marvel.

They all looked at him, Robert and Paula and his wife in horror, Plutarch with a kind of detached fascination.

"I've just been reading that Stassinopu-what's-it's book on Picasso, and that's not one," he added by way of explanation.

Hartford's arm flicked out and a waiter materialized out of thin air. "Ask Gregory to slip over for a second, would you."

The manager was there immediately.

"Who painted the picture over there? The one of the lady in red."

"That's a Picasso, sir."

"It doesn't look like a fucking Picasso," said Marvel truculently.

"Oh, but it does. It couldn't possibly be by anyone else," said Paula firmly.

"I gather from the reviews that Arianna's book is mainly about Picasso's sex life. Thinking of turning it into a skin flick, Hank?" added Robert.

"Can I get you all something to drink," said the waiter into the ugly silence.

"Champagne," said Marvel as if it were a response in church. Then, realizing that this was not a sufficient response, he cranked out, "Dom Pérignon or Cristal?" as he peered crossly around the table for dissension. In the Marvel world there was only one kind of champagne—the kind that cost the most.

"I think you'll find," said Robert carefully, "that they don't have the Cristal, and the Dom Pérignon is a little old, I see. Nothing the matter with that, but what I always do is have a carafe of champagne. I don't know anywhere else they do that, and it's rather good. It's French nonvintage, but totally acceptable, dry and not too acid. I think you'd like it."

"That sounds nice," said Marie-Lee Marvel, intrigued by the rubber necks that were zeroing in on her table, on Robert Hartford. However rich Hank and she got, nobody ever looked at *them.*

"Great," said Paula, adding her vote to the majority. Plutarch's nod was noncommittal, signaling that it was of no consequence at all to him what he drank. Three to one. Marvel looked like he was going to explode with anger.

"Shall I bring a carafe of the house champagne?" The waiter looked first to Robert, second to Marvel.

"Yes. And bring me a bottle of Dom, and make sure the damn thing's cold, okay?" barked Marvel. His face was on fire with fury but he fought to stay calm. Don't get mad. Get even. Forget even, get ahead. Way ahead.

"Hello luv," said Dudley Moore. Moore had walked across the room from superagent Sam Cohn's banquette opposite, where the two were dining with RTR regulars David Mamet and Joe Mantegna.

"Hi, Dudley," said Robert warmly. "Do you know Marie-Lee Marvel, Paula Hope, Hank Marvel, David Plutarch?"

Hank Marvel jumped up. Moore was a star with staying power. The audiences loved him, and they would forgive him anything. Even failures. That was real stardom. "I hope you will work for my studio someday," he said pompously.

Dudley caught the Hartford eye, but he was far too well trained in the Hollywood game to send up the studio head's pomposity. In England powerful people expected to be ridiculed. It was the national pastime, the price you paid for wanting a thing as disreputable as success. Here in America where success was godly, and where failure was frowned upon rather than celebrated, the famous expected to be taken very seriously indeed.

"I'd certainly like that, Mr. Marvel. I've heard Moviecom has some very good things in the pipeline."

"A few, a few," chuckled Marvel, his mood to some extent restored by the ego massage. *His* studio had some good things in development. The star had said so.

Robert couldn't resist it. Moore was big, but *he* was the biggest. He didn't have to play the Hollywood game. He was above it, and he liked Hank Marvel like he liked nuclear war.

"Mr. Marvel is a *business* genius," was what he said. "Mr. Marvel can take no artistic credit at all for any good things in the Moviecom pipeline," was what he meant.

Dudley Moore smiled nervously. "Well, anyway. Good luck. Good luck," he said, backing away from the table.

Marvel had been hot inside; now he was cold as the icy fingers of hatred plucked at his innards. He wondered if he should say it now, this minute, when he felt like saying it. Plutarch's voice, sharp, concerned, preempted him. "How's the picture deal with Galaxy going, Robert? You must be busy. Brave of you to take on the Sunset as well."

Robert watched him like a mongoose watches a snake. He sat there, so tight and so deadly, with his billions in his pocket—and all around him, hovering like an aura, was the fatal presence of Caroline Kirkegaard. He could sense her. Like Banquo's ghost, she was there at the feast.

Plutarch wasn't talking about the shortage of Robert's time. He was talking about the relative shortage in Robert's bank balance. He'd just paid $11.5 million into escrow as the ten percent deposit on the sale, with the balance due on closing in three months' time. The bank financing was in place, but his liquid assets were just about cleaned out, until he could complete the deal and get his hands on the Sunset's cash flow. In the meantime the income from the Galaxy contract would barely pay the mortgage and the borrowing costs. At the end of the eighties it was the American way. It was called gearing. Robert hadn't done a deal like this before. He was worried about it. He'd even lost a little sleep. There was very little margin for error.

"Oh, you know, David. There's only one life."

"Are you sure?" said David Plutarch, the wintery smile flicking around his cold-fish eyes.

Robert turned to Paula, and his laugh was dismissive. "David's into reincarnation, darling. He's very trendy, you know. I'm a little old for it myself."

"I'd never have guessed it." Again she pushed her leg against his under the table. The reference was to this afternoon. Everyone sensed that.

Hank Marvel's eyes were narrow as he watched Robert. He opened his mouth to say something but again from across the table the Plutarch eyes silenced him, his head moving almost imperceptibly from side to side.

"Are you ready to order, or would you like a few more minutes?" said the waiter. Dressed in a red Cossack-style tunic and black pants, he hovered solicitously by the number-one table.

"Are you all ready to order? Perhaps, Robert, you would suggest dinner for us. Obviously you are the regular here." The totally unexpected charm suddenly dripped from the Marvel lips.

Robert's head flipped back, on instant alert. "Well, everyone ought to try the borscht. You can have it cold but hot is best, and they serve it with delicious pastries, filled with meat. They call them 'pirojok.' It's a much better start than the caviar, which is the same as it is everywhere else. Otherwise the chicken Kiev is good, unusually moist inside. That's if you're not on a diet . . . or what about a good, traditional stroganoff? The beef is mixed with crunchy mushrooms in a terrific cream sauce . . ."

"Sounds wonderful," beamed the brand-new Hank Marvel.

"Delicious," twittered his wife.

Plutarch was silent.

"Mmmmmm," said Paula, squeezing Robert's leg.

They settled back in the new pseudoharmony and prepared to survive the evening. Then David Plutarch cleared his throat. "I think that perhaps this is the moment for my little announcement," he said. He leaned back in his chair, quiet, deadly. The loudest thing about him was his rather unfortunate tie.

Robert felt the surge of adrenaline. Next to him Paula felt him feel it. They both knew at once. Plutarch's prior detachment now suddenly made sense. He had been watching Robert and Paula dig holes. Now he was going to push them in.

"Hank and I are going to become partners, which is, I suppose, a way of saying that I have taken a controlling interest in Moviecom International."

That wasn't it. Robert knew that. A lot of superrich people put money into the movies. Hollywood was one of the few places on earth where cash could still be transferred into instant status of sorts. It meant that the two enemies he had at the table were now revealed as a team. But Plutarch's presence there had suggested that anyway. "How nice," he said.

Plutarch leaned forward into the patronization, his eyes narrow now, his face a killer's face.

Marvel's breath was coming faster. He'd wanted to do this himself, but at least it was getting done at last.

"The second half of my foray into Hollywood is Moviecom's agreed bid for control of Galaxy. I signed the papers this afternoon."

Robert felt the color leave his face. He tried to keep it there but it just drained away.

"So, basically, Robert, from today on you're working for me."

He paused before he added the fatal rider. "For now, that is."

All Robert knew was that a terrible thing had happened to him, and that it was impossible to remain sitting at the table in the face of it. He stood up slowly, his remote-control cool covering his retreat. His mouth was tight shut, a bloodless line of lips bisecting his jutting jaw. He said nothing. There was nothing that could, with dignity, be said.

He reached for Paula's hand and he pulled her up with him, and together they pushed into the body of the room.

The two men, wreathed in malicious smiles, watched them go.

"Oh, I almost forgot," said Plutarch as Robert backed away from him. "Caroline said to say hello."

PAULA LAY across the sofa of Robert's Carlyle apartment, slumped against the petit point cushions. She knew something dreadful had happened, but she couldn't understand its dimensions. Across the table, sunk in gloom against the Clarence House chintz of a fine Chippendale lug chair, Robert Hartford clearly could. He sipped pensively on a caramel-colored scotch.

"I can't tell you how bad the vibrations were. It was awful," said Paula, more to murder the nervous silence than for any other reason.

"Sounds like a *wonderful* evening," trilled Winthrop Tower valiantly. "My evenings never vibrate these days. Anyway, I love self-made billionaires. They're so . . . *raw*. And they do nothing but talk about money. Such a relief from art, don't you think?"

Robert smiled wanly, Paula bravely.

"The trouble was that Robert kept putting them down in this incredibly subtle way—so that they couldn't take offense openly. It drove them crazy."

Her voice was full of admiration as she watched him. It seemed to cheer him. He straightened himself up in the chair, and this time his smile had body.

"The only point in reaching the top in this goddamn country is not having to sniff around the guys who think they've made it. You don't see Winty brown-nosing the heavy hitters."

Winthrop paused as if in serious thought.

"There was a *certain* amount of sniffing around that milk-carton heir up on Laurel. He was *so* cute, stuck irretrievably in the closet door, not sure whether he was in or out. He changed the color of his drawing room three times in four weeks, or was it four times in three weeks. Anyway, I took it lying down. I *wish!*"

Robert scooped up the receiver and punched the numbers, reading them from the pad next to the telephone.

"It's Robert Hartford again. Is Mr. Liebowitz back yet?" His eyes narrowed and he leaned forward intently. He'd tried four times to reach the Galaxy CEO since they'd gotten back from the Russian Tea Room, but his car phone had been permanently engaged. Now, at last Liebowitz was home. He was being put through. "Bos? Robert."

"Robert, for chrissakes, where are you? I've left a hundred messages at the Sunset. We've got to meet. Like now." There was panic in Liebowitz's voice. It had happened. Robert had prayed, but never believed, that Plutarch had been bluffing.

"I'm in New York, at the Carlyle. What's up?" He knew, of course, but old habits died hard. Always hear the other man's information before you volunteered your own.

"You've got to get back here, Robert. What the hell's going on? It's chaos here. The whole thing's falling apart." He was babbling, his voice thick with fear.

"Bos, calm down. What is all this?"

"There's nothing to be fucking calm about," shouted Liebowitz. "For crying out loud, what has Marvel got against you? I'm fucking history around here, and the word is it's your fault."

Robert slipped into a more gentle mode as he tried to pry the information from the studio head. "So it's true that Galaxy has been reversed into Moviecom? That's final, is it?"

"You'd better believe it's final, and do you know how I heard about it— me, the guy who's supposed to run Galaxy? George Christy calls me up from the *Reporter* and tells me his inside man at Reuters says the wires are running the story in forty-five minutes. I call Hank Marvel and he confirms, and oh-by-the-way he says, the first thing they're going to do is junk your contract and the second thing they're going to do is to junk me. What's going down, Robert? What the hell's going down?"

"Try not to get upset, Bos. . . . I've just had dinner with . . ."

"I *am* upset, Robert. I'm on the street with nothing, and I've got payments, and Rachel won't understand. You've fucking destroyed me, Robert, and it's pissing me off . . . it's really pissing me off. . . ."

Robert waited. Across the room Paula's eyes were wide. Winthrop's head was cocked to one side, like a wise old owl's.

The broken voice at the end of the telephone was small now, like the career of its owner. "I've been sitting next to the fax, Robert. The documents are coming in nonstop. David Plutarch, the Stellar Communications guy, bought Marvel's sixty-two percent of Moviecom. As part of the same deal Moviecom bought the Wayco share of Galaxy, which gives it control. Marvel takes over the presidency and my job at Galaxy. The legal department has instructions to void the Galaxy deal with you, whatever it takes. They want you dead, Robert. It's almost as if the whole thing is about you. What did you do, Robert? What have you done to me . . . ?"

He started to whine, but Robert Hartford was no longer listening. He was thinking. As if in a dream, he put down the telephone in the middle of a Liebowitz sentence. Whatever details Bos had still to tell him were incidental. The deed had been done, as Plutarch had promised. The billionaire had paid maybe 150 million bucks for Moviecom and probably the best part of five hundred big ones for the controlling interest in Galaxy. And he had done it with the sole purpose of screwing Robert's career and finances. For the very first time in his life Robert saw a vision of the scenery on the other side of the hill.

He laughed the hollowest laugh in history. "He's done it," he said. "Plutarch's torn up my movie contract." There was an expression of total disbelief on his face.

"He can't do that. It was a legal contract. Galaxy signed it," said Paula, equally incredulous. She leaned forward—her eyes full of hurt and frustration at the affront to her lover.

Robert's voice was quiet. He had thought about that already. "I couldn't afford the court battle. Plutarch'd love it. His studio could bleed me white with every delaying tactic in the book. At the end of the day you can't make someone employ you if it's the last thing in the world he wants to do. The contract's just paper. Galaxy'll lose a fortune in potential profits when they blow this deal, and all the prestige that went with it. But the guy doesn't mind. He's more than happy to take a financial hit to get at me. Caroline Kirkegaard got him to do it, to pay me back for screwing up her blackmail attempt on Francisco. I can't believe she's got that much power over him. It's weird. It's frightening."

"Can't the studio management stand up to him? I mean, they wanted this deal. They were crazy for it," said Paula.

Robert smiled tenderly at her. There was so much she didn't know about Hollywood.

"The studio management," said Winthrop Tower, his voice laden with double entendre, "have been unable to stand for years."

Mist welled up in Paula's eyes. She jumped up and she walked slowly across to Robert. Kneeling down beside him, she threaded her hand into his in a gesture of solidarity that was also mixed with apology, as if to say, "I hope you don't think I'm bad luck." In answer, he squeezed her hand. "I know what you're thinking. Don't. This is my problem. You make it easier to bear," said his gentle touch.

"I think I might have another glass of whiskey," said Tower, more to himself than to anyone else as he moved toward the ship's decanter on the amboyna-inlaid library table. "I suppose," he added almost as an after-thought, "that the loss of the cash flow on the Galaxy contract might compli-cate the financing of the Sunset Hotel."

"That," said Robert simply, "is what the whole thing is about."

It was true. It was the double whammy. His career had suffered a major setback, but so had his finances. Without the income from the movie deal there was no way he could afford to borrow the money to buy the Sunset. Plutarch knew that. Caroline knew that. Together they had spent around 650 million dollars to get both their revenge and their own way. Now, with Rob-ert an impoverished spectator on the sidelines, Livingstone would almost certainly have to sell them the hotel.

Winthrop sloshed the scotch into the thick crystal glass. "Let's hope Fran-cisco gives you back your deposit," he said, his voice quietly ominous.

"What?"

Winthrop Tower's remark arrowed into Robert's brain. The deposit. There were eleven and a half million dollars sitting in escrow. Francisco Livingstone was not legally obliged to return his deposit if, as now seemed certain, he would have to back out of his commitment to buy the Sunset Hotel.

Robert's voice shook as he spoke. "I hadn't thought of that. He doesn't have to give me the money back, does he? That was the deal. Would you? Would I?"

Tower didn't know the answer to either question. There was friendship; there was honor; and there was decency. And there were eleven and a half million bucks.

"I'm sure he'd do the right thing," said Winthrop doubtfully.

Robert wasn't sure either. He'd always worked on the principle that no-body could be relied upon to "do the right thing," especially in Hollywood. That way occasionally you were pleasantly surprised. His mouth was dry. "He might. He's a good man, and he owes me one. But he's not a fool, and it wouldn't be a sensible thing to do, would it?"

He pushed back in the chair, his hand slipping from Paula's. He mur-mured to himself, to them. "If he takes the deposit, I'll have nothing left."

Winthrop walked over with the decanter. Without saying anything he poured four fingers of Glenfiddich into Robert's glass. No ice. No soda. Just sympathy. Robert lifted the malt whiskey to his lips, but he didn't drink it.

"Robert, it's not the end of the world." Paula reached out for his shoul-der. "You can earn a fortune anywhere. If Galaxy wanted you, then Para-mount will, and Universal, and all the others."

He looked up at her, but it was as if he wasn't really seeing her. Was it mere coincidence that his first love had coincided with the collapse of his life? Perhaps some people were just not meant to live in the world of emotions. When he spoke, the irritation coursed through the words, reflecting the illogical desire to hit out, to harm someone, to push part of the blame onto the only person in the world he was close to. "You don't understand these things, Paula," he said sharply. "Hollywood is sheep town. They follow each other. They'll all want to know why Galaxy pulled the contract, and nobody will guess or believe the real reason. The studio's new management will start a KGB-style disinformation service that'll fuel the rumor factory for months, coast to coast. Bits in Liz Smith, the trades out here—*Variety* and the *Reporter,* the celebrity mags like *Premiere* and *Us.* They'll say I'm over the hill, that I've peaked. They'll suggest I'm a megalomaniac, unreasonable in my demands, impossible to satisfy, a royal pain in the butt. You name it, they'll say it, up to and over the borders of libel, as long as it's damaging enough. They'll even pull in the Sunset deal. You can imagine the kind of thing . . . some crazy idea to buy a hotel he could never really afford . . . a sign of instability, of losing contact with reality. They might even bring you into it. . . ." His eyes glinted with the cruelty of the deeply wounded. "You know, involving himself with someone young enough to be his daughter. . . ."

He buried his head in his hands. Would the studio be so very wrong in all the things they would say?

Paula looked at Winthrop in desperation, wanting him to tell her that it wasn't true. But he just nodded at her. Up and down. Affirmative.

Robert's voice seemed to come from far away. ". . . I'm going down. That's the truth of it. My fee takes a nosedive, and second chances in that town are rarer than overnight success." Again he looked up at her, and this time there were tears in his eyes, tears of anger, of frustration as much as fear for his suddenly uncertain future. All he had worked for, all he had built, the extraordinary edifice of his brilliant career stood teetering above the abyss.

His reputation was in the bloodstained hands of a latter-day Jack the Ripper, and the witch who controlled him, and his food, warmth, and shelter were at the disposal of a capricious old man. And then there was Paula.

He had fallen in love with her. Brilliant! Perfect timing. At the height of his fame, poised for greater glory than he had ever known, he had met the only girl to whom he had ever opened his heart. And she loved him, too. He could see it in her eyes. He could feel it in the warmth of her tender heart. And *whom* did she love? The movie star, of course. The myth. Paula loved the man who dined with presidents and was courted by the candidates for his legendary fund-raising abilities. She loved the biggest name in the industry that epitomized America, the man who could charm women because of his beauty, self-confidence, and power. She hadn't fallen for a fading has-been. Few of those survived the rocket-ship reentry on the journey back from the stars. What was left of them was picked up at the Betty Ford, on "Hollywood Squares," in guest-star roles on the dreaded "Love Boat." No, Paula would not love him then, and he wouldn't blame her. He wouldn't even like himself.

"What will you do?" said Winthrop softly.

Robert splayed out his hands. "There's nothing for me to do. The others are in the driver's seat. Kirkegaard. Plutarch. Livingstone. Whoever. I can't change anything, and sure as hell I'm not going to beg. Who knows? Maybe Plutarch will be struck by lightning. God can't like him a whole lot." Robert laughed bitterly.

"Robert." Paula's voice was sharp, urgent. "This doesn't change anything, does it?" The "about us" was left hanging.

"I don't know," he said.

~14~

THE MOONLIGHT DANCED across the Pacific Ocean, picking out the dark rocks just off the shore, and the late gulls that scurried among them searching for food. The salmon sunset was over, but a pink-blue light stained the distant horizon and the line of the Malibu Hills still separated earth from sky. The desert wind moaned gently across the rapidly cooling sand, and the lights of the mainland across the Santa Monica bay and the distant planes rising from LAX were a frame for the picture of the lovers.

Hand in hand, Robert and Paula nuzzled close, protecting each other from a thousand make-believe demons, as they walked on the deserted private beach of the Malibu Colony toward the pier. They kicked contentedly at mounds of seaweed, they rolled up the legs of their jeans to ford the shallow rivulets that crisscrossed the sand, and they admired the myriad moonlit sandcastles left hostage by happy children to the ravages of the wind and sea. "It's so beautiful here. So perfect," she murmured, her words almost lost in the salt-stained breeze. He didn't answer but he held her tighter, and the strength of his arms said yes, he felt that. Despite everything. Despite the danger to the only world he had. The only world that had existed . . . before Paula.

Yesterday, in New York, when everything had been turned upside down, he had been unable to get things into perspective. Like a hound at bay, he had turned against the girl who loved him as instinct had told him to discard anything that might slow him down in the battle to preserve what he was in danger of losing.

Then, on the long flight back to L.A., lying beside her high in the night sky, he had realized that nothing mattered to him except this girl, this strange beautiful waif who had entered his life so late, and who had captured it so completely. Somewhere over the heartland of America he had discovered the extraordinary truth. Robert Hartford, the screen idol, was no longer alone—and he never need be again. The moment the plane had landed they had gone to the beach—some lunch at Michael's, drinks with Goldie Hawn and

Kurt Russell at Broad Beach—and now here they were, on the potent sands of Malibu.

She looked up into his eyes and smiled. "Nothing matters except us," she said. "There isn't anything else."

Paula had come to realize that he was like a Russian doll. Layer upon layer of carefully crafted sophistication had produced a lacquered exterior whose sole purpose was to hide the man inside. Slippery smooth, he wafted through life on the cloud of his own charisma, and no one had ever before plumbed the depths of him except her. She knew and loved the inner core. She loved the gentle child who had been starved of his parents' love, and who had fought and won the world's sham adoration as a pale substitute. She loved the loneliness of the superstar and the vulnerability of the lover who didn't know how to love, and she was sucked into his naïveté as it clutched so desperately at the blanket of worldly wisdom. Paula loved the delicious paradox of him. Nothing was as it seemed, the outward persona at war with the inner being.

"You know, before I met you, today would have been the worst day of my life. You've made it the best," he said. He bent toward her and for long seconds their breaths mingled, the scent of them exchanged with the happiness they shared, merging in the magic moonlight of the Pacific beach.

Then he kissed her. It was not the kiss of passion. Not the kiss of exploration, that first nervous step to the feast of bodies. Instead it was the kiss of love. His lips moved against hers in the twilight, reverently, as if he was taking the sacrament. It was a moment of shared wholeness, a holy moment of truth that only true lovers could feel. His lips brushed hers, too caring to crush them as he talked to her with his kiss. "I love you," it said. "I will always love you," it vowed. "All my life I will exist for you. You have made everything new again. You have given me a second chance."

Paula fought to stop time in its tracks and suspend the moment forever. All she had ever wanted was to be loved like this. Now, at last, she was fulfilled. Her lips were melting with the passivity of total love. She was his, and she was telling him that with the ultimate eloquence, more beautiful, more true by far than all the lies of language.

He pulled back, not because he wanted to stop but because more than that he wanted to watch her. He must fix her in his memory, now, at this precious time.

Like a frightened doe, infinitely vulnerable on the mighty plain of love, she stared up at him, her lips painted with moisture, her mouth parted to let the warm breath escape. Her eyes were wide with the glorious fear of decision, as she surrendered to him, body and soul, heart and mind, this day, and tomorrow and forever more.

"I love you, Paula," he said, his words thick on the night air, as he peered into her essence, plundering it of its sweet generosity, of its purity, its innocent strength.

A shuddering sigh rushed from her and her breasts thrust against his chest as she hugged him tight and the joy coursed through her. "Oh Robert, I love you too. God, how much. How very much," she whispered.

There were tears in his eyes as he heard her, and he fought to make sense of the crazy feelings. No longer was he Robert Hartford, the great lover. He was a child again, experiencing the awesome feeling of global newness, the thrill and the fear that came with the realization that everything would have to be learned. Here was the man who knew how to please a woman. And here on the cooling sand, with the wind in his hair and the so-young girl in his arms, was a teenage novice, lost in the mad glory of his own first love.

"Love me always. Whatever happens. Love only me," he said.

He could have laughed as he heard what he was asking, but he had never been more serious in his life. Never before had he revealed the desperate insecurity lurking beneath the superstar veneer.

"I do. I will. Of course I will."

She clung to him limpet tight as she promised the strange promise. She didn't hate his sudden doubt. She loved it. She didn't care that he was the movie star, or the millionaire. The first time she had met him she had felt the tug at her heart, and then he had been the busboy, the guy with the "hello" eyes she had tipped on that faraway first evening at the Sunset Hotel. It was wonderful that he wanted her to be faithful to him, because it meant that he cared, this supposedly casual, careless, carefree myth whose body was plastered warm against hers on the Malibu sand. How could he doubt her? How could he need to ask her about forever? But she understood, because those were the questions on *her* lips, asked and answered and asked yet again in the beauty of their kiss, and in all the kisses they would share. "Do you love me?" "Will you always love me?" "Promise never to love another." There would never be any escape from the fears that measured the strength of the feelings. The loss of such sublime happiness was too terrible to contemplate. Only when the flame flickered and began to die would the timeless questions at last become irrelevant.

But the intensity had not left his face. He needed more than her breathless agreement. "I want you to promise, Paula. Promise now that you will never be unfaithful to me. From this moment on. Promise."

The old Robert Hartford stood back shocked and shaken as he contemplated the new. Where did this terror come from? Had it all started with his father's casual promiscuity when he had learned the lessons of female infidelity, and had, at the same time, fallen in collective love with the unfaithful? Those soft sirens of long ago, romping silkily around the bungalows of the Sunset Hotel, had defined the impermanence of sexuality. They had been the stuff of it, and they had filled him up with it as they had turned him on, and molded him into the man he had become. His father had loved them and left them, and so had he. Left the leavers. Done it first. Stuck in the daggers that were planned for his own back. But what if you dared to care? What if you *loved?* What if you gave yourself to those unworthy of the gift? It had been far too awful to contemplate and so, through the long years, he had insulated himself from that, and instead perfected the skills of sterile lovemaking in the void where love itself was a stranger.

Now, it had happened, and with the cruelty of fate it had happened on the eve of his own destruction. With his riches stripped away and his fame in ruins, the "expert" was about to become a novice locked in the terminal angst of those who dared to put themselves on the line. In the affair of the heart, Robert Hartford was a gambler at last. And it scared the living daylights out of him.

So around his brain the word kept winging around and around. *Promise. Promise. Promise.*

He knelt down and his arms held her tight so that she knelt before him, too, and they faced each other, solemn, close.

Paula reached out and touched his cheek as if to soothe away the pain of doubt. "I promise you, Robert Hartford. On my life I promise I will always be faithful to you."

A tear rolled down the famous cheek.

"Make love to me," he said.

⟶

It was the end of a long day, but Francisco Livingstone's tiredness was not the normal kind. His illness was draining his energy.

He walked over to the Benjamin Burnham Connecticut block-front cherry desk and the typewritten document stared up at him. Thank God, his beloved hotel would be in good hands. Robert Hartford would make all sorts of mistakes, but then so had he in the early days. It didn't matter. It would be good for the Sunset to go through a few dramas. At least Robert's heart was in the right place, and most of all he had good taste, and the wisdom to hire people whose taste was better than his. The problems he would engineer would result from his standards being too high rather than too low, and at the end of the day those could always be overcome.

He brightened a little. At least he would get to see the Winthrop Tower-designed Sunset. That would be some memorial.

He sat down, pulled the silk dressing gown tightly around him, and picked up the telephone.

"Front desk? Whom am I speaking to?"

"John, Mr. Livingstone." They all recognized his voice.

"Oh, John, be a good fellow and send a bellboy down to my bungalow, will you? I want him to witness a signature. He'll bring you back a sealed envelope. Could you put it in the night safe and give it to the manager in the morning? Tell Brough I want it transferred to my own document safe tomorrow. Is that clear?"

"Quite clear, Mr. Livingstone."

Everyone knew that the hotel was in escrow and that Robert Hartford was the new owner, but equally everyone knew that while he was alive the Sunset would always belong to Francisco Livingstone.

"And, sir, there's a message just come in for you. Your masseuse telephoned to say she was sick. She's arranged a replacement who she says is very good indeed. If it's okay, she'll be there at the usual time. That's in about half an hour, sir."

Livingstone put down the receiver, irritated. His weekly massage was a ritual that he relied upon for its total regularity. Karen, the usual girl, knew exactly what he liked and disliked and they had evolved a clockwork procedure that reduced to a minimum all potential for discord. On the first day she had visited him she had asked how he liked to be massaged. "In total silence," he had replied, and that was how it had always occurred. Over the years they had refined the procedure. Knowing that he could set his watch by the punctuality of her arrival, he would have a ten-minute sauna, a twenty-minute bath, and would then take up his position on the permanent marble slab that was a feature of his cavernous bathroom. The sweating and the heat would relax him completely, and sometimes he would even doze off to awaken to the soothing caresses of Karen's practiced fingers. One hour's massage was always followed by a facial, manicure, pedicure, and a vigorous rubdown with a rough towel bathed in cologne. The whole business took about three hours, and it was the best part of Francisco Livingstone's week. On the very few occasions when Karen had canceled before, she had provided a replacement and briefed her on the plot of the massage. He hoped she'd done so this time.

The doorbell rang. He walked over and let the bellboy in.

"I just wanted you to witness my signature on this document." He scrawled his name in a spidery hand. The bellboy wrote his in big round letters beneath, purposefully not asking what it was he was signing. "Thank you. Now you be sure to give that to John and make sure he remembers to put it in the night safe. What's your name?"

"Walter."

To ask an employee's name was the equivalent of a tip. The impression was given that Walter would not be forgotten.

Well, that was one thing out of the way. Far better to be safe than sorry.

Now what should he do about the masseuse? Karen had a key. Had she given it to the new girl? Almost certainly not. Should he disrupt his usual schedule? No. He walked quickly to the door and placed it on the latch. The girl could let herself in. By that stage he'd be totally relaxed on the slab. That was the whole point of it all.

He had switched the sauna on earlier and it was creaking with heat when he opened the door, the scrubbed, faded wood hot to the touch, the coals glowing radiantly in the spotless, stainless-steel furnace. He reached inside and ladled some green-pine essence onto the coals, watching the steam heat hiss into the dry atmosphere. Quickly he checked the inventory. Six or seven crisp, clean towels, *The New Yorker, The Economist,* and *Vogue,* a Thermos of crushed ice for the delicious merger of heat and cold that was perhaps the best part of the sauna. He slipped off the dressing gown and stepped inside, being careful to avoid contact with any of the burning wooden surfaces. He stretched out full length and flicked the switch that controlled the piped music, a little Beethoven for the jangled nerves. Beneath him the towel sopped up the moisture springing from his back. He had to be careful at his age. Dehydration was a problem, and the heart was always threatening unpleasant surprises. Still, he breathed in deeply and sighed his contentment. Then, quite suddenly, there was a shift deep within him. In the middle of the carefully orchestrated comfort he felt the premonition. It tickled at the back of his spine where the sweat gathered, and it speeded his already racing heart. He hadn't the faintest idea what had caused it. He was wrapped in sensuous comfort, and yet suddenly he was thoroughly disturbed. It made no sense at all, and if there was one thing that Francisco Livingstone couldn't stand it was nonsense. He closed his eyes and hoped it would go away, as the timer ticked and the wooden walls of the sauna expanded and contracted to the conductor's baton of the thermostat.

He picked up a copy of *Vogue,* thumbed past an article on spa burn-out, and settled on a photospread of Jami Ramona! Her beauty and his memories wiped his mind clean. Had it really happened? He looked down at his own body, and a smile softened his crinkled features. The little girl had nearly destroyed him, but it had been worth it. Absentmindedly, he ladled some more pine essence onto the coals.

The small glass window in the wooden door of the sauna steamed up as he threw the pine liquid onto the coals. What made him think of *Psycho?* God, what a creepy film that was. The knife falling, falling, the outflow of the tub, the rusty water and poor Janet Leigh's lifeless eye. On an impulse he reached out to wipe the window clear with the corner of the towel, but only the tan marble of the bathroom wall stared back at him. Livingstone had had enough. Maybe the warm bubbles in the bath would help restore his equilibrium. But in the bath the silly mood persisted. He ladled out a more than generous quantity of Dior bath oil into the water, tipping it with abandon from the twenties cut-glass decanter. It was a superstitious gesture of sorts, as if conspicuous consumption would somehow protect him from the evil spirits that seemed to dance around the room. Livingstone sighed. He got out of the bath, pulled the Sunset Hotel bathrobe around him, and patted himself dry. Then he let the robe fall to the floor, walked to the massage table, and climbed on top of it. He lay face downward, adjusting a large towel over his lower back. The exertion of it all had exhausted him, as it was supposed to. He looked at his watch. Half past. The girl would be here any moment.

Good. That was better. The tension was easing at last.

He heard the girl then—soft, muffled sounds as she let herself in. She would be orienting herself from Karen's instructions, working out which door led to the hallway, which to the massage area that separated the vast clothes closet from the bathroom. He heard the door open, heard it close. The unseen girl walked toward him and stood by the side of his bed. A hand, cool, its touch light but knowing, landed in the small of his back.

"Hi," she said quietly.

He twisted around and peered upward, up the neat thighs, the short white skirt of the uniform, past the angled breasts to the girl's face. She smiled down at him, very pretty, very friendly, eager to please from the milk-white teeth to the retroussé nose, from the square dimpled chin to the gorgeous flame-red hair.

"Hi," grunted Livingstone. That should about do it for the conversation. He had no need whatsoever to know her name.

He could smell the almond oil as she poured it on her hands, and his skin waited in anticipation for the fingers that would charm him into the reverie of the no-man's-land between sleep and wakefulness.

She dug deep into his back, firm yet gentle in the perfect combination, up to the shoulders, thumbs to the base of the neck, kneading, testing, exploring his body as she felt for the right pace, the optimum degree of hardness.

Francisco Livingstone wafted in and out of sleep as he was supposed to do, unsure whether dropping off or coming around was more blissful. All life should be like this—responsibility banished; sensuality with no recriminations; nothing to catch, nobody to catch you. It must feel like this to be a violin, milked of your music, vibrating at the whim of another's fingers. How wonderfully passive he felt, and yet, paradoxically, it was he who was in control. With his barked command, the pace would slow or quicken, the hands reach deeper or less deep.

"Could you turn over, Mr. Livingstone." The request was a caress.

He rolled over, like an old log on a young river, adjusting immediately to his new position, and only marginally aware that he had exposed his nakedness to the young girl. He felt her hands reorganize the towel to cover his front, and once more he was flirting with sleep.

She bent in close to his ear and her breath went inside it with her words. "You just relax, Mr. Livingstone. I'll start your facial right after I finish the massage."

But Francisco Livingstone was already asleep.

The girl stopped. Her hands slipped away from him, and noiselessly she stood back from the table, watching him, gauging how far gone he was into sleep. For a minute or two she stood motionless in the quiet room, until his snores became stronger. Then, suddenly she seemed to decide. She walked quickly to the door, and she opened it carefully, her eyes never leaving her sleeping client.

A woman stood in the doorway, like an angel of death. She filled it up, from floor to ceiling, legs apart, hands on hips, her face hidden beneath the brim of a black leather peaked cap. Claude Montana clothed the broad shoulders, and the soft leather of the micro-skirt clung like wallpaper to the curves of her bottom. She wore leather boots, black as the devil's heart. A belt of wound thongs strangled her waspish waist, and a black cashmere polonecked sweater hugged her tall white neck. Lit from the back she stood there, surrounded by the aura of her terrible vengeance.

"He's asleep," said Kanga.

"Good," said Caroline Kirkegaard.

They passed each other, speaking no more, and the redhead's eyes fixed on the floor as she walked by the woman who owned her.

Caroline Kirkegaard glided into the room. He was snoring on the massage table, this puny obstacle to her purpose. Francisco Livingstone had tried to deliver up the Sunset to the man she loathed. Once Hartford had slithered from her trap. He would not do so again. For two delicious days she had reveled in Plutarch's and her revenge on Robert Hartford and the wonderful fact that he would no longer be able to afford the hotel that Livingstone so desperately wanted to sell to him. Once more she was so near. Yet nothing could be left to chance. Who could predict the caprice of a rich and dying man? Despite Hartford's cash crisis Livingstone might still find a way for his friend to buy the Sunset—at the very least he would search the ends of the earth for an acceptable alternative. But with Francisco dead, and Hartford unable to complete his deal, the Livingstone executors would sell immediately to the highest and most convenient bidder—to David Plutarch. And Robert Hartford would never see his eleven and a half million dollar deposit again. He would be penniless, in Beverly Hills, where poverty was a serious felony.

So she walked quietly toward the table and her heart laughed as she contemplated the marvelous thing she would do.

He wanted a facial. That was what he always had, according to the hotel gossip. He would get one. It had been simple to find the number of his masseuse, and no problem at all to cancel her. "Mr. Livingstone has asked me to cancel his appointment for this evening as he has an important business meeting. His secretary will call you tomorrow to reschedule." The message left at the reception had been equally straightforward. "This is Karen, Mr. Livingstone's masseuse. I'm unable to keep my appointment this evening, but I have organized a replacement in the usual way. Can you please pass the message on to Mr. Livingstone, as his private line has been engaged?"

She reached into her bag as she took up her position at the head of the table. A good facial should always begin with a thorough cleaning of the pores, shouldn't it? She drew out the bottle of astringent lotion and splashed some onto her hands, filling the room with the smell of jasmine.

She smoothed the lotion onto his parchment skin, taking care not to get it near his lips, his eyes, his nose. No sting must wake him.

Again she reached into her bag, but this time no potion, no sweet-smelling lotion, no soothing cream emerged. The tube was big and ugly, and it was painted a garish green. The letters in red were quite clear about its contents. CYANOACRYLATE, they said.

It was super glue.

She unscrewed the top, and she moved the tube toward Francisco Livingstone's jasmine-scented face. The pungent aroma of the industrial glue was lost, as it was supposed to be, in the heavy perfume.

First the mouth, parted a little as his meager breath escaped it. The dollops of clear liquid ran all over it, cascading between his thin lips, bonding eagerly onto his teeth. Quick, so quick the tube raced to his nose, and her hands squeezed tight as the glue invaded the nostrils, running, racing, sliding to fill the twin voids. And then, of course, his eyes. Not necessary, but such fun to block them up. One. Two. So easy as they wept the innocent liquid that was not tears. Nor ever would be.

She stood back, and a smile lit up her beautiful face as she surveyed her handiwork. The bits of him where the air entered, where the breath left him, were awash with the glue. The manufacturers were adamant about it. That was why it was "super." It set in seconds. And it bonded stronger than tempered steel.

She reached forward with her finger and thumb and she placed them on each side of the patrician nose. Then, as if picking a delicate flower, she nipped it tight.

Francisco Livingstone's dream was turning sour. The carpet on which he floated over the scented valley had turned into a bed of sharp nails. And now, worse, it was falling precipitously from the sky toward a black, dark lake he had not seen before. Down, down he went, and he braced himself for impact, and readied himself to swim for his life as the waters threatened to swallow him up. Splash. He must hold his breath in this foul-smelling water. He must get out of this suffocating blackness to the surface and the sunlight.

He sat bolt upright and fire filled his throat, as agony burned in his eyes and his nose. He tried to breathe in, but he couldn't breathe and he tried to open his eyes, but he couldn't see. His hands raced to his face to find out why. But his searching fingers found no answers. There was concrete at his lips, at his nostrils, in his eyes. He was blocked up with some strange substance that seared and burned at him, but the pain didn't matter because he couldn't *breathe*, and his world was deathly dark. A massage. A masseuse. There would be someone there to help him and he tried to scream in the soundless void as his lungs howled their protest in his chest and the panic squeezed the toothpaste of his brain. He tore at his mouth, ripping at his sealed lips, and he tried to push his fingers into the blocked nostrils, but there were no holes anymore. He was all stopped up. There was cement in his vital places, and, oh God, his eyes! Red pokers of white heat were stuck in them, but they merged with the rest of his face when he tried to find them. They were gone, lost in a featureless expanse of smooth, plastic nothingness. He fell sideways in the soundless chaos and his hand scratched at the air, his fingers brushing briefly at the hair of the person who had murdered him. Then he crashed headlong toward the marble floor.

Only his ears were still open. That she knew. That she intended. "Goodbye, Francisco Livingstone," she said. "When you get to wherever you're going, tell them that Caroline Kirkegaard sent you."

~15~

LIMOUSINES WERE LINED up outside the Church of the Good Shepherd like Russian tanks at a May Day parade. They stretched back down Bedford Drive as far as the eye could see, and they seemed to be disgorging their contents all at once.

Robert Hartford stood on the breezy sidewalk in front of the main doors of the church on Santa Monica Boulevard and shrank from the crowds that swirled all around him. He had never been to this particular church before, nor even known that Livingstone was a Catholic, but as he looked around, it appeared that God shared the preoccupations of all the other proprietors of Beverly Hills real estate. The United Artists building was just across the street, and so was the Wells Fargo bank, while outside the church a bright sign announced that it was protected by Selective Security. Clearly the Almighty was leaving nothing to either chance or the morals of those He had created, and He had taken care to position His house as close to Mammon and the movie industry as was decently possible in La-la Land.

Robert suppressed a bitter smile. He couldn't afford such cynicism. He had a more pressing problem. Two days before, the Galaxy press conference announcing the rescinding of his movie contract had cleaned the other news off the front page of every show-biz paper in America, and now the press was in a feeding frenzy.

The side streets around the Sunset Hotel were packed with paparazzi, and everywhere he went they lined up to humiliate him. In the whole of his life he had never experienced anything like it. Fame and money made you soft. You withdrew from the world behind your cash mountain and you threw bucks at your problems until all paths were smooth. Mentally flabby on the diet of sycophancy and luxury, you grew weak. Then the walls were ripped away. Like now. And the icy blast of cruel reality zipped through your unprepared body to freeze your heart. He should have been ready for the legendary impermanence of superstardom. Apparently he wasn't.

David Plutarch loomed up, welcome as an iceberg on a lonely sea at night. "Ah, Robert. My people have been trying to reach you. So sad about poor Francisco. Still, what a way to go! No pain. No misery. They found him in the tub, apparently. Out like a light." He flicked his fingers in the air. On his face was a mocking smile.

Robert stared back at him, the hatred blazing in his expression. Yet he knew he had to take it. The world was watching him. They wanted to know whether he would lose his cool along with everything else.

"Of course, it's an ill wind, isn't it, Robert? I mean, Livingstone being so implacably opposed to my buying the Sunset, and then this business . . . and your 'cash flow' problem on top . . ." He tailed off. What he was saying was that Robert Hartford was bust and that he, Plutarch, had done the busting. He smiled an oily smile, and he stood back to watch the effect on Robert.

"Closing isn't until the day after tomorrow," Robert replied, trying to make his voice sound relaxed and steely all at the same time. But this wasn't the movies, and Plutarch knew his way around a deal like a roach around a kitchen.

"Yes," Plutarch continued, "not really enough time to find someone to take you out of the contract by closing, so it's good-bye to your deposit, I imagine. I suppose the Livingstone estate will look quite kindly on my offer now." His eyes glinted. "Still, not to worry, Robert. It's only eleven-point-five that you lose. That's small change to you movie stars, isn't it? But I remember the days when I *thought* it was quite a lot of money, don't you?" He paused, allowing the irony to burn deep; then he turned and walked toward the church. "See you inside," he said cheerfully over his shoulder. "Oh, and watch out for Caroline. She'll be here soon, and she's just *dying* to see you."

Robert didn't often feel like a drink, but he did now. He shouldn't have come, let alone take it on himself to arrange the funeral. But there had been no one else to do it, and it had to be done. Why had Francisco chosen this time to die? At the back of his mind he had felt that the old boy would do the right thing by him and let him off the hook by paying him back his deposit. No way in a million light-years would the Livingstone executors—some hatchet-faced attorneys from Century City with shifting sand for souls and time clocks for hearts. Yet, even in his frustration at the timing of it, there was room for genuine sorrow. He had liked the old boy. They went back a long way, they were polite to each other, and when they met by chance each looked pleased. In Robert Hartford's book that just about defined friendship, but he was hardly an expert on the subject. In this life people were divided into those who worked on their careers, those who concentrated on their families, and those whose efforts went into their friends. Only one thing was certain. Juggling all three ended in balls on the floor.

He peered over the heads of the milling crowd. Where was Paula, and Kristina, and dear old Winty? Robert was already regretting that he had come on ahead to make sure that the Sunset Hotel people were organizing things properly.

"Robert Hartford, we meet again."

Hank Marvel was standing in front of Robert and apparently he, too, wanted to collect his pound of flesh.

"I've got nothing to say to you. Talk to my lawyers," snapped Robert. "We're here for a funeral, not a fight."

Hank Marvel was the sort of man who did not come singly. His entourage clustered around him like greedy puppies at a bitch's teat. Robert scanned them quickly. They were quite a high-powered bunch for hangers-on.

"Nobody's fighting. Nobody's fighting," lied a hotshot agent who had been courting Robert Hartford for the last five years, but whose face was alight with the realization that he would have to court him no more. "We're just business people trying to turn a buck."

Robert Hartford was there in a flash. Being an agent who doubled as an attorney was the preferred path to running a studio these days.

"Congratulations, Sam. I gather that you get to sit on the board at Galaxy. Wasn't it lucky I didn't sign with you, like you kept asking me to. I'd be clean out of an agent now, wouldn't I?"

"But will you be needing one?" barked Marvel.

They all laughed at that. Status changed fast in Beverly Hills. A week before and they'd have been clustering around the Hartford table at Spago like priests around a pope.

Robert bit his lip. Damn. He'd walked right into that one.

"So it's business as usual at Galaxy, is it? Making more bombs for the Pentagon!" Robert sneered the insult.

The agent-turned-studio-executive could cope with that one. "Oh, I think we'll be all right from now on. Poor old Bos lost the plot, I'm afraid. Your contract would have bled the studio white. Best to junk it. No point putting all one's eggs in one bastard," he said.

"Why on earth not?" blasted the icy tones of Winthrop Tower. "I mean, after all, you've crammed all the bastards into one Galaxy."

Robert spun around as Tower arrived, and the Marvel entourage took a metaphorical collective step backward. Open season might have been declared on Robert Hartford. It had certainly *not* been declared on Winthrop Tower. He was an intact Hollywood legend, standing foresquare on the crossroads where business met art; where money, often for the first time, met taste; and where the slow of tongue and the feeble of mind invariably met their Waterloo.

"I see the drinking men stand together," tried Hank, without conviction.

"Yes, better watch out in the gutter when we piss," said Winthrop cheerfully. Billionaires, studio heads, powerful attorneys meant nothing to him. The harder they fell.

They backed off at that. Nobody wanted to alienate Tower to the point of no return. One fine day he might be prevailed upon to make their homes look like they didn't own them, that ultimate signal of social arrival.

"See you in court," Robert shot at the retreating Marvel.

"If you can find a contingency lawyer," said Marvel loudly over his shoulder as he walked away.

"Where's Paula?" asked Robert.

"She's coming. She was driving with Kristina," said Winthrop.

Robert felt the relief run through him. "Thanks for the support there, Winty," he said, squeezing the Tower arm.

"Anytime, dear. Sitting ducks are *such* good sport, aren't they? Funny thing, isn't it, that the very last thing you need to make money in Beverly Hills is *brains.*"

Suddenly Paula was by his side. Her hand slipped into his, and she squeezed it tight.

"Well I think this is a *wonderful* funeral," Tower chimed in. "Haven't had so much fun at a Livingstone party for years. Come on, let's go and bury the dear old thing. I'm told the choirboys are a *dream.*" Tower shepherded them inside, his gimlet eyes frightening off any would-be Robert baiters who might be littering the steps of the church.

All around them the glorious sadness of Mozart's *Requiem* mass filled the air. The fragrant melody, heavy with heartache, burdened with grief, floated free. It rose to the high ceiling, climbed to the spires, and flew like a message to God through the Giorgio-scented air. But all the sorrow was in the music. Among the rubbernecking, lipo-sucked, tummy-tucked crowd there was only the mild exhilaration of finding themselves in the right place at the right time. As if aware it was carrying the entire burden of the mourning, the music crashed to a climax and stopped. In the loud silence that followed, Robert led the way down the long aisle toward the front pew. Arranging the funeral had given him a choice of a seat at it, and all around the tongues were murmuring that he had better enjoy his last shot at being first.

The Beverly Hills crowd saw the bravado of his stride. He was walking as if he wanted the world to know that he still knew where he was going, and his jaw was set pugnaciously like the sails of a small ship on a rough sea—defiant, proud, and worried all at the same time. It was a high-profile, stiff walk, too aware of the eyes that watched him, too determined not to care. The old Robert Hartford had padded about like a loose leopard, and the surrogate shyness, that potent signal of his temporal power, had beamed off him to cow the world and deter the would-be intimate. Now, the paradox was the give-away to the finely tuned antennae of the congregation. The word was out. Robert Hartford had peaked, and the valley yawned on the other side of the hill.

It wasn't totally certain, of course. Nothing in Hollywood was. But Galaxy had not only pulled the picture deal, they had gone out of their way to bad-mouth him, both privately and publicly. So the cognoscenti hurried to count him out, to start the trend of the self-fulfilling prophecy.

The stage whisper over to the right was hissingly sibilant. "God!" said somebody. "Nobody told me that Robert's new girl was a cripple."

Robert almost stopped as the verbal missile struck home. He faltered, and next to him he felt Paula shake suddenly as the vicious words roared into her brain. But the gauntlet had to be run. They both knew that. There could be no public response. Not now. So they marched on toward the front pew and the pain welled up inside along with the anger and the frustration and the mutual tenderness.

Into the breach of unnatural quiet, the priest moved toward the lectern. His voice—frail but rich, its accent softened by the hint of an Irish brogue—winged out over the scattered loudspeakers into the packed church. "Fellow mourners, we are gathered here today to say good-bye to someone we all loved. A servant of God, a child of America. In this time of great sadness words can seldom help, but I urge you today to remember that Francisco lives on, safe in the arms of Jesus. It is we who bear the burden of his passing. It is we who suffer . . ."

Robert Hartford wasn't listening, but he *was* suffering. How could he reach out to her, and tell her it was all right? How could he blot out the insult to her very essence, the wickedness that had basically been aimed at him and not at her? It felt as if his heart were bleeding. The sadness welled out of it, and the pool of pure love built within him, filling him up with desire for the woman he loved, and the need to comfort her.

And then he knew. It wasn't the first time that the idea had occurred to him, but it was the only time that it had seemed to be joined to action. He didn't think about it. He didn't have to. It was just so effortlessly right. He was on his knees. She was kneeling, too.

He leaned toward her, and there were tears in his eyes as he spoke. "Paula, will you marry me?" he said.

Paula's eyes opened wide as she watched him, and she traveled from the depths of despair to the sublime. The tracks of her tears were there already. Now it was joy, not pain, that fathered them.

"What?" she whispered back, her voice quivering with excitement.

He smiled at her, at himself, at the wonderful thing that was happening to them.

"Marry me!" It was a command, and he said it louder, not caring that this was a man's funeral, caring only that it was the future he wanted, the one he needed, the one he must have.

"Oh, Robert. Oh, Robert," she breathed his name, unsure how to respond. To say simply yes seemed so banal at this precious moment.

He didn't mind. Her eyes were saying all the things he wanted her to say. Her face, her body, her voice were joined in the chorus of commitment.

So he moved toward her, and his lips reached for hers to seal the life they would spend together.

At the lectern the priest, oblivious to the pocket of sudden happiness in the sea of surrogate sorrow, droned on. "Francisco Livingstone was above all a gentleman, a gentle man, courteous, chivalrous in an age when those qualities are so very hard to find . . ." He paused to allow the congregation to ponder the passage of chivalry, to contemplate its isolated existence in the persona of Francisco Livingstone. Then he began to warm to his theme. "Today, unfortunately, good manners are almost nonexistent, the elderly are no longer respected. . . ."

The crash from the back of the church stopped him in mid-cliché. Everyone turned to see what had happened.

Caroline Kirkegaard was what had happened. She had arrived. Flinging open the carved oak doors of the church as if they were papier-mâché stage furniture, she posed in the entrance, head flung back, lips parted in anticipation, as she gratefully received the eyes of the congregation. Silhouetted against the harsh vertical light of the early Beverly Hills afternoon, she was a Valkyrie from some Wagnerian opera, an Amazonian warrior hot from the hunting field, an avenging horseman posthaste from Hades. Everyone recognized her, but many had never really "seen" her until now. It was her moment. The ultimate arrival. Caroline Kirkegaard, queen of the New Age, paramour of the billionaire, and, it was rumored among those who knew, the brand-new owner-to-be of the Sunset Hotel.

With the majestic inevitability of a rocket blasting from the Cape, Caroline Kirkegaard set off down the aisle. She was huge, more than formidable, far more impressive than statuesque. She sailed, glided, poured herself toward the front of the church and the rustling of her viscose velour silk-satin Marc Bohan black tiered dress was the only sound that anyone could hear. In each ear a black satin bow was threaded through the black pearl-and-diamond earrings that had been given to the Duchess of Windsor by the duke, and on her head a rakish, wide-brimmed felt fedora reached to the line of the pads at her powerful shoulders.

A force field of Dior's Poison preceded her and she licked full, voluptuous lips as she basked in the almost palpable fascination of the mourners. On her face she wore a half smile, something between humility and graciousness, because although this was a funeral, it was also a coronation. As if to emphasize that fact, David Plutarch walked Prince Philip–style two paces behind her.

All around the wagging tongues told the story.

"Mistress . . . Moviecom and Galaxy . . . he's buying her the Sunset . . . power over him . . . Destiny cult . . . ruthless people . . ."

Like an arrow to the bull Caroline Kirkegaard made for the front pew across the aisle from the Hartford group. She didn't permit herself to think that there would be no place for her there. It was a trick she had learned early in life. Great expectations alone delivered greatness. Unto them that hath, it shall be given. Who dared, won.

The occupants of the front pew, ancient Southern California royalty, folded up before the Kirkegaard assault like a tattered concertina. "Hello, we're so sorry to disturb you," she lied, shoving the social heavy hitters up against each other like dates in a box.

The Pasadena family who'd been Livingstone's distant cousins grinned as they bore it. They weren't used to being exposed to people like Caroline. The whole of their sheltered lives was dedicated to the avoidance of that. It was what the old money was for, a moat against the meritocrats, a hedge against the horrible. "Quite all right," they muttered unconvincingly through stiffened upper lips as they crammed up to accommodate the interlopers in their midst.

Caroline stood back to allow Plutarch to enter the pew first. She wanted to be on the outside, where she could see and be seen, where Robert Hartford would be available to her.

On the outside of the Hartford pew, Kristina, like the rest of the congregation, had been submerged in the drama of Caroline Kirkegaard's theatrical entry. On her it had a special impact. In her life so far there had been few heroes, fewer heroines, but Caroline Kirkegaard was one. Kristina couldn't quite remember when she had begun to take the spiritual path. There had been no blinding light, no born-again experience, but gradually she had found herself gravitating toward the mystical and away from the material. It had started with a book or two from the Bodhi Tree, and progressed through Forum, Life Spring, and an Insight weekend, to a Destiny desert retreat via a couple of channelings and a private "reading." She had given up booze and learned to sneer at drugs, and slowly but surely she had dropped her old friends, knee-deep in materialism, and acquired new ones with their heads in the clouds. Bit by bit, Kristina had begun to accept not only that reality was unreal, but that the bizarre was in fact commonplace, the unusual not extraordinary at all. Truth, at a stroke, was reassigned to the realm of the emotions rather than the intellect, which made it infinitely more fun. This New Age world had its own gurus, and standing head and shoulders above them all—both literally and metaphorically—was Caroline Kirkegaard.

Now, from across the aisle, Caroline Kirkegaard was smiling directly at her.

It was an extraordinary smile, much deeper and more interesting than the normal smiles you might expect from someone you had met briefly at a party a few weeks before. Her ripe lips were pulled back from her fine teeth, and Kristina couldn't help noticing that they were damp, moist, wet actually. There was a quizzical component to the expression—as if Caroline Kirkegaard were questioning her. Her eyes sparkled and shone with an unmistakable warmth, and Kristina couldn't escape the feeling that this was the smile of an old friend, one that . . . you were rather attracted to, although you hadn't really worked out why. Had Caroline Kirkegaard remembered the evening of poor Livingstone's black ball, when they had sat at the same table and had a brief conversation beforehand about the power of amethysts? Certainly she could not know of the Destiny meetings that Kristina had attended —a fascinated disciple vibrating with wonder in the darkness of the room.

One thing, however, was clear. There was a contact between them at a spiritual level, and on a physical level, too. New and disturbing realities were taking shape.

The smile was going on too long. It was time to look away. It was like walking toward a stranger on a lonely street. Your eyes met his, untangled, hooked up again. It might be long seconds till you passed by him, but now you and he had made some tenuous contact and it was your decision, his too, whether you would nod and smile, and say hello—not because you wanted to but because it was difficult to do otherwise.

Kristina couldn't break the link of the smile. Instead, suddenly and inexplicably helpless in its bondage, she returned it—the silly, bemused expression sitting all over her own face like a fat cat on a baby.

At the very moment Kristina was about to give up her effort to interpret what she was feeling, her body began to speak. The whole of her seemed suddenly sensitized, the peculiar awareness that she possessed bodily parts that one seldom thought about in church, at funerals, while psychics smiled at you across the aisle. It started as a sensation of warmth, of fullness, and it proceeded to take on electrical form, a tingling, tickling feeling that was on the move, creeping, crawling, slowly at first then faster between her skin and the soft silk of her Dior panties. If she had a geographical center then it had begun there, but now it was wherever her blood was, rushing hither and thither, as if it couldn't make up its mind where to go or what to do. Only one thing was completely certain. It was mothered by Caroline Kirkegaard's deeply unsettling smile.

Kristina breathed in deeply as the weird feeling took her, and her breath shuddered out again. The church was disappearing, and Caroline's face was getting bigger, filling her mind with its sweet seduction, and crowding out all thought as it conjured up the ghostly music in her body. She was being played like an instrument, her heartstrings caressed by a silken bow, her tense skin stroked by a steady touch of deepening strength, and there was nothing at all that she could do about it, and still less that she wanted to do. She was sinking in the whirlpools of Caroline's eyes.

IN THE back of the parked limo outside the church on the corner of Bedford and Santa Monica, Graham stared moodily at the TV and wondered if he could be bothered to switch the channels. Which brand of soap would best clean off the depression that had settled over him like a fine layer of dust since his recent return from London. Maybe he should do a drink instead, something thoroughly British like warm lager, sticky-sweet sherry, or scotch and soda with no ice. He reached forward to the drinks tray and splashed a double measure of twelve-year-old Chivas Regal whiskey into the heavy Orrefors tumbler. Then he leaned back into the aggressively comfortable cushions as he sipped petulantly at the unappetizing drink. Was he glad to be back in Beverly Hills? It was impossible to say. One thing was for sure. The thing he had gone away to forget hadn't been forgotten.

And that was the problem. Paula wasn't a thing at all. Things could be got. They could be had. They could be bought and sold. In Graham's odd life people were categorized as "things." In the East End of London where he had been dragged up, there had never been time for the finer nuances of "feeling." Those, and the other luxuries of life, had been in short supply among the jellied eels, the creeping cold, and the mean streets of his cockney fish-and-chips childhood. Back then, within the sound of Bow Bells' chimes, sentiment was singing "Danny Boy" half pissed with your mates on the way back from the boozer at closing time. Politeness was not hitting a man with glasses. Sensitivity was bothering to get out of the tin tub by the fire to piss in the outside khazi. In the slums of East Ham there had been no crash course in romance. Everyone had been far too busy surviving.

It was funny how he felt about her, if *felt* was the right word. He wanted her, he desired her, and that meant that he must have her—in his bed, in his life, in his debt—doing the things he told her to do, saying the words he wanted to hear. She must think only about him, not recognizing others. She must come when he called, do what pleased him; and of course she should be loyal to him, because she would be his mistress and he would be her master, as proper men were to their proper women. In return he would take her as his wife, and he would fight any man that crossed her, and break the teeth and the arms and the legs of those who insulted him through her. In his fashion he would be faithful—in his own way he would be true to her—but when the time came to scratch the itch of maleness it would not threaten what they had, because he would never flaunt it, and what the eye didn't see . . . A man knew where he was in a relationship like that. It was how things were in the Old World, and it would have to be like that in the new one.

Deep down, however, he knew it was pure fantasy. Paula would never be that kind of a person, and it wasn't just because she was American. It was worse than that. On paper she should share his philosophy, but for some reason she was beyond him and his working-class attitudes and expectations. Her neck wasn't red and she had effortlessly transcended the world of the bumper sticker and the pickup truck, because, despite her small-town upbringing, there was nothing small about her dreams. In the ordinary way that wouldn't have mattered. It should have been simple. They were wrong for each other, so he should forget her. It was what he had gone to England to do—Tower had owed him a holiday and he had taken it—but it hadn't worked out as planned.

On his short vacation he had found that the old haunts hadn't changed much, and neither had the sharp-tongued, bleached-blond bints of Barking. They had laughed at his jokes and mocked the mid-Atlantic accent he'd developed and their brittle good humor and straightforward, no-nonsense sexual appetites had provided a test of sorts for his feelings for Paula. He had stood his rounds and slashed in the car parks, and he had indulged in knee tremblers outside the pubs in the old Kent Road, and slightly more up-market liaisons on half a dozen couches with sparky Aryan girls whose chirpy self-confidence papered over the sad limitations of their lives. But at night when he tumbled into bed through the bitter beer haze and wondered if the electric blanket would make it through the night, he could think only of Paula's angelic beauty, and her bright brilliance, and the terrible tragedies she had survived. He would fall asleep and his dreams would be alive with California and Paula.

So now he was back in L.A., and the evil mood persisted, knotting up his insides beneath the hard, flat stomach and poisoning his mind. He placed the glass on the steel muscle of his thigh and his face tightened and his body tensed as he thought of what he had discovered on his return.

Robert and Paula had gone to New York, and they had become lovers. Not for one second did he doubt it. Their every gesture, their every word, confirmed it. And it was eating away at his soul.

His mind roamed around like a hungry hyena on a snow-covered steppe. It wasn't the first time he had thought of it, but now the former daydream had the substance of a plan. Paula herself had given him the vital information, in the sweet-scented garden on the night of Livingstone's party, as the tears had bathed her beauty and she had told of the terrible night in a place called Placid when a man called Seth Baker had raped and murdered her friend and burned the twin brothers she worshiped. A powerless woman with an awesome desire for vengeance would look with all the favor in the world on an avenging angel. A girl would live for the man who killed for her. A girl would love the man that she lived for. It was so straightforward in his simple mind. Yes, Seth Baker was the open sesame to the future he wanted.

The knock on the window was sharp, and Graham reached forward to wind it down.

"Can you move the limo forward to the front entrance please, sir? They'll be out in a minute or two." The cop wasn't usually so deferential, but then limos weren't usually that long. Over the policeman's shoulder the ubiquitous Beverly Hills palm trees, fat ones alternating with thin, lined the street, their manicured orderliness a dramatic contrast to Graham's dangerous emotions.

"Okay," said Graham, thrusting the drink out of sight.

Mentally he braced himself. Paula had gone in with Robert Hartford. Soon she would be coming out with him, and the superstar's supercilious eyes would be all over him. "Hello, servant," they would say. "You dared to lust after my girl, didn't you? And you don't like me, do you, because I'm rich and successful, and I'm even better looking than you and I don't work for *anybody* but myself." It was small consolation that Hartford's career was in free fall. It would take a lifetime for it to reach the lowly level where Graham's bumped along.

He cleaned the glass quickly and opened the door, smoothing down the gray worsted of the uniform that was nearly a suit. He slipped into the driver's seat and did what the cop wanted. Then he was outside again, his peaked cap stuck awkwardly beneath his arm where it was less noticeable. Next he adjusted the Revo sunglasses for greater anonymity, and he leaned casually against the spit-and-polished coachwork of the stretch Mercedes.

The doors to the church were opening. From his position by the number-one car Graham could see right inside. The first few pews were disgorging their contents steadily into the aisle, as the organ ground and the mourners beamed and everyone wondered how long Livingstone would do in purgatory before they allowed the old lecher upstairs.

Robert Hartford and Paula seemed completely insulated from the tense group that had now arrived at the top of the steps. Wrapped in a cellophane of transcendent happiness, they stared into each other's eyes, their hands intertwined, their bodies so close that walking seemed a miracle. Hovering about them, like Indians around a well-defended wagon train, were a malevolent blond beauty and, swooping and darting at her side, the billionaire David Plutarch. Kristina, a dreamy, trancelike expression on her face, seemed locked in the blonde's gravitational field. Winthrop Tower and five classically dressed aristocrats made up the remainder of the extraordinary group. The blonde's voice floated toward Graham like a cloud of nuclear dust. "Robert. Robert! We'd just love to have you stay on at the Sunset, but we'd have to move you into something a little less spacious. Probably suit you now."

Robert Hartford didn't seem to hear her. Her sour sarcasm floated harmlessly over his head as he looked down tenderly at Paula.

Stung by his indifference, Caroline tried again, louder this time. "Perhaps you could move in with Mr. Tower. Yes, that's the best thing. The odd couple. A pair of 'confirmed bachelors.' We could use it in the advertising. Turn it into a tourist attraction. Isn't that a wonderful idea, David?"

Robert turned to look at her as if he was seeing her for the very first time. There was no hatred on his face. There was only undiluted pleasure. "Sorry to disappoint you, Caroline, but that wouldn't do at all. You see I won't *be* a bachelor, confirmed or otherwise."

Some got there faster than others. Tower was the first of all.

"Robert. Paula. That's *wonderful!*" he boomed.

Caroline Kirkegaard froze as the penny dropped. Her eyes, wide, incredulous, shot back and forth from Robert to Paula. Kristina, stunned, could say nothing at all. Graham had reached them now, but as he walked the information had been pouring into his protesting mind. The lovers, indecently happy on the steps of the church, were joined together, their postures emphasizing the closeness of their commitment. He was shut out. He didn't exist. They didn't even know he was there. He opened his mouth to say something—anything—to turn them away, however briefly, from each other, but the big blonde was talking and now Robert Hartford had just said the words that had stopped Graham's world in its tracks.

"Yes," said Robert. "Paula and I are going to get married."

"No!" said Graham. His voice was sharp, the desperate shout of the man who interrupted the reading of the banns in church. Robert couldn't marry her, because he wanted Paula for himself.

Everyone saw him for the very first time. Robert looked at him in intense surprise, and then his lip began to curl around the edges of the happiness on his face. "What do you mean 'no'?" he asked.

"I mean, you can't . . . get married . . . to Paula," Graham stammered, his face drained of blood, his hands clenched at his side.

The silence gathered strength. Robert's eyes were flashing.

Caroline Kirkegaard saw it in a second. The angelic-looking chauffeur loved Paula himself. The lord of the manor had pulled seigneurial rank on the vassal. It was a drama as old as life, and for a brief moment it sustained her in the midst of her disappointment.

"Who on *earth* says so?"

Graham was cornered. Caroline watched the Englishman carefully. He seemed to be undergoing an extraordinary change. He was shrinking, crouching down low, but at the same time his chest was expanding and his shoulders seemed to be broadening beneath her gaze. His eyes were small and his lips thin and the baby face was flat, the pale skin plastered tight across the perfect bone structure. His nostrils were flared and his fists were tight, and he was coiled up like a spring forced into a box, the one whose lid the child's fingers were beginning to loosen. . . .

"That's right, Graham," said Paula quickly. "This *is* a Tower Design corporate decision, isn't it, Winty? Only the full board can give me away. . . ." She laughed easily into the unbearable tension.

"Absolutely right. Board meeting convened. Over drinks. At the Sunset Hotel. Marriage motion to be laid before the board." Winthrop Tower backed her up, and the fuse spluttered out, millimeters from the bomb.

Graham backed away, unwinding slowly, and the furious fires died down in Robert's eyes. Paula and Winthrop exchanged lightning glances. Caroline Kirkegaard smiled as she made careful note of the incident.

"Come on, Paula. You're coming in my car," said Robert.

But apparently the Livingstone funeral was not quite over.

The two men who now approached looked like lawyers.

"Mr. Hartford?" said one.

Robert spun around, irritated, desperate to be out of it. "Yes, what is it?"

"I am Enthoven of Emory, Quiddick, Marshall, Maverick, Nolan and Enthoven. We are the attorneys for Mr. Livingstone's estate."

David Plutarch cut in rudely. "Why haven't you been answering my letters?" he barked.

The lawyer ignored him. It was to Robert Hartford that he continued to speak. "We need to discuss with you the contents of Mr. Livingstone's will."

"Livingstone's *will?*" said Caroline Kirkegaard in a voice that sounded as if it came from another world.

"Yes," said Enthoven. "We've found a new will. A very recent one." Now he turned to Plutarch. "I know, sir, that you've written letters expressing a willingness to buy the Sunset Hotel should Mr. Hartford's offer not be completed. I think it is important that you attend the reading of the will, along with Mr. Hartford. Would tomorrow morning be suitable for you all? Say at ten? Mr. Tower, too, sir, and Miss Kirkegaard, if it is at all convenient." The lawyer looked supremely doubtful. It seemed unlikely that everyone would have the time or inclination to attend the meeting he had suggested.

But Enthoven had overlooked one of the most powerful and least visible of human emotions—curiosity. The giant question mark hung over the group. One by one, quite quickly, they said that yes, why not, ten o'clock would be just fine.

—

"COFFEE. BLACK."

Somehow it wasn't the kind of place you said please.

The waitress didn't seem at all put out. Plain, her face pocked like a pineapple, she splashed the coffee into an almost clean cup, allowing it to overflow into a chipped saucer. Her movements were brisk, the irritation just beneath the surface. Folks who drifted in ten minutes before closing time were popular as palmetto bugs.

Graham shifted on the scuffed plastic of the bar stool and peered around the diner. It was "Happy Days" gone sour, all messed up by dirt, neglect, and by an unmistakable sense of all-pervasive gloom that hung over the restaurant. It was even possible to pinpoint the place the bad vibrations were coming from. They were beaming out from the corner. From the table at which the fat man sat. They were coming from the man who would be Seth Baker.

He was monumentally ugly, his stomach hanging over the edge of the table like a filthy cloth. A big pitcher of beer in front of him was nearly empty. His eyes were lost in the fleshy, parchment-colored folds of his face, and the stubble of his uneven beard, sometimes gray, sometimes black, was dotted with beads of booze and sweat. Graham wasn't near enough to smell him, but he knew from twenty feet what the smell would be. Sour, decaying, beer and body.

He turned back to face the front, and the music started somewhere in the depths of his brain. "Seth Baker?" he said quietly to the girl behind the bar, nodding his head backward over his shoulder.

She tried to summon up the energy to make a problem. "Who's askin'," something like that. He could see it in her irritable eyes. But she couldn't make it. In the Everglades problem creation took effort.

"Yeah," she mumbled.

Seth Baker. Graham could see him through the back of his head. This piece of human rubbish that had raped and killed Paula's friend—who had murdered Paula's beloved brothers in an attempt to kill her. He smiled at the grotesqueness of the thought, allowing it to stoke the fires of wrath that flickered deep within him. This diseased creature had raped a woman. He had tried to set Paula on fire to protect his foul secret. He wasn't a human being. He was a thing—but a thing that would make noises when the time came for it to be broken. He smiled, and this time a strange laugh slipped from the back of his throat.

The waitress watched him, suddenly in tune with the aura of menace that clung to him. "Just passin' through?" she said. He talked funny. Like an out-of-state trucker. There were a few of those.

He didn't reply. He just looked through her, as if she didn't exist. She shrugged. "Better finish your coffee. We're closin' in a minute or two," she managed in retaliation.

Graham felt the familiar chill in his fingers, the itch in the muscles of his forearms. It was wonderful, this, the heightened awareness, as the world danced in new colors, and his thoughts came crystal clear, and his nostrils flared to sniff at the adrenaline reality.

He reached inside the scruffy anorak and he pulled out his wallet. From it he took five single hundred-dollar bills. They were crisp, ironed, and he laid them on the counter like soldiers on the parade ground, perfectly symmetrical, side by side. The eyes of the waitress zeroed in on them.

"Step outside for ten minutes, honey, will you," said Graham. "Somethin' I got to talk about to the boss."

He could see the bills reflected in her pupils, and inside her brain the bells were ringing as the cash registered. One, two, three, four, five across the neuron mass, up and down and around the tangled undergrowth on the slow voyage to understanding. Before she arrived at the destination of meaning her fingers were reaching toward the money, drawn by a magnet far more powerful than the intellect. She placed them one on top of each other, carefully, and she drew them toward her with the reverence of the communicant placing the wafer to her lips. "You want me to get lost?" she said as the five hundred disappeared into the pocket of her Levi's. "You got it." She didn't bother to do any tidying up around the bar. The look on her face said she wasn't ever coming back. She was junk labor in a junk bar in a junk town, and she'd never been as close to five hundred as she was right now, nor would she ever be again. If walking was what the gentleman wanted, then walking was what he was going to get. An' the stranger looked like bad news to Seth Baker, and that was the second best news today.

"Where you goin'?" The gravelly roar cut through the gloom. It wasn't closing time. The girl owed him another five minutes. Some loser was still propping up the bar.

But she didn't turn to look at him. The slam of the door was all she left behind.

Baker growled to himself and reached for the beer. What the heck! They came and they went. He changed his pants less often.

Graham stood up and he ambled to the door. He reached for the sign marked OPEN and he twisted it around till it read CLOSED. Then he slipped the bolt across the door, and he turned, and very slowly he walked across the diner to the corner where Seth Baker sat.

Seth Baker stuck a fat finger inside his mouth and dislodged a piece of chili that was wedged beneath tooth and gum up there at the back. He swallowed it. Good chili. Fartin' burpin' good chili. What did the drifter want? A job most like. Well, if he could get into the dress he could wait the tables. Ha! Ha! Then the laughter died. Because now he could see the eyes of the stranger.

They were the eyes of winter. Not of the pale apology for a winter they had down here, but a real one, bleak, and angry, ice-cold cruel, a winter that could kill, a winter that loved nothing more. They were blue, the bluest blue he had ever seen, but there was no spark of life, nothing swimming in their clear, frozen depths. And they were deep, endlessly deep, passing through twin infinities and beyond, to the end of other worlds. They were forever eyes, unswervingly eternal, and suddenly the gas in his guts was exploding and the prickly heat was sizzling around the fat folds of his neck where the nape had once been.

Closer, he came closer, until he was on the edge of Seth Baker's space, where any more intrusion would be invasion. He stopped.

"What you want?" Baker's voice was nervous.

But Graham didn't answer. All around the loneliness was loud, amplifying the dread that built around the two men.

Graham watched him, and inside he played the heat against the cool, the flames of his hatred searing the freezing blocks of his resolve. Exterminators didn't feel. They walked among the creepy crawly things and they killed dispassionately, efficiently, fast. But this hideous thing was so very ugly and all his life he would have done horrible deeds. Like to Paula, the girl who would be his. And he laughed then, when he thought of that, because this filthy flesh mountain had wounded *him* by wounding her. It was personal. Not like the rivals of long ago on the wet streets, in the damp alleyways, in the cavernous lofts of the East End. He'd twisted flesh then in the business relationship that had sometimes been death, and the pain had been incidental, uninteresting, like the howling of the wind or the crackling of a fire. But this time it would be sweet music. Blissful music. Wedding music. Because of what would happen now, he would be given the key to Paula's heart. After this, she could refuse him nothing.

"Do you remember Paula?" His voice was featureless, matter-of-fact.

Seth Baker's head flipped back as he heard the name, and he knew he must lie as he knew that the eyes would not believe him. The name dried in his mouth, and his lips stuck firm together as he tried to force them apart. Paula! Paula, who'd frightened him, whom he'd tried to kill. Paula, whose little brothers had died in the fire he'd started. "I don' know no Paula."

Graham smiled at that, and his head moved slowly from side to side in the gesture of denial. "It doesn't matter," he said. It was true. It didn't matter, because for Seth Baker nothing mattered anymore. Soon, so soon, nothing would ever matter again.

He reached behind him, and the neon glow fell across the matte-black blade of the knife. He put it out in front of him, where Seth Baker could see it, and he turned it around slowly like a pig on a spit.

The threat was not in the action. The threat was everywhere. It hung in the still air, and it lurked in the foul smell that sprang in panic from beneath Seth Baker's arms. It clung to the ceiling and it sprang up from the floor, but mostly it lurked in the place where it had always been. In the terrible eyes of the stranger.

Seth Baker tried to get up. His knees, his legs could usually manage that, but not this time. He was halfway there when they let him down and so he sank back like a paralyzed man, and the sweat leaped to his forehead, and bubbled at his upper lip as his mind tumbled over itself in its rush for the exit.

"I never laid no finger on Paula," he babbled. No finger on the girl he didn't know. What would it take to close the eyes that watched him from the depths of his grave? He could see every detail of the knife. With the clarity of super-vision he knew it. It was a flat, dull thing, so undramatic for the horror it conjured up, and he could feel it on his skin as he focused on the space that separated him from it, as the cries for a mercy he wouldn't receive formed in his throat. Once more he tried to stand. He pressed down on the table with both hands, and one slid on a pool of beer, sending the pitcher crashing to the floor, but the diversion meant nothing, like the sound in the forest unheard. At last he was upright, his enormous belly weighing him down as his fear-weakened legs bowed beneath the strain. His hands made little pleading motions, funny, unambitious gestures, his pudgy fingers going around in circles as they sought to communicate with the emptiness in the stranger's head.

Graham took one step toward him. He did not draw back his arm. He did not push out with it. He simply laid the tip of the blade against the stomach of Seth Baker, right up against the grubby T-shirt, and for a second or two he did not move. There they stood, waiting for the music to start, waiting for the dance of death to begin.

A big tear squeezed from Seth Baker's eyes and rolled down his cheek, parting the grime, conquering the stubble.

"Please," he murmured.

"Okay," said Graham.

The knife seemed to have a life of its own. A magic knife, it sank sedately into the folds of fat, dragging the arm of the killer along with it. The blood rushed out to greet it, but it didn't stay for its warm welcome. It had embarked on a journey. Off it went, slowly, gracefully, like a sailing ship caught by a sudden breeze on a brisk sea. Once, twice it tacked as it sped through the yielding skin, and once, twice it shuddered as if catching a glancing blow on some submerged obstacle. But it didn't stop. On, on it went, the blood rushing past its bows, oozing, cascading as it hurried to form the bright, bubbling wake of the vessel that was the knife.

Seth Baker's features were still set in the look of supplication. Mercy was what he wanted, and it had hardly registered that it was too late. But there was a weird feeling in his gut, a tugging, a pulling, an experience that was on the verge of pain but not yet there. Should he continue his plea to the eyes that couldn't see him? Should he investigate the source of discomfort down below?

He looked down. Oh, the blood! Oh! Oh! Oh, the blood was all over him. He was a Jacuzzi spouting it, and the shark fin of the knife, that black knife, was swimming around in his guts. He heard himself screaming and he looked back to find the face laughing in his as he tried to make sense of it all. Paula. It had something to do with Paula, and the fire he'd set.

He sank down to the floor, because this was not something that should take place standing up, and the man who held the knife sank down with him.

"I'm bleeding," said Seth Baker.

"Oh yes, you are," agreed Graham. He drew his arm back, and the blade came with it, making a little sucking noise as it jumped from its temporary home. Graham laid it, dripping, on the scuffed linoleum floor of the diner.

Once again, his face wrapped in disbelief, Seth checked the place where his belly had been. It wasn't there anymore. His guts were. They had spilled out of him, and they showed no sign at all of wanting to stop. On and on they came, like the baloney he talked, great coils of them, bright brown and blood red, steaming in a growing pile on the floor.

Now, his mind said *pain.* It howled the message to his lungs and his lips drew back and his teeth bared as the roar of anguish cascaded from him. He threw back his head and he screamed the scream of the damned.

Graham moved with lightning speed. He scooped up a length of Seth Baker's bowel and he looped it around his exposed neck, once, twice. Then he pulled it tight.

In front of him, the scream died as he turned the tourniquet. Now Seth Baker's eyes were the eyes of fishes, popping, so big, in the blood-red face.

His hands tore at his misplaced guts, and the battle to express pain was now the struggle to breathe.

Tighter and tighter drew the noose. It bit into his neck, slippery, unyielding, and his head seemed to bulge as it filled with blood that could not escape. There was no room for his brain in the closed box, no room for thought, no place for the future. If only he could breathe. If he could do that then all the horror would go away. But there was no breath. No life. No nothing. There were only the eyes still peering into his, and a strange booming sound that seemed to be saying . . . Paula . . .

~*16*~

T HE TWO TEAMS faced each other across the shining mahogany of the Sunset Hotel's boardroom table, beneath the full-length portrait of Francisco Livingstone. He beamed down on them, and today the enigmatic, Mona Lisa smile on his face had a new significance.

"Let's get on with it," said Caroline Kirkegaard.

She wasn't dressed to be disobeyed. The Jean-Paul Gaultier sleek black molded leather "torso" jumpsuit was future shock. A black jersey top trans-formed at the nipples into front and back panels of softly dangerous black leather, held together at the side by an intricate wool cable weave. She wore short black PVC ankle boots, elbow-length black gloves, and a black leather skullcap pulled down over her forehead in the style of an Olympic swimmer.

Beside her, David Plutarch contributed to the tense atmosphere. His ner-vous eyes roamed the room. The aura of angst had already enveloped the three well-fed attorneys he had brought along to the meeting.

Enthoven, from the prestigious Century City law firm, sat at the head of the table. He arranged the papers into two neat rows in front of him, and he looked up solemnly in response to Caroline's suggestion.

"Are we all here?" he said.

Robert Hartford could not escape the feeling that this was in some way a deeply philosophical question. Were they all here? Or were they all some-where else? With an effort he straightened up his mind for the business at hand, and beneath the table his leg moved out to rest against Paula's knee, glad that it pushed back at his. He lay back in the chair, detached from the formality of the lawyers, in an open-neck Brooks Brothers shirt and loose navy-blue poplin pants that were distinctly more Palm Beach than Beverly Hills. For the first time in his life he found himself agreeing with Caroline Kirkegaard. His irritable cough said so.

"Ladies and gentlemen, it is very kind of you to spare us a little of your valuable time . . ." Enthoven paused as if calculating just how valuable that time actually was. Plutarch's hour was probably worth more than *he* would earn in an entire year. "I hope you won't feel that it has been wasted. As you already know, Mr. Livingstone has appointed the trust department of my firm to administer his estate. It is in that capacity that I appear before you today. It goes without saying that this is a very sad occasion. Mr. Livingstone was, I am proud to say, a personal friend of mine as well as a client, so I share your feelings. . . ." He lowered his head, rather dramatically, as if he felt that a tear might be appropriate at this point.

Why was it, thought Winthrop Tower, that even the supporting players in L.A.—the butchers, the bakers, and the candlestick makers—all wanted to be actors? God, the attorney was ugly. There should be a law against people looking like that. Perhaps one of the million lawyers on his letterhead could help draft it. He put both his hands up to his throbbing temples and wished he'd passed on the wine at Cha Cha Cha. The transcendent beauty of the owner had hardly made up for it. He couldn't for the life of him think why he was there. Presumably dear old Francisco had left him something personal. Hopefully not his dreadful collection of neckties in Gatsbyesque colors from increasingly garish Turnbull and Asser. Superrich old men, with or without relatives, left anything valuable to obscure charities. It was baked in the cake. You spent the rest of your days wondering what strange bond had been formed in his lifetime between Francisco Livingstone and the Bellringers Benevolent Society, or why at some moment of doubt he had imagined he had Von Recklinghausen's disease and in consequence left millions to the remote institute where they struggled to find a cure for it.

Winthrop groaned out loud and wished that his hangover would go away. And he wondered where the *hell* Graham had got to. He hadn't showed up for work that morning and Tower needed to be a hundred places later in the day. That meant some tired limo driver pitching him scripts despite Winthrop's disbelieved protestations that he had nothing to do with the movie business.

"But life must go on. Business must go on, and that's why Francisco hired us, and that's why we are here today." Enthoven brightened visibly to show that he had made a successful passage through the valley of the shadow of his personal grief, and that, brave and resilient, he was now able to carry on. "It's really a very simple will. Quite straightforward, and it has been carefully drafted, so I don't think there can be any doubts as to intention, nor . . ."— and he laughed now—"as to soundness of mind . . ."

The lawyer looked up quickly at the nest of Plutarch legal eagles. They looked evenly back at him. "So, if I may, I'll just read away. It is a new will, drafted, signed, and witnessed last Thursday, I think, yes, that's right."

"What?" said Caroline Kirkegaard. Her face was pale, and her question shot out across the table like a bullet from a gun. Her mind was racing. Livingstone had made a will on the day he had died. On the day of his last massage.

"Is there any problem with that?" asked Enthoven.

She climbed down fast, as she realized that there was nothing she could say. Plutarch's eyes were on her. "Oh no, I just didn't hear you properly. Last Thursday, you said."

"Last Thursday."

Paula watched her in fascination. She was so big, so deadly, and Robert had kissed her. Now she knew the whole story, of Caroline's attempted blackmail of Livingstone, of Jami Ramona, and of Robert's diversionary candlelit dinner for two while the incriminating photographs were being recovered. But still they had kissed. Had they *needed* to do that? Had Robert needed to? She tried to push the nasty thought out of her mind, and she wondered instead how Caroline had *dared* come to Livingstone's funeral. What in God's name could he possibly have left her in his will? One thing was certain. Kirkegaard was not her usual calm, evil self.

Pressing herself secretly against her lover, against her fiancé, Paula looked down happily at the beautiful ring. The single emerald was totally perfect, large but not too large, the classic marquise cut complementing its antique setting. Despite herself she had mixed feelings about the tearing-up of the Galaxy contract. Obviously she cared desperately about his happiness, but strangely it seemed to have survived the misfortune. She had been his safety net, and now on the edge of an eternity together she had picked him up and put him back on top, not of Hollywood, but of life. Nothing else mattered. Nothing except the Sunset Hotel. That had been a dream they had both shared. Together it would have been their life's work, as it had been Livingstone's, and she tried to suppress the sadness that bubbled up as she thought about how they had lost it.

At the table's head Enthoven was off and running. " 'I, Francisco Livingstone, being of sound mind, hereby declare this to be my last will and testament superseding all others. I have made this will because of the circumstances that have arisen during the last few months with regard to my principal asset, my one hundred percent holding in the private corporation, Sunset Hotel, Inc. On the first day of November of this year I signed a contract of sale in which I agreed to sell my shareholding to Robert Hartford. The contract stated that completion was to take place on the last day of January, of next year.' "

Caroline Kirkegaard began to settle down. This wasn't as bad as she thought. Livingstone was going to tell everyone that in the event of the deal not being completed then the lawyers were to sell it to the highest bidder, or perhaps he was even going to specify that the sale should be to Plutarch. The glint in Plutarch's eye said that was what he thought, too.

Robert Hartford sighed. It was so sad. So unnecessary. So terribly wrong. He, too, was wondering why he was there. Obviously Livingstone had left him something. Wine, maybe. The Canaletto of Westminster Bridge that was his pride and joy and which Robert had so often admired?

" 'It occurs to me as I write this document that I am in poor health. Death is a factor that should be taken into account in making my dispositions.' "

But you didn't know how soon, did you, Francisco Livingstone? thought Caroline. You didn't know that you had only hours to live as you wrote your boring will. I beat you, didn't I? If you had known Robert couldn't afford your precious hotel you might have given him back his deposit and left him a relatively rich man. And you might have hawked your hotel around until you found another buyer, some effete loser with more money than sense who shared your ancient ideas about class, your pretension and your hypocrisy.

Enthoven droned on. " 'In the event of my dying between the time of the signing of the contract and the completion of the sale, and in the event of Mr. Hartford for some unforeseen reason being unable to complete the purchase of my aforementioned shares, it occurs to me that the contract would become null and void and my executors would be legally bound, in the absence of any guidance from me, to sell to the highest bidder.' "

Tower pricked up his ears. Only one phrase so far had promised any fireworks at all. "In the absence of any guidance from me." Where would the executors be guided? He sat forward in his chair. Good old Livingstone. This was turning out to be quite fun. He must have one of these himself one day, but not just yet.

" 'It seems likely, given the interest already shown in the hotel, that the highest bidder would, in this situation, be David Plutarch, acting for and on behalf of his friend, Caroline Kirkegaard.' "

The lawyer managed to put question marks on either side of the word *friend*. As a professional actor, Robert had to admit it was quite well done.

The attorney paused. He looked up at Plutarch. At Livingstone's portrait. He turned to look at Robert Hartford. He looked down again. " 'Under no circumstances could I die in peace thinking that the Sunset Hotel might end up in the hands of Plutarch and Kirkegaard.' "

Not a muscle moved, not a face twitched as the news sank in.

" 'It is the purpose of this document to ensure that this dreadful hypothetical situation will never come to pass.' "

Fire burned high on David Plutarch's cheeks. The trio of his attorneys began to scribble on their yellow legal pads.

Caroline Kirkegaard stood up. Then she sat down. Then she stood up again. Her mouth opened, closed, opened once more. No sound came out. She looked like the Method acting school's prize-winning depiction of "shock."

Robert Hartford, too, fought back the desire to jump to his feet. It didn't matter that he had lost. At least Plutarch and Kirkegaard had been denied the prize.

"Bravo, Francisco," said Tower out loud.

But Livingstone was still speaking. " 'Because simple things work best, this is my solution. If I die before completion of the above-mentioned contract, I hereby will and bequeath my entire shareholding in the Sunset Hotel Corporation free and gratis and unencumbered to Robert Byron Hartford of the Sunset Hotel, Sunset Boulevard, Beverly Hills.' "

The Sunset Hotel. It was his. He had been given it. For nothing. One hundred and fifty million dollars. Maybe more.

He jumped up, and Paula, too, was on her feet. She rushed toward him and fell into his arms. "Darling, oh, my darling. You've won. You've *won*." He ran his fingers through her hair, and he looked down at her tenderly.

Then Robert turned toward Caroline Kirkegaard. At the other end of the table she stood facing him. The full length of the gleaming table separated them, but in reality they stood eyeball to eyeball, locked in a hatred that glued them together.

Paula took a deep breath. Never in her whole life had she seen a woman so dangerous. Caroline stood, vibrating her wrath, her huge chest rising and falling beneath the wicked jumpsuit. Around her muscular neck several single platinum chains nestled against the throbbing carotid arteries, and the cargo they carried, a cluster of assorted crystals, sparkled and shone beneath the bright boardroom lights. So much for the healing power of crystals. So much for their calming, soothing influence, the mystical ability they gave the wearer to transcend life's tricky moments. She was not cool. She was hot, hotter than the fires of hell, and she hadn't even *started* to burn. Paula watched in wonder as the natural rouge bloodied her cheeks, and she caught the twitching, clenching hands at the ends of arms that looked like they could kill. Instinctively Paula looked for missiles, ashtrays, anything that might be hurled at the man she loved. But there was none within range of Caroline Kirkegaard, and it didn't look as if it were earthly missiles she was after. She was searching for thunderbolts, weapons of awesome complexity and fiendish destruction, that could be used for the once-and-for-all demolition of the Teflon man.

Through the mist of her fury Caroline Kirkegaard saw him. He was standing before her, and he was laughing as he loathed her, smiling as he despised her. Around and around in her mind ran the words of the will. If she hadn't murdered Livingstone this would never have happened. Robert didn't know it, but it was *she* who had just handed him the Sunset Hotel. What he couldn't pay for she had given him for nothing.

"We shall contest this will," barked Plutarch.

"On what grounds?" drawled Robert Hartford.

Plutarch, cold and deadly, turned to his lawyers. Lawyers could always find "grounds" even when there weren't any.

"We shall want to interview the witness to the signature. Also, at Mr. Livingstone's advanced age there is the question of competency. Mr. Hartford is not a relative. It may be that undue influence . . ."

The lead Plutarch attorney talked fast, but not fast enough. Enthoven trumped his cards as he played them. Like a cardsharp on a Mississippi riverboat he floated his aces onto the table, throwing the documents so that they skidded along the smooth surface.

"One affidavit signed by the witness to the will and notarized . . . the report of two independent handwriting experts stating that the signature is indeed Francisco Livingstone's . . . a medical report signed by a board-certified neuropsychiatrist that at his last checkup one month ago Mr. Livingstone's mental status was normal in every way . . . a copy of a letter from Mr. Livingstone to Mr. Hartford saying how pleased he was that Mr. Hartford was the buyer of the Sunset Hotel because he could think of no one in whose hands the hotel would be safer. . . ."

Plutarch stood too. There was a time to give up. He nodded at his team and flicked his head toward the door. They were leaving. They had lost.

"Enjoy it while you can, Robert," Caroline snarled.

"Get the *hell* out of my hotel," he ordered. There was venom in his voice.

"Caroline!" Plutarch's voice was sharp. There would be other days, other times for revenge. Right now, they were beaten, and in enemy territory.

Caroline moved toward Plutarch, but her mind was roaring. Inside, she made the solemn promise. She would take his toy away from him. Whatever it took. Whatever price had to be paid. But in the meantime there was his happiness. How could she destroy that? She looked at Paula, and already she was thinking about the love-struck chauffeur at the funeral, with the vicious, haunted, hurting eyes. And, as it did at times like these, when the little people made her angry and the silly world messed up her brilliant schemes, her mind was already planning a terrible retribution.

—

PAULA LAY back on the sofa, yawned and stretched. She was in Robert's bungalow, watching MTV, and she had fallen fast asleep, all tubed out, after an incredible room-service dinner. She looked at her watch and rubbed sleep from her eyes. It was nearly midnight. She should drag herself into the bedroom and crash properly. Robert would be back tomorrow, and she wanted to look as good for him as she possibly could.

The thought of him finished the job of waking her up, and she smiled to his empty room—the one that so soon would be hers as well as his. He was in New York. Right now he would be all tucked up in the Carlyle double bed, the place where first they had made love, and tomorrow he would be back with her again. She hadn't realized until now that Hollywood had invented the roller-coaster ride. She and Robert had just ridden it. The news of Livingstone's will and Robert's windfall had traveled the grapevine at breakneck speed, and quite suddenly his injured career had staged a dramatic recovery. How many movie stars were worth a hundred and fifty big ones? How many strato-celebrities owned the best hotel in the world? Suddenly everyone believed the Hartford counterrumors, the ones that gave the lie to the Galaxy/Plutarch misinformation. Galaxy had dumped Robert because he had crossed the star-struck corporate Monopoly man and his sinister lover, and for no other reason. Well, good for Robert, Hollywood had concluded. In tearing up the Hartford contract the billionaire had been childishly cutting off his nose to spite his face.

Three studios had called to pick up the contract that Galaxy had dropped, and right now Robert was in New York discussing a new deal. When he had called earlier that day, the renegotiation with Horizon Pictures had been coming together like peaches and cream. By now it might even be signed, and the man she loved would be back in the pilot's seat.

In three short weeks they would be married. Christian Lacroix had designed the dress, an extravaganza of fluffy lightness and scintillating romance, and Kristina, who understood such things, was helping her with the arrangements for the wedding.

She shivered with delight and she leaped up, smoothing down the crumpled Georges Marciano denim skirt so that it just about covered what it was designed to just about cover, as the exhilaration coursed through her. She ran over to the full-length mirror in the entrance hall, the one that checked the legend on his forays into the outside world, and she pirouetted happily in front of it. She had never felt more beautiful. Her skin was glowing with a mad joy and her breasts pushed out straight against the navy-blue pullover, her hair shining with vitality, her teeth gleaming in the center of her smile.

She twirled around. "I feel pretty, oh, so pretty," she sang to herself and to the lover who couldn't hear her. "It's alarming how charming I feel." She was bubbling, a dancing caldron of pure bliss as she wondered if anyone, ever, had had such a perfect life, and if there was anything that could possibly make it better.

There was.

The telephone warbled its greeting. Eleven forty-five P.M. It was way past Beverly Hills' bedtime. It could only be one person. Leaping across the big sofa, dancing deliriously on the cushions, she ran toward it.

She would surprise him.

"Hello darling," she whispered provocatively. "I love you."

" 'allo, luv," said Graham's flat, featureless voice.

"Graham? Goodness, I thought you were Robert." Her voice was full of irrational reproach. He *should* have been Robert.

"Yeah, I thought that's what you thought."

"It's nearly midnight," she said, irritated.

"Yeah."

"What do you want, Graham?"

Her fabulous mood was going, going, gone.

"Listen, luv, I've got to talk to you."

"I was just going to bed. It'll have to wait until tomorrow."

"No!" His voice was suddenly sharp. "It's important, Paula. I need to see you now. Right away. Can I come on over? I'm calling from a phone on the Strip."

"No, you can't come over. This is Robert's home. I'm just staying here. He's in New York."

Graham got the picture. He wasn't welcome in Robert's house. Robert didn't like him. And it would be deeply inappropriate for Paula to entertain men of any sort in the middle of the night three weeks before her wedding— especially when it was an open secret that Graham had a crush on her.

"You gotta hear what I gotta say, luv. I mean you've *got* to."

It wasn't the desperate plea of a lovesick suitor. It was a plain statement of fact. Quite suddenly Paula picked up on the underlying vibrations. Graham had some bad news.

"Okay, we can talk now. You can't come over."

"I can't talk on the phone, luv."

"Oh, Graham, stop being so *dramatic*. What's so urgent in the middle of the night? I was just about to get into bed."

"I just got back from Florida. I been to Placid, luv."

Paula's heart stopped. When it started again, it was beating far faster than before. "What? Why? Why did you go to Placid, Graham?" Oh no! Oh dear *God* no! Not now. It was all *over*.

"I 'ad to see someone, didn't I? I 'ad to see someone 'bout somefink."

Paula's voice was quiet. "You'd better come on over," she said.

He put the telephone down quickly, as if worried that she'd change her mind.

She stood up and walked in a daze to the bathroom to splash some cold water on her face. Graham had gone to Placid. There was only one person he could have gone to see. Seth Baker, who had killed poor Laura and murdered her brothers. Seth Baker, whom she had hated with such a desperate loathing in those far-off days before she had fallen in love.

Almost before she had dared to dread it, the doorbell rang.

When she opened the door he was standing there, wreathed in shadows, and there was a look on his face that Paula had never seen before. For a second they stood watching each other, sizing each other up, like wild animals prepared to fight for their needs, to defend their territory whatever the cost. She didn't say "come in," but she stood back, and he slid past her into the bungalow, his movements somehow furtive, strangely threatening.

"I 'ad to see you Paula. I know it's late, but you'll understand."

She led the way into the drawing room, uncertain how best to do this. She had to hear the news he brought, and then she had to neutralize it. But at the same time she didn't want to hear it. Instead, she wanted it to be like the old times when she had laughed and joked with him, even relied on him. "What were you doing in Placid, Graham?"

" 'e was slime, Paula. 'e was rubbish."

He wasn't ashamed as he spoke. He was proud. He smiled to show her that.

Paula's hand flew to her mouth.

"I done 'im in, Paula. For wot 'e did to you an' your little ones. An' 'e didn't die nice—trust me—I gave 'im a right bad time." He sank down on the sofa and he watched her for her reaction as he delivered his gift, neatly wrapped, in the packet marked "vengeance."

"You killed him? You murdered Seth Baker?"

"I executed him, luv. 'e 'ad no right to be on the same planet as you."

"Oh, Graham, you *didn't!*" It was clear what had happened. In his crazed mind he expected her to be grateful. All the time her premonitions about him had been correct. There was a screw missing behind his impenetrable eyes. Immediately the thick fog of foreboding descended. She knew instinctively that a terrible thing was about to happen. She stood there, rigid with fright. Please God, she murmured to herself. I've suffered enough. Must I suffer more? Incredibly there was no part of her that was glad, despite all the nights she had lain awake and prayed to God for this moment. The thought that one day she might engineer the destruction of the man she loathed had given her the strength to carry on, and once she had been prepared to trade her life for his, in the knowledge that she would be meting out justice that the law would never provide. But now, as she heard of the revolting man's death, there was no pleasure in it. Her love for Robert had healed her hating heart, and in the love land there was no place for loathing and revenge. It was different because *she* was different. She was about to be married, and her past had melted away, bleached into insignificance by the bright sunlight of her future. In the slow fade, the scars had dimmed, and the brilliant colors of her pain, her hurt, and her hatred had metamorphosed into the uniform sepia of an old photograph. Before, she had nothing to lose but her own miserable life. Now all the happiness in the world was suddenly at risk. Graham had killed for her. How far was that from killing at her command? At the very least she was an accomplice to his crime. She would be guilty before the law, if and when the murder was discovered.

Graham tried to understand her feelings so that he could move on to the other things, to the claiming of the reward he was there to claim.

"Don't worry. They won't pin it on me . . . on us, Paula."

His reassurance shuddered against the implied threat.

"Why? Why did you kill him, Graham?" It was a ridiculous question, because of course she knew. She was playing for time. She had to know what all this meant to him. She had to understand what was going down in the vacant lot behind his eyes.

"I done 'im in for you, Paula. You told me 'ow much you wanted to 'urt 'im for wot 'e done. I did it for you, luv. I did it for us."

Again the "us." The conspiracy. She splayed out her hands and the tears sprang to her eyes as she realized the hopelessness of her position. He wanted something, this killer who sat with her in the dead of night. He wanted *her!* He had killed Seth Baker to get her.

"But, Graham, you're *crazy!*" The exasperation spilled out of her. "You're mad. I'm going to be married. I'm in love with Robert. I never wanted you to *kill* him. People don't kill people." The words were tumbling over themselves as she tried to deny the deed she knew had been performed.

"I love you, girl. You can learn to love me."

"I *can't* love you. I don't love you. What the *hell* are you talking about, Graham? You're mad. Do you hear? I love Robert. We're going to be married. Can't you understand that?" She was shouting at him, her voice breaking with the strain.

He stood up, quickly, and his face was changing. Anger scurried across it. He took hold of her arms, roughly, and his fingers closed tightly around them.

"Listen to me! Listen to me! Forget Robert bleedin' 'artford. 'e's over. 'e's 'istory. Talk like that again an' I'll 'urt 'im, too. You're not getting married to 'im. You're gettin' married to me! You got a choice. Live with me, or burn with me. Understand, darlin'. You 'earin' wot I'm sayin'?"

Paula was terrified. This man who held her was no longer Graham, her cockney friend. He was a cold-blooded psychopathic killer. Now at last her mind slowed down as she began to think. What she did now, what she said now, mattered more than thought and action had ever mattered before.

"Don't hurt me, Graham. I'm just confused, that's all," she said carefully. He would understand that: a poor confused woman, shocked and shaken by the violence of the all-male world.

"I won't 'urt you, doll. Just do right by me. Just 'ear me out. See it my way. I love you, doll."

His hands relaxed their steely grip, and she rubbed at the marks they left as her mind whirred on, and she tried to avoid his cold blue gaze. "Graham, we've got to talk," she said into the sudden quiet.

"Yeah, we can talk."

She sat down beside him on the sofa. Paula knew that she had to get rid of him. Nothing else was important. Once he had gone she could call Robert in New York. He would know what to do. He would get in touch with hotel security, call Winty, call the police, whatever. He would make it all right. But first she had to get rid of Graham. How? What would make him go? What did he have to hear before he would leave? Only lies could save her.

She turned toward him, and she prayed for her words to ring true. "I can't believe what you did for me. I just can't believe it." Stay as close to the truth as possible. Tears poured down her cheeks, fear posing as gratitude. "I hated him so much. He destroyed my life."

Graham waited and watched with the gutter cunning of his species. There was no trust in him. His life was lived in enemy territory. Even those he desired, especially those he desired, had the power to harm him.

"How could I possibly stop loving Robert and start loving you? I *like* you, Graham. I'm fond of you, but I'm not in love with you. And this whole thing. It's such a shock. I'm just so *confused*. I can't make any sense out of it."

The words said that she would never love him, but her confusion injected doubt into her message, and the liking she had for him would be a base on which to build. His expression said he had wanted more. But she had given him hope. It said that, too. "It'll just take time, girl. That's all." He sat there, not reaching for her, prim and proper on the edge of the sofa, like some suitor in a Victorian melodrama. If he'd had a hat it would have been on his knees, his fingers fiddling with its brim.

Paula leaped into the opportunity he had provided for her. "You're right. That's what I need, Graham. I need time to think. I'm tired. It's late. I need to sleep. I need to make sense of it all. Of what you say. Of what you've done for me."

"Come away with me now. To my place. We can send for your things in the morning." His voice was insistent, and he leaned forward.

"No! I have to be alone. I have to get my feelings straightened out. You can understand that, can't you? I must be alone."

Graham looked at her carefully, suspicion heavy on his face. His eyes roamed the room, taking in the heavy door, the shutters on the windows. If he left he would not be allowed to return. Where was Robert? Would she try to tell him what had happened? If so, his reaction would be violent and effective. No, she couldn't be trusted. She wanted him outside. She was playing for time. The hope she was giving him was counterfeit hope.

"You gotta come with me," he said.

The panic rushed up in the back of Paula's throat as she saw the door slamming shut on her plan. If she went with him anything might happen. He could kill her, when it sank in that she would never be his. He might go to the police and confess the murder, implicating her. He could rape her.

She had to get rid of him. Only then would Robert be able to save her. Paula's eyes flicked toward the telephone, and the number of the Carlyle flashed in her mind. He would be asleep, and she would wake him and all her troubles would be over as Robert Hartford roared into action.

But he had seen her eyes on the telephone, and he knew what she was thinking. "Come on," he said, and he stood up.

Again a surge of terror rushed through Paula. She had no weapon to fight him, and any resistance would make him angry. She must avoid that at all costs.

Then, at the moment of hopelessness, she remembered. She did have a weapon. The oldest one of all. The one that women had used against men since the dawn of time. She had her body. And he wanted it.

"Graham!" Her voice was husky, low pitched.

He paused, and his mind registered the new development as his body was caught in the tangled web of instant desire. She was going to give herself to him—in gratitude, perhaps; in lust possibly, if not in love. It was a victory that he had not dared to hope for. If they became lovers now, just once, here in Robert Hartford's home, everything would change. On Robert's sofa—in the lair of the man who despised him—he would make love to the woman he would marry and at a stroke all the jealousy and the hatred would melt away. He smiled at the thought of so much pleasure. Paula's sweet body, a mighty rival humiliated, his own way so comprehensively achieved. In the act of love the ghosts would be exorcised, and Paula would be pulled from the pedestal from which she taunted him, down low into the world of grunts and groans and taut, slippery flesh. And maybe then her spell over him would be broken, and the fatal attraction that plagued him would melt away in the groveling surrender of her hungry body.

He pushed his head to one side to indicate that he heard her message and that he wanted confirmation of it, and he smiled the cocky cockney smile of the small-time winner.

Paula swallowed hard. Was it the only way? If she allowed him this, he would have to trust her. In the lazy aftermath she would make him leave her, because he would believe that he could not lose her. Then, with the doors closed against him, she could be as unfair as he had been. Then she could fight him, accuse him of rape, of threatening her, expose him as the murderer he was, and throw herself on Robert's mercy. In one way or another he could be handled, but only if she survived this night.

So she stood up, and she watched him with what she hoped was a look of awakening desire and she pleaded with her body to help her do this thing. "Make love to me," she said.

Graham laughed. Already he could feel a new lightness inside him. At the end of the day she was just a doll like all the rest. The uncomfortable tenderness he had felt, the aching longing, all the bad times in London and before and since were beginning to blow away like a mist in a wind and he was glad. So he laughed again as he saw the subservience in her eyes, and at the moment of his triumph he wanted more. He wanted vengeance, too, as she had been avenged on Seth Baker. He wanted to be repaid for Robert Hartford's snotty looks and patronizing remarks, and he wanted to be recompensed for the misery of the past few weeks when he had felt an odd love so alien to his nature.

"Get undressed," he said.

Paula heard the new harshness in his voice and paradoxically it made it easier for her to do what had to be done. She reached for the edges of the sweater, and she tried to push the horror from her eyes.

"Take off your skirt first," he ordered, the dreamy expression of triumph and lust all mixed up with the cruelty on his face.

She moved quickly to obey him, as the hurry to be done with it masqueraded as enthusiasm.

He watched her as she unloosed her belt and wriggled free of the denim micro-skirt. It fell like a crumpled blue handkerchief around her ankle boots.

"That's better, ain't it, darlin'," he said, and she closed her eyes so as not to see him as he moved toward her. Greedily his hand reached for her, slipping roughly into her panties, ripping them away from her, defiling the desert dry heart of her with his rough fingers. At the same time, his mouth bowed down and his lips crushed against hers.

"Paula!"

Robert Hartford's voice exploded into the dreadful moment, freezing it in time, catching it forever in the photograph of his memory. He stood in the entrance of the room, and his face was already white. A dozen red roses drooped from his left hand and the key to his own front door stuck up from his right. Behind him was a single suitcase. He was no longer in New York.

Paula opened her eyes as Graham's face raced back from hers, as his hand fought to disentangle itself from her. Her mouth flew open, and she tried to speak, knowing as she did so that there was nothing to say. Her seminakedness spoke for her. Graham's hand was gabbling its message, her crushed lips, unmoving, were describing every detail of the disaster. On the floor, the crumpled skirt screamed its reproach, and her long legs, quivering with surprise, howled their complicity in the betrayal. In fascination she watched the pain splatter over Robert's face. His fists were clenched tight, his knuckles white with anguish, and still he was only halfway to the realization that his fiancée was making love, in his home, to a man who wasn't him.

Graham stepped back. The surprise on his face was fading fast. " 'allo, Robert," he said. "We wasn't 'spectin' you back so soon." There was a cheerfulness in his voice, absolutely horrible in its self-centered superiority. At last he had the drop on the man he hated. He had screwed the screwer. He, the lowly Graham, had shown the legend just who the real man was.

Paula felt the nausea well up within her—at what she'd done, at what had happened, at what would happen.

"Robert," she said, as her hands reached in vain to cover herself. But her voice died away. What could she possibly say? Later, when light-years had passed, there might be some way to make this right. First there would have to be hell on this earth, the hell that was starting now.

Robert's blazing eyes tore themselves away from the vision that was his wife-to-be, and they carried with them the portrait of treachery. Her naked legs were trembling, her panties lewdly askew as the alien fingers milked at her privacy, at the place that was his alone, that had been pledged to him forever. Her skirt was lying on the floor where it had been kicked down as lust had run too fast for decency.

Now his furious gaze centered on Graham and he dropped the roses, and he dropped the key, and he launched himself body and soul at the man he must kill.

The street fighter in Graham saw him move before Robert himself knew what he would do, and pleasure flickered in his ghostly eyes. He ducked, hardly seeming to do so, and Robert's flailing arms flew above his head. Then he hit him, hard, so hard, where his chest met his stomach, and the breath crunched out of the older man as he stopped in midair, impaled hopelessly on the spear of Graham's fist.

For a second he hung there. Then Graham's left hand smashed like a hard wave into the proud cliff of Robert Hartford's cheek. He staggered back, straightened up by the force of the blow, and then he fell backward, his legs leaderless, his mind scrambled.

"No! Graham, don't hurt him. Don't *hurt* him!" screamed Paula. But she was too late. Graham had hurt him more thoroughly and completely than he had ever been hurt before, than he ever would be again.

The desk hit Robert hard in the small of his back and his momentum sent him up and over it. For a second he hovered there, his legs pointing toward the ceiling, and then down he went, landing hard on his shoulder, his fall broken only by the wastepaper basket that crumpled like a beer can beneath his weight.

Graham had won, but he hadn't finished. He walked quickly to the prostrate figure of Robert Hartford and he kicked him, casually, once, twice and a third time in his side, in his ribs, and the last, contemptuously, on his rump. He turned once again to Paula. "Rude not to knock," he said. "Now, where was we?"

She screamed now with all the fury and the anguish and the horror of the death of her life. It was loud, the scream, so loud that it blocked out her mind as it went on, and on, and on.

Graham's back was toward his defeated rival. He had dismissed him, because he had beaten him and he had humiliated him. The movie weakling would not attack him again. All he could do now was watch the fun.

Robert hauled himself to his feet, his fingers grabbing at the edge of the desk. The room was spinning around him to the music of Paula's screams, and the nausea gripped at his stomach as he fought to stand. His eyes swam in his head and he tried desperately to focus, to stop the mad ringing in his ears. Then an awful roar of rage exploded in his throat and once again he threw himself at his mortal enemy.

Graham half turned, but slowly, languidly, and a smile of condescension flashed across his face.

Robert Hartford had ceased to be a human being. He had become a missile. In the core of him the demon had been unleashed and all the anger had jelled into a quivering mass of venomous hatred. Here were all his rivals for all the sweet goddesses, wrapped up in the disgusting form of a single man, his lewd fingers plucking at the embodiment of feminine beauty—the one who had promised herself so solemnly to him. From the bottom of the low life his essence was being insulted, and the terrible desire for revenge ran like high-octane fuel in his broken body, filling him up with mad energy and the strength of the damned. The power surged in his quadriceps, and flowed free in the muscles of his calves, and, both his hands rigid with fury, he flew like the spear he had become at Graham.

Both palms landed in the small of Graham's back, and behind them was the total mass of Robert's body. Graham flew forward, off balance, trying too late to push his feet forward to maintain equilibrium. They caught in the edge of the rug, and he pitched forward toward the thick glass coffee table that stood in front of the fireplace. Both shins hit the three-quarter-inch-thick glass at the same time, and the sickening sound of the collision cut the air like the crack of a bullwhip. But the awful blow didn't stop Graham. On and on he went, crashing down now on the slippery glass as he slid headfirst across the ice rink that was the table, scattering the blue-covered scripts, the art books, and the African sculptures in his wake. Still he didn't stop, and the pain from his legs and the surprise at his extraordinary predicament fought for control of the expression on his speeding face.

At the end of the table, to one side of the sofa, stood the Advent television. Black and superb, big and beautiful, it loomed like a sculpture from the hydraulic mahogany cabinet that was its home. It had always been Robert's pride and joy. The touch of a button and it sank gracefully from sight. The flick of another and it rose serenely to view and be viewed. Beneath it was the cavernous hole that was supposed to hold the videotapes that Robert had never bothered to collect. The studio sent over the movies he wanted to see, and later someone would pick them up. So the space beneath the forty-two-inch monitor screen was empty, a glistening black hole just longing to be filled.

Like a limo gliding into a garage, Graham's rocket-tip head, facedown, aimed itself toward the beckoning void. It was a tight fit. Not really technically a "fit" at all. His head collided with the opening, and the sharp edge of the cabinet smashed effortlessly through his nose and crushed up against his forehead as the bottom of the television casually scalped the back of his head.

He was half in, half out, wedged tight where the tapes should be, and his scream of shock and agony was muffled in the enclosed space. At last he had stopped, and apart from his hands, which pried frantically at the opening of the hole that trapped him, he was still.

Suddenly the room was quiet, the peace interrupted only by a regular, insistent drip, drip, drip. It was blood falling with the regularity of a metronome onto the immaculate glass table. Graham was not speaking, but he was bleeding.

Crouched like a wild animal where he had fallen from the force of his forward momentum, Robert Hartford watched the thing he had done. His eyes stared from his head, and on the famous cheek the red of the bruise was spreading upward, downward, sideways toward his pencil-thin mouth. The air rasped through flared nostrils and his chest rose and fell in heaving lurches as he struggled to get his breath. His head darted to Paula, frozen in horror and her seminakedness, and then to Graham, lying half conscious amidst the wreckage of the table—his damaged head wedged tight in the hydraulic TV console. Robert's eyes glinted their fury, and then deep in the depths of them, there was another emotion. It was only a spark at first, but a tiny flame in a scrubland of potential fire. It was the flame of pleasure. Brightly now it burned in the forests of Robert's eyes, and the light from it fanned outward to illuminate his face. The smile was small, growing, big, bigger, a horrible leering thing that mocked his beauty as it hinted at a new and terrible purpose. His lips relaxed over his teeth, and what had been thin and mean with hatred were suddenly full and voluptuous with the joy of cruelty to come. He crawled forward, and with his right hand he searched among the coffee-table detritus. He was looking for something, and he laughed now as he looked, and the maniacal sound filled up the room, background music to the devil's pact he had already signed in his heart. There it was. He'd found it, and his fingers clutched at it, drawing it toward his chest like a mother a newborn child. Small and flat it lay, innocent, in the palm of his hand, and he didn't even have to look closely at it to know how to use it. It was the remote-control device that operated his television set—the one that lifted it up from its box . . . the one that sent it sinking down, so smoothly, so gently, with such irresistible force.

He held it up high, at arm's length, like the magic sword of He-Man, Master of the Universe, and, still laughing, he pressed down hard on the button.

It was an old Whitney Houston video, on MTV, and although the sound was turned way down low, it was just possible to learn that she wanted to dance with somebody, wanted to feel the heat of somebody, needed only someone to love her. But now Whitney Houston was descending like a coffin at a cremation. The initial sound was something in between a crack and a crunch but almost immediately it merged into the noise of heavy feet marching relentlessly across softly packed gravel. At first it was all so effortless, so inexorable, but quite suddenly there were sounds of protest, of mechanical protest, of human protest. The TV seemed to realize that there was an obstacle to its sedate disappearing act, and in the bowels of the cabinetry the smooth hum of the engine turned nervous, high pitched, as it lost its rhythm. Now it whined and whirred and strained, but its noises were drowned by the gurgling, muffled, liquid scream that came from what was left of Graham's mouth. Whitney Houston reared in the middle of her song, up an inch, down two, as she shuddered sideways, her brilliant brown sugary legs dancing, dancing, dancing on the back of Graham's crushed and bleeding head.

For milliseconds the battle raged. The eggshell of Graham's skull, his slippery soft brain within, against the brute force of the expensive machine. Would Whitney Houston dance into the very center of Graham's mind? Was that where she would find the heat of somebody? In the mud of his gray matter would there be someone to love her?

Robert's thumb was white on the button as he vibrated to the wonderful music. His hand danced up and down as if he was conducting it, orchestrating the terror, the ultimate downfall of every man in the cosmos who wasn't him. He was all but oblivious to hands that wrestled with his, to the voice shouting in his ear for him to turn off the spigot of murder that spurted in his heart.

Paula tore at his knuckles, her naked legs brushing against his bleeding cheek as she tried to get him to stop the dreadful thing he was doing. Already she had forgotten herself. She was existing at a deeper level of humanity, the place where death was evil and life was sacred. Robert's blood was on her thigh, and his acrid sweat was in her nostrils as she fought with him to spare what was left of the life of the man who had destroyed hers.

"Robert, stop it. Stop it. For God's sake, stop it," she screamed.

And he did, eventually. His hand relaxed and the color returned to his snow-white knuckles, as his thumb lifted from the button at last.

There was a faraway look in Robert's eyes, the look of postcoital ecstasy that she had learned to love before, in the far distant land that was now her past. Then she turned to look at Graham. At what was left of him. He lay there, his mangled head stuffed into the inverted V of Whitney Houston's endless legs, and there was only one part of him that moved.

His left leg had a life of its own. It twitched convulsively, and the toe of his shoe beat out a truncated rhythm on the shiny glass. Slower, then more slowly and with less force, the limb kept up its inaccurate dance, scattering a book, an obelisk, a headhunter's dagger from West Irian. *Rat-a-tat-tat-a-tat* it went . . . before, at last, the silly mindless sound trailed off into the stillness of an apocalyptic silence.

~17~

WINTHROP TOWER SCURRIED along the path, his head down, and the folds of his sky-blue silk Alfred Dunhill dressing gown flared out in the cold night air. His hair stood up in uneven tufts and he screwed up his eyes in concentration as he tried to wake up, to make sense of the telephone conversation he had just had. Robert had been short, his voice clipped. There had been a terrible accident at his bungalow. For some extraordinary reason Graham had been badly injured and had already been taken to the hospital. The police were there now. Could Winthrop get over as soon as possible? At the interface of sleep and wakefulness, of drunkenness and sobriety, he had slammed down the telephone and thrown on the dressing gown over his pajamas. In the Sunset lobby the clock had said three in the morning, but the electricity in the atmosphere had hinted that the time was high noon. There had been all sorts of movement at the desk, a couple of tight knots of people, and two or three uniformed policemen standing about with the casual unconcern that hinted that something important had happened.

The policeman guarding the front door of the bungalow seemed to have been expecting him.

"Mr. Winthrop Tower?"

"I think so. I think so," muttered Winthrop, pushing past him. Hoping that curiosity would not kill the cat, he wondered what he would find. He could probably deal with anything but blood.

First he found Robert.

"God, Robert are you all right? You look as bad as I feel. What the hell's going on?"

"I caught Graham and Paula making love," he said with the suave calm of a matinee idol pouring tea. "On the carpet, in front of the fire," he added.

"Good God!"

Robert peered at him carefully. "Do you know Barton, from the Beverly Hills P.D.?" asked Robert suddenly. "Captain Barton, this is Winthrop Tower, he's . . . the . . . uh . . . the employer." He clearly couldn't bring himself to mention Graham's name.

537

"Making love?" said Winthrop Tower. It hadn't really sunk in.

"Mr. Hartford returned from New York unexpectedly," said the man called Barton. "It appears that Miss Hope, his fiancée, was in uh . . . uh . . . a compromising position with Ovenden, who works for you. Mr. Hartford asked the man to leave. He was attacked. There was a scuffle, and in the course of it, Mr. Ovenden's head was badly damaged in the hydraulic mechanism of the television over there." He pointed at the TV. It was covered with white dust and white masking tape and toward its base where it met the cabinet the laminated plastic had suffered some kind of trauma. That was where the red stuff was, rusty, flaky, caked. Winthrop's stomach did a practice roll.

"Is Graham going to be all right?"

"Not necessarily," said Robert.

Winthrop looked at him, a stupid expression of incredulity all over his face. God, he looked wonderful. Absolutely *tragic.* And his weird choice of words seemed to emphasize the utter transcendence of his grief.

"Mr. Ovenden's been taken to Cedars-Sinai, sir," the policeman said smoothly. "The paramedics seem to think he's suffered a serious head injury. A very serious one."

"He *attacked* you, Robert?"

"Yes, he did, sir, as you can see," said the policeman. "There was a struggle, and Ovenden fell across the table and collided with the underside of the television. The impact started up the mechanism that lowers the television into the cabinet. Ovenden's head got caught inside. Miss Hope confirmed the facts. She works for you, too, I think, sir. Is that right?"

"Yes. Yes, they both do," agreed Winthrop.

"Did," said Robert.

Winthrop suddenly realized he was going to have to take sides. He ran the unedited tape through his mind, trying to make sense of the disjointed plot. Graham and Paula had been caught two-timing Robert Hartford in the drawing room of his own home. In the fight that followed, his servant had been all but killed, and Paula had confirmed the story to the police. The fiancée had admitted the infidelity. The marriage was over before it had started.

But Paula simply couldn't have behaved like that. It wasn't just out of character; it was totally bizarre. Yet it seemed impossible to argue with the facts, and it was certainly true that Graham had wanted to be Paula's lover. At least one of the conspirators had the right motive.

"Did you know that your two employees were having a relationship, Mr. Tower?"

"No. Certainly not. I mean, I think I recognized that Graham was taken with Paula Hope. As far as I knew it certainly wasn't reciprocated. She regarded him as a friend. She was a very attractive woman. Men liked her." Winthrop was surprised to hear himself talking in the past tense. "Where is she now?" he asked.

"Back in the gutter where she belongs." Robert's lip curled with aggression as he spoke. He paced over to the window and stared out into the

blackness as if searching for Paula among the streets to which he had consigned her.

He turned back toward them. "Is there anything else I can help you with,
Captain Barton?"

"No, I think we have everything we need. Obviously we'd like a statement
from Ovenden, but it may be we won't be getting that. Otherwise we'll be
collating the fingerprint and photographic evidence, but I think yours and
Ms. Hope's statements will be more than enough for the file. Of course if
Ovenden dies then there would have to be an inquest, and a medical examiner's verdict, but as far as I'm concerned that's it for now. You maintain that
the batteries in the remote-control device had been dead for at least three
days?"

"At least."

"Well, Ms. Hope confirms that, and she had been using the television, and
the batteries we removed from the remote *are* nonfunctioning. So it really
just remains for me to say how very sorry I am, sir, that this unfortunate
business has happened."

"Thank you for your courtesy and your efficiency," said Robert with the
forced charm of a minor royal on a tour of the factory.

The policeman hovered, unwilling to take the ultimate step of actually
leaving. It wasn't every day he got to investigate the domestic violence of the
Robert Hartfords of this world, and he would have liked to linger. But there
was nothing else to do. The story just had to be true, for one reason and one
alone. The girl had corroborated the movie star's version. If he had killed her
lover in a fit of jealous rage she would hardly have allowed herself to become
an accomplice to the cover-up. And if she still loved Robert and was risking
jail to protect him, then there was no way she would have been so enthusiastically cheating on him in the first place. Her testimony had allowed Barton
to do professionally what he had wanted to do emotionally—to believe the
man it was so easy to believe.

"I'll do my best to keep the lid on this one, Mr. Hartford."

"I'd be extremely grateful if you could." Robert Hartford drooped with
weariness. His shoulders were bowed, his voice heavy, his lids hovering lead-
like over the amazing eyes.

"I'll let myself out. Good-bye, Mr. Tower."

He was gone.

Winthrop walked quickly over to his old friend and put out a hand to his
shoulder. "Robert, I'm most terribly sorry."

Robert smiled back wanly.

"Not your fault, Winty. Mine. I trusted her. She was so easy to trust. I've
never done it before."

"Can't there be any other explanation? I mean, she wasn't drunk or anything. Sort of a horseplay thing?"

Robert shook his head slowly. He walked to the sofa and flung himself
down on it. Then he fixed Winthrop with his eyes. When he spoke his voice
was far away, the tone plaintive. "I came back from New York and I didn't

tell her I was coming because I wanted to surprise her. I wanted to wake her up, and make love to her, and tell her about the new deal I'd just done because I was so happy and I wanted her to be happy for me. They were standing there"—and he nodded to the middle of the room by the fireplace —"and she was naked, more or less, below the waist and he had his fingers . . . inside her . . . while he was kissing her."

Winthrop Tower took a deep breath and winced as he imagined it—Graham, his hard body the stuff of countless of Winthrop's own fantasies, and Paula, the angelic daughter he had never had—the pair of them traitors, mocking and shaming the grown-ups who had dared to love them.

"I wanted to kill him," said Robert's defeated voice, "the little limey with his chirpy tongue and his cheap suits, and he turned around and he smiled, and do you know what he said? 'We weren't expecting you.' 'We,' Winty. '*We* weren't expecting you.' " Robert's face struggled with disbelief, and he propped himself up against the cushions as a shuddering sigh escaped him. He screwed up his eyes in pain.

"I tried to beat his brains out, but of course he was better at that sort of thing, wasn't he? He was walking back toward Paula, and he said something like, 'Let's finish it off.' . . . I don't know . . . and I . . . I just ran at him and he sort of fell forward and that thing just . . . swallowed him up."

Again Winthrop Tower twisted his eyes away from Robert's. There was a very nasty feeling inside his head—the one called responsibility, the one he always tried so hard to avoid. He had been the prime mover in all this. Graham was a Tower production. So was Paula. He had more or less invented them, and then injected them into Robert Hartford's world. Now Graham was fighting for his life on some operating table, and Paula, on whom all his hopes for the future had been pinned, was now a pariah. He tried to digest the last part. Yes, Paula would have to go. His loyalty to Robert demanded it. He had known Hartford for twenty years. He had known Paula for one. Then there was the design of the Sunset. Robert would never allow her near the place after his humiliation at her hands. Last but not least, there was Paula's extraordinary mind-bending lapse of taste. Standing up! With an employee! Without double locking the door from the inside! One expected more from protégés. Very much more. There was no doubt at all about it. Paula Hope had let him down badly.

"I mean," said Robert, and Winthrop couldn't help noticing the mist that had sprung up in the famous eyes, "she just took my feelings, in the palm of her hand . . . and she crushed them . . . just like that."

"It goes without saying, Robert, that Paula no longer works for me, and I can be pretty sure that she won't work for anyone else either. I imagine she won't hang around for long." Winthrop fought back the regret. The girl had revealed herself to be serious trouble. Nothing wrong with that in small doses —they were rather stimulating—but there was a limit, and she had leaped over it. And yet . . . and yet . . .

For a second or two Robert pondered Paula's fate. His face was inscrutable. It was impossible to know whether he wanted further revenge or whether, already, he, too, was beginning to miss her. And when at last he spoke his meaning was very far from clear. "I can't stop thinking about her limp," he said.

GRAHAM LAY quite still, his face and head swathed in bandages, the plastic tubes with their straw-colored liquid disappearing into the folds of crepe around the flat area where his nose should have been.

Winthrop Tower picked up the pale hand of his servant and squeezed it. "Can you hear me, Graham?" he said. "Not with this fucking bandage on, mate," was the answer for which he half hoped.

"I am afraid he can't," said the quiet voice from behind.

Winthrop turned around. The neurosurgeon's green smock was covered with blood, but his hand, lily white and talcum powdered, was clean. He held it out for Winthrop to shake. "I gather from the nurse you're Winthrop Tower, Ovenden's employer," he added.

Tower took a deep breath at the sight of the doctor's gory appearance. His hand flew to his suddenly sweat-soaked brow, and he staggered sideways.

"Are you all right?" asked the doctor sharply in the tone of voice the medical profession reserves for unreliable friends of the family.

"Sorry. Yes, I'm fine. Never very good with blood. Not even very fond of the color red," muttered Winthrop weakly.

"Oh," said the surgeon, looking down absentmindedly at his stained smock. "I think you'd better sit down," he added, his voice more kindly now.

Winthrop sat down in the chair next to the bed. Beside his face the EKG machine traced the regular pattern of Graham's heartbeat.

"How is he?"

"He's had a terrible injury to the head. Multiple compound fractures of the skull. Bone injected into the gray matter. Brain compression. Tearing of the arteries in the cerebral and cerebellar areas. I'm not sure he's going to make it. I'm not sure it would be the best thing in the world if he did."

"You mean, he'd . . ."

"Well, it's difficult to say. He's throwing off EEG activity. He's not brain dead, but he's in a deep coma. If we can keep his vital signs stable for the next few days, he might survive. But he might never regain consciousness. If he did, he might not be able to speak or move."

"Like poor Sunny Von Bülow."

"That's more than a possibility."

"If it came to that, I'd be happy to pay for it," said Winthrop. "I don't want anyone switching him off." He wanted that absolutely clear. Quite suddenly he felt sadness well up within him. Dear Graham, who'd made him laugh, who'd eased his life, who'd looked like wild dreams. What would he look like now, behind the crepe mask, after being eaten by a television? God, what a way to go! Graham had always thought of himself as being up-to-date, but that was ridiculous. Winthrop smiled wryly as he felt the sadness recede. If life was ridiculous, why couldn't death be? Any minute now it would be his turn. Graham might actually outlast him, locked in the twilight of his ruinously expensive coma.

"Well, I'll certainly make a note of that in the medical file. So, you're going to be financially responsible for him?"

"Yes, certainly."

"Good. Look, I've got to go. We'll talk again. In the meantime there's nothing to do but wait and hope, I'm afraid."

"Yes, thank you. Thank you very much." Alone in the dim religious light of the intensive care cubicle, Winthrop Tower buried his head in his hands, and he realized exactly what he needed—a great big drink.

The hand on his shoulder was light, tentative.

"Hello, Winty," said Paula.

He started up.

"Paula! What the *hell* are you doing here?"

She stood before him, proud and defiant, and she looked him straight in his bloodshot eyes. "I came to find out how Graham was."

"He's a fucking vegetable, and it's your fault," blurted Winthrop, conscious of the cruelty, meaning to be cruel.

Her face was white, drained of blood, but it didn't change when he spoke. She didn't flinch at his terrible words. "It's not my fault, Winty. I hoped I could make you believe that."

Again she looked at him, straight in the eye, and Winthrop had to admire her brazenness. "How can you talk like that, Paula? How can you have done what you did to Robert? How long had it been going on?"

She looked desperate now, at the mention of Robert's name. Her lips trembled, her eyes widened. She was pleading with him, but he knew that she wasn't going to beg. "Graham could tell you what happened."

"He's never going to be able to, Paula."

"You believed what Robert told you, I suppose. He didn't want to hear my side of the story. I thought you would." There was despair in her voice.

Winthrop tried to tell himself that she was a counterfeit, a forger of emotions. After all, she had misled him, cheated his friend, and enslaved poor Graham, and now here she was trying to escape the consequences of her actions. What explanation *could* there be? She herself had confirmed to the police Robert's story of her infidelity.

He thundered when he spoke, the violence of his expressed sentiment partly disguising the strange ambivalence he felt. "How dare you stand in front of me, here in this hospital, with Graham fighting for his life, and tell me you have a 'side of the story'? What possible side could there be? I fear you're a tramp, Paula Hope, who took us all for a ride. Well, from now on you're a nobody all over again. I say so. Robert says so. And that means *everybody* says so." He jumped up, and he thrust out his chin as his belligerence burst over her.

For a long time she held his gaze. She didn't look away, and she was silent. She made no attempt to justify herself in the face of his anger.

Quietly, and quite firmly, she said, "Fuck *you*, Winthrop Tower," and then she turned quickly and strode from the room.

IN THE Bel-Air Hotel, Paula Hope was falling apart. All around her lay the wreck of the once immaculate room—half-empty coffee cups, the dirty towels piled high on the floor, the unmade bed. She hadn't allowed housekeeping in for at least three days, nor room service to take away the old trays, and the congealed food—greasy burgers, exhausted lettuce, melted ice cream—gave off a smell that reminded her of the diner in Placid on the Sunday morning after a Saturday night. The Bel-Air, haughtily aristocratic, had understood. Their guests were always indulged, however outlandish their requests.

It had been a terrible three weeks since the night in the Sunset Hotel when first Robert, then Winty, had become her enemy. Since then she had had no more contact with her old world than had poor Graham, sunk deep in his coma. She had crashed out of their lives on a raging sea of anger and disappointment, furious that the man she loved and the friend she trusted had trusted and loved her so little in return. Even a common criminal had the right to be heard, but they hadn't allowed her to explain, and in the face of their prejudice she had told them both to go to hell. But it was she who had gone there. She had moved into the Bel-Air, and the depression had settled over her like a black cloud as she had wandered around the curtained room in the robe they provided, unable to wash, to eat, or to sleep. The flickering TV, tuned in to MTV with the sound turned down low, had been the backdrop to her sorrow, and her thoughts had slowed down, sinking into numbness, way past tears, into the unreality of nothingness.

Paula sat down on the end of the bed. They had won. The world had beaten her. She had traveled on a magic carpet from hell to heaven, and she had found the happiness she deserved in beautiful Beverly Hills. Now it was gone. And so, at five hundred bucks a night, was the money she'd saved. In the hotel lot, just beyond the bridge and the swans, was the rest of her capital —the 1966 classic convertible Mustang that would carry her away from the place and the people she had dared to love.

Then, quite suddenly, a molecular shift occurred. Was it thinking about the car? Or escape? Or her lack of money? No. It was the contemplation of losing. She was not prepared to be defeated. Others had gotten their own way when she wanted hers. It was intolerable, said her heart. It was disgusting, said her guts. It was impossible, screamed her newly discovered will. She stood up.

"Screw *you*!" she said.

"Screw *you*, Robert Hartford! Screw you, Winthrop Tower! Screw *YOU*, Beverly Hills!"

She ran to the bathroom, the cleanest part of her suite, and she threw off the bathrobe and turned on the COLD tap. The water shocked her, and her thoughts were speeding as she soaped away the sweat and the tears. She jumped out, turned up the MTV, and let the clean music blast at her, reminding her that she was still *alive*. She scooped up a bathing suit and climbed into it, and she ran out of the door into the sunshine, her eyes blinking at the light. She wasn't even sure what time of day it was, though it was early morning certainly from the cold and the dew on the grass. In the pale blue sky, the underside of the shallow clouds were painted pink by the rising sun, and the air was crisp as she hurried along the path toward the pool.

When she reached it, she threw off the gown and she dived in, and once again the fresh water baptized her. She broke the surface, reborn, her whole body tingling. She looked up as she swam, toward the pencil-thin petticoat palms and the tall cypresses that ringed the oval pool, and she vowed that from now on she would only look forward and never look back. Her muscles rejoiced and her heart sang as she planned her future. They wouldn't drive her away from Beverly Hills, as they had driven her from Placid. She would find a job. Her Filofax was full of numbers—rival designers, suppliers, clients, would-be clients, and just plain strangers who passed in the plutocratic night of uptown L.A. One of them would come up trumps for her. It was just a matter of trying. It was simply a question of not losing faith. She swam for half an hour, and then she hurried back to her room and opened the drawer of the desk. She sketched out her plans on the Bel-Air writing paper. At nine o'clock the telephone would open up her brand-new world.

—

"No way José, Paula Love. What did you do to them, dear? I mean, I had some birdbrained girl on the line from Tower Design saying that you'd been fired and that you were bad news. She actually said that the old boy would consider it a personal favor if we failed to help out should you make a call like this. You didn't hide his whiskey bottle did you, honey, or bad-mouth his English taste? Well, I told her to mind her own business, darling, didn't I, but it wouldn't really be minding mine to give you a job. Not that you'd enjoy mincing around with my lot. The camp around here's not so much 'haute' as stratospheric. If the wrists get any limper they'll fall off! Anyway, *fantastic* talking to you, and good luck, darling. Have you thought about Alaska? No, no, just joking, sweetheart. One's got to laugh, lovely. It's only life."

Paula put the phone down. There had been all sorts of different ways of saying it, but the message had been the same. Thanks, but no thanks. They had closed the town on her. She had never imagined it was possible. Now she knew it was. She'd made thirty calls, but Winty and Robert had apparently made more. She was an untouchable in the place in which she'd vowed to succeed.

But Paula had had enough of pessimism. She had one chance and she picked it up from the desk, running her thumb absentmindedly over the raised italic script of the invitation. Unlike those who sent it, it was a very stylish thing, totally correct in the tradition of understatement—black on the finest white cardboard, no color, no drawings, no mindless colloquial chatter. *Mrs. Antoine Coriarchi*, it read. *At home. Black tie.* And the date? Tonight. At the top of Benedict Canyon, in the sky above Beverly Hills.

PAULA SWUNG the wheel of the Mustang and took the turn off Sunset by the Beverly Hills Hotel. Soon she was speeding through the flats up into the canyon. The houses looked grander at night, as the floodlights picked out the plants that God created rather than the houses that the humans had made. She fed the Bob Seger tape into the deck and cranked up the volume of the Blaupunkt a notch or two, allowing the hard-rock music to merge with the night air. The singer was going on about diamonds and frills in the Hollywood Hills. She laughed out loud at the lyrics. The black Anouska Hempel evening dress would do for the frills, but forget the diamonds. For now! Up ahead were the hills, and on the scuffed plastic of the seat beside her was the invitation to the Coriarchi party. She glanced down at it, as her heart beat faster in time to the frantic rhythm of the Silver Bullet band. It seemed light-years since the time when the Coriarchis had played the role of doormat to Winty's Stanislavsky interpretation of filthy feet. Since that day their star had risen. Maybe the house she designed for them had helped. Anyway, someone had given them a proper movie to make—Patrick Swayze had said yes to a Bo Goldman script, which meant that tonight's party would be far from the social desert it would otherwise have been. That was lucky, because it would be her last chance to salvage something from the wreckage of her career.

On either side the houses flashed by—great stone estates, displaced Mediterranean villas, contemporary masterpieces glossy wall by mossy jowl with somebody's idea of French châteaux. She climbed the twisting, turning road, and the adrenaline began to pump inside her, as the breeze plucked at her hair, sending it streaming out into the darkness. It was going to be all right. Nowhere this beautiful could be that bad. She had felt it on Melrose on the day she'd arrived. She was feeling it now. The angst of L.A. was coursing in her blood, all mixed up with hope, and optimism, and a reckless determination to win, here on the edge of the world where the dreamers dreamed.

The torches blazed at the entrance to the Coriarchi driveway, and Paula sent the gravel blasting from the Mustang's tires as she screeched to a halt in front of the valet parkers' station.

The blond boy, whose hand was on the handle of the door, looked almost too good to eat. His California "hello" smile was wide open. Paula smiled back. He was her age, but he wasn't her speed. "Great car," he said. "Great owner," he added.

"Thanks," she said, smiling back. She knew L.A. well enough to know that compliments like that got passed around a *lot*.

Encouraged by her attitude he tried again. "Hey, you wanna take in Camp Hollywood soon as this shit is over?" he tried, deepening the smile.

"Bail out, dork dick," said Paula cheerfully, heading toward the front door of the house, and smiling over her shoulder at him to show that there were no hard feelings. The heavy-metal video and barbecue bar might have been fun.

In the Coriarchi hallway she had herself designed, people were standing patiently before a gilt desk at which an elderly lady checked their invitations against a list. God, how awful, thought Paula. It was fine at some charity ball where people were paying $250 a pop for the tickets, but at a private party it was unbearably pretentious, insinuating both that people would actually want to crash a Coriarchi function, and that the hosts didn't know the people they had invited. In Hollywood, however, nobody liked to step out of line for fear of insulting someone, so all were submitting gracefully to the interrogation.

In front of her in the line a Tower client, who had never before missed an opportunity to say hello, twisted and turned her head like an ostrich to avoid eye contact with Paula. Her bony back, draped in shimmering Adolfo, was arranged in Paula's face like a shield and she chattered away to her surprised husband of the moment as if she actually enjoyed talking to him.

"Winthrop did this house, Michael. Did you know that? Isn't it wonderful? Really he is *so* clever."

The carrot-shredder voice wafted back over the skeletal shoulders.

Paula fought back the desire to tap her on the arm, introduce herself, and lay claim to the decorative scheme that the Coriarchi cow had attributed to Tower. But there wasn't time. Paula was at the desk. Her invitation floated down onto the table.

"Paula Hope," said Paula.

The social secretary peered at the list. She looked at Paula. Then she stared once more at the list. "I don't have any Paula Hope here," she said in a definite voice.

"But this is my invitation." The line behind Paula had gone deathly quiet.

The guardian of the gate picked it up like a bank cashier inspecting a dubious hundred. "And you *are* Paula Hope?" she said at last.

"Yes, of course I am," said Paula. She was getting angry and nervous. Weird things were beginning to occur to her. Could this have been done on purpose, as some kind of cruel social punishment?

"I'm afraid my instructions are to admit no one who isn't on this list, whether they have an invitation or not." It was the voice of the universal bureaucrat.

"This is ridiculous," said Paula. "I worked for Winthrop Tower. I *designed* this house." The irritation rushed out of her. Watch it, or I'll redesign you, said her threatening eyes.

"I don't make the rules, I just carry them out," said the narc with the self-satisfaction of her species. It was the umbrella excuse of the led as they basked in their little moment of power, their brief excursion into the otherwise forbidden land of the leader.

"At Nuremberg they hanged people who said that," said Paula.

"Can't you just step aside and let the rest of us join the party?" said someone loudly from behind.

"I don't think she works for Tower anymore," said somebody else.

"What seems to be the problem?" said Antoine Coriarchi. He had emerged as if from nowhere, and now he hovered at the shoulder of his minion.

"Ms. Hope has an invitation but she isn't on my list, and Mrs. Coriarchi told me specifically that no one who isn't on the list . . ." mumbled the woman, hurrying to cover herself in case she seemed to be doing the wrong thing.

"Please explain that I should have been on the list," said Paula. Her voice was sharp, not placatory at all. She didn't bother to say hello to her host.

For a second Antoine Coriarchi smiled his greasy Levantine smile. He knew what had happened, of course. His wife had mentioned it to him. This was a party unlike any he had given before. His newfound success meant that he had graduated from the Z team to the A one, and, in Hollywood style, it had happened overnight as it was meant to. Somewhere along the line one of the power people had declared through their offices that Paula Hope, the pretty young designer who'd done their house and then graduated briefly to Robert Hartford live-in status, was no longer persona grata. Therefore, she had been removed from the list. Simple. QED. Quite easily done. But now he seemed to remember that the shaker who'd wanted the girl scrubbed was in fact Tower, her former employer—Tower, who'd humiliated him when he was merely another Arab semipornographer; Tower, who'd said things that in any civilized country would have had a man reaching for his knife.

"Miss Hope is always an honored guest in my home," he said, and he bowed and he smiled as he contemplated his little act of revenge.

"*Thank* you," said Paula, and she swept into the bowels of the party that she already knew would be a battleground.

Paula helped herself to a glass of champagne and wandered out toward the swimming pool, where people seemed to be congregating. All around her the spectacular landscape lighting that she had organized merged with the light from flickering Malibu torches to bathe the partygoers in a flattering, luminescent glow. She recognized an actress she'd met with Robert.

"Hello, Martha," said Paula.

The girl looked at her in horror, the expression she had used when the vampire was about to do the business on her neck in a Cannon movie. "God! Paula," she said. She peered around quickly. "What are you *doing* here?" she stage-whispered.

"What do you mean 'What am I doing here'? I was invited, just like you."

"Well . . . I just think . . . you're incredibly brave," said Martha, making *brave* sound exactly like *stupid*. Then she turned and scurried away into the safety of the crowd.

Paula took a deep breath. She looked around. How had the Coriarchis handled the hot potato of a noncharity Beverly Hills party? Well. The flowers were definitely David Jones and somehow they'd managed to get Wolfgang Puck to do the catering. The groaning buffet had his fingerprints all over it— smoked salmon pizza, cheesecakes, big bowls of crème brulée. That scored points. The only other viable alternatives would have been Party Planners, overused Rococo, or safe but unexciting Chasens. She'd already heard someone say the poolside ivories were to be tinkled by hot Michael Feinstein rather than the more usual Marvin Hamlisch. Then there were the two or three uniformed Beverly Hills policemen dotted strategically around the house and gardens. That was a first-tier party touch. The guests, too, were far from a disaster. Beverly Hills supporting cast, mainly, but with the odd truffle scattered among the pâté. She noticed psychiatrist to the stars and former president of the American Psychiatric Association, Judd Marmor, chatting animatedly to numerologist Michael Kassett, yogi Alan Finger, and psychic nutritionist Eileen Poole, in a poolside meeting of the minds. There were no "go" studio people, but Columbia mini-moguls Rob Fried and Amy Pascal were working the crowd, as was Lois Bonfiglio of Fonda Films. Sharp divorce lawyer Gary Hendler circled; wide-eyed, charismatic Insight guru and actress Leigh Taylor Young hovered; Marilyn Grabowski, Hollywood insider and power behind *Playboy,* was surrounded by three or four of the youngest and most beautiful women at the party.

That was the knot that Paula wandered toward.

"Hi, darling," said Marilyn as she approached, and Paula smiled in gratitude that there was someone there who was not afraid to talk to her.

"Hi, Marilyn. Did you ever find that house down in Malibu?"

"Not yet, but apparently when I do you're not allowed to design it." Marilyn laughed to show that she'd heard but she didn't care, that she didn't take orders from the Hartfords and Towers of this world. *Playboy* was an insulated world within the world of Hollywood, and that was the way Hef liked to keep it.

"Boy, I'm glad you're here. They tried to throw me out at the door. Wow, they sure marked my card in this town. Like the old 'you'll-never-work-again' is alive and *well.*"

Marilyn laughed. "Don't worry, honey. You've got the talent. They've just got the egos."

The teenager with the part on the hottest soap had had enough of Marilyn's attention being distracted. "If you could get someone like Bruce Weber, and it wasn't *total* nudity, I mean, like, it was tasteful, I *might* be interested. . . ."

Marilyn rolled her eyes toward the sky and turned toward the pouting beauty.

Paula wandered on.

She approached an outlying group, recognizing a packager from Creative Artists Agency whose house she'd helped do. "Hi, Mr. Stieglitz, how's that fabulous Jack Russell terrier of yours? Has he eaten the drapes yet?"

The man next to the agent spun around at the sound of her voice. His back had been toward her. The up-lighter at the base of a nearby royal palm lit his face from below.

"Paula!" exploded Robert Hartford.

Paula took one step back. She stopped breathing. Her heart sprinted.

Shadows flickered around Robert's cheekbones, the angle of the light bathing him in Boris Karloff shades. Even in the diffuse glow it was quite apparent that initial shock was already turning into white-hot fury. He clenched his fists by the side of his immaculate dinner jacket and his neck pulsated above the floppy black velvet of his double bow tie. His eyes, seemingly sunk in dark trenches, blazed their anger. His whole body leaned toward her like a tree on some blasted heath.

"Hello, Robert," said Paula's mangled voice.

"What the *hell* are you. . . . How *dare* you come here. . . ." He spluttered his rage.

Paula managed to swallow. How many emotions could you feel at once? She loved him. Still. That was number one, and there was no doubt about it. You had to love him. He was an infinitely wayward child who could be forgiven everything because of the divinity of his face and the wonder of his body. His fame, his reputation, his cool power, the laser of his concentration, his absolute desire to give pleasure, his inventive single-mindedness in receiving it; all were good reasons to love him, and for all of them, she hated him, too.

"I didn't know this was your party," she said. "I wouldn't have come if it was." Sarcasm dripped from her words.

The four other people in the conversational knot acquired glacial smiles, but to Paula and Robert they had ceased to exist.

"You . . . shouldn't be allowed to . . . *mix* with decent people. Do you hear me? Do you hear me?"

Everybody did. The babble of poolside conversation stilled as the realization filtered into a couple of hundred minds. There was going to be a spectacular row.

"And where," said Paula evenly, "are the 'decent' people?"

She looked into the twin blazes that were his eyes. They were as close now as they had ever been, locked in loathing as they had been locked in love. Both wanted desperately to hurt; both knew that they would be hurt in return.

"You little . . . hooker," shouted Robert.

"I've never thought of myself as that, but coming from the expert on hookers I suppose I ought to give it some consideration. Perhaps it was the quality that made you want to marry me."

"Just *what* do you mean by that?" Robert's voice was still loud, but now it was superconductor cold.

"I'm merely saying what everyone knows already, Robert, that if it's female and between sixteen and sixty you screw it, or try to."

A buzz of excitement zipped around the Coriarchi pool. Cabaret like this could not be bought with mere money. Poor Michael Feinstein, scheduled to perform later, had already been upstaged.

Robert shuddered beneath the blow like an oak ship receiving a broadside at sea. She stood so still and defiant before him, unafraid, brimful of courage. He must punish her.

"You," he hissed the words, "were the first and the very last time I have ever screwed a cripple."

The oohs and the aahs that rumbled around the pool were Richter-scale strength. It wasn't just the viciousness of the insult. It was much more than that. Most of the listeners had been in therapy. They spoke psychobabble as a second language. Already the theories were forming, all of them different, all of them arriving at the same destination. Hartford was overreacting because, for the very first time in his life, somebody had lit his flame, and that same somebody/nobody had also blown it out. But a cripple, no less. Name-calling had taken on a new dimension. Hell, was it *true*? Who cared? It was deeply, meaningfully wonderful.

The tears sprang to Paula's eyes, and she shook her head in disbelief. She clenched her fists and battled against the sadness as she tried to think of a reply.

"Only a crippled mind could possibly say anything so cruel," Paula said.

She turned around, and she walked away from him, the stunned, delighted onlookers parting silently like the Red Sea to let her by. She half ran to the drawing room in a silence so thick that her own steps rattled like castanets. The tears poured down her cheeks, and all the time she could think of only one thing. She was limping. From the back he could see that. They all could. Now they knew what he was talking about, and in Hollywood, where they dealt in physical perfection, they would know that Robert Hartford was right. At the end of the day she was not merely a nothing; not just another maid come to town to milk the dream; not just another loose screw in the sleek machinery of the L.A. scene machine—Oh no, when the day became the night, what Paula Hope *really* was, was a cripple.

～*18*～

T HE BREEZE THAT was trying to be a wind sent the swallows curling in a night sky still ablaze with the memory of the marmalade sun. On Melrose the lights of the cars merged with the glow of the sodium vapor street lamps, the man-made brightness at war with the afterburn of the Beverly Hills sunset. The hum of the traffic filtered through the thick glass and merged with the other mating calls of the city at the left edge of heaven—the siren of a cop car, the shriek of brakes, the raucous music from the stereos of the designer macho machines, open Jeeps, Samurais, Mitsubishis, and all the other latter-day horses of the endlessly wild west.

In the queen's chair, the place where it had all started, Paula curled her legs up beneath her, and wondered where on earth it would end. She shouldn't be here. It was a crazy idea, but in crazy city where only the weird was real, it was okay to act on impulse—*if* you were out of the mainstream. Anyway, tonight she would be leaving L.A., and she wanted to leave from the place where she had arrived.

She sighed loudly in the dark of the Tower emporium, and all around the beauty wrapped her up. She still had her keys, and they had neglected to change the locks, so she had waited until she knew the showrooms would be deserted before slipping in, switching off the alarm, and then wandering alone in the place that had been so briefly the rich backdrop to her life. She had checked out of the Bel-Air at lunchtime and had spent the afternoon driving around Beverly Hills, her mind numbed by Robert's terrible words at the party the night before. As evening descended, she had had the idea of going back to Tower Design to say good-bye—not to him, but to the magical things they had both loved. Then? God knew. A ride to the desert? To Arizona? To someplace south?

The big tear grew in Paula's eye, and she blinked as she thought of all the leaving that went by the name of life. Dear Daddy; poor, sad Laura; Cool Hand Luke and little Jake; and now Winty and Robert, who had learned how to love her, but who had never learned to forgive. Was it like this for all the Los Angelenos behind the masks they wore on the freeways, on the Santa

Monica sands, in all the humdrum places of the dreamland? Or did the drabness of their thoughts mirror the ordinariness of their outward appearance, and were the highs and lows hers alone, to be suffered and enjoyed in the roller-coaster ride between the warm womb and the grave's cold? There were no answers to questions like that. Instead there was just the ticking of the clock, the countdown to good-bye, and the brave hello to a storm-clouded future.

"I'll miss you all," she said out loud, and her words conjured up a bigger tear as her heart lurched in her chest. There was no good reason to miss them, godlike Robert with his angel's face and his hideous words; sharp-tongued Winty, who had revealed a bizarre talent for betrayal; and Graham, who had so casually destroyed her and paid for her destruction with his brain —but she *would* miss them, because she still loved them. Still loved *him*. Could she ever forget the man who had predicted with such accuracy that they would be lovers but failed to mention that he would break her heart?

The end and the new beginning were creeping nearer, and Paula crouched back against the upholstery to draw strength from the memories for the long journey into the night.

A new noise thrust into the muted sounds of evening L.A. A key was turning in the lock of the store. Paula sat up as a thrill of alarm rushed through her. Immediately she knew it wasn't a break-in. For some odd reason, it was Winthrop Tower. Crumpled and crouched, looking just like the Savile Row scarecrow she remembered so well, he shambled into the showroom.

She stood up, anxious, but at the same time strangely pleased that she would see him one last time. "Winty?" she said.

"Good God, who is it? Paula?" He peered through the gloom, advancing into the shop. "What on earth are you doing here?"

"Don't worry, Winty. I'm not stealing anything. I came here to say good-bye." There was weariness in her words.

"Good-bye, Paula," said Winthrop Tower.

"Just 'Good-bye.' No 'Good luck'? Is that all I deserve?"

"Damn it, Paula, don't you realize what you've done?" There was exasperation in Winthrop's voice.

"I know what you've all done to *me*. You've worked overtime to make sure that I can never do anything in this town. Maybe I can understand Robert, but you . . ." The aching sense of loss was alive in her voice.

"I simply took back what I gave you, Paula. The first time you sat in that chair you had nothing either."

His eyes seemed to mist over as he remembered. Like Robert, Paula had turned him into a giver, had taught his heart to love. Like Robert, she had made him see that to trust was dangerous. It was why he, too, had reacted so violently to her betrayal.

"Do you know why Graham was in the bungalow that night?" She would try just once, only once, to explain.

"Spare me the tearjerker about the heart overriding the head. I don't want to hear how it was bigger than both of you. The soaps on TV are bad enough."

The bitterness was everywhere, but he hadn't choked her off. He was still standing in front of her. Still listening.

"He murdered someone he thought I wanted dead."

The Tower eyebrows shot upward. He hadn't expected anything so inventive. It was a good line. He could never resist those. "Oh?"

"He went to Florida, to Placid where I lived, and he killed a man called Seth Baker. He said he loved me, and he wanted to take me away with him, and that if I didn't go then he'd say I had planned the killing with him."

"And why did this poor Mr. Baker have to die at Graham's hand?" The sarcasm was ladled over the Tower words, yet in the wise old eyes there was the spark of interest.

Paula stood still, her leaden words still ringing in her ears. She knew it sounded impossibly unbelievable. Only a lunatic would imagine murder to be the way to a young girl's heart, and Graham had never seemed to be crazy.

Winty was the nearest thing she had to a friend on earth, and she could see from his whole demeanor that he thought she was lying. The surge tide of despair crashed headlong into the flood of memories. Why had Baker died, Winty had asked.

"Because he raped my friend, and he murdered my little brothers," she howled at him, and she sank down to her knees as the tears came and the great white-topped waves of grief rolled over her. All the fighting and the struggling, all the desire and the ambition, all the hurt and the heartache flowed from her in a raging torrent of anguish. Her head fell forward onto her chest and she held it in her hands in a gesture of prayer as the tears oozed through her fingers and the sobs burst from her lips. Her chest heaved as she battled for air to fuel her sorrow, and the sounds of her misery filled up the room. All around the tapestries watched her, the eyes of the famous, the ancient Romans at whom she had once dared to stick out her tongue. Now they had their revenge. Paula was finished. The emotion was draining from her before their marbled gaze, the lifeblood of feeling seeping steadily from her broken heart. In the darkness beneath the ocean of tears she felt the rock bottom of her life, but, as she touched it, there was something else.

Around her shoulders there were arms, in her ears there was a dear old voice. "Darling, I believe you. Of course I believe you. It's going to be all right," said Winthrop Tower.

—

WINTHROP TOWER watched Robert closely over the rim of the glass of Glenlivet. Would he believe the story he had just heard? Paula's and Robert's own future happiness depended on it. Winthrop had left nothing out. He had told it, as Paula had told him—the rape of her friend, the murder of her little brothers, Graham's free-lance revenge on Seth Baker. He had spelled out the hitherto invisible details of Paula's seeming betrayal, and now he could only wait to see how Robert would react.

Robert shifted in the armchair, his face expressionless, only his clenched fists giving away the strength of his feelings. He crossed one leg over the other, saying nothing.

"So we're asked to believe that your servant Graham is some sort of a freak psychopath?" he asked in a detached voice.

Winthrop's heart sank. He had half hoped for a joyous reaction—the enthusiasm of the lover on learning that the loved had not been unfaithful after all. But he had only *half* hoped. Robert Hartford had been badly wounded. The injury would not heal overnight. "Well, yes, it seems I got him wrong. It seems we all did." Winthrop suppressed the frisson of guilt. How wrong had he really got Graham? He had always known that there was a violent element to him. It was what he had been attracted to in the first place, the out-to-lunch eyes in the angel's face, the ropelike muscles and angular bones at odds with the cheerful cockney-sparrow demeanor. It had been fun to have a chauffeur like that, almost like having your own personal bodyguard while avoiding the L.A. cliché of hiring the real thing.

"So I suppose now you'll be thinking about having him switched off that life-support system you're paying through the nose for." The cruel edge to Robert's voice was totally unexpected, the viciousness of his words doubly so.

Winthrop coughed nervously. The conversation was not going as he had planned. Robert preoccupied had given way to Robert in vengeance mode. "I hadn't really thought about that," he said.

"I think you should. Either way, he'd be better off dead."

There was color now high up on Robert's cheeks, near the yellowing bruises. He sipped determinedly on a tall glass of Corona.

" 'Either way' . . . ?" said Winthrop as a request for clarification. But Robert cut in. "Why do you believe her, Winty?" It was a schoolmaster's question of a lowly pupil.

Winthrop could feel himself warming up inside. Robert had been his friend for twenty years. They had always treated each other as equals. Now he was being patronized. He had been told what to do with Graham. He was being asked to justify his faith in Paula. It was becoming irritating.

"If you'd heard her tell her story you'd have believed her, Robert. You loved her. You wanted to marry her. You weren't wrong about her."

Robert cocked his head to one side and allowed himself a sad smile. "I wasn't wrong about her?" His tone was mildly incredulous, the kindly teacher surprised and a little hurt that a star pupil had let him down. "Winty, I'm not a man who trusts easily. Some might call that a weakness. *I've* always regarded it as a strength. Everything I've ever achieved, I've done on my own. You know better than most how difficult it is to make the dreams come true. With Paula I broke the golden rule. I loved her. I actually *loved* her." He shook his head from side to side as his whole face registered the disbelief at his own stupidity.

"I mean . . . there are the feelings . . ." He waved a dismissive hand to register the global unimportance of *those*. "And then there are the other inconveniences. Can you have any *idea*, Winty, what a thing like this does to an image like mine? The rumors are everywhere. The studio hears them. The public hear them. And they get magnified in the telling, don't they . . . not that the actual truth needs much magnification. The point is that a thing like this could have destroyed my *career.*" He leaned forward and thrust the last word at Winthrop like an ace of trumps.

Winthrop wasn't buying. He knew Robert's apparent concern with his image was an attempt to disguise his hurt pride.

"But if it wasn't her *fault,* Robert, then you have to forgive her. I mean, she did it for you. What would you have done in her position? She was just trying to get rid of Graham so that she could call you in New York, and get you to protect her." Winthrop's voice was patient now, its tone humoring, sad that anyone could be so desperately naïve.

"It's all lies, Winty. She's made it up. Can't you see what's happening? She's trying to get back, and she's dreamed up this . . . *incredible* story, and she's actually made you believe it." Suddenly, he was tired of all the meaningless words that would never alter the bottom line. "Anyway, whatever you care to believe, I don't want her in this hotel. Understood? So get rid of her, Winty. Do I make myself clear?" His voice had sharpened. His eyes had narrowed. His jaw jutted.

So did Winthrop's. "You don't tell me what to do, Robert."

"I do in this hotel. I own it, remember? And I don't want Paula Hope anywhere near it. Another thing . . . if you choose to believe her nonsense and take her back into your company then I suggest that we rethink our plans to work together on the redecoration of the Sunset."

Winthrop felt the bile rise within him. Nobody talked to him like that. Not *anybody.* For Paula's sake, he tried to hold on to his temper. "It hurt you that badly, did it, Robert? You can't forget the sight of it, and the pain has screwed up your thinking."

"Cut the psychojargon, Winthrop!" he exploded. "Just get her out of my hotel. Do you hear? Just do it!" Robert drew himself up in the chair as if it were a throne, wrapping himself in an aura of kingly arrogance.

"Robert Hartford, you are a self-centered, emotionally ugly, narcissistic bastard, and I suggest that by far the best person for you to go screw is yourself."

The color sprang to Robert's cheeks.

"I suggest you get out of here, Tower, and out of the Sunset as well. You're history, okay? You understand me?" His voice was quiet.

Winthrop pumped himself up. "If I'm history, Robert, then you, my love, are *ancient* history. People are going to have to learn an entirely new language just to *study* you, dear. And without Livingstone and without me, your precious Sunset Hotel is going to become a monument. You won't have guests, you'll have sightseers. Behold the glory that was Rome until the mad emperor blew it all away. Good-bye, darling, and, oh, try to stay 'up' without us all. I mean your *mood,* sweetheart. After all, we mustn't ask for miracles." He jumped up and headed for the door as the cluster bomb of abuse rained down on Robert Hartford's astonished head.

On the path outside he walked fast. Already he knew exactly what he would do. He rushed along the walkways and he pushed past room-service trolleys and hurrying waiters, past pink-aproned maids, green-clad Mexican gardeners, and the odd scurrying guest late for a Star Room power lunch. He swam past the pool on a cloud of fearsome resolve, and he bustled through the lobby to the bank of elevators.

He was furious with Robert, but he was also furious with himself. If only he had listened to Paula in the first place. Instead, he and Robert had been so full of their inflated importance that they had never bothered to get to know the angel they both loved. Her past had remained a mystery to them, because *they* had not been a part of it, and therefore it was by definition uninteresting. They had played along with her reticence, not out of delicacy, but because, in typical Hollywood style, it suited them to pose and strut and joke and play at the center of the stage, oblivious to the feelings of lesser mortals—to their sorrow, their sadness, the horror of their memories. Last night as she had sobbed in his arms and poured out the dreadful details of her story, there and then he had taken her back into his life, his home, and his heart.

He had driven her to the Sunset and put her to bed, with a gallon of tea and an ocean of sympathy, but he had hardly been able to stop the tears. He couldn't believe there could be so much moisture in a human being. Immediately he had wanted to go to Robert to tell him the extraordinary news, but he had been unwilling to leave her, and he had eventually asked one of the maids he knew well to sit with her while he went to arrange the reconciliation. Well, so much for *that* plan. Now Winthrop was a messenger bearing the worst news of all.

The elevator door opened and his irritable finger jabbed at the P. God *damn* it. In what mood of mischief had the Good Lord dreamed up sex?

He searched for his key in the high-class junkyard of his pocket, and he burst into the apartment. The maid Maria jumped up as he hurried into the bedroom. On the bed, Paula, pale and all cried out, sat up. Her eyes searched Winthrop's face for clues.

"You and I, darling, are leaving this dreadful hotel, and we are never, ever coming back," he said. He didn't stop. He made straight for the telephone and grabbed at it like an important letter in a high wind.

"Roger, Mr. Tower. Roger, I'm checking out. Yes, that's exactly what I'm doing, leaving, and if you have any sense at all you yourself will check out. King Lear has flipped. I want an army of valets up here to pack, cases, crates —the works."

He banged the telephone down, and he turned to face the incredulous Paula. "Now you, Paula, are going to have to be brave. And you are going to have to trust me. Both at the same time."

"What did he say?" asked Paula.

"This isn't the time to go into that. The important thing is we're leaving and we're leaving now."

"What did he *say*, Winty?"

"He didn't believe your story. He's drowning in ego. I think his nuts have fallen off."

Paula started to get out of bed. "I'm going to see him. I'm going to set this straight. He'll listen to me."

"Paula! *Forget* it. Listen to *me*. He's going crazy in there. Trust me."

"He'll take it from me. He loved me. He still loves me."

Winthrop took a deep breath. He would have to be cruel to be kind. That was usually *enormous* fun. It wasn't going to be now. "He doesn't love you, Paula. He *hates* you. He can't deal with what he saw. He's like a vicious, wounded animal. He wants to destroy you. That's all he wants."

Her shoulders began to shake, the tears squeezing from her eyes all over again.

But Tower's voice was diamond hard as he spoke. "Listen, Paula. *Listen* to me! There's no time for this. Not now. Maybe not ever. A terrible thing has happened. The worst. Now you have two options. You can use it, or you can let it use you. You can be the victim or you can make someone else be a victim. It's your choice. You've only got one thing in this life. Yourself and your pride in yourself. Lose that, and you lose everything. Robert Hartford is a bastard, and a cheap bastard. Don't chase him. Let him go. Don't let him humiliate you. Humiliate him. I'll help you. I promise. Just pick yourself up off the floor, and toughen up, and get the *hell* on with your life."

Her sobs died down as the words sank in. He was right. She was too poor, too alone to wallow in the luxury of going to pieces. She had no army of friends who would enjoy her tragedy on condition that she in turn enjoyed theirs. There would be no audience for her nervous breakdown, and without one of those nothing in Hollywood meant anything at all.

Slowly she stood up, and she brushed away the dust of pain, and she fought the tears back. "What are we going to do?"

Winthrop, tutor in adversity, beamed at his star pupil. "We're going to have *fun*," he promised. He picked up the telephone, flipped through the battered black Asprey Filofax, and punched out a long-distance number. "Mr. Tower calling for Mr. Adam Partridge."

He was through in seconds. "Mr. Partridge? Winthrop Tower. Very well indeed, thank you. Good. Good. Yes, I know, I have been a little slow in answering your letters. Well, I'll tell you."

He smiled reassuringly at Paula. "I wondered if the deal you offered was still open. Really? Good. Well, I accept it. Yes. Just like that. I propose that this telephone conversation constitute an agreement between gentlemen to proceed on the basis of your lawyer's letter—the one you sent toward the end of last year. Yes, Mr. Partridge, I share your opinion of lawyers, but once our minds meet then they can be told what to do. Precisely. Exactly. Now there is just one additional condition, which shouldn't be a problem—I want to move into the Château tomorrow morning—first thing. If you could have a penthouse or one of the bungalows prepared, and I'll need a personal office, and a construction office, and the architects will want somewhere to do their drawings or whatever it is they do . . . yes, yes. Good. Then we have a deal.

Yes, you'll have a long, dull letter confirming it tomorrow, and doubtless you will send me an even more boring one in return. Good-bye, Mr. Partridge. Good-bye, Adam . . ."

He put down the telephone.

"There," he said. "Now we have a roof over our heads. And do you know what we are going to do? You and I, sweet Paula, are going to take over the Château Madrid."

THE CHÂTEAU Madrid had seen the very best days of all, but it was so ancient it had forgotten them. It stood half a mile back from the Strip, nestled among the foothills, and it reached up to scratch the sky like an old, decaying tooth. Lost in its dreamy detachment, its mildly anxious disorientation, the Château creaked and crumbled and lost bits in the high winds as it waited in resignation for death by demolition. Time had not so much passed it by as blown through it, covering everything with the dust of ages, and loosening the cement of elegance that once held it together.

The Partridge family had owned the Madrid for as long as anyone could remember. As if it were an elderly relative in an old people's home, they visited from time to time and made the right noises, and they brought fruit and flowers in the form of the occasional coat of paint, the odd roof tile replaced, the odder sofa re-covered. Then they hurried back to Pasadena where their real world was, to their gigantic family trusts, their prize azaleas, their charitable foundations, and of course to the serious business of murdering things that flew, and several other inoffensive animals that didn't. They had held on to the Madrid because one didn't sell one's things. So there it remained, a broken toy in the attic of the Partridge dynasty, like that awful, common aeroplane that Uncle Freddie had bought, which now stood rusting in some hangar up north.

Adam Partridge sat on the board of the Met in New York. A Partridge usually did, and Adam had been selected for the job because he had once taken a fine arts course at Yale, and had bothered to amass the finest collection of Jasper Johns in America. This set him apart as the family member with modern "taste." One fine day he had had an *idea,* and there were some in the family who had not yet forgiven him this departure from Partridge tradition. The more aggressive family members, however—the ones who paid lip service to the existence of an outside world and as a result administered the family money—had been rather taken with Adam's plan. It had been suggested that the enormously respected Winthrop Tower, the rare designing bird that was taken as seriously on the East Coast as on the West, be asked to rebuild and redecorate the Madrid in return for a slice of its equity. The beauty of the scheme was that it did not require the Partridge family to spend a single cent of their indecently large fortune, and *that* was how the old money stayed old. The revamped hotel, presently worth nothing apart from the real estate on which it sat, could be turned into a money-spinner under the clever guidance of the most fashionable designer in America. The Partridges had been impressed most of all by the fact that Tower was the black sheep of a family to which they were distantly related, and also by the very large sum of money it was rumored he had been left by his disappointed father. They had agreed that he should be approached.

But Tower had told them he did not "do" hotels. With the bemused incredulity of their class that anybody, anywhere would refuse them anything, the Partridges redoubled their efforts to persuade him. True aristocrats, they courted mercilessly those who wanted nothing to do with them, while reserving their scorn and disdain for those unfortunate outsiders who aspired to their ranks. As a result Winthrop had come under siege from the Pasadena law firm that existed primarily to administer the Partridge family affairs. Like spoiled rich children unable to have their own way, they had progressively sweetened their offer, secure in the knowledge that everyone but they had a "price," and that it was just a question of finding out what it was. Their most recent offer, which Tower had not even bothered to answer, was that he would do up the hotel at his own expense in return for a twenty-five percent share of the equity. He would also be given the option to buy out the Partridge seventy-five percent stake at any time during a five-year period at a price twenty percent higher than the prevailing value of the real estate. Thus, in a worst-case scenario, with Tower buying them out, they would receive twenty percent more than the present value of their investment, and, if real estate continued its upward spiral, perhaps very much more. However, if Tower succeeded in turning the Madrid around and didn't exercise his option to buy them out, then they would own three-quarters of a valuable, successful hotel instead of a hundred percent of a worthless one. Either way they would retain their real-estate play, and it would cost them nothing.

Now, quite suddenly, Tower had telephoned out of the blue and changed his mind, and he had just signed the ultimately binding agreement, a gentleman's agreement between genuine gentlemen.

The limo that swept Winthrop and Paula up to the baroque entrance to the Château seemed to sense the importance of its cargo. It swooped down like a hawk on the deserted forecourt of the hotel and crunched to a halt, seemingly appalled by the lack of ceremony that greeted its arrival. The "valet parker" did not speak English. It was a forlorn entrance, no flowers, no doorman, and the carpet that led into the somber reception hall was so dirty that the newer stains looked clean.

Winthrop erupted from the backseat, unfazed by the enormity of the task ahead. "Whatever we do to it, Paula," he pronounced, "what*ever* we do, we must not banish entirely the marvelous *depression* of this entry." He charged inside, and Paula, brightening, followed in his wake.

"I see granite. Granite everywhere. Marble is over. Marble is dead," he warbled. "Black granite, gray granite, cream granite. My word," he sighed, "I feel a granite jag coming on."

At the reception desk they were almost ready for him.

"Welcome to the Château Madrid," said the old man behind the desk, his uniform shiny as black ice. "We have bungalow four reserved for you, Mr. Tower. That's the Jean Harlow bungalow, out by the pool."

"I hope they've changed the sheets since her day," muttered Tower. "I was always worried about the state of her underwear."

"Winty!" said Paula, beginning to lose herself in the excitement. She looked around with the eye of the professional stranger. First impressions were vital.

The proportions were perfect: high ceilings, a good strong rectangular shape, well-placed windows. Winty was right. It could take granite.

"Minimalist," said Winthrop. "Let the architecture do the talking. It needs some very good paintings, light but traditional. Boucher. Fragonard. Poussin. Isn't it *romantic*?"

Paula didn't let the word upset her. This could be made absolutely wonderful. "God, look at that ceiling. That mural's out of this world. Restore it, light it. Maybe even repeat it. Say in the restaurant. We could fly Willie Fielding over from London. He'd do it perfectly. Just his style."

Paula clapped her hands in glee. "Oh, Winty, I can't believe this. I see ancient and modern in perfect harmony. Yes, your granite, but perhaps Ron Rezek lamps, over monolithic boxlike sofas in strong, dark colors in something no-nonsense durable like sail cloth. Spotlit oils on the walls, I agree, but tapestries, too. Marvelous Morris floss-silk-on-damask tapestries over pale pink magnolia walls—a five-to-one white to pink, very subtle, very quiet. Those cornices need rebuilding, and the reception desk has to go, and that awful newsstand, and the porter's desk, and something must be made of those stairs. . . ."

He smiled gently at her, and again the wave of guilt broke over him. How could he have doubted her? He, Winthrop Tower, had played the alien roles of sheep, hypocrite, and Victorian moralist as if to the manner born, and yet Paula's undiluted talent alone should have been enough to convince him that she would never stoop to the kind of callous infidelity of which he had accused her. A part of him had always wanted to believe her, but that was a coward's excuse. He had allowed himself to be overruled by the force of Robert Hartford's personality, by the conventional response, by the insider's traditional mistrust for the outsider. Paula had been L.A.-ed, and he had done the L.A.-ing. So much for the Yale motto, *Lux et Veritas*. Light and Truth.

Well, now he had amends to make. He would see Paula through this one last tragedy, the one called Robert Hartford, and he would help her rebuild her broken life brick by brick. Already, thank God, the thrill of the work was beginning to damp down her misery, as he had hoped that it would.

"I told you we were going to have fun," he said. "And you ain't seen nuthin' yet."

～ *19* ～

ROBERT HARTFORD LOOKED down at the open copy of *Interior Design* magazine on his desk and once again anger rushed into the back of his throat. The timing was so perfect it had to have been done on purpose. On the very day that he was launching the revamped Sunset Hotel to the press of America, he had been scooped. The Château Madrid had gotten there first. The endless, gushing article in the intellectual *Interior Design,* the most sophisticated of the shelter magazines, declared the new Madrid a triumph. Tower and his brilliant young protégé Paula Hope had performed a miracle. It was a glittering example of understated good taste, a masterpiece of interior decoration that had the writer scurrying around his thesaurus to discover appropriate superlatives. Everywhere the obvious had been avoided for the innovative, and safety had been left behind in a celebration of artistic vision, bold and sure, dramatic yet practical, a perfect melding of the old and the new. The last paragraph had been the worst of all. Winthrop Tower had given the credit to Paula. "I merely held her hand," he said. "If I'd let it go, the Madrid would look even better than it does today." Then the writer had written the paragraph that had had Robert spinning sleepless in his bed for the last week.

It is rare to see such beauty in a redesigned building. For years the Madrid was an architectural gem waiting to be discovered. Now, the touch of the true artist has wakened it from its Rip Van Winkle sleep. And this was a gentle kiss, accurate, sensitive, effortlessly sure of its purpose. The extraordinary design triumph of the Château has at a stroke catapulted Paula Hope into the first rank of young designers. It is the beginning of what can only be a stupendously successful career. One last thought. We were lucky to have something with which to compare the new Madrid. This month Robert Hartford's famed Sunset Hotel has completed *its* refurbishment. What a disaster it has been. The design firm of Tanker, Voos and Foster, usually reliable if seldom exciting, have produced a monument to mediocrity. They have never fallen beneath a standard of universal dullness in their work on the

561

Sunset. Nor have they ever risen above it. The student of late-twenti-eth-century design would do well to ponder these two rival hotels. In traveling from the one to the other he will come to understand the true meaning of the phrase "from the sublime to the ridiculous."

Robert wondered how the hell he was going to get through the press conference. Some bright spark would have read the *Interior Design* piece, and he would be closely questioned about it. What could he say? It was true. The Madrid looked like God's house in heaven. The Sunset's "new" look was about as visually interesting as a shopping mall in Wisconsin. Would they have found out that Tower and Paula had been his first-choice designers and that he had thrown them off the job?

He stared down at the article but he wasn't seeing it. He was thinking as he always thought—about Paula, and the night she had betrayed him. His hand moved up to his face and he stroked the small scar he had never bothered to get the surgeons to remove. It lingered on, an aid to memory, and a backbone to resolve. He could still feel Graham's fist exploding against his cheek, but it was the vision in his eyes that hurt him. That hand. That dreadful, lewd hand roaming free where only his was allowed to be. What had she been feeling as those fingers had invaded her? Had she been hot for the Englishman's street body, and his gutter mind? Had she been thinking of him, Robert, safe in New York, as she readied herself to receive his rival? Had she been laughing inside at the treachery as she rushed to do it, standing up, like some cheap Strip hustler in a back alley? For a year and three months he had whipped himself with the questions that could never be ade-quately answered. Graham was sealed off from the world. Paula was gone. And why, anyway, should she ever tell him the truth? He shook his head to make the memories go away, but they didn't obey him. That skirt, so squalid on the floor, and her panties, pulled away from her, yet not removed. God, the horror of it. The betrayal. It was a cliché that love could turn to hate, but he hated her. So much. So strong. So deep. So wide. And now, beyond his reach, in the Winthrop Tower firmament, she continued to taunt him with her talent.

Kristina didn't bother to knock. She came in fast, and the look on her face said "more bad news." "André's leaving." She blurted it out fast. "He's just been to see me. Mason's has poached him, and he's taking Paul and Michelle with him."

Robert groaned out loud. His chef. His under-chef. His pastry chef. It was a disaster, but it was not the first disaster. "You offered them more?"

"Yes, of course. I told him to name it. He wouldn't. Same old thing. He says the atmosphere here is a nightmare. He says everybody's worried about the falling occupancy. Nobody believes the management's on top of it, and he's still bitter about you calling him a jumped-up frog."

"How long did they give?"

"A month."

"Christ. We can't get anyone good in that time."

"I've already put out ads in Paris and Brussels. I guess I ought to try New York, too."

"Well, pay them anything. We've got to keep the Century at the top. That and the Star Room are the only things holding the place together."

"It's not the money, Dad. You know that. It's the tension. Everyone's unhappy. Everyone's nervous."

Robert slammed his fist down on the color photographs of the new Château. "Goddamn it, they've got no *right* to be nervous. I'm not selling the place. I'll die here."

"It's your temper, Dad. That's what makes them nervous. You fired Von Hofstader and they liked him and trusted him. He was the link with Livingstone."

"The kraut was on the take. He was raiding the wine cellar."

"Who cares, Dad? In offices you take the paper clips and the Bics. It's called perks. The new guy's got the personality of a sheep on Valium. Morale is falling out of bed. The staff are snapping at the guests and the guests are complaining to the staff. It's a vicious circle. Now that the occupancy's down to fifty percent it's ten below break even, and it's trending lower."

"Maybe I should get them all together and talk to them again."

"No way. The malcontents leak it to the press, and they start up all those 'trouble at the Sunset' rumors. Then the staff gets even more anxious. Personally, I don't think it helped last time when you told everybody that you were Big Brother and you were watching them. I thought that was a little confrontational."

"Oh, so now you're the world's hotshot hotelier, are you?"

"No, of course I'm not, but they'd rather deal with me than you. André came to me, didn't he?"

"He came to you because you're marshmallow soft, Kristina. That French creep wouldn't have had the balls to come in here and tell me he was walking out with my entire kitchen leadership. I'd have threatened to sue him for breach of contract. He'd have to have flambéed a few frog's legs to finance that little action."

"He didn't *have* a contract, Dad. He and Livingstone had been friends for years. He used to cook the old guy dinner in his bungalow once a month, and then they'd sit down and eat it. They tried out new recipes for the menu. He actually wept when he told me about it."

"You're right, Kristina. I'm sorry. I'm just not very good at this."

"The Madrid hasn't helped," she said, her eyes wandering down to the open magazine on her father's desk.

"You'd better believe it hasn't helped," he growled. "They're filling their beds with Sunset guests. Your friend Hope has really stuck it to us."

The thundercloud floated across his brow.

Kristina watched him quizzically. It had all started to unravel from that long-ago night in her father's bungalow. She had believed his story of course, of Paula's infidelity and Graham's accidental injury and of Winthrop Tower's extraordinary decision to side with the cheating lovers. She had cut Paula out of her life, not that her former friend had ever tried to contact her, but in her heart she had found it difficult to believe the story of her treachery. Her father had been devastated by the ending of the only real relationship he had ever experienced, and now the Sunset was slowly sinking below the horizon, while the faded Château was fast rising in the Hollywood Hills.

Kristina wondered if her father was ready for the next bit of bad news. "I heard that the Madrid hired Alfredo."

"What?"

"He gave notice. Said he wanted to go to Santa Barbara. Now I hear he's running the bar at the Château."

"They poached him?"

"It's difficult to say. Anyway, he's there now. And he's taken a lot of the regulars. Business in the Star Room is way down, and a lot of the screenwriters have apparently gone with Alfredo. He actually used to *listen* to their sob stories about what the studios had done to their scripts. The gossip says he used to get them women to make them feel better. The new guy wouldn't know a woman if she sat on his face. You'd think twice about telling him the time of day, let alone pouring out your sorrows."

"Well, fire him for God's sake, Kristina."

"Listen, at least he knows a mimosa from a screwdriver, even if he is psychotoxic. The next guy'd probably be a dealer, or worse."

Robert let out a weary sigh. That was it in a nutshell. Kristina was the realist. He dealt in the raw emotion. She was right, of course. For now it was probably better to have the devil they knew behind the bar. At least people could still get a drink, even if sympathy was off the menu.

"Sometimes I wonder if I've got the right temperament for this. Of course, you're right, darling. Do whatever you think is best. The bar is the least of my problems." He massaged invisible furrows on his smooth brow.

"You look tired."

"Yeah, I guess I am. I go on location tomorrow, and the script's a mess."

"How long will you be away?"

"Oh God, I don't know. They've been shooting around me. I guess it could be a wrap in six weeks, if there are no ego problems." He watched Kristina closely. She looked relieved. No doubt about it. "So you'll be able to get on with running the place with no interference," he added to show that he knew.

"I'll keep you in touch with developments. For God's sake, give Suki Marlowe a night or two off. She's pale enough as it is, and you look as if you've given your last pint of blood. Remember it's supposed to be a horse opera, not a ghost movie."

He laughed at her irreverence, and Suki Marlowe's face, pixie sweet, wafted across his mind's eye. Yes, she would be a distraction of sorts. They usually were. It would be a relief to get back to the game he was really good at. Thank God the police and his litigious reputation had managed to keep the lid on the Graham thing. Horizon, the studio that had picked up the Galaxy contract, had been skittish as wild mustangs while the rumors had multiplied but they'd hung in there, and now the contracted movies were beginning to get made. Somehow the Sunset would struggle through. It could probably live for years on the fat of its former glory, until Kristina and her dull manager, the one who made the dial tone sound like Lloyd Webber in full flood, learned the ropes. And one fine day, somewhere out there in the misty future, he'd probably be able to forget Paula Hope.

He stood up. "Listen, darling. I've got to pack. What the hell do they all wear in Arizona?"

⸺

THE THREE or four people in the packed bar who had actually been born in Southern California could remember the Château from their childhood. It had been the place where Auntie stayed on her annual visit from Boston, and it had smelled a bit like her—fusty, musty, and dusty. It had been spooky to have tea in the vast reception hall, and later that night the Madrid would provide an appropriate backdrop for ghostly fantasies and nervous dreams at bedtime. Now, however, it had been born again, and the zealous light in the trendy eyes of 150 guests said so. If you were out with the in crowd, at this very second you were drinking in the Kennedy Room at the Château Madrid.

Like a modern-day Régine, Paula sat at the corner table and sipped on a spritzer as they lined up to pay homage. Residents of the City of Angels prided themselves on their ability to recognize new talent, and the word was out. Paula was the Tower heir apparent. She would have to do their houses— despite the fact that they had just been "done."

They had reacted to her rehabilitation in exactly the same way they had to her downfall—with lemminglike enthusiasm, with Gadarene gusto, and now that the once waned star was bright in the heavens, they fell over each other to follow it. Wise men, Bethlehem.

Paula looked around, and the success smiled back. It was funny how you could tell. There were crowded bars from the redwood forests to the New York island but this was different. These people had dedicated their lives and their vast talents to "knowing" and their presence there, at six o'clock on an ordinary day, with nothing special going on, was like a message from God. Certainly the press coverage had helped, but it was much more than that. All over the city the telephones were ringing off their hooks as it was casually dropped that the meeting should be at the Madrid, rather than the Sunset— "So dull, dear, now that Livingstone's gone—and while we're there why not let's try the restaurant. Carl's organized a table, and I hear they're quite busy." So Carl had managed a table at the Madrid, had he? The movie must be doing well, better than the returns hinted. Was there an Oscar in the air? Paula was learning every minute, and she found that she was as good at running a hotel as she was at designing one. In the end it required the same skills—a commitment to excellence, an unfailingly accurate sense of good taste, a certain showman's panache. If you had those three, then everything else fitted into place. The staff, seeing themselves part of something superb, became pussycats overnight. They didn't need top dollar, because they were getting top job satisfaction, and they pulled together as part of a winning team, forgetting petty jealousies and nit-picking demarcation disputes as they concentrated instead on the greater good, the success of the Château Madrid. The best people at the other hotels were flooding her offices with their résumés, like Alfredo, the head bartender at the Sunset. Right now he stood there like a king behind the polished mahogany dispensing cocktails, sublime mixtures of spirits and equal parts wisdom, laced with an acid wit, and topped with a heartwarming smile. That was brilliance. That was art. How the hell could Robert have let him go?

A frown flew across Paula's face as she thought of him. He had seldom been out of her mind, but she had walled him off in his own private cell and now he was a prisoner there, unable to escape. Each day, each minute, she added another brick to the wall that surrounded him, as she fortified herself against him and the harm he could do. From that dreadful night at the Coriarchi party to this moment she had not set eyes on him, and it was difficult to know anymore what she felt about him because she had taught herself not to confront that. But he was there, in chains in the prison of her mind, and occasionally the clanking sound would remind her of the disturbing presence.

In the frenzied excitement of the Château she had been reborn. It seemed the Madrid was on the other end of the scales from the Sunset. While the Château had risen the Sunset, fat and heavy and out of condition, had fallen. It wasn't done on purpose. She hadn't tried to poach Alfredo, for instance. He had just been drawn to the magnet of the Madrid's success. The design had been one factor. The papers had been full of the innovative brilliance of the Madrid's décor, and gleefully they had contrasted it with the pedestrian design of Robert's hotel. In his crumbling tower, Robert would not be thanking her for her victory. He would be cursing her for it. Part of her cared about that. The other part didn't give a damn.

Winthrop Tower was the diversion from the unsettling thoughts. He pushed through the crowd and headed straight for Paula's table. His eyes were wide and his hair was tousled and it was clear from forty feet that he was both sober and in an enormously good mood. From ten feet away, he boomed his greeting. "I've exercised," he shouted. "For the first time in my life I've exercised and I feel bloody *marvelous*."

Paula leaped up in mock alarm, and she pulled out a chair for him as someone at the bar actually began to clap and twenty or thirty people nearby joined in.

"Sit down before you fall down, Winty. What on earth have you been doing? You don't look as if you're dressed for aerobics. Are you sure that's wise at your age? Aren't you supposed to start gently?"

Winthrop collapsed into the chair. "I have exercised," he said. "I have exercised my option."

"Your *option*?"

"Yes, darling. I've just bought the rest of the sodding hotel." He beamed at her proudly.

"You *haven't*, Winty."

"I have. I've just this second completed the contract. The Partridges are sulking in a pear tree. They didn't believe I was the silk-purse-from-sow's-ear guru. It's mine. The whole thing. I can blow it up if I like." His face brightened at the thought.

"God, that's the deal of the century."

"Yes, I suppose it is," said Winthrop. The idea of doing something as unoriginal as making money seemed momentarily to depress him. "Well, never mind that. Let's celebrate. At least I'll never have to see Adam Partridge again. He's a very decent fellow, and I couldn't begin to kick him as far as I trust him, but he keeps talking about the responsibilities of his position, and family tradition and all that bullshit. I'd have thought that the only responsibility the Partridges had was to spread it about like muck so that the rest of us can wallow in it."

"What does it feel like to be a hotelier?"

"A bloody site better than it feels to poor old Robert." He watched her as he said that, but her enigmatic smile told him nothing. "Goodness, this joint is jumping, isn't it? These people actually look as if they're enjoying themselves. God knows how they do that on the Perrier they all drink."

"What made it happen? Why the Madrid? Why not the Sunset?" Paula was genuinely bemused by it all.

"It's all to do with old age, sweetheart. West Coast folk pretend to love anything that's old, but they don't really. While they like the *idea* of old things they can't stand the disadvantages that come with old age—the plumbing and waterworks problems, the dilapidations of the exterior, the deteriorating electrical circuits—I'm talking about the *people* of course. . . ."

He giggled, full of wicked malice, as he plowed on. "So you take somewhere like the Château that has the cachet of being old and you make it modern and fix it up and presto, you have a success. And it helps that one has a certain reputation on the *East* Coast. Westerners love nothing more than to impress Easterners with their taste, in the same way that Easterners love to flaunt their virility in front of Westerners. It isn't often that each gets a chance to do either."

"Winty, you don't have a drink. How can we celebrate without one of those?" Paula caught a passing waiter. "Stoli on the rocks, and hold the rocks," she said.

"Good girl," agreed Winthrop. He pushed himself back in the chair, and he smiled around the room. It was going to be a wonderful evening. Dinner with Paula in *his* restaurant. The shortest possible distance to bed afterward. And everyone within earshot desperate to be there, every servant in his personal employ. He felt the thrill course through him, a little adrenaline surge of pure pleasure.

"What on earth shall I do for an encore?" he said.

There were lots of possibilities on his list. Having a heart attack was not at the top of it.

It was a strange feeling. Like heartburn at first, high up in the chest. Then it changed. It was lower, in the middle, and it hurt. The pain struck him a crushing central blow in the chest that stayed and didn't go away. It was as if someone had lowered a weight onto him, and that someone else had decided to sit on it. A band tightened around him, tighter, and tighter, and he opened his mouth to breathe because his nose wasn't doing the job properly anymore. With the pain came the feeling of panic, and his brain started to jabber to him—"heart attack, heart attack, you're having a heart attack."

The panic made the pain worse and the increased pain deepened the panic, and both made breathing more difficult as the room swam around and he stiffened in his chair, both his fists clasped to the center of his chest where the agony was.

Paula was standing, and her face was in shock and he could hear her saying, "Winty, Winty. What is it? What's the matter?" And he couldn't tell her, but he knew that she knew. She knew everything. His Paula. She would look after him.

They were crowding around him now, and one mustached face was pushed up against his as a hand clasped his wrist, and another tore at his necktie. Winthrop recognized him. He knew this man. From the deep somewhere he managed a throaty stage whisper. "This man's not a doctor. He's a plastic surgeon."

The Beverly Hills face restorer was not put off by the vote of no confidence from the victim. "Call for an ambulance," he barked. He fished in his pocket for some keys. "There's a matte-black Ferrari Testarossa outside. On the backseat there's a Louis Vuitton briefcase. Somebody run and get it. Fast. I need some IV heroin."

"Drug addict!" Somehow Winthrop managed the joke through the waves of pain that engulfed him.

Paula stood quite still. She was praying as she had never prayed before. In front of her, cradled in a semisitting position in the doctor's arms, Winthrop Tower was white as winter snow. Sweat stood out on his face, which was twisted terribly. His eyes were screwed shut and his clenched fists were little balls at his chest as the doctor wrestled to take off his coat, to free the arm vein for the needle.

Suddenly the Vuitton case was there, and the diamorphine was bubbling into the syringe. The doctor didn't bother to clean the surface of the arm. He just jammed the needle in, pulling back first on the plunger to send the smoky wisp of blood into the clear liquid. Thank God the veins hadn't collapsed, and thank God he'd brought the vials of Omnopon back from England where they realized that it was the only stuff for situations like this. In America, heroin was still unavailable to doctors.

At the end of the needle there was a dramatic change in Winthrop Tower, as the most powerful painkiller in the world cut into the vicious circle of pain-anxiety-anxiety-pain. Winthrop felt the steel band that encircled him loosen a notch, and he managed to fill his lungs with air. He was soaked with sweat, his skin was clammy and cold, and the fingers of nausea pushed and pulled in his stomach. But the pain was going and the relief was a new life. He was going to be all right. The tummy tucker had saved him. He managed the faintest of smiles as he tried to speak. "Don't worry, Paula. It was the exercise . . . the exercise."

"Oh, Winty, oh, Winty . . ." She knelt by his side. "Don't speak. Don't say anything. I'm here. You're going to be all right."

The paramedics pushed through the crowd, and the doctor stood up to greet them. "He's had a coronary. I've given him five milligrams of intravenous diamorphine and he's got a regular tachycardia of one-ten. I haven't got a cuff but he's got perfusion pressure. He'll need an open line for access—I guess some dextrose. I'll come with you. Where does he go? ICU at Cedars? I'm on the staff there."

They carried Winthrop through the lobby he had so brilliantly designed, the drip attached to his arm, the defibrillator pack and the oxygen cylinders following him.

"Don't leave me, Paula." He held her hand tightly as she walked beside the stretcher, and she blinked back the tears.

"I'm not going to leave you. I'm coming with you in the ambulance."

They squeezed inside it, Paula, the doctor, the seen-it-all-before paramedics, and Winthrop cocooned in the red blanket, his dear face poking out at the top, determined to find something to laugh about in the middle of the tragedy.

"I wouldn't be seen dead in red," he muttered, "but won't it be *lovely* to start collecting on all that Blue Cross."

"Try not to speak too much, Mr. Tower," said the doctor.

The wail of the ambulance siren underlined the seriousness of it all, as they sped down the winding roads toward Sunset Boulevard.

"Paula. Paula!" Winthrop's voice was suddenly urgent as he called out to her and she leaned in close to comfort him.

"It's all right, Winthrop. Just relax. You're going to be all right."

The paramedic and the doctor exchanged glances, but said nothing.

"Listen, Paula. I'm sure this is a false alarm, but if it isn't there are some things you should know. First, you're my heir. I've left you everything, and it's quite a lot."

She shook her head, not wanting to hear him talk like that, and a tear broke out and started a drunken journey down her cheek.

"I never could think of anything to spend it on, and it just accumulated in all sorts of dull things like apartment blocks, and dreadful things called bonds. Someone told me it was about fifty million a little while ago, and of course now there's the Château and Tower Design. They'll be yours when I go, and I couldn't care less what you do with them as long as you have *fun* with them and always remember not to take them too seriously. It's all a joke, you know, Paula. The one thing God has is a sense of humor. Not a very *kind* sense of humor, but a sense of it nonetheless."

"Oh, please don't say things like that, Winty. Please don't. You're making me cry. You're not going anywhere."

"Nonsense, darling. We all are. We're just haggling over the time and place. And the second thing is much more important. You're the kindest, loveliest, most talented person I have ever met in my entire life and you're also far and away the most beautiful. There. How about that. And I didn't need any vino for the veritas."

She bent down and kissed him gently on the cheek, as the tears poured silently down hers. They looked at each other, and the knowledge came to each at the same time. The time for jokes was nearly over. It was almost the time for sorrow, the time, so soon, for mourning.

His voice was clear as a bell when he spoke. "I hope to heaven," he said, "that there's a bloody good barman in hell."

And then, quite suddenly, he was gone.

He didn't move. No sigh escaped him. No pain tormented him. Inside him, something that had been hanging by a thread gave way. So close to him, she felt his spirit slip away, its wings fluttering in relief at the endless freedom. And she rested her head down, on his dear cheek, and she whispered low, "Good-bye, my darling."

GRAHAM DIDN'T look beautiful anymore. He looked like a badly broken doll, and he lay motionless against the crisp white sheets. His eyes were closed, and someone had combed his hair, its fashionless tidiness mocking the memory of the man who had hummed with life. All the wires came out of him at one point, and it was easy to imagine the spaghetti junction of terminals feeding them beneath the plain hospital blankets that wrapped him in the cocoon of the living dead. Beside the bed was a bank of machinery, at the center point of which were the two screens tracing the patterns of both brain and heart. The bedside table was bare. No fruit, no magazines, no photographs of the friends and loved ones that Graham had never had.

"Hello, Graham," said Paula.

How did you speak to someone who couldn't hear, who couldn't feel, who didn't care? It wasn't the first time she had visited him, and so the problem was not new, but it didn't go away. She tried to visualize Graham in the old days, before the night of madness when he had so wantonly destroyed her world. She remembered that first night, when he had carried poor Winty across the parking lot at Morton's. "Never separate 'im from 'is drink," he'd said and he'd winked at her, beginning the conspiracy she had treasured, before it had turned to tragedy.

"I came to tell you that Winty died last night," she said. "It was very quick, and he was joking all the time. A heart attack, we think."

She swallowed as the lump in her throat pushed up against her pointless words. Who was she telling? What was she talking to? But of course she knew. She was talking to the only living friend she had in the entire world. There was no one else with whom she could share her sorrow. Just this broken collection of flesh and blood whose heart ticked meaninglessly in his chest.

"He was so lovely, Graham, wasn't he? You knew that. We both did. And he loved us. We were the only ones he loved, and he was so beastly to everyone else." She laughed in the middle of the tears, summoning up the vision of Winty and his whiplash tongue, the Winty who had left her his fortune, his talent, and the warmth of his memory.

She moved closer to the bed and she held the cool hand, its flesh flaccid against hers. "I'm all alone again now, Graham. It's just me, but I have all Winty's work to do, and I have the Château." She squeezed his hand to tell him that she was brave, and she chewed on her lower lip as she plowed on.

"I want you to see our Château Madrid someday, Graham. It's a marvelous hotel, and it's doing much better than the Sunset. Everybody says so. It must be driving poor Robert mad."

If on some astral plane he could understand, the news that Robert was having a bad time would please him. "He's always hated me since that night, you know, when the devil got into you. He never believed me when I told him what happened. And we loved each other *so* much, *so* much, and yet he didn't believe me. Can you understand that? *I've* never been able to." With her free hand she plucked distractedly at the blanket, as her sigh of despair filled the room.

"But I shouldn't moan on about myself. Look at you. Poor, poor Graham. All you did was love me. I wish I could have loved you back."

The big tear hurried out onto the lower lid of her eye. Then, like a suicide on the ledge of a skyscraper, it jumped, cascading down her cheek. "We were both outsiders, weren't we, and Winty took us in, and now he's gone. . . . So it's just us against everyone, and we'll *win*, Graham, won't we. We'll win."

A cough came from behind her shoulder, the announcement of someone's presence rather than the clearing of a throat.

The doctor was standing close behind her. "Miss Hope? I'm so sorry to hear the news about Mr. Tower."

She smiled wanly and wiped hard at her face, well aware that he would have seen her tears. "I can't really believe it yet," she said simply.

"There's a period of shock, when you feel like that," he replied, his voice kind.

"How's Mr. Ovenden?" She tried to change the subject.

"Oh, there's no change. There won't be, I'm afraid. He's completely stable, but deep in his coma. He could go on like this for years."

He looked down and studied his feet. There was a question hidden among his words. Tower had paid the bills. Tower was dead. What would happen now? Was Miss Hope the right person to ask?

She heard his thoughts. "I'm Mr. Tower's sole heir," she said. "I want everything to go on as before."

"It's my duty to tell you that the prognosis is very poor. His brain has some activity, but I'm all but certain he'll never regain consciousness. It'll cost a fortune to . . ."

"That doesn't matter," said Paula quickly. She waved a suddenly impatient hand. "There's a ton of money, a *ton* of it."

"Well, that's a very caring attitude. He's a . . . a very lucky . . ." The doctor trailed off as he looked down at the luckless Graham, then back at Paula. Somehow his sentence had gone wrong.

"He's the only one I have left," she said.

She had turned fully to face the doctor, determined to let him know how much his damaged patient meant to her. Keep him alive, said her earnest expression. Don't cut off the last lifeline to my past.

She didn't see the movement behind her, because her body was between the doctor and the bed. So neither of them saw Graham's hand—saw it clasp once, twice; saw it hover above the blanket like a wounded bird trying for flight; saw it fall back exhausted into the stillness of his coma.

———

"LISTEN, FORGET the small-print script bullshit, is the high concept 'fish-out-of-water' or not?"

In the ice-cold interior of his personal converted Winnebago, rented to the production company as a "perk," Robert Hartford's voice smashed into the moviebabble like a fist into flesh.

For a second or two there was silence.

"I think Robert's right," said Suki Marlowe, uncoiling the best legs in the business as she licked her lips and thought of the night before, of the night to come. The fact that Robert had asked a question rather than made a statement meant nothing. He was the bankable name. His was the bunkable bed. That made him right, even when he was wrong.

"Well, it *is* fish-out-of-water, Robert, but we can't make the guy a *complete* hick. I mean, by the end of the movie he's got to be swimming on land like he's never even *heard* of the fucking sea."

Robert Hartford's fingers stopped their drumming on the mahogany table beside his chair. "I wish you wouldn't use words like that in front of Suki," he said.

The brand-name scriptwriter looked sorry, at the rebuke from the star, at the mess they were making of his script, at the fact that he hadn't won the state lottery and therefore couldn't afford to tell this roomful of idiots what to do with their artistic presumption.

The director, in the referee role, pitched in on what would be the winning side. "I'm inclined to agree with Robert and Suki," he said slowly, as if he had bothered to think about it for more than a nanosecond. "Can you write it that way?"

The "If you can't, we can find someone who will" hung in the cold air, the eternal Damoclean sword hovering over the heads of all movie writers.

"Yes, of course I can write it that way. I can turn it around to a musical S.F. 'buddy' movie set in ancient Rome if you want, but I just wonder if they'd want to come and see it."

"One or two of us in this room have a little experience of what they want to come and see," Robert drawled.

Somehow he managed to wrap the word *what* in a question mark. It filtered through to everyone in the room that only modesty had prevented him using the word *who*. And it was true. *He* was the guarantee the movie would open, and open big. Compared to the power of his name the script was blowing in the wind.

"The only thing I know to be true about the future is that it is essentially unpredictable, especially where movies are concerned," said the writer. He was angry, and enough of an idealist, and more important with enough of a track record, to stand up to a star of Hartford's magnitude.

The temperature in the trailer notched down a point or two. It made everyone uncomfortable when someone offered up "the great truth."

Robert Hartford's voice was very quiet. "If you're right, then presumably you know nothing either."

There was a long silence.

"So in the absence of divine guidance and laying aside contractual rights, perhaps in this little democracy we could let the majority decide." The sarcasm dripped from his lips. He flicked a look at Suki. Another at the director.

"Robert's right," pouted his costar on cue. Actually she thought the writer was quite cute, but in the industry you balled busters if you wanted to get on, writers if you wanted to get off.

"So that's settled then, David. You let us have some 'make like a nerd' pages, and later we graft the underdog-becomes-overdog theme onto the original high concept. That was what you envisaged, wasn't it, Robert?" said the director.

Robert had won. He peered out of the window at the battleship-gray mountains through the sparkling champagne-clear air. It was about 110 out there in the high desert, but inside the trailer he was wearing his baby-blue cashmere Scotch House cardigan. He looked over toward Suki Marlowe, impossibly pretty in an all-black leotard, pink leggings, and beautiful bare brown feet. Then he turned back to the little group of courtiers who were waiting for his assent.

Script approval. That was what it was all about. And all the other approvals, too. Who was hired, fired, booed, sued; who was praised, hazed, raised, fazed.

Why couldn't it be like that at the Sunset? Why didn't the staff behave like these yes-men? They had for Livingstone. They'd fed from the hand of the decrepit old bird, the minions bowing and scraping before him, and in his entire life Robert had never heard him raise his voice. Here he could make or break careers; in the Sunset he couldn't even get the bartender to make a decent martini. At the last meal he'd eaten in the Century Room, the whole place had the feel of a terminal illness, the flowers not actually wilted but certainly no longer fresh; the tablecloths white, but not pristine; the cutlery clean but not gleaming. Nobody had laughed and the conversation had been low pitched, as the guests had muttered gloomily to themselves and wondered why on earth they'd come. The waiters had dispensed the thoroughly mediocre food and drink as if it was the absolution, gliding reverentially between the tables like priests officiating at some solemn last rite.

"Robert?"

"What? Oh yes, yeah. That's the way to do it."

Damn! He had to concentrate. He always gave himself totally to a movie during shooting. The brooding single-mindedness went straight onto the film stock. If it wasn't there the public would miss it. But the Sunset was distracting him. All week he had burned up the lines to L.A. as Kristina had given him the blow-by-blow of the hotel's ongoing dissolution, and the worry was getting to him. He was only half there, in the world where he needed to be one hundred percent present.

"This is tomorrow's shooting schedule, Robert. It's an early call, I'm afraid. Four o'clock wake-up, makeup, but the scene's got to be in the can by sunup. These desert dawns are really something. Better than L.A. sunsets."

The director leaned forward and passed the mimeographed schedule to

Robert. "We'll need Suki, too," he added. Please, please don't keep her up all night, was the unspoken request.

He took the pages but he was thinking of the maddening impossibility of running the Sunset Hotel. How *had* Livingstone managed it? Robert had never seen *him* struggling. He had floated above the whole thing like the conductor of a well-drilled orchestra. The martinis had never been less than perfect in Livingstone's day and it was impossible to imagine him sitting down to a dinner of the inferior quality that he and Kristina had endured on the night before he'd left for location. A raised eyebrow would have given the chef a nervous breakdown, a frown would have sent the bartender crying to his drink. Yet Robert could rant and rave and they looked at him as if *he* were crazy, as they continued to provide service, food, and drink about which the only thing first class was price.

"That okay for you, Robert? The start tomorrow?"

Again he snapped back into the here and now. "Yes, of course it is. No problem." But even as he spoke he knew that there *was* a problem—the oil-and-water mix of his movie career and the Sunset Hotel.

The telephone on the table next to him rang once. He reached for it.

"Mr. Hartford. Your daughter Kristina is here, at the main set office. I told her you were in conference but she wants to see you right away. She says it's important."

"Bring her over," snapped Robert. He put down the telephone carefully, in an effort to control the frustration that was already building inside him. Okay, so he'd had enough of the toads in his trailer, but Kristina, in *Arizona,* unannounced and unexpected and with a bagful of undreamed-of disasters from the Sunset Hotel—that he could do without.

He stood up. "I'm afraid I must ask you all to leave. I have a visitor from L.A. I think we've basically wrapped up all the outstanding points."

They hurried to obey, the writer and the director eager to leave the demanding presence of the superstar, Suki Marlowe signaling her disappointment and irritation at the arrival of the "visitor" from L.A.

Kristina came in fast, talking from the hip. "I'm sorry, Dad. I'm really sorry, but this wasn't a phone-call thing."

He offered her a distracted embrace.

"Roosevelt left," she said simply. "He walked yesterday. He's got a job as assistant manager, *assistant* manager, can you believe, at the Four Seasons."

"He wouldn't have the nerve," said Robert, his mouth quivering in disbelief. Roosevelt had made soggy pasta look like high-tensile steel wire.

"He's done it. He's history, packed and gone. He said it was a personality conflict with you."

"He didn't *have* a fucking personality!" shouted Robert.

Kristina looked away in exasperation. There was only one problem with the Sunset Hotel. Her father. "Maybe we should discuss what we do about it." She threw herself down into a chair.

"Listen, Kristina, believe it or not, I'm trying to make a movie here. It's big budget purely and simply because they are having to pay *me.* I had to throw the entire creative team out of here to make space for you and the Sunset. I can't handle this any longer. I'm an actor. I've got to *act*. It's not as easy as I make it look."

"Maybe you should have thought of that before you bid for the Sunset."

Robert weaved an elegant hand through immaculate hair. Yes, Kristina was right. His childhood obsession was turning into a nightmare. "Okay, what are we going to do? Advertise, I guess."

"The trade journals are carrying nothing else but help-wanted ads for the Sunset. Any minute now they're going to come out with a special Sunset classified section. People leaving is a symptom, Dad. You don't treat a bacterial infection with blood transfusions."

There was a silence. Something had definitely been said.

"And *I* am the bacterial infection?"

Kristina said nothing.

Robert Hartford sat quite still, as he adjusted to being a disease.

"Dad, maybe we should get in a management company and let them run things. We're out of our depth here."

"I'm not having outsiders fiddling around with the Sunset," snapped Robert. In his mind he could see them, all the ugly men in their boxlike suits sniffing around the hotel that he loved as much as beautiful women. Better by far that it should die than that it should suffer the fate far more terrible than death as the filthy fingers of the faceless ones rummaged through its secret places, breaking its quivering heart.

"We've got to do *something*," said Kristina.

He fixed her with the killer eyes. There *was* a way out.

"You run it, Kristina. Take over the whole thing. Run it yourself. I'll be in the background in an advisory capacity."

" 'Advisory capacity'?" Kristina's heart quickened. The idea had not been far from the center of her mind, but the suggestion had had to come from her father.

"Yes, a consultant, a sort of chairman of the board." He waved a hand to suggest that his actual title was of no importance, and he looked at her intently as he wondered why she hadn't jumped at his suggestion.

"If I'm going to run things, I think I should have the votes." Kristina's tone was determined. She didn't want her father criticizing, complaining, moaning, groaning. It would be worse than the status quo. At least now the responsibility for his own mess was his, not hers.

Robert's eyebrows shot upward. "You mean shares? A controlling interest?"

"Whatever."

Kristina set her Hartford jaw. If there was to be a battle, let it be now. Her father was ruining the hotel she was trying to run, and the atmosphere of uncertainty was poisoning the Sunset. There was only one chance. He must back out before it was too late. Either he had to hire someone else and give that person some sort of tenure, or he had to let her do the job. Either way he would have to give up *control*.

Robert laughed, and he shook his head. He was amazed yet not angered by her request. He had always loved Kristina, despite her mystical preoccupations and her tendency to float about in a high wind. Now she was giving him something to respect. There was actually something to be said for her brave, not to say foolhardy, suggestion. The staff liked her and trusted her, and she was learning fast. It was he who was making it all go wrong. He undercut her authority, and his nerve-racking hands-on/hands-off management style played havoc with that most delicate of flowers, employee confidence. The atmosphere of mistrust had seeped into the fabric of the Sunset Hotel. They thought of him as Lear, the mad, sad, unpredictable king, and now here, before him, was his daughter asking for a slice of the kingdom.

His voice was dreamily reflective, when at last he spoke. "And what guarantee would I have, if I was to give you fifty-one percent of the Sunset, that you would not use it against me at some unforeseeable time in the future?"

Lear had never thought of that. Robert just had.

"I wouldn't do anything to upset you, Dad. Surely you know that. I love you."

"Ah, love," he said, "the thing that herpes outlasts."

But despite his words he was in tune with Kristina's thinking. He needed psychologically to be free of the Sunset, and yet he wanted the cake to be there after he had consumed it. It was a human enough desire, and Kristina had suggested a way of achieving it. The hotel had after all been a gift, and where else would it eventually end up but in his only daughter's hands? By giving her control now, he would get rid of the responsibility, and yet still retain forty-nine percent of the shares. The world would still consider it "his" hotel, while the staff would know that he had zero control over their destinies. He would "save" the Sunset by giving it away to the only person in the world that he loved, and he would continue to live there into a ripe old . . . He forced the alien thought from his mind.

"Have you ever heard of Wittgenstein?" he said.

"Vaguely."

"He was perhaps the greatest philosopher of the twentieth century, and he lived in Cambridge. He was walking in a public park one day with a friend, and he 'gave' his friend one of the trees. Only he made the gift subject to all sorts of conditions. For instance his friend was never to climb the tree, never to cut it down, never to tell anyone else that he owned it, et cetera. He was a linguistic philosopher and he was making a point about language, and its meaning. When you took into account all the restrictions, he wasn't really giving the tree away at all. Genuine ownership implies the right to be able to dispose of the things you own."

"I don't get it," said Kristina, but she did.

Robert leaned forward in his chair. "I'll give you fifty-one percent of the Sunset on the single condition that you never, ever sell any of the shares and that in the unlikely event of your dying before me then I get them back."

"And I get to prune the tree, fertilize it, water it, spray it for pests—with no interference from you?"

"All of the above."

"You'd draw up a contract. . . ."

"Why, certainly we'd sign a contract."

She stood up. So did he.

They didn't shake hands on the deal, they hugged on it, and this time all the warmth in the world was in the embrace.

~ 20 ~

*I*N DAVID PLUTARCH'S tennis-court-size office the glass walls gave him views over the whole of Los Angeles, but what he could really see was the world. He didn't look out much. He looked in. That was where the high visibility was. On the flickering Quotron screens; on the New York Stock Exchange tape that ran the full length of the only wall that wasn't see-through; on the four clocks, their hands set to West Coast, East Coast, Tokyo and London time and with thick red bands showing the timing of the opening and closing of the major exchanges.

He sat at a monolithic desk, and his feet were up on the faded green leather, as he clipped immaculate nails, sending the chips spinning out to be lost in the inch-deep pile of the carpet.

"Lose those Chicago calls," he shouted suddenly. "I don't like them. Don't be careful about it. Be brutal. Christ, why the hell isn't there any decent way to short Tokyo direct?"

Across the room the tape recorder caught it. Everything in this room was recorded. Millions of dollars flew in and out of this office. Later, if there was a difference of opinion over what had been said, the tape could decide who got fired. But the recorder wasn't the only person listening. Management of the around two billion in liquid assets that were left after his movie deals was a twenty-four-hour business. Most of it went through Morgan Stanley in New York, the best-run bank in America, but Plutarch liked to do a little dealing himself, hence the hometown operation in Beverly Hills. In the room with the money hero were a Japanese-speaking dealer, a young attorney specializing in the tax law of mergers and acquisitions, and a secretary whose job it was to monitor the wire services—Reuters, Dow Jones, and the financial press generally—for bits of information that pertained to Plutarch and his actual or possible business dealings. Throughout the day Financial News Network and CNN ran permanently, as did other programs, recorded on VHS during the previous twenty-four hours—Louis Rukeyser's "Wall Street Week," "Moneyline," and "The Nightly Business Report." Nothing in the public domain passed Plutarch by, and not much in the private one either. The banks of telephones surrounding his desk like a stockade saw to that.

"Difficult to short Japan," the dealer shouted back. "They don't like foreigners selling shares they don't own."

"Can't we try it?" asked Plutarch. "Dump some Sony we haven't got, and wait for the tariff barriers to go up. There'll be blood on the walls in Tokyo when they figure out that gravity works for stocks, too. My Congress people don't want to solve the trade deficit by raising taxes. They want to do it the popular way and nix the Nissans and the Hondas and tailspin the dollar. Who the hell cares about the currency when only one in ten Americans has a passport?"

"You're right on the fundamentals, Taipan, but forget shorting Japan. We tried it before. They just close out the positions without consulting us whenever it suits them. The Finance Ministry gives the order. *Free market* is something they pretend not to understand."

"All I say is, when they go, they blow. We're zero Jap exposure, aren't we?"

The dealer picked up the phone. In seconds he was through to the duty CPA. "What's our Japanese exposure?"

"Securities, yen, and real estate?"

"Yup."

"Zero direct stocks. Around five million in Euroyen year maturities. Nil real estate. Ten million in Bank of Tokyo Eurobonds, five-year maturity. Minimal exposure."

Plutarch waved a dismissive arm, as the dealer repeated the information. "Yeah, it's peanuts and it's safe peanuts. Forget it."

He stood up. It was a dull market. Nil action. He should make some. Greenmail a sleepy industrial. Shake up a teetering S and L. Dream up a leveraged buyout of a food company, and put a spike in the Pepto Bismol sales.

He walked moodily to the window, and he peered down at the pool beneath. The site was balm for the billionaire's jaded eyes. Kanga was massaging Caroline Kirkegaard's back.

―

CAROLINE BREATHED IN deeply. It was called Shiatsu, and it felt sublime. Poolside at Plutarch's, the Kirkegaard mood was good. She lay back on the sun bed and let the rays soak through her as the clever fingers kneaded her rippling muscles. Mmmmmmmmm! Things were almost better again. Destiny was growing explosively, the members pouring in, donating outrageous gifts to the movement in exchange for the cradle-to-grave/grave-to-infinity guidance and protection it offered in return. Who needed an L.A. tract home in the cosmic blot that was this lifetime when it could be traded in for an eternal ticket to ride? Who cared about cash, about jewelry (apart from crystals), about cars, when there was the possibility of happiness without end on the millennial journey that Destiny promised? Nobody who had seen the light in the Kirkegaard eyes, shining like a beacon to the true believer, gave a damn about those mundane things. The Destiny funds, played brilliantly by Plutarch, were soaring giddily to heights of which Caroline had never dreamed. Already there was a Destiny building on Wilshire, and a brownstone in New York, a branch office in London, and another in Paris. And there was no stopping it. New Age was getting bigger, but it hadn't really started, and now there was Destiny incense, Destiny herb tea, Destiny music, and Destiny crystal jewelry, quite apart from the bestseller *March to Destiny,* and the videotapes of Kirkegaard channeling spirits, and preaching charismatic Destiny themes to the ecstatic faithful. Yes, she was a guru now, but she had built only the ground floor. One fine day she would raise the roof, and then go through the roof, and up into the heavens where God lived, and where she, Caroline Kirkegaard, would rule.

One thought killed her joy. Robert Hartford and the Sunset Hotel. When there was nothing left to want she would still want it. When there was nothing left to dream of she would dream of his destruction. The rumor that it was running down under his erratic management was beside the point. If revenge was to mean anything at all it would have to be *she* who caused his downfall. But he would never part with the hotel. He would demolish it rather than let it fall into her hands.

She looked up, aware suddenly that he was watching her from the window of his office, and she smiled at Destiny's most important member.

He smiled at her, aware that she had seen him. Maybe he should wander down, and watch them together, the two beautiful girls, and their two beautiful bodies. . . .

An assistant with a Harvard MBA wandered into the Plutarch office. "Are we still interested in the Sunset Hotel?" she asked.

Plutarch spun around. "For sure," he said quickly. "What you got?"

She held out a piece of Reuters tape. "Reuters is saying Robert Hartford's made over a controlling interest in the Sunset to his daughter, Kristina. He's called a press conference for sometime next week. Want me to check it out? Sunset Corporation is private, but if Reuters has it, it's no secret. Should be able to confirm or deny, no problem."

Plutarch walked over to her and tore the piece of tape from her hand. His greedy eyes devoured it. "Confirm it," he barked. "And if it's true I want an in-depth profile on the daughter. Twenty-four-hour surveillance. History. Everything. Okay?"

He ran from the room, taking the marble stairs two at a time, and he nearly tripped as he darted across the cavernous hall. As he erupted onto the terrace, he was already calling Caroline's name.

She sat up and twisted around to face him.

"Hartford's given the Sunset to his daughter," he blurted out as he cascaded across the patio.

"What!" It wasn't a question. She'd heard. She just needed a second or two for her mind to catch up with the explosive news.

"Her name's Kristina. I think we met at Livingstone's black ball."

A radiant smile lit up the Kirkegaard face.

"Oh yes, we did, David. And at the Livingstone funeral, too."

"Well, she owns the Sunset now."

"But for how long?" said Caroline.

❦

"WOULD YOU like some tea?" said Caroline.

"Oh no, I don't think so, thank you," said Kristina.

"Please do. Join me. It's special herb tea. No caffeine. It's very soothing."

"Oh, okay, I'll try it. Thanks."

She felt it again. That feeling at the funeral. Caroline Kirkegaard could not be resisted—not because she was so powerful, so strong, so dictatorial—but because you didn't *want* to resist her. Instead, Kristina wanted to please her. Being with her reminded Kristina of school, when she had developed a crush on the teacher. She wanted to be her pet. She wanted to be clever for her. She wanted to behave really well.

"I'm glad you came, Kristina. I'm not surprised you did, but I'm glad."

Kristina couldn't think of a reply. Caroline was right. There was an inevitability about it, even though she had waited until the last minute before deciding definitely to come. The telephone call had arrived out of the blue, and there had been no real reason given for it.

"Hello, Kristina? This is Caroline Kirkegaard."

The voice, relaxed, self-confident, had been totally natural. Kristina's nervous reply had not been. "Oh, goodness! Caroline! Hello."

"I've been thinking about you a lot since Francisco's funeral. I want to find out why."

"Oh."

"Can we meet?"

Kristina's throat had gone dry. Her fingers had tingled. At the other end of the telephone she had sensed the full lips, the compelling eyes.

" 'Meet'?"

"Come and have tea with me. Say tomorrow. At four. It's the last house on Callejuela Drive off Coldwater. We can talk."

Refusal hadn't seemed an option. Caroline's voice had been heavy with destiny.

"Okay," Kristina had mumbled. Too late she had remembered the restaurant staff meeting scheduled for three-fifteen—the one that would hardly have started by four o'clock. The line had gone dead and she was glad there hadn't been time for the excuse.

From that moment to this she had thought of nothing else except Caroline Kirkegaard. The straight world couldn't make up its mind about her and the Destiny movement. Some saw it as a band of harmless hippies, lost in an airhead sixties time warp, albeit a mercifully drug-free one. Others believed it to be a sinister cult—shades of Satanism and the worst excesses of Synanon, with the ghost of Manson hovering overhead for good measure. Either way they were suspicious of it, fearing its antifamily, antiestablishment bias, and worst of all its antieighties-style materialism—that prize that conservative America had worked so hard and so long to win.

The straight world's antipathy toward Destiny was for Kristina a powerful argument in its favor. Her grudge against conventional wisdom had been conditioned by a lifetime as the victim of her mother's shape-up-or-ship-out nastiness. But it was not the strongest reason for keeping an open mind. *That* was Caroline Kirkegaard herself. As the personification of Destiny she transcended it in the way that Christ transcended Christianity, Buddha Buddhism. Her whole startling personality challenged the observer to make the leap of faith onto her strong shoulders. Oh, there were words, but she *was* the word, and the way and the truth and the light, too. Kristina had read the book, seen the video, and even bought the incense—all available at the Bodhi Tree, and now at Waldenbooks and B. Dalton as well—and though she had been impressed by the tantalizing mysticism, it had been when she had stared into the Kirkegaard eyes at Livingstone's funeral that things had begun to happen. It hadn't been the light at the Damascus roadside, but it had been a turning point. There was the feeling that her life might easily divide into a before and after, if she would just allow herself to embrace the truth.

From that moment on the phrases of Destiny had begun to roll around like ripe seeds in her mind. "God is in the Good but God is also in the Evil because he created all things and he lives in them." "Through eternal lives we can perfect ourselves, but we must trust the Guide that first we must find." "Our lives are little, our lives are short, but there is time to put one foot upon the path of Destiny." "We must cast away possessions to make room for the belief in the eternal that alone we can carry from this life to the next."

"Kanga, can you get us some of the new herb tea? We'll sit in the bay window."

It was all so normal. The room was like a thousand others in Beverly Hills, but as Kristina followed her toward the window her heart was thumping in her chest.

"Sit down, Kristina."

Kristina did as she was told, unable to escape the feeling that this was not merely a polite invitation but a life-or-death command.

Caroline's eyes peered at her and she smiled nervously back at them, letting her own eyes fall away when the intensity got too great. It seemed Caroline was already inside her.

"You are afraid of yourself. You are fearful of the great power I sense within you."

Kristina swallowed. There was something incredibly personal about the remark. At a stroke the conversation had moved to a far deeper level of communication. She had been invited for tea, for no very clear reason except the odd one that since the funeral she had been on Caroline's mind. Now here she was, unsure what to expect, but expectant nonetheless.

" 'Great power'?" said Kristina.

"I know you, Kristina. I have watched you and known you through many lifetimes. We have been friends. We have been enemies. We have been lovers . . ."

A blush exploded over Kristina's cheeks at Caroline's words. Suddenly she understood the feeling inside her. It had been there at the funeral, and it had hovered in the atmosphere ever since. She hadn't faced it. She hadn't named it. Caroline had. She looked away, as the blush deepened. Caroline's lips were parted, and her eyes were questioning, pleased with the color her words had painted on Kristina's cheeks.

"Lovers," she repeated, and her hand reached out across the space that separated them and she touched Kristina's knee. "Lovers across time and space and in dimensions that you cannot understand."

Kristina looked helplessly at the fingers resting on her knee. She didn't move away. The mesmeric quality of Caroline's voice, and the hypnotic thought of supernatural love combined to paralyze her. But the feelings were not still. They raged and roared inside her and the Kirkegaard fingers could feel them, that she knew, that she was afraid, that she wanted.

"You are so nearly open. So nearly open to the truth. When you embrace it, it will make you invincible. But you are afraid. You are afraid to claim the power that will be yours."

"I don't really understand," said Kristina's distant voice.

Caroline laughed. She threw back her head so that the sunlight caught the sculpted head, the chiseled hair, the jutting chin.

"There is no understanding of Destiny," she said. "Touch it with reason and it is gone. The truths we know are our truths. They are our reality. Our creation. As gods of our infinite soul we master our Destiny. We have no need of understanding."

"I see," said Kristina.

"But I will teach you to feel." She leaned forward, far forward, "And I will teach you how to be, and how to become."

Her face filled up Kristina's visual field.

"And your worries and fears will fade on the horizon of many lives. I will travel with you through endless worlds and I will be your guide and you will be my companion on the journey toward perfect happiness. Will you come with me, Kristina, to the end of the future, and the beginning that starts there?"

Kristina could see Caroline's lips and the words they spoke, but the two were existing on separate levels. The words spoke to her mind, and there was frantic sense in them. She believed in reincarnation. The circle of rebirth. Each new life a refining of the previous one. Perfection, found on the endless path, through the seeing eyes of the spirit guide. Yes, she wanted that. She wanted Caroline Kirkegaard to banish the insecurities, and the misery, and the lack of self-confidence and to exchange it for the bright light of infinite bliss. But the lips had meaning apart from the words they spoke. It was to them that her body responded. They were alluring, softly voluptuous, daringly sensuous. They spoke the truth but they *were* the truth, and suddenly Kristina realized she wanted to kiss them.

They leaned in closer, and Kristina felt herself drawn to them.

In the kiss there would be so many answers. She would be filled up—

body and mind—with the sweet messages of Caroline's mouth. There she would find the pieces that had always been missing in her life. In those lips she would find her destiny.

So she moved forward, and her eyes were big as she watched herself flirting on the edge of intimacy.

"Shall I pour the tea now?" said Kanga.

Like a glass shattered into a thousand pieces by the blow of a hammer, the illusion vanished with the words.

Kanga knew what she had done and her shamed face said that she was not able to help it. The tea had been ordered, but light-years had passed since then. The whole room was full of the subtle rhythms of cosmic seduction and she more than anyone could sense them. Long ago, Kanga had starred in the leading role, and she had never forgotten the magic of the drama or its sublime conclusion.

In the slavery that had begun that day, she had found freedom from self. She had ceased to exist as a person, and she had become the creature of Caroline Kirkegaard. Now she was merely a body, a brain, an instrument, a tool. Orders were the substitute for motivation, commands the replacement for voluntary acts. But inside the shell that looked like a person, the random sparks of emotion could still crackle and dart. Like now, when another threatened to usurp her place.

"Leave it on the table," said Caroline. In her jealousy, Kanga had willfully sabotaged the moment. Now she placed the tray on the table and backed away, her eyes wide with panic as she contemplated her punishment.

"Drive over to Sherman Oaks. Do some shopping," said Caroline, the words sharp as a chilled wind, as she banished her assistant. The end of the earth was not farther than the shops of the San Fernando Valley that moment, and Kanga knew it, but she hurried to obey.

Caroline took a deep breath, as if composing herself after hearing of some terrible tragedy. Then she reached forward for the pot, and she poured the tea that had broken the spell. "You know of Destiny?" she said.

"Yes, I've read your book. I've seen the tape of you channeling. . . . I've been to the meetings and one of the seminars in the desert."

Caroline replaced the pot on the tray, and suddenly she reached across it, taking up Kristina's hands in hers and staring deep into her eyes.

"Oh, Kristina. How can I make you understand how strong you are going to be? You are full of doubt, but you will walk with gods. You will be among them, as an equal. If you could harness one iota of your future greatness in this life, you would rule this world that knows you not. You would walk across it like a Titan, and the people would bow down before you and pray to you for the salvation that you could provide. I know it seems impossible to you. I am inside your mind and I feel the disbelief, but I promise you this is your destiny. Let your heart believe me. Let your body trust what your brain cannot. You must have faith to liberate your power. Believe in me. Trust in me, so that your faith can move the mountains of the world."

Kristina could feel the fervor. It could be touched. It was an incredible outpouring of certainty that melted puny doubt and groveling intellect. The words did not fit Kristina's experience of herself. She had always been a nobody. Oh, she had been Robert Hartford's daughter, and her body was great, and there had been little triumphs dotted along the roadside of her unremarkable life, but basically she was a nothing like everyone else. So the words seemed to lie, but the words did not exist alone. They had become more than objects. They rolled over her, melting her insignificance and painting her in the proud colors of glory. Now, before her, this strange, wonderful woman was drawing pictures of a future more brilliant than she had dared to imagine, a future that could somehow trickle down to her present and change her life.

She wanted to believe so badly. It would be so easy. Only the thin thread of common sense separated her from the spiritual riches that were rightfully hers.

She was being asked to cut that thread. It was an offer that she could hardly refuse. "What do I have to do?" she said.

The triumph that blazed in Caroline's eyes wore the mask of pleasure.

"You only have to surrender. You have to surrender your old self to Destiny. Give away your fear and doubt. Cast off your uncertainty. Open the doors that are closed. Let the word into your life. Let me inside you, Kristina. Let me come in."

Again her face filled up Kristina's. The face of a savior; the face of a goddess; the face of a lover.

I want to be inside you, said the lips. I want to live inside your body, and I want you to live in mine.

"Ohhhhhhh!" Kristina's soft sound was the moan of acquiescence. There was no way of saying yes to the inevitable. There was only the bowing down before it. The bended knee. The surrendered heart. The whole of her body was full of the sound of trumpets as she passed over to the other side. This was it. Her life had changed. Now she walked with Destiny.

"Kiss me, Kristina," said Caroline Kirkegaard.

❦

"MAGIC, MAGIC, Magic."

The chant filled the Forum and Robert Hartford, sitting on the extreme edge of the cheap metal orange chair, was sucked into it. It wasn't remotely his style to be cheering somebody, cheering a *man* and in public, but a Lakers game was different. Earvin "Magic" Johnson, Lakers guard and spearhead of the team's fast-break offense, was different.

Johnson, tapeworm tall, shimmied down the court as if he were slam dancing at On the Rox. The fact that the entire Celtics team was there to take the ball away from him didn't seem to figure in his equation. The opposition scurried about like fourth-graders whose coach had decided on a whim to show them how it was *really* done. The ball yo-yoed from his sensitive fingers, seemingly attached to them by an invisible string, and the drumbeat of rubber on polished wood had a rhythm all of its own. The NBA's highest-paid player, with his own billboard on the Boulevard, and now signed by

Mike Ovitz, Hollywood's ultimate dealmonger, Johnson defined the word *star* and in the heavens where he shone the other luminaries were not ashamed to applaud him.

There were enough of them to do it. Ringside at the Forum, the industry was out in force, and they were just about the only people who could afford to be there. If you knew a friend of God's you could buy a season seat for around ten thousand dollars. If you were merely an acquaintance of St. Peter you could be scalped a thousand a game, more for the playoffs. Of course you didn't have to sit at courtside, but then you didn't *have* to breathe. Robert had been given the tickets by John McEnroe and Tatum O'Neal, season ticket holders up by the Laker bench, and McEnroe had gotten them from Dr. Buss, the Forum owner, in exchange for playing a demonstration match for which he would normally have charged a hundred grand. So there they were, he and Suki Marlowe, who didn't know a basketball from a testicle, where the "now" L.A. action was, screaming for Magic and getting it. Last night they had gone to the movie wrap party at Spago, and today, blinking in the arc lights, the two filmmaking hermits were back at last in what passed for the real world.

Out on the court Johnson deigned to score, but before he did so there was a beautiful moment when his stiltlike legs were set in cement. They were the only part of him that wasn't a ballet of liquid motion. He was a limbo dancer; a charmed snake; he was the belly button of some sinuous Turkish delight. He was a candle in a low wind, the rushes of a weaved basket, the leather thong of a cracking whip. He never got where he was going, and he never returned from where he had come, and the dizzy eyes of the Celtics and their darting, ineffectual arms were always seconds behind him, inches in front of the place where once he had been. For an age and an instant he tortured them, and then at last he tired of the mice to whom he had become the cat. His arm-without-end arced behind him, the ball superglued to the palm of his hand. Then it bowled forward on its pendulum course, and as it reached the level of his shoulders the glue dissolved. The ball sailed, impossibly high, over the heads of the defenders, up, up, up, down, down, down. As it made the basket it hardly seemed to touch the sides, so central was its triumphal entry.

Over to the right of Robert, Nicholson was on his feet and so were his guests, Harry Dean Stanton and Timothy Hutton. To the left, Walter Matthau, another season ticket holder, had jumped up, as had father and son Douglases and Sheens, who had been lent the Lorimar block of seats. In the president's box directly opposite, the boxers, too, were jumping for joy— Sugar Ray Leonard and Mike Tyson sandwiching Mike's date, Michael Jackson's sister LaToya. Whoopi Goldberg and Dyan Cannon bounced up and down in delight in their regular seats opposite the Celtics bench, while behind it Ovitz clients Dustin Hoffman and Bill Murray went quietly wild with glee. On the bench, Pat Riley, better looking by far than most of his actor fans, smiled the sexy soft smile of a star on the daytime soaps. Dapper in a sharp business suit, his hair slicked back with gel, he looked more like a gunslinging bond trader on Wall Street than the head coach of the best basketball team in the world.

"How much longer?" whispered Suki Marlowe.

Robert Hartford was probably the only man in the 17,500-seat stadium who didn't mind her asking. The reason was simple. It was a woman's remark, and he was the man who loved women. All around, the superstars—with varying degrees of enthusiasm—would have considered themselves fond of the opposite sex, but they had other loves too, like male camaraderie, and one-of-a-kind athletes, and the L.A. Lakers on a winning streak. Those, except possibly the last, Robert did not share. It was right and fitting that Suki Marlowe would be bored out of her microscopic mind by basketball, because it meant that what she liked far more was to step out of the confines of her microscopic skirt. Here in this arena she was nothing but a gorgeous prop, a brilliantly colored umbrella in the male rain.

"Not long now," he said simply, smiling to himself at her irreverence.

He looked at her surreptitiously out of the corner of his eye. She had made the movie bearable, and he had used her for the chemistry in the love scenes, as he had used all the others. In the sealed world of the location you needed a partner. The shoot was like a mini-lifetime with its births and deaths, its spring and its winter, its Borgia subplots and Machiavellian conspiracies. So for two short months in the heat of the desert he had "married" Suki Marlowe, and she, poor thing, was already falling into the role of wife just days away from the divorce. Maybe tomorrow he'd dump her. Maybe tonight. The old speech would do—the one about "We've shared something beautiful. Don't let's spoil it by not being able to let go." It never went down particularly well, but the "You can always count on me to help you with your career" invariably dried the tears and brought out the thin, silver-medal smiles. That was the good and the bad news about Hollywood. The girls were the real tough guys. They had to be.

The unwelcome thought suddenly lanced into his mind. Tough girls like Paula, the ragamuffin to riches, who had traveled from anonymity to fame and fortune with just a little help from her friends . . . and lovers. Would he *ever* be able to forget her? Tower's death and the emergence of Paula as his heir had been a media feast of gluttonous proportions. Oh, Tower had left his mark, but the Paula Hope inheritance had provided a topspin to the story that had lifted it bodily from the arts section to the entertainment pages. The articles had starred Paula and the extraordinary story of Winthrop Tower's undreamed-of cash mountain. Lip service was paid to his place in the design hierarchy, his East Coast reputation, and there were snippets of conversation with the odd celebrity whose houses he had designed, but the L.A. bottom line had been the money that he'd salted away and the beautiful nobody from nowhere who'd scored it. How had it been possible to keep so much money hidden in this material world? Had it been honestly obtained? Had taxes been paid on it? And who was Paula Hope, the girl with the limp and the beauty, who had somehow escaped the movies and the sexual magnetism of none other than Robert Hartford, to whom she had briefly been engaged?

What had been her hold on Tower, the "confirmed bachelor"—nudge, nudge, wink, wink—and what had precipitated the row between Tower and Hartford around the time of the mysterious accident to the chauffeur who still lingered on at Cedars-Sinai? The pieces had always concluded with the immediate present, the only thing Tinsel Town cared about more than the maddeningly unpredictable future. Paula Hope was chatelaine of the intriguing Château, having mouth-to-mouthed it back from the dead, and now the tunes of her pied-piper pipes were emptying the bedrooms and the ballrooms of the fast-fading Sunset Hotel—to the almost certain fury of the reclusive superstar who had once loved her.

"Ma*gic*, Ma*gic*, Ma*gic*," chanted the crowd.

"You want, we'll split right now," said Robert suddenly.

Suki Marlowe beamed her pleasure. Had she just controlled the controller? She was doing better than she'd thought. In this town you judged people by the quality of the people they walked out on, and *nobody* walked on the Lakers.

She jumped up in case he changed his mind. "Yeah, my ass went to sleep," she said.

The McEnroe seats were next to the gangway. Ducking down low to avoid obscuring the view of the lesser fans, they began their escape.

The Horizon production veep five rows back had other ideas. He had been working on the movie, and it was too recently over for Robert to ignore him. His hand snaked out for the Hartford sleeve. "Hi, Robert. You *leaving*?"

Robert cursed silently as he slipped his arm away from the unwanted embrace. "Suki's not feeling too good," he muttered.

"Great party last night, no?"

Robert knew the game. This was maximum industry visibility. The studio nobody was scoring more points than Magic Johnson by being seen talking to Robert Hartford. The longer the conversation lasted, the more points he would run up. Touching and holding on to Hartford flesh was bonus goodies. A bear hug would have been a knockout career move.

"It was fine," said Robert.

He was moving away. The executive's moment in the sun was nearly over. His mind worked overtime for something that would hold the movie star in his orbit. You could all but hear the grinding of his mental gears. "I saw your daughter, Kristina, at lunch yesterday," he blurted out, wondering if he'd found the flypaper that would make Hartford stick. "She was in Le Dôme with that guru figure, Caroline Kirkegaard. *What* a great-looking couple!" He squeezed on the compliment like icing on a cake.

"Are you coming, Robert?" said Suki, reveling in her unaccustomed role as prime mover of immovable objects.

But Robert had stopped. His body had stopped. His mind had stopped. His soul had stopped.

He sat down in the gangway, and the eyes of the studio executive opened wide as he caught a glimpse of paradise on earth.

"*What* did you just say?" asked Robert.

"Kristina. Caroline Kirkegaard. Eating in the Dôme. Didn't you know she was in town, or something?"

"Are you sure about that?" barked Robert.

"Yeah, sure I'm sure. My son goes to those Destiny seminars. He's got pictures of Caroline Kirkegaard all over his room. And I know Kristina. I've seen her at the Sunset several times." The studio exec was puzzled, but he was making out. The front people were turning around to watch them, that guy from Carson Productions, another from CBS. Christ, there was Irving Azoff, the MCA president, eyeballing the pair of them.

Slowly Robert Hartford stood up, and his face looked like he had seen not a loser but a ghost.

Kristina had been eating with Caroline Kirkegaard. His daughter and his enemy. The one who owned the Sunset Hotel, and the one who wanted it. It was as innocent and as appetizing as a Jonestown picnic. The worst thing of all was that it made sense of things that had been puzzling him. For the last two months since he had signed the controlling interest over to Kristina, he had hardly spoken to her. She had sent some profit-and-loss schedules, some occupancy rates, a few notes on this and that, and from them he had gained the impression that there had been a marginal improvement in the Sunset's fortunes. When he had telephoned to congratulate her, he had not been able to reach her, except once when she had been unusually distant and evasive. He hadn't thought much about it. After all, it had been what he wanted—to be allowed to get on with making his movie in relative peace, untroubled by the goings-on at the hotel. He'd imagined she was as preoccupied as he was, and that had been just fine. Or had it? Now he was far from sure, and a hideous thought kept bubbling to the surface of his mind. Thank *God*, he had tied up the shares.

Whatever Kristina was up to she wouldn't be able to sell them, anymore than Wittgenstein's friend could have sold his miserable tree.

He powered up the gangway, overtaking Suki Marlowe as he headed for the exit. "Where are we going?" she wailed at his wake.

"I'm going back to the Sunset," said Robert Hartford, without bothering to turn around.

⸺

ROBERT STORMED into his drawing room. It had not been made up. The cushions had not been plumped. An empty glass on a side table had not been cleared away. The curtains had not been drawn for the evening. He stalked through to the bedroom, his mind on red alert. Nobody had made the bed, changed the sheets, replaced the flowers. In the bathroom, a pile of towels lay on the still-wet floor, the bathwater in situ, the shaving paraphernalia, the Royal Yacht after-shave, the tube of toothpaste all exactly as he'd left them. A copy of the L.A. *Herald Examiner* had soaked up a puddle from the floor and now it lay in a nasty papier-mâché heap on the twisted bathmat. Even the bathroom television, its sound turned down low, still warbled on.

As he reached for the telephone, it rang.

"Mr. Hartford?"

"Who is it?" he barked.

"Front desk, Mr. Hartford . . ."

"My place hasn't been cleaned!" he exploded.

There was a silence.

"We have you down as a checkout, sir . . . twelve noon today . . . that was why I was ringing."

"Checkout? Checkout? What the *hell* are you talking about? This is Robert Hartford. I live here. This is *my* hotel."

Again, a pause. "It's quite clear, this note, sir. It says, 'Mr. Robert Hartford will be checking out at noon today.' That's why the room hasn't been done, sir. It's done after the guest leaves."

"I'm not a *guest*! Who the *fuck* are you? What's your name?"

"I'm Dale, sir. Front desk duty assistant manager."

"I don't know you. Who hired you?" rasped Robert.

"Miss Kristina, sir, three weeks ago."

"And who was the joker who wrote this ridiculous 'note'?"

"It's signed by Mr. Vierteli, sir, the new manager. I'm sorry if there's been some mistake, sir. We're all new around here. But the problem is a little difficult, sir, because your bungalow has been rebooked . . . to a Mr. Ben Gazi, sir, and the gentleman has just arrived with his family. They're waiting in the lobby."

Robert Hartford spoke very slowly. "Listen, Dale, you may be new, but get wise. I'm Robert Hartford. *The* Robert Hartford, not some unlucky namesake. I *own* this hotel, and you ought to know that. I live here. I've always lived here. I'm always going to live here. I am not—repeat not—a guest and I never, repeat never, 'check out.' So I suggest you pitch Mr. Ben Gazi *and* his family right out on their asses if you haven't got anywhere to put them, and I suggest you put me through to the manager so that he can explain personally to me just what the *hell* is going on around here. Then maybe, just maybe, we can try to forgive you for being the new kid on the block."

There was definite fear in the quiet at the other end of the telephone. Rocks and hard places, devils and deep blue seas—the unfortunate Dale was sandwiched between them.

"Mr. Vierteli is at a meeting, sir."

"Put me THROUGH to him!"

"I can't, sir. I had specific instructions not to disturb him."

Robert's voice was ice cold. It was true. It had happened. Or at least it was trying to happen. "Put me through to my daughter," he said.

"She's not here this evening, sir."

"Put me through to her office. *Do* it, Dale. Do it now." He dared the minion to disobey him. There was a long pause and then the extension began ringing.

Robert gripped the receiver tight in his fist as if it were a blunt instrument.

"Hello," said a woman's voice.

"Who *is* this?" he yelled down the line.

"Hello, Robert," said Caroline Kirkegaard.

—

ROBERT HARTFORD stood in the office that had once been Kristina's, in the office that before then had been his. He fought for breath because he had just run all the way from his bungalow and his rage made speech difficult.

"What are you doing in my hotel?" he screamed.

Caroline Kirkegaard, razor sharp in a Valentino double-breasted suit, didn't bother to get up from the desk at which she sat. She just looked at him, in frank amazement, a smile playing at the corners of her mouth.

"*Your* hotel?" she said.

"My hotel. Kristina's hotel. What in God's name are you doing here? I told you if you ever set foot in this place again . . ."

"You'd have me thrown out. Well, Robert, guess who's going to be doing the throwing."

He paused. He had gotten this far on a surge tide of adrenaline, but there were things he had to know. "Did Kristina give you permission to come here?"

"I don't get permission. I give it." Her voice was threatening, totally in control.

Robert Hartford felt the fingers of doubt probing at him. He leaned forward, menacing, his jaw pushing out at her. "Are you telling me you think you've bought Kristina's share in the Sunset?" he thundered. "Because you can't. She's not allowed to sell it. Any contract you've signed with her is null and void."

He smiled bitterly through his fury. Was it possible that yet once again Caroline Kirkegaard had underestimated him? If so it would be the last time. By God he swore it.

" 'Bought'?" said Caroline quietly. "Sold? Who mentioned buying and selling?"

He watched her, the understanding creeping into his eyes from the corners.

"No!" he gasped.

"Yes," said Caroline.

"Kristina *gave* me her fifty-one percent share in the Sunset Hotel, and this . . ."—she pushed a piece of paper across the desk at him—"is the deed of gift."

Robert Hartford stared down at it as if it were his own bleeding heart.

There would be no point reading it. Plutarch's lawyers would have done that, time and time again. A gift. A present. It was a Wittgenstein condition he hadn't thought to include in the contract with Kristina. It had never occurred to him. How could he have conceived of the impossible?

"What did you do to her?" His voice was breaking.

Caroline threw back her head and laughed. "It was more what she did to me."

The insinuation crawled through the words.

"I'll fight you, Caroline. No court will uphold this."

Her smile was the purest patronization now. "Fight me by all means, Robert, but I wouldn't bother with the courts. The 'understanding' that Kristina and I have is unshakable. There was no duress. All the 'persuasion' came exclusively from your daughter. So, this is my hotel now, Robert Hartford, which reminds me . . . I think my people have told you that we need your room and you're way past checkout time. I'm afraid we're going to have to charge you for a whole extra day."

He backed away from her, but already she was reaching for the telephone, talking into it, and as she did so her eyes locked onto his.

"Yes, Mr. Hartford will be leaving. Have security supervise it. Yes, now. This minute. No, I'm not at all sure where he's going. Just stack it up in the lobby. Wherever. That's right. And report back to me when it's done. Okay. Good. Yes, that's right. The Sunset won't be at *all* the same place without him."

—

SMOG HAD closed in on Los Angeles, a hazy layer of unfocused yellow, swathing the city in an acrid blanket of surreptitious poison. The Hollywood Hills, above and beyond it, shone bright in the late afternoon sun. From the position where Robert stood, his nose pushed close to the inch-thick glass of the Century City skyscraper, it seemed that he was peering across a sea of ocher cotton wool to the distant mountains.

He had stood up, because he couldn't sit down any longer, and because he could no longer endure the drip, drip, drip of undiluted pessimism that was costing him a thousand dollars an hour. In this mini-Manhattan with palm trees four top attorneys at $250 each would be at least that, without the extras. Not that money was the problem. Kristina was.

"We'd have to prove that her mental capacities were diminished at the time of the deed of gift. Not now, but then. That's notoriously difficult. It's the problem with the insanity defense. How do you prove a compromised mental state a year or two ago?"

Robert turned from the window. It had all been said before. Now it would all be said again.

"Listen, for God's sake. We're not talking a year ago. We're talking six weeks ago. And anyway the nature of the deed tells you she was out of her mind. She just gave away a fifty-one percent share in a hotel that's worth a hundred and fifty million bucks. For nothing. A gift. If that isn't crazy, what the hell is?"

"People give that sort of money away all the time. It's called charity," said one of the lawyers.

"Destiny is *not* a charity. It's a cult. My daughter has been brainwashed, and you'd better find a way to make some judge believe it, and you'd better start by believing it yourselves."

"I suppose we could ask for an injunction, or at least a restraining order preventing Kirkegaard from taking control of the hotel pending a hearing, but we'd still have to present evidence at this stage, and the problem is we haven't got any."

The senior partner tried to inject a little optimism into the proceedings. "The trouble is," he continued, "Plutarch's lawyers are on top of all this. Thom Craddock wasn't born yesterday. They could countersue. I can think of a half a dozen grounds for a complaint. I don't suppose there's any way we can get to your daughter, Robert?"

"She won't speak to me, and I can't get into the Sunset. They've got more security people in there than waiters and maids. It's like a fortress," he said bitterly.

"I guess we could subpoena her if we bring suit, but it guarantees her hostility. The bottom line is that if we don't have Kristina, we don't have a case. If they've got her in their pockets, and it looks as if they have, we'll have a devil of a time trying to prove her incompetence," said the attorney.

Robert turned back to the window and stared out morosely at the city. He couldn't see the Sunset, but he could see the Château Madrid. The top of its roof stuck up toward the sky like a finger raised in disdain.

The telephone warbled in the background.

One of the lawyers picked it up. "Yes, he's here. Hang on." He turned to Robert and held out the phone. "Mr. Hartford, it's for you. A doctor from Cedars-Sinai. Says it's very urgent that he speak to you."

Robert took the receiver. "Mr. Hartford. This is Dr. Peel. I believe you know of a patient here, a Mr. Graham Ovenden. He's been in a coma here for over a year."

"I know who you mean," said Robert irritably.

"Well, he's come out of his coma. I've never seen it happen before. He's talking, and he seems to be making sense, and he wants to see you."

"I have absolutely no interest in seeing him," said Robert dismissively.

"He has a remarkable story to tell, Mr. Hartford. I think you should hear it. It appears he's confessing to the murder of a man in Florida among other things . . . other things concerning you, Mr. Hartford, and your personal life. I couldn't urge you strongly enough to come right on down here. We have no way of knowing how long this lucid phase will last. He could easily slip right back into coma."

But Robert was no longer listening. He was running. He charged across the room, dropping the telephone on the edge of a desk as he ran. He barged through the door, and across the reception area to the elevators, and the words of the doctor rang in his ears. Graham was confessing to a murder. In Florida. Oh, God, dear God, could Paula's story have been true all along?

IT WAS a very nasty gym, and the smell of male new sweat, their old sweat, and the disturbing aroma of their intermediate secretions—was unequivocal. The stench was the thing you noticed first, because everything else was half hidden in the gloomy twilight that permeated the windowless room. When you walked across the ancient carpet, it pulled at your feet, not actually sticky but clinging, like yesterday's lover. Dotted around the dungeon were what seemed to be instruments of torture, wicked contraptions of chipped metal, rich with pulleys and mobile weights. Gloomy music wafted through the fetid air, Bach, or Handel in somber mood, the funereal dirge rich with the sense of ritual and the unmistakable message that here sacrifice would be required.

Caroline Kirkegaard slid through the empty room. Around her hourglass waist she wore a thick brown belt, six inches wide, strapped together in front by three silver buckles. Above, her mighty superstructure loomed like the bridge of an ocean liner, and below, the sheet steel of her abdominal musculature rippled beneath the jet-black high-cut leotard. Her da Vinci legs, anatomically perfect, were naked all the way down to her man-size feet, and they padded across the tacky carpet to the man who stood in the shadows by the wall.

"So!" she said.

He held his head down low as if too nervous to face the full frontal force of her gaze, and he found something dull to do with his hands, which were buried in the pockets of an expensive but too-well-cut Armani suit. He coughed to clear a clearly dry throat.

"The lawyers say it's watertight. They've talked to Hartford's people and they haven't got a case. They may bluster for a week or two, but they won't even get a holding injunction."

"Good." It was only a word, but why should she tell him of her joy? Why should she warble on about the glory of revenge and the sweetness of victory? It was no part of her plan to let him know she was grateful. It was her intention to show him.

He looked around him, blinking in the dim, religious light.

"It's not the L.A. Sports Club. It's where the *real* people work out." She laughed as she spoke at the expense of the committers of aerobicide in their sanitized, designer gyms, with their bonded teeth and odorless sweat, their smooth, useless muscles.

Plutarch could see that. He could also see that Caroline and he were the only people there, and that she was not a real person at all. She was a fabulous prototype for some new and deeply wonderful form of humanity, and there was no position in the world more exalted than to be her servant.

Again he cleared a thickening throat. "Where is everyone?"

"They're not here." It meant "They won't be."

He swallowed hard when he heard both messages. She knew what he was feeling. It was how it should be—the fear and the longing; the deep dive in the adrenaline sea to find the mystery at the bottom; and all the time the difficulty in breathing, the sensation of drowning in the saliva of your own anticipation.

"You want me, don't you, David Plutarch?"

She smiled at him cruelly, her mouth splitting open to show the glistening teeth. She put one hand on her hip and she thrust herself out toward him with all the haughty arrogance of the owner for the owned.

Again he could not face her, nor anymore could he speak. His head rose and fell in the hopeless gesture of assent.

"But if you want me you must work for me, mustn't you?"

His furtive eyes said he didn't know. At last the billionaire knew nothing except that he would obey. Since the first day he had seen her it had been coming to this. Early on he had resisted. But her blitzkrieg assault had defeated him, and in her triumph and his debasement he had found a perverse joy. In the topsy-turvy world of sadomasochism he had discovered the dark secrets of his soul.

"Take off your coat and shirt," she commanded.

He dropped them on the filthy floor, the two-thousand-dollar suit jacket, the four-hundred-dollar Sulka silk shirt.

His stringy chest blinked beneath the neon half glow, ashamed of itself in this temple of gutter narcissism. In his mind he could see them, all the grunting, groaning pumpers, their sleek pudding biceps wet with their male juices, their round featureless steroid faces red with the heat of their pointless exertion. Would Bach or Handel play for them, or would they perform their self-love in soundless privacy?

Again he gulped back the nonexistent saliva from his throat. If they had been here, they would laugh at him and his apology for a physique. Or maybe they would be too self-obsessed for that, as they strutted by and showed him their greasy bodies and smiled smiles of satisfaction as they watched him watch them.

"Take off your shoes and socks."

Cole-Haan loafers, black silk knee-length Bijan socks fell among the rest of the crumpled finery on the dingy floor.

"Over here," she said.

He shuffled behind her, his eyes glued to the swerving gluteal muscles, as she led him toward her objective. They passed posters of sculpted men, signed with cheerful, childish signatures, men whose jocks contained the minuscule appendages that alone they couldn't exercise. They passed notice boards full of cheap messages about cheaper apartments and worthless things for sale. They passed racks of dumbbells and gargantuan weights, and all the time they passed deeper into the conspiracy of minds that promised the alien communion of bodies.

She had reached her destination. She turned to face him. Both hands behind her, her face alight with the exhilaration of her power, she undid the buckles of her belt, letting it clatter to the floor. She filled her lungs, inflating the upturned triangle of her phenomenal torso, and she flexed her legs and rose up on tiptoe in the pose of a bodybuilder, her muscles rippling and bulging with the effort. She reached for the shoulder straps of the one-piece body suit, pulling down one and then the other, and then she swept them away in a single movement and her breasts stood there unveiled, gleaming white in the gloom, the vast circular areolae surrounding tense, spiked nipples.

His eyes bulged and his bare chest shuddered with the uneven rhythm of his breathing. His hands flicked by his side, wanting to move toward her.

"No!" she commanded quietly.

She pushed the black material down, revealing the vertical slash of her belly button, the scarcely believable evidence of her humanity. Then it was her hips, her lower stomach, the tantalizing borders of her blond pubic hairs. There she stopped, and she watched him, as he prayed for her final act.

Her voice was softly deadly. "This is what you want, isn't it? This is what you dream of."

He reached for her, unable to stop himself.

"Don't *touch* me." Her voice cut like a knife. His hovering hands fell back.

She stepped aside. Behind her the black leather platform stretched up from the floor at a forty-five-degree angle. At its top end a heavy leather strap lay unbuckled.

"Get onto the platform."

He hurried to obey. Face upward, head downward, he lay flat on the sloped bench. She moved toward its top end and, looping the strap across his ankles, she fastened the buckle around his legs, pulling it tight so that he couldn't move below the waist.

"Sit up," she commanded.

It was easy the first time. David Plutarch tensed his abdominal muscles and hauled himself up against gravity to a sitting position. But he couldn't see her anymore. She was somewhere behind his head, and he wanted so very much to see. . . . He twisted around.

"Lie down," she barked. "Then sit up. Do it till I tell you to stop."

Down he went, and up again, and down and up and up and down, until slowly but surely the muscles in his stomach began to complain. His smooth movements became more jerky, as the lactic acid built in his tissues and the merely uncomfortable merged into pain as his breathing speeded and his motion slowed.

"I have . . . to rest . . ." he grunted.

"Go ON!"

On. He had to do it. She commanded it. In the eyes of his mind he could see her, naked, magnificent, the extraordinary heart of her so near to him, so far. Red-hot pokers jabbed into his abdomen, and the impossible fullness throbbed between his legs as he prayed to be allowed to rest.

At last his strength had gone. He lay still.

"I'm sorry, I can't do any more," he murmured.

Caroline Kirkegaard stepped forward. She spun around and she backed up until her legs straddled Plutarch's resting head. Her crotch was directly above his staring eyes, maybe three feet above them, maybe more.

The vision exploded into his mind, banishing all thoughts of comfort or pain. The cruel predicament nipped him tight in the vise of its paradox. At long last she had given him the gift he had always dreamed of at the precise moment his body was all but incapable of accepting it. "If you want me you must work for me," she had said. Now he knew what she had meant.

Above him was the prize. In his body there was a new power; in his heart there was a wild joy. So he screamed to himself, and the reserves of strength uncoiled, and the muscles that had died were reborn in the reincarnation of passion.

Very slowly, like a pale ghost rising at midnight from an exposed grave, David Plutarch rose up from the black leather of the bench. His mouth was open, and his hungry tongue darted in the dryness, as his head arched toward the nirvana that lived between Caroline Kirkegaard's legs.

~ 21 ~

Alarm bells were ringing. They blared in Paula's mind as they summoned her up from the depths of sleep. She surfaced by stages, and the anxiety faded, to be replaced by irritation. Because it was only the telephone. She tried to focus her thoughts. Some idiot had disobeyed her standing instructions and put through a call to her bedroom in the middle of the night. It was a firable offense unless the hotel itself was on fire, or worse . . . whatever that might be.

She screwed up her eyes and tried to focus on the luminous dial of the Braun travel clock. Five to midnight. Great! Brilliant! Which particular well-drilled soldier of the switchboard had chosen this particular hour of the night to go crazy? She reached for the phone. It seemed like the only way to stop it.

"Paula!"

Oh God, not him. Not now! Not all over again. *Woof,* away went the bottom of her stomach. *Wham,* went the anguish and the excitement in her brain. *Pow,* the bat punch to the small of the back and all the other crazed, disorienting feelings that went by the name of shock.

"Who is it?" As if she didn't know, but she needed precious time. Was he about to scream at her all over again? Accuse her of stealing his staff? What did he want, in the middle of the godforsaken night when only bad things happened and bad vibrations vibrated? There was a shortage of air in her lungs as she practiced her counterwrath, and the insects banged up against each other in her floorless guts. You fucking bastard, was all she could think, why were you so beautiful to love?

"It's me, Robert."

It didn't sound angry, the silken pseudovoice that belonged in the junkyard where they crushed the secondhand hearts. It sounded friendly, this voice of the man who had no friends—only enemies and lovers.

"What is it, Robert?" In her voice there was the wariness of the abused child, and her tone was soft, too soft to be wise, in the face of cruel experience.

"I'm at Cedars-Sinai. I've just talked to Graham."

"Graham? You can't. He's in a coma." It came out like an excited question.

"He just talked to me. He talked to me, and he died."

Robert on the telephone. Graham dead. At five to midnight and out of the blue in the blackness.

"Wait! Wait, Robert, what are you saying?" Graham had died. He had talked to Robert. Robert was calling her. What had Graham *said*?

"Paula . . . I don't know what to do. . . . I mean, I didn't believe you. I'm so terribly sorry."

Oh, what?! Thank you, God, for so little so late. Too late, when love had gone, when it didn't matter anymore. Thank you, Robert, for calling me a crippled hooker and throwing me out of your life when I worshiped you and wanted to live with you forever.

Thank you, Graham, for your belated decency. Damn you for dying, and leaving me alone like all the others.

Her tears came fast; a bubble of grief had burst in her.

"Oh, Robert. Oh, Robert."

She curled up around the phone like a baby in the womb as she hovered on the brink of a new life.

"Paula. Paula. Don't cry. I'm sorry. I'm so terribly sorry. He told me everything. That what you said was true. That he loved you. He heard you once, talking to the doctor, but you didn't know he could hear. He wanted to die without telling me because he wanted me to hate you, and you to hate me. But he heard you, that day. It made the difference." His voice hurried on, eager not to be cut off.

At Paula's end of the telephone there were just the sobs—just the wild hope—just the frantic anger.

"Paula. Listen to me. Don't cry. Please don't cry."

Can you forgive me? He would ask that now. In the movies he would ask that as the housewives wept and the teenyboppers drooled and everyone wanted to forgive the man who had been given everything, but who had been born with a shriveled heart.

"Can you forgive me, Paula? Could you ever . . ."

"Oh, Robert, shut up. Shut UP!"

A helpless rage burst from her. Why? Because she loathed him. Because now she was an L.A. woman with the instincts of Attila, and God help the stragglers on the long march through the enemy territory of life. Oh yes? Oh really? Was she ever? Why did she want him to shut up? Because he was inside her again. Because he had never left. Because she could see at last that she no longer belonged to herself. She belonged to him.

He knew that. Somehow he knew.

"I must see you. I must say I'm sorry. I must . . ."

All those things he must do, and what must *she* do? Forgive him? Love him again? Marry him?

"Robert, I don't know . . ."

"Can I come over now?"

"No! I'm asleep. I mean, I'm in bed. . . ."

"Then tomorrow morning. Can I come to the Madrid? Can I come at nine? I must see you, Paula. I can't live with this. . . ."

Her whole body was in flames, but her voice was cold as charity. "Robert," she said, "you threw me out of your life once before. Now get the hell out of mine."

And she put the telephone down on the man she loathed, as the tears tumbled down her cheeks for the man she loved.

ROBERT PROWLED the lobby of the Château Madrid as if it were the dangerous no-man's-land between the trenches of the future and the blood-soaked emotional dugouts of his past. All around him was the success that spelled the failure of the Sunset—the beautiful people, the low-pitched hum of excitement, the rare combination of opulence and superb taste—but he hardly noticed it. He was thinking of Paula. She had refused to see him. He was here to change her mind. But why should she? Why should she change her mind about a harebrained Othello; a little boy lost inside the movie armor full of the sound and fury that signified nothing but the wounds of a tortured childhood, and the devastation of a world without parental love? What momentous event had occurred to make Paula forgive him? He had merely taken the spectacles of jealousy from the famous bedroom eyes. That was all. Nothing else. And with that she was supposed to roll over like an innocent puppy and pretend that the horrible words had never been spoken, that the dreadful behavior had never been behaved. He swallowed nervously as he thought of her pride, of her strength, of her screw-you arrogance when she was treated unfairly or underestimated. They were the things he loved about her. They were the part of her he knew best. They were the bits that threatened to wreck the delicate machinery of his feelings all over again.

He looked at his watch. It was five to nine. Five, possibly, to Paula. Five to a future he hardly dared to hope for. Five to a rejection that he hadn't the strength to face a second time.

He stalked over to the Château Madrid newsstand and picked up a magazine, staring at it intently without the faintest idea what he was seeing. Almost immediately he slammed it down, and his hunted eyes darted around the lobby. The reception desk, discreetly hidden from general view behind a dense bank of simple white daisies, was directly across from him. He took a deep breath and he walked toward it.

The charcoal-gray-suited assistant manager looked up as he approached. "Good morning, Mr. Hartford, sir." He had recognized him instantly.

"Morning. I'd very much like to see Ms. Hope," said Robert. His voice was as casual as he could make it. He'd never realized that acting could be so useful.

"Is she expecting you, sir?"

Robert's heart sank as he ran into the brick wall of a superbly trained male employee.

"Not exactly," said Robert.

"If you don't mind I'll just check with Ms. Hope, sir." He picked up the telephone.

Robert leaned nonchalantly against the desk. He eyed the elevator bank, and he wondered where the stairs were. Should he make a dash for it, like a groupie at a pop concert darting past the cordon to get where he wanted? He peered at the ceiling. Closely he observed the floor.

"Ms. Hope? Jenkins. Front desk. I have Mr. Robert Hartford here to see you. He doesn't have an appointment."

Jenkins smiled a reassuring smile at Robert as he spoke. He was simply playing it by the book. It had not occurred to him for a single second that his boss wouldn't see Robert Hartford, appointment or no appointment. This was, after all, Hollywood.

A puzzled expression replaced the smile. Ms. Hope had answered, but she wasn't answering. "Miss Hope?" he said.

Robert looked away. He couldn't bear this. He fought back the desire to snatch the phone and lay down the law about the seeing of Robert Hartford when he wanted to be seen.

The smile-turned-puzzled now became puzzled-turned-anxious. "You'd like him to wait?" he repeated in the tone of voice that suggested that he had either misheard or misunderstood. "Here in the lobby?" He flicked an uncertain glance at the back of Robert Hartford's head. In this town Robert Hartfords did not wait, and if, as the result of some monumental screw-up, waiting was required, it did not, repeat not, take place in public. The movie star would now walk straight out of the Château Madrid. It would be unlikely that he would ever set foot in it again.

But Robert Hartford did not walk. He turned around to confront the astonished employee, and he smiled one of his laziest smiles.

"I'll wait," he said. "Did Ms. Hope say how long?"

"I'm certain not long, sir. Are you sure you'll be all right there on the sofa? Can I get you anything to read, sir? Is your transport being taken care of . . ."

Even in his state of internal confusion Robert took time out to admire the performance of the Madrid front desk man. The solicitous attention, the polite efficiency, the determination not to give offense. The word *transport* was itself a work of art, covering everything from a self-driven Lamborghini, via a chauffeur-driven limo, to a bicycle. This was the way staff should behave, and Robert knew the blood, toil, sweat, and tears it must have cost Paula to achieve it. Paula, who was making him wait; who, right this minute, was trying to make up her mind whether or not to see him; who held his future in the palm of her hand, as he had once held hers.

He wandered over to the sofa, and he sat down as the horrified eyes of the assistant manager followed him. He took a deep breath and the old saying flashed into his mind, Everything comes to he who waits. It had *not* been his experience of life.

PAULA SAT behind the vast desk that usually made her feel very big, and she felt very, very small. She was a child once more after all the tragedies that had turned her into a bonafide grownup. She rearranged the pencils, fiddled with the blotter, flicked the switch of the dictating machine. On. Off. On again. She stared out of the big picture window in the search for inspiration, but Los Angeles, as always, had troubles of its own and provided no answers to the questions she was asking. What should she think? What should she feel? What in God's name should she *do?* The sleepless night hadn't helped, and, on the two or three occasions when she had managed to drop off, neither had the dreams. They had been a docudrama of her life so far, and they had left a legacy of total confusion. Prosecuting counsel and defense attorney had argued the case of Robert Hartford before the jury of her heart and the jury of her brain. Both verdicts were on the table. Not guilty. Guilty. It made sentencing impossible, abstention the only possible course. But how did you pass on the grand passion of your life?

She dipped her head into her hands and she looked at her watch. It was twenty minutes since she had told them to tell him to wait. Would he still be there, in the dock of the court? Would he be fuming deliciously in his unaccustomed dilemma, smoking like a trout as some poor penance for the agony he had caused her? She brightened at the thought. The bastard! The stuck-up, insensitive bastard, with his slimy sexuality and his box of cheap sensual tricks! He had elevated self-love to a fine art form. He was obsessed with himself, lost in the ultimate affair, as he compacted lovers like used cars and sold them off for scrap. Was he still there? The string pulled at her heart, and again the trapdoor opened in her belly. Had he left already? She had to know. The telephone would tell her.

"Is he still there, Jenkins?" she whispered as if afraid Robert might overhear.

"Yes, but I think he's getting a little impatient, madam."

ROBERT HARTFORD was no longer impatient. Ten minutes ago he had been that. Now he was angry, and it was getting worse. He crossed and uncrossed his legs, and he stared around the lobby, murdering with his eyes anyone who dared to catch them. He arched his long neck and he clenched his fists as he fidgeted against the rich upholstery of the Tower-designed sofa. This was deliberate. He was being punished, and although on paper maybe he deserved it, the reality was totally unacceptable. He was a grown-up man. Paula was a grown-up woman. Misunderstandings should be settled in an adult fashion. This was puerile. When he saw her he would say so to her face before he made his formal apology—if, indeed, one was technically needed. Once again he looked at his watch. Half an hour. He had actually been sitting there, on public display, doing nothing, for half a whole hour! If she was going to see him, why make him wait? If. The word ran around like a rabbit in his mind. If. What if she *wouldn't* see him? What then?

He jumped up. He sat down. Damn her! He was furious. She had misunderstood him. This was not the way to treat Robert Hartford. If she thought that then she didn't begin to know him.

Jenkins called out across the twenty-foot space.

"Ms. Hope will see you now, sir. You press *P* in the elevator, sir. I'm sorry you've been kept waiting."

The bell of the elevator sounded like a siren in Paula's mind. She stood up. She could feel him near. Not since the Coriarchis' party had she seen him in the flesh, but she had seen him in her dreams. He had played every role, from sadistic lover to gentle child-man. He had been tender and soft and his hands had played her until her body had cried out and she had awakened in soaked sheets to hear her own voice repeating his name as wakefulness banished the blissful illusion. He had been hard and vicious, foul-mouthed as he insulted her, and she had wept in her sleep as she had learned to loathe the one she had loved, and on waking, her fists tight with anger, she had vowed vengeance in the darkness on the man who had so capriciously given, and then taken away, her happiness. She had been sorry for him, feared him, laughed with him, made love to him, but she had never been indifferent to him. And there had never been anyone else—that, too—neither before nor after her life's one and only love.

She smoothed down the material of the Yves Saint Laurent navy-blue pencil skirt, and she took a deep breath as she tried to prepare for him. In seconds the doorbell would ring, and she would say, "Who is it?" and he would say, "It's me, Robert." That was all she knew.

When the doorbell rang, she said nothing. She simply walked across the room and she opened the door.

He charged into the room, pushing past her, not looking at her.

"I've been waiting in that lobby for the best part of an hour," he said.

"Maybe you'd like to go down and wait a little longer until you get yourself into a better mood," she replied.

The anger flashed in her eyes as she turned to face him. The irritation pulsed in his as he turned to confront her.

"I don't wait in lobbies."

He threw back his head in defiance and he stared straight at her, and it was there that she could see the change in him, in his dear, wonderful eyes. The light had gone from them. They were wounded eyes, defeated eyes. They had always been the gateways to his soul. Before they had danced to the music of desire, and they had been straight, no-nonsense eyes that flashed danger and demanded respect as they had gazed into the heart of her. Once they had beamed power and mastery, but she had taught them how to transmit love and tenderness, and how to be vulnerable. Now they were the sorrowing eyes of a man who had sinned against her but mostly against himself. And they were the eyes of a man who didn't know how to say sorry.

"I do apologize for keeping you waiting, Robert Hartford. I hadn't been expecting you."

Her words were heavy with sarcasm, but there was the beginning of a smile on her face. She was winning. She was in control. Of herself. Of him. Somehow that mattered more than anything.

His head flicked down, unable to hold her gaze. Then he looked up again, and he ran his hand through his hair in the gesture that signaled his acute unease. "I came to say sorry," he said. "I had to see you to say it. To say it to you directly . . . I mean."

"Oh . . . it was nothing, really." Paula flung out a dismissive hand and the laughter was almost there in the words, as her smile broadened.

He was thinner than he had been. God . . . she wanted to touch him. That *was* what she wanted.

He looked puzzled by her reaction. Where was the stream of abuse, the tears, the recrimination? Where were all the tricks of the feminine armory, the ones he knew how to neutralize so effortlessly? She seemed to be treating him as if he were a joke.

"Maybe I shouldn't have come. Maybe . . ." But her face had filled up his mind and siphoned the breath from his lungs. The curves of her body swept through his brain, and the scent of her, jasmine fresh, wafted into his soul. In his ears he could hear the howls of her desire and his arms could feel all the shuddering surrenders as their bodies had bathed in the liquid union of flesh. There was nothing else but those memories, nothing else but the desperate necessity for the past to become the future, to become the present.

"Robert!" It was her invitation.

"Paula," his voice was husky in its acceptance.

"Come here," she said.

—

SHE LAY across him, hot and wet, in the blissful interlude before the glory began all over again. Her blond hair lay across her sweat-soaked forehead, and she rested her cheek on his. He closed his eyes and he breathed in deeply, taking the wild scent of her deep within him, feeding from it, drinking it, loving it in the lungs that were so close to his heart. Robert's fingers traced the moisture on her cheek.

"I love you, little girl," he murmured, his voice the gentlest caress, softer, lighter than the pressure of his flesh against her face.

In answer she crushed her leg closer to his and she breathed out, fanning him with her warm breath. She reached down beneath the back of his neck and drew his wonderful face toward her, watching it closely like a connoisseur the finest of fine paintings.

He opened his eyes, unable any longer not to see her.

"Oh, Robert!" The love light in her eyes gave his name all the eloquence in the world, and the long, shuddering sigh of satisfaction rolled from her.

" 'Oh, Robert,' what?"

"I love you."

He smiled his own satisfaction. How little minds knew. How much bodies did.

"A year just disappeared." He rolled over onto one elbow, leaving his legs entangled in hers, and the fingers that had drawn on the wetness of her face traced the graceful line of her naked breast.

"One year, and three months, and two days," she said with a rueful smile.

"I knew that, too." He laughed as he became the competitor in the love game. He *had* known that.

"But it didn't disappear for Winty. It didn't disappear for Kristina." She looked away from him as if to break the spell of his body. They had made love. Soon they would have to talk.

The frown flew across his face. "You heard about Kristina."

"I think everybody did. What did Caroline Kirkegaard *do* to her?"

"God, I don't know. Kristina was always easily influenced, but I think Caroline had been working on her for ages. She took me to a Destiny meeting in the Sunset once and I was so appalled I got Livingstone to ban them. Kirkegaard was always evil. I just hadn't realized how powerful she was."

"I love Kristina. Isn't there anything we can do? Anything I can do?"

"I don't think so. She won't speak to me. I've written. I've called. I've even tried to get to her at the Sunset. There's no way. The place is like Fort Knox, and apparently Kristina has round-the-clock bodyguards. If I could just see her, maybe I could make a difference. . . ." His voice trailed off uncertainly. "Maybe not."

"God, how awful for you. How awful for her."

"*She* doesn't think so. She's got that Destiny stuff up to her eyeballs. She's just not my daughter anymore. She was the only person I had. . . ."

Paula clung close. But not anymore. Now you have me again. Now I have you.

"We might not be able to get to Kristina, but we can get to Caroline Kirkegaard. *I* can get to her. It would be the easiest thing in the world."

"To do what?"

"I don't know. Just to check her out. To find out about Kristina. Anything. Something. God knows what she might say."

"She's hardly likely to talk freely to the girl I'm going to marry."

Paula smiled fondly down at him. That was the second time he'd said it with his lips. The thousandth time in the lifetime of this morning's lovemaking that he'd said it with his body.

"But she doesn't know about this morning, does she?" said Paula. "I've hardly had time to know about it myself."

➤

CAROLINE KIRKEGAARD stood up, towering above the pink-clothed table, and everyone in the Star Room at the Sunset Hotel turned to look at its new owner. They had been sneaking glances at her from the moment she arrived, but she had been half hidden by the flowers, and the folded copy of the *Wall Street Journal* that for some extraordinary reason she appeared to be reading. Now that she was upright, it was all there to see, the bits of the channeler that the Chanel didn't cover, the powerful scent of power floating out into the room to merge with that of the bagels and bacon, the hash browns and the steaming coffee.

She put out her hand and flashed a warm smile of greeting. "Welcome back to the Sunset Hotel," she said. "I hope that the memories aren't too painful."

Paula took her hand. "Times pass, times change," she said. And then with a half smile. "People come. People go."

Caroline laughed, as the waiters hovered and the maître d' pulled out the table to allow Paula to sit down.

"We never really got to know each other, did we, Paula Hope? I hope we can change that now." Her tongue snaked out to moisten already moist lips, and she placed both her hands on the table in a gesture that said they contained no hidden cards.

"Coffee, madam?"

She nodded briskly.

"I apologize for the present sorry state of the hotel. Not up to the Château's high standards, I'm afraid, but we will put that right. Poor Robert had let things go. And dear Kristina lacked experience."

Caroline floated the bait over the water. Two names. What would be the reaction? It was common knowledge that Robert Hartford had thrown Paula out and broken her heart, and the popular wisdom was that she had never forgiven him for it.

Whatever her feelings she had certainly wreaked a poetic revenge. She had built the Château into the best hotel in Los Angeles and she had humiliated Robert Hartford and his beloved Sunset in the process, stealing his staff, hijacking his guests, and raping his reputation. It was difficult to believe that she had any feelings for him now but contempt, but in this life you could never be sure. Then there was Kristina. Paula and she had been friends, but the friendship had faded after the breakdown of Paula's engagement to her father. Later, running two competing establishments, they had been rivals but, according to Kristina, never enemies. What did Paula feel about Kristina now, and Kristina's close relationship with Caroline and Destiny? During the course of breakfast she would find out.

She looked carefully into Paula's eyes. It was important not to misread them.

"Never underestimate the egos of movie stars. Never overestimate their intelligence," said Paula.

There was a glint in the younger girl's eyes as she spoke. Caroline saw it. The words had a sharp edge, and Paula's tongue curled around them as her lips enjoyed the mouthing of them.

"Yes, he's made a terrible mess of the Sunset. There are horror stories of his behavior here. The staff couldn't wait to get rid of him."

Again the Kirkegaard eyes zeroed in for the wince of pain in Paula's that would ring alarm bells, but there was just the spark of flint, hard and cold and cruel.

"It's funny, isn't it," said Paula. "I was devastated when he broke off the engagement, but, looking back on it, it was the best thing that ever happened to me. I mean, the Château and Winty leaving me all his money, and Tower

Design . . ." She looked out across the room, the smile on her face Cheshire-cat wide, as she savored her good fortune.

Caroline watched her, almost convinced. Once again she floated the bait. "Do you remember that time I was having dinner with him and you caught him in the middle of one of his ridiculous passes. You were furious, but so was I. I was *dying* to experience his technique. You know, it would have been a bit like playing tennis with Steffi Graf!"

Caroline laughed as she joked, but there was a wistful look in her eye.

Paula laughed too. "You didn't miss much. Mostly it was done with mirrors."

"And Robert peering into them, I imagine." Caroline giggled.

All around the room the necks craned and the ears flapped to discover what two hundred million dollars' worth of feminine beauty had found so funny.

"God, if Robert could hear this conversation, he'd die. He'd just die." Paula laughed through tear-filled eyes.

"We'd better send him a tape." Caroline giggled again.

Gradually the laughter subsided.

"Goodness," said Caroline. "I haven't laughed so much since that movie he did—do you remember—the one when he was an angel, and somebody had told him to put on a British accent because they wouldn't speak English with an American accent in heaven?"

"You'd better believe I remember. I had to sit through all his old movies. That wasn't an accent, that was an accident!"

"Oh dear, you are funny, Paula."

"Well, *you* certainly had your revenge on Robert," said Paula. "How on earth did you persuade Kristina to give you the shares?"

Caroline paused, with the successful person's suspicion of a question that required an answer. She seemed to debate whether to deflect it. "You don't really understand about Destiny, do you?" she said at last.

"Not really." Paula sounded only marginally interested.

Caroline leaned forward, the convivial lunch partner no more. Her eyes sparkled with a wild enthusiasm, and she was suddenly charged with energy. "It's my dream. It's all our dreams. It should be yours, Paula. It can be, if you let it. Destiny is all there is, and some day the world will know it. It's why I wanted this hotel, to act as its headquarters, to use its reputation to spread the message to those who do not yet know the truth. Kristina opened her eyes to her Destiny. It was easy. I showed her how."

Her hand snaked across the table and caught Paula's arm. "I can show you," she breathed.

Paula could feel Caroline's strength throbbing against her skin.

She said nothing, anxious not to provide ammunition for the charms of the sorceress. She felt stripped of her resolve in the disturbing currents of power that had been so dramatically unleashed. There was no need to question anymore what had happened to Kristina. This had. She fought to concentrate, and she muttered to herself a mantra to protect herself from the swirling might of the wickedness that was alive in the room. Don't listen to this crap. Don't think about it. Don't even try to understand it.

"Women can do anything," whispered Caroline Kirkegaard. "We are so strong. We can join in the sisterhood of Destiny and the world will worship at our feet. Kristina understands that. You could, beautiful Paula."

"In a way, that was what I wanted to talk to you about." Paula forced out the words, knowing that she was not supposed to speak. The sound of her voice cut into the wave of hypnotic vibrations that threatened to engulf her. The shock registered in the Kirkegaard eyes. Paula could actually see the confusion as she lost the mesmeric concentration and the spell she was casting began visibly to fall apart.

But Caroline recovered quickly. She sat back in her seat, and her hand moved away from Paula's arm as the fires that had burned in her eyes began to dim.

"You had a reason for seeing me?" asked Caroline.

Paula tried to keep her voice matter-of-fact. Slowly, the otherworldly atmosphere of mystical coercion began to fade.

"Oh, it was nothing specific, but I just thought we ought to meet, and open up the lines of communication. I know the Sunset's been having problems, and I have to admit that I caused some of them, but I want you to know that's over now. Robert's Sunset isn't the same as your Sunset, Caroline. Okay, we're still rivals, but there's more than enough business for both of us. I just wanted to signal to you that from now on I'm happy to play softball rather than hardball. I mean, no poaching. No dirty tricks. Just straightforward, honest competition."

"I hoped you'd say that. I thought you would, but I wasn't certain. Kristina maintains you were never aiming at her." Caroline's tone was conversational. Her disturbing flexing of psychic muscles was apparently forgotten.

"I always liked Kristina. I have nothing against her. Or you," said Paula. "We should all be friends. If you want any help with design or running things, I wouldn't say no. You just have to ask, although I sense that you'll have it all back together in no time. That's what I wanted to say. We can help each other. For instance, the guy that heads up your computerized accounts department, Ferris, I think his name is, is talking to the Four Seasons. If he goes to them he'll probably take your programs, and he'll almost certainly raid your client list. I'd ax him, and get your attorneys to frighten him in the process."

"How did you know that?" Caroline's voice was sharp.

"You hear things. In this business everyone knows everything. Pretty soon you'll know things like that. Hang around the bar. Talk to the waiters. Listen to the gossip. That way you get to do things to people rather than have them do things to you."

Caroline simmered quietly inside. Ferris. She didn't even know the asshole's name but already she hated him. But there was another cause for irritation. She, Caroline Kirkegaard, whose enemies always perished in eternal flame, had taken a dent in her reputation. Paula had appeared tougher and more efficient than she.

"People who cross me live to regret it," she said ominously. "Francisco Livingstone would have told you that."

Paula didn't react, but she seemed to be listening . . . just. Caroline felt the humiliation rise within her. The younger girl would be thinking "talk is cheap"—something like that. Already she had showed considerable strength in resisting the Kirkegaard influence.

"Or should I say, die to regret it," added Caroline Kirkegaard.

"Yes, poor old Livingstone really went out the way he wanted to. I wonder what the hell he was doing in the bath to make him blow a fuse. Something pretty kinky, I expect. The old fart was into that," said Paula.

Caroline's face went knowing. "Let's just say," she said, "that it was a thoroughly sticky end. You have my word on that."

Paula cocked a quizzical head to one side, as Caroline beamed the telepathic message across to her. Don't underestimate me, said the Kirkegaard eyes. I'm lethal. I can be deadly. I have been. I will be.

"The old pervert got what was coming to him," said Paula at last. "He and Robert deserved each other."

"I expect they used to compare notes on young girls," said Caroline Kirkegaard, and her eyes swept speculatively over Paula as once again the unsettling tongue snaked out to wet her glistening lips.

~22~

"LET ME GET this absolutely straight, Robert. You and Ms. Hope are telling me that Caroline Kirkegaard had Francisco Livingstone murdered and you want me to arrest her for it."

The Beverly Hills police chief watched the movie star carefully as he summarized the story. He hadn't been at all prepared for what he had just been told. He had met Hartford once or twice before, and when he, and Paula Hope, the young and trendy owner of the Château Madrid, had asked to see him urgently he had jumped at the opportunity for a little mutual back scratching. Robert's political clout and his legendary fundraising abilities could help the police department in all sorts of different ways.

But Caroline Kirkegaard was also a somebody. What's more, she was a close friend of David Plutarch, who was friends with senators, and judges, and whose money meant that he could be friends with anybody . . . or their enemies. This whole thing would have to be handled with the greatest care. Already it was beginning to look like a "no win" situation for him. Who to offend? This heavy hitter, or that one.

Hartford seemed to be enjoying the role of D.A. He leaned forward emphatically toward the old policeman's desk, adjusting and readjusting the horn-rimmed glasses around the bridge of his nose in a gesture that emphasized the steel-blue eyes behind them. "No, Antonio, we're not saying that. What we're saying is that there may be probable cause here. Kirkegaard had the motive. She couldn't have known about Livingstone's will, and she knew he was implacably opposed to her buying his hotel. With Livingstone dead, and myself unable to complete the contract I had signed, she and Plutarch knew that the estate would fall over itself to sell the hotel to them. Now, on top of motive, we have Caroline Kirkegaard's intimation to Ms. Hope that she was responsible for Livingstone's death. Ms. Hope will sign a deposition regarding that. What we're asking for is an autopsy. There was no postmortem done on Livingstone. He was ill. He died in the bath. Natural causes were assumed, not proven. Now I think there is new evidence that justifies digging him up."

"You want me to ask for Livingstone to be exhumed, and a forensic investigation carried out on his body."

"That's *exactly* what we want."

The police chief looked at him doubtfully. Then at Paula. Then at the hangnail that had been irritating him all morning. "Isn't it a bit much to ask anyone to believe that a person like Ms. Kirkegaard would have someone murdered just so that she could buy his hotel?"

His words carried absolutely no conviction. In L.A. a dented car was a reason for murder. The Bloods and the Crips gunned down innocents in the street because they didn't like the color of their clothes. Gang violence was altering life-styles, even in Beverly Hills.

"Chief, I wish I could explain to you the kind of person she is," Paula said. "You can feel the evil in her. You can almost touch it. And the disgusting thing is it's actually attractive. You're drawn toward the rocks by the siren music. Look at the way she's taken over Robert's daughter. Your department must have had hundreds of complaints from the families of that Destiny cult she runs. She told me she'd killed Livingstone. She as good as spelled it out."

Terrlizese nodded. It was true there had been complaints about Destiny. Nothing dramatic, but they added up to a minor irritation. "Tell me again what she said. *Precisely* what she said."

"Well, I can't remember the precise words, but she said, 'I promise you he met a sticky end.' And before that she had said, 'People who cross me live to regret it,' and then she changed the 'live to regret it' to 'die to regret it.' But it was the *way* she said it, the expression on her face, the wicked glee. If you'd been there you'd have arrested her on the spot."

"You see, Ms. Hope, you can't use this evidence. She'll deny it, or she'll say she was joking and you took it the wrong way. Or she could say that it was just bravado. You know, she was trying to impress you with what a macho lady she is . . . you both being competitors in the hotel business."

He smiled carefully, not letting too much patronization out, but he was rather pleased with his speech. It had the virtue of being true, and it should go a long way to making them see that this was a long shot, hardly worth the trouble, certainly not worth the trouble he could be in if he irritated someone like Plutarch.

Robert put out a hand and rested it on Paula's knee, in a let-me-handle-this gesture. "Of course," he said, "nobody's going to *object* to a Livingstone exhumation because there's no next of kin except those distant cousins in Pasadena, and Livingstone hardly knew them. You dig him up quietly and see what the pathologists come up with. If it's nothing, forget it, sorry, I owe you one. If not, then of course it would be your duty to investigate his murder." He emphasized the word *duty*.

The chief of the Beverly Hills Police Department had seen carrots and sticks before, but few so neatly disguised. He pushed his fingers together and he looked at Robert, at Paula, and at Robert again. "No next of kin," he said.

"Precisely," said Robert Hartford.

"Dig him up, cut him up, and stick him back if everything's kosher?"

"In a nutshell, and no front-page ads in the *Herald-Examiner*."

"Nobody would know," said Terrlizese to himself.

"Except us, and we . . ."—he paused dramatically—"would be eternally grateful." Terrlizese allowed himself to dream of the Hartford/Hope gratitude. Dinners at the Château. His wife on the arm of the superstar at the odd premiere. The mayoral, the *presidential* candidate of the moment draped around Terrlizese's shoulders like a security blanket. Then there was the new police building in the grand Civic Center expansion on Santa Monica scheduled for completion in a year's time. Anything that could expedite *that* would be a help in getting him out of this inconvenient, makeshift office in City Hall. The new Charles Moore-designed police facility was going to be just about the most impressive building in Beverly Hills, as befitted a place where the liberal "haves" were more than usually interested in hanging on to what they'd got. More money would always be needed to get the Art Deco fountains to play, the mosaic tiles inlaid, the palm trees planted around the magnificent monument to law enforcement. Robert Hartford knew how the town worked. He wouldn't forget a favor. Kirkegaard and Plutarch could complain only if they were accused, and without the forensic evidence there would *be* no accusation. With it, they would be indicted murderers, and then it wouldn't matter what they felt.

"Well, Robert, it's not really 'by the book,' but from what you both say I think maybe we should have a look at poor old Livingstone. Of course the doctor who examined him at the time of death didn't smell a rat, but then he wasn't looking for one, was he?"

Robert stood up, and so did Paula. He put out his hand.

"Thank you, Antonio. I won't forget this. You've gone out on a limb for me. Let me know how I can do the same for you. Anytime. Anyplace. You'll keep me posted?"

"Yes, of course. By the way, where are you staying now? Not at the Sunset anymore."

"No, I've rented Rod Stewart's house in Bel-Air." He looked down, as several thoughts came to him at once. "Oh, and Antonio. No word of this to anyone. In particular I don't want people putting my name and Ms. Hope's together. Kirkegaard thinks we're hardly the best of friends. I want to keep it that way."

He smiled gently at Paula. Soon the world could know it all, and he would no longer live in a rented home. Together, he and Paula would march in triumph into the Sunset.

———

"How LONG does it *take*?"

Exasperation was alive in Paula's voice as she paced the Mexican-tiled floor of the bedroom in Robert's rented Spanish-mission-style mansion.

"Terrlizese said we would hear something this morning. They did the postmortem late last night."

Robert lay back on the bed and watched her. How had he ever let her go?

What, in the whole of his miserable life, had he ever done to deserve the second chance he had been given?

"I want her dead," said Paula. "I want to *be* the cyanide that crawls up her nose." The awful thought occurred to her. "They would gas her, wouldn't they?"

"With Plutarch's lawyers on her side? Forget it. They'll probably give her house arrest and community service." He laughed bitterly. "But that doesn't matter. Whatever happens, a guilty verdict would finish her. She'd have to do *some* time, and then we can get Kristina helped, and some judge to nullify the deed of gift on the Sunset shares. It would be easy to prove a convicted murderess used undue influence. My troubles would be over."

"I still want her dead. I had to sit through that lunch, Robert. I had to hear the things she said. I had to agree with them. I'll feel dirty about that forever. She's evil, you know. I've never met that kind of wickedness before . . . not even Seth Baker. . . ."

Robert sat up and the pain shot across his face, as he saw it pass across hers.

"Can you ever forgive me?" said Robert, and he got up and walked toward her, taking her hand.

"I forgave you," she said. "The other morning. Last night. Maybe twenty other times. I lost count." She smiled away the sadness as she joked with him. There had been so much sorrow, so much hatred. Now there would be love, and more love, all the love in the world.

She walked over to kiss him, to make it twenty-one, but the telephone interrupted them.

Robert reached for it, motioning to Paula to pick up the extension.

"Robert? Antonio." The policeman's voice was excited. "Goddamn it, you were right! Cause of death, suffocation. No doubt about it, even after a year and a bit in the ground. And listen to this. The forensic team found traces of cyanoacrylate in the mouth, nostrils, and eyes. That's super glue."

"Super glue?"

"Yeah, isn't it incredible? It seems someone glued up his nose and mouth so he couldn't breathe."

Paula couldn't hold it back. "That's what she meant. She said it. That was what she meant by 'sticky end.' "

"That's wonderful, Antonio. So you arrest her and charge her. Have you done it already?"

There was silence.

"It's not quite as easy as that, Robert. My legal people are all over me now. There's no evidence to tie Kirkegaard to the murder, apparently. Her remarks to Paula just aren't enough. She'd walk out of a courtroom, and they could probably do my department for wrongful arrest. I'm afraid the very best we can do is keep her under surveillance, interview her. Maybe persuade her to confess . . ."

"She's not going to *confess*, Antonio! Christ, the woman has brass balls. I'd rather try to intimidate the Ayatollah. What the hell is this, Antonio? Is this some kind of a cover-up? I'm sorry. I didn't mean that. Forget I said that. But it's just that we're so close, and we all know she did it. . . ."

"Robert, I could give you the names of a hundred murderers walking the streets of L.A. right this minute, and I don't mean the ones on furlough. It's called living in a free country. She's not guilty until she's proven guilty in a court of law, and nobody cares what you or I 'know.' Don't blame me, blame all the bleeding-heart liberals. They do their bleeding in the corridors of power, while my officers are doing the real thing out on the streets."

"There must be some proof. We've just got to find it."

"That's the worst part of all. There is."

"There is, and that's the worst part? What the hell do you mean?"

"Well, obviously the killer cleaned him up after he'd croaked. They used a solvent to wipe away the evidence of the glue, and the forensic boys have found traces of that. But more important, they've found a human hair in his nostril. A red one."

"A red one? But Caroline's hair is blond."

"And they found a blond hair under Livingstone's fingernail."

"Her assistant has red hair," said Paula, her voice bubbling with excitement.

"So do maybe a hundred thousand girls in Los Angeles," said Terrlizese. "That's most of the ones that aren't blond."

"And there's no way to identify the hair as positively belonging to Caroline and the girl who works for her?" Robert's voice was full of disappointment.

"Funnily enough, there is. It's a new technique that they've been using in England since 1985. It's called DNA fingerprinting. DNA forms the building blocks of the amino acids that make up the cells' protein. Identical twins have the same DNA structure. Nobody else does. The pathologists have a technique that can compare the DNA structure on two samples of tissue. If we could get one of Caroline's hairs, we could find out if it matched the hair beneath Livingstone's nail. Same with the girlfriend."

"And that evidence would stand up in court?"

"It's a definite 'maybe.' They convicted a rapist in Florida using the test late last year, and they've used it successfully in some paternity cases."

"It wouldn't matter that the hair's been in the ground all that time?"

"No, apparently not. Livingstone's coffin was lead lined, and DNA is tough stuff. They're using it to decide a ten-year-old rape case in Illinois. And anyway hair lasts longer than most body tissue. No, that's not the problem. The problem is that the D.A. won't have Kirkegaard arrested on the evidence so far obtained. I've argued it out with him, but he's adamant. Says he's not prepared to go up against Plutarch's girl. I think he's wrong, but it's his decision and he's made it. I'm very sorry."

"You're telling me that a sample of Caroline's hair would clinch it, but you can't ask her to provide a sample."

"I can ask but I can't get, without arresting her, and I'm not allowed to arrest her without more proof. It's Catch Twenty-two."

"Fuck Catch Twenty-two," said Robert, biting his tongue to avoid saying any more.

"I know you're disappointed. *I'm* disappointed, but that's the end of the story, I'm afraid."

"Like *hell* it is," said Robert as he slammed down the phone.

He looked helplessly at Paula. "How do we get a sample of Caroline Kirkegaard's hair?"

"Easy," said Paula. "We cut it off."

⟶

"YOU TOUCH my hair and I'll sue your faggot ass from the Redwood forests to the Gulf Stream waters, okay?"

In the mirror, the Kirkegaard eyes flashed as a backup to the message, and behind her the hairdresser wilted like a waterlogged houseplant. The makeup girl, her brush poised in midair, froze.

"You, too, Kanga," added Caroline Kirkegaard loudly. "We agreed to turn up for a disease, not amateur night at a stylists' convention. When I want my hair cut I'll get someone to do it who thinks hair is something more than a way to get a part on 'Knots Landing.' "

Giles Ramillies put down the scissors and wished he hadn't bothered. It should have been the best. Paula Hope's AIDS fashion show at the Château Madrid had been a crimper's dream. The word had spread like wildfire all over town and every makeup artist, every stylist, every color person in Los Angeles had been waiting patiently for the summons that would be the ultimate sign of acceptance among the people who really mattered. AIDS was the hot ticket to the charity circuit. Everyone would say yes, nobody would dare to say no, and that was what had happened. The usual AIDS people were out in force, the Liz Taylors, the Richard Geres, and the newer people too, whose hot box office opened charity doors as well as movie ones—dirty dancer Patrick Swayze, fatally attractive Glenn Close, cheerful Kirstie Alley. But poor Giles had had the rotten luck to draw Caroline Kirkegaard and her sidekick, Kanga. The woman was a deadly weapon, pointed right at him.

"Miss Hope asked that we tidy up everyone's hair." He nearly bit off his tongue as he heard his own implication, that the Kirkegaard hair was untidy. It wasn't even true. The stark geometry of the sculpted cut was formidably neat. But his instructions from Paula had been quite clear—"tidy it up."

Quite suddenly Caroline Kirkegaard reached out and put her hand on the makeup artist's chin, and she pushed. The girl, paintbrush in one hand, blusher in the other, wasn't expecting it. The Kirkegaard fury had seemed to be aimed at the hapless barber. In the world of "beauty," makeup artists were distinctly inferior to hairdressers and were often treated as such, so she had been rather enjoying the discomfort of her "superior." Now, however, her head traveled about a foot at the end of Caroline Kirkegaard's palm and as a result she fell back, lost her balance, and fell in a heap to the floor.

"Fuck!" she said.

"Problems?" asked Paula sweetly from the doorway.

The makeup girl, her legs in the air, lay covered by a fine dust of highlighters, blushers, and powders from her upended tray. Ramillies was white as a sheet, his sensitive face contorted with the pain of the Kirkegaard insult. Kanga, pouting, sultry, sat quietly at the dressing table next to Caroline. The leader of the pack, cheered by the distress she had so comprehensively caused, beamed into the mirror at Paula.

"No problems," she said sweetly. "I just told the gay boy to lay off my hair. And I was tired with the princess fiddling around with my face like this was a movie set. How are you, Paula? You look good enough to eat."

Paula smiled easily, as she took in the scene. "You're right, Caroline. Your hair is just great as it is. Better than great. Who does it for you?"

"Dan Galvin from London. David sends the jet for him once a week."

Paula walked toward her and stood behind her, right up close, as the makeup artist, mumbling unmentionables, picked herself up off the floor.

"I'm so glad you could come, Caroline . . . and Kanga," she added as an afterthought. "I really wanted this gala to be special, and you've made it that."

"Well, AIDS is AIDS, but you are you," said Caroline. The meaning was unmistakable, and despite herself Paula felt her face reddening.

To cover her sudden confusion she introduced the girl who was standing by her side. "Caroline. I don't think you know my assistant. This is Greta. Greta, this is Caroline Kirkegaard, and this is her assistant Kanga."

"Hi," said Greta, but nobody bothered to look at her.

"How's it going, Paula?" Caroline asked. "Are the stars shining bright? Are the glitterati oiling their checkbooks? Are they all making block bookings in your hotel?"

Paula caught the drift. Charity in Hollywood was a two-way street. Apart from tax deductions there were other kickbacks, social advances, career opportunities, business deals. But she smiled to herself. Her ulterior motive was as far from the obvious as it was possible to be. "I wish they could," Paula laughed easily, "but I'm booked solid for months."

"Don't worry. My new Sunset will relieve some of your strain."

"I'm counting on it. Running this place is too much like hard work."

"You should meditate. It's a whole new world."

"You should teach me."

"Maybe I will."

Again the electricity crackled and Caroline smiled into the mirror—the special smile, the one that melted souls.

Paula found herself caught by the eyes. They seemed to bore inside her. They were enormously compelling and the feeling that came with them was above and beyond such words as *pleasant* and *unpleasant*. It was impossible to say whether the sensation was nice or nasty, far more difficult to determine whether it was good or bad. With an effort she tore her eyes away from Caroline's reflection, glad as she did so that the full force of her eyes was diluted by the glass. Was this what had unhinged Kristina, and the girl called Kanga, who had killed for her?

"Caroline, I think your hair looks out of this world, but I wonder if Kanga would object to having hers piled up a bit for our eighteenth-century theme. She wouldn't have to have much actually cut, would she, Giles, just the smallest bit off the back."

"Okay," said Caroline easily. "I guess I can live with that." She spoke as if Kanga didn't exist.

Paula motioned toward the chastened hairdresser to get on with it. "It's going to be a wonderful show," she said. "Valentino and Armani. Johnny doing the commentary. I can't believe that everyone got it together at such short notice."

"It's your charm," said Caroline. "You could make people do anything."

"Anything?"

"Anything."

Caroline spun around in her seat and the dressing gown she wore flipped open, as the naked breast, iceberg magnificent, sailed into glorious sight.

Paula swallowed despite herself. Nobody should underestimate this woman. She had the devil within her, with all his power, and all his charm, and all his consummate wickedness. "I'll bet," Paula laughed, "you wouldn't allow me to cut just one lock of your hair."

"For your locket?" smiled Caroline. The air was suddenly sprayed with the fine mist of supersexuality.

"Maybe," breathed Paula.

"Take some," said Caroline.

In slow motion Paula moved forward and picked up the scissors from the table. She came closer, and every millimeter that she advanced she felt the aura of Caroline Kirkegaard closing in on her. She had turned once more to the front and there were two breasts now, dazzling in their awesome symmetry. Paula struggled to remember her purpose.

"Just a little bit," said Paula to cover her sudden confusion.

Caroline watched her. She didn't find the request strange. In her life the strange had changed into the commonplace. She had but to get close to people, and the magic began to work. Now it was Paula Hope, beautiful, influential, and the ruler of the Château Madrid, the deadly rival to her Sunset Hotel. The girl with the swimming-pool eyes wanted a lock of her hair. Soon she would be wanting other things.

Snip.

"There!" said Paula with a giggle of embarrassment. "Here, Greta, will you look after that for me." She handed it to her assistant like it was the Holy Grail.

"Sure," said Sergeant Greta Kandinsky of the Beverly Hills Police Department.

—

"You have the right to remain silent . . ."

The uniformed officer was playing it by the book, and he was not alone. This wasn't just a straightforward homicide arrest. The deputy D.A. was there, and a police department doctor, and even the guy who handled publicity for the Beverly Hills P.D. It was only with difficulty that the ones who had them had resisted the temptation to bring their agents.

Kanga sat quite still, her face stricken but together. She didn't cry and she didn't plead. She just endured it as they read her Miranda rights and charged her with murder in the first degree. Well before they had charged her, they had searched her apartment and they had gone through her drawers, and her address books, and they had put everything loose into big cardboard boxes, but first they had enclosed everything in plastic, wearing rubber gloves as they did so. She had seen it coming like a tornado across a rough sea, but still she could think only of Caroline. If they knew about Kanga and her part in the Livingstone killing, then the chances were that they knew about Caroline, too. But how, after all this time, could they possibly know what had happened?

"You have the right to an attorney. . . ."

"Can I call my lawyer?" she said.

"You are allowed one call," said the policeman. "You can make it from here, or from headquarters. Whatever. And you say you have no knowledge at all of the whereabouts of Ms. Kirkegaard?"

"None," said Kanga. It was true. She didn't know where Caroline was. Usually she would be at Plutarch's house this time of the late evening, but the police and a battery of warrant-toting lawyers from the D.A.'s office had apparently checked it out. Already the dragnet was in operation, and the all-points bulletins would be burning up the wires and the airwaves, but so far Caroline was at large in the big city, almost certainly oblivious to the tragedy that was about to engulf her. Kanga fought to think calmly as the room went spinning round. She had one call. One chance to warn the woman she worshiped of what was about to happen. If only she could sound the alarm, then Caroline would know what to do.

One call. One try. Plutarch's house with its live-in legal department? No, that would be wasted. The cops had been there. Plutarch, too, would be trying to alert Caroline. Then she remembered it. The car phone. The unlisted number that nobody else but she possessed. Was Caroline out there in the Mercedes somewhere? At nine o'clock at night? Hardly. But wait a minute. Tonight was the night of Emilio Steinbeck's dinner party at the Bel-Air Hotel. Caroline had been invited by the New York agent because he was handling the auction of the sequel to her best-selling book, *March to Destiny*. It was just possible that she was running late. Perhaps this very second she was handing the keys of her car to the Bel-Air's valet parkers.

She leaped to the phone, not caring that the policeman at her shoulder took down the numbers as she punched them out.

For an age it rang, and then, at last, there was the irritable voice. "Yes?" barked Caroline Kirkegaard.

"It's Kanga."

"Christ, Kanga, I'm late for Emilio's party. What the hell is it?"

Kanga knew she hadn't much time. The cop at her elbow had all but climbed inside the telephone. "I'm being arrested for the murder of

Francisco Livingstone," she blurted out. "The police are here now, and they're looking everywhere for you." She jammed the telephone down as they rushed at her.

"Did you get the number?"

"Yeah, Sarge. It's right here." The plainclothes cop started to punch frantically at digits.

"It's a cellular phone. Get a subscriber trace. It's probably her car. She's out there somewhere in a car. Feed it into the APB. Did they get a diary from the Plutarch house? Is there one here? She may have an engagement tonight. Find it, for chrissakes, don't just stand there."

He swung around to confront Kanga.

"Okay, wise-ass, you're deep in it, believe me. There's no holes in this case against you, or against Kirkegaard. You talk, you help me find her, and there's a good word in it for you. Hear what I'm saying?"

"Go fuck yourself," said Kanga.

CAROLINE KIRKEGAARD turned off the ignition, and she rolled up the window she had just rolled down. The small parking lot at the Bel-Air was full to the bursting point as the literary high rollers of Tinsel Town disgorged from their top-end cars for the Steinbeck dinner, and inside her car the telephone was still warbling. But she knew not to answer it anymore. Kanga's words had been shot from the barrel of a gun. Anybody else on the private line would be foe not friend.

It was quiet in the eye of her storm. Her mind ground on, steamroller smooth, in the preanger, prepanic phase where there was only information, only facts. Kanga had been arrested for Livingstone's murder. So what. Kanga wouldn't implicate her if they stretched her on a rack. But there was an arrest warrant for her, too. That meant there was evidence against her, good evidence, the kind that could convict. It was then that the drums began to beat within her. Convicted of murder. Found guilty. Sentenced to die. At the very least all her dreams would vanish in the messy trial—Destiny, the power and the glory, the Sunset Hotel. She might be freed through the contortions of the lawyers, but she would never, ever again be free to be what she had to be, to become what she had to become.

It was all unraveling. At the moment when she had climbed every mountain and achieved every objective, her carefully constructed world was about to fall apart.

She looked down at her frilly dress, Lacroix on a roll. The frothy exuberance of it, the black tulle, the ballerina tutu frame for her world-without-end legs was the cruellest paradox in the universe. It was created with only joy in mind, and now she wore it while all the frustration and fury were boiling deep within the cavity where her heart had once been. Her instinct screamed at her. Robert Hartford was behind this. There was nobody else. Somehow he had found out about Livingstone. The body had been dug up, the cause of death determined, and the link between her and the murder somehow established. Her mind raced over the last few weeks. When had she ever mentioned the long forgotten Livingstone?

Paula! "A sticky end" she had bragged to the seemingly guileless girl. The meeting had been a fishing trip, and she had risen like a greedy novice to the bait. She and Paula had laughed at Robert Hartford in the easy conspiracy of the feminine wronged. But all the time Paula had been in Robert's camp, his lover once more, and she, Caroline, had dug the ditch that threatened to become her grave. The events of the last few days flashed before her. The fashion show, arranged at such short notice at the Château Madrid. Would dear Caroline and beautiful Kanga model the clothes to save the sick, and cement the friendship between the two most exotic hoteliers in the world? Could Paula, Robert Hartford's Paula, have a lock of her hair?

Such a business had been made of it. The hair. Hers. Kanga's. Yes, that was it. That must be it. The hair had in some way tied them to the murder. The *New York Times* had carried a story on it a while back. Body tissue of any kind could be identified like fingerprints. Science had undone the perfect crime.

She reached out and she turned the key in the ignition and the engine roared into life. Emilio Steinbeck wouldn't be getting a book on reincarnation after all. He would get another book. A far better book. A book called *Revenge.*

As she headed out onto Sunset Boulevard a plan was forming in her mind. One phrase ran through it like a theme song. It was everything, a symbol of all she had ever wanted, a sign of the totality of what she was. It represented the desires of those she hated. It would be the weapon of her retribution. It was all she could think about, filling up her brain, expanding like a balloon full of the vapor of loathing. The Sunset Hotel. The place she had longed for. The place she would destroy.

The Mercedes screeched to a halt at the gas station, and she spoke fast to the Mexican on duty, well aware that the hundred-dollar-bill dangling from her hand was speaking faster. Two cans of gasoline. Yes, ninety-two octane, for the car of her friend, stranded, can you believe the luck, in Bel-Air.

Outside the Sunset the scene was as she imagined. It was swarming with police, the crackling of the radios merging with the flashing blue lights to create the sense of panic so dear to police forces all over the world. They were looking for her there. But they wouldn't find her.

She parked the car in the side street, and she slipped across the ice-smooth grass by the bungalows, weighed down by the twin cans of gasoline, the smell of the fuel warring with that of her Paloma Picasso scent. Nobody was watching. Nobody saw the Christian Lacroix superwoman and her bizarre cargo. She hurried along the path, then disappeared into the bushes where she would be least likely to be seen. Using her master key she unlocked the side door to the ballroom. She knew that there was no function planned for the evening. She opened the door and hurried up the steps, the heavy cans of high-octane fuel light as feathers in her powerful hands.

The ballroom stretched out before her, the heart of the Sunset Hotel. It was deserted, prostrate at the feet of the mistress of Destiny.

For fifty years the room had not changed because Livingstone had loved it as it was. The faded, polished wood of the ancient floor gleamed in the moonlight that flooded in from the high windows, its boards worn by the feet of a million dancers. Love had blossomed here and alliances had been forged, marriages ended, as happiness had lived and died. The curtains, heavy damask, ran from the floor to the high ceiling, and across the back of the wooden bandstand, rich tapestries hung proudly, a defiant statement that the new world was no less grand than the old one. The tables and the chairs were stored away, magnifying the vastness, and the memories scurried around, cavorting with the moonbeams like happy children playing in a deserted house.

But Caroline saw Robert Hartford's face, smiling at her in victory. She saw Paula, proud on the arm of the man who had won. She saw Kristina, saying the things that the shrinks wanted to hear, muttering the meaningless phrases that would result in the withdrawal of the gift of her shares. In the terrible eye of her mind she saw the door banging shut on her freedom, and she watched in fascination as the upturned pyramid that was Destiny crumbled at its shattered foundation.

She reached down and she undid the caps of the gasoline cans. She kicked one over and watched the juice of potential fire spreading out like a bloodstain over the old wood of the floor. Then she walked with the other across to the bandstand, climbed up, and splashed the tapestries and the drapes, and the dry boards of the platform with the petroleum. There was so much of it, and she poured as she walked, leaving a river of gas trailing behind her. The uneven boards channeled the liquid. This way and that it hurried, defining the low parts, leaving areas of relative high ground surrounded as it found its level. But Caroline didn't notice as the floor became a chain of scattered islands, enclosed by a sea of flammable wetness.

Whatever else happened, Robert Hartford would never own the Sunset Hotel. It would die. It would burn. It would be gone forever. The fiery furnace that she would start here could never be contained. The ballroom was the core of the hotel. Nothing would survive.

She bent down and she flicked at the lighter, and she dipped it into the gasoline.

The flame raced away from her, quicker, stronger than she had imagined. It darted to the left, and it scurried to the right, and it flew like an arrow to the bandstand. It jumped up the steps, scaled the walls, and ran crazily to the priceless tapestries. It seized greedily at the thick damask of the drapes. Already the flames were crackling as they ate at the floor. Caroline stared in fascination at the extraordinary destructive force she had unleashed. Then she turned around and looked toward the door through which she had entered. There was a corridor of dry wood between her and the escape route, covered only by tiny pools of fuel. She walked backward fast as all around the sheets of flames sprang up, not yet hot, but already high, already beginning to sizzle and fizz with the excitement of fire. She hurried toward the door, but she couldn't resist looking back, to savor the destruction she had wrought and to dream of the sadness it would bring to those she hated.

And then she slipped.

Her foot, neat in its Manolo Blahnik black satin shoe, the heel so high, the sole so smooth, stepped into the middle of a pool of gasoline. She slid a foot or two on the ice-rink floor, and her flailing arms kept her upright as they windmilled in the air. But she knew she was going to fall.

She went backward and she landed on her bottom, the frilly black tulle of the frivolous Lacroix skirt floating on the puddle of gasoline like a lily on a pond.

The flames saw her. Alligators on the edge of a jungle swamp, they eased themselves toward her. A tongue of flame darted across her escape route, cutting it off with a solid wall of fire. Another curled around her in a semicircle, hungry, stalking her, creeping close.

She tried to get up but she was slippery with gasoline, sliding, swimming on the polished floor. There was a pain where she had fallen, but there was a far worse one in her mind. Because now she knew what was going to happen to her. She was going to burn. She was going to *be* the bonfire that she had started. She herself was going to be the fuel that destroyed the Sunset Hotel.

At first her scream was not loud. It was a cross between a shout and a warning, devoid of agony, but its volume increased as it poured out of her.

"Noooooooooooooo!" she howled.

Yes, said the flames. They rushed at her, wanting the dress more than they wanted her. They were crazy for the flimsy material, like avaricious billion-airesses in the front row of the Paris collections. They walked all over it, licking it, loving it, making it their own. They didn't mind that they made the flesh on Caroline Kirkegaard's legs bubble like hot tar. They didn't care that they turned her skin red, and black and white and whole bits of her that had been firm hissing, liquid soft. They were fond of her hair, too, and they reached it from the back of the dress, bridging the gap of skin with no problem at all until she was nothing but a flaming torch as she sat, upright, on the burning floor of the ballroom of the Sunset Hotel.

Her tongue, still wet inside, wanted to speak through fiery lips—something about terror and a pain more horrible than pain could be, but it was warming up inside her skull, as the furnace wrapped her head in its embrace. So she forgot what it was she wanted to say as she toppled sedately over to one side and cocked a fiery leg at the ceiling. As she died there was one lingering message left inside.

"This is the last life, Caroline," said a hideous voice. "Only joking about rebirth."

~ *Epilogue* ~

THE GLOW FROM the setting sun sent the finger shadows dancing across the pool. Above, the sky was blazing with all the Los Angeles colors, the orange-yellows, the purple-browns, and the deep red-magentas, and all around the wind from the desert, warm, sensual, scurried through the canyon like a lover in the twilight.

Robert Hartford breathed in deeply, his head buried in his hands. Paula stood beside him in the fading light, tall and statuesque. She put out a hand to touch his shoulder, and, absentmindedly, he covered it with his. "Can you believe that Plutarch killed himself?" she asked, staring off into the distance. Billions couldn't protect you from obsession. Nothing could.

"Kanga would have done it, too, if they didn't have her locked up," said Robert, his voice full of awe as he contemplated the extraordinary power that Caroline Kirkegaard had wielded.

The silence closed in. The wind was gathering pace, rustling the pine trees, shaking their needles into the immaculate pool.

She sat down beside him and leaned against his shoulder. He leaned back at her, his body hard against hers, for support, in affection.

"Will Kristina get over her?" said Paula.

Robert sighed. Had his daughter and Caroline been lovers? He hadn't dared to ask the psychiatrist, and the doctor hadn't volunteered the information. Perhaps he'd never know. Perhaps that was the best way. "The doctors say yes. Apparently it has to do with time. The Kirkegaard influence didn't last long enough to be permanent. They have techniques to counter the effects of brainwashing. She'll remember it as a sort of bad dream."

"Poor, *poor* Kristina," said Paula.

"It's funny, even now I can't really forgive her for what she did. I know it wasn't her fault, that it was like an addiction. I know that intellectually, but I can't *feel* it. I *feel* she betrayed me."

"That's nonsense, Robert. If the courts say she wasn't in her right mind when she deeded the Sunset shares to Caroline, then that's the truth. It wasn't something she could help."

He rocked his head backward and forward. "I know. I know. I'm just telling you what's inside. I'm always going to do that from now on. You'd better get used to it."

He smiled and she felt his mood lighten, and hers with it. "Well, anyway, she burned on earth and she's burning in hellfire right this very minute."

"Only talk good of the dead," said Robert in mock solemnity.

"Good. She's dead," said Paula, laughing.

"I never thought I'd thank God for a sprinkler system," said Robert.

"It was the three-minute delay before it was activated that I'm thankful for. I wouldn't have wanted anything to put her out. She'd have never given up, you know. Whatever happened to her—jail, anything—she'd have been there somehow to harm us."

She stood up, and she reached for Robert's hand, pulling him up beside her. Over the sea, the orange sun was sitting on the pencil line of the horizon, and Paula linked her arm through his as she led him across the lawn to the edge of the pool terrace.

"Will they charge Kanga with Livingstone's murder?"

"She'll get off on an insanity defense, I guess, then get psychiatric help."

"An exorcism would be more effective," said Paula.

She shuddered as the memory of the Evil scudded across her mind like the clouds hurrying across the burning sky. Above her head the evening wind rustled the fronds of the palm trees. The Santa Ana was picking up—the wind from the desert that longed for the sea. "So the Sunset is safe," she said, and she cuddled in close to him to ward off the chill of the wickedness that had so very nearly destroyed the happiness they now shared.

"Yes, the deed of gift will definitely be nullified. It's safe. But not from me, and not from competition from that pushy old hotel run by that genius from the Florida Everglades." He turned toward her, and he laughed as he spoke.

She smiled back at him. "You mean the one that's about to change its name from the Château Madrid to the Sunset Hotel, run by that girl who's about to change her name from Hope to Hartford?"

"There's no answer to that. Winty would have had one, wouldn't he? He always did."

They laughed at the bittersweet memory as she melted into his arms, and the warm wind washed over them as if they were a single person, joined together at last for the wonderful future they would share.

PALM BEACH

To my friend Roxanne Pulitzer, with love

～ *Prologue* ～

*E*VERYONE AGREED IT was the grandest and most beautiful wedding in Palm Beach history, but nearly everybody also felt that something was terribly, dreadfully wrong. Whatever that was, it was nowhere near the surface. Rather, it bubbled around in the collective unconscious, mysterious and threatening, shadowy but undeniable. The alien feeling seemed to lurk in the cool, formidably air-conditioned atmosphere of the old Mizner mansion, scurrying about in the dark corners of the carved wood ceilings, insinuating its presence along the somber Spanish-tiled corridors and the bougainvillaea-bedecked cloisters. Nobody who felt it could ignore it, and yet it was too intangible to describe—an uninvited guest at the wedding feast.

Lisa Blass and Bobby Stansfield were unaware of the disturbing undercurrents. It was their wedding day. They were two people who in short minutes would become one, and the aura of their mutual happiness insulated them effortlessly from the mists of dread that swirled round about. They stood close together, like the intertwined figures on the top of a child's music box, preparing cheerfully to dance their way through an eternity of togetherness. Occasionally, as if in mutual reassurance that this was not the unreality of a dream, their hands would reach out for the comfort of touch. "To hold is to have," their gestures seemed to say.

Lisa Blass squeezed hard on her fiancé's hand and leaned in toward the strong shoulders.

"Not long now," she whispered.

But it had been so very, very long. Almost as long as memory itself. All her life it seemed she had been traveling toward this point, and it had been the hardest and most dangerous road imaginable. Only Maggie could begin to understand the sorrow and the tragedy, the despair and the hurt, the struggle and the strife she had suffered on the journey. Everyone else saw only the beautiful Lisa Blass, the girl of uncertain origins who had carved an empire and was now about to merge it with a dynasty. That was the *People* magazine version, and it would be the *Social Register*'s verdict, too. But Lisa alone knew that in the emotional roller-coaster ride that had been her life the dominant motive had been . . . not love, as this ceremony seemed to suggest . . . but another one altogether. Only Lisa could know that the years of her meteoric rise to fame and fortune had been clouded all the while by the mind-numbing fog of revenge.

Now, however, the metamorphosis was complete, and from the chrysalis of hate the butterfly of love had flown free. Love for the man she had wanted so much to destroy.

Bobby turned to look at her, straightening himself up and flexing his shoulders beneath the immaculately cut Anderson and Sheppard Savile Row-tailored morning coat. He took a deep breath. "It can't be soon enough," he whispered back.

He had never spoken a truer word. There had been so much wasted time. So many regrets since the decision he had made with such difficulty all those years ago. His prayers had been answered and he had been given a second chance, and now he wanted the deed done before once again capricious Fate could snatch it from him. It was not only a second chance to have the Lisa he had always loved, but a second chance for everything. Bobby's heart filled with happiness as he contemplated his future. With Lisa Blass at his side, her vast fortune allied to his political wealth, her calming, steadying influence available night and day, the shining vision was possible again. The presidency would still be his. The excited murmur of the crowd was the backdrop to Bobby's reawakened dream, and he turned to look at his wedding guests.

The town of Palm Beach itself seemed to be present in the mighty room. It stood there in all its awesome self-satisfied glory—proud and defiant, parading its ancient wealth and social power. They were all there—the Old Guard—Phippses, Munns, Wideners, Pulitzers, Kimberlys, and those who would one day become Old Guard—Loy Andersons, Leidys, Cushings, Hanleys. The Polo crowd had made it over from Wellington: meaty Argentinians with hungry eyes and bulging quadriceps; smooth-tongued silver-haired socialites with beautiful wives and speedy daughters; and dispossessed Englishmen with high handicaps and low morals. There were political allies, the occasional political enemy, a liberal sprinkling of Euro-trash. Descendants of German armaments tycoons, a smattering of pseudoroyalty from the Balkans, the inevitable gaggle of suave White Russians.

Yes, they were all there to see the marriage of the town's two most influential fortunes. To them it was not so much a wedding—it was a coronation. Palm Beach was about to have a new king and a new queen, and the courtiers had come to pay homage.

Scott Blass, however, was existing on his own private cloud of horror. Slumped in a tall-backed chair, his eyes darted nervously, away from the soon-to-be-married couple who stood together by the side of the orchid-covered rostrum, toward the white telephone inches below his hand. Despite the electric field of anxiety that hovered around him, he found time to think that he had never seen his mother look more beautiful. The pale ivory of the seventeenth-century Milanese lace Pat Kerr dress, its almost virginal halter neck studded with pearls, gave to her a spiritual grace that he had never seen before. The exquisite features had not changed, but the tension had gone from her face and had been replaced by a quiet peace. His mother, cleansed by the fire, had been reborn, and the light of love that shone from her eyes—the light that Scott had prayed in vain would one day shine on him—was focused adoringly on her husband-to-be. The wheel had turned its circle. Wrong was about to be made right, cold to be made warm. From the fields in which evil had been sown the harvest of happiness was about to be reaped. Or was it? Again Scott stared at the telephone. Daring it to ring. Defying it to do so. He pulled unhappily at his stiff collar to let the air at the damp sweat that discomforted him, knowing as he did so that it would bring no relief from the torment.

From either side of the room two women watched him suffer. Caroline Stansfield had never met Lisa Blass's son before, but he had been pointed out to her, and she liked what she saw. As the matriarch of the Stansfield political dynasty, and abiding pillar of Palm Beach high society, she knew a thing or two when it came to sizing up voter appeal. Really he was a remarkably fine specimen. Tall, clean-limbed, and with the vote-catching deep blue eyes of her own son, Bobby. Obviously the boy would have inherited intelligence from the mother. The son of a woman like Lisa who had come from nowhere to rule the only world that mattered would have the right political instincts. He could be trained. Maybe she would take him under her wing and teach him the art of winning, as she had taught her own children. But what on earth was he doing fidgeting around like that? A man should learn how to sit still and exude dignity. As it was, he looked as if he were about to appear before a firing squad rather than witness his mother's marriage to possibly the most eligible man in the world. With the ease born of eighty-five years of practice, Caroline Stansfield banished the jarring thought from her mind and smiled regally around the room.

Everything was really quite perfect. How very clever of Lisa to have learned the rules. Bobby would have helped of course, but his heart wasn't really in things like the organization of weddings. In her mind's eye she made a checklist of the details that top-notch Palm Beachers like herself loved to contemplate: morning clothes for the groom, a single white carnation worn in the English style—plain and unadorned with greenery or fussy sprigs of this and that—the reassuring Andover tie, pinstriped trousers beautifully pressed, the highly polished shoes that had seen at least thirty years of comfortable service. And Lisa? Really a superb compromise between virginal white and hypocrisy. The lace was more ivory than white, and yet it was a hymn to purity. Very well chosen. No color in the bouquet. That was a nice touch. Just plain white daisies hinting at the simplicity and the hatred of affectation that the very best people affected. Caroline's knowing, snobbish old eyes continued their appreciative tour of the arrangements. More than enough ushers, each in identical charcoal-gray cutaways, striped pants, stiff collars, ascots and pearl-gray gloves. Not a single dinner jacket in the room. She checked her watch. Nearly time. High noon, the only time to wed, in her opinion.

A few latecomers were still taking their seats, spirited smoothly from their

Rolls-Royces by the well-drilled boys from John Kavekos's Palm Beach Valet
Parking, ushered down the long, petal-strewn corridors of the fabulous old
house to the body of the room where their fellow guests were already craning
their necks like ostriches on amphetamine to check out who else was there,
and, more important, who wasn't. Caroline could have put them at rest. All
the "somebodies" were there. There were no "nobodies" in sight. Fords, du
Ponts, Meeks, Dudleys. And what looked like a whole cabbage patch of
Kennedys. The entire membership of the Coconuts, the elite club that met
but once a year on New Year's Eve, and whose invitations were more treasured than telephone calls from the president; the complete board of Poinciana Club Governors, the ever vigilant watchdogs of the Palm Beach social
scene; most of the Everglades Club, a judicious selection from the Bath and
Tennis Club. A handful from the Beach Club, and none at all, thank the
Lord, from the Palm Beach Country Club. Then there was the Hobe Sound
contingent, with Permelia Pryor Reed, the autocratic ruler of the Jupiter
Island Club, shepherding a small flock of Doubledays, Dillons, and Auchin-
closses.

The Stansfield roving eye returned to Scott, and once again the harmony
was replaced by discord. What on *earth* was he up to? He looked so incredibly—what was the silly word they used nowadays?—"uptight." And it was
round about that time that Caroline Stansfield's finely tuned antennae, legacy
of nearly a century of political and social intrigue, began to sense that there
was something horribly wrong with her world.

Fifty feet away her granddaughter Christie stood, surrounded by flowers
in what should have been paradise, but what felt like hell. On either side
great banks of white orchids framed her delicate beauty, mocking the agony
of her suspense with their majestic tranquillity. Her eyes, too, were on Scott
Blass. But unlike her grandmother, she knew exactly what he was thinking.
How much more time was there? What would they do when time ran out? In
the absence of God's guidance there would be nothing for it but to steal His
role. She tore her eyes away from the tormented figure by the telephone and
glanced at the ignorantly blissful couple. Could she do it to her father at this
late hour? Could Scott do it to his mother? She just didn't know, and she
knew that he didn't know either. Across the sea of expectant faces she managed to catch his darting eyes. Perhaps telepathy would strengthen him.
Christie concentrated hard and tried to send out the message of reassurance
she wanted so desperately to receive herself. The blue eyes thanked her, and
she managed a half smile. Scott. Poor Scott. He had been taken away from
her only to be given back by Fate in the wild paradox that went by the name
of Life. Scott who had abused her so dreadfully. Scott, who was now her
partner, who had been her lover, who was now so much more than that.

Father Bradley, rector of Bethesda-by-the-Sea, that colonnaded sanctuary
where Episcopalian Palm Beach was born and died, where it merged and
worshiped, was gearing himself up for the time-honored ritual. He looked
relaxed, suntanned, and at ease as he moved intimately among his phenomenally plutocratic congregation. He couldn't remember a wedding as

important as this one, and everything seemed to be under control; but even as he stood there, making polite small talk with the more influential wedding guests, he could not suppress the frisson of anxiety that kept coursing through him. He could do this thing in his sleep. Why should he be worried? Of course it was easier in church, but home was quite the right place for a second wedding, and especially the Stansfield home. Father Bradley looked at his watch. Two minutes to twelve and all was well. But why in God's *heaven* did he want to add the words "so far"?

Maggie had escaped briefly to a private world of memory. She was Lisa's oldest friend, but nowadays their worlds were far apart. This house, the grandeur of this wedding, symbolized the gap that had opened between them. In the old days it had been the sweat and the tears of the West Palm gym, the hurried hamburgers in the downtown delis, the joy and heartache of building a business that they had both loved so much, that she still loved. But now the delis had given way to catering by John Sunkel, the sumptuous food laid out lovingly on the white organdy and moiré-taffeta-covered buffet tables that lined the wall of the huge dining room next door. Years ago, in Lisa's apartment, long since transformed into the underground parking lot of a South Flagler skyscraper, there had been potted areca palms and the occasional impatients for color. Here there were deep purple and white orchids, and garlands of green vines snaking in breathtaking profusion over the buffet tables, running free over the spotless tablecloths, intertwining with the bowls of lush tropical fruits, kiwi, papaya, and muscat grapes. She had seen the small army of white-jacketed waiters as they prepared to receive the wedding throng; she had heard the ever green Peter Duchin, aristocratic spirit of Palm Beach parties, loosening his fingers on the Steinway piano; she had avoided the ubiquitous lens of Bob Davidoff, who had seen more society weddings than any other man alive, and she had noted the understated flowers on the four-tiered wedding cake, which replaced the tiny figures of bride and groom, which she, and the rest of America, would have unthinkingly preferred. They were perhaps little things in themselves, but they spoke volumes. They were all part of the silent language by which these people recognized each other. It was a secret society, full of signs and signals, of gestures and unspoken intimations. Things were "done." Things were "not done." Nobody taught you. Nobody could. You learned by osmosis. By being it. By living it. By the time you were a teenager you could pick an impostor from forty feet. It was as simple and as impossible as that. What rule dictated *eight* bridesmaids, all in identical pastel dresses? Who decided that the wedding presents should be laid out for all to see on white damask-covered tables in the library? Why Taittinger champagne? It was all a mystery, and Maggie couldn't help feeling totally shut out.

She turned to look at Lisa, and at once the familiar affection flooded back into her heart. Lisa, who had suffered so much and was, at last, poised on the brink of happiness. But why was Christie so white and Scott so deathly pale? And why was Caroline Stansfield watching them, her wise old face all wrinkled up with worry and alarm? And, as these unsettling thoughts came

winging into her suddenly active mind, Maggie picked up on the subterranean vibrations. Dear God, something awful was about to happen. She felt
her hand fly involuntarily to her mouth, the saliva dry on her tongue. No.
Surely not. Not at this late stage. Could the sins of the fathers be the last of
the wedding guests?

~ 1 ~

*B*OBBY STANSFIELD CAUGHT the wave and for a brief moment it was his world. Beneath his feet the surfboard leaped and reared, and inside his chest his heart went with it. It was getting late, and the sun was weary behind the palm trees, the dancing shadows of gold rushing across the surface of the sea. This would be the last breaker of the afternoon, and it looked like it was the day's best.

Like an avenging bird of prey he swooped down on the waiting beach, his body crouched in the classic surfer's pose, and as he sailed toward the sand his soul flew too—thankful for the day and for its beauty. In this life there were few moments like this, and although he was only thirteen he knew how to recognize them.

The wave was nearly spent now. Bobby would see it out in style. He arched his back and tensed his legs as he felt the board's energy running out, and then, with a shout of what might have been farewell he lunged up toward the pale blue of the Florida sky. His eyes followed the mad kaleidoscope of textured colors as his body embraced the chaos. Sky, scudding clouds, the pink beach cabana, the champagne bubbles of the surf before the warm darkness beneath the North End rollers. For a few seconds he allowed the current to take him, safe in the confidence of his strong arms and legs, buffeted by the undertow of the waves. He felt the rough sand against his chest, the popping in his ears as the pressure built, and then he was going upward to reclaim the world he had so recently departed. Bobby broke the surface. He was cleansed of the fantasy.

He had made the journey a thousand times. A hundred yards across the still-warm sand, a hundred more along the bleached-out boardwalk to the bubbling tarmac of the road. Sometimes it was a laughing, joking journey as the other surfers, their boards dangling from wiry, sun-bronzed arms, their salt-stained hair pulled and plucked by the late summer Palm Beach breeze, traveled homeward with him. Today, however, Bobby was alone and grateful for it. Soon he would be back in the great big throbbing house, the engines of its constant activity roaring and grinding, impossible to ignore or to escape.

He climbed onto his bicycle, slung his board casually beneath one arm, and set off down North Ocean Boulevard.

At the imposing gates of the big house, he decided on a whim to change the pattern of his journey. He'd take just one more look at the waves. Sometimes you could predict the next day's surf, from the sky, from the breeze, from the activity of the dive-bombing pelicans. So, leaving his board and his bike in their usual corner of the cavernous garage, he slipped along the side of the mighty house toward the breakwater that protected it from the unpredictable sea.

His father's den, a circular room, attached as a post-Mizner addition, was a feature on the journey. It was Bobby's habit to take a quick look through the window. The whole family was in awe of the imposing senator. Everyone, with the notable exception of his mother. Sometimes he would be dictating a speech at the big kneehole desk, his rich sonorous voice wrapping itself indulgently around the high-sounding platitudes, a smile of the purest pleasure on his face as he contemplated the reactions of some future audience. Or he might be catching a ball game, a thick cut-glass goblet in his right hand, sipping appreciatively at the dark amber bourbon he liked to drink in the evenings. Rarely, with his feet resting regally on a tapestry footstool, a crumpled copy of the *Wall Street Journal* across his still tight stomach, he would be snoring contentedly in the worn, chintz armchair. Today, however, he was doing none of those things. He was making love to someone on the sofa.

Bobby Stansfield froze, and his baby-blue eyes almost popped right out of his teenage head. The question of what to do did not for one moment arise. It wasn't every day that a son got to see his father on the job, and he wasn't going to miss a millisecond of it. Conflicting emotions coursed through him —fear, excitement, fascination, disgust—as intertwined as the unlikely lovers on the sofa of the den. Bobby was appalled, but the curiosity of youth held him rigidly in place.

Senator Stansfield was clearly no Rudolph Valentino. He was going at lovemaking with the same caution, sensitivity, and sophistication that had always characterized his immensely successful political career. It was a frontal assault, the position uncompromisingly missionary, the finer nuances of sensuality abandoned. The disturbing sounds of sexual activity drifted through the open window on the hot, liquid air to merge uneasily with the other sounds of the late Florida afternoon—the gentle hiss of the lawn sprinklers, the muted roar of the surf—and were to Bobby perhaps the most unsettling aspect of the whole remarkable business. Nobody had prepared him for this in the yard at school where "the facts of life" had been as available as booze and cigarettes.

Who on earth was the girl? The long suntanned legs provided a clue. The white shoes, still precariously in place, clinched it. It was Mary-Ellen. No question. His mother's maid. Christ! Bobby went hot and cold as his fevered mind considered the implications. First there was the matter of screwing the hired help. Second, and rather more pressing, was the question of jealousy.

As far as he was concerned Mary-Ellen had all the qualities of a beautiful angel, and Bobby was not a little in love with her. She was funny, bright, and vivacious—all the attributes that his three bun-faced sisters so conspicuously lacked—and the very last place in the world that Bobby had ever expected to see her was beneath his father on the sofa.

Bobby watched transfixed. Both lovers were still fully clothed. His father's bright green poplin trousers hung loosely around his knees, and the navy-blue Brooks Brothers shirt still hid the powerful frame of his upper body. Mary-Ellen, too, had not taken time out to undress—and through the wide-open window Bobby could see the white cotton uniform rucked up to the waist, caught a glimpse of candy-pink-striped cotton briefs. Again the disgust rushed through him, but the Stansfield blood told him there were all sorts of points to be picked up from a close observation of this scene. The emotions could be sorted out later. For now, the trick was to catch the action.

And then, quite suddenly, the thought crashed into his mind like a breaking tidal wave. Mother! Did mother know? Would mother know? What on God's earth would she do if and when she knew?

But while Bobby struggled to deal with the thought of his mother, the sofa's cargo was about to conclude its business. There was a frantic intensification of movement as the lovers danced in a maelstrom of flailing limbs. Suddenly Mary-Ellen's legs seemed to lose their coordination as they set off in a wild rhythm, thrashing the air, shaking, twitching, and vibrating as the shuddering feeling took her. For his father, too, the music had apparently stopped and he collapsed, exhausted, like a puppet on a suddenly severed string.

To Bobby—unwilling voyeur, witness to his father's infidelity, jilted by the Mary-Ellen of his fantasy—it seemed that in that brief moment his childhood had disappeared forever.

BOBBY STARED out moodily across the steam-ironed lawns to the glass-topped sea. It was only eleven o'clock but the sun was already imposing its will on Palm Beach, the beautiful town its slave and mistress. The early morning breeze had gone, and the lazy pelicans, content before to be passengers on the wind, now had to work for their prey. Theirs was the only sign of industry in the damp heat. Bobby himself lay propped up on the white-toweled sun bed, his thin, adolescent body baked honey brown by the southern sun. By his side the transistor radio played Connie Francis.

Caroline Stansfield's attitude toward direct sunlight was in contrast to her son's. Her skin a delicate, lily white, she sat shielded from the wrinkle-dispensing rays under a vast cream canvas umbrella. Her distaste for the sun was considered something of an eccentricity by the family and it was quite acceptable to make fun of it. Caroline would join in the somewhat stylized jokes at her expense and her small and precise features would light up with one of her rare, gracious smiles when the family made cautious fun of her. In many ways her preference for the shade was symbolic of her role within the Stansfield family. It was generally agreed that the limelight was the province of the gregarious, extrovert senator and, to a lesser extent, of the noisy children. But that did not diminish her undoubted authority. When Caroline Stansfield spoke, which was not often, everybody listened and nobody was quite sure why. Was it the pedigree stretching back to the eighteenth century? The extraordinarily substantial block holding in IBM? The quiet, unmistakable authority of her patrician voice? Nobody knew. One thing was certain; it was no longer her physical attraction. Perhaps she had once possessed a "fine" appearance—that euphemism among the rich and well-born for what the less fortunate might have described as "plain"—but the years had taken their toll. The generous childbearing hips had functioned well, but six children—two, like Macbeth, "untimely ripped" from her by Caesarean section—had not helped. Her bust, too, was large and formless, legacy of the religious breastfeeding her role of earth mother had demanded. In short, as a sexual object Caroline Stansfield left much to be desired, and, as a result, Senator Stansfield—who had always required a skinful of vodka before each dutiful procreative dance with his unalluring but phenomenally well connected wife—now avoided her bed completely. Most people didn't realize that Caroline herself preferred it that way.

Through the sultry night Bobby had been in an agony of indecision about what he should do, and the various elements of his personality were at war one with another. Part of him was sure that the thing to do was nothing. Hearts grieved only over what eyes saw and tongues repeated. Everyone knew that. By saying nothing he would save his mother pain and keep the faith with his adulterous father. On the other hand it could be argued that his duty was to tell his mother. Perhaps if she knew of her husband's extracurricular activities she would be able to nip them in the bud before unspeakable things like divorce or separation reared their ugly heads. But there was another element in the emotional equation, one that had been passed on in the blood, one that only a Stansfield could experience. For the very first time in his life Bobby found himself exposed to a commodity for which he had a genetically determined liking. Power. For a century the Stansfields had been addicted to it. They had fought for it, prayed for it, risked all for it, and they had never been able to get enough. The Senate, the Supreme Court, the great departments of government had all yielded up their fruits of office to generations of ambitious, cunning Stansfields. The presidency alone had escaped them, and, in their beds at night, all the family members worth their salt dreamed endlessly of this, the ultimate "fix" of power.

There was no escaping the fact that Bobby now possessed power. He had the drop on his mighty father at last. But here again there was a dilemma. On the one hand it was true that for thirteen years he had put up with the boisterous tyranny, the ceaseless exhortations to excel, the unthinking, almost casual cruelty, the scorn and humiliation when he, the eldest son, had failed to live up to the vaulting ambition of the Machiavellian senator. To that extent revenge would be welcome, and even intensely pleasurable. But at the same time, and despite the undeniable beauty of his predicament in that respect, Bobby didn't feel at all good about it. Okay, so his father had been an insensitive and demanding taskmaster, but he was a pretty impressive figure nonetheless and Bobby was enormously proud of him. Funnily enough this whole business hadn't really diminished his respect one iota. Quite the opposite. After all, making it with a gorgeous twenty-year-old two short weeks after one's sixtieth birthday just had to be pretty hot shit.

Then there was Mary-Ellen. Mary-Ellen, who'd been able to turn him on like an electric light when she sashayed across the room. Funny, kind Mary-Ellen who made him laugh, and who laughed at life. Suddenly her job security didn't look so good anymore. Part of him cared about that. With an effort he forced the thought from his mind. Stansfields had been programmed to control their emotions. Toughness was the quality they were supposed to value. Their hearts were allowed to bleed for America, for the poor, for the weak, for the hungry, but the needing friend came way down on the list of priorities. Too bad people would get hurt. People always got hurt. *He* had been hurt. What mattered was that he possessed power, and he had been taught that the thing you did with power was to *use* it. The only real question was how.

And so as the tough side of Bobby Stansfield warred with the tender he shifted uncomfortably on the formidably comfortable sun bed as the horns of his dilemma dug into him. Then, quite suddenly, the decision was made. It made itself. Life was like that. Half an hour deciding when one would get out of bed, and then the surprised realization that you have thrown back the blankets. Connie Francis's insistent plea for greater consideration from her lover died in midphrase as Bobby flicked the transistor's switch.

"Mother, there's something I've been wanting to say to you."

Caroline Stansfield looked up, a resigned, unflappable expression on her face. Speeches that started out like this often contained discouraging news. A dent in the car, in the boat, in the pride? There wasn't a lot that could faze her, few things that couldn't be straightened out one way or another. That was one of the advantages of being a Stansfield. Perhaps the most important advantage.

"What is it, dear?"

Bobby made his voice as serious as he could, the sort of voice you used when the early voting returns were unfavorable.

"Mother. I've thought a lot about whether I should tell you this. I'm in a pretty terrible position, and I don't want to be disloyal to dad . . ." His voice trailed off uncertainly.

Caroline Stansfield winced inwardly. The field of possible disasters had been narrowed down drastically. It began to look as if she were going to be embarrassed, and of all the feelings in the world that was the one she experienced least and disliked most.

"You know there are some things that are often best left unsaid, Bobby."

Bobby had reached the point of no return. "I think you have the right to know that father and Mary-Ellen are having an affair."

Pain and distaste fought for control of Caroline Stansfield's facial expression. It was not, however, the content of the news that upset her. That was about as interesting as yesterday's cold potatoes. Her husband had been chasing the prettier female staff for years now. Some of them had even found it necessary to leave, without of course mentioning the reason for their departure to Caroline. By her silence on the subject she had in effect condoned it. Really, it suited her quite well. Emotionally, Fred Stansfield was still a child. His sexual adventures were the adult equivalent of childhood candy, the pat on the head, mommy's good-night kiss. Sex and votes were his method of keeping the score, his way of knowing that he was still loved—and in both he dealt in quantity rather than quality. Certainly she knew all about Mary-Ellen. She rather liked her. Full of spirit, ambitious for the good things in life. What more natural than that she should let the senator seduce her, the man who was the symbol of all the money and power she coveted but could never hope to have?

No, the maddening thing was that now things were out in the open, where they had no right to be; and that meant something would have to be done about them.

Wearily she forced herself to confront the immediate problem. Appearances had to be kept up. She managed a watery laugh, and accompanied it with an amused, patronizing expression.

"Oh, really, Bobby. What can you mean? Where on earth did you get that extraordinary idea?" Had he caught the smoldering glances? Seen Fred goose Mary-Ellen in the corridor?

Bobby took a deep breath as he plowed on. "I saw them screwing on the sofa in his den."

In many ways Caroline Stansfield's whole life had consisted of an endless training program in how best to survive unfortunate situations such as this. At the rarefied heights of the social pyramid on which she existed the emotions had to be mastered, suppressed, controlled. People like her would always keep their cool because they had been so effectively tutored in hiding their feelings.

So, Caroline just said, "Oh, dear."

"The caterpillars have eaten the citrus. Oh, dear."

"The town council has refused the variance on the beach cabana. Oh, dear."

Whatever response Bobby had expected, this had for sure not been it. With the wind metaphorically billowing his sails, he had run slap bang into the doldrums of his mother's magnificent indifference.

There wasn't anything to say.

"I just thought you ought to know," he added lamely, to cover his confusion. It seemed the world was a more complicated place than he had ever imagined.

⟶

MARY-ELLEN WAS vaguely aware that trying on one's employer's clothes was a bit of a cliché, but she was enough of a dreamer to ignore that. Anyway, she saw it as one of the perks of the job. To Mary-Ellen, who loved the good things in life—and especially the expensive good things—Caroline

Stansfield's closet, scrupulously air-conditioned to protect against the ubiquitous Palm Beach mildew, was indeed a magical place. Swathed from head to toe in a full-length ranch mink, she stood back to admire the effect in the long mirror.

She was not Caroline Stansfield's size, but with mink that didn't seem to matter. Ball gowns were a different story. With them it was vital to get the measurements right, and Mary-Ellen knew that Mrs. Stansfield never had less than three fittings at Martha's, the chic Worth Avenue store where she bought many of her evening clothes. Mink, however, was not so much clothes as a statement, and this mink was a very substantial statement indeed —far more explicit than anything you get from a bank. Mary-Ellen gathered it around herself tightly, hugging the soft, warm fur to her tiny waist as she pirouetted, flicking her long black hair from side to side, experimenting with the effect. Outside the thermometer was way into the middle eighties as the unforgiving sun poured down on the hot sand, but in Mrs. Stansfield's bedroom the temperature was rock solid at seventy degrees, the colder air from the separate closet air-conditioning system wafting past Mary-Ellen as she modeled the fur in front of the mirrored door.

God, she was happy. Everything was happening for her. She loved this job. The vast, rambling old house with its Mizner architecture, the jewels, the servants, the exotic food, constant parties, the cars and the cheerful chauffeurs, famous guests, the shimmering Olympic-size pool, the ogling sons, the gracious mistress, the senator . . . Senator Fred Stansfield. His semen inside her. This all-powerful man, who lunched at the White House, headed the Senate Foreign Relations Committee—whatever that meant—who appeared on the cover of *Time* and *Newsweek*. Who cared that he was three times her age? She'd always been drawn to older men, to their worldly wisdom, their sophistication, to the security they symbolized.

Mary-Ellen's body began to tingle at the delicious thought of her lover, and she wrapped the coat around her more closely. Really she should be naked, the fur caressing her warm skin. That would be nice. The senator making love to her while she wore his wife's mink coat. For a split second she paused. Had Fred Stansfield been telling the truth when he had said that his wife and he had an "understanding," that actually she didn't mind him making love to her maid? It seemed pretty odd, but then these people were different. Wonderfully, gorgeously different. They were so much richer than anyone else. With an effort Mary-Ellen banished her doubt. She didn't like to hurt people, and she believed the senator when he told her that it was all right. That made it so much better. She was safe. Safe in her beautiful job— able to stand in the middle of a life she had always dreamed of having, and as a participant not just a spectator. There was a sense in which *she* was the senator's wife, that this was indeed *her* fur coat.

Once again the flame of sensuality flickered. She would allow herself to turn it up . . . just a bit. Still watching herself in the mirror, she let the coat hang open. Her legs were good—very good. Slowly she lifted up the knee-length white skirt of her uniform to show the cotton briefs, a dramatic contrast to the black stockings and brown mink. With her left hand she hitched the skirt up high, and with her right she drew down the panties to midthigh, admiring the visual effect of the collage she had created.

"Do you like that coat, Mary-Ellen?"

The voice was Caroline Stansfield's, and she was standing in the doorway to the bedroom. Her question was simple, direct. There was no edge to it. None at all. It appeared that she really wanted to know whether Mary-Ellen liked her coat.

Mary-Ellen felt the shock wave hit her. The rosy red flush of acute embarrassment invaded her cheeks. "Oh, Mrs. Stansfield, I'm so dreadfully sorry. I really shouldn't have . . . but it was just so beautiful. All your things are so beautiful."

"I'd like you to have it, Mary-Ellen."

"What?"

"It's yours. I'd like you to keep it. As a present."

Mary-Ellen wondered if in some mad way her mind was playing tricks on her. Was Mrs. Stansfield in fact screaming abuse at her, yelling at her to take off the coat, while her fevered brain misinterpreted the words, desire the mother of invention? "You mean it's mine? You want me to have it, to take away with me?"

Caroline Stansfield smiled a kindly smile. Really this was a very nice girl. Quite unspoiled. Fresh, vivacious—and very, very pretty. It was easy to see why her husband found her so irresistible. She had never understood what he had seen in some of the others, but there was no doubt that Mary-Ellen was uniquely desirable. Life was really so cruel. At times, the cruelty was so unnecessary. Why couldn't Fred draw the drapes like any other respectable man cheating on his wife? Really, it was most inconsiderate of him—especially as she was the one who had to clean up the mess, pick up the pieces. Strangely enough, she felt sorry for the lovely little maid. She'd been a real gem. Her clothes beautifully kept, suitcases perfectly packed, everything always in its place. Now of course she'd have to go. It was a question of form.

But it would have to be done carefully. There was only one really important thing on this earth and that was the Stansfield name. It must be safeguarded at all costs. This girl lived in West Palm Beach and West Palm was only a bridge away across the lake. It would not do to have her bad-mouthing the Stansfields. Wouldn't do at all. Not that she thought for one second that Mary-Ellen was that type of person. Far too nice.

A great tear of relief and joy began to form in the corner of Mary-Ellen's eye. Far from being berated she had just been given a present of incomparable beauty, a thing that never in her wildest dreams had she thought of possessing. Great waves of innocent affection shot out from her toward the cause of her happiness. Her mind raced as her lips tried to find the suitable words of thanks.

But Caroline Stansfield's upraised hand halted her fumbling speech before she could begin it. "Now, Mary-Ellen, there was one other thing I wanted to discuss," she said.

"IT LOOKS like our fine neighbor is going to run Nixon close. Gallup's got 'em neck and neck." The senator sat at the end of the long, highly polished mahogany dining table, the *Wall Street Journal* propped open in front of him. At the Stansfield family breakfast he was the only one allowed to read the daily newspapers, and this gave him a considerable advantage over everyone else. As usual he was making the most of his privileged position.

The Stansfield children groaned openly.

The Kennedys' Mizner on North Ocean Boulevard had gone up a year or two after the Stansfield home, and from the lawn of their house the ugly bulwarks of the massive Kennedy seawall could be seen pushing out aggressively over the North End beach.

"I think Kennedy can win." Bobby, sitting on his father's right in the traditional position of the eldest son, was playing devil's advocate. On occasions like this, only Senator Stansfield's opinions were "correct."

"Rubbish, Bobby. Shows how little you know. Nixon'll bury him. Kennedy gets Massachusetts, Maine, New York—the eastern liberal states. Nixon sweeps the South, the West, and the Midwest. No contest."

"Well, I certainly hope so," said Caroline Stansfield from the other end of the table. "It would be so inconvenient from the traffic point of view to have a president just up the road. There are quite enough sightseers from the mainland anyway."

Her husband grunted his agreement. "And all those Secret Service people crawling all over the beach and snooping into everything," he added gloomily. For the briefest of moments he allowed himself to dream. Twenty years ago there had been a chance at the presidency for him, but the glittering prize had escaped him. God, how he had wanted it, the power and the glory, and all the trappings of high office that went with it—Secret Servicemen included. He snapped back into optimism.

"It won't happen. Can't happen."

Caroline's quietly determined voice disagreed with him. "I'm not sure you're right, dear. You know, I saw Jack Kennedy and his wife in Green's last Sunday. They go in there after church at St. Edward's. My word, she's pretty, and with lots of style. And he's really very attractive. I'm afraid they make poor Nixon look like he's hustling real estate, or something worse. I think looks are getting so important nowadays. Especially with all that television. You're always saying that, dear."

Fred Stansfield put his cup down on the shimmering table rather harder than was strictly necessary. Both his wife and his son were contending with him openly at the breakfast table in an area in which he was considered the acknowledged expert. Far worse, they were suggesting that a Kennedy was about to make it to the White House.

To an outsider the Stansfields and the Kennedys appeared to have much in common. Both families were rich, had been Palm Beach neighbors for a quarter of a century, and now each had representatives in the most exclusive club in America, the United States Senate.

There, however, the similarities ended. Fred Stansfield was the epitome of the difference. From his silver gray, Brylcreemed patrician hair to his immaculately polished brown slip-on tassel loafers, worn of course with no socks, the senator was pure, old Palm Beach. The tattered, green Everglades club blazer, the deep, rich tan, and the cream linen shirt merely confirmed his aristocratic status.

As far as he was concerned the Kennedys were pushy social climbers— about as grand as Ole Opry. What was worse, they were northern Democrats who dared to live, at least part of the time, in a staunchly southern Republican town. To the Stansfields the Kennedys were class enemies, liberal poseurs who had sold out to the dreaded ethnic minorities, adventurers who had turned their backs on their own kind in order to achieve power. Okay, so he himself had occasionally to woo the Negro and Jewish vote, but he would encourage neither group to enter his front door. Then there was the whole Catholic thing. Bells and smells. Popery. That alone was the kiss of death in real Palm Beach high society. In this town the WASPs had stings and the Kennedys were thoroughly ostracized. The only galling aspect of the whole business was that since old Joe Kennedy had been turned down by the Everglades Club, the Kennedys had withdrawn from the game, refusing to show the slightest inclination to participate in the society that was so eager to exclude them.

The three Stansfield daughters, scenting the beginnings of a promising family argument, sided as always with their charismatic father. That was usually, at least in political matters, the winning team. Bunny Stansfield, nineteen and a prelaw student, chipped in. "They'll never elect a Catholic in preference to Eisenhower's veep. Anyway, we don't think he's so good looking. *We* think he's a creep."

Bunny Stansfield always spoke for the other girls, and the three tended to vote as a bloc.

It was a way to survive in the male-dominated Stansfield environment.

Fred Stansfield beamed his approval on his three unremarkable daughters. The politician in him was trained to accept support from wherever it came.

"Of course you're right, Louise. Obviously they're teaching you something up there in Charlottesville." He refused to call his children by their nicknames.

Caroline Stansfield stared dreamily down the ancient table. In many ways, she thought, the gleaming wood looked more permanent, more substantial than the entire assembled Stansfield clan. So for that matter did Brown, the ancient but distinguished English butler, who hovered ineffectually at the vast sideboard. For some reason, long since forgotten, it was traditional practice for him to pour the hot Kenya coffee. This he did with a shaky, uncertain hand, lending an element of danger to the family breakfast. Otherwise one helped oneself—kedgeree, bacon and eggs in a silver salver, Kellogg's corn flakes. Caroline liked this meal best. It was the one time everyone was guaranteed to be present—a sort of informal meeting at which family business could be discussed.

"I'm sure you're right, dear. You usually are." Caroline conceded defeat; Fred would need that victory to survive the next little missile.

Fred Stansfield beamed down the table at his wife. He stuffed a large piece of toast into his mouth and leaned back in his chair contentedly. It was going to be another good day. Some letters with the secretary. A game of golf at the club, followed by a heavy lunch. And then, in the late afternoon, perhaps a delicious action replay with Mary-Ellen. Lazily he pushed away the Limoges china plate, its contents half eaten. Must look after the waistline. He owed that to the pretty maid.

"I'm afraid I've had to let Mary-Ellen go," said Caroline Stansfield pleasantly to nobody in particular. She glanced around the table for a reaction to her news.

Bobby's head was low, his eyes apparently fascinated by the heavy linen napkin he saw every day of his life. He felt the color begin to rise up his cheeks.

"Ah," said the senator. Words for the first time in many years entirely failed him.

The girls were united in their approval. The sensationally attractive Mary-Ellen had put noses out of joint all over the place.

Joe, the youngest son, was totally unmoved. Nine was a bit too young to see the point of Mary-Ellen. Tom at twelve was the only one who spoke. He was not too young. "Oh, mom, why? I thought she was really neat."

"Well, yes, she was rather 'neat'—I'm sure we all thought that, didn't we, Fred? The fact is that just lately she hasn't been concentrating on her job, so I let her go."

Her tone was conversational, but not one single person at the table, her husband included, dared to question Caroline Stansfield's authority. Mary-Ellen would not reenter their universe.

FOR MARY-ELLEN, the last few days had been hell on earth, but now, as the wet heat of the humid summer gave way to the dry freshness of the Florida winter, there seemed to be new hope. The excitement of the election had helped. They had stayed up all night as the mighty electoral battle had raged. At seven fifteen in the evening with the CBS computer predicting a Nixon landslide, and with Tommy and her dad sunk in the depths of despair, Mary-Ellen had been rooting for a Republican victory, but strangely, when one hour later the forecast was revised to a Kennedy victory by 51 percent of the vote, she found herself joining in the cheers. Kennedy might live there but they had all hated him. The Stansfields in particular would be plunged into gloom at the thought of their neighbor in the White House, and paradoxically Mary-Ellen found herself wanting the thing they feared most. They had stayed up all night demolishing the six-packs, and cheering the Democrat victories until five forty-five in the morning when Michigan had put JFK over the top. It had been the dawn of a new day, and as West Palm had nursed its

hangover and the Negroes had gone wild with hope at the promise of the
New Frontier, Mary-Ellen's spirits had revived.

On the bottom of the bed, a living representation of Mary-Ellen's
changed attitude, lay Caroline Stansfield's fur coat. No longer was it an ankle-length testimony to a bygone era. It had updated itself, and like the
brand-new president, it was looking forward and not back. With the effrontery of the natural anarchist, Mary-Ellen had taken the scissors to it, and in a
daring morning it had been transformed to the new fashionable length just
above the knee. She had used the extra material provided by the radical
surgery to make a fur pill box hat just like the one she had seen Jackie
Kennedy wear on the news, and now it lay with an identical muff next to the
shortened coat on the bed.

Mary-Ellen peered out of the window hopefully. Was the freshness in the
air the first of the winter cold spells that could lower the temperature to the
forties and below? She prayed that it was. Screw the citrus crop. What she
wanted was to wear her coat. There were few enough days in Florida when
she could get away with it.

Impatiently she swept it up and put it on over the T-shirt and jeans,
fighting back the bittersweet memory of the Stansfield bedroom. It was hers
now. A bribe for her silence? An anesthetic for the pain? A hand-me-down
cast-off for a defeated rival? Whatever. It didn't matter anymore. There was a
life to live. Here. Now. At the beginning of the sixties. And the doctored fur
would be her talisman in the years ahead. When the blades of the scissors
had cut into it they had severed more than the skins. They had cut the
umbilical cord that had bound her to the past. She was free at last. Free to be
herself.

Mary-Ellen threw back her head and looked at herself in the mirror.
Screw them all. She could laugh at the world. She was young and very beautiful and if Palm Beach was not possible for her then West Palm was.

But even as she challenged fate with her beauty and her vitality she
nursed her secret thought. One fine day, if God blessed her with a daughter,
her child would be what she could never be. She would send her across the
bridge to conquer the promised land that had so cruelly expelled her.

THE MIND-BENDING, ear-shattering rock 'n roll blasted all thought from the
brain. Like a hurricane surge it blanketed everything around—people, machinery, the shimmering air in which it vibrated. There was no fighting it.
You had to give in, to surrender completely.

Like a ballet dancer performing his own intricate pas de deux, Jack Kent
weaved his magic on the railway roundabout. It was his best moment, repeated a couple of hundred times a day. The train started slowly on its
undulating course, and its human cargo, all souped up and ready to go, were
grooving on the excitement building within them. Shouting to friends in the
audience on the parched grass, to others in neighboring box cars, they
screamed to be heard above the wild, all-enveloping music as the train began
to accelerate. Supposedly Jack's job was to collect the tickets and to make

sure everyone was safely seated, but here he was the rodeo cowboy, the essence of the fairground, his every movement amplifying the tingling feelings of scarcely suppressed sexuality, of violent danger that were just below the surface in everyone. Holding on, and letting go. That was what it was all about. His ropelike muscles, smooth and shining with a thin film of axle grease, contracted and relaxed as, like Spiderman, he moved effortlessly among the howling passengers, launching himself bodily from the stationary boardwalk onto the speeding cars, only to return a second later, his short, powerful legs whacking solidly into the timbers of the platform. Pain and destruction hovered all around. One missed step, one tiny miscalculation and Jack Kent would have been the baloney he so often talked. To pile on the pressure he would make it more difficult for himself, light a cigarette, drink a can of beer, comb his black oiled hair—flicking it competently into the duck's-ass style as he diced with death.

All the time he kept up the dialogue with the paying customers. "Hey, honey. You's sure a cute little thing. You hang on tight now. Take care." That way they came back for more. Sometimes a great deal more. Jack Kent's darting, practiced eyes told him everything. He could see the love light start in the teeny-bopper eyes, the legs crushed close together, the tautness in the pubescent tits. He's gotten to need the tight little up-turned asses, the slinky soft teenage skin, the doelike eyes of the virgins as they took it from him on the grass or standing up in the generator shed. He'd rip the clinging jeans down like some spoiled child tearing open the last of too many Christmas presents, and sock it to them with no thought of their pleasure or pain. They merged into one. Warm quivering contraptions that existed only to make him feel terrific.

Mary-Ellen had lost count of the times she'd watched her father work, and she never tired of it. Throughout her childhood she had followed the fair. In the early days Jack Kent had done it all. Hustled the darts, flogged the cotton candy, even spieled on the "let me guess your weight" spot. But when he had hit the railway he had come home. He was a natural. In two short years he had tripled the roundabout's income, been taken into partnership, and then bought out his partner. The money wasn't that good, but he'd had the sense to buy the ramshackle old wooden house in West Palm that had always been the family's security. Constantly on the road himself, he had made a home for his wife and for Mary-Ellen. It wasn't much of a place with its faded, peeling paint, broken slats, and warped, uneven timbers, but it was full of love and life. At night when she would return home it would loom up out of the darkness like some tramp steamer out of a pea-soup fog, the kerosene lamp flickering its welcome on the porch. Her father, if he was in town at all, would be drinking at Roxy's bar with Willie Boy Willis and Tommy Starr, but her mother would be home—and there would be the smell of chili on the heavy night air, the soft sounds of the country music that she loved, and the shout of welcome as she trod the creaking floorboards of the veranda.

Breathing in deeply, Mary-Ellen gathered the strength to shout above the music. "Dad's sure in good form today," she yelled.

Tommy Starr smiled and made to reply. Then he gave up, splaying his big hands open in a gesture of defeat. He stuck two huge fingers in his ears to make the point.

He smiled fondly at her, his great big craggy face breaking up in a look of total adoration. He could hardly remember when he hadn't loved her, and every day when he woke and each evening when he fell asleep he had experienced the bitter pangs of her rejection. Now, he had almost come to terms with the reality. She was too good for him, and unfortunately she knew it. It wasn't that she was stuck up or snobbish, just that she had dared to dream the dream. The town across the water had gotten to her, and now Palm Beach and all it stood for pulsed in her blood. It had been like that from the moment the Stansfields had taken her on. She had seen paradise, and West Palm had been forgotten. A little while ago there had been a chance. The rich, pompous assholes had fired her. Why he would never know. Mary-Ellen had been devastated, plunged into the very depths of depression, and it had hurt like hell to see her so upset. He had tried to cheer her up, to take her mind off the rat pack across the bridge, but still she had refused to see herself as the West Palm girl she was.

Once, one drunken evening, he had persuaded her father to take him home after a hard session in Roxy's. As Jack had led the way across the creaking porch with its empty rocking chair and its unraveling wicker furniture, there had been the sound of crying from the house's interior. They had gone to investigate and there by the light of the soundless, flickering TV Tommy had seen the vision that would remain engraved on his memory forever. Like some discarded, sad rag doll, Mary-Ellen lay across the brass bed, its rumpled, untidy sheets framing her perfect body. Inhabiting that no-man's-land between sleep and wakefulness she lay still, her white dress crumpled and dirty, only partially clothing her. One of the straps had fallen away from the shoulder, and from the upper border of her dress, a pink nipple protruded innocently, the crowning glory to a perfect conical breast.

Across her upper chest and above her lip, a thin film of sweat glistened. Her tousled, untidy hair lay on the pillow, framing the open face whose honest, uncomplicated beauty had so enslaved him. As he had stood there, peering into Mary-Ellen's innermost life, into her torment and her misery, he had experienced the shocking realization that he could never have her. Her anguish and sorrow were too strong for him. He could not compete with whatever had caused this emotion.

Mary-Ellen looked at him quizzically, watching the replacement of the smile with the puzzled expression of contemplation. Dear Tommy. So big, and safe. He was built like a mountain, and he would be as constant. For so many years she had listened to her father sing the praises of the hardworking construction worker he wanted her to marry, but although she had heard she had never believed. Always the siren voices had lured her to the land across the water where the titans lived, men who in their sophistication and worldly wisdom dwarfed Tommy Starr. But that was then, and this was now. She had been thrown out by the world she wanted, and she had gotten over the pain. Only a masochist would wish to prolong it. So at last she slipped her small hand into Tommy's massive one and laughed as she pulled him away to escape from the prison of sound which had held them.

It was high noon, and the crowd was braving the unforgiving heat. Mary-Ellen seemed to be thriving on it. Like the most delicate, most delicious hibiscus blossom she was all opened up. The simple white cotton dress told the world almost all it needed to know about her breasts—the perfect geometry, the pointed aggressive nipples, the faultless superstructure that neither needed nor received any artificial support. A big conch belt, brought back by her father from Albuquerque and her most prized possession, surrounded the small waist that in turn led down to long, lingering brown legs. She wore no stockings or tights, and the silhouette of white panties encasing the firm, boyish bottom was just visible through the thin material of her frock.

From time to time Tommy stole a glance at her, as if to reassure himself he wasn't dreaming. He hardly dared to entertain the idea but it seemed there had been a dramatic change in Mary-Ellen. He had noticed it a few days before, but now it was undeniable. There was a new cheerfulness about her, and it appeared that he was its main beneficiary. Her attitude toward him was different, and somehow he was no longer merely the dependable elder brother, the arm's length friend. Their relationship seemed to be hovering on the brink of something else entirely.

"So what d'ya think of the fair?" Mary-Ellen squeezed on the outsize hand.

Tommy wasn't thinking about the fair at all, but he was probably as happy as he had ever been. For him magic danced in the air, the cheap, tacky side stalls a magnificent background to the main event—the drama of his love for the girl by his side.

Mary-Ellen wanted him to like it. It was her childhood, its atmosphere filtered into her blood. Tommy's emotions were at her beck and call, desiring only to please.

"I like it real fine, Mary-Ellen."

"I guess you oughta see the headless corpse, or would you prefer the fattest man in the world?"

"I think we should take a ride on that ghost train."

"Okay, but now you be sure an' keep your hands to yourself. I've had to fight for my life in that darn thing before now."

The laughter bubbled from her throat, but the message was ambiguous. Tommy felt the blood begin to move within him. It rushed up like a fountain into his cheeks, coloring up the skin. At the same time it roared south, and with that well-known feeling of helplessness he sensed the buildup in his distending penis.

Mary-Ellen saw his confusion, and laughed louder. Her arm snaked out around his waist, building up the pressure. She, too, felt the buzz begin. Flicking her tongue over suddenly dry lips she allowed her gaze to wander downward. She could see its outline clearly, and she watched fascinated as it grew and grew. With an effort she tore her eyes away, but the vision remained in her mind as she guided Tommy toward the ghost train's pay booth.

Now, as they boarded the open coach and braced themselves for the voyage of surrogate suspense, she leaned in toward him, pushed herself up, and whispered suggestively in his ear.

"I didn't mean that, Tommy. About keeping your hands to yourself."

With a clatter the coach shuddered off into the darkness, and to Tommy's extraordinary delight the soft words and warm breath in his ear were replaced by the exquisite wetness of a probing tongue. His low-pitched moan of desire was in dramatic contrast to the shrieks of nameless horror in the murky gloom, as skeletons and demons flashed and glowed.

He half-turned toward Mary-Ellen, and cupping her warm cheeks in his hands he moved her face toward his. As if taking the sacrament at a first communion he bent his mouth toward hers, full of reverence and awe at this their first kiss. Mary-Ellen's knowing lips rose hungrily to meet his. At first she played with him, the touch feathery light, occasionally withdrawing, to return once more. Mouth half open she covered him with her warm, sweet breath, letting him smell her scent, feel her passion.

Tommy shook with excitement. He had never dreamed it could be like this. So slow, so intense. Already he was on some private astral plane of ecstasy, and it was only a kiss. It must go on and on. Nothing must stop it. He pushed in toward her, his penis rock hard inside the tight jeans, thrusting his body against hers.

Mary-Ellen heard the messages of his body and responded with her own. First she took his lower lip between her teeth, nuzzling it gently, and then her tongue was there, the wet oasis in the parched desert of dry lips. At first it was careful explorer, cautious, an inquisitive traveler in a foreign country, but then as the orchestra of passion struck up within her, it discovered courage. Now Tommy could taste the saliva, feel the darting invader as it made free with his mouth—a conquistador now, relentless and unforgiving in its pursuit of pleasure.

His strong arms held her to him, and she clung to him desperately, her left hand at his neck, her right at his chest. And then her right hand was on the move. Suspended in his own world of joy Tommy both wanted and feared what he knew would happen.

Mary-Ellen's hand reached its destination, and for a second she held him tightly through the straining denim. Then, her tongue, intertwined in his, she began very gently to rub him, sometimes letting her fingers trace the outline of his erection, at others massaging firmly with the flat of her hand.

In Tommy's mind the crazy thoughts crashed against the messages that zoomed in from the mad environment. The rocking, roaring boxcar careered around ridiculous hairpin bends and collided endlessly with saloon bar doors on which skeletons and nameless demons danced. Screaming coyotes howled in the darkness and ghostly cobwebs plucked at his hair and face as the divine fingers of his lover encouraged his passion. Mary-Ellen was loving him. At last it was happening. After all the years of desperate wanting, and now, here, at last—in the chaotic darkness of a fairground ghost train— ecstasy had arrived. It seemed a cruel and wonderful trick of Fate, to be handed heaven in a place in which it was impossible to receive it.

Mary-Ellen too was half aware of the paradox. She hadn't known that desire would take over so effortlessly. For so long Tommy had been one thing. Now, for reasons she could not understand, he was another. It was as if a veil had lifted. She had been blinded by the vision of Palm Beach, and the real world—of warm flesh and rampant needs—had been beyond her touch. Somehow the events of the past few weeks had healed her. She was a prisoner no more, living no longer in the fairy castles of fantasy, a slave to her ambition and lust for betterment. In the heat of the early afternoon, the scent of corn dogs, kabobs and roasted peanuts in her nostrils, the wailing laments of the country music wafting into her ears, she had found herself once more and it was a wonderful feeling. Like a reprieved prisoner under sentence of death, she had been spared and the world was new. Now she wanted above all to live, and the best way to do that was to love. To love this good man, who wanted her so badly. Whom now she so desperately wanted.

She looked into his face, revealed intermittently in the ghostly light, its kind features bathed in oranges, purples, and vivid greens as the train passed through grottoes of dread, and headless corpses dripped blood round about. There was so much there. The almost stricken look of the man suspended above the ultimate abyss, uncomprehending, wondering, powerless in the grip of Destiny. His mouth was open and his eyes were gleaming, the breath coming fast through distended nostrils. The gales of crackling laughter mocked the savage intensity of feeling, but they accentuated it too, emphasizing the peculiar beauty of the moment when hearts met and souls touched. She whispered to him, her voice firm in the storm of horror that surrounded them.

"I want you to make love to me, Tommy."

His voice was drowned in the adrenaline surge that had engulfed him. Yes. To make love to her. The sacrament. The beauty of wholeness. All his life he had wanted that.

"Yes."

"I want it here. Right now." Mary-Ellen's voice was insistent, urgent. Her hand pressed down hard on him, emphasizing her unmistakable meaning, invading his essence with the spears of pleasure.

"How?"

And then Mary-Ellen smiled at him. She hadn't known until now, but now she knew.

There would be a place for them. Somewhere a place. The moment demanded it, and its request was granted. In her laughing eyes Tommy saw she wanted to forget the humiliation of the past in the abandonment of the present. And he longed only to join her. As the coach slowed down he stood as she stood, jumped as she jumped, and in seconds they were together, hidden in the darkness as the empty boxcar trundled out of sight.

There was no time to wonder about it. No time to worry. Only time to hear the gurgling, abandoned laughter, to see the beautiful head thrown back, the passion glittering in the sparkling eyes, to feel the soft body crushed against him. For an age he held her, smelling the warm scent of her, his fingers running in wonderment over the soft skin of her neck. She was his, and here in the anonymous blackness, as the other seekers of thrills rushed past a few feet away from where they stood, he reveled in the joy of possession.

Electric screams knifed through the air, drawing from the human voyagers delighted yells of conspiracy as they milked the moment of its terror, but Tommy could only hear the pounding of his heart, could only feel the cool hands that were drawing him toward the union of bliss. He watched her closely, trying to etch her beauty into his mind. For him, the black, dirty wall against which she leaned was a frame of monumental loveliness, the dusty air they breathed fresh and sparkling as the first day of spring. She held him in both hands, her eyes locked on to his as, slowly, gently she pulled him toward her. Tommy felt the weakness in his legs, the throbbing rhythm in his stomach as he followed where she led.

Mary-Ellen leaned toward him, her warm breath painted onto his cheek, and the white dress raced up eagerly toward her waist, the white cotton panties plunging gratefully downward. She was the high priestess controlling and guiding the ancient ritual of love.

Tommy tried to slow each moment, unwilling to let go, but he was unable to hold back.

"I love you Mary-Ellen, oh my God I love you."

Mary-Ellen took him into her, her warmth comforting him, wrapping him in her love, making the home in which he would always live. She let out a long, shuddering sigh of contentment at the joyful peace that his presence brought. It was so right. It was how it should be, how it always should have been. This was the moment. The timeless moment of unity. Later there would be the sweet conclusion as their souls communed, but now there was the reality of the only true togetherness—awe-inspiring in its simplicity and its beauty.

Like sleepwalkers they moved as one, dancing to an ancient rhythm that had never been taught, never explained. They held each other close, swaying, inclining in the little motions that conjured up the exquisite sensations, bathing their minds in the potent potion of the purest pleasure. Sometimes they stopped, hovering on the abyss's brink, staring down in wonder at the lush valley that would be their destination. At others they swooped down, brave hawks with the wild wind beneath their wings, soaring above the cool streams and the green pastures of the paradise where they would live. They muttered soundlessly to each other, their lips moving as they sought in vain to express the inexpressible, oblivious to the mad hell that surrounded them on every side. The make-believe hell that had made possible their heaven.

Together they seemed to decide when the voyage must end, its mystic conclusion negotiated at some magic place where no thought lived, no words were spoken. For an eternity of time each lover was still, paying homage to the force of life that soon would move through them, bathing the fires with its balm, signifying an end, the new beginning. And then, at last, it was upon them. Creation's act, accompanied by two lovers' screams of ecstasy, harrowing, piercing in their reality among the clamorous counterfeits on every side.

~2~

LISA STARR SLIPPED her mind into top gear and went for the burn. From the screaming, protesting muscles the messages flooded back to her racing mind—pain and ecstasy, ecstasy and pain. You had to feel it, to suffer it if you were to take the class along with you. That was the secret. The air waves of the small, stuffy gym reverberated with the insistent drum notes as thirty pairs of track shoes beat out the rhythm of the aerobics routine.

"Higher. Get 'em higher." Lisa's yell was lost in the raucous sound of the stereo, but everyone knew what she was saying. All round the room the piston action of the dancing legs intensified, as their owners searched for the reserves of strength.

Lisa saw the increased effort. Great. They were going with her. All the way. There was exhaustion in the dripping, glistening faces, but there was something else too. Admiration, and gratitude. Lisa was teaching them to do something difficult, to seek and find that little bit extra. They were being taken to the limit, and the feeling was good.

Time for a change of pace.

"Jumping jacks, and one and two and three and four . . ."

Lisa liked this one. There was something so satisfying about the regimented geometry of the movement, the hands clapping above the head as the ever-mobile legs sprang apart, and then together.

For her, and for many of the class, this was coasting. Relaxation in the midst of total activity. They had needed the rest after the frenetic exertion of the knee raising. But not everyone found it easy. Lisa's eyes sought out her friend. Poor Maggie. She came religiously to the classes, and tried harder than anyone, but somehow she always looked like a spastic. It wasn't that she was ugly, and piece by piece her body looked passable, but somehow the effect of the whole was aesthetic disaster.

Unbeknown to Lisa, Maggie's eyes told a very different story as she gazed in open admiration at her friend and teacher. Sometimes Maggie wondered just which bit of Lisa's superb body carried off the ultimate prize. Her bottom, turning up in the perfectly flowing line of one side of a heart before heading down to join the immaculately sculpted upper thigh? Her tits, push-ing out self-confidently, impervious to the forces of gravity, crowned by the assertive, conical nipples as they pushed impatiently against the already soaked pink leotard? Her silky dark hair, with its dancing fringe, the page-boy bob rising and falling on her muscular shoulders? Or, perhaps, it was the face itself. Great big saucer eyes, blue as the Coral Sea. Lisa could make them so much wider, when she wanted to look surprised or interested, and they seemed to work on men like twin magnets. The small pert nose, which could wrinkle up in distaste. The generous, welcoming lips, which, when she was feeling good, would part to show the perfect teeth. Whichever way you looked at it you had to admit there had been cheating in the lottery of life. Lisa Starr just had too much.

In front of the class, Lisa forced herself to concentrate. These people were giving their all, and they wanted to see the color of yours. A moment's loss of attention and she would lose them, blow their confidence in her total commitment to the physical experience. Other teachers made that mistake, and their students would begin inexorably to dwindle. Lisa for sure didn't have that problem, nor did she intend to. This evening class was bursting at the seams, the prancing bodies all but touching as they fought to make every inch of the small floor count.

"Okay now, knee raising one last time. Go for it now. Feel the pain . . ." Lisa screamed the last word at the top of her voice, and with the furtive joy of group masochism the class pushed into overdrive. Once again the staccato beat rocked the wooden floor of the West Palm gym. Before her eyes Lisa could see the calories burning. Smell them, too. Through the open door the humid air of the early Florida evening wafted into the small room where it hung immobile, saturated with the sea's moisture, resisting scornfully the feeble attempts of the ancient ceiling fan to circulate it. Sweat soaked the skin-tight leotards, revealing the contours of the firm, muscular bodies be-neath.

"And twenty, now twenty more, and one and two . . ."

"Lisa, you're *cruel*." Maggie's joking wail was lost in the force field of violent concentration as muscles were once again asked to do the impossible, to incur the mighty oxygen debt.

Now Lisa herself was almost there, at the magical moment of transcen-dence when body and soul merged, when delicious agony melted into the total experience—the exercise high. Her body suddenly light, she had reached the cloud on which, it seemed, she could float forever. But she was the teacher. She couldn't leave the class behind, a straggling convoy, leaderless and abandoned, their engines seizing as they fought to keep up.

"Now we ease," she shouted. "Don't stop. Keep jogging, but relax now."

Groans of relief greeted her words, but the atmosphere of mutual con-gratulation was almost palpable.

"Hey, Lisa, where did they train you, Dachau?" shouted a big, muscular girl from the back.

Lisa joined in the general laughter. "It'd take more than whips and jackboots to make you shift ass, Paulene." She felt good. This was what she was paid for, but it was more than that, much more. In the faces of these girls was a respect she had not seen before she had taken this job. And it wasn't just an ego trip. She was doing them good, helping them to do themselves good. The results were actually visible. In looking better they were actually feeling better, and it showed in a thousand little ways. In six short weeks she had seen body postures improving, walks becoming more confident, the formerly shy girls cracking jokes, becoming more extroverted as they learned to like themselves more. It was incredibly rewarding, and Lisa wanted it to go on and on.

"Okay, you guys, now for some leg work."

Leopardlike, Lisa stretched herself out on the rubber mat.

Knees together, the weight of her torso balancing on splayed fingertips, she looked up at the sea of expectant eyes. What was their average age? Thirty? Twenty-five? Something like that. It was a good feeling for a seventeen-year-old to have them literally dancing to her command, performing to the crack of her ringmaster's whip. What would they do for her? What could she make them do? The little thrill of power shot through her as she watched them love her, saw them admiring her splendid body, jealous of it, wanting to possess it—and in the eyes of some of the girls just the faintest hint of something scarcely admitted, barely available to conscious thought. Yes, it was unmistakable. Like a fine Scots mist, hovering ethereally in the damp atmosphere was the heady scent of physical desire. Nothing was said, no action taken, but it was there in the shining eyes, in the sometimes lingering glances, in the torrents of intermixed hormones that coursed vigorously in the pumping blood. Lisa smelled it, knew it, but like the others she rejected it, forcing it down into her subconscious by an effort of will. There it lived on, giving a delicious subterranean meaning to the agony and the ecstasy of the physical exertion.

"Now I want you to work those buns. Turn those asses into beautiful things. Right leg raising thirty times. Go for it, and one and two . . ."

The music was softer now—the mind-blowing heavy rock of the exercise routine replaced by a more subtle sound—urging, caressing, creamy. Each phase of the hour-and-a-quarter advanced routine had a different character, and Lisa's thought processes slipped into the appropriate gear to complement them. Somehow this was always the sensual bit. Here the pain was absent. The class could probably cope with fifty or sixty leg movements on each limb but Lisa could happily keep going for half an hour. So for her the stretching movements were like scratching an itch, the delicious feeling of squeezing muscles that were already in the peak of physical condition. Now as she lifted her right leg out high to the side she felt the tautness in the gluteals, the warm glow in her groin as her vagina opened up, its lips levered apart and then forced together by the piston action of her lower limb. At moments like this Lisa wondered what it must be like to be made love to by a man.

Usually she was far too busy for such thoughts, but there was something about the glorious physical abandonment of the workout that summoned them up from some vasty deep. Here, buried in the blood, the sweat, and the tears, the flame flickered. Lisa wanted to be held in warm, strong arms, by someone who belonged to her, to whom she belonged. She wanted to feel the hard body against the hardness of hers. A man who would love her and please her all at once. Tender, strong, sensitive, powerful. It was a fantasy that she was determined time would turn into reality. Not now, but later. Soon.

Careful Lisa. Stay with their minds. *Be* with them.

"Okay, you girls. Go for it. Left leg, and one, and two, and three . . ."

Ten minutes more and it was nearly over. First the vital relaxation movements. The gentle stretching, the slow measured breathing.

"Okay, guys. That's it. Thank you and see you tomorrow."

"Oh, Lisa, you killed me today. I think I'm actually dead. No, really!" Maggie's affection beamed out in waves as she rested her hand on Lisa's damp shoulder.

"Nonsense, Maggie. You were moving like a dream. I noticed you several times. You're getting there, for sure."

"Listen, Lisa, I love you anyway, but thanks for the encouragement." Maggie was under few illusions about her performance. Sacks of potatoes had a way of looking more graceful. It was just like Lisa to spare her feelings. As far as Maggie was concerned Lisa could do no wrong, and she was content to bask in the warm glow of her aura.

"Come on, Maggs, let's get some coffee and something to eat. I get so hungry around this time."

Neither girl bothered to shower. That could wait. If they cleaned up and cooled down now the Florida humidity would have melted them again before they got home. Somehow the sweaty Lisa looked infinitely more alluring than the perspiring Maggie.

In the diner on Clematis they ordered decaffeinated coffee and doughnuts.

Maggie made her face all serious. "You know, Lisa, really you are so *good* at teaching that exercise thing. I think you should seriously think of doing it full time."

Lisa laughed. "You just think I'm soft. They might replace me with somebody who calls for a little effort in there."

"No, Lisa, I mean it. You're a natural. None of the other teachers can touch you. And it's not just me. Everybody in the class says it. Ronnie is getting pissed off that his other girls haven't got anyone in their classes anymore."

Lisa's laugh was rather more thoughtful. It was true, and it was becoming a bit of a problem. She was miles better than the others, and the consumers, not unnaturally, had noticed it. Ronnie was the guy who owned the gym, and it was true that over the last few weeks he had begun to cool toward her. If the other instructors were into a whispering campaign, she might just end up a victim of her own success. "Yeah, those cats are just longing for me to burn myself out, screw a ligament or something. Well, for sure they've got a long wait. This body intends to hold together all the way."

Maggie saw the determination in her friend's eyes. Sometimes it seemed to her that Lisa was composed of the finest tempered steel. Nothing seemed to throw her. She was only a year away from the worst tragedy that could have befallen anyone, and yet she had bounced back, stronger than before, tested and not found wanting by the dreadful experience. It was not that she hadn't suffered the grief. She had felt the pain all right, because she was tough, not hard. There was a difference.

Maggie sowed the seed. "Me and a couple of the girls were saying you ought to branch out on your own. Start your own place. You'd strip Ronnie of all his customers if you did. We'd all go with you, to a man."

They both smiled at the reference to the opposite sex. Some habits didn't give up without a fight.

Lisa looked thoughtful as she spoke.

"But Maggie, love, starting a gym takes things like money. You remember the stuff. And you have to know about accounts, property, leases, and things. I can take class but those other things are for the birds. Jumping jacks and muscle burn are my field, not business."

"You could learn all that—and I could help. And perhaps some of the others would put up some money. I've got five hundred dollars. That might pay for some professional advice."

"I suppose there is the insurance money," said Lisa uncertainly. "But I was kinda relying on that to get me through college and possibly into a career in teaching."

Maggie saw that she was making progress. "Listen, honey. This world is full of teachers and they know shit-all, except what others have told them. What was it that artist Braque said when they asked him whether he had any talent as an art student? 'If I did, my teacher would have been the last to know.'"

Lisa could sympathize with that. In the teaching profession original thinking tended to go down like soul food at a Klan rally. But a career in teaching was security. Unexciting, perhaps, but a meal ticket for life. She would have a profession, a husband, 2.5 children, and she would help with the mortgage payments. It was the American dream. Lisa shuddered instinctively. She tried to put her dilemma into words.

"The teaching thing would be so easy, Maggie, so safe. It'd be tough to turn down all that steady money. The trouble is I know it'd be a cop-out. It'd be so much more fun to take life by the balls and give it a swing, like with the exercise trip. I guess I could always go back to teaching later . . ."

Lisa's voice faltered. Life wasn't quite like that and she knew it. Once you got off the conventional ladder, somebody else moved in to take your place. There would be new A students, teacher's pets with no suspicious gaps in their curricula vitae. And when Lisa tried to get her foot back on the lower rungs, their shoe leather, or worse, would be in her face. It was the way the system exacted obedience from the slaves who serviced it. Move out and the door slams in your face. Stay put and obey the rules and the addictive drug of security is dripped in increasing quantities into your veins, each additional fix carefully metered and spread out tantalizingly through time. The more you got the more you wanted—the higher the ladder the steeper the jump to get off. It was a trap into which Mr. and Mrs. Average were all too pleased to fall, willing junkies to the habit of conformity. The thought filled Lisa with horror. At the tender age of seventeen she had no idea of what she wanted to be, but she knew that whatever it was it would represent phenomenal success in one sense or another. For now she was ambitious in a vacuum, a rebel against mediocrity waiting for a cause; but it would not always be like that, and in her guts Lisa knew that the thing to do was to fly by the seat of your pants, letting instinct be the pilot.

Maggie licked the last of the doughnut's sugar off her stubby fingers. No way should she have eaten that, let alone be about to order another. Furtively, she caught the waitress's eye.

"Oh, no you don't, Maggie—it's not all muscle yet." Lisa laughed as she played the policeman. Maggie's fat cells were very far from transformation into muscular protein.

Maggie didn't put up a struggle. Not many did against Lisa. She had the sort of charm that magicians had in children's comic books, a kind of velvet-gloved force that you couldn't resist, and didn't want to. Maggie had often tried to analyze it, and on the whole she had failed. It had something, she had concluded, to do with motive. Lisa wanted the best for people.

"Hey, Lisa—you know I'm really high on this gym idea. You really ought to go for it. Make it happen." Visions of wizard's wands were conjured up. If Lisa wanted it she would have it.

For a second or two Lisa was silent. Both hands cupped around her chin, she stared thoughtfully at her friend.

At last she spoke. "You know, Maggs, I think I'm going to give it a try. I just want to say one thing. I really appreciate what you offered—you know, the five hundred bucks. It was really sweet of you, but when I do it I'm going to do it alone. Perhaps I can borrow from the bank, and use the insurance money. It'll be dangerous as hell, but it should be *real* fun."

Maggie couldn't contain a little yelp of enthusiasm. Great! Lisa was going to do it, and as always she would sweep her friend along in her wake. A thoughtful look swam into Maggie's big brown eyes and hovered there between the bright patches on the excited cheeks. What a friendship it had been. A cliché, of course. The wild-looking girl and her plain sidekick, but in these difficult days when fortune favored the beautiful rather than the brave it was a fact that the Maggies of this world tended to be wallflowers at life's party, watchers and waiters, while the Lisas twirled and pirouetted to the abandoned music. And she genuinely didn't mind. She was more than content to live vicariously, to experience Lisa's triumphs as her own and to be thrust down into the depths by Lisa's misfortunes. It had been like that for as long as Maggie could remember. Since those far-off days in the schoolyard when she never had to be told to share her candy and her cuddly toys with the little girl who was prettier by far than any Alexander doll; since the times when she had not minded that Lisa was the teacher's pet; since the steamy West Palm afternoons when she had been so proud to walk the streets with her, responding haughtily to the "come-ons" of the boys that "they" were not interested.

"Oh, Lisa, that's just *wonderful.* I just know you can make it work. You make everything work. Everyone'll come with you, and I just can't bear to think of you wasted in some dreary classroom." Maggie clapped her hands together in excitement. Then her expression of pure joy clouded over. "But you'll let me help, won't you? I don't mean with the money if you don't want that, but like with all the organization. I won't need wages. Well, not much anyway."

"Come *on,* Maggs. It's your idea. I couldn't possibly do it without you. I couldn't possibly do *anything* without you. Anyway, we've got to put the finishing touches on your new body."

They both laughed.

Maggie was under few illusions about where she stood in the beauty stakes. Her face wasn't so bad, and for sure she wasn't exactly *ugly,* although the bone structure lacked definition and the pasty color of the skin tended to merge without trace against the beige coloring of the gymnasium's walls. No, it was the body that let her down, and it needed far more than the "finishing touches" of which Lisa had spoken. But there had been a dramatic improvement, and although things still didn't hang together, at least they no longer *"hung."* At the beginning she had been unenthusiastic about Lisa's love affair with exercise, and she had wandered into the gym in a cynical frame of mind, with lots of jokes about body fascism and a cheerful irreverence about the almost religious faith in things physical that had surrounded her. As always, Lisa had won her over. Never once had she made fun of her, as so many "friends" would not have hesitated to do. Instead she had led her gently through the agonizing introduction classes, and Maggie's natural self-confidence, which had survived despite the handicap of her personal appearance, had received a massive transfusion as her body had begun the painful process of reorganizing itself before her eyes.

Now there was even a boyfriend, and there hadn't been one of those before.

"I promise you, Lisa. You won't believe this, but one of these days it'll be me up there in front of the class. You remember that."

"Listen, Maggs. I'm *counting* on it."

Maggie smiled. By saying things out loud like that it helped to make them come true. To have Lisa agree made it almost certain that they would.

"Okay, Lisa. Let's go right to work on it. The first thing we need is a space. There's a great one for rent on Clematis. I was just thinking the other day how perfect it would be for a gym. God knows how much they want for it. What are you doing right now, Lisa? Can I come home with you, and we can start making plans?"

Lisa cut into the bubbling enthusiasm. "I'm afraid it's no good tonight,

Maggie. Willie Boy Willis said he'd drop by at around five thirty to talk about old times. You know what he's like when he starts on the beer."

Maggie saw the veil of melancholy descend on Lisa as she spoke. Her shoulders sagged, her voice was heavy, eyes suddenly misty. Maggie knew what it was all about, and her hand sneaked out across the table to comfort her friend. "Oh, Lisa, baby. If only I could help. You're so brave. Keep fighting."

And Maggie watched the great big tear roll down the beautiful but now strangely haunted face.

—

The bags under Willie Boy's eyes were practically big enough to have contained bar trash, and there were times when, late at night, as he passed out among the Roxy's garbage containers, they were not far off doing just that. The beer belly hung down over his belt like some obscene apron, and between the sweat-stained T-shirt and the top of his equally unclean jeans a couple of inches of unhealthy skin protruded. His ginger beard looked as if it contained things, and the occasional foraging expedition of his blunt and blackened nails tended to confirm this disturbing possibility.

Lisa, however, didn't see or smell the Willie Boy Willis that others saw and smelled. For her he was faded dreams, bittersweet walks through her memories, a passport to the past where things had been so blissfully different.

"Yup, Lisa babe, I remember the time when your ol' man and your granpappy set to arm wrestling on the bar. Remember it like yesterday. Nobody in there that night wanted money on who'd win. Never seen nothing like it. You know they'd cuss and yell at each other like they was worst enemies, yet sure as I stand here now I've never seen two men more fond of each other."

Lisa knew. Her mother had always pretended to be infuriated by the alliance between her father and her husband, but secretly she was pleased by it.

"So what happened, Willie Boy?" Lisa tucked up her long legs beneath her on the threadbare sofa and fixed her eyes on her guest's face in studious attention.

Willie Boy burped theatrically. A lifetime tending bar at Roxy's had taught him a thing or two about storytelling. The trick was to tell it as slowly as the audience's attention span would permit. He drew hard and long on the can of beer as if to appease the complaining stomach gods with some valuable sacrificial offering.

"Well, there was money riding on it, fer sure. Big money as I recall. Fifty bucks at least—real money. An' your dad says to me, 'Now you hold this money, Willie Boy, 'cause ol' Jack's meaner'n mouse shit an' never done pay his debts.'"

In her mind's eye Lisa saw the scene, heard the beloved voices.

"Then they set to it. Well, I'll tell you this an' no mistake, in my time I seen arm wrestling—big uns, small uns, tall uns, short uns—but I never seen nothing like that match on the Roxy bar that night between old Jack Kent and young Tommy. You could have heard a roach fart in that room—sure as I'm alive."

Lisa could feel the tension in the steamy bar, as the hushed drinkers witnessed the battle of giants.

Willie Boy could see he was carrying his audience. No sweat. His memory wasn't too good anymore. The drink had seen to that, but he knew the value of exaggeration. "An' strike me down if I tell a lie, but I swear that match went on for fifteen minutes by the clock, an' in all that time I didn't see a drop of beer pass anybody's lips, they was so intent on that contest—and fer sure that ain't happened before or since in Roxy's during opening time."

Lisa was in there, too. Rooting for both sides. For the father who had loved her, protected her, given her the happiest home in the world, for the grandfather who had excited, amused, and frightened her, who had been the color, and the danger, and the adventure.

"You know, when old Jack's hand finally hit that bar there was a cheer went up like the ones you hear at the dogs. That cheer was for both of them, an' no mistake."

Willie Boy sat down heavily and reached for the Bud that was his reward for the story. Singing for a liquid supper was no new thing to him. The leathery hand transferred surplus beer and spit from his mouth to the leg of his once-blue jeans.

"How did Jack take being beaten?"

Willie Boy laughed. "Oh, Lisa. That was *Tommy* done beat him. Tell you something for nothing. Old Jack was a mean one. Real ornery. Seen him beat guys to pulp in that bar 'cause he didn't like their faces. Slapped me around more'n once. But that Tommy Starr could've cut off his balls an' he'd still have loved him. That's how close those two guys were."

For a second or two Willie Boy said nothing, as he appeared to weigh the advisability of his next remark.

"Then that Jack wanted to get drunk as a skunk, but Tommy all he wanted to do was get back to your momma. I never seen a man love a girl so much as young Tom loved Mary-Ellen. Never, an' that's the truth."

He looked across the small room to see its effect on Lisa, but he could see that she had gone, vanished to some private world of memory.

—

THE OLD rocking chair's creak was to Lisa the safest sound in the world, but it came as part of a package deal. It was attached firmly to other sensations— her mother's warm, hard thighs beneath Lisa's squirming legs, the opulent scent of the night flowering jasmine, the bittersweet complaints of the singer on the country station, the tricky light of the kerosene lamp. Sitting on her mother's lap on the porch of the old house, Lisa came closest to heaven— and it was always of paradise that Mary-Ellen spoke. Lisa Starr's five hectic years had not prepared her for the nuances of her mother's message, but there was no mistaking the gentle passion with which it was delivered—and Lisa could remember the words as if it were yesterday. Night after night they had tumbled out, seeping deep into Lisa's consciousness until they were a living part of her, sometimes, she felt, the most important part. The intense pleasure of the circumstances surrounding these conversations formed powerful associations for the young girl, and firmly but delicately, her mind had been washed clean of all heresy that might dilute the force of the gospel truth.

Never for one moment had the content of the message deviated. Across the bridge, a few hundred yards away, was a magical world peopled by gods and demigods, beautiful, kindly people who could do no wrong. Charming, urbane, witty, sophisticated, and thoroughly good, the citizens and part-time residents of Palm Beach inhabited a different planet, behaved and thought in a way alien to the mere mortals of West Palm. Theirs was a glittering life of music and dance, of genteel conversation, of culture and excellence far removed from the game of financial and moral survival that was played with such intensity on the other side of the coastal railroad. Her eyes glistening with the faith of the convert, Mary-Ellen had told and retold of the sumptuous banquets, the intricate arrangements of flowers, of the comings and goings of the rich and famous; and all the time Lisa had sat in wonderment, soothed and stimulated by her mother's lilting voice. Other children, her friends and adversaries of a hundred make-believe street battles, had other champions—Batman, Superman, and Captain Marvel—but to Lisa these were paper heroes, insubstantial specters who would melt away when confronted by the transcendent reality of a Stansfield, a Duke, or a Pulitzer. To Lisa's childlike questions the responses were patient, self-assured.

"Why don't we live in Palm Beach, mommy?"

"Folks like us just don't live there, honey."

"But *why* not?"

"It has to do with birth, Lisa. Some people are born to live like that."

"You lived there once, at the Stansfield house."

"Yes, but I *worked* there. I wasn't *really* there." Then her mother's eyes would film over as she dared to dream, and her voice would say cautiously, "But one day, Lisa, if you grow up to be very beautiful and very good, like a fairy princess, who knows but some prince might take you there. Across the bridge."

Far from wise in the ways of the world, Lisa had nonetheless picked up on the inconsistencies of her mother's logic, but it had not been enough to cause her to doubt the truth of her mother's words—nor did she want to. This was the realm of fantasy, of dreaming, of white knights and dashing ponies, of superhuman powers and ultimate wisdom—and Palm Beach was the mysterious universe in which mythical beings cavorted, in which deeds of derring-do were endlessly performed. And there was one shining belief that Lisa kept always to herself. In her dreams Lisa would one day be a part of it. She would be drawn across the bridge in a golden carriage, serenaded by a marching band, welcomed into heaven by a choir of angels, taking her mother and her family with her as she crossed in glory to the other side. And then her family's mighty gratitude would break all over her. She, Lisa, would have been the instrument for the attainment of the impossible dream, and could bask forever in the loving respect that such an achievement must bring.

WILLIE BOY'S gritty voice sawed itself into Lisa's consciousness, interrupting the sad, sweet memories.

"Seems like I lost you there, Lisa."

"Yeah, I was thinking of mom." Lisa smiled a wan smile.

"Sure was one hell of a lady. Best-looking lady in the county I ever saw. Yup, she had style—real style—your mom did, Lisa. Tommy was one lucky man."

They looked at each other warily. Both knew what would happen now. Both willed it. Each in a way dreaded it.

With fascination, a serpent in the grip of the charmer's spell, Lisa watched it start, having no power to stop the doomed attempt at exorcism, the futile longing to lay the ghosts to sleep.

"I'll never know how it happened. Never forgive myself for that night."

Willie Boy often started like that.

But Lisa knew. Knew every single detail—would carry it with her through her nights and her days forever.

Tommy and Jack. The drunken march home. Thoughts flying high, alcohol the wind beneath the wings of imagination. Arm in arm, the masculine smells, the comradeship of tried and trusting drinking partners. The old house, quiet but well lit. The giggled lip service to the necessity of silence. Creaking boards, unsteady feet, uncertain eyes. Whose unknowing elbow had dislodged the kerosene lamp, what extraneous sound had camouflaged its fall —a car? the wail of the train whistle? some needless joke?

The fire had started before each man had crawled beneath the hot sheets; it was gathering force as they slipped into drink's stupor. Racing hungrily through the willing timbers baked and cracked by the sun's heat, driven on by the capricious nocturnal breeze, it had enjoyed its wicked orgy of destruction. Lisa, sleeping fitfully, had heard and smelled it first. Throwing open her door, she was hit by the wall of heat, the snapping, hissing roar of the flames in her ears. Instinct alone had saved her. She had closed the door against the fire, and in the few seconds that the inspired action had bought her she had climbed out of her bedroom window into the dark safety of the backyard.

Standing alone, her senses in turmoil, scarcely aware of what was happening, Lisa had watched her world consumed. The time between sleep, wakefulness, and action had amounted to a few brief seconds. Now, the awful dread had welled up within her. Beyond the fence the neighbors were shouting, their urgent cries of alarm seeping into Lisa's half-awake mind.

Her father, her mother, her grandfather were in the roaring tinderbox. Had they, like her, escaped? Or had they already left her—gone forever, with no possibility of even a sad farewell? She had walked toward the pitiless flames, felt once again the merciless heat on her face, the suffocating fumes of the smoke. She had recoiled from it, from the singeing pain on her exposed and naked nipples, from the dreadful, nameless horror it represented. And then she had seen the specter.

From the midst of the conflagration, moving jerkily like a sleepwalker, the figure emerged.

Numb with horror, Lisa took a second or two to realize who it was. It was her mother, and she was burning. Mary-Ellen had emerged from the inferno, but she had not escaped it.

Lisa leaped forward, her stricken eyes on the dancing, darting flames that jumped and pranced from her mother's bare flesh. In her nostrils was the stench of burning skin, as the body which had borne her was consumed in front of her. In her heart was sick dread.

Already blinded by the fire, Mary-Ellen stumbled toward her, a dry, parched shout of pain and alarm seeping out between burned lips. Her arms made strange beseeching gestures, the movements of the blindfolded child playing blindman's buff, as she sought the comfort she would never find.

Oblivious to the flames, Lisa rushed into her arms, giving her naked body to her mother, as balm for the unhealable wounds, as an alternative source of fuel for the deadly fire. Roughly, she pushed Mary-Ellen to the ground and, straddling her, she offered her body as a blanket in her wild attempt to starve her mother's flesh of the oxygen without which the flames could not burn. She felt no pain as the fire sought to transfer its attentions, had no thought of the scars she might incur by her selfless action. She was an animal driven only by the power of instinct, by the power of love.

Together mother and daughter rolled on the parched, sparse grass of the backyard, their brains and bodies screaming. And then there were other hands, other voices, the rude shock of the cold water, muted exclamations of horror.

With Mary-Ellen cradled in Lisa's arms, their time-honored positions were reversed; mother and child clung together resisting the hands that sought to separate them. Tenderly Lisa looked down at the ravaged face, its beauty liquidized by the unforgiving fire, the well-remembered features twisted and tormented by the flames' force. Murmuring words of reassurance and desperate hope, she smoothed the stricken hair, but Lisa could feel the presence of death's angel hovering, swooping, backing away again—and she knew that her mother was dying.

And then the tears had found their strength as the emotion of sorrow burst through the raging torrent of fear and anger, the adrenaline surge of action.

"Oh, momma," she sobbed, as the big salty tears welled up in Lisa's eyes, cascading down dry cheeks, dripping steadily onto the swollen, discolored, and weeping skin.

"Oh, mom, stay with me. Don't go away. Please stay."

She hugged her dying mother, crushing her to her body, trying to merge with her—to force life into death, to stave off the inevitable moment of eternal emptiness. Mary-Ellen was unrecognizable, reduced to the wickedest caricature of her former beauty, but inside her ruined body the heart still beat, the lungs still breathed. For Lisa that was enough, and she prayed to her God not to take away the gift of existence without which nothing was possible, no future could be.

Through hurting lips Mary-Ellen had tried to speak, and Lisa had leaned down to listen to the pained words. They would never be forgotten, always respected, would be carried through life like a talisman—the magic charm that would show the way forward.

"Darling Lisa. I love you so much . . . so much."

"Oh, mom, I love you too. I love you. Stay with me. Stay with me."

"I went . . . to your room. But you're safe. I'm so happy." Her voice weaker now, she spoke again. "Lisa. Darling girl. All those evenings, on the porch. You remember those things I said. Don't throw it away like I did. You can do it. I know you can. Do you know what I'm saying. Oh. Lisa . . . hold me tight."

"Don't talk, mom. The doctors will be here soon. Don't try to talk." Now the waves of grief began to break all over Lisa, and she began to sob as in her arms she felt the shudder course through the broken body, as her mother fought to hold on to elusive life.

"I remember, mommy. I remember everything. Don't die. Mommy, please don't die."

Then in open defiance of her most fervent prayer, Mary-Ellen's back arched and her body contracted. Like a leaf carried on the wind, the message was borne on the sweet, dying air.

"Palm Beach . . . Lisa . . . it's only a bridge away . . ."

IT WAS twelve noon and the sun sliced down like a javelin, boring into the baked sidewalk, shimmering and quivering in still air. Lisa and Maggie, however, seemed to be in some way immune to it as, heads together, they talked intensely outside the bank.

"But what are you going to *say*, Lisa? These guys are real smart, you know. Pop always says they only lend money to the folks who don't need it."

"It'll be okay, Maggs. I can make the gym work. I know that, and I'll make him know that, too. We'll get a good deal. You'll see."

Maggie looked doubtful, but as always, Lisa's self-confidence was infectious. "You got all the paperwork."

Lisa waved the manila folder in her friend's face and laughed. "It's just props, Maggie. Bankers lend to people, not to scraps of paper. Do I look okay?"

It was Maggie's turn to laugh. As far as she was concerned Lisa always looked great. Loose, sky-blue linen jacket over white T-shirt. Long brown legs exploding out of the short, white, pleated cotton skirt, ankle socks, canvas lace-up shoes. But the clothes were really an irrelevance, a distraction from the main event—the superb body that they so ineffectively concealed. "Let's just hope the guy's happily married and a pillar of the church—otherwise you'll get molested in there."

"Don'tcha think of anything else, Maggs? Hey, it's late. I'd better get on in. Wish me luck."

In the elevator Lisa's self-confidence sank as she rose. It was a week or two since she had made her decision, and every day since her desire had grown geometrically. She was going to open the most successful gym the world had ever known—a center of bodily excellence whose reputation would spread far and wide. She would create it, shape it, be it, and in turn it would give her what she wanted. It would be her passport across the bridge, her posthumous gift to her dead mother. Soon the gods and goddesses would hear of her on the celestial grapevine, and, as the word filtered across the gleaming surface of the lake, the younger inhabitants of paradise would seek her out, give their bodies to her to shape, to sculpt, to condition. In their gratitude they would reward her by allowing her to move among them. Only one thing stood in Lisa's way. A banker by the name of Weiss. Without finance she would be nowhere, a nobody condemned forever to mediocrity.

Lisa allowed the gloomy thought to swirl around her mind. It was a trick she had learned. To get things in this life you had to want them like hell. That was the secret. If the desire wasn't there you were lost. And the way to tank up desire was to dwell on the consequences of failure, as she was doing now. By the time the elevator was ready to decant her Lisa Starr was gripped by a steely resolve. She would have her way no matter what. Weiss would give her the loan, and she would do whatever it took to get it. By fair means or foul she would win.

The hatchet-faced receptionist had not been encouraging when she had made the appointment, and she didn't seem to have changed her tune. Luckily there wasn't any waiting time. Throwing open the door to the office, she said briefly, "Ms. Lisa Starr, Mr. Weiss—your twelve o'clock appointment," as she ushered Lisa inside.

Weiss, small and owllike, leaped to his feet as Lisa entered, his face lighting up, the wizened features illuminated by the spark of instant lust. Lisa could almost hear what he was thinking as he beamed his welcome, and she could feel his eyes as they roamed over the pleasing contours of her body, lingering lasciviously on the erogenous zones, the full lips, the unrestrained nipples, darting down hungrily to speculate on the hidden Mecca barely covered by the short skirt.

"Ah, Ms. Starr." The pudgy hands spread in welcome. "Do please sit down." Weiss hovered at Lisa's shoulder. He didn't actually pull out the chair for her, as if unwilling to undertake so subservient an action despite the phenomenal physical charms of his young customer. Instead he angled his body from the waist, leaning over Lisa and making little darting movements with his arms as if orchestrating the complicated physical process of sitting down, a puppeteer attached to Lisa's limbs by unseen strings. Lizardlike, a small tongue darted out to wet dry lips as the restless eyes flickered over the highest point of the crossed thighs where the incompetent skirt did its best to cover Lisa Starr's candy-striped cotton briefs.

Reluctantly Weiss retreated behind the imposing desk and took up his position in the tall, dark green leather chair. The libidinous smile lost some of its intensity, as the fantasy visions faded and cold reality reasserted itself. Damn. Joseph Weiss—Casanova, Don Juan, lady's man—merged relentlessly into old Joe Weiss, sixty-two, with halitosis and fallen arches.

He peered down at his desk, staring intently at the almost blank sheet of paper. "Well, Ms. Starr. How can I help you?"

"What I really need, Mr. Weiss, is a loan of twenty thousand dollars to open an exercise studio here in West Palm." That was the bottom line. Lisa had considered all sorts of other possible beginnings, but had been congenitally drawn to the most straightforward one. "I have twenty thousand dollars of my own from an insurance policy, and I would be putting that into the venture, too," she added. Presumably bankers liked you to join them in the risk.

"Aaaaaaaah," said Weiss approvingly. That was better. She wanted something from him. People usually did, and it tended to make him feel good. Sometimes they were prepared to do things in return. It was far from unknown in his experience, and this girl was so young, so very pretty.

For a second Lisa waited, but Weiss added nothing to his enigmatic expression. Was this the moment to start the long speech—her credentials, her profit predictions, the already discovered premises on Clematis Street? Instinct told her no. She sat up as straight as she could in the high-backed chair and watched the banker evenly, noting the dramatic return of prurient interest in the restless eyes.

"That seems a lot of money, Ms. Starr," he said at last.

"It'd be a good investment for your bank," said Lisa brightly, letting the self-confidence show.

Weiss looked at her carefully. A good investment for the bank? Forget it. For himself in his capacity of lender of the bank's money? Maybe. Just maybe. He peered at the sharp nipples, blinked, and then swallowed nervously. There was a way of handling this one, but it was littered with minefields. One wrong foot and he'd blow it.

"Suppose you fill me in on some of the details of your business proposition." The avuncular look didn't quite come off. There was definitely some sort of a leer.

Lisa was well prepared. What bankers liked was sheets of paper. Things to look at that could be shown to other people. She'd brought plenty of that, character references, photographs of the prospective premises, estimates of probable income. She passed the envelope across to the banker with a few words of explanation. For a minute or two Weiss ran through them.

When he looked up his smile was sly. "This is pretty impressive, Lisa—if I can call you that—but what seems to me to be missing here is any reference to training in physical education." He waited for a split second before deciding to go for it. "Although I suppose one might say that your . . . aaaaaah . . . superb bodily condition is evidence of that."

Once again the creepy eyes lasered in on Lisa, darting around her breasts, aiming down to the flat stomach, heading lower still.

She was quite unable to control the blush. Christ, he was coming on like gangbusters.

She laughed nervously and played it as straight as hell. "I'm afraid they haven't gotten around to giving out diplomas in stretch and aerobics, but I could for sure get references from the place I teach now."

As she spoke she knew that Weiss's remark hadn't meant that at all.

Weiss's laugh crackled disconcertingly. "No, I'm sure that side of things isn't a problem. I'm certain the physical side of things would be no problem for you. No problem at all."

Inside he felt the adrenaline begin to hum. How much did this little fox want her gym? Because if she really wanted it there was only one way she was going to get it. One way alone. Twenty thousand bucks for some crappy studio that would close down in six months? It was laughable. But a twenty-thousand-dollar screw at the bank's expense—who knew, perhaps several screws—that might not be such a bad deal. It wouldn't be the first time, and, he fervently hoped, it wouldn't be the last. So what that it would be a bad loan, and he would lose a few points? Everyone was entitled to the odd mistake. He would be forgiven. No question. Anyway this girl was *young,* and *stacked.* He would use a modified version of the same basic speech, the one with the good track record.

"Lisa, I must be quite frank with you. I am afraid my experience tells me this loan wouldn't be at all safe. There are several reasons. You're young, very young, with no track record in business. And the exercise thing—fashionable though it may be at the moment—is hardly 'money in the bank.' "

Weiss laughed heartily at the weak joke, as he picked up on the disappointment in the beautiful eyes. The trick was to beat them down into the dust before picking up the pieces. "The truth of the matter is—and I am sorry to be so pessimistic—I can't see any bank taking on a loan like this." He shook his head sadly and made a little clicking noise with his tongue. "Can't see it at all," he added unnecessarily.

Lisa watched it slip away from her, as the dread welled up within her. She had been so certain, so sure. In the past, her desire for something had always been enough, the instant ticket to her destination. Ambition plus effort had equaled success. Now, for the first time in her life, she was about to be thwarted. This man Weiss was standing in her way, and predicting, quite plausibly, that there would be other Weisses who would do the same if she tried to go elsewhere. The worst thing of all was that Lisa *knew* the gym would be a success, but how on earth could she hope to convince a banker of that? All he could see was her inexperience and naiveté.

But Lisa was wrong. Weiss, his eyes blinking excitedly behind the thick glasses, could see a very great deal more than that. He leaned forward into Lisa's almost palpable disappointment and threw her the lifeline. "However." Weiss repeated the word. "However, I'll be quite honest and say that I like you, Lisa. I like you very much, and I admire . . . what you have done and what you plan to do."

The long pause was full of hidden meanings, as he willed Lisa to get the drift. "Perhaps I *can* help. Perhaps we can work together on this one," he said at last. Weiss smiled an oily smile. Still a bit too oblique. How much needed to be spelled out? He waited for a sign of encouragement.

Lisa's friendly smile was strictly neutral, but her mind was suddenly on red alert. Not yet in the forefront of consciousness she had a subterranean awareness of what was going on. Some atavistic instinct told her that Weiss was up to something, and that it was nasty.

"What I suppose I'm trying to say," Mr. Weiss murmured, "is that it would be nice if we could kinda keep in touch—maybe on a social basis—while we have the loan out to you. If, of course, I were to decide to go ahead." There. He'd done it. It was on the table. You screw me for twenty thousand. It was as clear as daylight.

Lisa watched the play and knew at once what he was saying. She wasn't surprised, and that in itself she found surprising. As little grenades of revulsion exploded deep within her, she kept her face deadpan for the reply. "Well, I'd certainly welcome some fatherly advice along the way. I'd be very grateful for it."

Immediately she regretted her remark. She was walking a tightrope, and the safety net was conspicuous by its absence. Weiss wanted her to come on to him, and she had more or less told him he was a dirty old man—old enough to be her grandfather. The twenty thousand, which a second before had dangled in front of her nose, had gone swinging away again.

Weiss laughed uncertainly. Could she be that innocent? Or was she saying "no way"? "What I really mean is, perhaps we could go out to dinner from time to time—get to know each other." There was a hint of desperation in his voice.

Lisa knew she was about to make one of the most important decisions of her life, and she hadn't a clue which way it was going to go. She had two alternatives. Either she sold herself to this ridiculous old man and got the money she needed, or she walked away empty-handed into a teaching career. Whore or respectable pillar of the establishment. Palm Beach or Minneapolis. Danger or safety. She hovered in an agony of indecision.

Through clenched teeth Weiss said, "What do you say?"

For what seemed like an age Lisa said absolutely nothing.

The thoughts came in like gunfire. His disgusting thing inside her proud body, polluting her, violating her, owning her forever as he took her virginity. But it would be only a short moment of time, gone, forgotten, erased from memory by a mighty act of will as the fruits of her ordeal smoothed the path ahead to victory and glory. Her self-respect lost forever as she sold herself to the devil to get what she wanted. But a solemn promise to her dead mother fulfilled as she moved toward paradise. "Only a bridge away . . . only a bridge away . . ." In her nostrils was the scent of burning flesh, as she peered through suddenly tear-filled eyes at her potential tormentor, at her potential savior. Devil or angel—which was he?

Weiss watched the turmoil in the liquid eyes as Lisa struggled with her conscience. The message had gotten across at last. It was out of his hands.

He had only to wait. In delicious anticipation he sat back in his chair and savored the delectable feeling that was beginning to course through him.

"I'm not quite sure what you have in mind," Lisa heard herself say. She was playing for time, fishing for anything that would help her to make the decision.

"I think you know what I have in mind," said Weiss quickly. She wasn't getting off the hook.

By fair means or foul. Lisa had promised herself that a few brief minutes before. Had fair means been exhausted? And, if so, how foul could you get?

A passionately interested observer of her own mental processes, Lisa watched herself in fascination to see what she would do. Her soul seemed to hover over her, a passive spectator as, like a sleepwalker, she stumbled onward.

The speech when it came was delivered in a firm, defiant voice. "Mr. Weiss, I think I *do* understand what you are saying to me. You're saying that you will lend me the money if I make love to you, and *only* if I make love to you." She stopped, and when she began again there was a catch in her voice. "Well, you must know that I don't want to do that and I think it's very wrong of you to ask it and to want it. But I do need the money—I need it desperately because I want so much from life. So if you want it I will make love to you, but on one condition—that we do it here, now, this very minute. And then you give me my money. All of it—in a certified banker's draft."

Slowly, deliberately, with her mind on fire, she stood up.

The mighty wave of guilt crashed over Joe Weiss, extinguishing the dancing flame of passion with the ease of a tornado blowing out a candle flame. Torrents of the purest shame rushed and raced, dampening his base desires. Joe Weiss, the father of his children, the husband of his wife, the son of his mother, was reincarnated and he struggled for the words that would best show his atonement. Before him Lisa Starr stood stock still, offering herself as a glorious sacrifice, an embodiment of magnificent determination and single-mindedness.

And then the guilt in old Joe Weiss was replaced with another feeling—admiration—and quite suddenly he laughed his first genuine laugh of the day.

He had been outmaneuvered, outgunned, outplayed by this beautiful seventeen-year-old girl—and he laughed because for some extraordinary reason he didn't mind a bit. That just had to be the definition of charm. Until this moment he hadn't thought for one second that her business had a snowdrop's chance in hell. Now suddenly he wasn't at all sure. The one thing he'd learned in the money-lending business was that you lent bucks to people, not to ideas, and this person had a bankable personality quite apart from the more obvious ready assets.

"Lisa Starr," he said, "you get the money, and let me tell you this for nothing: you're going to go one hell of a long way."

In all of his sixty-two years Joe Weiss had never been more right.

—

BOBBY STANSFIELD's face peered back at him from the hand-held mirror, and he liked what he saw. The Florida suntan seemed to have been painted on, a deep rich all-over brown relieved only by the tiny white streaks in the embryonic wrinkles around the shining, laughing eyes. From long practice Bobby made the inventory fast. Start at the top. The sandy hair, lustrous, exuberant, was suitably untidy—its self-confident, orderly chaos hinting at the harmonious marriage between boy and man that the voters had learned to love. He shook his head from side to side, encouraging the wayward curl to fall forward over the right eye before flicking it back again with the sweep of an impatient hand. The nose, cracked neatly by the side of a loose surfboard so many years before, gave an appealing lack of conformity to the otherwise all-too-perfect face. Endless Stansfield conferences, political and familial, had debated the advisability of plastic surgery. Now, and on a hundred previous occasions, he thanked God that the verdict had been no go. He needed the nose. It had become a trademark, a symbol of virility, a statement that Bobby Stansfield, despite all other appearances to the contrary, was very far from vanity. Mouth? Closed—just a little too thin, intimating the possibility of coldness, if not of cruelty. Open—incredible, a perfect frame for the sculpted, pure white teeth. The chin was smooth and square, with no hint of a vote-losing shadow. Great. The box of tricks was looking good. He allowed the face to smile its self-satisfaction, the smile widening in positive feedback as it contemplated itself.

"How do I look, Jimmy?"

"Knicker-wetting good," laughed the short, squat man by his side.

Despite the joke, Jimmy Baker's professional eyes checked the Stansfield visuals below the neck. Dark blue ribbed silk tie with a subdued crimson diagonal stripe; standard-issue Brooks Brothers suit, navy blue and not too well cut so as to avoid the aroma of smoothness that would be the kiss of death to the people's choice; black Gucci loafers, their leather soft as a baby's bottom. It was all there and all hanging together. Candidates had become instant history for crimes no more heinous than an unzipped fly. In this life there was no relaxing.

From the wings both men could see the stage and the rostrum. More important, they could both hear and feel the excitement building in the hotel auditorium. The characterless room, its decorations derived effortlessly from airports and waiting rooms all over the world, throbbed with eager anticipation as three thousand women, and a handful of males, prepared to meet their man of destiny. Over the stage somebody had hung a banner bearing the legend THE MAN YOU KNOW.

Standing at the rostrum, some faceless party hack was making his pitch, basking in the reflected glory of the bringer of good tidings.

"And now, ladies and gentlemen—the moment we have all been waiting for. It is for me the greatest pleasure to introduce you to a man who needs no introduction. Ladies and gentlemen, the man who—though he doesn't say it himself—will one day be president of these here United States, Senator *Bobby Stansfield!*"

At the mention of his name, Bobby took a deep breath and launched himself into the sea of noise that erupted all around him. Looking neither to right or left he negotiated the blinding lights and achieved the floodlit rostrum. Now at last he could make contact with the audience, begin the ritualized love-in that was so important to both him and them. The smile was deprecating, the head held low in the universal gesture of humility, but the thrill ran through him. In his ears ran the mealymouthed platitudes of the introduction. He had heard words like that a thousand times in a thousand dreary halls, but he never tired of them. As his father had before him, he loved every single one. Stansfields didn't need food, drink, and vitamins like other mortals; they ran on a different kind of fuel. What they needed was appreciation, noisy appreciation, public appreciation. It didn't matter what people said and it didn't matter who said it. The phrases and sentiments were meaningless and irrelevant. The vital thing was that they should be an expression, however inadequate and unimaginative, of unconditional love.

Bobby held up his hand wearily to stem the flood of enthusiastic approval. He didn't mean it to work and it didn't. The applause rolled on like a river, punctuated now by shouts and whoops as the women went into their act.

"We love ya, Bobby!"

"We're with you, Bobby. All the way. All the way to the White House!"

The boyish smile played hesitantly around his lips, turning up remorselessly the sexual rheostat of the audience. A quick movement of the head sent the curl downward on its predestined journey to meet the tidying fingers and, in the intensification of the applause that the gesture brought, he stared straight back at them, the suddenly glistening eyes showing that the love was getting to him, touching him, that he was *theirs*. Again the hand raised to stem the floodtide of adulation, the mouth opening and closing as if to speak. The smile again. The laugh. A sideways glance. A shake of the head.

He was talking to them, but he wasn't speaking. I'm overwhelmed by your welcome, said the body language. Overwhelmed and deeply touched. I've never been greeted like this. It's the first time. You're all special. Special people. Special friends. Together we will march to glory. Your glory, my glory.

This was the point when the aides got into the act. From either side of the stage, immaculately suited young men burst from the wings, gesticulating to the audience, pleading with them to allow the ritual to proceed to the next phase, the one in which the hero was actually going to *speak*.

Bobby played the resulting silence like a soundless Stradivarius violin. For long seconds he said nothing. The suspense built. Then from the back of the auditorium a lone female—fat, fair, and fifty—told it like it was.

"I love you, Bobby."

Now they could hear the laugh. It was a sort of a chuckle, deep, gurgling, reassuringly genuine, frighteningly charming.

"Well, thank you, ma'am," came the stylish reply. The syllables were cut short, except for the very last word, which went on forever, like a stripper's legs. Patrician, Old World, the gentleman from the southern plantation. Rhett Butler time.

Once again the audience dissolved in a demonstration of collective love. The wit of the man. The intelligence. The brilliance of the repartee. He would eat those Russian peasants for breakfast, castrate the international bankers, make Fidel Castro curse his mother for bearing him.

When the laughter and clapping died down at last, Bobby seemed hesitant, nervous, a little boy lost, tossed on the ocean of the audience's enthusiasm. He straightened the already straight tie and gripped the rostrum firmly in a gesture that said he was going to need all the help and support he could get. All around the crowded room maternal instincts made their appearance, merging in titillating alliance with the sexual ones.

The voice was pitched low, now—deliberately downbeat, leaving lots of space for the long journey to cataclysmic climax when he would make his audience explode in ecstatic joy as he loved them and left them.

"Ladies and gentlemen, you have made me very happy tonight . . . by the warmth of your welcome. I thank you all from the bottom of my heart." Head bowed, Bobby felt the love go out to them, feeling it, being it, as the delicious tears welled up in his shining eyes. The next words positively vibrated with the genuineness of his emotion.

"In Savannah one expects courtesy and good manners—sometimes seems to me Georgians invented those—but I get the feeling tonight I'm among close friends. And, if I may, that's the way I'd like to talk to you."

His voice firmer now, he mouthed the familiar words like a litany.

"The great thing about friends is that you can speak freely to them because you know that at heart they share your values, and that you will not be misunderstood. You may disagree over the little things, but deep down you know you are on the same side. I could give you a list right now of the truths you and I know. Self-evident truths in which we believe passionately . . . but which our enemies disavow."

Bobby loved the next bit. In a way it summed up his very essence. The strength of his belief illuminated the words, and in turn the words invigorated the sentiments.

"We believe in the sanctity of the family . . . in the greatness of our beloved country. We believe in God and in the Christian morality of the Bible. We believe in being strong so that we can protect freedom. We believe in the individual and in his right, unhindered, to do the best for himself and his loved ones."

One by one he ticked off the items on his beloved agenda, punctuating each one with the wave of an outstretched hand, his finger a stabbing emphasis of each point. In front of him the audience hummed with pent-up passion at this appeal to their most basic beliefs, feeding back the enthusiasm of the converted to the preacher.

First establish the mutual interest, the shared creed. Then to identify the enemy.

"But you and I know that some people . . . fellow Americans . . . are working day and night to undermine those institutions and beliefs that we hold so dear. They are the doubters, the pessimists who let no opportunity pass to sneer and scoff at our patriotism. They neglect our defenses, preferring to see us weak in the face of the threat from without. They seek to strip the religion from our schools, to allow the destruction of the innocent unborn, and everywhere they encourage perversion and pornography in the name of their beliefs. Professing faith in freedom, they strive night and day to take away our right to determine our own future—building always the government and the faceless bureaucracy which they themselves seek to control. We, however, are vigilant. We know of their ambitions. We understand Big Brother's plans."

The roar of the applause submerged the words. In the lull they allowed, Bobby searched the wings of the auditorium for Jimmy. Even the stupendous audience feedback was hardly enough for him. He wanted the professional's accolade, too.

Jimmy Baker caught his eye immediately and made the thumbs-up sign. If it was possible, he was somewhere above the seventh heaven. The whiskey sours before dinner may have helped, but it was the way these folk were going for the "candidate" that had provided most of the uplift. For a blissful moment earlier on he had wondered briefly if Bobby Stansfield might be able to get through the entire twenty-minute slot without actually saying anything at all except his courteous response to the lady in the audience. It would have gone down in the record books as the " 'Well, thank you, ma'am,' speech." Now, his professional campaign manager's mind was assessing the phenomenal vote-pulling power of the Stansfield persona.

Jimmy's restless eyes peered into the back of the hall and found the NBC crew. Great. They were catching the action, immortalizing on tape the throbbing excitement his boy could generate. It had taken some doing to persuade the network that the speech would contain a fireworks display that they would need to cover. They seemed to have gotten the message, if the quality of the field producer they had sent was anything to go by.

The speech was heading for its climax now, and all around the room the emotions surged and raged as Bobby took the audience with him. It was a virtuoso performance, and, suddenly, in the crash of thunderous applause it was over.

Bobby came off the platform almost at the run. All souped up on adrenaline, he was also bathed in sweat, overdosed on attention.

"Great, Bobby. That was just great. NBC got it all in the can. I've never seen an audience like it. Better than Orlando."

Bobby looked relieved. He wiped a weary hand across the famous brow. "They understood, Jim. My kind of people," he said. "Where is it we go tomorrow?"

~3~

T HE POWERFUL PROBING fingers darted mercilessly into the small of Jo-
Anne Duke's back, and the shock waves of exquisite pain went roaring
into her mind, cold, clean, and invigorating as a line of the purest pharma-
ceutical coke.

"Oh, Jane, baby, you're strong today," she moaned, half in reproach, half
in admiration.

The lithe, muscular masseuse didn't let up for a second. Biceps and triceps rippling, she played the sleek, oiled body like a musical instrument—
torturing it, caressing it, controlling it—oblivious to the pleasurable anguish
she was causing. Her laid-back voice, soft and confident, provided the running commentary. "What we're doing here is moving the tissues to a new
place—allowing the energy work to travel the body. We reorganize the tissues so that the gravity field reinforces the body rather than breaking it
down."

"Fer sure," murmured Jo-Anne, luxuriating in the feeling. "Feels like I'm
dancing the masochism tango."

Jane didn't laugh. Rolfing was no laughing matter. It was a religion, an
article of faith, a way of life. Jokes were just inappropriate.

Her right elbow replaced the unforgiving fingers as her chosen instrument, punishing Jo-Anne for her unwarranted levity, her insufficient respect
for the great Dr. Ida Rolf. She leaned in hard on the slippery, suntanned
back and smiled grimly as she elicited the first small squeak of pain.

"It's a question of alignment. The body must be aligned with gravity.
What we call 'grounding.' As the biological system becomes more stable and
orderly your emotions will become more fluid, more free."

The clipped, patrician voice cut into the psychobabble. "Surely you can't
believe all that crap."

Peter Duke had had enough. It was one thing to watch your wife being
massaged poolside in the open air by a long-legged girl with an ass like a
dream, but he didn't see why he should have to put up with all the verbal

shit. He clinked the ice in the tall glass and sipped moodily at the rum punch as he waited to see the effect of his observation.

Jane tossed her shoulder-length hair petulantly, but said nothing. She reached out for the bottle of moisturizing cream and poured a generous portion onto Jo-Anne's splendid back.

From the prone figure came Jo-Anne's languid drawl. "Oh, Peter, why is it that everything you don't understand always has to be described as *crap?* Couldn't it just be rubbish, or nonsense or something?" Jo-Anne felt like quarreling. It cleared the air like the late afternoon thunderstorms that dropped the unbearable temperatures of the Palm Beach summers. And afterward, sometimes, they would make love, angrily, hungrily, punishing each other's bodies as they ground themselves together. It was about the only time they got to do it nowadays.

"It's crap because it comes out all the time and because it stinks. That's why." Peter stood up. Like the spoiled child he was he wanted the last word. Turning on his heel he disappeared into the shady recesses of the vast house. Over his shoulder, winging like an arrow, came his Parthian shot. "I don't know why you two bull dykes don't just cut the cackle and get it on. That's what it's all about, isn't it?"

The muted whir of the pool filter was the only sound to disturb the lakeside silence as the two women digested Peter Duke's barbed verbal missile. For a minute or two neither spoke, as each wondered how best to use the remark to her own advantage.

"Don't take any notice of him. He's been in a filthy mood all day." It was a sort of apology, and an invitation to a female alliance against men in general and Peter in particular.

Jane was all too happy to join in on that.

She removed the elbow that had been wreaking such havoc with Jo-Anne's vertebrae, and with the flat of both hands swept up and down the statuesque back in the motions of Swedish massage. From her position beside the firm naked buttocks she leaned forward, sending her strong hands north to grip the square shoulders, drawing them back again down the full length of the spine, letting them linger briefly on the perfectly rounded cheeks of Jo-Anne's bottom.

"He seems a little hostile," she agreed. "But it doesn't worry me. I get that all the time."

The long slow strokes continued remorselessly, making twin tracks of oil on the supple, suntanned skin.

Jo-Anne moaned her pleasure.

The massage had surreptitiously changed its character. No longer were the fingers aggressive, invasive, cruel. Now they were capricious, daring, innovative, and Jo-Anne's appreciative response was asking that they stay that way.

Jane was intending to grant that request.

"You're not overheating, are you?" she asked solicitously, her voice warm and caring, wafted on the sandalwood-scented breeze.

"No. I'm fine. Just . . . fine." Jo-Anne drawled the words as she luxuriated in the delicious feeling. This was how she liked it best. Being massaged
in the direct sun was the ultimate experience as the ultraviolet rays merged
with the infrared ones to unknit the muscle knots and melt the tension. All
over her perfectly proportioned body the little beads of sweat fought to escape the thin film of oil that covered her, before exploding into nothingness
under Jane's powerful touch.

Sometimes Jane's long soft hair would fall forward like a waterfall onto Jo-
Anne's smooth hot skin, sending a tantalizingly ambiguous message into her
tingling psyche. Jo-Anne flowed with the rhythm of the massage, in perfect
harmony with the knowing hands that worked her body. At times like this she
knew she was in paradise and she would allow her spirits to fly away, soaring
like an eagle, free and unfettered while down below, spread out like some
exotic Persian carpet, lay her life.

In the bleak streets of the truculent city, it had been far from easy. Mostly
it was temperature rather than hunger that she remembered. In the Big
Apple you were always either too hot or too cold. In the unforgiving winter
everything froze and even the restless roaches slowed down. In the steaming
cauldron of summer, one's body became a sponge, enervated and flaccid, as
it indulged its voracious appetite for the liquid whose only purpose was immediate escape. The money to buy food had always been scarce, but the
fingers to take it had been nimble and Jo-Anne had never failed to find the
fuel for the awesomely beautiful body that she had somehow known from
the earliest times would be her salvation.

And so it had been. Of course, her stepfather had been first. Drunk and
horny he had taken her roughly, standing up against the living-room wall. It
was one of the great mysteries of her life that she had never suffered the
emotional pain that everyone assumed must flow from this presumably trau-
matic event. Even now she could remember the scene perfectly. It had hurt
a bit going in, but not as much as the other twelve-year-old street children
predicted. Once inside, it had been a little like having a mild itch scratched—
sort of nice but not terrific. The main problem had been her stepfather's
precarious balance, helped by neither the position nor the alcohol. Jo-Anne
remembered surreptitiously propping him up as she produced the dutiful
tears and protests that she felt the situation demanded. The worst thing of
the whole business had been the poisonous fumes of the stale breath that had
engulfed her; the best part had been the quality of the scene when her
mother had walked in to discover them. After that her stepfather had not
tried his luck again. For a week or two afterward she had been mildly disappointed. Had she been deficient in some way? Hadn't she given him a good
enough time?

Then the whole business had faded from her mind. In the ghetto you
didn't have the luxury of indulging in emotional amateur dramatics. There
was the business first of survival, and then, in Jo-Anne's case, of advancement. That was another mystery. Where the hell had she discovered ambition? Certainly she hadn't gotten it from her drunken stepfather, her

slatternly mother, or the two older brothers who had fingered her in exchange for candy and makeup before she finally walked out on the whole motley crew at the tender age of fourteen.

It had been one small step for Jo-Anne to prostitution, and she had worked her way through the business from the bottom up. In that brief year of scratched existence she had done it all, and in some remarkable way she had managed to keep her feelings out of it, had existed always on some emotional automatic pilot. Come to think of it, that had never changed. It was as true of her now as it had been then, and sometimes she wondered what this thing was that others called conscience. Certainly *she* had never found it a problem.

A pusher had put her in touch with the Upper East Side madam who had smartened her up and fed her before putting her to work in the city's high-class call-girl system. She had been a natural. Her fifteen-year-old tits, pink, pointed, perfect, had slain the businessmen in their hotel rooms, and as her percentage of the take mounted remorselessly she was increasingly able to call the tune from her pretty, one-room studio on Madison. The jocks got grander, the accents tighter, the pricks limper, and the tastes more jaded.

It was around that time, somewhere between the Madison Avenue studio and the apartment on Fifth with a view of the park, that she had discovered girls. The Racquet Club member whose request had resulted in Jo-Anne's first double act had one hell of a lot to answer for. In the musky, sweet scents of the female body, the silky softness of the warm flesh, in the gentle intimacy of a woman's arms, Jo-Anne had found herself. On leaving the Pierre suite where she had first experienced it, she had invited the svelte Jewish girl back to her apartment, and for the first time in her life Jo-Anne had made love with the earth-shattering intensity of the virgin who had discovered how to give not only her body but her soul. For two years she and Rachel had been lovers. By day they had worked as a team doing for money what at night they did freely for each other, and Jo-Anne had been faithful.

Ambition, however, had not slept. The modeling world was the passport to a different society. Men married models. Seldom did they knowingly marry prostitutes. Every afternoon, as Jo-Anne saw in a thousand hotel mirrors the superb body that she was selling for peanuts, she vowed that one day she would flog it for megabucks. One hundred dollars to make some middle-aged lush come. A million big ones to move the cosmetics of some tycoon like Estée Lauder off the drugstore shelf.

Well, she'd gotten there. Right now Estée Lauder's oceanfront estate was only a rifle shot away.

Breaking into the modeling world had been the second step. Jo-Anne had bided her time and sharpened her image. She had spent her money wisely on the right clothes, read everything she could on etiquette and manners, eaten clever food, gotten lots of sleep, exercised fanatically until she looked as good as the best of the girls who stared at her from the covers of *Vogue* and *Cosmo*. It had been a question then of getting the "in." Pauline Parker had been the passport. Something of an institution in the modeling world,

Pauline Parker was quite shameless about using her position as head of the prestigious Parker Agency to indulge her passion for beautiful women. Short and stocky, she scored zero out of ten for looks, but at the interview, as she sat in amazement behind the big desk, Jo-Anne had turned her on like a neon sign. Spoiled by oversupply, Pauline came across few enough girls who could do that. She had instantly taken the phenomenal-looking girl onto her books, and, in exchange for the ditching of Rachel, and her moving in as live-in lover, Pauline had set about turning her into a star.

The rest had been easy. A top model met anyone she liked. It was just a question of sorting out the sheep from the goats and not doing anything stupid like falling in love, or going for some cheap con man's line.

Peter Duke had not been a con man and was a card-carrying fully paid-up member of the sheep species. There hadn't been a goat in the Duke family since old Teddy Duke, who had bought the scrubland under which the large proportion of Louisiana's oil lay. Disgustingly rich, spoiled, and headstrong, Peter Duke had fallen hopelessly in love with Pauline Parker's girlfriend, and after a few short, spine-tingling weeks during which he had discovered the meaning of sexual ecstasy, he had proposed to her.

Fearing the overzealous investigations of more circumspect Duke relations, Jo-Anne had capitalized on Peter Duke's self-confident spontaneity. She had spirited him away to the Dominican Republic and married him the next day on the beach, to the exuberant strains of a mariachi band and to the congratulations of two Army generals, one owned by Gulf and Western, the other by the CIA.

The inquisitive finger, racing down the slippery back, seemingly overshot its destination. It plunged precipitously into the cleavage of the tight buttocks and hovered encouragingly on the edge of the erogenous zone—cutting short Jo-Anne's reverie and precipitating her back into the suddenly more interesting here and now.

Jane's voice cut through the mists of memory. "I thought I'd lost you there." Was there an iota of reproach in the remark?

"Just daydreaming. I'm back now."

"Sometimes the Rolfing gets you going down memory lane. Sort of lets you dare to remember." The gentle insinuation that Jo-Anne might need courage to remember was a shot in the dark, but Jane was intuitive. Massage made you like that. You got to know bodies, and from there it was a short step to getting to know minds.

Once again the fingers overstepped their mark in the ambiguous gesture. Was it a mistake or a mistake on purpose?

Jo-Anne pushed it.

"Mmmmmmmm. That was nice."

It was Jane's turn to think. What was she doing? What did she want? What did Mrs. Duke want?

She had been mildly irritated when her client had drifted away from her. Her fingers had summoned her back. But why had she chosen that particular method to regain her attention? Jane had worked the bodies of Palm Beach for nearly three years now, and she was far from insensitive about what was required of her. Massage was relaxing therapy, but beneath the surface, the spark of sensuality danced. Some people liked it to be ignored, others for it to be gently fanned, while a small, but far from insignificant minority wanted the spark to become a raging fire, stoked and banked by the masseuse's fingers until it burst through in the prancing flames of overt sexuality.

It was vital not to get it wrong. With some of her clients, but not all, Jane was more than prepared to go all the way. This was only the second time she had been to the Duke home, but with a little thrill of excitement Jane realized that Jo-Anne was indubitably in that last category. It wasn't her husband's scornful remark, not even the enthusiastic response to her hands' daring. There was something else. Something indefinable, yet instantly knowable. The exciting aura of a woman who liked women. It was as real and as alluring as the warm, perfumed air.

"Does your husband have a fantasy about women making it together? A lot of men do, you know." Somehow the time gap between Peter Duke's remark and the present didn't seem important.

Jo-Anne knew. Firsthand. That was nice. Jane was softening up. Jo-Anne squirmed obviously beneath the pleasing touch and laughed. Soon this thing could be out in the open.

On one level Jane's question had been irrelevant. She didn't really want to know the answer, but she was drawn toward a discussion of the topic. That was the oldest trick in the book. Thinking and talking about things was so often a prelude to action. But to Jo-Anne the question was interesting. What did her husband want?

In the early days in the Big Apple he had seemed so straightforward. Poor-little-rich-boy time. He was suntanned and sexy, preppy as hell, in love with vodka, in love with life, the accelerator firmly pressed to the floor. Like everyone else in his group he had been lazy, spoiled, was in love with his mother, and fought like a dog with the father whom he so exactly resembled. In short, Peter Duke had been typecast and Jo-Anne had made a special study of his category. There had been nothing she hadn't known about him, from the latent homosexuality to his abhorrence of men who wore white shoes and jewelry. In those days he had just loved to screw but he hadn't had a clue about how to do it, and he had never tried it when he was even halfway sober. She had been able to provide a crash course of instruction and he had gone for it.

Before she had scored the marriage certificate and the meal ticket for life, she had played it as straight as lace. No funny stuff to offend patrician susceptibilities. Later on, as the novelty of the toy had begun to wear off and boredom, the curse of his class, had showed its ugly head, Jo-Anne had begun to improvise. In those days he certainly had liked to watch her with girls, and he hadn't had to fantasize about it either—it had been gritty reality. But now? It was difficult to say.

One thing was certain. He wasn't into her anymore. For the last year or two there had been nothing but arguments. Only then did they have sex and on two occasions just a little bit of violence.

To Jo-Anne that was pretty much par for the course. She had never believed in such bourgeois concepts as married bliss, and in her experience knights on white chargers had a way of metamorphosing into bloated toads or worse. No, Peter Duke had already done his bit, and for that she would be eternally grateful. He had married her. She was a Duke. Could anything else possibly matter? And the Dukes were rich. Seriously rich, and certain to remain so. They had long since diversified out of oil and now the money was everywhere, woven into the very fabric of America, in rolling Texas acres, in rolling stock, in long-term Treasury bills, in Manhattan office blocks. The Duke position in General Motors alone would have financed the deficit of a medium-size banana republic, while the Palm Beach estate, stretching from ocean to lake at the southern end of the island below Worth Avenue, just had to be worth ten million. That wouldn't be a bad marital home to cop if it ever came to divorce. Not that Jo-Anne contemplated divorce. There was no way to follow a Peter Duke. Richer Americans could be counted on fingers, and mostly they were spoken for.

So Jo-Anne had been careful. In Palm Beach society, in which the Dukes were substantial stars, it didn't do to play around—at least with men. There was one thing alone that the American aristocracy could not stand and that was the thought of their wives getting it from another man. The Europeans didn't share that prejudice. For them a young lover and a lot of discretion was often more than acceptable. It took some of the heat off husbands in whom both the flesh *and* the desire had weakened.

So in Palm Beach if you wanted to stay close to the real money, you didn't mess with the tennis pro. Going up market was marginally less dangerous, on the principle that fraternity relationships were as thick if not thicker than blood, and that a man to whom you would cheerfully lend your golf clubs could probably be forgiven for borrowing your wife. Still, with a billion dollars at risk it didn't do to take chances. Which left a problem: what to do about the zipping hormones, the urges of incredible strength whose power could neither be repressed, sublimated, nor wished away.

Jo-Anne had found her solution, and it was the one that had always worked so well for her. Women. Now, in the heady social atmosphere of Palm Beach charity galas, in the smooth, slick ambiance of the Bath and Tennis Club, in the smartly decorated salons and bedrooms of the sleek oceangoing yachts, she indulged her illicit desires. Bored, underoccupied, neglected by their husbands, not daring to risk the divorce that a heterosexual affair might threaten, the wives of the richest society on earth succumbed in turn to Jo-Anne's charms.

Did Peter know about it? Jo-Anne had often wondered. If so, he was apparently more than prepared to turn a blind eye. Perhaps, as the masseuse had suggested, he still got a vicarious thrill out of imagining her with other girls. Certainly his last remark hinted at something like that. Whatever. By his silence he had condoned it. She was in the clear. Nothing else mattered.

Well, something else did.

In Jane's electric fingertips Jo-Anne could detect the early signs of panic. Floating, drifting up and down her back, the friction was now reduced, and her skin rather than the firm underlying muscle was the target. The nails touched her lightly and the center of operations moved inexorably lower as the fingers became more bold, roaming longingly over the proud upturned buttocks, sometimes pushing down hard, crushing Jo-Anne's pelvis against the black leather of the massage table.

Slowly, surely, Jo-Anne responded to the new meanings of the touch, allowing her firm rump to ride up to meet Jane's eager hands. At last the two bodies were speaking to each other directly. There would be no need of further conversation.

It was going to happen.

The Negro's deferential voice blew it all away.

"Mr. Duke says to tell you you're running late for the party." Standing at his mistress's head, seemingly oblivious of her nakedness, the white-coated servant delivered his message with total impassivity.

Suspended in space in the jingle-jangle moment of sexual arousal, Jo-Anne cursed openly. As the pile of carefully constructed bricks of passion toppled about her, irritation filled the gap so recently vacated by desire.

Screw them all. Peter, Jane, black servants, the world.

With a fluid, sinuous movement she slipped off the massage table, grabbed the monogrammed rough white terrycloth dressing gown from the hands of the servant, and stalked off toward the house. Over her shoulder, without smiling, she said, "Some other time, Jane. Okay?"

THE COLD carrara marble beneath her feet went some way toward calming Jo-Anne's suddenly foul temper. It was cool in here, the unrelenting sunlight blocked out, the air circulated by the eight large ceiling fans. For Jo-Anne it was the best room in the whole remarkable house—the deep, comfortable sofas, the inch-and-a-half-thick glass tables, great bowls of white gardenias— the whites and different shades of oatmeal saved from lack of adventure by the stunning colors of the paintings. Jackson Pollock, Rothko, de Kooning— the best examples of the greatest artists of the Abstract Expressionist move- ment chosen by her personally from the famed Duke collection in Houston. There was not a museum director in the world who would not cheerfully have given a testicle to possess one tenth of the room's paintings. The curator at Houston had been in tears as Jo-Anne had made her choice, stalking through the high-ceilinged, air-conditioned rooms, legal pad in hand, Tom Wesselman tits straining against a tight T-shirt, Allen Jones legs rearing sug- gestively out of dangerous Manolo Blahnik shoes. Unfailingly she had gone for the most important paintings—the ones that couldn't be replaced with mere money, and now the results of her expedition were all around her, existing solely for her private consumption, removed from the prying eyes of the Texan hoi polloi forever.

Casting herself down languorously on the welcoming sofa, she stretched herself out—a graceful feline, preening itself in blissful self-congratulation. It was a long way from the hungry, steamy streets. The whole western wall of the room was arranged as electrically operated sliding doors, the smoked-glass panels screening the ubiquitous sun. In the middle they were retracted and Jo-Anne's field of vision was clear to the sixty-foot pool with its separate cabana, the bright green lawns, smooth as the baize of a billiard table, the sensuously rounded Henry Moore bronze sculptures scattered on the grass like smooth pebbles dotted capriciously on a sea-washed beach. By the pool Jane was folding her table crossly—a nomadic Arab packing away her tent before moving on—her back bent in the graceful curve of a Modigliani line drawing.

Jo-Anne sighed appreciatively. It was good, all of it. The art, Jane's body, the landscape, the life she had won for herself. Nobody would take this away from her. Not a living soul. Certainly no soul who would not die in the attempt. That much she swore to herself. No, the problem, if there was one at all, was where to go from here. Hanging on to what you had was about as exciting as hearing her husband's views on the likely course of interest rates. Okay, so she tried to inject a little danger into the proceedings from time to time, but compared to the survival game on the Big Apple's streets, it was the softest of softball.

In Palm Beach the hottest game in town was social climbing. There at least people got hurt. They didn't bleed openly, but they made up for that in the quantity and quality of their tears. Jo-Anne had learned the game's rules in a long afternoon and was now a past mistress of it. The trick was to keep your ass and your shoe leather in the faces of the people on the rung below. A few rungs below that you could give people a leg up, aiming always for the downward displacement of those who aspired to one's own position. Once one had achieved that objective, the former allies would themselves become fierce adversaries as they tried with all their might to steal your rung. The higher you got the more difficult, and the more desirable, became the upward mobility. In that, the climbing game resembled real life. Peter and Jo-Anne Duke of course were already in the rarefied stratosphere when they had, at Jo-Anne's instigation, begun to play.

Still, once you were in the contest you had to struggle onward, bravely, courageously, employing cunning, dirty tricks, and very large quantities of money, ignoring the emotional or financial cost until the top of the mountain had been reached. And at the top of the mountain, high above the clouds, beyond the racing of the rats, at the right hand of God the Father Almighty, was Marjorie du Pont Donahue. The queen of Palm Beach. The one Jo-Anne Duke wanted to *be*.

Jo-Anne let out a deep sigh and hugged the dressing gown close to her. Some raddled old trout with varicose veins like a relief map of Europe and the mind of a black widow spider: Marjorie du Pont Donahue, the rat-bag with the fortune that made even the Dukes look like small time, the bag of bones held together by leather skin whose offhand remarks could cut an unlucky social mountaineer in two.

Nobody knew why she was the queen. Nobody knew how she had gotten there. But the players of the game all knew that she *was* the queen, and the only queen, and they all paid homage at her court. Marjorie Donahue was the first thing they thought about in the morning, and their last shining vision before they went to bed at night. In between the darkness and the dawn they would dream of her—of her dinner-party invitations arriving on the silver salver, of her crackling voice on their cordless telephones, of the rasping touch of her wrinkled hand.

Unbelievably, Jo-Anne herself had been drawn into the spider's web. The game was no longer absurd. Instead, it was all-consuming. As a fish swimming in Palm Beach waters, one became oblivious to the reality of the world outside. Jo-Anne was more than happy to be one of them, just as long as she was the hunter and not the hunted—that her teeth were sharper, her bite more deadly than that of the other inhabitants of the aquarium. So far it had been just that.

Tonight there would be another round. The Planned Parenthood Victorian Picnic. Jo-Anne didn't even try to suppress the smile at the thought of it. Charity dances were a joke in themselves, but Planned Parenthood? In a way she supposed she ought to have been considered a charter member. In prostitution there were two "no-no's"—pregnancy and the pox. Both reduced one's income-making capacity, that ultimate sin. Jo-Anne shuddered to think how many men had been inside her—a thousand, two thousand?—but not one of them had succeeded in impregnating her. Planned Parenthood indeed. Planned Parenthood owed her a medal. Perhaps she would arrange a special announcement. "Ladies and gentlemen. May I have your attention please. Jo-Anne Duke has had more screws than you've had hot dinners without getting pregnant. Planned Parenthood would like to recognize her services publicly by . . ."

Jo-Anne laughed out loud at the outrageous thought. Boy, that would really be dropping it on the fan. For years she had worked to bury her past, and she had been completely successful. Not a whisper had survived. Not a single rumor had found the fertile soil in which grew the Palm Beach grapevine, and she prayed that it would stay that way. She couldn't help feeling that now she was in the clear. The Duke name and her Donahue friendship were the most powerful possessions. With those two talismans a girl could enter the very gates of hell unafraid.

Contentedly Jo-Anne gazed up at the brilliant de Kooning. Why was the girl with the big tits smiling like that as she stood next to her bicycle? She looked mighty pleased with herself. Had she just spread her legs for the bank manager and bought the bicycle with the proceeds? Little things, little minds, she thought absent-mindedly. What was *her* bicycle? The sleek hundred-and-twenty-foot oceangoing Jon Bannenberg yacht bobbing on the waters of Lake Worth just the other side of the twelve-foot ficus hedge? The sky-blue Lear jet soaking up the sun in the Bennett Aviation compound at the West Palm International Airport? Or perhaps it was her splendid-looking husband himself, six feet of fifty-year-old muscle and breeding, and with just a touch of blood in his vodka-filled veins.

Damn. The thought of Peter clouded her mood. Really, he had been impossible lately, rude and indifferent, his previously reliable sense of humor absent. Perhaps it was the drink. *Palm Beach Life* said it made you irritable.

For sure it wasn't a shortage of sex. It was no secret that he screwed everything that moved and even, in Jo-Anne's opinion, one or two women for whom any movement at all had become difficult. But that had never been a problem. It was often irritating but not a problem problem. To hell with it. She needed a drink if she was going to get through this evening.

She hardly raised her voice. Certainly didn't bother to look around. There would be a servant there. Hopefully, Caesar. He seemed to understand about caiparinhos.

"Can somebody make me a caiparinho?"

A minute or two later the glass was in her hands. Sometimes she preferred the tequila base, but today she was glad it was white rum. The shiny green crushed limes nestled in among the chunks of ice and she drank deep on the bittersweet liquid. The Brazilians called it a peasant girl. Well, she liked the taste of peasant girls, Brazilian or otherwise. Taking a deep breath, and revitalized by the first warming sensations as the strong spirit hit her empty stomach, she stood up and walked toward the marble staircase.

In the master bedroom on the first floor the angry colors of the Abstract Expressionists were merely an exciting memory. Here all was pastel peace— gentle Renoirs, soothing Manets, a deeply relaxing Pissarro. The huge four-poster bed dominated the room, its football-field size allowing exotic acrobatics, or almost total privacy from one's bedmate. Recently it had been the latter.

Jo-Anne looked around. Peter was in here somewhere. In his dressing room? On the fifty-foot veranda with its view of Lake Worth and the mainland?

She heard the click of the replaced telephone receiver.

"There you are. About time. The cars are organized for six thirty. What a time to fix a massage." The aggressive, truculent voice drifted in through the open window.

"Oh, fuck off, Peter. Don't give me a hassle. Who the hell wants to get to this ridiculous party before eight o'clock anyway? Riding on carousels and having my fortune told I can do without. When I want to know my fortune I call the accountant."

Jo-Anne stalked through the open doors onto the balcony. Peter was all dressed up. Standard Palm Beach evening wear. Kilgour, French and Stanbury navy-blue double-breasted blazer, Everglades Club buttons, sky-blue-and-white dotted silk tie from Turnbull and Asser in London, Gucci loafers worn without socks, dark gray razor-creased worsted pants. The sunburned face, greased hair, graying slightly at the temples, and a vague but indefinable flavor of the most understated cologne made up the picture of plutocratic excellence.

He looked great. It was just a drag that there would be two hundred Identikit look-alikes under the big top at the Flagler Museum. Sartorial daring was no part of the Palm Beach picture, and people had been socially extinguished for crimes no greater than the wearing of white shoes or synthetic-fiber shirts.

Peter Duke snarled back, "Believe it or not I am not a carousel fiend either, but we are meeting Marjorie *and* Stansfield and we said we'd be there at seven. I realize of course that doing what you promise to do is not something you learned on mother's knee. However, I was always brought up to keep my word."

Bastard, thought Jo-Anne. That was hitting low. It wasn't like Peter to throw the class thing at her. Something was definitely up.

Still, trading insults was something of a specialty for her. She had for sure learned *that* from her mother. She let rip.

"Frankly, I'm surprised you have the nerve to bring *your* mother into all this. Everyone says the old lush hardly knew your name, and that you were farmed out to all those English nannies. The only thing you ever learned from her was to drink too much."

Peter stood stock still. Knuckles white, his face suffused with blood, he pulsated with anger and hatred.

Jo-Anne wondered momentarily if she had gone too far. Employing the old Arab ruse of insulting an adversary's mother could always be relied on for strong reactions, but she hadn't expected this.

"You tramp," he managed at last, spitting the words out through clamped teeth. "I'll bury you for that. Do you hear me? *Bury you.*" His voice rose to a crescendo, cracking with the strain of the violent emotion that shook him. "Don't you ever dare mention my mother again. Do you hear me? *Do you hear me?*"

Me and the rest of Palm Beach, thought Jo-Anne. "Oh, why are you always such a *child,* Peter," she said aloud, in apparent despair as she turned around and walked back into the bedroom.

—

JO-ANNE WAS laughing helplessly. Tears had appeared to order and her whole body shook with uncontrollable hilarity. But the really funny thing was that Marjorie's joke hadn't been funny at all. Marjorie Donahue had long since ceased to care about counterfeit emotions. She had been dealing in that currency for far too long, and now she had even lost the facility to recognize the real thing. For her the important element was power. When people failed to laugh at her dirty stories it didn't mean they were lacking in humor—that was irrelevant. The significant message would be that her power was on the wane, that her courtiers were on the verge of some violent palace coup. So, she laughed back at Jo-Anne and filed the information away in the ancient but still awesomely efficient filing cabinet that was her mind. Jo-Anne could be counted on. Jo-Anne was loyal. Jo-Anne would still get favors. Jo-Anne's enemies would be her enemies.

"Oh, Marjorie. Why can't I tell jokes like that?" Jo-Anne forced out the words through the gales of laughter.

Marjorie Donahue preened herself, while around the table the other dinner-party guests mentally reached for the vomit bag. They'd all laughed at the queen's joke too, but none of them had been as willing or as able to go so convincingly far over the top as Jo-Anne. All had made the fatal mistake of underestimating a successful person's vanity. Jo-Anne alone had recognized that in the department of flattery nothing succeeded like excess. It was only the moderately successful people in life who affected a dislike for sycophants. The real winners couldn't get enough of them.

The Duke table was very definitely the top spot for the top dogs, and all around the lesser players craned their necks to see what was going on and to identify those who by their presence among the mighty were on the up and up. Jo-Anne stared proudly back at the envious heads, shouting a welcome here, delivering a glassy rebuke there, as she reveled in the public demonstration of her social-climbing skills. The heady feeling gripped her, as she saw the envy in a hundred eyes. And not just any eyes. This was not the untutored, unconditional adoration of common people for some movie idol. These eyes had class. There were Vanderbilts out there, and Fords, as well as sleek counts of obscure Italian origin; the inevitable English, poor as church mice but dramatically well dressed, sponging like hell off everyone in return for a few finely turned phrases; and a group of truculent Frenchmen, perpetually irritated by the fact that nobody could or would speak their half-dead language. All of them would have given whatever they had to give to be sitting at Jo-Anne's table.

Marjorie Donahue peered suspiciously around the table at her courtiers— a bit like a lion tamer in a circus cage.

"I do so *enjoy* dirty jokes," she said to no one in particular. "Makes a change from talking about money and servants, although sometimes those are rather cruder topics."

Jo-Anne laughed loudly.

"You're so right, Marjorie. You should hear Peter on interest rates. It's positively disgusting."

She made a face that managed to suggest that her husband discussing any topic at all was positively disgusting.

He scowled across the table at her.

"Well, dear, if it *has* to be money I'd like to hear what the senator has to say about the budget deficit." Ostentatiously she stifled a yawn. At this table and in this town she was the boss and she wanted everyone to know it. If that meant poking a little gentle fun at the powerful senator, then so be it.

Bobby didn't mind one bit. The self-confidence was armor-plated.

"Funny you should say that, Marjorie." Bobby Stansfield's voice was calm, and around it danced the ghost of a dry humor. "You know, if you and

Jo-Anne got together and made a small contribution from your personal funds, I think we could solve the deficit problem right here."

That was nice. They were all rich as well. Rich, beautiful, and successful. The mood of mutual self-congratulation hung heavily in the air, merging easily with the scent of the fifty white gardenias that floated in the Irish Waterford glass bowl in the center of the table.

Bobby turned to Jo-Anne.

"Would you like to dance?"

"Why, thank you, senator."

Jo-Anne mimicked a Southern belle drawl.

He smiled across the table at Peter Duke.

"You don't mind if I borrow your wife? I might never bring her back."

Peter Duke joined in the general laughter, but inside he wasn't laughing. You can take the cunt. She's just about what you deserve, you self-satisfied, stuck-up, pompous ass, he wanted to say. Since childhood days Dukes and Stansfields had enjoyed an uneasy friendship. In many ways they had a lot in common—old, patrician, Republican Palm Beach families, with vast fortunes and shared prejudices. There were, however, two problems that tended inevitably to sour relationships. The first was that the Dukes were much, much richer than the Stansfields. The second was that the Stansfields were far, far more successful than the Dukes.

The bone of contention had two infinitely gnawable ends. Dukes were jealous of the Stansfields' power, and the attention that power brought. To compensate they accused the Stansfields of being common, lacking in class, courting media attention, being overactive philistines who didn't know how to behave. The Stansfields were envious of the phenomenal Duke wealth and of their nationwide reputation as sophisticated patrons of the arts. To get even, they accused the Dukes of being self-centered layabouts who asked not what they could do for their country, who drank too much and did too little, who thought a great deal of themselves for no better reason than that their ancestor had locked into Louisiana's oil.

That having been said, the families were too alike to afford to fall out openly. Palm Beach was a small town, and there were other enemies who could only profit from a Duke-Stansfield vendetta. Teddy Kennedy, for example. When old Stansfield had died, his eldest son Bobby had inherited his well-oiled political machine and, soon after, his Senate seat. Bobby was flashily good looking and the standard bearer of the Stansfield political dynasty; some of the more aware pundits were already muttering about his making a bid for the presidency. It was likely that in the future his Democratic opponent might be his North Ocean Boulevard neighbor, Teddy Kennedy—the memories of Chappaquiddick perhaps dulled by the passage of time and by sterling work in the Senate.

No true Palm Beacher who was welcome in the Everglades Club viewed the disturbing possibility of a second Kennedy presidency with anything but naked horror. Kennedys were Democrats and Democrats were socialists, who were, of course, the next best thing to communists. All ranks would have to be closed to defeat a Kennedy. The result of all this was that although Peter Duke's thoughts about Bobby Stansfield were seldom charitable, he had actually donated to his Senate election campaign. In turn Bobby had not only accepted the gift graciously; he had on more than one occasion intervened in Washington on behalf of Duke business interests, despite his personal dislike of Peter Duke—a dislike that in no way included his pretty, vivacious wife.

Bobby threaded his way between the closely packed tables toward the dance floor. It was a regal progress. Everyone fought for his attention—hands reaching out to grab the sleeve of his immaculately cut dinner jacket, the rasping welcomes of the gravelly voiced society matrons, the raucous jokes of the good-ol'-boy battalions, their tongues well oiled by the predinner martinis. Bobby swam effortlessly across the sea of popularity, an impressed Jo-Anne following in his wake. For every remark, he had the appropriate one-liner, pitched at just the right level, matching ounce for ounce the seriousness or frivolity of those who had made it. In the short time it took him to reach the floor he had smiled and frowned, charmed and flirted, made promises and accepted them. As Jo-Anne watched the strong back with its wide, sculpted shoulders, she was lost in admiration of the performance. This was the art of the born politician. He had offended no one, massaged egos, consolidated votes. In his position, Jo-Anne would not have resisted the temptation to spread a little pain with the pleasure. That was the difference between the professional and the amateur.

On the edge of the dance floor he turned toward her, his arms held out to take hers. The smile was warm but with an edge of humor. It said that he was attracted to her, and that she was about to have to deal with that fact.

Jo-Anne smiled right back. Handling men had never been a problem. In this case it was going to be a pleasure.

"Do you know this is the first time we've danced together?" Bobby pretended to be hurt.

"Surely you weren't too shy to ask. God knows you've had enough opportunity. Sometimes I think the only damn thing we do in this town is dance."

"Well, you know what they say—you don't go to a ball to dance. You go to look out for a wife, to look after a wife, or to look after somebody else's wife."

Bobby looked right into her eyes as he said that, and swirled her selfconfidently into the mainstream of dancers. On the bandstand, Joe Renée and his orchestra, veterans of a thousand Palm Beach balls, told Dolly for the umpteenth time that she was looking swell.

"Are you looking after somebody else's wife right now, Bobby?" She squeezed the strong hand and moved in a little bit closer, conscious of the eyes upon them. Flirting on the dance floor was permissible in Palm Beach. That was one of the reasons there were so many dances.

In answer, he bent forward and whispered in her ear. "We should have an affair, you know." That was the Stansfield way. Up front. No time wasted. The smell of self-confidence all over the place.

"I don't cheat on my husband." Jo-Anne laughed flirtatiously as she moved in closer.

"There's always a first time."

"Not for me. Until death us do part."

"Maybe we should try to arrange that."

They both laughed as he swung her exuberantly across the room. Both Joe Renée and the endless Dolly were still going strong.

God, you're attractive, thought Jo-Anne. Fabulous looking. Famous as hell. A man of the future who knew how to make the present sparkle like diamonds. But, compared to Peter Duke, a pauper. Richer by far than most Americans could ever hope to be, here in Palm Beach he was a financial minnow. What a pity. God, in his wisdom, had dealt fairly, and Bobby Stansfield missed by that all important card the royal straight flush. Which was why a flirtation was all he would ever get from her, as long as she was Mrs. Peter Duke.

"Come on, Bobby, stop practicing your charms on a married woman. Let's go and have a ride on the carousel. I'd never get Peter on it. He'd be sick, or something boring."

Outside the marquee, in the grounds of Henry Morrison Flagler's museum, a fairground setting had been created for the Planned Parenthood ball. There were jugs of ice-cold martinis on long, white-linen-covered trestle tables, a fortuneteller and a palmist, and a sparkling, magical carousel, its red-and-white horses rising and falling to the evocative sound of an old fairground organ. The cream of the town's society mingled beneath the palm trees, many of them dressed in the Victorian costume that was the "picnic's" theme, the men wearing the traditional straw boaters that had been given to them on arrival.

Jo-Anne had ignored the fancy dress on the principle that modern women had on the whole done better than Victorian ones. She wore a knee-length Anne Klein silk crepe dress of the purest white, slit to the calf on one side and covered in bugle beads that shimmered and shone as she moved. From time to time a long brown leg flashed interestingly, and the rest of her, dramatic and alluring, was hardly concealed at all by the flimsy material. Jo-Anne didn't detract from the beautiful sexual simplicity of the dress by wearing jewelry. In that she was almost alone. All around her the rocks of the plutocracy flashed and sparkled, but Jo-Anne, who could have afforded any of them and all of them, confined herself to simple one-carat diamond-stud earrings.

On the carousel, jammed tightly against her in the wooden saddle built for one, Bobby Stansfield didn't give up. Stansfields never gave up. "We bachelors get lonely, you know."

"That's not what I heard. Word is there's more ass up in the North End on the weekends than Heinz has varieties."

Bobby Stansfield's laugh was almost the best thing about him. It was wicked, and uninhibited, charming and totally real. Jo-Anne felt the danger signs within her. This man was just a bit too attractive, and the stakes were high. It would be safer back at the table.

When the music stopped she was firm. "Come on, Bobby. Time to eat. I could eat a horse, I'm so hungry."

Taking his hand in hers she lead him back to the marquee.

Horses not being evident among the courses on the menu, Jo-Anne had to struggle through a sumptuous cold buffet of Scots salmon flown in from the Dee that afternoon, Maine lobsters, Florida Bay prawns, cracked crab, sliced filet mignon, and crisp apple pie. There was a Bâtard Montrachet 1973 with the mollusks, the crustaceans, and the fish, a mouth-watering Chateau Beychevelle 1966 with the beef, and a Dom Pérignon '71 with the pie.

With the coffee the party began to go liquid in more senses of the word than one. During the "picnic" the tables had more or less hung together, the members of each dancing and talking among themselves. Now, as the alcohol liberated the party's collective psyche, lines of communication between the guests loosened up, and that well-known species, the table hopper, began to appear. The old hands recognized this as the most dangerous, but also the most promising, time of all for a little judicious social climbing. The booze had injected courage into the socially faint-hearted, but it had impaired judgment, too, and the floor of the tent was positively littered with banana skins for the unwary. During this stage the "haves" sat tight as they prepared to receive homage from the "have-nots." The aim of the upwardly mobile parvenus was to secure a seat at the table of a group of their social superiors. The game plan of the top dogs was to repel boarders as far as possible except in those cases where it had been decided that some protégé needed a visible "leg up" the ladder. The Duke party was the honey pot around which the most ambitious bees buzzed. Marjorie Donahue's presence always guaranteed that.

Two or three unlucky Palm Beachers had already gotten their coded messages to "walk on" by the time Eleanor Peacock arrived. Eleanor was a difficult one. A fully paid-up member of one of the town's oldest families, she had, however, never quite made it in the social swim. Her parties were unexciting, and her food and flower arrangements were as dull and lacking in inspiration as her placements. Also, the Peacocks were not rich. Well born certainly, and members of all the right clubs, but the North End house wasn't on the beach or the lake, and the summer trips to Connecticut were shorter than was strictly desirable. And Arch Peacock worked. That in itself was not a disaster, but it certainly didn't score bonus points in a town where the smart thing was to inherit old money and spend one's time looking after it, or rather supervising others as they looked after it.

The fact that she was not a top dog in Palm Beach society irritated Eleanor Peacock, and she had scratched at the itch until it had become an angry, livid sore, painfully obvious for all to see. Sometimes she would cover it over, all sweetness and light, as she fought for the place in the sun that she felt was rightfully hers. At others she would lapse into a cynical, explosive aggression during which her bile would be directed menacingly at those she felt had wrongfully taken her place. Jo-Anne was an obvious target. Obscure origins, and too good looking by half. On several occasions Eleanor had tried to take her on, but she had always come off the worse in the clinches.

Tonight, however, she reckoned she had some very special ammunition and she was going to fire it to maximum effect. Both Peter Duke and—far more important—Marjorie Donahue would be there to watch her deliver the broadside that would sink Jo-Anne Duke for good. All evening she had savored what she knew would be her triumph as she had tucked into the wine. Now in full sail, her white taffeta dress billowing in the breeze created by her confident approach, she bore down on the Duke table as heads craned to see whether she would do better than the three aspirants who had already failed.

Jo-Anne saw her old adversary coming and noted the red flush on the chest bone above the ample if shapeless bosom and beneath the rather mean diamond choker. Her nose scented trouble. A veteran of a thousand such skirmishes, Jo-Anne sought out her most powerful ally. Tonight Peter would be no help at all. He had been scowling at her all evening.

Leaning across the table she laid her hand on Marjorie's weatherbeaten forearm, kneading the wrinkled skin. "Oh, Marjorie, I'm *so* glad you could come tonight. I haven't laughed so much for *weeks*—since the Heart Ball."

Marjorie had been at their table at that one, too.

"Hello, everyone."

Eleanor Peacock's forced bonhomie broke over the table like a big wet wave. With various degrees of enthusiasm, none of them substantial, muttered welcomes were returned.

"Marjorie, you're looking wonderful as usual," Eleanor lied ingratiatingly. The old bag looked as if she had some terminal disease.

Taper at the ready, she prepared her salvo as she turned threateningly toward Jo-Anne.

"Oh, Jo-Anne, I didn't see you there," she lied. "Do you know I met the most *extraordinary* person in New York the other day? He said he used to know you really well." To everyone at the table with the glaring exception of Jo-Anne, Eleanor Peacock's words were completely innocent. It was a standard table hopper's opening gambit. Eleanor was about to ingratiate herself with her social superiors by claiming a shared friend. The more alert might have wondered about the word "extraordinary," but nobody did.

The effect on Jo-Anne, however, was electric. Any mention of New York made her nervous as hell, and from the lips of Eleanor Peacock the mention was grotesquely significant. Jo-Anne alone picked up on the cruel smile and the horrendous innuendos. The "know," for instance, had been given almost biblical connotations, and the "really well" meant *really* well.

For the first time in years, Jo-Anne Duke felt the emotion of fear. It rushed through her body like a tidal wave, blotting out everything, washing away all thought, paralyzing her with its dreadful force. Oh, God! Not now. Not here. In front of the queen. In front of her husband. In front of Senator Stansfield. She felt the blood drain from her face and watched her right hand move in slow motion toward her untouched glass of water as if by this unnecessary movement she was proving to herself that she still had some control over her destiny. In blissful ignorance of the drama that was being played, the rest of the table carried on as if nothing had happened. Eleanor Peacock was being "endured." General conversation wouldn't be interrupted for long before Marjorie Donahue would "move her on" with a few placating phrases. It was the sort of minor irritation that was part of the onerous burdens of social superstardom.

The thoughts were coming together again now and Jo-Anne fought to organize them in the milliseconds left before disaster struck. What did this dreadful woman know? How much, and in what detail? And if she knew it all would she say it now? All of it?

"Oh, really," her voice said.

As she spoke Jo-Anne took in the Teflon determination in the Peacock eyes, the glassy patina painted on by the white burgundy and the claret. Dear God. This was it. She was going to be exposed.

"Yes, it was really interesting. It was at a charity gala for the New York police department, and I found myself sitting next to this character called Krumpe . . ."

Krumpe. Krumpe. Krumpe. The name rolled around in Jo-Anne's mind like an undetonated mine. Krumpe. Fat and mean. Krumpe, cruel and revengeful. Krumpe who'd screwed her in exchange for his silence. Lieutenant Krumpe of Vice. On the wings of memory she soared like an eagle over the sordid fields of her past, and beneath her, scurrying about like a rat in a sewer, was Leo Krumpe. Krumpe had blown away the morals charges, tipped her off about the drug busts, protected her from violent pimps and outraged johns. But he had exacted a terrible payment. In exchange he had demanded and received the run of her body, and even now at the top of the Palm Beach pinnacle she could feel the fetid, alcohol-sodden breath on her skin, the rough touch of the stubbled cheek, the dreadful heaviness of the short, squat body as it straddled her. When Peter Duke had entered her life, she discarded Krumpe like a used condom, and almost certainly he had never forgiven her. Now from the grave of her past his evil finger was reaching out to touch her.

She was at the interface. Up till this second she was in the clear. A good friend in New York called Krumpe. Dear old Leo. I hope you gave him my love. No relation to the Palm Beach plumbers of the same name. Ha! Ha! Haven't seen him in years. Always remember his wonderful Polish jokes. But in a few seconds the cat would be out of the bag and a lifetime's work would be destroyed.

She must play for time, summon allies, call in I.O.U.'s.

Her unsteady hand found the glass of water, brushed against its side, and sent it crashing from the table to the floor. At the same time she turned to Marjorie Donahue and allowed her stricken face to do the talking. No actress had won an Oscar with a better performance than Jo-Anne's now. Everything was there in her eyes. The fear, the helplessness, the awful need. She was white as a sheet and her lip was trembling as her left hand felt for the scrawny forearm of the only person who could save her.

Marjorie Donahue saw it all, and the ancient mind weighed it up. Jo-Anne was in mortal danger. And the threat was coming from Eleanor Peacock. That much was immediately clear. But what threat? It was impossible to say. She hadn't really been listening. One never made a point of listening to Eleanor. Something about New York. Some mutual friend? The hand that gripped her and the face that beseeched spoke of the urgency. The urgency for her intervention. But why? What was to be said? Time was clearly of the essence. She would have to rely on her social instinct; seldom had it let her down. Jo-Anne was a friend. She laughed at her jokes; she flattered her extravagantly. At her age and in her position, what more could one ask for? Eleanor Peacock, however, had never been a fawning courtier. While far from being an enemy, she was a million miles from the inner circle. She had tried to play the game all right, but there had always been something held back—almost as if she subscribed to the heretical idea that there were other things in the world besides Palm Beach and its social scene. And no money to speak of. Perhaps if there had been charm and good looks in sufficient quantities to offset the disadvantage of relative poverty, she might have been forgiven. But in those departments she was deficient too. No, in the stone, paper, scissors game that they played in this town there could be only one winner in a confrontation between Peacocks and Dukes. Jo-Anne must prevail. No question.

Eleanor puffed herself up like a balloon as she prepared to launch the missiles that would destroy Jo-Anne. But before she could speak, the queen spoke, and it was with all the sweet reason of a nice old lady.

"Eleanor, dear. I'm glad you popped by. You remember I mentioned the possibility of your doing the junior chairman stint for the Red Cross Ball next year. Well, on more mature reflection I think you're a bit inexperienced for it. So I think we'd better forget it. Oh, and thank you for that invitation to drinks next week, but I'm afraid I won't be able to come. I'm surprised you chose next week for your party. What with everything else going on, I'd imagine quite a lot of people won't be able to make it."

Everyone saw the blood leave Eleanor Peacock's face as they witnessed the social execution. Apart from Jo-Anne, all were unaware of the cause. As far as the rest of the table were concerned this was public retribution for some prior crime, Marjorie Donahue's meting out justice for some peccadillo —Eleanor's befriending of a Donahue enemy, a treacherous remark of Eleanor's finding its way back to the Donahue ear. Something like that. All were far too caught up in the guts and the gore to recognize that Jo-Anne herself had had a significant part in it.

No ritually slaughtered lamb could have bled so fast and so comprehensively as Eleanor Peacock. The social lifeblood drained from her at the touch of Marjorie Donahue's deft dagger, and nobody doubted that her days in Palm Beach society were gone forever. Her "party" next week would be as well attended as a wife-swap evening given by a host who was rumored to have the clap.

In case there should be the merest shadow of doubt, the queen turned the knife in the wound. Overkill.

"Anyway, Eleanor dear, I'm sure we are all thrilled you enjoyed New York. I suspect that in the future you'll be spending *much* more time there."

~4~

THE EXCITEMENT IN the air crackled like electricity. On the surface nothing much was happening; the girls stood around on the wooden workout floor chatting nervously, giggling occasionally. From time to time there was an extravagant yawn—always a sign of tension.

Lisa was no exception. She, too, was affecting a nonchalance she didn't feel, a bravado she imagined the occasion demanded, but inside all was turmoil. Perched on the edge of the receptionist's desk, long legs dangling aimlessly, she smiled down at Maggie.

"Well, Maggs, a few more minutes and then . . . instant fame."

She laughed and looked at her watch for the hundredth time. They were ten and a half minutes late.

"You don't think they'll cancel," said Maggie dubiously.

"No way, sweetheart. My gym's news, and they need news. We're doing them a favor." Even Lisa had to admit that didn't ring true. West Palm TV's "Focus" program could almost certainly struggle on without Lisa Starr.

"Does everything look all right?" Maggie peered unhappily around the glittering, gleaming gymnasium. The question, of course, was superfluous, but at moments like this the free-floating anxiety needed a home and the mind searched desperately to find one.

"Oh, come on, Maggie. Everything's immaculate. You know it is."

That was true. Old Weiss's money was scattered all over the room, but it wasn't in dollar bills. The shining Nautilus machines, closely resembling fiendish instruments of cunning Medieval torture, took up the whole north wall of the oak-floored exercise area. They had been delivered factory fresh the week before—twenty thousand dollars' worth of mechanical pain. There were biceps machines, triceps machines, stomach flatteners, trapezius strengtheners, and all were arranged in strict scientific order, each of the body's muscle groups catered to in turn.

To reach them you had to cross the aerobics floor, its highly polished wood brand new, not yet scuffed and mellowed by the assault of a thousand pounding sneakers. All around, the mirrored walls threw back the reflections,

697

pandering to the narcissistic element that seemed such a vital part of all bodily endeavor. In corners, scattered in apparently orderly chaos, were piles of foam-rubber exercise mats, and stacks of dumb-bell-shaped weights for the aerobic routines.

In the back portion, entered by a long corridor, was a different world. If the front of the gym was blood, toil, sweat, and tears, in the back all was soft seduction, an air-conditioned retreat from the harsh realities of routine. The Finnish sauna was big enough to lie down in, welcoming and womblike. On its floor the wooden bucket was permanently filled with the delicious pine essence whose scent would fill the suddenly damp atmosphere as it was poured over the white-hot coals. Outside in the sitting area, there were oatmeal-colored deck chairs beside which lay columns of magazines, shamelessly up market: *New York* magazine, *Architectural Digest, Town and Country*. Rough, white towels lay in neat, serried ranks, a superabundance of plenty, giving an aura of effortless luxury. Farther down the narrow corridor, doors led to the soundproof massage area, and the mosaic-tiled Jacuzzi. The entrance foyer in which Lisa and Maggie sat doubled as a boutique for the dancewear. The sexy, skimpy, brightly colored workout clothes were everywhere—festooned from each available ledge and corner, their straps and bodices leaving nothing at all to be imagined, hymns of celebration to the beauty of the female body. There were leg warmers, flesh-colored body stockings, pastel-shaded dance shoes, pink plastic hair clips, hand weights, terrycloth head and wrist bands, and bottle after bottle of vitamin pills.

"I don't know how you do it, Lisa. I guess some people are just born lucky."

"Screw luck, Maggie. It wasn't just that. I telephoned that producer every day for a week, until he finally agreed to see me. And then he said no at first. So I hung around that sandwich shop he uses eating rubbish and drinking shit until he finally surrendered."

"And now he's in love with you, I suppose."

"Who knows or cares? I got the spot. This place is on the map and the paint's hardly dry." Lisa laughed at the sound of herself. So tough, so ballsy. But why the hell not? If you believed in yourself enough, then everything was up for grabs. It was a question of daring to reach for the sky, of blocking one's ears to the propaganda of those who believed that some things just weren't possible.

In her stomach, however, the butterflies were playing and her mouth was as dry as the desert. She mustn't blow it. She must get the message across.

The arrival of the mobile television crew was always something of a spectacle, enjoyed most of all by the TV people themselves. In latter-day America, media men were gods incarnate as the citizens fought tooth and nail for their fifteen minutes of instant fame. Jim Summerford, relaxed but businesslike, led the way. Behind him trooped a gang of laid-back professionals—cameramen, lighting men, sound men. The greetings were friendly but he obviously wanted to get down to work. "I thought we'd start by having the class work out with these hand-weight things. Then we could cut to you pumping iron on those machines. We wrap it up with the interview in which you lay down the philosophy of the gym and explain how it differs from the mainstream gyms. How does that grab you?"

"Sounds fine to me."

The film crew worked fast setting up their equipment, and soon everything was ready for Lisa to give the signal to begin.

Bathed in the unforgiving heat of the arc lights and pushing themselves to the maximum, Lisa's girls gave it their best shot. The cameras lingered lovingly on the dancing, waving bodies, tracing the erotic contours, peeping shamelessly into the wet feminine recesses, playing lasciviously over the thrashing limbs. Hungrily the tape recorders lapped up the slashing rhythm of the electrobeat music as the frenetic arms and legs whipped up their owners' sweat into a rich lather of effort and ecstasy.

Jim Summerford raised both thumbs in the air as his daring cameramen waded into the cauldron of bubbling feminine flesh, their phallic lenses leering lecherously at smooth damp cleavages, at parted lips, tasting the abandonment, the total commitment to movement and work. Across his face was the smile of a man who had gotten what he wanted—a turn-on for his male viewers to which wives and lovers could not possibly take exception.

"Okay. That's it. I think we have it," he screamed above the music. "Let's move on."

Coitus interruptus. The cameras withdrew at the conductor's command, leaving the collective female psyche stranded on a plateau of unfulfilled expectation. Somebody threw the switch on the music, and the dancing limbs began dejectedly to wind down, marionettes of whom the puppeteer had tired, clockwork figures whose time was up. This was television, and what television wanted television got.

To Lisa, strapped into the hip adducer machine, it seemed everything was going well. The girls had looked great, and the pretty ones in the front had, as was intended, gotten all the attention. Now it was her turn. First the visuals, then the verbals.

She had chosen the particular Nautilus machine carefully. Its purpose was to exercise the muscles that drew the legs together. Starting with her legs splayed wide apart she would draw the two platforms to which they were attached toward the midline against resistance, before allowing the force of the machine to snap them apart once again. The camera angle was full frontal, the camera lens peering unashamedly straight between her spread-eagled legs. The effect, blatantly erotic, was heightened by Lisa's choice of clothes. A daringly brief jet-black singlet, its tantalizingly thin strip of black cloth barely covering her crotch, was superimposed over a skin-colored one-piece body stocking.

To all but the exercise cognoscenti it looked as if she were wearing hardly anything at all.

Jim Summerford was not complaining. "Lisa, that looks wonderful. Tell us what you're doing. Let's have a commentary."

As Lisa's powerful legs opened and closed in front of the camera's unblinking eye, her voice was confident, assured, showing no evidence at all of physical exertion. "The basic difference between my studio and the others is that I have the Nautilus machines. I don't just rely on aerobics. The beauty of the Nautilus program is that you can complete the circuit in twenty minutes. Ideal for a lunch break. And you only need to do it three times a week. In fact, you shouldn't work out on the machines more than that."

Her legs scissored effortlessly in and out as she spoke, the sensuality of the movements seemingly at odds with the matter-of-fact delivery of her words.

"You start slowly, lifting only the weight you can manage. Then you build up gradually until you move mountains."

The dazzling smile burned into the videotape as Lisa's legs made short work of the formidable pile of iron ingots. "The circuit is arranged so that all the different muscle groups are dealt with in order. You keep a record of the weight you move on each machine, and increase it gradually as you get stronger. You do fifteen actions on each machine. No more. No less. I guess that's my fifteen now."

Languorously, she unstrapped herself from the Nautilus, disentangling her legs from the platforms, sitting upright now, hands clasped demurely in her lap, as she waited for Jim Summerford's approach.

"Well, Lisa Starr, that was pretty impressive. But I expect our viewers might wonder if this sort of body building gets one musclebound."

"Do I look musclebound?"

Lisa did not look musclebound. The fantasy of some daydreaming anatomist? Yes. The answered prayer of any heterosexual who liked his women fit? Certainly. Incredible hulk? No way.

"I think we'd all agree you look great, just great, Lisa."

The camera roamed lovingly over the magnificent body.

"What I am trying to do here is a whole new concept in body maintenance. I call it body sculpting. Being fit isn't enough anymore. It's good, essential even, but it's not enough. What we women need is to get strong as well as get fit. To be strong and beautiful. That's what we aim for here. When we do aerobics we carry weights—and every other day we work out on these machines. The body building helps with the exercise and stretch, and vice versa."

In Lisa's eyes shone the spark of the zealot, and for a second she stopped as the glorious vision played around in her mind. A sea change. A fundamental realignment of attitudes and expectations. Strong women. Physically strong women. The emotional and intuitive strength now allied to a firm, hard, efficient body—a body that could lift things, carry things, *do* things. And then it would be but a short step to real meaningful parity with men, and an end to second-class citizenship which at the bottom line stemmed from female weakness.

As if reading her thoughts Jim Summerford went for the obvious question.

"And what about us men? Are you hoping that women are going to make

some sort of takeover bid for territory that has always been ours?" Jim Summerford smiled to himself. That was a question that might have gotten him
fired in New York or Massachusetts. But you couldn't get farther south in the
U.S.A. than Florida. This was chauvinist country.

"I want women to compete with men, and on equal terms. I don't want
women to fight them. They're not our enemies. We love ya'll." The dazzling
smile cemented the truce between sexes.

No action in flogging that line, thought Summerford. "And I believe you
suggest that psychological problems respond to this fitness discipline. Could
you tell us about that?"

"Certainly they do. My program is guaranteed to cure the blues. Far
better than the couch or the medicine bottle. But it's not all work. We offer
saunas, Jacuzzi, steam heat, body massage. Once a month every woman
should take a morning off and really pamper herself."

Get in the sales pitch. Do the commercial. Christ, this was going to go out
into people's homes, into *Palm Beach* homes.

Then Lisa leaned in closer, and her eyes bored into the camera as she
forced her thoughts into the minds of her future listeners. "There's no doubt
at all. It can change your life," she said. "It's changed mine."

$-5-$

Jo-ANNE DUKE WAS having a very bad day indeed. Waking up had been a problem, opening her eyes an effort, getting out of bed a seemingly insuperable task. Now, as she sat moodily on the veranda still swathed in the pure silk Christian Dior negligée she had worn all day, she wondered why she had bothered. Sleepers and sedative antidepressants spaced out judiciously every few hours would have kept her near enough to unconsciousness to miss out on the angst that nagged and pulled at her. She could have given the whole damn day a miss. Passed on it. Started again with a clear slate tomorrow. The sun was getting low, its red fingers beginning to explore the surrounding sky. Usually the Lake Worth sunset was something that was guaranteed to lift her spirits. This evening it seemed to have all the soul of a gaudy picture postcard.

Jo-Anne wandered aimlessly back into the bedroom, and for a minute or two she stood in front of the long looking glass. God, she looked awful. The depression seemed to have painted her gray. Gray hair, gray face, gray eyes. Intellectually she knew that her mood's distorting spectacles were playing tricks with her perception, but intellect was the slave of emotion, and she felt that she looked awful. Nothing else mattered. In vain she concentrated on the jutting breasts, the billiard-table-flat stomach, the high, self-confident bottom. Filtered through the all pervading gloom that engulfed her, the body that could drive all humanity wild looked to be fit only for the glue factory.

Days like this happened from time to time and there was nothing that could be done about them. In the Big Apple the moods had sometimes lasted a whole week. She would shut herself up in the apartment, refuse to open the door, and take the greatest pleasure in living like a slut. She'd eat chocolate and junk food, let the dishes pile up in the sink, and wallow around in the slough of despond. Jo-Anne used to call it "housecoat weather." What was it now? Finest-silk-negligée weather? For sure the surroundings had changed, and the dishes got done. But feeling blue under a Renoir was much the same as feeling fed up under a bullfight poster.

It was pointless to speculate on what had caused the black mood. There

702

were several candidates: Peter's bloody-mindedness, the near disaster at the Planned Parenthood thing, and Mary d'Erlanger's failure to call up after the mind-bending afternoon in the rented room at the Brazilian Court. But on other days she could take little local difficulties like that in her stride. Today she felt she could have a nervous breakdown if she found a spider in the swimming pool.

A tiny squirt of energy appeared from nowhere and fed itself into her bloodstream. Almost as a disinterested observer she discovered that she was going to phone that bitch Mary. Talk about bad manners. The least she could have done was to call and say she'd enjoyed the screw. Moodily she drifted across toward the telephone and punched out the familiar number.

The strange metallic click had been there before. From time to time over the last few months it had been quite noticeable. A click, and a kind of a hollowness on the line, as if you were speaking in a public lavatory. There was obviously something wrong with the damn telephones. She kept meaning to mention it to the housekeeper.

Mary d'Erlanger's voice was just a little cool. Friendly, but at the same time distant. It hadn't sounded like that in the bedroom of the Brazilian Court. Jo-Anne pictured the long, thin fingers, the delicately manicured nails as they caressed the telephone. The ones that had left marks on her back.

"Jo-Anne, darling. How are you? I've been meaning to call you."

"What stopped you?" Jo-Anne wasn't in the mood to pussyfoot.

"Oh, you know how it is. I've been so busy. Sometimes I just don't know what happens to my day."

"Well we both know what happened to your day last Wednesday afternoon, don't we?" The anger and the irritation were right up there on the surface. Mary would already be dressed for the evening. A little Givenchy number. Black and simple. Great pearls, great legs. The ones that had wrapped themselves tightly around Jo-Anne's body when she'd come.

Mary d'Erlanger's sigh was one of resigned disappointment. Why was everything a problem? Why did *everything* have to be paid for? "Don't be like that, Jo-Anne. It was fun, but it was silly. I wouldn't want it to happen again."

Jo-Anne felt the fuse blow within her. The stupid, vacuous cow. Who the *hell* did she think she was playing with?

"Fun, but silly. *Fun but silly!*" she screamed into the telephone. "You lie there on that bed like some beached whale pleading with me to make you come and now you call it funny but silly? Well, let me tell you one thing, Mary d'Erlanger. In bed you stink. You couldn't fuck your way out of a paper bag. No wonder that impotent lush of a husband of yours can't get it up. If I was a man I wouldn't have been able to either."

Jo-Anne heard the gratifying gasp of horror at the other end of the telephone as she slammed the receiver down. "Okay, Mary d'Erlanger. You're history," she said out loud to herself. Great! That was better. Some of the angst was out of her. Suddenly there was a gap in the little black cloud that had been sitting on her head all day.

She stalked across the room to the drinks tray and paused for a minute. Decisions. Decisions. Why were they always more difficult when you were down? Scotch on the rocks? With water? With soda? With nothing. She splashed a generous measure of Glenfiddich into the bottom of the big crystal glass and walked over to the sofa. She looked at her watch. Cartier said it was 7 P.M. Cartier was never wrong.

Drawing up her long legs beneath her she nursed the drink. Damn. She had lied to Mary. It wasn't true that she was bad in bed. She had been unbelievable, amazing. Now she was over. Jo-Anne drank long and hard of the smooth amber liquid, allowing it to burn the back of her throat before swallowing it down, feeling the warmth of the malt whiskey as it hit her empty stomach. She exhaled and shuddered with the momentary pleasure. Leaning out she reached for the remote control device and touched the Channel 5 sensor. A few feet away the Sony Trinitron flickered into life.

God Almighty. Jo-Anne sat up straight. She was peering between the legs of the most attractive girl she'd ever seen in her life. With consummate ease the legs opened and closed, seemingly oblivious to the pile of black weights that tried pointlessly to impede their progress, as their owner extolled the virtues of the Nautilus program.

Eyes on stalks, Jo-Anne took in the earnest, enthusiastic message, the dramatic facial features of the messenger.

"Body sculpting . . . to get strong and beautiful . . . want women to compete with men, and on equal terms . . . guaranteed to cure the blues . . ."

Hey, this was exactly what she had been waiting for. This girl had it right. You only had to look at her, to listen to her, to know that. The vitality, the charm came beaming off the screen. It zapped you right between the eyes.

And then quite suddenly Jo-Anne realized that the cloud had lifted. It was gone, vanished into the heavy atmosphere, dispelled effortlessly by the vision in the black singlet. A thoughtful expression appeared in the beautiful eyes, and a smile of anticipation began to play around the full lips.

LISA STARR knew the very second she saw her. This girl was the *real* thing. It wasn't the cream-colored open Mercedes roadster, or the casual, even aggressive way it had been parked—one wheel on the pavement, the rear jutting dangerously into the road. Nor was it the quality and shape of the clothes—the almost square shoulders of the Calvin Klein jacket, the waspish waist, the matching oatmeal-colored linen skirt showing perfect, bronzed legs. It was none of these things, but at the same time it was all of them. The manner, too, screamed Palm Beach. Jo-Anne came in at a rush, her hair flying behind her, giving not a backward glance to the soon-to-be-ticketed car. Her whole attitude proclaimed that as far as the Mercedes was concerned any juggernaut was perfectly welcome to eat it for breakfast.

She walked right up to the receptionist's desk where Lisa sat, and her face dissolved into an enormously attractive smile.

"Hello, Lisa Starr. I'm Jo-Anne Duke and I saw you on television."

The thrill of adrenaline shot right through Lisa. To announce yourself as a Duke in this part of the world was like saying you were a Rockefeller in New York. Or a duke in England, for that matter. But somehow the girl's open manner, her transparent friendliness, forced all hierarchical thoughts out of mind.

Lisa laughed at the directness of the approach. "Welcome to my gym, Jo-Anne Duke," she said in mock formality, her smile encouraging, warm. "I won't ask which program, because I've only done one," she added.

Jo-Anne waved an arm in the air dismissively, and Lisa caught the flash of the four white-gold Cartier love bangles—the ones made to be screwed on by your lover with the sapphire-studded screwdriver.

"I've come to join your gym. I want you to cure my blues and to turn me into superwoman."

Lisa wasn't at all sure why that made her blush, but somehow it did. And when Lisa heard herself saying "Well, my initial impression is that it'll only take about ten minutes," she felt the color deepen.

"Thanks for the compliment," came Jo-Anne's straightforward reply. "But actually I feel like shit." Again the laughter bubbled and gurgled. Then it stopped. The next line came across dead straight.

"I want to look exactly like you."

Lisa couldn't think of any answer to that at all. Compliments she could usually handle—from men, from girls like Maggie. But coming from a girl who made a *Playboy* centerfold look like a secondhand rose, it was a fast ball. Clearly she had lost all control of her facial blood vessels. She could swear her cheeks were beginning to *pulsate*.

Again the laughter, the head thrown back, as the Duke girl enjoyed her confusion.

"Come on. I'm only joking . . . sort of, anyway."

The apparent disclaimer only served to reinforce the truth of her originally expressed desire, as it was meant to. Lisa covered her confusion by getting down to business.

"I'd sure like to have you as a member here. Would you let me show you around? Classes don't start for another half an hour, but you could look at the saunas and Jacuzzi."

"No, I don't need to see it. I just want to join it. Let's do it now."

"It's a hundred and twenty bucks a month, but you can take out a year's membership for nine hundred dollars. That's the best value." To a Duke that had to be insultingly little, thought Lisa. She didn't yet understand the habits and attitudes of the stinking rich.

"Hmm. Expensive," said Jo-Anne. "For West Palm," she added as an afterthought. "I'll take out a month's membership for now, and see how things go."

The gold American Express card floated down onto the desk, and Lisa thanked God that she had signed on with the company. She'd thought twice about it.

"Do I get you for that?" Both girls laughed at the apparently unintentional ambiguity. It was obvious what Jo-Anne meant, but on another level it wasn't clear at all.

"Oh yes, I'm here all the time," said Lisa, allowing herself a neutral smile.

"Great. Now let me tell you, Lisa. You were terrific on that show. I was feeling really low, and you picked me right up. This place is going to be a goldmine. All my friends will be screaming to get in. I'm going to pass the word. That's if you don't mind a whole lot of neurotic, sex-starved trouble-makers with more money than sense."

Lisa didn't mind. It was what she had prayed for, dreamed about, and now this fairy godmother was waving her magic wand and promising her paradise. And she liked her. They would be friends. Good friends. Her mother would have been so pleased, so proud.

Jo-Anne picked up on the suddenly wistful, distant expression, saw the mark of pain's touch. "They're not as bad as all that," she joked, well aware that it was not her disparaging remarks about her Palm Beach neighbors that had caused the momentary hurt.

"No. No. Of course not. I'd love to have any of them," said Lisa, forcing the sad thought from her mind. "Come on, Jo-Anne Duke," she said suddenly, springing up and taking her hand. "I'm going to put you on the rack— see what you're made of."

Jo-Anne smiled and ran a tongue over already moist lips. "Sugar and spice of course," she lied, "like all the very best little girls."

STRETCHED OUT on the Nautilus machine that specialized in quadriceps contractions, Jo-Anne, it turned out, was made chiefly of beautifully constructed, if a little underworked, muscle, ligament, tendon, and bone. Aerobics had kept her fit, massage had made her sleek and smooth, but she was short on strength.

"No problem. No problem at all," Lisa said. "Two weeks and you'll be pushing seven, maybe eight, weights on this one."

Lisa took her slowly through the circuit—demonstrating the exercises, making sure that Jo-Anne knew how to do each correctly. It was vital to get it right. Bad habits could creep in, and once one started cheating and the muscles did the wrong work then the whole carefully calculated program fell apart, and the beneficial effects were lost.

By the end of the course Jo-Anne knew she was hooked, and in more ways than one. Muscles she didn't know she even had were speaking to her at last. It would be a whole voyage of bodily self-discovery. Her posture would improve, and with it her spirits. The excitement that coursed through her had a focus, too. Lisa had been the pathfinder, the guide, and her almost obsessional attention to detail had been almost as impressive as her startling physique, as alluring as the coolness of her strong hands. And she had a terrific sense of humor too. Bright as a button, sharp as a knife, fresh as a daisy: the old phrases were always the best ones. It was a combination for which Jo-Anne had all the time in the world.

In the shower Jo-Anne had felt her spirits sing, had even managed a bar or two of the dreaded "Hello, Dolly," which Palm Beach bandleaders always insisted on playing. Was it imagination or could she see the protuberance of a new muscle high up there on her arm? The mirror said "yes," but then yesterday's mirror had told her she was gray all over. Mirrors, like men, could not be trusted. She dried and dressed quickly. Outside she found Lisa organizing the tapes for the first aerobics workout of the day, bending down low over the tape deck. She laid a hand on one of the rock-hard gluteal muscles.

"Lisa Starr, will you have lunch with me?" she asked.

Lisa turned and smiled. "Sure, I'd love to," she said, only subliminally aware that Jo-Anne's hand was still resting on her bottom.

—

"How DO I look, Maggs?" Lisa twirled in front of her girlfriend, half joking, half deadly serious. A Palm Beach lunch with Jo-Anne Duke was about as excitingly unpredictable as playing "lucky dip" with a diamond in one box and a rattlesnake in the other. Lisa hadn't a clue what to expect. She had remembered her mother's intense monologues, but they weren't any help; such vital details as what one wore to lunch and how one understood a French menu had been left out of the general and highly romanticized picture. Would it be a sit-down lunch for twelve in the Duke mansion, a buffet poolside with chicken legs and glasses of wine balanced precariously on knees—or perhaps it would be a restaurant thing? There was no way of knowing and Lisa had instinctively felt it would be desperately uncool to ask. So she had gone for the woman-of-all-seasons look, and she felt it worked. The faded blue jeans were immaculately pressed, downy soft, and offset perfectly by the expensive cream silk shirt and the wide-shouldered Diane Von Furstenberg jacket, which she had discovered on special sale at Burdine's. Including the black patent-leather pumps and the Christian Dior tights with the raised heart motif, the whole outfit had cost less than a hundred bucks, but the total effect was that of understated elegance, of throwaway cool. The Levi's were a bit of a gamble, but then so was life.

"You look like a dog. A great big, ugly dog." Maggie made a face. "Lisa, I really don't think you should go out like that. You might frighten the horses."

Through the skin-tight trousers the graceful limbs twisted and strained as Lisa struck a carefree pose, hands on hips, head thrown back, ass jutting up toward the ceiling. She laughed at her friend, and at her own silly feelings of insecurity. "Okay, Palm Beach. I'm ready for you. Do your worst," was what she said, and was trying to feel.

"What time is she picking you up?"

"Picking me up? Picking me up? The Dukes don't pick people up. They *have* them picked up. The limo comes at one."

Lisa bowed extravagantly from the waist, the years of stretching allowing the raven hair to sweep down low to the floor, the knees ramrod straight, the arm extended in the graceful gesture of a ballet dancer.

"Well, all I say is make sure you're back before the clock strikes midnight, Cinderella—and don't let Prince Charming screw you on day one."

Lisa went for the mock drop kick to Maggie's plump bottom, but the horseplay was cut short by the arrival outside of the biggest black limousine either girl had ever seen. The Dukes' stretched Mercedes was intimidating transport indeed, and was intended to be. Chivers, the dove-gray-uniformed English chauffeur, was no less impressive. Holding his peaked cap beneath his arm he oiled his way into the gym.

"Miss Elizabeth Starr?" The jaw dropped away as he drooled Lisa's last name, so that no possible hint of an *r* remained.

"I'm Lisa. Are you taking me to lunch with Jo-Anne Duke?"

"Mrs. Duke has asked that I take you to meet her at the Café L'Europe." He said that as if the restaurant were about as familiar as the Eiffel Tower to a Parisian, the sort of place Lisa ate every other day.

"Take me to your leader," said Lisa, winking hugely at Maggie as she set off toward the limo, trailing a marginally chastened Chivers in her wake.

In the air-conditioned womb of the mighty car Lisa stretched out her legs and tried to relax. That was what the damn thing had been designed for. No way could one have had an adequate game of mixed doubles in there, but eight people could happily sit down for after-dinner drinks. The cushions seemed to want to devour her. It was like quicksand—the sensation of being sucked down into a vortex of naked luxury.

Lisa laughed out loud at the theatricality of her thoughts, causing Chivers to chance a look over his shoulder to investigate the cause of the levity. Finding none, he slipped into the safety of the servant role. "Should you like some refreshment you'll find the bar in the cupboard in front of you. There's fresh ice in the bucket and mixers in the refrigerator."

Lisa's initial inclination was to refuse, but quite suddenly she changed her mind. Hell. Why not? If this was the *dolce vita* maybe she should make hay while the sun shone. Rich people had a way of tiring of new toys, even if she had scarcely been unwrapped.

She reached forward and opened the Aladdin's cave that was the bar. There wasn't a bottle in sight. Everything was decanted into flat-bottomed ship's decanters of the finest cut glass. Around the neck of each hung a silver label on which the contents were described in a rich, intricately engraved script. She poured a half inch of vodka into one of the heavy goblets and scooped a handful of ice on top. The color was confined to the cooler section below. Every conceivable drink was there. A jug of iced tomato juice, Miller's Lite, Carlsberg, what looked like fresh orange juice again in a tall jug, a bottle of Taittinger Rosé, another of hock, Tio Pepe sherry, a plate of sliced limes. Resisting the temptation to embark on the construction of a bloody mary, Lisa reached instead for the iced Martini and splashed a minimal amount onto the vodka. Ignoring the elegant silver stirrer she stuck her finger irreverently into the drink and whisked it around. Mustn't get too carried away.

The cold spirit on the warm stomach lining had messages for the brain. Lisa felt the rush almost immediately. Drinking was not really her bag, but today was special. She was going across the bridge at last and in the style of

which her beloved mother had dreamed. Okay, so white chargers were conspicuous by their absence, but since the first sip of the vodka martini she
could have sworn she'd heard a choir of angels warming up. Again she chuckled to herself as the golden-coach substitute purred down Royal Palm Way
into the heart of Palm Beach. The sign in the stockbroker's window in the
"400" building told her that the Dow was off 19.48 points. Oh, dear. What a
pity. The rich had gotten just a little poorer. Would that mean pasta for
lunch?

The crowd waiting to get into Doherty's as they made the right turn onto
South County hinted that the town's residents were putting a brave face on
the stock-market fall. Nor did the people on Worth Avenue look down-
hearted.

The big car swept into the Esplanade complex as if it was returning home;
a gaggle of valet parkers clustered around it. Chivers spoke imperiously. "If
you look after it for a minute or two I'll be back immediately." He decanted
himself from the front seat and opened the back door for Lisa. "If I may I'll
take you to Mrs. Duke."

Lisa was only dimly aware of her surroundings as she made her way up
the Spanish steps of the Esplanade's staircase, her eyes fixed on Chivers's
rather ungainly bottom. He looked a bit like a Confederate soldier in some
made-for-TV Civil War rehash, she couldn't help thinking. At the top of the
stairs the signs on the doors said Café L'Europe, and Lisa took a deep breath
and thanked God for the vodka as the improbable duo made it inside. The
maître d' seemed to have been waiting for them.

"Is this Mrs. Duke's luncheon guest?" asked the heavy French accent.
"Please follow me, mademoiselle."

Lisa fought back the idea that this seemingly endless process of being
transported into the hallowed presence of Jo-Anne Duke might well go on all
day. At the table there would be a black major-domo who would transport
her by waiting helicopter to a yacht where the bearded captain would sail her
to a submarine . . .

With the vague impression of mountains of colorful flowers and of even
more colorful people, Lisa allowed herself to be wafted across the beautiful
restaurant.

Jo-Anne was sitting alone at what was clearly the best table in the room.
She stood up at Lisa's approach and held out a long arm. The smile was
warm, but was there just a hint of patronization in her opening words?

"My teacher, my guru. Great to see you, Lisa."

"Wow," said Lisa, sitting down gratefully. "Are you in the magical mystery
tour business?"

Jo-Anne laughed.

"Yeah, the limo's a little far out, isn't it? Chivers, too, for that matter. Still,
I always say, if you've got it, flaunt it."

Jo-Anne did always say that, and as far as possible she always *did* that.
Maybe when she was old and gray she'd play the understated high-class

game, like the Hobe Sound crew, but for now she wanted to get as far from big-city blowjobs as it was possible to get.

"I'll drink to that," said Lisa, reaching for the glass of chilled champagne that seemed to have been poured her while she was midway between standing and sitting down. The bubbles went right up her nose. That was nice. It was funny, now that she was there all the doubts and fears were gone. Already she was enjoying herself. Just the two of them. Good. Jo-Anne seemed real nice. She peered around the room at the flora and fauna of Palm Beach, as the reality met her fantasy.

Jo-Anne looked at her proudly. Christ, she was a magnificent specimen. Ballsy as hell and with the looks of a goddess. What did she want from life? That was the secret it would be the luncheon's purpose to answer. If you knew what people wanted, where they went to in their beds at night as they dreamed their wildest dreams, then you were well on your way to controlling them.

Jo-Anne felt the throb of the engine inside her as the machinery started up. Control. Domination. The scheming of schemes. Forget the champagne, forget the beluga. They were sideshows to the main attraction. "So what do you think of the show so far?"

Lisa wasn't quite sure. "Who *are* all these people? Let's have the guided tour, Jo-Anne. You must know everybody."

"Are you really interested, Lisa? For sure they could all use a subscription to your gym."

"Oh, I'm just fascinated by the whole Palm Beach trip. Ever since I was a little girl I've felt like that. My mom used to work over here, as some sort of a ladies' maid for the Stansfield family—you know Senator Stansfield. She loved it so much and never really talked about anything else. So I guess I sort of inherited the interest."

"No, how *fascinating*. That's really interesting, Lisa." Jo-Anne's mind churned up the information as she fed it into her mind's computer. The girl was totally unaffected and refreshingly naive. The fact that your mother had been a maid was not something that most people would have wanted to advertise. Also it appeared she was a little star-struck; the brainwashing process seemed to have substituted the Palm Beach plutocracy for the celluloid meritocracy. She smiled to herself and then at Lisa. It was all encouraging information.

"Well, let's see. I guess you've heard of Estée Lauder. She's the lady in the sequinned top. Next to her is somebody called Helen Boehm. She makes porcelain and runs the most successful polo team. The good-looking guy on Boehm's right is quite interesting. He's Howard Oxenberg—very attractive to women. On his other side is his wife, Anne, who's a real doll—beautiful and charming. Howard used to be married to Princess Elizabeth of Yugoslavia; they have a wonderful-looking daughter, Catherine, who acts. The Oxenbergs live out at Wellington part of the year at a place called the Palm Beach Polo and Country Club."

Jo-Anne smiled at Lisa's look of total concentration. To anybody who knew the Oxenbergs intimately, as she did, they were lovely, ordinary people whose comings and goings were totally taken for granted—unremarkable, hardly worthy of comment. But as part of a *People* magazine-style commentary they sounded undeniably glamorous. Perhaps a little influenced by Lisa's powerful reactions, Jo-Anne's attitude toward her old friends underwent a subtle shift as she saw them anew in the light of Lisa's enthusiasm.

"Tell me about this Wellington place. I've seen all the TV ads for the polo. Who lives there, and why?"

Jo-Anne began to feel a bit like a sociology major. How to define the delicate difference between the Polo Club and Palm Beach proper? It took a remarkably gifted social animal with a nose closely attuned to the ever-changing scents and aromas of societal intercourse to pinpoint the characteristics that divided the two communities. But in a way she *was* the expert. Lisa couldn't have asked a better person, with the possible exception of Marjorie Donahue herself.

"The obvious differences aren't the important ones. Wellington is fifteen miles from the sea. The emphasis is heavily on sport—golf and tennis as well as polo. I guess it's a younger place. Certainly a newer one. And it's very pushy. They're spending a fortune trying to make it the slickest place in America for the young, sports-loving group, and they *are* succeeding. But they haven't *quite* succeeded. A hell of a lot of Palm Beachers go out each Sunday for the polo, but the rest of the week during the season the Wellington crowd is eating and swimming over here. Of course it's cheaper there. You can get something for around five hundred thousand that's halfway decent. At that price you'd get a rabbit hutch in Palm Beach.

"I think the real thing is the race thing. In this town the WASPs and the Jews don't mix. It's like apartheid. Estée Lauder wouldn't be welcome at the Bath and Tennis Club for instance, although B and T members would be more than happy to go and drink her champagne if she gives a big charity reception. The Polo Club is much more free and easy, more democratic, more liberal. Perhaps you'd like to come with us all this Sunday. You could meet my husband, Peter. We usually have a big lunch first, then there's a box in the grandstand where we drink too much Pimms and catch the action."

"That sounds great, Jo-Anne. I'd like to see that."

Lisa sat back on the comfortable banquette and allowed the relaxation and the champagne to flow through her. None of the feared horrors had materialized. The menu had turned out to be an easily negotiated hurdle—a mixed salad followed by a minute steak—and Jo-Anne, too, had been totally charming, with no sign of the airs and graces that could so easily have been a by-product of her almost indecent wealth. So far Palm Beach had certainly lived up to Lisa's inflated expectations.

It was just about to exceed them in a way that would change her life forever. "Hey, look, speak of the devil." Jo-Anne's voice was suddenly full of excitement as she gesticulated toward the door of the restaurant.

Lisa did as she was told, but Satan was not at all what she saw.

The initial reaction was almost entirely biochemical. Later there would be words to describe it, rationalizations to explain the great surge deep within her. But now there was just the rush of feeling, the weird shift of emotion as a hornet's nest seemed to empty itself into the center of her gut. Something was happening to her, she didn't know what, and the appearance of a remarkably attractive man in the doorway of the Café L'Europe was the cause of her discomfort.

As her shocked intellect began to reassert control over the raging torrent of body chemicals, Lisa tried to work out what it was she was seeing. There wasn't a satisfactory answer. Okay, so he was incredibly good looking, but that wasn't exactly unique. It was something much more important than that —something disturbing, dangerous, exciting, inevitable. And it wasn't just coming from him. It was an interaction—a reaction, something between her and this stranger that added up to a total greater than the sum of the individual parts. Far from sure what it was, Lisa watched and waited, Fate's hostage, as the man left his position at the door and headed into the restaurant.

One thing was immediately obvious. He had about him success's sweet smell, the heady aroma of concentrated charisma, and all about him lesser mortals were sniffing at it. The *maître d'*, businesslike on Lisa's arrival, had degenerated into a hand-wringing hunchback as he ushered the man between the tables. All around the crowded room necks of rubber twisted and turned as the Palm Beachers shamelessly eyeballed the handsome newcomer, and the clatter of conversation stilled noticeably as elbows dug into ribs and fingers found wrists to alert the unwary to the clearly formidable presence in their midst.

Lisa turned helplessly toward Jo-Anne. The question didn't need to be asked.

Jo-Anne smiled back at her. "Bobby Stansfield," she said simply. "And that's his mother, Caroline Stansfield, behind him."

Lisa felt the strength go out of her. This man was a Stansfield. *The* Bobby Stansfield. Impressive to anybody. A mythical superhero to Lisa—standard bearer of the Stansfield dynasty, that fabled collection of Titans that had populated her beloved mother's romantic fantasies. No wonder she had known him instantly, recognized immediately at a subconscious level his phenomenal importance for her. The inexplicable was instantly explained, but the knowledge was no help at all.

And then there was Caroline Stansfield. Her mother's employer. The spirit of Palm Beach, the epitome of the magical world across the bridge. God Almighty! The mixed emotions struck up their raucous cacophony. Lisa fought to make sense of them. Bobby Stansfield, this beautiful, desirable, famous man, who could one day be president. Caroline Stansfield, who had fired her mother and ruined her life, and had been turned into a goddess as reward for her lack of charity. Did Lisa worship or hate her? It was impossible to intuit the answer to the question. As the mighty adrenaline flow sucked the color from Lisa's cheeks, she sat stock still like some frightened animal hypnotized by the headlights of the oncoming car—unable to move, unable to think. Dimly, through the mists that had engulfed her, she took in the fact that the Stansfields were heading directly toward her.

"Jo-Anne Duke? A girl's lunch? Well, well, I should get out more often." The twinkle in the voice said much, much more than the words. The baby-blue eyes fastened on Lisa's. "And may I be introduced to your very beautiful friend?"

The smile was still there, but somehow the voice had gone deadly serious.

"Oh, Bobby, this is Lisa Starr. Senator Stansfield. Lisa has just opened the most marvelous gym over in West Palm. She's going to change my life, turn me into a female Adonis, if such a thing exists."

Both Lisa and Bobby missed the delicate flavor of patronization. There were other things on their minds.

"I'm very pleased to meet you, Lisa Starr. Maybe if you've any spare time you could change my life a bit, too."

Lisa blushed deeply at the suggestion as the wonderful eyes probed her soul. Dear *God,* he was attractive. Disgustingly attractive.

"Mother, you know Peter Duke's wife, Jo-Anne. And this is Lisa Starr, who, I'm ashamed and unhappy to say, I've never met before."

Like a conjurer revealing the rabbit, he stood back to display Caroline Stansfield. Her weary smile said it all. Table hopping at a thousand-dollar-a-plate political dinner was business; table hopping in a restaurant was a perversion.

Caroline Stansfield extended a frail hand and both Jo-Anne and Lisa stood to take it. Yes, she knew Jo-Anne Duke. Hooker with a heart of brass, or some other unpleasant metal. Lisa Starr? Sounded like an actress. Surely no relation to the Philadelphia Starrs. But those beautiful eyes, the high cheekbones. They were distinctly familiar. Reminded her very much of someone. Damn. Her memory was all shot to pieces these days. Who on *earth* was it?

"Lisa Starr," she said thoughtfully as she shook hands. "I feel sure I know you from somewhere. Have we met before?"

There was so much to say, a lifetime of anguish, ambition, of joy and heartache to discuss—but, of course all of it was impossible. "No, I am afraid we haven't," was the only possible reply, and so Lisa said just that.

"Come on, Bobby. I'm starving. Are you going to buy me lunch or not?" Caroline Stansfield's command, as always, was instantly obeyed.

Bobby's arm assumed the steering position as he gathered up his mother for the resumption of their journey. Over his shoulder he said insistently, "When are you going to invite me over, Jo-Anne, or are the Dukes economizing? Give me a call. Bye, Lisa Starr. I hope very much we meet again."

The throaty, bantering laugh crept right inside Lisa's heart and immediately made itself a home.

~6~

FOR THE FIRST time in weeks Lisa was totally relaxed. The sauna had taken all the surplus liquid from her body, had cleaned the pores and sucked the tension from her tired muscles. Now the Jacuzzi was rounding off the process. Warm jets of water played firmly over her, massaging, soothing, kneading the flesh. There was no sound except for the gentle rush of the scented water, and the lights were turned down low to minimize all sensory input. At last Lisa was free, free to unwind, to feel, to enjoy the delicious sensations of the present. But her restless thoughts refused to be still. So much had happened. In such a short time she had traveled from tragedy to the edge of sublimity, but it had been a tiger ride, exhilarating, frightening, dangerous—and she herself had been part driver, part driven.

Before there had been safety, comfort, love—and of course her parents, who had represented all three. The aching sense of loss had lessened now, as time's balm worked its healing way, but the memories lived on, real and alive. Mostly it was her mother whose presence she felt, whose warm, reassuring scents she missed. The flames had eaten away her dreams, but had they, in Lisa, lived on, transmuted, transplanted into the body and mind of a new and worthy standard bearer?

Lisa sighed as she wiped a bead of sweat from her brow. She had given up her ambition of going to college and becoming a teacher. Was her discarded life a cause for regret? In a vacuum, maybe. But the vacuum had been filled. Now she was queen of her own domain, not a lowly courtier in the kingdom of someone else. It was an infinitely smaller fiefdom, but she ruled it. That it was already a success was obvious for all to see. The membership applications were flooding in and the list was on the verge of closure. But it offered so very much more. It was a way to give to her mother the ultimate posthumous gift. On Sunday she would sit with the Dukes in their private box at Palm Beach polo, not as a servant but as an equal. At a stroke she had achieved Mary-Ellen's impossible dream. Okay, so for now it was only a tenuous foothold on the ladder, but for sure she hadn't started at the bottom.

Nor did she intend to rest on her laurels. She would consolidate her position like some invading army, build up her reserves, before breaking out of the beachhead on a campaign of conquest that would leave Palm Beach helpless at her feet, its unspecified delights surrendered unconditionally to Lisa Starr. She savored the delicious thought, but even as she did so sorrow crept in at the edges to sour its flavor. Damn. It was so unfair. If her mother could have lived to have seen it. If her father, and granddad. . . . But they were all gone away, and there was nobody to watch the first tentative steps.

She was all alone in the world of danger and difficulty with only her wits, her beauty, and her shining vision to help her. Suddenly Lisa felt the self-confidence slip from her tight grasp, and the lump in her throat found a companion with the emergence of the tears in her eyes. "Yours enemies, my's enemies"—that was what Grandpa Jack had liked to say. "Some boah don't treat you right, Lisa, you be tellin' me. He won' be chewing steak so good." And then they would always laugh, but the truth was Jack Kent had broken jaws before, and for some real or imagined slight to his beloved granddaughter he would probably have exacted a far more fearsome retribution. With that kind of man on your side there wasn't much to fear. With old Jack's meanness, and her father's enormous fists, Lisa's childhood had been totally secure. No fresh black boy along the block had ever dared to give her lip, no booze-sodden wino ever risked a suggestive remark when her tits had begun to sprout, no boyfriend had ever pushed his luck when the answer had been no. Then in a few wicked minutes they had all gone away and left her alone. A motherless, fatherless child.

A big tear rolled gently down Lisa's flushed cheek, picking up the moisture of her sweat, and she reached up to smooth it away. In Palm Beach nobody would use fists against her, but they would possess words as sharp as any dagger. Their defenses would be lawyers, money; their allies the cunning tongues of their friends. Competing in that world would be far from easy, very far from safe. Somehow that thought pleased Lisa. After all, Jack Kent's blood ran in her veins, and if there was one thing that invariably cheered him up it was the prospect of a good fight, preferably with the odds against him. Her father had not been quite like that, but she had seen his eyes light up in Roxy's when the beer had begun to flow and when some raw youngster had decided the time had come to chance his arm against his elders and betters. She would take them all on, and she would win in the process. No matter how big the guns she would find a way to return a more withering fire.

As if to exorcise the rapidly lifting despondency, she dipped down into the bubbles, lowering her head into the warmth. When she reemerged her old self-confidence was back.

She began to think about Sunday. What would it be like? Who would be there? Bobby Stansfield? The thought came through like the rays of the sun through a thick cloud—suddenly, unexpectedly, and with the same warming, uplifting effect. Stansfield. The name with the power to concentrate the mind, to tie the loose threads into the coherent whole. It was the code word for everything—for her past, for her present, and, she dared to hope, for her future. Maybe he was only a symbol for the world she sought, but his was a frighteningly potent image, one of flesh, and of blood.

Mmmmmmmmmmmmmmm. Now the sunlight played on Lisa as on the petals of a flower ready to open, and in response her legs splayed wide open, and she pushed her pelvis out toward the satisfying jets of water. In her mind was the memory of bright blue eyes and a lilting voice that had dared to admire that which she knew to be admirable. It was true, thank God, that she was beautiful, but then so was he. Everything her mother had predicted, and more. What would happen now? Would she see him again? On Sunday? If not, then maybe at another of Jo-Anne's parties. His last words at the restaurant had contained the unmistakable message that he was hoping for such a meeting.

Would he want her? Would he like her? Could he love her? Make love to her? The delicious speculation went on and on as the column of water pushed at her, playing delightfully with her most precious place.

Before now, her desire had not been for warm bodies, for the comforting touch of lovers. That sort of thing she had always thought of as a sideshow. It would happen when the rest of her life was in place. Then it would be an amusing, even a fascinating diversion, but it would be a leisure-time pursuit —somewhere between Tennessee Williams's plays and live country music on a Saturday night in the hierarchy of pleasure. Lisa had never been able to understand the people whose lives were controlled by love. It seemed so inefficient, so fundamentally self-indulgent. For her control was the thing. Control over herself. There had been boys, but they had never been her *life,* and their inexpert fumblings and unpracticed lips had never tempted her to let them have what they all so desperately desired. One day it would happen. But she was more curious than impatient.

Gently Lisa eased herself off the Jacuzzi's seat. She advanced delicately on the column of water, which pleased her, savoring the more insistent touch as she approached its source. Now, both hands on the side of the sunken tub, she pressed herself against the orifice, luxuriating in the delectable feeling of the water's pressure against her. She sought sweet words for the sexual poem she was about to compose. Hard and strong the water stroked her, long and lean it lapped at her, shameless, invading, it took her. Through parted lips Lisa breathed in deeply. Careful. Not too fast. Lisa swiveled her hips to disengage the instrument of pleasure, allowing the confident stream to play over her hard lower stomach, to hose the sweeping lines of her inner thighs.

Then, very slowly, as if unwilling to disturb or discourage her watery lover, she turned and gave it her back. It rushed in eager torrents into the welcoming cleavage of the rounded buttocks, searching out the shy entrance —loving it, pleasing it, with a firm touch. Little packets of explosive pleasure discharged their contents into Lisa's mind and she moved to intensify the feeling. Bending at the waist, her spine perfectly straight, she brought her chin to the level of the water's surface at the same time thrusting hard against the wall of the Jacuzzi. In blissful collusion with the daring water jet, she allowed it to ravish her. But in her mind she had achieved the fusion she sought. The lifeless, mechanical thing that thrust so aggressively at her had magically acquired life. It belonged to Bobby Stansfield.

Into the steamy vision, unwanted, unmistakable, intruded the doorbell's tactless ring.

Christ! Damn!

She tried to block it out, to hold on to the fragile fantasy that promised so much.

As she struggled to capture the elusive dream the ringing stopped. Great! A few more seconds and the moment would have been gone. Lisa repositioned herself to reclaim the divine stimulation, but even as she did so the unknown finger disturbed the work of the watery one. This time the bell was more intrusive. Its truncated rhythm said that the intruder knew there was somebody inside to open the door.

With a sinuous movement she extricated herself from the womblike waters, and grabbing a towel, she padded through the gym toward the street door. "Who on earth is it?" she shouted through the bolted door.

In West Palm you didn't open the door to strangers. "It's me—Jo-Anne," came the confident reply, unfazed by the distinctly irritable tone of the question.

"Oh, Jo-Anne. Hang on a second while I open up. You've got me out of the Jacuzzi."

Again Jo-Anne refused to be discouraged by the underwhelming enthusiasm of the greeting. Lisa Starr recently emerged from a Jacuzzi was to her a choice morsel indeed. As the door opened and the truth was confirmed she made her pitch. "I was just passing by, and I saw the lights on. Wondered what you were up to."

Jo-Anne looked straight at Lisa as she told the lie. This part of Clematis Street wasn't on the way to anywhere. During the last day or two she'd made a point of checking out the gym when she happened to be over the bridge. It looked as if her scouting efforts had paid off.

Lisa knew the geography; it was unlikely to be coincidental that Jo-Anne was standing on her doorstep, although the reason for her presence was far from clear.

"Well, aren't you going to ask me in? I could catch my death of cold out here."

They both laughed. The West Palm temperature was pushing eighty-eight degrees.

"Of course, come on in."

"Hey, Lisa, don't let me disturb you. You'd better get right back into the health-giving waters. Come to think of it, I might join you. That's if you don't mind, of course."

"No, I'd like that. You can fill me in on what to expect on Sunday." An uninvited guest in what was supposed to have been a solitary hot tub was *not* what she needed, but she hadn't forgotten that Jo-Anne was the open sesame to the Palm Beach cave. Better to give in with grace.

Purposefully, Jo-Anne lingered a step behind on the short walk to the

Jacuzzi. In front of her a dripping, betoweled Lisa led the way. Mentally Jo-Anne checked her out. Big, square shoulders, rounded muscular calves, delicate, beautifully arched feet, immaculately pedicured toes. The long, dark hair, wet and untidy, rushed over the shoulders on which beads of moisture —sweat? water?—still glistened. Lisa walked with a swinging, easy gait— perhaps just a tiny bit butch, certainly athletic, not typically feminine. Inside her Jo-Anne felt the little rush of excitement as the familiar feeling began to build. In a second or two the sculpture would be unveiled. It was not difficult to predict that it would win prizes.

It did. For one brief, blissful second as the white towel made it to the mosaic tiled floor Lisa Starr stood naked at the brink of the Jacuzzi. The lights, still dimmed, gave to the visual an ethereal, detached quality—a latter-day Victorian photograph, a bather caught unawares on the banks of some lazy Indian river at dusk. The body, of course, was magnificent and it was held momentarily in the relaxed pose of the professional athlete, one leg pushed forward in front of the other, the subdued light able to pick out the edge of the smooth quadriceps muscle group, the perfect triangle of dark and infinitely interesting hair, the undulating sweep of the tight stomach. Her right hand dangled delicately, fingers in the repose of some Greek goddess; the left was held up high at shoulder height attached by the well-formed pectoral to the sublime breast. Was it the heat or the pummeling of the water jets that had stimulated the erectile tissue in the delicate pink nipples—or did the girl always look like this, her breasts permanently conical, perfect pyramids, demanding attention, commanding admiration, haunting in their loveliness, daring the adventurous touch?

Jo-Anne's eyes lingered longingly over the transient vision, trying to capture it for the album of her mind. Then, it was taken from her as Lisa stepped into the foaming water.

As Lisa did so she was mystically aware of the greedy eyes that had fed from her. Far from conscious of the muted music of desire that all around her was beginning quietly to play, she somehow felt that the water was a safe haven from an alien, exotic thing at once alarming and alluring. Its bubbles touched the skin that Jo-Anne's eyes had touched and inexplicably sent little shivers up and down Lisa's graceful spine.

Lisa turned her face upward toward Jo-Anne, her expression curious, questioning. Women always had a passing interest in the appearance of each other's bodies, and Lisa, a professional in the field, was no exception. But somehow, somewhere there was something else. For a second she looked away as an inexplicable embarrassment gripped her, but then her eyes were drawn back again by some force field of magnetism of which she was only subliminally aware. Jo-Anne was staring at her, and there was a hypnotic quality in her gaze. It was lazy, laid back, reassuring, and yet frighteningly powerful, and impossible to ignore.

I'm fully clothed, and yet soon I'll be naked. I want you to watch me undress, said Jo-Anne's eyes—and unable, unwilling to resist, Lisa found herself obeying. On a thousand similar occasions she had witnessed the same happening, but now it was charged, invested with an altogether indefinable flavor of illicit voyeuristic coercion. Try as she might, Lisa could not get the idea out of her mind that she was peeping through a keyhole.

The fingers played with the big brass buckles of the two thick brown leather belts that straddled Jo-Anne's tiny waist. Patiently, gently she pushed downward, peeling back the blue denim trouser tops, easing down the white silk briefs. Her eyes were laughing, now, teasing, mocking, daring Lisa to transfer the center of her gaze from the knowing smile to her most secret place.

Lisa felt the moisture in her throat begin to dry. Self-consciously she tried to swallow, suddenly aware of a difficulty in doing so. Then, seemingly unable to resist the unspoken command, she looked down, her eyes playing helplessly over the pubic hairs, framed like some priceless painting by the turned-down jeans. Seemingly aware of the beauty of the effect, Jo-Anne made no effort to lower the jeans any farther. Instead her hands moved higher to the buttons of the sky-blue man's silk shirt against which her stiff nipples already strained. Dancing to the string of the expert puppeteer, Lisa's gaze was once again dragged upward to pay homage to the arrogant, self-confident breasts.

The silence had gone on too long for comfort, and yet somehow there was nothing to say. Already an unholy alliance was in its earliest stages of formation, but its purpose was ill defined, scarcely to be admitted. With mounting horror Lisa realized that the appalling dryness of her mouth was being balanced by the beginnings of wetness elsewhere.

Jo-Anne sensed it all, saw it in the confused eyes. So often it had happened like this. The alien act, undreamed of, unwanted, translated into abandoned desire by the art of the seductress. Quickly now, she slipped off her trousers, panties, and ankle-length cotton socks and slid smoothly into the water. Still she didn't speak. No words must disturb the magic.

Sitting opposite her prey in the bubbling foam, Jo-Anne waited and watched for the moment she knew so well how to recognize.

Slowly, like the rising sun, the realization of what was happening came to Lisa. For the very first time in her life she had been turned on by a woman, by a supremely beautiful and powerful naked woman who sat inches from her in the swirling, sweet-smelling currents of her own hot tub.

But why? Was it just a hangover from her own interrupted attempt at self-gratification, her aroused senses searching desperately for an object to focus on. No. It wasn't just her. Jo-Anne was a far from passive participant in whatever it was that was happening. Waves of sensuality were beaming from her, creeping under Lisa's skin, vitalizing her nerve endings. There was a fullness in her breasts, an empty void in her stomach and the far more significant feeling of emptiness between her legs.

Jo-Anne's laughing eyes bored into her, understanding her dilemma, mocking what was rapidly becoming her need, at the same time encouraging it. Then, with her reassuring, knowing smile still playing around her parted lips, Jo-Anne crossed the short space into intimacy.

The kiss was an age in coming. It started as a slow, lazy thing with all the time in the world. The nuzzling lips, warm, soft, and dry as the desert's air, did not touch her at first. They hovered, suspended in space and time, inches, and then less than inches, from Lisa's own. Through them came the hot, scented breath, fanning her face, creeping delightfully into her nostrils, evaporating the moisture on her skin. Then, in swoops and darts, they descended on her, delicate, calm, on their mission of mercy and conquest. Lisa felt her back turn to liquid as the extraordinary lips traced the borders of her own, exploring, curious, tenderly spelling out the unspoken language of love. Still it was not a kiss, but it was a treaty, an unbreakable alliance in what promised to be a voyage into the uncharted seas of sexual ecstasy. Soon, mercifully soon there would be the tongue. Lisa for the very first time in her life was a helpless passenger; whatever deed would be done, she had in some way agreed to it. The passive acceptance of these lips was final as the signature on some ghostly contract.

As if acknowledging the capitulation Jo-Anne moved to consolidate her position. Resting her lips on the corner of Lisa's half-open mouth, she licked at her, running a wet, sweet-tasting tongue along first the upper and then the lower lip, moistening the dry skin with saliva.

Lisa stifled her low moan of pleasure as the wetness exploded deep within her. She leaned back against the wall of the Jacuzzi and let her long legs stretch out before her as she opened herself up.

Jo-Anne saw the gesture of acquiescence and moved to take advantage of it. Beneath the water her fingers sought and found the rock-hard nipples, playing over the firm breasts in wondrous reverence as her mind's eye compared the messages of touch to the remembered vision. Gently, but insistently she squeezed the tight flesh between her thumb and forefinger as her tongue traced the contours of Lisa's teeth, before plunging in deep to taste the delicious secretions of this beautiful girl's mouth. Now she concentrated everything on the kiss. Jo-Anne's body had effectively disappeared. It was a mere appendage, a superfluous adjunct to her conquering mouth. Her hands moved gently to frame Lisa's flushed cheeks, and always her tongue, inventive, unpredictable, wise in the ways of arousal, moved subtly to fan the flames of Lisa's rampaging desire. Her forearms strongly flexed, she drew the younger girl in toward her, her right hand reaching behind Lisa's head, buried in the damp hair as she forced her mouth onto her own. Sometimes there was desperation in the embrace as the lips were crushed together, as the tongue sought to merge with the deepest recesses of Lisa's throat. Then it would be playful, teasing as it licked and tickled, luxuriating in the lascivious wetness. Occasionally there was the sharp touch of teeth, and the momentary excitement of delicious pain as Lisa fought back for her share of ecstasy, taking the aggressive tongue between the pure white teeth, nipping, nibbling, disciplining it before succumbing once again to its infinitely welcome dictates.

Lisa was lost hopelessly in the battlefield of the kiss. It was war, life, love. Nothing else mattered. No ambition, no memory, no happiness. It was not a prelude, not a conclusion. It was instead the only reality, the distillation of the present, the very essence of bliss.

Long, and thin, now Jo-Anne's tongue reached into her, its strokes slow and deliberate. Lisa loved it, braced herself to receive it as she tried to ease its pleasure-giving progress, willing it to penetrate her head, to creep further into her mind, to reinforce the wild riot of joyous feeling that roared out of control within her.

Jo-Anne sensed the approach to the plateau as she held the vibrating body in her arms. The fresh innocence of this girl had primed her for this head-long descent into abandonment. Lisa Starr, the ripest and the best. Her beautiful virginity there to be taken, wide open, asking, begging, demanding for satisfaction. She was a gift, a divine sacrifice to the passion gods, whom Jo-Anne Duke served.

Not yet. Not yet. Jo-Anne forced the decision, willing herself to do the impossible, to brake the careering, all but uncontrollable wagon of mutual desire. With very nearly every fiber of her being she wanted the sweet con-clusion, as Lisa jerked and twisted her way into ecstasy; but there was a sinewy, steel thread of determination in her as well.

With the effort of the superhuman she turned down the rheostat of raw desire and slowed the pace of the kiss, licking tenderly now at the hungry, suddenly insecure mouth. Jo-Anne moved the forefinger of her right hand to separate their lips, leaving it in place on Lisa's as she pulled hers away. She looked down tenderly at the eager face, allowing the love light to shine through concerned eyes. Then, still silent, she eased herself upward to a standing position on the ledge on which Lisa sat. Towering over her would-be lover, straddling her, she stood, tall and splendid, unpredictable, magnifi-cent.

Lisa felt the thrill of anticipation collide with the sudden doubt. Before her eyes was the prize and the cause of her predicament. The hairs shone with moisture, the pouting pink lips mimicking the promise of the ones she had loved but a few short seconds before. She lifted her head, her eyes questioning. In reply, Jo-Anne spoke for the very first time. "Not now, Lisa. Not now, my love."

In a second she was out of the water, once more the tantalizing but distant vision. She swooped down gracefully to pick up a towel, and in a few moments of mind-numbing disappointment she was gone.

As THE Duke limo sped along Forest Hill Boulevard toward the polo fields of Wellington, Lisa's thoughts were in turmoil. Things seemed to be happening too fast. Good things, strange things, frightening things. She herself all but seduced by the sweet-smelling, sweet-talking billionairess who now sat by her side. From the start Jo-Anne had played it cool. When Lisa had climbed into the cavernous limousine Jo-Anne had pecked at her cheek as if she were a favorite niece. Clearly the party line was to carry on as if nothing had hap-pened. That suited Lisa down to the ground. As far as she was concerned Jo-Anne Duke's lips had been revealed a dangerous weapon, and an action replay of her near fall from grace was the very last thing she wanted, now, or ever for that matter.

Lisa breathed in deeply and tried to keep the excitement inside her. She was riding in the fast lane at last, living in the middle of her Palm Beach dreams, and although it was wonderful it was terrifying, too. Bobby Stansfield had also been invited. She was going to meet him again. Please God he'd be there. A man like him was more than capable of canceling at the last moment. A crisis in South America. Some problems with interest rates, and maybe he'd be called away. Bobby Stansfield. In his eyes she had seen him want her, as in hers she had signaled her desire. When they met the heavens would move. It was as simple as that. Apart from one dreadful thing. She had been conned into wearing all the wrong clothes.

It was the oldest trick in the feminine book and Lisa had fallen for it. What should she wear, she had asked earlier in the week. "Oh, anything, darling. It's not at all smart. We don't dress up," had been Jo-Anne's confident reply. Lisa had taken her at her word. From her limited wardrobe she had picked out a simple cotton sundress, ending at mid-thigh. A pair of white rubber-soled dancing shoes and the faithful conch belt, once her mother's pride and joy, made up the formidably casual ensemble. Bare legs. No jewelry. In dramatic contrast was Jo-Anne's double-breasted Yves Saint Laurent suit. Tapering down from wide shoulders to a narrow waist, the navy-blue material hugged the curvaceous body, ending precipitously at the knees, where a frontal vee flashed visuals of the inner thigh. The big brass buttons, bright and gleaming, were offset beautifully by pure white gloves. The color was provided by two silk scarves of red, white, and blue—one peeping stylishly from beneath the coat just in front of the left hip and cascading down the upper thigh, the other knotted carefully around the neck, held in place by a vast amethyst brooch surrounded by an exuberant cluster of diamonds. The earrings were smaller versions of the same design, sparkling and shining against the background of a stunning red-and-black striped turban whose tail spread out in an Egyptian-style fan across the formidable shoulders.

She looked like far more than a million dollars.

The breathtaking outfit had taken the wind right out of Lisa's sails at the very moment when she most needed flying speed. At a stroke she had been relegated to country-cousin status. The initial feeling of panic had given way to mild irritation at being so comprehensively set up. Now it had been replaced by the to-hell-with-it attitude that was par for her course.

The enormous car sailed grandly through the gates of the Polo Club, the driver waving imperiously at the obsequious guard whose duty it was to vet intruders. There was the shortest of waits in the semicircular entrance driveway and then the valet parkers were clustering around like puppy dogs at a bitch's teat. In the cool of the foyer Lisa braced herself for the plunge into the deep end. Here it was at last. The gates of paradise. In the role of Archangel Peter, the maître d' rushed forward to greet the party, abandoning the lectern at which he presided over the table bookings.

"Mr. Duke, Mrs. Duke. Welcome. Your table is ready, and Senator

Stansfield arrived only a minute or two ago. I hope you enjoy your lunch. Follow me please."

Lisa was only vaguely aware of her surroundings. It was the sound of her heart leaping about in her chest that preoccupied her most. At the waiter's mention of Bobby's name it had started its wild war dance, and it showed no signs of slowing down. He was *here*. Over there by the window, already beginning to get up as he saw them across the crowded room. Some enchanted evening. It felt like that to Lisa. She had been cast headfirst into the romantic deep end, and all the clichés in the world had come true. So this is what it felt like to walk on air. On either side the bronzed and alabaster faces peered up at her—white for women, brown for men—with the interest of regulars for a stranger in their midst. But Lisa didn't see them. On remote control she steered herself around the groaning buffet and headed for the Duke table, the place of honor in the middle of the picture window with its panoramic view of the cool green polo fields.

Bobby Stansfield was on his feet to greet them.

His first words were infinitely reassuring. Dressed with confident casualness in an open-necked gray-and-white striped Lacoste shirt, gray worsted pants, and a pair of black Cole-Haan loafers, he fastened his disturbing eyes on Lisa. "How wonderful. Lisa Starr. The girl who changes lives."

He continued to watch her as he ladled out far less substantial greetings on the Dukes. Peter Duke in particular, immaculately blue blazered and white-duck trousered, scored a pointedly cool reception.

If Jo-Anne was undermined by the relative lack of warmth at her arrival she wasn't in the business of showing it. "Sorry we're late, senator. It's Peter's fault. He's so vain, you know. Takes far longer to dress than I do."

Both Lisa and Bobby laughed at that. Peter Duke looked as if he had just accepted the invitation to be pallbearer at a close friend's funeral. Lisa immediately stopped laughing when she saw that the butt of the joke wasn't enjoying it, but Bobby didn't. She got the picture right away. It wasn't going to be a cozy foursome at all. Bobby and Peter Duke were quite clearly in the middle of a cold war. Jo-Anne was at best neutral, but probably inclining against her husband. For Lisa herself, Bobby seemed already much more than an ally, and Jo-Anne was a far from certain friend if the dress ploy was anything to go by. Damn. She'd imagined that the tricky part would be relating to the outsiders. Now it looked as if the hard ball would be played right there at the table.

An uneasy truce descended as the wine waiter hovered over the table. It didn't last long.

Bobby turned toward Lisa, helpful, solicitous. "The champagne's fine with orange juice, but I wouldn't drink it on its own." Somehow the way he said it didn't sound pompous at all. At least that was what Lisa thought. To her champagne was fizzy, expensive stuff that you drank to celebrate something. But to people like Bobby, who obviously drank it all the time, it was presumably possible to make all sorts of subtle distinctions between one type and another.

"I wouldn't drink it at all, with orange juice or anything else for that matter," said Peter Duke grandly, his lip curling with acid condescension. "That Spanish rubbish produces the worst hangovers in the world. The next day is a total write-off. I'd stick to the bloody marys, Lisa."

His remark said a lot. In the Duke household the champagne was always French, invariably vintage—1971s and 1973s at the moment—and of the very finest marques—Krug, Louis Roederer, Bollinger. A bottle of the Spanish Cordorniu that was being served at the Palm Beach Polo and Country Club Sunday brunch would have been about as welcome in the Duke cellar as a cockroach in a jar of face-cream.

Peter Duke's purpose was not merely to establish himself as a connoisseur. What he meant was that Bobby Stansfield was not only a Philistine, but an impoverished one at that. Stansfield could not afford to buy his way out of vicious hangovers. He was prepared to drink filth and to hide its taste with orange juice. The nuance was there for all to see. Dukes could buy Stansfields at any hour of the day or night.

Bobby got the message. Politicians of his caliber, however, were not fazed by puny javelins of the type Peter Duke could throw. "Must be pretty vital, Peter, for you to be on top form first thing in the morning." Bobby Stansfield's apparently flattering observation was about as innocent as a Chicago politician counting dollar bills in a smoke-filled room.

Peter Duke's face reddened as he picked up on the rebuke. Mornings these days tended to start late, and it was a problem filling in the couple of hours before one could decently start to drink again. There was a limit to the amount of time that could be spent on the telephone to the broker finding out if the market movements of the day before had left you a few million dollars richer or poorer.

Jo-Anne didn't help matters by laughing outright. "Listen, Bobby. Poor Peter's mornings are a write-off anyway. I don't think it's the quality of what he drinks—more like the quantity."

Lisa fought back the desire to laugh. Already she had Peter Duke's drift. He was a lazy, pompous incompetent whose most significant achievement had been the accident of his birth. Money was all he had.

Nobody was prepared for Peter's reaction.

First he changed color completely. High up on his cheekbones twin dots of red began to spread like the bloodstains of a disemboweled Samurai warrior. Then, throwing the crumpled linen napkin onto the table in front of him, he stood up suddenly, shaking the china and the cutlery with the violence of the movement.

"Listen, you fucking cow. Don't you ever speak about me like that again. Especially in front of your gym mistress and some clapped-out poseur of a politician." He didn't speak at the top of his voice, but everyone within twenty feet with waxless ears caught the speech. Abruptly, he proceeded to withdraw facilities. Turning his back on the surprised trio, he stalked out of the crowded restaurant, ignoring the two or three would-be friends who tried to talk to him on the way.

For a brief moment the babble of conversation slowed. Not for long. The Polo Club crowd were used to this sort of thing. Too much booze? Somebody caught cheating on his wife? Coke paranoia? Whatever. In seconds they were concentrating on their own lives once again.

"I'm so sorry. I don't know what's gotten into Peter lately. He's as antsy as hell these days."

"He's an asshole," said Bobby simply, and Lisa was more than inclined to agree.

They all ordered champagne and orange juice as a gesture of solidarity.

"Come on, Lisa, let's get you some food. All that exercise you do you must burn a lot of fuel." Bobby Stansfield stood up, and he held Lisa's chair for her as she did the same. Jo-Anne had to make it on her own, and for the very first time her expression registered displeasure. Hey, wait a *minute*—it seemed to say. This hick kid is *my* production. You can look but don't touch —and don't forget *I'm* the star around here.

Bobby and Lisa didn't see it at all, and both were already at the stage where they wouldn't have cared if they did. As far as Lisa was concerned, he didn't have to do a thing, and anything he did would be all right. But Bobby wasn't used to the passive role. From the moment he had set eyes on the beautiful young girl, all his most potent instincts as a hunter had been aroused. Okay, so he had a lot going for him in the seduction stakes, but he couldn't know the conditioning process that this one had undergone. So he pulled out the stops and piled on the Stansfield charm, far from suspecting that it was overkill.

Several things were obvious to him. First, from the social point of view Lisa was in way over her head. The clothes said it, the manners confirmed it. But at the same time she was far from overawed. A little uncertain now and again maybe, but not thrown by the heavy hitters who now surrounded her. Then there was the unmistakable feeling of anarchic strength that hung around her like an aura. This girl would not be pushed around, by people, by conventions, by life itself. Bobby had always been drawn to that. Most politicians, adventurers at heart, were.

Standing in line at the magnificent buffet laid out on the vast T-shaped table Bobby protectively guided her through the social minefield.

"The thing to do is to make several expeditions. Start with some gazpacho maybe, and then come back for the shellfish. The cracked crab is just delicious. Some people just pile it all on their plate, and end up eating roast beef covered with apple pie."

Behind him Jo-Anne's temperature was beginning to rise. She had already lost her husband from this party. Now it looked as if she were in the process of losing one of the best-looking girls she had ever come across. It was time to reassert a bit of her authority, to crack the ringmistress's whip. She looked around for a blunt instrument.

A small man, looking a bit like a tired schoolmaster, scurried past. Snake-like, Jo-Anne's arm shot out to grab the only arm he possessed.

"John, wonderful to *see* you. I must introduce you to my new discovery.

Lisa, this is Lord Cowdray. He's on the board of governors here, and just about everywhere else I should imagine. You must have heard of Cowdray Park in England. That's really the Mecca of the polo world."

Lisa reached out a hand. She'd never heard of Cowdray, never met an English lord before, didn't at all like being introduced as Jo-Anne's "new discovery." Rubbing in salt, Jo-Anne bubbled on. "Yes, Lisa runs a little gym in West Palm. We all go there to work out. Isn't that cute?"

Behind the spectacles, John Cowdray had acquired a hunted look. He hardly knew Jo-Anne Duke, and what he had seen of her he was inclined to dislike. Nodding politely, he offered a word or two of small talk before engineering an escape.

Bobby Stansfield, busy plate filling, missed the exchange, but Lisa felt Jo-Anne's wave of patronization break all over her. For some reason the girl who a day or two before had almost seduced her clearly didn't like her at all. Mentally she put up her defenses. Jo-Anne was obviously a very dangerous lady.

Back at the table, Bobby Stansfield was on top of the world. "The thing I always feel is that the people here miss the point. I like to come out here to watch the polo, not the damn people. I can't think why everyone dresses up like it's some fashion parade. Now, you and I, Lisa, have it just right. Casual, nice and cool, comfortable. That's the way to dress in this weather."

"Oh, Jo-Anne told me to dress like this. I'm real glad she filled me in," said Lisa with the innocence of an asp.

Bobby looked at Jo-Anne first in disbelief and then with quizzical interest. Feminine games were clearly being played.

Jo-Anne, looking like she had just gotten off the runway at the Paris collections, stared back evenly. Touché.

"Senator, Jo-Anne, looking indecently lovely I may say. How are you all?"

"Hello, Merv," said Bobby. "Have you allowed yourself a weekend off? I thought you TV superstars were too busy making money to relax."

Merv Griffin laughed good-naturedly. He had been one of the first to buy into the Polo Club. "You're quite right, senator. Actually I'm working right now. Came over to ask you on the show. We need a class act to shore up the ratings." Both men laughed. It was only half a joke.

"Now, Merv, if you want to go through the top on the Nielsens, the person you want is sitting right here. Lisa Starr, meet Merv Griffin."

"Tell you what, senator. You marry her, and we'll have you both on as a double act. How about that."

Lisa felt the blush explode all over her cheeks.

Bobby threw back his head and let out the well-known Stansfield guffaw.

"Well, now we might just do that. Might just get around to that. What do you say, Lisa? Would you take on a confirmed old bachelor like me?"

It was with only the bare minimum of surprise that Lisa realized that, yes, that was exactly what she would be prepared to do.

～7～

T HE VEIN HIGH up on Peter Duke's forehead had quite definitely begun to pulsate. Jo-Anne had only seen that happen once before, and it was not a good omen.

"Shall I tell you what I want. *Exactly* what I want," he yelled at the top of his voice. "I want a fucking divorce, and I want it quick."

There weren't many words that Jo-Anne Duke found really dirty, but divorce was undoubtedly one of them. Divorce, from a Duke. That was a real obscenity. She felt the color drain from her face.

A distant voice, presumably hers, said, "Oh, don't be so silly, Peter. If there's a problem we can work it out. We always did before."

"You're a tramp, Jo-Anne. You know that. You were a whore when you hooked me, and you're still one today. I want out, and I want out now. Do you hear me?"

Jo-Anne struggled to make sense of the earth-shattering message she was receiving. If the decibels were anything to go by, it looked as if he were serious. The fact that it was ten o'clock in the morning meant that he wasn't drunk either.

Jo-Anne tried to lighten it up. That had worked before. It didn't now. She managed a hollow laugh. "You'd be lost without me. You know you would." Sitting on the end of the big bed, she languidly drew on a silk stocking.

Peter Duke took two steps toward his wife, until he towered over her, an unforgiving mountain of hate. The spit that cascaded from his mouth as he fought to wrap his tongue around the venomous syllables filled the air above Jo-Anne's head. "You filthy bitch. How dare you suggest I need you. I need you like I need brain cancer. I'll step on you like the roach you are. I'll bury you."

He was on the verge of physical violence. Jo-Anne knew the signs. In the old days the hookers who cared about their looks had learned to read their johns right.

She said nothing at all.

"And when I've gotten rid of you, I'll be free to marry someone who's as pure and clean as you are totally *disgusting*." He stepped back, a pleased look of neat spite all over his face.

Jo-Anne struggled for words. She could hardly believe her ears. This was the ultimate danger. Another woman? Who, what, where?

"You've got somebody else," she managed at last.

Peter smiled wickedly. "Pamela Whitney. We love one another. You were too busy whoring to notice."

Christ! Jo-Anne couldn't take much more of this. Pamela Whitney. Face like a doughnut, ass like a sponge pudding, pedigree as long as the yellow brick road. Of course, it made sense. A dynastic marriage, like the ones the medieval princes arranged. You take my daughter, and we merge our king-doms. Dimly, through the mists of horror, she began to see the enormity of what faced her. Together the Whitneys and the Dukes would eat her for breakfast. Between them they must own more lawyers than the Justice De-partment. She'd be lucky to get out of the marriage with anything more than the exotic underwear that had been her sole material contribution to it.

"Listen, Peter, I think we should talk about this."

"We *are* talking about it, sweetheart. At least I'm *telling* you about it. There's not a lot you can say that'll interest me."

Jo-Anne couldn't help herself. She just had to test the water, to see how bad things really were. "If we do split up, I guess there'll be some sort of settlement."

She sounded far from certain.

"Right on, there'll be a settlement. Do you want to know what it'll be? I can tell you right now. You get to pack a suitcase, just one, and you get to call a cab—and then you piss the hell out of my life, back to the gutter you came from. Understand? Maybe, just maybe, if you act real nice I may let you take the Mercedes."

It was Jo-Anne's turn to laugh. "You've got to be joking, Peter. This isn't the Dark Ages, you know, or Saudi Arabia. If I go, then I *take*. Do *you* understand? I'll cut your fucking fortune off at the knees."

"Hah." All the scorn in the world was packed into Peter Duke's derisive exclamation. He had the look of the man who was holding all the trumps. "That's for a court to decide, isn't it. And a *Florida* court. More specifically a Palm Beach County court. Do you know what that means, Jo-Anne? Dukes have been around here a long time. They've got some powerful friends, and in this part of the world the good ol' boys have a way of sticking closer together than copulating dogs—or haven't you noticed? When I said I'd bury you I wasn't joking. Sweetest thing is, you gave it to me on a plate."

Jo-Anne had never heard a nastier laugh. What the hell did he mean?

"Yes, sir, I'd sure like you to see what I've got sitting on old Ben Car-stairs's safe. Just about the juiciest dossier a man could read. If I ever get short of cash, I might just go right on and publish it. Should be worth mil-lions."

The dreadful fear rushed through Jo-Anne. "What dossier? Have you been spying on me?" Even as she asked the question, she knew the answer was yes. God! How could she have *been* so stupid? She'd thought she'd played it safe, covered her tracks, avoided the heterosexual affairs that were always supposed to be the dangerous ones. She had heard the metallic click of the telephone, the hollow sound when she spoke into the receiver. Peter had bugged it. For months all her most secret conversations had been going down on tape.

"I've got transcripts of conversations that would make a seventy-year-old judge's false teeth fall out. I swear I thought old Ben was going to come right there in his pants when he heard you sweet-talking that Mary d'Erlanger. And you know those photographs of the pair of you walking out of the Brazilian Court—boy, I've seen some wrecked ladies in my time, but you two looked as if you needed crutches. Somehow, I don't think the court is going to look too kindly on your claims on my assets."

Of course he was right. No way he wasn't. But suddenly Jo-Anne didn't mind at all. Already she was one step ahead of poor Peter. Always had been. Ice cold inside, she knew exactly what she would do.

"WHAT WAS he like, for chrissakes?" Maggie looked ready to explode with curiosity.

Lisa reached down and picked up her leg as if it were a totally foreign object. Putting her right knee on her cheekbone she straightened it and pointed the big toe directly at the ceiling. As she did so she thought about Maggie's question.

"I guess I'm in love," she laughed.

"Oh, I know that. Of course you are. But what the hell is he *like?*"

"Well, if you want me to be serious, let's see. He's incredibly good looking, which isn't exactly the latest news, I guess. He's kind, sort of sensitive. You know, puts you at ease. Protective, you could say. Oh, and he's funny, very funny—and incredibly self-confident. Like you know he wouldn't take any shit from anybody. He really carved up that Peter Duke guy. Put him through the mincer."

Maggie leaned forward. It wasn't nearly enough. "But did he come on to you? Is he going to *call,* for God's sake? How did you leave it?"

Lisa's expression was reflective. "He could call. I'm sure he liked me. But I just don't know if he has time. He must be worked off his feet."

Lisa retrieved her limb, removed her bottom from the corner of the desk, and stuck her foot in the small of her back.

Looking envious, Maggie went right back to gnawing the bone. "Listen, baby. It doesn't take that long."

Lisa laughed wickedly. "Yeah, maybe he'll stop by and try me out on the Nautilus machines."

"Okay. Well, I bet he makes a move. Anyone would."

"Thanks, Maggs. But seriously, I just can't be his type. You know, a guy like that. I mean he's so sophisticated. He knows everything, everyone. I mean he probably calls up the president to check what's on TV if he's lost the newspaper. What the hell have I got to offer him?"

"I can see a couple of things right now," Maggie said. "That body stocking is *evil*, Lisa."

"I think somebody like Bobby Stansfield is into minds more than bodies. All those political groupies, with their master's in philosophy and politics."

"I know we all try to forget brains around here, Lisa, but you're really bright."

"If he *does* call, he's going to wait a day or two, so there's no point us getting too excited just yet."

Six inches to the right of Lisa's crotch the telephone rang.

She smiled as she picked it up, flushed as she heard the voice.

"I can tell that's Lisa Starr I'm talking to. Bobby Stansfield. What are you doing for lunch?"

"Oh, goodness. Hello. How are you? Lunch. God! What's today? Yes, of course I'd like to."

"Great. We were all sitting here around the pool trying to think of what we needed to make good things even better, and I hit on you. Have you got wheels? I can send a car. Come as soon as you like—it's paradise over here, and we're drinking the neatest margaritas."

Lisa's head had begun to throb. The compliment was nice, but it was something else he'd said. Paradise over here. Paradise over here. Paradise over here. She opened her mouth to speak, but the words wouldn't come.

"Are you still there? Do you know where to come? You turn left at . . ."

"It's okay. I know the way. I can find it." I've been there a thousand times in my dreams.

"And you don't need transportation?"

"No. I'd like to cycle over."

"God! In this heat? Boy, are you exercise freaks into punishment. Anyway, hurry, and don't melt before you arrive. I want to see all of you."

"I'm on my way."

Lisa put down the telephone. For a second the two friends stared at each other, saying nothing.

Maggie broke the ice. In an exaggerated stage voice she intoned, "Ladies and gentlemen, please make way for Senator and Mrs. Robert Stansfield," as Lisa threw at her four pens, six paper clips, an eraser, and a small Japanese calculator.

—

LISA PEDALED hard as she crossed the dangerous North Flagler intersection. Her experience had been that accidents tended to take place around where she was; that she herself might possibly be the cause of them had not occurred to her. The disinterested observer would not have made that mistake. She was all in white, from her Adidas sneakers and ankle socks to the shorts and loose T-shirt under which her mindbending breasts surged and reared. Her long firm legs stroked the pedals with seemingly effortless ease.

Across her back was the white plastic beach bag, a rope from each end snaking out around Lisa's torso and plastering the T-shirt flat between the conical tits. There wasn't much inside. She had packed fast. The only real problem had been the swimsuit. The ones she possessed were just fine for the *Sports Illustrated* beachwear editions, but were hardly, she imagined, standard issue around the Stansfield swimming pool. Still, there hadn't been time for a shopping trip, or indeed the inclination. Lisa was intelligent enough to know that in this life you scored few points trying to pass yourself off as something you were not—especially to the Bobby Stansfields of this world.

The jet-black skin-tight suit she had selected would have been a wow on Copacabana and Ipanema. One piece, it was cut away sharply at the crotch, front and back, to show all but the most private aspects of the anatomy. So far she hadn't had any complaints, and she didn't anticipate any now.

Once across the bridge, she made the left turn onto the Palm Beach bicycle trail. Running along the borders of Lake Worth, the five-foot-wide tarmac pathway rambled for seven miles past some of the most beautiful, and expensive, houses in the world. It was a magical thoroughfare, closed strictly to motor vehicles of every kind and yet, despite its flavor of total exclusivity, it was open to the public. Here different worlds could meet as cyclists, joggers, and hikers were able to peer at the pools of the rich. Somehow, though, it never happened like that. The bicycle trail was a closely guarded secret, and those sophisticated enough to have discovered it were discreet enough to respect the rights of others. For Lisa it was enough to speed past the sleek yachts moored at the bottoms of their owners' gardens, past the thick banyan trees, the banks of sweet-smelling jasmine ivy, through the rich aroma of sandalwood and frangipani blossoms, past the tall ficus hedges of those who valued their privacy more than their view. She remembered her mother's words, "The higher the ficus, the richer the man." Would, one day, her ficus hedge be tall? The street names at the intersections said it all—Tangier Avenue, West Indies Drive, Bahama Lane. Farther north there would be Tradewind Drive, Orange Grove Road, and Mockingbird Trail. How easy it would be to love a place like this. How easy it *was* to love it. And the people who lived in it.

On purpose Lisa overshot the Garden Road turn that would have taken her directly to the Stansfield house. She often did that. Instead she took the right on Colonial that brought her to the gates of the Kennedy home. She paused briefly. Was Rose in there now, insulated at last from the ongoing tragedies that history seemed determined to heap on her family? In the parking lot stood the battered family Buick, desperately unpretentious. Who could have thought a few years ago the car park had been created as a helicopter pad for the most powerful man in the world? Even then Palm Beach had made it hard on the Kennedys, and it was only with the utmost reluctance that the town council had made a special exception to the strict rule that forbade any flying craft to land within the town's borders. The brick-red paint on the Mizner gem was peeling unselfconsciously, and the two signs that read hopefully NO TRESPASSERS and BEWARE OF THE DOG had long outlived their usefulness.

What trick of fate had thrown the Kennedys and the Stansfields together, separated by only half a dozen houses on the long, lonely beach? Two great political dynasties, one Democrat, one Republican, neighbors and foes, one day perhaps to be locked in battle for the greatest prize of all. It was a potent thought. The two potential opponents could near enough have enjoyed a game of Frisbee without ever leaving their respective front lawns. Within a few years, North Ocean Boulevard could once again number a president of the United States among its residents, and casual bicycle rides of this sort would be very strictly curtailed. Lisa allowed herself to imagine it: the traffic diversions, the lean, hard men with their suspicious eyes, the aura of latent excitement and danger. And maybe, God willing, it would be Bobby. Bobby Stansfield. Her host for lunch. She was to be an honored guest in the mansion where her mother had been so proud to work.

The police car rolled by, its driver checking her out quickly. She was used to that. Every other car in this town belonged to the police, and the three-and-a-half-mile strip of the North End was probably just about the only place on God's earth where *everybody* kept to the speed limit. Most of the residents liked it that way. People didn't lock their doors in this part of town. Lisa shook her head in disbelief, half admiration, half horror as she thought about the town's excesses. They'd recently passed a bylaw that made it compulsory for the people who worked in the town without living there—the gardeners, cleaners, etc.—to carry I.D. cards at all times and to give mandatory fingerprint samples. That just *had* to be unconstitutional. But Palm Beach didn't mind. Palm Beach did things its own way. Even now, some liberal was taking the town to court to contest the rule. Lisa hoped he had deep pockets; he'd need them. Then there was the jogger, arrested and charged for being indecently dressed. The poor guy had taken off his T-shirt. Perhaps if he'd been female . . . Lisa laughed out loud at the thought. Then the laugh died in her throat. She was cycling through the big gates of the Stansfield mansion.

—

LISA WAS hardly ready for the white-uniformed maid who opened the heavy, carved oak door. For a second she stood there, immobile, as the bittersweet memories came flooding back. How well she had grown to love that uniform. How proud her mother had been of its immaculate whiteness, of its symbolic meaning. All those years it had lain there in the closet, laundered faithfully from time to time and kept scrupulously pressed. Occasionally Mary-Ellen had taken it out and put it on to show the young Lisa the glories of her former position as trusted servant in the Stansfield house. Did the young girl in front of her feel the same way about her job? Unlikely. For a start she was black, and for blacks it was unwise and unprofitable to dream dreams in Palm Beach.

Lisa pushed the unwelcome thoughts from her mind. There were other emotions to be dealt with besides nostalgia. Life had to go on. To go upward. "I think Senator Stansfield is expecting me. I'm Lisa Starr."

The maid inclined her head backward and made a sort of a sniffing noise.

The look said, Senator Stansfield is always expecting pretty young girls. Don't you go getting ideas above your station.

"Theyse all out by the pool. Follow me, Miss Starr," was what she said.

Lisa was inside at last—a child in the toy shop of her dreams. Wide eyed, she tried to imprint everything on her memory as she followed the maid through the dark old house. They passed along a Spanish-tiled cloister, both sides of it opening through archways to immaculately landscaped terraces, thick with greenery—bougainvillaea, tecoma, and wild orchids nestling in Spanish moss—and the sound of tinkling water from cleverly placed fountains. Long oak sideboards, dark and intricately carved, containing silver bowls of long-stemmed flowers and smaller bowls of pink and white azaleas, lined the walls. A huge still life of fruit and flowers painted in the style of the Dutch School was lit by an ancient picture light.

Gloomy, thought Lisa. But incredibly stylish. Pure and unadulterated Mizner—the whole house reeking of twenties Palm Beach when its rich had ruled the world and imagined that they would do so forever.

Before her the soft-soled white shoes padded over the highly polished tiles as her mother's had once done; again Lisa fought back the wave of sadness that threatened to engulf her. At the end of the cloister was a big, black wrought-iron gate, its brass doorknob highly polished. Through the delicate patterns of its design Lisa could see a stretch of green lawn beyond which was the sea, its waves rolling in lazily toward the breakwater.

"I'll leave you here, Miss Starr. You'll find the senator and his friends over there by the pool."

As she approached, Bobby Stansfield uncoiled himself from a toweled sun bed, rising to greet her.

"Lisa. Lisa. Just what we needed." He turned to his friends. "There you are. I promised you an angel and now I deliver one." His smile was as warm and welcoming as sunlight on soft skin. "Lisa, this is Jimmy Baker. Knows everything in the world about politics. I hope! Not much about anything else."

Jimmy smiled carefully at the jocular introduction, as he stood to shake Lisa's hand, his cunning eyes reaching into her. How would she affect his boy? Was she good news or bad news? A cheap trick or a respectable girl? How could she be *used*?

Lisa looked him up and down in distaste. If he ever got around to shaving his chest he could go into the doormat business.

The other two men seemed to be less important, more deferential, eager to please.

"Now, Lisa, can you handle a margarita? I'm afraid we started without you—if I may understate the case a bit." He threw back his head and laughed. A little boy owning up to a raid on the cookie jar? A fun-loving man of the world who was not afraid to enjoy himself and needed a partner in crime? An old-style aristocrat who knew a thing or two when it came to mixing a cocktail? There was an element of all three in his remark and in his laughter, and Lisa wasn't at all sure which she found the most attractive.

He steered her toward the bar area of the poolside cabana. "The secret of a *really* good margarita is always to make it yourself," he said in mock seriousness. "Glass in the icebox, of course."

Like a conjurer he extracted two frosted, V-shaped cocktail glasses from the freezer compartment of the refrigerator. He emptied a pile of salt onto the white marble slab and smoothed it flat with his hand before dipping in the rim of each glass.

Bobby filled the two glasses from a large jug, and handed one to Lisa. "Tell me what you think of that." On his face was a playful expression of concern.

"Mmmmmmm. That's delicious," said Lisa. "What a way to go."

Bobby laughed as he led her away to a table some distance from the other three men. Lisa felt the alcohol pass straight through her stomach lining and into her bloodstream. He was even more attractive than she had remembered, if that was at all possible. Sort of craggy rather than muscular—a body that looked as if it had become fit by being used for things other than just constant exercise. There was enough hair on the chest, but not too much. Nice feet and, thank God, well-manicured toenails. Few men realized how important that was. The face of course won medals, but then that was common knowledge from the redwood forests to the Gulf Stream waters. It was difficult to separate the man from what he meant, from what it was possible he could mean. Bobby Stansfield wasn't just a good-looking jock hanging out poolside and getting gently stoned in the sun. He was a symbol. More self-confident than the old conservatism, the philosophy he embraced had struck a vein of feeling right across the country, and if he was able to mine it well he might draw the ultimate dividend. That made him a figure of awesome potential power, which acted in synergy with his abundant physical attractions. Anyone would have felt that. But Lisa wasn't just anyone: she was Mary-Ellen Starr's daughter, and if the pun could be forgiven, she saw him through starry eyes.

"Listen, did you bring some swimming things? If not, I'm sure we could fix you up. There's usually a pile of my sisters' stuff around."

"Sure. In here." Lisa patted the bag. "Where do I change?"

"Use the cabana."

By the time she had returned Bobby had stretched himself out on the sun bed and, eyes closed, was soaking up the sun.

Standing over him she cut out the sun's rays. Bobby sat up, aware of her presence from the sudden darkness. He opened his eyes, filling them up with the erotic vision of a lifetime. For the first time in an age he was at a loss for words. "Christ," he managed at last.

Lisa laughed, pleased at the effect she knew she was having.

For a second or two she let him feast upon her, his desperate eyes sliding all over her flowing body. Then she turned on her heel and ran the few steps to the pool's edge. In one liquid movement she arced through the air and, making no splash at all, disappeared into the drinkable blue water.

She knew he would follow her, that he would be drawn into the water by the magnet of her body. She had seen it all in the eager eyes. Lisa swam the length of the pool before breaking the surface, her lungs more than capable of providing the oxygen for her powerful underwater breast stroke. As she emerged from the depths she tossed back her head, sending the wet, black hair behind the strong shoulders. With her right hand she smoothed errant strands from her eyes as with her left she held on to the blue mosaic tiles of the pool's edge. She looked for Bobby. He had vanished.

For a second her heart skipped a beat. He'd gone. Gone to get himself another drink? To talk a little more politics with his poolside cronies? To answer the telephone?

Like an otter, slippery, muscular, the dark form rushed up between her legs. He was very close, his hands tracing the contours of her body, of her ankles, her calves, her outer thighs, the fine line of her buttocks, the sweep of her waist. In one lingering second of delight the confident hands touched the line of her breasts, before reaching for their final destination—in the pits of her arms.

The underwater lap of the sixty-foot pool had not caused Lisa to lose any breath at all, but she lost it now. As Bobby's head emerged into the sunshine inches from Lisa's own, his laughing smile promising the world, he lifted her up, strong and mischievous, until she herself was propelled from the pool by the crane of his arms, forced to sit on its side, her knees dangling in the water, framing Bobby's head as he smiled up at her.

There, silhouetted against the wild blue of the Florida sky, he allowed himself to worship at the altar of her teenage beauty as Lisa, the breath coming fast now through parted lips, gazed back at him, the excitement shining in her eyes at the contemplation of the desire in his.

Something would happen. Both knew it.

For an age they savored the moment—the first delicate moment of the journey to intimacy when everything is new, all is supercharged with the mystery and danger of passion.

Bobby's arms snaked upward to encircle each of Lisa's upper legs and he drew himself in toward her, forcing the delicious flesh hard against his head, his lips centimeters from the place she already wanted to be his. Again he looked up at her, his chin touching the material of the bathing suit, its delicious pressure caressing her at the most vulnerable part of her being. Once again the baby-blue eyes questioned her, reassured her, tantalized her. Then she was being pulled forward, her bottom losing its precarious seat at the pool's edge as he drew her toward him into the water. Her momentum carried her down deep, and Bobby went with her, his hard body plastered against hers, held rigidly against her by the ropelike arms.

Like the drowning man whose life is supposed to flash past in the seconds before destruction, Lisa's mind kaleidoscoped the events which had led to this most wanted moment. She was gone, lost, spinning in the vortex of lust, and love. That was it. She loved this man who held her. Loved him physically and mentally as she had been programmed to do. He was everything. Her mother, her ambition, her future. And he was here now. Holding her tightly in his arms beneath the surface of the Stansfield swimming pool a few feet away from his friends.

For a desperate moment she felt the need to escape, to collect her chaotic thoughts. Soon they would be lovers, but there was a no-man's-land to cross.

Like a mermaid she slipped away from him, searching for the safe haven where she could rediscover her mind, the clarity of her thoughts. Without looking back she was out of the pool, and running toward the cabana.

It was dark in the changing room. Cool and dark. As good a place as any to try to get a hold on runaway emotions. Lisa was wet, and she shook from head to foot. Every single nerve ending was shouting, screaming for some sort of release from the unbearable tension that gripped her body. She backed up against the white tile of the shower, grateful for its cold touch against her skin—for any touch at all. All the time she fought to grip the reins, to slow the chariot of desire that careened dangerously within her. On her thigh she could still feel the imprint of Bobby's urgent strength, the mind-stopping feeling of him crushed against her in the deep blue waters. God, how she wanted him. It was crazy to want like this, and so ludicrously sudden. Then, with the shock of joy she realized that she was no longer alone. Her eyes tightly closed, she felt his hand on hers, and her mind stopped as her body crashed on. It was a beautiful dream, a wonderful fantasy, as he placed her hand elsewhere. She could feel it throb, expanding, rearing, twitching beneath her hot fingers. Still she kept her eyes closed, unwilling to disturb the magic of the moment that she knew now would come. She heard her low moan of acquiescence, as the material of the swimsuit was drawn away from her body.

Beneath her hand the penis moved, a living, wanting thing, desiring conquest and possession. Lovingly she traced its contours from the proud, smooth head along the rock-hard shaft to the jungle abundance of its base. Still her eyes remained closed as she prepared herself to receive the offering. From her parted lips came a shuddering sigh of ecstasy as she readied herself, and she flexed her powerful pelvic muscles, bending very slightly at the knee as she pressed her back against the shower's wall.

The two hands of the lovers worked in union to guide the invader to its destination. Pausing for the briefest of moments at the wet, anxious entrance, it plunged gratefully into its rightful home.

Lisa let out a short, sharp cry as the delightful thing moved within her. Like a traveler in a strange land it was first cautious, unsure of itself as it explored the unfamiliar surroundings, but slowly it began to gain in confidence as it established a rhythm of its own.

Only now did she open her eyes.

"How did you know it was me?" he whispered tenderly.

Lisa tried to speak as she moistened dry lips with a partially dry tongue. She smiled back at him, saying nothing, as he pushed gently into her.

"I wanted you since the first time I saw you," Bobby said.

"You can have me. Like this. Anytime. Anywhere." Thrusting downward she gripped him in the vice of her passion, guarding the willing prisoner, crushing its abundant strength with the power of her own need.

Her tongue reached out for his, ravenous for him, hungry for his taste, as her mind willed the impossible merger of bodies, of souls. It seemed to Lisa as if whole parts of her had ceased to exist. From her mouth to her vagina, all the feeling, the wanting, the living and the loving concentrated at the point where Bobby had entered her.

"Do you want it here? Like this?"

The question was concerned, urgent.

Lisa felt the panic rush into the battlefield of her mind. "God yes. Don't stop, Bobby. Don't dare stop."

All she wanted was his climax. Later there would be time for anything and everything, but now she wanted his seed inside her. Nothing else mattered, not her own body's satisfaction, not tenderness, not understanding, not even love.

Her hands found the thrusting buttocks and she pulled at them in the desperation of desire, forcing him deeper inside her as she added her own strength to his. Her back jammed tight against the wall now slippery with her sweat, she withstood the heavenly onslaught as she prayed for its sweet end.

She saw it first in his eyes, the faraway look, the almost dreamy detachment, the intensification of the thrashing love dance in her belly. Like a clarion call from the clearest of trumpets it summoned the reaction in Lisa. Together. It would be together, and they would always be together. Locked in love. Locked in each other's bodies. She stood up on tiptoe, making him reach for her.

"Oh, Lisa."

"It's all right. I'm ready. I want you, Bobby. God, how I want you."

And then Lisa's mind took off, wandering, drifting, dreaming on the sea of detachment as the wave of sublimity engulfed her. Shaking with the rumbling tremors of her own orgasm, she tried, too, to experience his. Feverishly she attempted to call her brain to order, to shine the spotlight of sensation on the event that was happening inside her. She was being cleansed, washed clean of her past, as Bobby bathed her with his passion. Bucking, rearing, forcing himself deeper into her, he shouted triumphantly as Lisa's feet left the ground, a butterfly pinned to the wall by the exploding instrument of desire.

Head bowed on her streaming chest, Bobby shook in the aftermath of love.

Tenderly Lisa cradled the nuzzling head, as she felt the triumph in her soul. And there was another feeling too, mad, impossible, but absolutely certain. One fine day she would have this man. Have his love, his name, forever.

PETER DUKE could hardly believe it. Beneath the Egyptian cotton sheets his wife's hands were all over him. For a second or two he lay there like a log as he tried to make sense of it. It seemed to be about breakfast time from the chinks of sunlight visible through cracks in the heavy curtains. But why? They hadn't made it for months, except after quarrels. Giving Jo-Anne her marching orders was unlikely to have made him more attractive in her eyes. Masochism had never been her bag.

Then Peter Duke smiled to himself. Okay, he had her number. Boy, she must have thought he was a real sucker. She was trying to win him back by turning him on. He wanted to laugh out loud. God, the transparency of it. Jo-Anne was disappointing him. He'd expected more from her. Some smart legal moves, perhaps, and a brash determination to brazen it out, to drag the Duke name through the courts and, incidentally, the mud. To avoid that he'd certainly reach for his checkbook. The old Jo-Anne wouldn't have missed that sort of a move. But this? Wow.

Whatever the motive she certainly hadn't lost her touch, and it was impossible to avoid the comparison with Pamela Whitney, who'd never had the touch in the first place. Certainly the first time with his bride-to-be had been a complicated failure. He'd had all the potency of a noodle soaked overnight in condensed milk, and concluded that the act of lovemaking for a female Whitney was about as unimportant as forgetting to carry I.D. to the bank when cashing a check. No, Whitneys relied on other charms. Like money, superior genes, and all those extraordinary *horses*. Breeding horses and breeding children. Those were the sorts of things they were good at. Soon there would be a clan of pint-size Whitney Dukes, a gaggle of little preppies to run the businesses, join the clubs, and irritate the stockbrokers.

Jo-Anne Duke went about her work with the expertise of the true professional. There was no pleasure in it, none at all, but there *was* purpose. Afterward Peter Duke would unwind a bit, bend a little, be marginally more prepared to fit in with her suggestions. That was important if she was to avoid the ultimate disaster. Not for one moment did she imagine it would change his mind. Dynasties and dollars had been in his eyes when he had talked of divorce, and the cold, calculating way he had snooped on her over the months argued that the whole thing had been premeditated. Her objective was a lesser one.

After she had achieved it Peter Duke lay back on the pillows and watched his beautiful wife with suspicious eyes.

"Was that okay?" He couldn't resist fishing for the compliment.

"Only the greatest," she lied. Jo-Anne put out a hand and touched his arm. "You know, Peter, we shouldn't fight."

She laughed the attractive, flirtatious laugh.

Peter smiled back knowingly. It was bad manners to kick somebody in the mouth who had recently been the source of so much pleasure. He fought back the desire to tell her that nothing had changed, that she was still out on the street without a bean, that blowing him was blowing in the wind.

"I guess I can't argue with that," he said.

"You know, I've been thinking, Peter. I've been thinking a lot about everything. About us. The divorce." She watched the interest spark in him as he waited for her to make her pitch. It was clear that he expected bargaining. If you give me this, you can have that. In exchange for the jewels, I'll . . .

She went on. "I came to a strange conclusion, really. I think it's been my fault all along. I blew it. I guess I always have. Perhaps it's just the way I am. Anyway, what I want to say is that I'm sorry for everything. I'm not going to contest the divorce, and I don't want anything for me. I'm best like that, on my own, looking after myself, fighting my own battles. No responsibilities. Kind of like a child of the universe, doing my own thing."

Peter's eyes narrowed. He could hardly believe this. There just had to be an angle. No free lunches.

Jo-Anne plowed on in the pregnant silence.

"I guess I realize you're holding all the cards, but playing them would make a great big mess, for both of us really. It wouldn't help anyone. Who knows, maybe you'd think that was worth something."

Peter saw the play. It wasn't such a bad move, but it was a trusting one. She would go quietly, and in exchange he would do the decent thing and smooth her path with a generous settlement. Effectively, she was throwing herself on his mercy.

Peter Duke liked what he heard. He was at heart a bully, and there was nothing on this earth he enjoyed doing more than exploiting weakness. He would appear to fit in with her plans. Make her sign all sorts of things, and then, when it came to signing the settlement check he would laugh in her face, slam the door, then change the locks.

"That would be very decent of you, Jo-Anne. You could count on my recognizing that, once things had been sorted out."

Jo-Anne let the relief shine out through her eyes. "Oh, Peter, that's great. Just great. I hoped you'd see it like that. So we don't fight anymore. Okay? Listen, I've got a wonderful idea. Let's go waterskiing. Like we used to. I haven't driven the boat in an age, and the ocean's flat as a mill pond out there. I checked it earlier."

"Hell, why not. It might be fun," said Peter Duke.

———

"ARE YOU ready?" Jo-Anne shouted the words above the gentle thud of the Riva's powerful engine.

Across the smooth, still waters off the North End beach, Peter Duke's reply was clearly audible. His yes drifted through on the breezeless air.

Jo-Anne reached down, pulled hard at the throttle, and the great boat lurched forward as the engines let out a mighty roar.

Peter Duke arose from the calm waters with effortless ease, rock steady, hardly moving from side to side. Right away it was obvious to the lazy sun-worshippers of the nearby beach that this skier was no novice, and the impression was confirmed when he headed immediately toward the speedboat's wake. Arms stretched out fully in front of him, he leaned well back, body straight and inclined at a forty-five-degree angle to the sea surface. As his speed increased he hit the waves of the wash and was momentarily airborne, before crashing down into the flat water beyond. Now, almost parallel with the Riva's side, his forward velocity slowed, allowing him time for a cheery wave to Jo-Anne, before he braced his legs for the turn.

This was the part he liked. Beneath his feet he felt the enormous upward force as he twisted the ski in opposition to the water. The muscles of his forearms stood out like steel spans as the tow rope pulled at him, and the high column of seawater splayed out satisfactorily from the edge of the ski as he made the turn.

Now, he raced across the stern of the boat. Two wakes to jump as he crossed to the other side. He was dimly aware of his wife's long hair waving in the wind created by the Riva's speed.

This was what it was all about. A man pitting himself against the elements, using his skill and determination to stay upright in a situation in which all the cards were stacked against him. In this life the list of his achievements was not a long one, but he was good at this. No question. It had been a great idea of Jo-Anne's.

For a second as he sped along through the salt-sprayed air, he allowed himself the luxury of a moment's regret. Somehow he couldn't see Pamela Whitney in the role of furious chariot driver that Jo-Anne filled so well. She would have other charms, but driving his ski boat wouldn't be one of them. Still, it looked as if they would part as friends. Maybe he'd slip her a million or two for old times' sake. At least it would keep her off the streets—the cheaper ones anyway.

Hey, hang on there. Concentrate. Nearly lost that turn. Twisting and turning like an unleashed rocket on the Fourth of July, the Riva was tracing crazy patterns all over the sea. Peter smiled to himself. Good old Jo-Anne. This was the spirit he admired in her. Nothing she liked more than competition. Her powers as a driver against his as a skier. It was the best way. He gritted his teeth and tensed his muscles for the battle.

Jo-Anne's mouth, usually sensual and full, was now a thin pencil line across her face. Her eyes, normally sparkling, were cold and dead as she gripped the leather-clad wheel. This way and that she turned the sleek vessel, carving and churning at the soft ocean, like a Navy Phantom caught in the guidance system of a heat-seeking missile, she tried for the totally unpredictable turn, the cunningly deceptive change of speed.

Behind the boat Peter Duke held on grimly as he tried to anticipate her movements. As the minutes clicked by his muscles began to tire with the strain, and his mind to slow with the effort of bodily coordination. Okay, Jo-Anne, that's about it. Enough is enough. Don't let's overdo it.

But the boat didn't stop. If anything its movements had become even more frantic as it leaped and bounded over the sea surface in its effort to shake off its load. Peter Duke fought to stay with it, a fisherman determined not to lose a record catch, as it raced all over the ocean to defeat him. And then, quite suddenly, it was all over. As he went into a turn Jo-Anne cut the throttle. As he came out of it she opened right up again, wrenching the wheel to the right as she did so. Game, set, and match. With rueful resignation and not a little relief, Peter Duke let himself go, arcing gracefully through the air, as the smooth blue surface rushed up to meet his face.

Wipe-out. That was what the surfers said. Well, beneath the water it was cool and quiet, a welcome contrast to the struggle of the fifteen-minute contest. Lazily Peter Duke headed upward.

When he broke surface the boat was just finishing its turn, its bow settled in the water as the big propellers ground the seas at idling speed. Sixty, maybe seventy feet away, and the bow was now toward him. Lying on his back, kicking gently at the warm ocean, he planned his greeting.

Were you trying to kill me back there? Yes, that would do. A humorous response to his wife's little victory. Thirty feet away. Jo-Anne was totally invisible behind the looming prow of the boat with its steel-edged V and sloping mahogany walls.

Careful, Jo-Anne. You should be in neutral now. Swing around a bit to give me some room.

Peter Duke opened his mouth, "Were you trying to kill . . ."

With an angry roar the Riva's engines howled into life. Like an arrow the bow came at him. No time to act. No time to think. The gleaming wood smacked into his shoulder, and the shuddering shock of the terrific blow seemed to loosen all the connections in his body. Down, down he went, his senses pained by the drowsy numbness of a dimly remembered poem. Fractions of time away, the burnished, razor-sharp blades of the propellers churned in eager anticipation. It was a funny sensation. Jingle jangle—a bit like driving over a bumpy road. No pain. Just a strange whirring in the head as the screws rearranged his formerly neat body, spilling his blood, his tissues, and his guts all over the ocean. And then there was nothing really, except perhaps the mildest sense of irritation at the inefficiency of it all, as Peter Duke started out on his unplanned trip to eternity.

———

"Eternal father strong to save . . ."

Through the black lace veil, Jo-Anne could see that the whole of Palm Beach had turned out for the funeral. She had never seen Bethesda-by-the-Sea so packed. Not at the Phipps wedding, the winter fête—not ever. But then they would come, wouldn't they? After all, a Duke was a Duke. Of course, nobody had really *liked* Peter—except presumably for the grotesque Pamela Whitney, visible out of the corner of her eye, back as straight as that of any Marine honor guard, upper lip as stiff as a surfer's penis on Saturday night, as she "suffered in dignity." Christ! Those two sure deserved each other. They could have lain in bed for the rest of their lives playing with each other's pedigrees. Every now and again she would have turned on her back and thought of the flag while Peter grunted and groaned on top of her to produce a few more little Dukes for the *Social Register*.

". . . those in peril on the sea."

She had asked specially for the song. Good enough for President Kennedy. Good enough for poor old Peter. Apt, really.

She looked around. It was going off well. The Jackie Kennedy bit. The grieving widow. Jo-Anne didn't have to look behind her to know that there wasn't a dry eye in the church.

"Glad hymns of praise and victory . . ."

That was nice. Yes, it had been her victory all right. No other word for it. Victory snatched in the nick of time from the gaping cavern of defeat's halitosis-ridden jaws. Peter would have gotten his divorce, and she would have been drummed out of the town with hardly the price of a Greyhound bus ticket. From paradise to Queer Street at the direction of a good-ol'-boy judge. But now she was smiling beneath the black veil at his funeral, and maybe later, when no one was looking, she'd go out and dance on his grave. They had all underestimated her, her determination, her ruthlessness, her willingness to do whatever it took to maintain her position—and now they were all having to pay for their oversight. Jo-Anne Duke—the respected, grieving widow, overtaken by tragedy. Pure as the driven snow, a lady in white cruelly forced into the black of mourning.

Old Ben Carstairs had nearly had apoplexy at the reading of the will. A hooker had triumphed—but there was absolutely nothing he could do about it. Peter's last will and testament had been made years before in the halcyon days after the honeymoon. When she had asked exactly how many millions there were, nobody had been able to say. It apparently depended on all sorts of things like changing property valuations, exchange rates, and things like that. It was the moment Jo-Anne had known that she was seriously rich. If you couldn't count it you were in megabuck territory for sure.

Almost as an aside she had demanded Peter's dossier.

"Shortly before he died my husband told me you were holding a private and personal file of his. I gather from the will that all his personal possessions are now mine. Perhaps you could get it for me."

With a face as black as the late-afternoon thunderclouds of the Palm Beach summer, Carstairs had done as he was told. Jo-Anne had spent the whole afternoon going through it, playing the tapes, marveling at the efficiency of the detective work, the sound quality of the recorded telephone conversations. The Mary d'Erlanger one had made her quite horny. No wonder poor old Carstairs had gotten off on it. Mary d'Erlanger would have to be resurrected. No question. It had seemed such a pity to destroy it, but she knew how to learn from the mistakes of others. Getting anal about things like that hadn't done the Nixon presidency any good at all.

Jo-Anne's eyes rested briefly on the polished wood of the coffin, and she thought briefly of the grisly contents. Was there any regret? Any warmth, any tenderness toward the thing that had been her husband? No, there wasn't. Turning the other cheek was for girls who hadn't had to give blow jobs to tramps in exchange for a few miserable pieces of candy. When Peter Duke had used his power against her and tried to throw her back into the gutter from which she had crawled with such difficulty, she had positively enjoyed unzipping him like a banana with the Riva's propellers. He had never known who she really was, had never bothered to find out—and the oversight had turned him into underdone hamburger meat. There was poetry in the justice.

Things seemed to be winding down. It was time to face the people outside. The tear-stained eyes, the studies in sympathy—"If there's anything we can do, anything at all, please don't hesitate . . ."

Were there suspicions in the eyes of the milling, mourning-clothed crowds on the lawns outside the church? For the paranoid, undoubtedly. But Jo-Anne wasn't paranoid. She was deliriously, deliciously happy. "Accidental death" had been the verdict, and nothing else in the whole wide world mattered. Nothing at all. People could whisper to their hearts' content, but if Jo-Anne knew the fellow citizens of her town, nobody would argue with her Duke name, still less with her Duke fortune.

There was only one question of any importance at all. Where did she go from here? She was one of the richest and most powerful women in America, bearing the proud name of one of its oldest families. She was also single again. A glorious widow, her feet loose, her fancies free. What the hell did she do for an encore? For a second or two she stood there, oblivious to the mouthed condolences, as she pondered her enviable dilemma.

The voice cut into her reverie, the hand squeezed insistently at her arm. "Jo-Anne, I'm desperately sorry. I'm thinking of you."

It provided, of course, the simple answer to her simple question. It was easy, really. Why on earth hadn't she thought of it before? This man was the answer, with his soft voice and sexy eyes. There was only one person in Palm Beach, in the whole of America even, who would be at all possible after a Duke. After a decent interval, whatever that was, she would marry Bobby Stansfield.

~8~

T HE SETTING SUN had only about ten minutes to go before bedtime, and
at the controls of the twin-engine Beechcraft Baron Bobby Stansfield
was worried. He had no time to take in the haunting beauty of the sunlight
on the aquamarine sea between Bequia and St. Vincent, still less to pick out
and identify the extraordinary houses set like jewels in the rich landscape of
the island below. All he cared about was that the airstrip on Mustique had no
lights, and he had to land before dark. Damn. He was cutting it close. He
reached up to adjust the trim, cut back on the throttle, and twisted the stick
to the left as he went into the bank. Only one chance at the runway. Why the
hell hadn't they stayed in Barbados? They could have been hitting the plant-
ers' punches in Sandy Lane by now, not dicing with disaster in the depths of
the Caribbean. Pan Am and their damn scheduling; the flight from Miami
had given them the minimum possible time to reach Mustique before night-
fall. It was always a gamble, but this was the closest yet.

Next to him Lisa sensed the tension without knowing its cause. Bobby had
been quiet on the forty-five-minute flight from Barbados' Grantley Adams
airport. A couple of times he had spoken to draw her attention to a beautiful
cloud formation or a school of flying fishes frolicking in the warmth of the
pale blue ocean below, but he kept looking at his watch, and from time to
time a frown puckered the bronze skin of his forehead. Lisa was supremely
unworried. Bobby Stansfield was at the controls—of the airplane—of her life.
That was enough. And if the Lord in His wisdom decided to take them both
here and now, well, what a way to go—locked in the arms of a man she had
learned to love with an intensity she had never dreamed possible. Over the
last few weeks the Florida weather had gone over the top with record heat
and prize-winning humidity: she and Bobby had done little to cool things
down. From the first earth-moving lovemaking in the Stansfield cabana to
last night's mindbending sailboat ride on the edge of the Gulf Stream, their
bodies had fanned the furnace of the Florida heat wave, their sweat running
together as their minds clashed in the steambath of ecstasy. Even now Lisa
could feel her body humming like a taut clothesline in a high wind. She was

744

all tensed up, vibrating like a snare drum in response to the closeness of her lover. It was nothing less than a magic swirling trip of delight and she prayed to her God it would go on and on.

To cap it all, he had invited her to Mustique—the most exclusive private island in the world. And they wouldn't be staying in some hotel. It was incredible, almost totally unbelievable, but Lisa was on her way to stay with Princess Margaret, sister of the queen of England—and in her own house. She had known that the Stansfields mingled with the rich and famous, *were* the rich and famous, but this was ridiculous. Yet Lisa wasn't worried. She was so far removed from the social game she had never had a chance to cultivate a fear of the players. To her, foreign royalty were a different world, exotic animals who aroused curiosity rather than apprehension.

In case she was nervous Bobby had played the whole thing down.

"She's really not too bad when you get to know her. Rather more fond of amusing young men than good-looking girls like you, I'm afraid. We all have to sing for our supper, sometimes quite literally, but it's a beautiful house and it's a great opportunity for me to meet Mark Havers. I get these invitations from time to time. We all do. The bottom line is she just can't *bear* to be alone, and so if the house looks like it's going to be empty she puts out distress calls and we all have to rally round. Being close by in Florida often means I get the first call! Anyway, it'll be amusing. Quite an experience. And Havers is going places in England right now."

That, it transpired, had been the important factor. Mark Havers was the blond-haired, sharp-tongued rising star in Britain's Conservative Party, and a great favorite of Prime Minister Margaret Thatcher. He had been a friend of the princess's for many years and was to be a fellow house guest. It was an important opportunity for Bobby to meet him and vice versa. If the dreams of the two men were ever to become substance, they would then meet in very different circumstances. A friendship cemented here would stand each in good stead later.

There was, however, from Lisa's point of view, a fly in the ointment.

Behind the two lovers, legs stretched out over the neighboring seat, sat Jo-Anne Duke.

Lisa couldn't quite understand why Jo-Anne had been invited, but she was enough of an innocent and sufficiently in love not to question Bobby's motives. Actually, it was quite straightforward. When Bobby had received the princess's distress call to fend off loneliness he had been asked to bring people on a "more-the-merrier" basis. Feeling sorry for Jo-Anne in her supposed grief, and genetically attracted to fortunes of the size she now possessed, she had been the obvious person to invite. The fact that Lisa and she were friends and fellow exercise fanatics made it that much better.

Although Jo-Anne looked relaxed, actually she was hard at work, her mind racing as she schemed to catch her prey. This invitation had been an additional stroke of good luck, and everything else had dropped neatly into place: Peter's coffin into the soft earth of the cemetery, his stupendous fortune into her eager lap, his dangerous dossier into her fire.

Only one thing had gone wrong, but it was already beginning to look like a blooper of monumental proportions. The maddening thing was she had brought it entirely on herself, although even with the benefit of hindsight it was difficult to see how she could have predicted the disaster. Bobby Stansfield and Lisa Starr were busy screwing each other's brains out, and to Jo-Anne's practiced eye it looked like far more than a casual affair. In the ordinary way that would have been merely irritating. After all, she'd been planning Lisa for herself. On Bobby she had had no territorial ambitions. Not while her husband still wanted her to be his wife. Now, however, things had changed dramatically. Little bits of Peter Duke were still feeding the fishes off the North End beach. That left Bobby Stansfield—a great big target slap bang in the middle of her sights. Somehow she would have to have him. He would have to be persuaded to see things her way. After all, politicians needed two things—money and status—and she had bags of both. Luckily Bobby Stansfield had liquid ambition running in his veins. He was programmed to want, to need, to grasp at anything that would push him higher. Jo-Anne intended to be that object. Of course he would have to be reeducated with regard to Lisa Starr. He would have to realize exactly what she was. A passing ship in the middle of the night. Nothing more, nothing less. To Jo-Anne, Lisa was a nobody. A peasant with the body of an angel who would be cast aside like a broken doll, as Bobby and she marched on toward a White House destiny. At this most appealing thought Jo-Anne pushed out her long legs in front of her and eased herself backward in the comfortable seat.

Buffeted by the rising currents of hot air from the ground below, the Beechcraft bucked and reared as Bobby straightened her up for the landing. As he felt the wheels slap down on the tarmac he could sense the sun slipping below the horizon as dusk began to fall. He had made it with nothing at all to spare.

He taxied toward the thatched hut that served as the customs and immigration building. As he cut the engines and pushed open the door a tall, diffident, and effortlessly good-looking man walked across to greet them.

"Hi, Bobby. Welcome to Mustique."

The English accent was recognizably upper class.

"Only just made it. You know you've got to get this strip lit, Brian."

"Afraid the residents won't play. Frightened of being kept awake all night."

Bobby grunted. Screw the residents. He'd just had a hairy half hour. He made the introductions as Lisa and Jo-Anne clambered out onto the tarmac.

As he sipped the traditional Mustique welcoming drink—a pure white concoction on which an equally white hibiscus flower floated, he attempted to suppress his irritation with small talk.

"These white hibiscus are rare, Brian. Just like you English to go for the sophisticated understatement. White on white."

"Nothing sophisticated about the effect—white rum, dark rum, banana liqueur—it's all in there."

"Great," said Bobby, cutting him short. "Let's get this show on the road. I could use a shower, and I bet the girls could, too."

They piled into a red jeep, the luggage stacked in another one, and the convoy set off into the gathering dusk. It was an incredibly bumpy ride.

"Mustique Company doesn't run to tarmac yet I see," said Bobby.

"It's an effective speed limit, and the Europeans don't seem to mind. Probably because they're used to it."

Bobby changed the subject. "Have the Haverses arrived?"

"Yup, they came in yesterday morning. P.M.'s on good form, and Patrick Lichfield's here with a load of people, so your end of the island should be busy. Mick Jagger and Jerry are staying with Patrick for a couple of weeks. Mick's going to build here, you know."

Jo-Anne perked up at the mention of the rock star. To Lisa, Jagger was about as interesting as Bing Crosby, but Jo-Anne's age group had been weaned on Stones music.

"How did he come to invest here?"

"Quite interesting actually," said Brian. "Around the time he was getting rid of Bianca it looked for a moment as if he were going to get stuck for a load of alimony. Bianca had hired that Mitchelson chap. Mick's business adviser, a guy called Prince Loewenstein, was a friend of Colin Tennant, who used to own this island, and they got him residency of St. Vincent in ten days flat. Apparently it saved him a hell of a lot of money. He had to own a house here to satisfy the residency requirement, so he bought a plot on the beach at L'Ansecoy Bay, and lived in a run-down beach house that happened to be on it. Now he's building a fantastic Japanese-style house with a croquet lawn."

The night smells of the Caribbean drifted over them as they peered out into the blackness. Occasionally the car's headlights illuminated something, a shed full of bulldozers, a native family walking by the side of the road, banks of wild bougainvillaea. It looked far from the manicured paradise that Lisa and Jo-Anne had expected. A million miles from Palm Beach.

Then quite suddenly they were traveling up a steep incline that led to a straight road, on either side of which the land fell away into darkness. Over to the left were the sparkling lights of a rambling yellow-painted house, a feature of which was the large pagodalike building standing like a gatehouse guarding the causeway over which they were crossing. Directly ahead were the lights of another house. Low slung and built on one level, two symmetrical wings flanked a central terrace and courtyard that led up to the front door.

Lisa took in the flamingo-pink stucco exterior, the bugs dancing in the beams of the headlights, the faint sounds of big band music. So this was it. Princess Margaret's house. Her own home for the next three or four days. God!

Brian Alexander shut off the engine. "Here we are. Les Jolies Eaux."

"What does that mean?" said Jo-Anne. French had been in short supply on the streets of the Bronx. At least the *language* had.

"Beautiful waters." Lisa helped out.

The black servant opened the door.

"What the hell do I call her—'Princess'?" whispered Lisa urgently.

Bobby laughed as they were ushered into the living room, but he didn't answer.

Lisa looked around her. Not at all what she'd expected. Pretty, rather than formal or grand. Cane furniture with fitted cushions, two stainless-steel frame chairs—the sort of thing they had at Jefferson Ward, a light-colored wooden writing desk on which two colorful porcelain parrots stood guard. The lamps were standard island design, raffia shades, patterned coral bases. Over to the right of the room was a dining table, seating eight. Orange candles protruded from glass candle holders complementing, no doubt, the far from expert painting of an orange fish. Otherwise there were the sorts of things she had in *her* room—lots of tattered paperbacks in a bookshelf, a ton of music cassettes, a cheap and rather ancient black-and-white color television. The architecture was infinitely superior to the room's contents, from the concrete floor with its geometrical design, to the white bleached wood of the V-shaped ceiling. But the real point of the room was obviously its view. Lisa's eyes were drawn irresistibly through the theatrical French windows out toward the floodlit swimming pool—the one in which Prince Andrew had seduced Koo, or had it been the other way around?

"Bobby, how lovely to see you."

The voice was deep and throaty, legacy of too many cigarettes, the hint, perhaps, of the odd late night.

"Wonderful to see you, ma'am." Bobby leaned forward to brush the proffered cheek. One each side—European style.

"And these are my two friends. Jo-Anne Duke and Lisa Starr."

As she shook hands, Lisa tried to analyze her first impression. Petite, small, definitely—dare one even think it?—squat. Princess Margaret waved a long tortoiseshell cigarette holder from her left hand as she said her hellos.

"Well, ma'am, it's a great relief to be here. We only just made it before sunset."

"I'm glad you did. We are all going over to Patrick's for dinner. He's got a house full of people. Mick Jagger and his 'lady,' and lovely David Wogan. I can't remember whether you met him before." The Haverses are here, but they're resting. We had rather a hectic lunch down at Basil's."

⁓

LISA WAS prepared for the sleeping arrangements. There were only four bedrooms, and overt cohabitation of unmarrieds was apparently frowned on. She had to share with Jo-Anne.

Already she sensed a chill in the air. Since the lunch at the Polo Club, Jo-Anne had been less than friendly. She still came to the gym, but the girls' lunches had dried up, and when they spoke there was a reservation that had not been there before. Lisa had been too preoccupied to think much about it. After all, Jo-Anne had just lost her husband, and in the most horrific circumstances imaginable, and she herself had been far too busy falling in love to worry about anything at all. It was a big drag that Bobby had taken pity on her and invited her along to this party, but then that was just like him —kind, thoughtful, generous.

"I think she gave us the goddamn servants' room," said Jo-Anne, flicking the hair from her eyes in a gesture of irritation.

Lisa felt the sharp pang of hurt. She had moved so far and so fast, remarks like that really got to her. In her world there had been nothing wrong with being a servant. She had always seen it through her mother's eyes as a wonderful profession. Presumably people like Jo-Anne, probably even Bobby, had a different viewpoint. She felt almost furtive, an interloper who had infiltrated the ranks of the aristocracy by false pretenses. It was ridiculous and untrue, but for the very first time in her life she felt she had something to hide—a strange and alien emotion of shame at something of which she had formerly been proud. Was that what these people did to you? Was it the first subtle step in a campaign of humiliation that would leave her riddled with secret fears, her self-confidence destroyed as she fought to appear to be something she was not? No way. Not Lisa Starr.

She drank deep on the rich rum punch the black butler had poured for her and headed for the bathroom. If these were the servants' quarters she was going to apply for the job. The house seemed to be predominantly orange, which was clearly Princess Margaret's favorite color. The towels in the bathroom, however, were sludge green. Lisa let out a little yelp of glee.

"Oh, Jo-Anne, *look*. The label on these towels says 'Royal Family.' Look, right here. Cannon beach towels. Royal Family. That has to be some sort of a joke, doesn't it?"

She waltzed into the bedroom brandishing the exhibit.

Jo-Anne fired from the hip.

"Really, Lisa, I think you ought to try to have a bit more respect. I know it's a little strange for you to be here with us all, but it isn't a game you know." Jo-Anne's voice was heavy with patronization as she fiddled with Jeep curlers.

"Well, screw you," said Lisa shortly, and walked straight out of the door.

Bobby's room was directly opposite across the tiled terrace, both rooms having doors that opened outside the house. She didn't knock.

He was wet from the shower, a towel slung casually around his waist. Lisa felt her batteries recharge just looking at him. "Hi, senator—or should I say Mr. President. Thought you might need some assistance after your shower."

Bobby smiled his lazy, sexy smile. He placed a finger on his lips and pointed at the closed communicating door.

"I'm next to the master suite," he whispered.

As if in confirmation, the faintest sound of the royal baritone could be heard singing in the bath. "I'm siiiiiiiiinging in the rain, siiiiiiiinging in the rain. What a gloooooooorious feeling I'm haaaappy again . . ."

"I think she'd really like to have been a nightclub act," said Bobby. "In fact, in a way I guess she *is*."

Lisa smiled as she moved toward him. Gently, but firmly, she pushed him back onto the bed.

MARK HAVERS, his lustrous blond hair ruffling slightly in the welcome breeze, was making his point strongly. He waved his gin and tonic to emphasize the words.

"I just think it's a little naive to see the Soviets as being intent on world domination. History tells us they are terribly insecure. They're so frightened of being attacked that they have adopted offense as the best method of defense. By saber rattling we bolster that sense of insecurity, and turn them into some dangerous cornered animal. The other place we tend to take issue with you is the actual scale of the threat they pose. We see them as a nation with very serious problems—economic, political, and military. They haven't been very successful in the Third World, and if it's world domination they're after they appear to be blowing it."

Bobby leaned back in his chair and smiled gently. "Well, that sure seems to be the European position right now," he drawled. "I don't agree with any of it, but you put it very eloquently." He was formidably polite, the Stansfield charm wafting out across the space that divided the two men, to compete with the force field of Royal Yacht hair lotion that surrounded the Englishman. Havers wasn't sure whether he had been complimented or not.

"Of course from our vantage point here in the New World," Bobby continued, "we see you Europeans as being a little too obsessed with the so-called lessons of history. I tend to agree with the guy who said that history was bunk. You can read it any way you choose, just like statistics. To the average American, your so-called dialogue with the Russians smacks of appeasement. Quite rightly you're anxious that Europe shouldn't be turned into a nuclear waste dump. Talking endlessly to the Russians may not be the best way to avoid that."

"Better jaw-jaw than war-war."

Bobby leaned forward and fixed his blue eyes on the Englishman's. "Sometimes jaw-jaw is the very best way to get war-war. As an example of the lessons of history of which you're so fond, what about Munich? Talking to Hitler hardly led to 'peace in our time.' He took it as a sign of weakness and went right on building up his military machine."

The complacent smile that had been hovering around Havers's lips vanished in a hurry. This character was no pushover. He might have adopted the rather simplistic American right-wing position toward Russia, but he certainly knew how to argue his corner. Munich was always a sore point to an English Conservative. It had been far from their finest hour.

He fell back on his second position. "But it seems to us your position is a little paranoid. Russia simply doesn't have the resources to control the world, and if you look back over the last forty years you see that in fact their frontiers have remained static, with the exception of Afghanistan."

Bobby couldn't resist it. The politician in him produced a smile of dazzling brilliance to offset the unkindness of the words he was about to use. "I think you Europeans have every reason to be grateful for our so-called paranoia, even perhaps for our so-called naiveté. You're totally correct when you say that the Russians haven't been that successful so far. Let me tell you why: because of our half million men in Europe, and because of our nuclear umbrella, under which you people shelter. And I'll tell you another thing. Those defenses are paid for by American tax dollars, at a time when the budget deficit is causing high interest rates and widespread unemployment. The most difficult thing I ever have to do is to explain to my constituents why they have to pay out all that money to protect a whole load of foreigners who demonstrate against our missiles, bad-mouth us in their newspapers, and refuse to pay a reasonable contribution toward their own defense."

Havers gulped at his drink.

Seeing the effect of his words, Bobby moved fast to defuse any hostility they might cause. "Of course, you know and I know that our interests are your interests. I'm telling you this to give you an idea of public opinion in my country. As you know I was totally against the Senate threat to withdraw troops from Europe unless the Europeans contributed more to defense costs. I realize, too, that England is not guilty in that area. I'm a great admirer of your prime minister—Americans know she's not soft on communism, that she sees the threat."

By ending with a fulsome compliment Bobby poured soothing balm over any hurt feelings. It had been a useful conversation, since it was always as important to get your own view across as to listen to the other man's. Prime Minister Thatcher would get a report on this exchange of opinions. Bobby hoped the report would be that he was a man whose right-wing views were not only from the heart but had been well thought out, too.

Princess Margaret's voice cut into the debate. Framed in the French windows she shouted out to the thatched poolside gazebo in which the two politicians sat. "Come on, you men. We'll be late for dinner."

—

DINNER, AS far as Lisa was concerned, had not been a success, and just about everyone was to blame. Jo-Anne, for instance, was rapidly turning into Public Enemy Number One. She had been seated at Bobby's right and throughout the meal she had been all over him like a bad attack of hives. Her restless fingers had never left him alone for a minute. As she laughed up into his face at his every remark she had reached out constantly to touch him, caressing his wrist, grabbing enthusiastically at his arm to emphasize a point, and on at least one mind-stopping occasion she had allowed her fingertips to rest briefly on the nape of his neck. To Lisa she was as innocent as a fox in a chicken coop, and just about as welcome. At first she had hardly been able to believe her eyes. It was so totally unexpected. But then, as the outrageous flirting became more and more overt, she wondered why she had been so naive. It was obvious that Jo-Anne had engineered the whole thing. Her husband was still warm in his coffin, and she was busy on the trail of a replacement. It all made perfect sense. Bobby Stansfield was one of the most eligible bachelors in the universe. To somebody like Jo-Anne Duke, he would be the ultimate prize.

The whole business had put Lisa right off her food, as the alien emotion of jealousy had eaten away at her guts. Bobby had been hers, *was* hers. But it sure didn't look like it from where she sat. Jo-Anne Duke had acquired the capacity to make her blood run cold. Jo-Anne Duke, whose lips had brought Lisa to the verge of sexual surrender in the foaming waters of the Jacuzzi. Jo-Anne Duke, with the splendid body, the Midas fortune, the aristocratic name. It was difficult to conceive of a more dangerous and powerful rival. Damn it to hell. She had fallen in love for the first and only time in her life, and already it began to look as if she had a battle on her hands—and one in which the heavy artillery belonged to the opposition. Already it was possible to see the direction in which the enemy offensive might go. Bobby Stansfield's political ambitions.

From her position on Bobby's left, Princess Margaret had leaned across and said, "Tell me Jo-Anne, do you support Bobby politically? I'm told running for office in your country is ruinously expensive. You ought to make a campaign contribution."

It had been clear to Lisa that the princess was hoping to create a marginally difficult situation for the stunningly attractive Jo-Anne. Her remark had put Jo-Anne on the line. If she wanted to pass herself off as a political soulmate of Bobby's, she might now feel obliged to put her money where her mouth was. Unwittingly she had played right into Jo-Anne's hands. The gift horse had not been looked in the mouth.

"I'm glad you mentioned that, ma'am. Actually I haven't told Bobby yet, but I've been talking to the Duke Foundation about doing something clever for his campaign—that's if he decided to run of course."

Everybody laughed. Except Bobby. Stansfields didn't laugh about things like campaign contributions. After all, one didn't play touch football in church. For a long moment he had stared at her, as if seeing her for the very first time, in an entirely new and comprehensively favorable light. Across the table Lisa had watched it happen, and it had frightened the hell out of her. Straightaway afterward they had begun to talk serious turkey, as Jo-Anne had floated the megabuck bait at Bobby's voraciously eager mouth. Once or twice he had caught Lisa's eyes across the table and smiled the warm, reassuring Stansfield smile. All Lisa had been able to see in the baby-blue eyes had been dollar signs.

Mick Jagger, on Lisa's right, had been as much use as a fart in a four-acre field. For some extraordinary reason best known to himself he had imagined that Lisa might be interested in cricket, a passion of his. After forty minutes of her glacial disinterest, he had tried her on croquet instead. Wipe-out. On her left David Wogan had been much more use. A lovely, bubbling, gurgling Irishman well known to be Princess Margaret's best friend, or B.F. as he liked to describe it, he was in the process of doing what his countrymen did better than anyone. He was getting drunk. From what Lisa could gather, this had not been a process started during the course of dinner, or even during the cocktails that had preceded it. No, David's voyage into foothills of oblivion had apparently started with the Buck's fizz before lunch.

In a stage whisper David produced the lowdown on the cricket- and croquet-loving pop superstar.

"Somewhat inferior manners, me darlin'." He took a deep breath and burped theatrically, incurring a frosty glance from Princess Margaret. Unfazed, he continued. "Don't know why P.M. puts up with him. Probably 'cos her cousin was best man at his wedding to Bianca."

Lisa laughed, and the laugh made her feel just a little bit better, if such a thing was possible. The hell with it, nothing was lost yet. If Jo-Anne wanted to make a play for Bobby Stansfield then she would be given a run for her money that would leave her fighting for breath.

Lisa sipped at the red wine, sighed deeply, and tried to enjoy herself. This should have been paradise—mingling with the mighty in perhaps the prettiest home on the most beautiful island in the world. She looked around her. Patrick Lichfield's house was a jewel. Painted canary yellow, it was built in the Oliver Messel style—theatrical, wide open to the Caribbean breezes, and with stunning views and vistas. The house itself was constructed on several different levels, and so far four had been completed, although Patrick apparently had plans for more. At the pool level a large semicircular poolhouse had been fitted out as a video area, with a beige-cushioned half-moon banquette arranged around the Sony VHS system. Later that evening they would all watch a movie. Now, in the round dining gazebo she could look out at the lush, subtly lit landscape, the sparkling forty-foot pool, and smell the heady scents of the Grenadines, as she listened to the hum of polite conversation, the chink of fine china, the ceaseless sound of the crickets.

The booming voice picked her out like a searchlight on an escaping prisoner. "Tell me, Lucy, how exactly did you meet Bobby? I'm always so intrigued to know how people met."

Could one decently tell a princess she had gotten your name wrong? Lisa felt the answer was probably no, especially as the odds were it had been done on purpose.

Princess Margaret, wielding her tortoiseshell cigarette holder as if it were an offensive weapon, leaned across the table for her answer. The full lips, bright lipstick, and mahogany suntan made her look more like a Miami Beach manicurist than the queen of England's sister, thought Lisa.

"I was introduced to him by Jo-Anne." In retaliation Lisa had left out the "ma'am."

The royal eyes hardened at the oversight. Princess Margaret took a long sip at the dark brown malt whiskey which had appeared unbidden with the coffee. "Have you and Jo-Anne been friends for long?" The questioning was taking on a relentless quality. After this one there would be another, and another, until Lisa had been forced to say something embarrassing.

Pretending to be the friend she no longer was, Jo-Anne came to Lisa's aid. "Lisa runs a gymnasium in West Palm Beach, ma'am. We met there."

The laughter resembled the sound of a broken fingernail being drawn slowly over a microphone.

"A gymnasium? A gymnasium? What an *extraordinary* thing to do. And in Palm Beach, too. I thought everyone there was far too old to exercise."

Lisa took a deep breath.

Around the table two people tried to help out, with hopefully defusing exercise jokes.

"I'm with W. C. Fields. Whenever I get the urge to exercise I lie down until it goes away," said David Wogan, looking and sounding as if an hour or two on the horizontal were exactly what he needed.

"The only exercise I take is playing chess in front of an open window," offered Patrick Lichfield.

Lisa was grateful for the attempts, but she knew she mustn't avoid the confrontation. Any weakness now would be paid for with interest later on. "Exercise is very good for you, ma'am. You should try it sometime."

An ominous silence descended.

Mentally Lisa packed her bags. How did one get a flight out of Mustique? For a second her fate hovered in the balance. In this atmosphere, surrounded by her courtiers, the faithful members of her most recent "set," a heavy rebuke from "P.M." would transform her at a stroke into a nonperson, condemned to walk forever with the social "undead," an outcast, a pariah. If she was unable for some reason to fly away, she would be in for the stickiest few days of her life.

Princess Margaret let the malice flow from her eyes as she considered how best to deliver the *coup de grace.*

Lisa stared evenly back at her, defiant, unafraid. In the eyeball-to-eyeball confrontation it was the older woman who looked away.

"I've far better things to do with my time," she said at last, taking a petulant swig at the Famous Grouse Scotch.

The distraction from Lisa's small but far from insignificant victory was not long in coming.

Muttering, "I'm not feeling well. Not at all. Not at all," David Wogan struggled to his feet and, before anyone could come to his aid, lurched out into the night. A minute or two later a short sharp cry was followed by the sound of crackling vegetation and then complete silence.

It had taken the men ten minutes to find him in the darkness, fast asleep and lodged firmly in the branches of a deep purple bougainvillaea bush, fifty feet down the hillside.

Somehow, and none too soon as far as Lisa was concerned, that seemed to bring dinner to a close.

————

*"They all laughed at Chris-to-pher Co-lum-bus
When he said the world was round . . ."*

Lisa could hardly believe her eyes or her ears. The whole thing had clearly gone right over the top into the realms of black humor. And the funniest thing of all was that she seemed to be the only person who had noticed it.

The little group clustered around the piano in Basil's Bar on the Mustique beach of Britania Bay didn't see the joke at all. They, like the royal performer to whom they listened with such rapt attention, were playing it straight as hell.

"They told Mar-co-ni wire-less was a pho-ny
It's the same old cry . . ."

Princess Margaret was shamelessly soaking every last ounce of up-tempo jauntiness from the old Gershwin tune. She wrapped her full, ripe lips indulgently around the syllables, milking them of their humor, as she rolled her eyes toward the ceiling. Her voice was surprisingly, almost disturbingly deep —a bit like Betty Bacall on a bad day—and it tended to wander around like a leaf on a Chicago street when it went for the higher notes. The accompaniment was standard saloon strum, the left hand pumping backward and forward. There were missed notes, and missed words, and the two seldom coincided.

From the looks on the faces of the audience, however, this could well have been Rubinstein in full spate, Streisand in top gear. They crowded around deferentially, attempting to swing and sway in time to the uncertain rhythm, to catch the eye of the royal cabaret artiste as her turretlike eyes swirled and swiveled to identify who was with her, who against her.

On the top of the battered black piano stood the glass of Famous Grouse, the ashtray with its cargo of long cigarette holder and wispy, burning cigarette.

In midsyllable the maudlin song was interrupted. "Damn! I've forgotten the words."

Lisa's mouth dropped open. This just couldn't be for real. Could this *happen* in the twentieth century? She fought back the overwhelming desire to laugh.

"Something about Hershey inventing the chocolate bar, I think, ma'am."

"*Thank* you, Patrick." The tone was accusing. The schoolmistress irritated that the class had been slow in answering her question. Had they been *attending?*

Once again the assault on the soundwaves continued.

For a second Lisa allowed herself a guided tour of the company assembled around the piano. Royalty might not have much real power anymore, but clearly, like the Almighty, it moved in mysterious ways, its wonders to perform. An old Harrovian photographer aristocrat, an Irishman who, it was rumored, had once been the conductor of a London bus, a glamorous Texan model and a pop superstar, a British cabinet minister and his wife, an American heiress, and a potential contender for the Republican nomination for president of the United States. There had been two unlikely additions to the party who had made it down to the beach bar after the sumptuous dinner: a dusky South American called Julio, a regular at the bar, and a rather blowsy but pleasant redhead who had been introduced as Contessa Crespoli. Julio and Contessa Crespoli were clearly close "friends," leaning against each other for support as if each would be unable to remain upright without the other.

Lisa caught Bobby's eye, and seeing the look of amazed amusement on her face, he winked broadly at her. Lisa smiled back at him. Thank God somebody around here still had a sense of humor. On "Saturday Night Live" this would have brought down the house.

"*Who's got the last laugh now?*"

From the thunderous applause it was clear the song was at an end.

"My word, you sing that well, ma'am," said somebody, enthusiasm dripping from the syllables.

Quite suddenly Lisa had had more than enough. She wanted to be away from all these people with their alien values and weird attitudes. They were Martians to her. Well meaning, perhaps, but way beyond her experience. Their world wasn't her world, and she wanted out.

She moved quickly in the excited confusion caused by the agreement that the next song should be "Hello, Dolly." Apparently that was something of a royal show stopper.

Lisa hurried along the wooden catwalk, half expecting to hear barked commands in her wake as the hounds were sent chasing after the defector from the royal audience. What crime had she committed? *Lèse majesté?* Would they telegraph to prepare a room for her in the Tower?

She kicked off her shoes as she made it to the sand, still warm from the sun's heat. God! That was better. This was what it was all about. Soft sand, the gentle lapping sounds of the Caribbean, the smells of native cooking from the pine trees behind the beach. Seventy yards from the shore half a dozen yachts bobbed on the insistent swell. Some were lit up like Christmas trees, their owners dining ostentatiously in the stern as crewmen padded the decks, catering to their every whim. Others carried minimal navigation lights only, their passengers obviously dining ashore, with Colin Tennant perhaps, or one of the many Guinnesses who had houses there. Mustique. An island of crazy contradictions. Which was the real Mosquito Island? The jade-green mountains, the pearl-white beaches, the aquamarine sea, the pink conch shells littering the Caribbean-lapped shores? Or was the essence of the place best summed up by the uncertain strains of "Embraceable You," now unhappily audible on the scented night air—embodiment of all the worst excesses of English snobbery, as it polluted the natural beauty of the environment it had so capriciously taken over?

Lisa sat down on a piece of driftwood and tried to gather her surging thoughts. Where was she going? What was *happening?* Until this evening there had been no time and no reason to think, as she had immersed herself in passion, in her magnificent obsession. There had been no time to doubt whether her love had been returned. Lisa had, subconsciously, taken that for granted. Now, alone with her thoughts on a beach in the Grenadines, she dared to wonder if her oasis of ecstasy had been an illusion constructed from shimmering sand, about to vanish from view, leaving behind nothing but a bittersweet emptiness. From the corners of her eyes two large tears broke free and rolled down her cheeks at the awful thought.

The soft voice at her shoulder stole into her consciousness. "Lisa Starr, I had no idea you weren't a music lover."

Lisa had to smile through the tears, but it was gratitude more than humor that allowed her to do so. He had followed her. He cared. He loved her. "Oh, Bobby. Can we go back to the house now? Just you and me, and split this scene."

"We're on our way," he replied, and leaning forward tenderly, he licked away her tears.

LISA LOOKED up at the star-filled sky and breathed in deeply. The moon was almost full and it cast a magical light across the rippling waters of the pool. Bobby knelt beside her on the steps, his hand resting gently on her strong shoulders.

"I guess pools are a bit special for us," she said at last, and her laughter, soft, tinkling, carried with it hints of suggestion as well.

Bobby chuckled. "Moonlight swims. Sure takes me back."

Lisa aimed a mock blow at his arm. "I was talking about *us,* senator." She pretended the jealousy. "You know, this is the most beautiful place on the island. I mean right here in this pool. It's like swimming on the edge of a cliff. The house I don't really go for—although the commemoration plates of the family are quite sweet. She sure didn't have an interior decorator do it. White vinyl furniture and brass knobs. Yuk!"

"I don't think you'd make a good courtier," said Bobby. "Not enough *reverence.*"

"Doesn't it stick in your throat too?"

"Listen, when you're a politician you'd better be able to massage egos. Anyway, meeting Havers has been useful. That was the bottom line."

"Are we the bottom line, Bobby?"

He didn't answer her. Instead he reached for her.

Lisa tumbled into his arms, letting the water's buoyancy take her. She felt like a gift, a beautiful naked present, the sort that was far too good to be wrapped.

Bobby lifted her up toward him, bending down to receive the parted lips. His action would answer her question. There was no need for words. But he knew as he kissed her that the choice of words would not have been easy, that at some level he was avoiding them because he didn't know which ones to use. Lisa Starr. What was she to him? A lover certainly. Never before in his far from insubstantial experience had he enjoyed making love to somebody as much as he did to Lisa. And then there was her mind, pure, forceful, unsullied by the bitterness of life's defeats—a far from cockeyed optimist who saw the best in people because she chose not to dwell on the worst. Her vibrating enthusiasm had lifted him up, a tonic for his jaded palate, and he had felt the cloak of cynicism in which he so often wrapped himself fall away under her liberating influence. He had, during these last days, begun to see life anew as he peered at his world through her eager eyes. All that was true. But what did it amount to? Was this love? If so, it was his very first experience of it. Stansfields had never been encouraged to fall in love. That was rather an irresponsible thing to do, often unlocking a Pandora's box of nasty tricks that had a way of screwing up the really important things in life. Of course his father had "loved" his mother and vice versa. It went without saying. Husbands and wives loved each other until the divorce. Being "in love," however, was an entirely different ball game, a world of Barbara Cartland novels where handsome princes fell for servant girls and gave up their kingdoms for their passion. Yes, that was part of the definition. You had to be prepared to give something up. Something important. Something like his political ambition. As Lisa's tongue squirmed deliciously in his mouth Bobby felt the potent pang of guilt as he realized that his was a Judas kiss.

As Bobby wrestled with his doubt Lisa felt hers melt away. She would merge with this wonderful man, become him. Their bodies had already fused, two burning liquids joined in the same container, entering each other, passing through each other, pouring themselves into each other. In marriage the world would see the unnecessary evidence of the mystic, sweet communion that joined their souls and cemented their flesh. Someday, a child would come as the consummate blessing, the living proof of their need to become one. Her child, his child. Their child.

She wrapped her legs tightly around him, crushing herself against him as, in joy, she felt the familiar stirrings. Still she explored the well-known mouth, retracing lovingly the memory-illuminated paths, the little pockets of pleasure, the silky softness of his tongue. They would make love here, in the pool, her body light as a feather in the warm water, her soul soaring above them both, witnessing the desire, the need, and the passion.

Bobby hovered on the brink of her, feeling her open up to him, as he luxuriated in the delicious anticipation of entry. Then, unable any longer to prolong the sensation, he pushed himself upward into the depths of Lisa's being as she closed herself gratefully over him. For a second he didn't move as his mind received the delightful messages of pleasure, then as his senses acclimated to bliss, he began to move within her.

Lisa leaned back, her arms around his neck, her legs straddling his waist as he pushed at her. She wanted to watch his eyes, to see his face. In the moonlight she would experience it all, the love, the glory—as the life-giving fluid bathed her body.

As he thrust into her she rode him, her body reeling with the power of his rhythm, and all the time she watched his eyes as her muscles tensed around the pleasure source. It was the look of sleepiness that prepared her to receive the offering—the eyelids suddenly hooded, the gleam in the eyes dulled, the breath coming faster, lips parted, the tongue forming the shout of ecstasy. At her back she felt the desperate fingers bury themselves into her, beneath her heels she felt the buttocks harden, summoning their remaining strength for the star burst that would soak her soul.

She took his head between her hands, using her legs alone to hold him to her. Tenderness and force, the love light burning, the beauty of wholeness. He was almost there.

She felt his legs go weak, and she watched him intently, her eyes hungry, determined to capture this moment for eternity. Whatever happened, nobody could take this away.

Through the still night air the cry rose up to the cloudless sky, abandoned, shameless, unmistakable, as the two lovers howled their passion at the moon.

~9~

*F*OR JO-ANNE IT had been pretty much of a normal Palm Beach day. She had woken early, around seven o'clock, and breakfasted in bed. Earl Grey tea, a bowl of fresh fruit, some thinly sliced toast, a single pink hibiscus flower floating in a small Sèvres bowl as decoration for the tray. More important than the breakfast had been the immaculately folded copy of the Shiny Sheet. The blue and white *Palm Beach Daily News* that got its nickname from the high quality of its glossy paper was the most important single factor in the high-stakes social intercourse of Palm Beach, and had been ever since its establishment in 1894. There were three basic ways of playing the Shiny Sheet game, and Jo-Anne was thoroughly conversant with all of them. First, there was no other way to the top in the town's society than through constantly repeated presence in its columns. A thousand glazed expressions conjured up by a thousand impudent flashbulbs was the considerable price of social glory. In order to achieve that glory, the most important thing was "being there." Endless charity balls had to be religiously attended, some far grander and more prestigious than others. The Heart Ball, the Red Cross Ball, and the American Cancer Society Gala were the most important of all, and to miss them was socially irresponsible, but others were moving up fast —Planned Parenthood, for example, and the Norton Gallery dinner dance. As a rule of thumb for novice climbers, diseases ranked above culture—the Retina Research Institute Gala, known affectionately as "the Eyeball," for instance, counted for more than some orchestra or ballet benefit.

But being there was not enough. You could be there and yet not really "be there." No, the important thing was to be "seen" to have been there, and that meant celluloid evidence. Somehow the photographer had to take the picture. That was hurdle number one. Next, the photograph had to be selected to appear in the paper itself. That meant being favorably regarded by the powerful social editor, Shannon Donnelly, and the even more powerful publisher, Agnes Ash. In the very early days when Peter Duke had introduced his young bride to the deeply paranoid Palm Beachers, Jo-Anne had been considered guilty until proved innocent. That was par for the Palm

Beach course. Every social parvenu, gigolo, con man, and phony European aristocrat in the Western Hemisphere worth his salt had tried his luck on the WASP natives, and they were naturally suspicious. Starting at the bottom, Jo-Anne had begun work on the photographers. One in particular had been identified as a target. He had been young, gullible, and horny—a superb combination for a girl whose total experience had been exclusively in the art of turning men on. Poor John Destry had been a pushover. From the first mind-bending kiss behind the Henry Flagler railroad car on the grounds of the Flagler Museum, while Palm Beach society danced and pranced a few nerve-racking feet away, he had been in love with her. She had played him like a fish, keeping the line taut and the hook firmly in place, and throughout two seasons he had taken photographs of hardly anyone else. The social arbiters in the Royal Poinciana offices of the Shiny Sheet had been more or less forced to include her against their own better judgment, and by the time Destry's partiality had been exposed and he had been "let go," Jo-Anne's feet had been firmly on the ladder. From that moment on she had consolidated her position, dressing carefully, never deviating from the mainstream in public, keeping her makeup as simple and straightforward as her standard-issue right-wing Republican political views. Over the years the policy had paid off. No matter that from time to time the female chairmen of the charity galas— there being no chairpeople, chairwomen, or other such nonsense in Palm Beach—would occasionally drop their pants for her. What mattered was that in public Jo-Anne Duke's image remained as pure as a nun's underwear.

The next and ultimate step in Palm Beach society seemed on the surface to be somewhat paradoxical. In a few years she would resign from the Shiny Sheet's pages altogether. In the rarefied atmosphere at the very top of the tree where the Maddocks and the Phippses lived, all publicity was bad publicity—even in the otherwise hallowed pages of Agnes Ash's newspaper. It was strange, really, but in other ways it was a bit like life. You served your apprenticeship, immersed yourself in the rat race, desiring only to reach a position in which you could turn up your nose and scoff at the contestants whose ranks you had so recently deserted.

As a background to her professional analysis of the changing fortunes of the players of the Palm Beach social game, Jo-Anne had flicked capriciously backward and forward between "Today" and "Good Morning America." That was where she acquired most of her information. There and in the pages of *Town and Country*, *Vogue*, and *W*. She had dressed at a leisurely pace—a plain white Calvin Klein suit, perfectly tailored, a splash or two of Joy, chosen because she didn't want to smell like all the other Palm Beachers of her generation who seemed at the moment to favor Opium—and walked downstairs to the vast marble hallway where the head chef had been waiting for her. In her book-lined study they had gone over the menus for the evening's dinner party—a smoked salmon soufflé, beef Wellington, a mango sorbet. The head butler had joined them for a discussion of the wine. In that department she had to rely heavily on the Englishman's expertise—a dry Corton Charlemagne 1973 with the fish, Latour 1961 with the meat, a 1975 Krug with the dessert, or what the upper-class English and their servants preferred to call the pudding.

"I'll leave the flowers up to you," she had said over her shoulder as she made her way toward the Rolls. "Get them sent over from the Everglades Flower Shop. Those lilies were nice last week."

In the hallowed precincts of the world's finest jewelers at 340 Worth Avenue, Jo-Anne had not messed around. In thirty minutes in the private room at the back she had gone through three hundred seventy-five thousand dollars.

The Cartier manager, Jill Romeo, had not batted an eyelid when Jo-Anne had said she would wear the ring and the sapphire-and-diamond-studded leopard bracelet immediately. Nor had she asked for any payment, not even the signing of a receipt when Jo-Anne had gotten up to leave. As far as Cartier was concerned, knowing their customers was everything. A Duke could pay. A Duke would pay. Most important of all a Duke would come back . . . again and again.

On a whim she had decided to stop at the Armonds Nail Salon. She liked having her fingers fiddled with. An hour later, blood-red talons super-glued in place, she had been ready for the light Petite Marmite lunch—steamed stone crabs and a green salad with a genuine French vinaigrette dressing— with Inger Anderson and her attractive husband, Harry Loy.

By two o'clock it had been time to enjoy the high point of the day so far. So now here she was tucked comfortably into the red plastic swivel chair of the Domani hairdressing salon as Dino ran appreciative fingers through her long blond hair. Dino was great. He was above all safe, and he *understood*. What was it about hairdressers that made them so knowing? The fact that they saw the face behind the mask? That they caught you when you were most relaxed? The intimacy of the close bodily contact shorn of its sexuality? Most of it anyway. It was difficult to say. The smooth, firm fingers plowed knowingly through Jo-Anne's lustrous locks, occasionally catching an earlobe —the touch professional, totally expert. Sometimes Dino would gather up a whole bunch of hair and hold it up for a second as he watched the effect in the mirror before casting it down again, like the discards in a game of ca- nasta. Jo-Anne felt deliciously like an object, not really a person at all but more a collection of bits and pieces that needed to be rearranged to produce a more pleasing appearance. If any other man in the world had made her feel like that she would have gone for the jugular. With Dino it was just fine.

"I haven't seen you since the day of the funeral. You're looking very wonderful, Jo-Anne."

Jo-Anne appreciated that. It was charming. Delightfully European. *Bellissima signora* and all that jazz.

Boy, had Dino done her proud for the funeral. Everybody had agreed she looked the personification of widowhood, the hair piled up high, severe, minimalistic. But there was something else in his remark. He had picked up on the buoyant sense of freedom, of triumph, that bubbled throughout her soul. Some of it undoubtedly shone through her eyes. Perhaps some, too, was palpable beneath the practiced and mobile fingers. Dino was probing. He had her number. He knew the grieving-widow bit was window dressing. Jo-Anne's antennae sensed danger, but immediately she rejected the thought. She was safe. She had it all. The three hundred seventy-five thousand dollars' worth of Cartier jewelry was caressing her skin, the tangible proof of her victory.

She smiled a wicked smile and allowed the flavor of conspiracy to leak out. "One must struggle on," she said. "I'm sure Peter would have wanted that."

Like hell he would, ran the subterranean thought. He must be the unhappiest man in heaven right now. Fuming and spluttering with his mighty rage. The Cartier trip would have made that little vein in his forehead jump around like a jack-in-the-box.

"If this is you struggling, then I'm thinking when the sailing is plain you'll be looking a million dollars."

Jo-Anne laughed. "Only a million dollars, Dino? Forget it, baby, that's the small change in the Duke family."

It was the Italian's turn to laugh, but it was a respectful one. In this country, and especially in this town, one didn't laugh too loud and too long about money.

"So, what are we going to do with it today?"

"I want that Eton crop look. Short at the back, long and straight on top. Do you know the one I mean? Not very Palm Beach, but screw that."

"Sure, I know it. It'll suit you fine. Let's get you washed."

For Jo-Anne, Dino did his own washing. It was one of the subtle little messages that created a hierarchy among his customers. They liked that.

Back in the cutting chair, Jo-Anne was totally relaxed. Like some body slave in ancient Rome, Dino sensed what was needed. He sent his fingers into the firm back, pushing at the muscles of the shoulders, massaging away any lingering tightness.

Behind closed eyes Jo-Anne's mind worked on. Already she was looking forward to tonight. The telephone conversation last week still reverberated in her mind.

"Bobby? Jo-Anne. Listen, I've been doing some work on the campaign thing we discussed in Mustique. I wonder if you could make dinner one evening to discuss it. I have a couple of the Duke trustees staying, and I've done a little work on them. If you could come yourself, and perhaps bring some of your people, we might be able to get it all sewn up. I'm afraid that it'll be a dead loss socially. They're boring old farts. That's why I haven't invited Lisa. She'd feel pretty out of it."

"Sounds wonderful, Jo-Anne," Bobby had said. "I'll bring Baker if I may. Can't guarantee he'll know which knife and fork to use, but he's hot shit politically."

Tonight he would sit on her right-hand side at dinner. And Jo-Anne would buy him as she had bought the Cartier jewels. Oh, it wouldn't appear she was doing it. The language would be businesslike, the sentiments expressed lofty.

She would intimate that it would be in the very best interests of the Duke Foundation for it to find a way to support the Stansfield campaign with heavy cash. The Democratic threat, the debasement of American values, etc. But at the end of the day she would own a part of him and would be well positioned to make a takeover bid for the rest. And maybe, after dinner, when the exquisite Napoleon brandy, 1805, the Trafalgar year, made its appearance, Bobby Stansfield would be in a mellow mood. First she would let slip a couple of choice pieces of information about Lisa . . . and then, who knew?

As the hands moved from her back to take up the scissors, and as the gentle snip, snip, snip of the sharp blades sent her blond locks to the floor, Jo-Anne kept her eyes shut. She was far from being asleep, but she didn't want any words to disturb her delicious anticipation of what was to come.

BOBBY STANSFIELD held the paper-thin brandy balloon between thumb and forefinger and pressed gently around the rim. The glass bent satisfyingly in toward the center. He lowered his head appreciatively toward the rich amber liquid, taking in the smooth, caramel aroma. Unbelievable. Divine. Next he swirled the glass around, the heavy spirit clinging like glue to the walls, and only then did he allow himself to taste it.

Across the room Jo-Anne smiled back at him as she saw the enjoyment written all over his face. How handsome he was. The dinner jacket so very well cut, the bow tie small, hinting that it had belonged to his father, even his grandfather—the patent-leather opera pumps formidably correct. Even the cuff links, thin, plain gold, the initials RS engraved with understated elegance, were absolutely right. Bobby Stansfield had class. He would look terrific at the altar.

Jo-Anne waited for the moment. About the time the brandy hit the stomach wall. "I'm sorry Lisa couldn't be here tonight," she lied.

"Mmmm," agreed Bobby absent-mindedly. God, this brandy was good.

"Amazing girl, Lisa." Jo-Anne sharpened the knife.

"You'd better believe it," agreed Bobby with enthusiasm. "You sure did me a favor making that introduction."

"Yep, she's a surprising lady. I was really amazed to find out she cuts both ways."

"What do you mean?"

"You know, that she's AC/DC, bisexual."

"What!" Bobby sat up in his chair. "You're joking," he added.

"You mean you didn't know? I imagined it was part of the thing you had going together."

"Not only did I not know, but I don't believe it. Who on earth told you that?"

Jo-Anne had expected the irritation. She moved quickly to produce her "evidence."

"It's firsthand. Lisa tried to seduce me. It was quite embarrassing actually. You know—I almost felt it was rude to refuse." Jo-Anne laughed. The liberal lady. Intrigued, surprised but not shocked by another's little weakness.

Bobby could hardly believe his ears. He took a long hard swig on the brandy. The connoisseur had been replaced by the man who felt he needed a drink.

"When? Where? In Mustique? Are you sure you didn't get it wrong?"

Great, he wanted chapter and verse. "It was some time ago. When we first met. We were in the Jacuzzi, and she just asked me straight out if I wanted to screw her. You could have knocked me over with a feather. I said it wasn't my bag, and I was sorry, and she put her hand right between my legs —just like that. I gather she has quite a reputation at the gym. You know, 'we aim to please' taken just that little bit further."

Again she laughed, to avoid the suspicion she was dishing the dirt on Bobby's girl.

"I can't *believe* it."

"Do you mind?" Jo-Anne asked. "Surely it's no big deal." Was he ready for the double whammy?

"It's just an incredible surprise. I mean, I'm really close to Lisa. She never gave me any idea. I'm sure she'd have told me if she was gay." Unusually for him, Bobby's words didn't seem to be coming at all easily. He was obviously flabbergasted.

"God, Bobby—it sounds as if you've got it bad. I never thought I'd see you, of all people, go overboard for the daughter of the hired help."

"The hired *what?*" he spluttered.

"Christ, don't tell me she didn't mention *that?*" Jo-Anne looked incredulous. "You must know her mother used to be a maid working for your parents."

"Who on *earth* says so?"

"She does, Bobby. It was one of the very first things she told me. In fact I think she told me that day at lunch when we met up with you in the Café L'Europe. Don't you remember? You were there with your mother."

Jo-Anne looked down at her red nails as she spoke. They were a little too much really. Maybe she'd go back tomorrow and have them filed off. When her eyes locked back on Bobby's, the change in him was immediately apparent. He was slumped in his chair, his face a complex mixture of emotion. Most of the ones that Jo-Anne had intended were there—surprise, hurt, perhaps even the beginnings of anger—but there were other feelings, too: sorrow, disbelief, and, around the corners of the mouth, determination. Jo-Anne read them all. But what the hell was he going to do with that determination?

Jo-Anne moved toward him quickly, the ancient bottle in her hand.

"You look as if you could use another drink," she said, running a moist tongue over her lips.

CAROLINE STANSFIELD rather enjoyed old age. Not many people recommended it, but she found it restful. Most of the things it had forced her to give up she had given up anyway—through choice. Sex. Drinking and eating too much. Exercise. She didn't even mind the physical decline. She had never been vain, and the slack skin, liver spots, and gray hair didn't bother her at all. The failing eyesight was a bore, as that interfered with her tapestries, and so were the increasingly arthritic fingers—but those were small things. On the other hand the advantages of old age were quite substantial. She had always been the family's gray eminence, and now that she actually *looked* like one, her influence was even more powerful than it had been in her youth.

"What did you want to see me about, Bobby?" Her tone sounded positively matriarchal.

"I wanted some of your famous advice, mother."

She smiled back proudly at her eldest son. There was no mistaking his charisma. Even though she was his mother she could be objective enough to recognize that he possessed the X factor. Poor old Fred had never had it, and despite the energy and cunning with which he pursued his political career, he was never able to make it to the ultimate goal. But Bobby was different. He had star quality. Her bridge partners at the Everglades thought the sun shone out of his backside. They were always twittering on about a nephew who had heard him speak in Boston, a cousin who had read his book in Saratoga, a grandson who had been impressed by him on "60 Minutes." Yes, a shot at the presidency looked entirely possible. And yet . . . there was possibly a little something missing. Did he have the killer instinct? Or was he just a mite too gentle, a touch too sensitive? Fred Stansfield had done his best to thwart those instincts in him, and certainly he had been partially successful, but the doubt remained. Only time would tell.

Caroline Stansfield arranged the tapestry in her lap, and waited.

"I've fallen in love, mother."

"How very nice, dear." She plunged the needle into the beige background of the tapestry like a Sioux warrior dispatching a cavalry scout with his spear.

"Anyone we know?" she added as an afterthought.

Bobby felt the burst of irritation rush through him. His mother could produce this response in him with effortless ease. What the hell did she mean, "*we* know?" It was insufferably condescending, the more so because she had gone right to the core of the problem. "We" didn't know Lisa Starr. "We" wouldn't want to know Lisa Starr. "We" wouldn't cross the road to piss on Lisa Starr if she was on fire.

Damn. He wasn't going to get what he wanted. She was going to say it wasn't on, could never be on.

Bobby wished the color wasn't burning on his cheeks.

"Her name is Lisa Starr. I believe you met her once when lunching with me at the Café L'Europe. A very beautiful, wonderful young lady. I'm very fond of her, mother."

"Who is she?" Caroline Stansfield had had a lifetime's experience of cutting through the shit. He's going to get angry, she thought, picking up on the twin spots of red high up on her son's cheeks, and caring not a bit.

It was pointless to pretend to misunderstand the question, to reiterate that her name was Lisa Starr. His mother hadn't meant that at all. Bobby tried to minimize the damage. "She's from West Palm. Runs a business there." Even as he spoke he knew that, far from minimizing it, he had compounded it.

"Yes?" The word said it all. West Palm for a Palm Beacher had all sorts of hidden meanings. After all, the town across the bridge owed its existence to Palm Beach. It was where the black servants lived. Nowadays they had been joined by a crude assortment of carpetbagging riffraff, retirees from the North, the ubiquitous lawyers and dentists and God knows who else, but to Caroline Stansfield it was a ghost town, inhabited by specters, people without substance, without significance. Intellectually she knew that it was no big deal for a politician's wife to be born in a place like that. Americans in general wouldn't understand the significance. But emotionally the idea filled her with horror. A daughter-in-law from West Palm. It was unthinkable. She cocked her head to one side and repeated her loaded affirmative. "Yes?" she said again.

Bobby looked out of the window for inspiration, for rescue. A water skier, a man in a rowboat hauling in what looked like a pretty decent fish, two or three busy sea gulls. Hardly the Seventh Cavalry.

His mother was not about to be fobbed off. She wanted *information*—the page number of the *Social Register,* the Dun and Bradstreet report on the business, the brief biographies of the more substantial relatives, a thumbnail sketch of the most disreputable of the family black sheep. So far one thing was globally clear. She was not impressed. Apparently Lisa's face was not to be found in the Stansfield memory bank, and that was ominous. She had made it her life's work to know of everybody who was anybody, who had *been* anybody.

Caroline Stansfield explored one last cul-de-sac, knowing as she did so what the answer would be. "Nothing to do with the Philadelphia Starrs?"

"No."

For what seemed like an age his mother was silent. One thing was crystal clear. This was not the range. Discouraging words had been heard. At last she spoke, and as she did so, she single-handedly proved the validity of extrasensory perception.

"How old did you say she was?"

"I didn't," said Bobby unnecessarily. He paused. "She's very young, mother."

"Very young, and no money." It was a statement.

"Yes, she has no money, and I guess you'd have to say she's not exactly our class, but she has very many wonderful qualities and I love her. I'm thinking of marrying her. I believe she'd even be a great asset to my career. You know, the working-class vote, the young . . ." He petered out. He was scarcely convincing himself.

"Baloney." Caroline Stansfield didn't bother to hide her scorn. Bobby was talking nonsense. Marriage to a moneyless, familyless child bride from West Palm might just be all right for a Democrat, but for a right-wing Republican it would be political and social disaster, and Bobby knew it. It was insulting that he tried to pull the wool over her eyes.

She looked down and sent the needle darting into the material with renewed vigor, as if into the heart of the adventuress who had dared to make a play for the standard bearer of the Stansfield political dynasty.

"Love's one thing. Politics is another. Frankly, the money thing is the most powerful objection of all. To get to the Oval Office you need more than we Stansfields have. It cost me a small fortune to keep your father afloat, and there isn't enough left to give you the push you need. Don't kid yourself. Unless you can marry it you're not going to get it. Please yourself, but don't make the mistake of believing you can have your cake and eat it. That's just not practical."

Lack of practicality was for Caroline Stansfield a cardinal sin. Still, she had come on a bit strong. Bobby would have to be talked out of this. He was no longer a child, and although he would listen to her, he was headstrong. She would have to tread carefully. Her sixth sense, far better preserved than her failing eyesight, told her there was more. "Anything else I should know about her?"

"There *is* a slight problem." Bobby hesitated.

Caroline Stansfield watched and waited, fighting back the desire to say something like, "Go on, Bobby, cough it up. That's a good boy." How many times had she used those lines when he'd been sick as a child?

"It appears that her mother once worked for us as a servant. A maid, I think. I'm not sure what her name was."

Caroline Stansfield fought back the impulse to laugh out loud. That would be quite the wrong thing to do, but it was difficult to resist.

A Stansfield had never yet been president, and Bobby would look so good on the Capitol steps, taking the oath. He had such a marvelous speaking voice. And at the White House receptions everyone would say how distinguished she looked. She'd be where she belonged at last. Then, quite suddenly, it wasn't funny anymore. The glorious dream was in deadly danger. Marriage? To a penniless young girl from West Palm of all places, and the daughter of a former servant? It would be a disaster. But how to tell Bobby so that he believed her. That was a problem. He was already beginning to bristle at her lack of enthusiasm.

"Well, Bobby, how can I advise you about the person you love? Love is everything. You must follow your heart." Somehow she made love sound like a dangerous drug in which only the weak-willed and feebleminded indulged. Certainly Bobby picked up that message.

"What I meant, mother, was how do you think it would affect me politically?"

"Ah. That's quite a different thing altogether, isn't it? Well, she's poor apparently, and unknown. And very young, you say. The daughter of one of our servants. I wonder which one. Mmmmmmm. It doesn't sound as if it's the cleverest match in the world—politically speaking, of course. But then, does it matter, Bobby? Do you really want to go any higher than the Senate? It should be enough for most men. It was for your father. He got used to it in the end. We all did. You see, the presidency is a vocation. You have to want it, to need and to dream it if you are ever going to be it. And you have to put up with all the hardship and the sacrifice, because you know you can serve your country, your fellow Americans. That has always been the Stansfield way— but then you are already in service, Bobby. You have done enough. I don't think Lisa Starr would hurt your reelection chances in the Senate, and if you hang on long enough you should get the chairmanship of a good committee. Agriculture, or even Foreign Relations."

Bobby's face was going through the floor as Caroline spoke, and one by one, she watched her clever bombs strike home. Noblesse oblige. Ask not what your country can do for you. The greater good, the wider picture. Its significance in comparison to the paltry lusts and personal desires of the individual. She knew Bobby wanted the Oval Office the way he wanted air to breathe. She and Fred had personally supervised the placing of the desire in the depths of his mind. But how great was the need? Less than his need for Lisa Starr? More?

"You think she'd be no good for the presidential nomination."

"She wouldn't be any good for that. You know that, Bobby, don't you?"

"It would be the popular wisdom." Bobby sounded ungraceful on purpose.

His mother didn't care. The stakes were far too high to worry about little things like that. She played a trump. "Really, though, you shouldn't be asking me. What do I know about politics anymore? I'm old and passé. What does that awful Baker man say? I must say I can't stand his manners, but I've a healthy respect for his political judgment."

Bobby looked miserable. He had never met anyone with the political nose of his mother. Baker ran her a close second. He hadn't dared to ask Baker's opinion, because he knew in his heart exactly what it would be. He would have said what his mother had just said, with a piquant sauce of the more fashionable and cruder swear words thrown in for good measure.

Like a wise old owl Caroline Stansfield watched her son struggle on the horns of his dilemma.

"It would be political oblivion," said Bobby, almost to himself. Inside the questions milled around. Did that matter? Weren't there more important things in life? Like Lisa?

"It's one of the marks of greatness to have the ability to make sacrifices. We are all so unimportant in relation to the common good. It's the cross you have to bear in public life."

"You make yourself very clear, mother. I shall have to give this matter a great deal of thought."

Caroline Stansfield smiled her gracious smile, the one that went down so well at charity functions. It was not exactly a racing certainty, but she was pretty sure she had won. She shifted her tack. The negative must always be balanced by the positive. When you took something away you should always try to replace it with something of value. "I hope you won't mind my saying this, Bobby, but as you know, I've always spoken my mind. Too old to break the habit now." She laughed the tinkling laugh that all Stansfields had come to value for its rarity.

"It seems to me that poor Jo-Anne Duke is a marvelously attractive person. So dignified at the funeral. So *very* good looking. Apparently Peter Duke left her everything—control of the foundation, the entire fortune. And I'm told she's very ambitious . . ." She tailed off as she cast the seed. Would it fall on fertile ground? The ground on which she had just so effectively doused the flames of Lisa Starr.

Bobby managed a laugh. Really, his mother was incorrigible. He couldn't resist drawing her out a little more. "Mother, you're wonderful. But I can't say I know an awful lot about Jo-Anne Duke's past. Do you? Rumor has it she was some sort of model in New York when Peter Duke found her."

"The point is she was *found,* dear. And by a Duke. And what's more, he gave her his name. That makes her one of us. At a stroke. She bears his name, controls his money, and looks the part. I don't think one could ask for much more than that."

Bobby fell silent. The Duke money . . . and the Stansfield machine. The one oiling the other. It was quite a thought. Quite a thought indeed.

Caroline moved to consolidate her position; she seemed to be talking to herself. "So much sense," she murmured. "So much sense." Out loud she added, "But of course it's the heart that's important. One should always do what the heart dictates."

She watched her son carefully. What *did* his heart dictate? Were the genes, the careful upbringing strong enough to undermine his infatuation with the nobody who had captured him? Her instinct said they were. They had better be. Because around the corners of Caroline Stansfield's canny mind scurried a very disturbing idea.

~ 10 ~

*L*ISA AND MAGGIE peered into the mirror with a studied intensity that suggested that the secrets of life itself were about to be revealed.

"There's nothing there," said Lisa. It was difficult for her to catch the feeling conjured up by the words. Relief? Disappointment? Relief mixed with disappointment?

There was no doubt at all about Maggie's response. "Well, thank *God* for that."

Maggie's satisfaction seemed to push Lisa off the fence of indecision. "But I've *never* been late before. Usually you can set your watch by me. I know I'm pregnant. I can feel it. That time in the pool in Mustique. I just *know* it. Perhaps we did something wrong. Let me look at the instructions again."

Maggie laughed in disbelief.

"Lisa, really. You sound as if you *want* to be pregnant. You ought to be thanking God that the damn thing's not positive."

It had never crossed Maggie's practical mind that anyone who wasn't married or engaged to be married would actually want to be "in the club." She had seen more than enough soap operas to know that the traditional masculine response to learning that fatherhood was in the pipeline was shock/horror followed quickly by anger/irritation and blame/abuse. Somewhere around the third stage came the veiled accusations that some Machiavellian schemer was trying to trick him into marriage. Invariably it was followed by a dry little speech about getting rid of the baby, and then the relationship. That was the reaction ordinary people expected, and whatever else she wasn't, Maggie was certainly one of those.

The look on Lisa's face reflected the indecision in her heart, and Maggie's gut response amplified it.

Did she want to be pregnant? It was almost impossible to say. A beautiful baby by the man she loved. Her life changed at a stroke by the intervention of Fate's cruelty. Or was it kindness? Around and around the emotions whirled as intellect attempted to inject order into the chaos. One thing was certain: it had not been done on purpose. That was not her style. She simply hadn't considered the possibility. Of babies, of marriage. Of anything like that. In the awesome intensity of the love boat ride to bliss, such mundane things had been forgotten in the excitement of the glorious present. But now reality was intruding on the dream, with its own demands, and Lisa fought to make sense of it. But it was still uncertain. The bridge loomed up, but it had not been reached. Maybe it never would.

She didn't respond to Maggie. Instead, for the twentieth time that morning, they pored over the blue Daisy 2 booklet. They hadn't made a mistake. An imbecile couldn't have screwed up. Early morning urine specimen. Don't shake the tube after mixing the urine with the chemicals. Read the result only from the mirror on the test kit stand. Don't read the result until exactly forty-five minutes had passed. Well, of course they hadn't obeyed *that*. They had sat, side by side, eyes glued to the mirror, waiting for the black ring to appear from minute one.

"Maybe if it's going to appear at all it sort of comes suddenly at the end of the forty-fifth minute, and it's not a gradual thing at all," said Maggie.

Even as she spoke, she was aware that there had been a subtle shift in her attitude. Lisa could do things like that. Lisa had intimated that pregnancy would not necessarily be a total disaster and Maggie's psychology was already beginning to shift to accommodate the alien idea. But although emotion had moved, intellect was still rock solid. Bobby Stansfield would not like the idea of Lisa's carrying his child.

Lisa saw it first.

There was excitement in her voice, but a careful, reserved kind of excitement. The sort you experienced when something of awesome importance occurred whose effects were uncertain. Possibly good. Possibly bad.

"Look, Maggs, it's forming. Can you see it? Can you see it? There, that blackness. It's round isn't it? Like a halo? Christ!"

She turned to look at her friend, her expression questioning, as if she hoped for some lead as to how she ought to feel.

Maggie felt acutely uncomfortable. Should she share her misgivings? The bearers of bad tidings tended to get a bad press. Sometimes, as now, the duties of friendship could conflict. Should she be there with reassurance and support, or was a little reeducation in the unfortunate ways of the world in order? "Will Bobby be pleased?" she asked lamely, as a sort of a compromise.

Now Lisa's face registered open disbelief. Dear God, *that* wasn't the problem. It was *her* feelings she was worrying about, not Bobby's. She hadn't reckoned on being pregnant, and now she was. It took a bit of dealing with. "Maggie, what do you mean? Of course he'll be pleased. Surprised as hell, like me, but pleased for sure. It's *his* baby, silly."

The laugh was all mixed up with the words. It was unlike Maggie to fail to get the point.

Maggie couldn't give up just yet. "But . . . I mean . . . some men . . . feel, you know . . . that girls should be sort of responsible for taking precautions . . . and if they don't . . . well, you know, it's like a back-door way of getting them to the altar."

For a second Lisa looked thoughtful. She hadn't really confronted that one. Not consciously anyway.

"Oh, Maggie, Bobby's not like that. I mean, he loves me. We love each other. He'd never react like that. He just couldn't. Not Bobby. Anyway, he knows I'd never even *think* of doing a thing like that on purpose."

Maggie took a deep breath and plowed on. "You mean he'll marry you."

"Well, I guess so." Suddenly Lisa didn't sound quite so sure. "There isn't an alternative, is there?" she added quietly.

"Some people get rid of the baby."

"No!" The exclamation shot from Lisa's lips, and its force blew away the doubts and fears that had been hovering around the edges of consciousness. Maggie had voiced the unthinkable, and clarified the confusion in Lisa's mind.

She spoke fast. "Maggie, that's just ridiculous. Bobby and I aren't 'some people.' We never have been and we never will be. He's a totally responsible person, and so am I. He'd always do the right thing."

Maggie could feel herself giving in. Like Custer she had made her last stand against "head-in-the-clouds" attitudes, and now it was time to relinquish the role. Maybe Lisa was right, anyway. One thing was certain: Stansfield would have to be a moron to turn her away. The girl was as near to perfection as it was possible to be on this earth, and a man of his experience would recognize that. Wouldn't he?

"Of course he will, Lisa. Hey, this is *exciting*. You a senator's wife! Do I get to be maid of honor?" With a certain lack of conviction Maggie attempted the role change from doubting Thomas to cheerleader.

But Lisa was scarcely listening. She sat up straight and ran her hand over the superflat stomatch. "Bobby's baby. Growing in here. How *weird!*" The sudden thought rushed into her mind. "There's no chance it could be wrong, is there?"

"It says it's ninety-eight percent accurate." Maggie laughed in the more comforting part of co-conspirator.

Flinging her arms around her friend's neck, Lisa let it all surge out, and, as within the tube her human chorionic gonadotrophin, a special hormone of pregnancy, reacted with the HCG antibody of the test kit to form the black ring, she burst into floods of tears.

BOBBY STANSFIELD's heart was breaking. In front of him stood Lisa, her beautiful face beginning to drain of color, her hands gripped tightly, her knuckles white. God, how he loved her. He wanted her now, even this minute while his words tortured her, but there was the steely Stansfield part of his soul, and he was letting it ride roughshod over his emotions. Over the last few days he had rehearsed this moment in his mind, but he was still unprepared for the reality. Lisa was carrying his child. She had walked through the door as if floating on air and had told him the news with all the excitement and wonder of the young, and deeply in love. It had never occurred to her that he wouldn't share her joy. It was occurring to her now. Before his eyes she was teetering on the brink of tears.

"Lisa, I don't want you to think what we've had together hasn't been important to me. It has. We both know that. You're a sweet and wonderful person, and I'm very, very, fond of you . . ."

He moved to the window, and for a second his broad back was toward Lisa as he fought to find the words that would lessen the pain, that would excuse him from his dreadful guilt.

Lisa stared at him, her face blank with the beginnings of shock as she tried to understand what she didn't want to hear. There was something wrong with the script. She hadn't written it like this. Fond? A sweet and wonderful person? Like somebody's favorite great aunt. Christ! He was going to slam the door in her face at the precise moment he was supposed to take her into his heart.

Her voice, small and insecure, shook with words. "Bobby, I'm pregnant, I said. With our child." It was a plea as much as a statement. Maybe he hadn't quite understood what she'd said.

Bobby turned to face her. He splayed his hands open in a gesture of defeat. "I sort of imagined you'd ah . . ." His voice trailed off unhappily as he heard the indecision in it. God, this was awful. The guilt was creeping all over him, plucking at his skin with its sharp little fingers.

Lisa sat down heavily on the edge of the old chintz sofa, her knees up to her chin, her face startled, bemused, uncomprehending. She said nothing as she watched her world die before her eyes. He'd imagined she was on the pill. That she'd "taken precautions." What did he think she was now? A West Palm girl on the make. That her pregnancy was part of some deep-laid plot to hook the eligible senator. He was supposed to be ecstatic. She was supposed to be twirling in his arms as he whispered his promises of a lifetime together as parents of the child she would bear him. This wasn't Bobby. Her Bobby. She should call the police and have him arrested for impersonating the man who had fathered her baby.

Bobby tried desperately to find the tap that would turn on the ice-cold water to douse the emotional flames. He had wanted this girl. But her irresistible love had crashed up against the unmovable object of his ambition, and the mighty wave was about to be broken into a fine mist of spray on that massive breakwater. Cruel to be kind. It should be clean. It was the only way for her. He would not turn her into his mistress. He could not marry her. He belonged to America, to his vision of America's future. Lisa Starr would be replaced in his life, but perhaps never fully replaced in his heart. Like the child of Abraham she had to be sacrificed at the altar of the greater need, and Bobby prayed that both he and she would be able to survive it.

"Lisa, I'm afraid marriage is totally out of the question. It always was, and it was wrong of me not to make that clear. God knows I'm not a snob, but there are things that politically just don't make sense, and it's the politics that must always come first with me. Jo-Anne tells me that your mother used to work here in this house. I wish you'd felt able to tell me that yourself. In itself it's no big thing, but it was something I should have known about. The press could hurt me with a thing like that. Believe me, I know the sorts of things they can do. And then there's the whole family thing. My mother, and the Stansfield name. And you're so young. You have so much time. One day you'll find a better man than me and you'll look back on this . . ."

Bobby winced as he made the nasty little speech. Pushing the red button just might be preferable.

"What!" said Lisa.

It was the cruelest and most vicious thing she had ever heard, and it came from the lips of the man she loved. He was as good as telling her that she wasn't good enough to be the mother of his child. She had defiled the Stansfield bloodline, polluted it with her innocent baby. Surely he hadn't meant that.

"What?" she repeated, her mind woolly and numb with shock.

"I think you must know what I mean, Lisa."

He couldn't handle that all over again. He swallowed hard. He had to go the whole way. "And Jo-Anne tells me there's another problem, Lisa. I didn't know you were bisexual. It came as a great surprise. Both personally and politically I'm afraid that's a hot potato, too. As you know I take a firm stand against homosexuality, and I always have. I'd find that very difficult to deal with." That at least was true. In a way it was all true. But the words came from the mind and not from the heart.

A lesbian? Where? Why? How? Who? No answers, but the beginnings of anger. The birth of herself. The rebirth. She would nurture the emotion, cosset it, build it up to replace the numbing unreality that had gripped her.

"Bobby, what the *hell* are you saying to me?"

She stood up, her fingers pushing into her palms, the blood rushing in her ears. There was a funny feeling in her throat.

Bobby watched her. Inside he was beginning to uncoil. He had done the deed. The blood was on his hands. Christ, she was magnificent. The most beautiful woman he had ever seen. Never again would he be asked to make a sacrifice like this. He had given his all, and paradoxically there was pride to be found in that. It was the sort of thing that separated the sheep from the goats. To get there you had to want it enough. You had to be prepared to pay the price.

There was one last thing to be done. "As for the child, Lisa. Well, you know that my stand against abortion is a fundamental part of my beliefs. But the child will be well taken care of. There will be no financial problems for either of you. I promise you that."

Like a can of kerosene poured over a burning match Bobby's words amplified the fire in Lisa's soul. Now she saw it. Saw the snobbery, saw the callous indifference to her and to the truth, saw the hardness of heart. Her eyes rested on the naked ambition, the brutality, the single-minded, undistractible preoccupation with self, and her stomach turned as her mind exploded into hatred.

The rage hovered and slithered about her, creating sparks of electricity as it crackled through the atmosphere.

She took a step toward him. Bobby took one back.

"When I leave this dreadful house, Bobby, do you know what I'm going to do? I'm going to find the dirtiest and most disreputable doctor I can find. I'm going to have him rip this thing of yours out of me and flush it into the sewers. Along with all my memories of you."

~

LISA PARKED her bike right up against one of the immaculate white columns of the Duke mansion façade, taking care to chip the paint as she did so. She walked straight past the pin-stripe trousered, black-jacketed butler as if he didn't exist. In the marble entrance hall beneath the vast cut-glass Georgian chandelier she hesitated as she looked around. It was eight o'clock in the morning. She took the steps of the Carrara marble stairs two at a time. Jo-Anne's bedroom would not be hard to find.

Struggling in her wake, making little mutterings of protest, his arms waving ineffectually, followed the English butler.

The second door she tried led her to her quarry. Jo-Anne lay back queen-like in the huge bed, a Crown Derby cup of exquisite delicacy raised to her lips.

Lisa stood at the end of the bed white with fury, her body quivering with anger. Behind her the butler had made it to the door. "Madam, I'm so sorry. I wasn't able to stop her."

Jo-Anne put down the teacup. She was rather looking forward to this. It began to look as if she had won. Mrs. Bobby Stansfield's former name would be Duke, not Starr. Served the little girl right. Nobody got in her way. Nobody should dare to try. But what a pity she hadn't made hay while the sun had shone in that damn Jacuzzi. She'd never get around to experiencing that amazing body now.

"It's all right, Roberts. I think you'd better leave us alone. It looks as if Miss Starr has a thing or two on her mind."

"You're too right there's something on my mind. You set me up, you bitch. What the *hell* are you trying to do to me?"

"My dear Lisa, there's no need to be melodramatic. Listen, sweetheart, you've been setting *yourself* up ever since you set foot in this town. Who the hell do you think you are?"

"I know exactly who I am and I know exactly what you are. You're a vicious, disgusting liar. You told Bobby I was a lesbian. You know that's not true."

"Truth? Truth? You naive little fool. What the hell do I care about truth? Anyway, for someone who's not a lesbian, you sure kiss like one."

Lisa shook her head in disbelief. Somehow she hadn't expected this reaction. Jo-Anne was actually enjoying it, goading her, ready to add to her humiliation. She was totally at sea when confronted by the pulsating force of pure evil.

"Why did you do it to me, Jo-Anne? Did you want him for yourself? Or was it to get at me?" The anger was receding. Now she was puzzled, desperately hurt but wanting to know the reason why, to understand the wickedness that had broken her heart and ruined her life.

"Why did you lie to him, and why did you tell him about my mom? I wanted to do that myself. It was a terrible thing to do."

Jo-Anne lay back on the cushions as the purest malice shot from her eyes. The girl had shown weakness, and she was trained to go for the kill in its presence. Her voice was low as she spoke, but the words dripped with the poison of her sarcasm. "You really don't understand, do you? You walk into this town, all bright eyed and bushy tailed, and expect everyone to forget where you came from and what you stand for. Don't you realize, Lisa Starr, you're just a nobody, a great big zero with no past, no present, and no future? You don't count here. You come from a sleazy part of town, from sleazy parents, and yet you dare to walk into our world and pretend you're an equal. Bobby Stansfield is a prize around here, you know. He's ours. Or at least mine. Baby, you never had a chance. Okay, so I helped blow you out of the window, but you were never anything more than a slow, comfortable screw, so I didn't have to try very hard. Your grave had been dug before you were even born. You should have gotten wise and chosen less beat-up parents."

Lisa stood there as the acid words burned her soul. There and then she felt her world change. Nothing could ever be the same for her again. A metamorphosis had occurred and now she was different. Lisa Starr had died. Lisa Starr had risen.

Her voice was quiet when she spoke, but it turned Jo-Anne's stomach and sent icy fingers dancing up and down between her shoulder blades.

"For what you have just said, Jo-Anne Duke, I will bury you. I will destroy you and everyone and everything you love, if it takes me a lifetime to do it. Never, never forget this promise."

She turned and left, but when Jo-Anne had reached out for her tea, her fingers had seemed to have a mind of their own. The Crown Derby cup and its pretty saucer had gone crashing all over the place, leaving Jo-Anne with the discouraging thought that their destruction could just have been a symbol of Lisa Starr's spine-tingling vow of vengeance.

—

Jo-anne sipped gently on the ice-cold fino sherry, allowing the arid dryness to scourge her tongue. It was a delicious penance to drink it, atonement for more simple and straightforward pleasures. She kicked off her shoes and hoisted her bare legs onto the oatmeal hessian sofa, allowing her eyes to roam around the elegantly decorated Jon Bannenberg yacht. It had been a good move to get him to do the interior. He wasn't the most original choice, but more than any other boat designer in the world he knew how to achieve the delicate marriage of good taste and expediency that was so necessary in a private transoceanic vessel. Beneath her she could both sense and hear the reassuring throb of the twin 1,280-horsepower General Motors turbodiesels as the 120-foot motor yacht *Jo-Anne* edged out from the dock into the smooth waters of Lake Worth.

Absent-mindedly she reached out to the nearby brushed-chrome control panel and flicked casually at a switch. It took her three tries to score the Vivaldi. Just what one needed to complement a mood like this. Soothing, yet uplifting. A present for the senses of a hooker who was in the process of landing the biggest and best catch of them all.

Everything had gone like clockwork. A virtuoso performance, the logistics impeccably handled. God, she was a winner. She brought the treble up a bit, turned down the base. Mmmmmmmm. The sound was full and rich. Just like her. In the blue stateroom Bobby Stansfield would be changing for dinner. Slipping into that dinner jacket that he wore so well. Probably splashing on the Eau Sauvage that all men of his class seemed to prefer. Later they would drink the dryest of martinis, Tanqueray gin, a Spanish olive, on the afterdeck and watch the spectacular Lake Worth sunset. Oh yes, it had all been stage managed, the timing orchestrated by the conductress's baton with nothing left to chance. Dinner would be open air, *à deux*, bobbing on the Gulf Stream by the light of the silvery moon. Owl-and-pussycat time.

The white-coated steward cut into her reverie. "May I get you another glass of sherry, Mrs. Duke? Or perhaps a canapé."

"No thank you, James. I'll wait for the senator. Was the chef able to get the swordfish steaks I asked for?"

"He certainly was. And I think I can say that the sauce Bearnaise is the best I have ever tasted. Roberts has organized the wine. Le Montrachet 'seventy-six with the fish."

"Marvelous, James. Make sure you keep a close eye on the senator's glass. Oh, how are we doing for breakages on the blue Sèvres dinner service? I think it was for sixteen originally."

"It would certainly cover fourteen now. No problem. Tonight I laid out the Meissen. That was what you ordered."

"Yes, that's fine. Flowers?"

"Four single birds of paradise as a centerpiece. White orchids on the serving table."

Jo-Anne was really just checking. Everything was shipshape. The troops responding like automatons to her general's command. It was things like that that made the difference between success and failure. And tonight was special. Quite apart from anything else it was day fourteen of her menstrual cycle, and she fully intended to make maximum use of that.

She fingered the buff folder on the heavy glass table in front of her. No need for another look. She knew its contents intimately. Six legal methods of short-circuiting the rule that said no individual's contribution to a political campaign should be more than one thousand dollars. All skirted the borders of legality, obeying the letter if not the spirit of the law. As a result all were a little dubious, laying one open to the criticism that play had not been entirely fair. That could cost votes in a close-fought campaign. Jo-Anne's way was a better one altogether. It had the virtue of simplicity and it tied up all the loose ends. On the day of her marriage to Bobby Stansfield she would write him a check for five million dollars. A simple gift from a loving wife to her much-loved husband. That way he could spend it as he wished. No law forbade a rich man from financing his own run for the presidency. But although it was a "no-strings-attached" gift, it would also be a fee. Jo-Anne Duke would actually be buying the Stansfield name.

She stood up and walked over to the mirrored wall. A simple pure silk dress. A single strand of the Duke pearls. White shoes. No stockings, no bra. White silk briefs. Nothing else at all. He could have her wherever and whenever he wanted. As long as it happened, Jo-Anne didn't mind. Once the game was on, she was its mistress. She could do everything because she *had* done everything. Practice had made her perfect.

THE SWORDFISH, lightly grilled, had been a dream, its flesh firm yet moist. And the white burgundy had set it off to perfection. Bobby hadn't held back on the martinis and he hadn't held back on the classic wine either. Over the delicate, frothy chocolate mousse she had cast her fly and like a salmon on the rainswept Spey in August he had risen to take it. She hadn't actually proposed to him—some things, not many, a man had to do for himself. But she had put her proposal to him. The difference had been largely one of semantics. As the moonlight had caught the surface of the warm water, as the soft, salt breeze had played across their faces and the delicious wine mellowed them, she had leaned across the polished mahogany and let him see her tits as she had offered him the power of her huge fortune, and the delights of her voluptuous body. She had watched the mighty battle being fought in his eyes as his ambition had gone to war with his finer feelings, and she had known that she had won. The real decision had been made a day or so earlier when Bobby had sacrificed happiness for the ultimate goal.

Now he smiled across the table at her. Shy, debonair, infinitely appealing, he allowed her a sight of the Stansfield grin, universally described as boyish from *People* magazine to the acerbic pages of the *National Review*. But there was a sadness about him, too. Unmistakable, and appealing in its challenge. Lisa had gone. Clearly, though, she was not forgotten.

"I think we maybe should get married," he said at last.

"I think that certainly we should," agreed Jo-Anne. She stood up. The contract needed to be signed in the most meaningful way she knew how.

Holding his hand in hers, she took him below, steering him past the Erté watercolors and the gorgeous set of original Diaghilev stage designs, past the Epstein bronzes recessed in alcoves and lit by hidden spots, to the place where her best deals had always been made. Her bedroom.

~11~

L ISA WANTED TO be sick. She wanted to lie down right now on the polished wood boards with all the heaving flesh dancing around her and puke until her soul had come out of her. She wanted to spill her guts, vomit until she was empty, blow her insides all over the gym. And they called it morning sickness. What a grotesquely inadequate description for the hell on earth she had experienced these last few weeks. Why did women keep this one quiet? Were they frightened that if the truth came out the human race would end then and there, stopped in its tracks by the universal knowledge of this most dreadful experience? With quiet desperation she forced herself to concentrate on the music. They said the first three months were the worst. Well, it was almost twelve weeks since she had stared with such misplaced joy at that black ring and she had had enough.

"And eight more . . . one and two and three and four . . . Come on go for that extra bit . . . work those bodies . . ."

Lisa pushed herself harder. Maybe the exercise would do what she had found herself unable to do. Three times she had made the appointment. Three times she had canceled it as she had fought back the tempation to sacrifice the unborn child on the altar of her hate. Now it was too late. Bobby Stansfield's baby would see the light of day after all. Conceived in love, it would be born in an atmosphere thick with the smoke of loathing, the sky dimmed by the black cloud of revenge. Sometimes when she woke bathed in the swirling mists of nausea, Lisa Starr looked in horror at the person she saw in the mirror. Outwardly little had changed, but inside her mind it was another planet. There was a stranger there living in her brain, an alien creature, foreign and fearsome, feeding on bile. Already the invader was taking over, as it redesigned her memories, redefined her beliefs, recast her ambitions. Already the fruits of its handiwork were subtly visible.

In front of her the bodies tortured themselves, twisting and straining as they fought for physical glory. But they were not the same bodies. Cheap sweat shirts, torn tights, Swiss-cheese leotards, grubby sneakers were nowhere to be seen. Nor were haggard faces, cheap hairstyles, Timex watches.

The lingering smell of stale sweat was gone too, together with the cheap beach bags and dirty towels that previous patrons had left littered around the edge of the exercise floor as they sweated out their grinding routines. The colors now were brighter, the fabrics of the workout clothes of a noticeably higher quality—Barely Legal, Body Electric, Dance France. Through the air thick with the smell of Joy, Opium, and Giorgio, Cartier and Piaget watches flashed and darted in time to the rhythms belted out from the state-of-the-art Fisher sound system. A coal miner from Kentucky would have missed the point. To him it would have been a tits and ass show—"Solid Gold" dancers in the flesh. The point that he would have missed however was that this class was different in that it *had* class. Inside the tits the blood was blue, and the ass was pure old Palm Beach.

Lisa watched them as she orchestrated the group effort. It was working beautifully. From across the bridge the Palm Beachers were flocking to Clematis Street as she had intended: a few cunningly worded ads in the Shiny Sheet, her personal touch, and the word of mouth which crackled like wildfire around the tiny town. Already she was something of a celebrity. An outsider of course, and likely to remain one, but more than useful to make up numbers when house guests arrived in Palm Beach from the North, when nephews were on vacation from Princeton or the University of Virginia.

Lisa smiled grimly to herself as mercifully the nausea began to pass. She was getting there. Slowly but surely the first part of her life plan was coming together. Already she was learning the rules of the complicated social structure, her antennae sensitive to the vaguest nuance that could point the way forward. It was a deadly business and no book of etiquette was of the remotest use. You were allowed few mistakes, and beneath the precarious gangplank on which one walked, the water was stiff with the sharks, their razor teeth poised to rip the socially unwary wide open from top to toe.

The blood that had formerly run in her veins, warm and loving, had been replaced by another liquid, cold and unforgiving. It was exactly what was required for Palm Beach survival, and more important for Palm Beach advancement, and now she knew not only who was important to her, but, just as vitally, who was not. Now there were a group of people to whom she didn't talk; not large admittedly, but it was a start. The West Palm people, of course, had gone first. It had taken a few barbed comments, a few public quarrels, but they had been cleared out eventually to the continual protests of the ever-faithful Maggie. Into the vacuum created by their departure had come the "quality," with their high-pitched laughs, their "in" jokes, their endless gossip, their boundless self-confidence. Lisa knew them all—the girl with the funny name who was actually a Vanderbilt by birth, the one who was married to a Greek but whose children were called Phipps, the older woman with the toothpick tits whose daughter was a leading light on the junior committee of the Bath and Tennis Club.

They were a funny lot. Martians at first, but she was getting to know them —what they liked and didn't like. First, they didn't like any sign at all of weakness, of deference, which might hint that you needed them. The moment they sensed that, their lips would curl in condescension, as they sharpened their tongues for the slice-up job, an art they practiced effortlessly and with surgical precision. Second, they were more than prepared for a hard time, superb masochist material, quite happy to endure the pain and the insults as Lisa revved up their screaming bodies and forced them toward the muscle "burn." That had been unexpected. Somehow she imagined the upper classes to be without spines, effete and ineffectual. Maybe they were, but on the workout floor they went for it as if their lives depended on it, and she had to admire that.

Never for one moment, however, did Lisa make the mistake in believing that just because they allowed her to scream at them, that she was one of them. In Palm Beach nobody was given instant access. It took time. She would be on probation for years. There was one and only one way to shortcut the process, apart from marrying into the town's aristocracy. If she could somehow get hold of a sponsor—a patron who would look on her as a proté- gée, somebody powerful enough socially to insist that her friends became Lisa's friends. That was what she needed. She had found it briefly with Jo- Anne Duke, and it had ended in tragedy. But now Jo-Anne was a bitter enemy who could be relied upon to bad-mouth her at every opportunity, and the rumors of impending marriage to Bobby Stansfield had strengthened her already almost invincible position. Without a protector, Jo-Anne would murder her in Palm Beach society, and without her infiltration into its ranks revenge would be impossible.

More than anything, Lisa needed friends in the big league whose social cannons could outgun Jo-Anne's. But who? And how would she meet them? How could she befriend them? There were so many unanswerable questions.

"Okay you guys, let's unwind—relaxation, deep breathing, stretch it all out."

Lisa looked down at her forearms. Only the thinnest film of sweat. In front of her the class looked like it had been under a shower. That was what fitness was all about, and Christ, was she in top condition, her skin shining with the patina of robust health, her body a superb machine . . . with one small blemish. Damn. The child. How soon before it wrecked her body and disfigured her sculpted abdominal musculature? The child of the man who had more or less told her she was inferior goods, that his bloodline deserved a better baton carrier. Well, damn them all. She would work out until she dropped the little bastard.

THE CAKE was unashamedly traditional—huge, and layered—the initials of the happy couple intertwined on top. Apart from the size, a little too large for Palm Beach purists, it was understated. Snow white, the icing intricate, the proportions perfect. It stood all by itself on a long table at the end of the pink-and-white marquee that had been erected on the lawn of the Duke mansion, and many of the guests had already admired it as they had the ice sculptures that were scattered strategically among the groaning buffet tables. Typical of these was an enormous American eagle, powerful and predatory, which hovered over the white damask tablecloth as the tent's air conditioning fought a losing battle to keep it alive, its body dripping away gently onto the immaculate linen. The beluga had a separate table all to itself, and the finest Iranian caviar, both black and red, free of its unhappy homeland at last, lay in huge inviting mounds on ice beds in the silver serving salvers. It was here, and around the champagne bar, where a Taittinger Rosé 1976, the color of crushed rose petals, was being poured into elegant Baccarat wineglasses, that the crowds were thickest.

"Can I get you a little caviar, Aldo? Some chopped egg or chives with it?" Jo-Anne spooned a mound of the improbable delicacy onto a Limoges plate.

"Just a little lemon. Nothing else, thank you." The elegant old Italian showed his traditionalist colors. Dr. Aldo Gucci, like the merchandise he sold, was interested only in undiluted quality.

She looked around the tent. It was magnificent. The perfect wedding reception after the fairy-tale wedding. Even the hard-bitten Palm Beachers had been touched by the emergence of happiness from the ashes of tragedy, although there were more than a few who had commented on the indelicate speed of the process and others who had smiled behind their hands at the ostentation of the caviar and the ice sculptures. Whatever they thought, they had all showed up—the aristocrats, the politicians, the fashion people, the displaced Europeans. Palm Beach was on the map again, and nobody was quite sure why. It had never really changed, but the world around it had. Both money and conservatism were fashionable, and Palm Beach had buckets and buckets of both.

Across the room Jo-Anne saw Ralph Lauren locked in conversation with Laura Ashley, the hugely successful British designer who had recently bought a house in the town. Ralph, it was rumored, was planning a "Palm Beach look" for his next collection.

In another corner was Ted Kennedy, floating his formidable charm over house guest Beverly Sassoon. Bobby might despise him, but only a few hundred yards of North End beach separated the Kennedy house from the Stansfield home. It would have been impossibly churlish to have failed to send an invitation. Actually Jo-Anne herself was rather drawn to him—that braying self-confidence, the skill with the Frisbee in the surf, the eyes that said their owner liked women more than men. Whatever else you could say about the Kennedys and their socialist politics, you had to admit they had style. That was a cliché, but it was true. The North Ocean Boulevard home, for instance, was a tip. Jo-Anne had been there once with Peter in the days when Rose had given the occasional party. The carpets had been threadbare, the furniture damaged irreparably by the corrosive sea air, the ancient fifty-foot pool requiring all the considerable skills of C and P Maintenance to save it from algae, frog spawn, and nameless creepy-crawly things. The windows didn't open and close properly and the whole house needed a coat of paint. But the Kennedys didn't mind things like that. They were above it, no longer interested or aware of what others thought. And they displayed the true patrician disinterest in conspicuous materialism. Despite their wealth they looked after the pennies. In the kitchen the refrigerator was so old that once a week the maid had to defrost it by hand. To them the vast 1923 Mizner home on North Ocean Boulevard was just a beach house, and they treated it as such. She had to admire that.

Jo-Anne smoothed her hands over her stomach. It was such a funny feeling being pregnant. So much was going on in there, but there was so little to show for it. In vain she had waited for the morning sickness, for the food fads and all the other little happenings that seemed to figure so prominently in other people's pregnancies. It looked as if she were going to sail through her nine months with no problems and no discomfort at all. What had she done to deserve the prizes that were falling so readily into her lap? It was almost as if the Lord in His wisdom had decided to make it up to her for all the bad times, for the cold, for the hunger of the Big Apple days. She had wanted Bobby, and wanted to be pregnant as a method of increasing her hold over him, and she had gotten both. How lucky could you get?

Thank God she hadn't messed around with the wedding dress. She had played it straight and gone for Dior. Traditional elegance, sweeping lines, the finest stitching, obsessional attention to detail. If she was filling out below the waist it wouldn't show in this creation.

The voice whispering in her ear cut into her thoughts. "Congratulations, honey. 'Mrs. Robert Stansfield' sounds even better than 'Mrs. Peter Duke.' " Mary d'Erlanger smiled the smile of the person who had seen through the charade.

Jo-Anne laughed openly. What the hell did it matter anymore? She'd made the home run. She was the girl with the perfect batting score. There was only one important secret, and that had died as the blood had risen in Peter Duke's drowning throat. No longer did she have to play the part of the grieving widow. She didn't even have to pretend that she loved the man she had just married. At last she could let it all hang out. It was with a glorious feeling of liberation that Jo-Anne Duke Stansfield realized that she didn't give a fart.

"The problem is I have nothing left for the encore."

"Oh, come off it. Jo-Anne. I'm counting on you for the White House dinner parties. I've already started to read *Time* magazine at the hairdresser so that I'll know what to say to all those foreign politicians."

Again Jo-Anne laughed. People always got it wrong. The presidency was Bobby's trip, not hers. Nobody seemed to realize that. The truth was she was hooked on another game, the one they played here in the town of Palm Beach. For years she had crept higher up the social ladder, dislodging the incumbents on the rungs above as she sabotaged the progress of fellow-traveling glory seekers. It was in her blood now, an addictive drug whose withdrawal would be extraordinarily difficult if not impossible. There was absolutely no doubt about it. What she wanted right now was not the world-wide fame of the first ladyship. That could come later. Now she wanted the crown of Palm Beach. She wanted to park her pert rump on the throne on which Marjorie Donahue sat so regally. She wanted to pry the wily old bird's wizened fingers from the top-rung perch. For far too long she had been a princess, the jam promised tomorrow but never had today. But nothing lasted forever. It could be done. She could make it happen. The queen is dead. Long live the queen.

There was a wistful look in the eyes of Jo-Anne Duke Stansfield as she looked across to the corner in which Marjorie Donahue was holding court. Around her clustered half a dozen socially ambitious, attentive courtiers wrapping their tongues around the compliments—shameless in their syco-phancy. In a minute or two Jo-Anne herself would be among them. A first among equals maybe, but still nothing more than an ass-licking parasite.

Marjorie, what a *brilliant* dress. How dare you shame me on my wedding day? Where on earth did you get it? That would just about do for openers. Christ, what a terrible dress it was. The sort of thing you got in a thrift-shop clearance sale. Jo-Anne fervently wished it were a shroud. She turned to her "friend." "Come on, Mary, we'd better go pay our respects. A thousand dollars for the most flattering lie!"

As she walked toward her social superior, Jo-Anne felt the irritation rise within her. This was *her* day. *She* was the star. Why the hell was she doing the walking? Who did this superannuated geriatric think she was fooling? A chemical fortune married to department store megabucks was pretty impres-sive, especially when allied to a diamond-sharp tongue, but what right did she have to exact subservience and obedience from a person like Jo-Anne, who would spend the next forty years dancing on her grave? The feeling of dangerous exhilaration coursed through her as she realized what she was going to do. She would open hostilities. Fire the first shot in a long, cruel, but infinitely exhilarating campaign. Everyone would be forced to take sides, as the town split across the middle, like Virginia families in the Civil War.

The moment of truth was approaching, after which nothing would be the same again. Jo-Anne could feel the color rising in her cheeks as the burst of careless self-confidence exploded within her. Was it the wedding? The Tait-tinger? The hormones of pregnancy? Impossible to say. It was an emotional thing, not rational, hardly wise, but it was symbolic of her newfound power. For the first time she had the ammunition and big battalions on her side. The all important bit players who would be the troops in the coming conflict would expect payment and protection from their general. The Duke money and the Stansfield patronage would provide for them, and as her husband's star rose across the firmament of America, she would prevail in the real battle, in the one in which her heart was involved. It would start here. Now. She would insult the queen.

The gaggle of courtiers parted to allow Jo-Anne's approach.

"Jo-Anne dear. What a wonderful day. Such a brilliant wedding. A mar-velous day for us all, and for Palm Beach."

Jo-Anne's lip curled in condescension as she left fly the arrow. It was Pearl Harbor. The crucial element of surprise. All who were present at the opening skirmish of the war agreed later that Jo-Anne had been victorious. "My dear Marjorie, where on earth did you get that absolutely *dreadful* dress? The Church Mouse or that other little leukemia thrift shop in West Palm?"

Later opinions differed as to the nature of Marjorie du Pont Donahue's expression as the verbal missile struck home. Some said her mouth dropped open and her eyes widened. There were others, however, who told a different story. Some went for malice rather than surprise. A few for incredulous humor, at least one for a hint of tears. As always when momentous events occur unexpectedly, the reported details got blurred, but, strangely, most observers agreed on the substance of what had actually been said.

"What did you say?" had been the initial response as Marjorie had played for time to regain her composure.

Jo-Anne had just smiled back at her, enjoying the confusion.

Marjorie, however, was not the queen for nothing. In a split second she had seen it all. This was a palace revolution. A courtier had become too powerful, too successful, and was making a play for her title. It had happened before, but it always came with the element of surprise. Jo-Anne had been a favorite. Et tu, Brute? Damn. She had allowed herself to become too complacent, to be lulled by the flattery, to believe in her own P.R. That was how empires fell, as ancient rulers lost their grip and fell into bad habits, allowing the cutting edges of their swords to become blunted, the strength of their sword arms to wane.

She knew immediately that she had been badly wounded. This was all happening before a big audience, and deep down every single one of them wanted her to fall on her face. She had laid herself wide open by not anticipating the threat. She had given politeness and enthusiasm and received open hostility in return. That made her look weak and ingratiating. And any comeback now would be of necessity contrived and artless. Yet she would have to respond.

The ancient neurons worked at high speed as she sifted through her most potent armament—her global information system. "My dear Jo-Anne, I'm surprised you think I shop in West Palm. I haven't even thought of the place for years, although lately friends have been saying I ought to go and check out some gymnasium run by a very close friend of your husband's. Lisa Starr I think she's called."

She made the most of the "very close friend."

It wasn't the best she had ever done, but in the circumstances it was creditable.

But Jo-Anne was impervious to insult and insinuation. She was flying high on an adrenaline surge. Already she could see the admiration and wonder creeping around the mouths of the younger observers.

"God, Marjorie, you mustn't go anywhere near Lisa Starr's gym. At your advanced age you'd almost certainly drop down dead, and we'd all have to get out those dreary little black dresses for the funeral."

As she turned her back and walked away, Jo-Anne wondered if anybody would walk with her. Mary d'Erlanger was still by her side. So was Pauline Bismarck, and one of the Boardman girls. The queen would forgive none of them. They were bound to Jo-Anne at the hip. The Palm Beach wars had begun.

LISA POWERED the vintage 1966 Ford Mustang across the Southern Boulevard bridge. It had been her present to herself. Some small compensation for the collapse of her future. Charlie Stark from Mustang Paradise had picked it out at a bank foreclosure sale. It had been a bargain then at six thousand dollars, but her old friend had sharpened it up at no extra charge. Red leather upholstery, immaculate bright white body work, thin black stripes strategically placed to mark the aerodynamic flow of the wind. The expensive Sony sound system was tuned as always to the Country K and Emmylou Harris was telling the world it was going to be all right in her dreams. Well, for sure she was the lucky one. In Lisa's dreams things looked about as bleak as a nuclear winter.

Until last night's telephone call, that is.

The accent of the caller had been the purest of prep. Female. In her thirties. "I am calling on behalf of Mrs. Marjorie Donahue, for whom I work as social secretary. Mrs. Donahue has asked me to say that she has heard a great deal about you from mutual friends and would very much like to meet you. Would you be available at around eleven o'clock tomorrow morning?"

Like the offer from a godfather, it was not one that could be refused. Nor did Lisa want to refuse it. A royal command appearance. It just had to be significant. But what did it mean? What would the mighty Mrs. du Pont Donahue want with her? Hardly a course of aerobic instruction! Whatever, Lisa had agreed there and then. Somebody else could take her class. Yes, most certainly, she would be at the Bath and Tennis Club at eleven o'clock sharp.

She eased the convertible across the roundabout and through the gates of the B and T. It was the first time she had been through the portals of the Palm Beach social Mecca, but then the air was thick with "firsts" these days. Thank God the awful sickness seemed to have passed. Throwing up on the floor of one of Palm Beach's grandest clubs would score no points at all.

The bellhop who parked her car liked it as much as he liked its driver. But why the hell did everybody know she wasn't a fully paid-up member of the Palm Beach ruling class? Lisa would bet a hundred bucks he didn't wink at a Vanderbilt. Through the doors and up the steps, and the first hurdle. The lady with the severe glasses at the reception desk looked about as welcoming as a starved Doberman Pinscher. Like the parking attendant she seemed to have advance warning that Lisa didn't "belong."

"How can I help you, ma'am?" The tone was not nearly as deferential as the words implied. There was a definite note of irritability there, and a touch of mockery about the "ma'am." Christ! Was she wearing her "other side of the tracks" sign? Were the words flashing in neon across her chest? What was the matter with the open-necked cotton shirt and matching mid-calf-length skirt? She'd purposefully given the blue jeans a miss.

"I have an appointment to meet Mrs. Donahue here at eleven."

The words "open sesame" could scarcely have had greater impact. In the haughty receptionist there was a breathless change. Usually when strangers stated their name and business she would peer maddeningly at the crumpled pieces of paper in front of her as she pretended to look for the name of the visitor on some mythical list. That little charade could reduce even the most self-confident visitor to a twitching heap of groveling uncertainty as he or she contemplated the possibility of the oversight that could lead to instant rejection.

"Ah, Mrs. Donahue's guest. Of course, of course. Miss Starr. We've been expecting you. If you wouldn't mind just waiting here a minute, I'll call through to Mrs. Donahue's cabana and have somebody come down to pick you up." She spoke quickly into the telephone.

Within what seemed like seconds Lisa was following a Lilly Pulitzer wraparound skirt through the long green-carpeted corridor off the B and T main drag. A right turn took them out to the Olympic-size pool, its clear blue water sparkling like Evian. Delicately they threaded their way through the studious millionaire sunbathers as they picked over the by now bare bones of the previous night's party. In Palm Beach midnight was Cinderella time, and that allowed an early start the next day.

Up some stairs carpeted with Astroturf, a left turn along a balcony, and they had arrived. The Donahue cabana, or rather cabanas, were a completely different world. Lisa couldn't know of the years of political infighting that had allowed them to be so. The essence of a Palm Beach club was that within it all members were treated equally while collectively being able to look down their noses at outsiders. It hadn't been enough for Marjorie Donahue, who considered equality to be the enemy of her own excellence. So when she had asked the committee to allow her to knock three cabanas into one, they had refused. Over the next few years of social bloodletting, thirty percent of the committee had eventually been replaced by Donahue lapdogs. She had gotten her way. "If one can't have one's way over little things like that, then there's no point in having any influence in this town," she was fond of saying. She never referred to herself as the queen.

Lisa could hardly believe it. The green synthetic-grass-look-alike floor covering had been replaced with black and white marble, checkered like a chessboard. It was not impossible to imagine the floor being laid out, after lunch, perhaps, with social pawns, bishops, and knights as the queen herself dictated the play—the courtiers hopping lightly from square to square as they demolished the opposition. Black and white was clearly the theme of the décor. There were black-and-white awnings, black-and-white zebra-skin rugs, black-and-white coverings on the sofas and chairs. On the walls were the most extraordinary black-and-white paintings, in which twisted faces and scenes of dreadful carnage figured prominently. They looked vaguely familiar to Lisa.

Marjorie du Pont Donahue lay like a Dugong on a black-and-white terry-covered chaise longue basking in the direct sunlight. Clearly she was used to it. She looked like a raisin, a dried-up prune—black and baked by the years of exposure to the ultraviolet rays. There was not an inch of her body visible whose elasticity had not been eaten up by the sunlight, and any moisture or liquid that her skin contained quite obviously came out of bottles. Cactuslike, she could have existed for days out alone in the Sahara. Effortlessly she would have been the survivor on an unsheltered life raft after the shipwreck. She disproved by her very existence the link between sunbathing and skin cancer. Around her three or four women rushed about like roaches as they scurried and crept from the sunlight, hiding under huge hats and judiciously positioned parasols.

Lisa stood there and took it all in. Marjorie Donahue was talking on a white telephone. She had signaled for Lisa to wait. Nobody spoke while the queen spoke.

"Yes, Fran. The most extraordinary behavior. In all my years in this town I've never heard anything like it. One always gave poor Jo-Anne the benefit of the doubt with regard to her background—for Peter's sake as much as anything, but I am afraid this marriage to Stansfield has taken the lid off the can of worms. What was the name of that nice young man who always maintained he had seen her "perform" at some bachelor party up North? I am afraid I was rather harsh on him. I fear now he might have been right all the time. I'm sure we should all put him back on our party lists. I should tell you he's certainly back on mine. Yes, my dear, you're quite right. That's the point. What are we all going to do about it? Well, I'm sure the very first thing is for us all to cancel our tables at that ball she's running for the leukemia people. I think that between us we can guarantee that party will be the non-event of the year. I suppose it's a bit hard on the cancer people, but personally I'm going to make an anonymous donation to their central fund to make up for it. I don't think she'll be getting any ball chairmanships after *that*. Oh, yes, Fran, and I want you and your crowd to come to the drinks party I'm giving next week for Eleanor Peacock. *Such* a wonderful person, Eleanor, don't you think? Yes, dear, I do so agree. Such a *good* friend." As she spoke Marjorie stared hard at Lisa, who got the message loud and clear. This telephone conversation was in part directed at her.

"Good, darling. Marvelous. I knew I could count on you. You're a wonderful friend, Fran. In fact, the more I come to think of it, they should have asked you to do the leukemia thing in the first place. Let's see what we can do about that next year. Yes, I'm sure we could fix that up. No, you'd be perfect. A great pleasure. Yes, darling. And be sure to pass the word, won't you? I don't want any of our friends at that party of Jo-Anne's. I can't think that anybody who shows up will have any future in this town. None at all. All right, sweetheart. Bye, darling."

She banged the telephone down, a look of triumph on her face.

"Put Fran Dudley down on the 'definitely with us' list," she barked at a pale girl wielding a large yellow legal pad.

Once again the gimlet eyes fastened onto Lisa. "How very nice of you to come, Miss Starr. Your fame has spread across Lake Worth, and I wanted to meet you so that I should know firsthand who everybody is talking about."

There was a twinkle in the eyes. It was as clear as the sunlight that beat down on her tortured body that Marjorie Donahue was motivated by something more than just curiosity.

Lisa, whose training on the streets of West Palm as a child had taught her a thing or two about human nature, was beginning to get the drift. Marjorie Donahue and Jo-Anne Stansfield had, for some as yet unknown reason, fallen out in a substantial way. The cabana already resembled some command bunker in the front line. Reinforcements were being mobilized on the telephone, aides-de-camp were taking notes. It had the look of a pretty substantial operation. Somehow this cunning old fox had learned of Lisa's feelings about Jo-Anne. Most likely she knew too about Lisa's recent relationship with Bobby. Was it possible she even knew about the child? She had kept it secret from everyone except Maggie. But doctors at the Good Sam knew . . . and nurses . . . and presumably secretaries . . . maybe cleaners. Lisa didn't care, for in the back of her mind a particularly wonderful picture was beginning to form. In it she saw the beginnings of the most beautiful alliance. A friendship with Marjorie Donahue based on the total destruction of Jo-Anne Stansfield. It was exactly what she needed. With the Donahue protection she would possess an asset with which she could walk through the gates of hell unafraid. The queen's protégée would swim without a backward glance through the predator-infested Palm Beach waters, and she needed to do that before she could even contemplate the achievement of what had become her life's ambition—to revenge herself on the Stansfields who had so hurt and humiliated her.

"It's a great honor to meet you, Mrs. Donahue," said Lisa as she walked over to take the gnarled hand. Marjorie Donahue cocked her head to one side as she sized her up. Stunningly attractive. An open smile. Self-confident, yet sufficiently deferential. She would make a promising ally. Yes, a great deal could be done with this girl. Really, a very great deal.

"I'm surprised our paths haven't crossed before, Lisa. At the Stansfield wedding yesterday, for instance. It seems we have so many mutual friends."

Again Marjorie looked quizzical as she attempted to read the effect of her words in Lisa's eyes. That she and Bobby Stansfield had had an affair was common knowledge. How it had ended was not. It was far from impossible, however, to speculate on how things might have become unstuck. A young girl with more enthusiasm than experience caught in the spider's web of the Stansfield charm. A beautiful young innocent who had underestimated the power and cunning of a scheming rival. After all, Marjorie herself could still feel the mark of Jo-Anne's dagger between her shoulder blades. This girl would have had no chance at all.

Lisa stood her ground, but said nothing. There would be more cards laid on the table. Her eyes began to sparkle as she thought of what might happen.

"Yes," Marjorie continued reflectively. "So many mutual friends who go to your gym. I say they're committing aerobicide." She laughed a jolly laugh in which Lisa joined.

Any minute now it would come. Marjorie seemed to be talking almost to herself. "And possibly we may have shared enemies."

Suddenly the air was thick with the aroma of conspiracy, the sense of common purpose overpowering. Lisa knew she had been propositioned. It wouldn't be spelled out any clearer than this. She had to give some sign that she had accepted the terms of the alliance.

"I'd like to think that I see people the same way that you do, Mrs. Donahue."

But it was Lisa's expression more than her words that told Marjorie Donahue what she had wanted to hear.

One thing was crystal clear. This perfect-looking girl had learned how to hate. It was more than likely that Jo-Anne had taught her.

It was time for a little small talk, before the telephone marathon continued once more as the troops were summoned to do battle, and the social I.O.U.'s were called in. "Good, good, Lisa. Now tell me, what do you think of the throbbing heart of Palm Beach?" She flung out a scrawny arm to indicate her surroundings, the pool, the club, the people who inhabited them.

Lisa, whose mind was full of stimulating visions of fire and brimstone falling all over her enemies, was caught temporarily off guard. "I think these paintings are very interesting," she managed at last.

"Supposed to be Goya. His black period, you know. Aren't they wonderfully gloomy? Quite mad when he painted them. I just love depressing art, don't you? So uplifting. Of course they're all fakes. Everything I ever buy seems to turn out to be a fake in the end. One of the disadvantages of being so terribly rich. Not that I mind anymore. In fact, it's rather fun. I sold a Renoir I didn't like the other day, and it turned out to be genuine. For two whole weeks I was walking on air. Never would have gotten such a charge out of it if I didn't always expect the worst."

Lisa laughed at the cheerful irreverence and was at the same time awed by the vast wealth that allowed it. It was a side of Marjorie Donahue she had not imagined would exist. This old girl was formidable, but it seemed like she was fun, too.

"I'm afraid I've never been able to afford to buy a painting." The way Lisa said it didn't sound at all self-pitying.

"Ah, Lisa. When I was your age I'd never bought one either. But let me tell you something, my dear, and remember what I say . . . you will, you will."

It seemed to Lisa as much a promise as a prediction.

The audience was clearly at an end, but not the relationship. "Anyway, Lisa, I've very much enjoyed meeting you, as I imagined I would, which brings me to something else. I wondered if you would like to join my party to the first night of the new Neil Simon play at the Poinciana Theater. We all go on to dinner at Capriccio afterward. Cocktails at my house at six thirty sharp. Nothing dressy."

That was it. Passport to paradise. Multiple reentry visa to the Palm Beach inner sanctum. Lisa didn't have to ask where she lived. She could have walked there blindfolded. But it was with something close to desperation that she contemplated the "nothing dressy." She had been caught like that before. Where the hell in West Palm did you rent a tiara?

~ 12 ~

*I*T WAS ONLY the second time that Lisa had met Vernon Blass, but already she was beginning to warm to him. The first meeting, at the Donahue dinner party, had not been a success. During the cold Madras soup he had ogled her shamelessly, scarcely bothering to reply to her attempts at conversation. Over the broiled grouper he had propositioned her with all the delicacy of a New York taxi driver, and in response to her haughty and disdainful refusal, he had bided his time before plunging his hand between her legs as they prepared to attack the orange sorbet. Lisa had been appalled, not so much at his behavior, as at the fact that a seventy-one-year-old Palm Beacher of the most impeccable social credentials could stoop so low. On more mature reflection she had come to the conclusion that it wasn't so strange. JoAnne Duke, Bobby Stansfield, and now this Vernon Blass. It began to look as if her mother's P.R. had been the bummest of bum steers. She had delighted him, and incidentally her host, by responding in no-nonsense fashion. Without thinking twice she had emptied her gelatinous water ice into his lap, where for several blissful seconds it had clung to the immaculate navy-blue trousers in the region of his fly, its intense cold symbolically cooling his misplaced ardor.

From that moment on, his attitude toward her had changed dramatically. No longer did he see her as a cheap and cheerful import from the other side of the tracks who might provide some scratching for the endless itch that plagued him. The girl had spirit to go with the dangerously attractive body that so excited him. And, apparently, she had for some reason the most powerful of friends. As he had attempted to remove the sticky dessert from between his legs Marjorie du Pont Donahue had pitched into him, using humor and ridicule as her weapons.

"Lisa Starr, *now* I know where you got your marvelous name," she had boomed across the table so that everybody in the crowded Capriccio restaurant could hear. "I've been telling Vernon he should have an operation on that prostate gland of his for ages. If he'd have the damn thing out he might be able to keep his fingers to himself."

793

Vernon had joined in the general laughter at his expense. In part this was because it was almost a reflex action to laugh at Marjorie's jokes, but there was another reason. All his life he had been a bully. His immensely successful father had taught him that. Rich and pampered, he had been the classical spoiled only child, and the years that had passed hadn't changed that one iota. Most people he needed he had bought, and those he didn't need or couldn't buy he had avoided. To be confronted by a girl like Lisa, who had dared to stand up to him at considerable social risk to herself, was refreshing in the extreme. For the rest of the evening he had poured his not inconsiderable charm all over her and by its end he had been forgiven. Over the next few days he had found himself thinking of her all the time—so much so that he had called up Marjorie Donahue and requested a rematch.

This was it.

In the Donahue box at the Palm Beach Polo Club the Pimms was flowing free, and the atmosphere matched the fizzy, colorful drink. Lisa was thoroughly enjoying herself, and *that* was a relief. It had been a bad four months. Growing a child on a diet of hate didn't make for happy days. Still, there had been compensations, and most of them were called Marjorie Donahue. Since the meeting at the Bath and Tennis she had taken a rocket trip into the social stratosphere, and now, like Major Tom, she had almost lost touch with ground control. It had started with the gym. The queen had spoken, and, kamikazelike, the Palm Beach high flyers had responded, taking out memberships in droves. Lisa had kept the lists open to take them and was already negotiating for a lease on the adjoining building. Her stock was rising in every way.

"The thing to remember about polo handicaps is that it's the opposite of golf. The higher the better. That little fella hitting the ball now, is called Alonso Montoya. He's one of the only two ten-handicap players in the country." Vernon Blass leaned in toward Lisa as he spoke. For the past half an hour he had been teaching her the intricacies of polo, pointing out the superb horsemanship, the dangerous and illegal plays, providing biographies of the players seasoned with spicy details of their off-field activities.

"The Argentinians are the best. No doubt at all. And off the field they make love to anything in a skirt as long as it's got money in the bank. They'll go anywhere for a free meal, eat you out of house and home, and knock off your wife and daughter when you go to the men's room."

Lisa laughed. She had the measure of Blass now. He was a dirty old man, but at least he was an amusing one. She liked the way he dressed, too: the Panama hat from Lock's in St. James's, the worn but immaculate white linen suit, the faded, blue-spotted bow tie, the glasslike brown brogues.

"What about those two Englishmen? The Wentworths. I think I rather like the look of them," Lisa joked.

"My dear Lisa. Promise me—whatever you do, never go to bed with an Englishman," he intoned in mock horror. "They don't wash, it takes two minutes if you're unlucky, and afterward they're so proud of themselves they expect applause and a letter of thanks in triplicate they can show to their friends."

Lisa wagged a finger at him. "I hope you didn't find that out firsthand, Vernon."

It was Vernon's turn to laugh. "Never succumbed to the temptation. Mind you, it's been offered once or twice. Something to do with all those public schools, I believe."

Lisa looked around. The stand was packed for the final of the Piaget World Cup, and it looked as if everyone were there. Jo-Anne? Bobby? It seemed such an age since her first visit, when she had played Cinderella, dressed in rags at Jo-Anne's request. God, how naive she had been. Even then, while her husband was still alive, Jo-Anne Duke had been sabotaging the competition. Had she wanted Bobby then? With the benefit of hindsight it seemed far from impossible.

"Come on, Vernon. Tell me who all these people are. Who's that incredible-looking guy with the earring?"

"That's Jim Kimberly. He's my age—seventy-one, going on seventeen. His family founded Kimberly-Clark, so each time you blow your pretty little nose in a Kleenex you make Jim a cent or two richer. Poor old Jim's had a bit of trouble lately. He married a child bride, Jacquie—the one who starred in the Pulitzer divorce. She's just left him. There wasn't another man. She moved into the guest house, the one King Hussein owns, with the housekeeper!"

Vernon Blass's eyes were rolling at her again. The Kimberly marriage seemed to have set off a dangerous thought process.

"Now, now Vernon. Don't make me put the Pimms where the orange ice went."

A large blond woman shouted over from a neighboring box. "Vernon, you rat. Now I know why you skipped my lunch party. Don't you ever stop? Why don't you give in gracefully and let the younger men have a try?"

"Who is that?" whispered Lisa as Vernon Blass waved cheerfully, acknowledging the compliment.

"Sue Whitmore, the Listerine Queen. After you've wiped off your Estée Lauder makeup with one of Jim's Kleenexes you can have a crack at the halitosis with some of Sue's mouthwash. Sometimes I wonder what the rest of America would do without the inhabitants of this town."

"Thanks a lot, but I don't *have* halitosis," laughed Lisa.

"Prove it," said Vernon with a chuckle, lunging in toward her.

"Vernon, are you molesting my adopted daughter again?"

Lisa heard the music play within her. It was all coming together. All the loose ends. Now she was Marjorie Donahue's "adopted daughter," and this cheerful old lecher with his publishing company and his magnificent house on South Ocean Boulevard was eating out of her hand. And she smiled to herself grimly as she thought what she would do with her newfound power.

THIS WAS more like it. Lisa hadn't looked at the price tag yet. She was already learning that that tended to spoil the fun, but the dress was one of the most exciting things she had ever seen. It could have been made for her, apart from its understandable failure to accommodate her rapidly growing breasts. All morning she had traipsed around the "acceptable" Worth Avenue shops with Marjorie. She had been patronized by middle-aged matrons posing as shop assistants in the spacious marble halls of Martha's as she had tried on beautifully tailored dresses from Valentino and Geoffrey Beene. Later, in the Ralph Lauren boutique, which was Marjorie's idea of "young fun," she had been patronized by uniformed preppies as they went through the motions of selling the goods.

In desperation she had gone into Saint Laurent's Rive Gauche where the conspiracy to turn her into a forty-year-old had achieved mammoth proportions and she had been patronized by a French comtesse whose elegant fingers had plucked and picked at her as if she were merchandise at a Roman slave market. The Krizia shop in the Esplanade had provided an oasis of style and originality. The clothes were her age, daring, provocative. There was no built-in safety in the label, no passport to acceptance by the casual dropping of the designer name; only the truly avant garde knew all about Krizia, and when you were wearing one of their eye-catching creations you were out there on your own.

Lisa twirled in front of the long mirror. On paper, the dress didn't look like much. Hundreds of white plastic disks meticulously sewed together, mid-calf length, slit up the side to the thigh. A matching top, the generous slice of bronzed breast, the occasional sight of the already darkening pregnant nipple. God, it looked good. God, *she* looked good. Lisa smiled at her reflection. Marjorie, perched uncomfortably outside on some sharp edge, longing for the comfortable sofas and deferential homage of Martha's, would loathe it. They had had such a funny morning.

Since the meeting at the B and T, they had become close friends. Lisa had soon learned the measure of the tricky old socialite and had discovered the goldmine of her sense of humor. You couldn't hold back on the flattery, but if you looked around there were enough genuine things to flatter. No, the real point about Marjorie was that she was an anarchist at heart. Irreverence for everything and anything, her own person strictly excluded, was what she liked. In response to Lisa's anguished plea to be allowed to look her age, Marjorie Donahue had replied with world-weary wisdom that anyone under forty should be heard but not seen.

"Listen, darling," she had said. "It's difficult enough in this town to keep one's age under reasonable control, especially when one's nephews and nieces all need facelifts. The last thing we need is teeny-boppers with tits."

Well, this teeny-bopper's tits were available for the world to see. Thank God her stomach was still flat as a board. The unfortunate child must be paper thin in there, crushed by the iron wall of her ceaselessly exercised abdominal muscles. Praying that there would be no males in the shop to catch the potent visuals, Lisa shot out of the changing room with the high-powered velocity of a model hitting the catwalk at a Kenzo show.

Straight into Bobby Stansfield's arms.

For the split second that he was just a person, a man who had gotten lucky, she began to mumble her apology. It stopped when she saw the blue eyes and felt the strong arms on her shoulders, when she smelled the familiar smell of him, remembered the mind-bending taste of him. That was the part that came first. Apparently, for both of them. The first few bars were the New York Philharmonic on a good day, the music pure, clean, crisp, clear. On the waves of sound were borne the scent of the Caribbean night air, the moonlight's soft touch on the clear waters of the pool, the joyful cry of ecstasy as their baby had been created. Then, as if the conductor had tired capriciously of the beautiful harmonies, the music was sweet no more. It didn't stop suddenly. Instead it degenerated, falling apart bit by bit into cacophonous discord and, as Lisa's mind's ear heard the terrible words once again, she recoiled from him, pushing him away from her, tearing her eyes from his.

"Lisa."

Politicians weren't supposed to be lost for words. They were meant to be unflappable, suave, and urbane in the most trying of circumstances. The public demanded it. But Bobby was on the verge of losing his cool. Behind him somewhere was Jo-Anne, who could be expected to view Lisa about as favorably as a hole in a Renoir, and yet he was seized by an all but uncontrollable desire to run after her, to take her in his arms once again, to tell her he hadn't wanted it to end in the way that it had, to dare to hope that what was past had not ended a possible future. In short Bobby was in turmoil.

There was another problem. The logistics of the situation posed all sorts of potential difficulties. The Krizia boutique was in fact a cul-de-sac joined to a larger area by the narrow corridor that contained the two changing rooms and in which he and Lisa had just inadvertently embraced. Jo-Anne was hard on his heels, only having missed the emotion-laden meeting by seconds. Unless they turned back some sort of confrontation was now inevitable.

Marjorie Donahue stood up awkwardly from her cramped seat on the window ledge as Lisa cascaded into the room. Wise in the ways of the world, she saw immediately that the dress was no longer the point. Lisa was white as a sheet and, a second or two later as Bobby Stansfield loomed over her shoulder, she could see why. But her mind didn't stop there. Bobby Stansfield would not be cruising Worth Avenue dress shops by himself. Any minute now there would be Jo-Anne. A moment later there was.

The minimal advance warning allowed Marjorie Donahue the substantial advantage of first service.

"My, my, the Stansfields on a shopping expedition," she warbled. "How nice to see the two of you out and about. I thought you'd given up going out altogether, Jo-Anne. I never seem to see you at the parties anymore."

Marjorie's social blockade of Jo-Anne had been a conspicuous success. Her invitations had dried up like a fly's wings under a blowtorch as the queen had passed the word that she would not attend any party at which Jo-Anne Stansfield was present, and that she would never invite to her house a hostess who had allowed her through the front door. Within days Jo-Anne had discovered the full extent of her catastrophic miscalculation. Nobody of any importance had rallied to her banner, and those that had had rapidly been made to see the error of their ways. Cleverly Marjorie had outflanked her, concluding alliances with Jo-Anne's initial supporters and offering them a free pardon in exchange for the renewal of their allegiance. It had been a lightning campaign in which no mercy had been shown, and the few revolutionaries who had stayed loyal to Jo-Anne were now themselves outcasts, puttering about on the fringes of Palm Beach society.

To Jo-Anne it was a bit like being mugged from behind in church. She stopped dead in her tracks as the verbal missile snaked out toward her and could only watch in disbelief as it exploded in an air burst over her position. Lisa Starr, standing next to her arch enemy, looked good enough to eat, and her husband's eyes were registering that fact for all the world to see. And Marjorie Donahue was spitting venom from a position of unchallenged strength. There were few things on earth she needed less than that. Thank the Lord it was a small audience. There surely wasn't much else to thank Him for.

"Oh, Marjorie, you know how it is. Small-town politics are so provincial once you've had some experience of the big time. There's a whole world out there. You Palm Beachers are inclined to forget that."

Damn it to hell. If only she could *feel* that. It sounded so sensible, but without the emotion it was as transparent as a glass-bottom boat over the Pennekamp Reef.

"My word, Jo-Anne, it begins to sound as if you and Bobby are beginning to think of moving on. Back to New York, perhaps. One gathers you had a fairly 'colorful' upbringing there. Should be excellent for Bobby's political career."

Jo-Anne turned toward Bobby. It was about time he joined in the battle. After all, his wife had as good as been called a hooker who would destroy his political career. His "putdown" would have to be pretty neat to pull the bacon out of this fire.

But Bobby wasn't really listening. He was staring at Lisa as if he were a prep-school boy at his first strip show, and it wasn't just lust in his eyes. Jo-Anne felt the anger and irritation well up within her. What had happened to everybody? Had they all gone mad? Wasn't *she* the one with the pot of gold that made Croesus look like small time, with the body electric that could light men up like a beacon?

"Oh no, Marjorie, we wouldn't dream of *leaving*. But just because one has a house or two on the island, and the boat's here sometimes, it doesn't mean one *lives* here. Of course it's different for you. An old leopard can't change its spots, can it? But we just don't want to fall into the trap of thinking that the sun rises and sets in Palm Beach. That's all."

Marjorie Donahue changed tack. This was just too good to miss. "Bobby,

I was going to introduce you to my good friend Lisa Starr, but I can see from the look on your face that you've met her already. Isn't she just the prettiest girl you've ever seen?" She turned and shot a triumphant look at Jo-Anne.

"Yes, she is," said Bobby simply, turning his wife into an instant enemy. He knew what he was doing, and suddenly, he didn't mind. The hell with it. Lisa *was* the prettiest girl he had ever seen, and he didn't care who knew it. He was already fast tiring of his wife's ludicrous social ambitions. The words she had just been uttering expressed sentiments with which he heartily agreed. Who needed Palm Beach high society when one could be top dog of the whole Western world? But Jo-Anne had caught the Palm Beach bug and the disease looked to be fatal. She was a big girl now, and up to a point he didn't care what she did as long as it wasn't an embarrassment to him, but he was damned if he was going to be drawn into her spider webs. He had better things to do. Like looking at Lisa.

Jo-Anne had had quite enough. That was *it*. Damn Marjorie. Damn Lisa, and most of all damn Bobby. What an asshole! He had dropped her right in it at the moment when she had most needed his support. He'd never get a chance to do that again. And he'd be wiser to give up water skiing.

"Come on, Bobby, we're late. Let's go." She might just as well have run up the white flag. As she retreated she threw a parting shot over her shoulder.

"Love the dress, Lisa. But maybe you should think about having a breast reduction."

Outside on the terra-cotta tiles of the crowded Esplanade, Jo-Anne could keep it inside no longer. It was years since she had been humiliated like that, and the whole point of her enormously successful struggle toward riches beyond avarice's dreams had been to avoid such situations. The man she had married, the man who had been happy enough to share her bed, her body, and her mighty fortune, had stood by while her enemy had walked all over her and hadn't attempted to lift a finger. Worse, he had stared at the girl who had been his former lay as if all he wanted were for her to be his future one, and then had more or less admitted it in front of Jo-Anne.

"You filthy piece of shit," she screamed at the top of her voice. "How dare you treat me like that!"

Bobby's head shot back as if he had been hit on the jaw with a baseball bat. Hey, this was public! The political training flashed the danger signals, as he moved to contain the potentially damaging situation.

"Come on, Jo-Anne. You're overreacting, honey." He reached out for her forearm, as he saw a blue rinse and her portly husband stop and go into recognition mode. "Isn't that Senator Stansfield?" mouthed the pinched lips as, like a fairground lip reader, Bobby picked up the soundless message.

"Don't 'honey' me, you filthy pervert. Save it for when you're going down on that whore in there."

Jo-Anne's voice was now shrill and loud. Any minute now it would be a high-pitched scream. Bobby prayed as he thought of the information being fed into the wire services. Even now some bum was probably running to look for a telephone. Out of the corner of his eye he saw the crowd beginning to form like the concentric rings of a pearl growing from a grain of sand. The couple who had recognized him were now firmly rooted to the spot, all thought of continuation on their journey abandoned as they contemplated the delicious domestic accident they had stumbled across.

Bobby wondered briefly whether he could get away with slapping her. It might put out the fire before too much damage had been done, but then again it might be the equivalent of pouring kerosene over it. And zapping a woman in front of an audience, especially when the woman was your wife, tended to be a political no-no.

"Jo-Anne, you're being unreasonable. Let's discuss this at home." Once again he attempted to get hold of her arm to steer her toward the stairs.

" 'Discuss this at home.' What home? Do you mean that miserable mausoleum you occasionally come back to sleep in?"

The oohs and aahs whistled around like the wind in the willows. This was food and drink to the handful of tourists and shoppers who now stood two or three deep about the famous couple. The words "Senator Stansfield" and "wife" were now clearly audible. In his mind Bobby was already reading the news story. SENATOR IN FURIOUS PUBLIC ROW WITH WIFE. ACCUSED. OF ADULTERY. WIFE SAYS SENATOR A PERVERT. NEWLYWEDS LET IT ALL HANG OUT. A bit like the time Senator Ted Kennedy had left his weekend girlfriend stranded at West Palm International as he and an aide took the only two remaining seats to New York. The lady had not been pleased and had said so in public. Next day, Middle America had devoured the blow-by-blow account.

It was beginning to look as if he had miscalculated. Jo-Anne was unstable. If she could behave like this now, what the hell might she do on the campaign trail when the press would know how many times she changed her underwear? And what about her past? He had been so taken with the money he had ignored that, and turned down Baker's request for an "in-depth" investigation. Certainly the odd rumor had surfaced that suggested there were creepy-crawlies under the stone. Marjorie Donahue's most recent remark about a "colorful upbringing" was a case in point.

Bobby cut short the postmortem. The pressing consideration was how to dampen this thing down. Later he could make plans. Isolate Jo-Anne. Keep her under wraps. He could start to lead a much more separate life. Base himself in Washington and leave Jo-Anne to play her Palm Beach games on her own.

"Jo-Anne, you don't know what you're saying. I know you haven't been feeling well. Calm down." He knew as he spoke that he hadn't found the right button.

"Not feeling well. Not feeling well," screamed Jo-Anne like some demented parrot, as she searched her mind for the most damaging words. "How could anybody feel well with your stinking child inside them. Christ! If the poor little bastard's anything like you and your lecherous old father, he'll probably spend all his days in the state pen as a sex offender."

The red mist sprang up in front of Bobby Stansfield's eyes. More than anything else in the world he wanted to hit her, but he was enough of a politician to know the fatal effect of that, and wise enough, too, to know that it was just what Jo-Anne wanted him to do. The *Daily News* would say something like, SENATOR K.O.'S WIFE IN SHOPPING MALL. The others would dress it up a bit, but the effect would be the same. So he held on to the rage that bubbled within him as he vowed there and then to wipe Jo-Anne out of his life. He would not divorce her, but as a partner she was history. All his life he had dreamed of the presidency. He had given up everything for it. Nothing, no one, would stand in his way.

With bitter determination he turned away from his spitting wife and elbowed a passage through the small crowd.

IT HADN'T been the easiest of births. On examination, Lisa's hips had looked more than all right. Fetal skull measurements showed that the baby should sail through the birth canal with colors flying, but it hadn't happened like that at all. From the very beginnings Scott had proved a difficult individual. For a start he had decided to meet the world bottom first. For an encore he had gotten stuck fast in Lisa's pelvis like a too-new cork in a too-young bottle of wine.

The wrestling match that had followed had left Lisa as flat as a pancake, and propped up against the pillows in the private room of the Good Samaritan hospital, she looked as if she had gone ten rounds with Doctor Death. All around her the flowers competed for the oxygen, and they were just the tip of the floral iceberg. Palm Beach had emptied its shops of everything that was colored and alive, and there was hardly a patient in the hospital who hadn't benefited from the excess of well-wishing enthusiasm.

Lisa was under no illusions about all this. The reason for her popularity sat in the corner of the simple room, looking a bit like an expensive scarecrow in Adam and Eve's garden. Everyone who mattered knew the score. Lisa Starr was Marjorie du Pont Donahue's protégée and confidante. Some even used the words "crown princess." To ignore the birth of her illegitimate child would be an oversight that could turn the social ladder into a water slide to oblivion for the careless climber. Few had taken the chance, and they had been right not to. Marjorie Donahue had written the names of every flower sender in a little black book, much to Lisa's amusement.

"It may seem a little thing, Lisa," she had said. "But if you catch disrespect early, it's so much easier to nip it in the bud."

Lisa had laughed again, but she had gotten the point. In this life you couldn't be too careful if you wanted to get anywhere. You had to be ceaselessly on your guard, constantly attending to detail if you wanted to make things happen for you.

She looked down at the baby in her arms, and for the thousandth time tried to discover what she felt about him. He was kind of cute. Very little. Perfectly formed. Delicate, of course. Sort of dependent, and rather charming for that. In vain she tried to get past the clichés. There was a sense of having produced something, of having done something worthwhile, but there ought to be more . . . much more. Maybe it was just too soon. Did they call it the baby blues? But she didn't feel blue, just tired and very sore, and a bit empty. She smiled to herself at the thought of emptiness. That was really crass. The sort of thing people said on the TV soaps. "How do you feel, Mary-Lou?" "Empty, Craig. So *desperately* empty."

She allowed herself to think of the child's father. That was better. Firmer ground. Real emotions. The bastard and his bitch wife. What an incredible, unbelievable, hysterical coincidence that Jo-Anne should be in the room along the corridor teetering on the brink of labor. Two little Bobby Stansfields popping from neighboring pods with scarcely a day between them. It was a great big black joke. Funny and sick at the same time. Hers to all the world a fatherless child, while Jo-Anne's would be as legitimate as the Supreme Court, instantly rich and instantly famous as it choked on its silver spoon. Little Scott Starr, who would never be able to use the Stansfield name that meant so much in the world in which he would live.

Again Lisa permitted herself a bittersweet smile. On that extraordinarily convoluted plant, the nurses' grapevine, she had heard that Jo-Anne's room was as empty as hers was full. Even her husband hadn't bothered to visit. Bobby Stansfield. Okay, so he couldn't know about Scott, but surely he could have looked in on his wife. In the fatherhood stakes he rated top for virility but one great big zero for everything that mattered. Not that Jo-Anne deserved any better. She had gotten what she wanted. Now she would have to learn to like what she'd gotten. All the money in the world and no friends to send flowers. Married to a superstar, and yet with no love. Possessing the body of an angel and yet devoid of heart and soul. It was a topsy-turvy world as God played with his dice, taking with one hand as he gave with the other.

"A penny for your thoughts," said Marjorie.

Lisa sighed. "Oh, Marjorie, I don't know anymore. I was just thinking about Bobby and little Scott, and Jo-Anne all alone in that room along the corridor. It all seems such a mess. I guess the only good thing is that this little thing won't ever know what went down before he was born."

"Of course he won't," said Marjorie in a definite tone of voice. She peered carefully at Lisa. Was this the moment she had been waiting for to make her pitch?

"You know, Lisa my dear. What you need is a husband. In polite society anybody who has a child ought to have a husband."

"Marjorie, you've got to be *joking*. For a start, who'd have me with somebody else's bastard child? And second, the whole love business turns my stomach just to *think* about it."

"Don't be silly, dear. I'm talking about marriage—not love. It's naive to confuse the two. And I'm sure we can come up with somebody who'd be more than happy to have you, child or no child. Anyway, whoever it is can pretend the child is his. It's been done before, and it can be done again. Some nice old codger with a bankroll to match the size of his ego—that's what we need."

Lisa laughed outright. "Okay, Marjorie, who?" It sounded like quite an amusing game.

"I've been giving it some thought, dear. Quite a lot actually. And I have a short list of one. Vernon Blass."

Lisa hooted her reply. "Vernon *Blass*. But, Marjorie, he's *seventy-one*. He told me himself. That probably means he's eighty-five in this town."

Marjorie was not at all put out by the response. She hadn't expected to carry Lisa with her immediately. Like all the best things in life this would take time, careful manipulation.

"One can't have everything in this life, dear. He's old Palm Beach. Everglades Club, and so was his father. And the family publishing business is reasonably profitable, apparently. Nothing fantastic but solvent. Then there's that beautiful house on South Ocean. The business plus the house must be worth about twenty. He's a widower, no children yet that we know of, so you get it all when he goes. He's always banging on about how much he likes you. It would be perfect, darling—a match made in heaven. Can't miss."

By the end of her little speech the enthusiasm was positively dripping from Marjorie Donahue's lips as she contemplated the instant status that her projected match would bestow on Lisa. Mrs. Vernon Blass and her young son Scott Blass. It would be the foundation on which very nearly anything could be built. And it would give her, Marjorie Donahue, that most desirable commodity of old age—an heir presumptive. Lisa could be groomed to inherit her power. It would live on beyond the grave. Immortality. A hereditary monarchy. As senility set in, her crown would not be pried from her grip by upstarts like Jo-Anne Stansfield. She could die with the dignity of her position intact, awaiting the last trumpet in the secure knowledge that her kingdom would not be broken up after her demise—that, in Lisa's capable hands, it would survive unscathed as a monument to her memory.

Lisa had fallen silent. Of course it was all totally ridiculous—the most ridiculous thing she had ever heard. Two words, however, kept reverberating through her brain. Scott Blass.

WHILE YOUNG Scott Starr screamed and yelled his anger at the world in his mother's flower-bedecked room, little Christie Stansfield slept the sleep of the blessed in Jo-Anne's monastic suite. Her introduction to the land of the living had been quite unlike that of her half brother, and her birth, like her mother's pregnancy, had been totally without complications. Born in peace as Scott had been born in violence, her tiny face was a picture of serenity.

The scene that was being enacted over her sleeping head, however, was in direct contrast to her tranquillity. Jo-Anne was thoroughly annoyed.

"Listen, Bobby. I know we don't get along. Everyone knows that, and usually I don't ask for much. But I do think that when I'm bothering to go through the motions of bringing your daughter into the world, you might show up to see how things are going. Frankly, I couldn't give a damn, but you might just think about appearances at least. The nurses here can't believe it."

Bobby felt the anger rise in him once again. God, this woman knew how to irritate. Why the hell had he taken her on? Why the hell had he ever had anything to do with the female sex at all? They were nothing but trouble. Always screwing him around. There was a lot to be said for celibacy.

Jo-Anne changed tack. "I suppose you're upset that I didn't give you a boy. That's what you Stansfields always want, isn't it? Then at least when you fail there's someone else to keep alive the dream."

"You know I don't feel like that." But of course he did. Obviously he had wanted a son, and it *was* maddening that she had produced a girl. Typical, but infuriating.

He looked down at his sleeping daughter. A girl! God! Boyfriends and pregnancies. Girls' schools and Barbie dolls. Forget the touch football and fishing trips, the Racquet and the Senate.

There was a long silence as both digested their private thoughts. Jo-Anne broke it. "And to add insult to injury, can you imagine who just produced a son two or three rooms down the hall?"

Bobby wasn't in the mood for guessing games. He shook his head disinterestedly. Jo-Anne and her mindless Palm Beach gossip. She was looking at him strangely though. Somehow what she said next was going to be important.

"Lisa Starr."

"Lisa Starr?"

"Lisa Starr."

"Oh." For some reason, not entirely clear to himself, Bobby said it again. "Oh."

Lisa. Lisa who'd been pregnant with his child. Lisa who'd promised to flush it into the sewer. It had been a terrible, wicked thing to say. A dreadful, evil thing to do. How often during these last months he'd thought of it, and of Lisa. A son. Whose son? *His* son? No, impossible. No, not impossible.

"What do you think about that?" Jo-Anne watched him carefully, picking up on the confusion. During the course of her pregnancy, she had all but forgotten about her defeated rival. As far as she was concerned, Lisa Starr had dropped off the end of the world and been swallowed up in infinity. But for the last couple of days, after she had learned of Lisa's parallel pregnancy, all sorts of disturbing doubts had bubbled to the surface. Was it possible that Lisa had borne Bobby's child? The timing certainly was right. In the scheme of things it wouldn't be a total disaster. After all she was the legitimate wife, her daughter the legitimate Stansfield child, but it was something that needed to be cleared up. She didn't love her husband, but she was enough of a woman to know all about jealousy.

"I don't know what to think . . . I mean, I don't think anything. I'm glad for Lisa. Who's the father?" He tried to make the question as neutral as possible. Like . . . Who was at the party last night? Did the Munns enjoy Lyford Cay?

"Apparently nobody knows. Do you know, Bobby?"

"What do you mean?" Bobby tried to sound irritated.

"I mean . . . is that your baby, Bobby? That's what I mean. Is the little bastard your bastard? That's what I mean. You screwed her, after all, and we've just proved you work." Jo-Anne's voice dripped neat sarcasm as she flipped a casual hand in the direction of her daughter.

Bobby played for time. There were all sorts of ways to react to this. His child? Wonderful! No, a disaster. An illegitimate son. A son! The political fallout if it ever leaked. Some filthy West Palm surfer. His hands all over that amazing body. The love words in Lisa's ears. In the ears of *his* Lisa. The one he had so capriciously given away. The one who had been so terribly hurt.

The answer when it came was spoken with a soft voice. "No, it's not my child, Jo-Anne. It could have been, but it isn't. Lisa was pregnant by me, but she had a termination. I didn't want that, but she insisted. That's what happened."

It was the look of infinite sadness on his face as he spoke that made Jo-Anne believe him. And she did want to believe him.

She almost crowed her triumph. "So, who's the father then? Some cowboy with big balls, no money, and no class I suppose. Loser Lisa. Ha!"

Bobby's face was a mask. "I've got to go now, Jo-Anne. If you like I'll come back this evening. Is there anything you want?"

"Not a thing."

As he closed the door behind him Bobby knew exactly what he must do.

LISA LOOKED perfect. Fully recovered from the rigors of her labor, the color was back in her cheeks, the gloss in her hair, the glow on her skin. She was looking away from him, the radio playing softly the country music she had always loved.

Bobby stood there for a minute. It was time enough to take in the cot, Lisa's pink gingham nightdress, the sumptuous array of flowers, his own seething emotions.

At last she saw him.

Bobby didn't know how to describe her expression. Surprise, certainly. Confusion, too. Mostly, though, it was the intensity of the look that was its most powerful characteristic. One thing was obvious. She was not yet indifferent to his presence.

She turned off the radio and continued to look at him.

"Lisa. I just heard from Jo-Anne that you were here. I didn't know . . . you were having a baby . . . nobody told me . . ." Bobby searched for the words. "I wanted to know . . ."

"If it was yours?" She finished the sentence for him, her tone flat, matter-of-fact.

Bobby spread out his hands. He needed her answer. Lisa said nothing.

"May I look at him?"

"Yes."

There were no answers from the crib with its tiny bundle of life.

Again he turned to her. She had to let him off the hook. "Lisa?"

Scott started to cry.

Lisa stared back at him.

Her voice was ice cold as she said, "Don't worry, Bobby. He's not your child. After what you did I'd never have had your child. Never. You'll know who the father is soon enough. When we get married. So you needn't worry, I haven't polluted the famous Stansfield genes. I got rid of your thing just like I said I would. Now do me a favor and get the *hell* out of this room."

~13~

"*M*AGGIE," SHRIEKED LISA. "Help!"

Maggie rushed toward the bathroom. Over the last hour or two there had been half a dozen "crises," each more serious than the last. What would it be this time? A broken nail? Some mascara in the eye? A run in her stockings?

"Okay, Lisa Starr, the troubleshooter is here. Your worries are over."

"Like hell they are. This Carmen roller's stuck."

Stuck it was. The one that did the bangs. Somehow the hair and the plastic had become indissolubly wedded. "It sure is," Maggie said at last after two or three minutes of fruitless fingerwork. "Listen, we'll just have to wet it down, and start again."

"But I'm late already. The car's been outside for hours."

Maggie looked at her watch. Lisa was right. She was hopelessly late, or at least she would be if they started on the hair again from scratch.

The two friends stared at each other—the same thought in both their minds.

"Will you do it or shall I?" said Lisa with a laugh.

"I haven't got the nerve," said Maggie.

"Coward. Okay, Maggs, get the scissors."

Both peered into the mirror to observe the effect, the guilty Carmen with its cargo of hair lying abandoned on the scuffed Formica.

"It's sort of weird," said Maggie uncertainly.

"It sort of is," agreed Lisa.

"Maybe we could cover it up with flowers." Maggie was far from sure. Lisa was more optimistic.

"Don't worry, Maggs. The veil will cover it up until it's too late to matter."

It had been only a few short weeks since Marjorie Donahue had planted the seed of the idea in the Good Sam hospital room, and it had found fertile soil. As day succeeded day, it had grown and grown in the hospitable environment of Lisa's mind, and the more she had thought about it the more it had made sense. First, there had been Scott. His life would be hard enough without having to struggle through it as a penniless bastard. Lisa had been quite wrong to assume that no man would be willing to lend her son his name. Vernon Blass had been thrilled by the idea and had agreed to the match the moment Marjorie Donahue had suggested it. The beautiful Lisa Starr as his wife? What more could a seventy-one-year-old want, except maybe a strapping baby boy to show Palm Beach that there was life in the old dog yet.

"Are you all right, Lisa?"

"What? Oh, yes. I was just thinking about everything. Do you suppose Mrs. McTaggart has gotten Scott to the church yet? I bet he's howling up a storm in there."

"Aren't you supposed to worry about your husband turning up?"

"Oh, Vernon'll turn up all right. Let's try the veil."

For the tenth time they did just that. It looked like it had the other times. Lisa Starr in the softest of soft focus. A haunting beauty of dramatic loveliness, thought Maggie, about to be sacrificed to a man old enough to be her grandfather. Not for the first time since she had heard the terrible news of the engagement she fought back the revulsion. It wasn't too late. It hadn't happened yet. Her friend was still intact, but within hours Mrs. Vernon Blass!

"Lisa, are you sure this is wise? It's not too late, you know."

Lisa's voice was suddenly a little shaky. "We've been through all that a thousand times, Maggie. Don't bring it up again now . . . of all times."

Boy, had they been through it. Sometimes till all hours of the morning. But the logic had been unshakable. It wasn't just Scott; it was for Lisa, too. She lived now only to get her own back, and revenge she knew was a dish best served ice cold. Marriage to Vernon Blass was a step toward achieving it. That was the only thing that mattered.

Vernon Blass was an old man. He would not live forever. Another ten years? Fifteen? Whichever way you looked at it she would be mistress of the fabled Mizner house on South Ocean Boulevard. Geographically it was not far from West Palm and Roxy's Bar, but in all the ways that mattered it was a different planet. If she would not necessarily be a merry widow, she would be a rich one. Blass Publishing had quite a reputation, and presumably one day she would control it.

"No, you're right, Lisa," said Maggie with a watery smile. "I guess I just haven't gotten used to the idea of losing you." She put out a hand to touch her friend's arm. "You look wonderful, Lisa. Good enough to eat."

Lisa smiled back at her mistily through the delicate veil. "You're not going to lose me. God, Maggs, I'm going to need you more than ever. It's a snake pit over there. A great big beautiful snake pit, and you're the only real friend I've got."

"Better than Marjorie?" Maggie had always been competitive.

"Marjorie is Marjorie. She's more of an institution than a friend." They both laughed. Marjorie was a bit like that. A vast crumbling edifice, huge and awe-inspiring, housing a fiendishly efficient bureaucracy.

"Come on, let's go. Take me to my destiny." Lisa intoned the words in a theatrical voice, as Maggie manipulated her through the door of the tiny West Palm apartment that had been her home. Lisa didn't give it a backward glance. She was going forward.

In the car as she crossed the bridge to meet her bridegroom Lisa didn't say much, but her mind was far from still. Crossing the bridge to a Palm Beach wedding. Her very own. In the church still warm from a Stansfield wedding. The one when Bobby, her Bobby, had promised to love and honor the woman she despised and detested. How proud her mother would have been . . . of Vernon Blass? Lisa blotted her family from her mind. It wasn't efficient to be sentimental. She would have to grow up, to grow hard. It was too late now to protect herself from heartbreak, but at last she could see through her mother's naive and foolish vision. Palm Beach was paradise all right, but its inhabitants were very far from gods. All she had heard on those front-porch evenings had been myths and fairy tales from the mouth of a dreamer. Now Lisa knew the truth; but hadn't her mother's ignorant bliss been preferable to the folly of her own wisdom, born as it had been in the bitter pain of the cruelest rejection? Bobby Stansfield, who had been her love and was now her hate—who was still in his own way the center of her universe. She had sworn to destroy him as she had his wife, and the holy state of matrimony into which she was about to enter was nothing more nor less than a weapon of war.

The tall royal palms on either side of the road seemed to Maggie like a guard of honor as they drove into Palm Beach. Or were they the erect, well-drilled members of a firing squad? She was far from certain. As if to reassure herself she slipped her hand into Lisa's and squeezed, but Lisa was far away, confronting nameless dragons, anticipating the traps and snares that lay waiting for her.

They were there. Bethesda-by-the-Sea.

"Good luck, honey. I love ya," said Maggie.

"Thanks, Maggie. I've a feeling I'm going to need it."

━━

"OF COURSE they were all thinking that you married me for my money. But only *we* know it was really for my body."

It was the first time all day that Vernon Blass had referred in any way to sex, and Lisa heard herself laugh nervously. From the polished oak table whose ten feet separated husband from wife she could just see the ocean across the lawn. The waves were flecked with white. Wind must be getting up.

Vernon Blass eyed her speculatively. The first night wouldn't be easy. Was she a shallow- or a deep-end person? It was so difficult to know. Other people's feelings. How on earth did you ever know what they were? How did one drum up the enthusiasm to care? He toyed with the glass of claret in front of him. A marvelous wine—1961 Haut Brion. Somehow it never tasted so good here as in Europe. The distance? The humidity? It was impossible to say. But he was putting off the moment he had been waiting for. He had given Lisa and her son his name, and when he was dead they would have his money. There would have to be a little something in return. That was life. Maybe she understood that, but then again maybe she didn't. In his experience people seemed to have an insatiable desire to get something for nothing. Was his child bride one of those?

Lisa smiled back at him. With all his millions, Vernon Blass would not come cheap. It had been cloud cuckoo land to dare to dream otherwise. Thank God she hadn't held back on the champagne at the reception or the rather good red wine at dinner. It would be nasty, but it would probably be quick.

You might be called Mrs. Vernon Blass, but deep down you're just a hooker like all the others, thought Vernon Blass as he began to psych himself up for the main event. She might not be a slut but it sure as hell helped to get him up to imagine she was one. He felt the first vague stirrings. Good. That was better.

"If you've finished, my dear, I thought perhaps we would retire early to celebrate our wedding . . . if that is what you'd like, of course."

A headache? A migraine? Too much to drink? Lisa couldn't bring herself to be so banal. With my body I thee worship. It had been a contract all right. The minds had met, and she had as good as promised that the flesh would. She forced herself to think of something else. Of the Stansfields counting their money and dreaming their dreams of political and social glory. Enduring the gropings of a courteous old geriatric was a small price to pay for ruining them.

"I'll be in my room when you're ready," he said.

Lisa watched him go. Dark blue velvet smoking jacket, formal trousers, black velvet slippers with the leopard's head embossed in gold braid. The perfect gentleman. A kindly, generous old man. Why should he be denied his conjugal rights?

Lisa stared out across the lawns to the waving palm trees, their leaves indistinct in the gathering dusk. Storm clouds scudded across an irritable sky. Soon there would be the Florida rain, soothing the hot land, washing away the dust, cleansing the world. She suppressed an involuntary shudder. Would she herself soon need its healing balm? She drank long and hard on the glass of Hine brandy in front of her, grimacing at the unfamiliar strength of the hard liquor. She looked at her watch. How long should she give him? How long could she decently give herself? It could never be long enough. Like some victim of the Spanish Inquisition, Lisa tried to prepare herself for the ordeal—to separate her mind from her body, placing it in some neutral place where fortune's slings and arrows would pass it by. She could do that in the gym sometimes: the screaming, complaining body belonging to somebody else as the spirit soared above the physical, lost in the wonder of transcendence. And so the clock ticked away the minutes of her dying innocence as she sought to escape the implications of the march of time.

She was on her feet. Sleepwalking to the unwanted union. Across the room. Up the stairs. To the room which would be hers. Theirs. For a brief second, for an entire eternity she paused outside the door. She took one last inventory of her emotions and was surprised to find that pity was the most prominent of all. Poor Vernon. Already he would be tucked up in bed, his head poking nervously over clean, white sheets. His "dirty-old-man" role, strictly for public consumption, would be discarded, and now, about to be confronted by the wonders of his wife's body, he would be suitably chastened. Nervous even. He would need reassurance, to be coaxed toward some sort of satisfaction as the reward for the life he had made possible for her. She would turn out the lights for both their sakes, and do what had to be done to fulfill her part of the hard bargain she had struck.

Lisa Blass took the deepest of deep breaths and walked into the bedroom. Vernon Blass wasn't in bed. Somebody else was.

The girl was very pretty. A pixie face, no makeup, the soft-focus complexion, downy soft blond hair that had never seen the contents of a coloring bottle. The girl was very, very young. She sat there, calm and composed, the sheets covering the lower part of her flat, adolescent stomach, eyeing Lisa speculatively. With one hand she pushed a strand of hair away from one round blue eye, as she sucked contemplatively on a forefinger of the other.

Vernon Blass stood by the side of the bed, and he didn't look nervous at all. He looked absolutely and completely amazing. The pajamas were acceptable. They looked like standard Brooks Brothers, but his round little face had undergone the most startling transformation. It wasn't so much the heavy mascara, or even the hot pink of the lipstick. It wasn't really the faded ivory of the foundation, or the fact of the cheap costume earrings. It was his expression. It was pure. It was undiluted. It was the face of evil, and the horsewhip dangling from his hand emphasized it.

Lisa stood stock still, as she tried to take in the scene in front of her, and the breath she had taken before opening the door remained imprisoned in her lungs, waiting for the order for release. She had not stumbled on this happening by mistake. It had all been arranged for her benefit. The look on Vernon's face said it all. The expectant look on the teenager's merely confirmed it.

She opened her mouth to say words that didn't exist.

The child on the bed helped her out. "Welcome to your wedding night, Mrs. Blass." The voice was little-girl sexy, provocative, but matter-of-fact. She sounded like a marginally fresh bellhop—Welcome to the Hawaii Hilton. We hope you enjoy your stay.

Lisa found some words. Not the ones she really wanted, but the ones that seemed most available to her tongue. "What on *earth* are you doing here?" For some reason she looked at Vernon as she spoke.

The girl cocked her head to one side, a quizzical expression on a suddenly rather weary face. She, too, looked at Vernon. This was the trouble with all these rich weirdos, her look seemed to say. Too many games. You never knew what was real. What was fantasy. She gave voice to her thoughts. "You mean Vernon didn't let you in on all this? It's like a *surprise!*" Vernon Blass laughed. A nasty, crackling, cackling laugh.

The teenager saw it as her role to salvage what was fast turning into an unpromising situation. She tried to make her voice encouraging, sensual even. But it was the voice of a little girl wheedling. "Well, ma'am, the thing is, Vernon likes to watch. It'll be real fun. You and me, and he watches." Her voice trailed off. She wasn't carrying her audience with her. "The whip don't mean nuthin'. That's just for show," she added as an afterthought.

She apparently decided that actions spoke louder than words. Her trump card usually delivered the goods, and presumably this rich mother *was* into chicks. With a languid gesture she threw back the sheets to show exactly what was being offered.

For one second of concentrated ghastliness Lisa took it all in. The long brown legs, painted pink toenails, small and delicate to match the color of the pubescent nipples, the perfect blond triangle with its shy, half-hidden rose-bud lips. In desperation her eyes swiveled back to her husband, demanding, pleading for a lifeline. A dreadful mistake. An intruder. A very badly calcu-lated practical joke. Some amateur theatrical rehearsal. Anything.

Nothing, was the answer in the cruel eyes. It was for real. He'd wanted her to do it. To make love to girl jail bait while he watched, jerked off, and maybe flicked at them a bit with his whip.

Lisa grabbed the frame of the doorway as she backed toward it. In the corridor outside she walked fast, breaking quickly into a run. And after her, like the appalling odor of decay, came the fearsome sound of her husband's laughter.

~

OUTSIDE THE rain poured down in solid sheets, providing a double obstacle to vision. The tears and the rain on her wedding night. Christ! Lisa swore out loud as she ground the gears of her Mustang and tried to see the road. She'd had to get out of that dreadful house and away from the repulsive fiend she had married. How could she have made such a comprehensive and terrible mistake? Why the hell hadn't anybody *told* her? Wasn't Palm Beach sup-posed to *know* about its inhabitants? The anger and frustration rushed through her at the thought of her humiliation and its message for the future. She would have to break it up: the famous Lisa Starr marriage that made the *Guinness Book of Records.* Dead as a dodo in six hours flat. God, the disgust-ing little pervert, the wicked glee on his face as he had contemplated the horror in hers. She had seen evil tonight in the eyes of the man she had promised to obey and honor until death, in the eyes of the man whom the world now thought was the father of her son.

Over to her left Lisa saw the surf explode against the seawall on South Ocean Boulevard. Not long now and she would be there. The warming brandy, the words of comfort in Marjorie Donahue's snug den. Marjorie would know what to do. She would stay the night with her friend and tomor-row morning the telephone lines would burn as the Donahue lawyers were alerted, as Vernon Blass was exposed.

She peered out into the wet blackness. This was it. The driveway of the Donahue house. But it wasn't dark; it was floodlit, alive with people, and full of cars. A police car's blue light flashed, its driver huddled against its side, talking excitedly into a radio telephone. In the distance there was the sound of a siren, coming closer. Then, there it was. The ambulance, the paramedics jumping from the back. The stretcher. The bottles of plasma. Urgent shouts. The red light of the ambulance at war with the circulating blue one of the police car. And the rain. Slamming down in irritation on Lisa Blass's suddenly upside-down world.

In the house, the pandemonium continued. Lisa grabbed the forearm of a white-uniformed maid as she scurried past at high speed to nowhere.

"What's happened?" she shouted. But of course she knew.

"Oh, Miss Starr, it's madam. I think she's passed away. It was so sudden. When she was having dinner."

Lisa felt the blood run cold within her. Marjorie couldn't die. She wasn't allowed to. It was against the rules. Marjorie had been above such mundane things as life and death.

She took the steps of the big spiral staircase two at a time as the paramedics clattered in front of her. Please let her be alive. Please God. Dear God, please.

Somebody had put her into bed, and Marjorie Donahue was battling to hold on. One side of her face had fallen away like an eroded cliff and she was deathly pale, her breath coming in shallow gusts through the dry, blue lips.

"Looks like a CVA. Put up an IV line, Jim, and get some plasma expander in there. She's in shock. Let's get the vitals going. And whack her with some hydrocortisone. A hundred-twenty-five-milligram bolus into the line for starters."

Lisa stood there helpless as the paramedics went to work. In seconds the straw-colored liquid was pouring into an arm vein, the blood pressure cuff strapped on, the stethoscope taped into place just below the left breast.

The man in charge bent down with the ophthalmoscope. "We've got a chance here. Pupils are reacting to light. But she's bleeding in there. Bilateral papilledema. We may need some burr holes. The sooner we get her to intensive care the better."

Lisa felt the panic rush up inside her. They were going to take Marjorie away. She must be allowed to go too. To be with Marjorie in the ambulance.

"Can I come too? I'm her granddaughter," she lied.

In the back of the ambulance on the way to the Good Samaritan hospital Lisa cursed the snobbery that had not allowed Palm Beach a hospital of its own. The town was always so proud of things like that, but at moments like this when seconds made the difference, it seemed a dreadful and callous affectation.

In the semidarkness, the blue of the electrocardiograph line danced around on the monitor screen. Even Lisa could see it was irregular as hell, the QRS complexes all over the place like the frantic scribblings of a three-year-old let loose with a felt-tip pen on an immaculately painted wall.

Lisa was startled to hear the slurred whisper. "Is that you, Lisa? Why aren't you at home? It felt like somebody hit me on the head when I was having dinner. Where are they taking me?"

"Oh, Marjorie." Lisa cradled the ancient head in her arms. "Don't speak. Don't say a thing. It's all going to be all right. I promise you."

"I've had a stroke, dear. I must have, because I can't feel my right side." Despite the weakness of her voice, Marjorie sounded quite pleased with her diagnostic skills.

"Just a little one, perhaps. But you mustn't worry. It's going to be fine."

"Nonsense, darling . . . only big things happen to me."

There was a pause punctuated only by Marjorie's labored breathing. Lisa looked at the paramedic for guidance. He nodded to her. The message was unmistakable. Talk away while talking was still possible. It was a lucid interval; she would relapse again into unconsciousness.

Lisa smoothed the sparse gray hair of her friend away from the sweat-stained brow. Already the prayers were winging their way upward. "Don't die, Marjorie. Please, please don't die."

"I'm so glad you're here, Lisa. I feel safe with you." Marjorie's voice was a little stronger, but the words were indistinct and blurred. A drop of saliva formed at the edge of the paralyzed side of her mouth.

"Don't talk, Marjorie. Save your strength. You don't have to say anything."

The knowing eyes turned upward to find her own. The spark was still there, although it seemed to Lisa that a film had formed, a misty veil like a soft-focus lens, over the formerly clear pupils.

"Oh, but I do. I always needed . . . to talk. And I want to tell you something I've never said to you. Come closer."

Lisa leaned down toward the blue lips. With one hand she moved her hair aside to prevent its falling in the face of her stricken friend.

"I love you, Lisa. As I'd have loved a daughter. I admit that in the beginning I wanted to use you. But these last months have been wonderful. You showed me how to laugh . . . again. And how to have . . . dreams."

The voice trailed off. It seemed to be coming from some deeper place now, possessing a disembodied quality, still Marjorie's but traveling from some distance.

"I'm so glad I came to you tonight."

"What? They didn't call you? You came to see me?"

Lisa could have bitten off her tongue. Marjorie had been slipping into sleep. Her remark had been addressed mostly to herself. God! The cunning old fox had picked it up. Half paralyzed and yet still as sharp as a diamond.

"I was dropping by." In a thunderstorm, at ten o'clock on my wedding night. Oh, great, Lisa. Full marks for believability.

Again the restless eyes were searching for hers, peering into the depths of her, reading her like a picturebook. Marjorie had always been able to do that. It was useless to lie to her, and it was the only thing that made her cross. That couldn't happen now. She would play for time.

Through the windows of the ambulance she could see that they had crossed the Royal Palm Bridge and were already turning north on Flagler Drive. They would be in the Good Sam emergency room in about five minutes.

"Why did you come, Lisa? What happened with Vernon?"

"We had a bit of an argument. It was nothing. Don't let's talk about it now."

The stroke had clearly not affected the fabled Donahue antennae. A scrawny arm reached for the flesh of Lisa's strong forearm and the spindly fingers dug into her.

Once again Lisa was drawn in close. This time the voice was suspicious. "Lisa, tell me exactly . . . what happened." The tone said that time was precious and she would not be fobbed off.

It was pointless to resist. Lisa told her the truth.

"Ah. I see. Ah."

"It's simple," said Lisa. "I'll just get a divorce."

"No!" From somewhere Marjorie summoned the effort to shout the command. At the same time she tried in vain to sit up.

Her grip on Lisa's arm tightened, until the formerly frail fingers were biting into the skin.

The broken voice was difficult to hear, but it was totally insistent, the urgency dripping from the muffled words. "No divorce. No divorce, Lisa. Promise me . . . no divorce."

Lisa nodded her head helplessly. This was the last thing she wanted. The strain on the sick woman was building before her eyes and it was all Lisa's fault.

Marjorie Donahue was speaking from the heart. The physical apparatus was all but ruined, but the sentiments were as strong as ever. Lisa couldn't remember when she had seen her friend so determined to get her message across.

"Too soon . . . all this . . . too soon for you." The good arm waved weakly to encompass the ambulance, her stroke, the broken artery in her brain. "I can't protect you in this town anymore. They'll . . . kill you without me."

"What do you mean, Marjorie? You'll be here. You're not going anywhere. You'll be here."

Lisa repeated the words like an incantation. On the flickering screen the dancing blue lines fluttered nervously.

"Do a deal . . . with Blass. Leave him, but don't divorce him . . . Leave town . . . London, New York . . . Without me they're too strong for you . . . Jo-Anne . . . Revenge later . . . later . . . Revenge."

Two big tears rolled down Lisa's cheeks as her subconscious recognized the sound of the Horseman's clattering hooves. She gathered up the wise old head, cradling it in her arms, her tears splashing soundlessly onto the leathery skin.

"Don't leave me, Marjorie. Oh, please don't leave me all alone."

But Marjorie's effort to summon up the energy to impart the vital wisdom had drained her. Inside her head the aching suddenly became more intense, but mercifully she could feel a muzziness creeping through her mind. Like a fine morning mist in the Blue Ridge Mountains. Rather nice really. Its wet softness blurring the edges of the pain, drawing its sting. Floating, flying. Drifting on the tide. Or leaning on the reassuring arm of old Don Donahue in the stern of the *Bonaventure* in the moonlight off the Grenadines. It was such a relief to be going home at last.

Lisa recognized the insistent high-pitched whine of the EKG machine. And the blue line on the screen was flat, just as it should be when somebody had died.

~14~

IN THE PASSENGER seat of Maggie's battered Buick, Lisa was a bundle of contradictory emotions. It was impossible to talk, possible only to feel as the ancient car wound its way, tortoiselike, along the coast road to the Southern Boulevard bridge. The speed limit was twenty-five miles an hour, but they were doing less than that, the way forward blocked as usual by a carload of rubber-necking tourists checking out the mansions, living vicariously as they stared intently at what they could never hope to afford. Once Lisa had been one of them, but what was she now? Was she about to become a sightseer again? Certainly, like the outlaws of old, she was being ridden out of town. Or at least she was getting out while the getting was still good. But despite her tactical retreat from Palm Beach, she didn't feel like an outsider. She had tasted of the tree of the knowledge of good and evil, and she had been Marjorie du Pont Donahue's friend. After those experiences there was no going back.

Surreptitiously she wiped away a tear. Palm Beach. It was so powerful. She no longer idealized it, but it was still a monumental force. It had been her ambition and her dream, and it had turned on her, treated her cruelly, and now forced her away. But Lisa still loved it. She admired its capricious strength. Above all it was mysterious, a creature of infinite difficulty which defied predictions and refused lightly to surrender its prizes. That much she had learned as she had been defeated in the bloody battle. The war, however, was far from lost, and Lisa still had stomach for the fight.

"There's the John Lennon house," the tourists would be whispering to themselves in the car in front. That would be all they knew as they whistled and gasped and fantasized about the mythical superhero who had paced the floor of the first-floor ballroom. Lisa, however, was a member of the club. She could have filled them in on the spicy details. Such as the fact that Yoko Ono had bought the seaside Mizner house for eight hundred thousand dollars and had it on the market for an outrageous eight million. Like the fact that in the few short months he had lived there John Lennon had been having an affair with his secretary, and that the reconciliation with Yoko gave the world the haunting beauty of the song "Woman." Such as the fact that although the house had two swimming pools it had been built as the servants' quarters of the one next door.

Lisa sighed. Where she was going they wouldn't know about Palm Beach. Oh, they'd have heard of it, but they would have never seen the miles of deserted beaches in the North End of town, or walked beachcombing along the soft sand discovering exotic seashells, watching the scurrying crabs, communing with the ever-changing sea and sky, at one with the lazy pelicans as they soared overhead. They would never have cycled along the bicycle trail and experienced the heady scents of the flowers, as the water skiers carved their graceful patterns on the waters of the lake, and the oceangoing yachts drifted majestically down the intracoastal waterway. They would be strangers to the formidable neatness of the tamed jungle, the sparkling cleanliness of the streets and houses, the safety of a town in which to lock your door would be an affectation. Above all they would be oblivious to the undercurrents that swirled and twisted beneath the surface of this paradise on earth, that gave Palm Beach its excitement and its danger, that made the old young, and the young old, that made it the envy of towns like Beverly Hills and Palm Springs, where money and success were the only entrance tickets you needed for the game.

Maggie broke the silence as they approached the bridge. "I wonder what they'll have done to Mar-a-Lago by the time you get back."

She half turned to look at her friend. In some ways she had never seen her look more beautiful. Stricken, but serene. Her fine features colored by the pain, her character forged anew in the flames of the emotional holocaust that had engulfed her. It was one short week since her world had fallen apart for the third time. How much more could she take? Maggie had tried to understand the hurt, but, because she had never known the longing, it was out of her reach. The sympathy was there, but the experience of its cause was missing. All she knew was that for some essentially inexplicable reason Lisa was leaving, and that her interest in the gym that had meant so much to them both was dead. The day before she had signed it all over to Maggie for a nominal sum. It should have been for Maggie the dawn of a glorious new period in her life, but the joy was overshadowed by the sadness of the coming farewell.

Lisa made the effort to answer Maggie's valiant attempt at small talk. "For fifteen million they'll have to sell a lot of houses on the subdivision. Poor old Mrs. Post must be turning in her grave."

Mrs. Merriweather Post. Long before Marjorie Donahue *she* had once worn the crown. The Bath and Tennis loomed low and squat above the high wall on the left side of the road, and Lisa's mind wandered back to the time when she had been summoned for the audience that had had such dramatic effect on her life. Without that meeting her son would have no name, and she would have no future. It was a weird world.

Marjorie Donahue had given her friendship, and now death had taken it away. But she had left her most valuable legacy of all—her advice—and Lisa had followed it to the letter. She would not divorce Blass. Instead she would leave him and spend the days and the nights praying to the good Lord for his speedy destruction. She would exile herself voluntarily from Palm Beach, but, as she roamed the world, a dispossessed soul, she would use the time wisely and well, planning and scheming for a triumphant return. The thought of that would nourish and sustain her in the wilderness as she sought to master the intricacies of the publishing company that one fine day she would inherit. However long it took, Lisa would come to understand it—its weaknesses, its strengths. She would sniff around in its corners and backwaters and poke about in its closets and drawers. Then when the time came she herself would take over its reins, and bend it to her purpose. At the moment Blass Publishing was to her a blank sheet of paper. Soon it would be an open book.

Vernon Blass had been surprised when she had confronted him, coldly, and without apparent emotion. She hadn't tried to condemn his behavior either with a violent outburst of furious abuse or with a "more-in-sorrow-than-in-anger" approach. She had laid it on the line in matter-of-fact tones.

"I won't be living here, Vernon," she had said, forcing herself to look him directly in his gimlet eyes as the sticky fingers of nausea crawled through her. "I think it's best for both of us if I leave Palm Beach for some time. I want to learn about the publishing business. I thought that you could arrange for me to work in the Blass companies in New York and London. Obviously I'd pay my own way out of what I earned. I wouldn't be a drain on profits. I'm quite used to that."

For a second or two she had seen the conflict in the hated face. There was a part of him that wanted to keep her there. To plan new exercises in humiliation and degradation. At the same time he saw, too, that he had gotten her wrong. The girl from the other side of the tracks who might have learned to perform his tricks wasn't 'that sort of animal at all. He had miscalculated. The girl had balls. She wouldn't play, and she would make him pay. The divorce would be as messy as one could get. It would run on the networks for weeks. No, it was better to cut one's losses as cheaply as possible. To have her tucked away as an office girl or whatever in the furthest reaches of the family business seemed a very tidy deal. The charade of the marriage could be kept going, and people would even be impressed that his young wife was such a serious and hard-working person: "Won't take a penny from me. Insists on living like some student in rooms paid for out of her own salary. Wouldn't suit me, but you've got to admire the girl." The line would go down well at the Palm Beach dinner parties.

There and then he had agreed to write a letter of introduction to the man who ran Blass in New York.

There was also the question of the son. The boy that everybody thought was his. Little Scott Blass, just a month or two old.

He wanted to keep him. As a status symbol. Living evidence of his virility. Would Lisa want to schlep him around the world as she pursued her shadowy purpose?

"I think Scott and the nanny would be better off here, with me," he had said.

A few short weeks ago, knowing what now she knew, Lisa would have as soon left her son at the gates of hell as in Blass's custody, but she had changed. The child knew no one, loved no one. It was merely a bundle of physical needs. In Europe and New York it would be a distraction. Scott would be a weight around her neck far heavier than his few pounds. The Scots nanny was a gem, tough as old boots and yet kind and dependable. Even Vernon Blass was afraid of her sharp tongue. The boy would be safe and surrounded by luxury.

Of course mothers weren't supposed to abandon their young children. But then a lot of things had happened that weren't "supposed" to. Marjorie wasn't "supposed" to have bled all over her brain. Vernon wasn't "supposed" to hire hookers for his wedding night. Jo-Anne wasn't "supposed" to have told the man she loved that Lisa was a dyke. The dreadful cold had run through her veins as she had made the decision.

"Scott can stay," she had said at last as her heart plunged toward the floor. "But Vernon, there's a condition to all this. We both know you're getting off lightly. A divorce would cost you your reputation and a pile of money. If I walk away now and take nothing with me, I want your word that I inherit everything." Vernon Blass's word. It was about as impressive as his morals. Wills could always be changed, but she'd had to take the chance.

For a minute or two Vernon Blass had watched her carefully. There had been a strange look in his eye when he finally said, "I hear what you're saying, Lisa. You have my word."

So here she was flying away to a strange world with nothing but a letter, a Louis Vuitton carry-all, a promise, and a prayer.

On Southern Boulevard she felt the log jam break and the waters of loneliness flow into her soul, filling it with melancholy. Symbolically a dark cloud scudded across the sun, sending a long shadow across the road where they made the left into the airport.

As she turned to Maggie the floodgates opened and, with tears streaming down her face, she said, "Oh, Maggs, I'm going to miss you so much. It's like I'm heading into the darkness."

New York

LISA'S FIRST impression of Steven Cutting was that he was a closet queen, and nothing he said to her, and nothing she later heard about him, gave her any reason at all to change her mind. Behind the too large desk, in front of the thick glass picture window overlooking Madison Avenue, he shifted his thin ass in the green leather chair and twirled his tongue around the lisping syllables.

"Well, Mrs. Blass, it is indeed a pleasure to meet you at last. I wish I could say I knew all about you from Vernon, but I gather it was a whirlwind court-ship, and that he swept you off your feet."

The laugh was a cross between a snigger and a snort. The implication was unmistakable. She had hooked poor old Vernon. Taken advantage of a man old enough to be her grandfather. Used her obvious sexual appeal to do the dirty trick.

Lisa took him in: electric gray hair, a slight but well-exercised frame, horn-rimmed glasses, standard middle-aged preppy clothes. A personality as buttoned down as his white broadcloth shirt, on which the monogramed SC would be in maroon. This guy would belong to the Union, not the Knick; he would summer in Newport rather than the Hamptons, and suffer from piles rather than varicose veins.

Lisa couldn't remember when she had disliked someone so much at an initial meeting. Still, she mustn't let it show. This man was vital to her. He was the pilot of the Blass ship, and although Vernon had technical control, he wouldn't override Cutting. To do that might easily be to lose him, and the last thing that Vernon needed was the responsibility of running the company.

"What Vernon didn't mention in his telegram was the exact purpose of your visit." He placed his fingertips together and smiled a patronizing smile across the red leather surface of the empty desk.

"I'm very interested in the publishing business," Lisa said. "I thought I would take advantage of my husband's owning one to come and pick your brains. I gather you're the man who knows." The compliment went against the grain, and Lisa didn't quite manage the enthusiasm that she had intended to convey. She stared at him, her face like a mask.

"Let me think. What can I tell you about Blass Publishing that you'd be interested in?" Lisa crossed her legs and shifted position in the ladderback fake Chippendale chair. Usually that had the effect of increasing male confusion. Steven Cutting was clearly immune to that sort of thing. He didn't bat an eyelid as he began to warm to his theme.

"Blass Publishing is a wonderful little company. Vernon's grandfather started it around the turn of the century in England, and his father expanded here into America. Now of course the New York office is the tail that wags the dog. The London office is really a subsidiary, and the Paris offshoot is way down the line in terms of importance. The real action is right here." He waved an expansive hand to indicate what was supposed to be the spinning vortex of the humming Blass Publishing machine.

Lisa glanced around the bare room. It looked like Sunday in Philadelphia.

"Vernon, frankly, has never been particularly interested in publishing," Cutting continued, "and since his father's death the company has been pretty much run by 'professionals' like myself, although the traditions of the firm have been jealously guarded." His voice became suitably reverential as he said this. Keeper of the Faith. Champion of the True Religion. He managed to make "professional" a marginally dirty word that nonetheless possessed minimal entertainment value.

"And what are those traditions?" Lisa felt that she knew what was coming from her analysis of Steven Cutting's persona. Still, she had to keep him talking, had to soften him up for the pitch she would be making later.

Steven Cutting sat up a little straighter. He loved this bit.

He replaced the letter opener at an exact ninety-degree angle to the black, red, and blue pencils that were the only objects on the surface of his desk. As far as Lisa could see, the last thing they had needed was realignment.

"Most of the other publishers both here and in England have become disgustingly profit oriented," Steve Cutting said. "They'd publish Hitler's toilet paper if they thought it would sell. At Blass we're not interested in the bottom line. We publish books because they ought to be published and for no other reason, and we count our profits in terms of the quality of the reviews we get, not the number of books we sell. We feel that is the gentlemanly way. Quality before quantity. Not many people in this business can say that."

Lisa couldn't resist it. "I can't imagine many would want to."

Cutting flinched. He seemed to hiss his next words. "Ah, well, one can't expect outsiders to understand a business like Blass immediately. Vernon has the right instincts. He is in tune with our way of thinking. His heart is in the right place."

The message was clear. Lisa was a parvenu who should enjoy her brief strut center stage while she could. It wouldn't be long before good old Vernon threw her back into the garbage heap from which she had undoubtedly come.

The anger was boiling insistently now, the steam escaping, the lid of Lisa's kettle beginning to dance up and down.

"What people find most irritating is that we don't do so badly with this policy. We have total author loyalty, and we pay that back with interest. Once you are a Blass author you stay that way . . . even after death. And because we deal only with quality, we go to the top of the pile on every reviewer's desk, and our salesmen go to the front of the line when they visit the book sellers." He paused, wishing fervently that the second point was a fraction as true as the first.

It was time for the summary. "The great advantage of being privately owned by a family of what one might call enlightened absentee landlords is that you are free to avoid the strictures of the marketplace which so hamper our competitors."

Lisa had the picture. Blass was owned by snobs, run by snobs, and produced books written by snobs for a readership of snobs. The competitors must be crying all the way to the bank. "How much control does Vernon have?" How much control will I have when I inherit, was what Lisa meant.

How much money is the business worth, was how Steven Cutting read the question. "Vernon still has about sixty percent, but frankly we don't make large profits for the reasons I've described. Businesses like this tend to be valued on the amount of money they make, so his share would be difficult if not impossible to sell. Not that Vernon would contemplate getting rid of it."

He smiled a satisfied smile that said he was sure the information would be a big disappointment.

Lisa smiled back. Sixty percent was nine percent more than she needed.

"What kind of books do you publish? I know there are some poetry collections."

"Yes, we make a bit of a specialty of those, both here and in England. Poetry. Serious novels. Biographies of literary figures. Quite a lot of fine-art stuff, mainly in Paris. You can imagine the sort of thing. All top quality and a joy to produce."

"Joy to produce" had acquired a sonorous ring. Lisa judged that the time was ripe for her to make her move. "My reason for coming to see you was to ask for a job. Here, in New York."

"What?"

"A job."

For a second the blank amazement hovered over the thin, mean features. Then Lisa saw the lips begin to curl.

"Oh dear, no. No. No. Quite out of the question. Ha. Ha. A job? Dear me, no."

Lisa saw she had blown it. Now she would have to endure the explanation. The face in front of her was alive with a cruel pleasure.

"We at Blass believe in nepotism, of course, but we wouldn't consider carrying passengers. Our duty is to our authors and to the book-buying public, not to . . . dare I say it . . . bored housewives. Then there is the question of propriety. I don't think it fits the Blass image at all well to have the owner's wife *working*, even pretending to work. I can't believe Vernon really wants that, although I'm sure you've been very persuasive."

Lisa stood up. She had had enough. This man would die for what he had just done. The realist in her saw for now she would not get what she wanted. A man like Cutting would make every minute of her life a misery if she put herself for one second in his power. She had had to leave Palm Beach. Exile from America was next. She would have to crawl away to some quiet place to wait, and learn, to learn and wait. Somewhere like Paris, where they did the "art" books. That would do for starters. For finishers she personally promised there would be Steven Cutting's blue blood on the paneled walls of his patrician office, his guts hanging like Christmas decorations from the dangling bits of the cut-glass Georgian chandelier. He would be thrown out with his pencils and his letter openers to search for a job among the ranks of the publishers he scorned.

"Fix me up with a job in the Paris office," she said. "Do it today. In fact, do it now. If you don't, I will go back to Palm Beach immediately and spend the rest of my life bad-mouthing you to Vernon."

For a second or two Steven Cutting sat back in his chair. Fishlike, his mouth opened and closed as he sought the appropriate response. But he knew that he would have to do as Lisa said. The risk was too great. Who knew what control she had over the idiotic Vernon Blass?

He picked up the telephone from the side table by his desk, and his voice was high pitched as he shouted into the mouthpiece. "Get me Michel Dupré in Paris."

Lisa smiled. She was beginning to learn how to get her own way at last, and it felt wonderful.

~15~

MICHEL WAS TOTALLY still, his eyes tightly closed, legs clamped together, stretched out impassively on the already hot, damp sheets.
Deep within her Lisa loved the part of him which lived. Firm and hard it
moved against the walls of the prison she had created for it, testing strength,
probing for weakness, pushing insistently against the smooth slippery surface.
That was it. She was doing it all, having it all, selfish and yet generous in the
pleasure she was both giving and receiving. The delicious sensations floated
up in her mind. Where did they come from? Not alone from the obvious
place. On either side of her prostrate lover's hips Lisa's feet gripped the
mercifully hard mattress and her hamstring muscles groaned their pleasure
as they strained to lift and lower the full weight of her body over the rigid
invader. To Lisa the muscle pain, the oxygen debt of the "burning" tissues,
was a source of ecstasy inseparable from that provided by the alien that had
entered her.

Delicately she balanced herself as the warm wet lips at the core of her
being caressed the foreign skin, milking it, squeezing it, vibrating to its
rhythm, luxuriating in its arrogant self-confidence. Sometimes she would
hover, wrapped indulgently around its tip, daring it to try for escape, willing
it to break for freedom, to withdraw from the dark haven in which it pretended to be an unwilling prisoner. Then, hawklike, she would swoop down,
an unforgiving jailer, until the captive was forced into the innermost recesses
of the sweet dungeon, enveloped and controlled, humiliated and used, gloriously powerless.

Beneath her as he feigned the sleep of the grave, Michel Dupré clung to
the physical joy that splashed over him. Seeing nothing, the eyes of his mind,
clear and true, showed him the vision of bliss. His nostrils attuned to the
wonderful scents of unbridled passion, he allowed his lover to ride him, to
have him, to own him. On his hard, flat stomach he could feel the perfect
buttocks as they ground him down, could love the divine moisture that was

825

the undeniable evidence of Lisa's longing, and it seemed that his heart stood still as he contemplated the worship in his soul. Lisa. His Lisa. The goddess who in short minutes would journey with him to the gates of paradise in the shuddering truth of the orgasm. How many times like this? How many more times?

Above him Lisa was lost in ecstasy. But the beauty of passion was not all that she sought and found. Here, now, she was free of the disturbing longings that shaped and molded her existence. It was a moment of sublime forgetfulness, an oasis of heart-rending pleasure amid the desert of exile, the shifting sands of pain and anguish in which she remembered the world and the tiny helpless child she had left behind. As if to blot out the disturbing visions of Palm Beach and little Scott she quickened the pace, a furious horsewoman punishing the saddle of the mount she so effortlessly rode.

Lisa could feel the beginnings. Inside her the alien being was speaking its need, its earnest intention. Growing, pulsating, it called out to her for mercy, crying for release from the wonderful torment.

As it started Lisa stopped. This was the way she had learned to like it: soft, still, no motion distracting the awesome force as life flowed. There was no going back. The orgasm already had an existence of its own. It had had its beginnings. Nothing could prevent a middle and a sublime end. The wheels were turning, and the two lovers were now mere spectators, standing outside themselves, suspended in nothingness as they watched the chariot of happiness career toward the cliffs of abandonment.

She threw back her head and gasped as the familiar yet always unexpected feeling took her. It was only just inside her, quiet, yet ominous, its gentle whisperings muttering rumors of the storm to come. So fragile was the union. The chaste kiss of unpracticed lovers, the touch vulnerable, dangerous in its capricious wantonness. One careless move and contact would be lost and the precious moment destroyed in a travesty of wasted emotion and unconsummated love. But Lisa held her precarious position and was repaid by the sensations of the delectable twitchings, the lightning flashes that warned of the thunder to come. At the gates of her sexuality she loved the promising vibrations, and her muscles quivered in rhythm to the bearer of the gift she was about to receive.

Michel's desperate call of warning was unnecessary—a meaningless sound borne on the winds of passion, telling her only what her body already knew so well. The first offering of love bathed her hot body as it entered her mind. It came from below, but it was experienced above. Wet and rich, warm and fertile, soothing yet arousing, the sweet feed of masculinity.

In the presence of the catalyst that rushed into her, Lisa abandoned the fight for control. It was her turn now. The gates were opened; the pent-up longing was free. Down, down she sank, letting the muscles go, falling headlong, pushing the roaring, rearing pleasure machine into the heartland of her body. The long, lonely cry of anguish echoed around the small room as she howled her happiness at the uncaring heavens, the thrashing limbs, the twitching fingers clasping at the crumpled sheets, her head moving from side to side, eloquent testimony to the dreadful joy that coursed through her.

In the jingle-jangle aftermath, for long minutes there was silence. Only their thoughts spoke as the two lovers contemplated their journey to the mountaintop, and their descent to the valley on the other side. Leaning back heavily on him, her shoulder across his chest, her legs still holding him hostage inside her, Lisa spoke first.

"I'm going to miss you, Michel."

"You're determined to go?"

"You know I am."

"But London is so cold and wet. The people are all cold and wet. You'll hate it there away from me."

As she turned to look at him the Frenchman tried a watery smile. He only just made it.

It was true she was going to miss him. More true that he was going to miss her. Michel Dupré. Forty-two years of French charm, and a hard body that could distract her from the thoughts that plagued her. Lost and alone at Charles de Gaulle Airport, spat out from the mouth of the country that had borne her, she had needed somebody like Michel, and she had every cause to be grateful. Of course he had fallen in love with her, as he had stowed her Vuitton case in the back of his battered Citröen.

And later, over lunch at the Brasserie Lipp on the Boulevard St. Germain, he had already started to plan their future. Lisa had laughed at him then. At his charming self-confidence, at the occasional hints of the little boy inside the man, at his extravagant romanticism. For a few short weeks she had resisted him, but Paris had worked its magic and she had needed an antidote to the homesickness that gnawed away at her and the dull, aching desire for revenge that throbbed and burned within her. Now they were lovers, but she didn't love him—and she suspected that he knew that.

"But London is the place I have to be. From there I can see all the Blass operations."

"You're not happy with me and my art books?"

No, Lisa wasn't happy. A few minutes ago she had been, but reality had intruded itself into the dream, scattering the fabric of make-believe with its unforgiving winds. Paris was a marvelous, beautiful backwater. The French were proud of their decaying language and their artistic heritage and scorned the unashamed materialism of the Americans, and the self-centeredness of the British. The Blass books were indeed magnificent, their color rich, their paper fine, their cost exorbitant, their sales minimal.

She had used her Frenchman shamelessly. Used his body and used his mind. He had taught her to see with the eye of the French, to speak with the subtle accent of Aix, to understand about style—and above all he had told her everything he knew and all that he suspected about publishing. Michel had been a man of the world. He had dirtied his fingers in commercial publishing before seeking the safe haven of Blass, and now he had completed his retreat from a business for which temperamentally he had never been equipped. In the ivory towers of art-book publishing he was completely at home, cheerfully anachronistic, obsessed by quality and beauty, happily oblivious to the realities of the profit-and-loss statement. From time to time Lisa felt like Judas when she contemplated their mutual future, for it was obvious to her that Michel had dared to dream. To dream of a time when death would free Mrs. Vernon Blass from her extraordinary liaison. When she would turn to the man who had taught her, loved her, and pleased her.

Poor Michel. He couldn't know her, or understand the forces that had shaped her. He couldn't suspect that he was irrelevant, a pleasant interlude, nothing more nor less.

As if to emphasize this subterranean point Lisa withdrew from him, dangling her long legs over the side of the wrecked bed. She fought back the desire to say something cruel, something that would destroy the illusion she had allowed him to create.

She ran an impetuous hand through her sweat-soaked hair and tossed her head, shaking off the responsibility of love. In the shower later she would complete the process of dissociation.

What had he said? Was she happy with him and his art books?

She stood up. Dangerous, she knew, in her beauty. Love hurts. Love kills. Lost love needs so desperately to be avenged.

"I said I'd miss you, Michel," she said to his disappointed eyes.

But as she spoke the words Lisa was already walking in her mind on the wet damp streets, avoiding the blood-red buses and the odd-shaped taxis, picking her way slowly through the Bloomsbury squares, learning what she needed to know about the company she planned one day to own.

London

IT WAS one of those London days when the cold dampness creeps into the brain and invades the muscles, propelling everybody into a deep well of pessimism and lethargy. Outside the rain drifted down, quietly relentless, determined to sink the gray world on which it fell in a slough of despond. In the Bedford Square offices of Blass Publishing, most had effortlessly succumbed to the all pervading sense of gloom, as they had every day for the last two weeks while the dreadful weather had called the psychological tune to which they danced. Lisa was no exception. She sat moodily at the big desk in the small room and doodled on the blotter with a black felt-tip pen, occasionally looking out through the dirty window at the red brick wall that was her only view.

About ten times a day in situations like this, she thought wistfully of the Florida sunshine and compared the anemic, miserable London rain with the Palm Beach variety. There, rain was a cleansing experience. A short sharp blast of warm energy, chasing the humidity from the atmosphere, setting the stage for the triumphant return of the sun. Here the rain was an end in itself, a scourge of the spirit, a character-forming impediment to happiness whose main achievement was the creation of the Englishman's traditionally jaundiced eye. Worse, far worse, the poisonous environment it so callously conjured up was a superb habitat for some of the nastiest viruses the world had known. It had been five long years since Lisa had left Palm Beach, and during that time she reckoned she had experienced them all. With clockwork regularity they descended at the most cunningly inconvenient times, laying her low, filling her mind with cotton wool, sandpapering the back of her throat, clogging up her lungs with the accumulated rubbish of the unhappy city. She could swear that at this very moment they were breeding once more within her. Beneath the navy-blue cashmere sweater and the matching pleated wool skirt, she was already blowing hot and cold in a rhythm that didn't seem to coincide with the vagaries of the firm's ancient ventilation system.

She looked down at her Hublot watch, the one she ought to be diving with in the warm waters of the Gulf Stream. Eleven o'clock. That meant tea, and Mavis. For a brief second Lisa's spirits made it off the bottom. Tea wasn't really tea. It was a brown, plastic-tasting liquid that came in a cup designed specifically for the burning of fingers. Still it was usually warm and possessed a limited amount of caffeine value. Mavis, however, was the real thing, a genuine Cockney tea-lady with a philosophy of gloom that made the day-to-day weather-induced depressions seem like the emotional highs of an ecstatic manic. On the principle that there is always someone worse off than yourself and that realizing it is the first step to contentedness, Mavis's effect on the workers at Blass was a tonic indeed—of infinitely greater value than the insipid liquid she dispensed.

Lisa smiled as she heard the knock on the door. Oozing concentrated gloom from every pore, Mavis trudged into the room.

"Good morning, Mavis," offered Lisa brightly, knowing exactly the response she'd get.

"Nothing good about it," came the predictable reply. "Three killed in that train crash, and my Len's tooth's gone septic."

Mavis had a way of pulling together different strands of tragedy and weaving them together into a tapestry of doom. Everything was taken personally, whether it was a small earthquake in Chile or her cocker spaniel's tendency to shed on the sofa.

"Oh dear," said Lisa supportively. "Hope the tooth's okay."

"'Spect he'll get blood poisoning. Usually does. Of course, the doctor drinks. No bloody good at all."

Lisa sipped on the disgusting concoction. As usual Mavis's chapter of disasters was cheering her up.

"You know, Mavis, I'll have been away from home five years next month."

Mavis cocked her head to one side and looked at her suspiciously. "Seems more like ten," she said at last, her face as black as thunder. "Them's been a *terrible* five years. If the next five's like them five we might as well all give up. That's what I say."

She leaned phlegmatically on the tea trolley weighing up the advisability

of a guided tour of the five years of tragedy. Where to start? So many dreadful things. Something made her decide against it. "Oh, well. Struggle on,
that's what I say. Fight the good fight, though, Lord, sometimes I don't know
why we bothers."

Lisa laughed, but after Mavis had gone the words wouldn't go away. Five
terrible years. Five terrible years since that day when she had said good-bye
to Maggie, to little Scott, and to Palm Beach.

She looked down morosely at her desk. The engagement book, lying
open, caught her eye. Damn! She'd almost forgotten. She had a lunch date.
Charles Villiers. Le Caprice at one. Lisa felt her spirits lift. Normally the
thought of lunch with her boss would have had the opposite effect. But today
it would be a distraction. Anyway, there was something she wanted from him.
Very much indeed.

THE TRENDY Le Caprice restaurant in St. James's was humming like the busi-
est bumblebee, but Lisa was oblivious to the glitterati and the bustle all
around her. She was trying to sell something as if her life depended on it, and
already she could sense she was on the verge of failure.

"Charles, have you read it? I don't mean speedread it, I mean really *read*
it. I'm telling you this book will be number one forever. I promise you. I
know it."

Charles Villiers threw back his head and gave the whinnying laugh the
secretaries liked to copy. It was sort of a guffaw, but it was heavily involved
with the nose and it always ended in a kind of a snort.

"Yes, I did read it actually. One *can* read, you know."

Three years in London publishing had taught Lisa the significance of the
Old Etonian accent, the secret signals it could impart, its nationwide status as
a badge of privilege and high class, but she never ceased to marvel at it. It
was a phonetic work of art—no question—a cross between a high-pitched
nasal whine and the sort of sounds you might expect from a person with
lockjaw.

Charles Villiers's version of it was to Lisa the standard against which all
others were judged. Having no chin to speak of seemed to be a help, but
then so did the oily self-confidence, the aggressively Aryan face, the high
forehead, and the crinkly short blond hair. In fact the bits of Charles Villiers
were inseparable from each other. He was a job lot, the polka-dotted white
and blue Turnbull and Asser tie at one with the cream Harvie and Hudson
shirt, the wide-lapeled double-breasted gray flannel suit melding effortlessly
with the shiny black lace-up walking shoes from Lobb, which had clearly
made it through at least one generation. The inch of cuff; the thin, understated gold links bearing the faded family crest, worn away by the years; the
blood red suspenders, the black woollen socks, all were potent statements
about everything Charles Villiers stood for. From them one knew that he
shot grouse, holidayed in the mountains of Scotland rather than on the
beaches of Europe, "killed" salmon rather than caught them. One small
mistake—ornate cuff links, a neatly folded breast-pocket handkerchief, Gucci

shoes with buckles—would have revealed him instantly as an imposter, a posing parvenu, a minor public-school sham. But nothing spoiled the effortlessly patrician effect, no aftershave, no misplaced vowels, no warmth, no empathy.

He was a perfect specimen and Lisa disliked him with an intensity that bordered on paranoia.

Lisa leaned across the table and let the enthusiasm flow from her. She *had* to win this.

"Well, isn't it just terrific? I mean the hooks and the characterization. The girl's a genius. We've got to have her on the list."

"On a *Blass* list, Lisa? Remember the sort of company we're running here." Lisa didn't have to be reminded of that. Charles Villiers and Steven Cutting sang in unison, peas from the same disgusting pod.

"You're not going to go for it."

It was a statement. Charles Villiers never went for anything she suggested. It had been a forlorn hope. She slumped back in the chair. One more defeat. A brilliant author thrown away. Yet another golden opportunity missed. God, it was frustrating. Christ, she hated this apology for a man who understood so little. Since her arrival from the safe haven of Paris he had gone out of his way to make her life a misery.

He had started by attempting to patronize her, his natural chauvinism as much a part of his being as his Royal Yacht hair lotion and his membership of Whites and the Turf. Then, at an Eaton Square dinner party, his wife tucked away safely in the Lindo Wing of St. Mary's stoically producing their fourth child, and his high forehead glistening with the sweat induced by the consumption of too much after-dinner Kümmel on the rocks, he had propositioned her. Lisa hadn't minced her words. She had told him to his face that she found him both physically and morally disgusting, and she had not been forgiven. The physical bit he hadn't minded at all. An Old Etonian didn't rely much on things like that. But for Charles Villiers it was unforgivable to suggest that he had "behaved badly"—about as unacceptable as being called a "dangerous shot" or being accused of cheating at backgammon. Since that moment he had found it difficult to look her in the eye, and he had seen to it personally that her progress up through the ranks of Blass, London, had been along a path liberally coated with molasses.

Despite the obstacles so tenaciously placed in her way, Lisa had moved upward. In the early days she had done just about everything but make Mavis's tea. She had read proofs till she had thought her eyes would drop out, undergone months of numbing tedium in the accounts department, and put up with the blasé inefficiency of the Oxford undergraduates who pretended to be editors and the gushingly self-confident debs whose social training and "contacts" were thought to be of value in the P.R. department. In desperation she had volunteered to go out on the road as a sales rep, and had spent a soul-shattering three months among the dusty bookshops of the home counties attempting the all but insuperable task of selling the dreary Blass books to incompetent old men who had dreamed that bookselling would provide them with a "gentlemanly" way of making a living. So hard had she worked, so formidably efficient had she been, that even Charles Villiers had been unable to prevent her being given a job, first as an editor, and then as senior editor.

It had been as far as he was prepared to go. If she wanted to publish a book, then he didn't think it was suitable. It was as simple as that.

Lisa stared moodily around the restaurant. In three years a lot of things had changed, but a lot had remained the same. The David Bailey portraits were still on the wall—Mick Jagger, Roman Polanski, mythical heroes now, like the Harlows and Russells of old.

Charles Villiers was droning on, the platitudes dripping from his cotton-wool-filled mouth. "Really rather trite . . . can't write her way out of a paper bag . . . enough people about who want to publish trash . . ."

Lisa yawned rudely at him. She leaned back in the chair and looked down at her tits as they pushed out anxiously against the silk blouse.

"Now a *decent* writer . . . rely on sex . . . puerile ending . . ."

But Lisa wasn't listening. She had left him for the burning sand and the midday sun. And the unfortunate child she hadn't seen for so very long

———

MAVIS'S KNOCK on the door snapped Lisa out of her intercontinental reverie. Outside the rain beat against the window, drawing crazy patterns on the grime, supremely oblivious to Lisa's magical mystery tour of memory's lanes.

"Come in."

"Telegram, Lisa. Somebody's died, 'spect."

Lisa laughed. "Terminal pessimism, Mavis," she joked.

Terminal optimism, she should have said. The telegram was brief and to the point. REGRET TO INFORM YOU VERNON BLASS PASSED AWAY 7 P.M. LOCAL TIME, 14 DECEMBER. PLEASE CONTACT OFFICES OF BROWN, BAKER, MCKENZIE 305-555-3535. DEEPEST CONDOLENCES.

Things were supposed to swim before your eyes at moments like this. They didn't. Lisa had never seen anything in her life so clearly. She had bionic vision. It must be like this when you did coke. The words sparkled up at her as their message burrowed comfortably into her brain. It was over. The waiting was finished. Her husband was dead. She could go home at last.

Mavis, peering expectantly across the desk, could see at once that her worst suspicions were confirmed. Something of terrible importance had happened. A close relation at the very least, perhaps even a child. She braced herself for the ghastly information and prepared to etch the moment indelibly in her memory for later regurgitation at the pub.

It was to make quite a good story.

Lisa Blass came out of her chair like a punch-drunk fighter reacting reflexively to the ringing of a bell. She made it around the desk at light's speed and in a second Mavis was surrounded. Strong arms gripped her, and as her feet left the ground, the war whoop assaulted her ears.

The breath was crushed out of her by the exuberant bear hug, but she managed to get out the words, "Somebody died then."

"Yes, yes," came the joyous response. "My husband. He's dead. He's dead. Oh, Mavis, the filthy old bugger is dead at last."

THE TIME difference was just right for the opening of the Brown, Baker law offices. How convenient, she thought as she waited for the overseas telephone connection. How accommodating of old Vernon to do his dying at the right time.

Lisa cut right through the traditional responses.

". . . how very sorry we all are . . ."

"Did he leave me the Blass Publishing shares?" she barked into the grubby receiver.

"Why, yes, of course. Didn't you know? They were in joint names—yours and his. It means we don't have to wait for probate to arrange the transfer. As surviving co-owner you get immediate title."

"I can vote the stock now? This minute?"

"Technically from the legal pronouncement of death. That was last night."

"And the house?"

"You are the sole heir. About the funeral. Will you be returning . . ."

But Lisa had heard more than enough. "I'll call you back later," she said, and she put down the telephone. Oh, God, this was going to be good. So very, very good.

She didn't knock at Charles Villiers's door. She just walked straight in. It was pleasing to see that he looked suitably irritated by the infraction.

He was having some sort of a meeting. One of the ones that Lisa tended not to get told about. One thing was quite obvious. He had not heard about Blass's death.

"Hi, you guys," said Lisa as brightly as she felt.

The young woman from St. Mary's, Wantage, and the editor from Northfallen Lodge exchanged supercilious looks. The earl's daughter who headed up publicity smiled patronizingly.

Lisa hovered over them, languid hand on a jutting hip. In this life there were moments of rare beauty. This would be one of them.

"We were just going through the spring list," said Charles Villiers by way of explanation for what was clearly a clandestine meeting.

"Gee, how depressing," said Lisa with feeling.

"What on earth do you mean, 'depressing'?"

Lisa stared back at him. She hoped this would be like being shot in the stomach. A slow, lingering, painful death. "I mean how depressing to be even thinking about that miserable collection of pretentious junk that rejoices in the name of the 'spring list'—that's what I mean."

Around the conference table the mouths were beginning to drop open. A lid was clearly being flipped. Did Lisa Blass drink? Was she on some stuff?

Lisa toured the faces. Then, her eyes roamed the room. It was too good to be true. Behind the Villiers desk was the big empty red leather Villiers chair. He was sitting with the minions at the long mahogany table.

She sauntered slowly toward it, aware of the piercing eyes on her broad shoulders, her slender back, her prize-winning ass. As she moved she turned back to look at them over her shoulder, the glorious smile playing over her radiant face. "Yes," she mused as if to herself. "I don't think very many people are going to miss the spring list—outside this room, that is."

"Lisa, for goodness' sake, stop talking nonsense. Are you feeling all right?" The exasperation was palpable. Charles Villiers was thoroughly irritated.

" 'All right'?" said Lisa, her voice incredulous. "I can truthfully tell you I haven't felt this good in years." She reached the desk, and her destination. As she sat down heavily in the managing director's chair she added maliciously, "I think widowhood must suit me."

It seemed like an age as the bomb dropped. One by one her audience came to grips with the news. To give him his due, Charles Villiers was there first. His face was still whitening and his thoughts were racing ahead of the words when he said, "You mean . . . Vernon is . . ."

"Dead," said Lisa cheerfully. She swept both feet up onto the immaculate leather of the desktop, the one that Charles Villiers kept clear of all sharp objects to preserve the surface. "Yes," she repeated reflectively. "Dead as mutton. And the lawyers tell me I'm your new boss. Just like that."

Everyone was there now. Lined up in the sights of the firing squad. The spring list would not be the only casualty.

"And it gives me the very greatest pleasure to tell you kind people that you're all fired. Every damn one of you."

And with that, Lisa let out a sigh of the deepest contentment as she ran the sharp heel of her shoe in a ripping path of destruction along the previously immaculate red-leather surface of Charles Villiers's desk.

～

FOR WHAT seemed like an age the telephone rang unanswered. Please God, let her be there. Please God she hadn't signed with anyone else. Anne Liebermann. She thought of her disappointed eyes when Lisa had told her that Blass wouldn't be offering for *Big Apple,* her disbelieving eyes when Lisa had tried to tell her that the book was really a winner but that the head of Blass had overridden her, her great big brown eyes which would have mesmerized the coast-to-coast talk-show audiences and looked a dream on the cover of *People* magazine. Anne Liebermann with the potential to sell more books than the world had bricks.

The soft voice answered at last. "Anne Liebermann speaking."

"This is Lisa Blass of Blass Publishing."

"Hello."

The response was neutral.

"Listen, I'll get right to the point. There have been management changes here at Blass and I'm in a position now to make you an offer on your book. Is it still available?"

There was a long pause and what sounded like a sigh. "I am afraid it's sort of promised to Macmillan. They haven't actually *made* an offer, but they have promised to make one."

"Whatever it is, I'll double it and you can have a signed contract in the time it takes me to get to your flat in a taxi."

Anne Liebermann, whose characters were nothing if not decisive, showed that she prospected for source material within herself. "I accept," she said, almost before Lisa had stopped speaking.

"Would you be interested in a three-book deal—world rights—structured through Blass, New York?"

"Am I hearing this right?" laughed Anne Liebermann. "I've only had one gin and tonic."

"Don't move. I'm on my way with the contracts and the Moët," said Lisa as she slammed down the phone.

How was it the strings of your heart were supposed to go? *Zing.* That was it. They had just gone *zing.* God only knew what would happen to them when Anne Liebermann and Blass made it to the top of the *New York Times* best-sellers list.

Lisa reached into her drawer for a draft contract and some Blass letterheads. The lawyers could look it over later, but she just wanted something in writing.

For a second or two Lisa stood still trying to get a grip on her still surging thoughts. From the next room she heard what might easily have been the sound of tears, and of raised male voices. Boy, the hornets were stirred up in there. Any minute now they'd all come buzzing after her, threatening, cajoling, pleading, appealing to "better" instincts. Yes, any second and the whole motley crew would be creeping and crawling around as they tried to get a lick at her butt, feverishly trying to save their flats, and their mortgages, their mistresses, boyfriends, and wives, their pride and their prejudices. They would try collectively, and they would try singly. All but a very few would try in vain. She would play God with their futures and she would enjoy every minute of it in revenge for the slights and insults, for all the years of forced subjugation to terminal arrogance and amateur inefficiency, to glutinous hypocrisy and transcendental crassness. But right now there was another telephone call to make. She dialed 142 for information. "Pan American, please. Reservations," she said quickly. Lisa Blass could go home at last.

———

LISA CAME out of what the English called the "lift" like a human cannonball in the circuses of old. The momentum carried her effortlessly through the swinging doors into the Madison Avenue Blass offices, and the receptionist jumped up as if she had been shot.

Lisa wore skin-tight soft blue jeans, a T-shirt bearing the legend POVERTY SUCKS, and a full-length brown sable with big patch pockets. White ankle socks peeped out at the bottom of the jeans and disappeared into dark brown crocodile loafers. Her hair was swept back from her face and her whole ensemble screamed the self-confident style of Europe. Lisa Blass was home at last, and she was a girl no more. She had grown up.

The receptionist didn't recognize her at first. The energy of her arrival and her remarkable appearance had been the reason she had leaped to her feet.

Now, the truth dawned. The receptionist gushed nervously. "Oh, Mrs. Blass. I didn't recognize you. We were expecting you. How marvelous to see you again. Mr. Cutting has canceled all his morning appointments so that he could be available when you arrived."

Lisa was all fired up, running on the highest octane, and relishing the job that was about to be done.

"Do me a favor," said Lisa nastily, "and cancel all his afternoon appointments as well. In fact, while you're at it, you might like to toss the appointment book in the trash." She didn't wait to savor the confused and horrified expression on the old retainer's face. She knew the way. She'd been there before.

Steven Cutting stood up as Lisa crashed into his office. No condemned man due for lunchtime execution had had a worse morning than had the president of Blass Publishing. In his desperate attempt to produce order in his suddenly threatened world he had arranged and rearranged the pencils until they defined a right-angle triangle more accurately than any protractor. The look on Lisa's face did nothing to calm his shattered nerves.

"Lisa . . . after all these years . . . poor Vernon . . ." His hands tried to conduct the little mutterings.

"Bullshit," said Lisa loudly. She flung herself down in an armchair and cocked one long leg over its arm, letting a crocodile shoe dangle from her foot.

"Oh," said Steven Cutting.

Lisa felt a bit like the gunfighter in a saloon showdown. A girl could get hooked on this. It was better by far than sex.

Steven Cutting had a speech prepared. A bit like the last-minute application of the condemned man for a stay of execution. It even possessed a vaguely legalistic flavor. "Mrs. Blass, I would be foolish if I didn't admit that I made a mistake in underestimating your contribution to Blass. I have cause to regret that. Regret it very much. I hope you will give me an opportunity of rectifying that . . . of putting it right . . . I know we can work well together . . ."

"Hah," said Lisa, cutting him short.

She sent the other leg up onto the arm of the chair to join its fellow. "Do you have a contract with Blass?" she asked ominously.

"A contract? A contract with Blass." Cutting looked as if he were about to pass out, as if the word "contract" was entirely foreign to him—a verb, perhaps, in Swahili. "No. No contract. At Blass we never believed in contracts. A gentleman's word . . ."

"Is about as much use as a mixed metaphor," said Lisa, finishing off the Cutting sentence, and noting that he had used the past tense when referring to Blass. The worm was getting there, halfway up one side of the razor blade now. Lisa breathed in deeply. Was that the aroma of power mixed in with her Paloma Picasso? "Yup," she said reflectively, "gentlemen's agreements don't cut so much ice when the "gentleman" in question is measuring his length on the slab in the West Palm mortuary."

Steven Cutting drew himself up very straight, the way you did before the firing squad. "Am I to take it that you have decided to dispense with my services?" he asked unnecessarily. "If so, then I'm sure you'd agree that there should be some compensation. After all these years."

It was time for the *coup de grace.*

"Mr. Cutting, I want you out on the street in fifteen minutes flat, and you go with nothing. And let me tell you this. If you take one thing out of here, *including* those anal pencils, I will personally drag you through every court in the land, so help me God."

~16~

LITTLE SCOTT BLASS knew it was supposed to be an important day, but he wasn't at all sure why. Some frightening person called "mummy" was coming to disrupt his cozy world, and he wasn't very keen on the idea. He pressed his nose up tight against the wire fence that surrounded the airport, and he shivered involuntarily, part anticipation, part reaction to the chill morning air. His small hand burrowed into Mrs. McTaggart's big one. "Nanny, is mummy nice?" he said uncertainly.

"Of course mummy is nice." The reply lacked conviction, and Scott picked up on that. Mummy was nice like rice pudding was nice, like "greens" were nice, like hair-washing was "nice."

Feeling that perhaps she was failing to carry her audience with her, Mrs. McTaggart compounded her error. "All mummies are nice," she added half-heartedly.

"I wish I could have gone to school today." The Wee Wisdom Montessori school on Flagler and the tender ministrations of the divine Miss Heidi appeared infinitely preferable to this little expedition into the unknown. Still the airplanes were always fun.

"Is mummy in that one?"

"No, dear. That's a little one. Mummy is coming in a great big one."

That gelled with his expectations. Mummy was clearly a great big person who arrived in great big things and made a great big fuss. Otherwise what was he doing in his best gray flannel trousers and black walking shoes and the super-clean white shirt? He sighed and said what he thought. "I don't think I'm going to like mummy."

"Nonsense, dear. Everybody likes mummy." Except me, thought Mrs. McTaggart, adjusting the wide belt of her immaculate uniform. It was way beyond the ken of the kindly Scotswoman that anyone could treat a child the way Lisa had treated poor little Scott. To walk out on a husband after a week of marriage and to leave a child in someone else's care with no direct contact for five years seemed like a cruel, unusual, and totally unwarranted punishment. During that time she had herself learned a few things about daddy that

had made even her phlegmatic blood curdle. Perhaps that excused the parting, but it certainly didn't explain the callous indifference to the innocent
baby. Luckily she had been there to fill the gap, and now the child was hers
in love as if she had borne him herself. Daddy had kept out of their way, and
on the occasions he had attempted to exert an influence, he had felt the
sharp edge of her Celtic tongue, an experience for which, unlike Oliver
Twist, he had tended not to return for more.

So Scott had reached the age by which the Jesuits believed that the character had been formed without knowing his father or his mother, and despite
her valiant efforts as a surrogate, the scars showed. Scott's was a brittle self-
confidence, outwardly impressive but a whitewash job. He seemed to be a
leader, appeared to be ready for any adventure, but inside he was a fragile
little soul, vulnerable and alone, nursing the great void in his heart where his
mother and father should have been. For that, Nellie McTaggart could not
and would not forgive Lisa Blass. For that, and for her sudden and unwanted
return. If she walked in now and attempted to reclaim what she had so
wickedly and capriciously abandoned then it was entirely possible that Scottie
would be destroyed in the turmoil, chaos, and confusion.

Nanny's mouth hardened perceptibly at the dreadful thought, and the
blood of her combative race began to warm at the thought of the coming
conflict as she went out to fight for the little mite whose hand was so small in
hers. She might technically be a servant, but she was a proud standard bearer
of an ancient profession whose status was enshrined in the mists of mythol-
ogy. Not merely an English nanny, but a Scots nanny. Belted earls and strutting dukes, posing politicians and High Court judges had all been reduced to
nice, polite, clean little boys when confronted by the iron ruler of the nursery, the one who had potty trained them and taught them their p's and q's.

"Come on, darling. Let's go and stand at the bottom of the escalator. We
can watch mummy coming down."

Lisa Blass's homecoming was very different from her departure. First
there was the retinue. Two secretaries, neat and efficient, carried their Canon
electronic portables as well as Lisa's Vuitton hand luggage. On the escalator
they stood behind and on either side of her, like some latter-day Praetorian
guard, framing the main event.

Then there were the visuals. Lisa was not the great big person of Scott's
childlike imagination, but, her long hair swept back from her face, her wide-
shouldered Kenzo tweed coat and skirt accentuating the sweeping contours
of her body, she was clearly a formidable force to be reckoned with. She
appeared, thought Mrs. McTaggart, absolutely astounded to see them.

Lisa was astounded all right, but not by the fact of their presence. As she
glided down the short escalator a pint-size, perfectly formed Bobby Stansfield clone was staring up at her, his eyes unquestioningly following his
nanny's pointed finger.

Lisa had been ready for anything except that. Scott Starr? Scott Blass?
Oh, no. Her son was Scott Stansfield.

As the escalator deposited her in front of him, and he took a first awkward step toward her, his nanny's fingers pushing in the small of his back, Lisa found it difficult to catch her breath. Those piercing blue eyes, the identical sandy hair, the set of the mouth, the shape of the ears. God, how could she live with this while hating the man who had produced it?

"Welcome home, mummy," said Nellie McTaggart's accusing voice. "Kiss your mummy," she stage-whispered to Scott.

The Stansfield mouth went into a determined line. "I don't want to," he said.

"Of course you do, dear."

"I don't."

"It doesn't matter, nanny. There'll be time for that later," said Lisa, wondering as she spoke whether there ever would be.

What did she feel? Did the emotion fit with what she *should* feel? Not really. She was shocked by the extraordinary resemblance but that was just unsettling. It stirred her up, but it didn't turn her on to him. He was a little person. Pretty, beautiful even, but not hers, not part of her—even he seemed to know that. In a way it was the lack of feeling that worried her most, the void, the vacuum where the love should be. Somehow that brought home to her the damage the world had inflicted on her. Outwardly she had survived intact, but inside the wounds were horrendous, her personality scarred and twisted. To abolish the pain she had had to surrender her power of tender feeling, leaving only revenge in emotion's cupboard. Intellectually she knew what damage must have been done to the innocent who looked at her so accusingly, but emotionally she was hardly able to care.

"We've got to get to know each other right from the beginning, haven't we?" she said as much to herself as to anyone else, but even as the chauffeur moved forward to organize the baggage, she was thinking of something else —of the huge mortgage loan she had arranged against the freehold of the Madison Avenue offices, and of the four million she had borrowed from Citibank on the security of her Blass stock. Already the money was at work, and over a few short days the slickest editors and the hot-shot authors had received offers they were finding it difficult to refuse.

Geared up to the hilt, it was a dangerous, high-risk game that Lisa was playing, but the long years in the wilderness had made her hungry for success, and she wanted it now. As she had dreamed of the power she would one day inherit, Lisa had targeted the men and women she wanted. The plan had been there, needing only Vernon Blass's death and the keeping of his word for it to be put immediately into action.

As she stalked toward the Rolls, a curious son in tow, she was already talking over her shoulder to one of the secretaries.

"Get a memo off to Ken Farlow in Rights to auction the Liebermann book to the paperback houses the moment it's copy edited. And tell him I'm looking for a big price. I don't want chicken shit. Okay?"

"What should we do about the mini-series inquiry from HBO?"

"Screw the mini-series, let's sell the book big first. Sorry, nanny."

"Screw," said Scott and giggled.

"Nice little boys don't say naughty words like that," said nanny as much to Lisa as to Scott.

But Lisa had missed the putdown.

She was back, heading the right way this time, up the coast road from the Southern Boulevard bridge. Nannies and the activities of small children were already expunged from her mind. What she needed to do was to make a killing on the Liebermann book to provide cash flow for the new-look Blass. And then . . . and then. There would be time for the eating of that cold dish on which she had set her heart so long ago.

CHRISTIE STANSFIELD had eaten rather too much of granny's chocolate cake and now she was feeling slightly sick. But she wasn't going to let on, because that might spoil the event she looked forward to all week. So she sat there looking exactly like the little angel she was, all blond curls and blue eyes, and hoped that the funny feeling in her tummy would go away.

Bobby Stansfield stared fondly at her across the immaculate white linen of his mother's tea table. Some things could never be explained, and in his view his daughter was one of them. Whatever substances ran in his wife's blood, the milk of human kindness was conspicuous by its absence, and Bobby was enough of a realist to admit that neither parent qualified wholeheartedly for the adjective "good." By some extraordinary quirk of fate, however, they had produced Christie—the dearest, kindest child it was possible to imagine.

From the very earliest days Christie had been quite unlike other children. Placid and calm, she had hardly cried at all as a baby, and the terrible twos, that period of controlled horror that seemed to afflict most parents, had been a dreamy interlude of sweet reason and gentle learning. Christie had never had to be told to share her toys. Instead the problem was to stop her from giving them away. All she seemed to want was for the people around her to be happy, and she worked toward that end with the single-minded determination of the genuine child of God. Insofar as she had a vice at all, it was the one for which she now secretly suffered. She was very fond of her food and was totally addicted to anything covered in chocolate. So although her face would have made Botticelli drool, it was beginning to be clear that, in adolescence at least, baby fat might well be a problem. Bobby, who had desperately wanted a boy for traditional Stansfield reasons, was, with regard to his daughter, a born-again convert and he loved her with an intensity he had not dreamed possible. Loved her and was not a little in awe of her.

"Are you all right, darling?" he said unnecessarily across the table.

"Yes, thank you, daddy. I'm having a lovely tea," she lied. She felt a little guilty about the fib, but then she didn't want to upset the traditional calm of her father's and her grandmother's weekly tea. She knew how much they both looked forward to it.

"Another piece of cake, dear?" Caroline Stansfield had lost none of her uncanny ability to hover instinctively around the burning issues of the moment. The enormously rich cake from the hot Poinciana delicatessen,

Toojays, was affectionately known throughout Palm Beach as the "killer" cake.

"No thanks, gran, but I'd love another cup of tea."

Caroline Stansfield manipulated the Limoges china with the practiced ease of one to the manor born: cold milk first, tea through the Georgian strainer, a little hot water from the fine George III silver jug, the sugar bowl passed to her granddaughter with the cup and saucer. Her ancient hands worked smoothly, eloquent testimony to the continued high quality of the mind that age had not withered.

"I think we could do with some more hot water, Brown."

The creaky butler slunk awkwardly from the shadows of the terrace to do his mistress's bidding. The tea taken care of, it was time for politics. It usually was.

"How did your support look in Dallas?"

"What there is of it is dedicated. All the work over the years with the fundamentalists has paid off. Trouble is, their support is a double-edged weapon."

"For now that may be true," said Caroline reflectively. She fingered the double row of pearls on the wrinkled neck. "But I sense a new mood in America. Hungry for purpose, for spiritual rebirth. I think cars and washing machines have had their day. Politicians will ignore that need at their peril. Ten years down the road we may not recognize this country."

She paused, seemingly uncertain as to whether she wanted to be able to recognize it or not. She made her decision. Anything would be all right as long as a Stansfield was at the helm. "I think you should stick with the zealots, Bobby. They may sound a bit fanatical today, but the way things are going, yesterday's conservatives seem like closet socialists now."

"I'm inclined to agree, mother."

Whoops. Christie's stomach was on the move. The tea didn't seem to have helped. What had been an outside possibility was beginning to look distinctly probable. "Granny, please may I get down? I need to go to the bathroom." She prayed nobody would notice how white she was.

"Of course, dear."

Caroline Stansfield took the opportunity of Christie's absence to raise a delicate subject. In a way it was about politics, too. "Such a dear, sweet child, Bobby. How's her mother?" Caroline tended not to use Jo-Anne's actual name. She was always "your wife," "Christie's mother," or, occasionally, things less flattering.

Bobby laughed dismissively. "Oh, you know Jo-Anne. Busy playing the social game as if her life depended on it. Ever since Marjorie Donahue died she seems to have been right in the thick of it. If she spent an ounce as much energy on my political thing as she does on her charities and parties I'd be home and dry, no question."

Caroline's face had acquired a rather sly expression. She watched her son carefully. So very good looking. Presidential material definitely. A good chance. Better than poor old Fred's. There had been a time not so long ago when she had been far from sure whether or not he wanted it enough.

"I gather that Lisa Blass is back in town. Old Vernon left her everything, apparently. Not bad for five years' work."

The shadow passed briefly over Bobby's face. Lisa Starr. His Lisa. Married to a geriatric. Bearing him a son. Aborting Bobby's own child.

In his mind he saw the stricken face as his cruel words exploded into it, and he remembered her bitterness, the hatred eating up the beauty, the poison spilling from the eyes. He no longer knew what he felt about her, but he had never forgotten her, and his political training told him that in some subterranean way he had reason to fear her. Especially now that she was at last a woman of substance.

In the downstairs lavatory Christie Stansfield wasn't feeling well at all. Nobody must know. She would get this done, clean up, and go back as if nothing had happened. Chocolate cake. It was always her downfall. Chocolate cake. Oooooh. She placed her small head firmly over the bowl and waited for the inevitable, and while her father mused over the girl he had treated so badly, the woman who would now be a power in Palm Beach, she puked out her tiny heart into the sparkling waters of the immaculate toilet.

~17~

*S*COTT BLASS LOUNGED moodily on the slubbed silk sofa, as he watched his mother. His expression of sulky indifference was common to rich teenagers all over the globe, but it hid feelings that were far from usual. The emotions were conflicting, and extraordinarily tangled, a mass of barbed wire and roses, of sharpness and sweetness, of adoration and rage.

Oblivious to the effect she was having on her seventeen-year-old son, Lisa Blass talked into the telephone with the single-mindedness of the born dealer. Into it she poured her charm, her energy, and her desire, and Scott would have gladly settled for any of these. It had always been like that from the moment he remembered seeing her first, smelling like a sweet dream and looking like a startled goddess as she descended from the escalator at West Palm International. From that moment to this he had been in love with her, and from this moment to that his love had been unrequited. It was by far and away the most frustrating aspect of his life so far. Wasn't a mother supposed to *love* her son? Endlessly he had sought the reason for her indifference, and being unable to find one, he had concluded it must be some inadequacy on his part that had led to this unhappy state of affairs, some dreadful character deficiency that had in some mysterious way made him uniquely unlovable and unworthy of maternal affection. In the years of dreadful yearning, one thing had remained constant. He had never given up hope, never stopped trying. In bed at night, riding the waves by day, he schemed and planned to make her care, to force her to really love him.

"You ought to get a surfboard, darling. Such good exercise," she had said to him. He had been six at the time. Now he was Florida State Champion.

"I do so admire men who know about car engines." He had begged Charlie Stark to take him on as an unpaid mechanic the very next day and had worked all summer at Mustang Paradise until he could rebuild a '77 from scratch in the pitch dark with one hand tied behind his back.

"A boy brought up on the streets of West Palm is worth half a dozen of the pathetic specimens you see around here." For two straight years he had refused to talk to anyone with the right accent or clothes, and had mixed exclusively with the rough, tough kids from neighborhood bars like Roxy's and from the country-music dives on the other side of the coastal railroad.

But it had all been for nothing. His mother's glacial indifference, like the laws of the Medes and Persians, altered not. It wasn't that she was aggressive to him, or even that she ignored him. She was always ready with advice and encouragement. It was just that she didn't seem to *care,* and it drove him into a frenzy of frustration.

His mother was doing a lot of smiling at the mouthpiece, but Scott could tell she didn't like what she was hearing. "Well, Mort, you could knock me down with a feather. I had no *idea* Anne was unhappy with the contract. I mean, she's staying here this weekend. She's out by the pool right now. She never mentioned it to me. Not a hint."

Somebody at the other end did a lot of talking.

"No, no, of course not. We're all friends. Annie and I go back to the very beginnings. Together we put Blass on the map. The contract isn't the point. I wouldn't want to force anything on Annie if she's unhappy."

Lisa paused. She had made the point obliquely. The contract *could* be enforced if it came to that. But it would be the baddest of bad scenes, and Anne Liebermann was enough of a prima donna to ladle tons of it into the fan. Damn! Why did everybody have to get greedy? Five consecutive number-one best sellers all under the Blass imprint had made Anne Liebermann a multimillionairess, but she was apparently happy to blow the relationship to smithereens for that little bit more. Except that a million dollars wasn't such a little bit.

She looked up at the ceiling for inspiration as the New York agent made his pitch. Boy, he was good. Worth every dime of his fifteen percent commission. He'd taken the trouble to line up the other houses, and Lisa knew he wasn't bullshitting. By Monday morning Anne Liebermann could be a Random House author. So far Blass had never lost one and had successfully poached a score from the other publishers. If it was to lose the jewel in its crown, then maybe other authors would get ideas. It could be the beginning of a slippery slope, as others jumped on the bandwagon, and Lisa's heart went cold at the dreadful thought. No, Anne Liebermann would have to be bought off, but hopefully for far less than a million bucks.

"Look, Mort, darling. Give me the weekend to think about it. Can I call you on Monday morning—first thing? I'll see what I can do to soften Anne up. Break open my best claret. Ha, ha. Yup. Okay, Mort. Talk to you then. Bye, darling."

She slammed the telephone down hard. "Damn it to hell. That thieving, greedy *bitch!* Where is the fat, money-grubbing cow?"

Scott's ears pricked up. As always his mother made him disturbingly ambivalent. He was pleased somebody had irritated her, and yet agonized by it all at the same time. "What's up, mom?"

Lisa cast her eyes over her superb-looking son as if he were the third banana in the fruit scene. "That goddamn Anne Liebermann is trying to wangle out of her contract and score a whole lot more money."

"Can't you make her stick to the contract?" It seemed a reasonable question. That's what contracts were for.

"In this game, if you haven't got a happy author, you've had it, no matter what the contract says. Trying to chain her to a typewriter against her will would be bad news for everyone. No, I'll just have to pay her what she wants. Try and soften her up over the weekend, I guess."

In his mother's eyes there was suddenly a faraway, speculative look. "Perhaps you could be a help, darling. You know, flatter her a little. You're so good at that sort of thing. I thought at lunch she seemed rather taken with you."

Scott felt the warm glow explode through him. That was not a million miles from a compliment. His mother had just told him he was charming, and indirectly she had even asked for his *help*. God! That was *really* something.

He stood up, trying desperately to look as cool as he didn't feel. "Okay, mom. No sweat. I'll see what I can do. Did you say she was out by the pool?"

ANNE LIEBERMANN'S body was singing like a souped-up soprano on speed, and she didn't want the sublime feeling to stop. What a night! Two in a row, and she had hardly dreamed it could be possible. It was far from unusual in her books for the heroine to be pleasured by a blond-haired blue-eyed surfer Joe equivalent, but she had hardly been prepared for the reality of the experience. Next time she would set the typewriter on fire. It would be faction, not fiction. There was only one interesting question, and that was "why?" She was rich, she was famous, but she was under few illusions about where she came in in the beauty stakes, and Scott Blass was just about young enough to be her son. For the moment, however, that was of academic interest. The problem right now was how to get him back into bed for an action replay before breakfast.

She stared up at the intricate carved wood ceiling searching for inspiration in its colored patterns. But the ghost of Addison Mizner wasn't interested in her predicament. In fact the whole room, with its heavy furniture, somber paintings, and Andalusian "feel" seemed sexually sterile, globally unconcerned with such trivial pursuits.

Through the open window of the bedroom, Scott could see the white-topped rollers drifting in gently toward the beach. Great! The surf was up. Later he'd meet with the boys at the East Inlet and do some tube riding on the new Impact board. *If* he was allowed to tear himself away from the world's best-selling authoress.

"Penny for your thoughts, Scott." Anne Liebermann's voice and her sparkling brown eyes were by far her most appealing physical attributes. The rest of her was a federal disaster area, but it was mercifully hidden beneath the silk sheets that she had drawn up to her neck. She had a chance.

"Oh, nothing. I was just looking at the surf. Should be a good day out there later."

Anne said nothing. The fish wasn't biting. Damn! He wasn't really into her. There was no getting away from that. And after two nights of ecstasy she was well on the way to becoming addicted. Suddenly, getting him out of his blue jeans and back under the sheets was one of the more important things in her life. Like pushing the mini-series rights to ABC, or copping the *Cosmopolitan* serialization.

"Did you enjoy last night, Scott?" she heard herself say coquettishly. Damn it to hell. How come people still believed in free will? That was the last thing she'd intended to say.

Scott turned to look at her. Enjoyed it? He had endured it. Endured it for the mother he worshiped, to save her the money that she wanted saved. He had survived it somehow, but both his back and his mind bore the scars of the ultimate sacrifice. He had closed his mind off and thought of his mother, not his country. She had wanted him to be "nice" to Anne Liebermann, and boy, had he been "nice." He just hoped to God the results would filter down to the Blass bottom line. Maybe, just maybe, Anne would stay with Blass and drop her asking price from a million to five hundred thousand. If so, every single penny of the money saved would have been hard earned.

He fought back the irritation. "Oh. Yeah. Sure. I mean, of course I did." The lie didn't sound very convincing. What the *hell* did she want? A vote of thanks? A quote for the dust jacket of her next novel? In between the one from *People* and the one from *Newsweek:* "Anne Liebermann screws as well as she writes."—Scott Blass, surfer.

Anne Liebermann tried to believe him, but she had not written five consecutive number-one best sellers for nothing. For some reason Scott Blass was humoring her, and she was not a million miles from suspecting just what that reason was. She sat up in bed, taking care that the bedclothes covered her ample bosom. "Scott. Did your mother mention that there's a chance I might be leaving Blass?" Anne had never been spoiled as a child, but her phenomenal success over the last twelve years had enabled her to make up for lost time. She was direct, worldly-wise, and quite ruthless. She peered at him intently to see how he would react to her fast ball.

His face told her everything. Scott took it right on the point of his chin. That was the last thing he had expected. In the clinches, Anne Liebermann had abandoned herself to passion. Now it seemed her critical faculties had been placed only temporarily on ice. He felt the color rush up into the sunburned cheeks, and he prepared his fervent denial of what Anne Liebermann now knew to be true. "Oh no. She never mentioned that. How awful. Why would you want to do that?"

Anne Liebermann missed none of the confusion. Okay, so that was it. Lisa Blass had detailed her son off to sweeten her up with some sexual candy. Wow. That was pretty heavy. Mothers usually drew the line at that sort of thing. Or maybe young Scott had gone into private enterprise, and Lisa had been an unwitting co-conspirator. Whatever. One thing was for sure. Two nights of bliss had been offered to induce her to stay with Blass. She almost laughed out loud as she thought of the words. Bliss and Blass. Blass for Bliss. It sounded like a good slogan.

"Oh, I might not leave, Scott. I might just stay right where I am," she said cunningly. She rolled her eyes. The initial disappointment that she might not be loved for herself alone was fast fading. In this life precious few people were, and she was enough of a realist to realize that. No, on this earth you had to be prepared to use what you had to get what you wanted. It appeared she had something. It was certain that she wanted something. It would be a straight trade.

"I hope so."

"Do you really, Scott? I wonder how much you hope that."

"Well, of course I hope that, Anne. C'mon. I would, wouldn't I?" Scott wasn't at all sure he'd gotten away with it. It seemed to him that his plan had been uncovered. There was still hope, but it looked as if his investment were going to have to be increased.

"Why don't you come over here and prove it, Scott."

Scott's stomach headed downward. Oh no. Not before breakfast. There had to be a way out, and a polite one, too.

"Not now, Anne. We'd miss breakfast. And that really irritates mother. Later, maybe."

Mother. Even now, he couldn't get away from her. He had screwed for her, and now he was using her as his excuse. And all, almost certainly, for nothing. If he delivered the goods his contribution would be ignored. As always he would be discounted, overlooked, patronized, treated like some beautiful, but ultimately pointless Ming vase. A thing to be admired, valued even, but ultimately forgotten. If only there was a way to gain the spotlight, to hijack the dead center of the stage, so that his life could be played out before his mother, a captive audience of one in the front row. It was all he asked for. It was all he had never been given.

Suddenly Scott was tired of the whole business. Tired and hungry. In the dining room there would be hash browns and French toast, bacon and scrambled eggs. This thing needed to be wrapped up. He had done the best he could.

He threw what he hoped was a warm smile at Anne as he headed determinedly toward the door. "I'll make sure they save some breakfast for you. See you later," he managed as he fled the scene.

———

"How DARE you sit there like some chubby cherub and tell me how I ought to behave! Christ, Christie, that's a dangerous world out there. Believe me, I know. If you don't shoot first you end up in the shit."

Bobby Stansfield came off the sun bed in a shower of crumpled newspaper. Already his sunburned face was turning a dangerous cherry red.

"Don't you *dare* talk to my daughter like that," he screamed at the top of his voice, advancing menacingly on Jo-Anne. "Don't you dare. Do you hear? Do you *hear* me?"

In a second Christie was between them. Referee. Peacemaker. Conscientious objector to violence, disharmony, anger. Her long golden-blond hair ran free to her shoulders, bangs framed the round, appealing face. Freckled cheeks, blue eyes, a retroussé nose, full, generous lips. The effect was as fresh as new-mown hay, cuddly puppy dogs, the first taste of summer strawberries.

"Please don't fight. It was my fault. I didn't mean to sound pompous, mom, but I realize I must have. I'm sorry. Forgive me."

An apoplectic Bobby could hardly get the words out. "Don't apologize. There's no need to apologize. I heard what you said. You were absolutely right. There's more to life than social climbing. She's got no right to speak to you like that."

"She does because she's my mom, and because I love her very much." Big tears appeared in Christie's eyes.

Bobby deflated like a pricked balloon. Christie always did that. The talent for turning the other cheek. Where had she gotten it from? There had never been a Stansfield remotely like her, and from the precious little he knew about his wife's family it didn't appear they had been overburdened with people like Christie, either.

"Oh, that's a very sweet thing to say, darling." Jo-Anne felt the alien emotion of tenderness flow through her. In the presence of transcendent goodness she usually felt acutely uncomfortable, which was one of the reasons she found her daughter almost impossible to live with, but occasionally it struck a chord within her.

"I'm sorry I overreacted, dear," said Bobby at last, swirling in the currents of forgiveness that seemed so suddenly to have engulfed the trio.

Somehow the atmosphere seemed ripe for the confessional. "You're quite right, Christie, it is unChristian of me to hate Lisa Blass so much. I should be able to rise above it, but she's so damn full of herself since that company of hers hit the headlines, and she's made so much goddamned *money* it's just indecent. She sits there in that huge house and stuffs it with everyone one's ever wanted to meet, and lords it over the rest of us. People in this town will shed blood to get to one of her dinner parties. Apparently last week she even had Michael Jackson there, and this weekend she's got that guy who discovered the AIDS cure and Anne Liebermann." Jo-Anne mused gloomily over the unfairness of it all. Palm Beach wasn't *supposed* to be impressed by meritocrats. It was the only place in America where it was considered poor form to ask a person what he did. When the only truthful answer was "not very much," the question was thought to demonstrate insensitivity in the questioner. In fact Jo-Anne's voice had taken on such tones of utter dejection that all three of them had to laugh.

"Oh, mom, you are incorrigible. What does it matter? So what, she's a social gadfly. If it makes her happy there's no harm."

Bobby couldn't resist a contribution. "Lisa makes Palm Beach nervous. It can't control her, and yet it can't ignore her because she has the commodity it worships above all other things. Money."

Jo-Anne felt the juices begin to flow once more. "Well, all I can say is that she's an ungrateful bitch. She was my friend once and she sided with that ludicrous old bag of bones Marjorie Donahue against me. It's all your father's fault. He introduced her to everyone, and now she won't even talk to him."

Christie was determined to keep the flame of good humor alive, as Jo-Anne's venomous breath threatened to extinguish it. "Ah, *now* I get the picture. She had a fling with dad and you're jealous after all these years. Isn't that cute? For sure there must have been something good about her if she was a girlfriend of dad's." Christie was trying desperately to keep it light.

"Don't be ridiculous, Christie. How could I be jealous of a nobody like Lisa Blass? She hooked that myopic old fart Vernon and then left town a week after the wedding. I tell you, if you love me I don't want you mixing with that bitch or anyone who'll even speak to her."

"I wouldn't be disloyal to you, mom."

"Don't be," said Jo-Anne nastily.

"Frankly," said Bobby, disengaging himself from the family group and retreating to the sun bed to retrieve his drink, "I admire what Lisa Blass has done. She turned Blass into the money spinner it is today entirely on her own. She invented Anne Liebermann, whose books you seem to read so avidly, and she restored that magnificent house to its former glory—by all accounts."

He took a long, self-satisfied sip on his dark Dewar's and water, confident that his remarks would have hit the spot.

In many ways time had been kind to Bobby. The presidency had so far eluded him, although, like Ted Kennedy, he was constantly mentioned as a possible future contender, but in the Senate he was a formidable figure indeed, his seniority landing him the chairmanship of the Foreign Relations Committee. In that august institution he was a potent force, a leading light in the inner circle. He was the best of the good ol' boys, the man whose nod and wink could smooth the path of the most controversial bills, and as a result he walked the corridors of power with a measured, self-confident tread, the president's ear never more than a telephone call away, the mightiest media men hanging on his every word, fascinated by his cocktail-party asides. He wasn't the king but he was the maker of kings and it was almost . . . almost . . . enough.

There was nowhere on earth he wasn't welcome. No corner of the globe where the arms wouldn't have opened for him. With one glaring exception. The Villa Gloria on South Ocean Boulevard. Lisa Starr, Lisa Blass, had not forgiven him, and it rankled. It was easy to blame Jo-Anne for the bad feeling, but he knew in his heart that it was unfair. It was he who had insulted her and thrown her out cruelly when she had honored and loved him. It was he who had called her a lesbian on his wife's word and told her in effect that Stansfields didn't marry street trash. For some people, the years would have smoothed the jagged memory, but for someone of Lisa's spirit and self-respect the wounds would live on, still sore, never healing in the damp atmosphere of hatred. Lisa had lain in his arms in the moonlight and learned the language of passion, an eager student, a brilliant pupil who had surpassed the teacher in the creative innovation of her lovemaking. Even now after all these years the perfect body lived on in his mind: its curves, its secret places opened up to him, its wonderful aromas, its tantalizing textures. Never before or since had he had such a lover, and he never would again.

He was vaguely aware of Jo-Anne's bad-tempered withdrawal, the too loud slamming of a couple of doors. To hell with her. The bitch. All her cunning manipulations had failed to bring her happiness and satisfaction. Nobody could win the social-climbing game. There was always someone just a little bit higher than you.

But there was one thing Jo-Anne *had* done for him, and it had changed his life. Christie. Kind, wonderful, beautiful Christie. About her he could not be objective. She was the Mona Lisa, more beautiful than the most highly paid model or the most successful film star. To him she had it all. Miss Peaches and Cream. Miss Young America. The sort of girl the Marines would die for in some foreign field. The living embodiment of everything that was wholesome and wonderful about his country. Christie didn't drink. She didn't take drugs. She was an active member of her church. She honored and loved her parents. She worked hard at school. Christie didn't sleep around.

He smiled ruefully to himself as he thought about that one. Fathers always had that problem sooner or later. He hoped fervently he would avoid the possessive-father role, but he was far from sure he would be able to. Just thinking about Christie's future boyfriends made him anxious as hell. Please God it would be somebody who was kind to her. She surely deserved that, but in this life you didn't always get what you deserved. He blotted it all out. It hadn't happened. Yet. "Come on Chris, let's shoot a few Frisbees on the beach. My spinning wrist is itching like hell."

"You're on, dad."

The two looked more like brother and sister than father and daughter as they scampered out over the lush lawns toward the cooling sands of the early evening seashore.

NONE OF them, except Anne Liebermann, had really wanted to go, but she had been adamant. So they had gone, and now they were there.

It was Palm Beach in flagrante delicto.

The huge El Bravo Way house was throbbing like the tight skin of a big bass drum, throbbing, shining, and shaking with the mighty, roaring party that it harbored in its bowels. Lisa had promised that the Von Preussen party would be over the top, and she had been proved magnificently right. The valet parkers had set the scene. Usually they wore neat little uniforms, red waistcoats, clean open-necked shirts, black trousers, black shoes. Not tonight. Tonight they were stripped to the waist, their torsos glistening with oil, shining and shimmering in the light of the storm torches that each carried. They wore what looked like short, pleated white skirts ending just above the knee, and nothing else at all except for ankle-length boots laced up with leather thongs. There were two to each limo. One to hold the light, the other to park —and everyone was forced to remember that the great gold-embossed invitations, extravagantly engraved with the Von Preussen baronial crest, had mentioned that the theme of the party was to be "Ancient Rome."

Anne Liebermann roared her appreciation. "I told you all it would be marvelous. I met Heine Von Preussen in Venice once at the Biennale. He's completely mad. Deliciously, wonderfully mad. Really Lisa, you oughtn't to be so stuffy. It's just what this town needs—a bit of eccentricity."

Lisa laughed politely. Anne Liebermann was happy, then so was she. If a few descendants of German war manufacturers wanted to part with some of their ill-gotten gains and in the process entertain her star author, then she would try to get through the evening with her insides still inside.

Scott's thoughts were running along parallel lines. He knew some of these guys. The ones that rich guy had gotten to dress like this. A couple of them were pals, fellow surfers, and as far as he was concerned the whole thing so far was a sick joke. The skirts were bad enough, but the oiled skin was Technicolor yawn time. Of course it was supposed to be *haute* camp, a lovely jaded joke, but the bottom line had to do with bottoms. Von Preussen was a queer, and that was why the valet parkers looked like they did. It was the final straw that Anne Liebermann found the whole disgusting fantasy "wonderfully mad." He tried to control his temper. After all, he had lost points by opting out of the prebreakfast coupling. It would be a shame to have wasted two nasty nights.

The girl who sold the subsidiary rights for Blass was hovering in emotional uncertainty. Her genes told her that there was something sinister, something deeply disreputable about what she was about to experience. But she was young enough not to be immune to the sight of rippling young flesh and the conspicuous if possibly decadent consumption that she was about to be asked to enjoy. Also there was the Liebermann factor. It might be a house party, but for Blass employees life was work, and so it was also an office party. Liebermann was flirting with another publisher; she must be humored.

"I agree, Anne. I think it's going to be fun."

The house party—a hot plastic surgeon from Brazil and his starlet wife who doubled as an advertisement for his ability to hold back the tide of time; the Nobel Prize winner who'd discovered the AIDS vaccine and his incredulous, middle-American wife; a fashionable, "straight" novelist who Lisa had just poached from Knopf; the guy who bought the mini-series rights for ABC, and his fast-talking, faster-looking "friend"—were gathering in front of the wide-open iron-studded oak door beneath the towering white marble columns of the vast portico.

"I have a feeling," Lisa said to Anne, "that you ain't seen nuthin' yet."

Just inside the door were four very beautiful young boys. In the Von Preussen establishment there was nothing remarkable about that. The surprise value was that they made the parking boys look seriously overdressed. They wore absolutely nothing at all except for an apology for a G string and a thin coat of the finest white talcum powder that extended all over their fine "Roman" features. Each stood still, striking a sculptor's pose, and each held a short leash that attached them to four sleek, sharp-toothed cheetahs. Guests were thus channeled through a perverse tunnel of danger before being deposited in front of their host.

Heine Von Preussen was not outshone by his surroundings. Tall and thin, he seemed to hover over the proceedings like some wizard from a land of childish dreams. He was about thirty, maybe fifty, possibly in his early twenties. His face was feminine, with big, liquid eyes and a fine full mouth in which small white teeth flashed prettily. It was perfectly clear that he had made it a life's preoccupation to avoid the sun, and his alabaster skin, soft and delicate, mimicked the porcelain of a Meissen figure. Although he was six feet tall, all his gestures hinted at those of a tiny, delicate person, as did the width of his shoulders and the rather obscene bulge of his little stomach that protruded crossly beneath the tight white toga. His dainty feet, their toenails painted blood red, peeped from beneath the Egyptian cotton; his fluttering fingers danced and plucked at the air as his reedy voice warbled its welcome.

Lisa led the way, shepherding her flock toward their host.

"I thought this was supposed to be Roman," said Anne Liebermann loudly. "Why am I picking up Greek vibrations?"

"Catch the Caravaggio on the right," said Scott to the virologist.

"Good evening, baron," said Lisa Blass.

Heine Von Preussen's eyes mocked her hostility. He had been in Palm Beach long enough to know the score. The locals didn't understand parties like this. Or if they did, then they didn't approve of them. Okay, so a few young people like the Loy Andersons, who every year gave the wild, Bruce Sutka-designed Young Friends of the Red Cross Ball at the Henry Morrison Flagler Museum, knew how to let their hair down and have some real fun, but the Europeans did this sort of thing better, and gay Europeans did it best of all.

"Lisa Blass. How very kind of you all to come to my party." He bowed gracefully from the waist and held Lisa's hand the correct centimeter and a half from the deep red lips that matched the color of his pedicured toenails.

Lisa made the introductions, her tone formal. None of her party, despite the demands of Anne Liebermann, had made the effort to dress according to the theme. In the milling throng behind the baron, she could see that they would be in the minority, as she had hoped.

"If there is anything you want that you don't see, then promise me you will ask for it." The baron waved an all-encompassing hand, his eyes knowing. The coded message was not far from the surface. Substances were available. And possibly people, too. "First you must drink from the fountain of life." His words hung in the jasmine-impregnated air as he stood back to let them pass.

The "fountain of life" stood six feet tall. It was a real fountain in which stone cherubs endlessly urinated into a large marble cachment area on the surface of which floated the finest and most delicate pink hibiscus flowers. Every now and again the recycled liquid was replaced by a powdered, pomaded, white-wigged flunkey wearing white gloves and beauty spots in the

Versailles style. The liquid, it could be seen from the labels on the jereboam bottles was Pol Roger's 1975 Vintage Pink Champagne. The servant's job was endlessly to fill frosted Lalique champagne glasses from the "waters" of the fountain.

Scott fought back the desire to ask for a Bud. Lisa gasped at the vulgarity of the ostentation. Anne Liebermann howled her delight. The Nobel winner began to see how he might enjoy himself and vowed to tell no one how he had won his award. He might get mobbed in a place like this.

Apparently there was one more receiving line.

The two people who stood waiting for them now were an unlikely couple. One, tall and regal, looked like royalty, albeit minor royalty. She was straight as a die, wearing a tiara with stones the size of crown jewels, long white gloves, a classic full empire-line white dress, and a look of long-suffering dignity on her pleasant but far from beautiful face. Beside her, and half her size, stood a smiling, be-togaed Vietnamese.

The old ballroom had been extended by a giant white-and-gold marquee, and it was difficult to tell where the house ended and the grounds began, the more so because all doors and window frames had been removed to amplify the feeling of the party's theme.

Right now they appeared to be in the middle of a thriving and extremely active slave market. Around the walls were hay carts, with wooden spoked wheels, each guarded by a couple of stern centurions in period costume. Spread about on their surface were the most extraordinary cross section of humanity, many of them in heavy chains, that Lisa had ever seen. There were cheerful dwarfs, buxom old ladies, scantily clad maidens of decidedly specific charms, and cheeky black urchins, who looked like, and almost certainly were, the back street hustlers of the poorer areas of West Palm. From time to time a garrulous old man would stand on a stool and conduct a make-believe auction in which the Von Preussen guests would "pretend" to buy the slaves on offer. It was perfectly clear to Lisa that the enthusiasm with which the "sales" were being conducted was quite definitely in excess of that demanded by fantasy.

The one in progress was a case in point. The small black boy, a chain around each skinny leg, was standing center stage in the protective crook of the auctioneer's arms, smiling broadly at the descriptive extravagances that were being applied to him.

"A charming little chap to have around the house . . . instantly available to satisfy your every whim, and I mean *every* whim, fellow citizens. Now I am only asking ten pieces of gold. That's because he's so young. But the young can be trained, can't they? They can learn to do exactly what you like, can't they? Now who'll buy this polite little boy . . ."

Apparently several people. Lisa recognized one of the better connected Palm Beach realtors among the active bidders, locked in combat with a big, greasy German industrialist whose fortune apparently came from soap.

"Would you like to feel him, fellow citizens? Feel what he's made of?" To shrieks of delight the contestants leaped forward to experience their pound of flesh, and for one second Lisa allowed herself to wonder if it had really been like this in those far-off days before the empire, its strength sapped by hedonism, fell prey to the marauding hordes from the north. If so, was there a lesson to be learned from history? Was this party trying to tell the world something about latterday Western civilization? It was almost worth thinking about.

The dancing seemed to be a sideshow to the main attraction of the slave auction, but here, too, both money and creativity had been spent. The dance floor was the swimming pool. In itself that was far from the most original thing in the world; at lots of Palm Beach parties they boarded over the pool for dancing. It was standard procedure, especially for a town in which space was at a premium. The Von Preussen establishment, however, was not short of space, and the pool had been selected for more unusual reasons. The dance floor was not of wood but of transparent Perspex, and raised a few feet over the surface of the hundred-foot-long pool, it left plenty of room for people to swim beneath it while looking up at the dancers above. Huge water lilies floated beneath the dancing feet, and sylphlike water nymphs, both male and female, their diaphanous robes failing completely to hide their strategically revealed nakedness, cavorted in the ninety-degree water. Several of the braver guests had already joined them, and now, their faces pressed rudely to the underside of the dance floor, their features squashed against the Perspex, they shouted ribald remarks up the togas of the cheerful dancers, as they swung and swayed to the reassuring rhythms of the Mike Carney band.

Lisa, firm in her desire to avoid either buying a slave or providing a peep show for the hoi polloi, managed to get everyone to a table where both spectacles could be seen without being indulged in.

"Well, Anne—you wanted to see the soft underbelly of Palm Beach. Here it is."

Anne flung out an arm to embrace the scene. "Darling, it's wonderful. Just wonderful. *Forget* Fellini."

Lisa raised a casual eyebrow. Anne Liebermann was being uncharacteristically girlish, and it was not a pretty sight. Usually she liked to affect a hard-bitten, tough-as-nails personality, her conversation peppered with fruity swear words and references to bizarre and unusual sexual practices. Now, however, she was simpering and giggling like a teenager on her first date.

Lisa had already identified its cause. Scott. Anne Liebermann was all over her son like a hot rash. The worst part was that Lisa had a suspicion she herself just might be the cause. She had asked Scott to be nice to Anne Liebermann, and it appeared that he had taken her at her word. What was the name of the king who had asked his knights to rid him of a troublesome priest? He hadn't expected them to take him literally. Or had he? After all, he'd demanded to be punished for it afterward. Should she accept responsibility too? The boy worshiped her. That was his tragedy. And for some reason that she had never quite understood she appeared to be congenitally incapable of returning his affection. That was *her* tragedy. Time and time again she had tried to love him. The raw material was all there. He looked almost too good to be true. A Stansfield clone and a dream to behold. He was sophisticated and vulnerable, charming yet insecure—everything that a mother should be drawn to.

In vain, however, had she sought for the spark of maternal instinct. But where love should be there was only blackness, coldness where there should be warmth. As far as she was concerned, her indifference to her own son was more than a weakness; it hovered on the borders of illness. She knew, too, that there was no cure for the disease and no therapy that could make something of the nothingness in her soul. Maybe if he hadn't looked quite so much like Bobby . . . every day those steel-blue eyes reminding her of the one-time love and of the ever pressing necessity for revenge on the man who had fathered him, and on his dreadful wife.

She forced herself out of the uncomfortable reverie. Perhaps she had asked her son to do too much, but at least Anne Liebermann was having the weekend of a lifetime.

In the glittering candlelight Lisa watched with interest as Anne Liebermann's short fingers plucked at her son, her square chin hovering at the shoulders of his immaculate tuxedo. Doubtless beneath the table her ample thigh would be rubbing insistently against his.

"Lisa, I think your son is the most delicious thing I've ever seen. Do you know I saw him *surf* today? He's the best thing in the world. I sat on the beach transfixed. Literally transfixed."

Everyone laughed except Scott. He had just been referred to as a "thing." God, she was awful.

For the novelist who'd been with Knopf it was too much. Most of the things Anne said were too much for him. "Really, you should have more respect for language, Anne," he said. " '*Literally* transfixed' means you were impaled through and through."

"I choose my words *extremely* carefully," shrieked Anne Liebermann, rolling her eyes in a charade of lewdness, as she dropped a huge dollop of beluga and melba toast into her mouth.

Everyone was expected to get the message. Everyone did. There was embarrassed general laughter that Scott and Lisa did not join in. Anne gushed on, capitalizing on the spotlight's descent on her glistening face. "In fact, Lisa, I've had a wonderful idea for a new book. Surfing. Just like that. Surfing and surfers. What do you think?"

"I think we should know if it's going to be a Blass book," said Lisa slyly.

"Darling, of course it's going to be a Blass book, and Scott can help me with the research. I think this book is going to need an *awful* lot of research."

Her hand massaged Scott's on the white damask in full view of the assembled company. With a superhuman effort he managed to keep it on the table. The triumph in his mother's face was reward enough. There was nothing he wouldn't do to see that.

Lisa wanted the *t*'s crossed and the *i*'s dotted. "I'm sure we have a deal,

Anne. Scott's your researcher and Blass is your publisher. You'd better let that high-powered agent of yours know the score."

She turned to her son. It was time for a sugar lump. He'd just made Blass a million dollars. "We ought to give you a commission, darling. For helping our authors dream up their ideas."

But a twinge of guilt shot through her like a knife as she beheld the slavelike devotion in Scott's eyes.

～18～

I N THE NORTON Gallery, funded almost exclusively by Palm Beach money and yet situated unhappily on the wrong side of Lake Worth, East and West met in anxious union. Both inside and out it showed the class of its parentage, and its Neoclassical exterior enclosed one of the finest collections of modern art outside the major centers such as New York, Malibu, and Houston. The faded houses that surrounded it provided a complete contrast. West Palm Beach's bustling, thrusting expansion had, for some reason, been almost entirely toward the north, and the seedy, run-down apartment buildings and factory warehouses still clustered greedily around the Norton like some rusty scaffolding about a soon-to-be-renovated architectural gem. In the entrance foyer the names of its benefactors were advertised prominently on polished wooden panels on a list that could have been lifted almost unchanged from the shiny social pages of the *Palm Beach Daily News*. It was one of the very few places on earth where the Blass and Stansfield names attempted an uneasy coexistence, their closeness in dramatic contrast to the unbridgeable gulf that in reality separated them.

Even though he preferred the gaudy self-confidence of the gallery's famed Gilbert and George collection, Scott had to agree with his mother that the Picasso was rather magnificent.

"Some people still sneer at Picasso and say he was a rip-off merchant, but look at the date on this: 1924. That's three years *before* the Braque next to it, and yet the subject matter and the treatment of it is almost identical in both paintings. Amazing texture. Wonderfully rich colors."

Lisa spoke with the authority of an expert. In Europe it was not the publishing business alone that she had mastered. It had all started in Paris under the adoring and penetratingly perceptive guidance of Michel Dupré. In London she had been her own tutor, but after Paris, the foundation had been there. She had attacked the museums of Europe like a hungry lioness, devouring voraciously the contents of the Prado, the Hermitage in Leningrad, and the Florentine galleries. The Norton could not hope to compete with these, but it contained paintings that would not have been out of place in even the greatest museum. This Picasso was one of them.

Lisa waved her elegant fingers to demonstrate her point, and Scott watched her reverently. No painting could compare with his mother. No artist would have dared attempt a likeness. Even if one had managed to capture the outside, he would have missed the restless energy that beamed from within, the steely purpose that hung around her like an ice-cold aura. It was the motivation that was the mystery. What provided the force for her dynamism, the thrust to mighty endeavor that flattened obstacles in her path and banished all opposition to her purpose? He had never learned the answer to the fascinating question, although he had spent his life trying. Somehow, though, he knew that in the answering he would find the key to his own ambition. Once he knew the secret of his mother's needs, then his own desires would be hovering on the brink of actualization. Once he knew how, he would become her champion, make her dreams his dreams, and in turning her fantasies into reality he, Scott, would be able to bask forever in the warm rays of her gratitude. In that dawn of new light he would be born again, the loved and wanted son, a mother-and-child reunion promising an eternity of bliss.

His mother had moved on ahead to admire a fine Matisse and he had lingered over the unusual Picasso sculpted head. A female voice, icepick sharp, cut into his thoughts.

"Over on this side of the bridge again, Lisa? Can't drag yourself away from the back streets?" said the sneering voice. "Amazing what marriage to a geriatric can achieve, but you know what they say. Money doesn't bring happiness. And it never changes a tramp into a lady."

From his vantage point twenty feet away Scott felt the shock waves break over him. He couldn't believe his ears. Was this some bantering joke, the hilarious jibing of an old and trusted friend? The tone of the voice—cruel and supercilious—said "no-way," and the persona of the speaker backed that up. It was Jo-Anne Stansfield, wife of Senator Stansfield, patroness of the arts, looking good enough to eat, and spitting poison through clenched lips.

Scott's initial response was to walk forward and smash her instantly to the ground, but instead he stood rooted to the spot, a force far stronger than emotion freezing him, like Lot's wife, to the place where he stood. Deep in his guts the howling cats of curiosity had been let loose. He knew instinctively that he would learn something now which would be of vital importance to him. It was a strange feeling, of itching intuition, of the dawning of an awareness that he hovered on the brink of fundamental knowledge. Jo-Anne Stansfield and her husband Bobby. His mother disliked them both intensely, but he hadn't a clue as to why. She always avoided parties at which she knew they would be present, and she had never had them to her house even when the entertaining was some arm's length charity affair, and the guest list anything but hand picked. He had sometimes wondered about it, but had concluded it was unimportant. Some people you liked, and some you didn't. It was as simple as that. Until now.

Like a small child glued to the keyhole, Scott watched in horror as the scene unfolded before his eyes.

Reeling from the initial surprise of the verbal ambush, Lisa had initially gone white, but she recovered quickly and already the color was returning to her cheeks. She turned to face her foe, a tiger at bay, the hunted about to become the hunter. "You yourself are a marvelous example of the truth of what you say, Jo-Anne. Unlike you, however, I have absolutely no inclination at all to forget my origins. I'm proud of them."

Lisa stood perfectly straight, her head thrown back in defiance, as she moved into the counterattack. Proud and undaunted, she was not, however, unbloodied, and Scott could see that the attack had left its mark. Never before had he seen his mother at war like this. It was a weird and awesome sight, but one that had to be endured. Still, he didn't go to her, secure in the subconscious understanding that what he witnessed was a necessary prelude to a mighty and more effective intervention later. For the very first time his mother's ghosts were visible. He had to get to know them.

Looking Jo-Anne evenly in the eyes, Lisa gave her the second barrel. "The only thing that's changed about you, Jo-Anne, is that over the years your fee's gone up. The service hasn't changed one bit."

"What? *What?*" Jo-Anne screamed in disbelief. "You're calling me a hooker? You're daring to call *me* a hooker?"

On some astral plane of detachment Scott watched and waited.

"Listen, Jo-Anne, everybody knows the panties fit. You've been wearing them for years."

Lisa smiled a triumphant smile. The skirmish she hadn't sought was over, and she was its victor. It was time to withdraw, not to retreat. In front of her, Jo-Anne looked as if she were on the verge of some dreadful explosion that threatened to cover the entire Norton art collection with her bodily tissues.

Lisa turned and walked toward her son, her gait even, her step measured, as Jo-Anne's infuriated howl wafted after her. "You're nobody from nowhere, Lisa Starr. Nobody from nowhere."

Over her shoulder Scott took in the amazing visual. Jo-Anne Stansfield, her beautiful face twisted with her terrible rage, had sunk gently to her knees as if in prayer for the thunderbolt that would strike down her enemy. There in the middle of the empty gallery she was closed off to everything but hatred, the emotion pure and undiluted, beamed at his mother's back. Its strength was incapable of description.

As Lisa put out her hand for his, Scott could feel that it was shaking. Nobody could be unmoved by such phenomenal and naked aggression.

"Come on, darling, we're leaving." The voice was almost conversational. But as he was swept along in her wake its character changed. Small and still, its power equaled the passion of Jo-Anne Stansfield's anger. "I pray to my God that one day He will rid me of that dreadful woman," she said.

It seemed to Scott that it was the very first time his mother had ever spoken to him.

⁓

IN PALM BEACH, the beating heart of any house was divided not into four but into two. The dining room, of course. And the swimming pool. The Blass mansion, like many others on South Ocean Boulevard, boasted a couple of pools. One, salt water, nestling next to the beach cabana on the south side of the road above the sea, was considered the "casual" pool, for children and horse play, rubber rings and boats. But at the freshwater pool behind the house, protected from the sea breeze and hidden away among the pink grapefruit, banana, and lemon trees, formal elegance was the game's name, and nothing was allowed to interfere with the tranquil serenity and the formidable neatness of the ordered setting.

The pool was one hundred feet long and the clear blue water, disturbed by the powerful skimming system, was clean enough to drink. Intricate mosaic tiles of a Moorish design lined the edge of the uncompromising rectangular surface, and the eye was effortlessly drawn along the pool to the Doric-columned terrace that graced one end of it. Here, in the shade, four Tropitone sun beds were spaced in military line on the white Carrara marble floor. On the end one, flicking half-heartedly through the pages of *Surfer Magazine,* lay Scott Blass. From time to time he looked up, an expression of worried concentration on his face, unseeing eyes scanning the serried ranks of manicured citrus trees that fronted the formal gardens along the pool's west side, ranging without purpose over the gashes of red of the stone-potted geraniums, the strategically placed statues of cherubs and seraphs, the tiny white scented flowers of the sticky sweet jasmine bushes.

How could it be done? Since the day in the Norton when he had learned the secret of his mother's hatred the problem had gone around and around in his mind. A window of opportunity had opened for him, but try as he might he hadn't been able to figure a way of getting through it. Somehow, he must damage the Stansfields. Hurt them, and hurt them badly. They had been revealed as his mother's enemies, and it followed as the night the day that they were his, too. He had assumed the mantle of revenge effortlessly. It would be the way to his mother's heart, the combination to the lock on the gates of paradise, and he had schemed and searched for a way to touch them. But the Stansfields were inaccessible. They were rich and powerful, protected physically by guards and electronic devices, by armies of lawyers, by ingratiating friends and acquaintances, by a complex web of patronage, influence, and political and social prestige. He had sought the Achilles heel in vain, spending long hours in the library with back copies of the weekly news magazines as he hunted for signs of weakness, for skeletons whose existence he might exploit. He had come up with nothing. There was a daughter, who would be about his age, and it seemed that the Stansfields were a perfect caricature of Mr. and Mrs. America. She had been a Duke and he was a Stansfield, a family of fixers whose fingers had never been far from the wheels that controlled the direction of the country's political and social machines. Money and power. Power and money. The wall that surrounded them appeared to be impregnable.

The cheerful voice broke into his thoughts. "So this is how the idle rich live. Sure is fine for them as has it."

Scott sat up. "Hi, Dave baby. You made it just in time. Department of Sanitation was about to order this pool *closed*, it's so dirty."

The jokes were fine, but actually Scott felt a bit guilty when Dave came to do the pool. It wasn't just that they were the same age and were good friends —fellow surfers who shared the same waves on the North End beach even when the water temperature dipped down into the fifties during the December cold spells. It was more than that. It was the guilt the rich felt when their money was flaunted in the face of the poor. The pool at the Villa Gloria was the ultimate symbol of wealth. It looked as if it might have well belonged to some fabulously rich ancient Roman, possibly the emperor himself.

And Dave was undoubtedly a card-carrying member of the poor fraternity. No question. The truth of the matter was that Dave's three weekly visits were largely unnecessary. The chemicals these days were fed into the pool automatically and there was a continual automatic monitoring of water pH. That combined with the awesomely efficient filter meant that Dave had very little to do. However, in Palm Beach you had C and P do your pool, Boynton to maintain the gardens, and Cassidy to service the air conditioning. Everybody had them, and so you did, too. After all, it was a *very* traditional town.

"Shove it, and break me out a Bud."

Dave, a.k.a. Dave the Rave, was a marginally more rugged, slightly downmarket version of Scott himself. That is, his hair looked as if it had spent a year or two pickled in bleach, some of which had dripped unevenly over the sawed-off once-blue denim shorts. There were fine blond hairs on his craggy legs and scuffed Dexter ankle boots on his feet, worn with no socks. The clean white T-shirt read C AND P POOL MAINTENANCE.

Scott leaned down into the cavernous interior of the poolside cabana's refrigerator. He spoke over his shoulder. "Okay, Rave, how's business? And I don't mean chlorine an' filters an' all that crap."

It was a convention that Dave's friends half believed that the job of pool attendant came with "perks" in the shape of bored housewives and their college-kid daughters. It was a fantasy that from time to time had a happy knack of turning into reality—especially in Palm Beach.

Dave sniggered. Scott might be a rich mother, might *have* a rich mother, but he was a regular guy. He reached out to take the bottle of ice cold Beck's, noting phlegmatically that the Blass household clearly didn't deal in anything as mundane as Bud.

He flipped through the inventory of half-true pseudoseductions, of come-ons imagined, of flirtations dreamed about. Okay. Right. There was one juicy one, and it was real as a shark in the shallows on a rough day in summer. "Hey, Scott. You ready for this? I got a story for you."

"The two sisters on El Vedado? The ones with the teeth braces? Dave, you're really *gross*, you know. Did they come across? *Both* of them?"

"Naw, better'n that. Not something I done, something I saw."

He bent down, scooped up a sample of the immaculate water in his testing kit, and splashed in a few drops of hydrochloric acid.

Scott smiled his anticipation. This sounded good. Dave was a character. Poor as a church mouse, but hot shit on the aerials and a real stayer on a Saturday night. He usually helped him vacuum the pool—one of the few things he did that annoyed his mother.

"Yeah, Scottie boy. You heard of the Stansfields?"

Scott's mind stopped. Then it started again. "Sure. Everyone knows them. Up on North Ocean by the Kennedy house."

"Well, I do their pool, don't I?"

"I didn't know that." Scott's tone was sharp and inappropriate. There was an implication that Dave should have mentioned that before. He caught hold of himself. Careful. This conversation had started out light. If he wanted to milk it of all possibilities he should keep it that way.

"I'm so sorry I didn't mention it before." Dave laughed at the rebuke and Scott joined in.

"No, go on, Dave. Sure, I know the Stansfields."

"Well, I only just started there, but let me tell you, that wife is really something. I mean *real* neat. Like she's built, and stacked, and she sort of smells of it. You know. Just amazing."

"You mean you *made* it? With the senator's wife? I don't *believe* it!" Scott ladled on the enthusiasm. That was the way to get Dave to open right up.

"Listen, baby. Nobody gets to make it with Jo-Anne Stansfield. I mean, no fella, anyway."

Dave had assumed the inscrutability of a politician laying out his budget-cutting proposals. "What do you mean, Dave? C'mon. Lay it on the line."

"I mean, like she's into chicks. But *heavily* into chicks. There's a different one up there every day. Terrific-looking girls and they don't even 'see' me. Me. Can you believe that?"

"She's a dyke? How on earth do you *know?*"

"I saw her kiss one of them in the cabana." The look on Dave's face was pure triumph.

"You didn't."

"I swear it."

"Christ!" Scott could hardly believe his ears.

Already his thoughts were winging away. His mother's enemy was a lesbian. She was married to a rightwing senator with enormous political ambitions. It was dynamite. He could explode their lives with this. The *National Enquirer* in Lake Worth? One of the big nationally syndicated columns? No, that wasn't the way. Where was the proof? A poolman's testimony. And Dave would clam up tighter than a Jesuit's mind at the threat of losing his job. The Duke money and the Stansfield influence would make it a kamikaze trip for any journalist brave enough or stupid enough to print the rumor. No, there was only one thing to do. One intriguing possibility. He had to get inside the Stansfield house. Once inside the ramparts of the Stansfield world he would figure out a way of blowing it apart. Already it began to look as if he had discovered a Trojan horse.

How to handle this?

"Dave. You're a betting man, aren't you?" Dave would respond to a challenge like that.

"I'm listening."

"A thousand bucks says I can make it with her."

"What!" Dave was incredulous and amused all at the same time.

"You heard."

"Thousand 'gainst what."

"Your hundred says I can't."

"Ten to one. You gotta be joking. It's money in the bank. You're crazy. Anyway, how'd you get to her?"

"I take your place for a few weeks. You come by here first and loan me the van. Nobody would know. I can clean a pool as well as you. I've had enough practice cleaning this one."

"Ralph would blow me away if he found out." Dave looked doubtful. He really needed the work.

"C'mon, he's not going to find out. You know you guys are always changing around. Like that asshole of a geriatric who comes here when you're on vacation. I'll just say you're sick or something."

"What are you trying to prove, Scott?" Dave's expression was quizzical. It wasn't like Scott to be throwing his money around. Or to be playing superstud either. He got more than his fair share as it was. Still, a thousand bucks would get the bike all straightened out with enough left over for a trip to the islands with Karen. One thing was for sure: if Scott lost he would pay. And it looked certain he would do just that. It was tempting. Tempting enough not to get too involved with motives.

"I got my reasons," Scott answered the question enigmatically.

"Babe, you got yourself a deal." Dave put out his hand to cement it.

Scott took it. "Which are your days next week?"

"Monday, Wednesday, Friday. I usually get there in the early afternoon."

"Meet me here anytime after one, okay?" Scott picked up the pole and basket. "C'mon, Dave, I'll help you clean this mother. God knows though, I don't know why anyone bothers."

In his nostrils he could already smell the scent of victory.

SCOTT ATTACKED the wave as if it had just insulted him. He swooped down it, the edge of his board carving mercilessly at the smooth water, chopping it to pieces like a surgeon on angel dust. With the spray in his hair, the roar of the surf in his ears, and the exultation in his soul, it was a good day on the North End beach. The rollers were coming in smooth and strong, breaking to order, and the water between the frothy white heads of the waves was pancake flat. The board was doing everything right, too. Perfect balance, sharp and light, tight as a drum on the turns. All morning long he'd been riding the tubes, and now he wanted a few aerials to rap up the session before lunch. He gritted his teeth and braced his powerful legs against the rough surface of the Impact board as he rode up the wave toward the lip. The mechanics of the movement were old hat, but he needed to perfect the style. At Daytona a few weeks before he'd lost points there.

This wave was perfect. Four to five feet, a lot of power on a clean face and buckets of hollow. Scott pushed for speed. That was the secret of a good aerial. The lip rushed up toward him, and he extended the vertical takeoff by unweighting. Wow! That was it. Suddenly it was an upside-down world. Keep tucked. Keep tucked down. Don't let the hands go up. Don't reach for the rails. That was for the rookies. The world was righting itself. The position looked good for wave reentry. Except . . . Damn! The stupid bitch! The girl was right on his line. Slap bang in the middle of his own wave. The one he had just dominated, owned, created. The fierce possession of surfers for their own water didn't have a chance to express itself further. To avoid catastrophe Scott pushed down as hard as he could and jumped sideways into the cauldron of crashing white water. As he went down into the blackness his mind's eye replayed the perfect, screwed-up aerial. He'd been there. It had been *right*. Until some bitch . . .

In the dark anonymity beneath the waves Scott planned his revenge. The girl was about to get a tongue thrashing she would never be able to forget. His golden head burst through the surface into the sunlight, and he flicked it angrily from side to side, sending off a cascade of shining diamonds into the sticky air. There she was. Standing in the shallows and looking a bit like a doomed aristocrat awaiting the sharp kiss of the guillotine blade. His powerful arms devoured the few yards to the shore line, as his tongue rehearsed the syllables of abuse.

He waded straight toward her, and they both spoke at once:

"Look, I'm terribly sorry. It was all my fault. I didn't . . ."

"You goddamned amateur. You were riding my frigging . . ."

They both stopped for the same reason, but neither of them knew what it was.

To Scott it seemed as if he had walked into a mirror. The girl was him. It was almost as simple as that. Useless to insult yourself. And totally unsatisfying. He heard the words dying in his throat. The girl stood there, the water dripping from the lush brown body, her wet hair plastered down flat over the gorgeous face. She had stolen his hair color, his nose, the baby blue of his eyes, the fullness of his mouth. What was it called? Döppelganger? When you saw your double. His eyes wandered on down. The tits of a seventeen-year-old, the bra an irrelevance. Small but perfect. Stomach, just a little too full—hips just a little too wide with the baby fat of adolescence. But everything hard and firm. The body of a cheerleader, a baton twirler, the sort that drove the boys on the football team into a lather of sexual frustration. Ridiculous. She was incredibly pretty. Anytime she liked she could wreck his wave. Be my guest, amateur surfer. You can even try my board.

"Sorry," Scott heard himself mumble. "I guess I overreacted." He waved a hand in a gesture of apology.

Christie Stansfield had always believed in angels but hadn't expected to bump into one on the North End beach. The boy was insanely good looking. The tousled hair was matted by the sand and surf, curled and basted by the endless ultraviolet, crying out for the touch of fingers, of caring hands. And the face—open, wide open to emotion, to anger, to sudden and inexplicable embarrassment, hinting already of a desperate desire for the warmth of intimacy. Wide shoulders tapering to the cliché of a finely muscled and thin waist. Long, long legs, and the undeniable excitement of the bit in between, hidden from view by the torn and tattered white cutoffs.

"No. No. What I did was unforgivable. You're absolutely right to be angry." Somehow this boy's anger would be a wonderful thing. Paradoxically Christie wanted it and its intensity more than the mumbled small talk that threatened to replace it.

Scott bent down to escape the girl's intent gaze and pulled the board in toward him by the ankle cord. "You find some good waves this morning?" He tried to sound casual.

"I'm just a beginner. They're all good to me. All good, but totally impossible!"

The laugh was really neat. Open in the beginning then closing up tight at the end, as if she felt she hadn't really the right to laugh about a subject so serious. Scott smiled back at her reassuringly. She was a nice kid. A sweet turn-on. Far, far away from the West Palm girls with their dirty talk and wise bodies. Light years, too, from the Palm Beach variety with their whining self-confidence and their preciously guarded, milk-white complexions.

"Wanna beer?" Scott subconsciously stayed in surfer mode. From the flush on the beautiful rounded cheeks he reckoned he wasn't doing so badly.

"If you have one to spare. Thanks."

Together they walked across the sand to the Polystyrene freezer box, trailing their boards by the fins.

"My name's Scott."

"Hi, I'm Christie."

"That's a nice name."

"Thanks."

Scott turned to look at her. As intended, the twin specks of red were expanding nicely. The eyes were gratifyingly downcast.

He threw himself down on the hot sand, languid and abandoned, letting out a sigh of satisfaction, of ostentatious relaxation. Leaning on one elbow he reached inside the cooler for a cold beer, watching the girl carefully as he did so.

Christie squatted beside him, vaguely self-conscious, uncommitted yet already hopelessly compromised. It was a pickup pure and simple. Christie Stansfield picked up by a surfer in her own back yard, about to down a Budweiser with a Greek god whose ancestry would be anything but divine. She suppressed the uncharitable thought. Who cared about things like that? She was always trying to reeducate her parents in precisely that area. Not that she'd ever had much success.

She felt the unsettling eyes boring through the bikini top, sensed them creep all over the warm flesh around her nipples. It was a delicious feeling, but extraordinarily illicit, the heady scent of forbidden fruit wafting tantalizingly through her mind as she felt the hardening in her breasts. Suddenly her throat was dry, and she wanted to swallow badly. But he was looking straight into her eyes again now, temporarily abandoning her swelling breasts. He would know all about the hormones that were jumping around inside her. And then what would he do? Would he laugh at her and touch her leg as he did so? Would he pull her down on top of him there and then and taste her tongue, uninvited, needing no invitation?

Scott watched the parted lips and saw the breath coming faster, as the erotic moment built its power. Two beads of sweat lingered charmingly between her nose and upper lip, moisture he could wipe away with his finger, with his tongue. He'd never known it to happen so fast. Was it narcissism? Was he drawn to the face that looked so like his? Whatever. In his stomach the familiar flutterings began as the caged butterflies were released, and the first hesitant movements heralded arousal's dawn.

"Christie," he said reflectively. "Christie. I like that name a lot." On purpose he made the soft syllables sound like a caress. He reached out his hand, and for a second he let it rest on the soft skin of her knee.

"What's your second name?"

"Stansfield," came the murmured reply.

~ *19* ~

THERE WAS DEFINITELY something alluring about him from behind. Something very feminine, a strong resemblance to somebody. Who on *earth* was it?

Jo-Anne hitched herself up on both elbows to improve her view. Her full breasts jutted down, almost exposing the dark nipples. She had been sunbathing with the straps of her bikini top undone. Yes, from the back he could almost have been a girl, and an incredibly pretty one at that. Blond hair, all long and curly at the back, almost ringlets really. A slim frame, and a tight upturned ass like the aerobics girls had. She tried to remember the face. It had been sort of familiar, but at the same time she knew she hadn't seen him before. Well, it was definitely intriguing and a dramatic improvement on the faceless oaf who usually came to do the pool—all soulful gazes and macho poses. A right little turn-off.

It was the way he held himself she liked best: delicately, as if he were aware of his body and its perfect proportions, but at the same time was a little embarrassed by it. Almost as if he didn't want it to cause any harm, to inflame any passions—although he was more than conscious that that was what it tended to do. Mmmmmmmmmmmm. Very graceful, but naturally so. No poses. Just shapes that looked good for the task at hand, which right now was reaching out to flick a few hibiscus leaves from the center of the pool. Jo-Anne took in the ropelike muscles of his extended forearms, and the wide shoulders.

He was working down the side of the pool toward where she was lying. Jo-Anne was interested enough to try some conversation. For sure he would blow that. Pretty boys always did. "What happened to the regular guy?" she said to the suntanned back. As if she cared.

"Oh, he got sick, ma'am."

Scott turned to look at her. It was working like a dream, and it was far too good to be true. A little while ago he had about as much chance of getting to the Stansfields as being selected for the space shuttle, but now he was almost an insider. Two incredible coincidences had come right on top of each other:

Dave was their poolman and Christie Stansfield liked to watch the surfers on the beach. Neither in itself was that remarkable. After all, Palm Beach was a small town. But in terms of his plan those two events could well have been conceived in heaven . . . or rather in hell. Mother and daughter. Both were accessible to him now, and Christie had already shown the early signs of being a plum ripe for the picking. Right at this very minute and every week-day she was safely tucked away, hawking Polo sweaters to the yuppies in the Esplanade. It was mummy's turn.

At a glance one thing was obvious: Christie Stansfield's mom sure had it all. Had it, and clearly worked like hell to keep it. The tits were bigger by far than her daughter's, and from the way the nipples brushed the material of the undone bra, it was plain that in the normal way they would need a bit of support. But the legs looked powerful, the thighs muscular and the butt tight, from the generous portion of it that was visible for appreciation around the minimal thong-type bikini briefs. Face? Time had left its wrinkles around the steel-cold eyes, and the rather cruel mouth was wickedly determined, but it was still beautiful—if a million miles from Christie's angelic countenance, all wide-eyed innocence and pre-Raphaelite purity.

How should he play it? The softest of soft sells to be sure. This one was a huntress. She wouldn't want to be hunted. He turned away from her. Deferential. Humble. The lowly poolboy, who knew how to behave in the presence of his betters.

Jo-Anne eyed him speculatively. Okay, so far you haven't hanged yourself. How about some more rope?

"You look like you do some surfing. Are you one of those pests always disobeying the parking signs in the North End?"

Jo-Anne made it sound taunting, the hint of flirtation softening the abrasive content of the question. The relationship between the surfers, nearly all of whom came from across the lake, and the town of Palm Beach had been a disastrous one for years. The Palm Beachers, who themselves rarely visited the beach, nonetheless thought of it—when they bothered to think about it at all—as their own private property. Despite the fact that every beach in America to the high-water line was supposed to be open to the public, the inhabitants of the North End spent much of their time discouraging the presence of outsiders. This they achieved in two basic ways. One was to disallow parking on any of the town's roads within three miles of the North End breakers. The other was to enforce rigorously the trespass laws while failing to provide public beach access. Undaunted, the surfers would either walk for miles from the one public beach in the center of the town, or cheerfully disregard both private property and the town's no-parking signs, which a large portion of West Palm Beachers thought unconstitutional anyway.

Once again Scott turned toward her. He put a casual hand on a cocked hip and smiled what he hoped was his boyish smile. "Yes, ma'am. I mean I do some surfin', but mostly down at Deerfield, or up Jupiter way. You ever tried it?" he added daringly.

"Do I *look* as if I have?"

Jo-Anne smiled at the cheek of the question. This one had charm. A *lot* of it. He was really rather sweet. Almost coquettish. Who the hell *did* he remind her of?

"Well, you look in pretty good shape, ma'am. If you don't mind me saying so." He ran a hand nervously through his hair. He'd washed it the night before.

Jo-Anne peered up at him, lifting a hand to shield her eyes from the early afternoon sun. Scott loomed over her, silhouetted against the clear blue sky. Then, on an impulse which she didn't herself really understand, she hitched herself up farther on the Grossfillex sun bed, allowing both her breasts to fall free in front of her, totally exposed to the gaze of the young boy.

Whatever the effect the gesture had on him—difficult to judge against the bright sun—the effect on herself was dramatic.

The thought of his eyes roaming free all over her suddenly naked torso was for some extraordinary reason thoroughly erotic. Jo-Anne could hardly believe what was happening. It seemed literally light years ago that she had last been turned on by a member of the opposite sex. She couldn't even remember the occasion. Had there ever *been* one? Women were different—soft, and sweet smelling, gentle and giving, pretty and clean. Infinitely attractive. A man? It was ridiculous. But it was also undeniably real.

Hovering over her, Scott swallowed hard. He'd been quite wrong about the tits. Strong pectorals had scooped them up, winning effortlessly the battle against gravity. Now the twin orbs, glistening with a thin film of what smelled like the all-but-unobtainable Charles of the Ritz Bain de Soleil suntan gel, imprisoned his gaze and dried out his mouth. The ball had been returned to the baseline of his court and it had buckets and buckets of topspin.

Things were moving along faster than he had dared to hope, but strangely, as the goal got closer the stakes got higher and higher. One wrong move, one uncool gesture, and the moment would be vaporized. It was the oldest problem in the world, and even at his tender age Scott had experienced it: how to cross the border into intimacy. Would there be more talk? Should there be? So, not knowing what to do, Scott did nothing. He just stood there watching the things he was clearly supposed to watch.

The reality of the situation was enough for Jo-Anne. Her whole life she had been nothing if not a sexual adventurer, a pleasure voyager who grabbed at the moment the second it came within reach. Some were like that in business; they only had to see a cheap stock or an expensive currency and they moved like lightning. Well, bodies were Jo-Anne's equivalent of pork bellies, precious metals, and interest-rate futures. And when the time was right she *traded*. Right now it appeared she was confronted by an excellent buying opportunity. So, at the very time when Scott felt that he was a mere spectator to events, Jo-Anne Duke Stansfield moved impatiently into the driver's seat. This boy was young enough to be her son. Good! Great!

With all the time in the world she stood up, moving slowly, languidly. If she wanted this thing to pleasure her she shouldn't frighten it away. The trick was to get just the right mix of firmness and femininity. From Big Apple days she remembered that there was a thin line between ball breaking and passivity. You had to lead them, not force-feed them.

Scott, playing the unaccustomed role of hypnotized rabbit, let it happen. The body was now standing up straight, and it fulfilled all the promise of the one that had been lying down. Jo-Anne made Dave's description sound like the incoherent ramblings of a neutered blindman. Before his eyes he could actually *see* her tits hardening, the moisture appearing as if by magic as her tongue traced the contours of her upper lip. In reaction the band inside him had already started to tune up. There were the dancing insects in the pit of his stomach, the squirting of the stuff that sent the heart into overdrive. His plan was on the back burner now, crudely displaced from the front of his mind by the total intrusiveness of desire. This woman was going to use him. Later she would spit him out, throw him away, until it suited her to act the replay. He was about to be pulled like the cork on a bottle of indifferent Algerian burgundy—crudely, roughly, and with no ceremony at all.

Jo-Anne stepped right up to him, putting her face close to his. During her brief walk she had already seen the hardness move in the tight jeans and the pupils widen in the deep blue eyes that reminded her of someone. For what seemed like an age she stood stock still, breathing in the unaccustomed masculine scent and allowing it to go to work on her hormones and to make free with her mind. So *very* different. Variety's spice. With all the time in the world she reached downward and laid the flat of her hand on the no longer flat denim, enjoying the heat beneath her palm and the impatient movements of the young boy's need. It was all so deliciously unusual. Perhaps she had missed out on this for too long. The smile that mocked her own lips was saying it all.

"Lend me your body, toy-boy. I need it for a while. You can have it back later."

—

Christie stansfield had taken the plunge and worried about it all morning, but now she didn't care anymore. She was out there—dancing, feeling, being. There was a cotton-wool cloud under her feet. In her nostrils was animal heat, in her soul the steep banked fires of love. This workout suit was state-of-the-art, but state-of-the-art London rather than West Palm. As usual, the English had gone overboard to produce today's shocker but tomorrow's norm, and the sheer hot-pink creation looked more like bondage gear than the leotards of old.

During the five minutes of easy social intercourse that always preceded the workout the other girls had showed their envy by thinly veiled jokes and the occasional flashes of pure malice in their envious eyes. "Christie, sweetheart, you look like something out of an X-rated movie. You are 'brave.'" "My, my, Christie, I wish I had the nerve to turn up in that . . . whatever it is."

But Christie didn't care what they thought. She was dressed for one person only: the beautiful boy with the worried eyes who had come out of the sea. Scott Blass. He was meeting her here. In a few minutes *he* would be the judge. And he was a *man*.

Now the adrenaline was making her feel as good as a young girl in love and with a resting pulse of fifty could possibly feel. Christie flung her head to one side and caught her reflection in the mirrored wall, and with the narcissism of the very young she enjoyed what she saw.

It was all there to see, brown and firm, the sun-baked skin basted by the thin film of sweat, framed by the daring pink thongs of the workout suit. There were muscles in the strong back, upper arms and thighs, but they were rounded out with youth's young flesh—intensely feminine, universally alluring. Her breasts were not big but they hardly moved as her body powered through the routine, and the sweat-soaked low-cut bodice gave away the secret that the conical nipples were the salmon pink of late adolescence. Her abdomen was revealed from just about every angle—the top part of the suit being joined to the bottom by four single strands of material that left open panels at front and back, and at both sides. If there was a criticism, Christie guessed it was around the hips. Just a little bit too generous, but kind of voluptuous, sort of neat really, and as part of the total picture far more than passable. Anyway, it was all getting better every day. Especially her bottom. Now it was real firm, and hard. It would be her gift to Scott. A toy for him to play with, factory fresh, unsullied by the touch of a male hand. He could have it, and when he arrived to pick her up he would be able to see it first— heaving and straining beneath the skimpy material, her wild buttocks bisected by the thin strip of pink material lodged deep in their cleavage, barely covering her most secret places. Even if he was late, the class would still be in progress when he arrived. Christie had thought of that. Maybe after all there was a *tiny* part of her mother in her.

Maggie's voice cut into the voyeuristic reverie.

"Make it smooth. Stroke the rhythm out. Concentrate on the *timing*. Lose yourself in it. Let the body take over the mind. That's it. That's it."

Christie tried to do as she was told and to still the raging thoughts. "I am my body. My body is all I am," she tried to tell herself. That was the philosophy. That was the way you were supposed to go. She pumped out her long leg to the side and tried to lose herself in the delicious feeling of stretch and exertion, of squeeze and relaxation as her powerful gluteal muscles orchestrated the doggie lifts. Spine straight, head down. Pump easy, pump slow. Would Scott see this from behind? She imagined his eyes upon her. The night before in the country-and-western bar he had looked at her like that and so now she could imagine the dangerous eyes. Mmmmmmmmmmmmmm. It was so very nice. What had the world done before they had invented exercise? And had anybody *ever* been as much in love as this?

The beat of the rhythm was unashamedly repetitive now. For ten minutes it had pretended to possess melody, but its purpose was at last exposed. It was a metronome, no more a tune than the ticking of a clock, and its aim was to conduct the movement of bodies. No more, and no less. The bass was turned up high and from ten or twenty speakers around the vast penthouse studio of the pink Phillips Point building the drumming beat etched its message into those parts of the brain that lived below consciousness, below wisdom, below feeling. The fundamental message could not be disobeyed. To hear it was to obey it as it merged the class into one single entity, beyond pain, beyond individual existence. Then, there it was. Tiptoeing around the edges of the insistent beat and gaining in strength second by second were the clarion notes of the national anthem. That was another vital ingredient. They were all one now, one nation, one body, one bundle of purpose. Joy through strength. Power through beauty. Happiness through the physical in the dawn's early light.

Alone in the throbbing room Maggie remained inoculated against the fever of the wild, abandoned music. Twenty years of exercise had given her that freedom, and sometimes, like today, she wished for the slavery that bound her class. She could see the ecstasy on the sweat-stained faces, could imagine the purity of the pleasure they were experiencing from the peak exertion. But for her it was over. She was so far ahead of them all she had come out the other side, and the body that encased her spirit was the evidence of her journey. It would have been untrue to say that she looked good. "Looking good" had always escaped Maggie. What *was* true was that she looked extraordinary—her body constructed like a suspension bridge, a complex system of levers and struts, of steel hawsers and massive concrete supports. It looked as if it could perform any task that the most inventive of masters could dream up. It had endured, and it would endure. When she and Lisa had started the old gym on Clematis she had never dreamed it would develop into this. Lisa had left, but Maggie had not lost the faith, and in the exercise explosion of the following years she had followed the developing trends and started a few of her own, and now the gym had a nationwide reputation to match its height. And so did she. Now, there was young Christie Stansfield in her class. Bobby's girl. The one who should have had Lisa for her mother.

Lisa Starr. Lisa Blass. Her Lisa. A superstar now, shining brightly in the firmament of the highest society as Maggie had always known she would. They had grown apart, but Maggie still loved her. Her memory. Her brave spirit. Her seemingly endless zest for life. They saw each other occasionally, at the bigger parties, and they would both try to pretend that nothing had changed, while each knew that everything had. It was a different Lisa now, and probably a different Maggie too, but mainly a different Lisa. The charm was there, the incredible beauty—but the warmth was gone—all snuffed out by the bitter frost of too much heartache. The ice had touched poor Lisa's soul, and it had killed the part of her that Maggie had loved the most.

Maggie forced herself back to the here and now. In front of her the class members were hurting, losing themselves in the delicious pain, their wet faces and steaming bodies crying out for the relief that another part of them didn't want. She should commune with them as they indulged in the sacrament of physicality. She should be with them as they suffered in the name of beauty.

"Come with me, you guys. Come with me all the way. Lose your minds. *Become* your bodies."

Exercise was getting metaphysical these days.

Suddenly in the midst of the frenetic activity Christie experienced the quietness of the hurricane's eye. Scott was leaning in the doorway, his eyes lazily flicking over the seething mass of prime feminine flesh, his mouth parted in a half smile—of patronization? of shyness? It was difficult to tell. He looked as if he had come straight from the beach. The salt was still all over him, and the dirty gray T-shirt and baggy white canvas trousers had quite obviously spent long weeks in the back of the vintage Le Baron ragtop he always drove. That was all part of him. The "to-hell-with-everybody" attitude that raised the temperature of Christie's teenage dreams. As she watched him his eyes found her, and the flush on her already hot cheeks deepened as she felt the reality of what had been a few minutes before only imagination. She tried a smile. It was not returned, but he nodded to her.

"Finish your business," his look seemed to say. "You're doing something important. Don't let me distract you. I wouldn't give you a second thought if I was riding a wave."

Christie dropped her head in acknowledgment of the silent rebuke. Of course he was right. She tried to concentrate on the job at hand.

"Okay, you guys. On your backs now. Let's work away those buns."

Christie groaned inwardly. Oh God. Why did *this* exercise have to come now? She arched her back and thrust her pelvis into the air, the pink thong plastered tight against her wide-open vagina, the outermost blond hairs hardly hidden by the skimpy material.

"Come on now, squeeze it out, and in double time now, and one and two and one and two . . ."

She closed her eyes to hide her embarrassment, and tried to forget where she was, and who was there. But the movement kept reminding her. She was making love to the air. There was no other interpretation of the action. The only thing lacking was Scott on top of her, and try as she might she couldn't get that awesome thought out of her mind.

Inside her the funny feeling grew and grew. The more she rejected it, the stronger it became. She should stop, but she couldn't do that. So desperately uncool.

"Push upward, you guys. Go for it. Make it work for you."

Christie did as she was told, and as her buttocks alternately contracted and relaxed the strange tingling sensation ran up and down the inside of her long brown thighs. Oh no. Not now. Not here. That would be just totally impossible.

She opened her eyes. Could the reality stop it happening?

Scott had moved. He was no longer in the doorway. He was at the side of the gym, close to her, and there was an odd faraway look in his eyes as he peered intently at the all but naked body that thrust and reared at him.

She flicked her tongue nervously over her lips and tried a half smile that didn't quite work.

Which was the exact moment she saw it.

There, framed in the gunsight of her thighs, sitting at the bottom of the deep V of her crotch and barely ten feet away, was the sight that put her way over the top. Inside the crumpled white trousers Scott Blass was rock hard.

Christie let out a little gasp of surprise at the thing that was happening to her. She had time to close her eyes, and then she lost the coordination altogether. Her legs froze, her back locked, and her mind stopped.

"Ohhhhhhhhhhhhhh, dear," she heard somebody, who might easily have been herself, exclaim.

She sat down hard, allowing her bottom to whack into the boards in a forlorn attempt to camouflage the obvious, but the event inside her was undeterred. It had a life of its own now. It wouldn't answer to anybody. In the velvet underground it held sway, living its terrible moment to the full, singing its beautiful, crazy song. Gripped by the shuddering madness she could not control, Christie sunbathed on the bean-bag cloud of awkward ecstasy, as she played host to the transient visitor. Invisible, secret, it lived out its brief moment of cosmic time, selfish, unrepentant, unashamed. And then, at last it was gone, leaving nothing behind but the trace of memory . . . and, more pressing, the growing legacy of wet desire on the pink material that shielded her pulsating core from the outside world.

When she opened her eyes Scott was staring directly at it. It was the first secret they had shared. It would not be the last.

———

FOR THREE quarters of a century the Paramount had been a Palm Beach landmark. First a theater, and then for years the only cinema in town, it had fallen into disrepair in the sixties and seventies. But now it was back. Restored to its former glory, and by the light of its flickering screen it was impossible to miss the doe-eyed devotion beaming out from Christie Stansfield's face. Like a billion girls before her she snaked her hand out across the lush seat and wormed it gently into Scott's. Three short whirlwind weeks hovering on the brink of ecstasy had all but destroyed her resolve, and she knew that she was about to fall. Maybe tonight. Maybe tomorrow. She wasn't in love, she was obsessed. It was a grand passion, the headlong romantic involvement of adolescence, quivering, magnificent, awesome in its force and power. One by one, the guiding lights of her life were being flooded out by the intensity of the gleaming vision—the meeting of body and soul in the longed-for flesh dance that she had so far resisted. Perhaps later it would happen. On the floodlit beach where he had promised to take her after the movie. Whatever. Already the cloak of her firm personal morality, worn as always on her sleeve for the world to see, was wearing thin. Soon the threadbare garment would protect her from herself no more, and she would be free, free to feel, to enjoy, to want and to need.

She looked up at the beautiful face and refused to see the cruelty there, preferring to construe it as the capricious strength of the young at heart. Scott would look after her in her moment of weakness. He would know what to do. He would not let her down. God, she worshiped him. Never before had she seen such a specimen, never in her polite and correct world where everything was predictable, all was safe. Scott, like some wonderful creature from lost Atlantis, had come to her out of the sea with his easy laughter and his daring. Every emotion was alive, vibrant, a reaction to stimulus never its effect. First of course there was the surfing and the single-minded addiction to excellence that went with it. Christie, surrounded always by friends who worked hard at their affectation of boredom, found that enthusiasm the biggest turn-on of all. That, and the body that went with it, the godlike outer shell that was the instrument of his power over the sea.

But there was so much more. The rough friends from the mainland, and the even rougher places he would take her in the early hours when sedate Palm Beach slept. In the tough bars of Old Okeechobee, and in the hookers' haunts of Riviera Beach, Christie had her eyes opened for the first time to the throbbing reality of the other half's life-style. She had been plunged into the midst of Dante's inferno, but with Scott at her side she had felt as safe as in the smooth shiny pews of Bethesda-by-the-Sea. He knew them all, and not as some rich, barely tolerated outsider. He was one of them, at ease with their jokes, happy with their gestures, sharing effortlessly their accents and their prejudices. And when in the dark of the night tempers frayed and minds bent and unwise hands reached for her, his fists would clench and his jaw would set as the creatures of the twilight zone saw the error of their ways. She had felt like a medieval princess on the arm of her champion, deliciously safe in the midst of danger, like watching the snow fall against the windowpane while sitting snugly by a big log fire.

It had been several days before she had found out who he was, and by that stage she had bitten deep on his hook. Scott Blass. Lisa Blass's son. The son of her mother's enemy. Briefly there had been a moral dilemma. Was it disloyal to go out with him? Should she indulge herself in her mother's vendetta against her father's old flame? The baby-blue eyes that looked so like her own had made up her mind. The sins of the fathers and mothers *shouldn't* be visited on the children. Anyway, Scott didn't seem to have inherited the hatred. He knew she was a Stansfield, and was neither impressed nor put off. She had, however, made one concession to pragmatism. She had avoided telling her mother the identity of her persistent date. Jo-Anne, steadfastly self-centered and globally uninterested in the doings of others, hadn't bothered to ask anyway.

On the sidewalk outside the Paramount Scott took her hand again. He didn't speak. He didn't have to. In the warm still of the scented night they walked down Seminole Avenue to the beach. They slipped off their shoes when they reached the sand and looked up at the three-quarter moon. Christie's firm chin obeyed the command of Scott's forefinger, her eyes locked onto his in the moonlight, and her warm, uncertain breath bathed his face with its fresh fragrance. She felt her lips part, dry like the rustling fronds of the palms above. Soon he would kiss her and transfuse his wetness into her, bringing dampness and fertility to the desert of her longing. What was there in the eyes of this boy she had learned to love so completely? Was it sadness, a melancholy loneliness all mixed up with the hunger of desire? If so, she wanted to satisfy all his yearnings. She wanted to make him whole and to fill the void in his soul of which his eyes so eloquently spoke, to banish the loneliness, to slake the physical appetite with the generous gift of her own young body.

Christie reached around the thin waist and she pulled him in toward her, feeling the startling hardness of him, pushing shamelessly against it. Still he didn't kiss her. He watched her, strange emotions surging like wild surf behind the twin curtains of his eyes. Why did he hesitate?

Then he moved down toward her, tenderly, slowly, irresistibly. Christie closed her eyes and heard herself moan as she readied to receive him. With all her might she focused on her lips. That would be the first touch, the first feel of him.

His lips arrived on hers as uncertain strangers, curious, polite, attentive, tentative. They seemed at first to hover in space, like a humming bird at the mouth of a wide-open flower. Then, dry and warm, they nuzzled in. Up and down Christie's skin the feeling played over her, plucking at her, caressing her with its glorious subtlety and power. She could feel it in the throbbing tautness of her nipples, feel it crawling over the tight skin of her full buttocks, feel it soft, warm, and liquid deep between her legs. And then Scott's tongue made her mouth his. Wise and willful, it took her with its confident, infinitely knowledgeable touch, and the long shuddering sigh it pulled from her was eloquent testimony to its skill. Christie opened her eyes and the stars rushed in, as Scott, gentle no more, moved with the impatience of adolescent lust, his mouth darting at hers, devouring it, savoring it, as it tried to draw her lips, her tongue, her teeth into the heart of passion's hurricane.

Christie fought back with him. He wanted her mouth. She wanted him so desperately to have it. He wanted her taste. Her taste was his.

Scott's hands moved urgently behind her back until they found the skin they sought. He eased the plain white T-shirt away from the waist of the blue jeans and ran his fingers softly up the warm skin of Christie's back, searching for the strap of the bra that wasn't there.

Slowly he sank down to the sand, kneeling, as if in church, in front of her. Then, firmly he drew her down, too. With reverence, his hands lifted the soft cotton, unveiling her, exposing her, thrusting her into the no-man's land of nakedness, the place from which there was no turning back.

Scott looked down at his gift. Proud, almost defiant, Christie stared back at him as she tried to tell him with her eyes that she belonged to him, that she would not fight him, that her will was intertwined with his as their lips had been short seconds before. The strength of her emotion was already too great for fear, but uncertainty hovered uneasily in the still night air. Her breasts were small. Perfect, firm, but very far from large. Would Scott mind? God Almighty, could he see them *throb?*

In answer to the unspoken question Scott leaned forward. He took each hot, tense breast into the palms of his hands and for what seemed like an age he communed with their urgent fullness as if the desire that coursed in them was a palpable thing, stiff and alive with the energy of passion.

Then he moved into them, his tongue anxious for each pink nipple, for its soft innocence, and Christie's heart stopped as his mouth enclosed it. Her fingers found the back of his neck, and she held him close like a suckling child as she fed him the nourishment of her young body, matching his desire with the feverish intensity of her own. She ran her fingers through the blond hair, star of her dreams and crowning glory of her lover, and below, inside her, the waterfall of need roared and foamed. Christie heard her body's voice, shrill and wonderful, as it told her what was about to happen. She wasn't ready for it. She could hardly believe it. But it was a fact. Along the inside of her thighs the express train screamed its approach, and in her lower stomach the avalanche rumbled its advance warning. Her mind was a mere spectator to the glorious accident that was about to happen as the irresistible force and the immovable object prepared for their earth-shattering union. There was no time to warn Scott. Hardly time to ready herself. Just time to shout out to the stars and to the sky and to the sand of the deserted beach the mystical intensity of her experience.

Scott heard the messages of her body as inside his mouth the once-small nipple bucked and reared like some frightened colt, filling his mouth with its suddenly compromised sweet innocence. He knew what would happen and he wanted it. Through the tropical storm of her orgasm he held on to her, his arms around her as she shuddered her satisfaction. Wet and violent, vibrating with its raw energy, Christie's climax rocked on and on, and through the torrential chaos of feeling she knew but one thing. She was empty and she wanted to be filled.

In the aftermath of orgasm Christie felt the first impossible flutterings of panic. Had she frightened him away? Had her inexperienced lack of control undone his desire? She had to know. Had to save the moment that every atom of her body so feverishly wanted. With bold hands she reached for him, an innocent no more. Her fumbling fingers found the hardness, found the way to expose it, found the vision of which she had dreamed. In wonder she felt it, and as she willed it to take her, her fingers communicated their rampant longing.

She lay back on the sand and undid the belt of her tight blue jeans, pushing them down over the full hips, her panties peeled away by the hard denim to reveal the blond secret, glistening in the moon's pale light. In her moment of total abandonment came the flash of self-knowledge. Little Christie Stansfield. Round and sweet. Pretty and pure. Everybody's American dream. Lying on the sand wracked by lust. Demanding, screaming to be entered, to be filled up with a young boy's desire.

Above her Scott's body blotted out the sky. And then, quite suddenly, Christie saw the thing that should not be there. In the eyes, around the mouth, was the outline trace of the inappropriate emotion. For one single second she saw it—triumph? cruel victory? the flickering flame of hate?— and then it was gone. Inside her mind the warning bells clanged their alarm, and intellect's forces mobilized to explain the intuition. Then there it was. The knowledge. This was wrong. Deeply and fundamentally wrong. Something she and he would regret forever. A crime against the ocean, the fragrant air, against the star-spangled sky.

But it was far too late. Already there was the searing pain, the feel of the warm red blood on her thigh, and already there was the siren cry of physical desire blotting out all thought, all sense, all prudence. And at the very moment she knew she had sinned against God in His heaven, Christie Stansfield reached out to her lover and pushed her hips off the sand, forcing him deep into her body, and deeper into her mind.

JO-ANNE STRETCHED herself like some sleepy but contented cat on the white wicker chaise longue. Three times a week for the last three weeks she had experienced a beautiful dream and today she would dream again. This young boy had it all. He was not too proud to learn; he was obedient; he had stamina. For two blissful hours—Mondays, Wednesdays, and Fridays—he had made clockwork love to her in the early afternoon. He had been clean as a whistle, hadn't tried to hustle her for bread, and hadn't even bothered to ask her name. That, and a gravity-defying prick on the body of an Adonis, made him very special indeed. Now, for some reason, there was to be a change in the established pattern. He was coming over to "do the pool" on a Saturday, and at three thirty rather than the usual two o'clock. He had made a point of telling her, and Jo-Anne had made a point of listening. Who knew, maybe he had an earlier appointment farther down the beach. Well, as long as he was all tanked up and ready to go, who cared?

Jo-Anne flicked moodily through *House and Garden* and sipped petulantly on a spritzer. Twelve o'clock. Three and a half hours to go. Patience had never been her strongest suit. She looked around for somebody to irritate. Christie, looking pensive in the shallow end, would do. Damn! She'd almost forgotten. She'd have to get rid of Christie somehow. Usually she was safely tucked away on Worth Avenue, but on the weekend if the weather was good she tended to hang out poolside.

"What on earth is the matter with you these days, Christie? You're either manic or in the depths of despair. Don't say you're in love or something boring like that."

Christie's laugh was totally devoid of humor. Scott hadn't called for twenty-four hours, and it had been a very bad day indeed. Her mother's remark hadn't helped. But then her mother's remarks seldom did. It wasn't Jo-Anne's fault, and Christie was sure she didn't mean to be unkind. It was just that she had the unhappy knack of sowing little seeds of unpleasantness every time she opened her mouth.

She dunked her shoulders beneath the still surface of the pool as she planned her reply. "Maybe I am," she said mysteriously. Christ! How had she managed a lie like that. If love was an illness then she was ringing the doorbell at the Pearly Gates. She'd never known anything like this roller-coaster ride. Scott Blass was a nuclear explosion of pure wonder who had atomized her former world and left her oscillating frantically between the sumptuous delights of heaven and burning daggers of the most dreadful hell.

"Well, if you are, then I suggest you enjoy it and don't forget to take the pill. Can't think why you have to look so damn miserable."

The surfer stud hadn't made *her* miserable. Just a bit irritated that he couldn't have made it a little bit earlier than three thirty.

Christie groaned inwardly. Great! A mother's concern for a much-loved daughter. But she had more important things on her mind than her mother's lack of maternal affection. There was only one person on this earth whose affection at this moment she craved, and he hadn't picked up the telephone to tell her he loved her. A shuddering communion on the sand, followed by the silence of the grave. It was driving her quietly mad.

The butler's voice, coldly formal, came to her rescue. "Miss Christie. There's a telephone call for you. A gentleman who wouldn't leave his name. Would you like to take the call?"

Christie was out of the pool.

The butler passed over the cordless telephone as if it were the baton in a relay race.

"Hello." Christie panted the word. Her heart prayed it wasn't a junk call —a time share in Boynton Beach, the man from the Pru.

"Christie, this is Scott. Can you talk?"

"Sort of. Oh, I'm so glad you called."

"Listen, I need to see you."

"I need to see *you*."

"What about this afternoon?"

"Wonderful. Where? When?"

"Can you meet me at your cabana? Just after four o'clock. Not before."

"I guess so. What a funny place. Yes, sure, that's fine. I want to see you so much."

"Okay. Look, I've got to rush, but see you then. After four. Remember."

Christie flicked the switch on the telephone as her heart took flight.

Her mother's voice failed completely to dampen her soaring spirits. "I *suppose* that was Captain Fantastic," she said with all the sarcasm she could muster.

"You'd better believe it," bubbled Christie.

And then there was a silence, as mother and daughter retreated to their own private worlds. So much anticipation to be enjoyed. Waiting for three thirty. Waiting for four.

CHRISTIE WASN'T sure if she really wanted to die, but life had failed her and death couldn't be worse. She looked down at the big blown-up photograph of Scott on his surfboard, riding the North End rollers. She'd loved him then— so very, very much. And now despite the horror she had witnessed, despite the incredible, premeditated cruelty of what he had done, she loved him still. She reached out for the bottle and popped another of the yellow-and-black pills into her mouth. How many was that. Ten? Fifteen? She'd lost count, the bottle blurred through the tears. The celluloid of the photograph already wet with her grief.

In her mind once again the dreadful movie played. The open door. Calling out his name. Hearing something. Seeing it. He'd said just after four. He'd wanted her there. Wanted her to be his audience of one as he had broken her heart and expelled her from his life. Never before had she contemplated such wickedness. It seemed as if the naked force of evil had been unleashed, that it was washing over her, polluting her with its terrible stench. For a second she had stood there unable to believe her eyes. Her mother's back had been toward her. Scott's hands on her naked buttocks. Over Jo-Anne's shoulders, his eyes burning with the awesome mixture of hatred and cruel triumph, Scott's face had stared haughtily into hers. For long seconds she had endured the horrendous vision as she tried to understand it. But Scott's expression said it all, and it was more, far more, than she could stand.

Letting out her cry of anguish she had rushed from that terrible place. She had run through the house as the tears came and her wild mind tried ineffectually to handle the horror. The bottle of pills from her mother's cabinet. A can of soda from the fridge. The photograph from her room. The car keys from the hall table. Did one need anything else for a trip to eternity?

Through blurred eyes she had driven through the gates and made the right turn toward the North Inlet. The sparkling sea was calm that day, mocking her sorrow with its blue tranquillity, hinting at the peace which now she would attempt to find. She would need a quiet street.

Here, outside a storm-shuttered house on Arabian, she had found the spot that would be her springboard to a kinder world. They would find Christie Stansfield asleep forever, and nobody would know what had made her want to die. That much she would give them, for even now she wanted no harm for the mother she loved and the boy she idolized. No note. No last testament to turn their lives upside down at the hands of her avenging father.

"Oh, dad," she said aloud in the emptiness. "I love you so much. Don't be sad for me."

The bottle was empty now, but still the sleepiness wouldn't come. Had she taken enough? There was no way of knowing. It was a giant gamble, and one which she didn't care if she won or lost. She didn't even know what winning would be, or what it would be to lose. She just knew that things would change after this.

And then the still small voice spoke to her. Firm, insistent, it sent out its messages to her hands and feet. In response, the ignition key was turned and the engine fired. In response, her feet pushed down on the accelerator and her fingers found the gear stick. She had to do it. She had to save him from the evil in his soul. She had to protect him from the guilt that would surely follow from his deed. It was something atavistic. She was dying but it was Scott who needed help. He had been possessed, his wonderful mind and body hijacked by an alien invader. He needed desperately to be saved from himself. And there was nobody else on earth but her to do it.

Paradoxically as she found her resolve the dust storm of sleep blew toward her, and she felt the numbness as its grains touched her. It called to her at the moment she had stopped up her ears to its previously desired voice, and now she had to fight against it. She opened the windows of the car, flicked the air fan onto full blast, and turned on the radio for stimulus to her suddenly sluggish mind. How many times had she driven this coast road? She thanked God for that now, for it looked as if literally she might have to negotiate it in her sleep. Would Scott be there? Thrown out by her mother in the anger of her shame. If not she would wait. Wait outside the door of the cottage in the grounds of the Blass house where he lived. Perhaps he would find her. Asleep on the grass. Gone from his world. Her death the shock that would exorcise his demons and allow the kindness that she loved to own him once more.

She hardly made the left on Barton and narrowly missed the gatepost of the Blass home, but the adrenaline surge counterattacked sleep's vanguard when she saw his much-loved Le Baron in the drive.

SCOTT SLUMPED into the big armchair and tried to get a hold on his emotions. He'd done it. His dreadful plan had worked. He'd struck a blow against the Stansfields from which their family was unlikely to recover. Mother and daughter had shared his body, the one casually, the other with the shuddering intensity of first love. Christie would never forgive Jo-Anne. Neither, when she told him, would her father. At the very least there would be divorce. Almost certainly violence. Yes, he had confounded his mother's enemies and cast them down into the pit. For that she would have to be grateful. For that she would have to take notice of him. For that she would have to love him.

He drank deep on the dark beaker of Scotch. This was the moment of triumph. But it didn't feel like it. Again and again the stricken face swam before his eyes, haunting in the beauty of its sadness. Christie had been so very good. She had given herself to him—trusting, believing in him deeply, throbbingly in love. Shamelessly he had built her passion and kindled the fires of her devotion. He had laughed with her and chided her. He had taught her and flattered her. And then, on the moonlit beach he had taken her virginity and locked up her soul. To do what? To gain the love of a mother who was a stranger. For revenge against an innocent for some ancient and unknown wrong. The whiskey circulated in his mind but it didn't drown the whispering voices of guilt. He had exploded into her quiet, well-ordered world like a psychopathic killer, and he had wreaked havoc upon her and those she loved. There was no good in it. No good in him.

Outside the window the dusk was gathering and the lights of the main house were coming on one by one. Soon it would be time for the bars and the rock clubs. Lauderdale? Boca? But the bars without Christie. Without the fresh-faced angel to show around. To show off. Even when setting her up, he hadn't been able to dislike her. There had been something about her, something vulnerable and yet so strong, reassuring, and strangely familiar.

The doorbell rang and didn't stop ringing.

She was the very last person he had expected to see.

Her tear-stained face was deathly pale, and the beads of sweat stood out like dewdrops on the once-proud forehead. The usually wide-open eyes were hooded with lids made heavy by the forces of sleep, and as he opened the door to her she stumbled in the entrance. Christie's voice was slurred when she spoke and Scott could barely make out the words. "Scott. Help me . . . I took some pills." They were her last words to him.

Taking one step forward she collapsed unconscious into his arms.

IN THE white-walled emergency room of the Good Sam, the atmosphere was thick with the emotion of controlled panic. It was all action and no words. The white-uniformed nurses and fraught doctors were alone in their own world of dripping IV bags and life-support systems, priests of their own scientific religion muttering the jargon of their trade, oblivious to the desperation in Scott's heart and the wild tears in his eyes. Normal saline, Ryle's tubes, forced alkaline diuresis—that was what they cared about, not Christie, all alone in the darkness of her coma. Scott hovered on the brink of the life-and-death struggle—supremely ineffectual, desperately affected. Nobody seemed to mind that he was there on the periphery of the action. They were too busy for that. And so he watched the battle helplessly as the experts fought to save Christie's life.

Earlier, as he had rushed through the swinging doors with Christie in his arms, he had, briefly, a role to play. They had sat him down and tried to draw from him a coherent story of what had happened. In their cold eyes he could see that they had done all this before. Teenage suicide. The American epidemic. This would be the boyfriend. The unconscious girl would be his lover. His would-be lover. His ex-lover. The permutations were infinite, but they had been interested in only three things. What type and quantity of tablets had she taken? When had she swallowed them? For how long had she been unconscious? As Scott had tried to tell them they had hung on his every word, but the second they discovered that he did not know the answer to the first vital question they had discarded him like yesterday's newspaper.

The young doctor, harassed and unkempt, was thinking aloud. "We have arrhythmias on the EKG now. Could this be tricyclics?" Nobody answered. "Was she on antidepressants? For God's sake, somebody ask the boyfriend. Did she have access to antidepressants?"

The note of exasperation communicated itself to the team. "Stomach contents are on the way to the lab now. We should have an answer in ten minutes."

"Ten minutes and it'll be blowing in the wind. I'm getting ventricular tachycardia here. Get some lidocaine into the drip site, Sue, fifty-milligram bolus, and get another syringe with the same dose ready in case we need it. We've got sodium bicarb ready. Okay? What did the boyfriend say about the antidepressants?"

The boyfriend in his agony of ignorance had nothing to say. Christie hadn't been depressed until he'd crumpled her up like a blank sheet of paper. Maybe Jo-Anne had been on that sort of medication. It was more than unlikely that Senator Stansfield had.

"I just don't know. God. I don't know," he managed in despair as the accusing and questioning eyes fixed on him.

"How is she? Is she going to be all right?" he pleaded to the now deaf ears. But he was once again the invisible man. For now he could bleat out his remorse all by himself.

"Hit her with the lido again. This isn't working. Give me a BP."

"I'm getting seventy over fifty."

"Shit, I think this one's going. Hook her up to the ventilator. Come on, *shift* it. Is the DC converter ready? Hand me that electrode jelly, Sue. Tom, watch that EKG readout like a hawk. The moment we get ventricular fib we give her a squirt of juice. Okay?"

"I can't hear diastolic now. BP's going down out of sight."

Scott's heart felt like it was in worse shape than Christie's. He didn't understand most of what was being said, but there was no mistaking the urgency of the action. Someone was pushing a tube down Christie's throat, another hand was fiddling frantically with the knob controlling the IV inflow, and a nurse was winding at the lever that raised the end of the bed.

"Don't go, baby. Hang on in there. You can make it." The doctor was murmuring to himself again, willing the lidocaine to bite, to calm the wriggling, uncoordinated heart. Unless it could regain its smooth pumping action, the pressure of the blood in the arteries would fall away and the vital heart muscle would be starved of oxygen.

"She's so young," said somebody.

"Are we all plugged in?"

"Damn, I'm getting VF now. The trace is all over the place."

"BP unrecordable."

"Okay, folks, let's go for it. DC countershock. Four hundred watt-seconds."

In dumb horror Scott watched as Christie flirted with death. She was dying. All but dead, and he'd killed her. And that made him the world's most repulsive creature. Please, God, let her live. And now as the tears rolled down his cheeks he sank to his knees in prayer as around him the doctors hustled and the nurses ran.

"Please, God. Please, God," he heard himself say out loud to the uncomprehending white walls as the doctor leaned over Christie's proud pale breast with the electrodes.

"Ready everyone. Stand back."

Scott was hardly aware of Christie's body as it bucked and reared under the current from the defibrillator. He was talking to God. Pleading, promising, bargaining.

"What are you getting, Tom? Still VF?"

"Yes."

"We'll go again."

Again he leaned forward to administer the crude antidote. Again Christie's small body reeled under the shock.

"That's better. I'm seeing sinus rhythm. She's flipped back into sinus. Brilliant. *Brilliant!*"

"Are you getting pressure?"

"There's a few millimeters of mercury now. Yup, pressure's coming back."

"Goddamn. She nearly went there. That was *close.*"

"All the vital signs are stabilizing now. BP's coming up nicely. Rhythm looks rock solid. Bradycardia of fifty."

Shakily Scott stood up. The atmosphere had changed. The room was lighter. The cloven hoofs of the Horseman had clattered away. For the moment his prayers had been answered, but it was going to be a long night.

THEY HAD thrown him out at midnight with the consolation prize that Christie would make it, but mouths had gone all hard when he had pleaded to be able to see her. They hadn't wanted his desperate need for forgiveness to be satisfied, and already all sorts of pictures were beginning to emerge. This was a *Stansfield* daughter, while the boy looked like some cheap beach bum. The mother was on her way. Somebody was trying to contact the senator in Ohio. It was far better that this bit player be swept out into the wings before the principal actors arrived. In the rush nobody had even bothered to ask his name.

On the fetid West Palm streets Scott had been left alone with his relief, alone with his guilt, alone with his self-hatred. He had walked along the shores of the lake and tried to understand the things that had happened to him, the thing he had allowed himself to become. There had been no answers to the fevered questions. He had slipped into the role of monster with the ease of a quick-change artist. The motivation had been enough. To please his mother. To gain her love. But now in the cold reality of the warm night the force to action looked a sad, pathetic thing. He had always believed that he was unworthy of love, but Christie had loved him. Loved him enough to die if she couldn't have him.

Perhaps all along there had been another explanation, even now scarcely perceived, hardly perceivable. Maybe, just maybe, the fault was with his mother. Was it the void in *her* heart that had caused so much hatred, so much insecurity, and so much pain? Even now the thought was almost too hot to handle.

Scott wanted desperately to escape the war that raged within him and to hide from the unhappy emotions that chased him. There was a time-honored method of doing just that.

Roxy's Bar. In the brash new world of hustling West Palm Beach, where the buildings now fought each other for a patch of the sky to scrape, few things remained the same. Roxy's and its drink-sodden owner Willie Boy Willis were two that had. Willie, who had known his mother and her family in the days before she had married his father, monosyllabic Willie of the strange looks and the buttoned-up mouth. He would be a good enough partner for a few hours of oblivion.

In the dimly lit innards of Roxy's, Willie Boy's welcome was warm. As usual he inhabited the no-man's-land between drunkenness and sobriety that seemed to be the stamping ground of the genuine alcoholic. His lopsided grin and his filthy face, bemused and fuddled by the years of booze, tried to make sense of Scott's presence.

"Hi, Scottie boy. What brings you down here? Ain't seen you in months. You been neglectin' ol' friends?"

It was a friendly greeting. On the whole, Willie Boy was a friendly soul. Though sometimes, toward closing time, he could turn mean. Tonight, however, Scott was in no mood for charity. Already a dreadful anger, directed at himself, was beginning to form within him. There was more than enough to spill over.

"I haven't been neglecting anyone," he said shortly. "Hit me with a big Jack Daniel's, and, Willie, I mean *big*."

Willie Boy let it go. Scott wasn't usually so touchy. Pretty easy-going in the main. Still, everyone was entitled to a bad mood from time to time.

He reached for the bottle of bourbon and poured a generous measure into a far from clean glass.

"I said *big*, Willie." Scott's voice was tense. He'd had about as much as he could take. The pain needed anesthetic. Now.

Willie Boy felt the burst of irritation within him. Scott was pushing it. Usually he came in Roxy's with some surfers. He talked rough and joked rough like a regular guy. But today he seemed all Palm Beach. All tight-assed. Like some stuck-up rich kid. He kept pouring, but he couldn't resist the dig. "Big drink for a big man. Eh, Scottie?"

"What's that supposed to mean?" Anything to avoid thinking about himself. Any distraction. The drink. An argument. Anything.

"Means what you want it to mean."

Willie leered across the polished bar. Lines like these he'd exchanged a million times before. A few times a week there were fights in Roxy's. Some you won. Some you didn't. With Jack Kent and with Tommy Starr the trick had always been to apologize. There wouldn't be any need for that tonight.

"Means you talk a lot of shit, man," said Scott nastily, taking a long pull at the bourbon.

Willie Boy's narrow eyes narrowed further. The punk. The little stuck-up punk. He ought to slam him all around the room. But he looked pretty fit, and he was obviously pretty mean. And then, quite suddenly, the final straw descended on Willie Boy Willis's long suffering back. He'd always been a loser, a drunk. A prisoner in the cellar of life, condemned to scratch out his existence amid the sawdust, the sweat, and the beer. People came in through the door and pissed on him in his misery. Men like Jack Kent who'd treated him like the scum he knew he was. Men like Tommy Starr, who'd been too gentle to tell him what he was but who'd allowed the truth to shine out of his eyes. Women like Lisa Starr who'd pretended he was her friend until she'd passed across the bridge into glory. And now this. This wet-behind-the-ears preppy—coming on like a great big man and trying to push poor old Willie Boy around as his grandfather had in days gone by. Well, he shouldn't have done that. There were reasons why he'd regret it. Two mighty big reasons. And they weren't called fists.

The smile split Willie Boy's face from ear to ear. Most of his mind was gone now, all shot to pieces by the drink. But there were a couple of things he knew. A couple of little time bombs ticking away in the remains of his brain. They wouldn't last forever. Maybe he'd forget them. Maybe they'd melt when the liver went. He'd always thought of the bartender's role as being like the priest's. You heard everything, spoke nothing. But that was foolish, wasn't it? Nobody thanked you for keeping their confidence. They despised you for it and treated you like shit. Like young Scott was now.

He leaned across the bar. "How's that flashy father of yours?"

Scott waved his hand dismissively. Willie Boy was clearly out of it. His brains were a jar of pickles. It wouldn't even be diverting to fight with him. "Oh, forget it, Willie Boy. My old man's been dead for years. Leave it alone."

"He ain't."

Scott looked up. There had been something about the triumphant tone of Willie Boy's voice. It was matched by the triumphant smile that he now saw on Willie Boy's face. "Come on, Willie. Drink up and shut up. I don't feel like all this bad-vibe rap."

When Scott spoke there was uncertainty in his voice. Vernon Blass was just a name to him. He was vaguely proud of being a Blass and had often wondered about his father, but somehow it had been no big deal not having one around. It was his mother who had bestrode his world like a colossus. From the pictures and the stories, he had been able to piece together a portrait of a blemished Palm Beacher who, as a man, had been worse than some but better than others. In one area, however, his father had showed himself to be a total winner, and it was the only one that mattered. He had married Lisa Starr.

Willie's smile was cunning now. Sly and evil. He was going to go for it. He could feel it inside. He was going to right the wrongs. Wrong the rights.

Lisa Starr, who'd been his friend until she'd walked across the water. Lisa Blass, queen of the most successful publishing company in the land. Lisa loaded, loaded Lisa. She never came down to Roxy's. Old friends abandoned, old memories conveniently forgotten. No handouts. Nothing. But he knew her secret, and he knew the secret she didn't know. All his miserable life he had kept a secret, and for what? So that they would be boxed with him? Yeah, that would suit them all. The whole frigging lot of them. He had been loyal. He had kept his promise to Tommy Starr. And for what? So that he could die without a pot to piss in or the window to throw it out of? Now this rich kid could come in here and patronize him. Willie, who knew it all. Who knew the whole stinking rotten truth.

"I ain't rubbishing you, Scott, boy. I just wondered if you was strong

888 — *Pat Booth* —

'nough for a bit of truth to go with that bourbon. Truth 'bout your old man, an' your mom."

"What 'truth'?" Suddenly the warm fire in his stomach wasn't from the alcohol alone.

Across the polished bar there was wickedness in the drink-sodden eyes. "Well, for one thing, you ain't no right to call yourself Blass."

Willie paused briefly before plowing on. He leaned both gnarled hands on the shining wood, to catch the effect of his words. Through the swirling mists, Scott's face seemed to come and go. One thing was clear as it clicked in and out of focus. It had gone white.

Through his bent mind Willie tried to work out the advisability of what he was about to do. It could still be a joke. Just. The alcohol talking. But his tongue was already out of control. The hell with it. Screw 'em all. Everyone had always screwed *him*. They'd never reckoned poor ol' Willie Boy. But late at night when the Bud had loosened them all up there wasn't much they'd been able to keep to themselves. Like that night with Tommy. The one he'd got all liquored up and tried to talk in riddles, with the tears streaming down his great big dirty face. Then there was Lisa. All those times in her little apartment when she liked him to tell the tales of the golden days. He'd known she was pregnant, known that she was carrying the Stansfield child who now stood before him across the glistening bar. He'd been sober when she'd talked of her love for Bobby Stansfield. Sober enough to keep his mouth buttoned up tight on Tommy Starr's secret. Okay, so he had discouraged her. The likes of them never marry the likes of you. That sort of thing. But he hadn't expected their relationship to work, and it hadn't. When Stansfield threw her out she'd gone for Blass on the rebound—and from that moment to this, West Palm, Willie Boy, and Roxy's Bar had been painted out of her life as if they had never existed.

"Yeah, Scott boy. Your last name's Stansfield. You're the senator's son. Ha ha. Ain't that great? You're a rich bastard. Your mom had the hots for him, and when he didn't want to know, she gone and married ol' man Blass. Told me so herself. Never let you in on the secret, eh?"

Scott felt the room creeping all around him. Like an Indian around a cowboy's campfire, it seemed to come and go, circling, crawling about on the edge of vision, on the periphery of hearing. What was Willie Boy saying? He was drunk. But he had been his mother's friend. So often she had talked of him, and of her onetime friendship with this living link with the past, with those she had loved and lost. It wasn't the sort of thing you made up, drunk or sober, mad or sane. And it explained all sorts of things that were otherwise scarcely explicable. His beautiful mother in the arms of a man old enough to be her grandfather. The hatred for the Stansfields and particularly for Jo-Anne. That could have stemmed from the jealousy of the jilted. His own looks. Blond and blue eyed like the Senator Stansfield of the glossy magazines. Like the baby blue of Christie's . . .

He took a step back from the bar as the world began to roar inside his head. Christie Stansfield. On the sand. Christie Stansfield, bucking and rearing under the current as they tried to start the heart he had stopped. Christie Stansfield, who looked so very much like him, and who loved him in such a strange, compelling way. His hand flew to his mouth, as the blood drained from his cheeks and his mouth sought the words that would express the dreadful feelings he felt. He had met her in anger, but immediately he had liked her. Only his terrible mission had blinded him to a truth that was trying to be told.

He took another step back from the messenger who was grinding to powder the remainder of his universe.

But, unbelievably, Willie Boy had not finished. His face was flushed with the enormity of what he was doing, the adrenaline wiping out temporarily the dulling effects of the alcohol. His voice was almost clear and soft as silk as he embarked on the second half of his roller-coaster ride into horror.

"Strangest thing is something even your mom didn't know. Mary-Ellen kept it from everyone 'cep poor Tommy. When she married him, she was carrying Lisa then. An' you know who was the real father? Ol' man Stansfield. Mary-Ellen worked in the house, an' he got her in the worst kind of trouble. Best thing Tommy ever did taking her on. Sure as hell I never would. But he told me that night, and he couldn't hold back the tears when he did. Never seen him cry before. He wanted her so bad he'd have had her under any circumstances, loved her that much."

Uncomprehending at first, then with the dawning of awareness, stark in their terror and hurt. Scott's eyes stared back at the bringer of the dreadful tidings.

He walked backward, stumbling over the leg of a chair, the feet of a customer. His hands reached behind him for the door to the street, and still his stricken eyes stayed locked on Willie's. Brothers and sisters. Happy families.

And as Willie Boy watched, sobered by the enormity of his act, the West Palm night swallowed Scott up.

~ *20* ~

*A*LL HER LIFE Jo-Anne had dreamed of getting there, but now that she had arrived she couldn't help wondering whether the arduous journey had been worth it. The view from the throne had certainly been better in fantasy than it was in reality, and the Jupiter Island Garden Club Bazaar, perhaps the most chic garage sale in the world, was the example that proved it all. Hobe Sound. The grandest place in America, bar none. Grander by far than Newport, effortlessly superior to Scottsdale, the social mecca that relegated such down-market towns as Beverly Hills and Palm Springs to the status of sniveling also-rans. Hobe Sound, nestling against the white sand of the arrogant Atlantic, was the most secret bastion of the oldest money, where privacy ruled, and where the American aristocracy hid from the world of television and newspapers, which the lesser mortals they despised so desperately sought.

It was a place of contradictions. Called Hobe Sound, it wasn't really that at all. It was the town of Jupiter Island, or rather the residential portion of it. The real Hobe Sound was across the electrically monitored bridge, a run-down place where the rest of Florida lived, and where the mighty went to pick up their mail: the inconvenience was minor compared to having those dreadful mail vans buzzing about to remind them of the real world from which "the Island" was their escape. Sand, sea, and seclusion for the two hundred Old Guard families who wintered here from New Year's Eve to March, hidden away in the four hundred mansions they preferred to call "places." Mellons, Adamses, Roosevelts nestled snugly in the refined and reverent silence of the scented Australian pines; Scrantons, Searles, and Olins cavorted with decorum around the side-by-side rectangular and kidney-shaped swimming pools of the Jupiter Island Club, a place so formidably upper class that it could dare such brave experimentation with good taste; Pierreponts, Fieldses, and Weyerhaeusers peered serenely over snipped lawns at their sour-faced gardeners as they dusted dustless pathways and tended immaculate orchids; Paysons, Lamonts, and Coleses sipped Scotch as they grumbled about servants and groused over the unsatisfactory behavior of grandsons and Democratic politicians.

"Can I get you something to drink, Jo-Anne? Some lemonade, perhaps?"

Laura Hornblower was suitably solicitous. After all, she was in charge of entertaining visiting royalty. The kingdom of Palm Beach had sent its reigning monarch on a state visit to the smaller but enormously prestigious one of Hobe Sound, and as aide-de-camp to the autocratic but enlightened despot who ruled it, Laura was working hard.

Jo-Anne looked unenthusiastic. Eleven o'clock in the morning and what she really needed was a shot of something much stronger. There in a nutshell was the difference between the two towns. Hobe Sound: tea, early risers, spartan ascetics, and wall-to-wall environmentalists. Palm Beach: booze, late nights—by Hobe Sound standards at least—hedonists, and achievers.

"Yes, wonderful. Thanks." Jo-Anne groaned inwardly. Power brought responsibility, at least, like now, when the visibility was high. God, how the hell was she going to get through this without a real drink?

The sun beat down with an unseasonal intensity over the sparse crowd, as they picked their way suspiciously through the stalls. There was more money here than in a medium-size South American nation, but they were still on the lookout for a bargain: some Percale sheets at fifty cents, an old wicker chair at two bucks, a wrought-iron table cheap at fifteen dollars. They didn't haggle, but they fingered and felt, relishing the pretense that they were shopping for a bargain. Making believe they were ordinary people. Later in the afternoon they would put the receipts for the things they had bought into a long-playing record sleeve or a shirt box, and in due course the grubby scraps of paper would make it to New York to the offices of Price, Waterhouse where, spread out on polished mahogany desks, they would be turned into tax deductions. Deduct five hundred thousand dollars for the donation to the University of Virginia Law Library. Fifty cents for the used sheets. It was all an affectation, of course, but it meant everything.

The parsimony, the horror of ostentation were all part of the secret language by which these special people communicated. *National Enquirer* readers, brought up on a staple diet of trash people—actors and celebrities—thought that the point of being rich was to spend money extravagantly. But they had no conception of how the really rich behaved. Any one of these Hobe Sound plutocrats could have bought Elizabeth Taylor with the income on the income on the income, and yet they would carefully write each other a check for $1.50 if that was what they had won or lost at bridge and canasta. And they saved silver paper, and Christmas wrapping, and drove around in clean but old Ford "Woodies," leaving the navy-blue Rolls-Royces and the black vintage Bentleys in their commodious garages. Nobody "designed" their houses, their yachts were ancient, their food was plain, and their self-confidence was boundless.

Jo-Anne stared moodily at the nearest stall. She knew she should buy something. Nothing too expensive. That wouldn't do at all. Up here, Palm Beachers had a reputation for unacceptable extravagance. But something.

After all, there were gimlet eyes guarding the cash box, the all-seeing eyes of the most powerful person in Hobe Sound—its undisputed ruler and social arbiter—Permelia Pryor Reed herself. Permelia Reed owned the Jupiter Island Club and decided exactly who was allowed through its hallowed portals. She ruled the small community with an iron hand, keeping it small, select, and upper class, and nobody who aspired to be anything but a hermit could afford to ignore her. Once, it was rumored, an unwise girl had worn a too-brief bikini at the club, and the beady eyes of the queen had descended upon her. A waiter had been dispatched with a pink cashmere sweater to cover her unseemly nakedness. Ever after, the story went, bad behavior in Hobe Sound was rewarded by the gift of a similar garment, a potent symbol of social death, as the white feather had been of cowardice. Nobody who received the feared cardigan had remained in Hobe Sound to live the life of the social "undead."

Jo-Anne wondered briefly about a set of beautifully molded brown wood coat hangers, bearing the carved initials G.D.H. That would just about do. But a bit bulky.

"Aren't they wonderful, Mrs. Stansfield? I can't stand the modern ones, can you?"

The Jupiter Island Garden Club member who manned the stall went through the motions. Wasn't it fun being a saleswoman—or salesperson as she supposed they were called nowadays. The largest single block holding in Smithkline was pretending to sell things. For charity, of course. The Hobe Sound Nature Center this year.

Jo-Anne murmured her acquiescence as the blue-blood carefully calculated the change from the five-dollar bill. Jo-Anne took it religiously. God, even in Big Apple days she'd have said "keep the change." Now, for appearances' sake she wondered if she ought to count it.

Laura was back with the warm lemonade. "Would you like something to nibble on? I can recommend the spinach balls. I made them myself."

"No, thanks, Laura," said Jo-Anne shortly. This whole thing was turning into a nightmare. Thank the Lord, the Sothebys of garage sales only happened once every two years. In all those years of clawing her way to the top, Jo-Anne hadn't realized it would come to this—picking her way through the attic treasures of the wealthy to fund some charity that could have been as easily enriched by one meaty check. How many long hot nights had she lain awake longing to be asked to join the Palm Beach chapter of the Garden Club of America, that ultimate symbol of social "arrival"? Now she was its ruler and had discovered the numbing tedium of its functions. Here she was, sweating beneath the canopy of the Christ Memorial Parish House tent, playing charades with fuddy-duddy moldy oldies whose bank balances were only equalled by the length of their pedigrees.

"Oh, Jo-Anne, I'm so glad you're here. Lovely to see a Palm Beach face." The unctuous tones, heavy with flattery and groveling friendliness, belonged to none other than Eleanor Peacock.

Jo-Anne turned to look at her former enemy. She bit deep into the ice-cold cake of revenge. "Eleanor, dear. What on earth are you doing up here? Shopping for a few bargains? I suppose the quality of the rubbish is a bit better than the West Palm thrifts."

As she had done a thousand times before, Eleanor Peacock swallowed the insult with a good grace. She had never been forgiven for her attempt at social murder on the eve of the Planned Parenthood party, and she never expected to be. Marjorie Donahue had effectively written her off the face of the earth. Later, during her all too brief rehabilitation at the time of the Jo-Anne/Marjorie wars, she had been born again, only to be cast down once more by the Donahue death. As Jo-Anne had moved to fill the power vacuum, Eleanor's social stock had completed its roller-coaster ride to rock bottom. Then, when she had least expected it, and when she had been on the verge of persuading poor Arch to give up his job and move to Connecticut, the new queen had offered her an unspoken deal. It hadn't been a very good one, but it had been a sort of salvation. Jo-Anne was apparently prepared to allow her to survive. In exchange she must suffer all the insults and indignities that a cruel and clever mind could dream up. And she must never, *never* answer back.

"Oh, Jo-Anne, you *are* unkind," laughed Eleanor, the false smile plastered uncomfortably all over her face. She stood her ground, preparing to accept a few more verbal blows before the cat tired of playing with the mouse. She was almost used to it now, but not quite. Trading her pride for Palm Beach social survival. There was scarcely an hour of the day, of course, when she didn't bombard the Almighty with prayers for a thunderbolt to descend on her hated superior, but she had more or less given up hope of divine intervention.

"Well, I suppose it's nice to have a Palm Beach ally up here even if it's only you, Eleanor. These golden oldies give me the creeps. This place is Costa Geriatrica. I wonder how soon I can decently get away."

Get away. Yes, that was it. Escape. Escape from the half-dead crinkly-wrinklies. Escape from responsibility, from genteel conversation, from hypocrisy, from Hobe Sound. Jo-Anne was sick of it all. Sick of being the queen, of all the snobs, of all the money. Of everything. She experienced all at once the overwhelming desire to blot it all out, and to travel to the farthest corner of the earth where people did things differently, thought different things. But where? How? The answer, born of claustrophobia's panic, came through with the clarity of a still, small voice. There was another world. A dangerous, exciting, alluring world.

She would drive south on Dixie to the place where Riviera Beach met the outskirts of West Palm. It was a dirty run-down area of flyblown bars and broken-down shops. It was the place the black hookers hung out.

THE WEST PALM suburb was a steaming cauldron, and the air was like hot fudge, sweet, thick, and sticky as hell itself. It blanketed Jo-Anne's body, wrapping her up in a wet towel of humid heat as it bathed her in its dampness and drew the abundant moisture from her own pores. At the wheel of the convertible she gave herself up to the delicious tackiness of the experience. It wasn't that she didn't have an alternative. One flick of a switch and the convertible top would have covered her. The touch of another and the icy cold of the air conditioner would have brought everything back to normal. But Jo-Anne was luxuriating in the sensuality of her own body heat. The long white pleated skirt, unbuttoned now to midthigh, was already awash with sweat, and the Turnbull and Asser cream silk shirt clung to her chest, providing a delicious friction to her hardening nipples. She ran her tongue over her top lip, clearing away the salty dewdrops of moisture. Hey, this was great. Turkish-bath time. She must be losing pounds. That was it. That was what she was doing. Cruising and losing. What a way to go. The Hobe Sound Garden Club Bazaar seemed already a million miles away.

Now she was about to blot it out in the most dangerous and exciting way possible. Jo-Anne laughed out loud. She should never have deviated from the straight and narrow, never attempted the disastrous transition from pussy to prick: the scene with Christie and the blue-eyed blondie with the intense eyes had been the baddest of bad trips. She'd never understood her daughter; but to attempt to do yourself in because you caught your mother on the job with someone just a little younger was surely carrying straightness too far. Still, there was one hell of a lot to be grateful for. First, she had survived, apparently as good as new. Second, she had failed to tell the tale. That much at least had been predictable. Christie made Goldilocks look like a two-bit Times Square hustler. Anyway, it was a relief. Bobby Stansfield wouldn't have understood about a woman's needs and the necessity of satisfying them, and it was just as well that the ignorance of his bliss would not be replaced by the folly of needless wisdom.

Again and again Jo-Anne had tried to understand her daughter's weird motivation, despite the fact that speculating about the thoughts of others was not her specialty. Christie had been tight mouthed both in the hospital and, later, at home. She had tried to pass off the suicide attempt as a "terrible mistake," an overreaction to the shock of her experience, and she had been completely forgiving, and even understanding of Jo-Anne's predicament.

"Don't worry, mom. I won't tell dad. But please, please promise me you'll never be unfaithful to him again."

Words being cheap, Jo-Anne had promised. "I swear it, darling. On my life I promise you."

Did this little expedition count as marital infidelity?

The wild side demanded its own precautions. Jo-Anne had hidden in the trunk anything that could identify her. Platinum American Express card, Chase Manhattan "Thousand Club" card, checkbooks, driver's license. Blackmail was something she for sure didn't need right now. She had also tucked away the jewelry—the Van Cleef diamond-encrusted bracelet, the ruby-and-diamond lucky horseshoe brooch, and the pear-drop diamond earrings.

She checked herself in the rearview mirror. Damn. She'd almost forgotten. The twin ebony diamond-lined hair combs from Cartier. They would have signaled "retirement" to most of the inhabitants of this part of South

Dixie. Impatiently she swept them off and jammed them without ceremony into the glove compartment, letting her hair fall free over her shoulders—a symbolic loosening of restraints, an embracing of abandonment.

Jo-Anne wasn't at all sure how or where she would get it, but she knew exactly what she wanted. She wanted the lowest of the low. Some dirty, back-street black girl. Somebody whose edges were all rough, with no manners, no graces, nothing, except a willing body.

Mmmmmmmmmmmmmmmm. The thought was turning her on. Memory lane was all but impassable now, overgrown with undergrowth, but the idea had the power to shift juices. Jo-Anne, who had sold it, was about to become a buyer for the very first time. Yeah, it was a real nice idea. Haggling in some shady parking lot over the price of a girl's body. Then, once she'd handed over the bucks, the delicious thrill of knowing that for a brief time she would own it, that it would be hers to do with as she wished.

She had a vague idea where she was heading. The Port o' Call Bar looked like the sort of place she wanted. Several times as the Rolls had purred up North Dixie to Hobe Sound dinner parties she had noticed the gaggle of taut-assed black hookers hanging around on the pavement trolling for passing trade in the damp heat of the early evening. It was a bit early, but then early birds were supposed to be the ones that scored, weren't they?

The paint on the bar's sign had seen better days, but then so, presumably, had the bar itself. Jo-Anne drove straight past it, noting the open door, the silhouette of a pin-ball machine, the green light shining inside. She took a deep breath. God, how would she have the nerve to walk into a place like that, let alone make a deal in there?

To the honking of a couple of outraged motorists she made a U-turn and headed back, drawn to the danger like an insect to the flame. To the danger and the promise of alien delight.

She twirled the wheel and sent the big Mercedes roadster winging into the seedy parking lot. She caught sight of them immediately. Three of them, talking and hanging out against the peeling paint of the wall. Their clothes said nearly all of it; their lazy, wandering eyes said the rest. The two on the right were way past anything, flyblown, clapped-out junkies, blowsy and bat-tered by the "good-time" life.

Slack minds, slack bottoms, faded dreams, faded jeans.

But the third girl was *really* something. As she pulled up Jo-Anne took it all in. She was very young. Fifteen. Possibly a little older. Probably a bit younger. Everything was on show and it was all tingling tight. The tall ass sat at the top of long gangling legs, and the tits, mocking gravity, made the sharpest of angles with the thin torso, a living indictment of the toneless mounds that belonged to her two older colleagues. Her face was alert—cheeky and alive, the big brown eyes very far from jaded—ready for all the adventures that life around the Port o' Call Bar promised. Her hair had been ruthlessly straightened and back-combed to give the appearance of late teens, which the rest of her body and demeanor denied. She wore a skirt so short it looked like a wide belt, no stockings to hide the cool chocolate-brown skin of her legs, ankle-length white boots, and a long shoulder bag of black plastic. Across the front of her T-shirt, the large letters A and Y hovering uncertainly on the pointed nipples, was the word ANY. And as she turned casually to see who had arrived in the sharp convertible, Jo-Anne could see that across the shirt's back was written in bold capitals the word THING. Jo-Anne laughed out loud.

The spark of interest in the expensive car was not completely extinguished when it took in the sex of the owner. In the dead eyes of the other two girls, however, Jo-Anne clearly rated about as much importance as a body in the Hudson to a New York cop.

Jo-Anne was five feet away from the three girls. She didn't even have to get out of the car. "Hello," she said.

The old pros didn't blink . . . or answer. Taking her cue from her "elders," the fox didn't speak either. But she looked a lot.

"I was wondering if you could help me."

Jo-Anne wasn't daunted. She knew this scene. And it was promising as hell.

"An how we gonna help a rich whitey mother like you, honey? You lost or somethin'?"

The bewigged hulk on the left showed bad teeth and hinted at worse breath as she spoke. The fox kept looking, a marginally puzzled expression on the full mouth, a casual thumb stuck jauntily into the rim of the belt/skirt.

"Well, I hoped you might be able to help me spend some money." Jo-Anne made her voice go provocative. It wasn't hard. The palms of her hands were already moist. The rest of her was getting there fast.

In four of the eyes dawned the beginnings of comprehension. In the youngest pair there was surprise.

The sound of the original speaker laughing was not nice. Apparently it wasn't meant to be. "You tryin' to score chicks, honey, you in the wrong place. You even in the wrong *state*. You better hit New York or L.A. or one of them *dirty* places where they do all that *jazz*."

Jo-Anne looked long and hard at the one she wanted, ignoring the discouraging words from the shit bag. She'd gotten there at last, and the amusement was pushing the surprise right off her beautiful young face.

"I have three hundred dollars to spend," said Jo-Anne quickly, before positions became too entrenched.

She had center stage now, all right. As intended, three big ones was way, way over the top for this market, and money was the loudest language there was.

The spokesperson for the trio wavered visibly, and when at last she spoke there was an angry disappointment in her voice. In this neck of the woods you just didn't *do* dyke scenes if you wanted to stay healthy. The men that looked after you didn't understand about things like that. It was a tooth-losing trip. But three hundred bucks? Christ, the chick must want it bad.

"Get drivin', honey. We don' want your stinkin' bucks," she managed at last. "Hey, wait a minute." Like clockwork, thought Jo-Anne. The target had spoken. "What you wanna do for three hundred bucks?"

The young girl wanted an answer to the question. She understood folding money, but she had no idea what was expected from her in return. A kiss? Something else? "We could make it up as we went along. You'd get the money up front."

"Now don' you mess with it, Mona. You don' know nothing, sweetheart. This is bad news, man. Clive, he don' like this kind of thing. You'll go an' get yourself all sorts of trouble. Ain' that right, Suzie?"

Suzie, unaccustomed to the role of arbitrator and clearly not long on words, nodded her agreement vigorously.

The two beaten-down dogs were united. Selling yourself to chicks just wasn't done. A little like converting to Catholicism on the island maybe, or wearing rough-soled shoes to drinks on board a yacht. And Clive, whoever he was, shared the view that such behavior was a definite *faux-pas*. Jo-Anne laughed to herself. It was a topsy-turvy world and rules were different, but still, whatever they were they were meant to be obeyed.

Jo-Anne now addressed herself directly to the gorgeous little girl. She was halfway there. Halfway to paradise. "Listen. Why don't you hop in and we can discuss this, you and me. You get fifty for just hearing me out. No harm in that."

The girl let out a laugh of delight, all warm and funny from the back of her throat. Life was still fun for her. She was young enough for that. And enough of a child to take the risk and to scorn the nameless threat because it was a future thing.

She didn't hesitate, and without even looking at the colleagues who had been so free with their advice, she signed the unwritten contract by crossing the space to the now open door of Jo-Anne's car.

As her pert bottom hit the soft white leather, the skirt-belt ceased its hypocrisy. There were acres of long, black thigh and shocking-pink panties, and there was the smell too of the cheap scent and, beneath it, subtle, heady, a much more potent aroma, the mindbending perfume of hot little girl.

Jo-Anne didn't waste any time. The engines were already running inside her. She did the same for the car and was out of the lot before anybody was in the business of changing minds.

On the highway she turned to look at her catch, and as she did so her right hand was drawn to the magnetic skin of its exposed leg. She ran a tongue over her dessicated lips and tried to swallow as she felt the eager heat beneath her hand. Her voice when it came was positively quivering with anticipation. "Where to?"

The big full lips pouted back at her. "I ain' done this before."

Jo-Anne tried to make her smile reassuring. She'd heard the line before. The tones had been more patrician, but the sentiment was not new. Neither was the response. "Trust me. It's a whole new world."

The black girl liked the sound of new worlds, but of other things more. "You got the bucks?"

Jo-Anne smiled ruefully. She'd almost forgotten. This was a different trip. Business sex. Did the girl feel like Jo-Anne herself had felt in all those endless hotel rooms? Had the johns felt as she felt now? The tinge of disappointment that this whole thing wasn't being done just for the love of it. Then she laughed. No, the reality was the turn-on. She'd rented a body. For an hour or so she'd own it. There was no need for the seduction routine. The bucks cut right through all that shit.

"Take three hundred out of the bag, and let's have the directions." There was a new sharpness in her voice. "I want this show on the road," her tone seemed to say.

"How old are you, anyway? Tell me the truth. It makes no difference."

The liquid brown eyes went careful, but the three hundred in the long chocolate fingers blew away caution. "Fourteen," she said, as she moved around a bit beneath Jo-Anne's hovering hand. "That too young?" The question was provocative, even a dare.

"No, it's not too young." But it would be the youngest ever. By about three years. That was a nice touch. Fourteen, black, and, as far as women were concerned, a virgin. Why the hell hadn't she thought of this before?

"Hang a right at the next light and pull into the lot on the left. I got the use of a room at the Sea Grass motel."

Jo-Anne did as she was told, relinquishing her position on the young girl's leg with regret as she made the turn.

They didn't speak as they walked up the stairs of the run-down motel. Already Jo-Anne could picture the room. It would be a facsimile of a million such rooms all across America: plastic, cigarette burns, Dacron, rayon, or whatever other synthetic they made fabric out of these days. Somebody would have cleaned his shoes on the drapes; there would be a ring around the bathtub, and a monster TV with a crackling four-channel-only selection, a mean, foam-filled pillow, a lopsided standard lamp. But in front of her walked the tight, high bottom that she had hired. That was more than enough to send the heart into overdrive and to set the stomach whispering.

The room lived up to its promise. There had been no concessions to aesthetic susceptibilities. None at all—from the dented tin wastebasket with its white plastic liner to the pink-plastic-framed mirror that would catch the action over the single bed.

But the prettiest thing was emphasized by the seediness of the surroundings. The little-girl hooker slung the cheap bag onto the bed and tried to look as if she were in control. Turning to face her client, she attempted to sound businesslike. "Okay, how do you want it?" The truth was she really didn't know at all.

"Every way in the book," said Jo-Anne simply. "But we'll start right here. Standing up."

She crossed the three steps into the younger girl's space. "Stand quite still. Don't do a thing."

The girl watched her. The eyes were unsure, but there was interest, almost a sense of fascination in their depths. She looked as if she had been hypnotized—her will all gone as she prepared to surrender herself to Jo-Anne's superior power.

Not taking her eyes off the black girl's face, Jo-Anne reached down and gently lifted the skirt. Only when the panties were completely exposed did she look down to enjoy what she had unveiled.

The sigh rushed through her parted lips at the sight. The almost fluorescent pink briefs were a good size too small. They looked like they had been spray painted on, and the tense mound of the teenager's sex thrust anxiously against the skimpy material. Twin thongs raced away to the back, plastered tight over the delicious brown buttocks, while the third dived down deep into the infinitely alluring mystery that lurked between the firm flesh of the thighs.

Jo-Anne's fingers found the rim of the tight elastic and slowly, centimeter by centimeter, she eased them away.

Now Jo-Anne knelt down, her face level with the place she wanted. Radiating against her cheeks, the heat rushed toward her. This young girl was too new to the game to be in control of it. Her switch had been turned. Her motor was on. Jo-Anne could feel and smell it.

"Just relax, honey," she murmured more to herself than to the girl to whom she was about to make love.

The pants were away now. Slung across the curved thighs, they were a lewd hammock brushing against the skin of Jo-Anne's chin as her eyes devoured the vision they had revealed. Pink lips close to her lips, the demanding scent next to her nostrils, the warm soul of the young girl asking to be taken, quivering in anticipation in front of her eager mouth.

Jo-Anne heard the moan from above, as her lover gave her the permission to proceed. For one beautiful second she hesitated as she milked the moment for every ounce of its pleasure-giving potential. Then she moved forward.

Jo-Anne didn't hear the door open. But as her lips tenderly brushed against the lips before her she felt the rush of panic immediately. The slippery wetness against her mouth coincided with the explosion of rage.

"You *evil* girl! What you doin'? What you doin', you *evil* girl?"

The stinging blow caught Jo-Anne full across the left side of her face, sending the stars billowing through her head as her ear echoed with its force. She toppled sideways, crashing into the end of the bed.

Her almost lover, the pink pants pinioning her legs accusingly, stood stock still, a look of visceral fear contorting her formerly beautiful face. In the doorway stood a hundred and ninety pounds of muscled black hatred, disgust beaming from his eyes and murder humming in his heart.

"Clive, I didn' mean no harm. Clive . . ."

Somehow both girl and woman knew everything would be all right if this dreadful man could now be made to speak. But Clive was past speaking. He had seen his own private horror, and in his drugged, psychopathic eyes the emptiness said his girl had betrayed him. Not with the johns. They didn't count. They were income. His income. But with a white chick! With some white trash. Some cheap whitey whore. Some no-account pervert girl.

The switchblade knife was already gleaming in his palm.

Dear God. This was the pimp. The one called Clive. Clive, who didn't approve of the thing she had been trying to do. And in the mad, staring eyes, Jo-Anne could see what was going to happen. He was going to hurt her. She was going to be punished. After all the long, long years, retribution had finally arrived. All she could foresee was pain, pain and its roaring, gnawing aftermath. Disfigurement. By the foot of the bed she watched the actors in the drama. Three of them, herself included, strutting their brief moment on the boards.

She was literally outside herself, riding the frantic tide of adrenaline, suspended in time and space by pure panic. How could she stop what must be? Some clever word, some subtle gesture would stop the mad play in its tracks. She would lie back laughing and the horror would go away as everyone relaxed into the joke. All quite funny really. Scary but funny. But even as she allowed the hope to build, Jo-Anne knew that it had no substance. Born of the thirst for life, it would die in a desert of destruction.

Clive walked toward her and the knife was against her stomach, rucking up the material of the flimsy silk shirt as his anger beamed at her.

Her leathery tongue, shorn of moisture, tried to form a word of protest. "No," she murmured.

"Yes," he replied.

She dared to look down at the tightening fingers as she saw the ripple of muscle along the strong forearm, felt the cold splash of nausea in the pit of her stomach. And, as panic's fingers death-danced up and down her spine, Jo-Anne froze—as if through stillness she could be safe.

Like a sacrificial lamb she looked up into the eyes of the man who held the knife, but they were cold as the snows of winter, dead as the forest's dark. In that cosmic second they communed, sharing the intimacy of the damned as their souls touched at the edge of terror.

In vain Jo-Anne tried to make contact with the vacant eyes, but they did not respond. There was nobody there.

In her disjointed mind the frantic thoughts piled over themselves as they tumbled before the searchlight of consciousness. Presenting themselves in bits and pieces they were the jigsaw puzzle of her life. The New York streets, the strife and the struggle, the riches of the world dropped into her lap. Poor Peter's head and its red-vapor cloud, the senator's wife so cool and elegant at the rostrum. Fast food, slow food, cheap tricks, expensive ones—and always, ever present, the silky strains of the sexual background music, the ones that had been playing such a very short time before.

She should be thankful for the confusion of her thoughts. In the merciful haze of unreality there would be no pain. That was a relief. The pain would be for later. But for the sake of appearances really she ought to scream. In a situation like this any respectable person would certainly do that.

And so with a languid lack of enthusiasm, Jo-Anne Duke Stansfield began to scream as the knife turned into the fin of a shark. Northward it swam. Lazily, effortlessly across the tranquil sea of her lower stomach. Behind it there was the neat red line, at first thin and clean, then growing blurred and furry in an increasingly messy wake. It would swim right up to her face, between the twin breast mountains, along her beautiful neck, and across the promontory of her chin. Then at least she would have a little peace from the awful noise that somebody was making. But the peace was coming sooner than she thought. Wonderful sleepy peace. Just what a girl needed at the end of too long a life. And so with the sensation of amused surprise at the ease of it all, Jo-Anne let go, as she nosedived gracefully into nothingness.

~ 21 ~

I T WAS ONE of those Florida dog days when the irritable sky threatened all kinds of unpleasantness, and Bobby Stansfield felt totally in tune with the elements. It had been a disastrous six months. Christie's suicide attempt, followed closely by Jo-Anne's brutal murder. The first had affected him emotionally even more than the second, but it was Jo-Anne's death that threatened to change his life. Even now the media wouldn't leave him alone. They were still clustered in the driveway, with their cameras and their note pads. Always a celebrity, he had been precipitated by his wife's messy ending into the ranks of the notorious—a position which, for a Stansfield, was about as welcome as a spell on a Florida chain gang. His ever-brightening political prospects seemed totally ruined, and Jo-Anne had been the culprit. For that, more than for the almost casual and totally bizarre infidelity, he would never forgive her.

He stared out moodily at the angry sea and the acrobatic pelicans as they soared on the rushing air. Was there any way to salvage it? Time and time again he had gone over the options. After all, Teddy had recovered from Chappaquiddick, and Nixon had made more comebacks than Frank Sinatra. There had to be a way.

He turned around and his heart lit up like a shaft of sunlight piercing the slate-gray sky. He hadn't lost Christie. There she was—curled up tightly on the sofa—a good deed in a naughty world. From the moment she had recovered from her own ordeal she had been a tower of strength in his. The loss of her mother, on top of the mysterious sequence of events that had caused her own sorrow, would have sunk lesser mortals, but Christie had weathered the storm. Now there were just the two of them. Alone against the world. Bobby knew he would never understand her. She was so desperately unlike him, and light years removed from anything remotely resembling her mother. Whatever had propelled her into the emotional depths had never been revealed, despite the hectoring questioning of a far from stupid politician. Bobby only knew that she had loved someone, and that he had let her down.

Nothing more than that. Occasionally, from the wistful, faraway look in her eyes, it was obvious that whoever he was he was not forgotten.

"You know, dad, you mustn't give up. I know I've said that before, but it's true. Stansfields don't give up, do they? I think I've got that engraved on my heart."

Bobby laughed. It was supposed to be true. Certainly he'd always believed it. And his mother was still saying it. It was only the other day that she had made what she thought was an encouraging little speech. "Things change, dear. The time requires the man. Look at De Gaulle. Look at Churchill. When the world is running smoothly, they pick the man without Mafia connections who has the best teeth. But that's a luxury, dear. When the going gets tough they pick the man with the biggest balls. The dreadful business with Jo-Anne would be overlooked if times ever turned really hard. That would be your moment. It's not over yet."

Again Bobby laughed out loud as he thought of his mother's uncharacteristic crudeness. In a lifetime he had never heard her say anything like that, but it had had its intended effect. The message had been clear. There is a time for gentility and breeding, but when it's hitting the fan, a man must learn to shovel shit.

"It's true, Christie. I won't give up." The smile lit up the handsome face, backlighting the beautifully broken nose. In front of his audience of one he felt the familiar old confidence creeping back. He walked over to the sofa and threw himself down next to his daughter. "But if you were my campaign manager, what the hell would you advise me to *do?*"

"I know exactly what you should do."

"Tell me."

"You should remarry."

"My darling daughter . . . and who do you think I should marry?"

"You should marry Lisa Blass."

Like a red-hot needle the thought seared through Bobby Stansfield's brain. Lisa Blass. Lisa, who he'd never been able to forget. Lisa, who all through the years had never forgiven him for the ambition that had forced him away from her. Lisa of the hard body and the soft skin. Of the gentle sweetness and the cold revenge. Lisa Starr. She'd carried his child and thrown it away, as he had discarded her. A back-street girl who had risen to a prominence few women ever achieved. How many times had he remembered her, longed for her patience and understanding and for the mind-capturing excitement of her touch? Instead he had taken Jo-Anne Duke. Married a hooker for her millions to further his own ambitions. It was a choice he had never ceased to regret and one for which he had never imagined he could be forgiven.

"Christie, do you know what you're saying? Lisa Blass hates my guts. You didn't know that, but then how could you? I wasn't very good to her, I'm afraid. I treated her badly. I didn't want to, but I did, and for years she's hated both me and your mother. I was very fond of her . . ."

Bobby saw the cloud pass over Christie's face. Sadness? The sort of look you had when you began to understand something that had long troubled you.

"Has she ever tried to harm you? I mean, I guess with that business of hers she could have maybe done that. Do you remember that dreadful book they wrote about us? The one they sent you a few years ago? Nobody would publish it, but she could have done so if she'd wanted to hurt us that much."

Bobby looked thoughtful. "Well, that's true. Certainly. But she's always avoided us like the plague, and in this town you know how difficult that is."

"Did you love her?"

"What is this? The third degree?" Again the laugh. The one that turned the crowds on. Then, more reflectively, "Yes. Yes, I did love her. Very much. She's a wonderful person. She was a wonderful person."

"Mom was more difficult to love." Christie's statement was matter-of-fact.

"Yes. I think we all found that."

Bobby turned to his daughter. The tears were there again. Jo-Anne was difficult to love, but Christie had achieved it. Christie, who was so full of love there was enough for everyone. Christie, who had blown her love on some no-good creature of the wasteland who had never even showed up at the house to be introduced to her parents. Whoever he was, he deserved the fate of the freaked-out maniac who'd murdered Jo-Anne. He, Bobby, would have volunteered personally to administer the poison—and he would have taken all day about it, reveling in the boy's facial expressions as he fought off the sleep that would kill.

"She has a son now. I never see him around, but he must be your age. Blass, he'd be called. Can't remember his first name."

"Scott. Scott Blass."

Bobby stood up. "You know what I think we both need? A *fantastic* margarita. Come on, Christie, I'll make it myself. I used to be famous for them. Let's see if I still am."

Christie smiled through the mask of tears. Her father could be like that, with the infectious enthusiasm of the youngest child in the body of the famous politician. But she wasn't going to let him off the hook. Not totally.

"I think you still love her, dad. You should meet up with her. See what happens. I wouldn't mind. Remember, I suggested it. There's been so much sadness, so much bitterness."

Her reward was the look on her father's face.

LISA FLICKED morosely through the *New York* Times best-sellers lists. This should be best part of the week. They were all there. All the Blass books. The ones she had nurtured, the ones she had invented, the ones she had bought. But there was no joy in it. No excitement. No enthusiasm. No nothing. Just the emptiness all around. It had been six long months since Scott had left. He had gone like a thief in the night, stealing away for no apparent reason, and since his departure there had been only the sound of his silence. The earth had devoured him. He had vanished without trace.

How many times had she tried to understand the reason for his bitter departure? It was as if he wanted to hurt her for some terrible wrong. But what had she done? Nothing had changed. The note had been little help.

She could remember it by heart, but still she couldn't understand it: "I am going away, mother, and I am not coming back. Please don't try to find me. All my life I have tried to make you love me, but now I understand why you never could. It's nearly destroyed me, and others, too—so if I can't be part of your love I don't want to have anything to do with your hatred. I trusted you so much, but you lied to me. And everything you pretended to be you weren't. So I'm going away to learn to live with myself and to try to learn that what's happened was not my fault, but yours. You sent me away a long, long time ago."

Love? Hatred? It meant nothing. Nothing anyway that *he* could know or care about. Yes, she had been hatred's friend. It had sustained her through the years of struggle and been the mother of the phenomenal success that screamed itself from the black-and-white pages of the *New York Times*. But now, like some spent bullet, the emotion was all tired and worn out, and with Jo-Anne's dreadful death, it had plummeted thankfully to earth.

"How's Anne Liebermann's surfing book coming along?" asked Maggie brightly. Cheering up Lisa was getting to be a full-time occupation these days.

"Terrific," said Lisa without enthusiasm. "The synopsis and chapter break-down are just wonderful. Has to be another number one. No problem. Oh yes," she added wearily. "Still raking it in. Blass is still on top." She paused as the bittersweet thought crossed her mind. "I wonder what poor Scottie would have thought of it." The voice had a catch in it.

"It was his idea, wasn't it?"

"It was Anne Liebermann's screwy idea. Or I should say it was Anne Liebermann's idea of screwing. Scott was sleeping with her, you know."

"Good God! Was he really? What an extraordinary thing to want to do."

"He didn't want to, Maggie. He did it for me. Liebermann was cutting up rough on her contract. He sweet-talked her into staying with Blass. He paid in kind."

"Oh, Lisa, don't be so ridiculous."

"I'm *not* being ridiculous, Maggie." Lisa stood up abruptly, throwing the paper onto the floor with an impatient gesture. After all these years Maggie still treated her like she was an innocent teenager. People seemed to think she was the same old Lisa, but she wasn't. Things had changed. It was irritating that people didn't recognize that. Especially old friends.

For a second or two there was silence. It was the sort that gave birth to things. "He wanted so desperately for me to take notice of him. I never could. I tried but I couldn't. There wasn't anything there before. But there is now."

She turned to face her old friend, her beautiful face suddenly drawn, the tears glistening in her eyes. "I want him back, Maggs. So . . . much." She threw out her hands in a gesture of impotence and shook her head from side to side. "He was so much like Bobby. It was ridiculous. Every time I looked at him, all the hurt and the anger just bubbled up inside. Poor Scott. He never had any idea. I couldn't tell him. Even now he doesn't know."

"Perhaps if he knew . . ."

"He's gone, Maggs. He's just gone. And it's my fault."

Lisa was talking to herself now. "So very much hatred. It was everywhere. I took it with me. I smelled of it. I reeked of it, and it made me so *strong*. So *damned* strong. It was like a pact with the devil, wasn't it? I could have everything, even revenge, if I gave up my soul."

"You can get it back, Lisa. You can get everything back. Everyone back."

"No. It's too late, Maggie. They've all gone. All gone. And there's nothing left except me. And all this . . ."

Lisa flung out her hand in despair to the high-ceilinged room with its exquisite Old Masters, its superb jade collection, the miraculous Rodin sculpture poached at auction from the underbidding Louvre. But she meant more than just that. She was the survivor. She had inherited it all. Palm Beach. The most desired thing of all was hers now, to bend to her will, to humiliate if she wished, to have and to hold, from this day forth . . . Her only rival was not only dead, but desperately discredited by the manner of her dying. The field was clear to the social priestess who ran the most successful publishing empire in America and yet still had the time and the skill to play the Palm Beach game. So she had won the Pyrrhic victory, and the taste of the ashes in her mouth was turning her stomach. What would Marjorie have said? Dear, wise Marjorie who had hidden her kindness and her compassion beneath the mask of her social ambition?

"Contact Bobby, Lisa. He must be so alone. Just like you. It's all so long ago. So very far away. Tell him it's over. Understand him. Understand yourself."

Maggie's voice echoed her thoughts.

As she heard the words, Lisa knew she would do it.

It was like a revelation. So obvious, and yet an idea not entertained by consciousness. In the depths of her psyche, however, the need was there. Without Bobby there could be no new beginning.

And suddenly, and with the desperation of the soulsick, Lisa began to long for a new dawn.

━

CHRISTIE STOOD stock still as the words buzzed around and around her head like an angry swarm of bees. Occasionally some of them peeled off from the milling horde and flew right into her ear: on a one-way trip into consciousness: "Half sister." "Brother." "Forgive." "That night on the beach."

In disbelief she shook her head from side to side, sending little droplets of Madison Avenue rain all around the tiny third-floor apartment. But even as Christie reeled with the shock of the revelation, her mad refusal to accept the truth of Scott's words was already starting to weaken.

"You mean we're brother and sister. That dad is your dad, too," said her disembodied voice.

Scott, his head still buried deep in his hands, nodded bleakly. All crumpled up on the dirty sofa, he looked as if he had given up the fight. It wasn't just the stubble of the beard, the filthy fingernails, the tangled, tousled hair. They were just the clichés of defeat. His whole body spoke the language of despair. Scott looked like a cardboard man who had been left out in the rain.

Even as she tried to digest the fact that the man she had loved so completely, who had hurt her so deeply, was her own brother, Christie's great big heart was opening up all over again. Into it flooded both relief and compassion. "I'm glad, Scott. Do you hear? I'm glad you're my brother."

And as she said it she felt it. She had lost a lover, but now she was no longer alone. Suddenly there was so much understanding of emotions, which, previously, had been inexplicable. She had a brother, a dear, wonderful, crazy, sad brother to walk through life with. A brother who would join her in turning up a nose at a ludicrous world.

Through parted fingers Scott looked up at her in disbelief. "Christie, what on earth do you mean?"

The warm smile was all over her face as she tried to explain. "I mean it's all fine, Scott. I forgive you, and we can love each other again. When I was a little girl, I used to pray to God to give me a brother. He's just been a tiny bit late in answering my prayers."

"Then you don't hate me . . . even after what I did?" He needed more reassurance. It had never occurred to him that Christie would react like this. He had focused solely on the tragedy, and as a result he had not been able to hope. For the last dreadful six months he had hardly left the apartment that had been his hide-away. Endlessly he had examined his conscience as he had tried to scourge the evil from his soul, but there had been no solution. Always the conclusion had been the same. He was a warped, misshapen thing—a genetic accident who had expressed his twisted inheritance in the most diabolical of ways. He, the son of an incestuous relationship, had maimed and mutilated the happiness of his own flesh and blood. He had seen his own sister's heart stop as the direct result of his wicked love plot. He had taken her on the sand. He had hated she whom nature demanded he should love, and he had defiled her with his polluted genes. And at the end, when confronted with the enormity of his act, he hadn't even had the courage to kill himself. Whichever way he had looked at it, there was no health in him.

Christie melted down toward him. Sitting next to him she reached out to him, and there, on the threadbare sofa, he fell gratefully into her arms as she cradled his head comfortingly.

"Oh, Scott. Poor Scott. Poor baby. You've had such a terrible time. Poor baby. My poor baby." As his tears came she rocked him gently, allowing the grief to break through the log jam that had blocked up all his sorrow. For long minutes brother and sister did not speak.

Scott broke the silence. "Oh, Christie. I didn't know how you'd react. I felt so guilty. I had to tell someone. I had to tell you. When I wrote, I thought maybe you wouldn't answer. Or perhaps you'd not even open the letter. I was so ashamed."

Christie pulled him in toward her, holding him tightly, feeling the wet splash of her brother's tears on her brown forearm. "It's all over now, Scottie. It's gone. You did it because something had hurt you very much. I know that. I forgive you. Listen to me. I forgive you."

And she lifted up his face toward her and made him smile the uncertain smile, encouraging it with her own. There was more to say. She must say it all. Clear it all away—the debris, the baggage of the past. Only if directly confronted would the ghosts be laid to rest.

"I guess I sort of knew right from the start. When we met on that beach. It was so immediate. So incredibly natural. All the emotions were so mixed up, but so close. Mainly they were just *strong*, I guess. Okay, so now we know what it was all about, but there was a kind of a way I knew then. When you made love to me. Just before . . . it suddenly felt terribly wrong. Wonderful, but wrong at the same time. There was a part of me that didn't want to . . . but it just didn't have the votes. Do you know what? I don't even regret it. I remember it, and it was the best moment of my life so far. I loved making love to you because I loved you, Scott. And I still love you now. Right now. Do you hear?"

She turned the stricken tear-stained face toward her and wiped away the wetness with her fingers, watching the softening of the hurt as her words eased away the pain.

"But I was so cruel . . . so evil to you, Christie. How can you forgive that?"

"It was you who was the victim, Scott, not me. I was just the passer-by who got drawn in by Fate. All that hatred. Somebody had to get caught in the flame. It's amazing about your mother, and mom and dad. Why did she want to hurt them so very much? And why didn't she love you? I can't understand that. It seems so incredible."

"It *is* incredible, Christie. I'm afraid you've only heard half the story." Scott sat up and took his sister's hand in his. "I still don't know whether or not to believe it, but Willie Willis says that my mother and your father are half brother and sister, too."

"What?" Christie's face managed to mix incredulity and humor in equal proportions. If Scott could joke at a time like this, then that was progress of a sort, but he seemed to have a rather macabre sense of what was funny.

"I know, it's crazy, isn't it? Absolutely mad. Anyway, he told me that my grandma used to work in your grandfather's house. They had an affair, and mom was their child. That was what he said. Even mom didn't know. Nobody knew. If it's true, it means my mom and your dad are mirror images of us. History repeated itself."

"Could he have made it up? To hurt you for some reason?"

"I guess it's possible. It seems anything is possible. I just know he was right about us. I mean, we look like we've been photocopied."

Like the sun shining through the clouds of a gloomy sky, the mutual laughter filled the room. They were partners at last. Co-conspirators against life, the dealer of dirty cards.

It was true. They not only looked like brother and sister, but could have been taken for twins.

"But how can we find out? We ought to know for certain, I guess. About them I mean . . . not us. I want us to be brother and sister, even if we're not."

"God knows how we find out. But does it matter? Maybe we should spare them that. After all, both their lives are sort of ruined anyway. Maybe it's better they shouldn't know."

"You're right, Scott. It's far better buried . . . if there's anything to bury. God, it's amazing. All that venom when the blood was screaming for love and not war. What an incredible waste."

"What will we do now?" Scott looked wiped out, sponged clean of emotion. If there were feelings left to feel, he scarcely knew what they were.

"That's easy," said Christie brightly. "We're going home."

LISA BLASS was a child again. Uncertain, excited, peering up once more at an outsize world. For the hundredth time she stared impatiently at the seemingly sticky hands of the Piaget watch. Today, time was moving at a snail's pace.

What to wear had been a problem. What to think had been a problem. In a few minutes' time, how to behave would be a problem.

Fate had excelled itself in the role of conjuror. Egged on by Maggie in her quest for a new beginning, Lisa had actually been reaching for the telephone when it had rung. Bobby Stansfield's voice had been tentative, unsure, devoid of confidence, but it had been his voice. He had stumbled several times as he had attempted to give her the message she was on the verge of giving him, and her heart had flown back to the time when life had been alive, way before the laughter had died.

It had seemed too simple as the staccato words had dug hatred's grave. "So many years . . . so much sorrow. It would mean a lot . . . see you again . . ."

Precipitously she had rushed headlong across the bridge of souls, her flying feet devouring the years that had separated them. "Yes," her voice had said. "Yes, I would like to see you again, Bobby."

Now Lisa was nervous as hell. Try as she might, she didn't know whether she wanted the meeting with Bobby or not. Yesterday it had seemed like the most wonderful idea in the world. But today it was different. In some ways it seemed that everything had changed, in others that nothing had. She and Bobby were the same people. Could Scott's disappearance and Jo-Anne's extraordinary murder turn the world upside down? It was impossible to decide, and impossible to entangle the mess of rushing emotions that raged like a tornado through her heart. Was it possible that she was still bent on Bobby's destruction and that this decision to meet him was the prelude to yet another battle in an ongoing war? As the clock ticked away the minutes to the time when she would see him once more, her level of anxiety rose toward the heavens. If she didn't know what she wanted, how could she know how to behave? If she didn't know how to feel, how could she know how to think?

To cover her confusion she had telephoned to change the time of the meeting. Tea was so neutral. So English. So safe. At four o'clock the butler would show him in.

"Senator Stansfield, ma'am."

And she would put out a cool hand and say, "Bobby, it's been a long time," or some such appropriate remark. Sophisticated. Formidably self-controlled. Suitably distant.

The butler's knock on the door was deferential.

"Come in."

"Senator Stansfield, ma'am."

For a moment Bobby stood framed in the open doorway. Around his mouth played the easy, open smile, its creases well worn now with constant repetition. Bobby Stansfield, strong and reassuring, promising the world, demanding attention, beaming his charisma. So much for mental rehearsals. As her insides turned to water and her soul began to crack in the packed ice that had surrounded it for so long, Lisa managed a breathless, "Oh, Bobby."

Somehow she hadn't been quite prepared for this, and the shock was as real as if it had been a total surprise. It was as if she were standing outside herself, a separate person altogether, watching with interest how she would behave. The physical feelings could easily be understood—the chemical rush of fear, excitement, almost anger, the strange feeling that something of enormous importance was happening, something that would change you forever, the sensation that nothing would ever be quite the same after this moment. Perhaps a car accident was like this. No pain. Just the knowledge that you were at the turning point, that things could go either way, and that they were out of your hands. Unable to control events, the body lapsed automatically into spectator mode, as it passed over the reins to an infinitely more powerful destiny. The intellect was a sad, helpless thing at a time like this, and yet as always, it continued its feeble, doomed attempts to explain and to predict. Was the real Bobby causing all this confusion? Or was she reacting to a memory? If so, could mere memory possess such strength? Must it not then be reality in its own right?

They were together now. Close to each other, and for a long moment they held on tightly—to the past, to the present, to the might-have-been. There were tears in her eyes, and deep within her essence Lisa felt herself begin to melt. Had it all been for nothing? The struggle. The passion. The yearning for revenge. Had the tiger she had ridden for all these long years been another creature in disguise? In the forests of the night, had it all the time been love, not hatred, that had burned so brightly? It seemed so impossible. It was so very obvious.

They stood back to look at each other.

Bobby saw the glistening eyes, the perfect curve of the well-remembered chin. How many dreams? So many visions, but nothing compared to the raw beauty of the reality: the softness of the skin on the rounded neck, the sculpted lines of the strong shoulders, the mouth that no woman had the right to possess. The magic wafted out from her and billowed around him, bewitching the mind that had always been wide open to Lisa's spell. With God's help he would keep her now, and to emphasize his determination he took her in his arms once again, nuzzled his head down in her warm hair as he whispered gently, "Lisa, my Lisa."

But there was a part of her that was still fighting him. Habit. The unforgotten memory of his cruelty. Gently but firmly she pushed him away from her, looking up into the blue eyes. Time had been kind to him, but there was a legacy of sadness painted into the corners of the handsome face. He had suffered, too.

"I wanted to contact you when Jo-Anne . . ." Lisa spread her hands to signify the impossibility of it all. There were so many things to be said. But no place to begin.

"I know. I know."

"I hated her so much. Now it seems so very pointless."

"And you never forgave me, either."

"No, I never did. Now I'm not sure that there was anything to forgive."

"The son we could have had together?"

Lisa smiled back at him. It seemed to be the right moment. Scott was gone, but he was there. For too long his reality had been denied. Its denial had sent him away. Perhaps its affirmation would bring him back. "We have a son, Bobby."

She watched the incredulity creep into the well-known eyes. "My son, Scott, is your son too. I didn't want you to know. Ever. Even he doesn't know."

"But you said you'd . . . Vernon Blass . . . You mean that time in the hospital, when Christie was born . . ."

"Yes. Yes. Of course the child was yours. I couldn't kill it. God, I wanted to. To kill it because I couldn't kill you. But I never wanted to give you the satisfaction of knowing you had a child by me. A son."

Bobby put out his hand to touch her, to douse the flames of bitterness that crept around her words. "Oh, Lisa. I'm so sorry. I just didn't know."

"What do you feel now?"

Bobby looked down at her, at the beautiful, deeply wounded woman who had loved him too much, and he knew exactly what he felt. "I love you, Lisa," he said simply.

"Then kiss me," she said. And she smiled.

Their mouths were dry at first, tense and nervous, like the lips of first-time lovers, as they hovered fearfully, frightened that the moment would pass before the flower of passion could grow. But the escalation of desire, so long denied, so long dormant, had a momentum of its own. Effortlessly it rushed and roared as it sought expression, carrying all in its path as it consumed consciousness and devoured caution. Side by side it ran with tenderness in a wild conspiracy of souls, Bobby and Lisa, joined together, their hearts beating against each other as their strong arms cemented their commitment. For long moments they luxuriated in the well-remembered tastes of each other, crushing themselves together so that no one nor anything could drive them apart. Lisa could feel his hardness, and she loved him for it. Loved it, as she had loved it so many years before. They had reached beyond words now, to the land where emotion lived. There was no need to analyze, no need to explain. They needed only to feel, and to be felt. Once again they were lovers.

—

THE STRIDENT sounds of the busy airport forced Scott to shout into the receiver. Crammed into the telephone booth beside him, Christie tried to keep track of the dialogue by watching his face.

"It's me, Scott. Can you hear me? It's noisy as hell here." He crushed his hand over his other ear in a vain attempt to shut out the background.

Christie could imagine the response. From someone like Lisa Blass it would be as likely to be anger as anything else. Anger that she had been deserted. Anger that she had been worried. Anger that she had failed as a mother.

"I'm fine, mother. I'm calling to say that I'm coming home."

"We can discuss all that when I get there, mother. It's impossible now. I can barely hear what you're saying."

Christie squeezed his arm in support. She knew all about powerful parents. It wasn't all easy being a child.

"What. *What?* Oh, my God."

Christie saw Scott stiffen, saw the color fade from his face, saw the tentacles of shock crawl all over his body.

"What is it, Scott? What is it?"

Scott put his hand over the receiver. When he spoke his voice was shaking.

"They're going to get married, Christie. God Almighty, they're going to get married."

"Who? What do you mean?"

"My mom, and your old man."

"Oh, no. Oh, no. They can't do that."

And in the crowded airport brother and sister stared at each other in horror as they contemplated the impossible union.

～22～

CHRISTIE AND SCOTT sat side by side on the sand, staring out morosely at the velvet smooth sea. Sometimes it was like this on the North End beach, the waves gone, the water the aquamarine blue of the Caribbean—a surfer's nightmare, a beach person's dream.

Scott scooped up a handful of sand and allowed it to fall slowly through his fingers. It was a symbolic gesture; the sands of time were running out.

"If Willie Boy was telling the truth, we can't let them get married. It's as simple as that. They'd have more children like me—all screwed up, inbred. God knows what the problems would be. We just can't let them do it."

"But, Scottie, we don't know for certain. The old drunk could be lying. Or he could have gotten it wrong. Or maybe your grandma's husband, that Tom Starr, was paranoid. Maybe he was just jealous. You know how much drinking they're all supposed to have done, and you said yourself that Willie is zoned from dawn till dusk."

"Yup, I guess all that's possible," said Scott doubtfully. "And I guess it's *possible* that grandma herself wanted to believe she was pregnant by one of the mighty Stansfields. Mom said she was always going on about how wonderful your family was, and how Palm Beach was the best and most beautiful place in the world. Maybe she talked herself into believing that mom was a Stansfield because it was grander than being a Starr." He paused. "But that's the whole problem. We just don't know for *sure,* and we can't know. I don't think we can take the risk."

Christie's face reflected the heavy atmosphere of gloom. "But, Scott, surely we can't blow their happiness out of the window. They've both suffered so much pain. Most of their lives so far have been ruined one way or another. It's their last chance to make everything okay. In the last analysis, does it matter if they're sort of related? I mean if they didn't *know* . . . and if they had children then they'd be like you, and for sure that's no big disaster."

Scott smiled back at her. His own little sister, and as far as he was concerned the best and wisest person on earth. That was one thing that Willie

913

Boy had gotten right. They were in this together up to the hilt. Whatever was decided, it would be a family decision.

"We couldn't let them do it, Christie. It'd just be too irresponsible."

"Oh, God—and the wedding's tomorrow. Everybody's been invited. Imagine the chaos if it had to be canceled. I honestly think dad would die. He cares so much about what people think. It's the politician in him. And your mom—after all the hatred. Now at last she can rationalize it, exorcise it, and have a chance at living again—and we pull the plug on the whole thing."

"Is there any way at all that we can find out more?"

"It's all so long ago. Everybody's dead. I've been trying to remember all the things people told me, but it doesn't amount to much. I mean, if it took me this long to find out that Vernon Blass wasn't my dad, how many other things have I been kept in the dark about?"

Christie said nothing. It was true. How little the children knew of the sins of the fathers.

"Tommy Starr, Jack Kent, and Mary-Ellen were all dead before I was born. The only thing I have to go on is what mom has told me, which isn't much—and it seems that a lot of that was bullshit."

"I remember grandma saying once that grandpa was too friendly with the servants. I thought she meant not distant enough. I suppose it could have meant a little more."

"Hmm, hardly cast-iron proof, is it? What we need is something like a birth certificate."

"Yeah, but that's bound to say 'Starr,' isn't it? In those days you didn't advertise things like that. The only absolutely certain evidence would be a blood test. From what I remember from biology you can sometimes prove that people *aren't* related, but you can't prove for certain that they are."

Scott laughed. "Oh, Christie, that's great. I can just hear the conversation. Mom, can I borrow a bit of blood? Senator, could you let me have a bit of yours? I'd like to run a few tests. Just general interest. They'd probably arrange to have me admitted to the funny farm."

They turned to each other and their eyes locked. "Blood test," they both blurted out.

It was a federal law, wasn't it? Nobody could get married without a blood test. The idea was to stamp out syphilis, but the bottom line was that somewhere probably at this precise moment in time samples of Lisa's and Bobby's blood were sitting innocently in a test tube on the Formica counter of some West Palm laboratory.

"If I could find out where they sent it, I could telephone the lab, pretend to be the senator, and ask for them to run a blood-group test on each sample. People are always interested in their blood groups. It'd be a pretty reasonable request. It is blood groups you need, isn't it?"

Christie could hardly contain her excitement. "Yes, that's right. It's like when you're trying to prove fatherhood in a paternity case. It could be that my dad and your mom have blood groups that are incompatible with their having the same father. God knows what the odds are, but it's worth a try. If it's okay, we let everything go ahead, and if it's still doubtful then we stop everything."

Scott was on his feet.

"Great! That's what we'll do," Scott agreed.

"How will you find out the name of the lab?" asked Christie.

"I'll just ask mom. She wouldn't be remotely curious as to why I want to know. She's always much too preoccupied to worry about things like that."

"Oh, Scott—good luck. Pray like mad."

Christie rose up on tiptoe to kiss him good-bye. As she did so she felt the warm sand of the North End beach run through her toes—a potent reminder of the raw emotions that had raged and blown over two shattered families. Could the shipwrecked lives make it to the safe haven? It was up to them.

— Epilogue —

IT WAS TIME, and both Lisa and Bobby knew it. The confirmation was in the face of Father Bradley. He took a deep breath. "Well now, senator, Lisa. I think we should get things under way. Then we can get to all that champagne!" He laughed nervously, not a hundred percent sure that he had hit quite the right note.

Bobby and Lisa, however, weren't listening to his small talk. He was there as a symbol alone. As God's agent. He was there to do the job that both so fervently desired.

Lisa could almost hear the words she was about to say. They rolled around in her mind like sparkling marbles sending off starbursts of happiness as they jostled her soul.

"Do you, Elizabeth Starr Blass, take Robert Edward Stansfield to be your lawful wedded husband?"

"I do," sounded ridiculously inappropriate but wonderful all the same. There should be more. A few more sonorous sentences, filling in the details of the bare bones of the commitment:

"I have always wanted this marvelous man. Nothing on this earth would give me so much pleasure as to become his wife . . ." Something like that, and then Bobby would reply in similar fashion. It would be like a creative act at the beginning of their life together. The exchange of poetry as they made known the full extent of their love before the army of their friends.

Side by side they walked up the steps behind Father Bradley and took their places on the raised dais in full view of the assembled company. The rector turned to face them, with what he hoped was a reassuring smile on his lips. In his experience there was nobody in the world who was not a little nervous at this minute. He opened his prayerbook, without taking his eyes off Lisa and Bobby.

Inside the old ballroom the excitement was almost a visible thing. It crackled in the air, darting hither and thither with capricious abandon, infecting the players and the spectators with its heady drama.

Maggie, formidably neat in her subdued coat and skirt, was swept along in

916

its current. Her instinct must have been wrong. It was going to be all right after all. You could see it in Lisa's face. It wasn't just her look, it was her "feel." It was as if the most majestic sailing ship had turned the Cape at last. Battered and threatened by the storm, she had survived the elements and, tried and tested in the threshing sea, had emerged, stronger and more serene, into the calm waters on the other side. There was a radiance about Lisa, a glorious self-confidence, a deep peace that Maggie had not seen before, and her heart went out to her friend.

And yet, and yet . . . there was the sense that the menace had not passed. Try as she might, Maggie could not see the direction of the danger, could not know its nature or its cause, but around the edges of intuition the feeling was undeniable. It wafted gently, a sickly aroma of decay unsettling those who smelled it, subtle yet insistent, present yet invisible.

But nothing could go wrong. There was Bobby beaming good humor, eager and willing to make the commitment he should have made so many years ago. No impediment to bliss would come from his direction. Caroline Stansfield, too, looked worried but controlled. Any mother could expect to feel anxious at the wedding of her eldest son. Once before she had been Lisa's enemy, but she was one no longer. Old and bent, her mind was still robust, and in the short conversation Maggie had had with her earlier there had been no signs at all of opposition to the marriage.

Once again she turned to look at Scott, and immediately she realized that it was from him that the unsettling vibrations were beaming. From Scott, and from Christie. It wasn't just that they appeared nervous—everyone's nerves were on edge. It was something more. It was their pallor and the total absence of Scott's normal languid air of laid-back cool. All his gestures seemed abnormally jerky and forced, almost as if somebody had replaced the red blood in his veins with a strong solution of caffeine. He looked uncomfortable as hell in the formal clothes, but it was much, much more than that. And why did his furtive eyes keep darting toward the telephone that sat on the table by his side?

Christie could actually hear the hammering of her heart. She had never dreamed it would end like this. One dreadful problem had replaced another. At first the blood samples had been lost, and all through the long night she had lain awake in her bed, knowing that Scott would be tossing and turning on his. They had bombarded the Almighty with their prayers, that the samples be found, that they would be discovered in a refrigerator and not in some warm corner of a humid laboratory, the temperature having rendered them useless for blood grouping. At ten o'clock that morning the test tubes had been located, only two hours away from the ceremony that might prove a disaster. Even then fate had intervened. A multiple traffic accident had strained the resources of the Good Sam lab, where, as a special favor, the Stansfield/Blass samples were being processed. The surgeons were calling out for transfusable blood, and the technician had had to put the Stansfield request on the back burner. There was nothing left to do but to wait . . . to watch . . . and to listen.

"Dearly beloved . . . friends. We are gathered here today on this *very* happy occasion to witness the joining together in holy matrimony of Robert and Lisa . . ."

Scott's mind was numb. Although he heard the words that signified the beginning of the ceremony, there was nothing in his world but the telephone. It had taken over the room, a living, throbbing thing, far more alive than the players in the human drama. Soon it would speak to him. Across the room he saw Christie's worried, questioning eyes. Somebody, who might or might not have been him, smiled unhappily at her.

Father Bradley had allowed himself a few sentences before the main event as a warmup to his fifteen minutes of fame. "It is indeed a wonderful thing when the Lord seeks to bless two of His most worthy servants with the gift of eternal happiness . . ."

The congregation was quiet now. Sitting back, they could enjoy the platitudes as a tasty hors d'oeuvre to the ceremony itself.

Lisa thought of tonight when she and Bobby would make love, as they had done so long ago. The pages of time, dripping still with the blood of her emotional wounds, were to be wiped clean at last.

Bobby's heart filled with pride. It was true. The Lord had blessed him and would continue to do so. With Lisa at his side he could resume the march toward greatness. Higher and higher in the firmament of America.

The soft warbling of the telephone sounded to everybody in the room like the blast of a nuclear explosion.

Christie's hammering heart seemed to stop altogether.

"Oh, dear," said Father Bradley in mid-cliché. Surely somebody should have thought to disconnect the telephone?

Bobby, thinking exactly the same thing, fought back the irritation. "Wrong number!" he said loudly to general laughter.

Lisa was not to be outdone. "More like my office. One of the authors has writer's block and needs to be talked through it."

Scott's hand darted out with the power and precision of a striking rattlesnake, as, all around the crowded room, annoyance at the unwanted interruption wore the mask of humor.

Eight hundred eyes turned to watch him, eight hundred ears swiveled to listen to him.

"Yes," said Scott. "Yes, it is. Ah. I see. What precisely does that mean? Ah. You're sure? No possibility of a mistake? None at all? No. I see. Thank you. Thank you."

"Who on earth is it?" asked Caroline Stansfield querulously. Why did Scott look as if he had seen a ghost?

The sound of the receiver making it back to the telephone jangled in four hundred minds.

Christie's voice, quite loud, just said, "Scott."

For one single second of omnipotence Scott held his secret.

At last he spoke. "Do you know what I think?" he said. "I think we should get the hell on with this wedding."

ABOUT THE AUTHOR

PAT BOOTH is the author of numerous bestsellers. In addition to the three bestsellers in this collection, she has written *The Sisters, Miami,* and four other novels. A former high-fashion model in London, she is also an accomplished photojournalist, with three one-woman shows to her credit. She has published three books of photography: *Making Faces, Self-Portrait,* and *Master Photographers.* She, her husband, and their two children divide their time between homes in Palm Beach, London, and New York.